TWENTIETH-CENTURY CLASSICS

THE PENGUIN COMPLETE SAKI

Hector Hugh Munro was born in 1870 in Burma, the son of a senior official in the Burma police. He was brought up in Devonshire and went to school in Exmouth and at Bedford Grammar School; later his father retired and took over his education by travelling with him widely in Europe. He joined the Burma police, but resigned because of ill health after a year's service. He began his writing career with political sketches for the *Westminster Gazette* and then worked as a foreign correspondent for the *Morning Post* in the Balkans, Russia and Paris. During this time he brought out his first collection of short stories, *Reginald* (1904). This was followed by *Reginald in Russia* (1910), *The Chronicles of Clovis* (1911), *The Unbearable Bassington* (1912) and *Beasts and Superbeasts* (1914). In 1914 he published *When William Came*, a pro-war fantasy of England under German occupation; his 'patriotic' sketches from the Western Front were collected as *The Square Egg* (1924). He enlisted as a private in 1914, refused a commission, went to France and was killed in 1916 at Beaumont Hamel. His pseudonym 'Saki' is taken from the last stanza of *The Ruba'iyat of Omar Khayyam*.

THE PENGUIN COMPLETE

Saki

H. H. MUNRO

With an introduction by Noël Coward

PENGUIN BOOKS

PENGUIN BOOKS

Published by the Penguin Group
Penguin Books Ltd, 27 Wrights Lane, London W8 5TZ, England
Viking Penguin, a division of Penguin Books USA Inc.
375 Hudson Street, New York, New York 10014, USA
Penguin Books Australia Ltd, Ringwood, Victoria, Australia
Penguin Books Canada Ltd, 2801 John Street, Markham, Ontario, Canada L3R 1B4
Penguin Books (NZ) Ltd, 182–190 Wairau Road, Auckland 10, New Zealand

Penguin Books Ltd, Registered Offices: Harmondsworth, Middlesex, England

This edition first published by Doubleday & Company Inc., 1976
Published in Penguin Books 1982
9 10

Printed in England by Clays Ltd, St Ives plc

CONTENTS

I

THE SHORT STORIES

II

THE NOVELS

III

THE PLAYS

INTRODUCTION BY NOËL COWARD

Now, in the year 1967, I have been asked to write an introductory preface for a reissue of the works of Hector Munro, "Saki." This most definitely belongs to the "Who could have dreamed?" department. Who could have dreamed fifty-two years ago when, at the age of fifteen, I first read "Beasts and Super-Beasts," that I should one day be in a position to reintroduce him to a reading public many of whom possibly have never heard of him. Mrs. Astley Cooper, in whose house in Rutland I happened to be staying when I made this joyful discovery, was a character who might well have been invented by Saki himself. She was an articulate, faintly eccentric old lady whose witticisms exploded like firecrackers. The explanation of why an ambitious young actor in his teens should have found himself in the unlikely atmosphere of the hunting country is given in the first volume of my autobiography, *Present Indicative.* In any event there I was and there, lying on a round table in the hall, was a copy of "Beasts and Super-Beasts." I took it up to my bedroom, opened it casually and was unable to go to sleep until I had finished it. One is well accustomed to reading in the biographies of successful authors how they were discovered in their tender, formative years curled up on the branches of a tree with their young noses buried in *Oliver Twist* or Gibbon's *Decline and Fall of the Roman Empire.* This would have been difficult in my circumstances for, with the exception of rare visits to the country, the only trees shading my precocious childhood were those of Battersea Park or Clapham Common, and had I been caught perched in any of them, even with a copy of *Chums* or *The Boys Own Paper*, I should have been led away immediately to the nearest police station.

On looking back I realise that the two most significant influences on my career as a writer were Saki and E. Nesbit, whose children's books I can still read with undiminished enchantment. This, on the surface, may seem to be a naïf, almost trivial admission but it must be remembered that my formal education was abandoned when I went on the stage at the age of ten. I had never had the dubious advantage of being forced to plough through the classics when I was too young to be able to appreciate them. In fact it wasn't until my late teens and early twenties that I discovered, off my own bat, the delights of Dickens, Thackeray, the Brontës etc.: and the dazzling genius of my eminent colleague William Shakespeare. This, in my opinion, was all to the good. I accepted the revelation with an adult mind rather than with the grudging resentment of an adolescent who has been bludgeoned into reading the great masters as an educational necessity. I am not meaning to imply that I consider a "thorough grounding" in the classics to be a bad thing, on the contrary for the average boy, temperamentally unequipped to enjoy reading for the sheer pleasure of it, a certain amount of forcible feeding is essential if he hopes to carve a successful career for himself. But I was far from being an average boy. My passion for reading evinced itself early, when I was no more than six or seven years old, and has progressively increased until the present day when, I am happy to say, it shows no signs of abating. No superior intellect being available to regulate my choice and steer me into deeper waters, I was left to splash about in the shallows to my heart's content. These shallows consisted principally of the popular novels of the day. Apart from my beloved E. Nesbit and Saki I sped with uncritical enthusiasm through the erotic social jungles of Miss Cynthia Stockley, the romantic "cloak and dagger" bravuras of the Baroness Orczy, the somewhat ponderous and occasionally gory historical novels of S. R. Crockett, as well as his more whimsical excursions *Sir Toady Lion* and *Sir Toady Crusoe*, and the lighthearted adventures of Edgar Jepson's Lady Noggs and Baroness von Hutten's Pam. There seems to have been a preponderance of baronesses among the female writers of that period. In addition to these, the South Sea Island romances of Beatrice Grimshaw and Louis Tracy fascinated me and probably injected into me the first insidious drops of that wanderlust which has lured me in later years to so many remote corners of the world. In those adolescent days the French Revolution established a tenacious grip on my imagination, which up to date it has never entirely relinquished. The breath-taking exploits of the Scarlet Pimpernel, the lovely blood and thunder of *The Reign of Terror* by, of all unlikely authors, G. A. Henty, the hair-raising excitement of D. K. Broster's *Chantemerle* and *The Yellow Poppy* were so vividly stamped on my mind that when in 1920 I first visited the château of Versailles it seemed as familiar as the London Coliseum.

I am aware that this discussion has caused me to stray a long way from the initial subject of this preface but it is not quite so irrelevant as it appears to be for it explains the rather haphazard state of my literary education when the verbal adroitness of Saki's dialogue and the brilliance of his wit first captivated me. Many writers who raise youthful minds to a high pitch of enthusiasm are liable, when re-read in the cold remorseless light of middle age, to lose much of their original magic. The wit seems laboured and the language old-fashioned. Saki does not belong to this category. His stories and novels appear as delightful and, to use a much abused word, sophisticated, as they did when he first published them. They are dated only by the fact that they evoke an atmosphere and describe a society which vanished in the baleful summer of 1914. The Edwardian era, in spite of its political idiocies and a sinister sense of foreboding which, to intelligent observers, underlay the latter part of it, must have been, socially at least, very charming. It is this evanescent charm that Saki so effortlessly evoked. True, beneath the lightly satirical badinage of *When William Came* he sounds a prophetic note of warning which shows that he was by no means insensitive to the growing international tension. The idea of England being occupied by Germany, which I shamelessly borrowed for my play *Peace in Our Time* must have been fairly startling to the upper-middle-class complacency of 1912. It might have been more so if Saki had been more widely read, but alas he had only a limited public, possibly for the usual reason that he was ahead of his time. I don't feel, however, that this conclusion is really a valid one. At whatever time he had written, his talent, enchanting as it is to devotees like myself, lacks the necessary ingredients of a "best seller." It is too unsentimental and too superficially flippant. On the rare occasions, such as the end of *The Unbearable Bassington*, when he attempts tragedy, the result is unconvincing and disconcertingly abrupt. His essays in the macabre are more successful. The sinister quality of "Sredni Vashtar" and "The Easter Egg" can be remembered with an authentic shudder. High comedy was undoubtedly his greatest gift. "The Schartz-Metterklume Method," "The Unrest-Cure" and "Tobermory" and "The Open Window" are masterpieces. I have often wondered, if he had survived World War I, how he would have reacted to the years immediately following it, that much maligned period now glibly referred to as "the Hectic Twenties" when upstart Michael Arlens and Noël Cowards flourished like green bay trees in the frenzied atmosphere of cocktail parties, treasure hunts, Hawes and Curtis dressing gowns, long cigarette holders and enthusiastically publicised decadence. He would undoubtedly have found many targets for his sardonic wit in that gay decade but I have an instinctive feeling that it wouldn't really have been his cup of tea. His satire was based primarily on the assumption of a fixed social status quo which, although at the time he was writing may have been wobbling a bit, outwardly at least, betrayed few signs of its imminent collapse. His articulate duchesses sipping China tea on their impeccable lawns, his witty, effete young heroes Reginald, Clovis Sangrail, Comus Bassington, with their gaily irreverent persiflage and their preoccupation with oysters, caviar and personal adornment, finally disappeared in the gunsmoke of 1914. True, a few prototypes have appeared since but their elegance is more shrill and their quality less subtle. Present-day ideologies are impatient, perhaps rightly, with aestheticism. World democracy provides thin soil for the growing of green carnations, but the green carnations, long since withered, exuded in their brief day a special fragrance, which although it may have made the majority sneeze brought much pleasure to a civilised minority. In this latter group I am convinced that there will always be enough admirers of Saki to keep his memory fresh. I cannot feel that he would have wished for more.

The Complete Works of

SAKI

I
THE SHORT STORIES

Reginald

REGINALD

I DID it—I should have known better. I persuaded Reginald to go to the McKillops' garden-party against his will.

We all make mistakes occasionally. "They know you're here, and they'll think it so funny if you don't go. And I want particularly to be in with Mrs. McKillop just now."

"I know, you want one of her smoke Persian kittens as a prospective wife for Wumples—or a husband, is it?" (Reginald has a magnificent scorn for details, other than sartorial.) "And I am expected to undergo social martyrdom to suit the connubial exigencies—"

"Reginald! It's nothing of the kind, only I'm sure Mrs. McKillop would be pleased if I brought you. Young men of your brilliant attractions are rather at a premium at her garden-parties."

"Should be at a premium in heaven," remarked Reginald complacently.

"There will be very few of you there, if that is what you mean.

But seriously, there won't be any great strain upon your powers of endurance; I promise you that you shan't have to play croquet, or talk to the Archdeacon's wife, or do anything that is likely to bring on physical prostration. You can just wear your sweetest clothes and a moderately amiable expression, and eat chocolate-creams with the appetite of a *blasé* parrot. Nothing more is demanded of you."

Reginald shut his eyes. "There will be the exhaustingly up-to-date young women who will ask me if I have seen *San Toy;* a less progressive grade who will yearn to hear about the Diamond Jubilee —the historic event, not the horse. With a little encouragement, they will inquire if I saw the Allies march into Paris. Why are women so fond of raking up the past? They're as bad as tailors, who invariably remember what you owe them for a suit long after you've ceased to wear it."

"I'll order lunch for one o'clock; that will give you two and a half hours to dress in."

Reginald puckered his brow into a tortured frown, and I knew that my point was gained. He was debating what tie would go with which waistcoat.

Even then I had my misgivings.

During the drive to the McKillops' Reginald was possessed with a great peace, which was not wholly to be accounted for by the fact that he had inveigled his feet into shoes a size too small for them. I misgave more than ever, and having once launched Reginald on to the McKillops' lawn, I established him near a seductive dish of *marrons glacés,* and as far from the Archdeacon's wife as possible; as I drifted away to a diplomatic distance I heard with painful distinctness the eldest Mawkby girl asking him if he had seen *San Toy.*

It must have been ten minutes later, not more, and I had been having *quite* an enjoyable chat with my hostess, and had promised to lend her *The Eternal City* and my recipe for rabbit mayonnaise, and was just about to offer a kind home for her third Persian kitten, when I perceived, out of the corner of my eye, that Reginald was not where I had left him, and that the *marrons glacés* were untasted. At the same moment I became aware that old Colonel Mendoza was essaying to tell his classic story of how he introduced golf into India, and that Reginald was in dangerous proximity. There are occasions when Reginald is caviare to the Colonel.

"When I was at Poona in '76–"

"My dear Colonel," purred Reginald, "fancy admitting such a thing! Such a give-away for one's age! I wouldn't admit being on this planet in '76." (Reginald in his wildest lapses into veracity never admits to being more than twenty-two.)

The Colonel went to the colour of a fig that has attained great ripeness, and Reginald, ignoring my efforts to intercept him, glided away to another part of the lawn. I found him a few minutes later happily engaged in teaching the youngest Rampage boy the approved theory of mixing absinthe, within full earshot of his mother. Mrs. Rampage occupies a prominent place in local Temperance movements.

As soon as I had broken up this unpromising *tête-à-tête* and settled Reginald where he could watch the croquet players losing their tempers, I wandered off to find my hostess and renew the kitten negotiations at the point where they had been interrupted. I did not succeed in running her down at once, and eventually it was Mrs. McKillop who sought me out, and her conversation was not of kittens.

"Your cousin is discussing *Zaza* with the Archdeacon's wife; at least, he is discussing, she is ordering her carriage."

She spoke in the dry, staccato tone of one who repeats a French exercise, and I knew that as far as Millie McKillop was concerned, Wumples was devoted to a lifelong celibacy.

"If you don't mind," I said hurriedly, "I think we'd like our carriage ordered too," and I made a forced march in the direction of the croquet ground.

I found every one talking nervously and feverishly of the weather and the war in South Africa, except Reginald, who was reclining in a comfortable chair with the dreamy, far-away look that a volcano might wear just after it had desolated entire villages. The Archdeacon's wife was buttoning up her gloves with a concentrated deliberation that was fearful to behold. I shall have to treble my subscription to her Cheerful Sunday Evenings Fund before I dare set foot in her house again.

At that particular moment the croquet players finished their game, which had been going on without a symptom of finality during the whole afternoon. Why, I ask, should it have stopped precisely when a counter-attraction was so necessary? Every one seemed to drift towards the area of disturbance, of which the chairs of the Archdeacon's wife and Reginald formed the storm-centre. Conversation flagged, and there settled upon the company that expectant hush that precedes the dawn—when your neighbours don't happen to keep poultry.

"What did the Caspian Sea?" asked Reginald, with appalling suddenness.

There were symptoms of a stampede. The Archdeacon's wife looked at me. Kipling or some one has described somewhere the look a foundered camel gives when the caravan moves on and leaves it to its fate. The peptonized reproach in the good lady's eyes brought the passage vividly to my mind.

I played my last card.

"Reginald, it's getting late, and a sea-mist is coming on." I knew that the elaborate curl over his right eyebrow was not guaranteed to survive a sea-mist.

"Never, never again, will I take you to a garden-party. Never. . . . You behaved abominably. . . . What did the Caspian see?"

A shade of genuine regret for misused opportunities passed over Reginald's face.

"After all," he said, "I believe an apricot tie would have gone better with the lilac waistcoat."

REGINALD ON CHRISTMAS PRESENTS

I WISH it to be distinctly understood (said Reginald) that I don't want a "George, Prince of Wales" Prayer-book as a Christmas present. The fact cannot be too widely known.

There ought (he continued) to be technical education classes on the science of present-giving. No one seems to have the faintest notion of what any one else wants, and the prevalent ideas on the subject are not creditable to a civilized community.

There is, for instance, the female relative in the country who "knows a tie is always useful," and sends you some spotted horror that you could only wear in secret or in Tottenham Court Road. It *might* have been useful had she kept it to tie up currant bushes with, when it would have served the double purpose of supporting the branches and frightening away the birds—for it is an admitted fact that the ordinary tomtit of commerce has a sounder æsthetic taste than the average female relative in the country.

Then there are aunts. They are always a difficult class to deal with in the matter of presents. The trouble is that one never catches them really young enough. By the time one has educated them to an appreciation of the fact that one does not wear red woollen mittens in the West End, they die, or quarrel with the family, or do something equally inconsiderate. That is why the supply of trained aunts is always so precarious.

There is my Aunt Agatha, *par exemple*, who sent me a pair of gloves last Christmas, and even got so far as to choose a kind that was being worn and had the correct number of buttons. But—*they were nines!* I sent them to a boy whom I hated intimately: he didn't wear them, of course, but he could have—that was where the bitterness of death came in. It was nearly as consoling as sending white flowers to his funeral. Of course I wrote and told my aunt that they were the one thing that had been wanting to make existence blossom like a rose; I am afraid she thought me frivolous—she comes from the North, where they live in the fear of Heaven and the Earl of Durham. (Reginald affects an exhaustive knowledge of things political, which furnishes an excellent excuse for not discussing them.) Aunts with a dash of foreign extraction in them are the most satisfactory in the way of understanding these things; but if you can't choose your aunt, it is wisest in the long run to choose the present and send her the bill.

Even friends of one's own set, who might be expected to know better, have curious delusions on the subject. I am *not* collecting copies of the cheaper editions of Omar Khayyám. I gave the last four that I received to the lift-boy, and I like to think of him reading them, with FitzGerald's notes, to his aged mother. Lift-boys always have aged mothers; shows such nice feeling on their part, I think.

Personally, I can't see where the difficulty in choosing suitable presents lies. No boy who had brought himself up properly could fail to appreciate one of those decorative bottles of liqueurs that are so reverently staged in Morel's window—and it wouldn't in the least matter if one did get duplicates. And there would always be the supreme moment of dreadful uncertainty whether it was *crême de menthe* or Chartreuse—like the expectant thrill on seeing your partner's hand turned up at bridge. People may say what they like about the decay of Christianity; the religious system that produced green Chartreuse can never really die.

And then, of course, there are liqueur glasses, and crystallized fruits, and tapestry curtains, and heaps of other necessaries of life that make really sensible presents—not to speak of luxuries, such as having one's bills paid, or getting something quite sweet in the way of jewellery. Unlike the alleged Good Woman of the Bible, I'm not above rubies. When found, by the way, she must have been rather a problem at Christmas-time; nothing short of a blank cheque would have fitted the situation. Perhaps it's as well that she's died out.

The great charm about me (concluded Reginald) is that I am so easily pleased. But I draw the line at a "Prince of Wales" Prayer-book.

REGINALD ON THE ACADEMY

"One goes to the Academy in self-defence," said Reginald. "It is the one topic one has in common with the Country Cousins."

"It is almost a religious observance with them," said the Other. "A kind of artistic Mecca, and when the good ones die they go—"

"To the Chantrey Bequest. The mystery is *what* they find to talk about in the country."

"There are two subjects of conversation in the country: Servants, and Can fowls be made to pay? The first, I believe, is compulsory, the second optional."

"As a function," resumed Reginald, "the Academy is a failure."

"You think it would be tolerable without the pictures?"

"The pictures are all right, in their way; after all, one can always *look* at them if one is bored with one's surroundings, or wants to avoid an imminent acquaintance."

"Even that doesn't always save one. There is the inevitable female whom you met once in Devonshire, or the Matoppo Hills, or somewhere, who charges up to you with the remark that it's funny how one always meets people one knows at the Academy. Personally, I *don't* think it funny."

"I suffered in that way just now," said Reginald plaintively, "from a woman whose word I had to take that she had met me last summer in Brittany."

"I hope you were not too brutal?"

"I merely told her with engaging simplicity that the art of life was the avoidance of the unattainable."

"Did she try and work it out on the back of her catalogue?"

"Not there and then. She murmured something about being 'so clever.' Fancy coming to the Academy to be clever!"

"To be clever in the afternoon argues that one is dining nowhere in the evening."

"Which reminds me that I can't remember whether I accepted an invitation from you to dine at Kettner's tonight."

"On the other hand, I can remember with startling distinctness not having asked you to."

"So much certainty is unbecoming in the young; so we'll consider that settled. What were you talking about? Oh, pictures. Personally, I rather like them; they are so refreshingly real and probable, they take one away from the unrealities of life."

"One likes to escape from oneself occasionally."

"That is the disadvantage of a portrait; as a rule, one's bitterest friends can find nothing more to ask than the faithful unlikeness that goes down to posterity as oneself. I hate posterity—it's so fond of having the last word. Of course, as regards portraits, there are exceptions."

"For instance?"

"To die before being painted by Sargent is to go to heaven prematurely."

"With the necessary care and impatience, you may avoid that catastrophe."

"If you're going to be rude," said Reginald, "I shall dine with you tomorrow night as well. The chief vice of the Academy," he continued, "is its nomenclature. Why, for instance, should an obvious trout-stream with a palpable rabbit sitting in the foreground be called 'an evening dream of unbeclouded peace,' or something of that sort?"

"You think," said the Other, "that a name should economize description rather than stimulate imagination?"

"Properly chosen, it should do both. There is my lady kitten at home, for instance; I've called it Derry."

"Suggests nothing to my imagination but protracted sieges and religious animosities. Of course, I don't know your kitten–"

"Oh, you're silly. It's a sweet name, and it answers to it–when it wants to. Then, if there are any unseemly noises in the night, they can be explained succinctly: Derry and Toms."

"You might almost charge for the advertisement. But as applied to pictures, don't you think your system would be too subtle, say, for the Country Cousins?"

"Every reformation must have its victims. You can't expect the fatted calf to share the enthusiasm of the angels over the prodigal's return. Another darling weakness of the Academy is that none of its luminaries must 'arrive' in a hurry. You can see them coming for years, like a Balkan trouble or a street improvement, and by the time they have painted a thousand or so square yards of canvas, their work begins to be recognized."

"Some one who Must Not be Contradicted said that a man must be a success by the time he's thirty, or never."

"To have reached thirty," said Reginald, "is to have failed in life."

REGINALD AT THE THEATRE

"AFTER all," said the Duchess vaguely, "there are certain things you can't get away from. Right and wrong, good conduct and moral rectitude, have certain well-defined limits."

"So, for the matter of that," replied Reginald, "has the Russian Empire. The trouble is that the limits are not always in the same place."

Reginald and the Duchess regarded each other with mutual distrust, tempered by a scientific interest. Reginald considered that the Duchess had much to learn; in particular, not to hurry out of the Carlton as though afraid of losing one's last 'bus. A woman, he said, who is careless of disappearances is capable of leaving town before Goodwood, and dying at the wrong moment of an unfashionable disease.

The Duchess thought that Reginald did not exceed the ethical standard which circumstances demanded.

"Of course," she resumed combatively, "it's the prevailing fashion to believe in perpetual change and mutability, and all that sort of thing, and to say we are all merely an improved form of primeval ape—of course you subscribe to that doctrine?"

"I think it decidedly premature; in most people I know the process is far from complete."

"And equally of course you are quite irreligious?"

"Oh, by no means. The fashion just now is a Roman Catholic frame of mind with an Agnostic conscience: you get the mediæval picturesqueness of the one with the modern conveniences of the other."

The Duchess suppressed a sniff. She was one of those people who regard the Church of England with patronizing affection, as if it were something that had grown up in their kitchen garden.

"But there are other things," she continued, "which I suppose are to a certain extent sacred even to you. Patriotism, for instance, and Empire, and Imperial responsibility, and blood-is-thicker-than-water, and all that sort of thing."

Reginald waited for a couple of minutes before replying, while the Lord of Rimini temporarily monopolized the acoustic possibilities of the theatre.

"That is the worst of a tragedy," he observed, "one can't always hear oneself talk. Of course I accept the Imperial idea and the responsibility. After all, I would just as soon think in Continents as anywhere else. And some day, when the season is over and we have the time, you shall explain to me the exact blood-brotherhood and all that sort of thing that exists between a French Canadian and a mild Hindoo and a Yorkshireman, for instance."

"Oh, well, 'dominion over palm and pine,' you know," quoted the Duchess hopefully; "of course we mustn't forget that we're all part of the great Anglo-Saxon Empire."

"Which for its part is rapidly becoming a suburb of Jerusalem. A very pleasant suburb, I admit, and quite a charming Jerusalem. But still a suburb."

"Really, to be told one's living in a suburb when one is conscious of spreading the benefits of civilization all over the world! Philanthropy—I suppose you will say *that* is a comfortable delusion; and yet even you must admit that whenever want or misery or starvation is known to exist, however distant or difficult of access, we instantly organize relief on the most generous scale, and distribute it, if need be, to the uttermost ends of the earth."

The Duchess paused, with a sense of ultimate triumph. She had made the same observation at a drawing-room meeting, and it had been extremely well received.

"I wonder," said Reginald, "if you have ever walked down the Embankment on a winter night?"

"Gracious, no, child! Why do you ask?"

"I didn't; I only wondered. And even your philanthropy, practised in a world where everything is based on competition, must have a debit as well as a credit account. The young ravens cry for food."

"And are fed."

"Exactly. Which presupposes that something else is fed upon."

"Oh, you're simply exasperating. You've been reading Nietzsche till you haven't got any sense of moral proportion left. May I ask if you are governed by *any* laws of conduct whatever?"

"There are certain fixed rules that one observes for one's own comfort. For instance, never be flippantly rude to any inoffensive, grey-bearded stranger that you may meet in pine forests or hotel smoking-rooms on the Continent. It always turns out to be the King of Sweden."

"The restraint must be dreadfully irksome to you. When I was younger, boys of your age used to be nice and innocent."

"Now we are only nice. One must specialize in these days. Which reminds me of the man I read of in some sacred book who was given a choice of what he most desired. And because he didn't ask for titles and honours and dignities, but only for immense wealth, these other things came to him also."

"I am sure you didn't read about him in any sacred book."

"Yes; I fancy you will find him in Debrett."

REGINALD'S PEACE POEM

"I'm writing a poem on Peace," said Reginald, emerging from a sweeping operation through a tin of mixed biscuits, in whose depths a macaroon or two might yet be lurking.

"Something of the kind seems to have been attempted already," said the Other.

"Oh, I know; but I may never have the chance again. Besides, I've got a new fountain pen. I don't pretend to have gone on any very original lines; in writing about Peace the thing is to say what everybody else is saying, only to say it better. It begins with the usual ornithological emotion:

'When the widgeon westward winging
Heard the folk Vereeniginging,
Heard the shouting and the singing–'"

"Vereeniginging is good, but why widgeon?"

"Why not? Anything that winged westward would naturally begin with a *w*."

"Need it wing westward?"

"The bird must go somewhere. You wouldn't have it hang around and look foolish. Then I've brought in something about the heedless hartebeest galloping over the deserted veldt."

"Of course you know it's practically extinct in those regions?"

"I can't help *that*, it gallops so nicely. I make it have all sorts of unexpected yearnings:

'Mother, may I go and maffick,
Tear around and hinder traffic?'

Of course you'll say there would be no traffic worth bothering about on the bare and sun-scorched veldt, but there's no other word that rhymes with maffick."

"Seraphic?"

Reginald considered. "It might do, but I've got a lot about angels later on. You must have angels in a Peace poem; I know dreadfully little about their habits."

"They can do unexpected things, like the hartebeest."

"Of course. Then I turn on London, the City of Dreadful Nocturnes, resonant with hymns of joy and thanksgiving:

'And the sleeper, eye unlidding,
Heard a voice for ever bidding
Much farewell to Dolly Gray;
Turning weary on his truckle-
Bed he heard the honey-suckle
Lauded in apiarian lay.'

Longfellow at his best wrote nothing like that."

"I agree with you."

"I wish you wouldn't. I've a sweet temper, but I can't stand being agreed with. And I'm so worried about the aasvogel."

Reginald stared dismally at the biscuit-tin, which now presented an unattractive array of rejected cracknels.

"I believe," he murmured, "if I could find a woman with an unsatisfied craving for cracknels, I should marry her."

"What is the tragedy of the aasvogel?" asked the Other sympathetically.

"Oh, simply that there's no rhyme for it. I thought about it all the time I was dressing—it's dreadfully bad for one to think whilst one's dressing—and all lunch-time, and I'm still hung up over it. I feel like those unfortunate automobilists who achieve an unenviable notoriety by coming to a hopeless stop with their cars in the most crowded thoroughfares. I'm afraid I shall have to drop the aasvogel, and it did give such lovely local colour to the thing."

"Still you've got the heedless hartebeest."

"And quite a decorative bit of moral admonition—when you've worried the meaning out—

'Cease, War, thy bubbling madness that the wine shares,
And bid thy legions turn their swords to mine shares.'

Mine shares seems to fit the case better than ploughshares. There's lots more about the blessings of Peace, shall I go on reading it?"

"If I must make a choice, I think I would rather they went on with the war."

REGINALD'S CHOIR TREAT

"NEVER," wrote Reginald to his most darling friend, "be a pioneer. It's the Early Christian that gets the fattest lion."

Reginald, in his way, was a pioneer.

None of the rest of his family had anything approaching Titian hair or a sense of humour, and they used primroses as a table decoration.

It follows that they never understood Reginald, who came down late to breakfast, and nibbled toast, and said disrespectful things about the universe. The family ate porridge, and believed in everything, even the weather forecast.

Therefore the family was relieved when the vicar's daughter undertook the reformation of Reginald. Her name was Amabel; it was the vicar's one extravagance. Amabel was accounted a beauty and intellectually gifted; she never played tennis, and was reputed to have read Maeterlinck's *Life of the Bee*. If you abstain from tennis *and* read Maeterlinck in a small country village, you are of necessity intellectual. Also she had been twice to Fécamp to pick up a good French accent from the Americans staying there; consequently she had a knowledge of the world which might be considered useful in dealings with a worldling.

Hence the congratulations in the family when Amabel undertook the reformation of its wayward member.

Amabel commenced operations by asking her unsuspecting pupil to tea in the vicarage garden; she believed in the healthy influence of natural surroundings, never having been in Sicily, where things are different.

And like every woman who has ever preached repentance to unregenerate youth, she dwelt on the sin of an empty life, which always seems so much more scandalous in the country, where people rise early to see if a new strawberry has happened during the night.

Reginald recalled the lilies of the field, "which simply sat and looked beautiful, and defied competition."

"But that is not an example for us to follow," gasped Amabel.

"Unfortunately, we can't afford to. You don't know what a world of trouble I take in trying to rival the lilies in their artistic simplicity."

"You are really indecently vain of your appearance. A good life is infinitely preferable to good looks."

"You agree with me that the two are incompatible. I always say beauty is only sin deep."

Amabel began to realize that the battle is not always to the strong-minded. With the immemorial resource of her sex, she abandoned the frontal attack and laid stress on her unassisted labours in parish work, her mental loneliness, her discouragements—and at the right moment she produced strawberries and cream. Reginald was obviously affected by the latter, and when his preceptress suggested that he might begin the strenuous life by helping her to supervise the annual outing of the bucolic infants who composed the local choir, his eyes shone with the dangerous enthusiasm of a convert.

Reginald entered on the strenuous life alone, as far as Amabel was concerned. The most virtuous women are not proof against damp grass, and Amabel kept her bed with a cold. Reginald called it a dispensation; it had been the dream of his life to stage-manage a choir outing. With strategic insight, he led his shy, bullet-headed charges to the nearest woodland stream and allowed them to bathe; then he seated himself on their discarded garments and discoursed on their immediate future, which, he decreed, was to embrace a Bacchanalian procession through the village. Forethought had provided the occasion with a supply of tin whistles, but the introduction of a he-goat from a neighbouring orchard was a brilliant afterthought. Properly, Reginald explained, there should have been an outfit of panther skins; as it was, those who had spotted handkerchiefs were allowed to wear them, which they did with thankfulness. Reginald recognized the impossibility, in the time at his disposal, of teaching his shivering neophytes a chant in honour of Bacchus, so he started them off with a more familiar, if less appropriate, temperance hymn. After all, he said, it is the spirit of the thing that counts. Following the etiquette of dramatic authors on first nights, he remained discreetly in the background while the procession, with extreme diffidence and the goat, wound its way lugubriously towards the village. The singing had died down long before the main street was reached, but the miserable wailing of pipes brought the inhabitants to their doors. Reginald said he had seen something like it in pictures; the villagers had seen nothing like it in their lives, and remarked as much freely.

Reginald's family never forgave him. They had no sense of humour.

REGINALD ON WORRIES

I HAVE (said Reginald) an aunt who worries. She's not really an aunt—a sort of amateur one, and they aren't really worries. She is a social success, and has no domestic tragedies worth speaking of, so she adopts any decorative sorrows that are going, myself included. In that way she's the antithesis, or whatever you call it, to those sweet, uncomplaining women one knows who have seen trouble, and worn blinkers ever since. Of course, one just loves them for it, but I must confess they make me uncomfy; they remind one so of a duck that goes flapping about with forced cheerfulness long after its head's been cut off. Ducks have *no* repose. Now, my aunt has a shade of hair that suits her, and a cook who quarrels with the other servants, which is always a hopeful sign, and a conscience that's absentee for about eleven months of the year, and only turns up at Lent to annoy her husband's people, who are considerably Lower than the angels, so to speak: with all these natural advantages—she says her particular tint of bronze is a natural advantage, and there can be no two opinions as to the advantage—of course she has to send out for her afflictions, like those restaurants where they haven't got a licence. The system has this advantage, that you can fit your unhappinesses in with your other engagements, whereas real worries have a way of arriving at meal-times, and when you're dressing, or other solemn moments. I knew a canary once that had been trying for months and years to hatch out a family, and every one looked upon it as a blameless infatuation, like the sale of Delagoa Bay, which would be an annual loss to the Press agencies if it ever came to pass; and one day the bird really did bring it off, in the middle of family prayers. I say the middle, but it was also the end: you can't go on being thankful for daily bread when you are wondering what on earth very new canaries expect to be fed on.

At present she's rather in a Balkan state of mind about the treatment of the Jews in Roumania. Personally, I think the Jews have estimable qualities; they're so kind to their poor—and to our rich. I daresay in Roumania the cost of living beyond one's income isn't so great. Over here the trouble is that so many people who have money to throw about seem to have such vague ideas where to throw it. That fund, for instance, to relieve the victims of sudden disasters—what is a sudden disaster? There's Marion Mulciber, who *would* think she could play bridge, just as she would think she could ride down a hill on a bicycle; on that occasion she went to a hospital, now she's gone into a Sisterhood—lost all she had, you know, and gave the rest to Heaven. Still, you can't call it a sudden calamity; *that* occurred when poor dear Marion was born. The doctors said at the time that she couldn't live more than a fortnight, and she's been trying ever since to see if she could. Women are so opinionated.

And then there's the Education Question—not that I can see that there's anything to worry about in that direction. To my mind, education is an absurdly overrated affair. At least, one never took it very seriously at school, where everything was done to bring it prominently under one's notice. Anything that is worth knowing one practically teaches oneself, and the rest obtrudes itself sooner or later. The reason one's elders know so comparatively little is because they have to unlearn so much that they acquired by way of education before we were born. Of course I'm a believer in Nature-study; as I said to Lady Beauwhistle, if you want a lesson in elaborate artificiality, just watch the studied unconcern of a Persian cat entering a crowded salon, and then go and practise it for a fortnight. The Beauwhistles weren't born in the Purple, you know, but they're getting there on the instalment system—so much down, and the rest when you feel like it. They have kind hearts, and they never forget birthdays. I forget what he was, something in the City, where the patriotism comes from; and she—oh, well, her frocks are built in Paris, but she wears them with a strong English accent. So public-spirited of her. I think she must have been very strictly brought up, she's so desperately anxious to do the wrong thing correctly. Not that it really matters nowadays, as I told her: I know some perfectly virtuous people who are received everywhere.

REGINALD ON HOUSE-PARTIES

The drawback is, one never really *knows* one's hosts and hostesses. One gets to know their fox-terriers and their chrysanthemums, and whether the story about the go-cart can be turned loose in the drawing-room, or must be told privately to each member of the party, for fear of shocking public opinion; but one's host and hostess are a sort of human hinterland that one never has the time to explore.

There was a fellow I stayed with once in Warwickshire who farmed his own land, but was otherwise quite steady. Should never have suspected him of having a soul, yet not very long afterwards he eloped with a lion-tamer's widow and set up as a golf-instructor somewhere on the Persian Gulf; dreadfully immoral, of course, because he was only an indifferent player, but still, it showed imagination. His wife was really to be pitied, because he had been the only person in the house who understood how to manage the cook's temper, and now she has to put "D.V." on her dinner invitations. Still, that's better than a domestic scandal; a woman who leaves her cook never wholly recovers her position in Society.

I suppose the same thing holds good with the hosts; they seldom have more than a superficial acquaintance with their guests, and so often just when they do get to know you a bit better, they leave off knowing you altogether. There was *rather* a breath of winter in the air when I left those Dorsetshire people. You see, they had asked me down to shoot, and I'm not particularly immense at that sort of thing. There's such a deadly sameness about partridges; when you've missed one, you've missed the lot—at least, that's been my experience. And they tried to rag me in the smoking-room about not being able to hit a bird at five yards, a sort of bovine ragging that suggested cows buzzing round a gadfly and thinking they were teasing it. So I got up the next morning at early dawn—I know it was dawn, because there were lark-noises in the sky, and the grass looked as if it had been left out all night—and hunted up the most conspicuous thing in the bird line that I could find, and measured the distance, as nearly as it would let me, and shot away all I knew. They said afterwards that it was a tame bird; that's simply *silly*, because it was awfully wild at the first few shots. Afterwards it quieted down a bit, and when its legs had stopped waving farewells to the landscape I got a gardener-boy to drag it into the hall, where everybody must see it on their way to the breakfast-room. I breakfasted upstairs myself. I gathered afterwards that the meal was tinged with a very unchristian spirit. I suppose it's unlucky to bring peacock's feathers into a house; anyway, there was a blue-pencilly look in my hostess's eye when I took my departure.

Some hostesses, of course, will forgive anything, even unto pavonicide (is there such a word?), as long as one is nice-looking and sufficiently unusual to counterbalance some of the others; and there *are* others—the girl, for instance, who reads Meredith, and appears at meals with unnatural punctuality in a frock that's made at home and repented at leisure. She eventually finds her way to India and gets married, and comes home to admire the Royal

Academy, and to imagine that an indifferent prawn curry is for ever an effective substitute for all that we have been taught to believe is luncheon. It's then that she is really dangerous; but at her worst she is never quite so bad as the woman who fires *Exchange and Mart* questions at you without the least provocation. Imagine the other day, just when I was doing my best to understand half the things I was saying, being asked by one of those seekers after country home truths how many fowls she could keep in a run ten feet by six, or whatever it was! I told her whole crowds, as long as she kept the door shut, and the idea didn't seem to have struck her before; at least, she brooded over it for the rest of dinner.

Of course, as I say, one never really *knows* one's ground, and one may make mistakes occasionally. But then one's mistakes sometimes turn out assets in the long-run: if we had never bungled away our American colonies we might never have had the boy from the States to teach us how to wear our hair and cut our clothes, and we must get our ideas from somewhere, I suppose. Even the Hooligan was probably invented in China centuries before we thought of him. England must wake up, as the Duke of Devonshire said the other day, wasn't it? Oh, well, it was some one else. Not that I ever indulge in despair about the Future; there always have been men who have gone about despairing of the Future, and when the Future arrives it says nice, superior things about their having acted according to their lights. It is dreadful to think that other people's grandchildren may one day rise up and call one amiable.

There are moments when one sympathizes with Herod.

REGINALD AT THE CARLTON

"A MOST variable climate," said the Duchess; "and how unfortunate that we should have had that very cold weather at a time when coal was so dear! So distressing for the poor."

"Some one has observed that Providence is always on the side of the big dividends," remarked Reginald.

The Duchess ate an anchovy in a shocked manner; she was sufficiently old-fashioned to dislike irreverence towards dividends.

Reginald had left the selection of a feeding-ground to her womanly intuition, but he chose the wine himself, knowing that womanly intuition stops short at claret. A woman will cheerfully choose husbands for her less attractive friends, or take sides in a political controversy without the least knowledge of the issues involved—but no woman ever cheerfully chose a claret.

"Hors d'œuvres have always a pathetic interest for me," said Reginald: "they remind me of one's childhood that one goes through, wondering what the next course is going to be like—and during the rest of the menu one wishes one had eaten more of the hors d'œuvres. Don't you love watching the different ways people have of entering a restaurant? There is the woman who races in as though her whole scheme of life were held together by a one-pin despotism which might abdicate its functions at any moment; it's really a relief to see her reach her chair in safety. Then there are the people who troop in with an-unpleasant-duty-to-perform air, as if they were angels of Death entering a plague city. You see that type of Briton very much in hotels abroad. And nowadays there are always the Johannes-bourgeois, who bring a Cape-to-Cairo atmosphere with them—what may be called the Rand Manner, I suppose."

"Talking about hotels abroad," said the Duchess, "I am preparing notes for a lecture at the Club on the educational effects of modern travel, dealing chiefly with the moral side of the question. I was talking to Lady Beauwhistle's aunt the other day—she's just come back from Paris, you know. Such a sweet woman—"

"And so silly. In these days of the overeducation of women she's quite refreshing. They say some people went through the siege of Paris without knowing that France and Germany were at war; but the Beauwhistle aunt is credited with having passed the whole winter in Paris under the impression that the Humberts were a kind of bicycle. . . . Isn't there a bishop or somebody who believes we shall meet all the animals we have known on earth in another world? How frightfully embarrassing to meet a whole shoal of whitebait you had last known at Prince's! I'm sure in my nervousness I should talk of nothing but lemons. Still, I daresay they would be quite as offended if one hadn't eaten them. I know if I were served up at a cannibal feast I should be dreadfully annoyed if any one found fault with me for not being tender enough, or having been kept too long."

"My idea about the lecture," resumed the Duchess hurriedly,

"is to inquire whether promiscuous Continental travel doesn't tend to weaken the moral fibre of the social conscience. There are people one knows, quite nice people when they are in England, who are so *different* when they are anywhere the other side of the Channel."

"The people with what I call Tauchnitz morals," observed Reginald. "On the whole, I think they get the best of two very desirable worlds. And, after all, they charge so much for excess luggage on some of those foreign lines that it's really an economy to leave one's reputation behind one occasionally."

"A scandal, my dear Reginald, is as much to be avoided at Monaco or any of those places as at Exeter, let us say."

"Scandal, my dear Irene–I may call you Irene, mayn't I?"

"I don't know that you have known me long enough for that."

"I've known you longer than your god-parents had when they took the liberty of calling you that name. Scandal is merely the compassionate allowance which the gay make to the humdrum. Think how many blameless lives are brightened by the blazing indiscretions of other people. Tell me, who is the woman with the old lace at the table on our left? Oh, *that* doesn't matter; it's quite the thing nowadays to stare at people as if they were yearlings at Tattersall's."

"Mrs. Spelvexit? Quite a charming woman; separated from her husband–"

"Incompatibility of income?"

"Oh, nothing of that sort. By miles of frozen ocean, I was going to say. He explores ice-floes and studies the movements of herrings, and has written a most interesting book on the home-life of the Esquimaux; but naturally he has very little home-life of his own."

"A husband who comes home with the Gulf Stream *would* be rather a tied-up asset."

"His wife is exceedingly sensible about it. She collects postage-stamps. Such a resource. Those people with her are the Whimples, very old acquaintances of mine; they're always having trouble, poor things."

"Trouble is not one of those fancies you can take up and drop at any moment; it's like a grouse-moor or the opium-habit–once you start it you've got to keep it up."

"Their eldest son was such a disappointment to them; they wanted him to be a linguist, and spent no end of money on having him taught to speak—oh, dozens of languages!—and then he became a Trappist monk. And the youngest, who was intended for the American marriage market, has developed political tendencies, and writes pamphlets about the housing of the poor. Of course it's a most important question, and I devote a good deal of time to it myself in the mornings; but, as Laura Whimple says, it's as well to have an establishment of one's own before agitating about other people's. She feels it very keenly, but she always maintains a cheerful appetite, which I think is so unselfish of her."

"There are different ways of taking disappointment. There was a girl I knew who nursed a wealthy uncle through a long illness, borne by her with Christian fortitude, and then he died and left his money to a swine-fever hospital. She found she'd about cleared stock in fortitude by that time, and now she gives drawing-room recitations. That's what I call being vindictive."

"Life is full of its disappointments," observed the Duchess, "and I suppose the art of being happy is to disguise them as illusions. But that, my dear Reginald, becomes more difficult as one grows older."

"I think it's more generally practised than you imagine. The young have aspirations that never come to pass, the old have reminiscences of what never happened. It's only the middle-aged who are really conscious of their limitations—that is why one should be so patient with them. But one never is."

"After all," said the Duchess, "the disillusions of life may depend on our way of assessing it. In the minds of those who come after us we may be remembered for qualities and successes which we quite left out of the reckoning."

"It's not always safe to depend on the commemorative tendencies of those who come after us. There may have been disillusionments in the lives of the mediæval saints, but they would scarcely have been better pleased if they could have foreseen that their names would be associated nowadays chiefly with race-horses and the cheaper clarets. And now, if you can tear yourself away from the salted almonds, we'll go and have coffee under the palms that are so necessary for our discomfort."

REGINALD ON BESETTING SINS

THE WOMAN WHO TOLD THE TRUTH

There was once (said Reginald) a woman who told the truth. Not all at once, of course, but the habit grew upon her gradually, like lichen on an apparently healthy tree. She had no children—otherwise it might have been different. It began with little things, for no particular reason except that her life was a rather empty one, and it is so easy to slip into the habit of telling the truth in little matters. And then it became difficult to draw the line at more important things, until at last she took to telling the truth about her age; she said she was forty-two and five months—by that time, you see, she was veracious even to months. It may have been pleasing to the angels, but her elder sister was not gratified. On the Woman's birthday, instead of the opera-tickets which she had hoped for, her sister gave her a view of Jerusalem from the Mount of Olives, which is not quite the same thing. The revenge of an elder sister may be long in coming, but, like a South-Eastern express, it arrives in its own good time.

The friends of the Woman tried to dissuade her from over-indulgence in the practice, but she said she was wedded to the truth; whereupon it was remarked that it was scarcely logical to be so much together in public. (No really provident woman lunches regularly with her husband if she wishes to burst upon him as a revelation at dinner. He must have time to forget; an afternoon is not enough.) And after a while her friends began to thin out in patches. Her passion for the truth was not compatible with a large visiting-list. For instance, she told Miriam Klopstock *exactly* how she looked at the Ilexes' ball. Certainly Miriam had asked for her candid opinion, but the Woman prayed in church every Sunday for peace in our time, and it was not consistent.

It was unfortunate, every one agreed, that she had no family; with a child or two in the house, there is an unconscious check upon too free an indulgence in the truth. Children are given us to discourage our better emotions. That is why the stage, with all its efforts, can never be as artificial as life; even in an Ibsen drama one must reveal to the audience things that one would suppress before the children or servants.

Fate may have ordained the truth-telling from the commencement and should justly bear some of the blame; but in having no children the Woman was guilty, at least, of contributory negligence.

Little by little she felt she was becoming a slave to what had once been merely an idle propensity; and one day she knew. Every woman tells ninety per cent. of the truth to her dressmaker; the other ten per cent is the irreducible minimum of deception beyond which no self-respecting client trespasses. Madame Draga's establishment was a meeting-ground for naked truths and overdressed fictions, and it was here, the Woman felt, that she might make a final effort to recall the artless mendacity of past days. Madame herself was in an inspiring mood, with the air of a sphinx who knew all things and preferred to forget most of them. As a War Minister she might have been celebrated, but she was content to be merely rich.

"If I take it in here, and–Miss Howard, one moment, if you please–and there, and round like this–so–I really think you will find it quite easy."

The Woman hesitated; it seemed to require such a small effort to simply acquiesce in Madame's views. But habit had become too strong. "I'm afraid," she faltered, "it's just the least little bit in the world too–"

And by that least little bit she measured the deeps and eternities of her thraldom to fact. Madame was not best pleased at being contradicted on a professional matter, and when Madame lost her temper you usually found it afterwards in the bill.

And at last the dreadful thing came, as the Woman had foreseen all along that it must; it was one of those paltry little truths with which she harried her waking hours. On a raw Wednesday morning, in a few ill-chosen words, she told the cook that she drank. She remembered the scene afterwards as vividly as though it had been painted in her mind by Abbey. The cook was a good cook, as cooks go; and as cooks go she went.

Miriam Klopstock came to lunch the next day. Women and elephants never forget an injury.

REGINALD'S DRAMA

REGINALD closed his eyes with the elaborate weariness of one who has rather nice eyelashes and thinks it useless to conceal the fact.

"One of these days," he said, "I shall write a really great drama. No one will understand the drift of it, but every one will go back to their homes with a vague feeling of dissatisfaction with their lives and surroundings. Then they will put up new wall-papers and forget."

"But how about those that have oak panelling all over the house?" said the Other.

"They can always put down new stair-carpets," pursued Reginald, "and, anyhow, I'm not responsible for the audience having a happy ending. The play would be quite sufficient strain on one's energies. I should get a bishop to say it was immoral and beautiful—no dramatist has thought of that before, and every one would come to condemn the bishop, and they would stay on out of sheer nervousness. After all, it requires a great deal of moral courage to leave in a marked manner in the middle of the second act, when your carriage isn't ordered till twelve. And it would commence with wolves worrying something on a lonely waste—you wouldn't see them, of course; but you would hear them snarling and scrunching, and I should arrange to have a wolfy fragrance suggested across the footlights. It would look so well on the programmes, 'Wolves in the first act, by Jamrach.' And old Lady Whortleberry, who never misses a first night, would scream. She's always been nervous since she lost her first husband. He died quite abruptly while watching a county cricket match; two and a half inches of rain had fallen for seven runs, and it was supposed that the excitement killed him. Anyhow, it gave her quite a shock; it was the first husband she'd lost, you know, and now she always screams if anything thrilling happens too soon after dinner. And after the audience had heard the Whortleberry scream the thing would be fairly launched."

"And the plot?"

"The plot," said Reginald, "would be one of those little everyday tragedies that one sees going on all round one. In my mind's eye there is the case of the Mudge-Jervises, which in an unpretentious way has quite an Enoch Arden intensity underlying it. They'd only been married some eighteen months or so, and circumstances had prevented their seeing much of each other. With him there was always a foursome or something that had to be played and replayed in different parts of the country, and she went in for slumming quite as seriously as if it was a sport. With her, I suppose, it was. She belonged to the Guild of the Poor Dear Souls, and they hold the record for having nearly reformed a washerwoman. No one has ever really reformed a washerwoman, and that is why the competition is so keen. You can rescue charwomen by fifties with a little tea and personal magnetism, but with washerwomen it's different; wages are too high. This particular laundress, who came from Bermondsey or some such place, was really rather a hopeful venture, and they thought at last that she might be safely put in the window as a specimen of successful work. So they had her paraded at a drawing-room "At Home" at Agatha Camelford's; it was sheer bad luck that some liqueur chocolates had been turned loose by mistake among the refreshments—really liqueur chocolates, with very little chocolate. And of course the old soul found them out, and cornered the entire stock. It was like finding a whelk-stall in a desert, as she afterwards partially expressed herself. When the liqueurs began to take effect, she started to give them imitations of farmyard animals as they know them in Bermondsey. She began with a dancing bear, and you know Agatha doesn't approve of dancing, except at Buckingham Palace under proper supervision. And then she got up on the piano and gave them an organ monkey; I gather she went in for realism rather than a Maeterlinckian treatment of the subject. Finally, she fell into the piano and said she was a parrot in a cage, and for an impromptu performance I believe she was very word-perfect; no one had heard anything like it, except Baroness Boobelstein who has attended sittings of the Austrian Reichsrath. Agatha is trying the Rest-cure at Buxton."

"But the tragedy?"

"Oh, the Mudge-Jervises. Well, they were getting along quite happily, and their married life was one continuous exchange of picture-postcards; and then one day they were thrown together on some neutral ground where foursomes and washerwomen overlapped, and discovered that they were hopelessly divided on the Fiscal Question. They have thought it best to separate, and she is to have the custody of the Persian kittens for nine months in the year—they go back to him for the winter, when she is abroad. There you have the material for a tragedy drawn straight from life—and the piece could be called 'The Price They Paid for Empire.' And of course one would have to work in studies of the struggle of hereditary tendency against environment and all that sort of thing. The woman's father could have been an Envoy to some of the smaller German Courts; that's where she'd get her passion for visiting the poor, in spite of the most careful upbringing. *C'est le premier pa qui compte,* as the cuckoo said when it swallowed its foster-parent. That, I think, is quite clever."

"And the wolves?"

"Oh, the wolves would be a sort of elusive undercurrent in the background that would never be satisfactorily explained. After all, life teems with things that have no earthly reason. And whenever the characters could think of nothing brilliant to say about marriage or the War Office, they could open a window and listen to the howling of the wolves. But that would be very seldom."

REGINALD ON TARIFFS

I'M not going to discuss the Fiscal Question (said Reginald); I wish to be original. At the same time, I think one suffers more than one realizes from the system of free imports. I should like, for instance, a really prohibitive duty put upon the partner who declares on a weak red suit and hopes for the best. Even a free outlet for compressed verbiage doesn't balance matters. And I think there should be a sort of bounty-fed export (is that the right expression?) of the people who impress on you that you ought to take life seriously. There are only two classes that really can't help taking life seriously—schoolgirls of thirteen and Hohenzollerns; they might be exempt. Albanians come under another heading; they take life whenever they get the opportunity. The one Albanian that I was ever on speaking terms with was rather a decadent example. He was a Christian and a grocer, and I don't fancy he had ever killed anybody. I didn't like to question him on the subject—that showed my delicacy. Mrs. Nicorax says I have no delicacy; she hasn't forgiven me about the mice. You see, when I was staying down there, a mouse used to cake-walk about my room half the night, and none of their silly patent traps seemed to take its fancy as a bijou residence, so I determined to appeal to the better side of it–which with mice is the inside. So I called it Percy, and put little delicacies down near its hole every night, and that kept it quiet while I read Max Nordau's *Degeneration* and other reproving literature, and went to sleep. And now she says there is a whole colony of mice in that room.

That isn't where the indelicacy comes in. She went out riding with me, which was entirely her own suggestion, and as we were coming home through some meadows she made a quite unnecessary attempt to see if her pony would jump a rather messy sort of brook that was there. It wouldn't. It went with her as far as the water's edge, and from that point Mrs. Nicorax went on alone. Of course I had to fish her out from the bank, and my riding-breeches are not cut with a view to salmon-fishing–it's rather an art even to ride in them. Her habit-skirt was one of those open questions that need not be adhered to in emergencies, and on this occasion it remained behind in some water-weeds. She wanted me to fish about for that too, but I felt I had done enough Pharaoh's daughter business for an October afternoon, and I was beginning to want my tea. So I bundled her up on to her pony, and gave her a lead towards home as fast as I cared to go. What with the wet and the unusual responsibility, her abridged costume did not stand the pace particularly well, and she got quite querulous when I shouted back that I had no pins with me–and no string. Some women expect so much from a fellow. When we got into the drive she wanted to go up the back way to the stables, but the ponies *know* they always get sugar at the front door, and I never attempt to hold a pulling pony; as for Mrs. Nicorax it took her all she knew to keep a firm hand on her seceding garments, which, as her maid remarked afterwards, were more *tout* than *ensemble*. Of course nearly the whole house-party were out on the lawn watching the sunset–the only day this month that it's occurred to the sun to show itself, as Mrs. Nic. viciously observed–and I shall never forget the expression on her husband's face as we pulled up. "My darling, this is too much!" was his first spoken comment; taking into consideration the state of her toilet, it was the most brilliant thing I had ever heard him say, and I went into the library to be alone and scream. Mrs. Nicorax says I have no delicacy.

Talking about tariffs, the lift-boy, who reads extensively between the landings, says it won't do to tax raw commodities. What, exactly, is a raw commodity? Mrs. Van Challaby says men are raw commodities till you marry them; after they've struck Mrs. Van C., I can fancy they pretty soon become a finished article. Certainly she's had a good deal of experience to support her opinion. She lost one husband in a railway accident, and mislaid another in the Divorce Court, and the current one has just got himself squeezed in a Beef Trust. "What was he doing in a Beef Trust, anyway?" she asked tearfully, and I suggested that perhaps he had an unhappy home. I only said it for the sake of making conversation; which it did. Mrs. Van Challaby said things about me which in her calmer moments she would have hesitated to spell. It's a pity people can't discuss fiscal matters without getting wild. However, she wrote next day to ask if I could get her a Yorkshire terrier of the size and shade that's being worn now, and that's as near as a woman can be expected to get to owning herself in the wrong. And she will tie a salmon-pink bow to its collar, and call it "Reggie," and take it with her everywhere—like poor Miriam Klopstock, who *would* take her Chow with her to the bathroom, and while she was bathing it was playing at she-bears with her garments. Miriam is always late for breakfast, and she wasn't really missed till the middle of lunch.

However, I'm not going any further into the Fiscal Question. Only I should like to be protected from the partner with a weak red tendency.

REGINALD'S CHRISTMAS REVEL

THEY say (said Reginald) that there's nothing sadder than victory except defeat. If you've ever stayed with dull people during what is alleged to be the festive season, you can probably revise that saying. I shall never forget putting in a Christmas at the Babwolds'. Mrs. Babwold is some relation of my father's—a sort of to-be-left-till-called-for cousin—and that was considered sufficient reason for my having to accept her invitation at about the sixth time of asking; though why the sins of the father should be visited by the children—you won't find any notepaper in that drawer; that's where I keep old menus and first-night programmes.

Mrs. Babwold wears a rather solemn personality, and has never been known to smile, even when saying disagreeable things to her friends or making out the Stores list. She takes her pleasures sadly. A state elephant at a Durbar gives one a very similar impression. Her husband gardens in all weathers. When a man goes out in the pouring rain to brush caterpillars off rose trees, I generally imagine his life indoors leaves something to be desired; anyway, it must be very unsettling for the caterpillars.

Of course there were other people there. There was a Major Somebody who had shot things in Lapland, or somewhere of that sort; I forget what they were, but it wasn't for want of reminding. We had them cold with every meal almost, and he was continually giving us details of what they measured from tip to tip, as though he thought we were going to make them warm under-things for the winter. I used to listen to him with a rapt attention that I thought rather suited me, and then one day I quite modestly gave the dimensions of an okapi I had shot in the Lincolnshire fens. The Major turned a beautiful Tyrian scarlet (I remember thinking at the time that I should like my bathroom hung in that colour), and I think that at that moment he almost found it in his heart to dislike me. Mrs. Babwold put on a first-aid-to-the-injured expression, and asked him why he didn't publish a book of his sporting reminiscences; it would be *so* interesting. She didn't remember till afterwards that he had given her two fat volumes on the subject, with his portrait and autograph as a frontispiece and an appendix on the habits of the Arctic mussel.

It was in the evening that we cast aside the cares and distractions of the day and really lived. Cards were thought to be too frivolous and empty a way of passing the time, so most of them played what they called a book game. You went out into the hall—to get an inspiration, I suppose—then you came in again with a muffler tied round your neck and looked silly, and the others were supposed to guess that you were *Wee MacGreegor*. I held out against the inanity as long as I decently could, but at last, in a lapse of good-nature, I consented to masquerade as a book, only I warned them that it would take some time to carry out. They waited for the best part of forty minutes while I went and played wineglass skittles with the page-boy in the pantry; you play it with a champagne cork, you know, and the one who knocks down the most glasses without breaking them wins. I won, with four unbroken out of seven; I think William suffered from over-anxiousness. They were rather mad in the drawing-room at my not having come back, and they weren't a bit pacified when I told them afterwards that I was *At the end of the passage*.

"I never did like Kipling," was Mrs. Babwold's comment, when the situation dawned upon her. "I couldn't see anything clever in *Earthworms out of Tuscany*—or is that by Darwin?"

Of course these games are very educational, but, personally, I prefer bridge.

On Christmas evening we were supposed to be specially festive in the Old English fashion. The hall was horribly draughty, but it seemed to be the proper place to revel in, and it was decorated with Japanese fans and Chinese lanterns, which gave it a very Old English effect. A young lady with a confidential voice favoured us with a long recitation about a little girl who died or did something equally hackneyed, and then the Major gave us a graphic account of a struggle he had with a wounded bear. I privately wished that the bears would win sometimes on these occasions; at least they wouldn't go vapouring about it afterwards. Before we had time to recover our spirits, we were indulged with some thought-reading by a young man whom one knew instinctively had a good mother and an indifferent tailor—the sort of young man who talks unflaggingly through the thickest soup, and smooths his hair dubiously as though he thought it might hit back. The thought-reading was rather a success; he announced that the hostess was thinking about poetry, and she admitted that her mind was dwelling on one of Austin's odes. Which was near enough. I fancy she had been really wondering whether a scrag-end of mutton and some cold plum-pudding would do for the kitchen dinner next day. As a crowning dissipation, they all sat down to play progressive halma, with milk-chocolate for prizes. I've been carefully brought up, and I don't like to play games of skill for milk-chocolate, so I invented a headache and retired from the scene. I had been preceded a few minutes earlier by Miss Langshan-Smith, a rather formidable lady, who always got up at some uncomfortable hour in the morning, and gave you the impression that she had been in communication with most of the European Governments before breakfast. There was a paper pinned on her door with a signed request that she might be called particularly early on the morrow. Such an opportunity does not come twice in a lifetime. I covered up everything except the signature with another notice, to the effect that before these words should meet the eye she would have ended a misspent life, was sorry for the trouble she was giving, and would like a military funeral. A few minutes later I violently exploded an air-filled paper bag on the landing, and gave a stage moan that could have been heard in the cellars. Then I pursued my original intention and went to bed. The noise those people made in forcing open the good lady's door was positively indecorous; she resisted gallantly, but I believe they searched her for bullets for about a quarter of an hour, as if she had been a historic battlefield.

I hate travelling on Boxing Day, but one must occasionally do things that one dislikes.

REGINALD'S RUBAIYAT

THE other day (confided Reginald), when I was killing time in the bathroom and making bad resolutions for the New Year, it occurred to me that I would like to be a poet. The chief qualification, I understand, is that you must be born. Well, I hunted up my birth certificate, and found that I was all right on that score, and then I got to work on a Hymn to the New Year, which struck me as having possibilities. It suggested extremely unusual things to absolutely unlikely people, which I believe is the art of first-class catering in any department. Quite the best verse in it went something like this:

"Have you heard the groan of a gravelled grouse,
Or the snarl of a snaffled snail
(Husband or mother, like me, or spouse),
Have you lain a-creep in the darkened house
Where the wounded wombats wail?"

It was quite improbable that any one had, you know, and that's where it stimulated the imagination and took people out of their narrow, humdrum selves. No one has ever called me narrow or humdrum, but even I felt worked up now and then at the thought of that house with the stricken wombats in it. It simply wasn't nice. But the editors were unanimous in leaving it alone; they said the thing had been done before and done worse, and that the market for that sort of work was extremely limited.

It was just on the top of that discouragement that the Duchess wanted me to write something in her album—something Persian, you know, and just a little bit decadent—and I thought a quatrain on an unwholesome egg would meet the requirements of the case. So I started in with:

> "Cackle, cackle, little hen,
> How I wonder if and when
> Once you laid the egg that I
> Met, alas! too late. Amen."

The Duchess objected to the Amen, which I thought gave an air of forgiveness and *chose jugée* to the whole thing; also she said it wasn't Persian enough, as though I were trying to sell her a kitten whose mother had married for love rather than pedigree. So I recast it entirely, and the new version read:

> "The hen that laid three moons ago, who knows
> In what Dead Yesterday her shades repose;
> To some election turn thy waning span
> And rain thy rottenness on fiscal foes."

I thought there was enough suggestion of decay in that to satisfy a jackal, and to me there was something infinitely pathetic and appealing in the idea of the egg having a sort of St. Luke's summer of commercial usefulness. But the Duchess begged me to leave out any political allusions; she's the president of a Women's Something or other, and she said it might be taken as an endorsement of deplorable methods. I never can remember which Party Irene discourages with her support, but I shan't forget an occasion when I was staying at her place and she gave me a pamphlet to leave at the house of a doubtful voter, and some grapes and things for a woman who was suffering from a chill on the top of a patent medicine. I thought it much cleverer to give the grapes to the former and the political literature to the sick woman, and the Duchess was quite absurdly annoyed about it afterwards. It seems the leaflet was addressed "To those about to wobble"—I wasn't responsible for the silly title of the thing—and the woman never recovered; anyway, the voter was completely won over by the grapes and jellies, and I think that should have balanced matters. The Duchess called it bribery, and said it might have compromised the candidate she was supporting; he was expected to subscribe to church funds and chapel funds, and football and cricket clubs and regattas, and bazaars and beanfeasts and bell-ringers, and poultry shows and ploughing matches, and reading-rooms and choir outings, and shooting trophies and testimonials, and anything of that sort; but bribery would not have been tolerated.

I fancy I have perhaps more talent for electioneering than for poetry, and I was really getting extended over this quatrain business. The egg began to be unmanageable, and the Duchess suggested something with a French literary ring about it. I hunted back in my mind for the most familiar French classic that I could take liberties with, and after a little exercise of memory I turned out the following:

"Hast thou the pen that once the gardener had?
I have it not; and know, these pears are bad.
Oh, larger than the horses of the Prince
Are those the general drives in Kaikobad."

Even that didn't altogether satisfy Irene; I fancy the geography of it puzzled her. She probably thought Kaikobad was an unfashionable German spa, where you'd meet matrimonial bargain-hunters and emergency Servian kings. My temper was beginning to slip its moorings by that time. I look rather nice when I lose my temper. (I hoped you would say I lose it very often. I mustn't monopolize the conversation.)

"Of course, if you want something really Persian and passionate, with red wine and bulbuls in it," I went on to suggest; but she grabbed the book from me.

"Not for worlds. Nothing with red wine or passion in it. Dear Agatha gave me the album, and she would be mortified to the quick—"

I said I didn't believe Agatha had a quick, and we got quite heated in arguing the matter. Finally, the Duchess declared I shouldn't write anything nasty in her book, and I said I shouldn't write anything in her nasty book, so there wasn't a very wide point of difference between us. For the rest of the afternoon I pretended to be sulking, but I was really working back to that quatrain, like a fox-terrier that's buried a deferred lunch in a private flower-bed. When I got an opportunity I hunted up Agatha's autograph, which had the front page all to itself, and, copying her prim handwriting as well as I could, I inserted above it the following Thibetan fragment:

"With Thee, oh, my Beloved, to do a dâk
(a dâk I believe is a sort of uncomfortable post-journey)
On the pack-saddle of a grunting yak,
With never room for chilling chaperon,
'Twere better than a Panhard in the Park."

That Agatha would get on to a yak in company with a lover even in the comparative seclusion of Thibet is unthinkable. I very much doubt if she'd do it with her own husband in the privacy of the Simplon tunnel. But poetry, as I've remarked before, should always stimulate the imagination.

By the way, when you asked me the other day to dine with you on the 14th, I said I was dining with the Duchess. Well, I'm not. I'm dining with you.

THE INNOCENCE OF REGINALD

Reginald slid a carnation of the newest shade into the buttonhole of his latest lounge coat, and surveyed the result with approval. "I am just in the mood," he observed, "to have my portrait painted by some one with an unmistakable future. So comforting to go down to posterity as 'Youth with a Pink Carnation' in catalogue-company with 'Child with Bunch of Primroses,' and all that crowd."

"Youth," said the Other, "should suggest innocence."

"But never act on the suggestion. I don't believe the two ever really go together. People talk vaguely about the innocence of a little child, but they take mighty good care not to let it out of their sight for twenty minutes. The watched pot never boils over. I knew a boy once who really was innocent; his parents were in Society, but they never gave him a moment's anxiety from his infancy. He believed in company prospectuses, and in the purity of elections, and in women marrying for love, and even in a system for winning at roulette. He never quite lost his faith in it, but he dropped more money than his employers could afford to lose. When last I heard of him, he was believing in his innocence; the jury weren't. All the same, I really am innocent just now of something every one accuses me of having done, and so far as I can see, their accusations will remain unfounded."

"Rather an unexpected attitude for you."

"I love people who do unexpected things. Didn't you always adore the man who slew a lion in a pit on a snowy day? But about this unfortunate innocence. Well, quite long ago, when I'd been quarrelling with more people than usual, you among the number—it must have been in November, I never quarrel with you too near Christmas—I had an idea that I'd like to write a book. It was to be a book of personal reminiscences, and was to leave out nothing."

"Reginald!"

"Exactly what the Duchess said when I mentioned it to her. I was provoking and said nothing, and the next thing, of course, was that every one heard that I'd written the book and got it in the press. After that, I might have been a goldfish in a glass bowl for all the privacy I got. People attacked me about it in the most unexpected places, and implored or commanded me to leave out things that I'd forgotten had ever happened. I sat behind Miriam Klopstock one night in the dress-circle at His Majesty's, and she began at once about the incident of the Chow dog in the bathroom, which she insisted must be struck out. We had to argue it in a disjointed fashion, because some of the people wanted to listen to the play, and Miriam takes nines in voices. They had to stop her playing in the 'Macaws' Hockey Club because you could hear what she thought when her shins got mixed up in a scrimmage for half a mile on a still day. They are called the Macaws because of their blue-and-yellow costumes, but I understand there was nothing yellow about Miriam's language. I agreed to make one alteration, as I pretended I had got it a Spitz instead of a Chow, but beyond that I was firm. She megaphoned back two minutes later, 'You promised you would never mention it; don't you ever keep a promise?' When people had stopped glaring in our direction, I replied that I'd as soon think of keeping white mice. I saw her tearing little bits out of her programme for a minute or two, and then she leaned back and snorted, 'You're not the boy I took you for,' as though she were an eagle arriving at Olympus with the wrong Ganymede. That was her last audible remark, but she went on tearing up her programme and scattering the pieces around her, till one of her neighbours asked with immense dignity whether she should send for a wastepaper-basket. I didn't stay for the last act.

"Then there is Mrs.—oh, I never can remember her name; she lives in a street that the cabmen have never heard of, and is at home on Wednesdays. She frightened me horribly once at a private view by saying mysteriously, 'I oughtn't to be here, you know; this is one of my days.' I thought she meant that she was subject to periodical outbreaks and was expecting an attack at any moment. So embarrassing if she had suddenly taken it into her head that she was Cesare Borgia or St. Elizabeth of Hungary. That sort of thing would make one unpleasantly conspicuous even at a private view. However, she merely meant to say that it was Wednesday, which at the moment was incontrovertible. Well, she's on quite a different tack to the Klopstock. She doesn't visit anywhere very extensively, and, of course, she's awfully keen for me to drag in an incident that occurred at one of the Beauwhistle garden-parties, when she says she accidentally hit the shins of a Serene Somebody or other with a croquet mallet and that he swore at her in German. As a matter of fact, he went on discoursing on the Gordon-Bennett affair in French. (I never can remember if it's a new submarine or a divorce. Of course, how stupid of me!) To be disagreeably exact, I fancy she missed him by about two inches—over-anxiousness, probably—but she likes to think she hit him. I've felt that way with a partridge which I always imagine keeps on flying strong, out of false pride, till it's the other side of the hedge. She said she could tell me everything she was wearing on the occasion. I said I didn't want my book to read like a laundry list, but she explained that she didn't mean those sort of things.

"And there's the Chilworth boy, who can be charming as long as he's content to be stupid and wear what he's told to; but he gets the idea now and then that he'd like to be epigrammatic, and the result is like watching a rook trying to build a nest in a gale. Since he got wind of the book, he's been persecuting me to work in something of his about the Russians and the Yalu Peril, and is quite sulky because I won't do it.

"Altogether, I think it would be rather a brilliant inspiration if you were to suggest a fortnight in Paris."

Reginald in Russia

First Collected, 1910

REGINALD IN RUSSIA

REGINALD sat in a corner of the Princess's salon and tried to forgive the furniture, which started out with an obvious intention of being Louis Quinze, but relapsed at frequent intervals into Wilhelm II.

He classified the Princess with that distinct type of woman that looks as if it habitually went out to feed hens in the rain.

Her name was Olga; she kept what she hoped and believed to be a fox-terrier, and professed what she thought were Socialist opinions. It is not necessary to be called Olga if you are a Russian Princess; in fact, Reginald knew quite a number who were called Vera; but the fox-terrier and the Socialism are essential.

"The Countess Lomshen keeps a bull-dog," said the Princess suddenly. "In England is it more chic to have a bull-dog than a fox-terrier?"

Reginald threw his mind back over the canine fashions of the last ten years and gave an evasive answer.

"Do you think her handsome, the Countess Lomshen?" asked the Princess.

Reginald thought the Countess's complexion suggested an exclusive diet of macaroons and pale sherry. He said so.

"But that cannot be possible," said the Princess triumphantly; "I've seen her eating fish-soup at Donon's."

The Princess always defended a friend's complexion if it was really bad. With her, as with a great many of her sex, charity began at homeliness and did not generally progress much farther.

Reginald withdrew his macaroon and sherry theory, and became interested in a case of miniatures.

"That?" said the Princess; "that is the old Princess Lorikoff. She lived in Millionaya Street, near the Winter Palace, and was one of the Court ladies of the Old Russian school. Her knowledge of people and events was extremely limited; but she used to patronize every one who came in contact with her. There was a story that when she died and left the Millionaya for Heaven she addressed St. Peter in her formal staccato French: 'Je suis la Princesse Lor-i-koff. Il me donne grand plaisir à faire votre connaissance. Je vous en prie me présenter au Bon Dieu.' St. Peter made the desired introduction, and the Princess addressed le Bon Dieu: 'Je suis la Princesse Lor-i-koff. Il me donne grand plaisir à faire votre connaissance. On a souvent parlé de vous à l'église de la rue Million.'"

"Only the old and the clergy of Established churches know how to be flippant gracefully," commented Reginald; "which reminds me that in the Anglican Church in a certain foreign capital, which shall be nameless, I was present the other day when one of the junior chaplains was preaching in aid of distressed somethings or other, and he brought a really eloquent passage to a close with the remark, 'The tears of the afflicted, to what shall I liken them—to diamonds?' The other junior chaplain, who had been dozing out of professional jealousy, awoke with a start and asked hurriedly, 'Shall I play to diamonds, partner?' It didn't improve matters when the senior chaplain remarked dreamily but with painful distinctness, 'Double diamonds.' Every one looked at the preacher, half expecting him to redouble, but he contented himself with scoring what points he could under the circumstances."

"You English are always so frivolous," said the Princess. "In Russia we have too many troubles to permit of our being light-hearted."

Reginald gave a delicate shiver, such as an Italian greyhound might give in contemplating the approach of an ice age of which he personally disapproved, and resigned himself to the inevitable political discussion.

"Nothing that you hear about us in England is true," was the Princess's hopeful beginning.

"I always refused to learn Russian geography at school," observed Reginald; "I was certain some of the names must be wrong."

"Everything is wrong with our system of government," continued the Princess placidly. "The Bureaucrats think only of their pockets, and the people are exploited and plundered in every direction, and everything is mismanaged."

"With us," said Reginald, "a Cabinet usually gets the credit of being depraved and worthless beyond the bounds of human conception by the time it has been in office about four years."

"But if it is a bad Government you can turn it out at the election," argued the Princess.

"As far as I remember, we generally do," said Reginald.

"But here it is dreadful, every one goes to such extremes. In England you never go to extremes."

"We go to the Albert Hall," explained Reginald.

"There is always a see-saw with us between repression and violence," continued the Princess; "and the pity of it is the people are really not in the least inclined to be anything but peaceable. Nowhere will you find people more good-natured, or family circles where there is more affection."

"There I agree with you," said Reginald. "I know a boy who lives somewhere on the French Quay who is a case in point. His hair curls naturally, especially on Sundays, and he plays bridge well, even for a Russian, which is saying much. I don't think he has any other accomplishments, but his family affection is really of a very high order. When his maternal grandmother died he didn't go as far as to give up bridge altogether but he declared on nothing but black suits for the next three months. That, I think, was really beautiful."

The Princess was not impressed.

"I think you must be very self-indulgent and live only for amusement," she said. "A life of pleasure-seeking and card-playing and dissipation brings only dissatisfaction. You will find that out some day."

"Oh, I know it turns out that way sometimes," assented Reginald. "Forbidden fizz is often the sweetest."

But the remark was wasted on the Princess, who preferred champagne that had at least a suggestion of dissolved barley-sugar.

"I hope you will come and see me again," she said in a tone that prevented the hope from becoming too infectious; adding as a happy after-thought, "you must come to stay with us in the country."

Her particular part of the country was a few hundred versts the other side of Tamboff, with some fifteen miles of agrarian disturbance between her and the nearest neighbour. Reginald felt that there is some privacy which should be sacred from intrusion.

THE RETICENCE OF LADY ANNE

Egbert came into the large, dimly lit drawing-room with the air of a man who is not certain whether he is entering a dovecote or a bomb factory, and is prepared for either eventuality. The little domestic quarrel over the luncheon-table had not been fought to a definite finish, and the question was how far Lady Anne was in a mood to renew or forgo hostilities. Her pose in the arm-chair by the tea-table was rather elaborately rigid; in the gloom of a December afternoon Egbert's pince-nez did not materially help him to discern the expression of her face.

By way of breaking whatever ice might be floating on the surface he made a remark about a dim religious light. He or Lady Anne were accustomed to make that remark between 4.30 and 6 on winter and late autumn evenings; it was a part of their married life. There was no recognized rejoinder to it, and Lady Anne made none.

Don Tarquinio lay astretch on the Persian rug, basking in the firelight with superb indifference to the possible ill-humour of Lady Anne. His pedigree was as flawlessly Persian as the rug, and his ruff was coming into the glory of its second winter. The page-boy, who had Renaissance tendencies, had christened him Don Tarquinio. Left to themselves, Egbert and Lady Anne would unfailingly have called him Fluff, but they were not obstinate.

Egbert poured himself out some tea. As the silence gave no sign of breaking on Lady Anne's initiative, he braced himself for another Yermak effort.

"My remark at lunch had a purely academic application," he announced; "you seem to put an unnecessarily personal significance into it."

Lady Anne maintained her defensive barrier of silence. The bullfinch lazily filled in the interval with an air from *Iphigénie en Tauride*. Egbert recognized it immediately, because it was the only air the bullfinch whistled, and he had come to them with the reputation for whistling it. Both Egbert and Lady Anne would have preferred something from *The Yeoman of the Guard*, which was their favourite opera. In matters artistic they had a similarity of taste. They leaned towards the honest and explicit in art, a picture, for instance, that told its own story, with generous assistance from its title. A riderless warhorse with harness in obvious disarray, staggering into a courtyard full of pale swooning women, and marginally noted "Bad News," suggested to their minds a distinct interpretation of some military catastrophe. They could see what it was meant to convey, and explain it to friends of duller intelligence.

The silence continued. As a rule Lady Anne's displeasure became articulate and markedly voluble after four minutes of introductory muteness. Egbert seized the milk-jug and poured some of its contents into Don Tarquinio's saucer; as the saucer was already full to the brim an unsightly overflow was the result. Don Tarquinio looked on with a surprised interest that evanesced into elaborate unconsciousness when he was appealed to by Egbert to come and drink up some of the spilt matter. Don Tarquinio was prepared to play many rôles in life, but a vacuum carpet-cleaner was not one of them.

"Don't you think we're being rather foolish?" said Egbert cheerfully.

If Lady Anne thought so she didn't say so.

"I daresay the fault has been partly on my side," continued Egbert, with evaporating cheerfulness. "After all, I'm only human, you know. You seem to forget that I'm only human."

He insisted on the point, as if there had been unfounded suggestions that he was built on Satyr lines, with goat continuations where the human left off.

The bullfinch recommenced its air from *Iphigénie en Tauride.* Egbert began to feel depressed. Lady Anne was not drinking her tea. Perhaps she was feeling unwell. But when Lady Anne felt unwell she was not wont to be reticent on the subject. "No one knows what I suffer from indigestion" was one of her favourite statements; but the lack of knowledge can only have been caused by defective listening; the amount of information available on the subject would have supplied material for a monograph.

Evidently Lady Anne was not feeling unwell.

Egbert began to think he was being unreasonably dealt with; naturally he began to make concessions.

"I daresay," he observed, taking as central a position on the hearth-rug as Don Tarquinio could be persuaded to concede him, "I may have been to blame. I am willing, if I can thereby restore things to a happier standpoint, to undertake to lead a better life."

He wondered vaguely how it would be possible. Temptations came to him, in middle age, tentatively and without insistence, like a neglected butcher-boy who asks for a Christmas box in February for no more hopeful reason than that he didn't get one in December. He had no more idea of succumbing to them than he had of purchasing the fish-knives and fur boas that ladies are impelled to sacrifice through the medium of advertisement columns during twelve months of the year. Still, there was something impressive in this unasked-for renunciation of possibly latent enormities.

Lady Anne showed no sign of being impressed.

Egbert looked at her nervously through his glasses. To get the worst of an argument with her was no new experience. To get the worst of a monologue was a humiliating novelty.

"I shall go and dress for dinner," he announced in a voice into which he intended some shade of sternness to creep.

At the door a final access of weakness impelled him to make a further appeal.

"Aren't we being very silly?"

"A fool," was Don Tarquinio's mental comment as the door closed on Egbert's retreat. Then he lifted his velvet forepaws in the air and leapt lightly on to a bookshelf immediately under the bullfinch's cage. It was the first time he had seemed to notice the bird's existence, but he was carrying out a long-formed theory of action with the precision of mature deliberation. The bullfinch, who had fancied himself something of a despot, depressed himself of a sudden into a third of his normal displacement; then he fell to a helpless wing-beating and shrill cheeping. He had cost twenty-seven shillings without the cage, but Lady Anne made no sign of interfering. She had been dead for two hours.

THE LOST SANJAK

The prison Chaplain entered the condemned's cell for the last time, to give such consolation as he might.

"The only consolation I crave for," said the condemned, "is to tell my story in its entirety to some one who will at least give it a respectful hearing."

"We must not be too long over it," said the Chaplain, looking at his watch.

The condemned repressed a shiver and commenced.

"Most people will be of opinion that I am paying the penalty of my own violent deeds. In reality I am a victim to a lack of specialization in my education and character."

"Lack of specialization!" said the Chaplain.

"Yes. If I had been known as one of the few men in England familiar with the fauna of the Outer Hebrides, or able to repeat stanzas of Camoëns' poetry in the original, I should have had no difficulty in proving my identity in the crisis when my identity became a matter of life and death for me. But my education was merely a moderately good one, and my temperament was of the general order that avoids specialization. I know a little in a general way about gardening and history and old masters, but I could never tell you off-hand whether 'Stella van der Loopen' was a chrysanthemum or a heroine of the American War of Independence, or something by Romney in the Louvre."

The Chaplain shifted uneasily in his seat. Now that the alternatives had been suggested they all seemed dreadfully possible.

"I fell in love, or thought I did, with the local doctor's wife," continued the condemned. "Why I should have done so, I cannot say, for I do not remember that she possessed any particular attractions of mind or body. On looking back at past events it seems to me that she must have been distinctly ordinary, but I suppose the doctor had fallen in love with her once, and what man has done man can do. She appeared to be pleased with the attentions which

I paid her, and to that extent I suppose I might say she encouraged me, but I think she was honestly unaware that I meant anything more than a little neighbourly interest. When one is face to face with Death one wishes to be just."

The Chaplain murmured approval. "At any rate, she was genuinely horrified when I took advantage of the doctor's absence one evening to declare what I believed to be my passion. She begged me to pass out of her life and I could scarcely do otherwise than agree, though I hadn't the dimmest idea of how it was to be done. In novels and plays I knew it was a regular occurrence, and if you mistook a lady's sentiments or intentions you went off to India and did things on the frontier as a matter of course. As I stumbled along the doctor's carriage-drive I had no very clear idea as to what my line of action was to be, but I had a vague feeling that I must look at the *Times* Atlas before going to bed. Then, on the dark and lonely highway, I came suddenly on a dead body."

The Chaplain's interest in the story visibly quickened.

"Judging by the clothes it wore the corpse was that of a Salvation Army captain. Some shocking accident seemed to have struck him down, and the head was crushed and battered out of all human semblance. Probably, I thought, a motor-car fatality; and then, with a sudden overmastering insistence, came another thought, that here was a remarkable opportunity for losing my identity and passing out of the life of the doctor's wife for ever. No tiresome and risky voyage to distant lands, but a mere exchange of clothes and identity with the unknown victim of an unwitnessed accident. With considerable difficulty I undressed the corpse, and clothed it anew in my own garments. Any one who has valeted a dead Salvation Army captain in an uncertain light will appreciate the difficulty. With the idea, presumably, of inducing the doctor's wife to leave her husband's roof-tree for some habitation which would be run at my expense, I had crammed my pockets with a store of banknotes, which represented a good deal of my immediate worldly wealth. When, therefore, I stole away into the world in the guise of a nameless Salvationist, I was not without resources which would easily support so humble a rôle for a considerable period. I tramped to a neighbouring market-town, and, late as the hour was, the production of a few shillings procured me supper and a night's lodging in a cheap coffee-house. The next day I started forth on an aimless course of wandering from one small town to another. I was already somewhat digusted with the upshot of my sudden freak; in a few hours' time I was considerably more so. In the contents-bill of a local news sheet I read the announcement of my own murder at the hands of some person unknown; on buying a copy of the paper for a detailed account of the tragedy, which at first had aroused in me a certain grim amusement, I found that the deed was ascribed to a wandering Salvationist of doubtful antecedents, who had been seen lurking in the roadway near the scene of the crime. I was no longer amused. The matter promised to be embarrassing. What I had mistaken for a motor accident was evidently a case of savage assault and murder, and, until the real culprit was found, I should have much difficulty in explaining my intrusion into the affair. Of course I could establish my own identity; but how, without disagreeably involving the doctor's wife, could I give any adequate reason for changing clothes with the murdered man? While my brain worked feverishly at this problem, I subconsciously obeyed a secondary instinct—to get as far away as possible from the scene of the crime, and to get rid at all costs of my incriminating uniform. There I found a difficulty. I tried two or three obscure clothes shops, but my entrance invariably aroused an attitude of hostile suspicion in the proprietors, and on one excuse or another they avoided serving me with the now ardently desired change of clothing. The uniform that I had so thoughtlessly donned seemed as difficult to get out of as the fatal shirt of— You know, I forget the creature's name."

"Yes, yes," said the Chaplain hurriedly. "Go on with your story."

"Somehow, until I could get out of those compromising garments, I felt it would not be safe to surrender myself to the police. The thing that puzzled me was why no attempt was made to arrest me, since there was no question as to the suspicion which followed me, like an inseparable shadow, wherever I went. Stares, nudgings, whisperings, and even loud-spoken remarks of 'that's 'im' greeted my every appearance, and the meanest and most deserted eating-house that I patronized soon became filled with a crowd of furtively watching customers. I began to sympathize with the feelings of Royal personages trying to do a little private shopping under the unsparing scrutiny of an irrepressible public. And still, with all this inarticulate shadowing, which weighed on my nerves almost worse than open hostility would have done, no attempt was made to interfere with my liberty. Later on I discovered the reason. At the time of the murder on the lonely highway a series of important bloodhound trials had been taking place in the near neighbourhood, and some dozen and a half couples of trained animals had been put on the track of the supposed murderer—on my track. One of our most public-spirited London dailies had offered a princely prize to the owner of the pair that should first track me down, and betting on the chances of the respective competitors became rife throughout the land. The dogs ranged far and wide over about thirteen counties, and though my own movements had become by this time perfectly well known to police and public alike, the sporting instincts of the nation stepped in to prevent my premature arrest. 'Give the dogs a chance,' was the prevailing sentiment, whenever some ambitious local constable wished to put an end to my drawn-out evasion of justice. My final capture by the winning pair was not a very dramatic episode, in fact, I'm not sure that they would have taken any notice of me if I hadn't spoken to them and patted them, but the event gave rise to an extraordinary amount of partisan excitement. The owner of the pair who were next nearest up at the finish was an American, and he lodged a protest on the ground that an otterhound had married into the family of the winning pair six generations ago, and that the prize had been offered to the first pair of bloodhounds to capture the murderer, and that a dog that had one sixty-fourth part of otterhound blood in it couldn't technically be considered a bloodhound. I forget how the matter was ultimately settled, but it aroused a tremendous amount of acrimonious discussion on both sides of the Atlantic. My own contribution to the controversy consisted in pointing out that the whole dispute was beside the mark, as the actual murderer had not yet been captured; but I soon discovered that on this point there was not the least divergence of public or expert opinion. I had looked forward apprehensively to the proving of my identity and the establishment of my motives as a disagreeable necessity; I speedily found out that the most disagreeable part of the business was that it couldn't be done. When I saw in the glass the haggard and hunted expression which the experiences of the past few weeks had stamped on my erstwhile placid countenance, I could scarcely feel surprised that the few friends and relations I possessed refused to recognize me in my altered guise, and persisted in their obstinate but widely shared belief that it was I who had been done to death on the highway. To make matters worse, infinitely worse, an aunt of the really murdered man, an appalling female of an obviously low order of intelligence, identified me as her nephew, and gave the authorities a lurid account of my depraved youth and of her laudable but unavailing efforts to spank me into a better way. I believe it was even proposed to search me for finger-prints."

"But," said the Chaplain, "surely your educational attainments–"

"That was just the crucial point," said the condemned; "that was where my lack of specialization told so fatally against me. The dead Salvationist, whose identity I had so lightly and so disastrously adopted, had possessed a veneer of cheap modern education. It should have been easy to demonstrate that my learning was on altogether another plane to his, but in my nervousness I bungled miserably over test after test that was put to me. The little French I had ever known deserted me; I could not render a simple phrase about the gooseberry of the gardener into that language, because I had forgotten the French for gooseberry."

The Chaplain again wriggled uneasily in his seat. "And then," resumed the condemned, "came the final discomfiture. In our village we had a modest little debating club, and I remembered having promised, chiefly, I suppose, to please and impress the doctor's wife, to give a sketchy kind of lecture on the Balkan Crisis. I had relied on being able to get up my facts from one or two standard works, and the back-numbers of certain periodicals. The prosecution had made a careful note of the circumstance that the man whom I claimed to be–and actually was–had posed locally as some sort of second-hand authority on Balkan affairs, and, in the midst of a string of questions on indifferent topics, the examining counsel asked me with a diabolical suddenness if I could tell the Court the whereabouts of Novibazar. I felt the question to be a crucial one; something told me that the answer was St. Petersburg or Baker Street. I hesitated, looked helplessly round at the sea of tensely expectant faces, pulled myself together, and chose Baker Street. And then I knew that everything was lost. The prosecution had no difficulty in demonstrating that an individual, even moderately versed in the affairs of the Near East, could never have so unceremoniously dislocated Novibazar from its accustomed corner of the map. It was an answer which the Salvation Army captain might conceivably have made–and I had made it. The circumstantial evidence connecting the Salvationist with the crime was overwhelmingly convincing, and I had inextricably identified myself with the Salvationist. And thus it comes to pass that in ten minutes' time I shall be hanged by the neck until I am dead in expiation of the murder of myself, which murder never took place, and of which, in any case, I am necessarily innocent."

When the Chaplain returned to his quarters, some fifteen minutes later, the black flag was floating over the prison tower. Breakfast was waiting for him in the dining-room, but he first passed into his library, and, taking up the *Times* Atlas, consulted a map of the Balkan Peninsula. "A thing like that," he observed, closing the volume with a snap, "might happen to any one."

THE SEX THAT DOESN'T SHOP

THE opening of a large new centre for West End shopping, particularly feminine shopping, suggests the reflection, Do women ever really shop? Of course, it is a well-attested fact that they go forth shopping as assiduously as a bee goes flower-visiting, but do they shop in the practical sense of the word? Granted the money, time, and energy, a resolute course of shopping transactions would naturally result in having one's ordinary domestic needs unfailingly supplied, whereas it is notorious that women servants (and housewives of all classes) make it almost a point of honour not to be supplied with everyday necessities. "We shall be out of starch by Thursday," they say with fatalistic foreboding, and by Thursday they are out of starch. They have predicted almost to a minute the moment when their supply would give out, and if Thursday happens to be early closing day their triumph is complete. A shop where starch is stored for retail purposes possibly stands at their very door, but the feminine mind has rejected such an obvious source for replenishing a dwindling stock. "We don't deal there" places it at once beyond the pale of human resort. And it is noteworthy that just as a sheep-worrying dog seldom molests the flocks in his near neighbourhood, so a woman rarely deals with shops in her immediate vicinity. The more remote the source of supply the more fixed seems to be the resolve to run short of the commodity. The Ark had probably not quitted its last moorings five minutes before some feminine voice gloatingly recorded a shortage of birdseed. A few days ago two lady acquaintances of mine were confessing to some mental uneasiness because a friend had called just before lunch-time, and they had been unable to ask her to stop and share their meal, as (with a touch of legitimate pride) "there was nothing in the house." I pointed out that they lived in a street that bristled with provision shops and that it would have been easy to mobilize a very passable luncheon in less than five minutes. "That," they said, with quiet dignity, "would not have occurred to us," and I felt that I had suggested something bordering on the indecent.

But it is in catering for her literary wants that a woman's shopping capacity breaks down most completely. If you have perchance produced a book which has met with some little measure of success, you are certain to get a letter from some lady whom you scarcely know to bow to, asking you "how it can be got." She knows the name of the book, its author, and who published it, but how to get into actual contact with it is still an unsolved problem to her. You write back pointing out that to have recourse to an ironmonger or a corn-dealer will only entail delay and disappointment, and suggest an application to a bookseller as the most hopeful thing you can think of. In a day or two she writes again: "It is all right; I have borrowed it from your aunt." Here, of course, we have an example of the Beyond-Shopper, one who has learned the Better Way, but the helplessness exists even when such bypaths of relief are closed. A lady who lives in the West End was expressing to me the other day her interest in West Highland terriers, and her desire to know more about the breed, so when, a few days later, I came across an exhaustive article on that subject in the current number of one of our best known outdoor-weeklies, I mentioned the circumstance in a letter, giving the date of that number. "I cannot get the paper," was her telephoned response. And she couldn't. She lived in a city where news-agents are numbered, I suppose, by the thousand, and she must have passed dozens of such shops in her daily shopping excursions, but as far as she was concerned that article on West Highland terriers might as well have been written in a missal stored away in some Buddhist monastery in Eastern Thibet.

The brutal directness of the masculine shopper arouses a certain combative derision in the feminine onlooker. A cat that spreads one shrew-mouse over the greater part of a long summer afternoon, and then possibly loses him, doubtless feels the same contempt for the terrier who compresses his rat into ten seconds of the strenuous life. I was finishing off a short list of purchases a few afternoons ago when I was discovered by a lady of my acquaintance whom, swerving aside from the lead given us by her god-parents thirty years ago, we will call Agatha.

"You're surely not buying blotting-paper *here?*" she exclaimed in an agitated whisper, and she seemed so genuinely concerned that I stayed my hand.

"Let me take you to Winks and Pinks," she said as soon as we were out of the building: "they've got such lovely shades of blotting-paper—pearl and heliotrope and *momie* and crushed—"

"But I want ordinary white blotting-paper," I said.

"Never mind. They know me at Winks and Pinks," she replied inconsequently. Agatha apparently has an idea that blotting-paper is only sold in small quantities to persons of known reputation, who may be trusted not to put it to dangerous or improper uses. After walking some two hundred yards she began to feel that her tea was of more immediate importance than my blotting-paper.

"What do you want blotting-paper for?" she asked suddenly. I explained patiently.

"I use it to dry up the ink of wet manuscript without smudging the writing. Probably a Chinese invention of the second century before Christ, but I'm not sure. The only other use for it that I can think of is to roll it into a ball for a kitten to play with."

"But you haven't got a kitten," said Agatha, with a feminine desire for stating the entire truth on most occasions.

"A stray one might come in at any moment," I replied.

Anyway I didn't get the blotting-paper.

THE BLOOD-FEUD OF TOAD-WATER

A WEST-COUNTRY EPIC

THE Cricks lived at Toad-Water; and in the same lonely upland spot Fate had pitched the home of the Saunderses, and for miles around these two dwellings there was never a neighbour or a chimney or even a burying-ground to bring a sense of cheerful communion or social intercourse. Nothing but fields and spinneys and barns, lanes and waste-lands. Such was Toad-Water; and, even so, Toad-Water had its history.

Thrust away in the benighted hinterland of a scattered market district, it might have been supposed that these two detached items of the Great Human Family would have leaned towards one another in a fellowship begotten of kindred circumstances and a common isolation from the outer world. And perhaps it had been so once, but the way of things had brought it otherwise. Indeed, otherwise. Fate, which had linked the two families in such unavoidable association of habitat, had ordained that the Crick household should nourish and maintain among its earthly possessions sundry head of domestic fowls, while to the Saunderses was given a disposition towards the cultivation of garden crops. Herein lay the material, ready to hand, for the coming of feud and ill-blood. For the grudge between the man of herbs and the man of live stock is no new thing; you will find traces of it in the fourth chapter of Genesis. And one sunny afternoon in late spring-time the feud came—came, as such things mostly do come, with seeming aimlessness and triviality. One of the Crick hens, in obedience to the nomadic instincts of her kind, wearied of her legitimate scratching-grounds, and flew over the low wall that divided the holdings of the neighbours. And there, on the yonder side, with a hurried consciousness that her time and opportunities might be limited, the misguided bird scratched and scraped and beaked and delved in the soft yielding bed that had been prepared for the solace and well-being of a colony of seedling onions. Little showers of earth-mould and root-fibres went spraying before the hen and behind her, and every minute the area of her operations widened. The onions suffered considerably. Mrs. Saunders, sauntering at this luckless moment down the garden path, in order to fill her soul with reproaches at the iniquity of the weeds, which grew faster than she or her good man cared to remove them, stopped in mute discomfiture before the presence of a more magnificent grievance. And then, in the hour of her calamity, she turned instinctively to the Great Mother, and gathered in her capacious hands large clods of the hard brown soil that lay at her feet. With a terrible sincerity of purpose, though with a contemptible inadequacy of aim, she rained her earth bolts at the marauder, and the bursting pellets called forth a flood of cackling protest and panic from the hastily departing fowl. Calmness under misfortune is not an attribute of either henfolk or womenkind, and while Mrs. Saunders declaimed over her onion bed such portions of the slang dictionary as are permitted by the Nonconformist conscience to be said or sung, the Vasco da Gama fowl was waking the echoes of Toad-Water with crescendo bursts of throat music which compelled attention to her griefs. Mrs. Crick had a long family, and was therefore licensed, in the eyes of her world, to have a short temper, and when some of her ubiquitous offspring had informed her, with the authority of eye-witnesses, that her neighbour had so far forgotten herself as to heave stones at her hen—her best hen, the best layer in the countryside—her thoughts clothed themselves in language "unbecoming to a Christian woman"—so at least said Mrs. Saunders, to whom most of the language was applied. Nor was she, on her part, surprised at Mrs. Crick's conduct in letting her hens stray into other body's gardens, and then abusing of them, seeing as how she remembered things against Mrs. Crick—and the latter simultaneously had recollections of lurking episodes in the past of Susan Saunders that were nothing to her credit. "Fond memory, when all things fade we fly to thee," and in the paling light of an April afternoon the two women confronted each other from their respective sides of the party wall, recalling with shuddering breath the blots and blemishes of their neighbour's family record. There was that aunt of Mrs. Crick's who had died a pauper in Exeter workhouse—every one knew that Mrs. Saunders' uncle on her mother's side drank himself to death —then there was that Bristol cousin of Mrs. Crick's! From the shrill triumph with which his name was dragged in, his crime must have been pilfering from a cathedral at least, but as both remembrancers were speaking at once it was difficult to distinguish his infamy from the scandal which beclouded the memory of Mrs. Saunders' brother's wife's mother—who may have been a regicide, and was certainly not a nice person as Mrs. Crick painted her. And then, with an air of accumulating and irresistible conviction, each belligerent informed the other that she was no lady—after which they withdrew in a great silence, feeling that nothing further remained to be said. The chaffinches clinked in the apple trees and the bees droned round the berberis bushes, and the waning sunlight slanted pleasantly across the garden plots, but between the neighbour households had sprung up a barrier of hate, permeating and permanent.

The male heads of the families were necessarily drawn into the quarrel, and the children on either side were forbidden to have anything to do with the unhallowed offspring of the other party. As they had to travel a good three miles along the same road to school every day, this was awkward, but such things have to be. Thus all communication between the households was sundered. Except the cats. Much as Mrs. Saunders might deplore it, rumour persistently pointed to the Crick he-cat as the presumable father of sundry kittens of which the Saunders she-cat was indisputably the mother. Mrs. Saunders drowned the kittens, but the disgrace remained.

Summer succeeded spring, and winter summer, but the feud outlasted the waning seasons. Once, indeed, it seemed as though the healing influences of religion might restore to Toad-Water its erstwhile peace; the hostile families found themselves side by side in the soul-kindling atmosphere of a Revival Tea, where hymns were blended with a beverage that came of tea-leaves and hot water and took after the latter parent, and where ghostly counsel was tempered by garnishings of solidly fashioned buns—and here, wrought up by the environment of festive piety, Mrs. Saunders so far unbent as to remark guardedly to Mrs. Crick that the evening had been a fine one. Mrs. Crick, under the influence of her ninth cup of tea and her fourth hymn, ventured on the hope that it might continue fine, but a maladroit allusion on the part of the Saunders good man to the backwardness of garden crops brought the Feud stalking forth from its corner with all its old bitterness. Mrs. Saunders joined heartily in the singing of the final hymn, which told of peace and joy and archangels and golden glories; but her thoughts were dwelling on the pauper aunt of Exeter.

Years have rolled away, and some of the actors in this wayside drama have passed into the Unknown; other onions have arisen, have flourished, have gone their way, and the offending hen has long since expiated her misdeeds and lain with trussed feet and look of ineffable peace under the arched roof of Barnstaple market.

But the Blood-feud of Toad-Water survives to this day

A YOUNG TURKISH CATASTROPHE

IN TWO SCENES

THE Minister for Fine Arts (to whose Department had been lately added the new subsection of Electoral Engineering) paid a business visit to the Grand Vizier. According to Eastern etiquette they discoursed for a while on indifferent subjects. The Minister only checked himself in time from making a passing reference to the Marathon Race, remembering that the Vizier had a Persian grandmother and might consider any allusion to Marathon as somewhat tactless. Presently the Minister touched the subject of his interview.

"Under the new Constitution are women to have votes?" he asked suddenly.

"To have votes? Women?" exclaimed the Vizier in some astonishment. "My dear Pasha, the New Departure has a flavour of the absurd as it is; don't let's try and make it altogether ridiculous. Women have no souls and no intelligence; why on earth should they have votes?"

"I know it sounds absurd," said the Minister, "but they are seriously considering the idea in the West."

"Then they must have a larger equipment of seriousness than I gave them credit for. After a lifetime of specialized effort in maintaining my gravity I can scarcely restrain an inclination to smile at the suggestion. Why, our womenfolk in most cases don't know how to read or write. How could they perform the operation of voting?"

"They could be shown the names of the candidates and where to make their cross."

"I beg your pardon?" interrupted the Vizier.

"Their crescent, I mean," corrected the Minister. "It would be to the liking of the Young Turkish Party," he added.

"Oh, well," said the Vizier, "if we are to do the thing at all we may as well go the whole h–" he pulled up just as he was uttering the name of an unclean animal, and continued, "the complete camel. I will issue instructions that womenfolk are to have votes."

The poll was drawing to a close in the Lakoumistan division. The candidate of the Young Turkish Party was known to be three or four hundred votes ahead, and he was already drafting his address, returning thanks to the electors. His victory had been almost a foregone conclusion, for he had set in motion all the approved electioneering machinery of the West. He had even employed motor-cars. Few of his supporters had gone to the poll in these vehicles, but, thanks to the intelligent driving of his chauffeurs, many of his opponents had gone to their graves or to the local hospitals, or otherwise abstained from voting. And then something unlooked-for happened. The rival candidate, Ali the Blest, arrived on the scene with his wives and womenfolk, who numbered, roughly, six hundred. Ali had wasted little effort on election literature, but had been heard to remark that every vote given to his opponent meant another sack thrown into the Bosporus. The Young Turkish candidate, who had conformed to the Western custom of one wife and hardly any mistresses, stood by helplessly while his adversary's poll swelled to a triumphant majority.

"Cristabel Columbus!" he exclaimed, invoking in some confusion the name of a distinguished pioneer; "who would have thought it?"

"Strange," mused Ali, "that one who harangued so clamorously about the Secret Ballot should have overlooked the Veiled Vote."

And, walking homeward with his constituents, he murmured in his beard an improvisation on the heretic poet of Persia:

"One, rich in metaphors, his Cause contrives
To urge with edgèd words, like Kabul knives;
And I, who worst him in this sorry game,
Was never rich in anything but—wives."

JUDKIN OF THE PARCELS

A FIGURE in an indefinite tweed suit, carrying brown-paper parcels. That is what we met suddenly, at the bend of a muddy Dorsetshire lane, and the roan mare stared and obviously thought of a curtsy. The mare is road-shy, with intervals of stolidity, and there is no telling what she will pass and what she won't. We call her Redford. That was my first meeting with Judkin, and the next time the circumstances were the same; the same muddy lane, the same rather apologetic figure in the tweed suit, the same—or very similar—parcels. Only this time the roan looked straight in front of her.

Whether I asked the groom or whether he advanced the information, I forget; but someway I gradually reconstructed the life-history of this trudger of the lanes. It was much the same, no doubt, as that of many others who are from time to time pointed out to one as having been aforetime in crack cavalry regiments and noted performers in the saddle; men who have breathed into their lungs the wonder of the East, have romped through life as through a cotillon, have had a thrust perhaps at the Viceroy's Cup, and done fantastic horsefleshy things around the Gulf of Aden. And then a golden stream has dried up, the sunlight has faded suddenly out of things, and the gods have nodded "Go." And they have not gone. They have turned instead to the muddy lanes and cheap villas and the marked-down ills of life, to watch pear trees growing and to encourage hens for their eggs. And Judkin was even as these others; the wine had been suddenly spilt from his cup of life, and he had stayed to suck at the dregs which the wise throw away. In the days of his scorn for most things he would have stared the roan mare and her turn-out out of all pretension to smartness, as he would have frozen a cheap claret behind its cork, or a plain woman behind her veil; and now he was walking stoically through the mud, in a tweed suit that would eventually go on to the gardener's boy, and would perhaps fit him. The dear gods, who know the end before the beginning, were perhaps growing a gardener's boy somewhere to fit the garments, and Judkin was only a caretaker, inhabiting a portion of them. That is what I like to think, and I am probably wrong. And Judkin, whose clothes had been to him once more than a religion, scarcely less sacred than a family quarrel, would carry those parcels back to his villa and to the wife who awaited him and them—a wife who may, for all we know to the contrary, have had a figure once, and perhaps has yet a heart of gold—of nine-carat gold, let us say at the least—but assuredly a soul of tape. And he that has fetched and carried will explain how it had fared with him in his dealings, and if he has brought the wrong sort of sugar or thread he will wheedle away the displeasure from that leaden face as a pastrycook girl will drive bluebottles off a stale bun. And that man has known what it was to coax the fret of a thoroughbred, to soothe its toss and sweat as it danced beneath him in the glee and chafe of its pulses and the glory of its thews. He has been in the raw places of the earth, where the desert beasts have whimpered their unthinkable psalmody, and their eyes have shone back the reflex of the midnight stars—and he can immerse himself in the tending of an incubator. It is horrible and wrong, and yet when I have met him in the lanes his face has worn a look of tedious cheerfulness that might pass for happiness. Has Judkin of the Parcels found something in the lees of life that I have missed in going to and fro over many waters? Is there more wisdom in his perverseness than in the madness of the wise? The dear gods know.

I don't think I saw Judkin more than three times all told, and always the lane was our point of contact; but as the roan mare was taking me to the station one heavy, cloud-smeared day, I passed a dull-looking villa that the groom, or instinct, told me was Judkin's home. From beyond a hedge of ragged elder-bushes could be heard the thud, thud of a spade, with an occasional clink and pause, as if some one had picked out a stone and thrown it to a distance, and I knew that *he* was doing nameless things to the roots of a pear tree. Near by him, I felt sure, would be lying a large and late vegetable marrow, and its largeness and lateness would be a theme of conversation at luncheon. It would be suggested that it should grace the harvest thanksgiving service; the harvest having been so generally unsatisfactory, it would be unfair to let the farmers supply all the material for rejoicing.

And while I was speeding townwards along the rails Judkin would be plodding his way to the vicarage bearing a vegetable marrow and a basketful of dahlias. The basket to be returned.

GABRIEL-ERNEST

"There is a wild beast in your woods," said the artist Cunningham, as he was being driven to the station. It was the only remark he had made during the drive, but as Van Cheele had talked incessantly his companion's silence had not been noticeable.

"A stray fox or two and some resident weasels. Nothing more formidable," said Van Cheele. The artist said nothing.

"What did you mean about a wild beast?" said Van Cheele later, when they were on the platform.

"Nothing. My imagination. Here is the train," said Cunningham.

That afternoon Van Cheele went for one of his frequent rambles through his woodland property. He had a stuffed bittern in his study, and knew the names of quite a number of wild flowers, so his aunt had possibly some justification in describing him as a great naturalist. At any rate, he was a great walker. It was his custom to take mental notes of everything he saw during his walks, not so much for the purpose of assisting contemporary science as to provide topics for conversation afterwards. When the bluebells began to show themselves in flower he made a point of informing every one of the fact; the season of the year might have warned his hearers of the likelihood of such an occurrence, but at least they felt that he was being absolutely frank with them.

What Van Cheele saw on this particular afternoon was, however, something far removed from his ordinary range of experience. On a shelf of smooth stone overhanging a deep pool in the hollow of an oak coppice a boy of about sixteen lay asprawl, drying his wet brown limbs luxuriously in the sun. His wet hair, parted by a recent dive, lay close to his head, and his light-brown eyes, so light that there was an almost tigerish gleam in them, were turned towards Van Cheele with a certain lazy watchfulness. It was an unexpected apparition, and Van Cheele found himself engaged in the novel process of thinking before he spoke. Where on earth could this wild-looking boy hail from? The miller's wife had lost a child some two months ago, supposed to have been swept away by the mill-race, but that had been a mere baby, not a half-grown lad.

"What are you doing there?" he demanded.

"Obviously, sunning myself," replied the boy.

"Where do you live?"

"Here, in these woods."

"You can't live in the woods," said Van Cheele.

"They are very nice woods," said the boy, with a touch of patronage in his voice.

"But where do you sleep at night?"

"I don't sleep at night; that's my busiest time."

Van Cheele began to have an irritated feeling that he was grappling with a problem that was eluding him.

"What do you feed on?" he asked.

"Flesh," said the boy, and he pronounced the word with slow relish, as though he were tasting it.

"Flesh! What flesh?"

"Since it interests you, rabbits, wild-fowl, hares, poultry, lambs in their season, children when I can get any; they're usually too well locked in at night, when I do most of my hunting. It's quite two months since I tasted child-flesh."

Ignoring the chaffing nature of the last remark Van Cheele tried to draw the boy on the subject of possible poaching operations.

"You're talking rather through your hat when you speak of feeding on hares." (Considering the nature of the boy's toilet the simile was hardly an apt one.) "Our hillside hares aren't easily caught."

"At night I hunt on four feet," was the somewhat cryptic response.

"I suppose you mean that you hunt with a dog?" hazarded Van Cheele.

The boy rolled slowly over on to his back, and laughed a weird low laugh, that was pleasantly like a chuckle and disagreeably like a snarl.

"I don't fancy any dog would be very anxious for my company, especially at night."

Van Cheele began to feel that there was something positively uncanny about the strange-eyed, strange-tongued youngster.

"I can't have you staying in these woods," he declared authoritatively.

"I fancy you'd rather have me here than in your house," said the boy.

The prospect of this wild, nude animal in Van Cheele's primly ordered house was certainly an alarming one.

"If you don't go I shall have to make you," said Van Cheele.

The boy turned like a flash, plunged into the pool, and in a moment had flung his wet and glistening body half-way up the bank where Van Cheele was standing. In an otter the movement would not have been remarkable; in a boy Van Cheele found it sufficiently startling. His foot slipped as he made an involuntary backward movement, and he found himself almost prostrate on the slippery weed-grown bank, with those tigerish yellow eyes not very far from his own. Almost instinctively he half raised his hand to his throat. The boy laughed again, a laugh in which the snarl had nearly driven out the chuckle, and then, with another of his astonishing lightning movements, plunged out of view into a yielding tangle of weed and fern.

"What an extraordinary wild animal!" said Van Cheele as he picked himself up. And then he recalled Cunningham's remark, "There is a wild beast in your woods."

Walking slowly homeward, Van Cheele began to turn over in his mind various local occurrences which might be traceable to the existence of this astonishing young savage.

Something had been thinning the game in the woods lately, poultry had been missing from the farms, hares were growing unaccountably scarcer, and complaints had reached him of lambs being carried off bodily from the hills. Was it possible that this wild boy was really hunting the countryside in company with some clever poacher dog? He had spoken of hunting "four-footed" by night, but then, again, he had hinted strangely at no dog caring to come near him, "especially at night." It was certainly puzzling. And then, as Van Cheele ran his mind over the various depredations that had been committed during the last month or two, he came suddenly to a dead stop, alike in his walk and his speculations. The child missing from the mill two months ago—the accepted theory was that it had tumbled into the mill-race and been swept away; but the mother had always declared she had heard a shriek on the hill side of the house, in the opposite direction from the water. It was unthinkable, of course, but he wished that the boy had not made that uncanny remark about childflesh eaten two months ago. Such dreadful things should not be said even in fun.

Van Cheele, contrary to his usual wont, did not feel disposed to be communicative about his discovery in the wood. His position as a parish councillor and justice of the peace seemed somehow compromised by the fact that he was harbouring a personality of such doubtful repute on his property; there was even a possibility that a heavy bill of damages for raided lambs and poultry might be laid at his door. At dinner that night he was quite unusually silent.

"Where's your voice gone to?" said his aunt. "One would think you had seen a wolf."

Van Cheele, who was not familiar with the old saying, thought the remark rather foolish; if he *had* seen a wolf on his property his tongue would have been extraordinarily busy with the subject.

At breakfast next morning Van Cheele was conscious that his feeling of uneasiness regarding yesterday's episode had not wholly disappeared, and he resolved to go by train to the neighbouring cathedral town, hunt up Cunningham, and learn from him what he had really seen that had prompted the remark about a wild beast in the woods. With this resolution taken, his usual cheerfulness partially returned, and he hummed a bright little melody as he sauntered to the morning-room for his customary cigarette. As he entered the room the melody made way abruptly for a pious invocation. Gracefully asprawl on the ottoman, in an attitude of almost exaggerated repose, was the boy of the woods. He was drier than when Van Cheele had last seen him, but no other alteration was noticeable in his toilet.

"How dare you come here?" asked Van Cheele furiously.

"You told me I was not to stay in the woods," said the boy calmly.

"But not to come here. Supposing my aunt should see you!"

And with a view to minimizing that catastrophe Van Cheele hastily obscured as much of his unwelcome guest as possible under the folds of a *Morning Post*. At that moment his aunt entered the room.

"This is a poor boy who has lost his way—and lost his memory. He doesn't know who he is or where he comes from," explained Van Cheele desperately, glancing apprehensively at the waif's face to see whether he was going to add inconvenient candour to his other savage propensities.

Miss Van Cheele was enormously interested.

"Perhaps his underlinen is marked," she suggested.

"He seems to have lost most of that, too," said Van Cheele, making frantic little grabs at the *Morning Post* to keep it in its place.

A naked homeless child appealed to Miss Van Cheele as warmly as a stray kitten or derelict puppy would have done.

"We must do all we can for him," she decided, and in a very short time a messenger, dispatched to the rectory, where a page-boy was kept, had returned with a suit of pantry clothes, and the necessary accessories of shirt, shoes, collar, etc. Clothed, clean, and groomed, the boy lost none of his uncanniness in Van Cheele's eyes, but his aunt found him sweet.

"We must call him something till we know who he really is," she said. "Gabriel-Ernest, I think; those are nice suitable names."

Van Cheele agreed, but he privately doubted whether they were being grafted on to a nice suitable child. His misgivings were not diminished by the fact that his staid and elderly spaniel had bolted out of the house at the first incoming of the boy, and now obstinately remained shivering and yapping at the farther end of the orchard, while the canary, usually as vocally industrious as Van Cheele himself, had put itself on an allowance of frightened cheeps.

More than ever he was resolved to consult Cunningham without loss of time.

As he drove off to the station his aunt was arranging that Gabriel-Ernest should help her to entertain the infant members of her Sunday-school class at tea that afternoon.

Cunningham was not at first disposed to be communicative.

"My mother died of some brain trouble," he explained, "so you will understand why I am averse to dwelling on anything of an impossibly fantastic nature that I may see or think that I have seen."

"But what *did* you see?" persisted Van Cheele.

"What I thought I saw was something so extraordinary that no really sane man could dignify it with the credit of having actually happened. I was standing, the last evening I was with you, half-hidden in the hedgegrowth by the orchard gate, watching the dying glow of the sunset. Suddenly I became aware of a naked boy, a bather from some neighbouring pool, I took him to be, who was standing out on the bare hillside also watching the sunset. His pose was so suggestive of some wild faun of Pagan myth that I instantly wanted to engage him as a model, and in another moment I think I should have hailed him. But just then the sun dipped out of view, and all the orange and pink slid out of the landscape, leaving it cold and grey. And at the same moment an astounding thing happened—the boy vanished too!"

"What! vanished away into nothing?" asked Van Cheele excitedly.

"No; that is the dreadful part of it," answered the artist; "on the open hillside where the boy had been standing a second ago, stood a large wolf, blackish in colour, with gleaming fangs and cruel, yellow eyes. You may think—"

But Van Cheele did not stop for anything as futile as thought. Already he was tearing at top speed towards the station. He dismissed the idea of a telegram. "Gabriel-Ernest is a werewolf" was a hopelessly inadequate effort at conveying the situation, and his aunt would think it was a code message to which he had omitted to give her the key. His one hope was that he might reach home before sundown. The cab which he chartered at the other end of the railway journey bore him with what seemed exasperating slowness along the country roads, which were pink and mauve with the flush of the sinking sun. His aunt was putting away some unfinished jams and cake when he arrived.

"Where is Gabriel-Ernest?" he almost screamed.

"He is taking the little Toop child home," said his aunt. "It was getting so late, I thought it wasn't safe to let it go back alone. What a lovely sunset, isn't it?"

But Van Cheele, although not oblivious of the glow in the western sky, did not stay to discuss its beauties. At a speed for which he was scarcely geared he raced along the narrow lane that led to the home of the Toops. On one side ran the swift current of the mill-stream, on the other rose the stretch of bare hillside. A dwindling rim of red sun showed still on the skyline, and the next turning must bring him in view of the ill-assorted couple he was pursuing. Then the colour went suddenly out of things, and a grey light settled itself with a quick shiver over the landscape. Van Cheele heard a shrill wail of fear, and stopped running.

Nothing was ever seen again of the Toop child or Gabriel-Ernest, but the latter's discarded garments were found lying in the road, so it was assumed that the child had fallen into the water, and that the boy had stripped and jumped in, in a vain endeavour to save it. Van Cheele and some workmen who were near by at the time testified to having heard a child scream loudly just near the spot where the clothes were found. Mrs. Toop, who had eleven other children, was decently resigned to her bereavement, but Miss Van Cheele sincerely mourned her lost foundling. It was on her initiative that a memorial brass was put up in the parish church to "Gabriel-Ernest, an unknown boy, who bravely sacrificed his life for another."

Van Cheele gave way to his aunt in most things, but he flatly refused to subscribe to the Gabriel-Ernest memorial.

THE SAINT AND THE GOBLIN

THE little stone Saint occupied a retired niche in a side aisle of the old cathedral. No one quite remembered who he had been, but that in a way was a guarantee of respectability. At least so the Goblin said. The Goblin was a very fine specimen of quaint stone carving, and lived up in the corbel on the wall opposite the niche of the little Saint. He was connected with some of the best cathedral folk, such as the queer carvings in the choir stalls and chancel screen, and even the gargoyles high up on the roof. All the fantastic beasts and manikins that sprawled and twisted in wood or stone or lead overhead in the arches or away down in the crypt were in some way akin to him; consequently he was a person of recognized importance in the cathedral world.

The little stone Saint and the Goblin got on very well together, though they looked at most things from different points of view. The Saint was a philanthropist in an old-fashioned way; he thought the world, as he saw it, was good, but might be improved. In particular he pitied the church mice, who were miserably poor. The Goblin, on the other hand, was of opinion that the world, as he knew it, was bad, but had better be let alone. It was the function of the church mice to be poor.

"All the same," said the Saint, "I feel very sorry for them."

"Of course you do," said the Goblin; "it's *your* function to feel sorry for them. If they were to leave off being poor you couldn't fulfil your functions. You'd be a sinecure."

He rather hoped that the Saint would ask him what a sinecure meant, but the latter took refuge in a stony silence. The Goblin might be right, but still, he thought, he would like to do something for the church mice before winter came on; they were so very poor.

Whilst he was thinking the matter over he was startled by something falling between his feet with a hard metallic clatter. It was a bright new thaler; one of the cathedral jackdaws, who collected such things, had flown in with it to a stone cornice just above his niche, and the banging of the sacristy door had startled him into dropping it. Since the invention of gun powder the family nerves were not what they had been.

"What have you got there?" asked the Goblin.

"A silver thaler," said the Saint. "Really," he continued, "it is most fortunate; now I can do something for the church mice."

"How will you manage it?" asked the Goblin.

The Saint considered.

"I will appear in a vision to the vergeress who sweeps the floors. I will tell her that she will find a silver thaler between my feet, and that she must take it and buy a measure of corn and put it on my shrine. When she finds the money she will know that it was a true dream, and she will take care to follow my directions. Then the mice will have food all winter."

"Of course *you* can do that," observed the Goblin. "Now, *I* can only appear to people after they have had a heavy supper of indigestible things. My opportunities with the vergeress would be limited. There is some advantage in being a saint after all."

All this while the coin was lying at the Saint's feet. It was clean and glittering and had the Elector's arms beautifully stamped upon it. The Saint began to reflect that such an opportunity was too rare to be hastily disposed of. Perhaps indiscriminate charity might be harmful to the church mice. After all, it was their function to be poor; the Goblin had said so, and the Goblin was generally right.

"I've been thinking," he said to that personage, "that perhaps it would be really better if I ordered a thaler's worth of candles to be placed on my shrine instead of the corn."

He often wished, for the look of the thing, that people would sometimes burn candles at his shrine; but as they had forgotten who he was it was not considered a profitable speculation to pay him that attention.

"Candles would be more orthodox," said the Goblin.

"More orthodox, certainly," agreed the Saint, "and the mice could have the ends to eat; candle-ends are most fattening."

The Goblin was too well bred to wink; besides, being a stone goblin, it was out of the question.

"Well, if it ain't there, sure enough!" said the vergeress next morning. She took the shining coin down from the gusty niche and turned it over and over in her grimy hands. Then she put it to her mouth and bit it.

"She can't be going to eat it," thought the Saint, and fixed her with his stoniest stare.

"Well," said the woman, in a somewhat shriller key, "who'd have thought it! A saint, too!"

Then she did an unaccountable thing. She hunted an old piece of tape out of her pocket, and tied it crosswise, with a big loop, round the thaler, and hung it round the neck of the little Saint.

Then she went away.

"The only possible explanation," said the Goblin, "is that it's a bad one."

"What is that decoration your neighbour is wearing?" asked a wyvern that was wrought into the capital of an adjacent pillar.

The Saint was ready to cry with mortification, only, being of stone, he couldn't.

"It's a coin of—ahem!—fabulous value," replied the Goblin tactfully.

And the news went round the Cathedral that the shrine of the little stone Saint had been enriched by a priceless offering.

"After all, it's something to have the conscience of a goblin," said the Saint to himself.

The church mice were as poor as ever. But that was their function.

THE SOUL OF LAPLOSHKA

Laploshka was one of the meanest men I have ever met, and quite one of the most entertaining. He said horrid things about other people in such a charming way that one forgave him for the equally horrid things he said about oneself behind one's back. Hating anything in the way of ill-natured gossip ourselves, we are always grateful to those who do it for us and do it well. And Laploshka did it really well.

Naturally Laploshka had a large circle of acquaintances, and as he exercised some care in their selection it followed that an appreciable proportion were men whose bank balances enabled them to acquiesce indulgently in his rather one-sided views on hospitality. Thus, although possessed of only moderate means, he was able to live comfortably within his income, and still more comfortably within those of various tolerantly disposed associates.

But towards the poor or to those of the same limited resources as himself his attitude was one of watchful anxiety; he seemed to be haunted by a besetting fear lest some fraction of a shilling or franc, or whatever the prevailing coinage might be, should be diverted from his pocket or service into that of a hard-up companion. A two-franc cigar would be cheerfully offered to a wealthy patron, on the principle of doing evil that good may come, but I have known him indulge in agonies of perjury rather than admit the incriminating possession of a copper coin when change was needed to tip a waiter. The coin would have been duly returned at the earliest opportunity—he would have taken means to ensure against forgetfulness on the part of the borrower—but accidents might happen, and even the temporary estrangement from his penny or sou was a calamity to be avoided.

The knowledge of this amiable weakness offered a perpetual temptation to play upon Laploshka's fears of involuntary generosity. To offer him a lift in a cab and pretend not to have enough money to pay the fare, to fluster him with a request for a sixpence when his hand was full of silver just received in change, these were a few of the petty torments that ingenuity prompted as occasion afforded. To do justice to Laploshka's resourcefulness it must be admitted that he always emerged somehow or other from the most embarrassing dilemma without in any way compromising his reputation for saying "No." But the gods send opportunities at some time to most men, and mine came one evening when Laploshka and I were supping together in a cheap boulevard restaurant. (Except when he was the bidden guest of some one with an irreproachable income, Laploshka was wont to curb his appetite for high living; on such fortunate occasions he let it go on an easy snaffle.) At the conclusion of the meal a somewhat urgent message called me away, and without heeding my companion's agitated protest, I called back cruelly, "Pay my share; I'll settle with you tomorrow." Early on the morrow Laploshka hunted me down by instinct as I walked along a side street that I hardly ever frequented. He had the air of a man who had not slept.

"You owe me two francs from last night," was his breathless greeting.

I spoke evasively of the situation in Portugal, where more trouble seemed brewing. But Laploshka listened with the abstraction of the deaf adder, and quickly returned to the subject of the two francs.

"I'm afraid I must owe it to you," I said lightly and brutally. "I haven't a sou in the world," and I added mendaciously, "I'm going away for six months or perhaps longer."

Laploshka said nothing, but his eyes bulged a little and his cheeks took on the mottled hues of an ethnographical map of the Balkan Peninsula. That same day, at sundown, he died. "Failure of the heart's action" was the doctor's verdict; but I, who knew better, knew that he had died of grief.

There arose the problem of what to do with his two francs. To have killed Laploshka was one thing; to have kept his beloved money would have argued a callousness of feeling of which I am not capable. The ordinary solution, of giving it to the poor, would by no means fit the present situation, for nothing would have distressed the dead man more than such a misuse of his property. On the other hand, the bestowal of two francs on the rich was an operation which called for some tact. An easy way out of the difficulty seemed, however, to present itself the following Sunday, as I was wedged into the cosmopolitan crowd which filled the side-aisle of one of the most popular Paris churches. A collecting-bag, for "the poor of Monsieur le Curé," was buffeting its tortuous way across the seemingly impenetrable human sea, and a German in front of me, who evidently did not wish his appreciation of the magnificent music to be marred by a suggestion of payment, made audible criticisms to his companion on the claims of the said charity.

"They do not want money," he said; "they have too much money. They have no poor. They are all pampered."

If that were really the case my way seemed clear. I dropped Laploshka's two francs into the bag with a murmured blessing on the rich of Monsieur le Curé.

Some three weeks later chance had taken me to Vienna, and I sat one evening regaling myself in a humble but excellent little Gasthaus up in the Währinger quarter. The appointments were primitive, but the Schnitzel, the beer, and the cheese could not have been improved on. Good cheer brought good custom, and with the exception of one small table near the door every place was occupied. Half-way through my meal I happened to glance in the direction of that empty seat, and saw that it was no longer empty. Poring over the bill of fare with the absorbed scrutiny of one who seeks the cheapest among the cheap was Laploshka. Once he looked across at me, with a comprehensive glance at my repast, as though to say, "It is my two francs you are eating," and then looked swiftly away. Evidently the poor of Monsieur le Curé had been genuine poor. The Schnitzel turned to leather in my mouth, the beer seemed tepid; I left the Emmenthaler untasted. My one idea was to get away from the room, away from the table where *that* was seated; and as I fled I felt Laploshka's reproachful eyes watching the amount that I gave to the piccolo—out of his two francs. I lunched next day at an expensive restaurant which I felt sure that the living Laploshka would never have entered on his own account, and I hoped that the dead Laploshka would observe the same barriers. I was not mistaken, but as I came out I found him miserably studying the bill of fare stuck up on the portals. Then he slowly made his way over to a milk-hall. For the first time in my experience I missed the charm and gaiety of Vienna life.

After that, in Paris or London or wherever I happened to be, I continued to see a good deal of Laploshka. If I had a seat in a box at a theatre I was always conscious of his eyes furtively watching me from the dim recesses of the gallery. As I turned into my club on a rainy afternoon I would see him taking inadequate shelter in a doorway opposite. Even if I indulged in the modest luxury of a penny chair in the Park he generally confronted me from one of the free benches, never staring at me, but always elaborately conscious of my presence. My friends began to comment on my changed looks, and advised me to leave off heaps of things. I should have liked to have left off Laploshka.

On a certain Sunday–it was probably Easter, for the crush was worse than ever–I was again wedged into the crowd listening to the music in the fashionable Paris church, and again the collection-bag was buffeting its way across the human sea. An English lady behind me was making ineffectual efforts to convey a coin into the still distant bag, so I took the money at her request and helped it forward to its destination. It was a two-franc piece. A swift inspiration came to me, and I merely dropped my own sou into the bag and slid the silver coin into my pocket. I had withdrawn Laploshka's two francs from the poor, who should never have had that legacy. As I backed away from the crowd I heard a woman's voice say, "I don't believe he put my money in the bag. There are swarms of people in Paris like that!" But my mind was lighter than it had been for a long time.

The delicate mission of bestowing the retrieved sum on the deserving rich still confronted me. Again I trusted to the inspiration of accident, and again fortune favoured me. A shower drove me, two days later, into one of the historic churches on the left bank of the Seine, and there I found, peering at the old wood-carvings, the Baron R., one of the wealthiest and most shabbily dressed men in Paris. It was now or never. Putting a strong American inflection into the French which I usually talked with an unmistakable British accent, I catechized the Baron as to the date of the church's building, its dimensions, and other details which an American tourist would be certain to want to know. Having acquired such information as the Baron was able to impart on short notice, I solemnly placed the two-franc piece in his hand, with the hearty assurance that it was "pour vous," and turned to go. The Baron was slightly taken aback, but accepted the situation with a good grace. Walking over to a small box fixed in the wall, he dropped Laploshka's two francs into the slot. Over the box was the inscription, "Pour les pauvres de M. le Curé."

That evening, at the crowded corner by the Café de la Paix, I caught a fleeting glimpse of Laploshka. He smiled, slightly raised his hat, and vanished. I never saw him again. After all, the money had been *given* to the deserving rich, and the soul of Laploshka was at peace.

THE BAG

"THE Major is coming in to tea," said Mrs. Hoopington to her niece. "He's just gone round to the stables with his horse. Be as bright and lively as you can; the poor man's got a fit of the glooms."

Major Pallaby was a victim of circumstances, over which he had no control, and of his temper, over which he had very little. He had taken on the Mastership of the Pexdale Hounds in succession to a highly popular man who had fallen foul of his committee, and the Major found himself confronted with the overt hostility of at least half the hunt, while his lack of tact and amiability had done much to alienate the remainder. Hence subscriptions were beginning to fall off, foxes grew provokingly scarcer, and wire obtruded itself with increasing frequency. The Major could plead reasonable excuse for his fit of the glooms.

In ranging herself as a partisan on the side of Major Pallaby Mrs. Hoopington had been largely influenced by the fact that she had made up her mind to marry him at an early date. Against his notorious bad temper she set his three thousand a year, and his prospective succession to a baronetcy gave a casting vote in his favour. The Major's plans on the subject of matrimony were not at present in such an advanced stage as Mrs. Hoopington's, but he was beginning to find his way over to Hoopington Hall with a frequency that was already being commented on.

"He had a wretchedly thin field out again yesterday," said Mrs.

Hoopington. "Why you didn't bring one or two hunting men down with you, instead of that stupid Russian boy, I can't think."

"Vladimir isn't stupid," protested her niece; "he's one of the most amusing boys I ever met. Just compare him for a moment with some of your heavy hunting men—"

"Anyhow, my dear Norah, he can't ride."

"Russians never can; but he shoots."

"Yes; and what does he shoot? Yesterday he brought home a woodpecker in his game-bag."

"But he'd shot three pheasants and some rabbits as well."

"That's no excuse for including a woodpecker in his game-bag."

"Foreigners go in for mixed bags more than we do. A Grand Duke pots a vulture just as seriously as we should stalk a bustard. Anyhow, I've explained to Vladimir that certain birds are beneath his dignity as a sportsman. And as he's only nineteen, of course, his dignity is a sure thing to appeal to."

Mrs. Hoopington sniffed. Most people with whom Vladimir came in contact found his high spirits infectious, but his present hostess was guaranteed immune against infection of that sort.

"I hear him coming in now," she observed. "I shall go and get ready for tea. We're going to have it here in the hall. Entertain the Major if he comes in before I'm down, and, above all, be bright."

Norah was dependent on her aunt's good graces for many little things that made life worth living, and she was conscious of a feeling of discomfiture because the Russian youth whom she had brought down as a welcome element of change in the country-house routine was not making a good impression. That young gentleman, however, was supremely unconscious of any shortcomings, and burst into the hall, tired, and less sprucely groomed than usual, but distinctly radiant. His game-bag looked comfortably full.

"Guess what I have shot," he demanded.

"Pheasants, wood-pigeons, rabbits," hazarded Norah.

"No; a large beast; I don't know what you call it in English. Brown, with a darkish tail." Norah changed colour.

"Does it live in a tree and eat nuts?" she asked, hoping that the use of the adjective "large" might be an exaggeration.

Vladimir laughed.

"Oh, no; not a *biyelka.*"

"Does it swim and eat fish?" asked Norah, with a fervent prayer in her heart that it might turn out to be an otter.

"No," said Vladimir, busy with the straps of his game-bag; "it lives in the woods, and eats rabbits and chickens."

Norah sat down suddenly, and hid her face in her hands.

"Merciful Heaven!" she wailed; "he's shot a fox!"

Vladimir looked up at her in consternation. In a torrent of agitated words she tried to explain the horror of the situation. The boy understood nothing, but was thoroughly alarmed.

"Hide it, hide it!" said Norah frantically, pointing to the still unopened bag. "My aunt and the Major will be here in a moment. Throw it on the top of that chest; they won't see it there."

Vladimir swung the bag with fair aim; but the strap caught in its flight on the outstanding point of an antler fixed in the wall, and the bag, with its terrible burden, remained suspended just above the alcove where tea would presently be laid. At that moment Mrs. Hoopington and the Major entered the hall.

"The Major is going to draw our covers tomorrow," announced the lady, with a certain heavy satisfaction. "Smithers is confident that we'll be able to show him some sport; he swears he's seen a fox in the nut copse three times this week."

"I'm sure I hope so; I hope so," said the Major moodily. "I must break this sequence of blank days. One hears so often that a fox has settled down as a tenant for life in certain covers, and then when you go to turn him out there isn't a trace of him. I'm certain a fox was shot or trapped in Lady Widden's woods the very day before we drew them."

"Major, if any one tried that game on in my woods they'd get short shrift," said Mrs. Hoopington.

Norah found her way mechanically to the tea-table and made her fingers frantically busy in rearranging the parsley round the sandwich dish. On one side of her loomed the morose countenance of the Major, on the other she was conscious of the scared, miserable eyes of Vladimir. And above it all hung *that.* She dared not raise her eyes above the level of the tea-table, and she almost expected to see a spot of accusing vulpine blood drip down and stain the whiteness of the cloth. Her aunt's manner signalled to her the repeated message to "be bright"; for the present she was fully occupied in keeping her teeth from chattering.

"What did you shoot today?" asked Mrs. Hoopington suddenly of the unusually silent Vladimir.

"Nothing–nothing worth speaking of," said the boy.

Norah's heart, which had stood still for a space, made up for lost time with a most disturbing bound.

"I wish you'd find something that was worth speaking about," said the hostess; "every one seems to have lost their tongues."

"When did Smithers last see that fox?" said the Major.

"Yesterday morning; a fine dog-fox, with a dark brush," confided Mrs. Hoopington.

"Aha, we'll have a good gallop after that brush tomorrow," said the Major, with a transient gleam of good humour. And then gloomy silence settled again round the tea-table, a silence broken only by despondent munchings and the occasional feverish rattle of a teaspoon in its saucer. A diversion was at last afforded by Mrs. Hoopington's fox-terrier, which had jumped on to a vacant chair, the better to survey the delicacies of the table, and was now sniffing in an upward direction at something apparently more interesting than cold tea-cake.

"What is exciting him?" asked his mistress, as the dog suddenly broke into short, angry barks, with a running accompaniment of tremulous whines.

"Why," she continued, "it's your game-bag, Vladimir! What *have* you got in it?"

"By Gad," said the Major, who was now standing up; "there's a pretty warm scent!"

And then a simultaneous idea flashed on himself and Mrs. Hoopington. Their faces flushed to distinct but harmonious tones of purple, and with one accusing voice they screamed, "You've shot the fox!"

Norah tried hastily to palliate Vladimir's misdeed in their eyes, but it is doubtful whether they heard her. The Major's fury clothed and reclothed itself in words as frantically as a woman up in town for one day's shopping tries on a succession of garments. He reviled and railed at fate and the general scheme of things, he pitied himself with a strong, deep pity too poignant for tears, he condemned every one with whom he had ever come in contact to endless and abnormal punishments. In fact, he conveyed the impression that if a destroying angel had been lent to him for a week it would have had very little time for private study. In the lulls of his outcry could be heard the querulous monotone of Mrs. Hoopington and the sharp staccato barking of the fox-terrier. Vladimir, who did not understand a tithe of what was being said, sat fondling a cigarette and repeating under his breath from time to time a vigorous English adjective which he had long ago taken affectionately into his vocabulary. His mind strayed back to the youth in the old Russian folk-tale who shot an enchanted bird with dramatic results. Meanwhile, the Major, roaming round the hall like an imprisoned cyclone, had caught sight of and joyfully pounced on the telephone apparatus, and lost no time in ringing up the hunt secretary and announcing his resignation of the Mastership. A servant had by this time brought his horse round to the door, and in a few seconds Mrs. Hoopington's shrill monotone had the field to itself. But after the Major's display her best efforts at vocal violence missed their full effect; it was as though one had come straight out from a Wagner opera into a rather tame thunderstorm. Realizing, perhaps, that her tirades were something of an anticlimax, Mrs. Hoopington broke suddenly into some rather necessary tears and marched out of the room, leaving behind her a silence almost as terrible as the turmoil which had preceded it.

"What shall I do with–*that?*" asked Vladimir at last.

"Bury it," said Norah.

"Just plain burial?" said Vladimir, rather relieved. He had almost expected that some of the local clergy would have insisted on being present, or that a salute might have to be fired over the grave.

And thus it came to pass that in the dusk of a November evening the Russian boy, murmuring a few of the prayers of his Church for luck, gave hasty but decent burial to a large polecat under the lilac trees at Hoopington.

THE STRATEGIST

Mrs. Jallatt's young people's parties were severely exclusive; it came cheaper that way, because you could ask fewer to them. Mrs. Jallatt didn't study cheapness, but somehow she generally attained it.

"There'll be about ten girls," speculated Rollo, as he drove to the function, "and I suppose four fellows, unless the Wrotsleys bring their cousin, which Heaven forbid. That would mean Jack and me against three of them."

Rollo and the Wrotsley brethren had maintained an undying feud almost from nursery days. They only met now and then in the holidays, and the meeting was usually tragic for whichever happened to have the fewest backers on hand. Rollo was counting tonight on the presence of a devoted and muscular partisan to hold an even balance. As he arrived he heard his prospective champion's sister apologizing to the hostess for the unavoidable absence of her brother; a moment later he noted that the Wrotsleys *had* brought their cousin.

Two against three would have been exciting and possibly unpleasant; one against three promised to be about as amusing as a visit to a dentist. Rollo ordered his carriage for as early as was decently possible, and faced the company with a smile that he imagined the better sort of aristocrat would have worn when mounting to the guillotine.

"So glad you were able to come," said the elder Wrotsley heartily.

"Now, you children will like to play games, I suppose," said Mrs. Jallatt, by way of giving things a start, and as they were too well-bred to contradict her there only remained the question of what they were to play at.

"I know of a good game," said the elder Wrotsley innocently. "The fellows leave the room and think of a word; then they come back again, and the girls have to find out what the word is."

Rollo knew that game. He would have suggested it himself if his faction had been in the majority.

"It doesn't promise to be very exciting," sniffed the superior Dolores Sneep as the boys filed out of the room. Rollo thought differently. He trusted to Providence that Wrotsley had nothing worse than knotted handkerchiefs at his disposal.

The word-choosers locked themselves in the library to ensure that their deliberations should not be interrupted. Providence turned out to be not even decently neutral; on a rack on the library wall were a dog-whip and a whalebone riding switch. Rollo thought it criminal negligence to leave such weapons of precision lying about. He was given a choice of evils, and chose the dog-whip; the next minute or so he spent in wondering how he could have made such a stupid selection. Then they went back to the languidly expectant females.

"The word's 'camel,'" announced the Wrotsley cousin blunderingly.

"You stupid!" screamed the girls, "we've got to *guess* the word. Now you'll have to go back and think of another."

"Not for worlds," said Rollo; "I mean, the word isn't really camel; we were rotting. Pretend it's dromedary!" he whispered to the others.

"I heard them say 'dromedary'! I heard them. I don't care what you say; I heard them," squealed the odious Dolores. "With ears as long as hers one would hear anything," thought Rollo savagely.

"We shall have to go back, I suppose," said the elder Wrotsley resignedly.

The conclave locked itself once more into the library. "Look here, I'm not going through that dog-whip business again," protested Rollo.

"Certainly not, dear," said the elder Wrotsley; "we'll try the whalebone switch this time, and then you'll know which hurts most. It's only by personal experience that one finds out these things."

It was swiftly borne in upon Rollo that his earlier selection of the dog-whip had been a really sound one. The conclave gave his under-lip time to steady itself while it debated the choice of the necessary word. "Mustang" was no good, as half the girls wouldn't know what it meant; finally "quagga" was pitched on.

"You must come and sit down over here," chorused the investigating committee on their return; but Rollo was obdurate in insisting that the questioned person always stood up. On the whole, it was a relief when the game ended and supper was announced.

Mrs. Jallatt did not stint her young guests, but the more expensive delicacies of her supper-table were never unnecessarily duplicated, and it was usually good policy to take what you wanted while it was still there. On this occasion she had provided sixteen peaches to "go round" among fourteen children; it was really not her fault that the two Wrotsleys and their cousin, foreseeing the long foodless drive home, had each quietly pocketed an extra peach, but it was distinctly trying for Dolores and the fat and good-natured Agnes Blaik to be left with one peach between them.

"I suppose we had better halve it," said Dolores sourly.

But Agnes was fat first and good-natured afterwards; those were her guiding principles in life. She was profuse in her sympathy for Dolores, but she hastily devoured the peach, explaining that it would spoil it to divide it; the juice ran out so.

"Now what would you all like to do?" demanded Mrs. Jallatt by way of a diversion. "The professional conjurer whom I had engaged has failed me at the last moment. Can any of you recite?"

There were symptoms of a general panic. Dolores was known to recite "Locksley Hall" on the least provocation. There had been occasions when her opening line, "Comrades, leave me here a little," had been taken as a literal injunction by a large section of her hearers. There was a murmur of relief when Rollo hastily declared that he could do a few conjuring tricks. He had never done one in his life, but those two visits to the library had goaded him to unusual recklessness.

"You've seen conjuring chaps take coins and cards out of people," he announced; "well, I'm going to take more interesting things out of some of you. Mice, for instance."

"Not mice!"

A shrill protest rose, as he had foreseen, from the majority of his audience.

"Well, fruit, then."

The amended proposal was received with approval. Agnes positively beamed.

Without more ado Rollo made straight for his trio of enemies, plunged his hand successively into their breast-pockets, and produced three peaches. There was no applause, but no amount of hand-clapping would have given the performer as much pleasure as the silence which greeted his coup.

"Of course, we were in the know," said the Wrotsley cousin lamely.

"That's done it," chuckled Rollo to himself.

"If they *had* been confederates they would have sworn they knew nothing about it," said Dolores, with piercing conviction.

"Do you know any more tricks?" asked Mrs. Jallatt hurriedly.

Rollo did not. He hinted that he might have changed the three peaches into something else, but Agnes had already converted one into girl-food, so nothing more could be done in that direction.

"I know a game," said the elder Wrotsley heavily, "where the fellows go out of the room, and think of some character in history; then they come back and act him, and the girls have to guess who it's meant for."

"I'm afraid I must be going," said Rollo to his hostess.

"Your carriage won't be here for another twenty minutes," said Mrs. Jallatt.

"It's such a fine evening I think I'll walk and meet it."

"It's raining rather steadily at present. You've just time to play that historical game."

"We haven't heard Dolores recite," said Rollo desperately; as soon as he had said it he realized his mistake. Confronted with the alternative of "Locksley Hall," public opinion declared unanimously for the history game.

Rollo played his last card. In an undertone meant apparently for the Wrotsley boy, but carefully pitched to reach Agnes, he observed:

"All right, old man; we'll go and finish those chocolates we left in the library."

"I think it's only fair that the girls should take their turn in going out," exclaimed Agnes briskly. She was great on fairness.

"Nonsense," said the others; "there are too many of us."

"Well, four of us can go. I'll be one of them."

And Agnes darted off towards the library, followed by three less eager damsels.

Rollo sank into a chair and smiled ever so faintly at the Wrotsleys, just a momentary baring of the teeth; an otter, escaping from the fangs of the hounds into the safety of a deep pool, might have given a similar demonstration of its feelings.

From the library came the sound of moving furniture. Agnes was leaving nothing unturned in her quest for the mythical chocolates. And then came a more blessed sound, wheels crunching wet gravel.

"It has been a most enjoyable evening," said Rollo to his hostess.

CROSS CURRENTS

VANESSA PENNINGTON had a husband who was poor, with few extenuating circumstances, and an admirer who, though comfortably rich, was cumbered with a sense of honour. His wealth made him welcome in Vanessa's eyes, but his code of what was right impelled him to go away and forget her, or at the most to think of her in the intervals of doing a great many other things. And although Alaric Clyde loved Vanessa, and thought he should always go on loving her, he gradually and unconsciously allowed himself to be wooed and won by a more alluring mistress; he fancied that his continued shunning of the haunts of men was a self-imposed exile, but his heart was caught in the spell of the Wilderness, and the

Wilderness was kind and beautiful to him. When one is young and strong and unfettered the wild earth can be very kind and very beautiful. Witness the legion of men who were once young and unfettered and now eat out their souls in dustbins, because, having erstwhile known and loved the Wilderness, they broke from her thrall and turned aside into beaten paths.

In the high waste places of the world Clyde roamed and hunted and dreamed, death-dealing and gracious as some god of Hellas, moving with his horses and servants and four-footed camp followers from one dwelling ground to another, a welcome guest among wild primitive village folk and nomads, a friend and slayer of the fleet, shy beasts around him. By the shores of misty upland lakes he shot the wild fowl that had winged their way to him across half the old world; beyond Bokhara he watched the wild Aryan horsemen at their gambols; watched, too, in some dim-lit tea-house one of those beautiful uncouth dances that one can never wholly forget; or, making a wide cast down to the valley of the Tigris, swam and rolled in its snow-cooled racing waters. Vanessa, meanwhile, in a Bayswater back street, was making out the weekly laundry list, attending bargain sales, and, in her more adventurous moments, trying new ways of cooking whiting. Occasionally she went to bridge parties, where, if the play was not illuminating, at least one learned a great deal about the private life of some of the Royal and Imperial Houses. Vanessa, in a way, was glad that Clyde had done the proper thing. She had a strong natural bias towards respectability, though she would have preferred to have been respectable in smarter surroundings, where her example would have done more good. To be beyond reproach was one thing, but it would have been nicer to have been nearer to the Park.

And then of a sudden her regard for respectability and Clyde's sense of what was right were thrown on the scrapheap of unnecessary things. They had been useful and highly important in their time, but the death of Vanessa's husband made them of no immediate moment.

The news of the altered condition of things followed Clyde with leisurely persistence from one place of call to another, and at last ran him to a standstill somewhere in the Orenburg Steppe. He would have found it exceedingly difficult to analyze his feelings on receipt of the tidings. The Fates had unexpectedly (and perhaps just a little officiously) removed an obstacle from his path. He supposed he was overjoyed, but he missed the feeling of elation which he had experienced some four months ago when he had bagged a snow-leopard with a lucky shot after a day's fruitless stalking. Of course he would go back and ask Vanessa to marry him, but he was determined on enforcing a condition: on no account would he desert his newer love. Vanessa would have to agree to come out into the Wilderness with him.

The lady hailed the return of her lover with even more relief than had been occasioned by his departure. The death of John Pennington had left his widow in circumstances which were more straitened than ever, and the Park had receded even from her notepaper, where it had long been retained as a courtesy title on the principle that addresses are given to us to conceal our whereabouts. Certainly she was more independent now than heretofore, but independence, which means so much to many women, was of little account to Vanessa, who came under the heading of the mere female. She made little ado about accepting Clyde's condition, and announced herself ready to follow him to the end of the world; as the world was round she nourished a complacent idea that in the ordinary course of things one would find oneself in the neighbourhood of Hyde Park Corner sooner or later no matter how far afield one wandered.

East of Budapest her complacency began to filter away, and when she saw her husband treating the Black Sea with a familiarity which she had never been able to assume towards the English Channel, misgivings began to crowd in upon her. Adventures which would have presented an amusing and enticing aspect to a better-bred woman aroused in Vanessa only the twin sensations of fright and discomfort. Flies bit her, and she was persuaded that it was only sheer boredom that prevented camels from doing the same. Clyde did his best, and a very good best it was, to infuse something of the banquet into their prolonged desert picnics, but even snow-cooled Heidsieck lost its flavour when you were convinced that the dusky cupbearer who served it with such reverent elegance was only waiting a convenient opportunity to cut your throat. It was useless for Clyde to give Yussuf a character for devotion such as is rarely found in any Western servant. Vanessa was well enough educated to know that all dusky-skinned people take human life as unconcernedly as Bayswater folk take singing lessons.

And with a growing irritation and querulousness on her part

came a further disenchantment, born of the inability of husband and wife to find a common ground of interest. The habits and migrations of the sand grouse, the folklore and customs of Tartars and Turkomans, the points of a Cossack pony—these were matters which evoked only a bored indifference in Vanessa. On the other hand, Clyde was not thrilled on being informed that the Queen of Spain detested mauve, or that a certain Royal duchess, for whose tastes he was never likely to be called on to cater, nursed a violent but perfectly respectable passion for beef olives.

Vanessa began to arrive at the conclusion that a husband who added a roving disposition to a settled income was a mixed blessing. It was one thing to go to the end of the world; it was quite another thing to make oneself at home there. Even respectability seemed to lose some of its virtue when one practised it in a tent.

Bored and disillusioned with the drift of her new life, Vanessa was undisguisedly glad when distraction offered itself in the person of Mr. Dobrinton, a chance acquaintance whom they had first run against in the primitive hostelry of a benighted Caucasian town. Dobrinton was elaborately British, in deference perhaps to the memory of his mother, who was said to have derived part of her origin from an English governess who had come to Lemberg a long way back in the last century. If you had called him Dobrinski when off his guard he would probably have responded readily enough; holding, no doubt, that the end crowns all, he had taken a slight liberty with the family patronymic. To look at, Mr. Dobrinton was not a very attractive specimen of masculine humanity, but in Vanessa's eyes he was a link with that civilization which Clyde seemed so ready to ignore and forgo. He could sing "Yip-I-Addy" and spoke of several duchesses as if he knew them—in his more inspired moments almost as if they knew him. He even pointed out blemishes in the cuisine or cellar departments of some of the more august London restaurants, a species of Higher Criticism which was listened to by Vanessa in awestricken admiration. And, above all, he sympathized, at first discreetly, afterwards with more latitude, with her fretful discontent at Clyde's nomadic instincts. Business connected with oil-wells had brought Dobrinton to the neighbourhood of Baku; the pleasure of appealing to an appreciative female audience induced him to deflect his return journey so as to coincide a good deal with his new acquaintances' line of march. And while Clyde trafficked with Persian horse-dealers or hunted the wild grey pigs in their lairs and added to his notes on Central Asian game-fowl, Dobrinton and the lady discussed the ethics of desert respectability from points of view that showed a daily tendency to converge. And one evening Clyde dined alone, reading between the courses a long letter from Vanessa, justifying her action in flitting to more civilized lands with a more congenial companion.

It was distinctly evil luck for Vanessa, who really was thoroughly respectable at heart, that she and her lover should run into the hands of Kurdish brigands on the first day of their flight. To be mewed up in a squalid Kurdish village in close companionship with a man who was only your husband by adoption, and to have the attention of all Europe drawn to your plight, was about the least respectable thing that could happen. And there were international complications, which made things worse. "English lady and her husband, of foreign nationality, held by Kurdish brigands who demand ransom" had been the report of the nearest Consul. Although Dobrinton was British at heart, the other portions of him belonged to the Habsburgs, and though the Habsburgs took no great pride or pleasure in this particular unit of their wide and varied possessions, and would gladly have exchanged him for some interesting bird or mammal for the Schoenbrunn Park, the code of international dignity demanded that they should display a decent solicitude for his restoration. And while the Foreign Offices of the two countries were taking the usual steps to secure the release of their respective subjects a further horrible complication ensued. Clyde, following on the track of the fugitives, not with any special desire to overtake them, but with a dim feeling that it was expected of him, fell into the hands of the same community of brigands. Diplomacy, while anxious to do its best for a lady in misfortune, showed signs of becoming restive at this expansion of its task; as a frivolous young gentleman in Downing Street remarked, "Any husband of Mrs. Dobrinton's we shall be glad to extricate, but let us know how many there are of them." For a woman who valued respectability Vanessa really had no luck.

Meanwhile the situation of the captives was not free from embarrassment. When Clyde explained to the Kurdish headmen the nature of his relationship with the runaway couple they were gravely sympathetic, but vetoed any idea of summary vengeance, since the Habsburgs would be sure to insist on the delivery of Dobrinton alive, and in a reasonably undamaged condition. They did not object to Clyde administering a beating to his rival for half an hour every Monday and Thursday, but Dobrinton turned such a sickly green when he heard of this arrangement that the chief was obliged to withdraw the concession.

And so, in the cramped quarters of a mountain hut, the ill-assorted trio watched the insufferable hours crawl slowly by. Dobrinton was too frightened to be conversational, Vanessa was too mortified to open her lips, and Clyde was moodily silent. The little Lemberg *négociant* plucked up heart once to give a quavering rendering of "Yip-I-Addy," but when he reached the statement "home was never like this" Vanessa tearfully begged him to stop. And silence fastened itself with growing insistence on the three captives who were so tragically herded together; thrice a day they drew near to one another to swallow the meal that had been prepared for them, like desert beasts meeting in mute suspended hostility at the drinking-pool, and then drew back to resume the vigil of waiting.

Clyde was less carefully watched than the others. "Jealousy will keep him to the woman's side," thought his Kurdish captors. They did not know that his wilder, truer love was calling to him with a hundred voices from beyond the village bounds. And one evening, finding that he was not getting the attention to which he was entitled, Clyde slipped away down the mountain side and resumed his study of Central Asian game-fowl. The remaining captives were guarded henceforth with greater rigour, but Dobrinton at any rate scarcely regretted Clyde's departure.

The long arm, or perhaps one might better say the long purse, of diplomacy at last effected the release of the prisoners, but the Habsburgs were never to enjoy the guerdon of their outlay. On the quay of the little Black Sea Port, where the rescued pair came once more into contact with civilization, Dobrinton was bitten by a dog which was assumed to be mad, though it may only have been indiscriminating. The victim did not wait for symptoms of rabies to declare themselves, but died forthwith of fright, and Vanessa made the homeward journey alone, conscious somehow of a sense of slightly restored respectability. Clyde, in the intervals of correcting the proofs of his book on the game-fowl of Central Asia, found time to press a divorce suit through the Courts, and as soon as possible hied him away to the congenial solitudes of the Gobi Desert to collect material for a work on the fauna of that region. Vanessa, by virtue perhaps of her earlier intimacy with the cooking rites of the whiting, obtained a place on the kitchen staff of a West End Club. It was not brilliant, but at least it was within two minutes of the Park.

THE BAKER'S DOZEN

Characters:

MAJOR RICHARD DUMBARTON

MRS. CAREWE

MRS. PALY-PAGET

Scene—Deck of eastward-bound steamer. Major Dumbarton seated on deck-chair, another chair by his side, with the name "Mrs. Carewe" painted on it, a third near by.

(Enter, R., Mrs. Carewe, seats herself leisurely in her deck-chair, the Major affecting to ignore her presence.)

Major (turning suddenly): Emily! After all these years! This is fate!

Em.: Fate! Nothing of the sort; it's only me. You men are always such fatalists. I deferred my departure three whole weeks, in order to come out in the same boat that I saw you were travelling by. I bribed the steward to put our chairs side by side in an unfrequented corner, and I took enormous pains to be looking particularly attractive this morning, and then you say, "This is fate." I *am* looking particularly attractive, am I not?

Maj.: More than ever. Time has only added a ripeness to your charms.

Em.: I knew you'd put it exactly in those words. The phraseology of love-making is awfully limited, isn't it? After all, the chief charm is in the fact of being made love to. You *are* making love to me, aren't you?

Maj.: Emily dearest, I had already begun making advances, even before you sat down here. I also bribed the steward to put our seats together in a secluded corner. "You may consider it done, sir," was his reply. That was immediately after breakfast.

Em.: How like a man to have his breakfast first. I attended to the seat business as soon as I left my cabin.

Maj.: Don't be unreasonable. It was only at breakfast that I discovered your blessed presence on the boat. I paid violent and unusual attention to a flapper all through the meal in order to make you jealous. She's probably in her cabin writing reams about me to a fellow-flapper at this very moment.

Em.: You needn't have taken all that trouble to make me jealous, Dickie. You did that years ago, when you married another woman.

Maj.: Well, you had gone and married another man—a widower, too, at that.

Em.: Well, there's no particular harm in marrying a widower, I suppose. I'm ready to do it again, if I meet a really nice one.

Maj.: Look here, Emily, it's not fair to go at that rate. You're a lap ahead of me the whole time. It's my place to propose to you; all you've got to do is to say "Yes."

Em.: Well, I've practically said it already, so we needn't dawdle over that part.

Maj.: Oh, well—

(They look at each other, then suddenly embrace with considerable energy.)

Maj.: We dead-heated it that time. (Suddenly jumping to his feet.) Oh, d—— I'd forgotten!

Em.: Forgotten what?

Maj.: The children. I ought to have told you. Do you mind children?

Em.: Not in moderate quantities. How many have you got?

Maj. (counting hurriedly on his fingers): Five.

Em.: Five!

Maj. (anxiously): Is that too many?

Em.: It's rather a number. The worst of it is, I've some myself.

Maj.: Many?

Em.: Eight.

Maj.: Eight in six years! Oh, Emily!

Em.: Only four were my own. The other four were by my husband's first marriage. Still, that practically makes eight.

Maj.: And eight and five make thirteen. We can't start our married life with thirteen children; it would be most unlucky. (Walks up and down in agitation.) Some way must be found out of this. If we could only bring them down to twelve. Thirteen is so horribly unlucky.

Em.: Isn't there some way by which we could part with one or two? Don't the French want more children? I've often seen articles about it in the *Figaro.*

Maj.: I fancy they want French children. Mine don't even speak French.

Em.: There's always a chance that one of them might turn out depraved and vicious, and then you could disown him. I've heard of that being done.

Maj.: But, good gracious, you've got to educate him first. You can't expect a boy to be vicious till he's been to a good school.

Em.: Why couldn't he be naturally depraved? Lots of boys are.

Maj.: Only when they inherit it from depraved parents. You don't suppose there's any depravity in me, do you?

Em.: It sometimes skips a generation, you know. Weren't any of your family bad?

Maj.: There was an aunt who was never spoken of.

Em.: There you are!

Maj.: But one can't build too much on that. In mid-Victorian days they labelled all sorts of things as unspeakable that we should speak about quite tolerantly. I daresay this particular aunt had only married a Unitarian, or rode to hounds on both sides of her horse, or something of that sort. Anyhow, we can't wait indefinitely for one of the children to take after a doubtfully depraved great aunt. Something else must be thought of.

Em.: Don't people ever adopt children from other families?

Maj.: I've heard of it being done by childless couples, and those sort of people—

Em.: Hush! Some one's coming. Who is it?

Maj.: Mrs. Paly-Paget.

Em.: The very person!

Maj.: What, to adopt a child? Hasn't she got any?

Em.: Only one miserable hen-baby.

Maj.: Let's sound her on the subject.

(Enter Mrs. Paley-Paget, R.)

Ah, good morning, Mrs. Paly-Paget. I was just wondering at breakfast where did we meet last?

Mrs. P.-P.: At the Criterion, wasn't it? (Drops into vacant chair.)

Maj.: At the Criterion, of course.

Mrs. P.-P.: I was dining with Lord and Lady Slugford. Charming people, but so mean. They took us afterwards to the Velodrome, to see some dancer interpreting Mendelssohn's "songs without clothes." We were all packed up in a little box near the roof, and you may imagine how hot it was. It was like a Turkish bath. And, of course, one couldn't see anything.

Maj.: Then it was not like a Turkish bath.

Mrs. P.-P.: Major!

Em.: We were just talking of you when you joined us.

Mrs. P.-P.: Really! Nothing very dreadful, I hope.

Em.: Oh, dear, no! It's too early on the voyage for that sort of thing. We were feeling rather sorry for you.

Mrs. P.-P.: Sorry for me? Whatever for?

Maj.: Your childless hearth and all that, you know. No little pattering feet.

Mrs. P.-P.: Major! How dare you? I've got my little girl, I suppose you know. Her feet can patter as well as other children's.

Maj.: Only one pair of feet.

Mrs. P.-P.: Certainly. My child isn't a centipede. Considering the way they move us about in those horrid jungle stations, without a decent bungalow to set one's foot in, I consider I've got a hearthless child, rather than a childless hearth. Thank you for your sympathy all the same. I daresay it was well meant. Impertinence often is.

Em.: Dear Mrs. Paly-Paget, we were only feeling sorry for your sweet little girl when she grows older, you know. No little brothers and sisters to play with.

Mrs. P.-P.: Mrs. Carewe, this conversation strikes me as being indelicate, to say the least of it. I've only been married two and a half years, and my family is naturally a small one.

Maj.: Isn't it rather an exaggeration to talk of one little female child as a family? A family suggests numbers.

Mrs. P.-P.: Really, Major, your language is extraordinary. I daresay I've only got a little female child, as you call it, at present—

Maj.: Oh, it won't change into a boy later on, if that's what you're counting on. Take our word for it; we've had so much more experience in these affairs than you have. Once a female, always a female. Nature is not infallible, but she always abides by her mistakes.

Mrs. P.-P. (rising): Major Dumbarton, these boats are uncomfortably small, but I trust we shall find ample accommodation for avoiding each other's society during the rest of the voyage. The same wish applies to you, Mrs. Carewe.

(Exit Mrs. Paly-Paget, L.)

Maj.: What an unnatural mother! (Sinks into chair.)

Em.: I wouldn't trust a child with any one who had a temper like hers. Oh, Dickie, why did you go and have such a large family? You always said you wanted me to be the mother of your children.

Maj.: I wasn't going to wait while you were founding and fostering dynasties in other directions. Why you couldn't be content to have children of your own, without collecting them like batches of postage stamps I can't think. The idea of marrying a man with four children!

Em.: Well, you're asking me to marry one with five.

Maj.: Five! (Springing to his feet.) Did I say five?

Em.: You certainly said five.

Maj.: Oh, Emily, supposing I've miscounted them! Listen now, keep count with me. Richard—that's after me, of course.

Em.: One.

Maj.: Albert-Victor—that must have been in Coronation year.

Em.: Two!

Maj.: Maud. She's called after—

Em.: Never mind who she's called after. Three!

Maj.: And Gerald.

Em.: Four!

Maj.: That's the lot.

Em.: Are you sure?

Maj.: I swear that's the lot. I must have counted Albert-Victor as two.

Em.: Richard!

Maj.: Emily!

(They embrace.)

THE MOUSE

Theodoric Voler had been brought up, from infancy to the confines of middle age, by a fond mother whose chief solicitude had been to keep him screened from what she called the coarser realities of life. When she died she left Theodoric alone in a world that was as real as ever, and a good deal coarser than he considered it had any need to be. To a man of his temperament and upbringing even a simple railway journey was crammed with petty annoyances and minor discords, and as he settled himself down in a second-class compartment one September morning he was conscious of ruffled feelings and general mental discomposure. He had been staying at a country vicarage, the inmates of which had been certainly neither brutal nor bacchanalian, but their supervision of the domestic establishment had been of that lax order which invites disaster. The pony carriage that was to take him to the station had never been properly ordered, and when the moment for his departure drew near the handyman who should have produced the required article was nowhere to be found. In this emergency Theodoric, to his mute but very intense disgust, found himself obliged to collaborate with the vicar's daughter in the task of harnessing the pony, which necessitated groping about in an ill-lighted outhouse called a stable, and smelling very like one—except in patches where it smelt of mice. Without being actually afraid of mice, Theodoric classed them among the coarser incidents of life, and considered that Providence, with a little exercise of moral courage, might long ago have recognized that they were not indispensable, and have withdrawn them from circulation. As the train glided out of the station Theodoric's nervous imagination accused himself of exhaling a weak odour of stableyard, and possibly of displaying a mouldy straw or two on his usually well-brushed garments. Fortunately the only other occupant of the compartment, a lady of about the same age as himself, seemed inclined for slumber rather than scrutiny; the train was not due to stop till the terminus was reached, in about an hour's time, and the carriage was of the old-fashioned sort, that held no communication with a corridor, therefore no further travelling companions were likely to intrude on Theodoric's semi-privacy. And yet the train had scarcely attained its normal speed before he became reluctantly but vividly aware that he was not alone with the slumbering lady; he was not even alone in his own clothes. A warm, creeping movement over his flesh betrayed the unwelcome and highly resented presence, unseen but poignant, of a strayed mouse, that had evidently dashed into its present retreat during the episode of the pony harnessing. Furtive stamps and shakes and wildly directed pinches failed to dislodge the intruder, whose motto, indeed, seemed to be Excelsior; and the lawful occupant of the clothes lay back against the cushions and endeavoured rapidly to evolve some means for putting an end to the dual ownership. It was unthinkable that he should continue for the space of a whole hour in the horrible position of a Rowton House for vagrant mice (already his imagination had at least doubled the numbers of the alien invasion). On the other hand, nothing less drastic than partial disrobing would ease him of his tormentor, and to undress in the presence of a lady, even for so laudable a purpose, was an idea that made his eartips tingle in a blush of abject shame. He had never been able to bring himself even to the mild exposure of open-work socks in the presence of the fair sex. And yet—the lady in this case was to all appearances soundly and securely asleep; the mouse, on the other hand, seemed to be trying to crowd a Wanderjahr into a few strenuous minutes. If there is any truth in the theory of transmigration, this particular mouse must certainly have been in a former state a member of the Alpine Club. Sometimes in its eagerness it lost its footing and slipped for half an inch or so; and then, in fright, or more probably temper, it bit. Theodoric was goaded into the most audacious undertaking of his life. Crimsoning to the hue of a beetroot and keeping an agonized watch on his slumbering fellow-traveller, he swiftly and noiselessly secured the ends of his railway-rug to the racks on either side of the carriage, so that a substantial curtain hung athwart the compartment. In the narrow dressing-room that he had thus improvised he proceeded with violent haste to extricate himself partially and the mouse entirely from the surrounding casings of tweed and half-wool. As the unravelled mouse gave a wild leap to the floor, the rug, slipping its fastening at either end, also came down with a heart-curdling flop, and almost simultaneously the awakened sleeper opened her eyes. With a movement almost quicker than the mouse's, Theodoric pounced on the rug, and hauled its ample folds chin-high over his dismantled person as he collapsed into the further corner of the carriage. The blood raced and beat in the veins of his neck and forehead, while he waited dumbly for the communication-cord to be pulled. The lady, however, contented herself with a silent stare at her strangely muffled companion. How much had she seen, Theodoric queried to himself, and in any case what on earth must she think of his present posture?

"I think I have caught a chill," he ventured desperately.

"Really, I'm sorry," she replied. "I was just going to ask you if you would open this window."

"I fancy it's malaria," he added, his teeth chattering slightly, as much from fright as from a desire to support his theory.

"I've got some brandy in my hold-all, if you'll kindly reach it down for me," said his companion.

"Not for worlds—I mean, I never take anything for it," he assured her earnestly.

"I suppose you caught it in the Tropics?"

Theodoric, whose acquaintance with the Tropics was limited to an annual present of a chest of tea from an uncle in Ceylon, felt that even the malaria was slipping from him. Would it be possible, he wondered, to disclose the real state of affairs to her in small instalments?

"Are you afraid of mice?" he ventured, growing, if possible, more scarlet in the face.

"Not unless they came in quantities, like those that ate up Bishop Hatto. Why do you ask?"

"I had one crawling inside my clothes just now," said Theodoric in a voice that hardly seemed his own. "It was a most awkward situation."

"It must have been, if you wear your clothes at all tight," she observed; "but mice have strange ideas of comfort."

"I had to get rid of it while you were asleep," he continued; then, with a gulp, he added, "it was getting rid of it that brought me to—to this."

"Surely leaving off one small mouse wouldn't bring on a chill," she exclaimed, with a levity that Theodoric accounted abominable.

Evidently she had detected something of his predicament, and was enjoying his confusion. All the blood in his body seemed to have mobilized in one concentrated blush, and an agony of abasement, worse than a myriad mice, crept up and down over his soul. And then, as reflection began to assert itself, sheer terror took the place of humiliation. With every minute that passed the train was rushing nearer to the crowded and bustling terminus where dozens of prying eyes would be exchanged for the one paralyzing pair that watched him from the further corner of the carriage. There was one slender despairing chance, which the next few minutes must decide. His fellow-traveller might relapse into a blessed slumber. But as the minutes throbbed by that chance ebbed away. The furtive glance which Theodoric stole at her from time to time disclosed only an unwinking wakefulness.

"I think we must be getting near now," she presently observed.

Theodoric had already noted with growing terror the recurring stacks of small, ugly dwellings that heralded the journey's end. The words acted as a signal. Like a hunted beast breaking cover and dashing madly towards some other haven of momentary safety he threw aside his rug, and struggled frantically into his dishevelled garments. He was conscious of dull suburban stations racing past the window, of a choking, hammering sensation in his throat and heart, and of an icy silence in that corner towards which he dared not look. Then as he sank back in his seat, clothed and almost delirious, the train slowed down to a final crawl, and the woman spoke.

"Would you be so kind," she asked, "as to get me a porter to put me into a cab? It's a shame to trouble you when you're feeling unwell, but being blind makes one so helpless at a railway station."

The Chronicles of Clovis

First Collected, 1911

To the Lynx Kitten,
With His Reluctantly Given Consent,
This Book Is Affectionately
Dedicated

H. H. M.
August, 1911

ESMÉ

"ALL hunting stories are the same," said Clovis; "just as all Turf stories are the same, and all–"

"My hunting story isn't a bit like any you've ever heard," said the Baroness. "It happened quite a while ago, when I was about twenty-three. I wasn't living apart from my husband then; you see, neither of us could afford to make the other a separate allowance. In spite of everything that proverbs may say, poverty keeps together more homes than it breaks up. But we always hunted with different packs. All this has nothing to do with the story."

"We haven't arrived at the meet yet. I suppose there was a meet," said Clovis.

"Of course there was a meet," said the Baroness; "all the usual crowd were there, especially Constance Broddle. Constance is one of those strapping florid girls that go so well with autumn scenery or Christmas decorations in church. 'I feel a presentiment that something dreadful is going to happen,' she said to me; 'am I looking pale?'

"She was looking about as pale as a beetroot that has suddenly heard bad news.

"'You're looking nicer than usual,' I said, 'but that's so easy for you.' Before she had got the right bearings of this remark we had settled down to business; hounds had found a fox lying out in some gorse-bushes."

"I knew it," said Clovis; "in every fox-hunting story that I've ever heard there's been a fox and some gorse-bushes."

"Constance and I were well mounted," continued the Baroness serenely, "and we had no difficulty in keeping ourselves in the first flight, though it was a fairly stiff run. Towards the finish, however, we must have held rather too independent a line, for we lost the hounds, and found ourselves plodding aimlessly along miles away from anywhere. It was fairly exasperating, and my temper was beginning to let itself go by inches, when on pushing our way through an accommodating hedge we were gladdened by the sight of hounds in full cry in a hollow just beneath us.

"'There they go,' cried Constance, and then added in a gasp, 'In Heaven's name, what are they hunting?'

"It was certainly no mortal fox. It stood more than twice as high, had a short, ugly head, and an enormous thick neck.

"'It's a hyæna,' I cried; 'it must have escaped from Lord Pabham's Park.'

"At that moment the hunted beast turned and faced its pursuers, and the hounds (there were only about six couple of them) stood round in a half-circle and looked foolish. Evidently they had broken away from the rest of the pack on the trail of this alien scent, and were not quite sure how to treat their quarry now they had got him.

"The hyæna hailed our approach with unmistakable relief and demonstrations of friendliness. It had probably been accustomed to uniform kindness from humans, while its first experience of a pack of hounds had left a bad impression. The hounds looked more than ever embarrassed as their quarry paraded its sudden intimacy with us, and the faint toot of a horn in the distance was seized on as a welcome signal for unobtrusive departure. Constance and I and the hyæna were left alone in the gathering twilight.

"'What are we to do?' asked Constance.

"'What a person you are for questions,' I said.

"'Well, we can't stay here all night with a hyæna,' she retorted.

"'I don't know what your ideas of comfort are,' I said; 'but I shouldn't think of staying here all night even without a hyæna. My home may be an unhappy one, but at least it has hot and cold water laid on, and domestic service, and other conveniences which we shouldn't find here. We had better make for that ridge of trees to the right; I imagine the Crowley road is just beyond.'

"We trotted off slowly along a faintly marked cart-track, with the beast following cheerfully at our heels.

"'What on earth are we to do with the hyæna?' came the inevitable question.

"'What does one generally do with hyænas?' I asked crossly.

"'I've never had anything to do with one before,' said Constance.

"'Well, neither have I. If we even knew its sex we might give it a name. Perhaps we might call it Esmé. That would do in either case.'

"There was still sufficient daylight for us to distinguish wayside objects, and our listless spirits gave an upward perk as we came upon a small half-naked gipsy brat picking blackberries from a low-growing bush. The sudden apparition of two horsewomen and a hyæna set it off crying, and in any case we should scarcely have gleaned any useful geographical information from that source; but there was a probability that we might strike a gipsy encampment somewhere along our route. We rode on hopefully but uneventfully for another mile or so.

"'I wonder what the child was doing there,' said Constance presently.

"'Picking blackberries. Obviously.'

"'I don't like the way it cried,' pursued Constance; 'somehow its wail keeps ringing in my ears.'

"I did not chide Constance for her morbid fancies; as a matter of fact the same sensation, of being pursued by a persistent fretful wail, had been forcing itself on my rather over-tired nerves. For company's sake I hulloed to Esmé, who had lagged somewhat behind. With a few springy bounds he drew up level, and then shot past us.

"The wailing accompaniment was explained. The gipsy child was firmly, and I expect painfully, held in his jaws.

"'Merciful Heaven!' screamed Constance, 'what on earth shall we do? What are we to do?'

"I am perfectly certain that at the Last Judgment Constance will ask more questions than any of the examining Seraphs.

"'Can't we do something?' she persisted tearfully, as Esmé cantered easily along in front of our tired horses.

"Personally I was doing everything that occurred to me at the moment. I stormed and scolded and coaxed in English and French and gamekeeper language; I made absurd, ineffectual cuts in the air with my thongless hunting-crop; I hurled my sandwich case at the brute; in fact, I really don't know what more I could have done. And still we lumbered on through the deepening dusk, with that dark uncouth shape lumbering ahead of us, and a drone of lugubrious music floating in our ears. Suddenly Esmé bounded aside into some thick bushes, where we could not follow; the wail rose to a shriek and then stopped altogether. This part of the story I always hurry over, because it is really rather horrible. When the beast joined us again, after an absence of a few minutes, there was an air of patient understanding about him, as though he knew that he had done something of which we disapproved, but which he felt to be thoroughly justifiable.

"'How can you let that ravening beast trot by your side?' asked Constance. She was looking more than ever like an albino beetroot.

"'In the first place, I can't prevent it,' I said; 'and in the second place, whatever else he may be, I doubt if he's ravening at the present moment.'

"Constance shuddered. 'Do you think the poor little thing suffered much?' came another of her futile questions.

"'The indications were all that way,' I said; 'on the other hand, of course, it may have been crying from sheer temper. Children sometimes do.'

"It was nearly pitch-dark when we emerged suddenly into the high road. A flash of lights and the whir of a motor went past us at the same moment at uncomfortably close quarters. A thud and a sharp screeching yell followed a second later. The car drew up, and when I had ridden back to the spot I found a young man bending over a dark motionless mass lying by the roadside.

"'You have killed my Esmé,' I exclaimed bitterly.

"'I'm so awfully sorry,' said the young man; 'I keep dogs myself, so I know what you must feel about it. I'll do anything I can in reparation.'

"'Please bury him at once,' I said; 'that much I think I may ask of you.'

"'Bring the spade, William,' he called to the chauffeur. Evidently hasty roadside interments were contingencies that had been provided against.

"The digging of a sufficiently large grave took some little time. 'I say, what a magnificent fellow,' said the motorist as the corpse was rolled over into the trench. 'I'm afraid he must have been rather a valuable animal.'

"'He took second in the puppy class at Birmingham last year,' I said resolutely.

"Constance snorted loudly.

"'Don't cry, dear,' I said brokenly; 'it was all over in a moment. He couldn't have suffered much.'

"'Look here,' said the young fellow desperately, 'you simply must let me do something by way of reparation.'

"I refused sweetly, but as he persisted I let him have my address.

"Of course, we kept our own counsel as to the earlier episodes of the evening. Lord Pabham never advertised the loss of his hyæna; when a strictly fruit-eating animal strayed from his park a year or two previously he was called upon to give compensation in eleven cases of sheep-worrying and practically to re-stock his neighbours' poultry-yards, and an escaped hyæna would have mounted up to something on the scale of a Government grant. The gipsies were equally unobtrusive over their missing offspring; I don't suppose in large encampments they really know to a child or two how many they've got."

The Baroness paused reflectively, and then continued:

"There was a sequel to the adventure, though. I got through the post a charming little diamond brooch, with the name Esmé set in a sprig of rosemary. Incidentally, too, I lost the friendship of Constance Broddle. You see, when I sold the brooch I quite properly refused to give her any share of the proceeds. I pointed out that the Esmé part of the affair was my own invention, and the hyæna part of it belonged to Lord Pabham, if it really was his hyæna, of which, of course, I've no proof."

THE MATCH-MAKER

THE grill-room clock struck eleven with the respectful unobtrusiveness of one whose mission in life is to be ignored. When the flight of time should really have rendered abstinence and migration imperative the lighting apparatus would signal the fact in the usual way.

Six minutes later Clovis approached the supper-table, in the blessed expectancy of one who has dined sketchily and long ago.

"I'm starving," he announced, making an effort to sit down gracefully and read the menu at the same time.

"So I gathered," said his host, "from the fact that you were nearly punctual. I ought to have told you that I'm a Food Reformer. I've ordered two bowls of bread-and-milk and some health biscuits. I hope you don't mind."

Clovis pretended afterwards that he didn't go white above the collar-line for the fraction of a second.

"All the same," he said, "you ought not to joke about such things. There really are such people. I've known people who've met them. To think of all the adorable things there are to eat in the world, and then to go through life munching sawdust and being proud of it."

"They're like the Flagellants of the Middle Ages, who went about mortifying themselves."

"They had some excuse," said Clovis. "They did it to save their immortal souls, didn't they? You needn't tell me that a man who doesn't love oysters and asparagus and good wines has got a soul, or a stomach either. He's simply got the instinct for being unhappy highly developed."

Clovis relapsed for a few golden moments into tender intimacies with a succession of rapidly disappearing oysters.

"I think oysters are more beautiful than any religion," he resumed presently. "They not only forgive our unkindness to them; they justify it, they incite us to go on being perfectly horrid to them. Once they arrive at the supper-table they seem to enter thoroughly into the spirit of the thing. There's nothing in Christianity or Buddhism that quite matches the sympathetic unselfishness of an oyster. Do you like my new waistcoat? I'm wearing it for the first time tonight."

"It looks like a great many others you've had lately, only worse. New dinner waistcoats are becoming a habit with you."

"They say one always pays for the excesses of one's youth; mercifully that isn't true about one's clothes. My mother is thinking of getting married."

"Again!"

"It's the first time."

"Of course, you ought to know. I was under the impression that she'd been married once or twice at least."

"Three times, to be mathematically exact. I meant that it was the first time she'd thought about getting married; the other times she did it without thinking. As a matter of fact, it's really I who am doing the thinking for her in this case. You see, it's quite two years since her last husband died."

"You evidently think that brevity is the soul of widowhood."

"Well, it struck me that she was getting moped, and beginning to settle down, which wouldn't suit her a bit. The first symptom that I noticed was when she began to complain that we were living beyond our income. All decent people live beyond their incomes nowadays, and those who aren't respectable live beyond other people's. A few gifted individuals manage to do both."

"It's hardly so much a gift as an industry."

"The crisis came," returned Clovis, "when she suddenly started the theory that late hours were bad for one, and wanted me to be in by one o'clock every night. Imagine that sort of thing for me, who was eighteen on my last birthday."

"On your last two birthdays, to be mathematically exact."

"Oh, well, that's not my fault. I'm not going to arrive at nineteen as long as my mother remains at thirty-seven. One must have some regard for appearances."

"Perhaps your mother would age a little in the process of settling down."

"That's the last thing she'd think of. Feminine reformations always start in on the failings of other people. That's why I was so keen on the husband idea."

"Did you go as far as to select the gentleman, or did you merely throw out a general idea, and trust to the force of suggestion?"

"If one wants a thing done in a hurry one must see to it oneself.

I found a military Johnny hanging round on a loose end at the club, and took him home to lunch once or twice. He'd spent most of his life on the Indian frontier, building roads, and relieving famines and minimizing earthquakes, and all that sort of thing that one does do on frontiers. He could talk sense to a peevish cobra in fifteen native languages, and probably knew what to do if you found a rogue elephant on your croquet-lawn; but he was shy and diffident with women. I told my mother privately that he was an absolute woman-hater; so, of course, she laid herself out to flirt all she knew, which isn't a little."

"And was the gentleman responsive?"

"I hear he told some one at the club that he was looking out for a Colonial job, with plenty of hard work, for a young friend of his, so I gather that he has some idea of marrying into the family."

"You seem destined to be the victim of the reformation, after all."

Clovis wiped the trace of Turkish coffee and the beginnings of a smile from his lips, and slowly lowered his dexter eyelid. Which, being interpreted, probably meant, "I *don't* think!"

TOBERMORY

It was a chill, rain-washed afternoon of a late August day, that indefinite season when partridges are still in security or cold storage, and there is nothing to hunt—unless one is bounded on the north by the Bristol Channel, in which case one may lawfully gallop after fat red stags. Lady Blemley's house-party was not bounded on the north by the Bristol Channel, hence there was a full gathering of her guests round the tea-table on this particular afternoon. And, in spite of the blankness of the season and the triteness of the occasion, there was no trace in the company of that fatigued restlessness which means a dread of the pianola and a subdued hankering for auction bridge. The undisguised open-mouthed attention of the entire party was fixed on the homely negative personality of Mr. Cornelius Appin. Of all her guests, he was the one who had come to Lady Blemley with the vaguest reputation. Some one had said he was "clever," and he had got his invitation in the moderate expectation, on the part of his hostess, that some portion at least of his cleverness would be contributed to the general entertainment. Until tea-time that day she had been unable to discover in what direction, if any, his cleverness lay. He was neither a wit nor a croquet champion, a hypnotic force nor a begetter of amateur theatricals. Neither did his exterior suggest the sort of man in whom women are willing to pardon a generous measure of mental deficiency. He had subsided into mere Mr. Appin, and the Cornelius seemed a piece of transparent baptismal bluff. And now he was claiming to have launched on the world a discovery beside which the invention of gunpowder, of the printing-press, and of steam locomotion were inconsiderable trifles. Science had made bewildering strides in many directions during recent decades, but this thing seemed to belong to the domain of miracle rather than to scientific achievement.

"And do you really ask us to believe," Sir Wilfrid was saying, "that you have discovered a means for instructing animals in the art of human speech, and that dear old Tobermory has proved your first successful pupil?"

"It is a problem at which I have worked for the last seventeen years," said Mr. Appin, "but only during the last eight or nine months have I been rewarded with glimmerings of success. Of course I have experimented with thousands of animals, but latterly only with cats, those wonderful creatures which have assimilated themselves so marvellously with our civilization while retaining all their highly developed feral instincts. Here and there among cats one comes across an outstanding superior intellect, just as one does among the ruck of human beings, and when I made the acquaintance of Tobermory a week ago I saw at once that I was in contact with a 'Beyond-cat' of extraordinary intelligence. I had gone far along the road to success in recent experiments; with Tobermory, as you call him, I have reached the goal."

Mr. Appin concluded his remarkable statement in a voice which he strove to divest of a triumphant inflection. No one said "Rats," though Clovis's lips moved in a monosyllabic contortion which probably invoked those rodents of disbelief.

"And do you mean to say," asked Miss Resker, after a slight pause, "that you have taught Tobermory to say and understand easy sentences of one syllable?"

"My dear Miss Resker," said the wonder-worker patiently, "one teaches little children and savages and backward adults in that piecemeal fashion; when one has once solved the problem of making a beginning with an animal of highly developed intelligence one has no need for those halting methods. Tobermory can speak our language with perfect correctness."

This time Clovis very distinctly said, "Beyond-rats!" Sir Wilfrid was more polite, but equally sceptical.

"Hadn't we better have the cat in and judge for ourselves?" suggested Lady Blemley.

Sir Wilfrid went in search of the animal, and the company settled themselves down to the languid expectation of witnessing some more or less adroit drawing-room ventriloquism.

In a minute Sir Wilfrid was back in the room, his face white beneath its tan and his eyes dilated with excitement.

"By Gad, it's true!"

His agitation was unmistakably genuine, and his hearers started forward in a thrill of awakened interest.

Collapsing into an armchair he continued breathlessly: "I found him dozing in the smoking-room and called out to him to come for his tea. He blinked at me in his usual way, and I said, 'Come on, Toby; don't keep us waiting'; and, by Gad! he drawled out in a most horribly natural voice that he'd come when he dashed well pleased! I nearly jumped out of my skin!"

Appin had preached to absolutely incredulous hearers; Sir Wilfrid's statement carried instant conviction. A Babel-like chorus of startled exclamation arose, amid which the scientist sat mutely enjoying the first fruit of his stupendous discovery.

In the midst of the clamour Tobermory entered the room and made his way with velvet tread and studied unconcern across to the group seated round the tea-table.

A sudden hush of awkwardness and constraint fell on the company. Somehow there seemed an element of embarrassment in addressing on equal terms a domestic cat of acknowledged dental ability.

"Will you have some milk, Tobermory?" asked Lady Blemley in a rather strained voice.

"I don't mind if I do," was the response, couched in a tone of even indifference. A shiver of suppressed excitement went through the listeners, and Lady Blemley might be excused for pouring out the saucerful of milk rather unsteadily.

"I'm afraid I've spilt a good deal of it," she said apologetically.

"After all, it's not my Axminster," was Tobermory's rejoinder.

Another silence fell on the group, and then Miss Resker, in her best district-visitor manner, asked if the human language had been difficult to learn. Tobermory looked squarely at her for a moment and then fixed his gaze serenely on the middle distance. It was obvious that boring questions lay outside his scheme of life.

"What do you think of human intelligence?" asked Mavis Pellington lamely.

"Of whose intelligence in particular?" asked Tobermory coldly.

"Oh, well, mine for instance," said Mavis, with a feeble laugh.

"You put me in an embarrassing position," said Tobermory, whose tone and attitude certainly did not suggest a shred of embarrassment. "When your inclusion in this house-party was suggested Sir Wilfrid protested that you were the most brainless woman of his acquaintance, and that there was a wide distinction between hospitality and the care of the feeble-minded. Lady Blemley replied that your lack of brain-power was the precise quality which had earned you your invitation, as you were the only person she could think of who might be idiotic enough to buy their old car. You know, the one they call 'The Envy of Sisyphus,' because it goes quite nicely up-hill if you push it."

Lady Blemley's protestations would have had greater effect if she had not casually suggested to Mavis only that morning that the car in question would be just the thing for her down at her Devonshire home.

Major Barfield plunged in heavily to effect a diversion.

"How about your carryings-on with the tortoise-shell puss up at the stables, eh?"

The moment he had said it every one realized the blunder.

"One does not usually discuss these matters in public," said Tobermory frigidly. "From a slight observation of your ways since you've been in this house I should imagine you'd find it inconvenient if I were to shift the conversation on to your own little affairs."

The panic which ensued was not confined to the Major.

"Would you like to go and see if cook has got your dinner ready?" suggested Lady Blemley hurriedly, affecting to ignore the fact that it wanted at least two hours to Tobermory's dinner-time.

"Thanks," said Tobermory, "not quite so soon after my tea. I don't want to die of indigestion."

"Cats have nine lives, you know," said Sir Wilfrid heartily.

"Possibly," answered Tobermory; "but only one liver."

"Adelaide!" said Mrs. Cornett, "do you mean to encourage that cat to go out and gossip about us in the servants' hall?"

The panic had indeed become general. A narrow ornamental balustrade ran in front of most of the bedroom windows at the Towers, and it was recalled with dismay that this had formed a favourite promenade for Tobermory at all hours, whence he could watch the pigeons—and heaven knew what else besides. If he intended to become reminiscent in his present outspoken strain the effect would be something more than disconcerting. Mrs. Cornett, who spent much time at her toilet table, and whose complexion was reputed to be of a nomadic though punctual disposition, looked as ill at ease as the Major. Miss Scrawen, who wrote fiercely sensuous poetry and led a blameless life, merely displayed irritation; if you are methodical and virtuous in private you don't necessarily want every one to know it. Bertie van Tahn, who was so depraved at seventeen that he had long ago given up trying to be any worse, turned a dull shade of gardenia white, but he did not commit the error of dashing out of the room like Odo Finsberry, a young gentleman who was understood to be reading for the Church and who was possibly disturbed at the thought of scandals he might hear concerning other people. Clovis had the presence of mind to maintain a composed exterior; privately he was calculating how long it would take to procure a box of fancy mice through the agency of the *Exchange and Mart* as a species of hush-money.

Even in a delicate situation like the present, Agnes Resker could not endure to remain too long in the background.

"Why did I ever come down here?" she asked dramatically.

Tobermory immediately accepted the opening.

"Judging by what you said to Mrs. Cornett on the croquet-lawn yesterday, you were out for food. You described the Blemleys as the dullest people to stay with that you knew, but said they were clever enough to employ a first-rate cook; otherwise they'd find it difficult to get any one to come down a second time."

"There's not a word of truth in it! I appeal to Mrs. Cornett—" exclaimed the discomfited Agnes.

"Mrs. Cornett repeated your remark afterwards to Bertie van Tahn," continued Tobermory, "and said, 'That woman is a regular Hunger Marcher; she'd go anywhere for four square meals a day,' and Bertie van Tahn said—"

At this point the chronicle mercifully ceased. Tobermory had caught a glimpse of the big yellow Tom from the Rectory working his way through the shrubbery towards the stable wing. In a flash he had vanished through the open French window.

With the disappearance of his too brilliant pupil Cornelius Appin found himself beset by a hurricane of bitter upbraiding, anxious inquiry, and frightened entreaty. The responsibility for the situation lay with him, and he must prevent matters from becoming worse. Could Tobermory impart his dangerous gift to other cats? was the first question he had to answer. It was possible, he replied, that he might have initiated his intimate friend the stable puss into his new accomplishment, but it was unlikely that his teaching could have taken a wider range as yet.

"Then," said Mrs. Cornett, "Tobermory may be a valuable cat and a great pet; but I'm sure you'll agree, Adelaide, that both he and the stable cat must be done away with without delay."

"You don't suppose I've enjoyed the last quarter of an hour, do you?" said Lady Blemley bitterly. "My husband and I are very fond of Tobermory–at least, we were before this horrible accomplishment was infused into him; but now, of course, the only thing is to have him destroyed as soon as possible."

"We can put some strychnine in the scraps he always gets at dinner-time," said Sir Wilfrid, "and I will go and drown the stable cat myself. The coachman will be very sore at losing his pet, but I'll say a very catching form of mange has broken out in both cats and we're afraid of its spreading to the kennels."

"But my great discovery!" expostulated Mr. Appin; "after all my years of research and experiment–"

"You can go and experiment on the short-horns at the farm, who are under proper control," said Mrs. Cornett, "or the elephants at the Zoological Gardens. They're said to be highly intelligent, and they have this recommendation, that they don't come creeping about our bedrooms and under chairs, and so forth."

An archangel ecstatically proclaiming the Millennium, and then finding that it clashed unpardonably with Henley and would have to be indefinitely postponed, could hardly have felt more crestfallen than Cornelius Appin at the reception of his wonderful achievement. Public opinion, however, was against him–in fact, had the general voice been consulted on the subject it is probable that a strong minority vote would have been in favour of including him in the strychnine diet.

Defective train arrangements and a nervous desire to see matters brought to a finish prevented an immediate dispersal of the party, but dinner that evening was not a social success. Sir Wilfrid had had rather a trying time with the stable cat and subsequently with the coachman. Agnes Resker ostentatiously limited her repast to a morsel of dry toast, which she bit as though it were a personal enemy; while Mavis Pellington maintained a vindictive silence throughout the meal. Lady Blemley kept up a flow of what she hoped was conversation, but her attention was fixed on the doorway. A plateful of carefully dosed fish scraps was in readiness on the sideboard, but sweets and savoury and dessert went their way, and no Tobermory appeared either in the dining-room or kitchen.

The sepulchral dinner was cheerful compared with the subsequent vigil in the smoking-room. Eating and drinking had at least supplied a distraction and cloak to the prevailing embarrassment. Bridge was out of the question in the general tension of nerves and tempers, and after Odo Finsberry had given a lugubrious rendering of "Mélisande in the Wood" to a frigid audience, music was tacitly avoided. At eleven the servants went to bed, announcing that the small window in the pantry had been left open as usual for Tobermory's private use. The guests read steadily through the current batch of magazines, and fell back gradually on the "Badminton Library" and bound volumes of *Punch*. Lady Blemley made periodic visits to the pantry, returning each time with an expression of listless depression which forestalled questioning.

At two o'clock Clovis broke the dominating silence.

"He won't turn up tonight. He's probably in the local newspaper office at the present moment, dictating the first instalment of his reminiscences. Lady What's-her-name's book won't be in it. It will be the event of the day."

Having made this contribution to the general cheerfulness, Clovis went to bed. At long intervals the various members of the house-party followed his example.

The servants taking round the early tea made a uniform announcement in reply to a uniform question. Tobermory had not returned.

Breakfast was, if anything, a more unpleasant function than dinner had been, but before its conclusion the situation was relieved. Tobermory's corpse was brought in from the shrubbery, where a gardener had just discovered it. From the bites on his throat and the yellow fur which coated his claws it was evident that he had fallen in unequal combat with the big Tom from the Rectory.

By midday most of the guests had quitted the Towers, and after lunch Lady Blemley had sufficiently recovered her spirits to write an extremely nasty letter to the Rectory about the loss of her valuable pet.

Tobermory had been Appin's one successful pupil, and he was destined to have no successor. A few weeks later an elephant in the Dresden Zoological Garden, which had shown no previous signs of irritability, broke loose and killed an Englishman who had apparently been teasing it. The victim's name was variously reported in the papers as Oppin and Eppelin, but his front name was faithfully rendered Cornelius.

"If he was trying German irregular verbs on the poor beast," said Clovis, "he deserved all he got."

MRS. PACKLETIDE'S TIGER

It was Mrs. Packletide's pleasure and intention that she should shoot a tiger. Not that the lust to kill had suddenly descended on her, or that she felt that she would leave India safer and more wholesome than she had found it, with one fraction less of wild beast per million of inhabitants. The compelling motive for her sudden deviation towards the footsteps of Nimrod was the fact that Loona Bimberton had recently been carried eleven miles in an aeroplane by an Algerian aviator, and talked of nothing else; only a personally procured tiger-skin and a heavy harvest of Press photographs could successfully counter that sort of thing. Mrs. Packletide had already arranged in her mind the lunch she would give at her house in Curzon Street, ostensibly in Loona Bimberton's honour, with a tiger-skin rug occupying most of the foreground and all of the conversation. She had also already designed in her mind the tiger-claw brooch that she was going to give Loona Bimberton on her next birthday. In a world that is supposed to be chiefly swayed by hunger and by love Mrs. Packletide was an exception; her movements and motives were largely governed by dislike of Loona Bimberton.

Circumstances proved propitious. Mrs. Packletide had offered a thousand rupees for the opportunity of shooting a tiger without overmuch risk or exertion, and it so happened that a neighbouring village could boast of being the favoured rendezvous of an animal of respectable antecedents, which had been driven by the increasing infirmities of age to abandon game-killing and confine its appetite to the smaller domestic animals. The prospect of earning the thousand rupees had stimulated the sporting and commercial instinct of the villagers; children were posted night and day on the outskirts of the local jungle to head the tiger back in the unlikely event of his attempting to roam away to fresh hunting-grounds, and the cheaper kinds of goats were left about with elaborate carelessness to keep him satisfied with his present quarters. The one great anxiety was lest he should die of old age before the date appointed for the memsahib's shoot. Mothers carrying their babies home through the jungle after the day's work in the fields hushed their singing lest they might curtail the restful sleep of the venerable herd-robber.

The great night duly arrived, moonlit and cloudless. A platform had been constructed in a comfortable and conveniently placed tree, and thereon crouched Mrs. Packletide and her paid companion, Miss Mebbin. A goat, gifted with a particularly persistent bleat, such as even a partially deaf tiger might be reasonably expected to hear on a still night, was tethered at the correct distance. With an accurately sighted rifle and a thumb-nail pack of patience cards the sportswoman awaited the coming of the quarry.

"I suppose we are in some danger?" said Miss Mebbin.

She was not actually nervous about the wild beast, but she had a morbid dread of performing an atom more service than she had been paid for.

"Nonsense," said Mrs. Packletide; "it's a very old tiger. It couldn't spring up here even if it wanted to."

"If it's an old tiger I think you ought to get it cheaper. A thousand rupees is a lot of money."

Louisa Mebbin adopted a protective elder-sister attitude towards money in general, irrespective of nationality or denomination. Her energetic intervention had saved many a rouble from dissipating itself in tips in some Moscow hotel, and francs and centimes clung to her instinctively under circumstances which would have driven them headlong from less sympathetic hands. Her speculations as to the market depreciation of tiger remnants were cut short by the appearance on the scene of the animal itself. As soon as it caught sight of the tethered goat it lay flat on the earth, seemingly less from a desire to take advantage of all available cover than for the purpose of snatching a short rest before commencing the grand attack.

"I believe it's ill," said Louisa Mebbin, loudly in Hindustani, for the benefit of the village headman, who was in ambush in a neighbouring tree.

"Hush!" said Mrs. Packletide, and at that moment the tiger commenced ambling towards his victim.

"Now, now!" urged Miss Mebbin with some excitement; "if he doesn't touch the goat we needn't pay for it." (The bait was an extra.)

The rifle flashed out with a loud report, and the great tawny beast sprang to one side and then rolled over in the stillness of death. In a moment a crowd of excited natives had swarmed on to the scene, and their shouting speedily carried the glad news to the village, where a thumping of tom-toms took up the chorus of triumph. And their triumph and rejoicing found a ready echo in the heart of Mrs. Packletide; already that luncheon-party in Curzon Street seemed immeasurably nearer.

It was Louisa Mebbin who drew attention to the fact that the goat was in death-throes from a mortal bullet-wound, while no trace of the rifle's deadly work could be found on the tiger. Evidently the wrong animal had been hit, and the beast of prey had succumbed to heart-failure, caused by the sudden report of the rifle, accelerated by senile decay. Mrs. Packletide was pardonably annoyed at the discovery; but, at any rate, she was the possessor of a dead tiger, and the villagers, anxious for their thousand rupees, gladly connived at the fiction that she had shot the beast. And Miss Mebbin was a paid companion. Therefore did Mrs. Packletide face the cameras with a light heart, and her pictured fame reached from the pages of the *Texas Weekly Snapshot* to the illustrated Monday supplement of the *Novoe Vremya*. As for Loona Bimberton, she refused to look at an illustrated paper for weeks, and her letter of thanks for the gift of a tiger-claw brooch was a model of repressed emotions. The luncheon-party she declined; there are limits beyond which repressed emotions become dangerous.

From Curzon Street the tiger-skin rug travelled down to the Manor House, and was duly inspected and admired by the county, and it seemed a fitting and appropriate thing when Mrs. Packletide went to the County Costume Ball in the character of Diana. She refused to fall in, however, with Clovis's tempting suggestion of a primeval dance party, at which every one should wear the skins of beasts they had recently slain. "I should be in rather a Baby Bunting condition," confessed Clovis, "with a miserable rabbit-skin or two to wrap up in, but then," he added, with a rather malicious glance at Diana's proportions, "my figure is quite as good as that Russian dancing boy's."

"How amused every one would be if they knew what really happened," said Louisa Mebbin a few days after the ball.

"What do you mean?" asked Mrs. Packletide quickly.

"How you shot the goat and frightened the tiger to death," said Miss Mebbin, with her disagreeably pleasant laugh.

"No one would believe it," said Mrs. Packletide, her face changing colour as rapidly as though it were going through a book of patterns before post-time.

"Loona Bimberton would," said Miss Mebbin. Mrs. Packletide's face settled on an unbecoming shade of greenish white.

"You surely wouldn't give me away?" she asked.

"I've seen a week-end cottage near Dorking that I should rather like to buy," said Miss Mebbin with seeming irrelevance. "Six hundred and eighty, freehold. Quite a bargain, only I don't happen to have the money."

Louisa Mebbin's pretty week-end cottage, christened by her "Les Fauves," and gay in summer-time with its garden borders of tiger-lilies, is the wonder and admiration of her friends.

"It is a marvel how Louisa manages to do it," is the general verdict.

Mrs. Packletide indulges in no more big-game shooting.

"The incidental expenses are so heavy," she confides to inquiring friends.

THE STAMPEDING OF LADY BASTABLE

"It would be rather nice if you would put Clovis up for another six days while I go up north to the MacGregors'," said Mrs. Sangrail sleepily across the breakfast-table. It was her invariable plan to speak in a sleepy, comfortable voice whenever she was unusually keen about anything; it put people off their guard, and they frequently fell in with her wishes before they had realized that she was really asking for anything. Lady Bastable, however, was not so easily taken unawares; possibly she knew that voice and what it betokened—at any rate, she knew Clovis.

She frowned at a piece of toast and ate it very slowly, as though she wished to convey the impression that the process hurt her more than it hurt the toast; but no extension of hospitality on Clovis's behalf rose to her lips.

"It would be a great convenience to me," pursued Mrs. Sangrail, abandoning the careless tone. "I particularly don't want to take him to the MacGregors', and it will only be for six days."

"It will seem longer," said Lady Bastable dismally. "The last time he stayed here for a week—"

"I know," interrupted the other hastily, "but that was nearly two years ago. He was younger then."

"But he hasn't improved," said her hostess; "it's no use growing older if you only learn new ways of misbehaving yourself."

Mrs. Sangrail was unable to argue the point; since Clovis had reached the age of seventeen she had never ceased to bewail his irrepressible waywardness to all her circle of acquaintances, and a polite scepticism would have greeted the slightest hint at a prospective reformation. She discarded the fruitless effort at cajolery and resorted to undisguised bribery.

"If you'll have him here for these six days I'll cancel that outstanding bridge account."

It was only for forty-nine shillings, but Lady Bastable loved shillings with a great, strong love. To lose money at bridge and not to have to pay it was one of those rare experiences which gave the card-table a glamour in her eyes which it could never otherwise have possessed. Mrs. Sangrail was almost equally devoted to her card winnings, but the prospect of conveniently warehousing her offspring for six days, and incidentally saving his railway fare to the north, reconciled her to the sacrifice; when Clovis made a belated appearance at the breakfast-table the bargain had been struck.

"Just think," said Mrs. Sangrail sleepily; "Lady Bastable has very kindly asked you to stay on here while I go to the MacGregors'."

Clovis said suitable things in a highly unsuitable manner, and proceeded to make punitive expeditions among the breakfast dishes with a scowl on his face that would have driven the purr out of a peace conference. The arrangement that had been concluded behind his back was doubly distasteful to him. In the first place, he particularly wanted to teach the MacGregor boys, who could well afford the knowledge, how to play poker-patience; secondly, the Bastable catering was of the kind that is classified as a rude plenty, which Clovis translated as a plenty that gives rise to rude remarks. Watching him from behind ostentatiously sleepy lids, his mother realized, in the light of long experience, that any rejoicing over the success of her manœuvre would be distinctly premature. It was one thing to fit Clovis into a convenient niche of the domestic jigsaw puzzle; it was quite another matter to get him to stay there.

Lady Bastable was wont to retire in state to the morning-room immediately after breakfast and spend a quiet hour in skimming through the papers; they were there, so she might as well get their money's worth out of them. Politics did not greatly interest her, but she was obsessed with a favourite foreboding that one of these days there would be a great social upheaval, in which everybody would be killed by everybody else. "It will come sooner than we think," she would observe darkly; a mathematical expert of exceptionally high powers would have been puzzled to work out the approximate date from the slender and confusing groundwork which this assertion afforded.

On this particular morning the sight of Lady Bastable enthroned among her papers gave Clovis the hint towards which his mind had been groping all breakfast time. His mother had gone upstairs to supervise packing operations, and he was alone on the ground-floor with his hostess—and the servants. The latter were the key to the situation. Bursting wildly into the kitchen quarters, Clovis screamed a frantic though strictly non-committal summons: "Poor Lady Bastable! In the morning-room! Oh, quick!" The next moment the butler, cook, page-boy, two or three maids, and a gardener who had happened to be in one of the outer kitchens were following in a hot scurry after Clovis as he headed back for the morning-room. Lady Bastable was roused from the world of newspaper lore by hearing a Japanese screen in the hall go down with a crash. Then the door leading from the hall flew open and her young guest tore madly through the room, shrieked at her in passing, "The jacquerie! They're on us!" and dashed like an escaping hawk out through the

French window. The scared mob of servants burst in on his heels, the gardener still clutching the sickle with which he had been trimming hedges, and the impetus of their headlong haste carried them, slipping and sliding, over the smooth parquet flooring towards the chair where their mistress sat in panic-stricken amazement. If she had had a moment granted her for reflection she would have behaved, as she afterwards explained, with considerable dignity. It was probably the sickle which decided her, but anyway she followed the lead that Clovis had given her through the French window, and ran well and far across the lawn before the eyes of her astonished retainers.

Lost dignity is not a possession which can be restored at a moment's notice, and both Lady Bastable and the butler found the process of returning to normal conditions almost as painful as a slow recovery from drowning. A jacquerie, even if carried out with the most respectful of intentions, cannot fail to leave some traces of embarrassment behind it. By lunch-time, however, decorum had reasserted itself with enhanced rigour as a natural rebound from its recent overthrow, and the meal was served in a frigid stateliness that might have been framed on a Byzantine model. Half-way through its duration Mrs. Sangrail was solemnly presented with an envelope lying on a silver salver. It contained a cheque for forty-nine shillings.

The MacGregor boys learned how to play poker-patience; after all, they could afford to.

THE BACKGROUND

"THAT woman's art-jargon tires me," said Clovis to his journalist friend. "She's so fond of talking of certain pictures as 'growing on one,' as though they were a sort of fungus."

"That reminds me," said the journalist, "of the story of Henri Deplis. Have I ever told it you?"

Clovis shook his head.

"Henri Deplis was by birth a native of the Grand Duchy of Luxemburg. On maturer reflection he became a commercial traveller. His business activities frequently took him beyond the limits of the Grand Duchy, and he was stopping in a small town of Northern

Italy when news reached him from home that a legacy from a distant and deceased relative had fallen to his share.

"It was not a large legacy, even from the modest standpoint of Henri Deplis, but it impelled him towards some seemingly harmless extravagances. In particular it led him to patronize local art as represented by the tattoo-needles of Signor Andreas Pincini. Signor Pincini was, perhaps, the most brilliant master of tattoo craft that Italy had ever known, but his circumstances were decidedly impoverished, and for the sum of six hundred francs he gladly undertook to cover his client's back, from the collar-bone down to the waist-line, with a glowing representation of the Fall of Icarus. The design, when finally developed, was a slight disappointment to Monsieur Deplis, who had suspected Icarus of being a fortress taken by Wallenstein in the Thirty Years' War, but he was more than satisfied with the execution of the work, which was acclaimed by all who had the privilege of seeing it as Pincini's masterpiece.

"It was his greatest effort, and his last. Without even waiting to be paid, the illustrious craftsman departed this life, and was buried under an ornate tombstone, whose winged cherubs would have afforded singularly little scope for the exercise of his favourite art. There remained, however, the widow Pincini, to whom the six hundred francs were due. And thereupon arose the great crisis in the life of Henri Deplis, traveller of commerce. The legacy, under the stress of numerous little calls on its substance, had dwindled to very insignificant proportions, and when a pressing wine bill and sundry other current accounts had been paid, there remained little more than 430 francs to offer to the widow. The lady was properly indignant, not wholly, as she volubly explained, on account of the suggested writing-off of 170 francs, but also at the attempt to depreciate the value of her late husband's acknowledged masterpiece. In a week's time Deplis was obliged to reduce his offer to 405 francs, which circumstance fanned the widow's indignation into a fury. She cancelled the sale of the work of art, and a few days later Deplis learned with a sense of consternation that she had presented it to the municipality of Bergamo, which had gratefully accepted it. He left the neighbourhood as unobtrusively as possible, and was genuinely relieved when his business commands took him to Rome, where he hoped his identity and that of the famous picture might be lost sight of.

"But he bore on his back the burden of the dead man's genius. On presenting himself one day in the steaming corridor of a vapour bath, he was at once hustled back into his clothes by the proprietor, who was a North Italian, and who emphatically refused to allow the celebrated Fall of Icarus to be publicly on view without the permission of the municipality of Bergamo. Public interest and official vigilance increased as the matter became more widely known, and Deplis was unable to take a simple dip in the sea or river on the hottest afternoon unless clothed up to the collar-bone in a substantial bathing garment. Later on the authorities of Bergamo conceived the idea that salt water might be injurious to the masterpiece, and a perpetual injunction was obtained which debarred the muchly harassed commercial traveller from sea bathing under any circumstances. Altogether, he was fervently thankful when his firm of employers found him a new range of activities in the neighbourhood of Bordeaux. His thankfulness, however, ceased abruptly at the Franco-Italian frontier. An imposing array of official force barred his departure, and he was sternly reminded of the stringent law which forbids the exportation of Italian works of art.

"A diplomatic parley ensued between the Luxemburgian and Italian Governments, and at one time the European situation became overcast with the possibilities of trouble. But the Italian Government stood firm; it declined to concern itself in the least with the fortunes or even the existence of Henri Deplis, commercial traveller, but was immovable in its decision that the Fall of Icarus (by the late Pincini, Andreas) at present the property of the municipality of Bergamo, should not leave the country.

"The excitement died down in time, but the unfortunate Deplis, who was of a constitutionally retiring disposition, found himself a few months later once more the storm-centre of a furious controversy. A certain German art expert, who had obtained from the municipality of Bergamo permission to inspect the famous masterpiece, declared it to be a spurious Pincini, probably the work of some pupil whom he had employed in his declining years. The evidence of Deplis on the subject was obviously worthless, as he had been under the influence of the customary narcotics during the long process of pricking in the design. The editor of an Italian art journal refuted the contentions of the German expert and undertook to prove that his private life did not conform to any modern standard of decency. The whole of Italy and Germany were drawn into the dispute, and the rest of Europe was soon involved in the quarrel. There were stormy scenes in the Spanish Parliament, and the University of Copenhagen bestowed a gold medal on the German expert (afterwards sending a commission to examine his proofs on the spot), while two Polish schoolboys in Paris committed suicide to show what *they* thought of the matter.

"Meanwhile, the unhappy human background fared no better than before, and it was not surprising that he drifted into the ranks of Italian anarchists. Four times at least he was escorted to the frontier as a dangerous and undesirable foreigner, but he was always brought back as the Fall of Icarus (attributed to Pincini, Andreas, early Twentieth Century). And then one day, at an anarchist congress at Genoa, a fellow-worker, in the heat of debate, broke a phial full of corrosive liquid over his back. The red shirt that he was wearing mitigated the effects, but the Icarus was ruined beyond recognition. His assailant was severely reprimanded for assaulting a fellow-anarchist and received seven years' imprisonment for defacing a national art treasure. As soon as he was able to leave the hospital Henri Deplis was put across the frontier as an undesirable alien.

"In the quieter streets of Paris, especially in the neighbourhood of the Ministry of Fine Arts, you may sometimes meet a depressed, anxious-looking man, who, if you pass him the time of day, will answer you with a slight Luxemburgian accent. He nurses the illusion that he is one of the lost arms of the Venus de Milo, and hopes that the French Government may be persuaded to buy him. On all other subjects I believe he is tolerably sane."

HERMANN THE IRASCIBLE—A STORY OF THE GREAT WEEP

It was in the second decade of the Twentieth Century, after the Great Plague had devastated England, that Hermann the Irascible, nicknamed also the Wise, sat on the British throne. The Mortal Sickness had swept away the entire Royal Family, unto the third and fourth generations, and thus it came to pass that Hermann the Fourteenth of Saxe-Drachsen-Wachtelstein, who had stood thirtieth in the order of succession, found himself one day ruler of the British dominions within and beyond the seas. He was one of the unexpected things that happen in politics, and he happened with great thoroughness. In many ways he was the most progressive monarch who had sat on an important throne; before people knew where they were, they were somewhere else. Even his Ministers, progressive though they were by tradition, found it difficult to keep pace with his legislative suggestions.

"As a matter of fact," admitted the Prime Minister, "we are hampered by these votes-for-women creatures; they disturb our meetings throughout the country, and they try to turn Downing Street into a sort of political picnic-ground."

"They must be dealt with," said Hermann.

"Dealt with," said the Prime Minister; "exactly, just so; but how?"

"I will draft you a Bill," said the King, sitting down at his type-writing machine, "enacting that women shall vote at all future elections. *Shall* vote, you observe; or, to put it plainer, must. Voting will remain optional, as before, for male electors; but every woman between the ages of twenty-one and seventy will be obliged to vote, not only at elections for Parliament, county councils, district boards, parish councils, and municipalities, but for coroners, school inspectors, churchwardens, curators of museums, sanitary authorities, police-court interpreters, swimming-bath instructors, contractors, choir-masters, market superintendents, art-school teachers, cathedral vergers, and other local functionaries whose names I will add as they occur to me. All these offices will become elective, and failure to vote at any election falling within her area of residence will involve the female elector in a penalty of £10. Absence, unsupported by an adequate medical certificate, will not be accepted as an excuse. Pass this Bill through the two Houses of Parliament and bring it to me for signature the day after tomorrow."

From the very outset the Compulsory Female Franchise produced little or no elation even in circles which had been loudest in demanding the vote. The bulk of the women of the country had been indifferent or hostile to the franchise agitation, and the most fanatical Suffragettes began to wonder what they had found so attractive in the prospect of putting ballot-papers into a box. In the country districts the task of carrying out the provisions of the new Act was irksome enough; in the towns and cities it became an incubus. There seemed no end to the elections. Laundresses and seamstresses had to hurry away from their work to vote, often for a candidate whose name they hadn't heard before, and whom they selected at haphazard; female clerks and waitresses got up extra early to get their voting done before starting off to their places of business. Society women found their arrangements impeded and upset by the continual necessity for attending the polling stations, and week-end parties and summer holidays became gradually a masculine luxury. As for Cairo and the Riviera, they were possible only for genuine invalids or people of enormous wealth, for the accumulation of £10 fines during a prolonged absence was a contingency that even ordinarily wealthy folk could hardly afford to risk.

It was not wonderful that the female disfranchisement agitation became a formidable movement. The No-Votes-for-Women League numbered its feminine adherents by the million; its colours, citron and old Dutch-madder, were flaunted everywhere, and its battle hymn, "We Don't Want to Vote," became a popular refrain. As the Government showed no signs of being impressed by peaceful persuasion, more violent methods came into vogue. Meetings were disturbed, Ministers were mobbed, policemen were bitten, and ordinary prison fare rejected, and on the eve of the anniversary of Trafalgar women bound themselves in tiers up the entire length of the Nelson column so that its customary floral decoration had to be abandoned. Still the Government obstinately adhered to its conviction that women ought to have the vote.

Then, as a last resort, some woman wit hit upon an expedient which it was strange that no one had thought of before. The Great Weep was organized. Relays of women, ten thousand at a time, wept continuously in the public places of the Metropolis. They wept in railway stations, in tubes and omnibuses, in the National Gallery, at the Army and Navy Stores, in St. James's Park, at ballad concerts, at Prince's and in the Burlington Arcade. The hitherto unbroken success of the brilliant farcical comedy "Henry's Rabbit" was imperilled by the presence of drearily weeping women in stalls and circle and gallery, and one of the brightest divorce cases that had been tried for many years was robbed of much of its sparkle by the lachrymose behaviour of a section of the audience.

"What are we to do?" asked the Prime Minister, whose cook had wept into all the breakfast dishes and whose nursemaid had gone out, crying quietly and miserably, to take the children for a walk in the Park.

"There is a time for everything," said the King; "there is a time to yield. Pass a measure through the two Houses depriving women of the right to vote, and bring it to me for the Royal assent the day after tomorrow."

As the Minister withdrew, Hermann the Irascible, who was also nicknamed the Wise, gave a profound chuckle.

"There are more ways of killing a cat than by choking it with cream," he quoted, "but I'm not sure," he added, "that it's not the best way."

THE UNREST-CURE

On the rack in the railway carriage immediately opposite Clovis was a solidly wrought travelling bag, with a carefully written label, on which was inscribed, "J. P. Huddle, The Warren, Tilfield, near Slowborough." Immediately below the rack sat the human embodiment of the label, a solid, sedate individual, sedately dressed, sedately conversational. Even without his conversation (which was addressed to a friend seated by his side, and touched chiefly on such topics as the backwardness of Roman hyacinths and the prevalence of measles at the Rectory), one could have gauged fairly accurately the temperament and mental outlook of the travelling bag's owner. But he seemed unwilling to leave anything to the imagination of a casual observer, and his talk grew presently personal and introspective.

"I don't know how it is," he told his friend, "I'm not much over forty, but I seem to have settled down into a deep groove of elderly middle-age. My sister shows the same tendency. We like everything to be exactly in its accustomed place; we like things to happen exactly at their appointed times; we like everything to be usual, orderly, punctual, methodical, to a hair's breadth, to a minute. It distresses and upsets us if it is not so. For instance, to take a very trifling matter, a thrush has built its nest year after year in the catkin-tree on the lawn; this year, for no obvious reason, it is building in the ivy on the garden wall. We have said very little about it, but I think we both feel that the change is unnecessary, and just a little irritating."

"Perhaps," said the friend, "it is a different thrush."

"We have suspected that," said J. P. Huddle, "and I think it gives us even more cause for annoyance. We don't feel that we want a change of thrush at our time of life; and yet, as I have said, we have scarcely reached an age when these things should make themselves seriously felt."

"What you want," said the friend, "is an Unrest-cure."

"An Unrest-cure? I've never heard of such a thing."

"You've heard of Rest-cures for people who've broken down under stress of too much worry and strenuous living; well, you're suffering from overmuch repose and placidity, and you need the opposite kind of treatment."

"But where would one go for such a thing?"

"Well, you might stand as an Orange candidate for Kilkenny, or do a course of district visiting in one of the Apache quarters of Paris, or give lectures in Berlin to prove that most of Wagner's music was written by Gambetta; and there's always the interior of Morocco to travel in. But, to be really effective, the Unrest-cure ought to be tried in the home. How you would do it I haven't the faintest idea."

It was at this point in the conversation that Clovis became galvanized into alert attention. After all, his two days' visit to an elderly relative at Slowborough did not promise much excitement. Before the train had stopped he had decorated his sinister shirt-cuff with the inscription, "J. P. Huddle, The Warren, Tilfield, near Slowborough."

Two mornings later Mr. Huddle broke in on his sister's privacy as she sat reading *Country Life* in the morning room. It was her day and hour and place for reading *Country Life,* and the intrusion was absolutely irregular; but he bore in his hand a telegram, and in that household telegrams were recognized as happening by the hand of God. This particular telegram partook of the nature of a thunderbolt. "Bishop examining confirmation class in neighbourhood unable stay rectory on account measles invokes your hospitality sending secretary arrange."

"I scarcely know the Bishop; I've only spoken to him once," exclaimed J. P. Huddle, with the exculpating air of one who realizes too late the indiscretion of speaking to strange Bishops. Miss Huddle was the first to rally; she disliked thunderbolts as fervently as her brother did, but the womanly instinct in her told her that thunderbolts must be fed.

"We can curry the cold duck," she said. It was not the appointed day for curry, but the little orange envelope involved a certain departure from rule and custom. Her brother said nothing, but his eyes thanked her for being brave.

"A young gentleman to see you," announced the parlour-maid.

"The secretary!" murmured the Huddles in unison; they instantly stiffened into a demeanour which proclaimed that, though they held all strangers to be guilty, they were willing to hear anything they might have to say in their defence. The young gentleman, who came into the room with a certain elegant haughtiness, was not at all Huddle's idea of a bishop's secretary; he had not supposed that the episcopal establishment could have afforded such an expensively upholstered article when there were so many other claims on its resources. The face was fleetingly familiar; if he had bestowed more attention on the fellow-traveller sitting opposite him in the railway carriage two days before he might have recognized Clovis in his present visitor.

"You are the Bishop's secretary?" asked Huddle, becoming consciously deferential.

"His confidential secretary," answered Clovis. "You may call me Stanislaus; my other name doesn't matter. The Bishop and Colonel Alberti may be here to lunch. I shall be here in any case."

It sounded rather like the programme of a Royal visit.

"The Bishop is examining a confirmation class in the neighbourhood, isn't he?" asked Miss Huddle.

"Ostensibly," was the dark reply, followed by a request for a large-scale map of the locality.

Clovis was still immersed in a seemingly profound study of the map when another telegram arrived. It was addressed to "Prince Stanislaus, care of Huddle, The Warren, etc." Clovis glanced at the contents and announced: "The Bishop and Alberti won't be here till late in the afternoon." Then he returned to his scrutiny of the map.

The luncheon was not a very festive function. The princely secretary ate and drank with fair appetite, but severely discouraged conversation. At the finish of the meal he broke suddenly into a radiant smile, thanked his hostess for a charming repast, and kissed her hand with deferential rapture. Miss Huddle was unable to decide in her mind whether the action savoured of Louis Quatorzian courtliness or the reprehensible Roman attitude towards the Sabine women. It was not her day for having a headache, but she felt that the circumstances excused her, and retired to her room to have as much headache as was possible before the Bishop's arrival. Clovis, having asked the way to the nearest telegraph office, disappeared presently down the carriage drive. Mr. Huddle met him in the hall some two hours later, and asked when the Bishop would arrive.

"He is in the library with Alberti," was the reply.

"But why wasn't I told? I never knew he had come!" exclaimed Huddle.

"No one knows he is here," said Clovis; "the quieter we can keep matters the better. And on no account disturb him in the library. Those are his orders."

"But what is all this mystery about? And who is Alberti? And isn't the Bishop going to have tea?"

"The Bishop is out for blood, not tea."

"Blood!" gasped Huddle, who did not find that the thunderbolt improved on acquaintance.

"Tonight is going to be a great night in the history of Christendom," said Clovis. "We are going to massacre every Jew in the neighbourhood."

"To massacre the Jews!" said Huddle indignantly. "Do you mean to tell me there's a general rising against them?"

"No, it's the Bishop's own idea. He's in there arranging all the details now."

"But—the Bishop is such a tolerant, humane man."

"That is precisely what will heighten the effect of his action. The sensation will be enormous."

That at least Huddle could believe.

"He will be hanged!" he exclaimed with conviction.

"A motor is waiting to carry him to the coast, where a steam yacht is in readiness."

"But there aren't thirty Jews in the whole neighbourhood," protested Huddle, whose brain, under the repeated shocks of the day, was operating with the uncertainty of a telegraph wire during earthquake disturbances.

"We have twenty-six on our list," said Clovis, referring to a bundle of notes. "We shall be able to deal with them all the more thoroughly."

"Do you mean to tell me that you are meditating violence against a man like Sir Leon Birberry," stammered Huddle; "he's one of the most respected men in the country."

"He's down on our list," said Clovis carelessly; "after all, we've got men we can trust to do our job, so we shan't have to rely on local assistance. And we've got some Boy-scouts helping us as auxiliaries."

"Boy-scouts!"

"Yes; when they understood there was real killing to be done they were even keener than the men."

"This thing will be a blot on the Twentieth Century!"

"And your house will be the blotting-pad. Have you realized that half the papers of Europe and the United States will publish pictures of it? By the way, I've sent some photographs of you and your sister, that I found in the library, to the *Martin* and *Die Woche;* I hope you don't mind. Also a sketch of the staircase; most of the killing will probably be done on the staircase."

The emotions that were surging in J. P. Huddle's brain were almost too intense to be disclosed in speech, but he managed to gasp out: "There aren't any Jews in this house."

"Not at present," said Clovis.

"I shall go to the police," shouted Huddle with sudden energy.

"In the shrubbery," said Clovis, "are posted ten men, who have orders to fire on any one who leaves the house without my signal of permission. Another armed picquet is in ambush near the front gate. The Boy-scouts watch the back premises."

At this moment the cheerful hoot of a motor-horn was heard from the drive. Huddle rushed to the hall door with the feeling of a man half-awakened from a nightmare, and beheld Sir Leon Birberry, who had driven himself over in his car. "I got your telegram," he said; "what's up?"

Telegram? It seemed to be a day of telegrams.

"Come here at once. Urgent. James Huddle," was the purport of the message displayed before Huddle's bewildered eyes.

"I see it all!" he exclaimed suddenly in a voice shaken with agitation, and with a look of agony in the direction of the shrubbery he hauled the astonished Birberry into the house. Tea had just been laid in the hall, but the now thoroughly panic-stricken Huddle dragged his protesting guest upstairs, and in a few minutes' time the entire household had been summoned to that region of momentary safety. Clovis alone graced the tea-table with his presence; the fanatics in the library were evidently too immersed in their monstrous machinations to dally with the solace of teacup and hot toast. Once the youth rose, in answer to the summons of the front-door bell, and admitted Mr. Paul Isaacs, shoemaker and parish councillor, who had also received a pressing invitation to The Warren. With an atrocious assumption of courtesy, which a Borgia could hardly have outdone, the secretary escorted this new captive of his net to the head of the stairway, where his involuntary host awaited him.

And then ensued a long ghastly vigil of watching and waiting. Once or twice Clovis left the house to stroll across to the shrubbery, returning always to the library, for the purpose evidently of making a brief report. Once he took in the letters from the evening postman, and brought them to the top of the stairs with punctilious politeness. After his next absence he came half-way up the stairs to make an announcement.

"The Boy-scouts mistook my signal, and have killed the postman. I've had very little practice in this sort of thing, you see. Another time I shall do better."

The housemaid, who was engaged to be married to the evening postman, gave way to clamorous grief.

"Remember that your mistress has a headache," said J. P. Huddle. (Miss Huddle's headache was worse.)

Clovis hastened downstairs, and after a short visit to the library returned with another message:

"The Bishop is sorry to hear that Miss Huddle has a headache. He is issuing orders that as far as possible no firearms shall be used near the house; any killing that is necessary on the premises will be done with cold steel. The Bishop does not see why a man should not be a gentleman as well as a Christian."

That was the last they saw of Clovis; it was nearly seven o'clock, and his elderly relative liked him to dress for dinner. But, though he had left them for ever, the lurking suggestion of his presence haunted the lower regions of the house during the long hours of the wakeful night, and every creak of the stairway, every rustle of wind through the shrubbery, was fraught with horrible meaning. At about seven next morning the gardener's boy and the early postman finally convinced the watchers that the Twentieth Century was still unblotted.

"I don't suppose," mused Clovis, as an early train bore him townwards, "that they will be in the least grateful for the Unrest-cure."

THE JESTING OF ARLINGTON STRINGHAM

Arlington Stringham made a joke in the House of Commons. It was a thin House, and a very thin joke; something about the Anglo-Saxon race having a great many angles. It is possible that it was unintentional, but a fellow-member, who did not wish it to be supposed that he was asleep because his eyes were shut, laughed. One or two of the papers noted "a laugh" in brackets, and another, which was notorious for the carelessness of its political news, mentioned "laughter." Things often begin in that way.

"Arlington made a joke in the House last night," said Eleanor Stringham to her mother; "in all the years we've been married neither of us has made jokes, and I don't like it now. I'm afraid it's the beginning of the rift in the lute."

"What lute?" said her mother.

"It's a quotation," said Eleanor.

To say that anything was a quotation was an excellent method, in Eleanor's eyes, for withdrawing it from discussion, just as you could always defend indifferent lamb late in the season by saying "It's mutton."

And, of course, Arlington Stringham continued to tread the thorny path of conscious humour into which Fate had beckoned him.

"The country's looking very green, but, after all, that's what it's there for," he remarked to his wife two days later.

"That's very modern, and I daresay very clever, but I'm afraid it's wasted on me," she observed coldly. If she had known how much effort it had cost him to make the remark she might have greeted it in a kinder spirit. It is the tragedy of human endeavour that it works so often unseen and unguessed.

Arlington said nothing, not from injured pride, but because he was thinking hard for something to say. Eleanor mistook his silence for an assumption of tolerant superiority, and her anger prompted her to a further gibe.

"You had better tell it to Lady Isobel. I've no doubt she would appreciate it."

Lady Isobel was seen everywhere with a fawn-coloured collie at a time when every one else kept nothing but Pekinese, and she had once eaten four green apples at an afternoon tea in the Botanical Gardens, so she was widely credited with a rather unpleasant wit. The censorious said she slept in a hammock and understood Yeats's poems, but her family denied both stories.

"The rift is widening to an abyss," said Eleanor to her mother that afternoon.

"I should not tell that to any one," remarked her mother, after long reflection.

"Naturally, I should not talk about it very much," said Eleanor, "but why shouldn't I mention it to any one?"

"Because you can't have an abyss in a lute. There isn't room."

Eleanor's outlook on life did not improve as the afternoon wore on. The page-boy had brought from the library *By Mere and Wold* instead of *By Mere Chance*, the book which every one denied having read. The unwelcome substitute appeared to be a collection of nature notes contributed by the author to the pages of some Northern weekly, and when one had been prepared to plunge with disapproving mind into a regrettable chronicle of ill-spent lives it was intensely irritating to read "the dainty yellow-hammers are now with us, and flaunt their jaundiced livery from every bush and hillock." Besides, the thing was so obviously untrue; either there must be hardly any bushes or hillocks in those parts or the country must be fearfully overstocked with yellow-hammers. The thing scarcely seemed worth telling such a lie about. And the page-boy stood there, with his sleekly brushed and parted hair, and his air of chaste and callous indifference to the desires and passions of the world. Eleanor hated boys, and she would have liked to have whipped this one long and often. It was perhaps the yearning of a woman who had no children of her own.

She turned at random to another paragraph. "Lie quietly concealed in the fern and bramble in the gap by the old rowan tree, and you may see, almost every evening during early summer, a pair of lesser whitethroats creeping up and down the nettles and hedge-growth that mask their nesting-place."

The insufferable monotony of the proposed recreation! Eleanor would not have watched the most brilliant performance at His Majesty's Theatre for a single evening under such uncomfortable circumstances, and to be asked to watch lesser whitethroats creeping up and down a nettle "almost every evening" during the height of the season struck her as an imputation on her intelligence that was positively offensive. Impatiently she transferred her attention to the dinner menu, which the boy had thoughtfully brought in as an alternative to the more solid literary fare. "Rabbit curry," met her eye, and the lines of disapproval deepened on her already puckered brow. The cook was a great believer in the influence of environment, and nourished an obstinate conviction that if you brought rabbit and curry-powder together in one dish a rabbit curry would be the result. And Clovis and the odious Bertie van Tahn were coming to dinner. Surely, thought Eleanor, if Arlington knew how much she had had that day to try her, he would refrain from joke-making.

At dinner that night it was Eleanor herself who mentioned the name of a certain statesman, who may be decently covered under the disguise of X.

"X.," said Arlington Stringham, "has the soul of a meringue."

It was a useful remark to have on hand, because it applied equally well to four prominent statesmen of the day, which quadrupled the opportunities for using it.

"Meringues haven't got souls," said Eleanor's mother.

"It's a mercy that they haven't," said Clovis; "they would be always losing them, and people like my aunt would get up missions to meringues, and say it was wonderful how much one could teach them and how much more one could learn from them."

"What could you learn from a meringue?" asked Eleanor's mother.

"My aunt has been known to learn humility from an ex-Viceroy," said Clovis.

"I wish cook would learn to make curry, or have the sense to leave it alone," said Arlington, suddenly and savagely.

Eleanor's face softened. It was like one of his old remarks in the days when there was no abyss between them.

It was during the debate on the Foreign Office vote that Stringham made his great remark that "the people of Crete unfortunately make more history than they can consume locally." It was not brilliant, but it came in the middle of a dull speech, and the House was quite pleased with it. Old gentlemen with bad memories said it reminded them of Disraeli.

It was Eleanor's friend, Gertrude Ilpton, who drew her attention to Arlington's newest outbreak. Eleanor in these days avoided the morning papers.

"It's very modern, and I suppose very clever," she observed.

"Of course it's clever," said Gertrude; "all Lady Isobel's sayings are clever, and luckily they bear repeating."

"Are you sure it's one of her sayings?" asked Eleanor.

"My dear, I've heard her say it dozens of times."

"So that is where he gets his humour," said Eleanor slowly, and the hard lines deepened round her mouth.

The death of Eleanor Stringham from an overdose of chloral, occurring at the end of a rather uneventful season, excited a certain amount of unobtrusive speculation. Clovis, who perhaps exaggerated the importance of curry in the home, hinted at domestic sorrow.

And of course Arlington never knew. It was the tragedy of his life that he should miss the fullest effect of his jesting.

SREDNI VASHTAR

Conradin was ten years old, and the doctor had pronounced his professional opinion that the boy would not live another five years. The doctor was silky and effete, and counted for little, but his opinion was endorsed by Mrs. De Ropp, who counted for nearly everything. Mrs. De Ropp was Conradin's cousin and guardian, and in his eyes she represented those three-fifths of the world that are necessary and disagreeable and real; the other two-fifths, in perpetual antagonism to the foregoing, were summed up in himself and his imagination. One of these days Conradin supposed he would succumb to the mastering pressure of wearisome necessary things—such as illnesses and coddling restrictions and drawn-out dulness. Without his imagination, which was rampant under the spur of loneliness, he would have succumbed long ago.

Mrs. De Ropp would never, in her honestest moments, have confessed to herself that she disliked Conradin, though she might have been dimly aware that thwarting him "for his good" was a duty which she did not find particularly irksome. Conradin hated her with a desperate sincerity which he was perfectly able to mask. Such few pleasures as he could contrive for himself gained an added relish from the likelihood that they would be displeasing to his guardian, and from the realm of his imagination she was locked out—an unclean thing, which should find no entrance.

In the dull, cheerless garden, overlooked by so many windows that were ready to open with a message not to do this or that, or a reminder that medicines were due, he found little attraction. The few fruit-trees that it contained were set jealously apart from his plucking, as though they were rare specimens of their kind blooming in an arid waste; it would probably have been difficult to find a market-gardener who would have offered ten shillings for their entire yearly produce. In a forgotten corner, however, almost hidden behind a dismal shrubbery, was a disused tool-shed of respectable proportions, and within its walls Conradin found a haven, something that took on the varying aspects of a playroom and a cathedral. He had peopled it with a legion of familiar phantoms, evoked partly from fragments of history and partly from his own brain, but it also boasted two inmates of flesh and blood. In one corner lived a ragged-plumaged Houdan hen, on which the boy lavished an affection that had scarcely another outlet. Further back in the gloom stood a large hutch, divided into two compartments, one of which was fronted with close iron bars. This was the abode of a large polecat-ferret, which a friendly butcher-boy had once smuggled, cage and all, into its present quarters, in exchange for a long-secreted hoard of small silver. Conradin was dreadfully afraid of the lithe, sharp-fanged beast, but it was his most treasured possession. Its very presence in the tool-shed was a secret and fearful joy, to be kept scrupulously from the knowledge of the Woman, as he privately dubbed his cousin. And one day, out of Heaven knows what material, he spun the beast a wonderful name, and from that moment it grew into a god and a religion. The Woman indulged in religion once a week at a church near by, and took Conradin with her, but to him the church service was an alien rite in the House of Rimmon. Every Thursday, in the dim and musty silence of the tool-shed, he worshipped with mystic and elaborate ceremonial before the wooden hutch where dwelt Sredni Vashtar, the great ferret. Red flowers in their season and scarlet berries in the winter-time were offered at his shrine, for he was a god who laid some special stress on the fierce impatient side of things, as opposed to the Woman's religion, which, as far as Conradin could observe, went to great lengths in the contrary direction. And on great festivals powdered nutmeg was strewn in front of his hutch, an important feature of the offering being that the nutmeg had to be stolen. These festivals were of irregular occurrence, and were chiefly appointed to celebrate some passing event. On one occasion, when Mrs. De Ropp suffered from acute toothache for three days, Conradin kept up the festival during the entire three days, and almost succeeded in persuading himself that Sredni Vashtar was personally responsible for the toothache. If the malady had lasted for another day the supply of nutmeg would have given out.

The Houdan hen was never drawn into the cult of Sredni Vashtar. Conradin had long ago settled that she was an Anabaptist. He did not pretend to have the remotest knowledge as to what an Anabaptist was, but he privately hoped that it was dashing and not very respectable. Mrs. De Ropp was the ground plan on which he based and detested all respectability.

After a while Conradin's absorption in the tool-shed began to attract the notice of his guardian. "It is not good for him to be pottering down there in all weathers," she promptly decided, and at breakfast one morning she announced that the Houdan hen had been sold and taken away overnight. With her short-sighted eyes she peered at Conradin, waiting for an outbreak of rage and sorrow, which she was ready to rebuke with a flow of excellent precepts and reasoning. But Conradin said nothing: there was nothing to be said. Something perhaps in his white set face gave her a momentary qualm, for at tea that afternoon there was toast on the table, a delicacy which she usually banned on the ground that it was bad for him; also because the making of it "gave trouble," a deadly offence in the middle-class feminine eye.

"I thought you liked toast," she exclaimed, with an injured air, observing that he did not touch it.

"Sometimes," said Conradin.

In the shed that evening there was an innovation in the worship of the hutch-god. Conradin had been wont to chant his praises, tonight he asked a boon.

"Do one thing for me, Sredni Vashtar."

The thing was not specified. As Sredni Vashtar was a god he must be supposed to know. And choking back a sob as he looked at that other empty corner, Conradin went back to the world he so hated.

And every night, in the welcome darkness of his bedroom, and every evening in the dusk of the tool-shed, Conradin's bitter litany went up: "Do one thing for me, Sredni Vashtar."

Mrs. De Ropp noticed that the visits to the shed did not cease, and one day she made a further journey of inspection.

"What are you keeping in that locked hutch?" she asked. "I believe it's guinea-pigs. I'll have them all cleared away."

Conradin shut his lips tight, but the Woman ransacked his bedroom till she found the carefully hidden key, and forthwith marched down to the shed to complete her discovery. It was a cold afternoon, and Conradin had been bidden to keep to the house. From the furthest window of the dining-room the door of the shed could just be seen beyond the corner of the shrubbery, and there Conradin stationed himself. He saw the Woman enter, and then he imagined her opening the door of the sacred hutch and peering down with her short-sighted eyes into the thick straw bed where his god lay hidden. Perhaps she would prod at the straw in her clumsy impatience. And Conradin fervently breathed his prayer for the last time. But he knew as he prayed that he did not believe. He knew that the Woman would come out presently with that pursed smile he loathed so well on her face, and that in an hour or two the gardener would carry away his wonderful god, a god no longer, but a simple brown ferret in a hutch. And he knew that the Woman would triumph always as she triumphed now, and that he would grow ever more sickly under her pestering and domineering and superior wisdom, till one day nothing would matter much more with him, and the doctor would be proved right. And in the sting and misery of his defeat, he began to chant loudly and defiantly the hymn of his threatened idol:

> Sredni Vashtar went forth,
> His thoughts were red thoughts and his teeth were white.
> His enemies called for peace, but he brought them death.
> Sredni Vashtar the Beautiful.

And then of a sudden he stopped his chanting and drew closer to the window-pane. The door of the shed still stood ajar as it had been left, and the minutes were slipping by. They were long minutes, but they slipped by nevertheless. He watched the starlings running and flying in little parties across the lawn; he counted them over and over again, with one eye always on that swinging door. A sour-faced maid came in to lay the table for tea, and still Conradin stood and waited and watched. Hope had crept by inches into his heart, and now a look of triumph began to blaze in his eyes that had only known the wistful patience of defeat. Under his breath, with a furtive exultation, he began once again the pæan of victory and devastation. And presently his eyes were rewarded: out through that doorway came a long, low, yellow-and-brown beast, with eyes a-blink at the waning daylight, and dark wet stains around the fur of jaws and throat. Conradin dropped on his knees. The great polecat-ferret made its way down to a small brook at the foot of the garden, drank for a moment, then crossed a little plank bridge and was lost to sight in the bushes. Such was the passing of Sredni Vashtar.

"Tea is ready," said the sour-faced maid; "where is the mistress?"

"She went down to the shed some time ago," said Conradin.

And while the maid went to summon her mistress to tea, Conradin fished a toasting-fork out of the sideboard drawer and proceeded to toast himself a piece of bread. And during the toasting of it and the buttering of it with much butter and the slow enjoyment of eating it, Conradin listened to the noises and silences which fell in quick spasms beyond the dining-room door. The loud foolish screaming of the maid, the answering chorus of wondering ejaculations from the kitchen region, the scuttering footsteps and hurried embassies for outside help, and then, after a lull, the scared sobbings and the shuffling tread of those who bore a heavy burden into the house.

"Whoever will break it to the poor child? I couldn't for the life of me!" exclaimed a shrill voice. And while they debated the matter among themselves, Conradin made himself another piece of toast.

ADRIAN

A CHAPTER IN ACCLIMATIZATION

HIS baptismal register spoke of him pessimistically as John Henry, but he had left that behind with the other maladies of infancy, and his friends knew him under the front-name of Adrian. His mother lived in Bethnal Green, which was not altogether his fault; one can discourage too much history in one's family, but one cannot always prevent geography. And, after all, the Bethnal Green habit has this virtue—that it is seldom transmitted to the next generation. Adrian lived in a roomlet which came under the auspicious constellation of W.

How he lived was to a great extent a mystery even to himself; his struggle for existence probably coincided in many material details with the rather dramatic accounts he gave of it to sympathetic acquaintances. All that is definitely known is that he now and then emerged from the struggle to dine at the Ritz or Carlton, correctly garbed and with a correctly critical appetite. On these occasions he was usually the guest of Lucas Croyden, an amiable worldling, who had three thousand a year and a taste for introducing impossible people to irreproachable cookery. Like most men who combine three thousand a year with an uncertain digestion, Lucas was a Socialist, and he argued that you cannot hope to elevate the masses until you have brought plovers' eggs into their lives and taught them to appreciate the difference between coupe Jacques and Macédoine de fruits. His friends pointed out that it was a doubtful kindness to initiate a boy from behind a drapery counter into the blessedness of the higher catering, to which Lucas invariably replied that all kindnesses were doubtful. Which was perhaps true.

It was after one of his Adrian evenings that Lucas met his aunt, Mrs. Mebberley, at a fashionable teashop, where the lamp of family life is still kept burning and you meet relatives who might otherwise have slipped your memory.

"Who was that good-looking boy who was dining with you last night?" she asked. "He looked much too nice to be thrown away upon you."

Susan Mebberley was a charming woman, but she was also an aunt.

"Who are his people?" she continued, when the protégé's name (revised version) had been given her.

"His mother lives at Beth—"

Lucas checked himself on the threshold of what was perhaps a social indiscretion.

"Beth? Where is it? It sounds like Asia Minor. Is she mixed up with Consular people?"

"Oh, no. Her work lies among the poor."

This was a side-slip into truth. The mother of Adrian was employed in a laundry.

"I see," said Mrs. Mebberley, "mission work of some sort. And meanwhile the boy has no one to look after him. It's obviously my duty to see that he doesn't come to harm. Bring him to call on me."

"My dear Aunt Susan," expostulated Lucas, "I really know very little about him. He may not be at all nice, you know, on further acquaintance."

"He has delightful hair and a weak mouth. I shall take him with me to Homburg or Cairo."

"It's the maddest thing I ever heard of," said Lucas angrily.

"Well, there is a strong strain of madness in our family. If you haven't noticed it yourself all your friends must have."

"One is so dreadfully under everybody's eyes at Homburg. At least you might give him a preliminary trial at Etretat."

"And be surrounded by Americans trying to talk French? No, thank you. I love Americans, but not when they try to talk French. What a blessing it is that they never try to talk English. Tomorrow at five you can bring your young friend to call on me."

And Lucas, realizing that Susan Mebberley was a woman as well as an aunt, saw that she would have to be allowed to have her own way.

Adrian was duly carried abroad under the Mebberley wing; but as a reluctant concession to sanity Homburg and other inconveniently fashionable resorts were given a wide berth, and the Mebberley establishment planted itself down in the best hotel at Dohledorf, an Alpine townlet somewhere at the back of the Engadine. It was the usual kind of resort, with the usual type of visitors, that one finds over the greater part of Switzerland during the summer season, but to Adrian it was all unusual. The mountain air, the certainty of regular and abundant meals, and in particular the social atmosphere, affected him much as the indiscriminating fervour of a forcing-house might affect a weed that had strayed within its limits. He had been brought up in a world where breakages were regarded as crimes and expiated as such; it was something new and altogether exhilarating to find that you were considered rather amusing if you smashed things in the right manner and at the recognized hours. Susan Mebberley had expressed the intention of showing Adrian a bit of the world; the particular bit of the world represented by Dohledorf began to be shown a good deal of Adrian.

Lucas got occasional glimpses of the Alpine sojourn, not from his aunt or Adrian, but from the industrious pen of Clovis, who was also moving as a satellite in the Mebberley constellation.

"The entertainment which Susan got up last night ended in disaster. I thought it would. The Grobmayer child, a particularly loathsome five-year-old, had appeared as 'Bubbles' during the early part of the evening, and been put to bed during the interval. Adrian watched his opportunity and kidnapped it when the nurse was downstairs, and introduced it during the second half of the entertainment, thinly disguised as a performing pig. It certainly *looked* very like a pig, and grunted and slobbered just like the real article; no one knew exactly what it was, but every one said it was awfully clever, especially the Grobmayers. At the third curtain Adrian pinched it too hard, and it yelled 'Marmar'! I am supposed to be good at descriptions, but don't ask me to describe the sayings and doings of the Grobmayers at that moment; it was like one of the angrier Psalms set to Strauss's music. We have moved to an hotel higher up the valley."

Clovis's next letter arrived five days later, and was written from the Hotel Steinbock.

"We left the Hotel Victoria this morning. It was fairly comfortable and quiet—at least there was an air of repose about it when we arrived. Before we had been in residence twenty-four hours most of the repose had vanished 'like a dutiful bream,' as Adrian expressed it. However, nothing unduly outrageous happened till last night, when Adrian had a fit of insomnia and amused himself by unscrewing and transposing all the bedroom numbers on his floor. He transferred the bathroom label to the adjoining bedroom door, which happened to be that of Frau Hofrath Schilling, and this morning from seven o'clock onwards the old lady had a stream of involuntary visitors; she was too horrified and scandalized it seems to get up and lock her door. The would-be bathers flew back in confusion to their rooms, and, of course, the change of numbers led them astray again, and the corridor gradually filled with panic-stricken, scantily robed humans, dashing wildly about like rabbits in a ferret-infested warren. It took nearly an hour before the guests were all sorted into their respective rooms, and the Frau Hofrath's condition was still causing some anxiety when we left. Susan is beginning to look a little worried. She can't very well turn the boy adrift, as he hasn't got any money, and she can't send him to his people as she doesn't know where they are. Adrian says his mother moves about a good deal and he's lost her address. Probably, if the truth were known, he's had a row at home. So many boys nowadays seem to think that quarrelling with one's family is a recognized occupation."

Lucas's next communication from the travellers took the form of a telegram from Mrs. Mebberley herself. It was sent "reply prepaid," and consisted of a single sentence: "In Heaven's name, where is Beth?"

THE CHAPLET

A STRANGE stillness hung over the restaurant; it was one of those rare moments when the orchestra was not discoursing the strains of the Ice-cream Sailor waltz.

"Did I ever tell you," asked Clovis of his friend, "the tragedy of music at mealtimes?

"It was a gala evening at the Grand Sybaris Hotel, and a special dinner was being served in the Amethyst dining-hall. The Amethyst dining-hall had almost a European reputation, especially with that section of Europe which is historically identified with the Jordan Valley. Its cooking was beyond reproach, and its orchestra was sufficiently highly salaried to be above criticism. Thither came in shoals the intensely musical and the almost intensely musical, who are very many, and in still greater numbers the merely musical, who know how Tschaikowsky's name is pronounced and can recognize several of Chopin's nocturnes if you give them due warning; these eat in the nervous, detached manner of roebuck feeding in the open, and keep anxious ears cocked towards the orchestra for the first hint of a recognizable melody.

"'Ah, yes, Pagliacci,' they murmur, as the opening strains follow hot upon the soup, and if no contradiction is forthcoming from any better-informed quarter they break forth into subdued humming by way of supplementing the efforts of the musicians. Sometimes the melody starts on level terms with the soup, in which case the banqueters contrive somehow to hum between the spoonfuls; the facial expression of enthusiasts who are punctuating potage

St. Germain with Pagliacci is not beautiful, but it should be seen by those who are bent on observing all sides of life. One cannot discount the unpleasant things of this world merely by looking the other way.

"In addition to the aforementioned types the restaurant was patronized by a fair sprinkling of the absolutely non-musical; their presence in the dining-hall could only be explained on the supposition that they had come there to dine.

"The earlier stages of the dinner had worn off. The wine lists had been consulted, by some with the blank embarrassment of a schoolboy suddenly called on to locate a Minor Prophet in the tangled hinterland of the Old Testament, by others with the severe scrutiny which suggests that they have visited most of the higher-priced wines in their own homes and probed their family weaknesses. The diners who chose their wine in the latter fashion always gave their orders in a penetrating voice, with a plentiful garnishing of stage directions. By insisting on having your bottle pointing to the north when the cork is being drawn, and calling the waiter Max, you may induce an impression on your guests which hours of laboured boasting might be powerless to achieve. For this purpose, however, the guests must be chosen as carefully as the wine.

"Standing aside from the revellers in the shadow of a massive pillar was an interested spectator who was assuredly of the feast, and yet not in it. Monsieur Aristide Saucourt was the *chef* of the Grand Sybaris Hotel, and if he had an equal in his profession he had never acknowledged the fact. In his own domain he was a potentate, hedged around with the cold brutality that Genius expects rather than excuses in her children; he never forgave, and those who served him were careful that there should be little to forgive. In the outer world, the world which devoured his creations, he was an influence; how profound or how shallow an influence he never attempted to guess. It is the penalty and the safeguard of genius that it computes itself by troy weight in a world that measures by vulgar hundredweights.

"Once in a way the great man would be seized with a desire to watch the effect of his master-efforts, just as the guiding brain of Krupp's might wish at a supreme moment to intrude into the firing line of an artillery duel. And such an occasion was the present. For the first time in the history of the Grand Sybaris Hotel, he was presenting to its guests the dish which he had brought to that pitch of perfection which almost amounts to scandal. Canetons à la mode d'Amblève. In thin gilt lettering on the creamy white of the menu how little those words conveyed to the bulk of the imperfectly educated diners. And yet how much specialized effort had been lavished, how much carefully treasured lore had been ungarnered, before those six words could be written. In the Department of Deux-Sèvres ducklings had lived peculiar and beautiful lives and died in the odour of satiety to furnish the main theme of the dish; champignons, which even a purist for Saxon English would have hesitated to address as mushrooms, had contributed their languorous atrophied bodies to the garnishing, and a sauce devised in the twilight reign of the Fifteenth Louis had been summoned back from the imperishable past to take its part in the wonderful confection. Thus far had human effort laboured to achieve the desired result; the rest had been left to human genius–the genius of Aristide Saucourt.

"And now the moment had arrived for the serving of the great dish, the dish which world-weary Grand Dukes and market-obsessed money magnates counted among their happiest memories. And at the same moment something else happened. The leader of the highly salaried orchestra placed his violin caressingly against his chin, lowered his eyelids, and floated into a sea of melody.

"'Hark!' said most of the diners, 'he is playing "The Chaplet."'

"They knew it was 'The Chaplet' because they had heard it played at luncheon and afternoon tea, and at supper the night before, and had not had time to forget.

"'Yes, he is playing "The Chaplet,"' they reassured one another. The general voice was unanimous on the subject. The orchestra had already played it eleven times that day, four times by desire and seven times from force of habit, but the familiar strains were greeted with the rapture due to a revelation. A murmur of much humming rose from half the tables in the room, and some of the more overwrought listeners laid down knife and fork in order to be able to burst in with loud clappings at the earliest permissible moment.

"And the Canetons à la mode d'Amblève? In stupefied, sickened wonder Aristide watched them grow cold in total neglect, or suffer the almost worse indignity of perfunctory pecking and listless munching while the banqueters lavished their approval and applause on the music-makers. Calves' liver and bacon, with parsley sauce, could hardly have figured more ignominiously in the evening's entertainment. And while the master of culinary art leaned back against the sheltering pillar, choking with a horrible brain-searing rage that could find no outlet for its agony, the orchestra leader was bowing his acknowledgments of the hand-clappings that rose in a storm around him. Turning to his colleagues he nodded the signal for an encore. But before the violin had been lifted anew into position there came from the shadow of the pillar an explosive negative.

"'Noh! Noh! You do not play thot again!'

"The musician turned in furious astonishment. Had he taken warning from the look in the other man's eyes he might have acted differently. But the admiring plaudits were ringing in his ears, and he snarled out sharply, 'That is for me to decide.'

"'Noh! You play thot never again,' shouted the *chef*, and the next moment he had flung himself violently upon the loathed being who had supplanted him in the world's esteem. A large metal tureen, filled to the brim with steaming soup, had just been placed on a side table in readiness for a late party of diners; before the waiting staff or the guests had time to realize what was happening, Aristide had dragged his struggling victim up to the table and plunged his head deep down into the almost boiling contents of the tureen. At the further end of the room the diners were still spasmodically applauding in view of an encore.

"Whether the leader of the orchestra died from drowning by soup, or from the shock to his professional vanity, or was scalded to death, the doctors were never wholly able to agree. Monsieur Aristide Saucourt, who now lives in complete retirement, always inclined to the drowning theory."

THE QUEST

An unwonted peace hung over the Villa Elsinore, broken, however, at frequent intervals, by clamorous lamentations suggestive of bewildered bereavement. The Momebys had lost their infant child; hence the peace which its absence entailed; they were looking for it in wild, undisciplined fashion, giving tongue the whole time, which accounted for the outcry which swept through house and garden whenever they returned to try the home coverts anew.

Clovis, who was temporarily and unwillingly a paying guest at the villa, had been dozing in a hammock at the far end of the garden when Mrs. Momeby had broken the news to him.

"We've lost Baby," she screamed.

"Do you mean that it's dead, or stampeded, or that you staked it at cards and lost it that way?" asked Clovis lazily.

"He was toddling about quite happily on the lawn," said Mrs. Momeby tearfully, "and Arnold had just come in, and I was asking him what sort of sauce he would like with the asparagus—"

"I hope he said hollandaise," interrupted Clovis, with a show of quickened interest, "because if there's anything I hate—"

"And all of a sudden I missed Baby," continued Mrs. Momeby in a shriller tone. "We've hunted high and low, in house and garden and outside the gates, and he's nowhere to be seen."

"Is he anywhere to be heard?" asked Clovis; "if not, he must be at least two miles away."

"But where? And how?" asked the distracted mother.

"Perhaps an eagle or a wild beast has carried him off," suggested Clovis.

"There aren't eagles and wild beasts in Surrey," said Mrs. Momeby, but a note of horror had crept into her voice.

"They escape now and then from travelling shows. Sometimes I think they let them get loose for the sake of the advertisement. Think what a sensational headline it would make in the local papers: 'Infant son of prominent Nonconformist devoured by spotted hyæna.' Your husband isn't a prominent Nonconformist, but his mother came of Wesleyan stock, and you must allow the newspapers some latitude."

"But we should have found his remains," sobbed Mrs. Momeby.

"If the hyæna was really hungry and not merely toying with his food there wouldn't be much in the way of remains. It would be like the small-boy-and-apple story—there ain't going to be no core."

Mrs. Momeby turned away hastily to seek comfort and counsel in some other direction. With the selfish absorption of young motherhood she entirely disregarded Clovis's obvious anxiety about the asparagus sauce. Before she had gone a yard, however, the click of the side gate caused her to pull up sharp. Miss Gilpet, from the Villa Peterhof, had come over to hear details of the bereavement. Clovis was already rather bored with the story, but Mrs. Momeby was equipped with that merciless faculty which finds as much joy in the ninetieth time of telling as in the first.

"Arnold had just come in; he was complaining of rheumatism–"

"There are so many things to complain of in this household that it would never have occurred to me to complain of rheumatism," murmured Clovis.

"He was complaining of rheumatism," continued Mrs. Momeby, trying to throw a chilling inflection into a voice that was already doing a good deal of sobbing and talking at high pressure as well.

She was again interrupted.

"There is no such thing as rheumatism," said Miss Gilpet. She said it with the conscious air of defiance that a waiter adopts in announcing that the cheapest-priced claret in the wine-list is no more. She did not proceed, however, to offer the alternative of some more expensive malady, but denied the existence of them all.

Mrs. Momeby's temper began to shine out through her grief.

"I suppose you'll say next that Baby hasn't really disappeared."

"He has disappeared," conceded Miss Gilpet, "but only because you haven't sufficient faith to find him. It's only lack of faith on your part that prevents him from being restored to you safe and well."

"But if he's been eaten in the meantime by a hyæna and partly digested," said Clovis, who clung affectionately to his wild beast theory, "surely some ill-effects would be noticeable?"

Miss Gilpet was rather staggered by this complication of the question.

"I feel sure that a hyæna has not eaten him," she said lamely.

"The hyæna may be equally certain that it has. You see, it may have just as much faith as you have, and more special knowledge as to the present whereabouts of the baby."

Mrs. Momeby was in tears again. "If you have faith," she sobbed, struck by a happy inspiration, "won't you find our little Erik for us? I am sure you have powers that are denied to us."

Rose-Marie Gilpet was thoroughly sincere in her adherence to Christian Science principles; whether she understood or correctly expounded them the learned in such manners may best decide. In the present case she was undoubtedly confronted with a great opportunity, and as she started forth on her vague search she strenuously summoned to her aid every scrap of faith that she possessed. She passed out into the bare and open high road, followed by Mrs. Momeby's warning, "It's no use going there, we've searched there a dozen times." But Rose-Marie's ears were already deaf to all things save self-congratulation; for sitting in the middle of the highway, playing contentedly with the dust and some faded buttercups, was a white-pinafored baby with a mop of tow-coloured hair tied over one temple with a pale-blue ribbon. Taking first the usual feminine precaution of looking to see that no motor-car was on the distant horizon, Rose-Marie dashed at the child and bore it, despite its vigorous opposition, in through the portals of Elsinore. The child's furious screams had already announced the fact of its discovery, and the almost hysterical parents raced down the lawn to meet their restored offspring. The æsthetic value of the scene was marred in some degree by Rose-Marie's difficulty in holding the struggling infant, which was borne wrong-end foremost towards the agitated bosom of its family. "Our own little Erik come back to us," cried the Momebys in unison; as the child had rammed its fists tightly into its eye-sockets and nothing could be seen of its face but a widely gaping mouth, the recognition was in itself almost an act of faith.

"Is he glad to get back to Daddy and Mummy again?" crooned Mrs. Momeby; the preference which the child was showing for its dust and buttercup distractions was so marked that the question struck Clovis as being unnecessarily tactless.

"Give him a ride on the roly-poly," suggested the father brilliantly, as the howls continued with no sign of early abatement. In a moment the child had been placed astride the big garden roller and a preliminary tug was given to set it in motion. From the hollow depths of the cylinder came an earsplitting roar, drowning even the vocal efforts of the squalling baby, and immediately afterwards there crept forth a white-pinafored infant with a mop of tow-coloured hair tied over one temple with a pale blue ribbon. There was no mistaking either the features or the lung-power of the new arrival.

"Our own little Erik," screamed Mrs. Momeby, pouncing on him and nearly smothering him with kisses; "did he hide in the roly-poly to give us all a big fright?"

This was the obvious explanation of the child's sudden disappearance and equally abrupt discovery. There remained, however, the problem of the interloping baby, which now sat whimpering on the lawn in a disfavour as chilling as its previous popularity had been unwelcome. The Momebys glared at it as though it had wormed its way into their short-lived affections by heartless and unworthy pretences. Miss Gilpet's face took on an ashen tinge as she stared helplessly at the bunched-up figure that had been such a gladsome sight to her eyes a few moments ago.

"When love is over, how little of love even the lover understands," quoted Clovis to himself.

Rose-Marie was the first to break the silence.

"If that is Erik you have in your arms, who is—that?"

"That, I think, is for you to explain," said Mrs. Momeby stiffly.

"Obviously," said Clovis, "it's a duplicate Erik that your powers of faith called into being. The question is: What are you going to do with him?"

The ashen pallor deepened in Rose-Marie's cheeks. Mrs. Momeby clutched the genuine Erik closer to her side, as though she feared that her uncanny neighbour might out of sheer pique turn him into a bowl of gold-fish.

"I found him sitting in the middle of the road," said Rose-Marie weakly.

"You can't take him back and leave him there," said Clovis; "the highway is meant for traffic, not to be used as a lumber-room for disused miracles."

Rose-Marie wept. The proverb "Weep and you weep alone," broke down as badly on application as most of its kind. Both babies were wailing lugubriously, and the parent Momebys had scarcely recovered from their earlier lachrymose condition. Clovis alone maintained an unruffled cheerfulness.

"Must I keep him always?" asked Rose-Marie dolefully.

"Not always," said Clovis consolingly; "he can go into the Navy when he's thirteen." Rose-Marie wept afresh.

"Of course," added Clovis, "there may be no end of a bother about his birth certificate. You'll have to explain matters to the Admiralty, and they're dreadfully hidebound."

It was rather a relief when a breathless nursemaid from the Villa Charlottenburg over the way came running across the lawn to claim little Percy, who had slipped out of the front gate and disappeared like a twinkling from the high road.

And even then Clovis found it necessary to go in person to the kitchen to make sure about the asparagus sauce.

WRATISLAV

THE Gräfin's two elder sons had made deplorable marriages. It was, observed Clovis, a family habit. The youngest boy, Wratislav, who was the black sheep of a rather greyish family, had as yet made no marriage at all.

"There is certainly this much to be said for viciousness," said the Gräfin, "it keeps boys out of mischief."

"Does it?" asked the Baroness Sophie, not by way of questioning the statement, but with a painstaking effort to talk intelligently. It was the one matter in which she attempted to override the decrees of Providence, which had obviously never intended that she should talk otherwise than inanely.

"I don't know why I shouldn't talk cleverly," she would complain; "my mother was considered a brilliant conversationalist."

"These things have a way of skipping one generation," said the Gräfin.

"That seems so unjust," said Sophie; "one doesn't object to one's mother having outshone one as a clever talker, but I must admit that I should be rather annoyed if my daughters talked brilliantly."

"Well, none of them do," said the Gräfin consolingly.

"I don't know about that," said the Baroness, promptly veering round in defence of her offspring. "Elsa said something quite clever on Thursday about the Triple Alliance. Something about it being like a paper umbrella, that was all right as long as you didn't take it out in the rain. It's not every one who could say that."

"Every one has said it; at least every one that I know. But then I know very few people."

"I don't think you're particularly agreeable today."

"I never am. Haven't you noticed that women with a really perfect profile like mine are seldom even moderately agreeable?"

"I don't think your profile is so perfect as all that," said the Baroness.

"It would be surprising if it wasn't. My mother was one of the most noted classical beauties of her day."

"These things sometimes skip a generation, you know," put in the Baroness, with the breathless haste of one to whom repartee comes as rarely as the finding of a gold-handled umbrella.

"My dear Sophie," said the Gräfin sweetly, "that isn't in the least bit clever; but you do try so hard that I suppose I oughtn't to discourage you. Tell me something: has it ever occurred to you that Elsa would do very well for Wratislav? It's time he married somebody, and why not Elsa?"

"Elsa marry that dreadful boy!" gasped the Baroness.

"Beggars can't be choosers," observed the Gräfin.

"Elsa isn't a beggar!"

"Not financially, or I shouldn't have suggested the match. But she's getting on, you know, and has no pretensions to brains or looks or anything of that sort."

"You seem to forget that she's my daughter."

"That shows my generosity. But, seriously, I don't see what there is against Wratislav. He has no debts—at least, nothing worth speaking about."

"But think of his reputation! If half the things they say about him are true—"

"Probably three-quarters of them are. But what of it? You don't want an archangel for a son-in-law."

"I don't want Wratislav. My poor Elsa would be miserable with him."

"A little misery wouldn't matter very much with her; it would go so well with the way she does her hair, and if she couldn't get on with Wratislav she could always go and do good among the poor."

The Baroness picked up a framed photograph from the table.

"He certainly is very handsome," she said doubtfully; adding even more doubtfully, "I dare say dear Elsa might reform him."

The Gräfin had the presence of mind to laugh in the right key.

Three weeks later the Gräfin bore down upon the Baroness Sophie in a foreign bookseller's shop in the Graben, where she was, possibly, buying books of devotion, though it was the wrong counter for them.

"I've just left the dear children at the Rodenstahls'," was the Gräfin's greeting.

"Were they looking very happy?" asked the Baroness.

"Wratislav was wearing some new English clothes, so, of course, he was quite happy. I overheard him telling Toni a rather amusing story about a nun and a mousetrap, which won't bear repetition. Elsa was telling every one else a witticism about the Triple Alliance being like a paper umbrella—which seems to bear repetition with Christian fortitude."

"Did they seem much wrapped up in each other?"

"To be candid, Elsa looked as if she were wrapped up in a horse-rug. And why let her wear saffron colour?"

"I always think it goes with her complexion."

"Unfortunately it doesn't. It stays with it. Ugh. Don't forget, you're lunching with me on Thursday."

The Baroness was late for her luncheon engagement the following Thursday.

"Imagine what has happened!" she screamed as she burst into the room.

"Something remarkable, to make you late for a meal," said the Gräfin.

"Elsa has run away with the Rodenstahls' chauffeur!"

"Kolossal!"

"Such a thing as that no one in our family has ever done," gasped the Baroness.

"Perhaps he didn't appeal to them in the same way," suggested the Gräfin judicially.

The Baroness began to feel that she was not getting the astonishment and sympathy to which her catastrophe entitled her.

"At any rate," she snapped, "now she can't marry Wratislav."

"She couldn't in any case," said the Gräfin; "he left suddenly for abroad last night."

"For abroad! Where?"

"For Mexico, I believe."

"Mexico! But what for? Why Mexico?"

"The English have a proverb, 'Conscience makes cowboys of us all.'"

"I didn't know Wratislav had a conscience."

"My dear Sophie, he hasn't. It's other people's consciences that send one abroad in a hurry. Let's go and eat."

THE EASTER EGG

It was distinctly hard lines for Lady Barbara, who came of good fighting stock, and was one of the bravest women of her generation, that her son should be so undisguisedly a coward. Whatever good qualities Lester Slaggby may have possessed, and he was in some respects charming, courage could certainly never be imputed to him. As a child he had suffered from childish timidity, as a boy from unboyish funk, and as a youth he had exchanged unreasoning fears for others which were more formidable from the fact of having a carefully-thought-out basis. He was frankly afraid of animals, nervous with firearms, and never crossed the Channel without mentally comparing the numerical proportion of life belts to passengers. On horseback he seemed to require as many hands as a Hindu god, at least four for clutching the reins, and two more for patting the horse soothingly on the neck. Lady Barbara no longer pretended not to see her son's prevailing weakness; with her usual courage she faced the knowledge of it squarely, and, mother-like, loved him none the less.

Continental travel, anywhere away from the great tourist tracks, was a favoured hobby with Lady Barbara, and Lester joined her as often as possible. Eastertide usually found her at Knobaltheim, an upland township in one of those small princedoms that make inconspicuous freckles on the map of Central Europe.

A long-standing acquaintanceship with the reigning family made her a personage of due importance in the eyes of her old friend the Burgomaster, and she was anxiously consulted by that worthy on the momentous occasion when the Prince made known his intention of coming in person to open a sanatorium outside the town. All the usual items in a programme of welcome, some of them fatuous and commonplace, others quaint and charming, had been arranged for, but the Burgomaster hoped that the resourceful English lady might have something new and tasteful to suggest in the way of loyal greeting. The Prince was known to the outside world, if at all, as an old-fashioned reactionary, combating modern progress, as it were, with a wooden sword; to his own people he was known as a kindly old gentleman with a certain endearing stateliness which had nothing of standoffishness about it. Knobaltheim was anxious to do its best. Lady Barbara discussed the matter with Lester and one or two acquaintances in her little hotel, but ideas were difficult to come by.

"Might I suggest something to the gnädige Frau?" asked a sallow high-cheek-boned lady to whom the Englishwoman had spoken once or twice, and whom she had set down in her mind as probably a Southern Slav.

"Might I suggest something for the Reception Fest?" she went on, with a certain shy eagerness. "Our little child here, our baby, we will dress him in little white coat, with small wings, as an Easter angel, and he will carry a large white Easter egg, and inside shall be a basket of plover eggs, of which the Prince is so fond, and he shall give it to his Highness as Easter offering. It is so pretty an idea; we have seen it done once in Styria."

Lady Barbara looked dubiously at the proposed Easter angel, a fair, wooden-faced child of about four years old. She had noticed it the day before in the hotel, and wondered rather how such a tow-headed child could belong to such a dark-visaged couple as the woman and her husband; probably, she thought, an adopted baby, especially as the couple were not young.

"Of course Gnädige Frau will escort the little child up to the Prince," pursued the woman; "but he will be quite good, and do as he is told."

"We haf some pluffers' eggs shall come fresh from Wien," said the husband.

The small child and Lady Barbara seemed equally unenthusiastic about the pretty idea; Lester was openly discouraging, but when the Burgomaster heard of it he was enchanted. The combination of sentiment and plovers' eggs appealed strongly to his Teutonic mind.

On the eventful day the Easter angel, really quite prettily and quaintly dressed, was a centre of kindly interest to the gala crowd marshalled to receive his Highness. The mother was unobtrusive and less fussy than most parents would have been under the circumstances, merely stipulating that she should place the Easter egg herself in the arms that had been carefully schooled how to hold the precious burden. Then Lady Barbara moved forward, the child marching stolidly and with grim determination at her side. It had been promised cakes and sweeties galore if it gave the egg well and truly to the kind old gentleman who was waiting to receive it. Lester had tried to convey to it privately that horrible smackings would attend any failure in its share of the proceedings, but it is doubtful if his German caused more than an immediate distress. Lady Barbara had thoughtfully provided herself with an emergency supply of chocolate sweetmeats; children may sometimes be time-servers, but they do not encourage long accounts. As they approached nearer to the princely daïs Lady Barbara stood discreetly aside, and the stolid-faced infant walked forward alone, with staggering but steadfast gait, encouraged by a murmur of elderly approval. Lester, standing in the front row of the onlookers, turned to scan the crowd for the beaming faces of the happy parents. In a side-road which led to the railway station he saw a cab; entering the cab with every appearance of furtive haste were the dark-visaged couple who had been so plausibly eager for the "pretty idea." The sharpened instinct of cowardice lit up the situation to him in one swift flash. The blood roared and surged to his head as though thousands of floodgates had been opened in his veins and arteries, and his brain was the common sluice in which all the torrents met. He saw nothing but a blur around him. Then the blood ebbed away in quick waves, till his very heart seemed drained and empty, and he stood nervelessly, helplessly, dumbly watching the child, bearing its accursed burden with slow, relentless steps nearer and nearer to the group that waited sheep-like to receive him. A fascinated curiosity compelled Lester to turn his head towards the fugitives; the cab had started at hot pace in the direction of the station.

The next moment Lester was running, running faster than any of those present had ever seen a man run, and—he was not running away. For that stray fraction of his life some unwonted impulse beset him, some hint of the stock he came from, and he ran unflinchingly towards danger. He stooped and clutched at the Easter egg as one tries to scoop up the ball in Rugby football. What he meant to do with it he had not considered, the thing was to get it. But the child had been promised cakes and sweetmeats if it safely gave the egg into the hands of the kindly old gentleman; it uttered no scream, but it held to its charge with limpet grip. Lester sank to his knees, tugging savagely at the tightly clasped burden, and angry cries rose from the scandalized onlookers. A questioning, threatening ring formed round him, then shrank back in recoil as he shrieked out one hideous word. Lady Barbara heard the word and saw the crowd race away like scattered sheep, saw the Prince forcibly hustled away by his attendants; also she saw her son lying prone in an agony of overmastering terror, his spasm of daring shattered by the child's unexpected resistance, still clutching frantically, as though for safety, at that white-satin gew-gaw, unable to crawl even from its deadly neighbourhood, able only to scream and scream and scream. In her brain she was dimly conscious of balancing, or striving to balance, the abject shame which had him now in thrall against the one compelling act of courage which had flung him grandly and madly on to the point of danger. It was only for the fraction of a minute that she stood watching the two entangled figures, the infant with its woodenly obstinate face and body tense with dogged resistance, and the boy limp and already nearly dead with a terror that almost stifled his screams; and over them the long gala streamers flapping gaily in the sunshine. She never forgot the scene; but then, it was the last she ever saw.

Lady Barbara carries her scarred face with its sightless eyes as bravely as ever in the world, but at Eastertide her friends are careful to keep from her ears any mention of the children's Easter symbol.

FILBOID STUDGE, THE STORY OF A MOUSE THAT HELPED

"I WANT to marry your daughter," said Mark Spayley with faltering eagerness. "I am only an artist with an income of two hundred a year, and she is the daughter of an enormously wealthy man, so I suppose you will think my offer a piece of presumption."

Duncan Dullamy, the great company inflator, showed no outward sign of displeasure. As a matter of fact, he was secretly relieved at the prospect of finding even a two-hundred-a-year husband for his daughter Leonore. A crisis was rapidly rushing upon him, from which he knew he would emerge with neither money nor credit; all his recent ventures had fallen flat, and flattest of all had gone the wonderful new breakfast food, Pipenta, on the advertisement of which he had sunk such huge sums. It could scarcely be called a drug in the market; people bought drugs, but no one bought Pipenta.

"Would you marry Leonore if she were a poor man's daughter?" asked the man of phantom wealth.

"Yes," said Mark, wisely avoiding the error of over-protestation. And to his astonishment Leonore's father not only gave his consent, but suggested a fairly early date for the wedding.

"I wish I could show my gratitude in some way," said Mark with genuine emotion. "I'm afraid it's rather like the mouse proposing to help the lion."

"Get people to buy that beastly muck," said Dullamy, nodding savagely at a poster of the despised Pipenta, "and you'll have done more than any of my agents have been able to accomplish."

"It wants a better name," said Mark reflectively, "and something distinctive in the poster line. Anyway, I'll have a shot at it."

Three weeks later the world was advised of the coming of a new breakfast food, heralded under the resounding name of "Filboid Studge." Spayley put forth no pictures of massive babies springing up with fungus-like rapidity under its forcing influence, or of representatives of the leading nations of the world scrambling with fatuous eagerness for its possession. One huge sombre poster depicted the Damned in Hell suffering a new torment from their inability to get at the Filboid Studge which elegant young fiends held in transparent bowls just beyond their reach. The scene was rendered even more gruesome by a subtle suggestion of the features of leading men and women of the day in the portrayal of the Lost Souls; prominent individuals of both political parties, Society hostesses, well-known dramatic authors and novelists, and distinguished aeroplanists were dimly recognizable in that doomed throng; noted lights of the musical-comedy stage flickered wanly in the shades of the Inferno, smiling still from force of habit, but with the fearsome smiling rage of baffled effort. The poster bore no fulsome allusions to the merits of the new breakfast food, but a single grim statement ran in bold letters along its base: "They cannot buy it now."

Spayley had grasped the fact that people will do things from a sense of duty which they would never attempt as a pleasure. There are thousands of respectable middle-class men who, if you found them unexpectedly in a Turkish bath, would explain in all sincerity that a doctor had ordered them to take Turkish baths; if you told them in return that you went there because you liked it, they would stare in pained wonder at the frivolity of your motive. In the same way, whenever a massacre of Armenians is reported from Asia Minor, every one assumes that it has been carried out "under orders" from somewhere or another; no one seems to think that there are people who might *like* to kill their neighbours now and then.

And so it was with the new breakfast food. No one would have eaten Filboid Studge as a pleasure, but the grim austerity of its advertisement drove housewives in shoals to the grocers' shops to clamour for an immediate supply. In small kitchens solemn pig-tailed daughters helped depressed mothers to perform the primitive ritual of its preparation. On the breakfast-tables of cheerless parlours it was partaken of in silence. Once the womenfolk discovered that it was thoroughly unpalatable, their zeal in forcing it on their households knew no bounds. "You haven't eaten your Filboid Studge!" would be screamed at the appetiteless clerk as he hurried weariedly from the breakfast-table, and his evening meal would be prefaced by a warmed-up mess which would be explained as "your Filboid Studge that you didn't eat this morning." Those strange fanatics who ostentatiously mortify themselves, inwardly and outwardly, with health biscuits and health garments, battened aggressively on the new food. Earnest spectacled young men de-voured it on the steps of the National Liberal Club. A bishop who did not believe in a future state preached against the poster, and a peer's daughter died from eating too much of the compound. A further advertisement was obtained when an infantry regiment mutinied and shot its officers rather than eat the nauseous mess; fortunately, Lord Birrell of Blatherstone, who was War Minister at the moment, saved the situation by his happy epigram, that "Discipline to be effective must be optional."

Filboid Studge had become a household word, but Dullamy wisely realized that it was not necessarily the last word in breakfast dietary; its supremacy would be challenged as soon as some yet more unpalatable food should be put on the market. There might even be a reaction in favour of something tasty and appetizing, and the Puritan austerity of the moment might be banished from domestic cookery. At an opportune moment, therefore, he sold out his interests in the article which had brought him in colossal wealth at a critical juncture, and placed his financial reputation beyond the reach of cavil. As for Leonore, who was now an heiress on a far greater scale than ever before, he naturally found her something a vast deal higher in the husband market than a two-hundred-a-year poster designer. Mark Spayley, the brainmouse who had helped the financial lion with such untoward effect, was left to curse the day he produced the wonder-working poster.

"After all," said Clovis, meeting him shortly afterwards at his club, "you have this doubtful consolation, that 'tis not in mortals to countermand success."

THE MUSIC ON THE HILL

Sylvia Seltoun ate her breakfast in the morning-room at Yessney with a pleasant sense of ultimate victory, such as a fervent Ironside might have permitted himself on the morrow of Worcester fight. She was scarcely pugnacious by temperament, but belonged to that more successful class of fighters who are pugnacious by circumstance. Fate had willed that her life should be occupied with a series of small struggles, usually with the odds slightly against her, and usually she had just managed to come through winning. And now she felt that she had brought her hardest and certainly her most important struggle to a successful issue. To have married Mortimer Seltoun, "Dead Mortimer" as his more intimate enemies called him, in the teeth of the cold hostility of his family, and in spite of his unaffected indifference to women, was indeed an achievement that had needed some determination and adroitness to carry through; yesterday she had brought her victory to its concluding stage by wrenching her husband away from Town and its group of satellite watering-places and "settling him down," in the vocabulary of her kind, in this remote wood-girt manor farm which was his country house.

"You will never get Mortimer to go," his mother had said carpingly, "but if he once goes he'll stay; Yessney throws almost as much a spell over him as Town does. One can understand what holds him to Town, but Yessney—" and the dowager had shrugged her shoulders.

There was a sombre almost savage wildness about Yessney that was certainly not likely to appeal to town-bred tastes, and Sylvia, notwithstanding her name, was accustomed to nothing much more sylvan than "leafy Kensington." She looked on the country as something excellent and wholesome in its way, which was apt to become troublesome if you encouraged it overmuch. Distrust of town-life had been a new thing with her, born of her marriage with Mortimer, and she had watched with satisfaction the gradual fading of what she called "the Jermyn-Street-look" in his eyes as the woods and heather of Yessney had closed in on them yesternight. Her will-power and strategy had prevailed; Mortimer would stay.

Outside the morning-room windows was a triangular slope of

turf, which the indulgent might call a lawn, and beyond its low hedge of neglected fuschia bushes a steeper slope of heather and bracken dropped down into cavernous combes overgrown with oak and yew. In its wild open savagery there seemed a stealthy linking of the joy of life with the terror of unseen things. Sylvia smiled complacently as she gazed with a School-of-Art appreciation at the landscape, and then of a sudden she almost shuddered.

"It is very wild," she said to Mortimer, who had joined her; "one could almost think that in such a place the worship of Pan had never quite died out."

"The worship of Pan never has died out," said Mortimer. "Other newer gods have drawn aside his votaries from time to time, but he is the Nature-God to whom all must come back at last. He has been called the Father of all the Gods, but most of his children have been stillborn."

Sylvia was religious in an honest, vaguely devotional kind of way, and did not like to hear her beliefs spoken of as mere after-growths, but it was at least something new and hopeful to hear Dead Mortimer speak with such energy and conviction on any subject.

"You don't really believe in Pan?" she asked incredulously.

"I've been a fool in most things," said Mortimer quietly, "but I'm not such a fool as not to believe in Pan when I'm down here. And if you're wise you won't disbelieve in him too boastfully while you're in his country."

It was not till a week later, when Sylvia had exhausted the attractions of the woodland walks round Yessney, that she ventured on a tour of inspection of the farm buildings. A farmyard suggested in her mind a scene of cheerful bustle, with churns and flails and smiling dairymaids, and teams of horses drinking knee-deep in duck-crowded ponds. As she wandered among the gaunt grey buildings of Yessney manor farm her first impression was one of crushing stillness and desolation, as though she had happened on some lone deserted homestead long given over to owls and cobwebs; then came a sense of furtive watchful hostility, the same shadow of unseen things that seemed to lurk in the wooded combes and coppices. From behind heavy doors and shuttered windows came the restless stamp of hoof or rasp of chain halter, and at times a muffled bellow from some stalled beast. From a distant corner a shaggy dog watched her with intent unfriendly eyes; as she drew near it slipped quietly into its kennel, and slipped out again as noiselessly when she had passed by. A few hens, questing for food under a rick, stole away under a gate at her approach. Sylvia felt that if she had come across any human beings in this wilderness of barn and byre they would have fled wraith-like from her gaze. At last, turning a corner quickly, she came upon a living thing that did not fly from her. Astretch in a pool of mud was an enormous sow, gigantic beyond the town-woman's wildest computation of swine-flesh, and speedily alert to resent and if necessary repel the unwonted intrusion. It was Sylvia's turn to make an unobtrusive retreat. As she threaded her way past rickyards and cowsheds and long blank walls, she started suddenly at a strange sound—the echo of a boy's laughter, golden and equivocal. Jan, the only boy employed on the farm, a tow-headed, wizen-faced yokel, was visibly at work on a potato clearing half-way up the nearest hill-side, and Mortimer, when questioned, knew of no other probable or possible begetter of the hidden mockery that had ambushed Sylvia's retreat. The memory of that untraceable echo was added to her other impressions of a furtive sinister "something" that hung around Yessney.

Of Mortimer she saw very little; farm and woods and trout-streams seemed to swallow him up from dawn till dusk. Once, following the direction she had seen him take in the morning, she came to an open space in a nut copse, further shut in by huge yew trees, in the centre of which stood a stone pedestal surmounted by a small bronze figure of a youthful Pan. It was a beautiful piece of workmanship, but her attention was chiefly held by the fact that a newly cut bunch of grapes had been placed as an offering at its feet. Grapes were none too plentiful at the manor house, and Sylvia snatched the bunch angrily from the pedestal. Contemptuous annoyance dominated her thoughts as she strolled slowly homeward, and then gave way to a sharp feeling of something that was very near fright; across a thick tangle of undergrowth a boy's face was scowling at her, brown and beautiful, with unutterably evil eyes. It was a lonely pathway, all pathways round Yessney were lonely for the matter of that, and she sped forward without waiting to give a closer scrutiny to this sudden apparition. It was not till she had reached the house that she discovered that she had dropped the bunch of grapes in her flight.

"I saw a youth in the wood today," she told Mortimer that evening, "brown-faced and rather handsome, but a scoundrel to look at. A gipsy lad, I suppose."

"A reasonable theory," said Mortimer, "only there aren't any gipsies in these parts at present."

"Then who was he?" asked Sylvia, and as Mortimer appeared to have no theory of his own, she passed on to recount her finding of the votive offering.

"I suppose it was your doing," she observed; "it's a harmless piece of lunacy, but people would think you dreadfully silly if they knew of it."

"Did you meddle with it in any way?" asked Mortimer.

"I–I threw the grapes away. It seemed so silly," said Sylvia, watching Mortimer's impassive face for a sign of annoyance.

"I don't think you were wise to do that," he said reflectively. "I've heard it said that the Wood Gods are rather horrible to those who molest them."

"Horrible perhaps to those that believe in them, but you see I don't," retorted Sylvia.

"All the same," said Mortimer in his even, dispassionate tone, "I should avoid the woods and orchards if I were you, and give a wide berth to the horned beasts on the farm."

It was all nonsense, of course, but in that lonely wood-girt spot nonsense seemed able to rear a bastard brood of uneasiness.

"Mortimer," said Sylvia suddenly, "I think we will go back to Town some time soon."

Her victory had not been so complete as she had supposed; it had carried her on to ground that she was already anxious to quit.

"I don't think you will ever go back to Town," said Mortimer. He seemed to be paraphrasing his mother's prediction as to himself.

Sylvia noted with dissatisfaction and some self-contempt that the course of her next afternoon's ramble took her instinctively clear of the network of woods. As to the horned cattle, Mortimer's warning was scarcely needed, for she had always regarded them as of doubtful neutrality at the best: her imagination unsexed the most matronly dairy cows and turned them into bulls liable to "see red" at any moment. The ram who fed in the narrow paddock below the orchards she had adjudged, after ample and cautious probation, to be of docile temper; today, however, she decided to leave his docility untested, for the usually tranquil beast was roaming with every sign of restlessness from corner to corner of his meadow.

A low, fitful piping, as of some reedy flute, was coming from the depth of a neighbouring copse, and there seemed to be some subtle connection between the animal's restless pacing and the wild music from the wood. Sylvia turned her steps in an upward direction and climbed the heather-clad slopes that stretched in rolling shoulders high above Yessney. She had left the piping notes behind her, but across the wooded combes at her feet the wind brought her another kind of music, the straining bay of hounds in full chase. Yessney was just on the outskirts of the Devon-and-Somerset country, and the hunted deer sometimes came that way. Sylvia could presently see a dark body, breasting hill after hill, and sinking again and again out of sight as he crossed the combes, while behind him steadily swelled that relentless chorus, and she grew tense with the excited sympathy that one feels for any hunted thing in whose capture one is not directly interested. And at last he broke through the outermost line of oak scrub and fern and stood panting in the open, a fat September stag carrying a well-furnished head. His obvious course was to drop down to the brown pools of Undercombe, and thence make his way towards the red deer's favoured sanctuary, the sea. To Sylvia's surprise, however, he turned his head to the upland slope and came lumbering resolutely onward over the heather. "It will be dreadful," she thought, "the hounds will pull him down under my very eyes." But the music of the pack seemed to have died away for a moment, and in its place she heard again that wild piping, which rose now on this side, now on that, as though urging the failing stag to a final effort. Sylvia stood well aside from his path, half hidden in a thick growth of whortle bushes, and watched him swing stiffly upward, his flanks dark with sweat, the coarse hair on his neck showing light by contrast. The pipe music shrilled suddenly around her, seeming to come from the bushes at her very feet, and at the same moment the great beast slewed round and bore directly down upon her. In an instant her pity for the hunted animal was changed to wild terror at her own danger; the thick heather roots mocked her scrambling efforts at flight, and she looked frantically downward for a glimpse of oncoming hounds. The huge antler spikes were within a few yards of her, and in a flash of numbing fear she remembered Mortimer's warning, to beware of horned beasts on the farm. And then with a quick throb of joy she saw that she was not alone; a human figure stood a few paces aside, knee-deep in the whortle bushes.

"Drive it off!" she shrieked. But the figure made no answering movement.

The antlers drove straight at her breast, the acrid smell of the hunted animal was in her nostrils, but her eyes were filled with the horror of something she saw other than her oncoming death. And in her ears rang the echo of a boy's laughter, golden and equivocal.

THE STORY OF ST. VESPALUUS

"TELL me a story," said the Baroness, staring out despairingly at the rain; it was that light, apologetic sort of rain that looks as if it was going to leave off every minute and goes on for the greater part of the afternoon.

"What sort of story?" asked Clovis, giving his croquet mallet a valedictory shove into retirement.

"One just true enough to be interesting and not true enough to be tiresome," said the Baroness.

Clovis rearranged several cushions to his personal solace and satisfaction; he knew that the Baroness liked her guests to be comfortable, and he thought it right to respect her wishes in that particular.

"Have I ever told you the story of St. Vespaluus?" he asked.

"You've told me stories about grand-dukes and lion-tamers and financiers' widows and a postmaster in Herzegovina," said the Baroness, "and about an Italian jockey and an amateur governess who went to Warsaw, and several about your mother, but certainly never anything about a saint."

"This story happened a long while ago," he said, "in those uncomfortable piebald times when a third of the people were Pagan, and a third Christian, and the biggest third of all just followed whichever religion the Court happened to profess. There was a certain king called Hkrikros, who had a fearful temper and no immediate successor in his own family; his married sister, however, had provided him with a large stock of nephews from which to select his heir. And the most eligible and royally-approved of all these nephews was the sixteen-year-old Vespaluus. He was the best looking, and the best horseman and javelin-thrower, and had that priceless princely gift of being able to walk past a supplicant with an air of not having seen him, but would certainly have given something if he had. My mother has that gift to a certain extent; she can go smilingly and financially unscathed through a charity bazaar, and meet the organizers next day with a solicitous 'had I but known you were in need of funds' air that is really rather a triumph in audacity. Now Hkrikros was a Pagan of the first water, and kept the worship of the sacred serpents, who lived in a hallowed grove on a hill near the royal palace, up to a high pitch of enthusiasm. The common people were allowed to please themselves, within certain discreet limits, in the matter of private religion, but any official in the service of the Court who went over to the new cult was looked down on, literally as well as metaphorically, the looking down being done from the gallery that ran round the royal bear-pit. Consequently there was considerable scandal and consternation when the youthful Vespaluus appeared one day at a Court function with a rosary tucked into his belt, and announced in reply to angry questionings that he had decided to adopt Christianity, or at any rate to give it a trial. If it had been any of the other nephews the king would possibly have ordered something drastic in the way of scourging and banishment, but in the case of the favoured Vespaluus he determined to look on the whole thing much as a modern father might regard the announced intention of his son to adopt the stage as a profession. He sent accordingly for the Royal Librarian. The royal library in those days was not a very extensive affair, and the keeper of the king's books had a great deal of leisure on his hands. Consequently he was in frequent demand for the settlement of other people's affairs when these strayed beyond normal limits and got temporarily unmanageable.

"'You must reason with Prince Vespaluus,' said the king, 'and impress on him the error of his ways. We cannot have the heir to the throne setting such a dangerous example.'

"'But where shall I find the necessary arguments?' asked the Librarian.

"'I give you free leave to pick and choose your arguments in the royal woods and coppices,' said the king; 'if you cannot get together some cutting observations and stinging retorts suitable to the occasion you are a person of very poor resource.'

"So the Librarian went into the woods and gathered a goodly selection of highly argumentative rods and switches, and then proceeded to reason with Vespaluus on the folly and iniquity and above all the unseemliness of his conduct. His reasoning left a deep impression on the young prince, an impression which lasted for many weeks, during which time nothing more was heard about the unfortunate lapse into Christianity. Then a further scandal of the same nature agitated the Court. At a time when he should have been engaged in audibly invoking the gracious protection and patronage of the holy serpents, Vespaluus was heard singing a chant in honour of St. Odilo of Cluny. The king was furious at this new outbreak, and began to take a gloomy view of the situation; Vespaluus was evidently going to show a dangerous obstinacy in persisting in his heresy. And yet there was nothing in his appearance to justify such perverseness; he had not the pale eye of the fanatic or the mystic look of the dreamer. On the contrary, he was quite the best-looking boy at Court; he had an elegant, well-knit figure, a healthy complexion, eyes the colour of very ripe mulberries, and dark hair, smooth and very well cared for."

"It sounds like a description of what you imagine yourself to have been like at the age of sixteen," said the Baroness.

"My mother has probably been showing you some of my early photographs," said Clovis. Having turned the sarcasm into a compliment, he resumed his story.

"The king had Vespaluus shut up in a dark tower for three days, with nothing but bread and water to live on, the squealing and fluttering of bats to listen to, and drifting clouds to watch through one little window slit. The anti-Pagan section of the community began to talk portentously of the boy-martyr. The martyrdom was mitigated, as far as the food was concerned, by the carelessness of the tower warden, who once or twice left a portion of his own supper of broiled meat and fruit and wine by mistake in the prince's cell. After the punishment was over, Vespaluus was closely watched for any further symptom of religious perversity, for the king was determined to stand no more opposition on so important a matter, even from a favourite nephew. If there was any more of this nonsense, he said, the succession to the throne would have to be altered.

"For a time all went well; the festival of summer sports was approaching, and the young Vespaluus was too engrossed in wrestling and foot-running and javelin-throwing competitions to bother himself with the strife of conflicting religious systems. Then, however, came the great culminating feature of the summer festival, the ceremonial dance round the grove of the sacred serpents, and Vespaluus, as we should say, 'sat it out.' The affront to the State religion was too public and ostentatious to be overlooked, even if the king had been so minded, and he was not in the least so minded. For a day and a half he sat apart and brooded, and every one thought he was debating within himself the question of the young prince's death or pardon; as a matter of fact he was merely thinking out the manner of the boy's death. As the thing had to be done, and was bound to attract an enormous amount of public attention in any case, it was as well to make it as spectacular and impressive as possible.

"'Apart from his unfortunate taste in religions,' said the king, 'and his obstinacy in adhering to it, he is a sweet and pleasant youth, therefore it is meet and fitting that he should be done to death by the winged envoys of sweetness.'

"'Your Majesty means–?' said the Royal Librarian.

"'I mean,' said the king, 'that he shall be stung to death by bees. By the royal bees, of course.'

"'A most elegant death,' said the Librarian.

"'Elegant and spectacular, and decidedly painful,' said the king; 'it fulfills all the conditions that could be wished for.'

"The king himself thought out all the details of the execution ceremony. Vespaluus was to be stripped of his clothes, his hands were to be bound behind him, and he was then to be slung in a recumbent position immediately above three of the largest of the royal beehives, so that the least movement of his body would bring him in jarring contact with them. The rest could be safely left to the bees. The death throes, the king computed, might last anything from fifteen to forty minutes, though there was division of opinion and considerable wagering among the other nephews as to whether death might not be almost instantaneous, or, on the other hand, whether it might not be deferred for a couple of hours. Anyway, they all agreed, it was vastly preferable to being thrown down into an evil smelling bear-pit and being clawed and mauled to death by imperfectly carnivorous animals.

"It so happened, however, that the keeper of the royal hives had leanings towards Christianity himself, and moreover, like most of the Court officials, he was very much attached to Vespaluus. On the eve of the execution, therefore, he busied himself with removing the stings from all the royal bees; it was a long and delicate operation, but he was an expert beemaster, and by working hard nearly all night he succeeded in disarming all, or almost all, of the hive inmates."

"I didn't know you could take the sting from a live bee," said the Baroness incredulously.

"Every profession has its secrets," replied Clovis; "if it hadn't it wouldn't be a profession. Well, the moment for the execution arrived; the king and Court took their places, and accommodation was found for as many of the populace as wished to witness the unusual spectacle. Fortunately the royal bee-yard was of considerable dimensions, and was commanded, moreover, by the terraces that ran round the royal gardens; with a little squeezing and the erection of a few platforms room was found for everybody. Vespaluus was carried into the open space in front of the hives, blushing and slightly embarrassed, but not at all displeased at the attention which was being centred on him."

"He seems to have resembled you in more things than in appearance," said the Baroness.

"Don't interrupt at a critical point in the story," said Clovis. "As soon as he had been carefully adjusted in the prescribed position over the hives, and almost before the gaolers had time to retire to a safe distance, Vespaluus gave a lusty and well-aimed kick, which sent all three hives toppling one over another. The next moment he was wrapped from head to foot in bees; each individual insect nursed the dreadful and humiliating knowledge that in this supreme hour of catastrophe it could not sting, but each felt that it ought to pretend to. Vespaluus squealed and wriggled with laughter, for he was being tickled nearly to death, and now and again he gave a furious kick and used a bad word as one of the few bees that had escaped disarmament got its protest home. But the spectators saw with amazement that he showed no signs of approaching death agony, and as the bees dropped wearily away in clusters from his body his flesh was seen to be as white and smooth as before the ordeal, with a shiny glaze from the honey-smear of innumerable bee-feet, and here and there a small red spot where one of the rare stings had left its mark. It was obvious that a miracle had been performed in his favour, and one loud murmur, of astonishment or exultation, rose from the onlooking crowd. The king gave orders for Vespaluus to be taken down to await further orders, and stalked silently back to his midday meal, at which he was careful to eat heartily and drink copiously as though nothing unusual had happened. After dinner he sent for the Royal Librarian.

"'What is the meaning of this fiasco?' he demanded.

"'Your Majesty,' said that official, 'either there is something radically wrong with the bees—'

"'There is nothing wrong with my bees,' said the king haughtily, 'they are the best bees.'

"'Or else,' said the Librarian, 'there is something irremediably right about Prince Vespaluus.'

"'If Vespaluus is right I must be wrong,' said the king.

"The Librarian was silent for a moment. Hasty speech has been the downfall of many; ill-considered silence was the undoing of the luckless Court functionary.

"Forgetting the restraint due to his dignity, and the golden rule which imposes repose of mind and body after a heavy meal, the king rushed upon the keeper of the royal books and hit him repeatedly and promiscuously over the head with an ivory chess-board, a pewter wine-flagon, and a brass candlestick; he knocked him violently and often against an iron torch sconce, and kicked him thrice round the banqueting chamber with rapid, energetic kicks. Finally, he dragged him down a long passage by the hair of his head and flung him out of a window into the courtyard below."

"Was he much hurt?" asked the Baroness.

"More hurt than surprised," said Clovis. "You see, the king was notorious for his violent temper. However, this was the first time he had let himself go so unrestrainedly on the top of a heavy meal. The Librarian lingered for many days—in fact, for all I know, he may have ultimately recovered, but Hkrikros died that same evening. Vespaluus had hardly finished getting the honey stains off his body before a hurried deputation came to put the coronation oil on his head. And what with the publicly-witnessed miracle and the accession of a Christian sovereign, it was not surprising that there was a general scramble of converts to the new religion. A hastily consecrated bishop was overworked with a rush of baptisms in the hastily improvised Cathedral of St. Odilo. And the boy-martyr-that-might-have-been was transposed in the popular imagination into a royal boy-saint, whose fame attracted throngs of curious and devout sightseers to the capital. Vespaluus, who was busily engaged in organizing the games and athletic contests that were to mark the commencement of his reign, had no time to give heed to the religious fervour which was effervescing round his personality; the first indication he had of the existing state of affairs was when the Court Chamberlain (a recent and very ardent addition to the Christian community) brought for his approval the outlines of a projected ceremonial cutting-down of the idolatrous serpent-grove.

"'Your Majesty will be graciously pleased to cut down the first tree with a specially consecrated axe,' said the obsequious official.

"'I'll cut off your head first, with any axe that comes handy,' said Vespaluus indignantly; 'do you suppose that I'm going to begin my reign by mortally affronting the sacred serpents? It would be most unlucky.'

"'But your Majesty's Christian principles?' exclaimed the bewildered Chamberlain.

"'I never had any,' said Vespaluus; 'I used to pretend to be a Christian convert just to annoy Hkrikros. He used to fly into such delicious tempers. And it was rather fun being whipped and scolded and shut up in a tower all for nothing. But as to turning Christian in real earnest, like you people seem to do, I couldn't think of such a thing. And the holy and esteemed serpents have always helped me when I've prayed to them for success in my running and wrestling and hunting, and it was through their distinguished intercession that the bees were not able to hurt me with their stings. It would be black ingratitude to turn against their worship at the very outset of my reign. I hate you for suggesting it.'

"The Chamberlain wrung his hands despairingly.

"'But, your Majesty,' he wailed, 'the people are reverencing you as a saint, and the nobles are being Christianized in batches, and neighbouring potentates of that Faith are sending special envoys to welcome you as a brother. There is some talk of making you the patron saint of beehives, and a certain shade of honey-yellow has been christened Vespalussian gold at the Emperor's Court. You can't surely go back on all this.'

"'I don't mind being reverenced and greeted and honoured,' said Vespaluus; 'I don't even mind being sainted in moderation, as long as I'm not expected to be saintly as well. But I wish you clearly and finally to understand that I will *not* give up the worship of the august and auspicious serpents.'

"There was a world of unspoken bear-pit in the way he uttered those last words, and the mulberry-dark eyes flashed dangerously.

"'A new reign,' said the Chamberlain to himself, 'but the same old temper.'

"Finally, as a State necessity, the matter of the religions was compromised. At stated intervals the king appeared before his subjects in the national cathedral in the character of St. Vespaluus, and the idolatrous grove was gradually pruned and lopped away till nothing remained of it. But the sacred and esteemed serpents were removed to a private shrubbery in the royal gardens, where Vespaluus the Pagan and certain members of his household devoutly and decently worshipped them. That possibly is the reason why the boy-king's success in sports and hunting never deserted him to the end of his days, and that is also the reason why, in spite of the popular veneration for his sanctity, he never received official canonization."

"It has stopped raining," said the Baroness.

THE WAY TO THE DAIRY

THE Baroness and Clovis sat in a much-frequented corner of the Park exchanging biographical confidences about the long succession of passers-by.

"Who are those depressed-looking young women who have just gone by?" asked the Baroness; "they have the air of people who have bowed to destiny and are not quite sure whether the salute will be returned."

"Those," said Clovis, "are the Brimley Bomefields. I dare say you would look depressed if you had been through their experiences."

"I'm always having depressing experiences," said the Baroness, "but I never give them outward expression. It's as bad as looking one's age. Tell me about the Brimley Bomefields."

"Well," said Clovis, "the beginning of their tragedy was that they found an aunt. The aunt had been there all the time, but they had very nearly forgotten her existence until a distant relative refreshed their memory by remembering her very distinctly in his will; it is wonderful what the force of example will accomplish. The aunt, who had been unobtrusively poor, became quite pleasantly rich, and the Brimley Bomefields grew suddenly concerned at the loneliness of her life and took her under their collective wings. She had as many wings around her at this time as one of those beast-things in Revelation."

"So far I don't see any tragedy from the Brimley Bomefields' point of view," said the Baroness.

"We haven't got to it yet," said Clovis. "The aunt had been used to living very simply, and had seen next to nothing of what we should consider life, and her nieces didn't encourage her to do much in the way of making a splash with her money. Quite a good deal of it would come to them at her death, and she was a fairly old woman, but there was one circumstance which cast a shadow of gloom over the satisfaction they felt in the discovery and acquisition of this desirable aunt: she openly acknowledged that a comfortable slice of her little fortune would go to a nephew on the other side of her family. He was rather a deplorable thing in rotters, and quite hopelessly top-hole in the way of getting through money, but he had been more or less decent to the old lady in her unremembered days, and she wouldn't hear anything against him. At least, she wouldn't pay any attention to what she did hear, but her nieces took care that she should have to listen to a good deal in that line. It seemed such a pity, they said among themselves, that good money should fall into such worthless hands. They habitually spoke of their aunt's money as 'good money,' as though other people's aunts dabbled for the most part in spurious currency.

"Regularly after the Derby, St. Leger, and other notable racing events they indulged in audible speculations as to how much money Roger had squandered in unfortunate betting transactions.

"'His travelling expenses must come to a big sum,' said the eldest Brimley Bomefield one day; 'they say he attends every race-meeting in England, besides others abroad. I shouldn't wonder if he went all the way to India to see the race for the Calcutta Sweeptstake that one hears so much about.'

"'Travel enlarges the mind, my dear Christine,' said her aunt.

"'Yes, dear aunt, travel undertaken in the right spirit,' agreed Christine; 'but travel pursued merely as a means towards gambling and extravagant living is more likely to contract the purse than to enlarge the mind. However, as long as Roger enjoys himself, I suppose he doesn't care how fast or unprofitably the money goes, or where he is to find more. It seems a pity, that's all.'

"The aunt by that time had begun to talk of something else, and it was doubtful if Christine's moralizing had been even accorded a hearing. It was her remark, however—the aunt's remark, I mean—about travel enlarging the mind, that gave the youngest Brimley Bomefield her great idea for the showing-up of Roger.

"'If aunt could only be taken somewhere to see him gambling and throwing away money,' she said, 'it would open her eyes to his character more effectually than anything we can say.'

"'My dear Veronique,' said her sisters, 'we can't go following him to race-meetings.'

"'Certainly not to race-meetings,' said Veronique, 'but we might go to some place where one can look on at gambling without taking part in it.'

"'Do you mean Monte Carlo?' they asked her, beginning to jump rather at the idea.

"'Monte Carlo is a long way off, and has a dreadful reputation,' said Veronique; 'I shouldn't like to tell our friends that we were going to Monte Carlo. But I believe Roger usually goes to Dieppe about this time of year, and some quite respectable English people go there, and the journey wouldn't be expensive. If aunt could stand the Channel crossing the change of scene might do her a lot of good.'

"And that was how the fateful idea came to the Brimley Bomefields.

"From the very first set-off disaster hung over the expedition, as they afterwards remembered. To begin with, all the Brimley Bomefields were extremely unwell during the crossing, while the aunt enjoyed the sea air and made friends with all manner of strange travelling companions. Then, although it was many years since she had been on the Continent, she had served a very practical apprenticeship there as a paid companion, and her knowledge of colloquial French beat theirs to a standstill. It became increasingly difficult to keep under their collective wings a person who knew what she wanted and was able to ask for it and to see that she got it. Also, as far as Roger was concerned, they drew Dieppe blank; it turned out that he was staying at Pourville, a little watering-place a mile or two further west. The Brimley Bomefields discovered that Dieppe was too crowded and frivolous, and persuaded the old lady to migrate to the comparative seclusion of Pourville.

"'You won't find it dull, you know,' they assured her; 'there is a little casino attached to the hotel, and you can watch the people dancing and throwing away their money at *petits chevaux*.'

"It was just before *petits chevaux* had been supplanted by *boule*.

"Roger was not staying in the same hotel, but they knew that the casino would be certain of his patronage on most afternoons and evenings.

"On the first evening of their visit they wandered into the casino after a fairly early dinner, and hovered near the tables. Bertie van Tahn was staying there at the time, and he described the whole incident to me. The Brimley Bomefields kept a furtive watch on the doors as though they were expecting some one to turn up, and the aunt got more and more amused and interested watching the little horses whirl round and round the board.

"'Do you know, poor little number eight hasn't won for the last thirty-two times,' she said to Christine; 'I've been keeping count. I shall really have to put five francs on him to encourage him.'

"'Come and watch the dancing, dear,' said Christine nervously. It was scarcely a part of their strategy that Roger should come in and find the old lady backing her fancy at the *petits chevaux* table.

"'Just wait while I put five francs on number eight,' said the aunt, and in another moment her money was lying on the table. The horses commenced to move round; it was a slow race this time, and number eight crept up at the finish like some crafty demon and placed his nose just a fraction in front of number three, who had seemed to be winning easily. Recourse had to be had to measurement, and the number eight was proclaimed the winner. The aunt picked up thirty-five francs. After that the Brimley Bomefields would have had to have used concerted force to get her away from the tables. When Roger appeared on the scene she was fifty-two francs to the good; her nieces were hovering forlornly in the background, like chickens that have been hatched out by a duck and are despairingly watching their parent disporting herself in a dangerous and uncongenial element. The supper-party which Roger insisted on standing that night in honour of his aunt and the three Miss Brimley Bomefields was remarkable for the unrestrained gaiety of two of the participants and the funereal mirthlessness of the remaining guests.

"'I do not think,' Christine confided afterwards to a friend, who re-confided it to Bertie van Tahn, 'that I shall ever be able to touch *pâté de foie gras* again. It would bring back memories of that awful evening.'

"For the next two or three days the nieces made plans for returning to England or moving on to some other resort where there was no casino. The aunt was busy making a system for winning at *petits chevaux*. Number eight, her first love, had been running rather unkindly for her, and a series of plunges on number five had turned out even worse.

"'Do you know, I dropped over seven hundred francs at the tables this afternoon,' she announced cheerfully at dinner on the fourth evening of their visit.

"'Aunt! Twenty-eight pounds! And you were losing last night too.'

"'Oh, I shall get it all back,' she said optimistically; 'but not here. These silly little horses are no good. I shall go somewhere where one can play comfortably at roulette. You needn't look so shocked. I've always felt that, given the opportunity, I should be an inveterate gambler, and now you darlings have put the opportunity in my way. I must drink your very good healths. Waiter, a bottle of *Pontet Canet*. Ah, it's number seven on the wine list; I shall plunge on number seven tonight. It won four times running this afternoon when I was backing that silly number five.'

"Number seven was not in a winning mood that evening. The Brimley Bomefields, tired of watching disaster from a distance, drew near to the table where their aunt was now an honoured habituée, and gazed mournfully at the successive victories of one and five and eight and four, which swept 'good money' out of the purse of seven's obstinate backer. The day's losses totalled something very near two thousand francs.

"'You incorrigible gamblers,' said Roger chaffingly to them, when he found them at the tables.

"'We are not gambling,' said Christine freezingly; 'we are looking on.'

"'I *don't* think,' said Roger knowingly; 'of course you're a syndicate and aunt is putting the stakes on for all of you. Any one can tell by your looks when the wrong horse wins that you've got a stake on.'

"Aunt and nephew had supper alone that night, or at least they would have if Bertie hadn't joined them; all the Brimley Bomefields had headaches.

"The aunt carried them all off to Dieppe the next day and set cheerily about the task of winning back some of her losses. Her luck was variable; in fact, she had some fair streaks of good fortune, just enough to keep her thoroughly amused with her new distraction; but on the whole she was a loser. The Brimley Bomefields had a collective attack of nervous prostration on the day when she sold out a quantity of shares in Argentine rails. 'Nothing will ever bring that money back,' they remarked lugubriously to one another.

"Veronique at last could bear it no longer, and went home; you see, it had been her idea to bring the aunt on this disastrous expedition, and though the others did not cast the fact verbally in her face, there was a certain lurking reproach in their eyes which was harder to meet than actual upbraidings. The other two remained behind, forlornly mounting guard over their aunt until such time as the waning of the Dieppe season should at last turn her in the direction of home and safety. They made anxious calculations as to how little 'good money' might, with reasonable luck, be squandered in the meantime. Here, however, their reckoning went far astray; the close of the Dieppe season merely turned their aunt's thoughts in search of some other convenient gambling resort. 'Show a cat the way to the dairy—' I forget how the proverb goes on, but it summed up the situation as far as the Brimley Bomefields' aunt was concerned. She had been introduced to unexplored pleasures, and found them greatly to her liking, and she was in no hurry to forgo the fruits of her newly acquired knowledge. You see, for the first time in her life the old thing was thoroughly enjoying herself; she was losing money, but she had plenty of fun and excitement over the process, and she had enough left to do very comfortably on. Indeed, she was only just learning to understand the art of doing oneself well. She was a popular hostess, and in return her fellow-gamblers were always ready to entertain her to dinners and suppers when their luck was in. Her nieces, who still remained in attendance on her, with the pathetic unwillingness of a crew to leave a foundering treasure ship which might yet be steered into port, found little pleasure in these Bohemian festivities; to see 'good money' lavished on good living for the entertainment of a nondescript circle of acquaintances who were not likely to be in any way socially useful to them, did not attune them to a spirit of revelry. They contrived, whenever possible, to excuse themselves from participation in their aunt's deplored gaieties; the Brimley Bomefield headaches became famous.

"And one day the nieces came to the conclusion that, as they would have expressed it, 'no useful purpose would be served' by their continued attendance on a relative who had so thoroughly emancipated herself from the sheltering protection of their wings. The aunt bore the announcement of their departure with a cheerfulness that was almost disconcerting.

"'It's time you went home and had those headaches seen to by a specialist,' was her comment on the situation.

"The homeward journey of the Brimley Bomefields was a veritable retreat from Moscow, and what made it the more bitter was the fact that the Moscow, in this case, was not overwhelmed with fire and ashes, but merely extravagantly over-illuminated.

"From mutual friends and acquaintances they sometimes get glimpses of their prodigal relative, who has settled down into a confirmed gambling maniac, living on such salvage of income as obliging moneylenders have left at her disposal.

"So you need not be surprised," concluded Clovis, "if they do wear a depressed look in public."

"Which is Veronique?" asked the Baroness.

"The most depressed-looking of the three," said Clovis.

THE PEACE OFFERING

"I WANT you to help me in getting up a dramatic entertainment of some sort," said the Baroness to Clovis. "You see, there's been an election petition down here, and a member unseated and no end of bitterness and ill-feeling, and the County is socially divided against itself. I thought a play of some kind would be an excellent opportunity for bringing people together again, and giving them something to think of besides tiresome political squabbles."

The Baroness was evidently ambitious of reproducing beneath her own roof the pacifying effects traditionally ascribed to the celebrated Reel of Tullochgorum.

"We might do something on the lines of Greek tragedy," said

Clovis, after due reflection; "the Return of Agamemnon, for instance."

The Baroness frowned.

"It sounds rather reminiscent of an election result, doesn't it?"

"It wasn't that sort of return," explained Clovis; "it was a home-coming."

"I thought you said it was a tragedy."

"Well, it was. He was killed in his bathroom, you know."

"Oh, now I know the story, of course. Do you want me to take the part of Charlotte Corday?"

"That's a different story and a different century," said Clovis; "the dramatic unities forbid one to lay a scene in more than one century at a time. The killing in this case has to be done by Clytemnestra."

"Rather a pretty name. I'll do that part. I suppose you want to be Aga—whatever his name is?"

"Dear no. Agamemnon was the father of grown-up children, and probably wore a beard and looked prematurely aged. I shall be his charioteer or bath-attendant, or something decorative of that kind. We must do everything in the Sumurun manner, you know."

"I don't know," said the Baroness; "at least, I should know better if you would explain exactly what you mean by the Sumurun manner."

Clovis obliged: "Weird music, and exotic skippings and flying leaps, and lots of drapery and undrapery. Particularly undrapery."

"I think I told you the County are coming. The County won't stand anything very Greek."

"You can get over any objection by calling it Hygiene, or limb-culture, or something of that sort. After all, every one exposes their insides to the public gaze and sympathy nowadays, so why not one's outside?"

"My dear boy, I can ask the County to a Greek play, or to a costume play, but to a Greek-costume play, never. It doesn't do to let the dramatic instinct carry one too far; one must consider one's environment. When one lives among greyhounds one should avoid giving life-like imitations of a rabbit, unless one wants one's head snapped off. Remember, I've got this place on a seven years' lease. And then," continued the Baroness, "as to skippings and flying leaps; I must ask Emily Dushford to take a part. She's a dear good thing, and will do anything she's told, or try to; but can you imagine her doing a flying leap under any circumstances?"

"She can be Cassandra, and she need only take flying leaps into the future, in a metaphorical sense."

"Cassandra; rather a pretty name. What kind of character is she?"

"She was a sort of advance-agent for calamities. To know her was to know the worst. Fortunately for the gaiety of the age she lived in, no one took her very seriously. Still, it must have been fairly galling to have her turning up after every catastrophe with a conscious air of 'perhaps another time you'll believe what I say.'"

"I should have wanted to kill her."

"As Clytemnestra I believe you gratify that very natural wish."

"Then it has a happy ending, in spite of it being a tragedy?"

"Well, hardly," said Clovis; "you see, the satisfaction of putting a violent end to Cassandra must have been considerably damped by the fact that she had foretold what was going to happen to her. She probably dies with an intensely irritating 'what-did-I-tell-you' smile on her lips. By the way, of course all the killing will be done in the Sumurun manner."

"Please explain again," said the Baroness, taking out a notebook and pencil.

"Little and often, you know, instead of one sweeping blow. You see, you are at your own home, so there's no need to hurry over the murdering as though it were some disagreeable but necessary duty."

"And what sort of end do I have? I mean, what curtain do I get?"

"I suppose you rush into your lover's arms. That is where one of the flying leaps will come in."

The getting-up and rehearsing of the play seemed likely to cause, in a restricted area, nearly as much heart-burning and ill-feeling as the election petition. Clovis, as adapter and stage-manager, insisted, as far as he was able, on the charioteer being quite the most prominent character in the play, and his panther-skin tunic caused almost as much trouble and discussion as Clytemnestra's spasmodic succession of lovers, who broke down on probation with alarming uniformity. When the cast was at length fixed beyond hope of reprieve matters went scarcely more smoothly. Clovis and the Baroness rather overdid the Sumurun manner, while the rest of the company could hardly be said to attempt it at all. As for Cassandra, who was expected to improvise her own prophecies, she appeared to be as incapable of taking flying leaps into futurity as of executing more than a severely plantigrade walk across the stage.

"Woe! Trojans, woe to Troy!" was the most inspired remark she could produce after several hours of conscientious study of all the available authorities.

"It's no earthly use foretelling the fall of Troy," expostulated Clovis, "because Troy has fallen before the action of the play begins. And you mustn't say too much about your own impending doom either, because that will give things away too much to the audience."

After several minutes of painful brain-searching, Cassandra smiled reassuringly.

"I know. I'll predict a long and happy reign for George the Fifth."

"My dear girl," protested Clovis, "have you reflected that Cassandra specialized in foretelling calamities?"

There was another prolonged pause and another triumphant issue.

"I know. I'll foretell a most disastrous season for the foxhounds."

"On no account," entreated Clovis; "do remember that all Cassandra's predictions came true. The M.F.H. and the Hunt Secretary are both awfully superstitious, and they are both going to be present."

Cassandra retreated hastily to her bedroom to bathe her eyes before appearing at tea.

The Baroness and Clovis were by this time scarcely on speaking terms. Each sincerely wished their respective rôle to be the pivot round which the entire production should revolve, and each lost no opportunity for furthering the cause they had at heart. As fast as Clovis introduced some effective bit of business for the charioteer (and he introduced a great many), the Baroness would remorselessly cut it out, or more often dovetail it into her own part, while Clovis retaliated in a similar fashion whenever possible. The climax came when Clytemnestra annexed some highly complimentary lines, which were to have been addressed to the charioteer by a bevy of admiring Greek damsels, and put them into the mouth of her lover. Clovis stood by in apparent unconcern while the words:

"Oh, lovely stripling, radiant as the dawn," were transposed into:

"Oh, Clytemnestra, radiant as the dawn," but there was a dangerous glitter in his eye that might have given the Baroness warning. He had composed the verse himself, inspired and thoroughly carried away by his subject; he suffered, therefore, a double pang in beholding his tribute deflected from its destined object, and his words mutilated and twisted into what became an extravagant panegyric on the Baroness's personal charms. It was from this moment that he became gentle and assiduous in his private coaching of Cassandra.

The County, forgetting its dissensions, mustered in full strength to witness the much-talked-of production. The protective Providence that looks after little children and amateur theatricals made good its traditional promise that everything should be right on the night. The Baroness and Clovis seemed to have sunk their mutual differences, and between them dominated the scene to the partial eclipse of all the other characters, who, for the most part, seemed well content to remain in the shadow. Even Agamemnon, with ten years of strenuous life around Troy standing to his credit, appeared to be an unobtrusive personality compared with his flamboyant charioteer. But the moment came for Cassandra (who had been excused from any very definite outpourings during rehearsals) to support her rôle by delivering herself of a few well-chosen anticipations of pending misfortune. The musicians obliged with appropriately lugubrious wailings and thumpings, and the Baroness seized the opportunity to make a dash to the dressing-room to effect certain repairs in her make-up. Cassandra nervous but resolute, came down to the footlights and, like one repeating a carefully learned lesson, flung her remarks straight at the audience:

"I see woe for this fair country if the brood of corrupt, self-seeking, unscrupulous, unprincipled politicians" (here she named one of the two rival parties in the State) "continue to infest and poison our local councils and undermine our Parliamentary representation; if they continue to snatch votes by nefarious and discreditable means–"

A humming as of a great hive of bewildered and affronted bees drowned her further remarks and wore down the droning of the musicians. The Baroness, who should have been greeted on her return to the stage with the pleasing invocation, "Oh, Clytemnestra, radiant as the dawn," heard instead the imperious voice of Lady

Thistledale ordering her carriage, and something like a storm of open discord going on at the back of the room.

The social divisions in the County healed themselves after their own fashion; both parties found common ground in condemning the Baroness's outrageously bad taste and tactlessness.

She has been fortunate in sub-letting for the greater part of her seven years' lease.

THE PEACE OF MOWSLE BARTON

Crefton Lockyer sat at his ease, an ease alike of body and soul, in the little patch of ground, half-orchard and half-garden, that abutted on the farmyard at Mowsle Barton. After the stress and noise of long years of city life, the repose and peace of the hill-begirt homestead struck on his senses with an almost dramatic intensity. Time and space seemed to lose their meaning and their abruptness; the minutes slid away into hours, and the meadows and fallows sloped away into middle distance, softly and imperceptibly. Wild weeds of the hedgerow straggled into the flower-garden, and wallflowers and garden bushes made counter-raids into farmyard and lane. Sleepy-looking hens and solemn preoccupied ducks were equally at home in yard, orchard, or roadway; nothing seemed to belong definitely to anywhere; even the gates were not necessarily to be found on their hinges. And over the whole scene brooded the sense of a peace that had almost a quality of magic in it. In the afternoon you felt that it had always been afternoon, and must always remain afternoon; in the twilight you knew that it could never have been anything else but twilight. Crefton Lockyer sat at his ease in the rustic seat beneath an old medlar tree, and decided that here was the life-anchorage that his mind had so fondly pictured and that latterly his tired and jarred senses had so often pined for. He would make a permanent lodging-place among these simple friendly people, gradually increasing the modest comforts with which he would like to surround himself, but falling in as much as possible with their manner of living.

As he slowly matured this resolution in his mind an elderly woman came hobbling with uncertain gait through the orchard. He recognized her as a member of the farm household, the mother or possibly the mother-in-law of Mrs. Spurfield, his present landlady, and hastily formulated some pleasant remark to make to her. She forestalled him.

"There's a bit of writing chalked up on the door over yonder. What is it?"

She spoke in a dull impersonal manner, as though the question had been on her lips for years and has best be got rid of. Her eyes, however, looked impatiently over Crefton's head at the door of a small barn which formed the outpost of a straggling line of farm buildings.

"Martha Pillamon is an old witch" was the announcement that met Crefton's inquiring scrutiny, and he hesitated a moment before giving the statement wider publicity. For all he knew to the contrary, it might be Martha herself to whom he was speaking. It was possible that Mrs. Spurfield's maiden name had been Pillamon. And the gaunt, withered old dame at his side might certainly fulfil local conditions as to the outward aspect of a witch.

"It's something about some one called Martha Pillamon," he explained cautiously.

"What does it say?"

"It's very disrespectful," said Crefton; "it says she's a witch. Such things ought not to be written up."

"It's true, every word of it," said his listener with considerable satisfaction, adding as a special descriptive note of her own, "the old toad."

And as she hobbled away through the farmyard she shrilled out in her cracked voice, "Martha Pillamon is an old witch!"

"Did you hear what she said?" mumbled a weak, angry voice somewhere behind Crefton's shoulder. Turning hastily, he beheld another old crone, thin and yellow and wrinkled, and evidently in a high state of displeasure. Obviously this was Martha Pillamon in person. The orchard seemed to be a favourite promenade for the aged women of the neighbourhood.

"'Tis lies, 'tis sinful lies," the weak voice went on "'Tis Betsy Croot is the old witch. She an' her daughter, the dirty rat. I'll put a spell on 'em, the old nuisances."

As she limped slowly away her eye caught the chalk inscription on the barn door.

"What's written up there?" she demanded, wheeling round on Crefton.

"Vote for Soarker," he responded, with the craven boldness of the practised peacemaker.

The old woman grunted, and her mutterings and her faded red shawl lost themselves gradually among the tree-trunks. Crefton rose presently and made his way towards the farmhouse. Somehow a good deal of the peace seemed to have slipped out of the atmosphere.

The cheery bustle of tea-time in the old farm kitchen, which Crefton had found so agreeable on previous afternoons, seemed to have soured today into a certain uneasy melancholy. There was a dull, dragging silence around the board, and the tea itself, when Crefton came to taste it, was a flat, lukewarm concoction that would have driven the spirit of revelry out of a carnival.

"It's no use complaining of the tea," said Mrs. Spurfield hastily, as her guest stared with an air of polite inquiry at his cup. "The kettle won't boil, that's the truth of it."

Crefton turned to the hearth, where an unusually fierce fire was banked up under a big black kettle, which sent a thin wreath of steam from its spout, but seemed otherwise to ignore the action of the roaring blaze beneath it.

"It's been there more than an hour, an' boil it won't," said Mrs. Spurfield, adding, by way of complete explanation, "we're bewitched."

"It's Martha Pillamon as has done it," chimed in the old mother; "I'll be even with the old toad. I'll put a spell on her."

"It must boil in time," protested Crefton, ignoring the suggestions of foul influences. "Perhaps the coal is damp."

"It won't boil in time for supper, nor for breakfast tomorrow morning, not if you was to keep the fire a-going all night for it," said Mrs. Spurfield. And it didn't. The household subsisted on fried and baked dishes, and a neighbour obligingly brewed tea and sent it across in a moderately warm condition.

"I suppose you'll be leaving us now that things has turned up uncomfortable," Mrs. Spurfield observed at breakfast; "there are folks as deserts one as soon as trouble comes."

Crefton hurriedly disclaimed any immediate change of plans; he observed, however, to himself that the earlier heartiness of manner had in a large measure deserted the household. Suspicious looks, sulky silences, or sharp speeches had become the order of the day. As for the old mother, she sat about the kitchen or the garden all day, murmuring threats and spells against Martha Pillamon. There was something alike terrifying and piteous in the spectacle of these frail old morsels of humanity consecrating their last flickering energies to the task of making each other wretched. Hatred seemed to be the one faculty which had survived in undiminished vigour and intensity where all else was dropping into ordered and symmetrical decay. And the uncanny part of it was that some horrid unwholesome power seemed to be distilled from their spite and their cursings. No amount of sceptical explanation could remove the undoubted fact that neither kettle nor saucepan would come to boiling-point over the hottest fire. Crefton clung as long as possible to the theory of some defect in the coals, but a wood fire gave the same result, and when a small spirit-lamp kettle, which he ordered out by carrier, showed the same obstinate refusal to allow its contents to boil he felt that he had come suddenly into contact with some unguessed-at and very evil aspect of hidden forces. Miles away, down through an opening in the hills, he could catch glimpses of a road where motor-cars sometimes passed, and yet here, so little removed from the arteries of the latest civilization, was a bat-haunted old homestead, where something unmistakably like witchcraft seemed to hold a very practical sway.

Passing out through the farm garden on his way to the lanes beyond, where he hoped to recapture the comfortable sense of peacefulness that was so lacking around house and hearth–especially hearth–Crefton came across the old mother, sitting mumbling to herself in the seat beneath the medlar tree. "Let un sink as swims, let un sink as swims," she was repeating over and over again, as a child repeats a half-learned lesson. And now and then she would break off into a shrill laugh, with a note of malice in it that was not pleasant to hear. Crefton was glad when he found himself out of earshot, in the quiet and seclusion of the deep overgrown lanes that seemed to lead away to nowhere; one, narrower and deeper than the rest, attracted his footsteps, and he was almost annoyed when he found that it really did act as a miniature roadway to a human dwelling. A forlorn-looking cottage with a scrap of ill-tended cabbage garden and a few aged apple trees stood at an angle where a swift-flowing stream widened out for a space into a decent-sized pond before hurrying away again through the willows that had checked its course. Crefton leaned against a tree-trunk and looked across the swirling eddies of the pond at the humble little homestead opposite him; the only sign of life came from a small procession of dingy-looking ducks that marched in single file down to the water's edge. There is always something rather taking in the way a duck changes itself in an instant from a slow, clumsy waddler of the earth to a graceful, buoyant swimmer of the waters, and Crefton waited with a certain arrested attention to watch the leader of the file launch itself on to the surface of the pond. He was aware at the same time of a curious warning instinct that something strange and unpleasant was about to happen. The duck flung itself confidently forward into the water, and rolled immediately under the surface. Its head appeared for a moment and went under again, leaving a train of bubbles in its wake, while wings and legs churned the water in a helpless swirl of flapping and kicking. The bird was obviously drowning. Crefton thought at first that it had caught itself in some weeds, or was being attacked from below by a pike or water-rat. But no blood floated to the surface, and the wildly bobbing body made the circuit of the pond current without hindrance from any entanglement. A second duck had by this time launched itself into the pond, and a second struggling body rolled and twisted under the surface. There was something peculiarly piteous in the sight of the gasping beaks that showed now and again above the water, as though in terrified protest at this treachery of a trusted and familiar element. Crefton gazed with something like horror as a third duck poised itself on the bank and splashed in, to share the fate of the other two. He felt almost relieved when the remainder of the flock, taking tardy alarm from the commotion of the slowly drowning bodies, drew themselves up with tense outstretched necks, and sidled away from the scene of danger, quacking a deep note of disquietude as they went. At the same moment Crefton became aware that he was not the only human witness of the scene; a bent and withered old woman, whom he recognized at once as Martha Pillamon, of sinister reputation, had limped down the cottage path to the water's edge, and was gazing fixedly at the gruesome whirligig of dying birds that went in horrible procession round the pool. Presently her voice rang out in a shrill note of quavering rage:

"'Tis Betsy Croot adone it, the old rat. I'll put a spell on her, see if I don't."

Crefton slipped quietly away, uncertain whether or no the old woman had noticed his presence. Even before she had proclaimed the guiltiness of Betsy Croot, the latter's muttered incantation "Let un sink as swims" had flashed uncomfortably across his mind. But it was the final threat of a retaliatory spell which crowded his mind with misgiving to the exclusion of all other thoughts or fancies. His reasoning powers could no longer afford to dismiss these old-wives' threats as empty bickerings. The household at Mowsle Barton lay under the displeasure of a vindictive old woman who seemed able to materialize her personal spites in a very practical fashion, and there was no saying what form her revenge for three drowned ducks might not take. As a member of the household Crefton might find himself involved in some general and highly disagreeable visitation of Martha Pillamon's wrath. Of course he knew that he was giving way to absurd fancies, but the behaviour of the spirit-lamp kettle and the subsequent scene at the pond had considerably unnerved him. And the vagueness of his alarm added to its terrors; when once you have taken the Impossible into your calculations its possibilities become practically limitless.

Crefton rose at his usual early hour the next morning, after one of the least restful nights he had spent at the farm. His sharpened senses quickly detected that subtle atmosphere of things-being-not-altogether well that hangs over a stricken household. The cows had been milked, but they stood huddled about in the yard, waiting impatiently to be driven out afield, and the poultry kept up an importunate querulous reminder of deferred feeding-time; the yard pump, which usually made discordant music at frequent intervals during the early morning, was today ominously silent. In the house itself there was a coming and going of scuttering footsteps, a rushing and dying away of hurried voices, and long, uneasy stillnesses. Crefton finished his dressing and made his way to the head of a narrow staircase. He could hear a dull, complaining voice, a voice into which an awed hush had crept, and recognized the speaker as Mrs. Spurfield.

"He'll go away, for sure," the voice was saying; "there are those as runs away from one as soon as real misfortune shows itself."

Crefton felt that he probably was one of "those," and that there were moments when it was advisable to be true to type.

He crept back to his room, collected and packed his few belongings, placed the money due for his lodgings on a table, and made his way out by a back door into the yard. A mob of poultry surged expectantly towards him; shaking off their interested attentions he hurried along under cover of cowstall, piggery, and hayricks till he reached the lane at the back of the farm. A few minutes' walk, which only the burden of his portmanteaux restrained from developing into an undisguised run, brought him to a main road, where the early carrier soon overtook him and sped him onward to the neighbouring town. At a bend of the road he caught a last glimpse of the farm; the old gabled roofs and thatched barns, the straggling orchard, and the medlar tree, with its wooden seat, stood out with an almost spectral clearness in the early morning light, and over it all brooded that air of magic possession which Crefton had once mistaken for peace.

The bustle and roar of Paddington Station smote on his ears with a welcome protective greeting.

"Very bad for our nerves, all this rush and hurry," said a fellow-traveller; "give me the peace and quiet of the country."

Crefton mentally surrendered his share of the desired commodity. A crowded, brilliantly over-lighted music-hall, where an exuberant rendering of "1812" was being given by a strenuous orchestra, came nearest to his ideal of a nerve sedative.

THE TALKING-OUT OF TARRINGTON

"Heavens!" exclaimed the aunt of Clovis, "here's some one I know bearing down on us. I can't remember his name, but he lunched with us once in Town. Tarrington—yes, that's it. He's heard of the picnic I'm giving for the Princess, and he'll cling to me like a life-belt till I give him an invitation; then he'll ask if he may bring all his wives and mothers and sisters with him. That's the worst of these small watering-places; one can't escape from anybody."

"I'll fight a rearguard action for you if you like to do a bolt now," volunteered Clovis; "you've a clear ten yards start if you don't lose time."

The aunt of Clovis responded gamely to the suggestion, and churned away like a Nile steamer, with a long brown ripple of Pekingese spaniel trailing in her wake.

"Pretend you don't know him," was her parting advice, tinged with the reckless courage of the non-combatant.

The next moment the overtures of an affably disposed gentleman were being received by Clovis with a "silent-upon-a-peak-in-Darien" stare which denoted an absence of all previous acquaintance with the object scrutinized.

"I expect you don't know me with my moustache," said the new-comer; "I've only grown it during the last two months."

"On the contrary," said Clovis, "the moustache is the only thing about you that seemed familiar to me. I felt certain that I had met it somewhere before."

"My name is Tarrington," resumed the candidate for recognition.

"A very useful kind of name," said Clovis; "with a name of that sort no one would blame you if you did nothing in particular heroic or remarkable, would they? And yet if you were to raise a troop of light horse in a moment of national emergency, 'Tarrington's Light Horse' would sound quite appropriate and pulse-quickening; whereas if you were called Spoopin, for instance, the thing would be out of the question. No one, even in a moment of national emergency, could possibly belong to Spoopin's Horse."

The new-comer smiled weakly, as one who is not to be put off by mere flippancy, and began again with patient persistence:

"I think you ought to remember my name–"

"I shall," said Clovis, with an air of immense sincerity. "My aunt was asking me only this morning to suggest names for four young owls she's just had sent her as pets. I shall call them all Tarrington; then if one or two of them die or fly away, or leave us in any of the ways that pet owls are prone to, there will be always one or two left to carry on your name. And my aunt won't *let* me forget it; she will always be asking 'Have the Tarringtons had their mice?' and questions of that sort. She says if you keep wild creatures in captivity you ought to see after their wants, and of course she's quite right there."

"I met you at luncheon at your aunt's house once–" broke in Mr. Tarrington, pale but still resolute.

"My aunt never lunches," said Clovis; "she belongs to the National Anti-Luncheon League, which is doing quite a lot of good work in a quiet, unobtrusive way. A subscription of half a crown per quarter entitles you to go without ninety-two luncheons."

"This must be something new," exclaimed Tarrington.

"It's the same aunt that I've always had," said Clovis coldly.

"I perfectly well remember meeting you at a luncheon-party given by your aunt," persisted Tarrington, who was beginning to flush an unhealthy shade of mottled pink.

"What was there for lunch?" asked Clovis.

"Oh, well, I don't remember that—"

"How nice of you to remember my aunt when you can no longer recall the names of the things you ate. Now my memory works quite differently. I can remember a menu long after I've forgotten the hostess that accompanied it. When I was seven years old I recollect being given a peach at a garden-party by some Duchess or other; I can't remember a thing about her, except that I imagine our acquaintance must have been of the slightest, as she called me a 'nice little boy,' but I have unfading memories of that peach. It was one of those exuberant peaches that meet you halfway, so to speak, and are all over you in a moment. It was a beautiful unspoiled product of a hothouse, and yet it managed quite successfully to give itself the airs of a compote. You had to bite it and imbibe it at the same time. To me there has always been something charming and mystic in the thought of that delicate velvet globe of fruit, slowly ripening and warming to perfection through the long summer days and perfumed nights, and then coming suddenly athwart my life in the supreme moment of its existence. I can never forget it, even if I wished to. And when I had devoured all that was edible of it, there still remained the stone, which a heedless, thoughtless child would doubtless have thrown away; I put it down the neck of a young friend who was wearing a very *décolleté* sailor suit. I told him it was a scorpion, and from the way he wriggled and screamed he evidently believed it, though where the silly kid imagined I could procure a live scorpion at a garden-party I don't know. Altogether, that peach is for me an unfading and happy memory—"

The defeated Tarrington had by this time retreated out of earshot, comforting himself as best he might with the reflection that a picnic which included the presence of Clovis might prove a doubtfully agreeable experience.

"I shall certainly go in for a Parliamentary career," said Clovis to himself as he turned complacently to rejoin his aunt. "As a talker-out of inconvenient bills I should be invaluable."

THE HOUNDS OF FATE

In the fading light of a close dull autumn afternoon Martin Stoner plodded his way along muddy lanes and rut-seamed cart tracks that led he knew not exactly whither. Somewhere in front of him, he fancied, lay the sea, and towards the sea his footsteps seemed persistently turning; why he was struggling wearily forward to that goal he could scarcely have explained, unless he was possessed by the same instinct that turns a hard-pressed stag cliffward in its last extremity. In his case the hounds of Fate were certainly pressing him with unrelenting insistence; hunger, fatigue, and despairing hopelessness had numbed his brain, and he could scarcely summon sufficient energy to wonder what underlying impulse was driving him onward. Stoner was one of those unfortunate individuals who seem to have tried everything; a natural slothfulness and improvidence had always intervened to blight any chance of even moderate success, and now he was at the end of his tether, and there was nothing more to try. Desperation had not awakened in him any dormant reserve of energy; on the contrary, a mental torpor grew up round the crisis of his fortunes. With the clothes he stood up in, a halfpenny in his pocket, and no single friend or acquaintance to turn to, with no prospect either of a bed for the night or a meal for the morrow, Martin Stoner trudged stolidly forward, between moist hedgerows and beneath dripping trees, his mind almost a blank, except that he was subconsciously aware that somewhere in front of him lay the sea. Another consciousness obtruded itself now and then—the knowledge that he was miserably hungry. Presently he came to a halt by an open gateway that led into a spacious and rather neglected farm-garden; there was little sign of life about, and the farm-house at the further end of the garden looked chill and inhospitable. A drizzling rain, however, was setting in, and Stoner thought that here perhaps he might obtain a few minutes' shelter and buy a glass of milk with his last remaining coin. He turned slowly and wearily into the garden and followed a narrow, flagged path up to a side door. Before he had time to knock the door opened and a bent, withered-looking old man stood aside in the doorway as though to let him pass in.

"Could I come in out of the rain?" Stoner began, but the old man interrupted him.

"Come in, Master Tom. I knew you would come back one of these days."

Stoner lurched across the threshold and stood staring uncomprehendingly at the other.

"Sit down while I put you out a bit of supper," said the old man with quavering eagerness. Stoner's legs gave way from very weariness, and he sank inertly into the arm-chair that had been pushed up to him. In another minute he was devouring the cold meat, cheese, and bread, that had been placed on the table at his side.

"You'm little changed these four years," went on the old man, in a voice that sounded to Stoner as something in a dream, far away and inconsequent; "but you'll find us a deal changed, you will. There's no one about the place same as when you left; nought but me and your old Aunt. I'll go and tell her that you'm come; she won't be seeing you, but she'll let you stay right enough. She always did say if you was to come back you should stay, but she'd never set eyes on you or speak to you again."

The old man placed a mug of beer on the table in front of Stoner and then hobbled away down a long passage. The drizzle of rain had changed to a furious lashing downpour, which beat violently against door and windows. The wanderer thought with a shudder of what the sea-shore must look like under this drenching rainfall, with night beating down on all sides. He finished the food and beer and sat numbly waiting for the return of his strange host. As the minutes ticked by on the grandfather clock in the corner a new hope began to flicker and grow in the young man's mind; it was merely the expansion of his former craving for food and a few minutes' rest into a longing to find a night's shelter under this seemingly hospitable roof. A clattering of footsteps down the passage heralded the old farm servant's return.

"The old Missus won't see you, Master Tom, but she says you are to stay. 'Tis right enough, seeing the farm will be yours when she be put under earth. I've had a fire lit in your room, Master Tom, and the maids has put fresh sheets on to the bed. You'll find nought changed up there. Maybe you'm tired and would like to go there now."

Without a word Martin Stoner rose heavily to his feet and followed his ministering angel along a passage, up a short creaking stair, along another passage, and into a large room lit with a cheerfully blazing fire. There was but little furniture, plain, old-fashioned, and good of its kind; a stuffed squirrel in a case and a wall-calendar of four years ago were about the only symptoms of decoration. But Stoner had eyes for little else than the bed, and could scarce wait to tear his clothes off him before rolling in a luxury of weariness into its comfortable depths. The hounds of Fate seemed to have checked for a brief moment.

In the cold light of morning Stoner laughed mirthlessly as he slowly realized the position in which he found himself. Perhaps he might snatch a bit of breakfast on the strength of his likeness to this other missing ne'er-do-well, and get safely away before any one discovered the fraud that had been thrust on him. In the room downstairs he found the bent old man ready with a dish of bacon and fried eggs for "Master Tom's" breakfast, while a hard-faced elderly maid brought in a teapot and poured him out a cup of tea. As he sat at the table a small spaniel came up and made friendly advances.

"'Tis old Bowker's pup," explained the old man, whom the hard-faced maid had addressed as George. "She was main fond of you; never seemed the same after you went away to Australee. She died 'bout a year agone. 'Tis her pup."

Stoner found it difficult to regret her decease; as a witness for identification she would have left something to be desired.

"You'll go for a ride, Master Tom?" was the next startling proposition that came from the old man. "We've a nice little roan cob that goes well in saddle. Old Biddy is getting a bit up in years, though 'er goes well still, but I'll have the little roan saddled and brought round to door."

"I've got no riding things," stammered the castaway, almost laughing as he looked down at his one suit of well-worn clothes.

"Master Tom," said the old man earnestly, almost with an offended air, "all your things is just as you left them. A bit of airing before the fire an' they'll be all right. 'Twill be a bit of a distraction like, a little riding and wild-fowling now and agen. You'll find the folk around here has hard and bitter minds towards you. They hasn't forgotten nor forgiven. No one'll come nigh you, so you'd best get what distraction you can with horse and dog. They'm good company, too."

Old George hobbled away to give his orders, and Stoner, feeling more than ever like one in a dream, went upstairs to inspect "Master Tom's" wardrobe. A ride was one of the pleasures dearest to his heart, and there was some protection against immediate discovery of his imposture in the thought that none of Tom's aforetime companions were likely to favour him with a close inspection. As the interloper thrust himself into some tolerably well-fitting riding cords he wondered vaguely what manner of misdeed the genuine Tom had committed to set the whole countryside against him. The thud of quick, eager hoofs on damp earth cut short his speculations. The roan cob had been brought up to the side door.

"Talk of beggars on horseback," thought Stoner to himself, as he trotted rapidly along the muddy lanes where he had tramped yesterday as a down-at-heel outcast; and then he flung reflection indolently aside and gave himself up to the pleasure of a smart canter along the turf-grown side of a level stretch of road. At an open gateway he checked his pace to allow two carts to turn into a field. The lads driving the carts found time to give him a prolonged stare, and as he passed on he heard an excited voice call out, "'Tis Tom Prike! I knowed him at once; showing hisself here agen, is he?"

Evidently the likeness which had imposed at close quarters on a doddering old man was good enough to mislead younger eyes at a short distance.

In the course of his ride he met with ample evidence to confirm the statement that local folk had neither forgotten nor forgiven the bygone crime which had come to him as a legacy from the absent Tom. Scowling looks, mutterings, and nudgings greeted him whenever he chanced upon human beings; "Bowker's pup," trotting placidly by his side, seemed the one element of friendliness in a hostile world.

As he dismounted at the side door he caught a fleeting glimpse of a gaunt, elderly woman peering at him from behind the curtain of an upper window. Evidently this was his aunt by adoption.

Over the ample midday meal that stood in readiness for him Stoner was able to review the possibilities of his extraordinary situation. The real Tom, after four years of absence, might suddenly turn up at the farm, or a letter might come from him at any moment. Again, in the character of heir to the farm, the false Tom might be called on to sign documents, which would be an embarrassing predicament. Or a relative might arrive who would not imitate the aunt's attitude of aloofness. All these things would mean ignominious exposure. On the other hand, the alternatives was the open sky and the muddy lanes that led down to the sea. The farm offered him, at any rate, a temporary refuge from destitution; farming was one of the many things he had "tried," and he would be able to do a certain amount of work in return for the hospitality to which he was so little entitled.

"Will you have cold pork for your supper," asked the hard-faced maid, as she cleared the table, "or will you have it hotted up?"

"Hot, with onions," said Stoner. It was the only time in his life that he had made a rapid decision. And as he gave the order he knew that he meant to stay.

Stoner kept rigidly to those portions of the house which seemed to have been allotted to him by a tacit treaty of delimitation. When he took part in the farm-work it was as one who worked under orders and never initiated them. Old George, the roan cob, and Bowker's pup were his sole companions in a world that was otherwise frostily silent and hostile. Of the mistress of the farm he saw nothing. Once, when he knew she had gone forth to church, he made a furtive visit to the farm parlour in an endeavour to glean some fragmentary knowledge of the young man whose place he had usurped, and whose ill-repute he had fastened on himself. There were many photographs hung on the walls, or stuck in prim frames, but the likeness he sought for was not among them. At last, in an album thrust out of sight, he came across what he wanted. There was a whole series, labelled "Tom," a podgy child of three, in a fantastic frock, an awkward boy of about twelve, holding a cricket bat as though he loathed it, a rather good-looking youth of eighteen with very smooth, evenly parted hair, and, finally, a young man with a somewhat surly dare-devil expression. At this last portrait Stoner looked with particular interest; the likeness to himself was unmistakable.

From the lips of old George, who was garrulous enough on most subjects, he tried again and again to learn something of the nature of the offence which shut him off as a creature to be shunned and hated by his fellow-men.

"What do the folk around here say about me?" he asked one day as they were walking home from an outlying field.

The old man shook his head.

"They be bitter agen you, mortal bitter. Ay, 'tis a sad business, a sad business."

And never could he be got to say anything more enlightening.

On a clear frosty evening, a few days before the festival of Christmas, Stoner stood in a corner of the orchard which commanded a wide view of the countryside. Here and there he could see the twinkling dots of lamp or candle glow which told of human homes where the goodwill and jollity of the season held their sway. Behind him lay the grim, silent farm-house, where no one ever laughed, where even a quarrel would have seemed cheerful. As he turned to look at the long grey front of the gloom-shadowed building, a door opened and old George came hurriedly forth. Stoner heard his adopted name called in a tone of strained anxiety. Instantly he knew that something untoward had happened, and with a quick revulsion of outlook his sanctuary became in his eyes a place of peace and contentment, from which he dreaded to be driven.

"Master Tom," said the old man in a hoarse whisper, "you must slip away quiet from here for a few days. Michael Ley is back in the village, an' he swears to shoot you if he can come across you. He'll do it, too, there's murder in the look of him. Get away under cover of night, 'tis only for a week or so, he won't be here longer."

"But where am I to go?" stammered Stoner, who had caught the infection of the old man's obvious terror.

"Go right away along the coast to Punchford and keep hid there. When Michael's safe gone I'll ride the roan over to the Green Dragon at Punchford; when you see the cob stabled at the Green Dragon 'tis a sign you may come back agen."

"But—" began Stoner hesitatingly.

"'Tis all right for money," said the other; "the old Missus agrees you'd best do as I say, and she's given me this."

The old man produced three sovereigns and some odd silver.

Stoner felt more of a cheat than ever as he stole away that night from the back gate of the farm with the old woman's money in his pocket. Old George and Bowker's pup stood watching him a silent farewell from the yard. He could scarcely fancy that he would ever come back, and he felt a throb of compunction for those two humble friends who would wait wistfully for his return. Some day perhaps the real Tom would come back, and there would be wild wonderment among those simple farm folks as to the identity of the shadowy guest they had harboured under their roof. For his own fate he felt no immediate anxiety; three pounds goes but little way in the world when there is nothing behind it, but to a man who has counted his exchequer in pennies it seems a good starting-point. Fortune had done him a whimsically kind turn when last he trod these lanes as a hopeless adventurer, and there might yet be a chance of his finding some work and making a fresh start; as he got further from the farm his spirits rose higher. There was a sense of relief in regaining once more his lost identity and ceasing to be the uneasy ghost of another. He scarcely bothered to speculate about the implacable enemy who had dropped from nowhere into his life; since that life was now behind him one unreal item the more made little difference. For the first time for many months he began to hum a careless light-hearted refrain. Then there stepped out from the shadow of an overhanging oak tree a man with a gun. There was no need to wonder who he might be; the moonlight falling on his white set face revealed a glare of human hate such as Stoner in the ups and downs of his wanderings had never seen before. He sprang aside in a wild effort to break through the hedge that bordered the lane, but the tough branches held him fast. The hounds of Fate had waited for him in those narrow lanes, and this time they were not to be denied.

THE RECESSIONAL

Clovis sat in the hottest zone but two of a Turkish bath, alternately inert in statuesque contemplation and rapidly manœuvring a fountain-pen over the pages of a note-book.

"Don't interrupt me with your childish prattle," he observed to Bertie van Tahn, who had slung himself languidly into a neighbouring chair and looked conversationally inclined; "I'm writing deathless verse."

Bertie looked interested.

"I say, what a boon you would be to portrait painters if you really got to be notorious as a poetry writer. If they couldn't get your likeness hung in the Academy as 'Clovis Sangrail, Esq., at work on his latest poem,' they could slip you in as a Study of the Nude or Orpheus descending into Jermyn Street. They always complain that modern dress handicaps them, whereas a towel and a fountain-pen—"

"It was Mrs. Packletide's suggestion that I should write this thing," said Clovis, ignoring the bypaths to fame that Bertie van Tahn was pointing out to him. "You see, Loona Bimberton had a Coronation Ode accepted by the *New Infancy*, a paper that has been started with the idea of making the *New Age* seem elder and hidebound. 'So clever of you, dear Loona,' the Packletide remarked when she had read it; 'of course, any one could write a Coronation Ode, but no one else would have thought of doing it.' Loona protested that these things were extremely difficult to do, and gave us to understand that they were more or less the province of a gifted few. Now the Packletide has been rather decent to me in many ways, a sort of financial ambulance, you know, that carries you off the field when you're hard hit, which is a frequent occurrence with me, and I've no use whatever for Loona Bimberton, so I chipped in and said I could turn out that sort of stuff by the square yard if I gave my mind to it. Loona said I couldn't, and we got bets on, and between you and me I think the money's fairly safe. Of course, one of the conditions of the wager is that the thing has to be published in something or other, local newspapers barred; but Mrs. Packletide has endeared herself by many little acts of thoughtfulness to the editor of the *Smoky Chimney*, so if I can hammer out anything at all approaching the level of the usual Ode output we ought to be all right. So far I'm getting along so comfortably that I begin to be afraid that I must be one of the gifted few."

"It's rather late in the day for a Coronation Ode, isn't it?" said Bertie.

"Of course," said Clovis; "this is going to be a Durbar Recessional, the sort of thing that you can keep by you for all time if you want to."

"Now I understand your choice of a place to write it in," said Bertie van Tahn, with the air of one who has suddenly unravelled a hitherto obscure problem; "you want to get the local temperature."

"I came here to get freedom from the inane interruptions of the mentally deficient," said Clovis, "but it seems I asked too much of fate."

Bertie van Tahn prepared to use his towel as a weapon of

precision, but reflecting that he had a good deal of unprotected coast-line himself, and that Clovis was equipped with a fountain-pen as well as a towel, he relapsed pacifically into the depths of his chair.

"May one hear extracts from the immortal work?" he asked. "I promise that nothing that I hear now shall prejudice me against borrowing a copy of the *Smoky Chimney* at the right moment."

"It's rather like casting pearls into a trough," remarked Clovis pleasantly, "but I don't mind reading you bits of it. It begins with a general dispersal of the Durbar participants:

"'Back to their homes in Himalayan heights
The stale pale elephants of Cutch Behar
Roll like great galleons on a tideless sea—'"

"I don't believe Cutch Behar is anywhere near the Himalayan region," interrupted Bertie. "You ought to have an atlas on hand when you do this sort of thing; and why stale and pale?"

"After the late hours and the excitement, of course," said Clovis; "and I said their *homes* were in the Himalayas. You can have Himalayan elephants in Cutch Behar, I suppose, just as you have Irish-bred horses running at Ascot."

"You said they were going back to the Himalayas," objected Bertie.

"Well, they would naturally be sent home to recuperate. It's the usual thing out there to turn elephants loose in the hills, just as we put horses out to grass in this country."

Clovis could at least flatter himself that he had infused some of the reckless splendour of the East into his mendacity.

"Is it all going to be in blank verse?" asked the critic.

"Of course not; 'Durbar' comes at the end of the fourth line."

"That seems so cowardly; however, it explains why you pitched on Cutch Behar."

"There is more connection between geographical place-names and poetical inspiration than is generally recognized; one of the chief reasons why there are so few really great poems about Russia in our language is that you can't possibly get a rhyme to names like Smolensk and Tobolsk and Minsk."

Clovis spoke with the authority of one who has tried.

"Of course, you could rhyme Omsk with Tomsk," he continued;

"in fact, they seem to be there for that purpose, but the public wouldn't stand that sort of thing indefinitely."

"The public will stand a good deal," said Bertie malevolently, "and so small a proportion of it knows Russian that you could always have an explanatory footnote asserting that the last three letters in Smolensk are not pronounced. It's quite as believable as your statement about putting elephants out to grass in the Himalayan range."

"I've got rather a nice bit," resumed Clovis with unruffled serenity, "giving an evening scene on the outskirts of a jungle village:

"'Where the coiled cobra in the gloaming gloats,
And prowling panthers stalk the wary goats.'"

"There is practically no gloaming in tropical countries," said Bertie indulgently; "but I like the masterly reticence with which you treat the cobra's motive for gloating. The unknown is proverbially the uncanny. I can picture nervous readers of the *Smoky Chimney* keeping the light turned on in their bedrooms all night out of sheer sickening uncertainty as to *what* the cobra might have been gloating about."

"Cobras gloat naturally," said Clovis, "just as wolves are always ravening from mere force of habit, even after they've hopelessly overeaten themselves. I've got a fine bit of colour painting later on," he added, "where I describe the dawn coming up over the Brahmaputra river:

"'The amber dawn-drenched East with sun-shafts kissed,
Stained sanguine apricot and amethyst,
O'er the washed emerald of the mango groves
Hangs in a mist of opalescent mauves,
While painted parrot-flights impinge the haze
With scarlet, chalcedon and chrysoprase.'"

"I've never seen the dawn come up over the Brahma-putra river," said Bertie, "so I can't say if it's a good description of the event, but it sounds more like an account of an extensive jewel robbery. Anyhow, the parrots give a good useful touch of local colour. I suppose you've introduced some tigers into the scenery? An Indian landscape would have rather a bare, unfinished look without a tiger or two in the middle distance."

"I've got a hen-tiger somewhere in the poem," said Clovis, hunting through his notes. "Here she is:

> "'The tawny tigress 'mid the tangled teak
> Drags to her purring cubs' enraptured ears
> The harsh death-rattle in the pea-fowl's beak,
> A jungle lullaby of blood and tears.'"

Bertie van Tahn rose hurriedly from his recumbent position and made for the glass door leading into the next compartment.

"I think your idea of home life in the jungle is perfectly horrid," he said. "The cobra was sinister enough, but the improvised rattle in the tiger-nursery is the limit. If you're going to make me turn hot and cold all over I may as well go into the steam room at once."

"Just listen to this line," said Clovis; "it would make the reputation of any ordinary poet:

> "'and overhead
> The pendulum-patient Punkah, parent of stillborn breeze.'"

"Most of your readers will think 'punkah' is a kind of iced drink or half-time at polo," said Bertie, and disappeared into the steam.

The *Smoky Chimney* duly published the "Recessional," but it proved to be its swan song, for the paper never attained to another issue.

Loona Bimberton gave up her intention of attending the Durbar and went into a nursing-home on the Sussex Downs. Nervous breakdown after a particularly strenuous season was the usually accepted explanation, but there are three or four people who know that she never really recovered from the dawn breaking over the Brahma-putra river.

A MATTER OF SENTIMENT

It was the eve of the great race, and scarcely a member of Lady Susan's house-party had as yet a single bet on. It was one of those unsatisfactory years when one horse held a commanding market position, not by reason of any general belief in its crushing superiority, but because it was extremely difficult to pitch on any other candidate to whom to pin one's faith. Peradventure II was the favourite, not in the sense of being a popular fancy, but by virtue of a lack of confidence in any one of his rather undistinguished rivals. The brains of club-land were much exercised in seeking out possible merit where none was very obvious to the naked intelligence, and the house-party at Lady Susan's was possessed by the same uncertainty and irresolution that infected wider circles.

"It is just the time for bringing off a good coup," said Bertie van Tahn.

"Undoubtedly. But with what?" demanded Clovis for the twentieth time.

The women of the party were just as keenly interested in the matter, and just as helplessly perplexed; even the mother of Clovis, who usually got good racing information from her dressmaker, confessed herself fancy free on this occasion. Colonel Drake, who was professor of military history at a minor cramming establishment, was the only person who had a definite selection for the event, but as his choice varied every three hours he was worse than useless as an inspired guide. The crowning difficulty of the problem was that it could only be fitfully and furtively discussed. Lady Susan disapproved of racing. She disapproved of many things; some people went as far as to say that she disapproved of most things. Disapproval was to her what neuralgia and fancy needlework are to many other women. She disapproved of early morning tea and auction bridge, of ski-ing and the two-step, of the Russian ballet and the Chelsea Arts Club ball, of the French policy in Morocco and the British policy everywhere. It was not that she was particularly strict or narrow in her views of life, but she had been the eldest sister of a large family of self-indulgent children, and her particular form of indulgence had consisted in openly disapproving of the foibles of the others. Unfortunately the hobby had grown up with her. As she was rich, influential, and very, very kind, most people were content to count their early tea as well lost on her behalf. Still, the necessity for hurriedly dropping the discussion of an enthralling topic, and suppressing all mention of it during her presence on the scene, was an affliction at a moment like the present, when time was slipping away and indecision was the prevailing note.

After a lunch-time of rather strangled and uneasy conversation, Clovis managed to get most of the party together at the further end of the kitchen gardens, on the pretext of admiring the Himalayan pheasants. He had made an important discovery. Motkin, the butler, who (as Clovis expressed it) had grown prematurely grey in Lady Susan's service, added to his other excellent qualities an intelligent interest in matters connected with the Turf. On the subject of the forthcoming race he was not illuminating, except in so far that he shared the prevailing unwillingness to see a winner in Peradventure II. But where he outshone all the members of the house-party was in the fact that he had a second cousin who was head stable-lad at a neighbouring racing establishment, and usually gifted with much inside information as to private form and possibilities. Only the fact of her ladyship having taken it into her head to invite a house-party for the last week of May had prevented Mr. Motkin from paying a visit of consultation to his relative with respect to the big race; there was still time to cycle over if he could get leave of absence for the afternoon on some specious excuse.

"Let's jolly well hope he does," said Bertie van Tahn; "under the circumstances a second cousin is almost as useful as second sight."

"That stable ought to know something, if knowledge is to be found anywhere," said Mrs. Packletide hopefully.

"I expect you'll find he'll echo my fancy for Motorboat," said Colonel Drake.

At this moment the subject had to be hastily dropped. Lady Susan bore down upon them, leaning on the arm of Clovis's mother, to whom she was confiding the fact that she disapproved of the craze for Pekingese spaniels. It was the third thing she had found time to disapprove of since lunch, without counting her silent and permanent disapproval of the way Clovis's mother did her hair.

"We have been admiring the Himalayan pheasants," said Mrs. Packletide suavely.

"They went off to a bird-show at Nottingham early this morning," said Lady Susan, with the air of one who disapproves of hasty and ill-considered lying.

"Their house, I mean; such perfect roosting arrangements, and all so clean," resumed Mrs. Packletide, with an increased glow of enthusiasm. The odious Bertie van Tahn was murmuring audible prayers for Mrs. Packletide's ultimate estrangement from the paths of falsehood.

"I hope you don't mind dinner being a quarter of an hour late tonight," said Lady Susan; "Motkin has had an urgent summons to go and see a sick relative this afternoon. He wanted to bicycle there, but I am sending him in the motor."

"How very kind of you! Of course we don't mind dinner being put off." The assurances came with unanimous and hearty sincerity.

At the dinner-table that night an undercurrent of furtive curiosity directed itself towards Motkin's impassive countenance. One or two of the guests almost expected to find a slip of paper concealed in their napkins, bearing the name of the second cousin's selection. They had not long to wait. As the butler went round with the murmured question, "Sherry?" he added in an even lower tone the cryptic words, "Better not." Mrs. Packletide gave a start of alarm, and refused the sherry; there seemed some sinister suggestion in the butler's warning, as though her hostess had suddenly become addicted to the Borgia habit. A moment later the explanation flashed on her that "Better Not" was the name of one of the runners in the big race. Clovis was already pencilling it on his cuff, and Colonel Drake, in his turn, was signalling to every one in hoarse whispers and dumb-show the fact that he had all along fancied "B.N."

Early next morning a sheaf of telegrams went Townward, representing the market commands of the house-party and servants' hall.

It was a wet afternoon, and most of Lady Susan's guests hung about the hall, waiting apparently for the appearance of tea, though it was scarcely yet due. The advent of a telegram quickened every one into a flutter of expectancy; the page who brought the telegram to Clovis waited with unusual alertness to know if there might be an answer.

Clovis read the message and gave an exclamation of annoyance.

"No bad news, I hope," said Lady Susan. Every one else knew that the news was not good.

"It's only the result of the Derby," he blurted out; "Sadowa won; an utter outsider."

"Sadowa!" exclaimed Lady Susan; "you don't say so! How remarkable! It's the first time I've ever backed a horse; in fact I disapprove of horse-racing, but just for once in a way I put money on this horse, and it's gone and won."

"May I ask," said Mrs. Packletide, amid the general silence, "why you put your money on this particular horse? None of the sporting prophets mentioned it as having an outside chance."

"Well," said Lady Susan, "you may laugh at me, but it was the name that attracted me. You see, I was always mixed up with the Franco-German war; I was married on the day that the war was declared, and my eldest child was born the day that peace was signed, so anything connected with the war has always interested me. And when I saw there was a horse running in the Derby called after one of the battles in the Franco-German war, I said I *must* put some money on it, for once in a way, though I disapprove of racing. And it's actually won."

There was a general groan. No one groaned more deeply than the professor of military history.

THE SECRET SIN OF SEPTIMUS BROPE

"Who and what is Mr. Brope?" demanded the aunt of Clovis suddenly.

Mrs. Riversedge, who had been snipping off the heads of defunct roses, and thinking of nothing in particular, sprang hurriedly to mental attention. She was one of those old-fashioned hostesses who consider that one ought to know something about one's guests, and that the something ought to be to their credit.

"I believe he comes from Leighton Buzzard," she observed by way of preliminary explanation.

"In these days of rapid and convenient travel," said Clovis, who was dispersing a colony of green-fly with visitations of cigarette smoke, "to come from Leighton Buzzard does not necessarily denote any great strength of character. It might only mean mere restlessness. Now if he had left it under a cloud, or as a protest against the incurable and heartless frivolity of its inhabitants, that would tell us something about the man and his mission in life."

"What does he do?" pursued Mrs. Troyle magisterially.

"He edits the *Cathedral Monthly*," said her hostess, "and he's enormously learned about memorial brasses and transepts and the influence of Byzantine worship on modern liturgy, and all those sort of things. Perhaps he is just a little bit heavy and immersed in one range of subjects, but it takes all sorts to make a good house-party, you know. You don't find him *too* dull, do you?"

"Dulness I could overlook," said the aunt of Clovis: "what I cannot forgive is his making love to my maid."

"My dear Mrs. Troyle," gasped the hostess, "what an extraordinary idea! I assure you Mr. Brope would not dream of doing such a thing."

"His dreams are a matter of indifference to me; for all I care his slumbers may be one long indiscretion of unsuitable erotic advances, in which the entire servants' hall may be involved. But in his waking hours he shall not make love to my maid. It's no use arguing about it, I'm firm on the point."

"But you must be mistaken," persisted Mrs. Riversedge; "Mr. Brope would be the last person to do such a thing."

"He is the first person to do such a thing, as far as my information goes, and if I have any voice in the matter he certainly shall be the last. Of course, I am not referring to respectably-intentioned lovers."

"I simply cannot think that a man who writes so charmingly and informingly about transepts and Byzantine influences would behave in such an unprincipled manner," said Mrs. Riversedge; "what evidence have you that he's doing anything of the sort? I don't want to doubt your word, of course, but we mustn't be too ready to condemn him unheard, must we?"

"Whether we condemn him or not, he has certainly not been unheard. He has the room next to my dressing-room, and on two occasions, when I dare say he thought I was absent, I have plainly heard him announcing through the wall, 'I love you, Florrie.' Those partition walls upstairs are very thin; one can almost hear a watch ticking in the next room."

"Is your maid called Florence?"

"Her name is Florinda."

"What an extraordinary name to give a maid!"

"I did not give it to her; she arrived in my service already christened."

"What I mean is," said Mrs. Riversedge, "that when I get maids with unsuitable names I call them Jane; they soon get used to it."

"An excellent plan," said the aunt of Clovis coldly; "unfortunately I have got used to being called Jane myself. It happens to be my name."

She cut short Mrs. Riversedge's flood of apologies by abruptly remarking:

"The question is not whether I'm to call my maid Florinda,

but whether Mr. Brope is to be permitted to call her Florrie. I am strongly of opinion that he shall not."

"He may have been repeating the words of some song," said Mrs. Riversedge hopefully; "there are lots of those sorts of silly refrains with girls' names," she continued, turning to Clovis as a possible authority on the subject. "'You mustn't call me Mary—'"

"I shouldn't think of doing so," Clovis assured her; "in the first place, I've always understood that your name was Henrietta; and then I hardly know you well enough to take such a liberty."

"I mean there's a *song* with that refrain," hurriedly explained Mrs. Riversedge, "and there's 'Rhoda, Rhoda kept a pagoda,' and 'Maisie is a daisy,' and heaps of others. Certainly it doesn't sound like Mr. Brope to be singing such songs, but I think we ought to give him the benefit of the doubt."

"I had already done so," said Mrs. Troyle, "until further evidence came my way."

She shut her lips with the resolute finality of one who enjoys the blessed certainty of being implored to open them again.

"Further evidence!" exclaimed her hostess; "do tell me!"

"As I was coming upstairs after breakfast Mr. Brope was just passing my room. In the most natural way in the world a piece of paper dropped out of a packet that he held in his hand and fluttered to the ground just at my door. I was going to call out to him 'You've dropped something,' and then for some reason I held back and didn't show myself till he was safely in his room. You see it occurred to me that I was very seldom in my room just at that hour, and that Florinda was almost always there tidying up things about that time. So I picked up that innocent-looking piece of paper."

Mrs. Troyle paused again, with the self-applauding air of one who has detected an asp lurking in an apple-charlotte.

Mrs. Riversedge snipped vigorously at the nearest rose bush, incidentally decapitating a Viscountess Folkestone that was just coming into bloom.

"What was on the paper?" she asked.

"Just the words in pencil, 'I love you, Florrie,' and then underneath, crossed out with a faint line, but perfectly plain to read, 'Meet me in the garden by the yew.'"

"There *is* a yew tree at the bottom of the garden," admitted Mrs. Riversedge.

"At any rate he appears to be truthful," commented Clovis.

"To think that a scandal of this sort should be going on under my roof!" said Mrs. Riversedge indignantly.

"I wonder why it is that scandal seems so much worse under a roof," observed Clovis; "I've always regarded it as a proof of the superior delicacy of the cat tribe that it conducts most of its scandals above the slates."

"Now I come to think of it," resumed Mrs. Riversedge, "there are things about Mr. Brope that I've never been able to account for. His income, for instance: he only gets two hundred a year as editor of the *Cathedral Monthly*, and I know that his people are quite poor, and he hasn't any private means. Yet he manages to afford a flat somewhere in Westminster, and he goes abroad to Bruges and those sorts of places every year, and always dresses well, and gives quite nice luncheon-parties in the season. You can't do all that on two hundred a year, can you?"

"Does he write for any other papers?" queried Mrs. Troyle.

"No, you see he specializes so entirely on liturgy and ecclesiastical architecture that his field is rather restricted. He once tried the *Sporting and Dramatic* with an article on church edifices in famous fox-hunting centres, but it wasn't considered of sufficient general interest to be accepted. No, I don't see how he can support himself in his present style merely by what he writes."

"Perhaps he sells spurious transepts to American enthusiasts," suggested Clovis.

"How could you sell a transept?" said Mrs. Riversedge; "such a thing would be impossible."

"Whatever he may do to eke out his income," interrupted Mrs. Troyle, "he is certainly not going to fill in his leisure moments by making love to my maid."

"Of course not," agreed her hostess; "that must be put a stop to at once. But I don't quite know what we ought to do."

"You might put a barbed wire entanglement round the yew tree as a precautionary measure," said Clovis.

"I don't think that the disagreeable situation that has arisen is improved by flippancy," said Mrs. Riversedge; "a good maid is a treasure—"

"I am sure I don't know what I should do without Florinda," admitted Mrs. Troyle; "she understands my hair. I've long ago given up trying to do anything with it myself. I regard one's hair as I regard husbands: as long as one is seen together in public one's private divergences don't matter. Surely that was the luncheon gong."

Septimus Brope and Clovis had the smoking-room to themselves after lunch. The former seemed restless and preoccupied, the latter quietly observant.

"What is a lorry?" asked Septimus suddenly; "I don't mean the thing on wheels, of course I know what that is, but isn't there a bird with a name like that, the larger form of a lorikeet?"

"I fancy it's a lory, with one 'r,'" said Clovis lazily, "in which case it's no good to you."

Septimus Brope stared in some astonishment.

"How do you mean, no good to me?" he asked, with more than a trace of uneasiness in his voice.

"Won't rhyme with Florrie," explained Clovis briefly.

Septimus sat upright in his chair, with unmistakable alarm on his face.

"How did you find out? I mean how did you know I was trying to get a rhyme to Florrie?" he asked sharply.

"I didn't know," said Clovis, "I only guessed. When you wanted to turn the prosaic lorry of commerce into a feathered poem flitting through the verdure of a tropical forest, I knew you must be working up a sonnet, and Florrie was the only female name that suggested itself as rhyming with lorry."

Septimus still looked uneasy.

"I believe you know more," he said.

Clovis laughed quietly, but said nothing.

"How much do you know?" Septimus asked desperately.

"The yew tree in the garden," said Clovis.

"There! I felt certain I'd dropped it somewhere. But you must have guessed something before. Look here, you have surprised my secret. You won't give me away, will you? It is nothing to be ashamed of, but it wouldn't do for the editor of the *Cathedral Monthly* to go in openly for that sort of thing, would it?"

"Well, I suppose not," admitted Clovis.

"You see," continued Septimus, "I get quite a decent lot of money out of it. I could never live in the style I do on what I get as editor of the *Cathedral Monthly*."

Clovis was even more startled than Septimus had been earlier in the conversation, but he was better skilled in repressing surprise.

"Do you mean to say you get money out of—Florrie?" he asked.

"Not out of Florrie, as yet," said Septimus; "in fact, I don't mind saying that I'm having a good deal of trouble over Florrie. But there are a lot of others."

Clovis's cigarette went out.

"This is *very* interesting," he said slowly. And then, with Septimus Brope's next words, illumination dawned on him.

"There are heaps of others; for instance:

"'Cora with the lips of coral,
You and I will never quarrel.'

That was one of my earliest successes, and it still brings me in royalties. And then there is—'Esmeralda, when I first beheld her,' and 'Fair Teresa, how I love to please her,' both of those have been fairly popular. And there is one rather dreadful one," continued Septimus, flushing deep carmine, "which has brought me in more money than any of the others:

"'Lively little Lucie
With her naughty nez retrousee'.

Of course, I loathe the whole lot of them; in fact, I'm rapidly becoming something of a woman-hater under their influence, but I can't afford to disregard the financial aspect of the matter. And at the same time you can understand that my position as an authority on ecclesiastical architecture and liturgical subjects would be weakened, if not altogether ruined, if it once got about that I was the author of 'Cora with the lips of coral' and all the rest of them."

Clovis had recovered sufficiently to ask in a sympathetic, if rather unsteady, voice what was the special trouble with "Florrie."

"I can't get her into lyric shape, try as I will," said Septimus mournfully. "You see, one has to work in a lot of sentimental, sugary compliment with a catchy rhyme, and a certain amount of personal biography or prophecy. They've all of them got to have a long string of past successes recorded about them, or else you've got to foretell blissful things about them and yourself in the future. For instance, there is:

"'Dainty little girlie Mavis,
She is such a rara avis.
All the money I can save is
All to be for Mavis mine.'

It goes to a sickening namby-pamby waltz tune, and for months nothing else was sung and hummed in Blackpool and other popular centres."

This time Clovis's self-control broke down badly.

"Please excuse me," he gurgled, "but I can't help it when I remember the awful solemnity of that article of yours that you so kindly read us last night, on the Coptic Church in its relation to early Christian worship."

Septimus groaned.

"You see how it would be," he said; "as soon as people knew me to be the author of that miserable sentimental twaddle, all respect for the serious labours of my life would be gone. I dare say I know more about memorial brasses than any one living, in fact I hope one day to publish a monograph on the subject, but I should be pointed out everywhere as the man whose ditties were in the mouths of nigger minstrels along the entire coast-line of our Island home. Can you wonder that I positively hate Florrie all the time that I'm trying to grind out sugar-coated rhapsodies about her?"

"Why not give free play to your emotions, and be brutally abusive? An uncomplimentary refrain would have an instant success as a novelty if you were sufficiently outspoken."

"I've never thought of that," said Septimus, "and I'm afraid I couldn't break away from the habit of fulsome adulation and suddenly change my style."

"You needn't change your style in the least," said Clovis; "merely reverse the sentiment and keep to the inane phraseology of the thing. If you'll do the body of the song I'll knock off the refrain, which is the thing that principally matters, I believe. I shall charge half-shares in the royalties, and throw in my silence as to your guilty secret. In the eyes of the world you shall still be the man who has devoted his life to the study of transepts and Byzantine ritual; only sometimes, in the long winter evenings, when the wind howls drearily down the chimney and the rain beats against the windows, I shall think of you as the author of 'Cora with the lips of coral.' Of course, if in sheer gratitude at my silence you like to take me for a much-needed holiday to the Adriatic or somewhere equally interesting, paying all expenses, I shouldn't dream of refusing."

Later in the afternoon Clovis found his aunt and Mrs. Riversedge indulging in gentle exercise in the Jacobean garden.

"I've spoken to Mr. Brope about F.," he announced.

"How splendid of you! What did he say?" came in a quick chorus from the two ladies.

"He was quite frank and straightforward with me when he saw that I knew his secret," said Clovis, "and it seems that his intentions were quite serious, if slightly unsuitable. I tried to show him the impracticability of the course that he was following. He said he wanted to be understood, and he seemed to think that Florinda would excel in that requirement, but I pointed out that there were probably dozens of delicately nurtured, pure-hearted young English girls who would be capable of understanding him, while Florinda was the only person in the world who understood my aunt's hair. That rather weighed with him, for he's not really a selfish animal, if you take him in the right way, and when I appealed to the memory of his happy childish days, spent amid the daisied fields of Leighton Buzzard (I suppose daisies do grow there), he was obviously affected. Anyhow, he gave me his word that he would put Florinda absolutely out of his mind, and he has agreed to go for a short trip abroad as the best distraction for his thoughts. I am going with him as far as Ragusa. If my aunt should wish to give me a really nice scarf-pin (to be chosen by myself), as a small recognition of the very considerable service I had done her, I shouldn't dream of refusing. I'm not one of those who think that because one is abroad one can go about dressed anyhow."

A few weeks later in Blackpool and places where they sing, the following refrain held undisputed sway:

"How you bore me, Florrie,
With those eyes of vacant blue;
You'll be very sorry, Florrie,
If I marry you.
Though I'm easy-goin', Florrie,
This I swear is true,
I'll throw you down a quarry, Florrie,
If I marry you."

"MINISTERS OF GRACE"

ALTHOUGH he was scarcely yet out of his teens, the Duke of Scaw was already marked out as a personality widely differing from others of his caste and period. Not in externals; therein he conformed correctly to type. His hair was faintly reminiscent of Houbigant, and at the other end of him his shoes exhaled the right *soupçon* of harness-room; his socks compelled one's attention without losing one's respect; and his attitude in repose had just that suggestion of Whistler's mother, so becoming in the really young. It was within that the trouble lay, if trouble it could be accounted, which marked him apart from his fellows. The Duke was religious. Not in any of the ordinary senses of the word; he took small heed of High Church or Evangelical standpoints, he stood outside of all the movements and missions and cults and crusades of the day, uncaring and uninterested. Yet in a mystical-practical way of his own, which had served him unscathed and unshaken through the fickle years of boyhood, he was intensely and intensively religious. His family were naturally, though unobtrusively, distressed about it. "I am so afraid it may affect his bridge," said his mother.

The Duke sat in a pennyworth of chair in St. James's Park, listening to the pessimisms of Belturbet, who reviewed the existing political situation from the gloomiest of standpoints.

"Where I think you political spade-workers are so silly," said the Duke, "is in the misdirection of your efforts. You spend thousands of pounds of money, and Heaven knows how much dynamic force of brain power and personal energy, in trying to elect or displace this or that man, whereas you could gain your ends so much more simply by making use of the men as you find them. If they don't suit your purpose as they are, transform them into something more satisfactory."

"Do you refer to hypnotic suggestion?" asked Belturbet, with the air of one who is being trifled with.

"Nothing of the sort. Do you understand what I mean by the verb to koepenick? That is to say, to replace an authority by a spurious imitation that would carry just as much weight for the moment as the displaced original; the advantage, of course, being that the koepenick replica would do what you wanted, whereas the original does what seems best in its own eyes."

"I suppose every public man has a double, if not two or three," said Belturbet; "but it would be a pretty hard task to koepenick a whole bunch of them and keep the originals out of the way."

"There have been instances in European history of highly successful koepenickery," said the Duke dreamily.

"Oh, of course, there have been False Dimitris and Perkin Warbecks, who imposed on the world for a time," assented Belturbet, "but they personated people who were dead or safely out of the way. That was a comparatively simple matter. It would be far easier to pass oneself off as dead Hannibal than as living Haldane, for instance."

"I was thinking," said the Duke, "of the most famous case of all, the angel who koepenicked King Robert of Sicily with such brilliant results. Just imagine what an advantage it would be to have angels deputizing, to use a horrible but convenient word, for Quinston and Lord Hugo Sizzle, for example. How much smoother the Parliamentary machine would work than at present!"

"Now you're talking nonsense," said Belturbet; "angels don't exist nowadays, at least, not in that way, so what is the use of dragging them into a serious discussion? It's merely silly."

"If you talk to me like that I shall just *do* it," said the Duke.

"Do what?" asked Belturbet. There were times when his young friend's uncanny remarks rather frightened him.

"I shall summon angelic forces to take over some of the more troublesome personalities of our public life, and I shall send the ousted originals into temporary retirement in suitable animal organisms. It's not every one who would have the knowledge or the power necessary to bring such a thing off—"

"Oh, stop that inane rubbish," said Belturbet angrily; "it's getting wearisome. Here's Quinston coming," he added, as there approached along the almost deserted path the well-known figure of a young Cabinet Minister, whose personality evoked a curious mixture of public interest and unpopularity.

"Hurry along, my dear man," said the young Duke to the Minister, who had given him a condescending nod; "your time is running short," he continued in a provocative strain; "the whole inept crowd of you will shortly be swept away into the world's waste-paper basket."

"You poor little strawberry-leafed nonentity," said the Minister, checking himself for a moment in his stride and rolling out his words spasmodically; "who is going to sweep us away, I should like to know? The voting masses are on our side, and all the ability and administrative talent is on our side too. No power of earth or Heaven is going to move us from our place till we choose to quit it. No power of earth or—"

Belturbet saw, with bulging eyes, a sudden void where a moment earlier had been a Cabinet Minister; a void emphasized rather than relieved by the presence of a puffed-out bewildered-looking sparrow, which hopped about for a moment in a dazed fasion and then fell to a violent cheeping and scolding.

"If we could understand sparrow-language," said the Duke serenely, "I fancy we should hear something infinitely worse than 'strawberry-leafed nonentity.'"

"But good Heavens, Eugène," said Belturbet hoarsely, "what has become of— Why, there he is! How on earth did he get there?" And he pointed with a shaking finger towards a semblance of the vanished Minister, which approached once more along the unfrequented path.

The Duke laughed.

"It is Quinston to all outward appearance," he said composedly, "but I fancy you will find, on closer investigation, that it is an angel under-study of the real article."

The Angel-Quinston greeted them with a friendly smile.

"How beastly happy you two look sitting there!" he said wistfully.

"I don't suppose you'd care to change places with poor little us," replied the Duke chaffingly.

"How about poor little me?" said the Angel modestly. "I've got to run about behind the wheels of popularity, like a spotted dog behind a carriage, getting all the dust and trying to look as if I was an important part of the machine. I must seem a perfect fool to you onlookers sometimes."

"I think you are a perfect angel," said the Duke.

The Angel-that-had-been-Quinston smiled and passed on his way, pursued across the breadth of the Horse Guards Parade by a tiresome little sparrow that cheeped incessantly and furiously at him.

"That's only the beginning," said the Duke complacently; "I've made it operative with all of them, irrespective of parties."

Belturbet made no coherent reply; he was engaged in feeling his pulse. The Duke fixed his attention with some interest on a black swan that was swimming with haughty, stiff-necked aloofness amid the crowd of lesser water-fowl that dotted the ornamental water. For all its pride of bearing, something was evidently ruffling and enraging it; in its way it seemed as angry and amazed as the sparrow had been.

At the same moment a human figure came along the pathway. Belturbet looked up apprehensively.

"Kedzon," he whispered briefly.

"An Angel-Kedzon, if I am not mistaken," said the Duke. "Look, he is talking affably to a human being. That settles it."

A shabbily dressed lounger had accosted the man who had been Viceroy in the splendid East, and who still reflected in his mien some of the cold dignity of the Himalayan snow-peaks.

"Could you tell me, sir, if them white birds is storks or halbatrosses? I had an argyment—"

The cold dignity thawed at once into genial friendliness.

"Those are pelicans, my dear sir. Are you interested in birds? If you would join me in a bun and a glass of milk at the stall yonder, I could tell you some interesting things about Indian birds. Right oh! Now the hill-mynah, for instance—"

The two men disappeared in the direction of the bun stall, chatting volubly as they went, and shadowed from the other side of the railed enclosure by a black swan, whose temper seemed to have reached the limit of inarticulate rage.

Belturbet gazed in an open-mouthed wonder after the retreating couple, then transferred his attention to the infuriated swan, and finally turned with a look of scared comprehension at his young friend lolling unconcernedly in his chair. There was no longer any room to doubt what was happening. The "silly talk" had been translated into terrifying action.

"I think a prairie oyster on the top of a stiffish brandy-and-soda might save my reason," said Belturbet weakly, as he limped towards his club.

It was late in the day before he could steady his nerves sufficiently to glance at the evening papers. The Parliamentary report proved significant reading, and confirmed the fears that he had been trying to shake off. Mr. Ap Dave, the Chancellor, whose lively controversial style endeared him to his supporters and embittered him, politically speaking, to his opponents, had risen in his place to make an unprovoked apology for having alluded in a recent speech to certain protesting taxpayers as "skulkers." He had realized on reflection that they were in all probability perfectly honest in their inability to understand certain legal technicalities of the new finance laws. The House had scarcely recovered from this sensation when Lord Hugo Sizzle caused a further flutter of astonishment by going out of his way to indulge in an outspoken appreciation of the fairness, loyalty, and straightforwardness not only of the Chancellor, but of all the members of the Cabinet. A wit had gravely suggested moving the adjournment of the House in view of the unexpected circumstances that had arisen.

Belturbet anxiously skimmed over a further item of news printed immediately below the Parliamentary report: "Wild cat found in an exhausted condition in Palace Yard."

"Now I wonder which of them–" he mused, and then an appalling idea came to him. "Supposing he's put them both into the same beast!" He hurriedly ordered another prairie oyster.

Belturbet was known in his club as a strictly moderate drinker; his consumption of alcoholic stimulants that day gave rise to considerable comment.

The events of the next few days were piquantly bewildering to the world at large; to Belturbet, who knew dimly what was happening, the situation was fraught with recurring alarms. The old saying that in politics it's the unexpected that always happens received a justification that it had hitherto somewhat lacked, and the epidemic of startling personal changes of front was not wholly confined to the realm of actual politics. The eminent chocolate magnate, Sadbury, whose antipathy to the Turf and everything connected with it was a matter of general knowledge, had evidently been replaced by an Angel-Sadbury, who proceeded to electrify the public by blossoming forth as an owner of race-horses, giving as a reason his matured conviction that the sport was, after all, one which gave healthy open-air recreation to large numbers of people drawn from all classes of the community, and incidentally stimulated the important industry of horse-breeding. His colours, chocolate and cream hoops spangled with pink stars, promised to become as popular as any on the Turf. At the same time, in order to give effect to his condemnation of the evils resulting from the spread of the gambling habit among wage-earning classes, who lived for the most part from hand to mouth, he suppressed all betting news and tipsters' forecasts in the popular evening paper that was under his control. His action received instant recognition and support from the Angel-proprietor of the *Evening Views*, the principal rival evening halfpenny paper, who forthwith issued an ukase decreeing a similar ban on betting news, and in a short while the regular evening Press was purged of all mention of starting prices and probable winners. A considerable drop in the circulation of all these papers was the immediate result, accompanied, of course, by a falling-off in advertisement value, while a crop of special betting broadsheets sprang up to supply the newly created want. Under their influence the betting habit became if anything rather more widely diffused than before. The Duke had possibly overlooked the futility of koepenicking the leaders of the nation with excellently intentioned angel under-studies, while leaving the mass of the people in its original condition.

Further sensation and dislocation was caused in the Press world by the sudden and dramatic *rapprochement* which took place between the Angel-Editor of the *Scrutator* and the Angel-Editor of the *Anglian Review*, who not only ceased to criticize and disparage the tone and tendencies of each other's publication, but agreed to exchange editorships for alternating periods. Here again public support was not on the side of the angels; constant readers of the *Scrutator* complained bitterly of the strong meat which was thrust upon them at fitful intervals in place of the almost vegetarian diet to which they had become confidently accustomed; even those who were not mentally averse to strong meat as a separate course were pardonably annoyed at being supplied with it in the pages of the *Scrutator*. To be suddenly confronted with a pungent herring salad when one had attuned oneself to tea and toast, or to discover a richly truffled segment of *pâté de foie* dissembled in a bowl of bread and milk, would be an experience that might upset the equanimity of the most placidly disposed mortal. An equally vehement outcry arose from the regular subscribers of the *Anglian Review*, who protested against being served from time to time with literary fare which no young person of sixteen could possibly want to devour in secret. To take infinite precautions, they complained, against the juvenile perusal of such eminently innocuous literature was like reading the Riot Act on an uninhabited island. Both reviews suffered a serious falling-off in circulation and influence. Peace hath its devastations as well as war.

The wives of noted public men formed another element of discomfiture which the young Duke had almost entirely left out of his calculations. It is sufficiently embarrassing to keep abreast of the possible wobblings and veerings-round of a human husband, who, from the strength or weakness of his personal character, may leap over or slip through the barriers which divide the parties; for this reason a merciful politician usually marries late in life, when he has definitely made up his mind on which side he wishes his wife to be socially valuable. But these trials were as nothing compared to the bewilderment caused by the Angel-husbands who seemed in some cases to have revolutionized their outlook on life in the interval between breakfast and dinner, without premonition or preparation of any kind, and apparently without realizing the least need for subsequent explanation. The temporary peace which brooded over the Parliamentary situation was by no means reproduced in the home circles of the leading statesmen and politicians. It had been frequently and extensively remarked of Mrs. Exe that she would try the patience of an angel; now the tables were reversed, and she unwittingly had an opportunity for discovering that the capacity for exasperating behaviour was not all on one side.

And then, with the introduction of the Navy Estimates, Parliamentary peace suddenly dissolved. It was the old quarrel between Ministers and the Opposition as to the adequacy or the reverse of the Government's naval programme. The Angel-Quinston and the Angel-Hugo-Sizzle contrived to keep the debates free from personalities and pinpricks, but an enormous sensation was created when the elegant lackadaisical Halfan Halfour threatened to bring up fifty thousand stalwarts to wreck the House if the Estimates were not forthwith revised on a Two-Power basis. It was a memorable scene when he rose in his place, in response to the scandalized shouts of his opponents, and thundered forth, "Gentlemen, I glory in the name of Apache."

Belturbet, who had made several fruitless attempts to ring up his young friend since the fateful morning in St. James's Park, ran him to earth one afternoon at his club, smooth and spruce and unruffled as ever.

"Tell me, what on earth have you turned Cocksley Coxon into?" Belturbet asked anxiously, mentioning the name of one of the pillars of unorthodoxy in the Anglican Church. "I don't fancy he *believes* in angels, and if he finds an angel preaching orthodox sermons from his pulpit while he's been turned into a fox-terrier, he'll develop rabies in less than no time."

"I rather think it was a fox-terrier," said the Duke lazily.

Belturbet groaned heavily, and sank into a chair.

"Look here, Eugène," he whispered hoarsely, having first looked well round to see that no one was within hearing range, "you've got to stop it. Consols are jumping up and down like bronchos, and that speech of Halfour's in the House last night has simply startled everybody out of their wits. And then on the top if it, Thistlebery—"

"What has he been saying?" asked the Duke quickly.

"Nothing. That's just what's so disturbing. Every one thought it was simply inevitable that he should come out with a great epoch-making speech at this juncture, and I've just seen on the tape that he has refused to address any meetings at present, giving as a reason his opinion that something more than mere speech-making was wanted."

The young Duke said nothing, but his eyes shone with quiet exultation.

"It's so unlike Thistlebery," continued Belturbet; "at least," he said suspiciously, "it's unlike the *real* Thistlebery—"

"The real Thistlebery is flying about somewhere as a vocally industrious lapwing," said the Duke calmly; "I expect great things of the Angel-Thistlebery," he added.

At this moment there was a magnetic stampede of members towards the lobby, where the tape-machines were ticking out some news of more than ordinary import.

"*Coup d'état* in the North. Thistlebery seizes Edinburgh Castle. Threatens civil war unless Government expands naval programme."

In the babel which ensued Belturbet lost sight of his young friend. For the best part of the afternoon he searched one likely haunt after another, spurred on by the sensational posters which the evening papers were displaying broadcast over the West End. "General Baden-Baden mobilizes Boy-Scouts. Another *coup d'état* feared. Is Windsor Castle safe?" This was one of the earlier posters, and was followed by one of even more sinister purport: "Will the Test-match have to be postponed?" It was this disquietening question which brought home the real seriousness of the situation to the London public, and made people wonder whether one might not pay too high a price for the advantages of party government. Belturbet, questing round in the hope of finding the originator of the trouble, with a vague idea of being able to induce him to restore matters to their normal human footing, came across an elderly club acquaintance who dabbled extensively in some of the more sensitive market securities. He was pale with indignation, and his pallor deepened as a breathless newsboy dashed past with a poster inscribed: "Premier's constituency harried by moss-troopers. Halfour sends encouraging telegram to rioters. Letchworth Garden City threatens reprisals. Foreigners taking refuge in Embassies and National Liberal Club."

"This is devils' work!" he said angrily.

Belturbet knew otherwise.

At the bottom of St. James's Street a newspaper motor-cart, which had just come rapidly along Pall Mall, was surrounded by a knot of eagerly talking people, and for the first time that afternoon Belturbet heard expressions of relief and congratulation.

It displayed a placard with the welcome announcement: "Crisis ended. Government gives way. Important expansion of naval programme."

There seemed to be no immediate necessity for pursuing the quest of the errant Duke, and Belturbet turned to make his way homeward through St. James's Park. His mind, attuned to the alarums and excursions of the afternoon, became dimly aware that some excitement of a detached nature was going on around him. In spite of the political ferment which reigned in the streets, quite a large crowd had gathered to watch the unfolding of a tragedy that had taken place on the shore of the ornamental water. A large black swan, which had recently shown signs of a savage and dangerous disposition, had suddenly attacked a young gentleman who was walking by the water's edge, dragged him down under the surface, and drowned him before any one could come to his assistance. At the moment when Belturbet arrived on the spot several park-keepers were engaged in lifting the corpse into a punt. Belturbet stooped to pick up a hat that lay near the scene of the struggle. It was a smart soft felt hat, faintly reminiscent of Houbigant.

More than a month elapsed before Belturbet had sufficiently recovered from his attack of nervous prostration to take an interest once more in what was going on in the world of politics. The Parliamentary Session was still in full swing, and a General Election was looming in the near future. He called for a batch of morning papers and skimmed rapidly through the speeches of the Chancellor, Quinston, and other Ministerial leaders, as well as those of the principal Opposition champions, and then sank back in his chair with a sigh of relief. Evidently the spell had ceased to act after the tragedy which had overtaken its invoker. There was no trace of angel anywhere.

THE REMOULDING OF GROBY LINGTON

"A man is known by the company he keeps."

In the morning-room of his sister-in-law's house Groby Lington fidgeted away the passing minutes with the demure restlessness of advanced middle age. About a quarter of an hour would have to elapse before it would be time to say his good-byes and make his way across the village green to the station, with a selected escort of nephews and nieces. He was a good-natured, kindly dispositioned man, and in theory he was delighted to pay periodical visits to the wife and children of his dead brother William; in practice, he infinitely preferred the comfort and seclusion of his own house and garden, and the companionship of his books and his parrot to these rather meaningless and tiresome incursions into a family circle with which he had little in common. It was not so much the spur of his own conscience that drove him to make the occasional short journey by rail to visit his relatives, as an obedient concession to the more insistent but vicarious conscience of his brother, Colonel John, who was apt to accuse him of neglecting poor old William's family. Groby usually forgot or ignored the existence of his neighbour kinsfolk until such time as he was threatened with a visit from the Colonel, when he would put matters straight by a hurried pilgrimage across the few miles of intervening country to renew his acquaintance with the young people and assume a kindly if rather forced interest in the well-being of his sister-in-law. On this occasion he had cut matters so fine between the timing of his exculpatory visit and the coming of Colonel John, that he would scarcely be home before the latter was due to arrive. Anyhow, Groby had got it over, and six or seven months might decently elapse before he need again sacrifice his comforts and inclinations on the altar of family sociability. He was inclined to be distinctly cheerful as he hopped about the room, picking up first one object, then another, and subjecting each to a brief bird-like scrutiny.

Presently his cheerful listlessness changed sharply to an attitude of vexed attention. In a scrap-book of drawings and caricatures belonging to one of his nephews he had come across an unkindly clever sketch of himself and his parrot, solemnly confronting each other in postures of ridiculous gravity and repose, and bearing a likeness to one another that the artist had done his utmost to accentuate. After the first flush of annoyance had passed away, Groby laughed good-naturedly and admitted to himself the cleverness of the drawing. Then the feeling of resentment repossessed him, resentment not against the caricaturist who had embodied the idea in pen and ink, but against the possible truth that the idea represented. Was it really the case that people grew in time to resemble the animals they kept as pets, and had he unconsciously become more and more like the comically solemn bird that was his constant companion? Groby was unusually silent as he walked to the train with his escort of chattering nephews and nieces, and during the short railway journey his mind was more and more possessed with an introspective conviction that he had gradually settled down into a sort of parrot-like existence. What, after all, did his daily routine amount to but a sedate meandering and pecking and perching, in his garden, among his fruit trees, in his wicker chair on the lawn, or by the fireside in his library? And what was the sum total of his conversation with chance-encountered neighbours? "Quite a spring day, isn't it?" "It looks as though we should have some rain." "Glad to see you about again; you must take care of yourself." "How the young folk shoot up, don't they?" Strings of stupid, inevitable perfunctory remarks came to his mind, remarks that were certainly not the mental exchange of human intelligences, but mere empty parrot-talk. One might really just as well salute one's acquaintances with "Pretty Polly. Puss, puss, miaow!" Groby began to fume against the picture of himself as a foolish feathered fowl which his nephew's sketch had first suggested, and which his own accusing imagination was filling in with such unflattering detail.

"I'll give the beastly bird away," he said resentfully; though he knew at the same time that he would do no such thing. It would look so absurd after all the years that he had kept the parrot and made much of it suddenly to try and find it a new home.

"Has my brother arrived?" he asked of the stable-boy, who had come with the pony-carriage to meet him.

"Yessir, came down by the two-fifteen. Your parrot's dead." The boy made the latter announcement with the relish which his class finds in proclaiming a catastrophe.

"My parrot dead?" said Groby. "What caused its death?"

"The ipe," said the boy briefly.

"The ipe?" queried Groby. "Whatever's that?"

"The ipe what the Colonel brought down with him," came the rather alarming answer.

"Do you mean to say my brother is ill?" asked Groby. "Is it something infectious?"

"Th' Colonel's so well as ever he was," said the boy; and as no further explanation was forthcoming Groby had to possess himself in mystified patience till he reached home. His brother was waiting for him at the hall door.

"Have you heard about the parrot?" he asked at once. "'Pon my soul I'm awfully sorry. The moment he saw the monkey I'd brought down as a surprise for you he squawked out, 'Rats to you, sir!' and the blessed monkey made one spring at him, got him by the neck and whirled him round like a rattle. He was as dead as mutton by the time I'd got him out of the little beggar's paws. Always been such a friendly little beast, the monkey has, should never have thought he'd got it in him to see red like that. Can't tell you how sorry I feel about it, and now of course you'll hate the sight of the monkey."

"Not at all," said Groby sincerely. A few hours earlier the tragic end which had befallen his parrot would have presented itself to him as a calamity; now it arrived almost as a polite attention on the part of the Fates.

"The bird was getting old, you know," he went on, in explanation of his obvious lack of decent regret at the loss of his pet. "I was really beginning to wonder if it was an unmixed kindness to let him go on living till he succumbed to old age. What a charming little monkey!" he added, when he was introduced to the culprit.

The new-comer was a small, long-tailed monkey from the Western Hemisphere, with a gentle, half-shy, half-trusting manner that instantly captured Groby's confidence; a student of simian character might have seen in the fitful red light in its eyes some indication of the underlying temper which the parrot had so rashly put to the test with such dramatic consequences for itself. The servants, who had come to regard the defunct bird as a regular member of the household, and one who gave really very little trouble, were scandalized to find his bloodthirsty aggressor installed in his place as an honoured domestic pet.

"A nasty heathen ipe what don't never say nothing sensible and cheerful, same as pore Polly did," was the unfavourable verdict of the kitchen quarters.

One Sunday morning, some twelve or fourteen months after the visit of Colonel John and the parrot-tragedy, Miss Wepley sat decorously in her pew in the parish church, immediately in front of that occupied by Groby Lington. She was, comparatively speaking, a new-comer in the neighbourhood, and was not personally acquainted with her fellow-worshipper in the seat behind, but for the past two years the Sunday morning service had brought them regularly within each other's sphere of consciousness. Without having paid particular attention to the subject, she could probably have given a correct rendering of the way in which he pronounced certain words occurring in the responses, while he was well aware of the trivial fact that, in addition to her prayer book and handkerchief, a small paper packet of throat lozenges always reposed on the seat beside her. Miss Wepley rarely had recourse to her lozenges, but in case she should be taken with a fit of coughing she wished to have the emergency duly provided for. On this particular Sunday the lozenges occasioned an unusual diversion in the even tenor of her devotions, far more disturbing to her personally than a prolonged attack of coughing would have been. As she rose to take part in the singing of the first hymn, she fancied that she saw the hand of her neighbour, who was alone in the pew behind her, make a furtive downward grab at the packet lying on the seat; on turning sharply round she found that the packet had certainly disappeared, but Mr. Lington was to all outward seeming serenely intent on his hymn-book. No amount of interrogatory glaring on the part of the despoiled lady could bring the least shade of conscious guilt to his face.

"Worse was to follow," as she remarked afterwards to a scandalized audience of friends and acquaintances. "I had scarcely knelt in prayer when a lozenge, one of *my* lozenges, came whizzing into the pew, just under my nose. I turned round and stared, but Mr. Lington had his eyes closed and his lips moving as though engaged in prayer. The moment I resumed my devotions another lozenge came rattling in, and then another. I took no notice for a while, and then turned round suddenly just as the dreadful man was about to flip another one at me. He hastily pretended to be turning over the leaves of his book, but I was not to be taken in that time. He saw that he had been discovered and no more lozenges came. Of course I have changed my pew."

"No gentleman would have acted in such a disgraceful manner," said one of her listeners; "and yet Mr. Lington used to be so respected by everybody. He seems to have behaved like a little ill-bred schoolboy."

"He behaved like a monkey," said Miss Wepley.

Her unfavourable verdict was echoed in other quarters about the same time. Groby Lington had never been a hero in the eyes of his personal retainers, but he had shared the approval accorded to his defunct parrot as a cheerful, well-dispositioned body, who gave no particular trouble. Of late months, however, this character would hardly have been endorsed by the members of his domestic establishment. The stolid stable-boy, who had first announced to him the tragic end of his feathered pet, was one of the first to give voice to the murmurs of disapproval which became rampant and general in the servants' quarters, and he had fairly substantial grounds for his disaffection. In a burst of hot summer weather he had obtained permission to bathe in a modest-sized pond in the orchard, and thither one afternoon Groby had bent his steps, attracted by loud imprecations of anger mingled with the shriller chattering of monkey-language. He beheld his plump diminutive servitor, clad only in a waistcoat and a pair of socks, storming ineffectually at the monkey which was seated on a low branch of an apple tree, abstractedly fingering the remainder of the boy's outfit, which he had removed just out of his reach.

"The ipe's been an' took my clothes," whined the boy, with the passion of his kind for explaining the obvious. His incomplete toilet effect rather embarrassed him, but he hailed the arrival of Groby with relief, as promising moral and material support in his efforts to get back his raided garments. The monkey had ceased its defiant jabbering, and doubtless with a little coaxing from its master it would hand back the plunder.

"If I lift you up," suggested Groby, "you will just be able to reach the clothes."

The boy agreed, and Groby clutched him firmly by the waistcoat, which was about all there was to catch hold of, and lifted him clear of the ground. Then, with a deft swing he sent him crashing into a clump of tall nettles, which closed receptively round him. The victim had not been brought up in a school which teaches one to repress one's emotions—if a fox had attempted to gnaw at his vitals he would have flown to complain to the nearest hunt committee rather than have affected an attitude of stoical indifference. On this occasion the volume of sound which he produced under the stimulus of pain and rage and astonishment was generous and sustained, but above his bellowings he could distinctly hear the triumphant chattering of his enemy in the tree, and a peal of shrill laughter from Groby.

When the boy had finished an improvised St. Vitus caracole, which would have brought him fame on the boards of the Coliseum, and which indeed met with ready appreciation and applause from the retreating figure of Groby Lington, he found that the monkey had also discreetly retired, while his clothes were scattered on the grass at the foot of the tree.

"They'm two ipes, that's what they be," he muttered angrily, and if his judgment was severe, at least he spoke under the sting of considerable provocation.

It was a week or two later that the parlour-maid gave notice, having been terrified almost to tears by an outbreak of sudden temper on the part of the master anent some under done cutlets. "'E gnashed 'is teeth at me, 'e did reely," she informed a sympathetic kitchen audience.

"I'd like to see 'im talk like that to me, I would," said the cook defiantly, but her cooking from that moment showed a marked improvement.

It was seldom that Groby Lington so far detached himself from his accustomed habits as to go and form one of a house-party, and he was not a little piqued that Mrs. Glenduff should have stowed him away in the musty old Georgian wing of the house, in the next room, moreover, to Leonard Spabbink, the eminent pianist.

"He plays Liszt like an angel," had been the hostess's enthusiastic testimonial.

"He may play him like a trout for all I care," had been Groby's mental comment, "but I wouldn't mind betting that he snores. He's just the sort and shape that would. And if I hear him snoring through those ridiculous thin-panelled walls, there'll be trouble."

He did, and there was.

Groby stood it for about two and a quarter minutes, and then made his way through the corridor into Spabbink's room. Under

Groby's vigorous measures the musician's flabby, redundant figure sat up in bewildered semi-consciousness like an ice-cream that has been taught to beg. Groby prodded him into complete wakefulness, and then the pettish self-satisfied pianist fairly lost his temper and slapped his domineering visitant on the hand. In another moment Spabbink was being nearly stifled and very effectually gagged by a pillow-case tightly bound round his head, while his plump pyjama'd limbs were hauled out of bed and smacked, pinched, kicked, and bumped in a catch-as-catch-can progress across the floor, towards the flat shallow bath in whose utterly inadequate depths Groby perseveringly strove to drown him. For a few moments the room was almost in darkness: Groby's candle had overturned in an early stage of the scuffle, and its flicker scarcely reached to the spot where splashings, smacks, muffled cries, and splutterings, and a chatter of ape-like rage told of the struggle that was being waged round the shores of the bath. A few instants later the one-sided combat was brightly lit up by the flare of blazing curtains and rapidly kindling panelling.

When the hastily aroused members of the house-party stampeded out on to the lawn, the Georgian wing was well alight and belching forth masses of smoke, but some moments elapsed before Groby appeared with the half-drowned pianist in his arms, having just bethought him of the superior drowning facilities offered by the pond at the bottom of the lawn. The cool night air sobered his rage, and when he found that he was innocently acclaimed as the heroic rescuer of poor Leonard Spabbink, and loudly commended for his presence of mind in tying a wet cloth round his head to protect him from smoke suffocation, he accepted the situation, and subsequently gave a graphic account of his finding the musician asleep with an overturned candle by his side and the conflagration well started. Spabbink gave *his* version some days later, when he had partially recovered from the shock of his midnight castigation and immersion, but the gentle pitying smiles and evasive comments with which his story was greeted warned him that the public ear was not at his disposal. He refused, however, to attend the ceremonial presentation of the Royal Humane Society's life-saving medal.

It was about this time that Groby's pet monkey fell a victim to the disease which attacks so many of its kind when brought under the influence of a northern climate. Its master appeared to be profoundly affected by its loss, and never quite recovered the level of spirits that he had recently attained. In company with the tortoise, which Colonel John presented to him on his last visit, he potters about his lawn and kitchen garden, with none of his erstwhile sprightliness; and his nephews and nieces are fairly well justified in alluding to him as "Old Uncle Groby."

Beasts and Super-Beasts

First Collected, 1914

THE SHE-WOLF

LEONARD BILSITER was one of those people who have failed to find this world attractive or interesting, and who have sought compensation in an "unseen world" of their own experience or imagination—or invention. Children do that sort of thing successfully, but children are content to convince themselves, and do not vulgarize their beliefs by trying to convince other people. Leonard Bilsiter's beliefs were for "the few," that is to say, any one who would listen to him.

His dabblings in the unseen might not have carried him beyond the customary platitudes of the drawing-room visionary if accident had not reinforced his stock-in-trade of mystical lore. In company with a friend, who was interested in a Ural mining concern, he had made a trip across Eastern Europe at a moment when the great Russian railway strike was developing from a threat to a reality; its outbreak caught him on the return journey, somewhere on the further side of Perm, and it was while waiting for a couple of days at a wayside station in a state of suspended locomotion that he made the acquaintance of a dealer in harness and metalware, who profitably whiled away the tedium of the long halt by initiating his English travelling companion in a fragmentary system of folk-lore that he had picked up from Trans-Baikal traders and natives. Leonard returned to his home circle garrulous about his Russian strike experiences, but oppressively reticent about certain dark mysteries, which he alluded to under the resounding title of Siberian Magic. The reticence wore off in a week or two under the influence of an entire lack of general curiosity, and Leonard began to make more detailed allusions to the enormous powers which this new esoteric force, to use his own description of it, conferred on the initiated few who knew how to wield it. His aunt, Cecilia Hoops, who loved sensation perhaps rather better than she loved the truth, gave him as clamorous an advertisement as any one could wish for by retailing an account of how he had turned a vegetable marrow into a wood-pigeon before her very eyes. As a manifestation of the possession of supernatural powers, the story was discounted in some quarters by the respect accorded to Mrs. Hoops' powers of imagination.

However divided opinion might be on the question of Leonard's status as a wonder-worker or a charlatan, he certainly arrived at Mary Hampton's house-party with a reputation for pre-eminence in one or other of those professions, and he was not disposed to shun such publicity as might fall to his share. Esoteric forces and unusual powers figured largely in whatever conversation he or his aunt had a share in, and his own performances, past and potential, were the subject of mysterious hints and dark avowals.

"I wish you would turn me into a wolf, Mr. Bilsiter," said his hostess at luncheon the day after his arrival.

"My dear Mary," said Colonel Hampton, "I never knew you had a craving in that direction."

"A she-wolf, of course," continued Mrs. Hampton; "it would be too confusing to change one's sex as well as one's species at a moment's notice."

"I don't think one should jest on these subjects," said Leonard.

"I'm not jesting, I'm quite serious, I assure you. Only don't do it today; we have only eight available bridge players, and it would break up one of our tables. Tomorrow we shall be a larger party. Tomorrow night, after dinner—"

"In our present imperfect understanding of these hidden forces I think one should approach them with humbleness rather than mockery," observed Leonard, with such severity that the subject was forthwith dropped.

Clovis Sangrail had sat unusually silent during the discussion on the possibilities of Siberian magic; after lunch he side-tracked Lord Pabham into the comparative seclusion of the billiard-room and delivered himself of a searching question.

"Have you such a thing as a she-wolf in your collection of wild animals? A she-wolf of moderately good temper?"

Lord Pabham considered. "There is Louisa," he said, "a rather fine specimen of the timber-wolf. I got her two years ago in exchange for some Arctic foxes. Most of my animals get to be fairly tame before they've been with me very long; I think I can say Louisa has an angelic temper, as she-wolves go. Why do you ask?"

"I was wondering whether you would lend her to me for tomorrow night," said Clovis, with the careless solicitude of one who borrows a collar stud or a tennis racquet.

"Tomorrow night?"

"Yes, wolves are nocturnal animals, so the late hours won't hurt her," said Clovis, with the air of one who has taken everything into consideration; "one of your men could bring her over from Pabham Park after dusk, and with a little help he ought to be able to smuggle her into the conservatory at the same moment that Mary Hampton makes an unobtrusive exit."

Lord Pabham stared at Clovis for a moment in pardonable bewilderment; then his face broke into a wrinkled network of laughter.

"Oh, that's your game, is it? You are going to do a little Siberian magic on your own account. And is Mrs. Hampton willing to be a fellow-conspirator?"

"Mary is pledged to see me through with it, if you will guarantee Louisa's temper."

"I'll answer for Louisa," said Lord Pabham.

By the following day the house-party had swollen to larger proportions, and Bilsiter's instinct for self-advertisement expanded duly under the stimulant of an increased audience. At dinner that evening he held forth at length on the subject of unseen forces and untested powers, and his flow of impressive eloquence continued unabated while coffee was being served in the drawing-room preparatory to a general migration to the card-room. His aunt ensured a respectful hearing for his utterances, but her sensation-loving soul hankered after something more dramatic than mere vocal demonstration.

"Won't you do something to *convince* them of your powers, Leonard?" she pleaded. "Change something into another shape. He can, you know, if he only chooses to," she informed the company.

"Oh, do," said Mavis Pellington earnestly, and her request was echoed by nearly every one present. Even those who were not open to conviction were perfectly willing to be entertained by an exhibition of amateur conjuring.

Leonard felt that something tangible was expected of him.

"Has any one present," he asked, "got a three-penny bit or some small object of no particular value—?"

"You're surely not going to make coins disappear, or something primitive of that sort?" said Clovis contemptuously.

"I think it very unkind of you not to carry out my suggestion of turning me into a wolf," said Mary Hampton, as she crossed over to the conservatory to give her macaws their usual tribute from the dessert dishes.

"I have already warned you of the danger of treating these powers in a mocking spirit," said Leonard solemnly.

"I don't believe you can do it," laughed Mary provocatively from the conservatory; "I dare you to do it if you can. I defy you to turn me into a wolf."

As she said this she was lost to view behind a clump of azaleas.

"Mrs. Hampton—" began Leonard with increased solemnity, but he got no further. A breath of chill air seemed to rush across the room, and at the same time the macaws broke forth into ear-splitting screams.

"What on earth is the matter with those confounded birds, Mary?" exclaimed Colonel Hampton; at the same moment an even more piercing scream from Mavis Pellington stampeded the entire company from their seats. In various attitudes of helpless horror or instinctive defence they confronted the evil-looking grey beast that was peering at them from amid a setting of fern and azalea.

Mrs. Hoops was the first to recover from the general chaos of fright and bewilderment.

"Leonard!" she screamed shrilly to her nephew, "turn it back into Mrs. Hampton at once! It may fly at us at any moment. Turn it back!"

"I—I don't know how to," faltered Leonard, who looked more scared and horrified than any one.

"What!" shouted Colonel Hampton, "you've taken the abominable liberty of turning my wife into a wolf, and now you stand there calmly and say you can't turn her back again!"

To do strict justice to Leonard, calmness was not a distinguishing feature of his attitude at the moment.

"I assure you I didn't turn Mrs. Hampton into a wolf; nothing was farther from my intentions," he protested.

"Then where is she, and how came that animal into the conservatory?" demanded the Colonel.

"Of course we must accept your assurance that you didn't turn Mrs. Hampton into a wolf," said Clovis politely, "but you will agree that appearances are against you."

"Are we to have all these recriminations with that beast standing there ready to tear us to pieces?" wailed Mavis indignantly.

"Lord Pabham, you know a good deal about wild beasts—" suggested Colonel Hampton.

"The wild beasts that I have been accustomed to," said Lord Pabham, "have come with proper credentials from well-known dealers, or have been bred in my own menagerie. I've never before been confronted with an animal that walks unconcernedly out of an azalea bush, leaving a charming and popular hostess unaccounted for. As far as one can judge from *outward* characteristics," he continued, "it has the appearance of a well-grown female of the North American timber-wolf, a variety of the common species *canis lupus*."

"Oh, never mind its Latin name," screamed Mavis, as the beast came a step or two further into the room; "can't you entice it away with food, and shut it up where it can't do any harm?"

"If it is really Mrs. Hampton, who has just had a very good dinner, I don't suppose food will appeal to it very strongly," said Clovis.

"Leonard," beseeched Mrs. Hoops tearfully, "even if this *is* none of your doing can't you use your great powers to turn this dreadful beast into something harmless before it bites us all—a rabbit or something?"

"I don't suppose Colonel Hampton would care to have his wife turned into a succession of fancy animals as though we were playing a round game with her," interposed Clovis.

"I absolutely forbid it," thundered the Colonel.

"Most wolves that I've had anything to do with have been inordinately fond of sugar," said Lord Pabham; "if you like I'll try the effect on this one."

He took a piece of sugar from the saucer of his coffee cup and flung it to the expectant Louisa, who snapped it in mid-air. There was a sigh of relief from the company; a wolf that ate sugar when it might at the least have been employed in tearing macaws to pieces had already shed some of its terrors. The sigh deepened to a gasp of thanksgiving when Lord Pabham decoyed the animal out of the room by a pretended largesse of further sugar. There was an instant rush to the vacated conservatory. There was no trace of Mrs. Hampton except the plate containing the macaws' supper.

"The door is locked on the inside!" exclaimed Clovis, who had deftly turned the key as he affected to test it.

Every one turned towards Bilsiter.

"If you haven't turned my wife into a wolf," said Colonel Hampton, "will you kindly explain where she has disappeared to, since she obviously could not have gone through a locked door? I will not press you for an explanation of how a North American timber-wolf suddenly appeared in the conservatory, but I think I have some right to inquire what has become of Mrs. Hampton."

Bilsiter's reiterated disclaimer was met with a general murmur of impatient disbelief.

"I refuse to stay another hour under this roof," declared Mavis Pellington.

"If our hostess has really vanished out of human form," said Mrs. Hoops, "none of the ladies of the party can very well remain. I absolutely decline to be chaperoned by a wolf!"

"It's a she-wolf," said Clovis soothingly.

The correct etiquette to be observed under the unusual circumstances received no further elucidation. The sudden entry of Mary Hampton deprived the discussion of its immediate interest.

"Some one has mesmerized me," she exclaimed crossly; "I found myself in the game larder, of all places, being fed with sugar by Lord Pabham. I hate being mesmerized, and the doctor has forbidden me to touch sugar."

The situation was explained to her, as far as it permitted of anything that could be called explanation.

"Then you *really* did turn me into a wolf, Mr. Bilsiter?" she exclaimed excitedly.

But Leonard had burned the boat in which he might now have embarked on a sea of glory. He could only shake his head feebly.

"It was I who took that liberty," said Clovis; "you see, I happen to have lived for a couple of years in North-eastern Russia, and I have more than a tourist's acquaintance with the magic craft of that region. One does not care to speak about these strange powers, but once in a way, when one hears a lot of nonsense being talked about them, one is tempted to show what Siberian magic can accomplish in the hands of some one who really understands it. I yielded to that temptation. May I have some brandy? the effort has left me rather faint."

If Leonard Bilsiter could at that moment have transformed Clovis into a cockroach and then have stepped on him he would gladly have performed both operations.

LAURA

"You are not really dying, are you?" asked Amanda.

"I have the doctor's permission to live till Tuesday," said Laura.

"But today is Saturday; this is serious!" gasped Amanda.

"I don't know about it being serious; it is certainly Saturday," said Laura.

"Death is always serious," said Amanda.

"I never said I was going to die. I am presumably going to leave off being Laura, but I shall go on being something. An animal of some kind, I suppose. You see, when one hasn't been very good in the life one has just lived, one reincarnates in some lower organism. And I haven't been very good, when one comes to think of it. I've been petty and mean and vindictive and all that sort of thing when circumstances have seemed to warrant it."

"Circumstances never warrant that sort of thing," said Amanda hastily.

"If you don't mind my saying so," observed Laura, "Egbert is a circumstance that would warrant any amount of that sort of thing.

You're married to him—that's different; you've sworn to love, honour, and endure him: I haven't."

"I don't see what's wrong with Egbert," protested Amanda.

"Oh, I dare say the wrongness has been on my part," admitted Laura dispassionately; "he has merely been the extenuating circumstance. He made a thin, peevish kind of fuss, for instance, when I took the collie puppies from the farm out for a run the other day."

"They chased his young broods of speckled Sussex and drove two sitting hens off their nests, besides running all over the flower beds. You know how devoted he is to his poultry and garden."

"Anyhow, he needn't have gone on about it for the entire evening and then have said, 'Let's say no more about it' just when I was beginning to enjoy the discussion. That's where one of my petty vindictive revenges came in," added Laura with an unrepentant chuckle; "I turned the entire family of speckled Sussex into his seedling shed the day after the puppy episode."

"How could you?" exclaimed Amanda.

"It came quite easy," said Laura; "two of the hens pretended to be laying at the time, but I was firm."

"And we thought it was an accident!"

"You see," resumed Laura, "I really *have* some grounds for supposing that my next incarnation will be in a lower organism. I shall be an animal of some kind. On the other hand, I haven't been a bad sort in my way, so I think I may count on being a nice animal, some thing elegant and lively, with a love of fun. An otter, perhaps."

"I can't imagine you as an otter," said Amanda.

"Well, I don't suppose you can imagine me as an angel, if it comes to that," said Laura.

Amanda was silent. She couldn't.

"Personally I think an otter life would be rather enjoyable," continued Laura; "salmon to eat all the year around, and the satisfaction of being able to fetch the trout in their own homes without having to wait for hours till they condescend to rise to the fly you've been dangling before them; and an elegant svelte figure—"

"Think of the other hounds," interposed Amanda; "how dreadful to be hunted and harried and finally worried to death!"

"Rather fun with half the neighbourhood looking on, and anyhow not worse than this Saturday-to-Tuesday business of dying by inches; and then I should go on into something else. If I had been a moderately good otter I suppose I should get back into human shape of some sort; probably something rather primitive—a little brown, unclothed Nubian boy, I should think."

"I wish you would be serious," sighed Amanda; "you really ought to be if you're only going to live till Tuesday."

As a matter of fact Laura died on Monday.

"So dreadfully upsetting," Amanda complained to her uncle-in-law, Sir Lulworth Quayne. "I've asked quite a lot of people down for golf and fishing, and the rhododendrons are just looking their best."

"Laura always was inconsiderate," said Sir Lulworth; "she was born during Goodwood week, with an Ambassador staying in the house who hated babies."

"She had the maddest kind of ideas," said Amanda; "do you know if there was any insanity in her family?"

"Insanity? No, I never heard of any. Her father lives in West Kensington, but I believe he's sane on all other subjects."

"She had an idea that she was going to be reincarnated as an otter," said Amanda.

"One meets with those ideas of reincarnation so frequently, even in the West," said Sir Lulworth, "that one can hardly set them down as being mad. And Laura was such an unaccountable person in this life that I should not like to lay down definite rules as to what she might be doing in an after state."

"You think she really might have passed into some animal form?" asked Amanda. She was one of those who shape their opinions rather readily from the standpoint of those around them.

Just then Egbert entered the breakfast-room, wearing an air of bereavement that Laura's demise would have been insufficient, in itself, to account for.

"Four of my speckled Sussex have been killed," he exclaimed; "the very four that were to go to the show on Friday. One of them was dragged away and eaten right in the middle of that new carnation bed that I've been to such trouble and expense over. My best flower bed and my best fowls singled out for destruction; it almost seems as if the brute that did the deed had special knowledge how to be as devastating as possible in a short space of time."

"Was it a fox, do you think?" asked Amanda.

"Sounds more like a polecat," said Sir Lulworth.

"No," said Egbert, "there were marks of webbed feet all over the place, and we followed the tracks down to the stream at the bottom of the garden; evidently an otter."

Amanda looked quickly and furtively across at Sir Lulworth.

Egbert was too agitated to eat any breakfast, and went out to superintend the strengthening of the poultry yard defences.

"I think she might at least have waited till the funeral was over," said Amanda in a scandalized voice.

"It's her own funeral, you know," said Sir Lulworth; "it's a nice point in etiquette how far one ought to show respect to one's own mortal remains."

Disregard for mortuary convention was carried to further lengths next day; during the absence of the family at the funeral ceremony the remaining survivors of the speckled Sussex were massacred. The marauder's line of retreat seemed to have embraced most of the flower beds on the lawn, but the strawberry beds in the lower garden had also suffered.

"I shall get the otter hounds to come here at the earliest possible moment," said Egbert savagely.

"On no account! You can't dream of such a thing!" exclaimed Amanda. "I mean, it wouldn't do, so soon after a funeral in the house."

"It's a case of necessity," said Egbert; "once an otter takes to that sort of thing it won't stop."

"Perhaps it will go elsewhere now that there are no more fowls left," suggested Amanda.

"One would think you wanted to shield the beast," said Egbert.

"There's been so little water in the stream lately," objected Amanda; "it seems hardly sporting to hunt an animal when it has so little chance of taking refuge anywhere."

"Good gracious!" fumed Egbert, "I'm not thinking about sport. I want to have the animal killed as soon as possible."

Even Amanda's opposition weakened when, during church time on the following Sunday, the otter made its way into the house, raided half a salmon from the larder and worried it into scaly fragments on the Persian rug in Egbert's studio.

"We shall have it hiding under our beds and biting pieces out of our feet before long," said Egbert, and from what Amanda knew of this particular otter she felt that the possibility was not a remote one.

On the evening preceding the day fixed for the hunt Amanda

spent a solitary hour walking by the banks of the stream, making what she imagined to be hound noises. It was charitably supposed by those who overheard her performance, that she was practising for farmyard imitations at the forthcoming village entertainment.

It was her friend and neighbour, Aurora Burret, who brought her news of the day's sport.

"Pity you weren't out; we have quite a good day. We found it at once, in the pool just below your garden."

"Did you—kill?" asked Amanda.

"Rather. A fine she-otter. Your husband got rather badly bitten in trying to 'tail it.' Poor beast, I felt quite sorry for it, it had such a human look in its eyes when it was killed. You'll call me silly, but do you know who the look reminded me of? My dear woman, what is the matter?"

When Amanda had recovered to a certain extent from her attack of nervous prostration Egbert took her to the Nile Valley to recuperate. Change of scene speedily brought about the desired recovery of health and mental balance. The escapades of an adventurous otter in search of a variation of diet were viewed in their proper light. Amanda's normally placid temperament reasserted itself. Even a hurricane of shouted curses, coming from her husband's dressing-room, in her husband's voice, but hardly in his usual vocabulary, failed to disturb her serenity as she made a leisurely toilet one evening in a Cairo hotel.

"What is the matter? What has happened?" she asked in amused curiosity.

"The little beast has thrown all my clean shirts into the bath! Wait till I catch you, you little—"

"What little beast?" asked Amanda, suppressing a desire to laugh; Egbert's language was so hopelessly inadequate to express his outraged feelings.

"A little beast of a naked brown Nubian boy," spluttered Egbert.

And now Amanda is seriously ill.

THE BOAR-PIG

"There is a back way on to the lawn," said Mrs. Philidore Stossen to her daughter, "through a small grass paddock and then through a walled fruit garden full of gooseberry bushes. I went all over the place last year when the family were away. There is a door that opens from the fruit garden into a shrubbery, and once we emerge from there we can mingle with the guests as if we had come in by the ordinary way. It's much safer than going in by the front entrance and running the risk of coming bang up against the hostess; that would be so awkward when she doesn't happen to have invited us."

"Isn't it a lot of trouble to take for getting admittance to a garden party?"

"To a garden party, yes; to *the* garden party of the season, certainly not. Every one of any consequence in the county, with the exception of ourselves, has been asked to meet the Princess, and it would be far more troublesome to invent explanations as to why we weren't there than to get in by a roundabout way. I stopped Mrs. Cuvering in the road yesterday and talked very pointedly about the Princess. If she didn't choose to take the hint and send me an invitation it's not my fault, is it? Here we are: we just cut across the grass and through that little gate into the garden."

Mrs. Stossen and her daughter, suitably arrayed for a county garden party function with an infusion of Almanack de Gotha, sailed through the narrow grass paddock and the ensuing gooseberry garden with the air of state barges making an unofficial progress along a rural trout stream. There was a certain amount of furtive haste mingled with the stateliness of their advance as though hostile searchlights might be turned on them at any moment; and, as a matter of fact, they were not unobserved. Matilda Cuvering, with the alert eyes of thirteen years and the added advantage of an exalted position in the branches of a medlar tree, had enjoyed a good view of the Stossen flanking movement and had foreseen exactly where it would break down in execution.

"They'll find the door locked, and they'll jolly well have to go back the way they came," she remarked to herself. "Serves them right for not coming in by the proper entrance. What a pity Tarquin Superbus isn't loose in the paddock. After all, as every one else is enjoying themselves, I don't see why Tarquin shouldn't have an afternoon out."

Matilda was of an age when thought is action; she slid down from the branches of the medlar tree, and when she clambered back again, Tarquin, the huge white Yorkshire boar-pig, had exchanged the narrow limits of his sty for the wider range of the grass paddock. The discomfited Stossen expedition, returning in recriminatory but otherwise orderly retreat from the unyielding obstacle of the locked door, came to a sudden halt at the gate dividing the paddock from the gooseberry garden.

"What a villainous-looking animal," exclaimed Mrs. Stossen; "it wasn't there when we came in."

"It's there now, anyhow," said her daughter. "What on earth are we to do? I wish we had never come."

The boar-pig had drawn nearer to the gate for a closer inspection of the human intruders, and stood champing his jaws and blinking his small red eyes in a manner that was doubtless intended to be disconcerting, and, as far as the Stossens were concerned, thoroughly achieved that result.

"Shoo! Hish! Hish! Shoo!" cried the ladies in chorus.

"If they think they're going to drive him away by reciting lists of the kings of Israel and Judah they're laying themselves out for disappointment," observed Matilda from her seat in the medlar tree. As she made the observation aloud Mrs. Stossen became for the first time aware of her presence. A moment or two earlier she would have been anything but pleased at the discovery that the garden was not as deserted as it looked, but now she hailed the fact of the child's presence on the scene with absolute relief.

"Little girl, can you find some one to drive away—" she began hopefully.

"*Comment? Comprends pas,*" was the response.

"Oh, are you French? *Êtes vous française?*"

"*Pas de tous. 'Suis anglaise.*"

"Then why not talk English? I want to know if—"

"*Permettez-moi expliquer.* You see, I'm rather under a cloud," said Matilda. "I'm staying with my aunt, and I was told I must behave particularly well today, as lots of people were coming for a garden party, and I was told to imitate Claude, that's my young cousin, who never does anything wrong except by accident, and then is always apologetic about it. It seems they thought I ate too much raspberry trifle at lunch, and they said Claude never eats too much raspberry trifle. Well, Claude always goes to sleep for half an hour after lunch, because he's told to, and I waited till he was asleep, and tied his hands and started forcible feeding with a whole bucketful of raspberry trifle that they were keeping for the garden party. Lots of it went on to his sailor-suit and some of it on to the bed, but a good deal went down Claude's throat, and they can't say again that he has never been known to eat too much raspberry trifle. That is why I am not allowed to go to the party, and as an additional punishment I must speak French all the afternoon. I've had to tell you all this in English, as there were words like 'forcible feeding' that I didn't know the French for; of course I could have invented them, but if I had said *nourriture obligatoire* you wouldn't have had the least idea what I was talking about. *Mais maintenant, nous parlons français.*"

"Oh, very well, *très bien,*" said Mrs. Stossen reluctantly; in moments of flurry such French as she knew was not under very good control. *"Là, à l'autre côté de la porte, est un cochon—"*

"Un cochon? Ah, le petit charmant!" exclaimed Matilda with enthusiasm.

"Mais non, pas du tout petit, et pas du tout charmant; un bête féroce—"

"Une bête," corrected Matilda, "a pig is masculine as long as you call it a pig, but if you lose your temper with it and call it a ferocious beast it becomes one of us at once. French is a dreadfully unsexing language."

"For goodness' sake let us talk English then," said Mrs. Stossen. "Is there any way out of this garden except through the paddock where the pig is?"

"I always go over the wall, by way of the plum tree," said Matilda.

"Dressed as we are we could hardly do that," said Mrs. Stossen; it was difficult to imagine her doing it in any costume.

"Do you think you could go and get some one who would drive the pig away?" asked Miss Stossen.

"I promised my aunt I would stay here till five o'clock; it's not four yet."

"I am sure, under the circumstances, your aunt would permit—"

"My conscience would not permit," said Matilda with cold dignity.

"We can't stay here till five o'clock," exclaimed Mrs. Stossen with growing exasperation.

"Shall I recite to you to make the time pass quicker?" asked Matilda obligingly. " 'Belinda, the little Breadwinner,' is considered my best piece, or, perhaps, it ought to be something in French. Henri Quatre's address to his soldiers is the only thing I really know in that language."

"If you will go and fetch some one to drive that animal away I will give you something to buy yourself a nice present," said Mrs. Stossen.

Matilda came several inches lower down the medlar tree.

"That is the most practical suggestion you have made yet for getting out of the garden," she remarked cheerfully; "Claude and I are collecting money for the Children's Fresh Air Fund, and we are seeing which of us can collect the biggest sum."

"I shall be very glad to contribute half a crown, very glad indeed," said Mrs. Stossen, digging that coin out of the depths of a receptacle which formed a detached outwork of her toilet.

"Claude is a long way ahead of me at present," continued Matilda, taking no notice of the suggested offering; "you see, he's only eleven, and has golden hair, and those are enormous advantages when you're on the collecting job. Only the other day a Russian lady gave him ten shillings. Russians understand the art of giving far better than we do. I expect Claude will net quite twenty-five shillings this afternoon; he'll have the field to himself, and he'll be able to do the pale, fragile, not-long-for-this-world business to perfection after his raspberry trifle experience. Yes, he'll be *quite* two pounds ahead of me by now."

With much probing and plucking and many regretful murmurs the beleaguered ladies managed to produce seven-and-sixpence between them.

"I am afraid this is all we've got," said Mrs. Stossen.

Matilda showed no sign of coming down either to the earth or to their figure.

"I could not do violence to my conscience for anything less than ten shillings," she announced stiffly.

Mother and daughter muttered certain remarks under their breath, in which the word "beast" was prominent, and probably had no reference to Tarquin.

"I find I *have* got another half-crown," said Mrs. Stossen in a shaking voice; "here you are. Now please fetch some one quickly."

Matilda slipped down from the tree, took possession of the donation, and proceeded to pick up a handful of over-ripe medlars from the grass at her feet. Then she climbed over the gate and addressed herself affectionately to the boar-pig.

"Come, Tarquin, dear old boy; you know you can't resist medlars when they're rotten and squashy."

Tarquin couldn't. By dint of throwing the fruit in front of him at judicious intervals Matilda decoyed him back to his sty, while the delivered captives hurried across the paddock.

"Well, I never! The little minx!" exclaimed Mrs. Stossen when she was safely on the high road. "The animal wasn't savage at all, and as for the ten shillings, I don't believe the Fresh Air Fund will see a penny of it!"

There she was unwarrantably harsh in her judgment. If you examine the books of the fund you will find the acknowledgment: "Collected by Miss Matilda Cuvering, 2s. 6d."

THE BROGUE

THE hunting season had come to an end, and the Mullets had not succeeded in selling the Brogue. There had been a kind of tradition in the family for the past three or four years, a sort of fatalistic hope, that the Brogue would find a purchaser before the hunting was over; but seasons came and went without anything happening to justify such ill-founded optimism. The animal had been named Berserker in the earlier stages of its career; it had been rechristened the Brogue later on, in recognition of the fact that, once acquired, it was extremely difficult to get rid of. The unkinder wits of the neighbourhood had been known to suggest that the first letter of its name was superfluous. The Brogue had been variously described in sale catalogues as a light-weight hunter, a lady's hack, and, more simply, but still with a touch of imagination, as a useful brown gelding, standing 15.1. Toby Mullet had ridden him for four seasons with the West Wessex; you can ride almost any sort of horse with the West Wessex as long as it is an animal that knows the country. The Brogue knew the country intimately, having personally created most of the gaps that were to be met with in banks and hedges for many miles round. His manners and characteristics were not ideal in the hunting field, but he was probably rather safer to ride to hounds than he was as a hack on country roads. According to the Mullet family, he was not really road-shy, but there were one or two objects of dislike that brought on sudden attacks of what Toby called swerving sickness. Motors and cycles he treated with tolerant disregard, but pigs, wheelbarrows, piles of stones by the roadside, perambulators in a village street, gates painted too aggressively white, and sometimes, but not always, the newer kind of beehives, turned him aside from his tracks in vivid imitation of the zigzag course of forked lightning. If a pheasant rose noisily from the other side of a hedgerow the Brogue would spring into the air at the same moment, but this may have been due to a desire to be companionable. The Mullet family contradicted the widely prevalent report that the horse was a confirmed crib-biter.

It was about the third week in May that Mrs. Mullet, relict of the late Sylvester Mullet, and mother of Toby and a bunch of daughters, assailed Clovis Sangrail on the outskirts of the village with a breathless catalogue of local happenings.

"You know our new neighbour, Mr. Penricarde?" she vociferated; "awfully rich, owns tin mines in Cornwall, middle-aged and rather quiet. He's taken the Red House on a long lease and spent a lot of money on alterations and improvements. Well, Toby's sold him the Brogue!"

Clovis spent a moment or two in assimilating the astonishing news; then he broke out into unstinted congratulation. If he had belonged to a more emotional race he would probably have kissed Mrs. Mullet.

"How wonderful lucky to have pulled it off at last! Now you can buy a decent animal. I've always said that Toby was clever. Ever so many congratulations."

"Don't congratulate me. It's the most unfortunate thing that could have happened!" said Mrs. Mullet dramatically.

Clovis stared at her in amazement.

"Mr. Penricarde," said Mrs. Mullet, sinking her voice to what she imagined to be an impressive whisper, though it rather resembled a hoarse, excited squeak, "Mr. Penricarde has just begun to pay attentions to Jessie. Slight at first, but now unmistakable. I was a fool not to have seen it sooner. Yesterday, at the Rectory garden party, he asked her what her favourite flowers were, and she told him carnations, and today a whole stack of carnations has arrived, clove and malmaison and lovely dark red ones, regular exhibition blooms, and a box of chocolates that he must have got on purpose from London. And he's asked her to go round the links with him tomorrow. And now, just at this critical moment, Toby has sold him that animal. It's a calamity!"

"But you've been trying to get the horse off your hands for years," said Clovis.

"I've got a houseful of daughters," said Mrs. Mullet, "and I've been trying—well, not to get them off my hands, of course, but a husband or two wouldn't be amiss among the lot of them; there are six of them, you know."

"I don't know," said Clovis, "I've never counted, but I expect you're right as to the number; mothers generally know these things."

"And now," continued Mrs. Mullet, in her tragic whisper, "when there's a rich husband-in-prospect imminent on the horizon Toby goes and sells him that miserable animal. It will probably kill him if he tries to ride it; anyway it will kill any affection he might have felt towards any member of our family. What is to be done? We can't very well ask to have the horse back; you see, we praised it up like anything when we thought there was a chance of his buying it, and said it was just the animal to suit him."

"Couldn't you steal it out of his stable and send it to grass at some farm miles away?" suggested Clovis. "Write 'Votes for Women' on the stable door, and the thing would pass for a Suffragette outrage. No one who knew the horse could possibly suspect you of wanting to get it back again."

"Every newspaper in the country would ring with the affair," said Mrs. Mullet; "can't you imagine the headline, 'Valuable Hunter Stolen by Suffragettes'? The police would scour the countryside till they found the animal."

"Well, Jessie must try and get it back from Penricarde on the plea that it's an old favourite. She can say it was only sold because the stable had to be pulled down under the terms of an old repairing lease, and that now it has been arranged that the stable is to stand for a couple of years longer."

"It sounds a queer proceeding to ask for a horse back when you've just sold him," said Mrs. Mullet, "but something must be done, and done at once. The man is not used to horses, and I believe I told him it was as quiet as a lamb. After all, lambs go kicking and twisting about as if they were demented, don't they?"

"The lamb has an entirely unmerited character for sedateness," agreed Clovis.

Jessie came back from the golf links next day in a state of mingled elation and concern.

"It's all right about the proposal," she announced, "he came out with it at the sixth hole. I said I must have time to think it over. I accepted him at the seventh."

"My dear," said her mother, "I think a little more maidenly reserve and hesitation would have been advisable, as you've known him so short a time. You might have waited till the ninth hole."

"The seventh is a very long hole," said Jessie; "besides, the tension was putting us both off our game. By the time we'd got to the ninth hole we'd settled lots of things. The honeymoon is to be spent in Corsica, with perhaps a flying visit to Naples if we feel like it, and a week in London to wind up with. Two of his nieces are to be asked to be bridesmaids, so with our lot there will be seven, which is rather a lucky number. You are to wear your pearl grey, with any amount of Honiton lace jabbed into it. By the way, he's coming over this evening to ask your consent to the whole affair. So far all's well, but about the Brogue it's a different matter. I told him the legend about the stable, and how keen we were about buying the horse back, but he seems equally keen on keeping it. He said he must have horse exercise now that he's living in the country, and he's going to start riding tomorrow. He's ridden a few times in the Row on an animal that was accustomed to carry octogenarians and people undergoing rest cures, and that's about all his experience in the saddle–oh, and he rode a pony once in Norfolk, when he was fifteen and the pony twenty-four; and tomorrow he's going to ride the Brogue! I shall be a widow before I'm married, and I do so want to see what Corsica's like; it looks so silly on the map."

Clovis was sent for in haste, and the developments of the situation put before him.

"Nobody can ride that animal with any safety," said Mrs. Mullet, "except Toby, and he knows by long experience what it is going to shy at, and manages to swerve at the same time."

"I did hint to Mr. Penricarde–to Vincent, I should say–that the Brogue didn't like white gates," said Jessie.

"White gates!" exclaimed Mrs. Mullet; "did you mention what effect a pig has on him? He'll have to go past Lockyer's farm to get to the high road, and there's sure to be a pig or two grunting about in the lane."

"He's taken rather a dislike to turkeys lately," said Toby.

"It's obvious that Penricarde mustn't be allowed to go out on that animal," said Clovis, "at least not till Jessie has married him, and tired of him. I tell you what: ask him to a picnic tomorrow, starting at an early hour; he's not the sort to go out for a ride before breakfast. The day after I'll get the rector to drive him over to Crowleigh before lunch, to see the new cottage hospital they're building there. The Brogue will be standing idle in the stable and Toby can offer to exercise it; then it can pick up a stone or something of the sort and go conveniently lame. If you hurry on the wedding a bit the lameness fiction can be kept up till the ceremony is safely over."

Mrs. Mullet belonged to an emotional race, and she kissed Clovis.

It was nobody's fault that the rain came down in torrents the next morning, making a picnic a fantastic impossibility. It was also nobody's fault, but sheer ill-luck, that the weather cleared up sufficiently in the afternoon to tempt Mr. Penricarde to make his first essay with the Brogue. They did not get as far as the pigs at Lockyer's farm; the rectory gate was painted a dull unobtrusive green, but it had been white a year or two ago, and the Brogue never forgot that he had been in the habit of making a violent curtsey, a back-pedal and a swerve at this particular point of the road. Subsequently, there being apparently no further call on his services, he broke his way into the rectory orchard, where he found a hen turkey in a coop; later visitors to the orchard found the coop almost intact, but very little left of the turkey.

Mr. Penricarde, a little stunned and shaken, and suffering from a bruised knee and some minor damages, good-naturedly ascribed the accident to his own inexperience with horses and country roads, and allowed Jessie to nurse him back into complete recovery and golf-fitness within something less than a week.

In the list of wedding presents which the local newspaper published a fortnight or so later appeared the following item:

"Brown saddle-horse, 'The Brogue,' bridegroom's gift to bride."

"Which shows," said Toby Mullet, "that he knew nothing."

"Or else," said Clovis, "that he has a very pleasing wit."

THE HEN

"Dora Bittholz is coming on Thursday," said Mrs. Sangrail.

"This next Thursday?" asked Clovis.

His mother nodded.

"You've rather done it, haven't you?" he chuckled. "Jane Martlet has only been here five days, and she never stays less than a fortnight, even when she's asked definitely for a week. You'll never get her out of the house by Thursday."

"Why should I?" asked Mrs. Sangrail. "She and Dora are good friends, aren't they? They used to be, as far as I remember."

"They used to be; that's what makes them all the more bitter now. Each feels that she has nursed a viper in her bosom. Nothing fans the flame of human resentment so much as the discovery that one's bosom has been utilized as a snake sanatorium."

"But what has happened? Has some one been making mischief?"

"Not exactly," said Clovis; "a hen came between them."

"A hen? What hen?"

"It was a bronze Leghorn or some such exotic breed, and Dora sold it to Jane at a rather exotic price. They both go in for prize poultry, you know, and Jane thought she was going to get her money back in a large family of pedigree chickens. The bird turned out to be an abstainer from the egg habit, and I'm told that the letters which passed between the two women were a revelation as to how much invective could be got on to a sheet of notepaper."

"How ridiculous!" said Mrs. Sangrail. "Couldn't some of their friends compose the quarrel?"

"People tried," said Clovis, "but it must have been rather like composing the storm music of the 'Fliegende Holländer.' Jane was willing to take back some of her most libellous remarks if Dora would take back the hen, but Dora said that would be owning herself in the wrong, and you know she'd as soon think of owning slum property in Whitechapel as do that."

"It's a most awkward situation," said Mrs. Sangrail. "Do you suppose they won't speak to one another?"

"On the contrary, the difficulty will be to get them to leave off. Their remarks on each other's conduct and character have hitherto been governed by the fact that only four ounces of plain speaking can be sent through the post for a penny."

"I can't put Dora off," said Mrs. Sangrail. "I've already postponed her visit once, and nothing short of a miracle would make Jane leave before her self-allotted fortnight is over."

"Miracles are rather in my line," said Clovis. "I don't pretend to be very hopeful in this case, but I'll do my best."

"As long as you don't drag me into it—" stipulated his mother.

"Servants are a bit of a nuisance," muttered Clovis, as he sat in the smoking-room after lunch, talking fitfully to Jane Martlet in the intervals of putting together the materials of a cocktail, which he had irreverently patented under the name of an Ella Wheeler Wilcox. It was partly compounded of old brandy and partly of curaçao; there were other ingredients, but they were never indiscriminately revealed.

"Servants a nuisance!" exclaimed Jane, bounding into the topic with the exuberant plunge of a hunter when it leaves the high road and feels turf under its hoofs; "I should think they were! The trouble I've had in getting suited this year you would hardly believe. But I don't see what you have to complain of—your mother is so wonderfully lucky in her servants. Sturridge, for instance—he's been with you for years, and I'm sure he's a paragon as butlers go."

"That's just the trouble," said Clovis. "It's when servants have been with you for years that they become a really serious nuisance. The 'here today and gone tomorrow' sort don't matter—you've simply got to replace them; it's the stayers and the paragons that are the real worry."

"But if they give satsifaction—"

"That doesn't prevent them from giving trouble. Now, you've mentioned Sturridge—it was Sturridge I was particularly thinking of when I made the observation about servants being a nuisance."

"The excellent Sturridge a nuisance! I can't believe it."

"I know he's excellent, and we just couldn't get along without him; he's the one reliable element in this rather haphazard household. But his very orderliness has had an effect on him. Have you ever considered what it must be like to go on unceasingly doing the correct thing in the correct manner in the same surroundings for the greater part of a lifetime? To know and ordain and superintend exactly what silver and glass and table linen shall be used and set out on what occasions, to have cellar and pantry and plate-cupboard under a minutely devised and undeviating administration, to be noiseless, impalpable, omnipresent, and, as far as your own department is concerned, omniscient?"

"I should go mad," said Jane with conviction.

"Exactly," said Clovis thoughtfully, swallowing his completed Ella Wheeler Wilcox.

"But Sturridge hasn't gone mad," said Jane with a flutter of inquiry in her voice.

"On most points he's thoroughly sane and reliable," said Clovis, "but at times he is subject to the most obstinate delusions, and on those occasions he becomes not merely a nuisance but a decided embarrassment."

"What sort of delusions?"

"Unfortunately they usually centre round one of the guests of the house party, and that is where the awkwardness comes in. For instance, he took it into his head that Matilda Sheringham was the Prophet Elijah, and as all that he remembered about Elijah's history was the episode of the ravens in the wilderness he absolutely declined to interfere with what he imagined to be Matilda's private catering arrangements, wouldn't allow any tea to be sent up to her in the morning, and if he was waiting at table he passed her over altogether in handing round the dishes."

"How very unpleasant. Whatever did you do about it?"

"Oh, Matilda got fed, after a fashion, but it was judged to be best for her to cut her visit short. It was really the only thing to be done," said Clovis with some emphasis.

"I shouldn't have done that," said Jane, "I should have humoured him in some way. I certainly shouldn't have gone away."

Clovis frowned.

"It is not always wise to humour people when they get these ideas into their heads. There's no knowing to what lengths they may go if you encourage them."

"You don't mean to say he might be dangerous, do you?" asked Jane with some anxiety.

"One can never be certain," said Clovis; "now and then he gets some idea about a guest which *might* take an unfortunate turn. That is precisely what is worrying me at the present moment."

"What, has he taken a fancy about some one here now?" asked Jane excitedly. "How thrilling! Do tell me who it is."

"You," said Clovis briefly.

"Me?"

Clovis nodded.

"Who on earth does he think I am?"

"Queen Anne," was the unexpected answer.

"Queen Anne! What an idea. But, anyhow, there's nothing dangerous about her; she's such a colourless personality."

"What does posterity chiefly say about Queen Anne?" asked Clovis rather sternly.

"The only thing that I can remember about her," said Jane, "is the saying 'Queen Anne's dead.'"

"Exactly," said Clovis, staring at the glass that had held the Ella Wheeler Wilcox, "dead."

"Do you mean he takes me for the ghost of Queen Anne?" asked Jane.

"Ghost? Dear no. No one ever heard of a ghost that came down to breakfast and ate kidneys and toast and honey with a healthy appetite. No, it's the fact of you being so very much alive and flourishing that perplexes and annoys him. All his life he has been accustomed to look on Queen Anne as the personification of everything that is dead and done with, 'as dead as Queen Anne,' you know; and now he has to fill your glass at lunch and dinner and listen to your accounts of the gay time you had at the Dublin Horse Show, and naturally he feels that something's very wrong with you."

"But he wouldn't be downright hostile to me on that account, would he?" Jane asked anxiously.

"I didn't get really alarmed about it till lunch today," said Clovis; "I caught him glowering at you with a very sinister look and muttering: 'Ought to be dead long ago, she ought, and some one should see to it.' That's why I mentioned the matter to you."

"This is awful," said Jane; "your mother must be told about it at once."

"My mother mustn't hear a word about it," said Clovis earnestly; "it would upset her dreadfully. She relies on Sturridge for everything."

"But he might kill me at any moment," protested Jane.

"Not at any moment; he's busy with the silver all the afternoon."

"You'll have to keep a sharp look-out all the time and be on your guard to frustrate any murderious attack," said Jane, adding in a tone of weak obstinacy: "It's a dreadful situation to be in, with a mad butler dangling over you like the sword of What's-his-name, but I'm certainly not going to cut my visit short."

Clovis swore horribly under his breath; the miracle was an obvious misfire.

It was in the hall the next morning after a late breakfast that Clovis had his final inspiration as he stood engaged in coaxing rust spots from an old putter.

"Where is Miss Martlet?" he asked the butler, who was at that moment crossing the hall.

"Writing letters in the morning-room, sir," said Sturridge, announcing a fact of which his questioner was already aware.

"She wants to copy the inscription on that old basket-hilted sabre," said Clovis, pointing to a venerable weapon hanging on the wall. "I wish you'd take it to her; my hands are all over oil. Take it without the sheath, it will be less trouble."

The butler drew the blade, still keen and bright in its well-cared-for old age, and carried it into the morning-room. There was a door near the writing-table leading to a back stairway; Jane vanished through it with such lightning rapidity that the butler doubted whether she had seen him come in. Half an hour later Clovis was driving her and her hastily packed luggage to the station.

"Mother will be awfully vexed when she comes back from her ride and finds you have gone," he observed to the departing guest, "but I'll make up some story about an urgent wire having called you away. It wouldn't do to alarm her unnecessarily about Sturridge."

Jane sniffed slightly at Clovis' ideas of unnecessary alarm, and was almost rude to the young man who came round with thoughtful inquiries as to luncheon-baskets.

The miracle lost some of its usefulness from the fact that Dora wrote the same day postponing the date of her visit, but, at any rate, Clovis holds the record as the only human being who ever hustled Jane Martlet out of the time-table of her migrations.

THE OPEN WINDOW

"My aunt will be down presently, Mr. Nuttel," said a very self-possessed young lady of fifteen; "in the meantime you must try and put up with me."

Framton Nuttel endeavoured to say the correct something which should duly flatter the niece of the moment without unduly discounting the aunt that was to come. Privately he doubted more than ever whether these formal visits on a succession of total strangers would do much towards helping the nerve cure which he was supposed to be undergoing.

"I know how it will be," his sister had said when he was preparing to migrate to this rural retreat; "you will bury yourself down there and not speak to a living soul, and your nerves will be worse than ever from moping. I shall just give you letters of introduction to all the people I know there. Some of them, as far as I can remember, were quite nice."

Framton wondered whether Mrs. Sappleton, the lady to whom he was presenting one of the letters of introduction, came into the nice division.

"Do you know many of the people round here?" asked the niece, when she judged that they had had sufficient silent communion.

"Hardly a soul," said Framton. "My sister was staying here, at the rectory, you know, some four years ago, and she gave me letters of introduction to some of the people here."

He made the last statement in a tone of distinct regret.

"Then you know practically nothing about my aunt?" pursued the self-possessed young lady.

"Only her name and address," admited the caller. He was wondering whether Mrs. Sappleton was in the married or widowed state. An undefinable something about the room seemed to suggest masculine habitation.

"Her great tragedy happened just three years ago," said the child; "that would be since your sister's time."

"Her tragedy?" asked Framton; somehow in this restful country spot tragedies seemed out of place.

"You may wonder why we keep that window wide open on an October afternoon," said the niece, indicating a large French window that opened on to a lawn.

"It is quite warm for the time of the year," said Framton; "but has that window got anything to do with the tragedy?"

"Out through that window, three years ago to a day, her husband and her two young brothers went off for their day's shooting. They never came back. In crossing the moor to their favourite snipe-shooting ground they were all three engulfed in a treacherous piece of bog. It had been that dreadful wet summer, you know, and places that were safe in other years gave way suddenly without warning. Their bodies were never recovered. That was the dreadful part of it." Here the child's voice lost its self-possessed note and became falteringly human. "Poor aunt always thinks that they will come back some day, they and the little brown spaniel that was lost with them, and walk in at that window just as they used to do. That is why the window is kept open every evening till it is quite dusk. Poor dear aunt, she has often told me how they went out, her husband with his white waterproof coat over his arm, and Ronnie, her youngest brother, singing, 'Bertie, why do you bound?' as he always did to tease her, because she said it got on her nerves. Do you know, sometimes on still, quiet evenings like this, I almost get a creepy feeling that they will all walk in through that window–"

She broke off with a little shudder. It was a relief to Framton when the aunt bustled into the room with a whirl of apologies for being late in making her appearance.

"I hope Vera has been amusing you?" she said.

"She has been very interesting," said Framton.

"I hope you don't mind the open window," said Mrs. Sappleton briskly; "my husband and brothers will be home directly from shooting, and they always come in this way. They've been out for snipe in the marshes today, so they'll make a fine mess over my poor carpets. So like you men-folk, isn't it?"

She rattled on cheerfully about the shooting and the scarcity of birds, and the prospects for duck in the winter. To Framton, it was all purely horrible. He made a desperate but only partially successful effort to turn the talk on to a less ghastly topic; he was conscious that his hostess was giving him only a fragment of her attention, and her eyes were constantly straying past him to the open window and the lawn beyond. It was certainly an unfortunate coincidence that he should have paid his visit on this tragic anniversary.

"The doctors agree in ordering me complete rest, an absence of mental excitement, and avoidance of anything in the nature of violent physical exercise," announced Framton, who laboured under the tolerably wide-spread delusion that total strangers and chance acquaintances are hungry for the least detail of one's ailments and infirmities, their cause and cure. "On the matter of diet they are not so much in agreement," he continued.

"No?" said Mrs. Sappleton, in a voice which only replaced a yawn at the last moment. Then she suddenly brightened into alert attention–but not to what Framton was saying.

"Here they are at last!" she cried. "Just in time for tea, and don't they look as if they were muddy up to the eyes!"

Framton shivered slightly and turned towards the niece with a look intended to convey sympathetic comprehension. The child was staring out through the open window with dazed horror in her eyes. In a chill shock of nameless fear Framton swung round in his seat and looked in the same direction.

In the deepening twilight three figures were walking across the lawn towards the window; they all carried guns under their arms, and one of them was additionally burdened with a white coat hung over his shoulders. A tired brown spaniel kept close at their heels. Noiselessly they neared the house, and then a hoarse young voice chanted out of the dusk: "I said, Bertie, why do you bound?"

Framton grabbed wildly at his stick and hat; the hall-door, the gravel-drive, and the front gate were dimly noted stages in his headlong retreat. A cyclist coming along the road had to run into the hedge to avoid imminent collision.

"Here we are, my dear," said the bearer of the white mackintosh, coming in through the window; "fairly muddy, but most of it's dry. Who was that who bolted out as we came up?"

"A most extraordinary man, a Mr. Nuttel," said Mrs. Sappleton; "could only talk about his illnesses, and dashed off without a word of good-bye or apology when you arrived. One would think he had seen a ghost."

"I expect it was the spaniel," said the niece calmly; "he told me he had a horror of dogs. He was once hunted into a cemetery somewhere on the banks of the Ganges by a pack of pariah dogs, and had to spend the night in a newly dug grave with the creatures snarling and grinning and foaming just above him. Enough to make any one lose their nerve."

Romance at short notice was her speciality.

THE TREASURE-SHIP

THE great galleon lay in semi-retirement under the sand weed and water of the northern bay where the fortune of war and weather had long ago ensconced it. Three and a quarter centuries had passed since the day when it had taken the high seas as an important unit of a fighting squadron—precisely which squadron the learned were not agreed. The galleon had brought nothing into the world, but it had, according to tradition and report, taken much out of it. But how much? There again the learned were in disagreement. Some were as generous in their estimate as an income-tax assessor, others applied a species of higher criticism to the submerged treasure chests, and debased their contents to the currency of goblin gold. Of the former school was Lulu, Duchess of Dulverton.

The Duchess was not only a believer in the existence of a sunken treasure of alluring proportions; she also believed that she knew of a method by which the said treasure might be precisely located and cheaply disembedded. An aunt on her mother's side of the family had been Maid of Honour at the Court of Monaco, and had taken a respectful interest in the deep-sea researches in which the Throne of that country, impatient perhaps of its terrestrial restrictions, was wont to immerse itself. It was through the instrumentality of this relative that the Duchess learned of an invention, perfected and very nearly patented by a Monegaskan savant, by means of which the home-life of the Mediterranean sardine might be studied at a depth of many fathoms in a cold white light of more than ball-room brilliancy. Implicated in this invention (and, in the Duchess's eyes, the most attractive part of it) was an electric suction dredge, specially designed for dragging to the surface such objects of interest and value as might be found in the more accessible levels of the ocean-bed. The rights of the invention were to be acquired for a matter of eighteen hundred francs, and the apparatus for a few thousand more. The Duchess of Dulverton was rich, as the world counted wealth; she nursed the hope of being one day rich at her own computation. Companies had been formed and efforts had been made again and again during the course of three centuries to probe for the alleged treasures of the interesting galleon; with the aid of this invention she considered that she might go to work on the wreck privately and independently. After all, one of her ancestors on her mother's side was descended from Medina Sidonia, so she was of opinion that she had as much right to the treasure as any one. She acquired the invention and bought the apparatus.

Among other family ties and encumbrances, Lulu possessed a nephew, Vasco Honiton, a young gentleman who was blessed with a small income and a large circle of relatives, and lived impartially and precariously on both. The name Vasco had been given him possibly in the hope that he might live up to its adventurous tradition, but he limited himself strictly to the home industry of adventurer, preferring to exploit the assured rather than to explore the unknown. Lulu's intercourse with him had been restricted of recent years to the negative processes of being out of town when he called on her, and short of money when he wrote to her. Now, however, she bethought herself of his eminent suitability for the direction of a treasure-seeking experiment; if any one could extract gold from an unpromising situation it would certainly be Vasco—of course, under the necessary safeguards in the way of supervision. Where money was in question Vasco's conscience was liable to fits of obstinate silence.

Somewhere on the west coast of Ireland the Dulverton property included a few acres of shingle, rock, and heather, too barren to support even an agrarian outrage, but embracing a small and fairly deep bay where the lobster yield was good in most seasons. There was a bleak little house on the property, and for those who liked lobsters and solitude, and were able to accept an Irish cook's ideas as to what might be perpetrated in the name of mayonnaise, Innisgluther was a tolerable exile during the summer months. Lulu seldom went there herself, but she lent the house lavishly to friends and relations. She put it now at Vasco's disposal.

"It will be the very place to practise and experiment with the salvage apparatus," she said; "the bay is quite deep in places, and you will be able to test everything thoroughly before starting on the treasure hunt."

In less than three weeks Vasco turned up in town to report progress.

"The apparatus works beautifully," he informed his aunt; "the deeper one got the clearer everything grew. We found something in the way of a sunken wreck to operate on, too!"

"A wreck in Innisgluther Bay!" exclaimed Lulu.

"A submerged motor-boat, the *Sub-Rosa,*" said Vasco.

"No! really?" said Lulu; "poor Billy Yuttley's boat. I remember it went down somewhere off that coast some three years ago. His body was washed ashore at the Point. People said at the time that the boat was capsized intentionally—a case of suicide, you know. People always say that sort of thing when anything tragic happens."

"In this case they were right," said Vasco.

"What do you mean?" asked the Duchess hurriedly. "What makes you think so?"

"I know," said Vasco simply.

"Know? How can you know? How can any one know? The thing happened three years ago."

"In a locker of the *Sub-Rosa* I found a water-tight strong-box. It contained papers." Vasco paused with dramatic effect and searched for a moment in the inner breast-pocket of his coat. He drew out a folded slip of paper. The Duchess snatched at it in almost indecent haste and moved appreciably nearer the fireplace.

"Was this in the *Sub-Rosa*'s strong-box?" she asked.

"Oh, no," said Vasco carelessly, "that is a list of the well-known people who would be involved in a very disagreeable scandal if the *Sub-Rosa*'s papers were made public. I've put you at the head of it, otherwise it follows alphabetical order."

The Duchess gazed helplessly at the string of names, which seemed for the moment to include nearly every one she knew. As a matter of fact, her own name at the head of the list exercised an almost paralyzing effect on her thinking faculties.

"Of course you have destroyed the papers?" she asked, when she had somewhat recovered herself. She was conscious that she made the remark with an entire lack of conviction.

Vasco shook his head.

"But you should have," said Lulu angrily; "if, as you say, they are highly compromising—"

"Oh, they are, I assure you of that," interposed the young man.

"Then you should put them out of harm's way at once. Supposing anything should leak out, think of all these poor, unfortunate people who would be involved in the disclosures," and Lulu tapped the list with an agitated gesture.

"Unfortunate, perhaps, but not poor," corrected Vasco; "if you read the list carefully you'll notice that I haven't troubled to include any one whose financial standing isn't above question."

Lulu glared at her nephew for some moments in silence. Then she asked hoarsely: "What are you going to do?"

"Nothing—for the remainder of my life," he answered meaningly. "A little hunting, perhaps," he continued, "and I shall have a villa at Florence. The Villa Sub-Rosa would sound rather quaint and picturesque, don't you think, and quite a lot of people would be able to attach a meaning to the name. And I suppose I must have a hobby; I shall probably collect Raeburns."

Lulu's relative, who lived at the Court of Monaco, got quite a snappish answer when she wrote recommending some further invention in the realm of marine research.

THE COBWEB

The farmhouse kitchen probably stood where it did as a matter of accident or haphazard choice; yet its situation might have been planned by a master-strategist in farmhouse architecture. Dairy and poultry-yard, and herb garden, and all the busy places of the farm seemed to lead by easy access into its wide flagged haven, where there was room for everything and where muddy boots left traces that were easily swept away. And yet, for all that it stood so well in the centre of human bustle, its long, latticed window, with the wide window-seat, built into an embrasure beyond the huge fireplace, looked out on a wild spreading view of hill and heather and wooded combe. The window nook made almost a little room in itself, quite the pleasantest room in the farm as far as situation and capabilities went. Young Mrs. Ladbruk, whose husband had just come into the farm by way of inheritance, cast covetous eyes on this snug corner, and her fingers itched to make it bright and cozy with chintz curtains and bowls of flowers, and a shelf or two of old china. The musty farm parlour, looking out to a prim, cheerless garden imprisoned within high, blank walls, was not a room that lent itself readily either to comfort or decoration.

"When we are more settled I shall work wonders in the way of making the kitchen habitable," said the young woman to her occasional visitors. There was an unspoken wish in those words, a wish which was unconfessed as well as unspoken. Emma Ladbruk was the mistress of the farm; jointly with her husband she might have her say, and to a certain extent her way, in ordering its affairs. But she was not mistress of the kitchen.

On one of the shelves of an old dresser, in company with chipped sauce-boats, pewter jugs, cheese-graters, and paid bills, rested a worn and ragged Bible, on whose front page was the record, in faded ink, of a baptism dated ninety-four years ago. "Martha Crale" was the name written on that yellow page. The yellow, wrinkled old dame who hobbled and muttered about the kitchen, looking like a dead autumn leaf which the winter winds still pushed hither and thither, had once been Martha Crale; for seventy odd years she had been Martha Mountjoy. For longer than any one could remember she had pattered to and fro between oven and wash-house and dairy, and out to chicken-run and garden, grumbling and muttering and scolding, but working unceasingly. Emma Ladbruk, of whose coming she took as little notice as she would of a bee wandering in at a window on a summer's day, used at first to watch her with a kind of frightened curiosity. She was so old and so much a part of the place, it was difficult to think of her exactly as a living thing. Old Shep, the white-nozzled, stiff-limbed collie, waiting for his time to die, seemed almost more human than the withered, dried-up old woman. He had been a riotous, roystering puppy, mad with the joy of life, when she was already a tottering, hobbling dame; now he was just a blind, breathing carcase, nothing more, and she still worked with frail energy, still swept and baked and washed, fetched and carried. If there were something in these wise old dogs that did not perish utterly with death, Emma used to think to herself, what generations of ghost-dogs there must be out on those hills, that Martha had reared and fed and tended and spoken a last good-bye word to in that old kitchen. And what memories she must have of human generations that had passed away in her time. It was difficult for any one, let alone a stranger like Emma, to get her to talk of the days that had been; her shrill, quavering speech was of doors that had been left unfastened, pails that had got mislaid, calves whose feeding-time was overdue, and the various little faults and lapses that chequer a farmhouse routine. Now and again, when election time came round, she would unstore her recollections of the old names round which the fight had waged in the days gone by. There had been a Palmerston, that had been a name down Tiverton way; Tiverton was not a far journey as the crow flies, but to Martha it was almost a foreign country. Later there had been Northcotes and Aclands, and many other newer names that she had forgotten; the names changed, but it was always Libruls and Toories, Yellows and Blues. And they always quarrelled and shouted as to who was right and who was wrong. The one they quarrelled about most was a fine old gentleman with an angry face—she had seen his picture on the walls. She had seen it on the floor too, with a rotten apple squashed over it, for the farm had changed its politics from time to time. Martha had never been on one side or the other; none of "they" had ever done the farm a stroke of good. Such was her sweeping verdict, given with all a peasant's distrust of the outside world.

When the half-frightened curiosity had somewhat faded away, Emma Ladbruk was uncomfortably conscious of another feeling towards the old woman. She was a quaint old tradition, lingering about the place, she was part and parcel of the farm itself, she was something at once pathetic and picturesque—but she was dreadfully in the way. Emma had come to the farm full of plans for little reforms and improvements, in part the result of training in the newest ways and methods, in part the outcome of her own ideas and fancies. Reforms in the kitchen region, if those deaf ears could have been induced to give them even a hearing, would have met with short shrift and scornful rejection, and the kitchen region spread over the zone of dairy and market business and half the work of the household. Emma, with the latest science of dead-poultry dressing at her fingertips, sat by, an unheeded watcher, while old Martha trussed the chickens for the market-stall as she had trussed them for nearly fourscore years—all leg and no breast. And the hundred hints anent effective cleaning and labour-lightening and the things that make for wholesomeness which the young woman was ready to impart or to put into action dropped away into nothingness before that wan, muttering, unheeding presence. Above all, the coveted window corner, that was to be a dainty, cheerful oasis in the gaunt old kitchen, stood now choked and lumbered with a litter of odds and ends that Emma, for all her nominal authority, would not have dared or cared to displace; over them seemed to be spun the protection of something that was like a human cobweb. Decidedly Martha was in the way. It would have been an unworthy meanness to have wished to see the span of that brave old life shortened by a few paltry months, but as the days sped by Emma was conscious that the wish was there, disowned though it might be, lurking at the back of her mind.

She felt the meanness of the wish come over her with a qualm of self-reproach one day when she came into the kitchen and found an unaccustomed state of things in that usually busy quarter. Old Martha was not working. A basket of corn was on the floor by her side, and out in the yard the poultry were beginning to clamour a protest of overdue feeding-time. But Martha sat huddled in a shrunken bunch on the window seat, looking out with her dim old eyes as though she saw something stranger than the autumn landscape.

"Is anything the matter, Martha?" asked the young woman.

"'Tis death, 'tis death a-coming," answered the quavering voice; "I knew 'twere coming. I knew it. 'Tweren't for nothing that old Shep's been howling all morning. An' last night I heard the screech-owl give the death-cry, and there were something white as run across the yard yesterday; 'tweren't a cat nor a stoat, 'twere something. The fowls knew 'twere something; they all drew off to one side. Ay, there's been warnings. I knew it were a-coming."

The young woman's eyes clouded with pity. The old thing sitting there so white and shrunken had once been a merry, noisy child, playing about in lanes and hay-lofts and farmhouse garrets; that had been eighty odd years ago, and now she was just a frail old body cowering under the approaching chill of the death that was coming at last to take her. It was not probable that much could be done for her, but Emma hastened away to get assistance and counsel. Her husband, she knew, was down at a tree-felling some little distance off, but she might find some other intelligent soul who knew the old woman better than she did. The farm, she soon found out, had that faculty common to farmyards of swallowing up and losing its human population. The poultry followed her in interested fashion, and swine grunted interrogations at her from behind the bars of their sties, but barnyard and rickyard, orchard and stables and dairy, gave no reward to her search. Then, as she retraced her steps towards the kitchen, she came suddenly on her cousin, young Mr. Jim, as every one called him, who divided his time between amateur horse-dealing, rabbit-shooting, and flirting with the farm maids.

"I'm afraid old Martha is dying," said Emma. Jim was not the sort of person to whom one had to break news gently.

"Nonsense," he said; "Martha means to live to a hundred. She told me so, and she'll do it."

"She may be actually dying at this moment, or it may just be the beginning of the break-up," persisted Emma, with a feeling of contempt for the slowness and dulness of the young man.

A grin spread over his good-natured features.

"It don't look like it," he said, nodding towards the yard. Emma turned to catch the meaning of his remark. Old Martha stood in the middle of a mob of poultry scattering handfuls of grain around her. The turkey-cock, with the bronzed sheen of his feathers and the purple-red of his wattles, the game-cock with the glowing metallic lustre of his Eastern plumage, the hens, with their ochres and buffs and umbers and their scarlet combs, and the drakes, with their bottle-green heads, made a medley of rich colour, in the centre of which the old woman looked like a withered stalk standing amid the riotous growth of gaily-hued flowers. But she threw the grain deftly amid the wilderness of beaks, and her quavering voice carried as far as the two people who were watching her. She was still harping on the theme of death coming to the farm.

"I knew 'twere a-coming. There's been signs an' warnings."

"Who's dead, then, old Mother?" called out the young man.

"'Tis young Mister Ladbruk," she shrilled back; "they've just a-carried his body in. Run out of the way of a tree that was coming down an' ran hisself on to an iron post. Dead when they picked un up. Ay, I knew 'twere coming."

And she turned to fling a handful of barley at a belated group of guinea-fowl that came racing toward her.

The farm was a family property, and passed to the rabbit-shooting cousin as the next-of-kin. Emma Ladbruk drifted out of its history as a bee that had wandered in at an open window might flit its way out again. On a cold grey morning she stood waiting with her boxes already stowed in the farm cart, till the last of the market produce should be ready, for the train she was to catch was of less importance than the chickens and butter and eggs that were to be offered for sale. From where she stood she could see an angle of the long latticed window that was to have been cozy with curtains and gay with bowls of flowers. Into her mind came the thought that for months, perhaps for years, long after she had been utterly forgotten, a white, unheeding face would be seen peering out through those latticed panes, and a weak muttering voice would be heard quavering up and down those flagged passages. She made her way to a narrow barred casement that opened into the farm larder. Old Martha was standing at a table trussing a pair of chickens for the market stall as she had trussed them for nearly fourscore years.

THE LULL

"I've asked Latimer Springfield to spend Sunday with us and stop the night," announced Mrs. Durmot at the breakfast-table.

"I thought he was in the throes of an election," remarked her husband.

"Exactly; the poll is on Wednesday, and the poor man will have worked himself to a shadow by that time. Imagine what electioneering must be like in this awful soaking rain, going along slushy country roads and speaking to damp audiences in draughty schoolrooms, day after day for a fortnight. He'll have to put in an appearance at some place of worship on Sunday morning, and he can come to us immediately afterwards and have a thorough respite from everything connected with politics. I won't let him even think of them. I've had the picture of Cromwell dissolving the Long Parliament taken down from the staircase, and even the portrait of Lord Rosebery's 'Ladas' removed from the smoking-room. And, Vera," added Mrs. Durmot, turning to her sixteen-year-old niece, "be careful what colour ribbon you wear in your hair; not blue or yellow on any account; those are the rival party colours, and emerald green or orange would be almost as bad, with this Home Rule business to the fore."

"On state occasions I always wear a black ribbon in my hair," said Vera with crushing dignity.

Latimer Springfield was a rather cheerless, oldish young man, who went into politics somewhat in the spirit in which other people might go into half mourning. Without being an enthusiast, however, he was a fairly strenuous plodder, and Mrs. Durmot had been reasonably near the mark in asserting that he was working at high pressure over this election. The restful lull which his hostess enforced on him was decidedly welcome, and yet the nervous excitement of the contest had too great a hold on him to be totally banished.

"I know he's going to sit up half the night working up points for his final speeches," said Mrs. Durmot regretfully; "however, we've kept politics at arm's length all the afternoon and evening. More than that we cannot do."

"That remains to be seen," said Vera, but she said it to herself.

Latimer had scarcely shut his bedroom door before he was immersed in a sheaf of notes and pamphlets, while a fountain-pen and pocket-book were brought into play for the due marshalling of useful facts and discreet fictions. He had been at work for perhaps thirty-five minutes, and the house was seemingly consecrated to the healthy slumber of country life, when a stifled squealing and scuffling in the passage was followed by a loud tap at his door. Before he had time to answer, a much-encumbered Vera burst into the room with the question: "I say, can I leave these here?"

"These" were a small black pig and a lusty specimen of black-red gamecock.

Latimer was moderately fond of animals, and particularly interested in small livestock rearing from the economic point of view; in fact, one of the pamphlets on which he was at that moment engaged warmly advocated the further development of the pig and poultry industry in our rural districts; but he was pardonably unwilling to share even a commodious bedroom with samples of henroost and sty products.

"Wouldn't they be happier somewhere outside?" he asked, tactfully expressing his own preference in the matter in an apparent solicitude for theirs.

"There is no outside," said Vera impressively, "nothing but a waste of dark, swirling waters. The reservoir at Brinkley has burst."

"I didn't know there was a reservoir at Brinkley," said Latimer.

"Well, there isn't now, it's jolly well all over the place, and as we stand particularly low we're the centre of an inland sea just at present. You see the river has overflowed its banks as well."

"Good gracious! Have any lives been lost?"

"Heaps, I should say. The second housemaid has already identified three bodies that have floated past the billiard-room window as being the young man she's engaged to. Either she's engaged to a large assortment of the population round here or else she's very careless at identification. Of course it may be the same body coming round again and again in a swirl; I hadn't thought of that."

"But we ought to go out and do rescue work, oughtn't we?" said Latimer, with the instinct of a Parliamentary candidate for getting into the local limelight.

"We can't," said Vera decidedly, "we haven't any boats and we're cut off by a raging torrent from any human habitation. My aunt particularly hoped you would keep to your room and not add to the confusion, but she thought it would be so kind of you if you would take in Hartlepool's Wonder, the gamecock, you know, for the night. You see, there are eight other gamecocks, and they fight like furies if they get together, so we're putting one in each bedroom. The fowl-houses are all flooded out, you know. And then I thought perhaps you wouldn't mind taking in this wee piggie; he's rather a little love, but he has a vile temper. He gets that from his mother—not that I like to say things against her when she's lying dead and drowned in her sty, poor thing. What he really wants is a man's firm hand to keep him in order. I'd try and grapple with him myself, only I've got my chow in my room, you know, and he goes for pigs wherever he finds them."

"Couldn't the pig go in the bathroom?" asked Latimer faintly, wishing that he had taken up as determined a stand on the subject of bedroom swine as the chow had.

"The bathroom?" Vera laughed shrilly. "It'll be full of Boy Scouts till morning if the hot water holds out."

"Boy Scouts?"

"Yes, thirty of them came to rescue us while the water was only waist-high; then it rose another three feet or so and we had to rescue them. We're giving them hot baths in batches and drying their clothes in the hot-air cupboard, but, of course, drenched clothes don't dry in a minute, and the corridor and staircase are beginning to look like a bit of coast scenery by Tuke. Two of the boys are wearing your Melton overcoat; I hope you don't mind."

"It's a new overcoat," said Latimer, with every indication of minding dreadfully.

"You'll take every care of Hartlepool's Wonder, won't you?" said Vera. "His mother took three firsts at Birmingham, and he was second in the cockerel class last year at Gloucester. He'll probably roost on the rail at the bottom of your bed. I wonder if he'd feel more at home if some of his wives were up here with him? The hens are all in the pantry, and I think I could pick out Hartlepool Helen; she's his favourite."

Latimer showed a belated firmness on the subject of Hartlepool Helen, and Vera withdrew without pressing the point, having first settled the gamecock on his extemporized perch and taken an affectionate farewell of the pigling. Latimer undressed and got into bed with all due speed, judging that the pig would abate its inquisitorial restlessness once the light was turned out. As a substitute for a cozy, straw-bedded sty the room offered, at first inspection, few attractions, but the disconsolate animal suddenly discovered an appliance in which the most luxuriously contrived piggeries were notably deficient. The sharp edge of the underneath part of the bed was pitched at exactly the right elevation to permit the pigling to scrape himself ecstatically backwards and forwards, with an artistic humping of the back at the crucial moment and an accompanying gurgle of long-drawn delight. The gamecock, who may have fancied that he was being rocked in the branches of a pine-tree, bore the motion with greater fortitude than Latimer was able to command. A series of slaps directed at the pig's body were accepted more as an additional and pleasing irritant than as a criticism of conduct or a hint to desist; evidently something more than a man's firm hand was needed to deal with the case. Latimer slipped out of bed in search of a weapon of dissuasion. There was sufficient light in the room to enable the pig to detect this manœuvre, and the vile temper, inherited from the drowned mother, found full play. Latimer bounded back into bed, and his conqueror, after a few threatening snorts and champings of its jaws, resumed its massage operations with renewed zeal. During the long wakeful hours which ensued Latimer tried to distract his mind from his own immediate troubles by dwelling with decent sympathy on the second housemaid's bereavement, but he found himself more often wondering how many Boy Scouts were sharing his Melton overcoat. The rôle of Saint Martin *malgré lui* was not one which appealed to him.

Towards dawn the pigling fell into a happy slumber, and Latimer might have followed its example, but at about the same time Stupor Hartlepooli gave a rousing crow, clattered down to the floor and forthwith commenced a spirited combat with his reflection in the wardrobe mirror. Remembering that the bird was more or less under his care Latimer performed Hague Tribunal offices by draping a bath-towel over the provocative mirror, but the ensuing peace was local and short-lived. The deflected energies of the gamecock found new outlet in a sudden and sustained attack on the sleeping and temporarily inoffensive pigling, and the duel which followed was desperate and embittered beyond any possibility of effective intervention. The feathered combatant had the advantage of being able, when hard pressed, to take refuge on the bed, and freely availed himself of this circumstance; the pigling never quite succeeded in hurling himself on to the same eminence, but it was not from want of trying.

Neither side could claim any decisive success, and the struggle had been practically fought to a standstill by the time that the maid appeared with the early morning tea.

"Lor, sir," she exclaimed in undisguised astonishment, "do you want those animals in your room?"

Want!

The pigling, as though aware that it might have outstayed its welcome, dashed out at the door, and the gamecock followed it at a more dignified pace.

"If Miss Vera's dog sees that pig–!" exclaimed the maid, and hurried off to avert such a catastrophe.

A cold suspicion was stealing over Latimer's mind; he went to the window and drew up the blind. A light, drizzling rain was falling, but there was not the faintest trace of any inundation.

Some half-hour later he met Vera on the way to the breakfast-room.

"I should not like to think of you as a deliberate liar," he observed coldly, "but one occasionally has to do things one does not like."

"At any rate I kept your mind from dwelling on politics all the night," said Vera.

Which was, of course, perfectly true.

THE UNKINDEST BLOW

THE season of strikes seemed to have run itself to a standstill. Almost every trade and industry and calling in which a dislocation could possibly be engineered had indulged in that luxury. The last and least successful convulsion had been the strike of the World's Union of Zoological Garden attendants, who, pending the settlement of certain demands, refused to minister further to the wants of the animals committed to their charge or to allow any other keepers to take their place. In this case the threat of the Zoological Gardens authorities that if the men "came out" the animals should come out also had intensified and precipitated the crisis. This imminent prospect of the larger carnivores, to say nothing of rhinoceroses and bull bison, roaming at large and unfed in the heart of

London, was not one which permitted of prolonged conferences. The Government of the day, which from its tendency to be a few hours behind the course of events had been nicknamed the Government of the afternoon, was obliged to intervene with promptitude and decision. A strong force of Blue-jackets was despatched to Regent's Park to take over the temporarily abandoned duties of the strikers. Blue-jackets were chosen in preference to land forces, partly on account of the traditional readiness of the British Navy to go anywhere and do anything, partly by reason of the familiarity of the average sailor with monkeys, parrots, and other tropical fauna, but chiefly at the urgent request of the First Lord of the Admiralty, who was keenly desirous of an opportunity for performing some personal act of unobtrusive public service within the province of his department.

"If he insists on feeding the infant jaguar himself, in defiance of its mother's wishes, there may be another by-election in the north," said one of his colleagues, with a hopeful inflection in his voice. "By-elections are not very desirable at present, but we must not be selfish."

As a matter of fact the strike collapsed peacefully without any outside intervention. The majority of the keepers had become so attached to their charges that they returned to work of their own accord.

And then the nation and the newspapers turned with a sense of relief to happier things. It seemed as if a new era of contentment was about to dawn. Everybody had struck who could possibly want to strike or who could possibly be cajoled or bullied into striking, whether they wanted to or not. The lighter and brighter side of life might now claim some attention. And conspicuous among the other topics that sprang into sudden prominence was the pending Falvertoon divorce suit.

The Duke of Falvertoon was one of those human *hors d'œuvres* that stimulate the public appetite for sensation without giving it much to feed on. As a mere child he had been precociously brilliant; he had declined the editorship of the *Anglian Review* at an age when most boys are content to have declined *mensa*, a table, and though he could not claim to have originated the Futurist movement in literature, his "Letters to a Possible Grandson," written at the age of fourteen, had attracted considerable notice. In later days his brilliancy had been less conspicuously displayed. During a debate in the House of Lords on affairs in Morocco, at a moment when that country, for the fifth time in seven years, had brought half Europe to the verge of war, he had interpolated the remark "a little Moor and how much it is," but in spite of the encouraging reception accorded to this one political utterance he was never tempted to a further display in that direction. It began to be generally understood that he did not intend to supplement his numerous town and country residences by living overmuch in the public eye.

And then had come the unlooked-for tidings of the imminent proceedings for divorce. And such a divorce! There were cross-suits and allegations and counter-allegations, charges of cruelty and desertion, everything in fact that was necessary to make the case one of the most complicated and sensational of its kind. And the number of distinguished people involved or cited as witnesses not only embraced both political parties in the realm and several Colonial governors, but included an exotic contingent from France, Hungary, the United States of North America, and the Grand Duchy of Baden. Hotel accommodation of the more expensive sort began to experience a strain on its resources. "It will be quite like the Durbar without the elephants," exclaimed an enthusiastic lady who, to do her justice, had never seen a Durbar. The general feeling was one of thankfulness that the last of the strikes had been got over before the date fixed for the hearing of the great suit.

As a reaction from the season of gloom and industrial strife that had just passed away the agencies that purvey and stage-manage sensations laid themselves out to do their level best on this momentous occasion. Men who had made their reputations as special descriptive writers were mobilized from distant corners of Europe and the further side of the Atlantic in order to enrich with their pens the daily printed records of the case; one word-painter, who specialized in descriptions of how witnesses turn pale under cross-examination, was summoned hurriedly back from a famous and prolonged murder trial in Sicily, where indeed his talents were being decidedly wasted. Thumb-nail artists and expert kodak manipulators were retained at extravagant salaries, and special dress reporters were in high demand. An enterprising Paris firm of costume builders presented the defendant Duchess with three special creations, to be worn, marked, learned, and extensively reported at various critical stages of the trial; and as for the cinematograph agents, their industry and persistence was untiring. Films representing the Duke saying good-bye to his favourite canary on the eve of the trial were in readiness weeks before the event was due to take place; other films depicted the Duchess holding imaginary consultations with fictitious lawyers or making a light repast off specially advertised vegetarian sandwiches during a supposed luncheon interval. As far as human foresight and human enterprise could go nothing was lacking to make the trial a success.

Two days before the case was down for hearing the advance reporter of an important syndicate obtained an interview with the Duke for the purpose of gleaning some final grains of information concerning his Grace's personal arrangements during the trial.

"I suppose I may say this will be one of the biggest affairs of its kind during the lifetime of a generation," began the reporter as an excuse for the unsparing minuteness of detail that he was about to make quest for.

"I suppose so—if it comes off," said the Duke lazily.

"If?" queried the reporter, in a voice that was something between a gasp and a scream.

"The Duchess and I are both thinking of going on strike," said the Duke.

"Strike!"

The baleful word flashed out in all its old hideous familiarity. Was there to be no end to its recurrence?

"Do you mean," faltered the reporter, "that you are contemplating a mutual withdrawal of the charges?"

"Precisely," said the Duke.

"But think of the arrangements that have been made, the special reporting, the cinematographs, the catering for the distinguished foreign witnesses, the prepared music-hall allusions; think of all the money that has been sunk—"

"Exactly," said the Duke coldly, "the Duchess and I have realized that it is we who provide the material out of which this great far-reaching industry has been built up. Widespread employment will be given and enormous profits made during the duration of the case, and we, on whom all the stress and racket falls, will get—what? An unenviable notoriety and the privilege of paying heavy legal expenses whichever way the verdict goes. Hence our decision to strike. We don't wish to be reconciled; we fully realize that it is a grave step to take, but unless we get some reasonable consideration out of this vast stream of wealth and industry that we have called into being we intend coming out of court and staying out. Good afternoon."

The news of this latest strike spread universal dismay. Its inaccessibility to the ordinary methods of persuasion made it peculiarly formidable. If the Duke and Duchess persisted in being reconciled the Government could hardly be called on to interfere. Public opinion in the shape of social ostracism might be brought to bear on them, but that was as far as coercive measures could go. There was nothing for it but a conference, with powers to propose liberal terms. As it was, several of the foreign witnesses had already departed and others had telegraphed cancelling their hotel arrangements.

The conference, protracted, uncomfortable, and occasionally acrimonious, succeeded at last in arranging for a resumption of litigation, but it was a fruitless victory. The Duke, with a touch of his earlier precocity, died of premature decay a fortnight before the date fixed for the new trial.

THE ROMANCERS

It was autumn in London, that blessed season between the harshness of winter and the insincerities of summer; a trustful season when one buys bulbs and sees to the registration of one's vote, believing perpetually in spring and a change of Government.

Morton Crosby sat on a bench in a secluded corner of Hyde Park, lazily enjoying a cigarette and watching the slow grazing promenade of a pair of snow-geese, the male looking rather like an albino edition of the russet-hued female. Out of the corner of his eye Crosby also noted with some interest the hesitating hoverings of a human figure, which had passed and repassed his seat two or three times at shortening intervals, like a wary crow about to alight near some possibly edible morsel. Inevitably the figure came to an anchorage on the bench, within easy talking distance of its original occupant. The uncared-for clothes, the aggressive, grizzled beard, and the furtive, evasive eye of the new-comer bespoke the professional cadger, the man who would undergo hours of humiliating tale-spinning and rebuff rather than adventure on half a day's decent work.

For a while the new-comer fixed his eyes straight in front of him in a strenuous, unseeing gaze; then his voice broke out with the insinuating inflection of one who has a story to retail well worth any loiterer's while to listen to.

"It's a strange world," he said.

As the statement met with no response he altered it to the form of a question.

"I dare say you've found it to be a strange world, mister?"

"As far as I am concerned," said Crosby, "the strangeness has worn off in the course of thirty-six years."

"Ah," said the greybeard, "I could tell you things that you'd hardly believe. Marvellous things that have really happened to me."

"Nowadays there is not demand for marvellous things that have really happened," said Crosby discouragingly; "the professional writers of fiction turn these things out so much better. For instance, my neighbours tell me wonderful, incredible things that their Aberdeens and chows and borzois have done; I never listen to them. On the other hand, I have read *The Hound of the Baskervilles* three times."

The greybeard moved uneasily in his seat; then he opened up new country.

"I take it that you are a professing Christian," he observed.

"I am a prominent and I think I may say an influential member of the Mussulman community of Eastern Persia," said Crosby, making an excursion himself into the realms of fiction.

The greybeard was obviously disconcerted at this new check of introductory conversation, but the defeat was only momentary.

"Persia. I should never have taken you for a Persian," he remarked, with a somewhat aggrieved air.

"I am not," said Crosby; "my father was an Afghan."

"An Afghan!" said the other, smitten into bewildered silence for a moment. Then he recovered himself and renewed his attack.

"Afghanistan. Ah! We've had some wars with that country; now, I dare say, instead of fighting it we might have learned something from it. A very wealthy country, I believe. No real poverty there."

He raised his voice on the word "poverty" with a suggestion of intense feeling. Crosby saw the opening and avoided it.

"It possesses, nevertheless, a number of highly talented and ingenious beggars," he said; "if I had not spoken so disparagingly of marvellous things that have really happened I would tell you the story of Ibrahim and the eleven camel-loads of blotting-paper. Also I have forgotten exactly how it ended."

"My own life-story is a curious one," said the stranger, apparently stifling all desire to hear the history of Ibrahim; "I was not always as you see me now."

"We are supposed to undergo complete change in the course of every seven years," said Crosby, as an explanation of the foregoing announcement.

"I mean I was not always in such distressing circumstances as I am at present," pursued the stranger doggedly.

"That sounds rather rude," said Crosby stiffly, "considering that you are at present talking to a man reputed to be one of the most gifted conversationalists of the Afghan border."

"I don't mean in that way," said the greybeard hastily; "I've been very much interested in your conversation. I was alluding to my unfortunate financial situation. You mayn't hardly believe it, but at the present moment I am absolutely without a farthing. Don't see any prospect of getting any money, either, for the next few days. I don't suppose you've ever found yourself in such a position," he added.

"In the town of Yom," said Crosby, "which is in Southern Afghanistan, and which also happens to be my birthplace, there was a Chinese philosopher who used to say that one of the three chiefest human blessings was to be absolutely without money. I forget what the other two were."

"Ah, I dare say," said the stranger, in a tone that betrayed no enthusiasm for the philosopher's memory; "and did he practice what he preached? That's the test."

"He lived happily with very little money or resources," said Crosby.

"Then I expect he had friends who would help him liberally whenever he was in difficulties, such as I am in at present."

"In Yom," said Crosby, "it is not necessary to have friends in order to obtain help. Any citizen of Yom would help a stranger as a matter of course."

The greybeard was now genuinely interested. The conversation had at last taken a favourable turn.

"If some one, like me, for instance, who was in undeserved difficulties, asked a citizen of that town you speak of for a small loan to tide over a few days' impecuniosity–five shillings, or perhaps a rather larger sun–would it be given to him as a matter of course?"

"There would be a certain preliminary," said Crosby; "one would take him to a wine-shop and treat him to a measure of wine, and then, after a little high-flown conversation, one would put the desired sum in his hand and wish him good-day. It is a roundabout way of performing a simple transaction, but in the East all ways are roundabout."

The listener's eyes were glittering.

"Ah," he exclaimed, with a thin sneer ringing meaningly through his words, "I suppose you've given up all those generous customs since you left your town. Don't practise them now, I expect."

"No one who has lived in Yom," said Crosby fervently, "and remembers its green hills covered with apricot and almond trees, and the cold water that rushes down like a caress from the upland snows and dashes under the little wooden bridges, no one who remembers these things and treasures the memory of them would ever give up a single one of its unwritten laws and customs. To me they are as binding as though I still lived in that hallowed home of my youth."

"Then if I was to ask you for a small loan–" began the greybeard fawningly, edging nearer on the seat and hurriedly wondering how large he might safely make his request, "if I was to ask you for, say–"

"At any other time, certainly," said Crosby; "in the months of November and December, however, it is absolutely forbidden for any one of our race to give or receive loans or gifts; in fact, one does not willingly speak of them. It is considered unlucky. We will therefore close this discussion."

"But it is still October!" exclaimed the adventurer with an eager, angry whine, as Crosby rose from his seat; "wants eight days to the end of the month!"

"The Afghan November began yesterday," said Crosby severely, and in another moment he was striding across the Park, leaving his recent companion scowling and muttering furiously on the seat.

"I don't believe a word of his story," he chattered to himself; "pack of nasty lies from beginning to end. Wish I'd told him so to his face. Calling himself an Afghan!"

The snorts and snarls that escaped from him for the next quarter of an hour went far to support the truth of the old saying that two of a trade never agree.

THE SCHARTZ-METTERKLUME METHOD

Lady Carlotta stepped out on to the platform of the small wayside station and took a turn or two up and down its uninteresting length, to kill time till the train should be pleased to proceed on its way. Then, in the roadway beyond, she saw a horse struggling with a more than ample load, and a carter of the sort that seems to bear a sullen hatred against the animal that helps him to earn a living. Lady Carlotta promptly betook her to the roadway, and put rather a different complexion on the struggle. Certain of her acquaintances were wont to give her plentiful admonition as to the undesirability of interfering on behalf of a distressed animal, such interference being "none of her business." Only once had she put the doctrine of non-interference into practice, when one of its most eloquent exponents had been besieged for nearly three hours in a small and extremely uncomfortable may-tree by an angry boar-pig, while Lady Carlotta, on the other side of the fence, had proceeded with the water-colour sketch she was engaged on, and refused to interfere between the boar and his prisoner. It is to be feared that she lost the friendship of the ultimately rescued lady. On this occasion she merely lost the train, which gave way to the first sign of impatience it had shown throughout the journey, and steamed off without her. She bore the desertion with philosophical indifference; her friends and relations were thoroughly well used to the fact of her luggage arriving without her. She wired a vague non-committal message to her destination to say that she was coming on "by another train." Before she had time to think what her next move might be she was confronted by an imposingly attired lady, who seemed to be taking a prolonged mental inventory of her clothes and looks.

"You must be Miss Hope, the governess I've come to meet," said the apparition, in a tone that admitted of very little argument.

"Very well, if I must I must," said Lady Carlotta to herself with dangerous meekness.

"I am Mrs. Quabarl," continued the lady; "and where, pray, is your luggage?"

"It's gone astray," said the alleged governess, falling in with the excellent rule of life that the absent are always to blame; the luggage had, in point of fact, behaved with perfect correctitude. "I've just telegraphed about it," she added, with a nearer approach to truth.

"How provoking," said Mrs. Quabarl; "these railway companies are so careless. However, my maid can lend you things for the night," and she led the way to her car.

During the drive to the Quabarl mansion Lady Carlotta was impressively introduced to the nature of the charge that had been thrust upon her; she learned that Claude and Wilfrid were delicate, sensitive young people, that Irene had the artistic temperament highly developed, and that Viola was something or other else of a mould equally commonplace among children of that class and type in the twentieth century.

"I wish them not only to be *taught*," said Mrs. Quabarl, "but *interested* in what they learn. In their history lessons, for instance, you must try to make them feel that they are being introduced to the life-stories of men and women who really lived, not merely committing a mass of names and dates to memory. French, of course, I shall expect you to talk at mealtimes several days in the week."

"I shall talk French four days of the week and Russian in the remaining three."

"Russian? My dear Miss Hope, no one in the house speaks or understands Russian."

"That will not embarrass me in the least," said Lady Carlotta coldly.

Mrs. Quabarl, to use a colloquial expression, was knocked off her perch. She was one of those imperfectly self-assured individuals who are magnificent and autocratic as long as they are not seriously opposed. The least show of unexpected resistance goes a long way towards rendering them cowed and apologetic. When the new governess failed to express wondering admiration of the large newly purchased and expensive car, and lightly alluded to the superior advantages of one or two makes which had just been put on the market, the discomfiture of her patroness became almost abject. Her feelings were those which might have animated a general of ancient warfaring days, on beholding his heaviest battle-elephant ignominiously driven off the field by slingers and javelin throwers.

At dinner that evening, although reinforced by her husband, who usually duplicated her opinions and lent her moral support generally, Mrs. Quabarl regained none of her lost ground. The governess not only helped herself well and truly to wine, but held forth with considerable show of critical knowledge on various vintage matters, concerning which the Quabarls were in no wise able to pose as authorities. Previous governesses had limited their conversation on the wine topic to a respectful and doubtless sincere expression of a preference for water. When this one went as far as to recommend a wine firm in whose hands you could not go very far wrong Mrs. Quabarl thought it time to turn the conversation into more usual channels.

"We got very satisfactory references about you from Canon Teep," she observed; "a very estimable man, I should think."

"Drinks like a fish and beats his wife, otherwise a very lovable character," said the governess imperturbably.

"My *dear* Miss Hope! I trust you are exaggerating," exclaimed the Quabarls in unison.

"One must in justice admit that there is some provocation," continued the romancer. "Mrs. Teep is quite the most irritating bridge-player that I have ever sat down with; her leads and declarations would condone a certain amount of brutality in her partner, but to souse her with the contents of the only soda-water syphon in the house on a Sunday afternoon, when one couldn't get another, argues an indifference to the comfort of others which I cannot altogether overlook. You may think me hasty in my judgments, but it was practically on account of the syphon incident that I left."

"We will talk of this some other time," said Mrs. Quabarl hastily.

"I shall never allude to it again," said the governess with decision.

Mr. Quabarl made a welcome diversion by asking what studies the new instructress proposed to inaugurate on the morrow.

"History to begin with," she informed him.

"Ah, history," he observed sagely; "now in teaching them history you must take care to interest them in what they learn. You must make them feel that they are being introduced to the life-stories of men and women who really lived—"

"I've told her all that," interposed Mrs. Quabarl.

"I teach history on the Schartz-Metterklume method," said the governess loftily.

"Ah, yes," said her listeners, thinking it expedient to assume an acquaintance at least with the name.

"What are you children doing out here?" demanded Mrs. Quabarl the next morning, on finding Irene sitting rather glumly at the head of the stairs, while her sister was perched in an attitude of depressed discomfort on the window-seat behind her, with a wolf-skin rug almost covering her.

"We are having a history lesson," came the unexpected reply. "I am supposed to be Rome, and Viola up there is the she-wolf; not a real wolf, but the figure of one that the Romans used to set store by —I forget why. Claude and Wilfrid have gone to fetch the shabby women."

"The shabby women?"

"Yes, they've got to carry them off. They didn't want to, but Miss Hope got one of father's fives-bats and said she'd give them a number nine spanking if they didn't, so they've gone to do it."

A loud, angry screaming from the direction of the lawn drew Mrs. Quabarl thither in hot haste, fearful lest the threatened castigation might even now be in process of infliction. The outcry, however, came principally from the two small daughters of the lodge-keeper, who were being hauled and pushed towards the house by the panting and dishevelled Claude and Wilfrid, whose task was rendered even more arduous by the incessant, if not very effectual, attacks of the captured maidens' small brother. The governess, fives-bat in hand, sat negligently on the stone balustrade, presiding over the scene with the cold impartiality of a Goddess of Battles. A furious and repeated chorus of "I'll tell muvver" rose from the lodge children, but the lodge-mother, who was hard of hearing, was for the moment immersed in the preoccupation of her washtub. After an apprehensive glance in the direction of the lodge (the good woman was gifted with the highly militant temper which is sometimes the privilege of deafness) Mrs. Quabarl flew indignantly to the rescue of the struggling captives.

"Wilfrid! Claude! Let those children go at once. Miss Hope, what on earth is the meaning of this scene?"

"Early Roman history; the Sabine women, don't you know? It's the Schartz-Metterklume method to make children understand history by acting it themselves; fixes it in their memory, you know. Of course, if, thanks to your interference, your boys go through life thinking that the Sabine women ultimately escaped, I really cannot be held responsible."

"You may be very clever and modern, Miss Hope," said Mrs. Quabarl firmly, "but I should like you to leave here by the next train. Your luggage will be sent after you as soon as it arrives."

"I'm not certain exactly where I shall be for the next few days," said the dismissed instructress of youth; "you might keep my luggage till I wire my address. There are only a couple of trunks and some golf-clubs and a leopard cub."

"A leopard cub!" gasped Mrs. Quabarl. Even in her departure this extraordinary person seemed destined to leave a trail of embarrassment behind her.

"Well, it's rather left off being a cub; it's more than half-grown, you know. A fowl every day and a rabbit on Sundays is what it usually gets. Raw beef makes it too excitable. Don't trouble about getting the car for me, I'm rather inclined for a walk."

And Lady Carlotta strode out of the Quabarl horizon.

The advent of the genuine Miss Hope, who had made a mistake as to the day on which she was due to arrive, caused a turmoil which that good lady was quite unused to inspiring. Obviously the Quabarl family had been woefully befooled, but a certain amount of relief came with the knowledge.

"How tiresome for you, dear Carlotta," said her hostess, when the overdue guest ultimately arrived; "how very tiresome losing your train and having to stop overnight in a strange place."

"Oh, dear, no," said Lady Carlotta; "not at all tiresome—for me."

THE SEVENTH PULLET

"It's not the daily grind that I complain of," said Blenkinthrope resentfully; "it's the dull grey sameness of my life outside of office hours. Nothing of interest comes my way, nothing remarkable or out of the common. Even the little things that I do try to find some interest in don't seem to interest other people. Things in my garden, for instance."

"The potato that weighed just over two pounds," said his friend Gorworth.

"Did I tell you about that?" said Blenkinthrope; "I was telling the others in the train this morning. I forgot if I'd told you."

"To be exact you told me that it weighed just under two pounds, but I took into account the fact that abnormal vegetables and fresh-water fish have an after-life, in which growth is not arrested."

"You're just like the others," said Blenkinthrope sadly, "you only make fun of it."

"The fault is with the potato, not with us," said Gorworth; "we are not in the least interested in it because it is not in the least interesting. The men you go up in the train with every day are just in the same case as yourself; their lives are commonplace and not very interesting to themselves, and they certainly are not going to wax enthusiastic over the commonplace events in other men's lives. Tell them something startling, dramatic, piquant, that has happened to yourself or to some one in your family, and you will capture their interest at once. They will talk about you with a certain personal pride to all their acquaintances. 'Man I know intimately, fellow called Blenkinthrope, lives down my way, had two of his fingers clawed clean off by a lobster he was carrying home to supper. Doctor says entire hand may have to come off.' Now that is conversation of a very high order. But imagine walking into a tennis club with the remark: 'I know a man who has grown a potato weighing two and a quarter pounds.' "

"But hang it all, my dear fellow," said Blenkinthrope impatiently, "haven't I just told you that nothing of a remarkable nature ever happens to me?"

"Invent something," said Gorworth. Since winning a prize for excellence in Scriptural knowledge at a preparatory school he had felt licensed to be a little more unscrupulous than the circle he moved in. Much might surely be excused to one who in early life could give a list of seventeen trees mentioned in the Old Testament.

"What sort of thing?" asked Blenkinthrope, somewhat snappishly.

"A snake got into your hen-run yesterday morning and killed six out of seven pullets, first mesmerizing them with its eyes and then biting them as they stood helpless. The seventh pullet was one of that French sort, with feathers all over its eyes, so it escaped the mesmeric snare, and just flew at what it could see of the snake and pecked it to pieces."

"Thank you," said Blenkinthrope stiffly; "it's a very clever invention. If such a thing had really happened in my poultry-run I admit I should have been proud and interested to tell people about it. But I'd rather stick to fact, even if it is plain fact." All the same his mind dwelt wistfully on the story of the Seventh Pullet. He could picture himself telling it in the train amid the absorbed interest of his fellow-passengers. Unconsciously all sorts of little details and improvements began to suggest themselves.

Wistfulness was still his dominant mood when he took his seat in the railway carriage the next morning. Opposite him sat Stevenham, who had attained to a recognized brevet of importance through the fact of an uncle having dropped dead in the act of voting at a Parliamentary election. That had happened three years ago, but Stevenham was still deferred to on all questions of home and foreign politics.

"Hullo, how's the giant mushroom, or whatever it was?" was all the notice Blenkinthrope got from his fellow travellers.

Young Duckby, whom he mildly disliked, speedily monopolized the general attention by an account of a domestic bereavement.

"Had four young pigeons carried off last night by a whacking big rat. Oh, a monster he must have been; you could tell by the size of the hole he made breaking into the loft."

No moderate-sized rat ever seemed to carry out any predatory operations in these regions; they were all enormous in their enormity.

"Pretty hard lines that," continued Duckby, seeing that he had secured the attention and respect of the company; "four squeakers carried off at one swoop. You'd find it rather hard to match that in the way of unlooked-for bad luck."

"I had six pullets out of a pen of seven killed by a snake yesterday afternoon," said Blenkinthrope, in a voice which he hardly recognized as his own.

"By a snake?" came in excited chorus.

"It fascinated them with its deadly, glittering eyes, one after the other, and struck them down while they stood helpless. A bedridden neighbour, who wasn't able to call for assistance, witnessed it all from her bedroom window."

"Well, I never!" broke in the chorus, with variations.

"The interesting part of it is about the seventh pullet, the one that didn't get killed," resumed Blenkinthrope, slowly lighting a cigarette. His diffidence had left him, and he was beginning to realize how safe and easy depravity can seem once one has the courage to begin. "The six dead birds were Minorcas; the seventh was a Houdan with a mop of feathers all over its eyes. It could hardly see the snake at all, so of course it wasn't mesmerized like the others. It just could see something wriggling on the ground, and went for it and pecked it to death."

"Well, I'm blessed!" exclaimed the chorus.

In the course of the next few days Blenkinthrope discovered how little the loss of one's self-respect affects one when one has gained the esteem of the world. His story found its way into one of the poultry papers, and was copied thence into a daily news-sheet as a matter of general interest. A lady wrote from the North of Scotland recounting a similar episode which she had witnessed as occurring between a stoat and a blind grouse. Somehow a lie seems so much less reprehensible when one can call it a lee.

For a while the adapter of the Seventh Pullet story enjoyed to the full his altered standing as a person of consequence, one who had had some share in the strange events of his times. Then he was thrust once again into the cold grey background by the sudden blossoming into importance of Smith-Paddon, a daily fellow-traveller, whose little girl had been knocked down and nearly hurt by a car belonging to a musical-comedy actress. The actress was not in the car at the time, but she was in numerous photographs which appeared in the illustrated papers of Zoto Dobreen inquiring after the well-being of Maisie, daughter of Edmund Smith-Paddon, Esq. With this new human interest to absorb them the travelling companions were almost rude when Blenkinthrope tried to explain his contrivance for keeping vipers and peregrine falcons out of his chicken-run.

Gorworth, to whom he unburdened himself in private, gave him the same counsel as theretofore.

"Invent something."

"Yes, but what?"

The ready affirmative coupled with the question betrayed a significant shifting of the ethical standpoint.

It was a few days later that Blenkinthrope revealed a chapter of family history to the customary gathering in the railway carriage.

"Curious thing happened to my aunt, the one who lives in Paris," he began. He had several aunts, but they were all geographically distributed over Greater London.

"She was sitting on a seat in the Bois the other afternoon, after lunching at the Roumanian Legation."

Whatever the story gained in picturesqueness for the dragging-in of diplomatic "atmosphere," it ceased from that moment to command any acceptance as a record of current events. Gorworth had warned his neophyte that this would be the case, but the traditional enthusiasm of the neophyte had triumphed over discretion.

"She was feeling rather drowsy, the effect probably of the champagne, which she's not in the habit of taking in the middle of the day."

A subdued murmur of admiration went round the company. Blenkinthrope's aunts were not used to taking champagne in the middle of the year, regarding it exclusively as a Christmas and New Year accessory.

"Presently a rather portly gentleman passed by her seat and paused an instant to light a cigar. At that moment a youngish man came up behind him, drew the blade from a swordstick, and stabbed him half a dozen times through and through. 'Scoundrel,' he cried to his victim, 'you do not know me. My name is Henri Leturc.' The elder man wiped away some of the blood that was spattering his clothes, turned to his assailant, and said: 'And since when has an attempted assassination been considered an introduction?' Then he finished lighting his cigar and walked away. My aunt had intended screaming for the police, but seeing the indifference with which the principal in the affair treated the matter she felt that it would be an impertinence on her part to interfere. Of course I need hardly say she put the whole thing down to the effects of a warm, drowsy afternoon and the Legation champagne. Now comes the astonishing part of my story. A fortnight later a bank manager was stabbed to death with a swordstick in that very part of the Bois. His assassin was the son of a charwoman formerly working at the bank, who had been dismissed from her job by the manager on account of chronic intemperance. His name was Henri Leturc."

From that moment Blenkinthrope was tacitly accepted as the

Munchausen of the party. No effort was spared to draw him out from day to day in the exercise of testing their powers of credulity, and Blenkinthrope, in the false security of an assured and receptive audience, waxed industrious and ingenious in supplying the demand for marvels. Duckby's satirical story of a tame otter that had a tank in the garden to swim in, and whined restlessly whenever the water-rate was overdue, was scarcely an unfair parody of some of Blenkinthrope's wilder efforts. And then one day came Nemesis.

Returning to his villa one evening Blenkinthrope found his wife sitting in front of a pack of cards, which she was scrutinizing with unusual concentration.

"The same old patience-game?" he asked carelessly.

"No, dear; this is the Death's Head patience, the most difficult of them all. I've never got it to work out, and somehow I should be rather frightened if I did. Mother only got it out once in her life; she was afraid of it, too. Her great-aunt had done it once and fallen dead from excitement the next moment, and mother always had a feeling that she would die if she ever got it out. She died the same night that she did it. She was in bad health at the time, certainly, but it was a strange coincidence."

"Don't do it if it frightens you," was Blenkinthrope's practical comment as he left the room. A few minutes later his wife called to him.

"John, it gave me such a turn, I nearly got it out. Only the five of diamonds held me up at the end. I really thought I'd done it."

"Why, you can do it," said Blenkinthrope, who had come back to the room; "if you shift the eight of clubs on to that open nine the five can be moved on to the six."

His wife made the suggested move with hasty, trembling fingers, and piled the outstanding cards on to their respective packs. Then she followed the example of her mother and great-grand-aunt.

Blenkinthrope had been genuinely fond of his wife, but in the midst of his bereavement one dominant thought obtruded itself. Something sensational and real had at last come into his life; no longer was it a grey, colourless record. The headlines which might appropriately describe his domestic tragedy kept shaping themselves in his brain. "Inherited presentiment comes true." "The Death's Head patience: Card-game that justified its sinister name in three generations." He wrote out a full story of the fatal occurrence for the *Essex Vedette*, the editor of which was a friend of his, and to another friend he gave a condensed account, to be taken up to the office of one of the halfpenny dailies. But in both cases his reputation as a romancer stood fatally in the way of the fulfilment of his ambitions. "Not the right thing to be Munchausening in a time of sorrow," agreed his friends among themselves, and a brief note of regret at the "sudden death of the wife of our respected neighbour, Mr. John Blenkinthrope, from heart failure," appearing in the news column of the local paper was the forlorn outcome of his visions of widespread publicity.

Blenkinthrope shrank from the society of his erstwhile travelling companions and took to travelling townwards by an earlier train. He sometimes tries to enlist the sympathy and attention of a chance acquaintance in details of the whistling prowess of his best canary or the dimensions of his largest beetroot; he scarcely recognizes himself as the man who was once spoken about and pointed out as the owner of the Seventh Pullet.

THE BLIND SPOT

"YOU'VE just come back from Adelaide's funeral, haven't you?" said Sir Lulworth to his nephew; "I suppose it was very like most other funerals?"

"I'll tell you all about it at lunch," said Egbert.

"You'll do nothing of the sort. It wouldn't be respectful either to your great-aunt's memory or to the lunch. We begin with Spanish olives, then a borsch, then more olives and a bird of some kind, and a rather enticing Rhenish wine, not at all expensive as wines go in this country, but still quite laudable in its way. Now there's absolutely nothing in that menu that harmonizes in the least with the subject of your great-aunt Adelaide or her funeral. She was a charming woman, and quite as intelligent as she had any need to be, but somehow she always reminded me of an English cook's idea of a Madras curry."

"She used to say you were frivolous," said Egbert. Something in his tone suggested that he rather endorsed the verdict.

"I believe I once considerably scandalized her by declaring that clear soup was a more important factor in life than a clear conscience. She had very little sense of proportion. By the way, she made you her principal heir, didn't she?"

"Yes," said Egbert, "and executor as well. It's in that connection that I particularly want to speak to you."

"Business is not my strong point at any time," said Sir Lulworth, "and certainly not when we're on the immediate threshold of lunch."

"It isn't exactly business," explained Egbert, as he followed his uncle into the dining-room. "It's something rather serious. Very serious."

"Then we can't possibly speak about it now," said Sir Lulworth; "no one could talk seriously, during a borsch. A beautifully constructed borsch, such as you are going to experience presently, ought not only to banish conversation but almost to annihilate thought. Later on, when we arrive at the second stage of olives, I shall be quite ready to discuss that new book on Borrow, or, if you prefer it, the present situation in the Grand Duchy of Luxemburg. But I absolutely decline to talk anything approaching business till we have finished with the bird."

For the greater part of the meal Egbert sat in an abstracted silence, the silence of a man whose mind is focussed on one topic. When the coffee stage had been reached he launched himself suddenly athwart his uncle's reminiscences of the Court of Luxemburg.

"I think I told you that great-aunt Adelaide had made me her executor. There wasn't very much to be done in the way of legal matters, but I had to go through her papers."

"That would be a fairly heavy task in itself. I should imagine there were reams of family letters."

"Stacks of them, and most of them highly uninteresting. There was one packet, however, which I thought might repay a careful perusal. It was a bundle of correspondence from her brother Peter."

"The Canon of tragic memory," said Lulworth.

"Exactly, of tragic memory, as you say; a tragedy that has never been fathomed."

"Probably the simplest explanation was the correct one," said Sir Lulworth; "he slipped on the stone staircase and fractured his skull in falling."

Egbert shook his head. "The medical evidence all went to prove that the blow on the head was struck by some one coming up behind him. A wound caused by violent contact with the steps could not possibly have been inflicted at that angle of the skull. They experimented with a dummy figure falling in every conceivable position."

"But the motive?" exclaimed Sir Lulworth; "no one had any interest in doing away with him, and the number of people who destroy Canons of the Established Church for the mere fun of killing must be extremely limited. Of course there are individuals of weak mental balance who do that sort of thing, but they seldom conceal their handiwork; they are more generally inclined to parade it."

"His cook was under suspicion," said Egbert shortly.

"I know he was," said Sir Lulworth, "simply because he was about the only person on the premises at the time of the tragedy. But could anything be sillier than trying to fasten a charge of murder on to Sebastien? He had nothing to gain, in fact, a good deal to lose, from the death of his employer. The Canon was paying him quite as good wages as I was able to offer him when I took him over into my service. I have since raised them to something a little more in accordance with his real worth, but at the time he was glad to find a new place without troubling about an increase of wages. People were fighting rather shy of him, and he had no friends in this country. No; if any one in the world was interested in the prolonged life and unimpaired digestion of the Canon it would certainly be Sebastien."

"People don't always weigh the consequences of their rash acts," said Egbert, "otherwise there would be very few murders committed. Sebastien is a man of hot temper."

"He is a southerner," admitted Sir Lulworth; "to be geographically exact I believe he hails from the French slopes of the Pyrenees. I took that into consideration when he nearly killed the gardener's boy the other day for bringing him a spurious substitute for sorrel. One must always make allowances for origin and locality and early environment; 'Tell me your longitude and I'll know what latitude to allow you,' is my motto."

"There, you see," said Egbert, "he nearly killed the gardener's boy."

"My dear Egbert, between nearly killing a gardener's boy and altogether killing a Canon there is a wide difference. No doubt you have often felt a temporary desire to kill a gardener's boy; you have never given way to it, and I respect you for your self-control.

But I don't suppose you have ever wanted to kill an octogenarian Canon. Besides, as far as we know, there had never been any quarrel or disagreement between the two men. The evidence at the inquest brought that out very clearly."

"Ah!" said Egbert, with the air of a man coming at last into a deferred inheritance of conversational importance, "that is precisely what I want to speak to you about."

He pushed away his coffee cup and drew a pocket-book from his inner breast-pocket. From the depths of the pocket-book he produced an envelope, and from the envelope he extracted a letter, closely written in a small, neat handwriting.

"One of the Canon's numerous letters to Aunt Adelaide," he explained, "written a few days before his death. Her memory was already failing when she received it, and I dare say she forgot the contents as soon as she had read it; otherwise, in the light of what subsequently happened, we should have heard something of this letter before now. If it had been produced at the inquest I fancy it would have made some difference in the course of affairs. The evidence, as you remarked just now, choked off suspicion against Sebastien by disclosing an utter absence of anything that could be considered a motive or provocation for the crime, if crime there was."

"Oh, read the letter," said Sir Lulworth impatiently.

"It's a long rambling affair, like most of his letters in his later years," said Egbert. "I'll read the part that bears immediately on the mystery.

"'I very much fear I shall have to get rid of Sebastien. He cooks divinely, but he has the temper of a fiend or an anthropoid ape, and I am really in bodily fear of him. We had a dispute the other day as to the correct sort of lunch to be served on Ash Wednesday, and I got so irritated and annoyed at his conceit and obstinacy that at last I threw a cupful of coffee in his face and called him at the same time an impudent jackanapes. Very little of the coffee went actually in his face, but I have never seen a human being show such deplorable lack of self-control. I laughed at the threat of killing me that he spluttered out in his rage, and thought the whole thing would blow over, but I have several times since caught him scowling and muttering in a highly unpleasant fashion, and lately I have fancied that he was dogging my footsteps about the grounds, particularly when I walk of an evening in the Italian Garden.'

"It was on the steps in the Italian Garden that the body was found," commented Egbert, and resumed reading.

"'I dare say the danger is imaginary; but I shall feel more at ease when he has quitted my service.'"

Egbert paused for a moment at the conclusion of the extract; then, as his uncle made no remark, he added: "If lack of motive was the only factor that saved Sebastien from prosecution I fancy this letter will put a different complexion on matters."

"Have you shown it to any one else?" asked Sir Lulworth, reaching out his hand for the incriminating piece of paper.

"No," said Egbert, handing it across the table, "I thought I would tell you about it first. Heavens, what are you doing?"

Egbert's voice rose almost to a scream. Sir Lulworth had flung the paper well and truly into the glowing centre of the grate. The small, neat handwriting shrivelled into black flaky nothingness.

"What on earth did you do that for?" gasped Egbert. "That letter was our one piece of evidence to connect Sebastien with the crime."

"That is why I destroyed it," said Sir Lulworth.

"But why should you want to shield him?" cried Egbert; "the man is a common murderer."

"A common murderer, possibly, but a very uncommon cook."

DUSK

NORMAN GORTSBY sat on a bench in the Park, with his back to a strip of bush-planted sward, fenced by the park railings, and the Row fronting him across a wide stretch of carriage drive. Hyde Park Corner, with its rattle and hoot of traffic, lay immediately to his right. It was some thirty minutes past six on an early March evening, and dusk had fallen heavily over the scene, dusk mitigated by some faint moonlight and many street lamps. There was a wide emptiness over road and sidewalk, and yet there were many unconsidered figures moving silently through the half-light or dotted unobtrusively on bench and chair, scarcely to be distinguished from the shadowed gloom in which they sat.

The scene pleased Gortsby and harmonized with his present

mood. Dusk, to his mind, was the hour of the defeated. Men and women, who had fought and lost, who hid their fallen fortunes and dead hopes as far as possible from the scrutiny of the curious, came forth in this hour of gloaming, when their shabby clothes and bowed shoulders and unhappy eyes might pass unnoticed, or, at any rate, unrecognized.

> A king that is conquered must see strange looks,
> So bitter a thing is the heart of man.

The wanderers in the dusk did not choose to have strange looks fasten on them, therefore they came out in this bat-fashion, taking their pleasure sadly in a pleasure-ground that had emptied of its rightful occupants. Beyond the sheltering screen of bushes and palings came a realm of brilliant lights and noisy, rushing traffic. A blazing, many-tiered stretch of windows shone through the dusk and almost dispersed it, marking the haunts of those other people, who held their own in life's struggle, or at any rate had not had to admit failure. So Gortsby's imagination pictured things as he sat on his bench in the almost deserted walk. He was in the mood to count himself among the defeated. Money troubles did not press on him; had he so wished he could have strolled into the thoroughfares of light and noise, and taken his place among the jostling ranks of those who enjoyed prosperity or struggled for it. He had failed in a more subtle ambition, and for the moment he was heart sore and disillusionized, and not disinclined to take a certain cynical pleasure in observing and labelling his fellow wanderers as they went their ways in the dark stretches between the lamp-lights.

On the bench by his side sat an elderly gentleman with a drooping air of defiance that was probably the remaining vestige of self-respect in an individual who had ceased to defy successfully anybody or anything. His clothes could scarcely be called shabby, at least they passed muster in the half-light, but one's imagination could not have pictured the wearer embarking on the purchase of a half-crown box of chocolates or laying out ninepence on a carnation buttonhole. He belonged unmistakably to that forlorn orchestra to whose piping no one dances; he was one of the world's lamenters who induces no responsive weeping. As he rose to go Gortsby imagined him returning to a home circle where he was snubbed and of no account, or to some bleak lodging where his ability to pay a weekly bill was the beginning and end of the interest he inspired. His retreating figure vanished slowly into the shadows, and his place on the bench was taken almost immediately by a young man, fairly well dressed but scarcely more cheerful of mien than his predecessor. As if to emphasize the fact that the world went badly with him the new-comer unburdened himself of an angry and very audible expletive as he flung himself into the seat.

"You don't seem in a very good temper," said Gortsby, judging that he was expected to take due notice of the demonstration.

The young man turned to him with a look of disarming frankness which put him instantly on his guard.

"You wouldn't be in a good temper if you were in the fix I'm in," he said; "I've done the silliest thing I've ever done in my life."

"Yes?" said Gortsby dispassionately.

"Came up this afternoon, meaning to stay at the Patagonian Hotel in Berkshire Square," continued the young man; "when I got there I found it had been pulled down some weeks ago and a cinema theatre run up on the site. The taxi driver recommended me to another hotel some way off and I went there. I just sent a letter to my people, giving them the address, and then I went out to buy some soap—I'd forgotten to pack any and I hate using hotel soap. Then I strolled about a bit, had a drink at a bar and looked at the shops, and when I came to turn my steps back to the hotel I suddenly realized that I didn't remember its name or even what street it was in. There's a nice predicament for a fellow who hasn't any friends or connections in London! Of course I can wire to my people for the address, but they won't have got my letter till to-morrow; meantime I'm without any money, came out with about a shilling on me, which went in buying the soap and getting the drink, and here I am, wandering about with twopence in my pocket and nowhere to go for the night."

There was an eloquent pause after the story had been told. "I suppose you think I've spun you rather an impossible yarn," said the young man presently, with a suggestion of resentment in his voice.

"Not at all impossible," said Gortsby judicially; "I remember doing exactly the same thing once in a foreign capital, and on that occasion there were two of us, which made it more remarkable. Luckily we remembered that the hotel was on a sort of canal, and when we struck the canal we were able to find our way back to the hotel."

The youth brightened at the reminiscence. "In a foreign city I wouldn't mind so much," he said; "one could go to one's Consul and get the requisite help from him. Here in one's own land one is far more derelict if one gets into a fix. Unless I can find some decent chap to swallow my story and lend me some money I seem likely to spend the night on the Embankment. I'm glad, anyhow, that you don't think the story outrageously improbable."

He threw a good deal of warmth into the last remark, as though perhaps to indicate his hope that Gortsby did not fall far short of the requisite decency.

"Of course," said Gortsby slowly, "the weak point of your story is that you can't produce the soap."

The young man sat forward hurriedly, felt rapidly in the pockets of his overcoat, and then jumped to his feet.

"I must have lost it," he muttered angrily.

"To lose an hotel and a cake of soap on one afternoon suggests wilful carelessness," said Gortsby, but the young man scarcely waited to hear the end of the remark. He flitted away down the path, his head held high, with an air of somewhat jaded jauntiness.

"It was a pity," mused Gortsby; "the going out to get one's own soap was the one convincing touch in the whole story, and yet it was just that little detail that brought him to grief. If he had had the brilliant forethought to provide himself with a cake of soap, wrapped and sealed with all the solicitude of the chemist's counter, he would have been a genius in his particular line. In his particular line genius certainly consists of an infinite capacity for taking precautions."

With that reflection Gortsby rose to go; as he did so an exclamation of concern escaped him. Lying on the ground by the side of the bench was a small oval packet, wrapped and sealed with the solicitude of a chemist's counter. It could be nothing else but a cake of soap, and it had evidently fallen out of the youth's overcoat pocket when he flung himself down on the seat. In another moment Gortsby was scudding along the dusk-shrouded path in anxious quest for a youthful figure in a light overcoat. He had nearly given up the search when he caught sight of the object of his pursuit standing irresolutely on the border of the carriage drive, evidently uncertain whether to strike across the Park or make for the bustling pavements of Knightsbridge. He turned round sharply with an air of defensive hostility when he found Gortsby hailing him.

"The important witness to the genuineness of your story has turned up," said Gortsby, holding out the cake of soap; "it must have slid out of your overcoat pocket when you sat down on the seat. I saw it on the ground after you left. You must excuse my disbelief, but appearances were really rather against you, and now, as I appealed to the testimony of the soap I think I ought to abide by its verdict. If the loan of a sovereign is any good to you–"

The young man hastily removed all doubt on the subject by pocketing the coin.

"Here is my card with my address," continued Gortsby; "any day this week will do for returning the money, and here is the soap –don't lose it again; it's been a good friend to you."

"Lucky thing your finding it," said the youth, and then, with a catch in his voice, he blurted out a word or two of thanks and fled headlong in the direction of Knightsbridge.

"Poor boy, he as nearly as possible broke down," said Gortsby to himself. "I don't wonder either; the relief from his quandary must have been acute. It's a lesson to me not to be too clever in judging by circumstances."

As Gortsby retraced his steps past the seat where the little drama had taken place he saw an elderly gentleman poking and peering beneath it and on all sides of it, and recognized his earlier fellow occupant.

"Have you lost anything, sir?" he asked.

"Yes, sir, a cake of soap."

A TOUCH OF REALISM

"I HOPE you've come full of suggestions for Christmas," said Lady Blonze to her latest arrived guest; "the old-fashioned Christmas and the up-to-date Christmas are both so played out. I want to have something really original this year."

"I was staying with the Mathesons last month," said Blanche Boveal eagerly, "and we had such a good idea. Every one in the house-party had to be a character and behave consistently all the time, and at the end of the visit one had to guess what every one's character was. The one who was voted to have acted his or her character best got a prize."

"It sounds amusing," said Lady Blonze.

"I was St. Francis of Assisi," continued Blanche; "we hadn't got to keep to our right sexes. I kept getting up in the middle of a meal and throwing out food to the birds; you see, the chief thing that one remembers of St. Francis is that he was fond of the birds. Every one was so stupid about it, and thought that I was the old man who feeds the sparrows in the Tuileries Gardens. Then Colonel Pentley was the Jolly Miller on the banks of Dee."

"How on earth did he do that?" asked Bertie van Tahn.

"'He laughed and sang from morn till night,'" explained Blanche.

"How dreadful for the rest of you," said Bertie; "and anyway he wasn't on the banks of Dee."

"One had to imagine that," said Blanche.

"If you could imagine all that you might as well imagine cattle on the further bank and keep on calling them home, Mary-fashion, across the sands of Dee. Or you might change the river to the Yarrow and imagine it was on the top of you, and say you were Willie, or whoever it was, drowned in Yarrow."

"Of course it's easy to make fun of it," said Blanche sharply, "but it was extremely interesting and amusing. The prize was rather a fiasco, though. You see, Millie Matheson said her character was Lady Bountiful, and as she was our hostess, of course we all had to vote that she carried out her character better than any one. Otherwise I ought to have got the prize."

"It's quite an idea for a Christmas party," said Lady Blonze; "we must certainly do it here."

Sir Nicholas was not so enthusiastic. "Are you quite sure, my dear, that you're wise in doing this thing?" he said to his wife when they were alone together. "It might do very well at the Mathesons', where they had rather a staid, elderly house-party, but here it will be a different matter. There is the Durmot flapper, for instance, who simply stops at nothing, and you know what Van Tahn is like. Then there is Cyril Skatterly; he has madness on one side of his family and a Hungarian grandmother on the other."

"I don't see what they could do that would matter," said Lady Blonze.

"It's the unknown that is to be dreaded," said Sir Nicholas. "If Skatterly took it into his head to represent a Bull of Bashan, well, I'd rather not be here."

"Of course we shan't allow any Bible characters. Besides, I

don't know what the Bulls of Bashan really did that was so very dreadful; they just came round and gaped, as far as I remember."

"My dear, you don't know what Skatterly's Hungarian imagination mightn't read into the part; it would be small satisfaction to say to him afterwards: 'You've behaved as no Bull of Bashan would have behaved.'"

"Oh, you're an alarmist," said Lady Blonze; "I particularly want to have this idea carried out. It will be sure to be talked about a lot."

"That is quite possible," said Sir Nicholas.

Dinner that evening was not a particularly lively affair; the strain of trying to impersonate a self-imposed character or to glean hints of identity from other people's conduct acted as a check on the natural festivity of such a gathering. There was a general feeling of gratitude and acquiescence when good-natured Rachel Klammerstein suggested that there should be an hour or two's respite from "the game" while they all listened to a little piano-playing after dinner. Rachel's love of piano music was not indiscriminate, and concentrated itself chiefly on selections rendered by her idolized offspring, Moritz and Augusta, who, to do them justice, played remarkably well.

The Klammersteins were deservedly popular as Christmas guests; they gave expensive gifts lavishly on Christmas Day and New Year, and Mrs. Klammerstein had already dropped hints of her intention to present the prize for the best enacted character in the game competition. Every one had brightened at this prospect; if it had fallen to Lady Blonze, as hostess, to provide the prize, she would have considered that a little souvenir of some twenty or twenty-five shillings' value would meet the case, whereas coming from a Klammerstein source it would certainly run to several guineas.

The close time for impersonation efforts came to an end with the final withdrawal of Moritz and Augusta from the piano. Blanche Boveal retired early, leaving the room in a series of laboured leaps that she hoped might be recognized as a tolerable imitation of Pavlova. Vera Durmot, the sixteen-year-old flapper, expressed her confident opinion that the performance was intended to typify Mark Twain's famous jumping frog, and her diagnosis of the case found general acceptance. Another guest to set an example of early bed-going was Waldo Plubley, who conducted his life on a minutely regulated system of time-tables and hygienic routine. Waldo was a plump, indolent young man of seven-and-twenty, whose mother had early in his life decided for him that he was unusually delicate, and by dint of much coddling and homekeeping had succeeded in making him physically soft and mentally peevish. Nine hours' unbroken sleep, preceded by elaborate breathing exercises and other hygienic ritual, was among the indispensable regulations which Waldo imposed on himself, and there were innumerable small observances which he exacted from those who were in any way obliged to minister to his requirements; a special teapot for the decoction of his early tea was always solemnly handed over to the bedroom staff of any house in which he happened to be staying. No one had ever quite mastered the mechanism of this precious vessel, but Bertie van Tahn was responsible for the legend that its spout had to be kept facing north during the process of infusion.

On this particular night the irreducible nine hours were severely mutilated by the sudden and by no means noiseless incursion of a pyjama-clad figure into Waldo's room at an hour midway between midnight and dawn.

"What is the matter? What are you looking for?" asked the awakened and astonished Waldo, slowly recognizing Van Tahn, who appeared to be searching hastily for something he had lost.

"Looking for sheep," was the reply.

"Sheep?" exclaimed Waldo.

"Yes, sheep. You don't suppose I'm looking for giraffes, do you?"

"I don't see why you should expect to find either in my room," retorted Waldo furiously.

"I can't argue the matter at this hour of the night," said Bertie, and began hastily rummaging in the chest of drawers. Shirts and underwear went flying on to the floor.

"There are no sheep here, I tell you," screamed Waldo.

"I've only got your word for it," said Bertie, whisking most of the bedclothes on to the floor; "if you weren't concealing something you wouldn't be so agitated."

Waldo was by this time convinced that Van Tahn was raving mad, and made an anxious effort to humour him.

"Go back to bed like a dear fellow," he pleaded, "and your sheep will turn up all right in the morning."

"I dare say," said Bertie gloomily, "without their tails. Nice fool I shall look with a lot of Manx sheep."

And by way of emphasizing his annoyance at the prospect he sent Waldo's pillows flying to the top of the wardrobe.

"But *why* no tails?" asked Waldo, whose teeth were chattering with fear and rage and lowered temperature.

"My dear boy, have you never heard the ballad of Little Bo-Peep?" said Bertie with a chuckle. "It's my character in the Game, you know. If I didn't go hunting about for my lost sheep no one would be able to guess who I was; and now go to sleepy weeps like a good child or I shall be cross with you."

"I leave you to imagine," wrote Waldo in the course of a long letter to his mother, "how much sleep I was able to recover that night, and you know how essential nine uninterrupted hours of slumber are to my health."

On the other hand he was able to devote some wakeful hours to exercises in breathing wrath and fury against Bertie van Tahn.

Breakfast at Blonzecourt was a scattered meal, on the "come when you please" principle, but the house-party was supposed to gather in full strength at lunch. On the day after the "Game" had been started there were, however, some notable absentees. Waldo Plubley, for instance, was reported to be nursing a headache. A large breakfast and an "A.B.C." had been taken up to his room, but he had made no appearance in the flesh.

"I expect he's playing up to some character," said Vera Durmot; "isn't there a thing of Molière's, '*Le Malade Imaginaire*'? I expect he's that."

Eight or nine lists came out, and were duly pencilled with the suggestion.

"And where are the Klammersteins?" asked Lady Blonze; "they're usually so punctual."

"Another character pose, perhaps," said Bertie van Tahn; " 'the Lost Ten Tribes.' "

"But there are only three of them. Besides, they'll want their lunch. Hasn't any one seen anything of them?"

"Didn't you take them out in your car?" asked Blanche Boveal, addressing herself to Cyril Skatterly.

"Yes, took them out to Slogberry Moor immediately after breakfast. Miss Durmot came too."

"I saw you and Vera come back," said Lady Blonze, "but I didn't see the Klammersteins. Did you put them down in the village?"

"No," said Skatterly shortly.

"But where are they? Where did you leave them?"

"We left them on Slogberry Moor," said Vera calmly.

"On Slogberry Moor? Why, it's more than thirty miles away! How are they going to get back?"

"We didn't stop to consider that," said Skatterly; "we asked them to get out for a moment, on the pretence that the car had stuck, and then we dashed off full speed and left them there."

"But how dare you do such a thing? It's most inhuman! Why, it's been snowing for the last hour."

"I expect there'll be a cottage or farmhouse somewhere if they walk a mile or two."

"But why on earth have you done it?"

The question came in a chorus of indignant bewilderment.

"*That* would be telling what our characters are meant to be," said Vera.

"Didn't I warn you?" said Sir Nicholas tragically to his wife.

"It's something to do with Spanish history; we don't mind giving you that clue," said Skatterly, helping himself cheerfully to salad, and then Bertie van Tahn broke forth into peals of joyous laughter.

"I've got it! Ferdinand and Isabella deporting the Jews! Oh lovely! Those two have certainly won the prize; we shan't get anything to beat that for thoroughness."

Lady Blonze's Christmas party was talked about and written about to an extent that she had not anticipated in her most ambitious moments. The letters from Waldo's mother would alone have made it memorable.

COUSIN TERESA

BASSET HARROWCLUFF returned to the home of his fathers, after an absence of four years, distinctly well pleased with himself. He was only thirty-one, but he had put in some useful service in an out-of-the-way, though not unimportant, corner of the world. He had quieted a province, kept open a trade route, enforced the tradition of respect which is worth the ransom of many kings in out-of-the-way regions, and done the whole business on rather less expenditure than would be requisite for organizing a charity in the home country. In Whitehall and places where they think, they doubtless thought well of him. It was not inconceivable, his father allowed himself to imagine, that Basset's name might figure in the next list of Honours.

Basset was inclined to be rather contemptuous of his half-brother, Lucas, whom he found feverishly engrossed in the same medley of elaborate futilities that had claimed his whole time and energies, such as they were, four years ago, and almost as far back before that as he could remember. It was the contempt of the man of action for the man of activities, and it was probably reciprocated. Lucas was an over-well nourished individual, some nine years Basset's senior, with a colouring that would have been accepted as a sign of intensive culture in an asparagus, but probably meant in this case mere abstention from exercise. His hair and forehead furnished a recessional note in a personality that was in all other respects obtrusive and assertive. There was certainly no Semitic blood in Lucas's parentage, but his appearance contrived to convey at least a suggestion of Jewish extraction. Clovis Sangrail, who knew most of his associates by sight, said it was undoubtedly a case of protective mimicry.

Two days after Basset's return, Lucas frisked in to lunch in a state of twittering excitement that could not be restrained even for the immediate consideration of soup, but had to be verbally discharged in spluttering competition with mouthfuls of vermicelli.

"I've got hold of an idea for something immense," he babbled, "something that is simply It."

Basset gave a short laugh that would have done equally well as a snort, if one had wanted to make the exchange. His half-brother was in the habit of discovering futilities that were "simply It" at frequently recurring intervals. The discovery generally meant that he flew up to town, preceded by glowingly worded telegrams, to see some one connected with the stage or the publishing world, got together one or two momentous luncheon parties, flitted in and out of "Gambrinus" for one or two evenings, and returned home with an air of subdued importance and the asparagus tint slightly intensified. The great idea was generally forgotten a few weeks later in the excitement of some new discovery.

"The inspiration came to me whilst I was dressing," announced Lucas; "it will be *the* thing in the next music-hall *revue*. All London will go mad over it. It's just a couplet; of course there will be other words, but they won't matter. Listen:

Cousin Teresa takes out Cæsar,
Fido, Jock, and the big borzoi.

A lilting, catchy sort of refrain, you see, and big-drum business on the two syllables of bor-zoi. It's immense. And I've thought out all the business of it; the singer will sing the first verse alone, then during the second verse Cousin Teresa will walk through, followed by four wooden dogs on wheels; Cæsar will be an Irish terrier, Fido a black poodle, Jock a fox-terrier, and the borzoi, of course, will be a borzoi. During the third verse Cousin Teresa will come on alone, and the dogs will be drawn across by themselves from the opposite wing; then Cousin Teresa will catch on to the singer and go off-stage in one direction, while dogs' procession goes off in the other, crossing *en route*, which is always very effective. There'll be a lot of applause there, and for the fourth verse Cousin Teresa will come on in sables and the dogs will all have coats on. Then I've got a great idea for the fifth verse; each of the dogs will be led on by a Nut, and Cousin Teresa will come on from the opposite side, crossing *en route*, always effective, and then she turns round and leads the whole lot of them off on a string, and all the time every one singing like mad:

Cousin Teresa takes out Cæsar,
Fido, Jock, and the big borzoi.

Tum-Tum! Drum business on the two last syllables. I'm so excited, I shan't sleep a wink tonight. I'm off tomorrow by the ten-fifteen. I've wired to Hermanova to lunch with me."

If any of the rest of the family felt any excitement over the creation of Cousin Teresa, they were signally successful in concealing the fact.

"Poor Lucas does take his silly little ideas seriously," said Colonel Harrowcluff afterwards in the smoking-room.

"Yes," said his younger son, in a slightly less tolerant tone, "in a day or two he'll come back and tell us that his sensational masterpiece is above the heads of the public, and in about three weeks' time he'll be wild with enthusiasm over a scheme to dramatize the poems of Herrick or something equally promising."

And then an extraordinary thing befell. In defiance of all precedent Lucas's glowing anticipations were justified and endorsed by the course of events. If Cousin Teresa was above the heads of the public, the public heroically adapted itself to her altitude. Introduced as an experiment at a dull moment in a new *revue,* the success of the item was unmistakable; the calls were so insistent and uproarious that even Lucas's ample devisings of additional "business" scarcely sufficed to keep pace with the demand. Packed houses on successive evenings confirmed the verdict of the first night audience, stalls and boxes filled significantly just before the turn came on, and emptied significantly after the last *encore* had been given. The manager tearfully acknowledged that Cousin Teresa was It. Stage hands and supers and programme sellers acknowledged it to one another without the least reservation. The name of the *revue* dwindled to secondary importance, and vast letters of electric blue blazoned the words "Cousin Teresa" from the front of the great palace of pleasure. And of course, the magic of the famous refrain laid its spell all over the Metropolis. Restaurant proprietors were obliged to provide the members of their orchestras with painted wooden dogs on wheels, in order that the much-demanded and always conceded melody should be rendered with the necessary spectacular effects, and the crash of bottles and forks on the tables at the mention of the big borzoi usually drowned the sincerest efforts of drum or cymbals. Nowhere and at no time could one get away from the double thump that brought up the rear of the refrain; revellers reeling home at night banged it on doors and hoardings, milkmen clashed their cans to its cadence, messenger boys hit smaller messenger boys resounding double smacks on the same principle. And the more thoughtful circles of the great city were not deaf to the claims and significance of the popular melody. An enterprising and emancipated preacher discoursed from his pulpit on the inner meaning of "Cousin Teresa," and Lucas Harrowcluff was invited to lecture on the subject of his great achievement to members of the Young Men's Endeavour League, the Nine Arts Club, and other learned and willing-to-learn bodies. In Society it seemed to be the one thing people really cared to talk about; men and women of middle age and average education might be seen together in corners earnestly discussing, not the question whether Servia should have an outlet on the Adriatic, or the possibilities of a British success in international polo contests, but the more absorbing topic of the problematic Aztec or Nilotic origin of the Teresa *motif*.

"Politics and patriotism are so boring and so out of date," said a revered lady who had some pretensions to oracular utterance; "we are too cosmopolitan nowadays to be really moved by them. That is why one welcomes an intelligible production like 'Cousin Teresa,' that has a genuine message for one. One can't understand the message all at once, of course, but one felt from the very first that it was there. I've been to see it eighteen times and I'm going again tomorrow and on Thursday. One can't see it often enough."

"It would be rather a popular move if we gave this Harrowcluff person a knighthood or something of the sort," said the Minister reflectively.

"Which Harrowcluff?" asked his secretary.

"Which? There is only one, isn't there?" said the Minister; "the 'Cousin Teresa' man, of course. I think every one would be pleased if we knighted him. Yes, you can put him down on the list of certainties—under the letter L."

"The letter L," said the secretary, who was new to his job: "does that stand for Liberalism or liberality?"

Most of the recipients of Ministerial favour were expected to qualify in both of those subjects.

"Literature," explained the Minister.

And thus, after a fashion, Colonel Harrowcluff's expectation of seeing his son's name in the list of Honours was gratified.

THE YARKAND MANNER

Sir Lulworth Quayne was making a leisurely progress through the Zoological Society's Gardens in company with his nephew, recently returned from Mexico. The latter was interested in comparing and contrasting allied types of animals occurring in the North American and Old World fauna.

"One of the most remarkable things in the wanderings of species," he observed, "is the sudden impulse to trek and migrate that breaks out now and again, for no apparent reason, in communities of hitherto stay-at-home animals."

"In human affairs the same phenomenon is occasionally noticeable," said Sir Lulworth; "perhaps the most striking instance of it occurred in this country while you were away in the wilds of Mexico. I mean the wander fever which suddenly displayed itself in the managing and editorial staffs of certain London newspapers. It began with the stampede of the entire staff of one of our most brilliant and enterprising weeklies to the banks of the Seine and the heights of Montmartre. The migration was a brief one, but it heralded an era of restlessness in the Press world which lent quite a new meaning to the phrase 'newspaper circulation.' Other editorial staffs were not slow to imitate the example that had been set them. Paris soon dropped out of fashion as being too near home; Nürnberg, Seville, and Salonica became more favoured as planting-out grounds for the personnel of not only weekly but daily papers as well. The localities were perhaps not always well chosen; the fact of a leading organ of Evangelical thought being edited for two successive fortnights from Trouville and Monte Carlo was generally admitted to have been a mistake. And even when enterprising and adventurous editors took themselves and their staffs further afield there were some unavoidable clashings. For instance, the *Scrutator*, *Sporting Bluff* and *The Damsels' Own Paper* all pitched on Khartoum for the same week. It was, perhaps, a desire to out-distance all possible competition that influenced the management of the *Daily Intelligencer*, one of the most solid and respected organs of Liberal opinion, in its decision to transfer its offices for three or four weeks from Fleet Street to Eastern Turkestan, allowing, of course, a necessary margin of time for the journey there and back. This was, in many respects, the most remarkable of all the Press stampedes that were experienced at this time. There was no make-believe about the undertaking; proprietor, manager, editor, sub-editors, leader-writers, principal reporters, and so forth, all took part in what was popularly alluded to as the *Drang nach Osten;* an intelligent and efficient office-boy was all that was left in the deserted hive of editorial industry."

"That was doing things rather thoroughly, wasn't it?" said the nephew.

"Well, you see," said Sir Lulworth, "the migration idea was falling somewhat into disrepute from the half-hearted manner in which it was occasionally carried out. You were not impressed by the information that such and such a paper was being edited and brought out at Lisbon or Innsbruck if you chanced to see the principal leader-writer or the art editor lunching as usual at their accustomed restaurants. The *Daily Intelligencer* was determined to give no loophole for cavil at the genuineness of its pilgrimage, and it must be admitted that to a certain extent the arrangements made for transmitting copy and carrying on the usual features of the paper during the long outward journey worked smoothly and well. The series of articles which commenced at Baku on 'What Cobdenism might do for the camel industry' ranks among the best of the recent contributions to Free Trade literature, while the views on foreign policy enunciated 'from a roof in Yarkand' showed at least as much grasp of the international situation as those that had germinated within half a mile of Downing Street. Quite in keeping, too, with the older and better traditions of British journalism was the manner of the home-coming; no bombast, no personal advertisement, no flamboyant interviews. Even a complimentary luncheon at the Voyagers' Club was courteously declined. Indeed, it began to be felt that the self-effacement of the returned pressmen was being carried to a pedantic length. Foreman compositors, advertisement clerks, and other members of the non-editorial staff, who had, of course, taken no part in the great trek, found it as impossible to get into direct communication with the editor and his satellites now that they had returned as when they had been excusably inaccessible in Central Asia. The sulky, overworked office-boy, who was the one connecting link between the editorial brain and the business departments of the paper, sardonically explained the new aloofness as the 'Yarkand manner.' Most of the reporters and sub-editors seemed to have been dismissed in autocratic fashion since their return and new ones engaged by letter; to these the editor and his immediate associates remained an unseen presence, issuing its instructions solely through the medium of curt type-written notes. Something mystic and Tibetan and forbidden had replaced the human bustle and democratic simplicity of pre-migration days, and the same experience was encountered by those who made social overtures to the returned wanderers. The most brilliant hostess of Twentieth Century London flung the pearl of her hospitality into the unresponsive trough of the editorial letter-box; it seemed as if nothing short of a Royal command would drag the hermit-souled *revenants* from their self-imposed seclusion. People began to talk unkindly of the effect of high altitudes and

Eastern atmosphere on minds and temperaments unused to such luxuries. The Yarkand manner was not popular."

"And the contents of the paper," said the nephew, "did they show the influence of the new style?"

"Ah!" said Sir Lulworth, "that was the exciting thing. In home affairs, social questions, and the ordinary events of the day not much change was noticeable. A certain Oriental carelessness seemed to have crept into the editorial department, and perhaps a note of lassitude not unnatural in the work of men who had returned from what has been a fairly arduous journey. The aforetime standard of excellence was scarcely maintained, but at any rate the general lines of policy and outlook were not departed from. It was in the realm of foreign affairs that a startling change took place. Blunt, forcible, outspoken articles appeared, couched in language which nearly turned the autumn manœuvres of six important Powers into mobilizations. Whatever else the *Daily Intelligencer* had learned in the East, it had not acquired the art of diplomatic ambiguity. The man in the street enjoyed the articles and bought the paper as he had never bought it before; the men in Downing Street took a different view. The Foreign Secretary, hitherto accounted a rather reticent man, became positively garrulous in the course of perpetually disavowing the sentiments expressed in the *Daily Intelligencer*'s leaders; and then one day the Government came to the conclusion that something definite and drastic must be done. A deputation, consisting of the Prime Minister, the Foreign Secretary, four leading financiers, and a well-known Nonconformist divine, made its way to the offices of the paper. At the door leading to the editorial department the way was barred by a nervous but defiant office-boy.

"'You can't see the editor nor any of the staff,' he announced.

"'We insist on seeing the editor or some responsible person,' said the Prime Minister, and the deputation forced its way in. The boy had spoken truly; there was no one to be seen. In the whole suite of rooms there was no sign of human life.

"'Where is the editor?' 'Or the foreign editor?' 'Or the chief leader-writer?' 'Or anybody?'

"In answer to the shower of questions the boy unlocked a drawer and produced a strange-looking envelope, which bore a Khokand postmark, and a date of some seven or eight months back. It contained a scrap of paper on which was written the following message:

> "'Entire party captured by brigand tribe on homeward journey. Quarter of million demanded as ransom, but would probably take less. Inform Government, relations, and friends.'

"There followed the signatures of the principal members of the party and instructions as to how and where the money was to be paid.

"The letter had been directed to the office-boy-in-charge, who had quietly suppressed it. No one is a hero to one's own office-boy, and he evidently considered that a quarter of a million was an unwarrantable outlay for such a doubtfully advantageous object as the repatriation of an errant newspaper staff. So he drew the editorial and other salaries, forged what signatures were necessary, engaged new reporters, did what sub-editing he could, and made as much use as possible of the large accumulation of special articles that was held in reserve for emergencies. The articles on foreign affairs were entirely his own composition.

"Of course the whole thing had to be kept as quiet as possible; an interim staff, pledged to secrecy, was appointed to keep the paper going till the pining captives could be sought out, ransomed, and brought home, in twos and threes to escape notice, and gradually things were put back on their old footing. The articles on foreign affairs reverted to the wonted traditions of the paper."

"But," interposed the nephew, "how on earth did the boy account to the relatives all those months for the non-appearance—"

"That," said Sir Lulworth, "was the most brilliant stroke of all. To the wife or nearest relative of each of the missing men he forwarded a letter, copying the handwriting of the supposed writer as well as he could, and making excuses about vile pens and ink; in each letter he told the same story, varying only the locality, to the effect that the writer, alone of the whole party, was unable to tear himself away from the wild liberty and allurements of Eastern life, and was going to spend several months roaming in some selected region. Many of the wives started off immediately in pursuit of their errant husbands, and it took the Government a considerable time and much trouble to reclaim them from their fruitless quests along the banks of the Oxus, the Gobi Desert, the Orenburg steppe, and other outlandish places. One of them, I believe, is still lost somewhere in the Tigris Valley."

"And the boy?"

"Is still in journalism."

THE BYZANTINE OMELETTE

Sophie Chattel-Monkheim was a Socialist by conviction and a Chattel-Monkheim by marriage. The particular member of that wealthy family whom she had married was rich, even as his relatives counted riches. Sophie had very advanced and decided views as to the distribution of money: it was a pleasing and fortunate circumstance that she also had the money. When she inveighed eloquently against the evils of capitalism at drawing-room meetings and Fabian conferences she was conscious of a comfortable feeling that the system, with all its inequalities and iniquities, would probably last her time. It is one of the consolations of middle-aged reformers that the good they inculcate must live after them if it is to live at all.

On a certain spring evening, somewhere towards the dinner-hour, Sophie sat tranquilly between her mirror and her maid, undergoing the process of having her hair built into an elaborate reflection of the prevailing fashion. She was hedged round with a great peace, the peace of one who has attained a desired end with much effort and perseverance, and who has found it still eminently desirable in its attainment. The Duke of Syria had consented to come beneath her roof as a guest, was even now installed beneath her roof, and would shortly be sitting at her dining-table. As a good Socialist, Sophie disapproved of social distinctions, and derided the idea of a princely caste, but if there were to be these artificial gradations of rank and dignity she was pleased and anxious to have an exalted specimen of an exalted order included in her house-party. She was broad-minded enough to love the sinner while hating the sin—not that she entertained any warm feeling of personal affection for the Duke of Syria, who was a comparative stranger, but still, as Duke of Syria, he was very, very welcome beneath her roof. She could not have explained why, but no one was likely to ask her for an explanation, and most hostesses envied her.

"You must surpass yourself tonight, Richardson," she said complacently to her maid; "I must be looking my very best. We must all surpass ourselves."

The maid said nothing, but from the concentrated look in her eyes and the deft play of her fingers it was evident that she was beset with the ambition to surpass herself.

A knock came at the door, a quiet but peremptory knock, as of some one who would not be denied.

"Go and see who it is," said Sophie; "it may be something about the wine."

Richardson held a hurried conference with an invisible messenger at the door; when she returned there was noticeable a curious listlessness in place of her hitherto alert manner.

"What is it?" asked Sophie.

"The household servants have 'downed tools,' madame," said Richardson.

"Downed tools!" exclaimed Sophie; "do you mean to say they've gone on strike?"

"Yes, madame," said Richardson, adding the information: "It's Gaspare that the trouble is about."

"Gaspare?" said Sophie wonderingly; "the emergency chef! The omelette specialist!"

"Yes, madame. Before he became an omelette specialist he was a valet, and he was one of the strike-breakers in the great strike at Lord Grimford's two years ago. As soon as the household staff here learned that you had engaged him they resolved to 'down tools' as a protest. They haven't got any grievance against you personally, but they demand that Gaspare should be immediately dismissed."

"But," protested Sophie, "he is the only man in England who understands how to make a Byzantine omelette. I engaged him specially for the Duke of Syria's visit, and it would be impossible to replace him at short notice. I should have to send to Paris, and the Duke loves Byzantine omelettes. It was the one thing we talked about coming from the station."

"He was one of the strike-breakers at Lord Grimford's," reiterated Richardson.

"This is too awful," said Sophie; "a strike of servants at a moment like this, with the Duke of Syria staying in the house. Something must be done immediately. Quick, finish my hair and I'll go and see what I can do to bring them round."

"I can't finish your hair, madame," said Richardson quietly, but with immense decision. "I belong to the union and I can't do another half-minute's work till the strike is settled. I'm sorry to be disobliging."

"But this is inhuman!" exclaimed Sophie tragically; "I've always been a model mistress and I've refused to employ any but union servants, and this is the result. I can't finish my hair myself; I don't know how to. What am I to do? It's wicked!"

"Wicked is the word," said Richardson; "I'm a good Conservative, and I've no patience with this Socialist foolery, asking your pardon. It's tyranny, that's what it is, all along the line, but I've my living to make, same as other people, and I've got to belong to the union. I couldn't touch another hairpin without a strike permit, not if you was to double my wages."

The door burst open and Catherine Malsom raged into the room.

"Here's a nice affair," she screamed, "a strike of household servants without a moment's warning, and I'm left like this! I can't appear in public in this condition."

After a very hasty scrutiny Sophie assured her that she could not.

"Have they *all* struck?" she asked her maid.

"Not the kitchen staff," said Richardson, "they belong to a different union."

"Dinner at least will be assured," said Sophie, "that is something to be thankful for."

"Dinner!" snorted Catherine, "what on earth is the good of dinner when none of us will be able to appear at it? Look at your hair—and look at me! or rather, don't."

"I know it's difficult to manage without a maid; can't your husband be any help to you?" asked Sophie despairingly.

"Henry? He's in worse case than any of us. His man is the only person who really understands that ridiculous new-fangled Turkish bath that he insists on taking with him everywhere."

"Surely he could do without a Turkish bath for one evening," said Sophie; "I can't appear without hair, but a Turkish bath is a luxury."

"My good woman," said Catherine, speaking with a fearful intensity, "Henry was *in* the bath when the strike started. *In* it, do you understand? He's there now."

"Can't he get out?"

"He doesn't know how to. Every time he pulls the lever marked 'release' he only releases hot steam. There are two kinds of steam in the bath, 'bearable' and 'scarcely bearable'; he has released them both. By this time I'm probably a widow."

"I simply can't send away Gaspare," wailed Sophie; "I should never be able to secure another omelette specialist."

"Any difficulty that I may xperience in securing another husband is of course a trifle beneath any one's consideration," said Catherine bitterly.

Sophie capitulated. "Go," she said to Richardson, "and tell the Strike Committee, or whoever are directing this affair, that Gaspare is herewith dismissed. And ask Gaspare to see me presently in the library, when I will pay him what is due to him and make what excuses I can; and then fly back and finish my hair."

Some half an hour later Sophie marshalled her guests in the Grand Salon preparatory to the formal march to the dining-room. Except that Henry Malsom was of the ripe raspberry tint that one sometimes sees at private theatricals representing the human complexion, there was little outward sign among those assembled of the crisis that had just been encountered and surmounted. But the tension had been too stupefying while it lasted not to leave some mental effects behind it. Sophie talked at random to her illustrious guest, and found her eyes straying with increasing frequency towards the great doors through which would presently come the blessed announcement that dinner was served. Now and again she glanced mirror-ward at the reflection of her wonderfully coiffed hair, as an insurance underwriter might gaze thankfully at an overdue vessel that had ridden safely into harbour in the wake of a devastating hurricane. Then the doors opened and the welcome figure of the butler entered the room. But he made no general announcement of a banquet in readiness, and the doors closed behind him; his message was for Sophie alone.

"There is no dinner, madame," he said gravely; "the kitchen staff have 'downed tools.' Gaspare belongs to the Union of Cooks and Kitchen Employés, and as soon as they heard of his summary dismissal at a moment's notice they struck work. They demand his instant reinstatement and an apology to the union. I may add, madame, that they are very firm; I've been obliged even to hand back the dinner rolls that were already on the table."

After the lapse of eighteen months Sophie Chattel-Monkheim is beginning to go about again among her old haunts and associates, but she still has to be very careful. The doctors will not let her attend anything at all exciting, such as a drawing-room meeting or a Fabian conference; it is doubtful, indeed, whether she wants to.

THE FEAST OF NEMESIS

"It's a good thing that Saint Valentine's Day has dropped out of vogue," said Mrs. Thackenbury; "what with Christmas and New Year and Easter, not to speak of birthdays, there are quite enough remembrance days as it is. I tried to save myself trouble at Christmas by just sending flowers to all my friends, but it wouldn't work; Gertrude has eleven hot-houses and about thirty gardeners, so it would have been ridiculous to send flowers to her, and Milly has just started a florist's shop, so it was equally out of the question there. The stress of having to decide in a hurry what to give to Gertrude and Milly just when I thought I'd got the whole question nicely off my mind completely ruined my Christmas, and then the awful monotony of the letters of thanks: 'Thank you so much for your lovely flowers. It was so good of you to think of me.' Of course in the majority of cases I hadn't thought about the recipients at all; their names were down in my list of 'people who must not be left out.' If I trusted to remembering them there would be some awful sins of omission."

"The trouble is," said Clovis to his aunt, "all these days of intrusive remembrance harp so persistently on one aspect of human nature and entirely ignore the other; that is why they become so perfunctory and artificial. At Christmas and New Year you are emboldened and encouraged by convention to send gushing messages of optimistic goodwill and servile affection to people whom you would scarcely ask to lunch unless some one else had failed you at the last moment; if you are supping at a restaurant on New Year's Eve you are permitted and expected to join hands and sing 'For Auld Land Syne' with strangers whom you have never seen before and never want to see again. But no licence is allowed in the opposite direction."

"Opposite direction; what opposite direction?" queried Mrs. Thackenbury.

"There is no outlet for demonstrating your feelings towards people whom you simply loathe. That is really the crying need of our modern civilization. Just think how jolly it would be if a recognized day were set apart for the paying off of old scores and grudges, a day when one could lay oneself out to be gracefully vindictive to a carefully treasured list of 'people who must not be let off.' I remember when I was at a private school we had one day, the last Monday of the term I think it was, consecrated to the settlement of feuds and grudges; of course we did not appreciate it as much as it deserved, because after all, any day of the term could be used for that purpose. Still, if one had chastised a smaller boy for being cheeky weeks before, one was always permitted on that day to recall the episode to his memory by chastising him again. That is what the French call reconstructing the crime."

"I should call it reconstructing the punishment," said Mrs. Thackenbury; "and, anyhow, I don't see how you could introduce a system of primitive school-boy vengeance into civilized adult life. We haven't outgrown our passions, but we are supposed to have learned how to keep them within strictly decorous limits."

"Of course the thing would have to be done furtively and politely," said Clovis; "the charm of it would be that it would never be perfunctory like the other thing. Now, for instance, you say to yourself: 'I must show the Webleys some attention at Christmas, they were kind to dear Bertie at Bournemouth,' and you send them a calendar, and daily for six days after Christmas the male Webley asks the female Webley if she has remembered to thank you for the calendar you sent them. Well, transplant that idea to the other and more human side of your nature, and say to yourself: 'Next Thursday is Nemesis Day; what on earth can I do to those odious people next door who made such an absurd fuss when Ping Yang bit their youngest child?' Then you'd get up awfully early on the allotted day and climb over into their garden and dig for truffles on their tennis court with a good gardening fork, choosing, of course, that part of the court that was screened from observation by the laurel bushes. You wouldn't find any truffles but you would find a great peace, such as no amount of present-giving could ever bestow."

"I shouldn't," said Mrs. Thackenbury, though her air of protest sounded a bit forced, "I should feel rather a worm for doing such a thing."

"You exaggerate the power of upheaval which a worm would be

able to bring into play in the limited time available," said Clovis; "if you put in a strenuous ten minutes with a really useful fork, the result ought to suggest the operations of an unusually masterful mole or a badger in a hurry."

"They might guess I had done it," said Mrs. Thackenbury.

"Of course they would," said Clovis; "that would be half the satisfaction of the thing, just as you like people at Christmas to know what presents or cards you've sent them. The thing would be much easier to manage, of course, when you were on outwardly friendly terms with the object of your dislike. That greedy little Agnes Blaik, for instance, who thinks of nothing but her food, it would be quite simple to ask her to a picnic in some wild woodland spot and lose her just before lunch was served; when you found her again every morsel of food could have been eaten up."

"It would require no ordinary human strategy to lose Agnes Blaik when luncheon was imminent: in fact, I don't believe it could be done."

"Then have all the other guests, people whom you dislike, and lose the luncheon. It could have been sent by accident in the wrong direction."

"It would be a ghastly picnic," said Mrs. Thackenbury.

"For them, but not for you," said Clovis; "you would have had an early and comforting lunch before you started, and you could improve the occasion by mentioning in detail the items of the missing banquet—the lobster Newburg and the egg mayonnaise, and the curry that was to have been heated in a chafing-dish. Agnes Blaik would be delirious long before you got to the list of wines, and in the long interval of waiting, before they had quite abandoned hope of the lunch turning up, you could induce them to play silly games, such as that idiotic one of 'the Lord Mayor's dinner-party,' in which every one has to choose the name of a dish and do something futile when it is called out. In this case they would probably burst into tears when their dish is mentioned. It would be a heavenly picnic."

Mrs. Thackenbury was silent for a moment; she was probably making a mental list of the people she would like to invite to the Duke Humphrey picnic. Presently she asked: "And that odious young man, Waldo Plubley, who is always coddling himself—have you thought of anything that one could do to him?" Evidently she was beginning to see the possibilities of Nemesis Day.

"If there was anything like a general observance of the festival," said Clovis, "Waldo would be in such demand that you would have to bespeak him weeks beforehand, and even then, if there were an east wind blowing or a cloud or two in the sky he might be too careful of his precious self to come out. It would be rather jolly if you could lure him into a hammock in the orchard, just near the spot where there is a wasps' nest every summer. A comfortable hammock on a warm afternoon would appeal to his indolent tastes, and then, when he was getting drowsy, a lighted fusee thrown into the nest would bring the wasps out in an indignant mass, and they would soon find a 'home away from home' on Waldo's fat body. It takes some doing to get out of a hammock in a hurry."

"They might sting him to death," protested Mrs. Thackenbury.

"Waldo is one of those people who would be enormously improved by death," said Clovis; "but if you didn't want to go as far as that, you could have some wet straw ready to hand, and set it alight under the hammock at the same time that the fusee was thrown into the nest; the smoke would keep all but the most militant of the wasps just outside the stinging line, and as long as Waldo remained within its protection he would escape serious damage, and could be eventually restored to his mother, kippered all over and swollen in places, but still perfectly recognizable."

"His mother would be my enemy for life," said Mrs. Thackenbury.

"That would be one greeting less to exchange at Christmas," said Clovis.

THE DREAMER

It was the season of sales. The august establishment of Walpurgis and Nettlepink had lowered its prices for an entire week as a concession to trade observances, much as an Archduchess might protestingly contract an attack of influenza for the unsatisfactory reason that influenza was locally prevalent. Adela Chemping, who considered herself in some measure superior to the allurements of an ordinary bargain sale, made a point of attending the reduction week at Walpurgis and Nettlepink's.

"I'm not a bargain hunter," she said, "but I like to go where bargains are."

Which showed that beneath her surface strength of character there flowed a gracious undercurrent of human weakness.

With a view to providing herself with a male escort Mrs. Chemping had invited her youngest nephew to accompany her on the first day of the shopping expedition, throwing in the additional allurement of a cinematograph theatre and the prospect of light refreshment. As Cyprian was not yet eighteen, she hoped he might not have reached that stage in masculine development when parcel-carrying is looked on as a thing abhorrent.

"Meet me just outside the floral department," she wrote to him, "and don't be a moment later than eleven."

Cyprian was a boy who carried with him through early life the wondering look of a dreamer, the eyes of one who sees things that are not visible to ordinary mortals, and invests the commonplace things of this world with qualities unsuspected by plainer folk—the eyes of a poet or a house agent. He was quietly dressed—that sartorial quietude which frequently accompanies early adolescence, and is usually attributed by novel-writers to the influence of a widowed mother. His hair was brushed back in a smoothness as of ribbon seaweed and seamed with a narrow furrow that scarcely aimed at being a parting. His aunt particularly noted this item of his toilet when they met at the appointed rendezvous, because he was standing waiting for her bareheaded.

"Where is your hat?" she asked.

"I didn't bring one with me," he replied.

Adela Chemping was slightly scandalized.

"You are not going to be what they call a Nut, are you?" she inquired with some anxiety, partly with the idea that a Nut would be an extravagance which her sister's small household would scarcely be justified in incurring, partly, perhaps, with the instinctive apprehension that a Nut, even in its embryo stage, would refuse to carry parcels.

Cyprian looked at her with his wondering, dreamy eyes.

"I didn't bring a hat," he said, "because it is such a nuisance when one is shopping; I mean it is so awkward if one meets any one one knows and has to take one's hat off when one's hands are full of parcels. If one hasn't got a hat on one can't take it off."

Mrs. Chemping sighed with great relief; her worst fear had been laid at rest.

"It is more orthodox to wear a hat," she observed, and then turned her attention briskly to the business in hand.

"We will go first to the table-linen counter," she said, leading the way in that direction; "I should like to look at some napkins."

The wondering look deepened in Cyprian's eyes as he followed his aunt; he belonged to a generation that is supposed to be over-fond of the rôle of mere spectator, but looking at napkins that one did not mean to buy was a pleasure beyond his comprehension. Mrs. Chemping held one or two napkins up to the light and stared fixedly at them, as though she half expected to find some revolutionary cypher written on them in scarcely visible ink; then she suddenly broke away in the direction of the glassware department.

"Millicent asked me to get her a couple of decanters if there were any going really cheap," she explained on the way, "and I really do want a salad bowl. I can come back to the napkins later on."

She handled and scrutinized a large number of decanters and a long series of salad bowls, and finally bought seven chrysanthemum vases.

"No one uses that kind of vase nowadays," she informed Cyprian, "but they will do for presents next Christmas."

Two sunshades that were marked down to a price that Mrs. Chemping considered absurdly cheap were added to her purchases.

"One of them will do for Ruth Colson; she is going out to the Malay States, and a sunshade will always be useful there. And I must get her some thin writing paper. It takes up no room in one's baggage."

Mrs. Chemping bought stacks of writing paper; it was so cheap, and it went so flat in a trunk or portmanteau. She also bought a few envelopes—envelopes somehow seemed rather an extravagance compared with notepaper.

"Do you think Ruth will like blue or grey paper?" she asked Cyprian.

"Grey," said Cyprian, who had never met the lady in question.

"Have you any mauve notepaper of this quality?" Adela asked the assistant.

"We haven't any mauve," said the assistant, "but we've two shades of green and a darker shade of grey."

Mrs. Chemping inspected the greens and the darker grey, and chose the blue.

"Now we can have some lunch," she said.

Cyprian behaved in an exemplary fashion in the refreshment department, and cheerfully accepted a fish cake and a mince pie and a small cup of coffee as adequate restoratives after two hours of concentrated shopping. He was adamant, however, in resisting his aunt's suggestion that a hat should be bought for him at the counter where men's head-wear was being disposed of at temptingly reduced prices.

"I've got as many hats as I want at home," he said, "and besides, it rumples one's hair so, trying them on."

Perhaps he was going to develop into a Nut after all. It was a disquieting symptom that he left all the parcels in charge of the cloak-room attendant.

"We shall be getting more parcels presently," he said, "so we need not collect these till we have finished our shopping."

His aunt was doubtfully appeased; some of the pleasure and excitement of a shopping expedition seemed to evaporate when one was deprived of immediate personal contact with one's purchases.

"I'm going to look at those napkins again," she said, as they descended the stairs to the ground floor. "You need not come," she added, as the dreaming look in the boy's eyes changed for a moment into one of mute protest, "you can meet me afterwards in the cutlery department; I've just remembered that I haven't a corkscrew in the house that can be depended on."

Cyprian was not to be found in the cutlery department when his aunt in due course arrived there, but in the crush and bustle of anxious shoppers and busy attendants it was an easy matter to miss any one. It was in the leather goods department some quarter of an hour later that Adela Chemping caught sight of her nephew, separated from her by a rampart of suitcases and portmanteaux and hemmed in by the jostling crush of human beings that now invaded every corner of the great shopping emporium. She was just in time to witness a pardonable but rather embarrassing mistake on the part of a lady who had wriggled her way with unstayable determination towards the bareheaded Cyprian, and was now breathlessly demanding the sale price of a handbag which had taken her fancy.

"There now," exclaimed Adela to herself, "she takes him for one of the shop assistants because he hasn't got a hat on. I wonder it hasn't happened before."

Perhaps it had. Cyprian, at any rate, seemed neither startled nor embarrassed by the error into which the good lady had fallen. Examining the ticket on the bag, he announced in a clear, dispassionate voice:

"Black seal, thirty-four shillings marked down to twenty-eight. As a matter of fact, we are clearing them out at a special reduction price of twenty-six shillings. They are going off rather fast."

"I'll take it," said the lady, eagerly digging some coins out of her purse.

"Will you take it as it is?" asked Cyprian; "it will be a matter of a few minutes to get it wrapped up, there is such a crush."

"Never mind, I'll take it as it is," said the purchaser, clutching her treasure and counting the money into Cyprian's palm.

Several kind strangers helped Adela into the open air.

"It's the crush and the heat," said one sympathizer to another; "it's enough to turn any one giddy."

When she next came across Cyprian he was standing in the crowd that pushed and jostled around the counters of the book department. The dream look was deeper than ever in his eyes. He had just sold two books of devotion to an elderly Canon.

THE QUINCE TREE

"I've just been to see old Betsy Mullen," announced Vera to her aunt, Mrs. Bebberly Cumble; "she seems in rather a bad way about her rent. She owes about fifteen weeks of it, and says she doesn't know where any of it is to come from."

"Betsy Mullen always is in difficulties with her rent, and the more people help her with it the less she troubles about it," said the aunt. "I certainly am not going to assist her any more. The fact is, she will have to go into a smaller and cheaper cottage; there are several to be had at the other end of the village for half the rent that she is paying, or supposed to be paying, now. I told her a year ago that she ought to move."

"But she wouldn't get such a nice garden anywhere else," protested Vera, "and there's such a jolly quince tree in the corner. I don't suppose there's another quince tree in the whole parish. And she never makes any quince jam; I think to have a quince tree and not to make quince jam shows such strength of character. Oh, she can't possibly move away from that garden."

"When one is sixteen," said Mrs. Bebberly Cumble severely, "one talks of things being impossible which are merely uncongenial. It is not only possible but it is desirable that Betsy Mullen should move into smaller quarters; she has scarcely enough furniture to fill that big cottage."

"As far as value goes," said Vera after a short pause, "there is more in Betsy's cottage than in any other house for miles round."

"Nonsense," said the aunt; "she parted with whatever old china ware she had long ago."

"I'm not talking about anything that belongs to Betsy herself," said Vera darkly; "but of course, you don't know what I know, and I don't suppose I ought to tell you."

"You must tell me at once," exclaimed the aunt, her senses leaping into alertness like those of a terrier suddenly exchanging a bored drowsiness for the lively anticipation of an immediate rat hunt.

"I'm perfectly certain that I oughtn't to tell you anything about it," said Vera, "but, then, I often do things that I oughn't to do."

"I should be the last person to suggest that you should do anything that you ought not to do–" began Mrs. Bebberly Cumble impressively.

"And I am always swayed by the last person who speaks to me," admitted Vera, "so I'll do what I ought not to do and tell you."

Mrs. Bebberly Cumble thrust a very pardonable sense of exasperation into the background of her mind and demanded impatiently:

"What is there in Betsy Mullen's cottage that you are making such a fuss about?"

"It's hardly fair to say that *I've* made a fuss about it," said Vera; "this is the first I've mentioned the matter, but there's been no end of trouble and mystery and newspaper speculation about it. It's rather amusing to think of the columns of conjecture in the Press and the police and detectives hunting about everywhere at home and abroad, and all the while that innocent-looking little cottage has held the secret."

"You don't mean to say it's the Louvre picture, La Something or other, the woman with the smile, that disappeared about two years ago?" exclaimed the aunt with rising excitement.

"Oh, no, not that," said Vera, "but something quite as important and just as mysterious–if anything, rather more scandalous."

"Not the Dublin–?"

Vera nodded.

"The whole jolly lot of them."

"In Betsy's cottage? Incredible!"

"Of course Betsy hasn't an idea as to what they are," said Vera; "she just knows that they are something valuable and that she must keep quiet about them. I found out quite by accident what they were and how they came to be there. You see, the people who had them were at their wits' end to know where to stow them away for safe keeping, and some one who was motoring through the village was struck by the snug loneliness of the cottage and thought it would be just the thing. Mrs. Lamper arranged the matter with Betsy and smuggled the things in."

"Mrs. Lamper?"

"Yes; she does a lot of district visiting, you know."

"I am quite aware that she takes soup and flannel and improving literature to the poorer cottages," said Mrs. Bebberly Cumble, "but that is hardly the same sort of thing as disposing of stolen goods, and she must have known something about their history; any one who reads the papers, even casually, must have been aware of the theft, and I should think the things were not hard to recognize. Mrs. Lamper has always had the reputation of being a very conscientious woman."

"Of course she was screening some one else," said Vera. "A remarkable feature of the affair is the extraodinary number of quite respectable people who have involved themselves in its meshes by trying to shield others. You would be really astonished if you knew some of the names of the individuals mixed up in it, and I don't suppose a tithe of them knew who the original culprits were; and now I've got you entangled in the mess by letting you into the secret of the cottage."

"You most certainly have not entangled me," said Mrs. Bebberly Cumble indignantly. "I have no intention of shielding anybody. The police must know about it at once; a theft is a theft, whoever is involved. If respectable people choose to turn themselves into receivers and disposers of stolen goods, well, they've ceased to be respectable, that's all. I shall telephone immediately—"

"Oh, aunt," said Vera reproachfully, "it would break the poor Canon's heart if Cuthbert were to be involved in a scandal of this sort. You know it would."

"Cuthbert involved! How can you say such things when you know how much we all think of him?"

"Of course I know you think a lot of him, and that he's engaged to marry Beatrice, and that it will be a frightfully good match, and that he's your ideal of what a son-in-law ought to be. All the same, it was Cuthbert's idea to stow the things away in the cottage, and it was his motor that brought them. He was only doing it to help his friend Pegginson, you know—the Quaker man, who is always agitating for a smaller Navy. I forget how he got involved in it. I warned you that there were lots of quite respectable people mixed up in it, didn't I? That's what I meant when I said it would be impossible for old Betsy to leave the cottage; the things take up a good bit of room, and she couldn't go carrying them about with her other goods and chattels without attracting notice. Of course if she were to fall ill and die it would be equally unfortunate. Her mother lived to be over ninety, she tells me, so with due care and an absence of worry she ought to last for another dozen years at least. By that time perhaps some other arrangements will have been made for disposing of the wretched things."

"I shall speak to Cuthbert about it—after the wedding," said Mrs. Bebberly Cumble.

"The wedding isn't till next year," said Vera, in recounting the story to her best girl friend, "and meanwhile old Betsy is living rent free, with soup twice a week and my aunt's doctor to see her whenever she has a finger ache."

"But how on earth did you get to know about it all?" asked her friend, in admiring wonder.

"It was a mystery—" said Vera.

"Of course it was a mystery, a mystery that baffled everybody. What beats me is how you found out—"

"Oh, about the jewels? I invented that part," explained Vera; "I mean the mystery was where old Betsy's arrears of rent were to come from; and she would have hated leaving that jolly quince tree."

THE FORBIDDEN BUZZARDS

"Is matchmaking at all in your line?"

Hugo Peterby asked the question with a certain amount of personal interest.

"I don't specialize in it," said Clovis; "it's all right while you're doing it, but the after-effects are sometimes so disconcerting—the mute reproachful looks of the people you've aided and abetted in matrimonial experiments. It's as bad as selling a man a horse with half a dozen latent vices and watching him discover them piecemeal in the course of the hunting season. I suppose you're thinking of the Coulterneb girl. She's certainly jolly, and quite all right as far as looks go, and I believe a certain amount of money adheres to her. What I don't see is how you will ever manage to propose to her. In all the time I've known her I don't remember her to have stopped talking for three consecutive minutes. You'll have to race her six times round the grass paddock for a bet, and then blurt your proposal out before she's got her wind back. The paddock is laid up for hay, but if you're really in love with her you won't let a consideration of that sort stop you, especially as it's not your hay."

"I think I could manage the proposing part right enough," said Hugo, "if I could count on being left alone with her for four or five hours. The trouble is that I'm not likely to get anything like that amount of grace. That fellow Lanner is showing signs of interesting himself in the same quarter. He's quite heartbreakingly rich and is rather a swell in his way; in fact, our hostess is obviously a bit flattered at having him here. If she gets wind of the fact that he's inclined to be attracted by Betty Coulterneb she'll think it a splendid match and throw them into each other's arms all day long, and then where will my opportunities come in? My one anxiety is to keep him out of the girl's way as much as possible, and if you could help me—"

"If you want me to trot Lanner round the countryside, inspecting alleged Roman remains and studying local methods of bee culture and crop raising, I'm afraid I can't oblige you," said Clovis. "You see, he's taken something like an aversion to me since the other night in the smoking-room."

"What happened in the smoking-room?"

"He trotted out some well-worn chestnut as the latest thing in good stories, and I remarked, quite innocently, that I never could remember whether it was George II. or James II. who was so fond of that particular story, and now he regards me with politely draped dislike. I'll do my best for you, if the opportunity arises, but it will have to be in a roundabout, impersonal manner."

"It's so nice having Mr. Lanner here," confided Mrs. Olston to Clovis the next afternoon; "he's always been engaged when I've asked him before. Such a nice man; he really ought to be married to some nice girl. Between you and me, I have an idea that he came down here for a certain reason."

"I've had much the same idea," said Clovis, lowering his voice; "in fact, I'm almost certain of it."

"You mean he's attracted by—" began Mrs. Olston eagerly.

"I mean he's here for what he can get," said Clovis.

"For what he can *get?*" said the hostess with a touch of indignation in her voice; "what do you mean? He's a very rich man. What should he want to get here?"

"He has one ruling passion," said Clovis, "and there's something he can get here that is not to be had for love nor for money anywhere else in the country, as far as I know."

"But what? Whatever do you mean? What is his ruling passion?"

"Egg-collecting," said Clovis. "He has agents all over the world getting rare eggs for him, and his collection is one of the finest in Europe; but his great ambition is to collect his treasures personally. He stops at no expense nor trouble to achieve that end."

"Good heavens! The buzzards, the rough-legged buzzards!" exclaimed Mrs. Olston; "you don't think he's going to raid their nest?"

"What do you think yourself?" asked Clovis; "the only pair of rough-legged buzzards known to breed in this country are nesting in your woods. Very few people know about them, but as a member of the league for protecting rare birds that information would be at his disposal. I came down in the train with him, and I noticed that a bulky volume of Dresser's *Birds of Europe* was one of the requisites that he had packed in his travelling-kit. It was the volume dealing with short-winged hawks and buzzards."

Clovis believed that if a lie was worth telling it was worth telling well.

"This is appalling," said Mrs. Olston; "my husband would never forgive me if anything happened to those birds. They've been seen about the woods for the last year or two, but this is the first time they've nested. As you say, they are almost the only pair known to be breeding in the whole of Great Britain; and now their nest is going to be harried by a guest staying under my roof. I must do something to stop it. Do you think if I appealed to him—?"

Clovis laughed.

"There is a story going about, which I fancy is true in most of its details, of something that happened not long ago somewhere on the coast of the Sea of Marmora, in which our friend had a hand. A Syrian nightjar, or some such bird, was known to be breeding in the olive gardens of a rich Armenian, who for some reason or other wouldn't allow Lanner to go in and take the eggs though he offered cash down for the permission. The Armenian was found beaten near to death a day or two later, and his fences levelled. It was assumed to be a case of Mussulman aggression, and noted as such in all the Consular reports, but the eggs are in the Lanner collection. No, I don't think I should appeal to his better feelings if I were you."

"I must do something," said Mrs. Olston tearfully; "my husband's parting words when he went off to Norway were an injunction to see that those birds were not disturbed, and he's asked about them every time he's written. Do suggest something."

"I was going to suggest picketing," said Clovis.

"Picketing! You mean setting guards round the birds?"

"No; round Lanner. He can't find his way through those woods by night, and you could arrange that you or Evelyn or Jack or the German governess should be by his side in relays all day long. A fellow guest he could get rid of, but he couldn't very well shake off members of the household, and even the most determined collector would hardly go climbing after forbidden buzzards' eggs with a German governess hanging round his neck, so to speak."

Lanner, who had been lazily watching for an opportunity for prosecuting his courtship of the Coulterneb girl, found presently that his chances of getting her to himself for ten minutes even were non-existent. If the girl was ever alone he never was. His hostess had changed suddenly, as far as he was concerned, from the desirable type that lets her guests do nothing in the way that best pleases them, to the sort that drags them over the ground like so many harrows. She showed him the herb garden and the greenhouses, the village church, some water-colour sketches that her sister had done in Corsica, and the place where it was hoped that celery would grow later in the year. He was shown all the Aylesbury ducklings and the row of wooden hives where there would have been bees if there had not been bee disease. He was also taken to the end of a long lane and shown a distant mound whereon local tradition reported that the Danes had once pitched a camp. And when his hostess had to desert him temporarily for other duties he would find Evelyn walking solemnly by his side. Evelyn was fourteen and talked chiefly about good and evil, and of how much one might accomplish in the way of regenerating the world if one was thoroughly determined to do one's utmost. It was generally rather a relief when she was displaced by Jack, who was nine years old, and talked exclusively about the Balkan War without throwing any fresh light on its political or military history. The German governess told Lanner more about Schiller than he had ever heard in his life about any one person; it was perhaps his own fault for having told her that he was not interested in Goethe. When the governess went off picket duty the hostess was again on hand with a not-to-be-gainsaid invitation to visit the cottage of an old woman who remembered Charles James Fox; the woman had been dead for two or three years, but the cottage was still there. Lanner was called back to town earlier than he had originally intended.

Hugo did not bring off his affair with Betty Coulterneb. Whether she refused him or whether, as was more generally supposed, he did not get a chance of saying three consecutive words, has never been exactly ascertained. Anyhow, she is still the jolly Coulterneb girl.

The buzzards successfully reared two young ones, which were shot by a local hairdresser.

THE STAKE

"Ronnie is a great trial to me," said Mrs. Attray plaintively. "Only eighteen years old last February and already a confirmed gambler. I am sure I don't know where he inherits it from; his father never touched cards, and you know how little I play—a game of bridge on Wednesday afternoons in the winter, for threepence a hundred, and even that I shouldn't do if it wasn't that Edith always wants a fourth and would be certain to ask that detestable Jenkinham woman if she couldn't get me. I would much rather sit and talk any day than play bridge; cards are such a waste of time, I think. But as to Ronnie, bridge and baccarat and poker-patience are positively all that he thinks about. Of course I've done my best to stop it; I've asked the Norridrums not to let him play cards when he's over there, but you might as well ask the Atlantic Ocean to keep quiet for a crossing as expect them to bother about a mother's natural anxieties."

"Why do you let him go there?" asked Eleanor Saxelby.

"My dear," said Mrs. Attray, "I don't want to offend them. After all, they are my landlords and I have to look to them for anything I want done about the place; they were very accommodating about the new roof for the orchid house. And they lend me one of their cars when mine is out of order; you know how often it gets out of order."

"I don't know how often," said Eleanor, "but it must happen very frequently. Whenever I want you to take me anywhere in your car I am always told that there is something wrong with it, or else that the chauffeur has got neuralgia and you don't like to ask him to go out."

"He suffers quite a lot from neuralgia," said Mrs. Attray hastily. "Anyhow," she continued, "you can understand that I don't want to offend the Norridrums. Their household is the most rackety one in the county, and I believe no one even knows to an hour or two when any particular meal will appear on the table or what it will consist of when it does appear."

Eleanor Saxelby shuddered. She liked her meals to be of regular occurrence and assured proportions.

"Still," pursued Mrs. Attray, "whatever their own home life may be, as landlords and neighbours they are considerate and obliging, so I don't want to quarrel with them. Besides, if Ronnie didn't play cards there he'd be playing somewhere else."

"Not if you were firm with him," said Eleanor; "I believe in being firm."

"Firm? I am firm," exclaimed Mrs. Attray; "I am more than firm —I am farseeing. I've done everything I can think of it to prevent Ronnie from playing for money. I've stopped his allowance for the rest of the year, so he can't even gamble on credit, and I've subscribed a lump sum to the church offertory in his name instead of giving him instalments of small silver to put in the bag on Sundays. I wouldn't even let him have the money to tip the hunt servants with, but sent it by postal order. He was furiously sulky about it, but I reminded him of what happened to the ten shillings that I gave him for the Young Men's Endeavour League 'Self-Denial Week.'"

"What did happen to it?" asked Eleanor.

"Well, Ronnie did some preliminary endeavouring with it, on his own account, in connection with the Grand National. If it had come off, as he expressed it, he would have given the League twenty-five shillings and netted a comfortable commission for himself; as it was, that ten shillings was one of the things the League had to deny itself. Since then I've been careful not to let him have a penny piece in his hands."

"He'll get round that in some way," said Eleanor with quiet conviction; "he'll sell things."

"My dear, he's done all that is to be done in that direction already. He's got rid of his wrist-watch and his hunting flask and both his cigarette cases, and I shouldn't be surprised if he's wearing imitation-gold sleeve links instead of those his Aunt Rhoda gave him on his seventeenth birthday. He can't sell his clothes, of course, except his winter overcoat, and I've locked that up in the camphor cupboard on the pretext of preserving it from moth. I really don't see what else he can raise money on. I consider that I've been both firm and farseeing."

"Has he been at the Norridrums lately?" asked Eleanor.

"He was there yesterday afternoon and stayed to dinner," said Mrs. Attray. "I don't quite know when he came home, but I fancy it was late."

"Then depend on it he was gambling," said Eleanor, with the assured air of one who has few ideas and makes the most of them. "Late hours in the country always mean gambling."

"He can't gamble if he has no money and no chance of getting any," argued Mrs. Attray; "even if one plays for small stakes one must have a decent prospect of paying one's losses."

"He may have sold some of the Amherst pheasant chicks," suggested Eleanor; "they would fetch about ten or twelve shillings each, I dare say."

"Ronnie wouldn't do such a thing," said Mrs. Attray; "and anyhow I went and counted them this morning and they're all there. No," she continued, with the quiet satisfaction that comes from a sense of painstaking and merited achievement, "I fancy that Ronnie had to content himself with the rôle of onlooker last night, as far as the card-table was concerned."

"Is that clock right?" asked Eleanor, whose eyes had been straying restlessly towards the mantelpiece for some little time; "lunch is usually so punctual in your establishment."

"Three minutes past the half-hour," exclaimed Mrs. Attray; "cook must be preparing something unusually sumptuous in your honour. I am not in the secret; I've been out all the morning, you know."

Eleanor smiled forgivingly. A special effort by Mrs. Attray's cook was worth waiting a few minutes for.

As a matter of fact, the luncheon fare, when it made its tardy appearance, was distinctly unworthy of the reputation which the justly treasured cook had built up for herself. The soup alone would have sufficed to cast a gloom over any meal that it had inaugurated, and it was not redeemed by anything that followed. Eleanor said little, but when she spoke there was a hint of tears in her voice that was far more eloquent than outspoken denunciation would have been, and even the insouciant Ronald showed traces of depression when he tasted the rognons Saltikoff.

"Not quite the best luncheon I've enjoyed in your house," said Eleanor at last, when her final hope had flickered out with the savoury.

"My dear, it's the worst meal I've sat down to for years," said her hostess; "that last dish tasted principally of red pepper and wet toast. I'm awfully sorry. Is anything the matter in the kitchen, Pellin?" she asked of the attendant maid.

"Well, ma'am, the new cook hadn't hardly time to see to things properly, coming in so sudden–" commenced Pellin by way of explanation.

"The *new* cook!" screamed Mrs. Attray.

"Colonel Norridrum's cook, ma'am," said Pellin.

"What on earth do you mean? What is Colonel Norridrum's cook doing in my kitchen–and where is *my* cook?"

"Perhaps I can explain better than Pellin can," said Ronald hurriedly; "the fact is, I was dining at the Norridrum's yesterday, and they were wishing they had a swell cook like yours, just for today and tomorrow, while they've got some gourmet staying with them; their own cook is no earthly good–well, you've seen what she turns out when she's at all flurried. So I thought it would be rather sporting to play them at baccarat for the loan of our cook against a money stake, and I lost, that's all. I have had rotten luck at baccarat all this year."

The remainder of his explanation, of how he had assured the cooks that the temporary transfer had his mother's sanction, and had smuggled the one out and the other in during the maternal absence, was drowned in the outcry of scandalized upbraiding.

"If I had sold the woman into slavery there couldn't have been a bigger fuss about it," he confided afterwards to Bertie Norridrum, "and Eleanor Saxelby raged and ramped the louder of the two. I tell you what, I'll bet you two of the Amherst pheasants to five shillings that she refuses to have me as a partner at the croquet tournament. We're drawn together, you know."

This time he won his bet.

CLOVIS ON PARENTAL RESPONSIBILITIES

MARION EGGELBY sat talking to Clovis on the only subject that she ever willingly talked about—her offspring and their varied perfections and accomplishments. Clovis was not in what could be called a receptive mood; the younger generation of Eggelby, depicted in the glowing improbable colours of parent impressionism, aroused in him no enthusiasm. Mrs. Eggelby, on the other hand, was furnished with enthusiasm enough for two.

"You would like Eric," she said, argumentatively rather than hopefully. Clovis had intimated very unmistakably that he was unlikely to care extravagantly for either Amy or Willie. "Yes, I feel sure you would like Eric. Every one takes to him at once. You know, he always reminds me of that famous picture of the youthful David—I forget who it's by, but it's very well known."

"That would be sufficient to set me against him, if I saw much of him," said Clovis. "Just imagine at auction bridge, for instance, when one was trying to concentrate one's mind on what one's partner's original declaration had been, and to remember what suits one's opponents had originally discarded, what it would be like to have some one persistently reminding one of a picture of the youthful David. It would be simply maddening. If Eric did that I should detest him."

"Eric doesn't play bridge," said Mrs. Eggelby with dignity.

"Doesn't he?" asked Clovis; "why not?"

"None of my children have been brought up to play card games," said Mrs. Eggelby; "draughts and halma and those sorts of games I encourage. Eric is considered quite a wonderful draughts-player."

"You are strewing dreadful risks in the path of your family," said Clovis; "a friend of mine who is a prison chaplain told me that among the worst criminal cases that have come under his notice, men condemned to death or to long periods of penal servitude, there was not a single bridge-player. On the other hand, he knew at least two expert draughts-players among them."

"I really don't see what my boys have got to do with the criminal classes," said Mrs. Eggelby resentfully. "They have been most carefully brought up, I can assure you that."

"That shows that you were nervous as to how they would turn out," said Clovis. "Now, my mother never bothered about bringing me up. She just saw to it that I got whacked at decent intervals and was taught the difference between right and wrong; there is some difference, you know, but I've forgotten what it is."

"Forgotten the difference between right and wrong!" exclaimed Mrs. Eggelby.

"Well, you see, I took up natural history and a whole lot of other subjects at the same time, and one can't remember everything, can one? I used to know the difference between the Sardinian dormouse and the ordinary kind, and whether the wryneck arrives at our shores earlier than the cuckoo, or the other way round, and how long the walrus takes in growing to maturity; I dare say you knew all those sorts of things once, but I bet you've forgotten them."

"Those things are not important," said Mrs. Eggelby, "but—"

"The fact that we've both forgotten them proves that they *are* important," said Clovis; "you must have noticed that it's always the important things that one forgets, while the trivial, unnecessary facts of life stick in one's memory. There's my cousin, Editha Clubberly, for instance; I can never forget that her birthday is on the 12th of October. It's a matter of utter indifference to me on what date her birthday falls, or whether she was born at all; either fact seems to me absolutely trivial, or unnecessary—I've heaps of other cousins to go on with. On the other hand, when I'm staying with Hildegarde Shrubley I can never remember the important circumstance whether her first husband got his unenviable reputation on the Turf or the Stock Exchange, and that uncertainty rules Sport and Finance out of the conversation at once. One can never mention travel, either, because her second husband had to live permanently abroad."

"Mrs. Shrubley and I move in very different circles," said Mrs. Eggelby stiffly.

"No one who knows Hildegarde could possibly accuse her of

moving in a circle," said Clovis; "her view of life seems to be a non-stop run with an inexhaustible supply of petrol. If she can get some one else to pay for the petrol so much the better. I don't mind confessing to you that she has taught me more than any other woman I can think of."

"What kind of knowledge?" demanded Mrs. Eggelby, with the air a jury might collectively wear when finding a verdict without leaving the box.

"Well, among other things, she's introduced me to at least four different ways of cooking lobster," said Clovis gratefully. "That, of course, wouldn't appeal to you; people who abstain from the pleasures of the card-table never really appreciate the finer possibilities of the dining-table. I suppose their powers of enlightened enjoyment get atrophied from disuse."

"An aunt of mine was very ill after eating a lobster," said Mrs. Eggelby.

"I dare say, if we knew more of her history, we should find out that she'd often been ill before eating the lobster. Aren't you concealing the fact that she'd had measles and influenza and nervous headache and hysteria, and other things that aunts do have, long before she ate the lobster? Aunts that have never known a day's illness are very rare; in fact, I don't personally know of any. Of course if she ate it as a child of two weeks old it might have been her first illness—and her last. But if that was the case I think you should have said so."

"I must be going," said Mrs. Eggelby, in a tone which had been thoroughly sterilized of even perfunctory regret.

Clovis rose with an air of graceful reluctance.

"I have so enjoyed our little talk about Eric," he said; "I quite look forward to meeting him some day."

"Good-bye," said Mrs. Eggelby frostily; the supplementary remark which she made at the back of her throat was—

"I'll take care that you never shall!"

A HOLIDAY TASK

Kenelm Jerton entered the dining-hall of the Golden Galleon Hotel in the full crush of the luncheon hour. Nearly every seat was occupied, and small additional tables had been brought in, where floor space permitted, to accommodate late-comers, with the result that many of the tables were almost touching each other. Jerton was beckoned by a waiter to the only vacant table that was discernible, and took his seat with the uncomfortable and wholly groundless idea that every one in the room was staring at him. He was a youngish man of ordinary appearance, quiet of dress and unobtrusive of manner, and he could never wholly rid himself of the idea that a fierce light of public scrutiny beat on him as though he had been a notability or a super-nut. After he had ordered his lunch there came the unavoidable interval of waiting, with nothing to do but to stare at the flower-vase on his table and to be stared at (in imagination) by several flappers, some maturer beings of the same sex, and a satirical-looking Jew. In order to carry off the situation with some appearance of unconcern he became spuriously interested in the contents of the flower-vase.

"What is the name of those roses, d'you know?" he asked the waiter. The waiter was ready at all times to conceal his ignorance concerning items of the wine-list or *menu;* he was frankly ignorant as to the specific name of the roses.

"*Amy Silvester Partington,*" said a voice at Jerton's elbow.

The voice came from a pleasant-faced, well-dressed young woman who was sitting at a table that almost touched Jerton's. He thanked her hurriedly and nervously for the information, and made some inconsequent remark about the flowers.

"It is a curious thing," said the young woman, "that I should be able to tell you the name of those roses without an effort of memory, because if you were to ask me my name I should be utterly unable to give it to you."

Jerton had not harboured the least intention of extending his thirst for name-labels to his neighbour. After her rather remarkable announcement, however, he was obliged to say something in the way of polite inquiry.

"Yes," answered the lady, "I suppose it is a case of partial loss of memory. I was in the train coming down here; my ticket told me that I had come from Victoria and was bound for this place. I had a couple of five-pound notes and a sovereign on me, no visiting cards or any other means of identification, and no idea as to who I am. I can only hazily recollect that I have a title; I am Lady Somebody—beyond that my mind is a blank."

"Hadn't you any luggage with you?" asked Jerton.

"That is what I didn't know. I knew the name of this hotel and made up my mind to come here, and when the hotel porter who meets the trains asked if I had any luggage I had to invent a dressing-bag and dress-basket; I could always pretend that they had gone astray. I gave him the name of Smith, and presently he emerged from a confused pile of luggage and passengers with a dressing-bag and dress-basket labelled Kestrel-Smith. I had to take them; I don't see what else I could have done."

Jerton said nothing, but he rather wondered what the lawful owner of the baggage would do.

"Of course it was dreadful arriving at a strange hotel with the name of Kestrel-Smith, but it would have been worse to have arrived without luggage. Anyhow, I hate causing trouble."

Jerton had visions of harassed railway officials and distraught Kestrel-Smiths, but he made no attempt to clothe his mental picture in words. The lady continued her story.

"Naturally, none of my keys would fit the things, but I told an intelligent page boy that I had lost my key-ring, and he had the locks forced in a twinkling. Rather too intelligent, that boy; he will probably end in Dartmoor. The Kestrel-Smith toilet tools aren't up to much, but they are better than nothing."

"If you feel sure that you have a title," said Jerton, "why not get hold of a peerage and go right through it?"

"I tried that. I skimmed through the list of the House of Lords in 'Whitaker,' but a mere printed string of names conveys awfully little to one, you know. If you were an army officer and had lost your identity you might pore over the Army List for months without finding out who you were. I'm going on another tack; I'm trying to find out by various little tests who I am *not*—that will narrow the range of uncertainty down a bit. You may have noticed, for instance, that I'm lunching principally off lobster Newburg."

Jerton had not ventured to notice anything of the sort.

"It's an extravagance, because it's one of the most expensive dishes on the menu, but at any rate it proves that I'm not Lady Starping; she never touches shell-fish, and poor Lady Braddleshrub has no digestion at all; if I am *her* I shall certainly die in agony in the course of the afternoon, and the duty of finding out who I am will devolve on the press and the police and those sort of people; I shall be past caring. Lady Knewford doesn't know one rose from another and she hates men, so she wouldn't have spoken to you in any case; and Lady Mousehilton flirts with every man she meets—I haven't flirted with you, have I?"

Jerton hastily gave the required assurance.

"Well, you see," continued the lady, "that knocks four off the list at once."

"It'll be rather a lengthy process bringing the list down to one," said Jerton.

"Oh, but, of course, there are heaps of them that I couldn't possibly be—women who've got grandchildren or sons old enough to have celebrated their coming of age. I've only got to consider the ones about my own age. I tell you how you might help me this afternoon, if you don't mind; go through any of the back numbers of *Country Life* and those sort of papers that you can find in the smoking-room, and see if you come across my portrait with infant son or anything of that sort. It won't take you ten minutes. I'll meet you in the lounge about tea-time. Thanks awfully."

And the Fair Unknown, having graciously pressed Jerton into the search for her lost identity, rose and left the room. As she passed the young man's table she halted for a moment and whispered:

"Did you notice that I tipped the waiter a shilling? We can cross Lady Ulwight off the list; she would have died rather than do that."

At five o'clock Jerton made his way to the hotel lounge; he had spent a diligent but fruitless quarter of an hour among the illustrated weeklies in the smoking-room. His new acquaintance was seated at a small tea-table, with a waiter hovering in attendance.

"China tea or Indian?" she asked as Jerton came up.

"China, please, and nothing to eat. Have you discovered anything?"

"Only negative information. I'm not Lady Befnal. She disapproves dreadfully at any form of gambling, so when I recognized a well-known book-maker in the hotel lobby I went and put a tenner on an unnamed filly by William the Third out of Mitrovitza for the three-fifteen race. I suppose the fact of the animal being nameless was what attracted me."

"Did it win?" asked Jerton.

"No, came in fourth, the most irritating thing a horse can do when you've backed it win or place. Anyhow, I know now that I'm not Lady Befnal."

"It seems to me that the knowledge was rather dearly bought," commented Jerton.

"Well, yes, it has rather cleared me out," admitted the identity-seeker; "a florin is about all I've got left on me. The lobster Newburg made my lunch rather an expensive one, and, of course, I had to tip that boy for what he did to the Kestrel-Smith locks. I've got rather a useful idea, though. I feel certain that I belong to the Pivot Club; I'll go back to town and ask the hall porter there if there are any letters for me. He knows all the members by sight, and if there are any letters or telephone messages waiting for me, of course that will solve the problem. If he says there aren't any, I shall say: 'You know who I am, don't you?' so I'll find out anyway."

The plan seemed a sound one; a difficulty in its execution suggested itself to Jerton.

"Of course," said the lady, when he hinted at the obstacle, "there's my fare back to town, and my bill here and cabs and things. If you lend me three pounds that ought to see me through comfortably. Thanks ever so. Then there is the question of that luggage: I don't want to be saddled with that for the rest of my life. I'll have it brought down to the hall and you can pretend to mount guard over it while I'm writing a letter. Then I shall just slip away to the station, and you can wander off to the smoking-room, and they can do what they like with the things. They'll advertise them after a bit and the owner can claim them."

Jerton acquiesced in the manœuvre, and duly mounted guard over the luggage while its temporary owner slipped unobtrusively out of the hotel. Her departure was not, however, altogether unnoticed. Two gentlemen were strolling past Jerton, and one of them remarked to the other:

"Did you see that tall young woman in grey who went out just now? She is the Lady–"

His promenade carried him out of earshot at the critical moment when he was about to disclose the elusive identity. The Lady Who? Jerton could scarcely run after a total stranger, break into his conversation, and ask him for information concerning a chance passer-by. Besides, it was desirable that he should keep up the appearance of looking after the luggage. In a minute or two, however, the important personage, the man who knew, came strolling back alone. Jerton summoned up all his courage and waylaid him.

"I think I heard you say you knew the lady who went out of the hotel a few minutes ago, a tall lady, dressed in grey. Excuse me for asking if you could tell me her name; I've been talking to her for half an hour; she—er—she knows all my people and seems to know me, so I suppose I've met her somewhere before, but I'm blest if I can put a name to her. Could you—?"

"Certainly. She's a Mrs. Stroope."

"*Mrs.?*" queried Jerton.

"Yes, she's the Lady Champion at golf in my part of the world. An awful good sort, and goes about a good deal in Society, but she has an awkward habit of losing her memory every now and then, and gets into all sorts of fixes. She's furious, too, if you make any allusion to it afterwards. Good day, sir."

The stranger passed on his way, and before Jerton had had time to assimilate his information he found his whole attention centred on an angry-looking lady who was making loud and fretful-seeming inquiries of the hotel clerks.

"Has any luggage been brought here from the station by mistake, a dress-basket and dressing-case, with the name Kestrel-Smith? It can't be traced anywhere. I saw it put in at Victoria, that I'll swear. Why—there *is* my luggage! and the locks have been tampered with!"

Jerton heard no more. He fled down to the Turkish bath, and stayed there for hours.

THE STALLED OX

THEOPHIL ESHLEY was an artist by profession, a cattle painter by force of environment. It is not to be supposed that he lived on a ranch or a dairy farm, in an atmosphere pervaded with horn and hoof, milking-stool, and branding-iron. His home was in a park-like, villa-dotted district that only just escaped the reproach of being suburban. On one side of his garden there abutted a small, picturesque meadow, in which an enterprising neighbour pastured some small picturesque cows of the Channel Island persuasion. At noonday in summertime the cows stood knee-deep in tall meadow-grass under the shade of a group of walnut trees, with the sunlight falling in dappled patches on their mouse-sleek coats. Eshley had conceived and executed a dainty picture of two reposeful milch-cows in a setting of walnut tree and meadow-grass and filtered sunbeam, and the Royal Academy had duly exposed the same on the walls of its Summer Exhibition. The Royal Academy encourages orderly, methodical habits in its children. Eshley had painted a successful and acceptable picture of cattle drowsing picturesquely under walnut trees, and as he had begun, so, of necessity, he went on. His "Noontide Peace," a study of two dun cows under a walnut tree, was followed by "A Mid-day Sanctuary," a study of a walnut tree, with two dun cows under it. In due succession there came "Where the Gad-Flies Cease from Troubling," "The Haven of the Herd," and "A Dream in Dairyland," studies of walnut trees and dun cows. His two attempts to break away from his own tradition were signal failures: "Turtle Doves Alarmed by Sparrow-hawk" and "Wolves on the Roman Campagna" came back to his studio in the guise of abominable heresies, and Eshley climbed back into grace and the public gaze with "A Shaded Nook Where Drowsy Milkers Dream."

On a fine afternoon in late autumn he was putting some finishing touches to a study of meadow weeds when his neighbour, Adela Pingsford, assailed the outer door of his studio with loud peremptory knockings.

"There is an ox in my garden," she announced, in explanation of the tempestuous intrusion.

"An ox," said Eshley blankly, and rather fatuously; "what kind of ox?"

"Oh, I don't know what kind," snapped the lady. "A common or garden ox, to use the slang expression. It is the garden part of it that I object to. My garden has just been put straight for the winter, and an ox roaming about in it won't improve matters. Besides, there are the chrysanthemums just coming into flower."

"How did it get into the garden?" asked Eshley.

"I imagine it came in by the gate," said the lady impatiently; "it couldn't have climbed the walls, and I don't suppose any one dropped it from an aeroplane as a Bovril advertisement. The immediately important question is not how it got in, but how to get it out."

"Won't it go?" said Eshley.

"If it was anxious to go," said Adela Pingsford rather angrily, "I should not have come here to chat with you about it. I'm practically all alone; the housemaid is having her afternoon out and the cook is lying down with an attack of neuralgia. Anything that I may have learned at school or in after life about how to remove a large ox from a small garden seems to have escaped from my memory now. All I could think of was that you were a near neighbour and a cattle painter, presumably more or less familiar with the subjects that you painted, and that you might be of some slight assistance. Possibly I was mistaken."

"I paint dairy cows, certainly," admitted Eshley, "but I cannot claim to have had any experience in rounding up stray oxen. I've seen it done on a cinema film, of course, but there were always horses and lots of other accessories; besides, one never knows how much of those pictures are faked."

Adela Pingsford said nothing, but led the way to her garden. It was normally a fair-sized garden, but it looked small in comparison with the ox, a huge mottled brute, dull red about the head and shoulders, passing to dirty white on the flanks and hind-quarters, with shaggy ears and large blood-shot eyes. It bore about as much resemblance to the dainty paddock heifers that Eshley was accustomed to paint as the chief of a Kurdish nomad clan would to a Japanese tea-shop girl. Eshley stood very near the gate while he studied the animal's appearance and demeanour. Adela Pingsford continued to say nothing.

"It's eating a chrysanthemum," said Eshley at last, when the silence had become unbearable.

"How observant you are," said Adela bitterly. "You seem to notice everything. As a matter of fact, it has got six chrysanthemums in its mouth at the present moment."

The necessity for doing something was becoming imperative. Eshley took a step or two in the direction of the animal, clapped his hands, and made noises of the "Hish" and "Shoo" variety. If the ox heard them it gave no outward indication of the fact.

"If any hens should ever stray into my garden," said Adela, "I should certainly send for you to frighten them out. You 'shoo' beautifully. Meanwhile, do you mind trying to drive that ox away? That is a *Mademoiselle Louise Bichot* that he's begun on now," she added in icy calm, as a glowing orange head was crushed into the huge munching mouth.

"Since you have been so frank about the variety of the chrysanthemum," said Eshley, "I don't mind telling you that this is an Ayrshire ox."

The icy calm broke down; Adela Pingsford used language that sent the artist instinctively a few feet nearer to the ox. He picked up a pea-stick and flung it with some determination against the animal's mottled flanks. The operation of mashing *Mademoiselle Louise Bichot* into a petal salad was suspended for a long moment, while the ox gazed with concentrated inquiry at the stick-thrower. Adela gazed with equal concentration and more obvious hostility at the same focus. As the beast neither lowered its head nor stamped its feet Eshley ventured on another javelin exercise with another pea-stick. The ox seemed to realize at once that it was to go; it gave a hurried final pluck at the bed where the chrysanthemums had been, and strode swiftly up the garden. Eshley ran to head it towards the gate, but only succeeded in quickening its pace from a walk to a lumbering trot. With an air of inquiry, but with no real hesitation, it crossed the tiny strip of turf that the charitable called the croquet lawn, and pushed its way through the open French window into the morning-room. Some chrysanthemums and other autumn herbage stood about the room in vases, and the animal resumed its browsing operations; all the same, Eshley fancied that the beginnings of a hunted look had come into its eyes, a look that counselled respect. He discontinued his attempt to interfere with its choice of surroundings.

"Mr. Eshley," said Adela in a shaking voice, "I asked you to drive that beast out of my garden, but I did not ask you to drive it into my house. If I must have it anywhere on the premises I prefer the garden to the morning-room."

"Cattle drives are not in my line," said Eshley; "if I remember I told you so at the outset."

"I quite agree," retorted the lady, "painting pretty pictures of pretty little cows is what you're suited for. Perhaps you'd like to do a nice sketch of that ox making itself at home in my morning-room?"

This time it seemed as if the worm had turned; Eshley began striding away.

"Where are you going?" screamed Adela.

"To fetch implements," was the answer.

"Implements? I won't have you use a lasso. The room will be wrecked if there's a struggle."

But the artist marched out of the garden. In a couple of minutes he returned, laden with easel, sketching-stool, and painting materials.

"Do you mean to say that you're going to sit quietly down and paint that brute while it's destroying my morning-room?" gasped Adela.

"It was your suggestion," said Eshley, setting his canvas in position.

"I forbid it; I absolutely forbid it!" stormed Adela.

"I don't see what standing you have in the matter," said the artist; "you can hardly pretend that it's your ox, even by adoption."

"You seem to forget that it's in my morning-room, eating my flowers," came the raging retort.

"You seem to forget that the cook has neuralgia," said Eshley; "she may be just dozing off into a merciful sleep and your outcry will waken her. Consideration for others should be the guiding principle of people in our station of life."

"The man is mad!" exclaimed Adela tragically. A moment later it was Adela herself who appeared to go mad. The ox had finished the vase-flowers and the cover of *Israel Kalisch,* and appeared to be thinking of leaving its rather restricted quarters. Eshley noticed its restlessness and promptly flung it some bunches of Virginia creeper leaves as an inducement to continue the sitting.

"I forget how the proverb runs," he observed; "something about 'better a dinner of herbs than a stalled ox where hate is.' We seem to have all the ingredients for the proverb ready to hand."

"I shall go to the Public Library and get them to telephone for the police," announced Adela, and, raging audibly, she departed.

Some minutes later the ox, awakening probably to the suspicion that oil cake and chopped mangold was waiting for it in some appointed byre, stepped with much precaution out of the morning-room, stared with grave inquiry at the no longer obtrusive and pea-stick-throwing human, and then lumbered heavily but swiftly out of the garden. Eshley packed up his tools and followed the animal's example and "Larkdene" was left to neuralgia and the cook.

The episode was the turning-point in Eshley's artistic career. His remarkable picture, "Ox in a Morning-room, Late Autumn," was one of the sensations and successes of the next Paris Salon, and when it was subsequently exhibited at Munich it was bought by the Bavarian Government, in the teeth of the spirited bidding of three meat-extract firms. From that moment his success was continuous and assured, and the Royal Academy was thankful, two years later, to give a conspicuous position on its walls to his large canvas "Barbary Apes Wrecking a Boudoir."

Eshley presented Adela Pingsford with a new copy of *Israel Kalisch,* and a couple of finely flowering plants of *Madame André Blusset,* but nothing in the nature of a real reconciliation has taken place between them.

THE STORY-TELLER

It was a hot afternoon, and the railway carriage was correspondingly sultry, and the next stop was at Templecombe, nearly an hour ahead. The occupants of the carriage were a small girl, and a smaller girl, and a small boy. An aunt belonging to the children occupied one corner seat, and the further corner seat on the opposite side was occupied by a bachelor who was a stranger to their party, but the small girls and the small boy emphatically occupied the compartment. Both the aunt and the children were conversational in a limited, persistent way, reminding one of the attentions of a housefly that refused to be discouraged. Most of the aunt's remarks seemed to begin with "Don't," and nearly all of the children's remarks began with "Why?" The bachelor said nothing out loud.

"Don't, Cyril, don't," exclaimed the aunt, as the small boy began smacking the cushions of the seat, producing a cloud of dust at each blow.

"Come and look out of the window," she added.

The child moved reluctantly to the window. "Why are those sheep being driven out of that field?" he asked.

"I expect they are being driven to another field where there is more grass," said the aunt weakly.

"But there is lots of grass in that field," protested the boy; "there's nothing else but grass there. Aunt, there's lots of grass in that field."

"Perhaps the grass in the other field is better," suggested the aunt fatuously.

"Why is it better?" came the swift, inevitable question.

"Oh, look at those cows!" exclaimed the aunt. Nearly every field along the line had contained cows or bullocks, but she spoke as though she were drawing attention to a rarity.

"Why is the grass in the other field better?" persisted Cyril.

The frown on the bachelor's face was deepening to a scowl. He was a hard, unsympathetic man, the aunt decided in her mind. She was utterly unable to come to any satisfactory decision about the grass in the other field.

The smaller girl created a diversion by beginning to recite "On the Road to Mandalay." She only knew the first line, but she put her limited knowledge to the fullest possible use. She repeated the line over and over again in a dreamy but resolute and very audible voice; it seemed to the bachelor as though some one had had a bet with her that she could not repeat the line aloud two thousand times without stopping. Whoever it was who had made the wager was likely to lose his bet.

"Come over here and listen to a story," said the aunt, when the bachelor had looked twice at her and once at the communication cord.

The children moved listlessly towards the aunt's end of the carriage. Evidently her reputation as a story-teller did not rank high in their estimation.

In a low, confidential voice, interrupted at frequent intervals by loud, petulant questions from her listeners, she began an unenterprising and deplorably uninteresting story about a little girl who was good, and made friends with every one on account of her goodness, and was finally saved from a mad bull by a number of rescuers who admired her moral character.

"Wouldn't they have saved her if she hadn't been good?" demanded the bigger of the small girls. It was exactly the question that the bachelor had wanted to ask.

"Well, yes," admitted the aunt lamely, "but I don't think they would have run quite so fast to her help if they had not liked her so much."

"It's the stupidest story I've ever heard," said the bigger of the small girls, with immense conviction.

"I didn't listen after the first bit, it was so stupid," said Cyril.

The smaller girl made no actual comment on the story, but she had long ago recommenced a murmured repetition of her favourite line.

"You don't seem to be a success as a story-teller," said the bachelor suddenly from his corner.

The aunt bristled in instant defence at this unexpected attack.

"It's a very difficult thing to tell stories that children can both understand and appreciate," she said stiffly.

"I don't agree with you," said the bachelor.

"Perhaps *you* would like to tell them a story," was the aunt's retort.

"Tell us a story," demanded the bigger of the small girls.

"Once upon a time," began the bachelor, "there was a little girl called Bertha, who was extraordinarily good."

The children's momentarily-aroused interest began at once to flicker; all stories seemed dreadfully alike, no matter who told them.

"She did all that she was told, she was always truthful, she kept her clothes clean, ate milk puddings as though they were jam tarts, learned her lessons perfectly, and was polite in her manners."

"Was she pretty?" asked the bigger of the small girls.

"Not as pretty as any of you," said the bachelor, "but she was horribly good."

There was a wave of reaction in favour of the story; the word horrible in connection with goodness was a novelty that commended itself. It seemed to introduce a ring of truth that was absent from the aunt's tales of infant life.

"She was so good," continued the bachelor, "that she won several medals for goodness, which she always wore, pinned on to her dress. There was a medal for obedience, another medal for punctuality, and a third for good behaviour. They were large metal medals and they clicked against one another as she walked. No other child in the town where she lived had as many as three medals, so everybody knew that she must be an extra good child."

"Horribly good," quoted Cyril.

"Everybody talked about her goodness, and the Prince of the country got to hear about it, and he said that as she was so very good she might be allowed once a week to walk in his park, which was just outside the town. It was a beautiful park, and no children were ever allowed in it, so it was a great honour for Bertha to be allowed to go there."

"Were there any sheep in the park?" demanded Cyril.

"No," said the bachelor, "there were no sheep."

"Why weren't there any sheep?" came the inevitable question arising out of that answer.

The aunt permitted herself a smile, which might almost have been described as a grin.

"There were no sheep in the park," said the bachelor, "because the Prince's mother had once had a dream that her son would either be killed by a sheep or else by a clock falling on him. For that reason the Prince never kept a sheep in his park or a clock in his palace."

The aunt suppressed a gasp of admiration.

"Was the Prince killed by a sheep or by a clock?" asked Cyril.

"He is still alive, so we can't tell whether the dream will come true," said the bachelor unconcernedly; "anyway, there were no sheep in the park, but there were lots of little pigs running all over the place."

"What colour were they?"

"Black with white faces, white with black spots, black all over, grey with white patches, and some were white all over."

The story-teller paused to let a full idea of the park's treasures sink into the children's imaginations; then he resumed:

"Bertha was rather sorry to find that there were no flowers in the park. She had promised her aunts, with tears in her eyes, that she would not pick any of the kind Prince's flowers, and she had meant to keep her promise, so of course it made her feel silly to find that there were no flowers to pick."

"Why weren't there any flowers?"

"Because the pigs had eaten them all," said the bachelor promptly. "The gardeners had told the Prince that you couldn't have pigs and flowers, so he decided to have pigs and no flowers."

There was a murmur of approval at the excellence of the Prince's decision; so many people would have decided the other way.

"There were lots of other delightful things in the park. There were ponds with gold and blue and green fish in them, and trees with beautiful parrots that said clever things at a moment's notice, and humming birds that hummed all the popular tunes of the day. Bertha walked up and down and enjoyed herself immensely, and thought to herself: 'If I were not so extraordinarily good I should not have been allowed to come into this beautiful park and enjoy all that there is to be seen in it,' and her three medals clinked against one another as she walked and helped to remind her how very good she really was. Just then an enormous wolf came prowling into the park to see if it could catch a fat little pig for its supper."

"What colour was it?" asked the children, amid an immediate quickening of interest.

"Mud-colour all over, with a black tongue and pale grey eyes that gleamed with unspeakable ferocity. The first thing that it saw in the park was Bertha; her pinafore was so spotlessly white and clean that it could be seen from a great distance. Bertha saw the wolf and saw that it was stealing towards her, and she began to wish that she had never been allowed to come into the park. She ran as hard as she could, and the wolf came after her with huge leaps and bounds. She managed to reach a shrubbery of myrtle bushes and she hid herself in one of the thickest of the bushes. The wolf came sniffing among the branches, its black tongue lolling out of its mouth and its pale grey eyes glaring with rage. Bertha was terribly frightened, and thought to herself: 'If I had not been so extraordinarily good I should have been safe in the town at this moment.' However, the scent of the myrtle was so strong that the wolf could not sniff out where Bertha was hiding, and the bushes were so thick that he might have hunted about in them for a long time without catching sight of her, so he thought he might as well go off and catch a little pig instead. Bertha was trembling very much at having the wolf prowling and sniffing so near her, and as she trembled the medal for obedience clinked against the medals for good conduct and punctuality. The wolf was just moving away when he heard the sound of the medals clinking and stopped to listen; they clinked again in a bush quite near him. He dashed into the bush, his pale grey eyes gleaming with ferocity and triumph, and dragged Bertha out and devoured her to the last morsel. All that was left of her were her shoes, bits of clothing, and the three medals for goodness."

"Were any of the little pigs killed?"

"No, they all escaped."

"The story began badly," said the smaller of the small girls, "but it had a beautiful ending."

"It is the most beautiful story that I ever heard," said the bigger of the small girls, with immense decision.

"It is the *only* beautiful story I have ever heard," said Cyril.

A dissentient opinion came from the aunt.

"A most improper story to tell young children! You have undermined the effect of years of careful teaching."

"At any rate," said the bachelor, collecting his belongings preparatory to leaving the carriage, "I kept them quiet for ten minutes, which was more than you were able to do."

"Unhappy woman!" he observed to himself as he walked down the platform of Templecombe station; "for the next six months or so those children will assail her in public with demands for an improper story!"

A DEFENSIVE DIAMOND

TREDDLEFORD sat in an easeful arm-chair in front of a slumberous fire, with a volume of verse in his hand and the comfortable consciousness that outside the club windows the rain was dripping and pattering with persistent purpose. A chill, wet October afternoon was emerging into a black, wet October evening, and the club smoking-room seemed warmer and cozier by contrast. It was an afternoon on which to be wafted away from one's climatic surroundings, and *The Golden Journey to Samarkand* promised to bear Treddleford well and bravely into other lands and under other skies. He had already migrated from London the rain-swept to Bagdad the Beautiful, and stood by the Sun Gate "in the olden time" when an icy breath of imminent annoyance seemed to creep between the book and himself. Amblecope, the man with the restless, prominent eyes and the mouth ready mobilized for conversational openings, had planted himself in a neighbouring arm-chair. For a twelvemonth and some odd weeks Treddleford had skilfully avoided making the acquaintance of his voluble fellow-clubman; he had marvellously escaped from the infliction of his relentless record of tedious personal achievements, or alleged achievements, on golf links, turf, and gaming table, by flood and field and covert-side. Now his season of immunity was coming to an end. There was no escape; in another moment he would be numbered among those who knew Amblecope to speak to—or rather, to suffer being spoken to.

The intruder was armed with a copy of *Country Life*, not for purposes of reading, but as an aid to conversational ice-breaking.

"Rather a good portrait of Throstlewing," he remarked explosively, turning his large challenging eyes on Treddleford; "somehow it reminds me very much of Yellowstep, who was supposed to be such a good thing for the Grand Prix in 1903. Curious race that was; I suppose I've seen every race for the Grand Prix for the last–"

"Be kind enough never to mention the Grand Prix in my hearing," said Treddleford desperately; "it awakens acutely distressing memories. I can't explain why without going into a long and complicated story."

"Oh, certainly, certainly," said Amblecope hastily; long and complicated stories that were not told by himself were abominable in his eyes. He turned the pages of *Country Life* and became spuriously interested in the picture of a Mongolian pheasant.

"Not a bad representation of the Mongolian variety," he exclaimed, holding it up for his neighbour's inspection. "They do very well in some covers. Take some stopping too once they're fairly on the wing. I suppose the biggest bag I ever made in two successive days–"

"My aunt, who owns the greater part of Lincolnshire," broke in Treddleford, with dramatic abruptness, "possesses perhaps the most remarkable record in the way of a pheasant bag that has ever been achieved. She is seventy-five and can't hit a thing, but she always goes out with the guns. When I say she can't hit a thing, I don't mean to say that she doesn't occasionally endanger the lives of her fellow-guns, because that wouldn't be true. In fact, the chief Government Whip won't allow Ministerial M.P.'s to go out with her; 'We don't want to incur by-elections needlessly,' he quite reasonably observed. Well, the other day she winged a pheasant, and brought it to earth with a feather or two knocked out of it; it was a runner, and my aunt saw herself in danger of being done out of about the only bird she'd hit during the present reign. Of course she wasn't going to stand that; she followed it through bracken and brushwood, and when it took to the open country and started across a ploughed field she jumped on to the shooting pony and went after it. The chase was a long one, and when my aunt at last ran the bird to a standstill she was nearer home than she was to the shooting party; she had left that some five miles behind her."

"Rather a long run for a wounded pheasant," snapped Amblecope.

"The story rests on my aunt's authority," said Treddleford coldly, "and she is local vice-president of the Young Women's Christian Association. She trotted three miles or so to her home, and it was not till the middle of the afternoon that it was discovered that the lunch for the entire shooting party was in a pannier attached to the pony's saddle. Anyway, she got her bird."

"Some birds, of course, take a lot of killing," said Amblecope; "so do some fish. I remember once I was fishing in the Exe, lovely trout stream, lots of fish, though they don't run to any great size—"

"One of them did," announced Treddleford, with emphasis. "My uncle, the Bishop of Southmolton, came across a giant trout in a pool just off the main stream of the Exe near Ugworthy; he tried it with every kind of fly and worm every day for three weeks without an atom of success, and then Fate intervened on his behalf. There was a low stone bridge just over this pool, and on the last day of his fishing holiday a motor van ran violently into the parapet and turned completely over; no one was hurt, but part of the parapet was knocked away, and the entire load that the van was carrying was pitched over and fell a little way into the pool. In a couple of minutes the giant trout was flapping and twisting on bare mud at the bottom of a waterless pool, and my uncle was able to walk down to him and fold him to his breast. The van-load consisted of blotting-paper, and every drop of water in that pool had been sucked up into the mass of spilt cargo."

There was silence for nearly half a minute in the smoking-room, and Treddleford began to let his mind steal back towards the golden road that led to Samarkand. Amblecope, however, rallied, and remarked in a rather tired and dispirited voice:

"Talking of motor accidents, the narrowest squeak I ever had was the other day, motoring with old Tommy Yarby in North Wales. Awfully good sort, old Yarby, thorough good sportsman, and the best—"

"It was in North Wales," said Treddleford, "that my sister met with her sensational carriage accident last year. She was on her way to a garden-party at Lady Nineveh's, about the only garden-party that ever comes to pass in those parts in the course of the year, and therefore a thing that she would have been very sorry to miss.

She was driving a young horse that she'd only bought a week or two previously, warranted to be perfectly steady with motor traffic, bicycles, and other common objects of the roadside. The animal lived up to its reputation, and passed the most explosive of motor-bikes with an indifference that almost amounted to apathy. However, I suppose we all draw the line somewhere, and this particular cob drew it at travelling wild beast shows. Of course my sister didn't know that, but she knew it very distinctly when she turned a sharp corner and found herself in a mixed company of camels, piebald horses, and canary-coloured vans. The dog-cart was overturned in a ditch and kicked to splinters, and the cob went home across country. Neither my sister nor the groom was hurt, but the problem of how to get to the Nineveh garden-party, some three miles distant, seemed rather difficult to solve; once there, of course, my sister would easily find some one to drive her home. 'I suppose you wouldn't care for the loan of a couple of my camels?' the showman suggested, in humorous sympathy. 'I would,' said my sister, who had ridden camel-back in Egypt, and she overruled the objections of the groom, who hadn't. She picked out two of the most presentable-looking of the beasts and had them dusted and made as tidy as was possible at short notice, and set out for the Nineveh mansion. You may imagine the sensation that her small but imposing caravan created when she arrived at the hall door. The entire garden-party flocked up to gape. My sister was rather glad to slip down from her camel, and the groom was thankful to scramble down from his. Then young Billy Doulton, of the Dragoon Guards, who has been a lot at Aden and thinks he knows camel-language backwards, thought he would show off by making the beasts kneel down in orthodox fashion. Unfortunately camel words-of-command are not the same all the world over; these were magnificent Turkestan camels, accustomed to stride up the stony terraces of mountain passes, and when Doulton shouted at them they went side by side up the front steps, into the entrance hall, and up the grand staircase. The German governess met them just at the turn of the corridor. The Ninevehs nursed her with devoted attention for weeks, and when I last heard from them she was well enough to go about her duties again, but the doctor says she will always suffer from Hagenbeck heart."

Amblecope got up from his chair and moved to another part of the room. Treddleford reopened his book and betook himself once more across

> The dragon-green, the luminous, the dark, the serpent-haunted sea.

For a blessed half-hour he disported himself in imagination by the "gay Aleppo-Gate," and listened to the bird-voiced singing-man. Then the world of today called him back; a page summoned him to speak with a friend on the telephone.

As Treddleford was about to pass out of the room he encountered Amblecope, also passing out, on his way to the billiard-room, where, perchance, some luckless wight might be secured and held fast to listen to the number of his attendances at the Grand Prix, with subsequent remarks on Newmarket and the Cambridgeshire. Amblecope made as if to pass out first, but a new-born pride was surging in Treddleford's breast and he waved him back.

"I believe I take precedence," he said coldly; "you are merely the club Bore; I am the club Liar."

THE ELK

TERESA, Mrs. Thropplestance, was the richest and most intractable old woman in the county of Woldshire. In her dealings with the world in general her manner suggested a blend between a Mistress of the Robes and a Master of Fox-hounds, with the vocabulary of both. In her domestic circle she comported herself in the arbitrary style that one attributes, probably without the least justification, to an American political Boss in the bosom of his caucus. The late Theodore Thropplestance had left her, some thirty-five years ago, in absolute possession of a considerable fortune, a large landed property, and a gallery full of valuable pictures. In those intervening years she had outlived her son and quarrelled with her elder grandson, who had married without her consent or approval. Bertie Thropplestance, her younger grandson, was the heir-designate to her property, and as such he was a centre of interest and concern to some half-hundred ambitious mothers with daughters of marriageable age. Bertie was an amiable, easy-going young man, who was quite ready to marry any one who was favourably recommended to his notice, but he was not going to waste his time in falling in love with any one who would come under his grandmother's veto. The favourable recommendation would have to come from Mrs. Thropplestance.

Teresa's house-parties were always rounded off with a plentiful garnishing of presentable young women and alert, attendant mothers, but the old lady was emphatically discouraging whenever any one of her girl guests became at all likely to outbid the others as a possible granddaughter-in-law. It was the inheritance of her fortune and estate that was in question, and she was evidently disposed to exercise and enjoy her powers of selection and rejection to the utmost. Bertie's preferences did not greatly matter; he was of the sort who can be stolidly happy with any kind of wife; he had cheerfully put up with his grandmother all his life, so he was not likely to fret and fume over anything that might befall him in the way of a helpmate.

The party that gathered under Teresa's roof in Christmas week of the year nineteen-hundred-and-something was of smaller proportions than usual, and Mrs. Yonelet, who formed one of the party, was inclined to deduce hopeful augury from this circumstance. Dora Yonelet and Bertie were so obviously made for one another, she confided to the vicar's wife, and if the old lady were accustomed to seeing them about a lot together she might adopt the view that they would make a suitable married couple.

"People soon get used to an idea if it is dangled constantly before their eyes," said Mrs. Yonelet hopefully, "and the more often Teresa sees those young people together, happy in each other's company, the more she will get to take a kindly interest in Dora as a possible and desirable wife for Bertie."

"My dear," said the vicar's wife resignedly, "my own Sybil was thrown together with Bertie under the most romantic circumstances–I'll tell you about it some day–but it made no impression whatever on Teresa; she put her foot down in the most uncompromising fashion, and Sybil married an Indian civilian."

"Quite right of her," said Mrs. Yonelet with vague approval; "it's what any girl of spirit would have done. Still, that was a year or two ago, I believe; Bertie is older now, and so is Teresa. Naturally she must be anxious to see him settled."

The vicar's wife reflected that Teresa seemed to be the one person who showed no immediate anxiety to supply Bertie with a wife, but she kept the thought to herself.

Mrs. Yonelet was a woman of resourceful energy and generalship; she involved the other members of the house-party, the deadweight, so to speak, in all manner of exercises and occupations that segregated them from Bertie and Dora, who were left to their own devisings—that is to say, to Dora's devisings and Bertie's accommodating acquiescence. Dora helped in the Christmas decorations of the parish church, and Bertie helped her to help. Together they fed the swans, till the birds went on a dyspepsia-strike, together they played billiards, together they photographed the village almshouses, and, at a respectful distance, the tame elk that browsed in solitary aloofness in the park. It was "tame" in the sense that it had long ago discarded the least vestige of fear of the human race; nothing in its record encouraged its human neighbours to feel a reciprocal confidence.

Whatever sport or exercise or occupation Bertie and Dora indulged in together was unfailingly chronicled and advertised by Mrs. Yonelet for the due enlightenment of Bertie's grandmother.

"Those two inseparables have just come in from a bicycle ride," she would announce; "quite a picture they make, so fresh and glowing after their spin."

"A picture needing words," would be Teresa's private comment, and as far as Bertie was concerned she was determined that the words should remain unspoken.

On the afternoon after Christmas Day Mrs. Yonelet dashed into the drawing-room, where her hostess was sitting amid a circle of guests and tea-cups and muffin-dishes. Fate had placed what seemed like a trump-card in the hands of the patiently manœuvring mother. With eyes blazing with excitement and a voice heavily escorted with exclamation marks she made a dramatic announcement.

"Bertie has saved Dora from the elk!"

In swift, excited sentences, broken with maternal emotion, she gave supplementary information as to how the treacherous animal had ambushed Dora as she was hunting for a strayed golf ball, and how Bertie had dashed to her rescue with a stable fork and driven the beast off in the nick of time.

"It was touch and go! She threw her niblick at it, but that didn't stop it. In another moment she would have been crushed beneath its hoofs," panted Mrs. Yonelet.

"The animal is not safe," said Teresa, handing her agitated guest a cup of tea. "I forget if you take sugar. I suppose the solitary life it leads has soured its temper. There are muffins in the grate. It's not my fault; I've tried to get it a mate for ever so long. You don't know of any one with a lady elk for sale or exchange, do you?" she asked the company generally.

But Mrs. Yonelet was in no humour to listen to talk of elk marriages. The mating of two human beings was the subject uppermost in her mind, and the opportunity for advancing her pet project was too valuable to be neglected.

"Teresa," she exclaimed impressively, "after those two young people have been thrown together so dramatically, nothing can be quite the same again between them. Bertie has done more than save Dora's life; he has earned her affection. One cannot help feeling that Fate has consecrated them for one another."

"Exactly what the vicar's wife said when Bertie saved Sybil from the elk a year or two ago," observed Teresa placidly; "I pointed out to her that he had rescued Mirabel Hicks from the same predicament a few months previously, and that priority really belonged to the gardener's boy, who had been rescued in the January of that year. There is a good deal of sameness in country life, you know."

"It seems to be a very dangerous animal," said one of the guests.

"That's what the mother of the gardener's boy said," remarked Teresa; "she wanted me to have it destroyed, but I pointed out to her that she had eleven children and I had only one elk. I also gave her a black silk skirt; she said that though there hadn't been a funeral in her family, she felt as if there had been. Anyhow, we parted friends. I can't offer you a silk skirt, Emily, but you may have another cup of tea. As I have already remarked, there are muffins in the grate."

Teresa closed the discussion, having deftly conveyed the impression that she considered the mother of the gardener's boy had shown a far more reasonable spirit than the parents of other elk-assaulted victims.

"Teresa is devoid of feeling," said Mrs. Yonelet afterwards to the vicar's wife; "to sit there, talking of muffins, with an appalling tragedy only narrowly averted–"

"Of course you know whom she really intends Bertie to marry?" asked the vicar's wife; "I've noticed it for some time. The Bickelbys' German governess."

"A German governess! What an idea!" gasped Mrs. Yonelet.

"She's of quite good family, I believe," said the vicar's wife, "and not at all the mouse-in-the-background sort of person that governesses are usually supposed to be. In fact, next to Teresa, she's about the most assertive and combative personality in the neighbourhood. She's pointed out to my husband all sorts of errors in his sermons, and she gave Sir Laurence a public lecture on how he ought to handle the hounds. You know how sensitive Sir Laurence is about any criticism of his Mastership, and to have a governess laying down the law to him nearly drove him into a fit. She's behaved like that to every one, except, of course, Teresa, and every one has been defensively rude to her in return. The Bickelbys are simply too afraid of her to get rid of her. Now isn't that exactly the sort of woman whom Teresa would take a delight in installing as her successor? Imagine the discomfort and awkwardness in the county if we suddenly found that she was to be the future hostess at the Hall. Teresa's only regret will be that she won't be alive to see it."

"But," objected Mrs. Yonelet, "surely Bertie hasn't shown the least sign of being attracted in that quarter?"

"Oh, she's quite nice-looking in a way, and dresses well, and plays a good game of tennis. She often comes across the park with messages from the Bickelby mansion, and one of these days Bertie will rescue her from the elk, which has become almost a habit with him, and Teresa will say that Fate has consecrated them to one another. Bertie might not be disposed to pay much attention to the consecrations of Fate, but he would not dream of opposing his grandmother."

The vicar's wife spoke with the quiet authority of one who has intuitive knowledge, and in her heart of hearts Mrs. Yonelet believed her.

Six months later the elk had to be destroyed. In a fit of exceptional moroseness it had killed the Bickelbys' German governess. It was an irony of its fate that it should achieve popularity in the last moments of its career; at any rate, it established the record of being the only living thing that had permanently thwarted Teresa Thropplestance's plans.

Dora Yonelet broke off her engagement with an Indian civilian, and married Bertie three months after his grandmother's death—Teresa did not long survive the German governess fiasco. At Christmas time every year young Mrs. Thropplestance hangs an extra large festoon of evergreens on the elk horns that decorate the hall.

"It was a fearsome beast," she observes to Bertie, "but I always feel that it was instrumental in bringing us together."

Which, of course, was true.

"DOWN PENS"

"HAVE you written to thank the Froplinsons for what they sent us?" asked Egbert.

"No," said Janetta, with a note of tired defiance in her voice; "I've written eleven letters today expressing surprise and gratitude for sundry unmerited gifts, but I haven't written to the Froplinsons."

"Some one will have to write to them," said Egbert.

"I don't dispute the necessity, but I don't think the some one should be me," said Janetta. "I wouldn't mind writing a letter of angry recrimination or heartless satire to some suitable recipient; in fact, I should rather enjoy it, but I've come to the end of my capacity for expressing servile amiability. Eleven letters today and nine yesterday, all couched in the same strain of ecstatic thankfulness: really, you can't expect me to sit down to another. There is such a thing as writing oneself out."

"I've written nearly as many," said Egbert, "and I've had my usual business correspondence to get through too. Besides, I don't know what it was that the Froplinsons sent us."

"A William the Conqueror calendar," said Janetta, "with a quotation of one of his great thoughts for every day in the year."

"Impossible," said Egbert; "he didn't have three hundred and sixty-five thoughts in the whole of his life, or, if he did, he kept them to himself. He was a man of action, not of introspection."

"Well, it was William Wordsworth, then," said Janetta; "I know William came into it somewhere."

"That sounds more probable," said Egbert; "well, let's collaborate on this letter of thanks and get it done. I'll dictate, and you can scribble it down. 'Dear Mrs. Froplinson—thank you and your husband so much for the very pretty calendar you sent us. It was very good of you to think of us.'"

"You can't possibly say that," said Janetta, laying down her pen.

"It's what I always do say, and what every one says to me," protested Egbert.

"We sent them something on the twenty-second," said Janetta, "so they simply *had* to think of us. There was no getting away from it."

"What did we send them?" asked Egbert gloomily.

"Bridge-markers," said Janetta, "in a cardboard case, with some inanity about 'digging for fortune with a royal spade' emblazoned on the cover. The moment I saw it in the shop I said to myself 'Froplinsons' and to the attendant 'How much?' When he said 'Ninepence,' I gave him their address, jabbed our card in, paid tenpence or elevenpence to cover the postage, and thanked heaven. With less sincerity and infinitely more trouble they eventually thanked me."

"The Froplinsons don't play bridge," said Egbert.

"One is not supposed to notice social deformities of that sort," said Janetta; "it wouldn't be polite. Besides, what trouble did they take to find out whether we read Wordsworth with gladness? For all they knew or cared we might be frantically embedded in the belief that all poetry begins and ends with John Masefield, and it might infuriate or depress us to have a daily sample of Wordsworthian products flung at us."

"Well, let's get on with the letter of thanks," said Egbert.

"Proceed," said Janetta.

"'How clever of you to guess that Wordsworth is our favourite poet,'" dictated Egbert.

Again Janetta laid down her pen.

"Do you realize what that means?" she asked; "a Wordsworth booklet next Christmas, and another calendar the Christmas after, with the same problem of having to write suitable letters of thankfulness. No, the best thing to do is to drop all further allusion to the calendar and switch off on to some other topic."

"But what other topic?"

"Oh, something like this: 'What do you think of the New Year Honours List? A friend of ours made such a clever remark when he read it.' Then you can stick in any remark that comes into your head; it needn't be clever. The Froplinsons won't know whether it is or isn't."

"We don't even know on which side they are in politics," objected Egbert; "and anyhow you can't suddenly dismiss the subject of the calendar. Surely there must be some intelligent remark that can be made about it."

"Well, we can't think of one," said Janetta wearily; "the fact is, we've both written ourselves out. Heavens! I've just remembered Mrs. Stephen Ludberry. I haven't thanked her for what she sent."

"What did she send?"

"I forget; I think it was a calendar."

There was a long silence, the forlorn silence of those who are bereft of hope and have almost ceased to care.

Presently Egbert started from his seat with an air of resolution. The light of battle was in his eyes.

"Let me come to the writing-table," he exclaimed.

"Gladly," said Janetta. "Are you going to write to Mrs. Ludberry or the Froplinsons?"

"To neither," said Egbert, drawing a stack of notepaper towards him; "I'm going to write to the editor of every enlightened and influential newspaper in the Kingdom. I'm going to suggest that there should be a sort of epistolary Truce of God during the festivities of Christmas and New Year. From the twenty-fourth of December to the third or fourth of January it shall be considered an offence against good sense and good feeling to write or expect any letter or communication that does not deal with the necessary events of the moment. Answers to invitations, arrangements about trains, renewal of club subscriptions, and, of course, all the ordinary everyday affairs of business, sickness, engaging new cooks, and so forth, these will be dealt with in the usual manner as something inevitable, a legitimate part of our daily life. But all the devastating accretions of correspondence, incident to the festive season, these should be swept away to give the season a chance of being really festive, a time of untroubled, unpunctuated peace and good will."

"But you would have to make some acknowledgment of presents received," objected Janetta; "otherwise people would never know whether they had arrived safely."

"Of course, I have thought of that," said Egbert; "every present that was sent off would be accompanied by a ticket bearing the date of dispatch and the signature of the sender, and some conventional hieroglyphic to show that it was intended to be a Christmas or New Year gift; there would be a counterfoil with space for the recipient's name and the date of arrival, and all you would have to do would be to sign and date the counterfoil, add a conventional hieroglyphic indicating heartfelt thanks and gratified surprise, put the thing into an envelope and post it."

"It sounds delightfully simple," said Janetta wistfully, "but people would consider it too cut-and-dried, too perfunctory."

"It is not a bit more perfunctory than the present system," said Egbert; "I have only the same conventional language of gratitude at my disposal with which to thank dear old Colonel Chuttle for his perfectly delicious Stilton, which we shall devour to the last morsel, and the Froplinsons for their calendar, which we shall never look at. Colonel Chuttle knows that we are grateful for the Stilton, without having to be told so, and the Froplinsons know that we are bored with their calendar, whatever we may say to the contrary, just as we know that they are bored with the bridge-markers in spite of their written assurance that they thanked us for our charming little gift. What is more, the Colonel knows that even if we had taken a sudden aversion to Stilton or been forbidden it by the doctor, we should still have written a letter of hearty thanks around it. So you see the present system of acknowledgment is just as perfunctory and conventional as the counterfoil business would be, only ten times more tiresome and brain-racking."

"Your plan would certainly bring the ideal of a Happy Christmas a step nearer realization," said Janetta.

"There are exceptions, of course," said Egbert, "people who really try to infuse a breath of reality into their letters of acknowledgment. Aunt Susan, for instance, who writes: 'Thank you very much for the ham; not such a good flavour as the one you sent last year, which itself was not a particularly good one. Hams are not what they used to be.' It would be a pity to be deprived of her Christmas comments, but that loss would be swallowed up in the general gain."

"Meanwhile," said Janetta, "what *am* I to say to the Froplinsons?"

THE NAME-DAY

ADVENTURES, according to the proverb, are to the adventurous. Quite as often they are to the non-adventurous, to the retiring, to the constitutionally timid. John James Abbleway had been endowed by Nature with the sort of disposition that instinctively avoids

Carlist intrigues, slum crusades, the tracking of wounded wild beasts, and the moving of hostile amendments at political meetings. If a mad dog or a Mad Mullah had come his way he would have surrendered the way without hesitation. At school he had unwillingly acquired a thorough knowledge of the German tongue out of deference to the plainly expressed wishes of a foreign-languages master, who, though he taught modern subjects, employed old-fashioned methods in driving his lessons home. It was this enforced familiarity with an important commercial language which thrust Abbleway in later years into strange lands where adventures were less easy to guard against than in the ordered atmosphere of an English country town. The firm that he worked for saw fit to send him one day on a prosaic business errand to the far city of Vienna, and, having sent him there, continued to keep him there, still engaged in humdrum affairs of commerce, but with the possibilities of romance and adventure, or even misadventure, jostling at his elbow. After two and a half years of exile, however, John James Abbleway had embarked on only one hazardous undertaking, and that was of a nature which would assuredly have overtaken him sooner or later if he had been leading a sheltered, stay-at-home existence at Dorking or Huntingdon. He fell placidly in love with a placidly lovable English girl, the sister of one of his commercial colleagues, who was improving her mind by a short trip to foreign parts, and in due course he was formally accepted as the young man she was engaged to. The further step by which she was to become Mrs. John Abbleway was to take place a twelvemonth hence in a town in the English midlands, by which time the firm that employed John James would have no further need for his presence in the Austrian capital.

It was early in April, two months after the installation of Abbleway as the young man Miss Penning was engaged to, when he received a letter from her, written from Venice. She was still peregrinating under the wing of her brother, and as the latter's business arrangements would take him across to Fiume for a day or two, she had conceived the idea that it would be rather jolly if John could obtain leave of absence and run down to the Adriatic coast to meet them. She had looked up the route on the map, and the journey did not appear likely to be expensive. Between the lines of her communication there lay a hint that if he really cared for her—

Abbleway obtained leave of absence and added a journey to

Fiume to his life's adventures. He left Vienna on a cold, cheerless day. The flower shops were full of spring blooms, and the weekly organs of illustrated humour were full of spring topics, but the skies were heavy with clouds that looked like cotton-wool that has been kept over long in a shop window.

"Snow comes," said the train official to the station officials; and they agreed that snow was about to come. And it came, rapidly, plenteously. The train had not been more than an hour on its journey when the cotton-wool clouds commenced to dissolve in a blinding downpour of snowflakes. The forest trees on either side of the line were speedily coated with a heavy white mantle, the telegraph wires became thick glistening ropes, the line itself was buried more and more completely under a carpeting of snow, through which the not very powerful engine ploughed its way with increasing difficulty. The Vienna-Fiume line is scarcely the best equipped of the Austrian State railways, and Abbleway began to have serious fears for a breakdown. The train had slowed down to a painful and precarious crawl and presently came to a halt at a spot where the drifting snow had accumulated in a formidable barrier. The engine made a special effort and broke through the obstruction, but in the course of another twenty minutes it was again held up. The process of breaking through was renewed and the train doggedly resumed its way, encountering and surmounting fresh hindrances at frequent intervals. After a standstill of unusually long duration in a particularly deep drift the compartment in which Abbleway was sitting gave a huge jerk and a lurch, and then seemed to remain stationary; it undoubtedly was not moving, and yet he could hear the puffing of the engine and the slow rumbling and jolting of wheels. The puffing and rumbling grew fainter, as though it were dying away through the agency of intervening distance. Abbleway suddenly gave vent to an exclamation of scandalized alarm, opened the window, and peered out into the snowstorm. The flakes perched on his eyelashes and blurred his vision, but he saw enough to help him to realize what had happened. The engine had made a mighty plunge through the drift and had gone merrily forward, lightened of the load of its rear carriage, whose coupling had snapped under the strain. Abbleway was alone, or almost alone, with a derelict railway waggon, in the heart of some Styrian or Croatian forest. In the third-class compartment next to his own he remembered to have seen a peasant woman, who had entered the train at a small wayside station. "With the exception of that woman," he exclaimed dramatically to himself, "the nearest living beings are probably a pack of wolves."

Before making his way to the third-class compartment to acquaint his fellow-traveller with the extent of the disaster Abbleway hurriedly pondered the question of the woman's nationality. He had acquired a smattering of Slavonic tongues during his residence in Vienna, and felt competent to grapple with several racial possibilities.

"If she is Croat or Serb or Bosniak I shall be able to make her understand," he promised himself. "If she is Magyar, heaven help me! We shall have to converse entirely by signs."

He entered the carriage and made his momentous announcement in the best approach to Croat speech that he could achieve.

"The train has broken away and left us!"

The woman shook her head with a movement that might be intended to convey resignation to the will of heaven, but probably meant noncomprehension. Abbleway repeated his information with variations of Slavonic tongues and generous displays of pantomime.

"Ah," said the woman at last in German dialect, "the train has gone? We are left. Ah, so."

She seemed about as much interested as though Abbleway had told her the result of the municipal elections in Amsterdam.

"They will find out at some station, and when the line is clear of snow they will send an engine. It happens that way sometimes."

"We may be here all night!" exclaimed Abbleway.

The woman looked as though she thought it possible.

"Are there wolves in these parts?" asked Abbleway hurriedly.

"Many," said the woman; "just outside this forest my aunt was devoured three years ago, as she was coming home from market. The horse and a young pig that was in the cart were eaten too. The horse was a very old one, but it was a beautiful young pig, oh, so fat. I cried when I heard that it was taken. They spare nothing."

"They may attack us here," said Abbleway tremulously; "they could easily break in, these carriages are like matchwood. We may both be devoured."

"You, perhaps," said the woman calmly; "not me."

"Why not you?" demanded Abbleway.

"It is the day of Saint Mariä Kleophä, my name-day. She would not allow me to be eaten by wolves on her day. Such a thing could not be thought of. You, yes, but not me."

Abbleway changed the subject.

"It is only afternoon now; if we are to be left here till morning we shall be starving."

"I have here some good eatables," said the woman tranquilly; "on my festival day it is natural that I should have provision with me. I have five good blood-sausages; in the town shops they cost twenty-five heller each. Things are dear in the town shops."

"I will give you fifty heller apiece for a couple of them," said Abbleway with some enthusiasm.

"In a railway accident things become very dear," said the woman; "these blood-sausages are four kronen apiece."

"Four kronen!" exclaimed Abbleway; "four kronen for a blood-sausage!"

"You cannot get them any cheaper on this train," said the woman, with relentless logic, "because there aren't any others to get. In Agram you can buy them cheaper, and in Paradise no doubt they will be given to us for nothing, but here they cost four kronen each. I have a small piece of Emmenthaler cheese and a honey-cake and a piece of bread that I can let you have. That will be another three kronen, eleven kronen in all. There is a piece of ham, but that I cannot let you have on my name-day."

Abbleway wondered to himself what price she would have put on the ham, and hurried to pay her the eleven kronen before her emergency tariff expanded into a famine tariff. As he was taking possession of his modest store of eatables he suddenly heard a noise which set his heart thumping in a miserable fever of fear. There was a scraping and shuffling as of some animal or animals trying to climb up to the foot-board. In another moment, through the snow-encrusted glass of the carriage window, he saw a gaunt prick-eared head, with gaping jaw and lolling tongue and gleaming teeth; a second later another head shot up.

"There are hundreds of them," whispered Abbleway; "they have scented us. They will tear the carriage to pieces. We shall be devoured."

"Not me, on my name-day. The holy Mariä Kleophä would not permit it," said the woman with provoking calm.

The heads dropped down from the window and an uncanny silence fell on the beleaguered carriage. Abbleway neither moved nor spoke. Perhaps the brutes had not clearly seen or winded the human occupants of the carriage, and had prowled away on some other errand of rapine.

The long torture-laden minutes passed slowly away.

"It grows cold," said the woman suddenly, crossing over to the far end of the carriage, where the heads had appeared. "The heating apparatus does not work any longer. See, over there beyond the trees, there is a chimney with smoke coming from it. It is not far, and the snow has nearly stopped. I shall find a path through the forest to that house with the chimney."

"But the wolves!" exclaimed Abbleway; "they may–"

"Not on my name-day," said the woman obstinately, and before he could stop her she had opened the door and climbed down into the snow. A moment later he hid his face in his hands; two gaunt lean figures rushed upon her from the forest. No doubt she had courted her fate, but Abbleway had no wish to see a human being torn to pieces and devoured before his eyes.

When he looked at last a new sensation of scandalized astonishment took possession of him. He had been straitly brought up in a small English town, and he was not prepared to be the witness of a miracle. The wolves were not doing anything worse to the woman than drench her with snow as they gambolled round her.

A short, joyous bark revealed the clue to the situation.

"Are those–dogs?" he called weakly.

"My cousin Karl's dogs, yes," she answered; "that is his inn, over beyond the trees. I knew it was there, but I did not want to take you there; he is always grasping with strangers. However, it grows too cold to remain in the train. Ah, ah, see what comes!"

A whistle sounded, and a relief engine made its appearance, snorting its way sulkily through the snow. Abbleway did not have the opportunity for finding out whether Karl was really avaricious.

THE LUMBER-ROOM

The children were to be driven, as a special treat, to the sands at Jagborough. Nicholas was not to be of the party; he was in disgrace. Only that morning he had refused to eat his wholesome bread-and-milk on the seemingly frivolous ground that there was a frog in it. Older and wiser and better people had told him that there could not possibly be a frog in his bread-and-milk and that he was not to talk nonsense; he continued, nevertheless, to talk what seemed the veriest nonsense, and described with much detail the colouration and markings of the alleged frog. The dramatic part of the incident was that there really was a frog in Nicholas' basin of bread-and-milk; he had put it there himself, so he felt entitled to know something about it. The sin of taking a frog from the garden and putting it into a bowl of wholesome bread-and-milk was enlarged on at great length, but the fact that stood out clearest in the whole affair, as it presented itself to the mind of Nicholas, was that the older, wiser and better people had been proved to be profoundly in error in matters about which they had expressed the utmost assurance.

"You said there couldn't possibly be a frog in my bread-and-milk; there *was* a frog in my bread-and-milk," he repeated, with the insistence of a skilled tactician who does not intend to shift from favourable ground.

So his boy-cousin and girl-cousin and his quite uninteresting younger brother were to be taken to Jagborough sands that afternoon and he was to stay at home. His cousins' aunt, who insisted, by an unwarranted stretch of imagination, in styling herself his aunt also, had hastily invented the Jagborough expedition in order to impress on Nicholas the delights that he had justly forfeited by his disgraceful conduct at the breakfast-table. It was her habit, whenever one of the children fell from grace, to improvise something of a festival nature from which the offender would be rigorously debarred; if all the children sinned collectively they were suddenly informed of a circus in a neighbouring town, a circus of unrivalled merit and uncounted elephants, to which, but for their depravity, they would have been taken that very day.

A few decent tears were looked for on the part of Nicholas when the moment for the departure of the expedition arrived. As a matter of fact, however, all the crying was done by his girl-cousin, who scraped her knee rather painfully against the step of the carriage as she was scrambling in.

"How she did howl," said Nicholas cheerfully, as the party drove off without any of the elation of high spirits that should have characterized it.

"She'll soon get over that," said the *soi-disant* aunt; "it will be a glorious afternoon for racing about over those beautiful sands. How they will enjoy themselves!"

"Bobby won't enjoy himself much, and he won't race much either," said Nicholas with a grim chuckle; "his boots are hurting him. They're too tight."

"Why didn't he tell me they were hurting?" asked the aunt with some asperity.

"He told you twice, but you weren't listening. You often don't listen when we tell you important things."

"You are not to go into the gooseberry garden," said the aunt, changing the subject.

"Why not?" demanded Nicholas.

"Because you are in disgrace," said the aunt loftily.

Nicholas did not admit the flawlessness of the reasoning; he felt perfectly capable of being in disgrace and in a gooseberry garden at the same moment. His face took on an expression of considerable obstinacy. It was clear to his aunt that he was determined to get into the gooseberry garden, "only," as she remarked to herself, "because I have told him he is not to."

Now the gooseberry garden had two doors by which it might be entered, and once a small person like Nicholas could slip in there he could effectually disappear from view amid the masking growth of artichokes, raspberry canes, and fruit bushes. The aunt had many other things to do that afternoon, but she spent an hour or two in trivial gardening operations among flower beds and shrubberies, whence she could keep a watchful eye on the two doors that led to the forbidden paradise. She was a woman of few ideas, with immense powers of concentration.

Nicholas made one or two sorties into the front garden, wriggling his way with obvious stealth of purpose towards one or other of the doors, but never able for a moment to evade the aunt's watchful eye. As a matter of fact, he had no intention of trying to get into the gooseberry garden, but it was extremely convenient for him that his aunt should believe that he had; it was a belief that would keep her on self-imposed sentry-duty for the greater part of the afternoon. Having thoroughly confirmed and fortified her suspicions, Nicholas slipped back into the house and rapidly put into execution a plan of action that had long germinated in his brain. By standing on a chair in the library one could reach a shelf on which reposed a fat, important-looking key. The key was as important as it looked; it was the instrument which kept the mysteries of the lumber-room secure from unauthorized intrusion, which opened a way only for aunts and such-like privileged persons. Nicholas had not much experience of the art of fitting keys into keyholes and turning locks, but for some days past he had practised with the key of the school-room door; he did not believe in trusting too much to luck and accident. The key turned stiffly in the lock, but it turned. The door opened, and Nicholas was in an unknown land, compared with which the gooseberry garden was a stale delight, a mere material pleasure.

Often and often Nicholas had pictured to himself what the lumber-room might be like, that region that was so carefully sealed from youthful eyes and concerning which no questions were ever answered. It came up to his expectations. In the first place it was large and dimly lit, one high window opening on to the forbidden garden being its only source of illumination. In the second place it was a storehouse of unimagined treasures. The aunt-by-assertion was one of those people who think that things spoil by use and consign them to dust and damp by way of preserving them. Such parts of the house as Nicholas knew best were rather bare and cheerless, but here there were wonderful things for the eye to feast on. First and foremost there was a piece of framed tapestry that was evidently meant to be a fire-screen. To Nicholas it was a living, breathing story; he sat down on a roll of Indian hangings, glowing in wonderful colours beneath a layer of dust, and took in all the details of the tapestry picture. A man, dressed in the hunting costume of some remote period, had just transfixed a stag with an arrow; it could not have been a difficult shot because the stag was only one or two paces away from him; in the thickly growing vegetation that the picture suggested it would not have been difficult to creep up to a feeding stag, and the two spotted dogs that were springing forward to join in the chase had evidently been trained to keep to heel till the arrow was discharged. That part of the picture was simple, if interesting, but did the huntsman see, what Nicholas saw, that four galloping wolves were coming in his direction through the wood? There might be more than four of them hidden behind the trees, and in any case would the man and his dogs be able to cope with the four wolves if they made an attack? The man had only two arrows left in his quiver, and he might miss with one or both of them; all one knew about his skill in shooting was that he could hit a large stag at a ridiculously short range. Nicholas sat for many golden minutes revolving the possibilities of the scene; he was inclined to think that there were more than four wolves and that the man and his dogs were in a tight corner.

But there were other objects of delight and interest claiming his instant attention: here were quaint twisted candlesticks in the shape of snakes, and a teapot fashioned like a china duck, out of whose open beak the tea was supposed to come. How dull and shapeless the nursery teapot seemed in comparison! And there was a carved sandal-wood box packed tight with aromatic cotton-wool, and between the layers of cotton-wool were little brass figures, hump-necked bulls, and peacocks and goblins, delightful to see and to handle. Less promising in appearance was a large square book with plain black covers; Nicholas peeped into it, and, behold, it was full of coloured pictures of birds. And such birds! In the garden, and in the lanes when he went for a walk, Nicholas came across a few birds, of which the largest were an occasional magpie or wood-pigeon; here were herons and bustards, kites, toucans, tiger-bitterns, brush turkeys, ibises, golden pheasants, a whole portrait gallery of undreamed-of creatures. And as he was admiring the colouring of the mandarin duck and assigning a life-history to it, the voice of his aunt in shrill vociferation of his name came from the gooseberry garden without. She had grown suspicious at his long disappearance, and had leapt to the conclusion that he had climbed over the wall behind the sheltering screen of the lilac bushes; she was now engaged in energetic and rather hopeless search for him among the artichokes and raspberry canes.

"Nicholas, Nicholas!" she screamed, "you are to come out of this at once. It's no use trying to hide there; I can see you all the time."

It was probably the first time for twenty years that any one had smiled in that lumber-room.

Presently the angry repetitions of Nicholas' name gave way to a shriek, and a cry for somebody to come quickly. Nicholas shut the book, restored it carefully to its place in a corner, and shook some dust from a neighbouring pile of newspapers over it. Then he crept from the room, locked the door, and replaced the key exactly where he had found it. His aunt was still calling his name when he sauntered into the front garden.

"Who's calling?" he asked.

"Me," came the answer from the other side of the wall; "didn't you hear me? I've been looking for you in the gooseberry garden, and I've slipped into the rain-water tank. Luckily there's no water in it, but the sides are slippery and I can't get out. Fetch the little ladder from under the cherry tree—"

"I was told I wasn't to go into the gooseberry garden," said Nicholas promptly.

"I told you not to, and now I tell you that you may," came the voice from the rain-water tank, rather impatiently.

"Your voice doesn't sound like aunt's," objected Nicholas; "you may be the Evil One tempting me to be disobedient. Aunt often tells me that the Evil One tempts me and that I always yield. This time I'm not going to yield."

"Don't talk nonsense," said the prisoner in the tank; "go and fetch the ladder."

"Will there be strawberry jam for tea?" asked Nicholas innocently.

"Certainly there will be," said the aunt, privately resolving that Nicholas should have none of it.

"Now I know that you are the Evil One and not aunt," shouted Nicholas gleefully; "when we asked aunt for strawberry jam yesterday she said there wasn't any. I know there are four jars of it in the store cupboard, because I looked, and of course you know it's there, but *she* doesn't, because she said there wasn't any. Oh, Devil, you *have* sold yourself!"

There was an unusual sense of luxury in being able to talk to an aunt as though one was talking to the Evil One, but Nicholas knew, with childish discernment, that such luxuries were not to be over-indulged in. He walked noisily away, and it was a kitchenmaid, in search of parsley, who eventually rescued the aunt from the rain-water tank.

Tea that evening was partaken of in a fearsome silence. The tide had been at its highest when the children had arrived at Jagborough Cove, so there had been no sands to play on—a circumstance that the aunt had overlooked in the haste of organizing her punitive expedition. The tightness of Bobby's boots had had disastrous effect on his temper the whole of the afternoon, and altogether the children could not have been said to have enjoyed themselves. The aunt maintained the frozen muteness of one who has suffered undignified and unmerited detention in a rain-water tank for thirty-five minutes. As for Nicholas, he, too, was silent, in the absorption of one who has much to think about; it was just possible, he considered, that the huntsman would escape with his hounds while the wolves feasted on the stricken stag.

FUR

"You look worried, dear," said Eleanor.

"I am worried," admitted Suzanne; "not worried exactly, but anxious. You see, my birthday happens next week—"

"You lucky person," interrupted Eleanor; "my birthday doesn't come till the end of March."

"Well, old Bertram Kneyght is over in England just now from the Argentine. He's a kind of distant cousin of my mother's, and so enormously rich that we've never let the relationship drop out of sight. Even if we don't see him or hear from him for years he is always Cousin Bertram when he does turn up. I can't say he's ever been of much solid use to us, but yesterday the subject of my birthday cropped up, and he asked me to let him know what I wanted for a present."

"Now I understand the anxiety," observed Eleanor.

"As a rule when one is confronted with a problem like that," said Suzanne, "all one's ideas vanish; one doesn't seem to have a desire in the world. Now it so happens that I have been very keen on a little Dresden figure that I saw somewhere in Kensington; about thirty-six shillings, quite beyond my means. I was very nearly describing the figure, and giving Bertram the address of the shop. And then it suddenly struck me that thirty-six shillings was such a ridiculously inadequate sum for a man of his immense wealth to spend on a birthday present. He could give thirty-six pounds as easily as you or I could buy a bunch of violets. I don't want to be greedy, of course, but I don't like being wasteful."

"The question is," said Eleanor, "what are his ideas as to present-giving? Some of the wealthiest people have curiously cramped views on that subject. When people grow gradually rich their requirements and standard of living expand in proportion, while their present-giving instincts often remain in the undeveloped condition of their earlier days. Something showy and not-too-expensive in a shop is their only conception of the ideal gift. That is why even quite good shops have their counters and windows crowded with things worth about four shillings that look as if they might be worth seven-and-six, and are priced at ten shillings and labelled 'seasonable gifts.'"

"I know," said Suzanne; "that is why it is so risky to be vague when one is giving indications of one's wants. Now if I say to him: 'I am going out to Davos this winter, so anything in the travelling line would be acceptable,' he *might* give me a dressing-bag with gold-mounted fittings, but, on the other hand, he might give me Baedeker's *Switzerland,* or *Ski-ing without Tears,* or something of that sort."

"He would be more likely to say: 'She'll be going to lots of dances, a fan will be sure to be useful.'"

"Yes, and I've got tons of fans, so you see where the danger and anxiety lies. Now if there is one thing more than another that I really urgently want it is furs. I simply haven't any. I'm told that Davos is full of Russians, and they are sure to wear the most lovely sables and things. To be among people who are smothered in furs when one hasn't any oneself makes one want to break most of the Commandments."

"If it's furs that you're out for," said Eleanor, "you will have to superintend the choice of them in person. You can't be sure that your cousin knows the difference between silver-fox and ordinary squirrel."

"There are some heavenly silver-fox stoles at Goliath and Mastodon's," said Suzanne, with a sigh; "if I could only inveigle Bertram into their building and take him for a stroll through the fur department!"

"He lives somewhere near there, doesn't he?" said Eleanor. "Do you know what his habits are? Does he take a walk at any particular time of day?"

"He usually walks down to his club about three o'clock, if it's a fine day. That takes him right past Goliath and Mastodon's."

"Let us two meet him accidentally at the street corner tomorrow," said Eleanor; "we can walk a little way with him, and with luck we ought to be able to side-track him into the shop. You can say you want to get a hair-net or something. When we're safely there I can say: 'I wish you'd tell me what you want for your birthday.' Then you'll have everything ready to hand—the rich cousin, the fur department, and the topic of birthday presents."

"It's a great idea," said Suzanne; "you really are a brick. Come round tomorrow at twenty to three; don't be late, we must carry out our ambush to the minute."

At a few minutes to three the next afternoon the fur-trappers walked warily towards the selected corner. In the near distance rose the colossal pile of Messrs. Goliath and Mastodon's famed establishment. The afternoon was brilliantly fine, exactly the sort of weather to tempt a gentleman of advancing years into the discreet exercise of a leisurely walk.

"I say, dear, I wish you'd do something for me this evening," said Eleanor to her companion; "just drop in after dinner on some pretext or other, and stay on to make a fourth at bridge with Adela and the aunts. Otherwise I shall have to play, and Harry Scarisbrooke is going to come in unexpectedly about nine-fifteen, and I particularly wanted to be free to talk to him while the others are playing."

"Sorry, my dear, no can do," said Suzanne; "ordinary bridge at threepence a hundred, with such dreadfully slow players as your aunts, bores me to tears. I nearly go to sleep over it."

"But I most particularly want an opportunity to talk with Harry," urged Eleanor, an angry glint coming into her eyes.

"Sorry, anything to oblige, but not that," said Suzanne cheerfully; the sacrifices of friendship were beautiful in her eyes as long as she was not asked to make them.

Eleanor said nothing further on the subject, but the corners of her mouth rearranged themselves.

"There's our man!" exclaimed Suzanne suddenly; "hurry!"

Mr. Bertram Kneyght greeted his cousin and her friend with genuine heartiness, and readily accepted their invitation to explore the crowded mart that stood temptingly at their elbow. The plate-glass doors swung open and the trio plunged bravely into the jostling throng of buyers and loiterers.

"Is it always as full as this?" asked Bertram of Eleanor.

"More or less, and autumn sales are on just now," she replied.

Suzanne, in her anxiety to pilot her cousin to the desired haven of the fur department, was usually a few paces ahead of the others, coming back to them now and then if they lingered for a moment at some attractive counter, with the nervous solicitude of a parent rook encouraging its young ones on their first flying expedition.

"It's Suzanne's birthday on Wednesday next," confided Eleanor to

Bertram Kneyght at a moment when Suzanne had left them unusually far behind; "my birthday comes the day before, so we are both on the look-out for something to give each other."

"Ah," said Bertram. "Now, perhaps you can advise me on that very point. I want to give Suzanne something, and I haven't the least idea what she wants."

"She's rather a problem," said Eleanor. "She seems to have everything one can think of, lucky girl. A fan is always useful; she'll be going to a lot of dances at Davos this winter. Yes, I should think a fan would please her more than anything. After our birthdays are over we inspect each other's muster of presents, and I always feel dreadfully humble. She gets such nice things, and I never have anything worth showing. You see, none of my relations or any of the people who give me presents are at all well off, so I can't expect them to do anything more than just remember the day with some little trifle. Two years ago an uncle on my mother's side of the family, who had come into a small legacy, promised me a silver-fox stole for my birthday. I can't tell you how excited I was about it, how I pictured myself showing it off to all my friends and enemies. Then just at that moment his wife died, and, of course, poor man, he could not be expected to think of birthday presents at such a time. He has lived abroad ever since, and I never got my fur. Do you know, to this day I can scarcely look at a silver-fox pelt in a shop window or round any one's neck without feeling ready to burst into tears. I suppose if I hadn't had the prospect of getting one I shouldn't feel that way. Look, there is the fan counter, on your left; you can easily slip away in the crowd. Get her as nice a one as you can see—she is such a dear, dear girl."

"Hullo, I thought I had lost you," said Suzanne, making her way through an obstructive knot of shoppers. "Where is Bertram?"

"I got separated from him long ago. I thought he was on ahead with you," said Eleanor. "We shall never find him in this crush."

Which turned out to be a true prediction.

"All our trouble and forethought thrown away," said Suzanne sulkily, when they had pushed their way fruitlessly through half a dozen departments.

"I can't think why you didn't grab him by the arm," said Eleanor; "I would have if I'd known him longer, but I'd only just been introduced. It's nearly four now, we'd better have tea."

Some days later Suzanne rang Eleanor up on the telephone.

"Thank you very much for the photograph frame. It was just what I wanted. Very good of you. I say, do you know what that Kneyght person has given me? Just what you said he would—a wretched fan. What? Oh, yes, quite a good enough fan in its way, but still . . ."

"You must come and see what he's given me," came in Eleanor's voice over the 'phone.

"You! Why should he give you anything?"

"Your cousin appears to be one of those rare people of wealth who take a pleasure in giving good presents," came the reply.

"I wondered why he was so anxious to know where she lived," snapped Suzanne to herself as she rang off.

A cloud has arisen between the friendships of the two young women; as far as Eleanor is concerned the cloud has a silver-fox lining.

THE PHILANTHROPIST AND THE HAPPY CAT

JOCANTHA BESSBURY was in the mood to be serenely and graciously happy. Her world was a pleasant place, and it was wearing one of its pleasantest aspects. Gregory had managed to get home for a hurried lunch and a smoke afterwards in the little snuggery; the lunch had been a good one, and there was just time to do justice to the coffee and cigarettes. Both were excellent in their way, and Gregory was, in his way, an excellent husband. Jocantha rather suspected herself of making him a very charming wife, and more than suspected herself of having a first-rate dressmaker.

"I don't suppose a more thoroughly contented personality is to be found in all Chelsea," observed Jocantha in allusion to herself; "except perhaps Attab," she continued, glancing towards the large tabby-marked cat that lay in considerable ease in a corner of the divan. "He lies there, purring and dreaming, shifting his limbs now and then in an ecstasy of cushioned comfort. He seems the incarnation of everything soft and silky and velvety, without a sharp edge in his composition, a dreamer whose philosophy is sleep and let sleep; and then, as evening draws on, he goes out into the garden with a red glint in his eyes and slays a drowsy sparrow."

"As every pair of sparrows hatches out ten or more young ones in the year, while their food supply remains stationary, it is just as well that the Attabs of the community should have that idea of how to pass an amusing afternoon," said Gregory. Having delivered himself of this sage comment he lit another cigarette, bade Jocantha a playfully affectionate good-bye, and departed into the outer world.

"Remember, dinner's a wee bit earlier tonight, as we're going to the Haymarket," she called after him.

Left to herself, Jocantha continued the process of looking at her life with placid, introspective eyes. If she had not everything she wanted in this world, at least she was very well pleased with what she had got. She was very well pleased, for instance, with the snuggery, which contrived somehow to be cozy and dainty and expensive all at once. The porcelain was rare and beautiful, the Chinese enamels took on wonderful tints in the firelight, the rugs and hangings led the eye through sumptuous harmonies of colouring. It was a room in which one might have suitably entertained an ambassador or an archbishop, but it was also a room in which one could cut out pictures for a scrap-book without feeling that one was scandalizing the deities of the place with one's litter. And as with the snuggery, so with the rest of the house, and as with the house, so with the other departments of Jocantha's life; she really had good reason for being one of the most contented women in Chelsea.

From being in a mood of simmering satisfaction with her lot she passed to the phase of being generously commiserating for those thousands around her whose lives and circumstances were dull, cheap, pleasureless, and empty. Work girls, shop assistants and so forth, the class that have neither the happy-go-lucky freedom of the poor nor the leisured freedom of the rich, came specially within the range of her sympathy. It was sad to think that there were young people who, after a long day's work, had to sit alone in chill, dreary bedrooms because they could not afford the price of a cup of coffee and a sandwich in a restaurant, still less a shilling for a theatre gallery.

Jocantha's mind was still dwelling on this theme when she started forth on an afternoon campaign of desultory shopping; it would be rather a comforting thing, she told herself, if she could do something, on the spur of the moment, to bring a gleam of pleasure and interest into the life of even one or two wistful-hearted, empty-pocketed workers; it would add a good deal to her sense of enjoyment at the theatre that night. She would get two upper circle tickets for a popular play, make her way into some cheap tea-shop, and present the tickets to the first couple of interesting work girls with whom she could casually drop into conversation. She could explain matters by saying that she was unable to use the tickets herself and did not want them to be wasted, and, on the other hand, did not want the trouble of sending them back. On further reflection she decided that it might be better to get only one ticket and give it to some lonely-looking girl sitting eating her frugal meal by herself; the girl might scrape acquaintance with her next-seat neighbour at the theatre and lay the foundations of a lasting friendship.

With the Fairy Godmother impulse strong upon her, Jocantha marched into a ticket agency and selected with immense care an upper circle seat for the "Yellow Peacock," a play that was attracting a considerable amount of discussion and criticism. Then she went forth in search of a tea-shop and philanthropic adventure, at about the same time that Attab sauntered into the garden with a mind attuned to sparrow stalking. In a corner of an A.B.C. shop she found an unoccupied table, whereat she promptly installed herself, impelled by the fact that at the next table was sitting a young girl, rather plain of feature, with tired, listless eyes and a general air of uncomplaining forlornness. Her dress was of poor material, but aimed at being in the fashion, her hair was pretty, and her complexion bad; she was finishing a modest meal of tea and scone, and she was not very different in her way from thousands of other girls who were finishing, or beginning, or continuing their teas in London tea-shops at that exact moment. The odds were enormously in favour of the supposition that she had never seen the "Yellow Peacock"; obviously she supplied excellent material for Jocantha's first experiment in haphazard benefaction.

Jocantha ordered some tea and a muffin, and then turned a friendly scrutiny on her neighbour with a view to catching her eye. At that precise moment the girl's face lit up with sudden pleasure, her eyes sparkled, a flush came into her cheeks, and she looked almost pretty. A young man, whom she greeted with an affectionate "Hullo, Bertie" came up to her table and took his seat in a chair facing her. Jocantha looked hard at the new-comer; he was in appearance a few years younger than herself, very much better looking than Gregory, rather better looking, in fact, than any of the young men of her set. She guessed him to be a well-mannered young clerk in some wholesale warehouse, existing and amusing himself as best he might on a tiny salary, and commanding a holiday of about two weeks in the year. He was aware, of course, of his good looks, but with the shy self-consciousness of the Anglo-Saxon, not the blatant complacency of the Latin or Semite. He was obviously on terms of friendly intimacy with the girl he was talking to, probably they were drifting towards a formal engagement. Jocantha pictured the boy's home, in a rather narrow circle, with a tiresome mother who always wanted to know how and where he spent his evenings. He would exchange that humdrum thraldom in due course for a home of his own, dominated by a chronic scarcity of pounds, shillings, and pence, and a dearth of most of the things that made life attractive or comfortable. Jocantha felt extremely sorry for him. She wondered if he had seen the "Yellow Peacock"; the odds were enormously in favour of the supposition that he had not. The girl had finished her tea, and would shortly be going back to her work; when the boy was alone it would be quite easy for Jocantha to say: "My husband has made other arrangements for me this evening; would you care to make use of this ticket, which would otherwise be wasted?" Then she could come there again one afternoon for tea, and, if she saw him, ask him how he liked the play. If he was a nice boy and improved on acquaintance he could be given more theatre tickets and perhaps asked to come one Sunday to tea at Chelsea. Jocantha made up her mind that he would improve on acquaintance, and that Gregory would like him, and that the Fairy Godmother business would prove far more entertaining than she had originally anticipated. The boy was distinctly presentable; he knew how to brush his hair, which was possibly an imitative faculty; he knew what colour of tie suited him, which might be intuition; he was exactly the type that Jocantha admired, which of course was accident. Altogether she was rather pleased when the girl looked at the clock and bade a friendly but hurried farewell to her companion. Bertie nodded "good-bye," gulped down a mouthful of tea, and then produced from his overcoat pocket a paper-covered book, bearing the title *Sepoy and Sahib, a Tale of the Great Mutiny*.

The laws of tea-shop etiquette forbid that you should offer theatre tickets to a stranger without having first caught the stranger's eye. It is even better if you can ask to have a sugar basin passed to you, having previously concealed the fact that you have a large and well-filled sugar basin on your own table; this is not difficult to manage, as the printed menu is generally nearly as large as the table, and can be made to stand on end. Jocantha set to work hopefully; she had a long and rather high-pitched discussion with the waitress concerning alleged defects in an altogether blameless muffin, she made loud and plaintive inquiries about the tube service to some impossibly remote suburb, she talked with brilliant insincerity to the tea-shop kitten, and as a last resort she upset a milk-jug and swore at it daintily. Altogether she attracted a good deal of attention, but never for a moment did she attract the attention of the boy with the beautifully brushed hair, who was some thousands of miles away in the baking plains of Hindostan, amid deserted bungalows, seething bazaars, and riotous barrack squares, listening to the throbbing of tom-toms and the distant rattle of musketry.

Jocantha went back to her house in Chelsea, which struck her for the first time as looking dull and over-furnished. She had a resentful conviction that Gregory would be uninteresting at dinner, and that the play would be stupid after dinner. On the whole her frame of mind showed a marked divergence from the purring complacency of Attab, who was again curled up in his corner of the divan with a great peace radiating from every curve of his body.

But then he had killed his sparrow.

ON APPROVAL

Of all the genuine Bohemians who strayed from time to time into the would-be-Bohemian circle of the Restaurant Nuremberg, Owl Street, Soho, none was more interesting and more elusive than Gebhard Knopfschrank. He had no friends, and though he treated all the restaurant frequenters as acquaintances he never seemed to wish to carry the acquaintanceship beyond the door that led into Owl Street and the outer world. He dealt with them all rather as a market woman might deal with chance passers-by, exhibiting her wares and chattering about the weather and the slackness of business, occasionally about rheumatism, but never showing a desire to penetrate into their daily lives or to dissect their ambitions.

He was understood to belong to a family of peasant farmers, somewhere in Pomerania; some two years ago, according to all that was known of him, he had abandoned the labours and responsibilities of swine tending and goose rearing to try his fortune as an artist in London.

"Why London and not Paris or Munich?" he had been asked by the curious.

Well, there was a ship that left Stolpmünde for London twice a month, that carried few passengers, but carried them cheaply; the railway fares to Munich or Paris were not cheap. Thus it was that he came to select London as the scene of his great adventure.

The question that had long and seriously agitated the frequenters of the Nuremberg was whether this goose-boy migrant was really a soul-driven genius, spreading his wings to the light, or merely an enterprising young man who fancied he could paint and was pardonably anxious to escape from the monotony of rye bread diet and the sandy, swine-bestrewn plains of Pomerania. There was reasonable ground for doubt and caution; the artistic groups that foregathered at the little restaurant contained so many young women with short hair and so many young men with long hair, who supposed themselves to be abnormally gifted in the domain of music, poetry, painting, or stagecraft, with little or nothing to support the supposition, that a self-announced genius of any sort in their midst was inevitably suspect. On the other hand, there was the ever-imminent danger of entertaining, and snubbing, an angel unawares. There had been the lamentable case of Sledonti, the dramatic poet, who had been belittled and cold-shouldered in the Owl Street hall of judgment, and had been afterwards hailed as a master singer by the Grand Duke Constantine Constantinovitch—"the most educated of the Romanoffs," according to Sylvia Strubble, who spoke rather as one who knew every individual member of the Russian imperial family; as a matter of fact, she knew a newspaper correspondent, a young man who ate borsch with the air of having invented it. Sledonti's *Poems of Death and Passion* were now being sold by the thousand in seven European languages, and were about to be translated into Syrian, a circumstance which made the discerning critics of the Nuremberg rather shy of maturing their future judgments too rapidly and too irrevocably.

As regards Knopfschrank's work, they did not lack opportunity for inspecting and appraising it. However resolutely he might hold himself aloof from the social life of his restaurant acquaintances, he was not minded to hide his artistic performances from their inquiring gaze. Every evening, or nearly every evening, at about seven o'clock, he would make his appearance, sit himself down at his accustomed table, throw a bulky black portfolio on to the chair opposite him, nod round indiscriminately at his fellow-guests, and commence the serious business of eating and drinking. When the coffee stage was reached he would light a cigarette, draw the portfolio over to him, and begin to rummage among its contents. With slow deliberation he would select a few of his more recent studies and sketches, and silently pass them round from table to table, paying especial attention to any new diners who might be present. On the back of each sketch was marked in plain figures the announcement "Price ten shillings."

If his work was not obviously stamped with the hall-mark of genius, at any rate it was remarkable for its choice of an unusual and unvarying theme. His pictures always represented some well-known street or public place in London, fallen into decay and denuded of its human population, in the place of which there roamed a wild fauna, which, from its wealth of exotic species, must have originally escaped from Zoological Gardens and travelling beast shows. "Giraffes drinking at the fountain pools, Trafalgar Square," was one of the most notable and characteristic of his studies, while even more sensational was the gruesome picture of "Vultures attacking dying camel in Upper Berkeley Street." There were also photographs of the large canvas on which he had been engaged for some months, and which he was now endeavouring to sell to some enterprising dealer or adventurous amateur. The subject was "Hyænas asleep in Euston Station," a composition that left nothing to be desired in the way of suggesting unfathomed depths of desolation.

"Of course it may be immensely clever, it may be something epoch-making in the realm of art," said Sylvia Strubble to her own particular circle of listeners, "but, on the other hand, it may be merely mad. One mustn't pay too much attention to the commercial aspect of the case, of course, but still, if some dealer would make a bid for that hyæna picture, or even for some of the sketches, we should know better how to place the man and his work."

"We may all be cursing ourselves one of these days," said Mrs. Nougat-Jones, "for not having bought up his entire portfolio of sketches. At the same time, when there is so much real talent going about, one does not feel like planking down ten shillings for what looks like a bit of whimsical oddity. Now that picture that he showed us last week, 'Sand-grouse roosting on the Albert Memorial,' was very impressive, and of course I could see there was good workmanship in it and breadth of treatment; but it didn't in the least convey the Albert Memorial to me, and Sir James Beanquest tells me that sand-grouse don't roost, they sleep on the ground."

Whatever talent or genius the Pomeranian artist might possess, it certainly failed to receive commercial sanction. The portfolio remained bulky with unsold sketches, and the "Euston Siesta," as the wits of the Nuremberg nicknamed the large canvas, was still in the market. The outward and visible signs of financial embarrassment began to be noticeable; the half-bottle of cheap claret at dinner-time gave way to a small glass of lager, and this in turn was displaced by water. The one-and-sixpenny set dinner receded from an everyday event to a Sunday extravagance; on ordinary days the artist contented himself with a sevenpenny omelette and some bread and cheese, and there were evenings when he did not put in an appearance at all. On the rare occasions when he spoke of his own affairs it was observed that he began to talk more about Pomerania and less about the great world of art.

"It is a busy time there now with us," he said wistfully; "the schwines are driven out into the fields after harvest, and must be looked after. I could be helping to look after if I was there. Here it is difficult to live; art is not appreciate."

"Why don't you go home on a visit?" some one asked tactfully.

"Ah, it cost money! There is the ship passage to Stolpmünde, and there is money that I owe at my lodgings. Even here I owe a few schillings. If I could sell some of my sketches—"

"Perhaps," suggested Mrs. Nougat-Jones, "if you were to offer them for a little less, some of us would be glad to buy a few. Ten shillings is always a consideration, you know, to people who are not over well off. Perhaps if you were to ask six or seven shillings—"

Once a peasant, always a peasant. The mere suggestion of a bargain to be struck brought a twinkle of awakened alertness into the artist's eyes, and hardened the lines of his mouth.

"Nine schilling, nine pence each," he snapped, and seemed disappointed that Mrs. Nougat-Jones did not pursue the subject further. He had evidently expected her to offer seven-and-fourpence.

The weeks sped by, and Knopfschrank came more rarely to the restaurant in Owl Street, while his meals on those occasions became more and more meagre. And then came a triumphal day, when he appeared early in the evening in a high state of elation, and ordered an elaborate meal that scarcely stopped short of being a banquet. The ordinary resources of the kitchen were supplemented by an imported dish of smoked goosebreast, a Pomeranian delicacy that was luckily procurable at a firm of *delikatessen* merchants in Coventry Street, while a long-necked bottle of Rhine wine gave a finishing touch of festivity and good cheer to the crowded table.

"He has evidently sold his masterpiece," whispered Sylvia Strubble to Mrs. Nougat-Jones, who had come in late.

"Who has bought it?" she whispered back.

"Don't know; he hasn't said anything yet, but it must be some American. Do you see, he has got a little American flag on the dessert dish, and he has put pennies in the music box three times, once to play the 'Star-spangled Banner,' then a Sousa march, and then the 'Star-spangled Banner' again. It must be an American millionaire, and he's evidently got a big price for it; he's just beaming and chuckling with satisfaction."

"We must ask him who has bought it," said Mrs. Nougat-Jones.

"Hush! no, don't. Let's buy some of his sketches, quick, before we are supposed to know that he's famous; otherwise he'll be doubling the prices. I *am* so glad he's had a success at last. I always believed in him, you know."

For the sum of ten shillings each Miss Strubble acquired the drawings of the camel dying in Upper Berkeley Street and of the giraffes quenching their thirst in Trafalgar Square; at the same price Mrs. Nougat-Jones secured the study of roosting sand-grouse. A more ambitious picture, "Wolves and wapiti fighting on the steps of the Athenæum Club," found a purchaser at fifteen shillings.

"And now what are your plans?" asked a young man who contributed occasional paragraphs to an artistic weekly.

"I go back to Stolpmünde as soon as the ship sails," said the artist, "and I do not return. Never."

"But your work? Your career as painter?"

"Ah, there is nossing in it. One starves. Till today I have sold not one of my sketches. Tonight you have bought a few, because I am going away from you, but at other times, not one."

"But has not some American—?"

"Ah, the rich American," chuckled the artist. "God be thanked. He dash his car right into our herd of schwines as they were being driven out to the fields. Many of our best schwines he killed, but he paid all damages. He paid perhaps more than they were worth, many times more than they would have fetched in the market after a month of fattening, but he was in a hurry to get on to Danzig. When one is in a hurry one must pay what one is asked. God be thanked for rich Americans, who are always in a hurry to get somewhere else. My father and mother, they have now so plenty of money; they send me some to pay my debts and come home. I start on Monday for Stolpmünde and I do not come back. Never."

"But your picture, the hyænas?"

"No good. It is too big to carry to Stolpmünde. I burn it."

In time he will be forgotten, but at present Knopfschrank is almost as sore a subject as Sledonti with some of the frequenters of the Nuremberg Restaurant, Owl Street, Soho.

The Toys of Peace

First Collected, 1923

TO

THE 22ND ROYAL FUSILIERS

Thanks are due to the Editors of the *Morning Post*, the *Westminster Gazette*, and the *Bystander* for their amiability in allowing tales that appeared in these journals to be reproduced in the present volume.

THE TOYS OF PEACE

"HARVEY," said Eleanor Bope, handing her brother a cutting from a London morning paper[1] of the 19th of March, "just read this about children's toys, please; it exactly carries out some of our ideas about influence and upbringing."

"In the view of the National Peace Council," ran the extract, "there are grave objections to presenting our boys with regiments of fighting men, batteries of guns, and squadrons of 'Dreadnoughts.' Boys, the Council admits, naturally love fighting and all the panoply of war . . . but that is no reason for encouraging, and perhaps giving permanent form to, their primitive instincts. At the Children's Welfare Exhibition, which opens at Olympia in three weeks' time, the Peace Council will make an alternative suggestion to parents in the shape of an exhibition of 'peace toys.' In front of a specially painted representation of the Peace Palace at The Hague

[1] An actual extract from a London paper of March 1914.

will be grouped, not miniature soldiers but miniature civilians, not guns but ploughs and the tools of industry. . . . It is hoped that manufacturers may take a hint from the exhibit, which will bear fruit in the toy shops."

"The idea is certainly an interesting and very well-meaning one," said Harvey; "whether it would succeed well in practice—"

"We must try," interrupted his sister; "you are coming down to us at Easter, and you always bring the boys some toys, so that will be an excellent opportunity for you to inaugurate the new experiment. Go about in the shops and buy any little toys and models that have special bearing on civilian life in its more peaceful aspects. Of course you must explain the toys to the children and interest them in the new idea. I regret to say that the 'Siege of Adrianople' toy, that their Aunt Susan sent them, didn't need any explanation; they knew all the uniforms and flags, and even the names of the respective commanders, and when I heard them one day using what seemed to be the most objectionable language they said it was Bulgarian words of command; of course it *may* have been, but at any rate I took the toy away from them. Now I shall expect your Easter gifts to give quite a new impulse and direction to the children's minds; Eric is not eleven yet, and Bertie is only nine-and-a-half, so they are really at a most impressionable age."

"There is primitive instinct to be taken into consideration, you know," said Harvey doubtfully, "and hereditary tendencies as well. One of their great-uncles fought in the most intolerant fashion at Inkerman—he was specially mentioned in dispatches, I believe—and their great-grandfather smashed all his Whig neighbours' hothouses when the great Reform Bill was passed. Still, as you say, they are at an impressionable age. I will do my best."

On Easter Saturday Harvey Bope unpacked a large, promising-looking red cardboard box under the expectant eyes of his nephews. "Your uncle has brought you the newest thing in toys," Eleanor had said impressively, and youthful anticipation had been anxiously divided between Albanian soldiery and a Somali camel-corps. Eric was hotly in favour of the latter contingency. "There would be Arabs on horseback," he whispered; "the Albanians have got jolly uniforms, and they fight all day long, and all night too, when there's a moon, but the country's rocky, so they've got no cavalry."

A quantity of crinkly paper shavings was the first thing that met the view when the lid was removed; the most exciting toys always began like that. Harvey pushed back the top layer and drew forth a square, rather featureless building.

"It's a fort!" exclaimed Bertie.

"It isn't, it's the palace of the Mpret of Albania," said Eric, immensely proud of his knowledge of the exotic title; "it's got no windows, you see, so that passers-by can't fire in at the Royal Family."

"It's a municipal dust-bin," said Harvey hurriedly; "you see all the refuse and litter of a town is collected there, instead of lying about and injuring the health of the citizens."

In an awful silence he disinterred a little lead figure of a man in black clothes.

"That," he said, "is a distinguished civilian, John Stuart Mill. He was an authority on political economy."

"Why?" asked Bertie.

"Well, he wanted to be; he thought it was a useful thing to be."

Bertie gave an expressive grunt, which conveyed his opinion that there was no accounting for tastes.

Another square building came out, this time with windows and chimneys.

"A model of the Manchester branch of the Young Women's Christian Association," said Harvey.

"Are there any lions?" asked Eric hopefully. He had been reading Roman history and thought that where you found Christians you might reasonably expect to find a few lions.

"There are no lions," said Harvey. "Here is another civilian, Robert Raikes, the founder of Sunday schools, and here is a model of a municipal wash-house. These little round things are loaves baked in a sanitary bakehouse. That lead figure is a sanitary inspector, this one is a district councillor, and this one is an official of the Local Government Board."

"What does he do?" asked Eric wearily.

"He sees to things connected with his Department," said Harvey. "This box with a slit in it is a ballot-box. Votes are put into it at election times."

"What is put into it at other times?" asked Bertie.

"Nothing. And here are some tools of industry, a wheelbarrow and a hoe, and I think these are meant for hop-poles. This is a model beehive, and that is a ventilator, for ventilating sewers. This seems to be another municipal dust-bin—no, it is a model of a school of art and a public library. This little lead figure is Mrs. Hemans, a poetess, and this is Rowland Hill, who introduced the system of penny postage. This is Sir John Herschel, the eminent astrologer."

"Are we to play with these civilian figures?" asked Eric.

"Of course," said Harvey, "these are toys; they are meant to be played with."

"But how?"

It was rather a poser. "You might make two of them contest a seat in Parliament," said Harvey, "and have an election—"

"With rotten eggs, and free fights, and ever so many broken heads!" exclaimed Eric.

"And noses all bleeding and everybody drunk as can be," echoed Bertie, who had carefully studied one of Hogarth's pictures.

"Nothing of the kind," said Harvey, "nothing in the least like that. Votes will be put in the ballot-box, and the Mayor will count them—the district councillor will do for the Mayor—and he will say which has received the most votes, and then the two candidates will thank him for presiding, and each will say that the contest has been conducted throughout in the pleasantest and most straightforward fashion, and they part with expressions of mutual esteem. There's a jolly game for you boys to play. I never had such toys when I was young."

"I don't think we'll play with them just now," said Eric, with an entire absence of the enthusiasm that his uncle had shown; "I think perhaps we ought to do a little of our holiday task. It's history this time; we've got to learn up something about the Bourbon period in France."

"The Bourbon period," said Harvey, with some disapproval in his voice.

"We've got to know something about Louis the Fourteenth," continued Eric; "I've learnt the names of all the principal battles already."

This would never do. "There were, of course, some battles fought during his reign," said Harvey, "but I fancy the accounts of them were much exaggerated; news was very unreliable in those days, and there were practically no war correspondents, so generals and commanders could magnify every little skirmish they engaged in till they reached the proportions of decisive battles. Louis was really famous, now, as a landscape gardener; the way he laid out Versailles was so much admired that it was copied all over Europe."

"Do you know anything about Madame Du Barry?" asked Eric; "didn't she have her head chopped off?"

"She was another great lover of gardening," said Harvey evasively; "in fact, I believe the well-known rose Du Barry was named after her, and now I think you had better play for a little and leave your lessons till later."

Harvey retreated to the library and spent some thirty or forty minutes in wondering whether it would be possible to compile a history, for use in elementary schools, in which there should be no prominent mention of battles, massacres, murderous intrigues, and violent deaths. The York and Lancaster period and the Napoleonic era would, he admitted to himself, present considerable difficulties, and the Thirty Years' War would entail something of a gap if you left it out altogether. Still, it would be something gained if, at a highly impressionable age, children could be got to fix their attention on the invention of calico printing instead of the Spanish Armada or the Battle of Waterloo.

It was time, he thought, to go back to the boys' room, and see how they were getting on with their peace toys. As he stood outside the door he could hear Eric's voice raised in command; Bertie chimed in now and again with a helpful suggestion.

"That is Louis the Fourteenth," Eric was saying, "that one in knee-breeches, that Uncle said invented Sunday schools. It isn't a bit like him, but it'll have to do."

"We'll give him a purple coat from my paintbox by and by," said Bertie.

"Yes, an' red heels. That is Madame de Maintenon, that one he called Mrs. Hemans. She begs Louis not to go on this expedition, but he turns a deaf ear. He takes Marshal Saxe with him, and we must pretend that they have thousands of men with them. The watchword is *Qui vive?* and the answer is *L'état c'est moi*—that was one of his favourite remarks, you know. They land at Manchester in the dead of night, and a Jacobite conspirator gives them the keys of the fortress."

Peeping in through the doorway Harvey observed that the municipal dust-bin had been pierced with holes to accommodate the muzzles of imaginary cannon, and now represented the principal fortified position in Manchester; John Stuart Mill had been dipped in red ink, and apparently stood for Marshal Saxe.

"Louis orders his troops to surround the Young Women's Christian

Association and seize the lot of them. 'Once back at the Louvre and the girls are mine,' he exclaims. We must use Mrs. Hemans again for one of the girls; she says 'Never,' and stabs Marshal Saxe to the heart."

"He bleeds dreadfully," exclaimed Bertie, splashing red ink liberally over the façade of the Association building.

"The soldiers rush in and avenge his death with the utmost savagery. A hundred girls are killed"—here Bertie emptied the remainder of the red ink over the devoted building—"and the surviving five hundred are dragged off to the French ships. 'I have lost a Marshal,' says Louis, 'but I do not go back empty-handed.'"

Harvey stole away from the room, and sought out his sister.

"Eleanor," he said, "the experiment—"

"Yes?"

"Has failed. We have begun too late."

LOUISE

"The tea will be quite cold, you'd better ring for some more," said the Dowager Lady Beanford.

Susan Lady Beanford was a vigorous old woman who had coquetted with imaginary ill-health for the greater part of a lifetime; Clovis Sangrail irreverently declared that she had caught a chill at the Coronation of Queen Victoria and had never let it go again. Her sister, Jane Thropplestance, who was some years her junior, was chiefly remarkable for being the most absent-minded woman in Middlesex.

"I've really been unusually clever this afternoon," she remarked gaily, as she rang for the tea. "I've called on all the people I meant to call on, and I've done all the shopping that I set out to do. I even remembered to try and match that silk for you at Harrod's, but I'd forgotten to bring the pattern with me, so it was no use. I really think that was the only important thing I forgot during the whole afternoon. Quite wonderful for me, isn't it?"

"What have you done with Louise?" asked her sister. "Didn't you take her out with you? You said you were going to."

"Good gracious," exclaimed Jane, "what *have* I done with Louise? I must have left her somewhere."

"But where?"

"That's just it. Where have I left her? I can't remember if the Carrywoods were at home or if I just left cards. If they were at home I may have left Louise there to play bridge. I'll go and telephone to Lord Carrywood and find out."

"Is that you, Lord Carrywood?" she queried over the telephone; "it's me, Jane Thropplestance. I want to know, have you seen Louise?"

"'Louise,'" came the answer, "it's been my fate to see it three times. At first, I must admit, I wasn't impressed by it, but the music grows on one after a bit. Still, I don't think I want to see it again just at present. Were you going to offer me a seat in your box?"

"Not the opera 'Louise'–my niece, Louise Thropplestance. I thought I might have left her at your house."

"You left cards on us this afternoon, I understand, but I don't think you left a niece. The footman would have been sure to have mentioned it if you had. Is it going to be a fashion to leave nieces on people as well as cards? I hope not; some of these houses in Berkeley Square have practically no accommodation for that sort of thing."

"She's not at the Carrywoods'," announced Jane, returning to her tea; "now I come to think of it, perhaps I left her at the silk counter at Selfridge's. I may have told her to wait there a moment while I went to look at the silks in a better light, and I may easily have forgotten about her when I found I hadn't your pattern with me. In that case she's still sitting there. She wouldn't move unless she was told to; Louise has no initiative."

"You said you tried to match the silk at Harrod's," interjected the dowager.

"Did I? Perhaps it was Harrod's. I really don't remember. It was one of those places where every one is so kind and sympathetic and devoted that one almost hates to take even a reel of cotton away from such pleasant surroundings."

"I think you might have taken Louise away. I don't like the idea of her being there among a lot of strangers. Supposing some unprincipled person was to get into conversation with her."

"Impossible. Louise has no conversation. I've never discovered a single topic on which she'd anything to say beyond 'Do you think so? I dare say you're right.' I really thought her reticence about the fall of the Ribot Ministry was ridiculous, considering how much her dear mother used to visit Paris. This bread and butter is cut far too thin; it crumbles away long before you can get it to your mouth. One feels so absurd, snapping at one's food in mid-air, like a trout leaping at may-fly."

"I am rather surprised," said the dowager, "that you can sit there making a hearty tea when you've just lost a favourite niece."

"You talk as if I'd lost her in a churchyard sense, instead of having temporarily mislaid her. I'm sure to remember presently where I left her."

"You didn't visit any place of devotion, did you? If you've left her mooning about Westminster Abbey or St. Peter's, Eaton Square, without being able to give any satisfactory reason why she's there, she'll be seized under the Cat and Mouse Act and sent to Reginald McKenna."

"That would be extremely awkward," said Jane, meeting an irresolute piece of bread and butter halfway; "we hardly know the McKennas, and it would be very tiresome having to telephone to some unsympathetic private secretary, describing Louise to him and asking to have her sent back in time for dinner. Fortunately, I didn't go to any place of devotion, though I did get mixed up with a Salvation Army procession. It was quite interesting to be at close quarters with them, they're so absolutely different to what they used to be when I first remember them in the 'eighties. They used to go about then unkempt and dishevelled, in a sort of smiling rage with the world, and now they're spruce and jaunty and flamboyantly decorative, like a geranium bed with religious convictions. Laura Kettleway was going on about them in the lift of the Dover Street Tube the other day, saying what a lot of good work they did, and what a loss it would have been if they'd never existed. 'If they had never existed,' I said, 'Granville Barker would have been certain to have invented something that looked exactly like them.' If you say things like that, quite loud, in a Tube lift, they always sound like epigrams."

"I think you ought to do something about Louise," said the dowager.

"I'm trying to think whether she was with me when I called on Ada Spelvexit. I rather enjoyed myself there. Ada was trying, as usual, to ram that odious Koriatoffski woman down my throat, knowing perfectly well that I detest her, and in an unguarded moment she said: 'She's leaving her present house and going to Lower Seymour Street.' 'I dare say she will, if she stays there long enough,' I said. Ada didn't see it for about three minutes, and then she was positively uncivil. No, I am certain I didn't leave Louise there."

"If you could manage to remember where you *did* leave her, it would be more to the point than these negative assurances," said Lady Beanford; "so far, all that we know is that she is not at the Carrywoods', or Ada Spelvexit's, or Westminister Abbey."

"That narrows the search down a bit," said Jane hopefully; "I rather fancy she must have been with me when I went to Mornay's. I know I went to Mornay's, because I remember meeting that delightful Malcolm What's-his-name there–you know whom I mean. That's the great advantage of people having unusual first names, you needn't try and remember what their other name is. Of course I know one or two other Malcolms, but none that could possibly be described as delightful. He gave me two tickets for the Happy Sunday Evenings in Sloane Square. I've probably left them at Mornay's, but still it was awfully kind of him to give them to me."

"Do you think you left Louise there?"

"I might telephone and ask. Oh, Robert, before you clean the tea-things away I wish you'd ring up Mornay's, in Regent Street, and ask if I left two theatre tickets and one niece in their shop this afternoon."

"A niece, ma'am?" asked the footman.

"Yes, Miss Louise didn't come home with me, and I'm not sure where I left her."

"Miss Louise has been upstairs all the afternoon, ma'am, reading to the second kitchenmaid, who has the neuralgia. I took up tea to Miss Louise at a quarter to five o'clock, ma'am."

"Of course, how silly of me. I remember now, I asked her to read the *Faërie Queene* to poor Emma, to try to send her to sleep. I always get some one to read the *Faërie Queene* to me when I have neuralgia, and it usually sends me to sleep. Louise doesn't seem to have been successful, but one can't say she hasn't tried. I expect after the first hour or so the kitchenmaid would rather have been left alone with her neuralgia, but of course Louise wouldn't leave off till some one told her to. Anyhow, you can ring up Mornay's, Robert, and ask whether I left two theatre tickets there. Except for your silk, Susan, those seem to be the only things I've forgotten this afternoon. Quite wonderful for me."

TEA

James Cushat-Prinkly was a young man who had always had a settled conviction that one of these days he would marry; up to the age of thirty-four he had done nothing to justify that conviction. He liked and admired a great many women collectively and dispassionately without singling out one for especial matrimonial consideration, just as one might admire the Alps without feeling that one wanted any particular peak as one's own private property. His lack of initiative in this matter aroused a certain amount of impatience among the sentimentally minded women-folk of his home circle; his mother, his sisters, an aunt-in-residence, and two or three intimate matronly friends regarded his dilatory approach to the married state with a disapproval that was far from being inarticulate. His most innocent flirtations were watched with the straining eagerness which a group of unexercised terriers concentrates on the slightest movements of a human being who may be reasonably considered likely to take them for a walk. No decent-souled mortal can long resist the pleading of several pairs of walk-beseeching dog-eyes; James Cushat-Prinkly was not sufficiently obstinate or indifferent to home influences to disregard the obviously expressed wish of his family that he should become enamoured of some nice marriageable girl, and when his Uncle Jules departed this life and bequeathed him a comfortable little legacy it really seemed the correct thing to do to set about discovering some one to share it with him. The process of discovery was carried on more by the force of suggestion and the weight of public opinion than by any initiative of his own; a clear working majority of his female relatives and the aforesaid matronly friends had pitched on Joan Sebastable as the most suitable young woman in his range of acquaintance to whom he might propose marriage, and James became gradually accustomed to the idea that he and Joan would go together through the prescribed stages of congratulations, present-receiving, Norwegian or Mediterranean hotels, and eventual domesticity. It was necessary, however, to ask the lady what she thought about the matter; the family had so far conducted and directed the flirtation with ability and discretion, but the actual proposal would have to be an individual effort.

Cushat-Prinkly walked across the Park towards the Sebastable residence in a frame of mind that was moderately complacent. As the thing was going to be done he was glad to feel that he was going to get it settled and off his mind that afternoon. Proposing marriage, even to a nice girl like Joan, was a rather irksome business, but one could not have a honeymoon in Minorca and a subsequent life of married happiness without such preliminary. He wondered what Minorca was really like as a place to stop in; in his mind's eye it was an island in perpetual half-mourning, with black or white Minorca hens running all over it. Probably it would not be a bit like that when one came to examine it. People who had been in Russia had told him that they did not remember having seen any Muscovy ducks there, so it was possible that there would be no Minorca fowls on the island.

His Mediterranean musings were interrupted by the sound of a clock striking the half-hour. Half-past four. A frown of dissatisfaction settled on his face. He would arrive at the Sebastable mansion just at the hour of afternoon tea. Joan would be seated at a low table, spread with an array of silver kettles and cream-jugs and delicate porcelain teacups, behind which her voice would tinkle pleasantly in a series of little friendly questions about weak or strong tea, how much, if any, sugar, milk, cream, and so forth. "Is it one lump? I forgot. You do take milk, don't you? Would you like some more hot water, if it's too strong?"

Cushat-Prinkly had read of such things in scores of novels, and hundreds of actual experiences had told him that they were true to life. Thousands of women, at this solemn afternoon hour, were sitting behind dainty porcelain and silver fittings, with their voices tinkling pleasantly in a cascade of solicitous little questions. Cushat-Prinkly detested the whole system of afternoon tea. According to his theory of life a woman should lie on a divan or couch, talking with incomparable charm or looking unutterable thoughts, or merely silent as a thing to be looked on, and from behind a silken curtain a small Nubian page should silently bring in a tray with cups and dainties, to be accepted silently, as a matter of course, without drawn-out chatter about cream and sugar and hot water. If one's soul was really enslaved at one's mistress's feet, how could one talk coherently about weakened tea? Cushat-Prinkly had never expounded his views on the subject to his mother; all her life she had been accustomed to tinkle pleasantly at tea-time behind dainty porcelain and silver, and if he had spoken to her about divans and Nubian pages she would have urged him to take a week's holiday at the seaside. Now, as he passed through a tangle of small streets that led indirectly to the elegant Mayfair terrace for which he was bound, a horror at the idea of confronting Joan Sebastable at her tea-table seized on him. A momentary deliverance presented itself; on one floor of a narrow little house at the noisier end of Esquimault Street lived Rhoda Ellam, a sort of remote cousin, who made a living by creating hats out of costly materials. The hats really looked as if they had come from Paris; the cheques she got for them unfortunately never looked as if they were going to Paris. However, Rhoda appeared to find life amusing and to have a fairly good time in spite of her straitened circumstances. Cushat-Prinkly decided to climb up to her floor and defer by half-an-hour or so the important business which lay before him; by spinning out his visit he could contrive to reach the Sebastable mansion after the last vestiges of dainty porcelain had been cleared away.

Rhoda welcomed him into a room that seemed to do duty as workshop, sitting-room, and kitchen combined, and to be wonderfully clean and comfortable at the same time.

"I'm having a picnic meal," she announced. "There's caviare in that jar at your elbow. Begin on that brown bread-and-butter while I cut some more. Find yourself a cup; the teapot is behind you. Now tell me about hundreds of things."

She made no other allusion to food, but talked amusingly and made her visitor talk amusingly too. At the same time she cut the bread-and-butter with a masterly skill and produced red pepper and sliced lemon, where so many women would merely have produced reasons and regrets for not having any. Cushat-Prinkly found that he was enjoying an excellent tea without having to answer as many questions about it as a Minister for Agriculture might be called on to reply to during an outbreak of cattle plague.

"And now tell me why you have come to see me," said Rhoda suddenly. "You arouse not merely my curiosity but my business instincts. I hope you've come about hats. I heard that you had come into a legacy the other day, and, of course, it struck me that it would be a beautiful and desirable thing for you to celebrate the event by buying brilliantly expensive hats for all your sisters. They may not have said anything about it, but I feel sure the same idea has occurred to them. Of course, with Goodwood on us, I am rather rushed just now, but in my business we're accustomed to that; we live in a series of rushes—like the infant Moses."

"I didn't come about hats," said her visitor. "In fact, I don't think I really came about anything. I was passing and I just thought I'd look in and see you. Since I've been sitting talking to you, however, a rather important idea has occurred to me. If you'll forget Goodwood for a moment and listen to me, I'll tell you what it is."

Some forty minutes later James Cushat-Prinkly returned to the bosom of his family, bearing an important piece of news.

"I'm engaged to be married," he announced.

A rapturous outbreak of congratulation and self-applause broke out.

"Ah, we knew! We saw it coming! We foretold it weeks ago!"

"I'll bet you didn't," said Cushat-Prinkly. "If any one had told me at lunch-time today that I was going to ask Rhoda Ellam to marry me and that she was going to accept me, I would have laughed at the idea."

The romantic suddenness of the affair in some measure compensated James's women-folk for the ruthless negation of all their patient effort and skilled diplomacy. It was rather trying to have to deflect their enthusiasm at a moment's notice from Joan Sebastable to Rhoda Ellam; but, after all, it was James's wife who was in question, and his tastes had some claim to be considered.

On a September afternoon of the same year, after the honeymoon in Minorca had ended, Cushat-Prinkly came into the drawing-room of his new house in Granchester Square. Rhoda was seated at a low table, behind a service of dainty porcelain and gleaming silver. There was a pleasant tinkling note in her voice as she handed him a cup.

"You like it weaker than that, don't you? Shall I put some more hot water to it? No?"

THE DISAPPEARANCE OF CRISPINA UMBERLEIGH

In a first-class carriage of a train speeding Balkanward across the flat, green Hungarian plain, two Britons sat in friendly, fitful converse. They had first foregathered in the cold grey dawn at the frontier line, where the presiding eagle takes on an extra head and Teuton lands pass from Hohenzollern to Habsburg keeping—and where a probing official beak requires to delve in polite and perhaps perfunctory, but always tiresome, manner into the baggage of sleep-hungry passengers. After a day's break of their journey at Vienna the travellers had again foregathered at the trainside and paid one another the compliment of settling instinctively into the same carriage. The elder of the two had the appearance and manner of a diplomat; in point of fact he was the well-connected foster-brother of a wine business. The other was certainly a journalist. Neither man was talkative and each was grateful to the other for not being talkative. That is why from time to time they talked.

One topic of conversation naturally thrust itself forward in front of all others. In Vienna the previous day they had learned of the mysterious vanishing of a world-famous picture from the walls of the Louvre.

"A dramatic disappearance of that sort is sure to produce a crop of imitations," said the Journalist.

"It has had a lot of anticipations, for the matter of that," said the Wine-brother.

"Oh, of course there have been thefts from the Louvre before."

"I was thinking of the spiriting away of human beings rather than pictures. In particular I was thinking of the case of my aunt, Crispina Umberleigh."

"I remember hearing something of the affair," said the Journalist, "but I was away from England at the time. I never quite knew what was supposed to have happened."

"You may hear what really happened if you will respect it as a confidence," said the Wine Merchant. "In the first place I may say that the disappearance of Mrs. Umberleigh was not regarded by the family entirely as a bereavement. My uncle, Edward Umberleigh, was not by any means a weak-kneed individual, in fact in the world of politics he had to be reckoned with more or less as a strong man, but he was unmistakably dominated by Crispina; indeed I never met any human being who was not frozen into subjection when brought into prolonged contact with her. Some people are born to command; Crispina Mrs. Umberleigh was born to legislate, codify, administrate, censor, license, ban, execute, and sit in judgment generally. If she was not born with that destiny she adopted it at an early age. From the kitchen regions upwards every one in the household came under her despotic sway and stayed there with the submissiveness of molluscs involved in a glacial epoch. As a nephew on a footing of only occasional visits she affected me merely as an epidemic, disagreeable while it lasted, but without any permanent effect; but her own sons and daughters stood in mortal awe of her; their studies, friendships, diet, amusements, religious observances, and way of doing their hair were all regulated and ordained according to the august lady's will and pleasure. This will help you to understand the sensation of stupefaction which was caused in the family when she unobtrusively and inexplicably vanished. It was as though St. Paul's Cathedral or the Piccadilly Hotel had disappeared in the night, leaving nothing but an open space to mark where it had stood. As far as was known nothing was troubling her; in fact there was much before her to make life particularly well worth living. The youngest boy had come back from school with an unsatisfactory report, and she was to have sat in judgment on him the very afternoon of the day she disappeared—if it had been he who had vanished in a hurry one could have supplied the motive. Then she was in the middle of a newspaper correspondence with a rural dean in which she had already proved him guilty of heresy, inconsistency, and unworthy quibbling, and no ordinary consideration would have induced her to discontinue the controversy. Of course the matter was put in the hands of the police, but as far as possible it was kept out of the papers, and the generally accepted explanation of her withdrawal from her social circle was that she had gone into a nursing home."

"And what was the immediate effect on the home circle?" asked the Journalist.

"All the girls bought themselves bicycles; the feminine cycling craze was still in existence, and Crispina had rigidly vetoed any participation in it among the members of her household. The youngest boy let himself go to such an extent during his next term that it had to be his last as far as that particular establishment was concerned. The elder boys propounded a theory that their mother might be wandering somewhere abroad, and searched for her assiduously, chiefly, it must be admitted, in a class of Montmartre resort where it was extremely improbable that she would be found."

"And all this while couldn't your uncle get hold of the least clue?"

"As a matter of fact he had received some information, though of course I did not know of it at the time. He got a message one day telling him that his wife had been kidnapped and smuggled out of the country; she was said to be hidden away, in one of the islands off the coast of Norway I think it was, in comfortable surroundings and well cared for. And with the information came a demand for money; a lump sum was to be handed over to her kidnappers and a further sum of £2,000 was to be paid yearly. Failing this she would be immediately restored to her family."

The Journalist was silent for a moment, and then began to laugh quietly.

"It was certainly an inverted form of holding to ransom," he said.

"If you had known my aunt," said the Wine Merchant, "you would have wondered that they didn't put the figure higher."

"I realize the temptation. Did your uncle succumb to it?"

"Well, you see, he had to think of others as well as himself. For the family to have gone back into the Crispina thraldom after having tasted the delights of liberty would have been a tragedy, and there were even wider considerations to be taken into account. Since his bereavement he had unconsciously taken up a far bolder and more initiatory line in public affairs, and his popularity and influence had increased correspondingly. From being merely a strong man in the political world he began to be spoken of as *the* strong man. All this he knew would be jeopardized if he once more dropped into the social position of the husband of Mrs. Umberleigh. He was a rich man, and the £2,000 a year, though not exactly a fleabite, did not seem an extravagant price to pay for the boarding-out of Crispina. Of course, he had severe qualms of conscience about the arrangement. Later on, when he took me into his confidence, he told me that in paying the ransom, or hush-money as I should have called it, he was partly influenced by the fear that if he refused it the kidnappers might have vented their rage and disappointment on their captive. It was better, he said, to think of her being well cared for as a highly valued paying-guest in one of the Lofoden Islands than to have her struggling miserably home in a maimed and mutilated condition. Anyway he paid the yearly instalment as punctually as one pays a fire insurance, and with equal promptitude there would come an acknowledgment of the money and a brief statement to the effect that Crispina was in good health and fairly cheerful spirits. One report even mentioned that she was busying herself with a scheme for proposed reforms in Church management to be pressed on the local pastorate. Another spoke of a rheumatic attack and a journey to a 'cure' on the mainland, and on that occasion an additional eighty pounds was demanded and conceded. Of course it was to the interest of the kidnappers to keep their charge in good health, but the secrecy with which they managed to shroud their arrangements argued a really wonderful organization. If my uncle was paying a rather high price, at least he could console himself with the reflection that he was paying specialists' fees."

"Meanwhile had the police given up all attempts to track the missing lady?" asked the Journalist.

"Not entirely; they came to my uncle from time to time to report on clues which they thought might yield some elucidation as to her fate or whereabouts, but I think they had their suspicions that he was possessed of more information than he had put at their disposal. And then, after a disappearance of more than eight years, Crispina returned with dramatic suddenness to the home she had left so mysteriously."

"She had given her captors the slip?"

"She had never been captured. Her wandering away had been caused by a sudden and complete loss of memory. She usually dressed in the style of a superior kind of charwoman, and it was not so very surprising that she should have imagined that she was one, and still less that people should accept her statement and help her to get work. She had wandered as far afield as Birmingham, and found fairly steady employment there, her energy and enthusiasm in putting people's rooms in order counter-balancing her obstinate and domineering characteristics. It was the shock of being patronizingly addressed as 'my good woman' by a curate, who was disputing with her where the stove should be placed in a parish concert hall, that led to the sudden restoration of her memory. 'I think you forget who you are speaking to,' she observed crushingly, which was rather unduly severe, considering she had only just remembered it herself."

"But," exclaimed the Journalist, "the Lofoden Island people! Who had they got hold of?"

"A purely mythical prisoner. It was an attempt in the first place by some one who knew something of the domestic situation, probably a discharged valet, to bluff a lump sum out of Edward Umberleigh before the missing woman turned up; the subsequent yearly instalments were an unlooked-for increment to the original haul.

"Crispina found that the eight years' interregnum had materially weakened her ascendency over her now grown-up offspring. Her husband, however, never accomplished anything great in the political world after her return; the strain of trying to account satisfactorily for an unspecified expenditure of sixteen thousand pounds spread over eight years sufficiently occupied his mental energies. Here is Belgrad and another custom house."

THE WOLVES OF CERNOGRATZ

"Are there any old legends attached to the castle?" asked Conrad of his sister. Conrad was a prosperous Hamburg merchant, but he was the one poetically-dispositioned member of an eminently practical family.

The Baroness Gruebel shrugged her plump shoulders.

"There are always legends hanging about these old places. They are not difficult to invent and they cost nothing. In this case there is a story that when any one dies in the castle all the dogs in the village and the wild beasts in the forest howl the night long. It would not be pleasant to listen to, would it?"

"It would be weird and romantic," said the Hamburg merchant.

"Anyhow, it isn't true," said the Baroness complacently; "since we bought the place we have had proof that nothing of the sort happens. When the old mother-in-law died last spring-time we all listened, but there was no howling. It is just a story that lends dignity to the place without costing anything."

"The story is not as you have told it," said Amalie, the grey old governess. Every one turned and looked at her in astonishment. She was wont to sit silent and prim and faded in her place at table, never speaking unless some one spoke to her, and there were few who troubled themselves to make conversation with her. Today a sudden volubility had descended on her; she continued to talk, rapidly and nervously, looking straight in front of her and seeming to address no one in particular.

"It is not when *any one* dies in the castle that the howling is heard. It was when one of the Cernogratz family died here that the wolves came from far and near and howled at the edge of the forest just before the death hour. There were only a few couple of wolves that had their lairs in this part of the forest, but at such a time the keepers say there would be scores of them, gliding about in the shadows and howling in chorus, and the dogs of the castle and the village and all the farms round would bay and howl in fear and anger at the wolf chorus, and as the soul of the dying one left its body a tree would crash down in the park. That is what happened when a Cernogratz died in his family castle. But for a stranger dying here, of course no wolf would howl and no tree would fall. Oh, no."

There was a note of defiance, almost of contempt, in her voice as she said the last words. The well-fed, much-too-well-dressed Baroness stared angrily at the dowdy old woman who had come forth from her usual and seemly position of effacement to speak so disrespectfully.

"You seem to know quite a lot about the von Cernogratz legends, Fräulein Schmidt," she said sharply; "I did not know that family histories were among the subjects you are supposed to be proficient in."

The answer to her taunt was even more unexpected and astonishing than the conversational outbreak which had provoked it.

"I am a von Cernogratz myself," said the old woman, "that is why I know the family history."

"You a von Cernogratz? You!" came in an incredulous chorus.

"When we became very poor," she explained, "and I had to go out and give teaching lessons, I took another name; I thought it would be more in keeping. But my grandfather spent much of his time as a boy in this castle, and my father used to tell me many stories about it, and, of course, I knew all the family legends and stories. When one has nothing left to one but memories, one guards and dusts them with especial care. I little thought when I took service with you that I should one day come with you to the old home of my family. I could wish it had been anywhere else."

There was silence when she finished speaking, and then the Baroness turned the conversation to a less embarrassing topic than family histories. But afterwards, when the old governess had slipped away quietly to her duties, there arose a clamour of derision and disbelief.

"It was an impertinence," snapped out the Baron, his protruding eyes taking on a scandalized expression; "fancy the woman talking like that at our table. She almost told us we were nobodies, and I don't believe a word of it. She is just Schmidt and nothing more. She has been talking to some of the peasants about the old Cernogratz family, and raked up their history and their stories."

"She wants to make herself out of some consequence," said the Baroness; "she knows she will soon be past work and she wants to appeal to our sympathies. Her grandfather, indeed!"

The Baroness had the usual number of grandfathers, but she never, never boasted about them.

"I dare say her grandfather was a pantry boy or something of the sort in the castle," sniggered the Baron; "that part of the story may be true."

The merchant from Hamburg said nothing; he had seen tears in the old woman's eyes when she spoke of guarding her memories—or, being of an imaginative disposition, he thought he had.

"I shall give her notice to go as soon as the New Year festivities are over," said the Baroness; "till then I shall be too busy to manage without her."

But she had to manage without her all the same, for in the cold biting weather after Christmas, the old governess fell ill and kept to her room.

"It is most provoking," said the Baroness, as her guests sat round the fire on one of the last evenings of the dying year; "all the time that she has been with us I cannot remember that she was ever seriously ill, too ill to go about and do her work, I mean. And now, when I have the house full, and she could be useful in so many ways, she goes and breaks down. One is sorry for her, of course, she looks so withered and shrunken, but it is intensely annoying all the same."

"Most annoying," agreed the banker's wife sympathetically; "it is the intense cold, I expect, it breaks the old people up. It has been unusually cold this year."

"The frost is the sharpest that has been known in December for many years," said the Baron.

"And, of course, she is quite old," said the Baroness; "I wish I had given her notice some weeks ago, then she would have left before this happened to her. Why, Wappi, what is the matter with you?"

The small, woolly lapdog had leapt suddenly down from its cushion and crept shivering under the sofa. At the same moment an outburst of angry barking came from the dogs in the castle-yard, and other dogs could be heard yapping and barking in the distance.

"What is disturbing the animals?" asked the Baron.

And then the humans, listening intently, heard the sound that had roused the dogs to their demonstrations of fear and rage; heard a long-drawn whining howl, rising and falling, seeming at one moment leagues away, at others sweeping across the snow until it appeared to come from the foot of the castle walls. All the starved, cold misery of a frozen world, all the relentless hunger-fury of the wild, blended with other forlorn and haunting melodies to which one could give no name, seemed concentrated in that wailing cry.

"Wolves!" cried the Baron.

Their music broke forth in one raging burst, seeming to come from everywhere.

"Hundreds of wolves," said the Hamburg merchant, who was a man of strong imagination.

Moved by some impulse which she could not have explained, the Baroness left her guests and made her way to the narrow, cheerless room where the old governess lay watching the hours of the dying year slip by. In spite of the biting cold of the winter night, the window stood open. With a scandalized exclamation on her lips, the Baroness rushed forward to close it.

"Leave it open," said the old woman in a voice that for all its weakness carried an air of command such as the Baroness had never heard before from her lips.

"But you will die of cold!" she expostulated.

"I am dying in any case," said the voice, "and I want to hear their music. They have come from far and wide to sing the death-music of my family. It is beautiful that they have come; I am the last von Cernogratz that will die in our old castle, and they have come to sing to me. Hark, how loud they are calling!"

The cry of the wolves rose on the still winter air and floated round the castle walls in long-drawn piercing wails; the old woman lay back on her couch with a look of long-delayed happiness on her face.

"Go away," she said to the Baroness; "I am not lonely any more. I am one of a great old family. . . ."

"I think she is dying," said the Baroness when she had rejoined her guests; "I suppose we must send for a doctor. And that terrible howling! Not for much money would I have such death-music."

"That music is not to be bought for any amount of money," said Conrad.

"Hark! What is that other sound?" asked the Baron, as a noise of splitting and crashing was heard.

It was a tree falling in the park.

There was a moment of constrained silence, and then the banker's wife spoke.

"It is the intense cold that is splitting the trees. It is also the cold that has brought the wolves out in such numbers. It is many years since we have had such a cold winter."

The Baroness eagerly agreed that the cold was responsible for these things. It was the cold of the open window, too, which caused the heart failure that made the doctor's ministrations unnecessary for the old Fräulein. But the notice in the newspapers looked very well—

"On December 29th, at Schloss Cernogratz, Amalie von Cernogratz, for many years the valued friend of Baron and Baroness Gruebel."

LOUIS

"It would be jolly to spend Easter in Vienna this year," said Strudwarden, "and look up some of my old friends there. It's about the jolliest place I know of to be at for Easter—"

"I thought we had made up our minds to spend Easter at Brighton," interrupted Lena Strudwarden, with an air of aggrieved surprise.

"You mean that you had made up your mind that we should spend Easter there," said her husband; "we spent last Easter there, and Whitsuntide as well, and the year before that we were at Worthing, and Brighton again before that. I think it would be just as well to have a real change of scene while we are about it."

"The journey to Vienna would be very expensive," said Lena.

"You are not often concerned about economy," said Strudwarden, "and in any case the trip to Vienna won't cost a bit more than the rather meaningless luncheon parties we usually give to quite meaningless acquaintances at Brighton. To escape from all that set would be a holiday in itself."

Strudwarden spoke feelingly; Lena Strudwarden maintained an equally feeling silence on that particular subject. The set that she gathered round her at Brighton and other South Coast resorts was composed of individuals who might be dull and meaningless in themselves, but who understood the art of flattering Mrs. Strudwarden. She had no intention of foregoing their society and their homage and flinging herself among unappreciative strangers in a foreign capital.

"You must go to Vienna alone if you are bent on going," she said; "I couldn't leave Louis behind, and a dog is always a fearful nuisance in a foreign hotel, besides all the fuss and separation of the quarantine restrictions when one comes back. Louis would die if he was parted from me for even a week. You don't know what that would mean to me."

Lena stooped down and kissed the nose of the diminutive brown Pomeranian that lay, snug and irresponsive, beneath a shawl on her lap.

"Look here," said Strudwarden, "this eternal Louis business is getting to be a ridiculous nuisance. Nothing can be done, no plans can be made, without some veto connected with that animal's whims or convenience being imposed. If you were a priest in attendance on some African fetish you couldn't set up a more elaborate code of restrictions. I believe you'd ask the Government to put off a General Election if you thought it would interfere with Louis's comfort in any way."

By way of answer to this tirade Mrs. Strudwarden stooped down again and kissed the irresponsive brown nose. It was the action of a woman with a beautifully meek nature, who would, however, send the whole world to the stake sooner than yield an inch where she knew herself to be in the right.

"It isn't as if you were in the least bit fond of animals," went on Strudwarden, with growing irritation; "when we are down at Kerryfield you won't stir a step to take the house dogs out, even if they're dying for a run, and I don't think you've been in the stables twice in your life. You laugh at what you call the fuss that's being made over the extermination of plumage birds, and you are quite indignant with me if I interfere on behalf of an ill-treated, over-driven animal on the road. And yet you insist on every one's plans being made subservient to the convenience of that stupid little morsel of fur and selfishness."

"You are prejudiced against my little Louis," said Lena, with a world of tender regret in her voice.

"I've never had the chance of being anything else but prejudiced against him," said Strudwarden; "I know what a jolly responsive companion a doggie can be, but I've never been allowed to put a finger near Louis. You say he snaps at any one except you and your maid, and you snatched him away from old Lady Peterby the other day, when she wanted to pet him, for fear he would bury his teeth in her. All that I ever see of him is the tip of his unhealthy-looking little nose, peeping out from his basket or from your muff, and I occasionally hear his wheezy little bark when you take him for a walk up and down the corridor. You can't expect one to get extravagantly fond of a dog of that sort. One might as well work up an affection for the cuckoo in a cuckoo-clock."

"He loves me," said Lena, rising from the table, and bearing the shawl-swathed Louis in her arms. "He loves only me, and perhaps that is why I love him so much in return. I don't care what you say against him, I am not going to be separated from him. If you insist on going to Vienna you must go alone, as far as I am concerned. I think it would be much more sensible if you were to come to Brighton with Louis and me, but of course you must please yourself."

"You must get rid of that dog," said Strudwarden's sister when Lena had left the room; "it must be helped to some sudden and merciful end. Lena is merely making use of it as an instrument for getting her own way on dozens of occasions when she would otherwise be obliged to yield gracefully to your wishes or to the general convenience. I am convinced that she doesn't care a brass button about the animal itself. When her friends are buzzing round her at Brighton or anywhere else and the dog would be in the way, it has to spend whole days alone with the maid, but if you want Lena to go with you anywhere where she doesn't want to go instantly she trots out the excuse that she couldn't be separated from her dog. Have you ever come into a room unobserved and heard Lena talking to her beloved pet? I never have. I believe she only fusses over it when there's some one present to notice her."

"I don't mind admitting," said Strudwarden, "that I've dwelt more than once lately on the possibility of some fatal accident putting an end to Louis's existence. It's not very easy, though, to arrange a fatality for a creature that spends most of its time in a muff or asleep in a toy kennel. I don't think poison would be any good; it's obviously horribly over-fed, for I've seen Lena offer it dainties at table sometimes, but it never seems to eat them."

"Lena will be away at church on Wednesday morning," said Elsie Strudwarden reflectively; "she can't take Louis with her there, and she is going on to the Dellings for lunch. That will give you several hours in which to carry out your purpose. The maid will be flirting with the chauffeur most of the time, and, anyhow, I can manage to keep her out of the way on some pretext or other."

"That leaves the field clear," said Strudwarden, "but unfortunately my brain is equally a blank as far as any lethal project is concerned. The little beast is so monstrously inactive; I can't pretend that it leapt into the bath and drowned itself, or that it took on the butcher's mastiff in unequal combat and got chewed up. In what possible guise could death come to a confirmed basket-dweller? It would be too suspicious if we invented a Suffragette raid and pretended that they invaded Lena's boudoir and threw a brick at him. We should have to do a lot of other damage as well, which would be rather a nuisance, and the servants would think it odd that they had seen nothing of the invaders."

"I have an idea," said Elsie; "get a box with an air-tight lid, and bore a small hole in it, just big enough to let in an india-rubber tube. Pop Louis, kennel and all, into the box, shut it down, and put the other end of the tube over the gas-bracket. There you have a perfect lethal chamber. You can stand the kennel at the open window afterwards, to get rid of the smell of the gas, and all that Lena will find when she comes home late in the afternoon will be a placidly defunct Louis."

"Novels have been written about women like you," said Strudwarden; "you have a perfectly criminal mind. Let's come and look for a box."

Two mornings later the conspirators stood gazing guiltily at a stout square box, connected with the gas-bracket by a length of india-rubber tubing.

"Not a sound," said Elsie; "he never stirred; it must have been quite painless. All the same I feel rather horrid now it's done."

"The ghastly part has to come," said Strudwarden, turning off the gas. "We'll lift the lid slowly, and let the gas out by degrees. Swing the door to and fro to send a draught through the room."

Some minutes later, when the fumes had rushed off, he stooped down and lifted out the little kennel with its grim burden. Elsie gave an exclamation of terror. Louis sat at the door of his dwelling, head erect and ears pricked, as coldly and defiantly inert as when they had put him into his execution chamber. Strudwarden dropped the kennel with a jerk, and stared for a long moment at the miracle-dog; then he went into a peal of chattering laughter.

It was certainly a wonderful imitation of a truculent-looking toy Pomeranian, and the apparatus that gave forth a wheezy bark when you pressed it had materially helped the imposition that Lena, and Lena's maid, had foisted on the household. For a woman who disliked animals, but liked getting her own way under a halo of unselfishness, Mrs. Strudwarden had managed rather well.

"Louis is dead," was the curt information that greeted Lena on her return from her luncheon party.

"Louis *dead!*" she exclaimed.

"Yes, he flew at the butcher-boy and bit him, and he bit me too, when I tried to get him off, so I had to have him destroyed. You warned me that he snapped, but you didn't tell me that he was down-right dangerous. I shall have to pay the boy something heavy by way of compensation, so you will have to go without those buckles that you wanted to have for Easter; also I shall have to go to Vienna to consult Dr. Schroeder, who is a specialist on dogbites, and you will have to come too. I have sent what remains of Louis to Rowland Ward to be stuffed; that will be my Easter gift to you instead of the buckles. For Heaven's sake, Lena, weep, if you really feel it so much; anything would be better than standing there staring as if you thought I had lost my reason."

Lena Strudwarden did not weep, but her attempt at laughing was an unmistakable failure.

THE GUESTS

"THE landscape seen from our windows is certainly charming," said Annabel; "those cherry orchards and green meadows, and the river winding along the valley, and the church tower peeping out among the elms, they all make a most effective picture. There's something dreadfully sleepy and languorous about it, though; stagnation seems to be the dominant note. Nothing ever happens here; seedtime and harvest, an occasional outbreak of measles or a mildly destructive thunderstorm, and a little election excitement about once in five years, that is all that we have to modify the monotony of our existence. Rather dreadful, isn't it?"

"On the contrary," said Matilda, "I find it soothing and restful; but then, you see, I've lived in countries where things do happen, ever so many at a time, when you're not ready for them happening all at once."

"That, of course, makes a difference," said Annabel.

"I have never forgotten," said Matilda, "the occasion when the Bishop of Bequar paid us an unexpected visit; he was on his way to lay the foundation-stone of a mission-house or something of the sort."

"I thought that out there you were always prepared for emergency guests turning up," said Annabel.

"I was quite prepared for half a dozen bishops," said Matilda, "but it was rather disconcerting to find out after a little conversation that this particular one was a distant cousin of mine, belonging to a branch of the family that had quarrelled bitterly and offensively with our branch about a Crown Derby dessert service; they got it, and we ought to have got it, in some legacy, or else we got it and they thought they ought to have it, I forget which; anyhow, I know they behaved disgracefully. Now here was one of them turning up in the odour of sanctity, so to speak, and claiming the traditional hospitality of the East."

"It was rather trying, but you could have left your husband to do most of the entertaining."

"My husband was fifty miles up-country, talking sense, or what he imagined to be sense, to a village community that fancied one of their leading men was a were-tiger."

"A what tiger?"

"A were-tiger; you've heard of were-wolves, haven't you, a mixture of wolf and human being and demon? Well, in those parts they have were-tigers, or think they have, and I must say that in this case, so far as sworn and uncontested evidence went, they had every ground for thinking so. However, as we gave up witchcraft prosecutions about three hundred years ago, we don't like to have other people keeping on our discarded practices; it doesn't seem respectful to our mental and moral position."

"I hope you weren't unkind to the Bishop," said Annabel.

"Well, of course he was my guest, so I had to be outwardly polite to him, but he was tactless enough to rake up the incidents of the old quarrel, and to try to make out that there was something to be said for the way his side of the family had behaved; even if there was, which I don't for a moment admit, my house was not the place in which to say it. I didn't argue the matter, but I gave my cook a holiday to go and visit his aged parents some ninety miles away. The emergency cook was not a specialist in curries; in fact, I don't think cooking in any shape or form could have been one of his strong points. I believe he originally came to us in the guise of a gardener, but as we never pretended to have anything that could be considered a garden he was utilized as assistant goatherd, in which capacity, I understand, he gave every satisfaction. When the Bishop heard that I had sent away the cook on a special and unnecessary holiday, he saw the inwardness of the manœuvre, and from that moment we were scarcely on speaking terms. If you have ever had a Bishop with whom you were not on speaking terms staying in your house, you will appreciate the situation."

Annabel confessed that her life-story had never included such a disturbing experience.

"Then," continued Matilda, "to make matters more complicated, the Gwadlipichee overflowed its banks, a thing it did every now and then when the rains were unduly prolonged, and the lower part of the house and all the out-buildings were submerged. We managed to get the ponies loose in time, and the syce swam the whole lot of them off to the nearest rising ground. A goat or two, the chief goatherd, the chief goatherd's wife, and several of their babies came to anchorage in the verandah. All the rest of the available space was filled up with wet, bedraggled-looking hens and chickens; one never really knows how many fowls one possesses till the servants' quarters are flooded out. Of course, I had been through something of the sort in previous floods, but never before had I had a houseful of goats and babies and half-drowned hens, supplemented by a Bishop with whom I was hardly on speaking terms."

"It must have been a trying experience," commented Annabel.

"More embarrassments were to follow. I wasn't going to let a mere ordinary flood wash out the memory of that Crown Derby dessert service, and I intimated to the Bishop that his large bedroom, with a writing table in it, and his small bathroom, with a sufficiency of cold-water jars in it, was his share of the premises, and that space was rather congested under the existing circumstances. However, at about three o'clock in the afternoon, when he had awakened from his midday sleep, he made a sudden incursion into the room that was normally the drawing-room, but was now dining-room, storehouse, saddle-room, and half a dozen other temporary premises as well. From the condition of my guest's costume he seemed to think it might also serve as his dressing-room.

"'I'm afraid there is nowhere for you to sit,' I said coldly; 'the verandah is full of goats.'

"'There is a goat in my bedroom,' he observed with equal coldness, and more than a suspicion of sardonic reproach.

"'Really,' I said, 'another survivor! I thought all the other goats were done for.'

"'This particular goat is quite done for,' he said; 'it is being devoured by a leopard at the present moment. That is why I left the room; some animals resent being watched while they are eating.'

"The leopard, of course, was easily explained; it had been hanging round the goat-sheds when the flood came, and had clambered up by the outside staircase leading to the Bishop's bath-room, thoughtfully bringing a goat with it. Probably it found the bath-room too damp and shut-in for its taste, and transferred its banqueting operations to the bedroom while the Bishop was having his nap."

"What a frightful situation!" exclaimed Annabel; "fancy having a ravening leopard in the house, with a flood all round you."

"Not in the least ravening," said Matilda; "it was full of goat, had any amount of water at its disposal if it felt thirsty, and probably had no more immediate wish than a desire for uninterrupted sleep. Still, I think any one will admit that it was an embarrassing predicament to have your only available guest-room occupied by a leopard, the verandah choked up with goats and babies and wet hens, and a Bishop with whom you were scarcely on speaking terms planted down in your only sitting-room. I really don't know how I got through those crawling hours, and of course meal-times only made matters worse. The emergency cook had every excuse for sending in watery soup and sloppy rice, and as neither the chief goatherd nor his wife were expert divers, the cellar could not be reached. Fortunately the Gwadlipichee subsides as rapidly as it rises, and just before dawn the syce came splashing back, with the ponies only fetlock deep in water. Then there arose some awkwardness from the fact that the Bishop wished to leave sooner than the leopard did, and as the latter was ensconced in the midst of the former's personal possessions there was an obvious difficulty in altering the order of departure. I pointed out to the Bishop that a leopard's habits and tastes are not those of an otter, and that it naturally preferred walking to wading, and that in any case a meal of an entire goat, washed down with tub-water, justified a certain amount of repose; if I had had guns fired to frighten the animal away, as the Bishop suggested, it would probably merely have left the bedroom to come into the already overcrowded drawing-room. Altogether it was rather a relief when they both left. Now, perhaps, you can understand my appreciation of a sleepy countryside where things don't happen."

THE PENANCE

Octavian Ruttle was one of those lively cheerful individuals on whom amiability had set its unmistakable stamp, and, like most of his kind, his soul's peace depended in large measure on the unstinted approval of his fellows. In hunting to death a small tabby cat he had done a thing of which he scarcely approved himself, and he was glad when the gardener had hidden the body in its hastily dug grave under a lone oak tree in the meadow, the same tree that the hunted quarry had climbed as a last effort towards safety. It had been a distasteful and seemingly ruthless deed, but circumstances had demanded the doing of it. Octavian kept chickens; at least he kept some of them; others vanished from his keeping, leaving only a few bloodstained feathers to mark the manner of their going. The tabby cat from the large grey house that stood with its back to the meadow had been detected in many furtive visits to the hen-coops, and after due negotiation with those in authority at the grey house a sentence of death had been agreed on: "The children will mind, but they need not know," had been the last word on the matter.

The children in question were a standing puzzle to Octavian; in the course of a few months he considered that he should have known their names, ages, the dates of their birthdays, and have been introduced to their favourite toys. They remained, however, as non-committal as the long blank wall that shut them off from the meadow, a wall over which their three heads sometimes appeared at odd moments. They had parents in India—that much Octavian had learned in the neighbourhood; the children, beyond grouping themselves garmentwise into sexes, a girl and two boys, carried their life-story no further on his behoof. And now it seemed he was engaged in something which touched them closely, but must be hidden from their knowledge.

The poor helpless chickens had gone one by one to their doom, so it was meet that their destroyer should come to a violent end, yet Octavian felt some qualms when his share of the violence was ended. The little cat, headed off from its wonted tracks of safety, had raced unfriended from shelter to shelter, and its end had been rather piteous. Octavian walked through the long grass of the meadow with a step less jaunty than usual. And as he passed beneath the shadow of the high blank wall he glanced up and became aware that his hunting had had undesired witnesses. Three white set faces were looking down at him, and if ever an artist wanted a threefold study of cold human hate, impotent yet unyielding, raging yet masked in stillness, he would have found it in the triple gaze that met Octavian's eye.

"I'm sorry, but it had to be done," said Octavian, with genuine apology in his voice.

"Beast!"

The answer came from three throats with startling intensity.

Octavian felt that the blank wall would not be more impervious to his explanations than the bunch of human hostility that peered over its coping; he wisely decided to withhold his peace overtures till a more hopeful occasion.

Two days later he ransacked the best sweet-shop in the neighbouring market town for a box of chocolates that by its size and contents should fitly atone for the dismal deed done under the oak tree in the meadow. The two first specimens that were shown him he hastily rejected; one had a group of chickens pictured on its lid, the other bore the portrait of a tabby kitten. A third sample was more simply bedecked with a spray of painted poppies, and Octavian hailed the flowers of forgetfulness as a happy omen. He felt distinctly more at ease with his surroundings when the imposing package had been sent across to the grey house, and a message returned to say that it had been duly given to the children. The next morning he sauntered with purposeful steps past the long blank wall on his way to the chicken-run and piggery that stood at the bottom of the meadow. The three children were perched at their accustomed look-out, and their range of sight did not seem to concern itself with Octavian's presence. As he became depressingly aware of the aloofness of their gaze he also noted a strange variegation in the herbage at his feet; the greensward for a considerable space around was strewn and speckled with a chocolate-coloured hail, enlivened here and there with gay tinsel-like wrappings or the glistening mauve of crystallized violets. It was as though the fairy paradise of a greedy-minded child had taken shape and substance in the vegetation of the meadow. Octavian's blood-money had been flung back at him in scorn.

To increase his discomfiture the march of events tended to shift the blame of ravaged chicken-coops from the supposed culprit who had already paid full forfeit; the young chicks were still carried off, and it seemed highly probable that the cat had only haunted the chicken-run to prey on the rats which harboured there. Through the flowing channels of servant talk the children learned of this belated revision of verdict, and Octavian one day picked up a sheet of copy-book paper on which was painstakingly written: "Beast. Rats eated your chickens." More ardently than ever did he wish for an opportunity for sloughing off the disgrace that enwrapped him, and earning some happier nickname from his three unsparing judges.

And one day a chance inspiration came to him. Olivia, his two-year-old daughter, was accustomed to spend the hour from high noon till one o'clock with her father while the nursemaid gobbled and digested her dinner and novelette. About the same time the blank wall was usually enlivened by the presence of its three small wardens. Octavian, with seeming carelessness of purpose, brought Olivia well within hail of the watchers and noted with hidden delight the growing interest that dawned in that hitherto sternly hostile quarter. His little Olivia, with her sleepy placid ways, was going to succeed where he, with his anxious well-meant overtures, had so signally failed. He brought her a large yellow dahlia, which she grasped tightly in one hand and regarded with a stare of benevolent boredom, such as one might bestow on amateur classical dancing performed in aid of a deserving charity. Then he turned shyly to the group perched on the wall and asked with affected carelessness, "Do you like flowers?" Three solemn nods rewarded his venture.

"Which sorts do you like best?" he asked, this time with a distinct betrayal of eagerness in his voice.

"Those with all the colours, over there." Three chubby arms pointed to a distant tangle of sweet-pea. Child-like, they had asked for what lay farthest from hand, but Octavian trotted off gleefully to obey their welcome behest. He pulled and plucked with unsparing hand, and brought every variety of tint that he could see into his bunch that was rapidly becoming a bundle. Then he turned to retrace his steps, and found the blank wall blanker and more deserted than ever, while the foreground was void of all trace of Olivia. Far down the meadow three children were pushing a go-cart at the utmost speed they could muster in the direction of the piggeries; it was Olivia's go-cart and Olivia sat in it, somewhat bumped and shaken by the pace at which she was being driven, but apparently retaining her wonted composure of mind. Octavian stared for a moment at the rapidly moving group, and then started in hot pursuit, shedding as he ran sprays of blossom from the mass of sweet-pea that he still clutched in his hands. Fast as he ran the children had reached the piggery before he could overtake them, and he arrived just in time to see Olivia, wondering but unprotesting, hauled and pushed up to the roof of the nearest sty. They were old buildings in some need of repair, and the rickety roof would certainly not have borne Octavian's weight if he had attempted to follow his daughter and her captors on their new vantage ground.

"What are you going to do with her?" he panted. There was no mistaking the grim trend of mischief in those flushed but sternly composed young faces.

"Hang her in chains over a slow fire," said one of the boys. Evidently they had been reading English history.

"Frow her down and the pigs will d'vour her, every bit 'cept the palms of her hands," said the other boy. It was also evident that they had studied Biblical history.

The last proposal was the one which most alarmed Octavian,

since it might be carried into effect at a moment's notice; there had been cases, he remembered, of pigs eating babies.

"You surely wouldn't treat my poor little Olivia in that way?" he pleaded.

"You killed our little cat," came in stern reminder from three throats.

"I'm very sorry I did," said Octavian, and if there is a standard of measurement in truths Octavian's statement was assuredly a large nine.

"We shall be very sorry when we've killed Olivia," said the girl, "but we can't be sorry till we've done it."

The inexorable child-logic rose like an unyielding rampart before Octavian's scared pleadings. Before he could think of any fresh line of appeal his energies were called out in another direction. Olivia had slid off the roof and fallen with a soft, unctuous splash into a morass of muck and decaying straw. Octavian scrambled hastily over the pigsty wall to her rescue, and at once found himself in a quagmire that engulfed his feet. Olivia, after the first shock of surprise at her sudden drop through the air, had been mildly pleased at finding herself in close and unstinted contact with the sticky element that oozed around her, but as she began to sink gently into the bed of slime a feeling dawned on her that she was not after all very happy, and she began to cry in the tentative fashion of the normally good child. Octavian, battling with the quagmire, which seemed to have learned the rare art of giving way at all points without yielding an inch, saw his daughter slowly disappearing in the engulfing slush, her smeared face further distorted with the contortions of whimpering wonder, while from their perch on the pigsty roof the three children looked down with the cold unpitying detachment of the Parcæ Sisters.

"I can't reach her in time," gasped Octavian, "she'll be choked in the muck. Won't you help her?"

"No one helped our cat," came the inevitable reminder.

"I'll do anything to show you how sorry I am about that," cried Octavian, with a further desperate flounder, which carried him scarcely two inches forward.

"Will you stand in a white sheet by the grave?"

"Yes," screamed Octavian.

"Holding a candle?"

"An' saying, 'I'm a miserable Beast'?"

Octavian agreed to both suggestions.

"For a long, long time?"

"For half an hour," said Octavian. There was an anxious ring in his voice as he named the time-limit; was there not the precedent of a German king who did open-air penance for several days and nights at Christmas-time clad only in his shirt? Fortunately the children did not appear to have read German history, and half an hour seemed long and goodly in their eyes.

"All right," came with threefold solemnity from the roof, and a moment later a short ladder had been laboriously pushed across to Octavian, who lost no time in propping it against the low pigsty wall. Scrambling gingerly along its rungs he was able to lean across the morass that separated him from his slowly foundering offspring and extract her like an unwilling cork from its slushy embrace. A few minutes later he was listening to the shrill and repeated assurances of the nursemaid that her previous experience of filthy spectacles had been on a notably smaller scale.

That same evening when twilight was deepening into darkness Octavian took up his position as penitent under the lone oak tree, having first carefully undressed the part. Clad in a zephyr shirt, which on this occasion thoroughly merited its name, he held in one hand a lighted candle and in the other a watch, into which the soul of a dead plumber seemed to have passed. A box of matches lay at his feet and was resorted to on the fairly frequent occasions when the candle succumbed to the night breezes. The house loomed inscrutable in the middle distance, but as Octavian conscientiously repeated the formula of his penance he felt certain that three pairs of solemn eyes were watching his moth-shared vigil.

And the next morning his eyes were gladdened by a sheet of copy-book paper lying beside the blank wall, on which was written the message "Un-Beast."

THE PHANTOM LUNCHEON

"The Smithly-Dubbs are in Town," said Sir James. "I wish you would show them some attention. Ask them to lunch with you at the Ritz or somewhere."

"From the little I've seen of the Smithly-Dubbs I don't think I want to cultivate their acquaintance," said Lady Drakmanton.

"They always work for us at election times," said her husband; "I don't suppose they influence very many votes, but they have an uncle who is on one of my ward committees, and another uncle speaks sometimes at some of our less important meetings. Those sort of people expect some return in the shape of hospitality."

"Expect it!" exclaimed Lady Drakmanton; "the Misses Smithly-Dubb do more than that; they almost demand it. They belong to my club, and hang about the lobby just about lunch-time, all three of them, with their tongues hanging out of their mouths and the six-course look in their eyes. If I were to breathe the word 'lunch' they would hustle me into a taxi and scream 'Ritz' or 'Dieudonné's' to the driver before I knew what was happening."

"All the same, I think you ought to ask them to a meal of some sort," persisted Sir James.

"I consider that showing hospitality to the Smithly-Dubbs is carrying Free Food principles to a regrettable extreme," said Lady Drakmanton; "I've entertained the Joneses and the Browns and the Snapheimers and the Lubrikoffs, and heaps of others whose names I forget, but I don't see why I should inflict the society of the Misses Smithly-Dubb on myself for a solid hour. Imagine it, sixty minutes, more or less, of unrelenting gobble and gabble. Why can't *you* take them on, Milly?" she asked, turning hopefully to her sister.

"I don't know them," said Milly hastily.

"All the better; you can pass yourself off as me. People say that we are so alike that they can hardly tell us apart, and I've only spoken to these tiresome young women about twice in my life, at committee-rooms, and bowed to them in the club. Any of the club page-boys will point them out to you; they're always to be found lolling about the hall just before lunch-time."

"My dear Betty, don't be absurd," protested Milly; "I've got some people lunching with me at the Carlton tomorrow, and I'm leaving Town the day afterwards."

"What time is your lunch tomorrow?" asked Lady Drakmanton reflectively.

"Two o'clock," said Milly.

"Good," said her sister; "the Smithly-Dubbs shall lunch with me tomorrow. It shall be rather an amusing lunch-party. At least, I shall be amused."

The last two remarks she made to herself. Other people did not always appreciate her ideas of humour. Sir James never did.

The next day Lady Drakmanton made some marked variations in her usual toilet effects. She dressed her hair in an unaccustomed manner, and put on a hat that added to the transformation of her appearance. When she had made one or two minor alterations she was sufficiently unlike her usual smart self to produce some hesitation in the greeting which the Misses Smithly-Dubb bestowed on her in the club lobby. She responded, however, with a readiness which set their doubts at rest.

"What is the Carlton like for lunching in?" she asked breezily.

The restaurant received an enthusiastic recommendation from the three sisters.

"Let's go and lunch there, shall we?" she suggested, and in a few minutes' time the Smithly-Dubb mind was contemplating at close quarters a happy vista of baked meats and approved vintage.

"Are you going to start with caviare? I am," confided Lady Drakmanton, and the Smithly-Dubbs started with caviare. The subsequent dishes were chosen in the same ambitious spirit, and by the time they had arrived at the wild duck course it was beginning to be a rather expensive lunch.

The conversation hardly kept pace with the brilliancy of the menu. Repeated references on the part of the guests to the local political conditions and prospects in Sir James's constituency were met with vague "ahs" and "indeeds" from Lady Drakmanton, who might have been expected to be specially interested.

"I think when the Insurance Act is a little better understood it will lose some of its present unpopularity," hazarded Cecilia Smithly-Dubb.

"Will it? I dare say. I'm afraid politics don't interest me very much," said Lady Drakmanton.

The three Miss Smithly-Dubbs put down their cups of Turkish coffee and stared. Then they broke into protesting giggles.

"Of course, you're joking," they said.

"Not me," was the disconcerting answer; "I can't make head or tail of these bothering old politics. Never could, and never want to. I've quite enough to do to manage my own affairs, and that's a fact."

"But," exclaimed Amanda Smithly-Dubb, with a squeal of bewilderment breaking into her voice, "I was told you spoke so informingly about the Insurance Act at one of our social evenings."

It was Lady Drakmanton who stared now. "Do you know," she

said, with a scared look around her, "rather a dreadful thing is happening. I'm suffering from a complete loss of memory. I can't even think who I am. I remember meeting you somewhere, and I remember you asking me to come and lunch with you here, and that I accepted your kind invitation. Beyond that my mind is a positive blank."

The scared look was transferred with intensified poignancy to the faces of her companions.

"*You* asked *us* to lunch," they exclaimed hurriedly. That seemed a more immediately important point to clear up than the question of identity.

"Oh, no," said the vanishing hostess, "*that* I do remember about. You insisted on my coming here because the feeding was so good, and I must say it comes up to all you said about it. A very nice lunch it's been. What I'm worrying about is, who on earth am I? I haven't the faintest notion."

"You are Lady Drakmanton," exclaimed the three sisters in chorus.

"Now, don't make fun of me," she replied crossly. "I happen to know her quite well by sight, and she isn't a bit like me. And it's an odd thing you should have mentioned her, for it so happens she's just come into the room. That lady in black with the yellow plume in her hat, there over by the door."

The Smithly-Dubbs looked in the indicated direction, and the uneasiness in their eyes deepened into horror. In outward appearance the lady who had just entered the room certainly came rather nearer to their recollection of their Member's wife than the individual who was sitting at table with them.

"Who *are* you, then, if that is Lady Drakmanton?" they asked in panic-stricken bewilderment.

"That is just what I don't know," was the answer; "and you don't seem to know much better than I do."

"You came up to us in the club—"

"In what club?"

"The New Didactic, in Calais Street."

"The New Didactic!" exclaimed Lady Drakmanton with an air of returning illumination; "thank you so much. Of course, I remember now who I am. I'm Ellen Niggle, of the Ladies' Brass-polishing Guild. The Club employs me to come now and then and see to the polishing of the brass fittings. That's how I came to know Lady

Drakmanton by sight; she's very often in the Club. And you are the ladies who so kindly asked me out to lunch. Funny how it should all have slipped my memory, all of a sudden. The unaccustomed good food and wine must have been too much for me; for the moment I really couldn't call to mind who I was. Good gracious," she broke off suddenly, "it's ten past two; I should be at a polishing job in Whitehall. I must scuttle off like a giddy rabbit. Thanking you ever so."

She left the room with a scuttle sufficiently suggestive of the animal she had mentioned, but the giddiness was all on the side of her involuntary hostesses. The restaurant seemed to be spinning round them, and the bill when it appeared did nothing to restore their composure. They were as nearly in tears as it is permissible to be during the luncheon hour in a really good restaurant. Financially speaking, they were well able to afford the luxury of an elaborate lunch, but their ideas on the subject of entertaining differed very sharply, according to the circumstances of whether they were dispensing or receiving hospitality. To have fed themselves liberally at their own expense was, perhaps, an extravagance to be deplored, but, at any rate, they had had something for their money; to have drawn an unknown and socially unremunerative Ellen Niggle into the net of their hospitality was a catastrophe that they could not contemplate with any degree of calmness.

The Smithly-Dubbs never quite recovered from their unnerving experience. They have given up politics and taken to doing good.

A BREAD AND BUTTER MISS

"Starling Chatter and Oakhill have both dropped back in the betting," said Bertie van Tahn, throwing the morning paper across the breakfast table.

"That leaves Nursery Tea practically favourite," said Odo Finsberry.

"Nursery Tea and Pipeclay are at the top of the betting at present," said Bertie, "but that French horse, Le Five O'Clock, seems to be fancied as much as anything. Then there is Whitebait, and the Polish horse with a name like some one trying to stifle a sneeze in church; they both seem to have a lot of support."

"It's the most open Derby there's been for years," said Odo.

"It's simply no good trying to pick the winner on form," said Bertie; "one must just trust to luck and inspiration."

"The question is whether to trust to one's own inspiration, or somebody else's. *Sporting Swank* gives Count Palatine to win, and Le Five O'Clock for a place."

"Count Palatine—that adds another to our list of perplexities. Good morning, Sir Lulworth; have you a fancy for the Derby by any chance?"

"I don't usually take much interest in turf matters," said Sir Lulworth, who had just made his appearance, "but I always like to have a bet on the Guineas and the Derby. This year, I confess, it's rather difficult to pick out anything that seems markedly better than anything else. What do you think of Snow Bunting?"

"Snow Bunting?" said Odo, with a groan, "there's another of them. Surely, Snow Bunting has no earthly chance?"

"My housekeeper's nephew, who is a shoeing-smith in the mounted section of the Church Lads' Brigade, and an authority on horseflesh, expects him to be among the first three."

"The nephews of housekeepers are invariably optimists," said Bertie; "it's a kind of natural reaction against the professional pessimism of their aunts."

"We don't seem to get much further in our search for the probable winner," said Mrs. de Claux; "the more I listen to you experts the more hopelessly befogged I get."

"It's all very well to blame us," said Bertie to his hostess; "*you* haven't produced anything in the way of an inspiration."

"My inspiration consisted in asking you down for Derby week," retorted Mrs. de Claux; "I thought you and Odo between you might throw some light on *the* question of the moment."

Further recriminations were cut short by the arrival of Lola Pevensey, who floated into the room with an air of gracious apology.

"So sorry to be so late," she observed, making a rapid tour of inspection of the breakfast dishes.

"Did you have a good night?" asked her hostess with perfunctory solicitude.

"Quite, thank you," said Lola; "I dreamt a most remarkable dream."

A flutter, indicative of general boredom, went round the table.

Other people's dreams are about as universally interesting as accounts of other people's gardens, or chickens, or children.

"I dreamt about the winner of the Derby," said Lola.

A swift reaction of attentive interest set in.

"Do tell us what you dreamt," came in a chorus.

"The really remarkable thing about it is that I've dreamt it two nights running," said Lola, finally deciding between the allurements of sausages and kedgeree; "that is why I thought it worth mentioning. You know, when I dream things two or three nights in succession, it always means something; I have special powers in that way. For instance, I once dreamed three times that a winged lion was flying through the sky and one of his wings dropped off, and he came to the ground with a crash; just afterwards the Campanile at Venice fell down. The winged lion is the symbol of Venice, you know," she added for the enlightenment of those who might not be versed in Italian heraldry. "Then," she continued, "just before the murder of the King and Queen of Servia I had a vivid dream of two crowned figures walking into a slaughter-house by the banks of a big river, which I took to be the Danube; and only the other day–"

"Do tell us what you've dreamt about the Derby," interrupted Odo impatiently.

"Well, I saw the finish of the race as clearly as anything; and one horse won easily, almost in a canter, and everybody cried out 'Bread and Butter wins! Good old Bread and Butter.' I heard the name distinctly, and I've had the same dream two nights running."

"Bread and Butter," said Mrs. de Claux, "now, whatever horse can that point to? Why–of course; Nursery Tea!"

She looked round with the triumphant smile of a successful unraveller of mystery.

"How about Le Five O'Clock?" interposed Sir Lulworth.

"It would fit either of them equally well," said Odo; "can you remember any details about the jockey's colours? That might help us."

"I seem to remember a glimpse of lemon sleeves or cap, but I can't be sure," said Lola, after due reflection.

"There isn't a lemon jacket or cap in the race," said Bertie, referring to a list of starters and jockeys; "can't you remember anything about the appearance of the horse? If it were a thick-set animal, thick bread and butter would typify Nursery Tea; and if it were thin, of course, it would mean Le Five O'Clock."

"That seems sound enough," said Mrs. de Claux; "do think, Lola dear, whether the horse in your dream was thin or stoutly built."

"I can't remember that it was one or the other," said Lola; "one wouldn't notice such a detail in the excitement of a finish."

"But this was a symbolic animal," said Sir Lulworth; "if it were to typify thick or thin bread and butter, surely it ought to have been either as bulky and tubby as a shire cart-horse, or as thin as a heraldic leopard."

"I'm afraid you are rather a careless dreamer," said Bertie resentfully.

"Of course, at the moment of dreaming I thought I was witnessing a real race, not the portent of one," said Lola; "otherwise I should have particularly noticed all helpful details."

"The Derby isn't run till tomorrow," said Mrs. de Claux; "do you think you are likely to have the same dream again tonight? If so, you can fix your attention on the important detail of the animal's appearance."

"I'm afraid I shan't sleep at all tonight," said Lola pathetically; "every fifth night I suffer from insomnia, and it's due tonight."

"It's most provoking," said Bertie; "of course, we can back both horses, but it would be much more satisfactory to have all our money on the winner. Can't you take a sleeping-draught, or something?"

"Oakleaves, soaked in warm water and put under the bed, are recommended by some," said Mrs. de Claux.

"A glass of Benedictine, with a drop of eau-de-Cologne—" said Sir Lulworth.

"I have tried every known remedy," said Lola, with dignity; "I've been a martyr to insomnia for years."

"But now we are being martyrs to it," said Odo sulkily; "I particularly want to land a big coup over this race."

"I don't have insomnia for my own amusement," snapped Lola.

"Let us hope for the best," said Mrs. de Claux soothingly; "tonight may prove an exception to the fifth-night rule."

But when breakfast time came round again Lola reported a blank night as far as visions were concerned.

"I don't suppose I had as much as ten minutes' sleep, and, certainly, no dreams."

"I'm so sorry, for your sake in the first place, and ours as well," said her hostess; "do you think you could induce a short nap after breakfast? It would be so good for you–and you *might* dream something. There would still be time for us to get our bets on."

"I'll try if you like," said Lola; "it sounds rather like a small child being sent to bed in disgrace."

"I'll come and read the *Encyclopædia Britannica* to you if you think it will make you sleep any sooner," said Bertie obligingly.

Rain was falling too steadily to permit of outdoor amusement, and the party suffered considerably during the next two hours from the absolute quiet that was enforced all over the house in order to give Lola every chance of achieving slumber. Even the click of billiard balls was considered a possible factor of disturbance, and the canaries were carried down to the gardener's lodge, while the cuckoo clock in the hall was muffled under several layers of rugs. A notice, "Please do not Knock or Ring," was posted on the front door at Bertie's suggestion, and guests and servants spoke in tragic whispers as though the dread presence of death or sickness had invaded the house. The precautions proved of no avail: Lola added a sleepless morning to a wakeful night, and the bets of the party had to be impartially divided between Nursery Tea and the French Colt.

"So provoking to have to split our bets," said Mrs. de Claux, as her guests gathered in the hall later in the day, waiting for the result of the race.

"I did my best for you," said Lola, feeling that she was not getting her due share of gratitude; "I told you what I had seen in my dreams, a brown horse, called Bread and Butter, winning easily from all the rest."

"What?" screamed Bertie, jumping up from his seat, "a *brown* horse! Miserable woman, you never said a word about it's being a brown horse."

"Didn't I?" faltered Lola. "I thought I told you it was a brown horse. It was certainly brown in both dreams. But I don't see what colour has got to do with it. Nursery Tea and Le Five O'Clock are both chestnuts."

"Merciful Heaven! Doesn't brown bread and butter with a sprinkling of lemon in the colours suggest anything to you?" raged Bertie.

A slow, cumulative groan broke from the assembly as the meaning of his words gradually dawned on his hearers.

For the second time that day Lola retired to the seclusion of her room; she could not face the universal looks of reproach directed at her when Whitebait was announced winner at the comfortable price of fourteen to one.

BERTIE'S CHRISTMAS EVE

It was Christmas Eve, and the family circle of Luke Steffink, Esq., was aglow with the amiability and random mirth which the occasion demanded. A long and lavish dinner had been partaken of, waits had been round and sung carols, the house-party had regaled itself with more carolling on its own account, and there had been romping which, even in a pulpit reference, could not have been condemned as ragging. In the midst of the general glow, however, there was one black unkindled cinder.

Bertie Steffink, nephew of the aforementioned Luke, had early in life adopted the profession of ne'er-do-weel; his father had been something of the kind before him. At the age of eighteen Bertie had commenced that round of visits to our Colonial possessions, so seemly and desirable in the case of a Prince of the Blood, so suggestive of insincerity in a young man of the middle-class. He had gone to grow tea in Ceylon and fruit in British Columbia, and to help sheep to grow wool in Australia. At the age of twenty he had just returned from some similar errand in Canada, from which it may be gathered that the trial he gave to these various experiments was of the summary drum-head nature. Luke Steffink, who fulfilled the troubled rôle of guardian and deputy-parent to Bertie, deplored the persistent manifestation of the homing instinct on his nephew's part, and his solemn thanks earlier in the day for the blessing of reporting a united family had no reference to Bertie's return.

Arrangements had been promptly made for packing the youth off to a distant corner of Rhodesia, whence return would be a difficult matter; the journey to this uninviting destination was imminent, in fact a more careful and willing traveller would have already begun to think about his packing. Hence Bertie was in no mood to share in the festive spirit which displayed itself around him, and resentment smouldered within him at the eager, self-absorbed discussion of social plans for the coming months which he heard on all sides. Beyond depressing his uncle and the family circle generally by singing "Say au revoir, and not good-bye," he had taken no part in the evening's conviviality.

Eleven o'clock had struck some half-hour ago, and the elder Steffinks began to throw out suggestions leading up to that process which they called retiring for the night.

"Come, Teddie, it's time you were in your little bed, you know," said Luke Steffink to his thirteen-year-old son.

"That's where we all ought to be," said Mrs. Steffink.

"There wouldn't be room," said Bertie.

The remark was considered to border on the scandalous; everybody ate raisins and almonds with the nervous industry of sheep feeding during threatening weather.

"In Russia," said Horace Bordenby, who was staying in the house as a Christmas guest, "I've read that the peasants believe that if you go into a cow-house or stable at midnight on Christmas Eve you will hear the animals talk. They're supposed to have the gift of speech at that one moment of the year."

"Oh, *do* let's *all* go down to the cow-house and listen to what they've got to say?" exclaimed Beryl, to whom anything was thrilling and amusing if you did it in a troop.

Mrs. Steffink made a laughing protest, but gave a virtual consent by saying, "We must all wrap up well, then." The idea seemed a scatterbrained one to her, and almost heathenish, but it afforded an opportunity for "throwing the young people together," and as such she welcomed it. Mr. Horace Bordenby was a young man with quite substantial prospects, and he had danced with Beryl at a local subscription ball a sufficient number of times to warrant the authorized inquiry on the part of the neighbours whether "there was anything in it." Though Mrs. Steffink would not have put it in so many words, she shared the idea of the Russian peasantry that on this night the beast might speak.

The cow-house stood at the junction of the garden with a small paddock, an isolated survival, in a suburban neighbourhood, of what had once been a small farm. Luke Steffink was complacently proud of his cow-house and his two cows; he felt that they gave him a stamp of solidity which no number of Wyandottes or Orpingtons could impart. They even seemed to link him in a sort of inconsequent way with those patriarchs who derived importance from their floating capital of flocks and herds, he-asses and she-asses. It had been an anxious and momentous occasion when he had had to decide definitely between "the Byre" and "the Ranch" for the naming of his villa residence. A December midnight was hardly the moment he would have chosen for showing his farm-building to visitors, but since it was a fine night, and the young people were anxious for an excuse for a mild frolic, Luke consented to chaperon the expedition. The servants had long since gone to bed, so the house was left in charge of Bertie, who scornfully declined to stir out on the pretext of listening to bovine conversation.

"We must go quietly," said Luke, as he headed the procession of giggling young folk, brought up in the rear by the shawled and hooded figure of Mrs. Steffink; "I've always laid stress on keeping this a quiet and orderly neighbourhood."

It was a few minutes to midnight when the party reached the cow-house and made its way in by the light of Luke's stable lantern. For a moment every one stood in silence, almost with a feeling of being in church.

"Daisy—the one lying down—is by a shorthorn bull out of a Guernsey cow," announced Luke in a hushed voice, which was in keeping with the foregoing impression.

"Is she?" said Bordenby, rather as if he had expected her to be by Rembrandt.

"Myrtle is—"

Myrtle's family history was cut short by a little scream from the women of the party.

The cow-house door had closed noiselessly behind them and the key had turned gratingly in the lock; then they heard Bertie's voice pleasantly wishing them good night and his footsteps retreating along the garden path.

Luke Steffink strode to the window; it was a small square opening of the old-fashioned sort, with iron bars let into the stonework.

"Unlock the door this instant," he shouted, with as much air of menacing authority as a hen might assume when screaming through the bars of a coop at a marauding hawk. In reply to his summons the hall-door closed with a defiant bang.

A neighbouring clock struck the hour of midnight. If the cows had received the gift of human speech at that moment they would not have been able to make themselves heard. Seven or eight other voices were engaged in describing Bertie's present conduct and his general character at a high pressure of excitement and indignation.

In the course of half an hour or so everything that it was permissible to say about Bertie had been said some dozens of times, and other topics began to come to the front—the extreme mustiness of the cow-house, the possibility of it catching fire, and the probability of it being a Rowton House for the vagrant rats of the neighbourhood. And still no sign of deliverance came to the unwilling vigil-keepers.

Towards one o'clock the sound of rather boisterous and undisciplined carol-singing approached rapidly, and came to a sudden anchorage, apparently just outside the garden-gate. A motor-load of youthful "bloods," in a high state of conviviality, had made a temporary halt for repairs; the stoppage, however, did not extend to the vocal efforts of the party, and the watchers in the cow-shed were treated to a highly unauthorized rendering of "Good King Wenceslas," in which the adjective "good" appeared to be very carelessly applied.

The noise had the effect of bringing Bertie out into the garden, but he utterly ignored the pale, angry faces peering out at the cow-house window, and concentrated his attention on the revellers outside the gate.

"Wassail, you chaps!" he shouted.

"Wassail, old sport!" they shouted back; "we'd jolly well drink y'r health, only we've nothing to drink it in."

"Come and wassail inside," said Bertie hospitably; "I'm all alone, and there's heaps of 'wet.'"

They were total strangers, but his touch of kindness made them instantly his kin. In another moment the unauthorized version of King Wenceslas, which, like many other scandals, grew worse on repetition, went echoing up the garden path; two of the revellers gave an impromptu performance on the way by executing the staircase waltz up the terraces of what Luke Steffink, hitherto with some justification, called his rock-garden. The rock part of it was still there when the waltz had been accorded its third encore. Luke, more than ever like a cooped hen behind the cow-house bars, was in a position to realize the feelings of concert-goers unable to countermand the call for an encore which they neither desire nor deserve.

The hall door closed with a bang on Bertie's guests, and the sounds of merriment became faint and muffled to the weary watchers at the other end of the garden. Presently two ominous pops, in quick succession, made themselves distinctly heard.

"They've got at the champagne!" exclaimed Mrs. Steffink.

"Perhaps it's the sparkling Moselle," said Luke hopefully.

Three or four more pops were heard.

"The champagne *and* the sparkling Moselle," said Mrs. Steffink.

Luke uncorked an expletive which, like brandy in a temperance household, was only used on rare emergencies. Mr. Horace Bordenby had been making use of similar expressions under his breath for a considerable time past. The experiment of "throwing the young people together" had been prolonged beyond a point when it was likely to produce any romantic result.

Some forty minutes later the hall door opened and disgorged a crowd that had thrown off any restraint of shyness that might have influenced its earlier actions. Its vocal efforts in the direction of carol-singing were now supplemented by instrumental music; a Christmas-tree that had been prepared for the children of the gardener and other household retainers had yielded a rich spoil of tin trumpets, rattles, and drums. The life-story of King Wenceslas had been dropped, Luke was thankful to notice, but it was intensely irritating for the chilled prisoners in the cow-house to be told that it was "a hot time in the old town tonight," together with some accurate but entirely superfluous information as to the imminence of Christmas morning. Judging by the protests which began to be shouted from the upper windows of neighbouring houses, the sentiments prevailing in the cow-house were heartily echoed in other quarters.

The revellers found their car, and, what was more remarkable, managed to drive off in it, with a parting fanfare of tin trumpets. The lively beat of a drum disclosed the fact that the master of the revels remained on the scene.

"Bertie!" came in an angry, imploring chorus of shouts and screams from the cow-house window.

"Hullo," cried the owner of the name, turning his rather errant steps in the direction of the summons; "are you people still there? Must have heard everything cows got to say by this time. If you haven't, no use waiting. After all, it's a Russian legend, and

Russian Chrismush Eve not due for 'nother fortnight. Better come out."

After one or two ineffectual attempts he managed to pitch the key of the cow-house door in through the window. Then, lifting his voice in the strains of "I'm afraid to go home in the dark," with a lusty drum accompaniment, he led the way back to the house. The hurried procession of the released that followed in his steps came in for a good deal of the adverse comment that his exuberant display had evoked.

It was the happiest Christmas Eve he had ever spent. To quote his own words, he had a rotten Christmas.

FOREWARNED

ALETHIA DEBCHANCE sat in a corner of an otherwise empty railway carriage, more or less at ease as regarded body, but in some trepidation as to mind. She had embarked on a social adventure of no little magnitude as compared with the accustomed seclusion and stagnation of her past life. At the age of twenty-eight she could look back on nothing more eventful than the daily round of her existence in her aunt's house at Webblehinton, a hamlet four and a half miles distant from a country town and about a quarter of a century removed from modern times. Their neighbours had been elderly and few, not much given to social intercourse, but helpful or politely sympathetic in times of illness. Newspapers of the ordinary kind were a rarity; those that Alethia saw regularly were devoted exclusively either to religion or to poultry, and the world of politics was to her an unheeded unexplored region. Her ideas on life in general had been acquired through the medium of popular respectable novel-writers, and modified or emphasized by such knowledge as her aunt, the vicar, and her aunt's housekeeper had put at her disposal. And now, in her twenty-ninth year, her aunt's death had left her well provided for as regards income, but somewhat isolated in the matter of kith and kin and human companionship. She had some cousins who were on terms of friendly, though infrequent, correspondence with her, but as they lived permanently in Ceylon, a locality about which she knew little, beyond the assurance contained in the missionary hymn that the human element there was vile, they were not of much immediate use to her. Other cousins she also possessed, more distant as regards relationship, but not quite so geographically remote, seeing that they lived somewhere in the Midlands. She could hardly remember ever having met them, but once or twice in the course of the last three or four years they had expressed a polite wish that she should pay them a visit; they had probably not been unduly depressed by the fact that her aunt's failing health had prevented her from accepting their invitation. The note of condolence that had arrived on the occasion of her aunt's death had included a vague hope that Alethia would find time in the near future to spend a few days with her cousins, and after much deliberation and many hesitations she had written to propose herself as a guest for a definite date some weeks ahead. The family, she reflected with relief, was not a large one; the two daughters were married and away, there was only old Mrs. Bludward and her son Robert at home. Mrs. Bludward was something of an invalid, and Robert was a young man who had been at Oxford and was going into Parliament. Further than that Alethia's information did not go; her imagination, founded on her extensive knowledge of the people one met in novels, had to supply the gaps. The mother was not difficult to place; she would either be an ultra-amiable old lady, bearing her feeble health with uncomplaining fortitude, and having a kind word for the gardener's boy and a sunny smile for the chance visitor, or else she would be cold and peevish, with eyes that pierced you like a gimlet, and an unreasoning idolatry of her son. Alethia's imagination rather inclined her to the latter view. Robert was more of a problem. There were three dominant types of manhood to be taken into consideration in working out his classification; there was Hugo, who was strong, good, and beautiful, a rare type and not very often met with; there was Sir Jasper, who was utterly vile and absolutely unscrupulous; and there was Nevil, who was not really bad at heart, but had a weak mouth and usually required the life-work of two good women to keep him from ultimate disaster. It was probable, Alethia considered, that Robert came into the last category, in which case she was certain to enjoy the companionship of one or two excellent women, and might possibly catch glimpses of undesirable adventuresses or come face to face with reckless admiration-seeking married women. It was altogether an exciting prospect, this sudden venture into an unexplored world of unknown human beings, and

Alethia rather wished that she could have taken the vicar with her; she was not, however, rich or important enough to travel with a chaplain, as the Marquis of Moystoncleugh always did in the novel she had been reading, so she recognized that such a proceeding was out of the question.

The train which carried Alethia towards her destination was a local one, with the wayside station habit strongly developed. At most of the stations no one seemed to want to get into the train or to leave it, but at one there were several market folk on the platform, and two men, of the farmer or small cattle-dealer class, entered Alethia's carriage. Apparently they had just foregathered, after a day's business, and their conversation consisted of a rapid exchange of short friendly inquiries as to health, family, stock, and so forth, and some grumbling remarks on the weather. Suddenly, however, their talk took a dramatically interesting turn, and Alethia listened with wide-eyed attention.

"What do you think of Mister Robert Bludward, eh?"

There was a certain scornful ring in the question.

"Robert Bludward? An out-an'-out rotter, that's what he is. Ought to be ashamed to look any decent man in the face. Send him to Parliament to represent us—not much! He'd rob a poor man of his last shilling, he would."

"Ah, that he would. Tells a pack of lies to get our votes, that's all that he's after, damn him. Did you see the way the *Argus* showed him up this week? Properly exposed him, hip and thigh, I tell you."

And so on they ran, in their withering indictment. There could be no doubt that it was Alethia's cousin and prospective host to whom they were referring; the allusion to a Parliamentary candidature settled that. What could Robert Bludward have done, what manner of man could he be, that people should speak of him with such obvious reprobation?

"He was hissed down at Shoalford yesterday," said one of the speakers.

Hissed! Had it come to that? There was something dramatically biblical in the idea of Robert Bludward's neighbours and acquaintances hissing him for very scorn. Lord Hereward Stranglath had been hissed, now Alethia came to think of it, in the eighth chapter of *Matterby Towers,* while in the act of opening a Wesleyan bazaar, because he was suspected (unjustly as it turned out afterwards) of having beaten the German governess to death. And in *Tainted*

Guineas Roper Squenderby had been deservedly hissed, on the steps of the Jockey Club, for having handed a rival owner a forged telegram, containing false news of his mother's death, just before the start for an important race, thereby ensuring the withdrawal of his rival's horse. In placid Saxon-blooded England people did not demonstrate their feelings lightly and without some strong compelling cause. What manner of evildoer was Robert Bludward?

The train stopped at another small station, and the two men got out. One of them left behind him a copy of the *Argus,* the local paper to which he had made reference. Alethia pounced on it, in the expectation of finding a cultured literary endorsement of the censure which these rough farming men had expressed in their homely, honest way. She had not far to look; "Mr. Robert Bludward, Swanker," was the title of one of the principal articles in the paper. She did not exactly know what a swanker was, probably it referred to some unspeakable form of cruelty, but she read enough in the first few sentences of the article to discover that her cousin Robert, the man at whose house she was about to stay, was an unscrupulous, unprincipled character, of a low order of intelligence, yet cunning withal, and that he and his associates were responsible for most of the misery, disease, poverty, and ignorance with which the country was afflicted; never, except in one or two of the denunciatory Psalms, which she had always supposed to have been written in a spirit of exaggerated Oriental imagery, had she read such an indictment of a human being. And this monster was going to meet her at Derrelton Station in a few short minutes. She would know him at once; he would have the dark beetling brows, the quick, furtive glance, the sneering, unsavoury smile that always characterized the Sir Jaspers of this world. It was too late to escape; she must force herself to meet him with outward calm.

It was a considerable shock to her to find that Robert was fair, with a snub nose, merry eye, and rather a schoolboy manner. "A serpent in duckling's plumage," was her private comment; merciful chance had revealed him to her in his true colours.

As they drove away from the station a dissipated-looking man of the labouring class waved his hat in friendly salute. "Good luck to you, Mr. Bludward," he shouted; "you'll come out on top! We'll break old Chobham's neck for him."

"Who was that man?" asked Alethia quickly.

"Oh, one of my supporters," laughed Robert; "a bit of a poacher and a bit of a pub-loafer, but he's on the right side."

So these were the sort of associates that Robert Bludward consorted with, thought Alethia.

"Who is the person he referred to as old Chobham?" she asked.

"Sir John Chobham, the man who is opposing me," answered Robert; "that is his house away there among the trees on the right."

So there was an upright man, possibly a very Hugo in character, who was thwarting and defying the evildoer in his nefarious career, and there was a dastardly plot afoot to break his neck! Possibly the attempt would be made within the next few hours. He must certainly be warned. Alethia remembered how Lady Sylvia Broomgate, in *Nightshade Court*, had pretended to be bolted with by her horse up to the front door of a threatened county magnate, and had whispered a warning in his ear which saved him from being the victim of foul murder. She wondered if there was a quiet pony in the stables on which she would be allowed to ride out alone. The chances were that she would be watched. Robert would come spurring after her and seize her bridle just as she was turning in at Sir John's gates.

A group of men that they passed in a village street gave them no very friendly looks, and Alethia thought she heard a furtive hiss; a moment later they came upon an errand-boy riding a bicycle. He had the frank open countenance, neatly brushed hair and tidy clothes that betoken a clear conscience and a good mother. He stared straight at the occupants of the car, and, after he had passed them, sang in his clear, boyish voice:

"We'll hang Bobby Bludward on the sour apple tree."

Robert merely laughed. That was how he took the scorn and condemnation of his fellow-men. He had goaded them to desperation with his shameless depravity till they spoke openly of putting him to a violent death, and he laughed.

Mrs. Bludward proved to be of the type that Alethia had suspected, thin-lipped, cold-eyed, and obviously devoted to her worthless son. From her no help was to be expected. Alethia locked her door that night, and placed such ramparts of furniture against it that the maid had great difficulty in breaking in with the early tea in the morning.

After breakfast Alethia, on the pretext of going to look at an outlying rose-garden, slipped away to the village through which they had passed on the previous evening. She remembered that Robert had pointed out to her a public reading-room, and here she considered it possible that she might meet Sir John Chobham, or some one who knew him well and would carry a message to him. The room was empty when she entered it; a *Graphic*, twelve days old, a yet older copy of *Punch*, and one or two local papers lay upon the central table; the other tables were stacked for the most part with chess and draughts-boards, and wooden boxes of chessmen and dominoes. Listlessly she picked up one of the papers, the *Sentinel*, and glanced at its contents. Suddenly she started, and began to read with breathless attention a prominently printed article, headed "A Little Limelight on Sir John Chobham." The colour ebbed away from her face, a look of frightened despair crept into her eyes. Never, in any novel that she had read, had a defenceless young woman been confronted with a situation like this. Sir John, the Hugo of her imagination, was, if anything, rather more depraved and despicable than Robert Bludward. He was mean, evasive, callously indifferent to his country's interests, a cheat, a man who habitually broke his word, and who was responsible, with his associates, for most of the poverty, misery, crime, and national degradation with which the country was afflicted. He was also a candidate for Parliament, it seemed, and as there was only one seat in this particular locality, it was obvious that the success of either Robert or Sir John would mean a check to the ambitions of the other, hence, no doubt, the rivalry and enmity between these otherwise kindred souls. One was seeking to have his enemy done to death, the other was apparently trying to stir up his supporters to an act of "Lynch law." All this in order that there might be an unopposed election, that one or other of the candidates might go into Parliament with honeyed eloquence on his lips and blood on his heart. Were men really so vile?

"I must go back to Webblehinton at once," Alethia informed her astonished hostess at lunch-time; "I have had a telegram. A friend is very seriously ill, and I have been sent for."

It was dreadful to have to concoct lies, but it would be more dreadful to have to spend another night under that roof.

Alethia reads novels now with even greater appreciation than before. She has been herself in the world outside Webblehinton, the world where the great dramas of sin and villainy are played unceasingly. She had come unscathed through it, but what might have happened if she had gone unsuspectingly to visit Sir John Chobham and warn him of his danger? What indeed! She had been saved by the fearless outspokenness of the local Press.

THE INTERLOPERS

In a forest of mixed growth somewhere on the eastern spurs of the Carpathians, a man stood one winter night watching and listening, as though he waited for some beast of the woods to come within the range of his vision, and, later, of his rifle. But the game for whose presence he kept so keen an outlook was none that figured in the sportsman's calendar as lawful and proper for the chase; Ulrich von Gradwitz patrolled the dark forest in quest of a human enemy.

The forest lands of Gradwitz were of wide extent and well stocked with game; the narrow strip of precipitous woodland that lay on its outskirt was not remarkable for the game it harboured or the shooting it afforded, but it was the most jealously guarded of all its owner's territorial possessions. A famous lawsuit, in the days of his grandfather, had wrested it from the illegal possession of a neighbouring family of petty landowners; the dispossessed party had never acquiesced in the judgment of the Courts, and a long series of poaching affrays and similar scandals had embittered the relationships between the families for three generations. The neighbour feud had grown into a personal one since Ulrich had come to be head of his family; if there was a man in the world whom he detested and wished ill to it was Georg Znaeym, the inheritor of the quarrel and the tireless game-snatcher and raider of the disputed border-forest. The feud might, perhaps, have died down or been compromised if the personal ill-will of the two men had not stood in the way; as boys they had thirsted for one another's blood, as men each prayed that misfortune might fall on the other, and this wind-scourged winter night Ulrich had banded together his foresters to watch the dark forest, not in quest of four-footed quarry, but to keep a look-out for the prowling thieves whom he suspected of being afoot from across the land boundary. The roebuck, which usually kept in the sheltered hollows during a storm-wind, were running like driven things tonight, and there was movement and unrest among the creatures that were wont to sleep through the dark hours. Assuredly there was a disturbing element in the forest, and Ulrich could guess the quarter from whence it came.

He strayed away by himself from the watchers whom he had placed in ambush on the crest of the hill, and wandered far down the steep slopes amid the wild tangle of undergrowth, peering through the tree-trunks and listening through the whistling and skirling of the wind and the restless beating of the branches for sight or sound of the marauders. If only on this wild night, in this dark, lone spot, he might come across Georg Znaeym, man to man, with none to witness—that was the wish that was uppermost in his thoughts. And as he stepped round the trunk of a huge beech he came face to face with the man he sought.

The two enemies stood glaring at one another for a long silent moment. Each had a rifle in his hand, each had hate in his heart and murder uppermost in his mind. The chance had come to give full play to the passions of a lifetime. But a man who has been brought up under the code of a restraining civilization cannot easily nerve himself to shoot down his neighbour in cold blood and without word spoken, except for an offence against his hearth and honour. And before the moment of hesitation had given way to action a deed of Nature's own violence overwhelmed them both. A fierce shriek of the storm had been answered by a splitting crash over their heads, and ere they could leap aside a mass of falling beech tree had thundered down on them. Ulrich von Gradwitz found himself stretched on the ground, one arm numb beneath him and the other held almost as helplessly in a tight tangle of forked branches, while both legs were pinned beneath the fallen mass. His heavy shooting-boots had saved his feet from being crushed to pieces, but if his fractures were not as serious as they might have been, at least it was evident that he could not move from his present position till some one came to release him. The descending twigs had slashed the skin of his face, and he had to wink away some drops of blood from his eyelashes before he could take in a general view of the disaster. At his side, so near that under ordinary circumstances he could almost have touched him, lay Georg Znaeym, alive and struggling, but obviously as helplessly pinioned down as himself. All round them lay a thick-strewn wreckage of splintered branches and broken twigs.

Relief at being alive and exasperation at his captive plight brought a strange medley of pious thank-offerings and sharp curses to Ulrich's lips. Georg, who was nearly blinded with the blood which trickled across his eyes, stopped his struggling for a moment to listen, and then gave a short, snarling laugh.

"So you're not killed, as you ought to be, but you're caught, anyway," he cried; "caught fast. Ho, what a jest, Ulrich von Gradwitz snared in his stolen forest. There's real justice for you!"

And he laughed again, mockingly and savagely.

"I'm caught in my own forest-land," retorted Ulrich. "When my men come to release us you will wish, perhaps, that you were in a better plight than caught poaching on a neighbour's land, shame on you."

Georg was silent for a moment; then he answered quietly:

"Are you sure that your men will find much to release? I have men, too, in the forest tonight, close behind me, and *they* will be here first and do the releasing. When they drag me out from under these damned branches it won't need much clumsiness on their part to roll this mass of trunk right over on the top of you. Your men will find you dead under a fallen beech tree. For form's sake I shall send my condolences to your family."

"It is a useful hint," said Ulrich fiercely. "My men had orders to follow in ten minutes' time, seven of which must have gone by already, and when they get me out—I will remember the hint. Only as you will have met your death poaching on my lands I don't think I can decently send any message of condolence to your family."

"Good," snarled Georg, "good. We fight this quarrel out to the death, you and I and our foresters, with no cursed interlopers to come between us. Death and damnation to you, Ulrich von Gradwitz."

"The same to you, Georg Znaeym, forest-thief, game-snatcher."

Both men spoke with the bitterness of possible defeat before them, for each knew that it might be long before his men would seek him out or find him; it was a bare matter of chance which party would arrive first on the scene.

Both had now given up the useless struggle to free themselves from the mass of wood that held them down; Ulrich limited his endeavours to an effort to bring his one partially free arm near enough to his outer coat-pocket to draw out his wine-flask. Even when he had accomplished that operation it was long before he could manage the unscrewing of the stopper or get any of the liquid down his throat. But what a Heaven-sent draught it seemed! It was an open winter, and little snow had fallen as yet, hence the captives suffered less from the cold than might have been the case at that season of the year; nevertheless, the wine was warming and reviving to the wounded man, and he looked across with something like a throb of pity to where his enemy lay, just keeping the groans of pain and weariness from crossing his lips.

"Could you reach this flask if I threw it over to you?" asked Ulrich suddenly; "there is good wine in it, and one may as well be as comfortable as one can. Let us drink, even if tonight one of us dies."

"No, I can scarcely see anything; there is so much blood caked round my eyes," said Georg, "and in any case I don't drink wine with an enemy."

Ulrich was silent for a few minutes, and lay listening to the weary screeching of the wind. An idea was slowly forming and growing in his brain, an idea that gained strength every time that he looked across at the man who was fighting so grimly against pain and exhaustion. In the pain and languor that Ulrich himself was feeling the old fierce hatred seemed to be dying down.

"Neighbour," he said presently, "do as you please if your men come first. It was a fair compact. But as for me, I've changed my mind. If my men are the first to come you shall be the first to be helped, as though you were my guest. We have quarrelled like devils all our lives over this stupid strip of forest, where the trees can't even stand upright in a breath of wind. Lying here tonight, thinking, I've come to think we've been rather fools; there are better things in life than getting the better of a boundary dispute. Neighbour, if you will help me to bury the old quarrel I—I will ask you to be my friend."

Georg Znaeym was silent for so long that Ulrich thought, perhaps, he had fainted with the pain of his injuries. Then he spoke slowly and in jerks.

"How the whole region would stare and gabble if we rode into the market-square together. No one living can remember seeing a Znaeym and a von Gradwitz talking to one another in friendship. And what peace there would be among the forester folk if we ended our feud tonight. And if we choose to make peace among our people there is none other to interfere, no interlopers from outside. . . . You would come and keep the Sylvester night beneath my roof, and I would come and feast on some high day at your castle. . . . I would never fire a shot on your land, save when you invited me as a guest; and you should come and shoot with me down in the marshes where the wildfowl are. In all the countryside there are none that could hinder if we willed to make peace. I never thought to have wanted to do other than hate you all my life, but I think I have changed my mind about things too, this last half-hour. And you offered me your wine-flask. . . . Ulrich von Gradwitz, I will be your friend."

For a space both men were silent, turning over in their minds the wonderful changes that this dramatic reconciliation would bring about. In the cold, gloomy forest, with the wind tearing in fitful gusts through the naked branches and whistling round the tree-trunks, they lay and waited for the help that would now bring release and succour to both parties. And each prayed a private prayer that his men might be the first to arrive, so that he might be the first to show honourable attention to the enemy that had become a friend.

Presently, as the wind dropped for a moment, Ulrich broke silence.

"Let's shout for help," he said; "in this lull our voices may carry a little way."

"They won't carry far through the trees and undergrowth," said Georg, "but we can try. Together, then."

The two raised their voices in a prolonged hunting call.

"Together again," said Ulrich a few minutes later, after listening in vain for an answering halloo.

"I heard something that time, I think," said Ulrich.

"I heard nothing but the pestilential wind," said Georg hoarsely.

There was silence again for some minutes, and then Ulrich gave a joyful cry.

"I can see figures coming through the wood. They are following in the way I came down the hillside."

Both men raised their voices in as loud a shout as they could muster.

"They hear us! They've stopped. Now they see us. They're running down the hill towards us," cried Ulrich.

"How many of them are there?" asked Georg.

"I can't see distinctly," said Ulrich; "nine or ten."

"Then they are yours," said Georg; "I had only seven out with me."

"They are making all the speed they can, brave lads," said Ulrich gladly.

"Are they your men?" asked Georg. "Are they your men?" he repeated impatiently as Ulrich did not answer.

"No," said Ulrich with a laugh, the idiotic chattering laugh of a man unstrung with hideous fear.

"Who are they?" asked Georg quickly, straining his eyes to see what the other would gladly not have seen.

"*Wolves.*"

QUAIL SEED

"THE outlook is not encouraging for us smaller businesses," said Mr. Scarrick to the artist and his sister, who had taken rooms over his suburban grocery store. "These big concerns are offering all sorts of attractions to the shopping public which we couldn't afford to imitate, even on a small scale—reading-rooms and play-rooms and gramophones and Heaven knows what. People don't care to buy half a pound of sugar nowadays unless they can listen to Harry Lauder and have the latest Australian cricket scores ticked off before their eyes. With the big Christmas stock we've got in we ought to keep half a dozen assistants hard at work, but as it is my nephew Jimmy and myself can pretty well attend to it ourselves. It's a nice stock of goods, too, if I could only run it off in a few weeks' time, but there's no chance of that—not unless the London line was to get snowed up for a fortnight before Christmas. I did have a sort of idea of engaging Miss Luffcombe to give recitations during afternoons; she made a great hit at the Post Office entertainment with her rendering of 'Little Beatrice's Resolve.'"

"Anything less likely to make your shop a fashionable shopping centre I can't imagine," said the artist, with a very genuine shudder; "if I were trying to decide between the merits of Carlsbad plums and confected figs as a winter dessert it would infuriate me to have my train of thought entangled with little Beatrice's resolve to be an Angel of Light or a girl scout. No," he continued, "the desire to get something thrown in for nothing is a ruling passion with the feminine shopper, but you can't afford to pander effectively to it. Why not appeal to another instinct, which dominates not only the woman shopper but the male shopper—in fact, the entire human race?"

"What is that instinct, sir?" said the grocer.

Mrs. Greyes and Miss Fritten had missed the 2.18 to Town, and as there was not another train till 3.12 they thought that they might as well make their grocery purchases at Scarrick's. It would not be sensational, they agreed, but it would still be shopping.

For some minutes they had the shop almost to themselves, as far as customers were concerned, but while they were debating the respective virtues and blemishes of two competing brands of anchovy paste they were startled by an order, given across the counter, for six pomegranates and a packet of quail seed. Neither commodity was in general demand in that neighbourhood. Equally unusual was the style and appearance of the customer; about sixteen years old, with dark olive skin, large dusky eyes, and thick, low-growing, blue-black hair, he might have made his living as an artist's model. As a matter of fact he did. The bowl of beaten brass that he produced for the reception of his purchases was distinctly the most astonishing variation on the string bag or marketing basket of suburban civilization that his fellow-shoppers had ever seen. He threw a gold piece, apparently of some exotic currency, across the counter, and did not seem disposed to wait for any change that might be forthcoming.

"The wine and figs were not paid for yesterday," he said; "keep what is over of the money for our future purchases."

"A very strange-looking boy?" said Mrs. Greyes interrogatively to the grocer as soon as his customer had left.

"A foreigner, I believe," said Mr. Scarrick, with a shortness that was entirely out of keeping with his usually communicative manner.

"I wish for a pound and a half of the best coffee you have," said an authoritative voice a moment or two later. The speaker was a tall, authoritative-looking man of rather outlandish aspect, remarkable among other things for a full black beard, worn in a style more in vogue in early Assyria than in a London suburb of the present day.

"Has a dark-faced boy been here buying pomegranates?" he asked suddenly, as the coffee was being weighed out to him.

The two ladies almost jumped on hearing the grocer reply with an unblushing negative.

"We have a few pomegranates in stock," he continued, "but there has been no demand for them."

"My servant will fetch the coffee as usual," said the purchaser, producing a coin from a wonderful metal-work purse. As an apparent afterthought he fired out the question: "Have you, perhaps, any quail seed?"

"No," said the grocer, without hesitation, "we don't stock it."

"What will he deny next?" asked Mrs. Greyes under her breath. What made it seem so much worse was the fact that Mr. Scarrick had quite recently presided at a lecture on Savonarola.

Turning up the deep astrachan collar of his long coat, the stranger swept out of the shop, with the air, as Miss Fritten afterwards described it, of a Satrap proroguing a Sanhedrin. Whether such a pleasant function ever fell to a Satrap's lot she was not quite certain, but the simile faithfully conveyed her meaning to a large circle of acquaintances.

"Don't let's bother about the 3.12," said Mrs. Greyes; "let's go and talk this over at Laura Lipping's. It's her day."

When the dark-faced boy arrived at the shop next day with his brass marketing bowl there was quite a fair gathering of customers, most of whom seemed to be spinning out their purchasing operations with the air of people who had very little to do with their time. In a voice that was heard all over the shop, perhaps because everybody was intently listening, he asked for a pound of honey and a packet of quail seed.

"More quail seed!" said Miss Fritten. "Those quails must be voracious, or else it isn't quail seed at all."

"I believe it's opium, and the bearded man is a detective," said Mrs. Greyes brilliantly.

"I don't," said Laura Lipping; "I'm sure it's something to do with the Portuguese Throne."

"More likely to be a Persian intrigue on behalf of the ex-Shah," said Miss Fritten; "the bearded man belongs to the Government Party. The quail seed is a countersign, of course; Persia is almost next door to Palestine, and quails come into the Old Testament, you know."

"Only as a miracle," said her well-informed younger sister; "I've thought all along it was part of a love intrigue."

The boy who had so much interest and speculation centred on him was on the point of departing with his purchases when he was waylaid by Jimmy, the nephew-apprentice, who, from his post at the cheese and bacon counter, commanded a good view of the street.

"We have some very fine Jaffa oranges," he said hurriedly, pointing to a corner where they were stored, behind a high rampart of biscuit tins. There was evidently more in the remark than met the ear. The boy flew at the oranges with the enthusiasm of a ferret finding a rabbit family at home after a long day of fruitless subterranean research. Almost at the same moment the bearded stranger stalked into the shop, and flung an order for a pound of dates and a tin of the best Smyrna halva across the counter. The most adventurous housewife in the locality had never heard of halva, but Mr. Scarrick was apparently able to produce the best Smyrna variety of it without a moment's hesitation.

"We might be living in the Arabian Nights," said Miss Fritten excitedly.

"Hush! Listen," beseeched Mrs. Greyes.

"Has the dark-faced boy, of whom I spoke yesterday, been here today?" asked the stranger.

"We've had rather more people than usual in the shop today," said Mr. Scarrick, "but I can't recall a boy such as you describe."

Mrs. Greyes and Miss Fritten looked round triumphantly at their friends. It was, of course, deplorable that any one should treat the truth as an article temporarily and excusably out of stock, but they felt gratified that the vivid accounts they had given of Mr. Scarrick's traffic in falsehoods should receive confirmation at first hand.

"I shall never again be able to believe what he tells me about the absence of colouring matter in the jam," whispered an aunt of Mrs. Greyes tragically.

The mysterious stranger took his departure; Laura Lipping distinctly saw a snarl of baffled rage reveal itself behind his heavy moustache and upturned astrachan collar. After a cautious interval the seeker after oranges emerged from behind the biscuit tins, having apparently failed to find any individual orange that satisfied his requirements. He, too, took his departure, and the shop was slowly emptied of its parcel and gossip laden customers. It was Emily Yorling's "day," and most of the shoppers made their way to her drawing-room. To go direct from a shopping expedition to a tea-party was what was known locally as "living in a whirl."

Two extra assistants had been engaged for the following afternoon, and their services were in brisk demand; the shop was crowded. People bought and bought, and never seemed to get to the end of their lists. Mr. Scarrick had never had so little difficulty in persuading customers to embark on new experiences in grocery wares. Even those women whose purchases were of modest proportions dawdled over them as though they had brutal, drunken husbands to go home to. The afternoon had dragged uneventfully on, and there was a distinct buzz of unpent excitement when a dark-eyed boy carrying a brass bowl entered the shop. The excitement seemed to have communicated itself to Mr. Scarrick; abruptly deserting a lady who was making insincere inquiries about the home life of the Bombay duck, he intercepted the newcomer on his way to the accustomed counter and informed him, amid a deathlike hush, that he had run out of quail seed.

The boy looked nervously round the shop, and turned hesitatingly to go. He was again intercepted, this time by the nephew, who darted out from behind his counter and said something about a better line of oranges. The boy's hesitation vanished; he almost scuttled into the obscurity of the orange corner. There was an expectant turn of public attention towards the door, and the tall, bearded stranger made a really effective entrance. The aunt of Mrs. Greyes declared afterwards that she found herself subconsciously repeating "The Assyrian came down like a wolf on the fold" under her breath, and she was generally believed.

The newcomer, too, was stopped before he reached the counter, but not by Mr. Scarrick or his assistant. A heavily veiled lady, whom no one had hitherto noticed, rose languidly from a seat and greeted him in a clear, penetrating voice.

"Your Excellency does his shopping himself?" she said.

"I order the things myself," he explained; "I find it difficult to make my servants understand."

In a lower, but still perfectly audible, voice the veiled lady gave him a piece of casual information.

"They have some excellent Jaffa oranges here." Then with a tinkling laugh she passed out of the shop.

The man glared all round the shop, and then, fixing his eyes instinctively on the barrier of biscuit tins, demanded loudly of the grocer: "You have, perhaps, some good Jaffa oranges?"

Every one expected an instant denial on the part of Mr. Scarrick of any such possession. Before he could answer, however, the boy had broken forth from his sanctuary. Holding his empty brass bowl before him he passed out into the street. His face was variously described afterwards as masked with studied indifference, overspread with ghastly pallor, and blazing with defiance. Some said that his teeth chattered, others that he went out whistling the Persian National Hymn. There was no mistaking, however, the effect produced by the encounter on the man who had seemed to force it. If a rabid dog or a rattlesnake had suddenly thrust its companionship on him he could scarcely have displayed a greater access of terror. His air of authority and assertiveness had gone, his masterful stride had given way to a furtive pacing to and fro, as of an animal seeking an outlet for escape. In a dazed perfunctory manner, always with his eyes turning to watch the shop entrance, he gave a few random orders, which the grocer made a show of entering in his book. Now and then he walked out into the street, looked anxiously in all directions, and hurried back to keep up his pretence of shopping. From one of these sorties he did not return; he had dashed away into the dusk, and neither he nor the dark-faced boy nor the veiled lady were seen again by the expectant crowds that continued to throng the Scarrick establishment for days to come.

"I can never thank you and your sister sufficiently," said the grocer.

"We enjoyed the fun of it," said the artist modestly, "and as for the model, it was a welcome variation on posing for hours for 'The Lost Hylas.'"

"At any rate," said the grocer, "I insist on paying for the hire of the black beard."

CANOSSA

Demosthenes Platterbaff, the eminent Unrest Inducer, stood on his trial for a serious offence, and the eyes of the political world were focussed on the jury. The offence, it should be stated, was serious for the Government rather than for the prisoner. He had blown up the Albert Hall on the eve of the great Liberal Federation Tango Tea, the occasion on which the Chancellor of the Exchequer was expected to propound his new theory: "Do partridges spread infectious diseases?" Platterbaff had chosen his time well; the Tango Tea had been hurriedly postponed, but there were other political fixtures which could not be put off under any circumstances. The day after the trial there was to be a by-election at Nemesis-on-Hand, and it had been openly announced in the division that if Platterbaff were languishing in gaol on polling day the Government candidate would be "outed" to a certainty. Unfortunately, there could be no doubt or misconception as to Platterbaff's guilt. He had not only pleaded guilty, but had expressed his intention of repeating his escapade in other directions as soon as circumstances permitted; throughout the trial he was busy examining a small model of the Free Trade Hall in Manchester. The jury could not possibly find that the prisoner had not deliberately and intentionally blown up the Albert Hall; the question was: Could they find any extenuating circumstances which would permit of an acquittal? Of course any sentence which the law might feel compelled to inflict would be followed by an immediate pardon, but it was highly desirable, from the Government's point of view, that the necessity for such an exercise of clemency should not arise. A headlong pardon, on the eve of a by-election, with threats of a heavy voting defection if it were withheld or even delayed, would not necessarily be a surrender, but it would look like one. Opponents would be only too ready to attribute ungenerous motives. Hence the anxiety in the crowded Court, and in the little groups gathered round the tape-machines in Whitehall and Downing Street and other affected centres.

The jury returned from considering their verdict; there was a flutter, an excited murmur, a death-like hush. The foreman delivered his message:

"The jury find the prisoner guilty of blowing up the Albert Hall. The jury wish to add a rider drawing attention to the fact that a by-election is pending in the Parliamentary division of Nemesis-on-Hand."

"That, of course," said the Government Prosecutor, springing to his feet, "is equivalent to an acquittal?"

"I hardly think so," said the Judge coldly: "I feel obliged to sentence the prisoner to a week's imprisonment."

"And may the Lord have mercy on the poll," a Junior Counsel exclaimed irreverently.

It was a scandalous sentence, but then the Judge was not on the Ministerial side in politics.

The verdict and sentence were made known to the public at twenty minutes past five in the afternoon; at half-past five a dense crowd was massed outside the Prime Minister's residence lustily singing, to the air of "Trelawney":

"And should our Hero rot in gaol,
For e'en a single day,
There's Fifteen Hundred Voting Men
Will vote the other way."

"Fifteen hundred," said the Prime Minister, with a shudder; "it's too horrible to think of. Our majority last time was only a thousand and seven."

"The poll opens at eight tomorrow morning," said the Chief Organizer; "we must have him out by 7 a.m."

"Seven-thirty," amended the Prime Minister; "we must avoid any appearance of precipitancy."

"Not later than seven-thirty, then," said the Chief Organizer; "I have promised the agent down there that he shall be able to display posters announcing 'Platterbaff is Out,' before the poll opens. He said it was our only chance of getting a telegram 'Radprop is In' tonight."

At half-past seven the next morning the Prime Minister and the Chief Organizer sat at breakfast, making a perfunctory meal, and awaiting the return of the Home Secretary, who had gone in person to superintend the releasing of Platterbaff. Despite the earliness of the hour, a small crowd had gathered in the street outside, and the horrible menacing Trelawney refrain of the "Fifteen Hundred Voting Men" came in a steady, monotonous chant.

"They will cheer presently when they hear the news," said the Prime Minister hopefully. "Hark! They are booing some one now! That must be McKenna."

The Home Secretary entered the room a moment later, disaster written on his face.

"He won't go!" he exclaimed.

"Won't go? Won't leave gaol?"

"He won't go unless he has a brass band. He says he never has left prison without a brass band to play him out, and he's not going to go without one now."

"But surely that sort of thing is provided by his supporters and admirers?" said the Prime Minister; "we can hardly be supposed to supply a released prisoner with a brass band. How on earth could we defend it on the Estimates?"

"His supporters say it is up to us to provide the music," said the Home Secretary; "they say we put him in prison, and it's our affair to see that he leaves it in a respectable manner. Anyway, he won't go unless he has a band."

The telephone squealed shrilly; it was a trunk call from Nemesis.

"Poll opens in five minutes. Is Platterbaff out yet? In Heaven's name, why–"

The Chief Organizer rang off.

"This is not a moment for standing on dignity," he observed bluntly; "musicians must be supplied at once. Platterbaff must have his band."

"Where are you going to find the musicians?" asked the Home Secretary wearily; "we can't employ a military band; in fact, I don't think he'd have one if we offered it, and there aren't any others. There's a musicians' strike on, I suppose you know."

"Can't you get a strike permit?" asked the Organizer.

"I'll try," said the Home Secretary, and went to the telephone.

Eight o'clock struck. The crowd outside chanted with an increasing volume of sound:

"Will vote the other way."

A telegram was brought in. It was from the central committee rooms at Nemesis. "Losing twenty votes per minute," was its brief message.

Ten o'clock struck. The Prime Minister, the Home Secretary, the Chief Organizer, and several earnest helpful friends were gathered in the inner gateway of the prison, talking volubly to Demosthenes Platterbaff, who stood with folded arms and squarely planted feet, silent in their midst. Golden-tongued legislators whose eloquence had swayed the Marconi Inquiry Committee, or at any rate the greater part of it, expended their arts of oratory in vain on this stubborn unyielding man. Without a band he would not go; and they had no band.

A quarter-past ten, half-past. A constant stream of telegraph boys poured in through the prison gates.

"Yamley's factory hands just voted you can guess how," ran a despairing message, and the others were all of the same tenor. Nemesis was going the way of Reading.

"Have you any band instruments of an easy nature to play?" demanded the Chief Organizer of the Prison Governor; "drums, cymbals, those sort of things?"

"The warders have a private band of their own," said the Governor, "but of course I couldn't allow the men themselves—"

"Lend us the instruments," said the Chief Organizer.

One of the earnest helpful friends was a skilled performer on the cornet, the Cabinet Ministers were able to clash cymbals more or less in tune, and the Chief Organizer had some knowledge of the drum.

"What tune would you prefer?" he asked Platterbaff.

"The popular song of the moment," replied the Agitator after a moment's reflection.

It was a tune they had all heard hundreds of times, so there was no difficulty in turning out a passable imitation of it. To the improvised strains of "I didn't want to do it" the prisoner strode forth to freedom. The words of the song had reference, it was understood, to the incarcerating Government and not to the destroyer of the Albert Hall.

The seat was lost, after all, by a narrow majority. The local Trade Unionists took offence at the fact of Cabinet Ministers having personally acted as strike-breakers, and even the release of Platterbaff failed to pacify them.

The seat was lost, but Ministers had scored a moral victory. They had shown that they knew when and how to yield.

THE THREAT

Sir Lulworth Quayne sat in the lounge of his favourite restaurant, the Gallus Bankiva, discussing the weaknesses of the world with his nephew, who had lately returned from a much-enlivened exile in the wilds of Mexico. It was that blessed season of the year when the asparagus and the plover's egg are abroad in the land, and the oyster has not yet withdrawn into its summer entrenchments, and Sir Lulworth and his nephew were in that enlightened after-dinner mood when politics are seen in their right perspective, even the politics of Mexico.

"Most of the revolutions that take place in this country nowadays," said Sir Lulworth, "are the product of moments of legislative panic. Take, for instance, one of the most dramatic reforms that has been carried through Parliament in the lifetime of this generation. It happened shortly after the coal strike, of unblessed memory. To you, who have been plunged up to the neck in events of a more tangled and tumbled description, the things I am going to tell you of may seem of secondary interest, but after all we had to live in the midst of them."

Sir Lulworth interrupted himself for a moment to say a few kind words to the liqueur brandy he had just tasted, and then resumed his narrative.

"Whether one sympathizes with the agitation for female suffrage or not one has to admit that its promoters showed tireless energy and considerable enterprise in devising and putting into action new methods for accomplishing their ends. As a rule they were a nuisance and a weariness to the flesh, but there were times when they verged on the picturesque. There was the famous occasion when they enlivened and diversified the customary pageantry of the Royal progress to open Parliament by letting loose thousands of parrots, which had been carefully trained to scream 'Votes for women,' and which circled round his Majesty's coach in a clamorous cloud of green, and grey and scarlet. It was really rather a striking episode from the spectacular point of view; unfortunately, however, for its devisers, the secret of their intentions had not been well kept, and their opponents let loose at the same moment a rival swarm of parrots, which screeched 'I *don't* think' and other hostile cries, thereby robbing the demonstration of the unanimity which alone could have made it politically impressive. In the process of recapture the birds learned a quantity of additional language which unfitted them for further service in the Suffragette cause; some of the green ones were secured by ardent Home Rule propagandists and trained to disturb the serenity of Orange meetings by pessimistic reflections on Sir Edward Carson's destination in the life to come. In fact, the bird in politics is a factor that seems to have come to stay; quite recently, at a political gathering held in a dimly lighted place of worship, the congregation gave a respectful hearing for nearly ten minutes to a jackdaw from Wapping, under the impression that they were listening to the Chancellor of the Exchequer, who was late in arriving."

"But the Suffragettes," interrupted the nephew; "what did they do next?"

"After the bird fiasco," said Sir Lulworth, "the militant section made a demonstration of a more aggressive nature; they assembled in force on the opening day of the Royal Academy Exhibition and destroyed some three or four hundred of the pictures. This proved an even worse failure than the parrot business; every one agreed that there were always far too many pictures in the Academy Exhibition, and the drastic weeding out of a few hundred canvases was regarded as a positive improvement. Moreover, from the artists' point of view it was realized that the outrage constituted a sort of compensation for those whose works were persistently 'skied,' since out of sight meant also out of reach. Altogether it was one of the most successful and popular exhibitions that the Academy had held for many years. Then the fair agitators fell back on some of their earlier methods; they wrote sweetly argumentative plays to prove that they ought to have the vote, they smashed windows to show that they must have the vote, and they kicked Cabinet Ministers to demonstrate that they'd better have the vote, and still the coldly reasoned or unreasoned reply was that they'd better not. Their plight might have been summed up in a perversion of Gilbert's lines—

> "'Twenty voteless millions we,
> Voteless all against our will,
> Twenty years hence we shall be
> Twenty voteless millions still.'

And of course the great idea for their master-stroke of strategy came from a masculine source. Lena Dubarri, who was the captain-general of their thinking department, met Waldo Orpington in the Mall one afternoon, just at a time when the fortunes of the Cause were at their lowest ebb. Waldo Orpington is a frivolous little fool who chirrups at drawing-room concerts and can recognize bits from different composers without referring to the programme, but all the same he occasionally has ideas. He didn't care a twopenny fiddlestring about the Cause, but he rather enjoyed the idea of having his finger in the political pie. Also it is possible, though I should think highly improbable, that he admired Lena Dubarri. Anyhow, when Lena gave a rather gloomy account of the existing state of things in the Suffragette world, Waldo was not merely sympathetic but ready with a practical suggestion. Turning his gaze westward along the Mall, towards the setting sun and Buckingham Palace, he was silent for a moment, and then said significantly, 'You have expended your energies and enterprise on labours of destruction; why has it never occurred to you to attempt something far more terrific?'

"'What do you mean?' she asked him eagerly.

"'Create.'

"'Do you mean create disturbances? We've been doing nothing else for months,' she said.

"Waldo shook his head, and continued to look westward along the Mall. He's rather good at acting in an amateur sort of fashion. Lena followed his gaze, and then turned to him with a puzzled look of inquiry.

"'Exactly,' said Waldo, in answer to her look.

"'But—how can we create?' she asked; 'it's been done already.'

"'Do it *again*,' said Waldo, 'and again and again—'

"Before he could finish the sentence she had kissed him. She declared afterwards that he was the first man she had ever kissed, and he declared that she was the first woman who had ever kissed him in the Mall, so they both secured a record of a kind.

"Within the next day or two a new departure was noticeable in Suffragette tactics. They gave up worrying Ministers and Parliament and took to worrying their own sympathizers and supporters —for funds. The ballot-box was temporarily forgotten in the cult of the collecting-box. The daughters of the horseleech were not more persistent in their demands, the financiers of the tottering *ancien régime* were not more desperate in their expedients for raising money than the Suffragist workers of all sections at this juncture, and in one way and another, by fair means and normal, they really got together a very useful sum. What they were going to do with it no one seemed to know, not even those who were most active in collecting work. The secret on this occasion had been well kept. Certain transactions that leaked out from time to time only added to the mystery of the situation.

"'Don't you long to know what we are going to do with our treasure hoard?' Lena asked the Prime Minister one day when she happened to sit next to him at a whist drive at the Chinese Embassy.

"'I was hoping you were going to try a little personal bribery,' he responded banteringly, but some genuine anxiety and curiosity lay behind the lightness of his chaff; 'of course I know,' he added, 'that you have been buying up building sites in commanding situations in and around the Metropolis. Two or three, I'm told, are on the road to Brighton, and another near Ascot. You don't mean to fortify them, do you?'

"'Something more insidious than that,' she said; 'you could prevent us from building forts; you can't prevent us from erecting an exact replica of the Victoria Memorial on each of those sites. They're all private property, with no building restrictions attached.'

"'Which memorial?' he asked; 'not the one in front of Buckingham Palace? Surely not that one?'

"'That one,' she said.

"'My dear lady,' he cried, 'you can't be serious. It is a beautiful and imposing work of art—at any rate, one is getting accustomed to it, and even if one doesn't happen to admire it one can always look in another direction. But imagine what life would be like if one saw that erection confronting one wherever one went. Imagine the effect on people with tired, harassed nerves who saw it three times on the way to Brighton and three times again on the way back. Imagine seeing it dominate the landscape at Ascot, and trying to keep your eye off it on the Sandwich golf-links. What have your countrymen done to deserve such a thing?'

"'They have refused us the vote,' said Lena bitterly.

"The Prime Minister always declared himself an opponent of anything savouring of panic legislation, but he brought a Bill into Parliament forthwith and successfully appealed to both Houses to pass it through all its stages within the week. And that is how we got one of the most glorious measures of the century."

"A measure conferring the vote on women?" asked the nephew.

"Oh, dear, no. An act which made it a penal offence to erect commemorative statuary anywhere within three miles of a public highway."

EXCEPTING MRS. PENTHERBY

It was Reggie Bruttle's own idea for converting what had threatened to be an albino elephant into a beast of burden that should help him along the stony road of his finances. "The Limes," which had come to him by inheritance without any accompanying provision for its upkeep, was one of those pretentious, unaccommodating mansions which none but a man of wealth could afford to live in, and which not one wealthy man in a hundred would choose on its merits. It might easily languish in the estate market for years, set round with notice-boards proclaiming it, in the eyes of a sceptical world, to be an eminently desirable residence.

Reggie's scheme was to turn it into the headquarters of a prolonged country-house party, in session during the months from October till the end of March—a party consisting of young or youngish people of both sexes, too poor to be able to do much hunting or shooting on a serious scale, but keen on getting their fill of golf, bridge, dancing, and occasional theatre-going. No one was to be on the footing of a paying guest, but every one was to rank as a paying host; a committee would look after the catering and expenditure, and an informal sub-committee would make itself useful in helping forward the amusement side of the scheme.

As it was only an experiment, there was to be a general agreement on the part of those involved in it to be as lenient and mutually helpful to one another as possible. Already a promising nucleus, including one or two young married couples, had been got together, and the thing seemed to be fairly launched.

"With good management and a little unobtrusive hard work, I think the thing ought to be a success," said Reggie, and Reggie was one of those people who are painstaking first and optimistic afterwards.

"There is one rock on which you will unfailingly come to grief, manage you never so wisely," said Major Dagberry cheerfully; "the women will quarrel. Mind you," continued this prophet of disaster, "I don't say that some of the men won't quarrel too, probably they will; but the women are bound to. You can't prevent it; it's in the nature of the sex. The hand that rocks the cradle rocks the world, in a volcanic sense. A woman will endure discomforts, and make sacrifices, and go without things to an heroic extent, but the one luxury she will not go without is her quarrels. No matter where she may be, or how transient her appearance on a scene, she will instal her feminine feuds as assuredly as a Frenchman would concoct soup in the waste of the Arctic regions. At the commencement of a sea voyage, before the male traveller knows half a dozen of his fellow-passengers by sight, the average woman will have started a couple of enmities, and laid in material for one or two more—provided, of course, that there are sufficient women aboard to permit quarrelling in the plural. If there's no one else she will quarrel with the stewardess. This experiment of yours is to run for six months; in less than five weeks there will be war to the knife declaring itself in half a dozen different directions."

"Oh, come, there are only eight women in the party; they won't all pick quarrels quite so soon as that," protested Reggie.

"They won't all originate quarrels, perhaps," conceded the Major, "but they will all take sides, and just as Christmas is upon you, with its conventions of peace and good will, you will find yourself in for a glacial epoch of cold, unforgiving hostility, with an occasional Etna flare of open warfare. You can't help it, old boy; but, at any rate, you can't say you were not warned."

The first five weeks of the venture falsified Major Dagberry's prediction and justified Reggie's optimism. There were, of course, occasional small bickerings, and the existence of certain jealousies might be detected below the surface of everyday intercourse; but, on the whole, the womenfolk got on remarkably well together. There was, however, a notable exception. It had not taken five weeks for Mrs. Pentherby to get herself cordially disliked by the members of her own sex; five days had been amply sufficient. Most of the women declared that they had detested her the moment they set eyes on her; but that was probably an afterthought.

With the menfolk she got on well enough, without being of the type of woman who can only bask in male society; neither was she lacking in the general qualities which make an individual useful and desirable as a member of a co-operative community. She did not try to "get the better of" her fellow-hosts by snatching little advantages or cleverly evading her just contributions; she was not inclined to be boring or snobbish in the way of personal reminiscence. She played a fair game of bridge, and her card-room manners were irreproachable. But wherever she came in contact with her own sex the light of battle kindled at once; her talent for arousing animosity seemed to border on positive genius.

Whether the object of her attentions was thick-skinned or sensitive, quick-tempered or good-natured, Mrs. Pentherby managed to achieve the same effect. She exposed little weaknesses, she prodded sore places, she snubbed enthusiasms, she was generally right in a matter of argument, or, if wrong, she somehow contrived to make her adversary appear foolish and opinionated. She did, and said, horrible things in a matter-of-fact innocent way, and she did, and said, matter-of-fact innocent things in a horrible way. In short, the unanimous feminine verdict on her was that she was objectionable.

There was no question of taking sides, as the Major had anticipated; in fact, dislike of Mrs. Pentherby was almost a bond of union between the other women, and more than one threatening disagreement had been rapidly dissipated by her obvious and malicious attempts to inflame and extend it; and the most irritating thing about her was her successful assumption of unruffled composure at moments when the tempers of her adversaries were with difficulty kept under control. She made her most scathing remarks in the tone of a tube conductor announcing that the next station is Brompton Road—the measured, listless tone of one who knows he is right, but is utterly indifferent to the fact that he proclaims.

On one occasion Mrs. Val Gwepton, who was not blessed with the most reposeful of temperaments, fairly let herself go, and gave Mrs. Pentherby a vivid and truthful *résumé* of her opinion of her. The object of this unpent storm of accumulated animosity waited patiently for a lull, and then remarked quietly to the angry little woman—

"And now, my dear Mrs. Gwepton, let me tell you something that I've been wanting to say for the last two or three minutes, only you wouldn't give me a chance; you've got a hairpin dropping out on the left side. You thin-haired women always find it difficult to keep your hairpins in."

"What can one do with a woman like that?" Mrs. Val demanded afterwards of a sympathizing audience.

Of course, Reggie received numerous hints as to the unpopularity of this jarring personality. His sister-in-law openly tackled him on the subject of her many enormities. Reggie listened with the attenuated regret that one bestows on an earthquake disaster in Bolivia or a crop failure in Eastern Turkestan, events which seem so distant that one can almost persuade oneself they haven't happened.

"That woman has got some hold over him," opined his sister-in-law darkly; "either she is helping him to finance the show, and presumes on the fact, or else, which Heaven forbid, he's got some queer infatuation for her. Men do take the most extraordinary fancies."

Matters never came exactly to a crisis. Mrs. Pentherby, as a source of personal offence, spread herself over so wide an area that no one woman of the party felt impelled to rise up and declare that she absolutely refused to stay another week in the same house with her. What is everybody's tragedy is nobody's tragedy. There was ever a certain consolation in comparing notes as to specific acts of offence. Reggie's sister-in-law had the added interest of trying to discover the secret bond which blunted his condemnation of Mrs. Pentherby's long catalogue of misdeeds. There was little to go on from his manner towards her in public, but he remained obstinately unimpressed by anything that was said against her in private.

With the one exception of Mrs. Pentherby's unpopularity, the house-party scheme was a success on its first trial, and there was no difficulty about reconstructing it on the same lines for another winter session. It so happened that most of the women of the party, and two or three of the men, would not be available on this occasion, but Reggie had laid his plans well ahead and booked plenty of "fresh blood" for the new departure. It would be, if anything, rather a larger party than before.

"I'm so sorry I can't join this winter," said Reggie's sister-in-law, "but we must go to our cousins in Ireland; we've put them off so often. What a shame! You'll have none of the same women this time."

"Excepting Mrs. Pentherby," said Reggie demurely.

"Mrs. Pentherby! *Surely*, Reggie, you're not going to be so idiotic as to have that woman again! She'll set all the women's backs up just as she did this time. What *is* this mysterious hold she's got over you?"

"She's invaluable," said Reggie; "she's my official quarreller."

"Your—what did you say?" gasped his sister-in-law.

"I introduced her into the house-party for the express purpose of concentrating the feuds and quarrelling that would otherwise have broken out in all directions among the womenkind. I didn't need the advice and warning of sundry friends to foresee that we shouldn't get through six months of close companionship without a certain amount of pecking and sparring, so I thought the best thing was to localize and sterilize it in one process. Of course, I made it well worth the lady's while, and as she didn't know any of you from Adam, and you don't even know her real name, she didn't mind getting herself disliked in a useful cause."

"You mean to say she was in the know all the time?"

"Of course she was, and so were one or two of the men, so she was able to have a good laugh with us behind the scenes when she'd done anything particularly outrageous. And she really enjoyed herself. You see, she's in the position of poor relation in a rather pugnacious family, and her life has been largely spent in smoothing over other people's quarrels. You can imagine the welcome relief of being able to go about saying and doing perfectly exasperating things to a whole houseful of women—and all in the cause of peace."

"I think you are the most odious person in the whole world," said Reggie's sister-in-law. Which was not strictly true; more than anybody, more than ever she disliked Mrs. Pentherby. It was impossible to calculate how many quarrels that woman had done her out of.

MARK

AUGUSTUS MELLOWKENT was a novelist with a future; that is to say, a limited but increasing number of people read his books, and there seemed good reason to suppose that if he steadily continued to turn out novels year by year a progressively increasing circle of readers would acquire the Mellowkent habit, and demand his works from the libraries and bookstalls. At the instigation of his publisher he had discarded the baptismal Augustus and taken the front name of Mark.

"Women like a name that suggests some one strong and silent, able but unwilling to answer questions. Augustus merely suggests idle splendour, but such a name as Mark Mellowkent, besides being alliterative, conjures up a vision of some one strong and beautiful and good, a sort of blend of Georges Carpentier and the Reverend What's-his-name."

One morning in December Augustus sat in his writing-room, at work on the third chapter of his eighth novel. He had described at some length, for the benefit of those who could not imagine it, what a rectory garden looks like in July; he was now engaged in describing at greater length the feelings of a young girl, daughter of a long line of rectors and archdeacons, when she discovers for the first time that the postman is attractive.

"Their eyes met, for a brief moment, as he handed her two circulars and the fat wrapper-bound bulk of the *East Essex News*. Their eyes met, for the merest fraction of a second, yet nothing could ever be quite the same again. Cost what it might she felt that she must speak, must break the intolerable, unreal silence that had fallen on them. 'How is your mother's rheumatism?' she said."

The author's labours were cut short by the sudden intrusion of a maidservant.

"A gentleman to see you, sir," said the maid, handing a card with the name Caiaphas Dwelf inscribed on it; "says it's important."

Mellowkent hesitated and yielded; the importance of the visitor's mission was probably illusory, but he had never met any one with the name Caiaphas before. It would be at least a new experience.

Mr. Dwelf was a man of indefinite age; his high, narrow forehead, cold grey eyes, and determined manner bespoke an unflinching purpose. He had a large book under his arm, and there seemed every probability that he had left a package of similar volumes in the hall. He took a seat before it had been offered him, placed the book on the table, and began to address Mellowkent in the manner of an "open letter."

"You are a literary man, the author of several well-known books–"

"I am engaged on a book at the present moment–rather busily engaged," said Mellowkent pointedly.

"Exactly," said the intruder; "time with you is a commodity of considerable importance. Minutes, even, have their value."

"They have," agreed Mellowkent, looking at his watch.

"That," said Caiaphas, "is why this book that I am introducing to your notice is not a book that you can afford to be without. *Right Here* is indispensable for the writing man; it is no ordinary encyclopædia, or I should not trouble to show it to you. It is an inexhaustible mine of concise information–"

"On a shelf at my elbow," said the author, "I have a row of reference books that supply me with all the information I am likely to require."

"Here," persisted the would-be salesman, "you have it all in one compact volume. No matter what the subject may be which you wish to look up, or the fact you desire to verify, *Right Here* gives you all that you want to know in the briefest and most enlightening form. Historical reference, for instance; career of John Huss, let us say. Here we are: 'Huss, John, celebrated religious reformer. Born 1369, burned at Constance 1415. The Emperor Sigismund universally blamed.'"

"If he had been burnt in these days every one would have suspected the Suffragettes," observed Mellowkent.

"Poultry-keeping, now," resumed Caiaphas, "that's a subject that might crop up in a novel dealing with English country life. Here we have all about it: 'The Leghorn as egg-producer. Lack of maternal instinct in the Minorca. Gapes in chickens, its cause and cure. Ducklings for the early market, how fattened.' There, you see, there it all is, nothing lacking."

"Except the maternal instinct in the Minorca, and that you could hardly be expected to supply."

"Sporting records, that's important too; now how many men, sporting men even, are there who can say off-hand what horse won the Derby in any particular year? Now it's just a little thing of that sort–"

"My dear sir," interrupted Mellowkent, "there are at least four men in my club who can not only tell me what horse won in any given year, but what horse ought to have won and why it didn't. If your book could supply a method for protecting one from information of that sort, it would do more than anything you have yet claimed for it."

"Geography," said Caiaphas imperturbably; "that's a thing that a busy man, writing at high pressure, may easily make a slip over. Only the other day a well-known author made the Volga flow into the Black Sea instead of the Caspian; now, with this book–"

"On a polished rose-wood stand behind you there reposes a reliable and up-to-date atlas," said Mellowkent; "and now I must really ask you to be going."

"An atlas," said Caiaphas, "gives merely the chart of the river's course, and indicates the principal towns that it passes. Now *Right Here* gives you the scenery, traffic, ferry-boat charges, the prevalent types of fish, boatmen's slang terms, and hours of sailing of the principal river steamers. It gives you–"

Mellowkent sat and watched the hard-featured, resolute, pitiless salesman, as he sat doggedly in the chair wherein he had installed himself, unflinchingly extolling the merits of his undesired wares. A spirit of wistful emulation took possession of the author. Why could he not live up to the cold stern name he had adopted?

Why must he sit here weakly and listen to this weary, unconvincing tirade? Why could he not be Mark Mellowkent for a few brief moments, and meet this man on level terms?

A sudden inspiration flashed across him.

"Have you read my last book, *The Cageless Linnet?*" he asked.

"I don't read novels," said Caiaphas tersely.

"Oh, but you ought to read this one, every one ought to," exclaimed Mellowkent, fishing the book down from a shelf; "published at six shillings, you can have it at four-and-six. There is a bit in chapter five that I feel sure you would like, where Emma is alone in the birch copse waiting for Harold Huntingdon—that is the man her family want her to marry. She really wants to marry him too, but she does not discover that till chapter fifteen. Listen: 'Far as the eye could stretch rolled the mauve and purple billows of heather, lit up here and there with the glowing yellow of gorse and broom, and edged round with the delicate greys and silver and green of the young birch trees. Tiny blue and brown butterflies fluttered above the fronds of heather, revelling in the sunlight, and overhead the larks were singing as only larks can sing. It was a day when all Nature—'"

"In *Right Here* you have full information on all branches of Nature study," broke in the book-agent, with a tired note sounding in his voice for the first time; "forestry, insect life, bird migration, reclamation of waste lands. As I was saying, no man who has to deal with the varied interests of life—"

"I wonder if you would care for one of my earlier books, *The Reluctance of Lady Cullumpton,*" said Mellowkent, hunting again through the bookshelf; "some people consider it my best novel. Ah, here it is. I see there are one or two spots on the cover, so I won't ask more than three-and-ninepence for it. Do let me read you how it opens:

"'Beatrice Lady Cullumpton entered the long, dimly lit drawing-room, her eyes blazing with a hope that she guessed to be groundless, her lips trembling with a fear that she could not disguise. In her hand she carried a small fan, a fragile toy of lace and satinwood. Something snapped as she entered the room; she had crushed the fan into a dozen pieces.'

"There, what do you think of that for an opening? It tells you at once that there's something afoot."

"I don't read novels," said Caiaphas sullenly.

"But just think what a resource they are," exclaimed the author, "on long winter evenings, or perhaps when you are laid up with a strained ankle—a thing that might happen to any one; or if you were staying in a house-party with persistent wet weather and a stupid hostess and insufferably dull fellow-guests, you would just make an excuse that you had letters to write, go to your room, light a cigarette, and for three-and-ninepence you could plunge into the society of Beatrice Lady Cullumpton and her set. No one ought to travel without one or two of my novels in their luggage as a stand-by. A friend of mine said only the other day that he would as soon think of going into the tropics without quinine as of going on a visit without a couple of Mark Mellowkents in his kit-bag. Perhaps sensation is more in your line. I wonder if I've got a copy of *The Python's Kiss.*"

Caiaphas did not wait to be tempted with selections from that thrilling work of fiction. With a muttered remark about having no time to waste on monkey-talk, he gathered up his slighted volume and departed. He made no audible reply to Mellowkent's cheerful "Good morning," but the latter fancied that a look of respectful hatred flickered in the cold, grey eyes.

THE HEDGEHOG

A "Mixed Double" of young people were contesting a game of lawn tennis at the Rectory garden party; for the past five-and-twenty years at least mixed doubles of young people had done exactly the same thing on exactly the same spot at about the same time of year. The young people changed and made way for others in the course of time, but very little else seemed to alter.

The present players were sufficiently conscious of the social nature of the occasion to be concerned about their clothes and appearance, and sufficiently sport-loving to be keen on the game. Both their efforts and their appearance came under the four-fold scrutiny of a quartet of ladies sitting as official spectators on a bench immediately commanding the court. It was one of the accepted conditions of the Rectory garden party that four ladies, who usually knew very little about tennis and a great deal about the players, should sit at that particular spot and watch the game. It had also come to be almost a tradition that two ladies should be amiable, and that the other two should be Mrs. Dole and Mrs. Hatch-Mallard.

"What a singularly unbecoming way Eva Jonelet has taken to doing her hair in," said Mrs. Hatch-Mallard; "it's ugly hair at the best of times, but she needn't make it look ridiculous as well. Some one ought to tell her."

Eva Jonelet's hair might have escaped Mrs. Hatch-Mallard's condemnation if she could have forgotten the more glaring fact that Eva was Mrs. Dole's favourite niece. It would, perhaps, have been a more comfortable arrangement if Mrs. Hatch-Mallard and Mrs. Dole could have been asked to the Rectory on separate occasions, but there was only one garden party in the course of the year, and neither lady could have been omitted from the list of invitations without hopelessly wrecking the social peace of the parish.

"How pretty the yew trees look at this time of year," interposed a lady with a soft, silvery voice that suggested a chinchilla muff painted by Whistler.

"What do you mean by this time of year?" demanded Mrs. Hatch-Mallard. "Yew trees look beautiful at all times of the year. That is their great charm."

"Yew trees never look anything but hideous under any circumstances or at any time of year," said Mrs. Dole, with the slow, emphatic relish of one who contradicts for the pleasure of the thing. "They are only fit for graveyards and cemeteries."

Mrs. Hatch-Mallard gave a sardonic snort, which, being translated, meant that there were some people who were better fitted for cemeteries than for garden parties.

"What is the score, please?" asked the lady with the chinchilla voice.

The desired information was given her by a young gentleman in spotless white flannels, whose general toilet effect suggested solicitude rather than anxiety.

"What an odious young cub Bertie Dykson has become!" pronounced Mrs. Dole, remembering suddenly that Bertie was rather a favourite with Mrs. Hatch-Mallard. "The young men of today are not what they used to be twenty years ago."

"Of course not," said Mrs. Hatch-Mallard; "twenty years ago Bertie Dykson was just two years old, and you must expect some difference in appearance and manner and conversation between those two periods."

"Do you know," said Mrs. Dole confidentially, "I shouldn't be surprised if that was intended to be clever."

"Have you any one interesting coming to stay with you, Mrs. Norbury?" asked the chinchilla voice hastily; "you generally have a house-party at this time of year."

"I've got a most interesting woman coming," said Mrs. Norbury, who had been mutely struggling for some chance to turn the conversation into a safe channel; "an old acquaintance of mine, Ada Bleek—"

"What an ugly name," said Mrs. Hatch-Mallard.

"She's descended from the de la Bliques, an old Huguenot family of Touraine, you know."

"There weren't any Huguenots in Touraine," said Mrs. Hatch-Mallard, who thought she might safely dispute any fact that was three hundred years old.

"Well, anyhow, she's coming to stay with me," continued Mrs. Norbury, bringing her story quickly down to the present day; "she arrives this evening and she's highly clairvoyante, a seventh daughter of a seventh daughter, you know, and all that sort of thing."

"How very interesting," said the chinchilla voice; "Exwood is just the right place for her to come to, isn't it? There are supposed to be several ghosts there."

"That is why she was so anxious to come," said Mrs. Norbury; "she put off another engagement in order to accept my invitation. She's had visions and dreams, and all those sort of things, that have come true in a most marvellous manner, but she's never actually seen a ghost, and she's longing to have that experience. She belongs to that Research Society, you know."

"I expect she'll see the unhappy Lady Cullumpton, the most famous of all the Exwood ghosts," said Mrs. Dole; "my ancestor, you know, Sir Gervase Cullumpton, murdered his young bride in a fit of jealousy while they were on a visit to Exwood. He strangled her in the stables with a stirrup leather, just after they had come in from riding, and she is seen sometimes at dusk going about the lawns and the stable yard, in a long green habit, moaning and trying to get the thong from round her throat. I shall be most interested to hear if your friend sees—"

"I don't know why she should be expected to see a trashy, traditional apparition like the so-called Cullumpton ghost, that is only vouched for by house-maids and tipsy stable-boys, when my uncle, who was the owner of Exwood, committed suicide there under the most tragical circumstances, and most certainly haunts the place."

"Mrs. Hatch-Mallard has evidently never read *Popple's County History,*" said Mrs. Dole icily, "or she would know that the Cullumpton ghost has a wealth of evidence behind it—"

"Oh, Popple!" exclaimed Mrs. Hatch-Mallard scornfully; "any rubbishy old story is good enough for him. Popple, indeed! Now my uncle's ghost was seen by a Rural Dean, who was also a Justice of the Peace. I should think that would be good enough testimony for any one. Mrs. Norbury, I shall take it as a deliberate personal affront if your clairvoyante friend sees any other ghost except that of my uncle."

"I dare say she won't see anything at all; she never has yet, you know," said Mrs. Norbury hopefully.

"It was a most unfortunate topic for me to have broached," she lamented afterwards to the owner of the chinchilla voice; "Exwood belongs to Mrs. Hatch-Mallard, and we've only got it on a short lease. A nephew of hers has been wanting to live there for some time, and if we offend her in any way she'll refuse to renew the lease. I sometimes think these garden parties are a mistake."

The Norburys played bridge for the next three nights till nearly one o'clock; they did not care for the game, but it reduced the time at their guest's disposal for undesirable ghostly visitations.

"Miss Bleek is not likely to be in a frame of mind to see ghosts," said Hugo Norbury, "if she goes to bed with her brain awhirl with royal spades and no trumps and grand slams."

"I've talked to her for hours about Mrs. Hatch-Mallard's uncle," said his wife, "and pointed out the exact spot where he killed himself, and invented all sorts of impressive details, and I've found an old portrait of Lord John Russell and put it in her room, and told her that it's supposed to be a picture of the uncle in middle age. If Ada does see a ghost at all it certainly ought to be old Hatch-Mallard's. At any rate, we've done our best."

The precautions were in vain. On the third morning of her stay Ada Bleek came down late to breakfast, her eyes looking very tired, but ablaze with excitement, her hair done anyhow, and a large brown volume hugged under her arm.

"At last I've seen something supernatural!" she exclaimed, and gave Mrs. Norbury a fervent kiss, as though in gratitude for the opportunity afforded her.

"A ghost!" cried Mrs. Norbury, "not really!"

"Really and unmistakably!"

"Was it an oldish man in the dress of about fifty years ago?" asked Mrs. Norbury hopefully.

"Nothing of the sort," said Ada; "it was a white hedgehog."

"A white hedgehog!" exclaimed both the Norburys, in tones of disconcerted astonishment.

"A huge white hedgehog with baleful yellow eyes," said Ada; "I was lying half asleep in bed when suddenly I felt a sensation as of something sinister and unaccountable passing through the room. I sat up and looked round, and there, under the window, I saw an evil, creeping thing, a sort of monstrous hedgehog, of a dirty white colour, with black, loathsome claws that clicked and scraped along the floor, and narrow, yellow eyes of indescribable evil. It slithered along for a yard or two, always looking at me with its cruel, hideous eyes, then, when it reached the second window, which was open, it clambered up the sill and vanished. I got up at once and went to the window; there wasn't a sign of it anywhere. Of course, I knew it must be something from another world, but it was not till I turned up Popple's chapter on local traditions that I realized what I had seen."

She turned eagerly to the large brown volume and read: "'Nicholas Herison, an old miser, was hung at Batchford in 1763 for the murder of a farm lad who had accidentally discovered his secret hoard. His ghost is supposed to traverse the countryside, appearing sometimes as a white owl, sometimes as a huge white hedgehog.'"

"I expect you read the Popple story overnight, and that made you *think* you saw a hedgehog when you were only half awake," said Mrs. Norbury, hazarding a conjecture that probably came very near the truth.

Ada scouted the possibility of such a solution of her apparition.

"This must be hushed up," said Mrs. Norbury quickly; "the servants—"

"Hushed up!" exclaimed Ada, indignantly; "I'm writing a long report on it for the Research Society."

It was then that Hugo Norbury, who is not naturally a man of brilliant resource, had one of the really useful inspirations of his life.

"It was very wicked of us, Miss Bleek," he said, "but it would be a shame to let it go further. That white hedgehog is an old joke of ours; stuffed albino hedgehog, you know, that my father brought home from Jamaica, where they grow to enormous size. We hide it in the room with a string on it, run one end of the string through the window; then we pull it from below and it comes scraping along the floor, just as you've described, and finally jerks out of the window. Taken in heaps of people; they all read up Popple and think it's old Harry Nicholson's ghost; we always stop them from writing to the papers about it, though. That would be carrying matters too far."

Mrs. Hatch-Mallard renewed the lease in due course, but Ada Bleek has never renewed her friendship.

THE MAPPINED LIFE

"These Mappin Terraces at the Zoological Gardens are a great improvement on the old style of wild-beast age," said Mrs. James Gurtleberry, putting down an illustrated paper; "they give one the illusion of seeing the animals in their natural surroundings. I wonder how much of the illusion is passed on to the animals?"

"That would depend on the animal," said her niece; "a jungle-fowl, for instance, would no doubt think its lawful jungle surroundings were faithfully reproduced if you gave it a sufficiency of wives, a goodly variety of seed food and ants' eggs, a commodious bank of loose earth to dust itself in, a convenient roosting tree, and a rival or two to make matters interesting. Of course there ought to be jungle-cats and birds of prey and other agencies of sudden death to add to the illusion of liberty, but the bird's own imagination is capable of inventing those—look how a domestic fowl will squawk an alarm note if a rook or wood-pigeon passes over its run when it has chickens."

"You think, then, they really do have a sort of illusion, if you give them space enough—"

"In a few cases only. Nothing will make me believe that an acre or so of concrete enclosure will make up to a wolf or a tiger-cat for the range of night prowling that would belong to it in a wild state. Think of the dictionary of sound and scent and recollection that unfolds before a real wild beast as it comes out from its lair every evening, with the knowledge that in a few minutes it will be hieing along to some distant hunting ground where all the joy and fury of the chase awaits it; think of the crowded sensations of the brain when every rustle, every cry, every bent twig, and every whiff across the nostrils means something, something to do with life and death and dinner. Imagine the satisfaction of stealing down to your own particular drinking spot, choosing your own particular tree to scrape your claws on, finding your own particular bed of dried grass to roll on. Then, in the place of all that, put a concrete promenade, which will be of exactly the same dimensions whether you race or crawl across it, coated with stale, unvarying scents and surrounded with cries and noises that have ceased to have the least meaning or interest. As a substitute for a narrow cage the new enclosures are excellent, but I should think they are a poor imitation of a life of liberty."

"It's rather depressing to think that," said Mrs. Gurtleberry; "they look so spacious and so natural, but I suppose a good deal of what seems natural to us would be meaningless to a wild animal."

"That is where our superior powers of self-deception come in," said the niece; "we are able to live our unreal, stupid little lives on our particular Mappin terrace, and persuade ourselves that we really are untrammelled men and women leading a reasonable existence in a reasonable sphere."

"But good gracious," exclaimed the aunt, bouncing into an attitude of scandalized defence, "we are leading reasonable existences! What on earth do you mean by trammels? We are merely trammelled by the ordinary decent conventions of civilized society."

"We are trammelled," said the niece, calmly and pitilessly, "by restrictions of income and opportunity, and above all by lack of initiative. To some people a restricted income doesn't matter a bit, in fact it often seems to help as a means for getting a lot of reality out of life; I am sure there are men and women who do their shopping in little back streets of Paris, buying four carrots and a shred of beef for their daily sustenance, who lead a perfectly real and eventful existence. Lack of initiative is the thing that really cripples one, and that is where you and I and Uncle James are so hopelessly shut in. We are just so many animals stuck down on a Mappin terrace, with this difference in our disfavour, that the animals are there to be looked at, while nobody wants to look at us. As a matter of fact there would be nothing to look at. We get colds in winter and hay-fever in summer, and if a wasp happens to sting one of us, well, that is the wasp's initiative, not ours; all we do is to wait for the swelling to go down. Whenever we do climb into local fame and notice, it is by indirect methods; if it happens to be a good flowering year for magnolias the neighbourhood observes, 'Have you seen the Gurtleberrys' magnolia? It is a perfect mass of flowers,' and we go about telling people that there are fifty-seven blossoms as against thirty-nine the previous year."

"In Coronation year there were as many as sixty," put in the aunt; "your uncle has kept a record for the last eight years."

"Doesn't it ever strike you," continued the niece relentlessly, "that if we moved away from here or were blotted out of existence our local claim to fame would pass on automatically to whoever happened to take the house and garden? People would say to one another, 'Have you seen the Smith-Jenkins' magnolia? It is a perfect mass of flowers,' or else, 'Smith-Jenkins tells me there won't be a single blossom on their magnolia this year; the east winds have turned all the buds black.' Now if, when we had gone, people still associated our names with the magnolia tree, no matter who temporarily possessed it, if they said, 'Ah, that's the tree on which the Gurtleberrys hung their cook because she sent up the wrong kind of sauce with the asparagus,' that would be something really due to our own initiative, apart from anything east winds or magnolia vitality might have to say in the matter."

"We should never do such a thing," said the aunt. The niece gave a reluctant sigh.

"I can't imagine it," she admitted. "Of course," she continued, "there are heaps of ways of leading a real existence without committing sensational deeds of violence. It's the dreadful little everyday acts of pretended importance that give the Mappin stamp to our life. It would be entertaining, if it wasn't so pathetically tragic, to hear Uncle James fuss in here in the morning and announce, 'I must just go down into the town and find out what the men there are saying about Mexico. Matters are beginning to look serious there.' Then he patters away into the town, and talks in a highly serious voice to the tobacconist, incidentally buying an ounce of tobacco; perhaps he meets one or two others of the world's thinkers and talks to them in a highly serious voice, then he patters back here and announces with increased importance, 'I've just been talking to some men in the town about the condition of affairs in Mexico. They agree with the view that I have formed, that things there will have to get worse before they get better.' Of course nobody in the town cared in the least little bit what his views about Mexico were or whether he had any. The tobacconist wasn't even fluttered at his buying the ounce of tobacco; he knows that he purchases the same quantity of the same sort of tobacco every week. Uncle James might just as well have lain on his back in the garden and chattered to the lilac tree about the habits of caterpillars."

"I really will not listen to such things about your uncle," protested Mrs. James Gurtleberry angrily.

"My own case is just as bad and just as tragic," said the niece dispassionately; "nearly everything about me is conventional make-believe. I'm not a good dancer, and no one could honestly call me good-looking, but when I go to one of our dull little local dances I'm conventionally supposed to 'have a heavenly time,' to attract the ardent homage of the local cavaliers, and to go home with my head awhirl with pleasurable recollections. As a matter of fact, I've merely put in some hours of indifferent dancing, drunk some badly made claret cup, and listened to an enormous amount of laborious light conversation. A moonlight hen-stealing raid with the merry-eyed curate would be infinitely more exciting; imagine the pleasure of carrying off all those white Minorcas that the Chibfords are always bragging about. When we had disposed of them we could give the proceeds to a charity, so there would be nothing really wrong about it. But nothing of that sort lies within the Mappined limits of my life. One of these days somebody dull and decorous and undistinguished will 'make himself agreeable' to me at a tennis party, as the saying is, and all the dull old gossips of the neighbourhood will begin to ask when we are to be engaged, and at last we shall be engaged, and people will give us butter-dishes and blotting-cases and framed pictures of young women feeding swans. Hullo, Uncle, are you going out?"

"I'm just going down to the town," announced Mr. James Gurtleberry, with an air of some importance: "I want to hear what people are saying about Albania. Affairs there are beginning to take on a very serious look. It's my opinion that we haven't seen the worst of things yet."

In this he was probably right, but there was nothing in the immediate or prospective condition of Albania to warrant Mrs. Gurtleberry in bursting into tears.

FATE

Rex Dillot was nearly twenty-four, almost good-looking and quite penniless. His mother was supposed to make him some sort of an allowance out of what her creditors allowed her, and Rex occasionally strayed into the ranks of those who earn fitful salaries as secretaries or companions to people who are unable to cope unaided with their correspondence or their leisure. For a few months he had been assistant editor and business manager of a paper devoted to fancy mice, but the devotion had been all on one side, and the paper disappeared with a certain abruptness from club reading-rooms and other haunts where it had made a gratuitous appearance. Still, Rex lived with some air of comfort and well-being, as one can live if one is born with a genius for that sort of thing, and a kindly Providence usually arranged that his week-end invitations coincided with the dates on which his one white dinner-waistcoat was in a laundry-returned condition of dazzling cleanness. He played most games badly, and was shrewd enough to recognize the fact, but he had developed a marvellously accurate judgment in estimating the play and chances of other people, whether in a golf match, billiard handicap, or croquet tournament. By dint of parading his opinion of such and such a player's superiority with a sufficient degree of youthful assertiveness he usually succeeded in provoking a wager at liberal odds, and he looked to his week-end winnings to carry him through the financial embarrassments of his mid-week existence. The trouble was, as he confided to Clovis Sangrail, that he never had enough available or even prospective cash at his command to enable him to fix the wager at a figure really worth winning.

"Some day," he said, "I shall come across a really safe thing, a bet that simply can't go astray, and then I shall put it up for all I'm worth, or rather for a good deal more than I'm worth if you sold me up to the last button."

"It would be awkward if it didn't happen to come off," said Clovis.

"It would be more than awkward," said Rex; "it would be a tragedy. All the same, it would be extremely amusing to bring it off. Fancy awaking in the morning with about three hundred pounds standing to one's credit. I should go and clear out my hostess's pigeon-loft before breakfast out of sheer good-temper."

"Your hostess of the moment mightn't have a pigeon-loft," said Clovis.

"I always choose hostesses that have," said Rex; "a pigeon-loft is indicative of a careless, extravagant, genial disposition, such as I like to see around me. People who strew corn broadcast for a lot of feathered inanities that just sit about cooing and giving each other the glad eye in a Louis Quatorze manner are pretty certain to do you well."

"Young Strinnit is coming down this afternoon," said Clovis reflectively; "I dare say you won't find it difficult to get him to back himself at billiards. He plays a pretty useful game, but he's not quite as good as he fancies he is."

"I know one member of the party who can walk round him," said Rex softly, an alert look coming into his eyes; "that cadaverous-looking Major who arrived last night. I've seen him play at St. Moritz. If I could get Strinnit to lay odds on himself against the Major the money would be safe in my pocket. This looks like the good thing I've been watching and praying for."

"Don't be rash," counselled Clovis, "Strinnit may play up to his self-imagined form once in a blue moon."

"I intend to be rash," said Rex quietly, and the look on his face corroborated his words.

"Are you all going to flock to the billiard-room?" asked Teresa Thundleford, after dinner, with an air of some disapproval and a good deal of annoyance. "I can't see what particular amusement you find in watching two men prodding little ivory balls about on a table."

"Oh, well," said her hostess, "it's a way of passing the time, you know."

"A very poor way, to my mind," said Mrs. Thundleford; "now I was going to have shown all of you the photographs I took in Venice last summer."

"You showed them to us last night," said Mrs. Cuvering hastily.

"Those were the ones I took in Florence. These are quite a different lot."

"Oh, well, some time tomorrow we can look at them. You can leave them down in the drawing-room, and then every one can have a look."

"I should prefer to show them when you are all gathered together, as I have quite a lot of explanatory remarks to make, about Venetian art and architecture, on the same lines as my remarks last night on the Florentine galleries. Also, there are some verses of mine that I should like to read you, on the rebuilding of the Campanile. But, of course, if you all prefer to watch Major Latton and Mr. Strinnit knocking balls about on a table—"

"They are both supposed to be first-rate players," said the hostess.

"I have yet to learn that my verses and my art *causerie* are of second-rate quality," said Mrs. Thundleford with acerbity. "However, as you all seem bent on watching a silly game, there's no more to be said. I shall go upstairs and finish some writing. Later on, perhaps, I will come down and join you."

To one, at least, of the onlookers the game was anything but silly. It was absorbing, exciting, exasperating, nerve-stretching, and finally it grew to be tragic. The Major with the St. Moritz reputation was playing a long way below his form, young Strinnit was playing slightly above his, and had all the luck of the game as well. From the very start the balls seemed possessed by a demon of contrariness; they trundled about complacently for one player, they would go nowhere for the other.

"A hundred and seventy, seventy-four," sang out the youth who was marking. In a game of two hundred and fifty up it was an enormous lead to hold. Clovis watched the flush of excitement die away from Dillot's face, and a hard white look take its place.

"How much have you got on?" whispered Clovis. The other whispered the sum through dry, shaking lips. It was more than he or any one connected with him could pay; he had done what he had said he would do. He had been rash.

"Two hundred and six, ninety-eight."

Rex heard a clock strike ten somewhere in the hall, then another somewhere else, and another, and another; the house seemed full of striking clocks. Then in the distance the stable clock chimed in. In another hour they would all be striking eleven, and he would be listening to them as a disgraced outcast, unable to pay, even in part, the wager he had challenged.

"Two hundred and eighteen, a hundred and three." The game was as good as over. Rex was as good as done for. He longed desperately for the ceiling to fall in, for the house to catch fire, for anything to happen that would put an end to that horrible rolling to and fro of red and white ivory that was jostling him nearer and nearer to his doom.

"Two hundred and twenty-eight, a hundred and seven."

Rex opened his cigarette-case; it was empty. That at least gave him a pretext to slip away from the room for the purpose of refilling it; he would spare himself the drawn-out torture of watching that hopeless game played out to the bitter end. He backed away from the circle of absorbed watchers and made his way up a short stairway to a long, silent corridor of bedrooms, each with a guest's name written in a little square on the door. In the hush that reigned in this part of the house he could still hear the hateful click-click of the balls; if he waited for a few minutes longer he would hear the little outbreak of clapping and buzz of congratulation that would hail Strinnit's victory. On the alert tension of his nerves there broke another sound, the aggressive, wrath-inducing breathing of one who sleeps in heavy after-dinner slumber. The sound came from a room just at his elbow; the card on the door bore the announcement. "Mrs. Thundleford." The door was just slightly ajar; Rex pushed it open an inch or two more and looked in. The august Teresa had fallen asleep over an illustrated guide to Florentine art-galleries; at her side, somewhat dangerously near the edge of the table, was a reading-lamp. If Fate had been decently kind to him, thought Rex, bitterly, that lamp would have been knocked over by the sleeper and would have given them something to think of besides billiard matches.

There are occasions when one must take one's Fate in one's hands. Rex took the lamp in his.

"Two hundred and thirty-seven, one hundred and fifteen." Strinnit was at the table, and the balls lay in good position for him; he had a choice of two fairly easy shots, a choice which he was never to decide. A sudden hurricane of shrieks and a rush of stumbling feet sent every one flocking to the door. The Dillot boy crashed into the room, carrying in his arms the vociferous and somewhat dishevelled Teresa Thundleford; her clothing was certainly not a mass of flames, as the more excitable members of the party afterwards declared, but the edge of her skirt and part of the table-cover in which she had been hastily wrapped were alight in a flickering, half-hearted manner. Rex flung his struggling burden on to the billiard table, and for one breathless minute the work of beating out the sparks with rugs and cushions and playing on them with soda-water syphons engrossed the energies of the entire company.

"It was lucky I was passing when it happened," panted Rex; "some one had better see to the room. I think the carpet is alight."

As a matter of fact the promptitude and energy of the rescuer had prevented any great damage being done, either to the victim or her surroundings. The billiard table had suffered most, and had to be laid up for repairs; perhaps it was not the best place to have chosen for the scene of salvage operations; but then, as Clovis remarked, when one is rushing about with a blazing woman in one's arms one can't stop to think out exactly where one is going to put her.

THE BULL

Tom Yorkfield had always regarded his half-brother, Laurence, with a lazy instinct of dislike, toned down, as years went on, to a tolerant feeling of indifference. There was nothing very tangible to dislike him for; he was just a blood-relation, with whom Tom had no single taste or interest in common, and with whom, at the same time, he had had no occasion for quarrel. Laurence had left the farm early in life, and had lived for a few years on a small sum of money left him by his mother; he had taken up painting as a profession, and was reported to be doing fairly well at it, well enough, at any rate, to keep body and soul together. He specialized in painting animals, and he was successful in finding a certain number of people to buy his pictures. Tom felt a comforting sense of assured superiority in contrasting his position with that of his half-brother; Laurence was an artist-chap, just that and nothing more, though you might make it sound more important by calling him an animal painter; Tom was a farmer, not in a very big way, it was true, but the Helsery farm had been in the family for some generations, and it had a good reputation for the stock raised on it. Tom had done his best, with the little capital at his command, to maintain and improve the standard of his small herd of cattle, and in Clover Fairy he had bred a bull which was something rather better than any that his immediate neighbours could show. It would not have made a sensation in the judging-ring at an important cattle show, but it was as vigorous, shapely, and healthy a young animal as any small practical farmer could wish to possess. At the King's Head on market days Clover Fairy was very highly spoken of, and Yorkfield used to declare that he would not part with him for a hundred pounds; a hundred pounds is a lot of money in the small farming line, and probably anything over eighty would have tempted him.

It was with some especial pleasure that Tom took advantage of one of Laurence's rare visits to the farm to lead him down to the enclosure where Clover Fairy kept solitary state—the grass widower of a grazing harem. Tom felt some of his old dislike for his half-brother reviving; the artist was becoming more languid in his manner, more unsuitably turned-out in attire, and he seemed inclined to impart a slightly patronizing tone to his conversation. He took no heed of a flourishing potato crop, but waxed enthusiastic over a clump of yellow-flowering weed that stood in a corner by a gateway, which was rather galling to the owner of a really very well weeded farm; again, when he might have been duly complimentary about a group of fat, black-faced lambs, that simply cried aloud for admiration, he became eloquent over the foliage tints of an oak copse on the hill opposite. But now he was being taken to inspect the crowning pride and glory of Helsery; however grudging he might be in his praises, however backward and niggardly with his congratulations, he would have to see and acknowledge the many excellencies of that redoubtable animal. Some weeks ago, while on a business journey to Taunton, Tom had been invited by his half-brother to visit a studio in that town, where Laurence was exhibiting one of his pictures, a large canvas representing a bull standing knee-deep in some marshy ground; it had been good of its kind, no doubt, and Laurence had seemed inordinately pleased with it; "the best thing I've done yet," he had said over and over again, and Tom had generously agreed that it was fairly life-like. Now, the man of pigments was going to be shown a real picture, a living model of strength and comeliness, a thing to feast the eyes on, a picture that exhibited new pose and action with every shifting minute, instead of standing glued into one unvarying attitude between the four walls of a frame. Tom unfastened a stout wooden door and led the way into a straw-bedded yard.

"Is he quiet?" asked the artist, as a young bull with a curly red coat came inquiringly towards them.

"He's playful at times," said Tom, leaving his half-brother to wonder whether the bull's ideas of play were of the catch-as-catch-can order. Laurence made one or two perfunctory comments on the animal's appearance and asked a question or so as to his age and such-like details; then he coolly turned the talk into another channel.

"Do you remember the picture I showed you at Taunton?" he asked.

"Yes," grunted Tom; "a white-faced bull standing in some slush. Don't admire those Herefords much myself; bulky-looking brutes, don't seem to have much life in them. Daresay they're easier to paint that way; now, this young beggar is on the move all the time, aren't you, Fairy?"

"I've sold that picture," said Laurence, with considerable complacency in his voice.

"Have you?" said Tom; "glad to hear it, I'm sure. Hope you're pleased with what you've got for it."

"I got three hundred pounds for it," said Laurence.

Tom turned towards him with a slowly rising flush of anger in his face. Three hundred pounds! Under the most favourable market conditions that he could imagine his prized Clover Fairy would hardly fetch a hundred, yet here was a piece of varnished canvas, painted by his half-brother, selling for three times that sum. It was a cruel insult that went home with all the more force because it emphasized the triumph of the patronizing, self-satisfied Laurence. The young farmer had meant to put his relative just a little out of conceit with himself by displaying the jewel of his possessions, and now the tables were turned, and his valued beast was made to look cheap and insignificant beside the price paid for a mere picture. It was so monstrously unjust; the painting would never be anything more than a dexterous piece of counterfeit life, while Clover Fairy was the real thing, a monarch in his little world, a personality in the countryside. After he was dead, even, he would still be something of a personality; his descendants would graze in those valley meadows and hillside pastures, they would fill stall and byre and milking-shed, their good red coats would speckle the landscape and crowd the market-place; men would note a promising heifer or a well-proportioned steer, and say: "Ah, that one comes of good old Clover Fairy's stock." All that time the picture would be hanging, lifeless and unchanging, beneath its dust and varnish, a chattel that ceased to mean anything if you chose to turn it with its back to the wall. These thoughts chased themselves angrily through Tom Yorkfield's mind, but he could not put them into words. When he gave tongue to his feelings he put matters bluntly and harshly.

"Some soft-witted fools may like to throw away three hundred pounds on a bit of paintwork; can't say as I envy them their taste. I'd rather have the real thing than a picture of it."

He nodded towards the young bull, that was alternately staring at them with nose held high and lowering its horns with a half-playful, half-impatient shake of the head.

Laurence laughed a laugh of irritating, indulgent amusement.

"I don't think the purchaser of my bit of paintwork, as you call it, need worry about having thrown his money away. As I get to be better known and recognized my pictures will go up in value. That particular one will probably fetch four hundred in a sale-room five or six years hence; pictures aren't a bad investment if you know enough to pick out the work of the right men. Now you can't say your precious bull is going to get more valuable the longer you keep him; he'll have his little day, and then, if you go on keeping him, he'll come down at last to a few shillingsworth of hoofs and hide, just at a time, perhaps, when *my* bull is being bought for a big sum for some important picture gallery."

It was too much. The united force of truth and slander and insult put over heavy a strain on Tom Yorkfield's powers of restraint. In his right hand he held a useful oak cudgel, with his left he made a grab at the loose collar of Laurence's canary-coloured silk shirt. Laurence was not a fighting man; the fear of physical violence threw him off his balance as completely as overmastering indignation had thrown Tom off his, and thus it came to pass that Clover Fairy was regaled with the unprecedented sight of a human being scudding and squawking across the enclosure, like the hen that would persist in trying to establish a nesting-place in the manger. In another crowded happy moment the bull was trying to jerk Laurence over his left shoulder, to prod him in the ribs while still in the air, and to kneel on him when he reached the ground. It was only the vigorous intervention of Tom that induced him to relinquish the last item of his programme.

Tom devotedly and ungrudgingly nursed his half-brother to a complete recovery from his injuries, which consisted of nothing more serious than a dislocated shoulder, a broken rib or two, and a little nervous prostration. After all, there was no further occasion for rancour in the young farmer's mind; Laurence's bull might sell for three hundred, or for six hundred, and be admired by thousands in some big picture gallery, but it would never toss a man over one shoulder and catch him a jab in the ribs before he had fallen on the other side. That was Clover Fairy's noteworthy achievement, which could never be taken away from him.

Laurence continues to be popular as an animal artist, but his subjects are always kittens or fawns or lambkins—never bulls.

MORLVERA

THE Olympic Toy Emporium occupied a conspicuous frontage in an important West End street. It was happily named Toy Emporium, because one would never have dreamed of according it the familiar and yet pulse-quickening name of toyshop. There was an air of cold splendour and elaborate failure about the wares that were set out in its ample windows; they were the sort of toys that a tired shop-assistant displays and explains at Christmas-time to exclamatory parents and bored, silent children. The animal toys looked more like natural history models than the comfortable, sympathetic companions that one would wish, at a certain age, to take to bed with one, and to smuggle into the bath-room. The mechanical toys incessantly did things that no one could want a toy to do more than half a dozen times in its lifetime; it was a merciful reflection that in any right-minded nursery the lifetime would certainly be short.

Prominent among the elegantly dressed dolls that filled an entire section of the window frontage was a large hobble-skirted lady in a confection of peach-coloured velvet, elaborately set off with leopard-skin accessories, if one may use such a conveniently comprehensive word in describing an intricate feminine toilette. She lacked nothing that is to be found in a carefully detailed fashion-plate—in fact, she might be said to have something more than the average fashion-plate female possesses; in place of a vacant, expressionless stare she had character in her face. It must be admitted that it was bad character, cold, hostile, inquisitorial, with a sinister lowering of one eyebrow and a merciless hardness about the corners of the mouth. One might have imagined histories about her by the hour, histories in which unworthy ambition, the desire for money, and an entire absence of all decent feeling would play a conspicuous part.

As a matter of fact, she was not without her judges and biographers, even in this shop-window stage of her career. Emmeline, aged ten, and Bert, aged seven, had halted on the way from their obscure back street to the minnow-stocked water of St. James's Park, and were critically examining the hobble-skirted doll, and dissecting her character in no very tolerant spirit. There is probably a latent enmity between the necessarily under-clad and the unnecessarily over-dressed, but a little kindness and good-fellowship on the part of the latter will often change the sentiment to admiring devotion; if the lady in peach-coloured velvet and leopard skin had worn a pleasant expression in addition to her other elaborate furnishings, Emmeline at least might have respected and even loved her. As it was, she gave her a horrible reputation, based chiefly on a second-hand knowledge of gilded depravity derived from the conversation of those who were skilled in the art of novelette reading; Bert filled in a few damaging details from his own limited imagination.

"She's a bad lot, that one is," declared Emmeline, after a long unfriendly stare; "'er 'usbind 'ates 'er."

"'E knocks 'er abart," said Bert with enthusiasm.

"No, 'e don't, cos 'e's dead; she poisoned 'im slow and gradual, so that nobody didn't know. Now she wants to marry a lord, with 'eaps and 'eaps of money. 'E's got a wife already, but she's going to poison 'er, too."

"She's a bad lot," said Bert with growing hostility.

"'Er mother 'ates her, and she's afraid of 'er, too, cos she's got a serkestic tongue; always talking serkesms, she is. She's greedy, too; if there's fish going, she eats 'er own share and 'er little girl's as well, though the little girl is dellikit."

"She 'ad a little boy once," said Bert, "but she pushed 'im into the water when nobody wasn't looking."

"No, she didn't," said Emmeline, "she sent 'im away to be kep' by poor people, so 'er 'usbind wouldn't know where 'e was. They ill-treat 'im somethink cruel."

"Wot's 'er nime?" asked Bert, thinking that it was time that so interesting a personality should be labelled.

"'Er nime?" said Emmeline, thinking hard, "'er nime's Morlvera." It was as near as she could get to the name of an adventuress who figured prominently in a cinema drama. There was silence for a moment while the possibilities of the name were turned over in the children's minds.

"Those clothes she's got on ain't paid for, and never won't be," said Emmeline; "she thinks she'll get the rich lord to pay for 'em, but 'e won't. 'E's given 'er jools, 'underds of pounds' worth."

"'E won't pay for the clothes," said Bert with conviction. Evidently there was some limit to the weak good nature of wealthy lords.

At that moment a motor carriage with liveried servants drew up at the emporium entrance; a large lady, with a penetrating and rather hurried manner of talking, stepped out, followed slowly and sulkily by a small boy, who had a very black scowl on his face and a very white sailor suit over the rest of him. The lady was continuing an argument which had probably commenced in Portman Square.

"Now, Victor, you are to come in and buy a nice doll for your cousin Bertha. She gave you a beautiful box of soldiers on your birthday, and you must give her a present on hers."

"Bertha is a fat little fool," said Victor, in a voice that was as loud as his mother's and had more assurance in it.

"Victor, you are not to say such things. Bertha is not a fool, and she is not in the least fat. You are to come in and choose a doll for her."

The couple passed into the shop, out of view and hearing of the two back-street children.

"My, he is in a wicked temper," exclaimed Emmeline, but both she and Bert were inclined to side with him against the absent Bertha, who was doubtless as fat and foolish as he had described her to be.

"I want to see some dolls," said the mother of Victor to the nearest assistant; "it's for a little girl of eleven."

"A fat little girl of eleven," added Victor by way of supplementary information.

"Victor, if you say such rude things about your cousin, you shall go to bed the moment we get home, without having any tea."

"This is one of the newest things we have in dolls," said the assistant, removing a hobble-skirted figure in peach-coloured velvet from the window; "leopard-skin toque and stole, the latest fashion. You won't get anything newer than that anywhere. It's an exclusive design."

"Look!" whispered Emmeline outside; "they've bin and took Morlvera."

There was a mingling of excitement and a certain sense of bereavement in her mind; she would have liked to gaze at that embodiment of overdressed depravity for just a little longer.

"I 'spect she's going away in a kerridge to marry the rich lord," hazarded Bert.

"She's up to no good," said Emmeline vaguely.

Inside the shop the purchase of the doll had been decided on.

"It's a beautiful doll, and Bertha will be delighted with it," asserted the mother of Victor loudly.

"Oh, very well," said Victor sulkily; "you needn't have it stuck into a box and wait an hour while it's being done up into a parcel. I'll take it as it is, and we can go round to Manchester Square and give it to Bertha, and get the thing done with. That will save me the trouble of writing, 'For dear Bertha, with Victor's love,' on a bit of paper."

"Very well," said his mother, "we can go to Manchester Square on our way home. You must wish her many happy returns of tomorrow, and give her the doll."

"I won't let the little beast kiss me," stipulated Victor.

His mother said nothing; Victor had not been half as troublesome as she had anticipated. When he chose he could really be dreadfully naughty.

Emmeline and Bert were just moving away from the window when Morlvera made her exit from the shop, very carefully held in Victor's arms. A look of sinister triumph seemed to glow in her hard, inquisitorial face. As for Victor, a certain scornful serenity had replaced the earlier scowls; he had evidently accepted defeat with a contemptuous good grace.

The tall lady gave a direction to the footman and settled herself in the carriage. The little figure in the white sailor suit clambered in beside her, still carefully holding the elegantly garbed doll.

The car had to be backed a few yards in the process of turning. Very stealthily, very gently, very mercilessly Victor sent Morlvera flying over his shoulder, so that she fell into the road just behind the retrogressing wheel. With a soft, pleasant-sounding scrunch the car went over the prostrate form, then it moved forward again with another scrunch. The carriage moved off and left Bert and Emmeline gazing in scared delight at a sorry mess of petrol-smeared velvet, sawdust, and leopard skin, which was all that remained of the hateful Morlvera. They gave a shrill cheer, and then raced away shuddering from the scene of so much rapidly enacted tragedy.

Later that afternoon, when they were engaged in the pursuit of minnows by the waterside in St. James's Park, Emmeline said in a solemn undertone to Bert—

"I've bin finking. Do you know oo 'e was? 'E was 'er little boy wot she'd sent away to live wiv poor folks. 'E come back and done that."

SHOCK TACTICS

On a late spring afternoon Ella McCarthy sat on a green-painted chair in Kensington Gardens, staring listlessly at an uninteresting stretch of park landscape, that blossomed suddenly into tropical radiance as an expected figure appeared in the middle distance.

"Hullo, Bertie!" she exclaimed sedately, when the figure arrived at the painted chair that was the nearest neighbour to her own, and dropped into it eagerly, yet with a certain due regard for the set of its trousers; "hasn't it been a perfect spring afternoon?"

The statement was a distinct untruth as far as Ella's own feelings were concerned; until the arrival of Bertie the afternoon had been anything but perfect.

Bertie made a suitable reply, in which a questioning note seemed to hover.

"Thank you ever so much for those lovely handkerchiefs," said Ella, answering the unspoken question; "they were just what I've been wanting. There's only one thing spoilt my pleasure in your gift," she added, with a pout.

"What was that?" asked Bertie anxiously, fearful that perhaps he had chosen a size of handkerchief that was not within the correct feminine limit.

"I should have liked to have written and thanked you for them as soon as I got them," said Ella, and Bertie's sky clouded at once.

"You know what mother is," he protested; "she opens all my

letters, and if she found I'd been giving presents to any one there'd have been something to talk about for the next fortnight."

"Surely, at the age of twenty—" began Ella.

"I'm not twenty till September," interrupted Bertie.

"At the age of nineteen years and eight months," persisted Ella, "you might be allowed to keep your correspondence private to yourself."

"I ought to be, but things aren't always what they ought to be. Mother opens every letter that comes into the house, whoever it's for. My sisters and I have made rows about it time and again, but she goes on doing it."

"I'd find some way to stop her if I were in your place," said Ella valiantly, and Bertie felt that the glamour of his anxiously deliberated present had faded away in the disagreeable restriction that hedged round its acknowledgment.

"Is anything the matter?" asked Bertie's friend Clovis when they met that evening at the swimming-bath.

"Why do you ask?" said Bertie.

"When you wear a look of tragic gloom in a swimming-bath," said Clovis, "it's especially noticeable from the fact that you're wearing very little else. Didn't she like the handkerchiefs?"

Bertie explained the situation.

"It is rather galling, you know," he added, "when a girl has a lot of things she wants to write to you and can't send a letter except by some roundabout, underhand way."

"One never realizes one's blessings while one enjoys them," said Clovis; "now I have to spend a considerable amount of ingenuity inventing excuses for not having written to people."

"It's not a joking matter," said Bertie resentfully: "you wouldn't find it funny if your mother opened all your letters."

"The funny thing to me is that you should let her do it."

"I can't stop it. I've argued about it—"

"You haven't used the right kind of argument, I expect. Now, if every time one of your letters was opened you lay on your back on the dining-table during dinner and had a fit, or roused the entire family in the middle of the night to hear you recite one of Blake's 'Poems of Innocence,' you would get a far more respectful hearing for future protests. People yield more consideration to a mutilated mealtime or a broken night's rest, than ever they would to a broken heart."

"Oh, dry up," said Bertie crossly, inconsistently splashing Clovis from head to foot as he plunged into the water.

It was a day or two after the conversation in the swimming-bath that a letter addressed to Bertie Heasant slid into the letter-box at his home, and thence into the hands of his mother. Mrs. Heasant was one of those empty-minded individuals to whom other people's affairs are perpetually interesting. The more private they are intended to be the more acute is the interest they arouse. She would have opened this particular letter in any case; the fact that it was marked "private," and diffused a delicate but penetrating aroma, merely caused her to open it with headlong haste rather than matter-of-course deliberation. The harvest of sensation that rewarded her was beyond all expectations.

"Bertie, carissimo," it began, "I wonder if you will have the nerve to do it: it will take some nerve, too. Don't forget the jewels. They are a detail, but details interest me.

"Yours as ever,

"CLOTILDE.

"Your mother must not know of my existence. If questioned swear you never heard of me."

For years Mrs. Heasant had searched Bertie's correspondence diligently for traces of possible dissipation or youthful entanglements, and at last the suspicions that had stimulated her inquisitorial zeal were justified by this one splendid haul. That any one wearing the exotic name "Clotilde" should write to Bertie under the incriminating announcement "as ever" was sufficiently electrifying, without the astounding allusion to the jewels. Mrs. Heasant could recall novels and dramas wherein jewels played an exciting and commanding rôle, and here, under her own roof, before her very eyes as it were, her own son was carrying on an intrigue in which jewels were merely an interesting detail. Bertie was not due home for another hour, but his sisters were available for the immediate unburdening of a scandal-laden mind.

"Bertie is in the toils of an adventuress," she screamed; "her name is Clotilde," she added, as if she thought they had better know the worst at once. There are occasions when more harm than good is done by shielding young girls from a knowledge of the more deplorable realities of life.

By the time Bertie arrived his mother had discussed every possible and improbable conjecture as to his guilty secret; the girls limited themselves to the opinion that their brother had been weak rather than wicked.

"Who is Clotilde?" was the question that confronted Bertie almost before he had got into the hall. His denial of any knowledge of such a person was met with an outburst of bitter laughter.

"How well you have learned your lesson!" exclaimed Mrs. Heasant. But satire gave way to furious indignation when she realized that Bertie did not intend to throw any further light on her discovery.

"You shan't have any dinner till you've confessed everything," she stormed.

Bertie's reply took the form of hastily collecting material for an impromptu banquet from the larder and locking himself into his bedroom. His mother made frequent visits to the locked door and shouted a succession of interrogations with the persistence of one who thinks that if you ask a question often enough an answer will eventually result. Bertie did nothing to encourage the supposition. An hour had passed in fruitless one-sided palaver when another letter addressed to Bertie and marked "private" made its appearance in the letterbox. Mrs. Heasant pounced on it with the enthusiasm of a cat that has missed its mouse and to whom a second has been unexpectedly vouchsafed. If she hoped for further disclosures assuredly she was not disappointed.

"So you have really done it!" the letter abruptly commenced; "Poor Dagmar. Now she is done for I almost pity her. You did it very well, you wicked boy, the servants all think it was suicide, and there will be no fuss. Better not touch the jewels till after the inquest.

"CLOTILDE."

Anything that Mrs. Heasant had previously done in the way of outcry was easily surpassed as she raced upstairs and beat frantically at her son's door.

"Miserable boy, what have you done to Dagmar?"

"It's Dagmar now, is it?" he snapped; "it will be Geraldine next."

"That it should come to this, after all my efforts to keep you at home of an evening," sobbed Mrs. Heasant; "it's no use you trying to hide things from me; Clotilde's letter betrays everything."

"Does it betray who she is?" asked Bertie. "I've heard so much about her, I should like to know something about her home-life. Seriously, if you go on like this I shall fetch a doctor; I've often enough been preached at about nothing, but I've never had an imaginary harem dragged into the discussion."

"Are these letters imaginary?" screamed Mrs. Heasant. "What about the jewels, and Dagmar, and the theory of suicide?"

No solution of these problems was forthcoming through the bedroom door, but the last post of the evening produced another letter for Bertie, and its contents brought Mrs. Heasant that enlightenment which had already dawned on her son.

> "DEAR BERTIE," it ran; "I hope I haven't distracted your brain with the spoof letters I've been sending in the name of a fictitious Clotilde. You told me the other day that the servants, or somebody at your home, tampered with your letters, so I thought I would give any one that opened them something exciting to read. The shock might do them good.
>
> "Yours,
> "CLOVIS SANGRAIL."

Mrs. Heasant knew Clovis slightly, and was rather afraid of him. It was not difficult to read between the lines of his successful hoax. In a chastened mood she rapped once more at Bertie's door.

"A letter from Mr. Sangrail. It's all been a stupid hoax. He wrote those other letters. Why, where are you going?"

Bertie had opened the door; he had on his hat and overcoat.

"I'm going for a doctor to come and see if anything's the matter with you. Of course it was all a hoax, but no person in his right mind could have believed all that rubbish about murder and suicide and jewels. You've been making enough noise to bring the house down for the last hour or two."

"But what was I to think of those letters?" whimpered Mrs. Heasant.

"I should have known what to think of them," said Bertie; "if you choose to excite yourself over other people's correspondence it's your own fault. Anyhow, I'm going for a doctor."

It was Bertie's great opportunity, and he knew it. His mother was conscious of the fact that she would look rather ridiculous if the story got about. She was willing to pay hush-money.

"I'll never open your letters again," she promised.

And Clovis has no more devoted slave than Bertie Heasant.

THE SEVEN CREAM JUGS

"I SUPPOSE we shall never see Wilfrid Pigeoncote here now that he has become heir to the baronetcy and to a lot of money," observed Mrs. Peter Pigeoncote regretfully to her husband.

"Well, we can hardly expect to," he replied, "seeing that we always choked him off from coming to see us when he was a prospective nobody. I don't think I've set eyes on him since he was a boy of twelve."

"There was a reason for not wanting to encourage his acquaintanceship," said Mrs. Peter. "With that notorious failing of his he was not the sort of person one wanted in one's house."

"Well, the failing still exists, doesn't it?" said her husband; "or do you suppose a reform of character is entailed along with the estate?"

"Oh, of course, there is still that drawback," admitted the wife, "but one would like to make the acquaintance of the future head of the family, if only out of mere curiosity. Besides, cynicism apart, his being rich *will* make a difference in the way people will look at his failing. When a man is absolutely wealthy, not merely well-to-do, all suspicion of sordid motive naturally disappears; the thing becomes merely a tiresome malady."

Wilfrid Pigeoncote had suddenly become heir to his uncle, Sir Wilfrid Pigeoncote, on the death of his cousin, Major Wilfrid Pigeoncote, who had succumbed to the after-effects of a polo accident. (A Wilfrid Pigeoncote had covered himself with honours in the course of Marlborough's campaigns, and the name Wilfrid had been a baptismal weakness in the family ever since.) The new heir to the family dignity and estates was a young man of about five-and-twenty, who was known more by reputation than by person to a wide circle of cousins and kinsfolk. And the reputation was an unpleasant one. The numerous other Wilfrids in the family were distinguished one from another chiefly by the names of their residences or professions, as Wilfrid of Hubbledown, and young Wilfrid the Gunner, but this particular scion was known by the ignominious and expressive label of Wilfrid the Snatcher. From his late schooldays onward he had been possessed by an acute and obstinate form of kleptomania; he had the acquisitive instinct of the collector without any of the collector's discrimination. Anything that was smaller and more portable than a sideboard, and above the value of ninepence, had an irresistible attraction for him, provided that it fulfilled the necessary condition of belonging to some one else. On the rare occasions when he was included in a country-house party, it was usual and almost necessary for his host, or some member of the family, to make a friendly inquisition through his baggage on the eve of his departure, to see if he had packed up "by mistake" any one else's property. The search usually produced a large and varied yield.

"This is funny," said Peter Pigeoncote to his wife, some half-hour after their conversation; "here's a telegram from Wilfrid, saying he's passing through here in his motor, and would like to stop and pay us his respects. Can stay for the night if it doesn't inconvenience us. Signed 'Wilfrid Pigeoncote.' Must be the Snatcher; none of the others have a motor. I suppose he's bringing us a present for the silver wedding."

"Good gracious!" said Mrs. Peter, as a thought struck her; "this is rather an awkward time to have a person with his failing in the house. All those silver presents set out in the drawing-room, and others coming by every post; I hardly know what we've got and what are still to come. We can't lock them all up; he's sure to want to see them."

"We must keep a sharp look-out, that's all," said Peter reassuringly.

"But these practised kleptomaniacs are so clever," said his wife apprehensively, "and it will be so awkward if he suspects that we are watching him."

Awkwardness was indeed the prevailing note that evening when the passing traveller was being entertained. The talk flitted nervously and hurriedly from one impersonal topic to another. The guest had none of the furtive, half-apologetic air that his cousins had rather expected to find; he was polite, well-assured, and, perhaps, just a little inclined to "put on side." His hosts, on the other hand, wore an uneasy manner that might have been the hallmark of conscious depravity. In the drawing-room, after dinner, their nervousness and awkwardness increased.

"Oh, we haven't shown you the silver-wedding presents," said Mrs.

Peter suddenly, as though struck by a brilliant idea for entertaining the guest; "here they all are. Such nice, useful gifts. A few duplicates, of course."

"Seven cream jugs," put in Peter.

"Yes, isn't it annoying," went on Mrs. Peter; "seven of them. We feel that we must live on cream for the rest of our lives. Of course, some of them can be changed."

Wilfrid occupied himself chiefly with such of the gifts as were of antique interest, carrying one or two of them over to the lamp to examine their marks. The anxiety of his hosts at these moments resembled the solicitude of a cat whose newly born kittens are being handed round for inspection.

"Let me see; did you give me back the mustard-pot? This is its place here," piped Mrs. Peter.

"Sorry. I put it down by the claret-jug," said Wilfrid, busy with another object.

"Oh, just let me have that sugar-sifter again," asked Mrs. Peter, dogged determination showing through her nervousness. "I must label it who it comes from before I forget."

Vigilance was not completely crowned with a sense of victory. After they had said "Good night" to their visitor, Mrs. Peter expressed her conviction that he had taken something.

"I fancy, by his manner, that there was something up," corroborated her husband. "Do you miss anything?"

Mrs. Peter hastily counted the array of gifts.

"I can only make it thirty-four, and I think it should be thirty-five," she announced. "I can't remember if thirty-five includes the Archdeacon's cruet-stand that hasn't arrived yet."

"How on earth are we to know?" said Peter. "The mean pig hasn't brought us a present, and I'm hanged if he shall carry one off."

"Tomorrow, when he's having his bath," said Mrs. Peter excitedly, "he's sure to leave his keys somewhere, and we can go through his portmanteau. It's the only thing to do."

On the morrow an alert watch was kept by the conspirators behind half-closed doors, and when Wilfrid, clad in a gorgeous bath-robe, had made his way to the bath-room, there was a swift and furtive rush by two excited individuals towards the principal guest-chamber. Mrs. Peter kept guard outside, while her husband first made a hurried and successful search for the keys, and then plunged at the portmanteau with the air of a disagreeably conscientious Customs official. The quest was a brief one; a silver cream jug lay embedded in the folds of some zephyr shirts.

"The cunning brute," said Mrs. Peter; "he took a cream jug because there were so many; he thought one wouldn't be missed. Quick, fly down with it and put it back among the others."

Wilfrid was late in coming down to breakfast, and his manner showed plainly that something was amiss.

"It's an unpleasant thing to have to say," he blurted out presently, "but I'm afraid you must have a thief among your servants. Something's been taken out of my portmanteau. It was a little present from my mother and myself for your silver wedding. I should have given it to you last night after dinner, only it happened to be a cream jug, and you seemed annoyed at having so many duplicates, so I felt rather awkward about giving you another. I thought I'd get it changed for something else, and now it's gone."

"Did you say it was from your *mother* and yourself?" asked Mr. and Mrs. Peter almost in unison. The Snatcher had been an orphan these many years.

"Yes, my mother's at Cairo just now, and she wrote to me at Dresden to try and get you something quaint and pretty in the old silver line, and I pitched on this cream jug."

Both the Pigeoncotes had turned deadly pale. The mention of Dresden had thrown a sudden light on the situation. It was Wilfrid the Attaché, a very superior young man, who rarely came within their social horizon, whom they had been entertaining unawares in the supposed character of Wilfrid the Snatcher. Lady Ernestine Pigeoncote, his mother, moved in circles which were entirely beyond their compass or ambitions, and the son would probably one day be an Ambassador. And they had rifled and despoiled his portmanteau! Husband and wife looked blankly and desperately at one another. It was Mrs. Peter who arrived first at an inspiration.

"How dreadful to think there are thieves in the house! We keep the drawing-room locked up at night, of course, but anything might be carried off while we are at breakfast."

She rose and went out hurriedly, as though to assure herself that the drawing-room was not being stripped of its silverware, and returned a moment later, bearing a cream jug in her hands.

"There are eight cream jugs now, instead of seven," she cried;

"this one wasn't there before. What a curious trick of memory, Mr. Wilfrid! You must have slipped downstairs with it last night and put it there before we locked up, and forgotten all about having done it in the morning."

"One's mind often plays one little tricks like that," said Mr. Peter, with desperate heartiness. "Only the other day I went into the town to pay a bill, and went in again next day, having clean forgotten that I'd—"

"It is certainly the jug that I brought for you," said Wilfrid, looking closely at it; "it was in my portmanteau when I got my bath-robe out this morning, before going to my bath, and it was not there when I unlocked the portmanteau on my return. Some one had taken it while I was away from the room."

The Pigeoncotes had turned paler than ever. Mrs. Peter had a final inspiration.

"Get me my smelling-salts, dear," she said to her husband; "I think they're in the dressing-room."

Peter dashed out of the room with glad relief; he had lived so long during the last few minutes that a golden wedding seemed within measurable distance.

Mrs. Peter turned to her guest with confidential coyness.

"A diplomat like you will know how to treat this as if it hadn't happened. Peter's little weakness; it runs in the family."

"Good Lord! Do you mean to say he's a kleptomaniac, like Cousin Snatcher?"

"Oh, not exactly," said Mrs. Peter, anxious to whitewash her husband a little greyer than she was painting him. "He would never touch anything he found lying about, but he can't resist making a raid on things that are locked up. The doctors have a special name for it. He must have pounced on your portmanteau the moment you went to your bath, and taken the first thing he came across. Of course, he had no motive for taking a cream jug; we've already got *seven*, as you know—not, of course, that we don't value the kind gift you and your mother— Hush, here's Peter coming."

Mrs. Peter broke off in some confusion, and tripped out to meet her husband in the hall.

"It's all right," she whispered to him; "I've explained everything. Don't say anything more about it."

"Brave little woman," said Peter, with a gasp of relief; "I could never have done it."

Diplomatic reticence does not necessarily extend to family affairs. Peter Pigeoncote was never able to understand why Mrs. Consuelo van Bullyon, who stayed with them in the spring, always carried two very obvious jewel-cases with her to the bath-room, explaining them to any one she chanced to meet in the corridor as her manicure and face-massage set.

THE OCCASIONAL GARDEN

"DON'T talk to me about town gardens," said Elinor Rapsley; "which means, of course, that I want you to listen to me for an hour or so while I talk about nothing else. 'What a nice-sized garden you've got,' people said to us when we first moved here. What I suppose they meant to say was what a nice-sized site for a garden we'd got. As a matter of fact, the size is all against it; it's too large to be ignored altogether and treated as a yard, and it's too small to keep giraffes in. You see, if we could keep giraffes or reindeer or some other species of browsing animal there we could explain the general absence of vegetation by a reference to the fauna of the garden: 'You can't have wapiti *and* Darwin tulips, you know, so we didn't put down any bulbs last year.' As it is, we haven't got the wapiti, and the Darwin tulips haven't survived the fact that most of the cats of the neighbourhood hold a parliament in the centre of the tulip bed; that rather forlorn-looking strip that we intended to be a border of alternating geranium and spiræa has been utilized by the cat-parliament as a division lobby. Snap divisions seem to have been rather frequent of late, far more frequent than the geranium blooms are likely to be. I shouldn't object so much to ordinary cats, but I do complain of having a congress of vegetarian cats in my garden; they must be vegetarians, my dear, because, whatever ravages they may commit among the sweet-pea seedlings, they never seem to touch the sparrows; there are always just as many adult sparrows in the garden on Saturday as there were on Monday, not to mention newly fledged additions. There seems to have been an irreconcilable difference of opinion between sparrows and Providence since the beginning of time as to whether a crocus looks best standing upright with its roots in the earth or in a recumbent posture with its stem neatly severed; the sparrows always have the last word in the matter, at least in our garden they do. I fancy that Providence must have originally intended to bring in an amending Act, or whatever it's called, providing either for a less destructive sparrow or a more indestructible crocus. The one consoling point about our garden is that it's not visible from the drawing-room or the smoking-room, so unless people are dining or lunching with us they can't spy out the nakedness of the land. That is why I am so furious with Gwenda Pottingdon, who has practically forced herself on me for lunch on Wednesday next; she heard me offer the Paulcote girl lunch if she was up shopping on that day, and, of course, she asked if she might come too. She is only coming to gloat over my bedraggled and flowerless borders and to sing the praises of her own detestably over-cultivated garden. I'm sick of being told that it's the envy of the neighbourhood; it's like everything else that belongs to her—her car, her dinner-parties, even her headaches, they are all superlative; no one else ever had anything like them. When her eldest child was confirmed it was such a sensational event, according to her account of it, that one almost expected questions to be asked about it in the House of Commons, and now she's coming on purpose to stare at my few miserable pansies and the gaps in my sweet-pea border, and to give me a glowing, full-length description of the rare and sumptuous blooms in her rose-garden."

"My dear Elinor," said the Baroness, "you would save yourself all this heart-burning and a lot of gardener's bills, not to mention sparrow anxieties, simply by paying an annual subscription to the O.O.S.A."

"Never heard of it," said Elinor; "what is it?"

"The Occasional-Oasis Supply Association," said the Baroness; "it exists to meet cases exactly like yours, cases of backyards that are of no practical use for gardening purposes, but are required to blossom into decorative scenic backgrounds at stated intervals, when a luncheon or dinner-party is contemplated. Supposing, for instance, you have people coming to lunch at one-thirty; you just ring up the Association at about ten o'clock the same morning, and say, 'Lunch garden.' That is all the trouble you have to take. By twelve forty-five your yard is carpeted with a strip of velvety turf, with a hedge of lilac or red may, or whatever happens to be in season, as a background, one or two cherry trees in blossom, and clumps of heavily flowered rhododendrons filling in the odd corners; in the foreground you have a blaze of carnations or Shirley poppies, or tiger lilies in full bloom. As soon as the lunch is over and your guests have departed the garden departs also, and all the cats in Christendom can sit in council in your yard without causing you a moment's anxiety. If you have a bishop or an antiquary or something of that sort coming to lunch you just mention the fact when you are ordering the garden, and you get an old-world pleasaunce, with clipped yew hedges and a sun-dial and hollyhocks, and perhaps a mulberry tree, and borders of sweet-williams and Canterbury bells, and an old-fashioned beehive or two tucked away in a corner. Those are the ordinary lines of supply that the Oasis Association undertakes, but by paying a few guineas a year extra you are entitled to its emergency E.O.N. service."

"What on earth is an E.O.N. service?"

"It's just like a conventional signal to indicate special cases like the incursion of Gwenda Pottingdon. It means you've got some one coming to lunch or dinner whose garden is alleged to be 'the envy of the neighbourhood.'"

"Yes," exclaimed Elinor, with some excitement, "and what happens then?"

"Something that sounds like a miracle out of the Arabian Nights. Your backyard becomes voluptuous with pomegranate and almond trees, lemon groves, and hedges of flowering cactus, dazzling banks of azaleas, marble-basined fountains, in which chestnut-and-white pond-herons step daintily amid exotic water-lilies, while golden pheasants strut about on alabaster terraces. The whole effect rather suggests the idea that Providence and Norman Wilkinson have dropped mutual jealousies and collaborated to produce a background for an open-air Russian Ballet; in point of fact, it is merely the background to your luncheon party. If there is any kick left in Gwenda Pottingdon, or whoever your E.O.N. guest of the moment may be, just mention carelessly that your climbing putella is the only one in England, since the one at Chatsworth died last winter. There isn't such a thing as a climbing putella, but Gwenda Pottingdon and her kind don't usually know one flower from another without prompting."

"Quick," said Elinor, "the address of the Association."

Gwenda Pottingdon did not enjoy her lunch. It was a simple

yet elegant meal, excellently cooked and daintily served, but the piquant sauce of her own conversation was notably lacking. She had prepared a long succession of eulogistic comments on the wonders of her town garden, with its unrivalled effects of horticultural magnificence, and, behold, her theme was shut in on every side by the luxuriant hedge of Siberian berberis that formed a glowing background to Elinor's bewildering fragment of fairyland. The pomegranate and lemon trees, the terraced fountain, where golden carp slithered and wriggled amid the roots of gorgeous-hued irises, the banked masses of exotic blooms, the pagoda-like enclosure, where Japanese sand-badgers disported themselves, all these contributed to take away Gwenda's appetite and moderate her desire to talk about gardening matters.

"I can't say I admire the climbing putella," she observed shortly, "and anyway it's not the only one of its kind in England; I happen to know of one in Hampshire. How gardening is going out of fashion. I suppose people haven't the time for it nowadays."

Altogether it was quite one of Elinor's most successful luncheon parties.

It was distinctly an unforeseen catastrophe that Gwenda should have burst in on the household four days later at lunch-time and made her way unbidden into the dining-room.

"I thought I must tell you that my Elaine has had a water-colour sketch accepted by the Latent Talent Art Guild; it's to be exhibited at their summer exhibition at the Hackney Gallery. It will be the sensation of the moment in the art world— Hullo, what on earth has happened to your garden? It's not there!"

"Suffragettes," said Elinor promptly; "didn't you hear about it? They broke in and made hay of the whole thing in about ten minutes. I was so heartbroken at the havoc that I had the whole place cleared out; I shall have it laid out again on rather more elaborate lines.

"That," she said to the Baroness afterwards, "is what I call having an emergency brain."

THE SHEEP

The enemy had declared "no trumps." Rupert played out his ace and king of clubs and cleared the adversary of that suit; then the Sheep, whom the Fates had inflicted on him for a partner, took the third round with the queen of clubs, and, having no other club to lead back, opened another suit. The enemy won the remainder of the tricks—and the rubber.

"I had four more clubs to play; we only wanted the odd trick to win the rubber," said Rupert.

"But I hadn't another club to lead you," exclaimed the Sheep, with his ready, defensive smile.

"It didn't occur to you to throw your queen away on my king and leave me with the command of the suit," said Rupert, with polite bitterness.

"I suppose I ought to have—I wasn't certain what to do. I'm awfully sorry," said the Sheep.

Being awfully and uselessly sorry formed a large part of his occupation in life. If a similar situation had arisen in a subsequent hand he would have blundered just as certainly, and he would have been just as irritatingly apologetic.

Rupert stared gloomily across at him as he sat smiling and fumbling with his cards. Many men who have good brains for business do not possess the rudiments of a card-brain, and Rupert would not have judged and condemned his prospective brother-in-law on the evidence of his bridge play alone. The tragic part of it was that he smiled and fumbled through life just as fatuously and apologetically as he did at the card-table. And behind the defensive smile and the well-worn expressions of regret there shone a scarcely believable but quite obvious self-satisfaction. Every sheep of the pasture probably imagines that in an emergency it could become terrible as an army with banners—one has only to watch how they stamp their feet and stiffen their necks when a minor object of suspicion comes into view and behaves meekly. And probably the majority of human sheep see themselves in imagination taking great parts in the world's more impressive dramas, forming swift, unerring decisions in moments of crisis, cowing mutinies, allaying panics, brave, strong, simple, but, in spite of their natural modesty, always slightly spectacular.

"Why in the name of all that is unnecessary and perverse should Kathleen choose this man for her future husband?" was the question that Rupert asked himself ruefully. There was young Malcolm Athling, as nice-looking, decent, level-headed a fellow as any one could wish to meet, obviously her very devoted admirer, and yet she must throw herself away on this pale-eyed, weak-mouthed embodiment of self-approving ineptitude. If it had been merely Kathleen's own affair Rupert would have shrugged his shoulders and philosophically hoped that she might make the best of an undeniably bad bargain. But Rupert had no heir; his own boy lay underground somewhere on the Indian frontier, in goodly company. And the property would pass in due course to Kathleen and Kathleen's husband. The Sheep would live there in the beloved old home, rearing up other little Sheep, fatuous and rabbit-faced and self-satisfied like himself, to dwell in the land and possess it. It was not a soothing prospect.

Towards dusk on the afternoon following the bridge experience Rupert and the Sheep made their way homeward after a day's mixed shooting. The Sheep's cartridge bag was nearly empty, but his game bag showed no signs of overcrowding. The birds he had shot at had seemed for the most part as impervious to death or damage as the hero of a melodrama. And for each failure to drop his bird he had some explanation or apology ready on his lips. Now he was striding along in front of his host, chattering happily over his shoulder, but obviously on the look-out for some belated rabbit or wood-pigeon that might haply be secured as an eleventh-hour addition to his bag. As they passed the edge of a small copse a large bird rose from the ground and flew slowly towards the trees, offering an easy shot to the oncoming sportsmen. The Sheep banged forth with both barrels, and gave an exultant cry.

"Hooray! I've shot a thundering big hawk."

"To be exact, you've shot a honey-buzzard. That is the hen bird of one of the few pairs of honey-buzzards breeding in the United Kingdom. We've kept them under the strictest preservation for the last four years; every gamekeeper and village gun loafer for twenty miles round has been warned and bribed and threatened to respect their sanctity, and egg-snatching agents have been carefully guarded against during the breeding season. Hundreds of lovers of rare birds have delighted in seeing their snap-shotted portraits in *Country Life*, and now you've reduced the hen bird to a lump of broken feathers."

Rupert spoke quietly and evenly, but for a moment or two a gleam of positive hatred shone in his eyes.

"I say, I'm so sorry," said the Sheep, with his apologetic smile. "Of course I remember hearing about the buzzards, but somehow I didn't connect this bird with them. And it was such an easy shot—"

"Yes," said Rupert; "that was the trouble."

Kathleen found him in the gun-room smoothing out the feathers of the dead bird. She had already been told of the catastrophe.

"What a horrid misfortune," she said sympathetically.

"It was my dear Robbie who first discovered them the last time he was home on leave. Don't you remember how excited he was about them? Let's go and have some tea."

Both bridge and shooting were given a rest for the next two or three weeks. Death, who enters into no compacts with party whips, had forced a Parliamentary vacancy on the neighbourhood at the least convenient season, and the local partisans on either side found themselves immersed in the discomforts of a mid-winter election. Rupert took his politics seriously and keenly. He belonged to that type of strangely but rather happily constituted individuals which these islands seem to produce in a fair plenty; men and women who for no personal profit or gain go forth from their comfortable firesides or club card-rooms to hunt to and fro in the mud and rain and wind for the capture or tracking of a stray vote here and there on their party's behalf—not because they think they ought to, but because they want to. And his energies were welcome enough on this occasion, for the seat was a closely disputed possession, and its loss or retention would count for much in the present position of the Parliamentary game. With Kathleen to help him, he had worked his corner of the constituency with tireless, well-directed zeal, taking his share of the dull routine work as well as of the livelier episodes. The talking part of the campaign wound up on the eve of the poll with a meeting in a centre where more undecided votes were supposed to be concentrated than anywhere else in the division. A good final meeting here would mean everything. And the speakers, local and imported, left nothing undone to improve the occasion. Rupert was down for the unimportant task of moving the complimentary vote to the chairman which should close the proceedings.

"I'm so hoarse," he protested, when the moment arrived; "I don't believe I can make my voice heard beyond the platform."

"Let me do it," said the Sheep; "I'm rather good at that sort of thing."

The chairman was popular with all parties, and the Sheep's opening words of complimentary recognition received a round of applause. The orator smiled expansively on his listeners and seized the opportunity to add a few words of political wisdom on his own account. People looked at the clock or began to grope for umbrellas and discarded neck-wraps. Then, in the midst of a string of meaningless platitudes, the Sheep delivered himself of one of those blundering remarks which travel from one end of a constituency to the other in half an hour, and are seized on by the other side as being more potent on their behalf than a ton of election literature. There was a general shuffling and muttering across the length and breadth of the hall, and a few hisses made themselves heard. The Sheep tried to whittle down his remark, and the chairman unhesitatingly threw him over in his speech of thanks, but the damage was done.

"I'm afraid I lost touch with the audience rather over that remark," said the Sheep afterwards, with his apologetic smile abnormally developed.

"You lost us the election," said the chairman, and he proved a true prophet.

A month or so of winter sport seemed a desirable pick-me-up after the strenuous work and crowning discomfiture of the election. Rupert and Kathleen hied them away to a small Alpine resort that was just coming into prominence, and thither the Sheep followed them in due course, in his rôle of husband-elect. The wedding had been fixed for the end of March.

It was a winter of early and unseasonable thaws, and the far end of the local lake, at a spot where swift currents flowed into it, was decorated with notices, written in three languages, warning skaters not to venture over certain unsafe patches. The folly of approaching too near these danger spots seemed to have a natural fascination for the Sheep.

"I don't see what possible danger there can be," he protested, with his inevitable smile, when Rupert beckoned him away from the proscribed area; "the milk that I put out on my window-sill last night was frozen an inch deep."

"It hadn't got a strong current flowing through it," said Rupert; "in any case, there is not much sense in hovering round a doubtful piece of ice when there are acres of good ice to skate over. The secretary of the ice-committee has warned you once already."

A few minutes later Rupert heard a loud squeal of fear, and saw a dark spot blotting the smoothness of the lake's frozen surface. The Sheep was struggling helplessly in an ice-hole of his own making. Rupert gave one loud curse, and then dashed full tilt for the shore;

outside a low stable building on the lake's edge he remembered having seen a ladder. If he could slide it across the ice-hole before the Sheep went under the rescue would be comparatively simple work. Other skaters were dashing up from a distance, and, with the ladder's help, they could get him out of his death-trap without having to trust themselves on the margin of rotten ice. Rupert sprang on to the surface of lumpy, frozen snow, and staggered to where the ladder lay. He had already lifted it when the rattle of a chain and a furious outburst of growls burst on his hearing, and he was dashed to the ground by a mass of white and tawny fur. A sturdy young yard-dog, frantic with the pleasure of performing his first piece of active guardian service, was ramping and snarling over him, rendering the task of regaining his feet or securing the ladder a matter of considerable difficulty. When he had at last succeeded in both efforts he was just by a hair's-breadth too late to be of any use. The Sheep had definitely disappeared under the ice-rift.

Kathleen Athling and her husband stay the greater part of the year with Rupert, and a small Robbie stands in some danger of being idolized by a devoted uncle. But for twelve months of the year Rupert's most inseparable and valued companion is a sturdy tawny and white yard-dog.

THE OVERSIGHT

"IT's like a Chinese puzzle," said Lady Prowche resentfully, staring at a scribbled list of names that spread over two or three loose sheets of notepaper on her writing-table. Most of the names had a pencil mark running through them.

"What is like a Chinese puzzle?" asked Lena Luddleford briskly; she rather prided herself on being able to grapple with the minor problems of life.

"Getting people suitably sorted together. Sir Richard likes me to have a house party about this time of year, and gives me a free hand as to whom I should invite; all he asks is that it should be a peaceable party, with no friction or unpleasantness."

"That seems reasonable enough," said Lena.

"Not only reasonable, my dear, but necessary. Sir Richard has his literary work to think of; you can't expect a man to concentrate on the tribal disputes of Central Asian clansmen when he's got social feuds blazing under his own roof."

"But why should they blaze? Why should there be feuds at all within the compass of a house party?"

"Exactly; why should they blaze or why should they exist?" echoed Lady Prowche. "The point is that they always do. We have been unlucky; persistently unlucky, now that I come to look back on things. We have always got people of violently opposed views under our roof, and the result has been not merely unpleasantness but explosion."

"Do you mean people who disagree on matters of political opinion and religious views?" asked Lena.

"No, not that. The broader lines of political or religious difference don't matter. You can have Church of England and Unitarian and Buddhist under the same roof without courting disaster; the only Buddhist I ever had down here quarrelled with everybody, but that was on account of his naturally squabblesome temperament; it had nothing to do with his religion. And I've always found that people can differ profoundly about politics and meet on perfectly good terms at breakfast. Now, Miss Larbor Jones, who was staying here last year, worships Lloyd George as a sort of wingless angel, while Mrs. Walters, who was down here at the same time, privately considers him to be—an antelope, let us say."

"An antelope?"

"Well, not an antelope exactly, but something with horns and hoofs and tail."

"Oh, I see."

"Still, that didn't prevent them from being the chummiest of mortals on the tennis court and in the billiard-room. They did quarrel finally, about a lead in a doubled hand of no trumps, but that of course is a thing that no amount of judicious guest-grouping could prevent. Mrs. Walters had got king, knave, ten, and seven of clubs—"

"You were saying that there were other lines of demarcation that caused the bother," interrupted Lena.

"Exactly. It is the minor differences and side-issues that give so much trouble," said Lady Prowche; "not to my dying day shall I forget last year's upheaval over the Suffragette question. Laura Henniseed left the house in a state of speechless indignation, but before she had reached that state she had used language that would not have been tolerated in the Austrian Reichsrath. Intensive bear-gardening was Sir Richard's description of the whole affair, and I don't think he exaggerated."

"Of course the Suffragette question is a burning one, and lets loose the most dreadful ill-feeling," said Lena; "but one can generally find out beforehand what people's opinions—"

"My dear, the year before it was worse. It was Christian Science. Selina Goobie is a sort of High Priestess of the Cult, and she put down all opposition with a high hand. Then one evening, after dinner, Clovis Sangrail put a wasp down her back, to see if her theory about the non-existence of pain could be depended on in an emergency. The wasp was small, but very efficient, and it had been soured in temper by being kept in a paper cage all the afternoon. Wasps don't stand confinement well, at least this one didn't. I don't think I ever realized till that moment what the word 'invective' could be made to mean. I sometimes wake in the night and think I still hear Selina describing Clovis's conduct and general character. That was the year that Sir Richard was writing his volume on *Domestic Life in Tartary*. The critics all blamed it for a lack of concentration."

"He's engaged on a very important work this year, isn't he?" asked Lena.

"*Land-tenure in Turkestan,*" said Lady Prowche; "he is just at work on the final chapters and they require all the concentration he can give them. That is why I am so very anxious not to have any unfortunate disturbance this year. I have taken every precaution I can think of to bring non-conflicting and harmonious elements together; the only two people I am not quite easy about are the Atkinson man and Marcus Popham. They are the two who will be down here longest together, and if they are going to fall foul of one another about any burning question, well, there will be more unpleasantness."

"Can't you find out anything about them? About their opinions, I mean."

"Anything? My dear Lena, there's scarcely anything that I haven't found out about them. They're both of them moderate Liberal, Evangelical, mildly opposed to female suffrage, they approve of the Falconer Report, and the Stewards' decision about

Craganour. Thank goodness in this country we don't fly into violent passions about Wagner and Brahms and things of that sort. There is only one thorny subject that I haven't been able to make sure about, the only stone that I have left unturned. Are they unanimously anti-vivisectionist or do they both uphold the necessity for scientific experiment? There has been a lot of correspondence on the subject in our local newspapers of late, and the vicar is certain to preach a sermon about it; vicars are dreadfully provocative at times. Now, if you could only find out for me whether these two men are divergently for or against—"

"I!" exclaimed Lena; "how am I to find out? I don't know either of them to speak to."

"Still, you might discover, in some roundabout way. Write to them, under an assumed name, of course, for subscriptions to one or other cause—or, better still, send a stamped typewritten reply postcard, with a request for a declaration for or against vivisection; people who would hesitate to commit themselves to a subscription will cheerfully write Yes or No on a prepaid postcard. If you can't manage it that way, try and meet them at some one's house and get into argument on the subject. I think Milly occasionally has one or other of them at her at-homes; you might have the luck to meet both of them there the same evening. Only it must be done soon. My invitations ought to go out by Wednesday or Thursday at the latest, and today is Friday."

"Milly's at-homes are not very amusing, as a rule," said Lena; "and one never gets a chance of talking uninterruptedly to any one for a couple of minutes at a time; Milly is one of those restless hostesses who always seem to be trying to see how you look in different parts of the room, in fresh grouping effects. Even if I got to speak to Popham or Atkinson I couldn't plunge into a topic like vivisection straight away. No, I think the postcard scheme would be more hopeful and decidedly less tiresome. How would it be best to word them?"

"Oh, something like this: 'Are you in favour of experiments on living animals for the purpose of scientific research—Yes or No?' That is quite simple and unmistakable. If they don't answer it will at least be an indication that they are indifferent about the subject, and that is all I want to know."

"All right," said Lena, "I'll get my brother-in-law to let me have them addressed to his office, and he can telephone the result of the plebiscite direct to you."

"Thank you ever so much," said Lady Prowche gratefully, "and be sure to get the cards sent off as soon as possible."

On the following Tuesday the voice of an office clerk, speaking through the telephone, informed Lady Prowche that the postcard poll showed unanimous hostility to experiments on living animals.

Lady Prowche thanked the office clerk, and in a louder and more fervent voice she thanked Heaven. The two invitations, already sealed and addressed, were immediately dispatched; in due course they were both accepted. The house party of the halcyon hours, as the prospective hostess called it, was auspiciously launched.

Lena Luddleford was not included among the guests, having previously committed herself to another invitation. At the opening day of a cricket festival, however, she ran across Lady Prowche, who had motored over from the other side of the county. She wore the air of one who is not interested in cricket and not particularly interested in life. She shook hands limply with Lena, and remarked that it was a beastly day.

"The party, how has it gone off?" asked Lena quickly.

"Don't speak of it!" was the tragical answer; "why do I always have such rotten luck?"

"But what has happened?"

"It has been awful. Hyænas could not have behaved with greater savagery. Sir Richard said so, and he has been in countries where hyænas live, so he ought to know. They actually came to blows!"

"Blows?"

"Blows and curses. It really might have been a scene from one of Hogarth's pictures. I never felt so humiliated in my life. What the servants must have thought!"

"But who were the offenders?"

"Oh, naturally the very two that we took all the trouble about."

"I thought they agreed on every subject that one could violently disagree about—religion, politics, vivisection, the Derby decision, the Falconer Report; what else was there left to quarrel about?"

"My dear, we were fools not to have thought of it. One of them was Pro-Greek and the other Pro-Bulgar."

HYACINTH

"The new fashion of introducing the candidate's children into an election contest is a pretty one," said Mrs. Panstreppon; "it takes away something from the acerbity of party warfare, and it makes an interesting experience for the children to look back on in after years. Still, if you will listen to my advice, Matilda, you will not take Hyacinth with you down to Luffbridge on election day."

"Not take Hyacinth!" exclaimed his mother; "but why not? Jutterly is bringing his three children, and they are going to drive a pair of Nubian donkeys about the town, to emphasize the fact that their father has been appointed Colonial Secretary. We are making the demand for a strong Navy a special feature in *our* campaign, and it will be particularly appropriate to have Hyacinth dressed in his sailor suit. He'll look heavenly."

"The question is, not how he'll look, but how he'll behave. He's a delightful child, of course, but there is a strain of unbridled pugnacity in him that breaks out at times in a really alarming fashion. You may have forgotten the affair of the little Gaffin children; I haven't."

"I was in India at the time, and I've only a vague recollection of what happened; he was very naughty, I know."

"He was in his goat-carriage, and met the Gaffins in their perambulator, and he drove the goat full tilt at them and sent the perambulator spinning. Little Jacky Gaffin was pinned down under the wreckage, and while the nurse had her hands full with the goat Hyacinth was laying into Jacky's legs with his belt like a small fury."

"I'm not defending him," said Matilda, "but they must have done something to annoy him."

"Nothing intentionally, but some one had unfortunately told him that they were half French—their mother was a Duboc, you know—and he had been having a history lesson that morning, and had just heard of the final loss of Calais by the English, and was furious about it. He said he'd teach the little toads to go snatching towns from us, but we didn't know at the time that he was referring to the Gaffins. I told him afterwards that all bad feeling between the two nations had died out long ago, and that anyhow the Gaffins were only half French, and he said that it was only the French half of Jacky that he had been hitting; the rest had been buried under the perambulator. If the loss of Calais unloosed such fury in him, I tremble to think what the possible loss of the election might entail."

"All that happened when he was eight; he's older now and knows better."

"Children with Hyacinth's temperament don't know better as they grow older; they merely know more."

"Nonsense. He will enjoy the fun of the election, and in any case he'll be tired out by the time the poll is declared, and the new sailor suit that I've had made for him is just in the right shade of blue for our election colours, and it will exactly match the blue of his eyes. He will be a perfectly charming note of colour."

"There is such a thing as letting one's æsthetic sense override one's moral sense," said Mrs. Panstreppon. "I believe you would have condoned the South Sea Bubble and the persecution of the Albigenses if they had been carried out in effective colour schemes. However, if anything unfortunate should happen down at Luffbridge, don't say it wasn't foreseen by one member of the family."

The election was keenly but decorously contested. The newly appointed Colonial Secretary was personally popular, while the Government to which he adhered was distinctly unpopular, and there was some expectancy that the majority of four hundred, obtained at the last election, would be altogether wiped out. Both sides were hopeful, but neither could feel confident. The children were a great success; the little Jutterlys drove their chubby donkeys solemnly up and down the main streets, displaying posters which advocated the claims of their father on the broad general grounds that he was their father, while as for Hyacinth, his conduct might have served as a model for any seraph-child that had strayed unwittingly on to the scene of an electoral contest. Of his own accord, and under the delighted eyes of half a dozen camera operators, he had gone up to the Jutterly children and presented them with a packet of butterscotch; "we needn't be enemies because we're wearing the opposite colours," he said with engaging friendliness, and the occupants of the donkey-cart accepted his offering with polite solemnity. The grown-up members of both political camps were delighted at the incident—with the exception of Mrs. Panstreppon, who shuddered.

"Never was Clytemnestra's kiss sweeter than on the night she slew me," she quoted, but made the quotation to herself.

The last hour of the poll was a period of unremitting labour for both parties; it was generally estimated that not more than a dozen votes separated the candidates, and every effort was made to bring up obstinately wavering electors. It was with a feeling of relaxation and relief that every one heard the clocks strike the hour for the close of the poll. Exclamations broke out from the tired workers, and corks flew out from bottles.

"Well, if we haven't won, we've done our level best." "It has been a clean, straight fight, with no rancour." "The children were quite a charming feature, weren't they?"

The children? It suddenly occurred to everybody that they had seen nothing of the children for the last hour. What had become of the three little Jutterlys and their donkey-cart, and, for the matter of that, what had become of Hyacinth? Hurried, anxious embassies went backwards and forwards between the respective party headquarters and the various committee-rooms, but there was blank ignorance everywhere as to the whereabouts of the children. Every one had been too busy in the closing moments of the poll to bestow a thought on them. Then there came a telephone call at the Unionist Women's Committee-rooms, and the voice of Hyacinth was heard demanding when the poll would be declared.

"Where are you, and where are the Jutterly children?" asked his mother.

"I've just finished having high-tea at a pastry-cook's," came the answer; "and they let me telephone. I've had a poached egg and a sausage roll and four meringues."

"You'll be ill. Are the little Jutterlys with you?"

"Rather not. They're in a pigsty."

"A pigsty? Why? What pigsty?"

"Near the Crawleigh Road. I met them driving about a back road, and told them they were to have tea with me, and put their donkeys in a yard that I knew of. Then I took them to see an old sow that had got ten little pigs. I got the sow into the outer sty by giving her bits of bread, while the Jutterlys went in to look at the litter, then I bolted the door and left them there."

"You wicked boy, do you mean to say you've left those poor children there alone in the pigsty?"

"They're not alone, they've got ten little pigs in with them;

they're jolly well crowded. They were pretty mad at being shut in, but not half as mad as the old sow is at being shut out from her young ones. If she gets in while they're there she'll bite them into mincemeat. I can get them out by letting a short ladder down through the top window, and that's what I'm going to do *if we win.* If their blighted father gets in, I'm just going to open the door for the sow, and let her do what she dashed well likes to them. That's why I want to know when the poll will be declared."

Here the narrator rang off. A wild stampede and a frantic sending-off of messengers took place at the other end of the telephone. Nearly all the workers on either side had disappeared to their various club-rooms and public-house bars to await the declaration of the poll, but enough local information could be secured to determine the scene of Hyacinth's exploit. Mr. John Ball had a stable yard down near the Crawleigh Road, up a short lane, and his sow was known to have a litter of ten young ones. Thither went in headlong haste both the candidates, Hyacinth's mother, his aunt (Mrs. Panstreppon), and two or three hurriedly summoned friends. The two Nubian donkeys, contentedly munching at bundles of hay, met their gaze as they entered the yard. The hoarse savage grunting of an enraged animal and the shriller note of thirteen young voices, three of them human, guided them to the sty, in the outer yard of which a huge Yorkshire sow kept up a ceaseless raging patrol before a closed door. Reclining on the broad ledge of an open window, from which point of vantage he could reach down and shoot the bolt of the door, was Hyacinth, his blue sailor-suit somewhat the worse for wear, and his angel smile exchanged for a look of demoniacal determination.

"If any of you come a step nearer," he shouted, "the sow will be inside in half a jiffy."

A storm of threatening, arguing, entreating expostulation broke from the baffled rescue party, but it made no more impression on Hyacinth than the squealing tempest that raged within the sty.

"If Jutterly heads the poll I'm going to let the sow in. I'll teach the blighters to win elections from us."

"He means it," said Mrs. Panstreppon; "I feared the worst when I saw that butterscotch incident."

"It's all right, my little man," said Jutterly, with the duplicity to which even a Colonial Secretary can sometimes stoop, "your father has been elected by a large majority."

"Liar!" retorted Hyacinth, with the directness of speech that is not merely excusable, but almost obligatory, in the political profession; "the votes aren't counted yet. You won't gammon me as to the result, either. A boy that I've palled with is going to fire a gun when the poll is declared; two shots if we've won, one shot if we haven't."

The situation began to look critical. "Drug the sow," whispered Hyacinth's father.

Some one went off in the motor to the nearest chemist's shop and returned presently with two large pieces of bread, liberally dosed with narcotic. The bread was thrown deftly and unostentatiously into the sty, but Hyacinth saw through the manœuvre. He set up a piercing imitation of a small pig in Purgatory, and the infuriated mother ramped round and round the sty; the pieces of bread were trampled into slush.

At any moment now the poll might be declared. Jutterly flew back to the Town Hall, where the votes were being counted. His agent met him with a smile of hope.

"You're eleven ahead at present, and only about eighty more to be counted; you're just going to squeak through."

"I mustn't squeak through," exclaimed Jutterly hoarsely. "You must object to every doubtful vote on our side that can possibly be disallowed. I must *not* have the majority."

Then was seen the unprecedented sight of a party agent challenging the votes on his own side with a captiousness that his opponents would have hesitated to display. One or two votes that would have certainly passed muster under ordinary circumstances were disallowed, but even so Jutterly was six ahead with only thirty more to be counted.

To the watchers by the sty the moments seemed intolerable. As a last resort some one had been sent for a gun with which to shoot the sow, though Hyacinth would probably draw the bolt the moment such a weapon was brought into the yard. Nearly all the men were away from their homes, however, on election night, and the messenger had evidently gone far afield in his search. It must be a matter of minutes now to the declaration of the poll.

A sudden roar of shouting and cheering was heard from the direction of the Town Hall. Hyacinth's father clutched a pitchfork and prepared to dash into the sty in the forlorn hope of being in time.

A shot rang out in the evening air. Hyacinth stooped down from his perch and put his finger on the bolt. The sow pressed furiously against the door.

"Bang!" came another shot.

Hyacinth wriggled back, and sent a short ladder down through the window of the inner sty.

"Now you can come up, you unclean little blighters," he sang out; "my daddy's got in, not yours. Hurry up, I can't keep the sow waiting much longer. And don't you jolly well come butting into any election again where I'm on the job."

In the reaction that set in after the deliverance furious recriminations were indulged in by the lately opposed candidates, their women folk, agents, and party helpers. A recount was demanded, but failed to establish the fact that the Colonial Secretary had obtained a majority. Altogether the election left a legacy of soreness behind it, apart from any that was experienced by Hyacinth in person.

"It is the last time I shall let him go to an election," exclaimed his mother.

"There I think you are going to extremes," said Mrs. Panstreppon; "if there should be a general election in Mexico I think you might safely let him go there, but I doubt whether our English politics are suited to the rough and tumble of an angel-child."

THE IMAGE OF THE LOST SOUL[1]

THERE were a number of carved stone figures placed at intervals along the parapets of the old Cathedral; some of them represented angels, others kings and bishops, and nearly all were in attitudes of pious exaltation and composure. But one figure, low down on the cold north side of the building, had neither crown, mitre, nor nimbus, and its face was hard and bitter and downcast; it must be a demon, declared the fat blue pigeons that roosted and sunned themselves all day on the ledges of the parapet; but the old belfry jackdaw, who was an authority on ecclesiastical architecture, said it was a lost soul. And there the matter rested.

One autumn day there fluttered on to the Cathedral roof a

[1] Written in 1891.

slender, sweet-voiced bird that had wandered away from the bare fields and thinning hedgerows in search of a winter roosting-place. It tried to rest its tired feet under the shade of a great angel-wing or to nestle in the sculptured folds of a kingly robe, but the fat pigeons hustled it away from wherever it settled, and the noisy sparrow-folk drove it off the ledges. No respectable bird sang with so much feeling, they cheeped one to another, and the wanderer had to move on.

Only the effigy of the Lost Soul offered a place of refuge. The pigeons did not consider it safe to perch on a projection that leaned so much out of the perpendicular, and was, besides, too much in the shadow. The figure did not cross its hands in the pious attitude of the other graven dignitaries, but its arms were folded as in defiance and their angle made a snug resting-place for the little bird. Every evening it crept trustfully into its corner against the stone breast of the image, and the darkling eyes seemed to keep watch over its slumbers. The lonely bird grew to love its lonely protector, and during the day it would sit from time to time on some rain-shoot or other abutment and trill forth its sweetest music in grateful thanks for its nightly shelter. And, it may have been the work of wind and weather, or some other influence, but the wild drawn face seemed gradually to lose some of its hardness and unhappiness. Every day, through the long monotonous hours, the song of his little guest would come up in snatches to the lonely watcher, and at evening, when the vesper-bell was ringing and the great grey bats slid out of their hiding-places in the belfry roof, the bright-eyed bird would return, twitter a few sleepy notes, and nestle into the arms that were waiting for him. Those were happy days for the Dark Image. Only the great bell of the Cathedral rang out daily its mocking message, "After joy . . . sorrow."

The folk in the verger's lodge noticed a little brown bird flitting about the Cathedral precincts, and admired its beautiful singing. "But it is a pity," said they, "that all that warbling should be lost and wasted far out of hearing up on the parapet." They were poor, but they understood the principles of political economy. So they caught the bird and put it in a little wicker cage outside the lodge door.

That night the little songster was missing from its accustomed haunt, and the Dark Image knew more than ever the bitterness of loneliness. Perhaps his little friend had been killed by a prowling cat or hurt by a stone. Perhaps . . . perhaps he had flown elsewhere. But when morning came there floated up to him, through the noise and bustle of the Cathedral world, a faint heart-aching message from the prisoner in the wicker cage far below. And every day, at high noon, when the fat pigeons were stupefied into silence after their midday meal and the sparrows were washing themselves in the street-puddles, the song of the little bird came up to the parapets—a song of hunger and longing and hopelessness, a cry that could never be answered.

The pigeons remarked, between mealtimes, that the figure leaned forward more than ever out of the perpendicular.

One day no song came up from the little wicker cage. It was the coldest day of the winter, and the pigeons and sparrows on the Cathedral roof looked anxiously on all sides for the scraps of food which they were dependent on in hard weather.

"Have the lodge-folk thrown out anything on to the dust-heap?" inquired one pigeon of another which was peering over the edge of the north parapet.

"Only a little dead bird," was the answer.

There was a crackling sound in the night on the Cathedral roof and a noise as of falling masonry. The belfry jackdaw said the frost was affecting the fabric, and as he had experienced many frosts it must have been so. In the morning it was seen that the Figure of the Lost Soul had toppled from its cornice and lay now in a broken mass on the dust-heap outside the verger's lodge.

"It is just as well," cooed the fat pigeons, after they had peered at the matter for some minutes; "now we shall have a nice angel put up there. Certainly they will put an angel there."

"After joy . . . sorrow," rang out the great bell.

THE PURPLE OF THE BALKAN KINGS[1]

LUITPOLD WOLKENSTEIN, financier and diplomat on a small, obtrusive, self-important scale, sat in his favoured café in the worldwise Habsburg capital, confronted with the *Neue Freie Presse* and the cup of cream-topped coffee and attendant glass of water that

1 This and the following tale were written during the Balkan war.

a sleek-headed piccolo had just brought him. For years longer than a dog's lifetime sleek-headed piccolos had placed the *Neue Freie Presse* and a cup of cream-topped coffee on his table; for years he had sat at the same spot, under the dust-coated, stuffed eagle, that had once been a living, soaring bird on the Styrian mountains, and was now made monstrous and symbolical with a second head grafted on to its neck and a gilt crown planted on either dusty skull. Today Luitpold Wolkenstein read no more than the first article in his paper, but he read it again and again.

"The Turkish fortress of Kirk Kilisseh has fallen. . . . The Serbs, it is officially announced, have taken Kumanovo. . . . The fortress of Kirk Kilisseh lost, Kumanovo taken by the Serbs, these are tidings for Constantinople resembling something out of Shakespeare's tragedies of the kings. . . . The neighbourhood of Adrianople and the Eastern region, where the great battle is now in progress, will not reveal merely the future of Turkey, but also what position and what influence the Balkan States are to have in the world."

For years longer than a dog's lifetime Luitpold Wolkenstein had disposed of the pretensions and strivings of the Balkan States over the cup of cream-topped coffee that sleek-headed piccolos had brought him. Never travelling farther eastward than the horse-fair at Temesvar, never inviting personal risk in an encounter with anything more potentially desperate than a hare or partridge, he had constituted himself the critical appraiser and arbiter of the military and national prowess of the small countries that fringed the Dual Monarchy on its Danube border. And his judgment had been one of unsparing contempt for small-scale efforts, of unquestioning respect for the big battalions and full purses. Over the whole scene of the Balkan territories and their troubled histories had loomed the commanding magic of the words "the Great Powers"—even more imposing in their Teutonic rendering, "Die Grossmächte."

Worshipping power and force and money-mastery as an elderly nerve-ridden woman might worship youthful physical energy, the comfortable, plump-bodied café-oracle had jested and gibed at the ambitions of the Balkan kinglets and their peoples, had unloosed against them that battery of strange lip-sounds that a Viennese employs almost as an auxiliary language to express the thoughts when his thoughts are not complimentary. British travellers had visited the Balkan lands and reported high things of the Bulgarians and their future, Russian officers had taken peeps at their army and confessed "this is a thing to be reckoned with, and it is not we who have created it, they have done it by themselves." But over his cups of coffee and his hour-long games of dominoes the oracle had laughed and wagged his head and distilled the worldly wisdom of his caste. The Grossmächte had not succeeded in stifling the roll of the war-drum, that was true; the big battalions of the Ottoman Empire would have to do some talking, and then the big purses and big threatenings of the Powers would speak and the last word would be with them. In imagination Luitpold heard the onward tramp of the red-fezzed bayonet bearers echoing through the Balkan passes, saw the little sheepskin-clad mannikins driven back to their villages, saw the augustly chiding spokesmen of the Powers dictating, adjusting, restoring, settling things once again in their allotted places, sweeping up the dust of conflict, and now his ears had to listen to the war-drum rolling in quite another direction, had to listen to the tramp of battalions that were bigger and bolder and better skilled in warcraft than he had deemed possible in that quarter; his eyes had to read in the columns of his accustomed newspaper a warning to the Grossmächte that they had something new to learn, something new to reckon with, much that was time-honoured to relinquish. "The Great Powers will have no little difficulty in persuading the Balkan States of the inviolability of the principle that Europe cannot permit any fresh partition of territory in the East without her approval. Even now, while the campaign is still undecided, there are rumours of a project of fiscal unity, extending over the entire Balkan lands, and further of a constitutional union in imitation of the German Empire. That is perhaps only a political straw blown by the storm, but it is not possible to dismiss the reflection that the Balkan States leagued together command a military strength with which the Great Powers will have to reckon. . . . The people who have poured out their blood on the battlefields and sacrificed the available armed men of an entire generation in order to encompass a union with their kinsfolk will not remain any longer in an attitude of dependence on the Great Powers or on Russia, but will go their own ways. . . . The blood that has been poured forth today gives for the first time a genuine tone to the purple of the Balkan Kings. The Great Powers cannot overlook the fact that a people that has tasted victory will not let itself be driven back again within its former limits. Turkey has lost today not only Kirk Kilisseh and Kumanovo, but Macedonia also."

Luitpold Wolkenstein drank his coffee, but the flavour had somehow gone out of it. His world, his pompous, imposing, dictating world, had suddenly rolled up into narrower dimensions. The big purses and the big threats had been pushed unceremoniously on one side; a force that he could not fathom, could not comprehend, had made itself rudely felt. The august Cæsars of Mammon and armament had looked down frowningly on the combat, and those about to die had *not* saluted, had no intention of saluting. A lesson was being imposed on unwilling learners, a lesson of respect for certain fundamental principles, and it was not the small struggling States who were being taught the lesson.

Luitpold Wolkenstein did not wait for the quorum of domino players to arrive. They would all have read the article in the *Freie Presse*. And there are moments when an oracle finds its greatest salvation in withdrawing itself from the area of human questioning.

THE CUPBOARD OF THE YESTERDAYS

"War is a cruelly destructive thing," said the Wanderer, dropping his newspaper to the floor and staring reflectively into space.

"Ah, yes, indeed," said the Merchant, responding readily to what seemed like a safe platitude; "when one thinks of the loss of life and limb, the desolated homesteads, the ruined—"

"I wasn't thinking of anything of the sort," said the Wanderer; "I was thinking of the tendency that modern war has to destroy and banish the very elements of picturesqueness and excitement that are its chief excuse and charm. It is like a fire that flares up brilliantly for a while and then leaves everything blacker and bleaker than before. After every important war in South-East Europe in recent times there has been a shrinking of the area of chronically disturbed territory, a stiffening of frontier lines, an intrusion of civilized monotony. And imagine what may happen at the conclusion of this war if the Turk should really be driven out of Europe."

"Well, it would be a gain to the cause of good government, I suppose," said the Merchant.

"But have you counted the loss?" said the other. "The Balkans have long been the last surviving shred of happy hunting-ground for the adventurous, a playground for passions that are fast becoming atrophied for want of exercise. In old bygone days we had the wars in the Low Countries always at our doors, as it were; there was no need to go far afield into malaria-stricken wilds if one wanted a life of boot and saddle and licence to kill and be killed. Those who wished to see life had a decent opportunity for seeing death at the same time."

"It is scarcely right to talk of killing and bloodshed in that way," said the Merchant reprovingly; "one must remember that all men are brothers."

"One must also remember that a large percentage of them are younger brothers; instead of going into bankruptcy, which is the usual tendency of the younger brother nowadays, they gave their families a fair chance of going into mourning. Every bullet finds a billet, according to a rather optimistic proverb, and you must admit that nowadays it is becoming increasingly difficult to find billets for a lot of young gentlemen who would have adorned, and probably thoroughly enjoyed, one of the old-time happy-go-lucky wars. But that is not exactly the burden of my complaint. The Balkan lands are especially interesting to us in these rapidly moving days because they afford us the last remaining glimpse of a vanishing period of European history. When I was a child one of the earliest events of the outside world that forced itself coherently under my notice was a war in the Balkans; I remember a sunburnt, soldierly man putting little pin-flags in a war-map, red flags for the Turkish forces and yellow flags for the Russians. It seemed a magical region, with its mountain passes and frozen rivers and grim battlefields, its drifting snows, and prowling wolves; there was a great stretch of water that bore the sinister but engaging name of the Black Sea—nothing that I ever learned before or after in a geography lesson made the same impression on me as that strange-named inland sea, and I don't think its magic has ever faded out of my imagination. And there was a battle called Plevna that went on and on with varying fortunes for what seemed like a great part of a lifetime; I remember the day of wrath and mourning when the little red flag had to be taken away from Plevna—like other maturer judges, I was backing the wrong horse, at any rate the losing horse. And now today we are putting little pin-flags again into maps of the Balkan region, and the passions are being turned loose once more in their playground."

"The war will be localized," said the Merchant vaguely; "at least every one hopes so."

"It couldn't wish for a better locality," said the Wanderer; "there is a charm about those countries that you find nowhere else in Europe, the charm of uncertainty and landslide, and the little dramatic happenings that make all the difference between the ordinary and the desirable."

"Life is held very cheap in those parts," said the Merchant.

"To a certain extent, yes," said the Wanderer. "I remember a man at Sofia who used to teach me Bulgarian in a rather inefficient manner, interspersed with a lot of quite wearisome gossip. I never knew what his personal history was, but that was only because I didn't listen; he told it to me many times. After I left Bulgaria he used to send me Sofia newspapers from time to time. I felt that he would be rather tiresome if I ever went there again. And then I heard afterwards that some men came in one day from Heaven knows where, just as things do happen in the Balkans, and murdered him in the open street, and went away as quietly as they had come. You will not understand it, but to me there was something rather piquant in the idea of such a thing happening to such a man; after his dulness and his long-winded small-talk it seemed a sort of brilliant *esprit d'escalier* on his part to meet with an end of such ruthlessly planned and executed violence."

The Merchant shook his head; the piquancy of the incident was not within striking distance of his comprehension.

"I should have been shocked at hearing such a thing about any one I had known," he said.

"The present war," continued his companion, without stopping to discuss two hopelessly divergent points of view, "may be the beginning of the end of much that has hitherto survived the resistless creeping-in of civilization. If the Balkan lands are to be finally parcelled out between the competing Christian Kingdoms and the haphazard rule of the Turk banished to beyond the Sea of Marmora, the old order, or disorder if you like, will have received its death-blow. Something of its spirit will linger perhaps for a while in the old charmed regions where it bore sway; the Greek villagers will doubtless be restless and turbulent and unhappy where the Bulgars rule, and the Bulgars will certainly be restless and turbulent and unhappy under Greek administration, and the rival flocks of the Exarchate and Patriarchate will make themselves intensely disagreeable to one another wherever the opportunity offers; the habits of a lifetime, of several lifetimes, are not laid aside all at once. And the Albanians, of course, we shall have with us still, a troubled Moslem pool left by the receding wave of Islam in Europe. But the old atmosphere will have changed, the glamour will have gone; the dust of formality and bureaucratic neatness will slowly settle down over the time-honoured landmarks; the Sanjak of Novi Bazar, the Muersteg Agreement, the Komitadje bands, the Vilayet of Adrianople, all those familiar outlandish names and things and places, that we have known so long as part and parcel of the Balkan Question, will have passed away into the cupboard of yesterdays, as completely as the Hansa League and the wars of the Guises.

"They were the heritage that history handed down to us, spoiled and diminished no doubt, in comparison with yet earlier days that we never knew, but still something to thrill and enliven one little corner of our Continent, something to help us to conjure up in our imagination the days when the Turk was thundering at the gates of Vienna. And what shall we have to hand down to our children? Think of what their news from the Balkans will be in the course of another ten or fifteen years. Socialist Congress at Uskub, election riot at Monastir, great dock strike at Salonika, visit of the Y.M.C.A. to Varna. Varna—on the coast of that enchanted sea! They will drive out to some suburb for tea, and write home about it as the Bexhill of the East.

"War is a wickedly destructive thing."

"Still, you must admit—" began the Merchant. But the Wanderer was not in the mood to admit anything. He rose impatiently and walked to where the tape-machine was busy with the news from Adrianople.

FOR THE DURATION OF THE WAR[1]

THE Rev. Wilfrid Gaspilton, in one of those clerical migrations inconsequent-seeming to the lay mind, had removed from the moderately fashionable parish of St. Luke's, Kensingate, to the immoderately rural parish of St. Chuddock's, somewhere in Yondershire. There were doubtless substantial advantages connected with the move, but there were certainly some very obvious drawbacks. Neither the migratory clergyman nor his wife were able to adapt themselves naturally and comfortably to the conditions of country life. Beryl, Mrs. Gaspilton, had always looked indulgently on the country as a place where people of irreproachable income and hospitable instincts cultivated tennis-lawns and rose-gardens and Jacobean pleasaunces, wherein selected gatherings of interested week-end guests might disport themselves. Mrs. Gaspilton considered herself as distinctly an interesting personality, and from a limited standpoint she was doubtless right. She had indolent dark eyes and a comfortable chin, which belied the slightly plaintive inflection which she threw into her voice at suitable intervals. She was tolerably well satisfied with the smaller advantages of life, but she regretted that Fate had not seen its way to reserve for her some of the ampler successes for which she felt herself well qualified. She would have liked to be the centre of a literary, slightly political salon, where discerning satellites might have recognized the breadth of her outlook on human affairs and the undoubted smallness of her feet. As it was, Destiny had chosen for her that she should be the wife of a rector, and had now further decreed that a country rectory should be the background to her existence. She rapidly made up her mind that her surroundings did not call for exploration: Noah had predicted the Flood, but no one expected him to swim about in it. Digging in a wet garden or trudging through muddy lanes were exertions which she did not propose to undertake. As long as the garden produced asparagus and carnations at pleasingly frequent intervals Mrs. Gaspilton was content to approve of its expense and otherwise ignore its existence. She would fold herself up, so to speak, in an elegant,

[1] Written at the Front.

indolent little world of her own, enjoying the minor recreations of being gently rude to the doctor's wife and continuing the leisurely production of her one literary effort, *The Forbidden Horsepond*, a translation of Baptiste Lepoy's *L'Abreuvoir interdit*. It was a labour which had already been so long drawn-out that it seemed probable that Baptiste Lepoy would drop out of vogue before her translation of his temporarily famous novel was finished. However, the languid prosecution of the work had invested Mrs. Gaspilton with a certain literary dignity, even in Kensingate circles, and would place her on a pinnacle in St. Chuddock's, where hardly any one read French, and assuredly no one had heard of *L'Abreuvoir interdit*.

The Rector's wife might be content to turn her back complacently on the country; it was the Rector's tragedy that the country turned its back on him. With the best intention in the world and the immortal example of Gilbert White before him, the Rev. Wilfrid found himself as bored and ill at ease in his new surroundings as Charles II would have been at a modern Wesleyan Conference. The birds that hopped across his lawn hopped across it as though it were their lawn, and not his, and gave him plainly to understand that in their eyes he was infinitely less interesting than a garden worm or the rectory cat. The hedgeside and meadow flowers were equally uninspiring; the lesser celandine seemed particularly unworthy of the attention that English poets had bestowed on it, and the Rector knew that he would be utterly miserable if left alone for a quarter of an hour in its company. With the human inhabitants of his parish he was no better off; to know them was merely to know their ailments, and the ailments were almost invariably rheumatism. Some, of course, had other bodily infirmities, but they always had rheumatism as well. The Rector had not yet grasped the fact that in rural cottage life not to have rheumatism is as glaring an omission as not to have been presented at Court would be in more ambitious circles. And with all this dearth of local interest there was Beryl shutting herself off with her ridiculous labours on *The Forbidden Horsepond.*

"I don't see why you should suppose that any one wants to read Baptiste Lepoy in English," the Reverend Wilfrid remarked to his wife one morning, finding her surrounded with her usual elegant litter of dictionaries, fountain pens, and scribbling paper; "hardly any one bothers to read him now in France."

"My dear," said Beryl, with an intonation of gentle weariness, "haven't two or three leading London publishers told me they wondered no one had ever translated *L'Abreuvoir interdit,* and begged me–"

"Publishers always clamour for the books that no one has ever written, and turn a cold shoulder on them as soon as they're written. If St. Paul were living now they would pester him to write an Epistle to the Esquimaux, but no London publisher would dream of reading his Epistle to the Ephesians."

"Is there any asparagus anywhere in the garden?" asked Beryl; "because I've told cook–"

"Not anywhere in the garden," snapped the Rector, "but there's no doubt plenty in the asparagus-bed, which is the usual place for it."

And he walked away into the region of fruit trees and vegetable beds to exchange irritation for boredom. It was there, among the gooseberry bushes and beneath the medlar trees, that the temptation to the perpetration of a great literary fraud came to him.

Some weeks later the *Bi-Monthly Review* gave to the world, under the guarantee of the Rev. Wilfrid Gaspilton, some fragments of Persian verse, alleged to have been unearthed and translated by a nephew who was at present campaigning somewhere in the Tigris valley. The Rev. Wilfrid possessed a host of nephews, and it was, of course, quite possible that one or more of them might be in military employ in Mesopotamia, though no one could call to mind any particular nephew who could have been suspected of being a Persian scholar.

The verses were attributed to one Ghurab, a hunter, or, according to other accounts, warden of the royal fishponds, who lived, in some unspecified century, in the neighbourhood of Karmanshah. They breathed a spirit of comfortable, even-tempered satire and philosophy, disclosing a mockery that did not trouble to be bitter, a joy in life that was not passionate to the verge of being troublesome.

"A Mouse that prayed for Allah's aid
 Blasphemed when no such aid befell:
A Cat, who feasted on that mouse,
 Thought Allah managed vastly well.

Pray not for aid to One who made
  A set of never-changing Laws,
But in your need remember well
  He gave you speed, or guile—or claws.

Some laud a life of mild content:
  Content may fall, as well as Pride.
The Frog who hugged his lowly Ditch
  Was much disgruntled when it dried.

'You are not on the Road to Hell,'
  You tell me with fanatic glee:
Vain boaster, what shall that avail
  If Hell is on the road to thee?

A Poet praised the Evening Star,
  Another praised the Parrot's hue:
A Merchant praised his merchandise,
  And he, at least, praised what he knew."

It was this verse which gave the critics and commentators some clue as to the probable date of the composition; the parrot, they reminded the public, was in high vogue as a type of elegance in the days of Hafiz of Shiraz; in the quatrains of Omar it makes no appearance.

The next verse, it was pointed out, would apply to the political conditions of the present day as strikingly as to the region and era for which it was written—

"A Sultan dreamed day-long of Peace,
  The while his Rivals' armies grew:
They changed his Day-dreams into sleep
  —The Peace, methinks, he never knew."

Woman appeared little, and wine not at all in the verse of the hunter-poet, but there was at least one contribution to the love-philosophy of the East—

"O Moon-faced Charmer, with Star-drownèd Eyes,
  And cheeks of soft delight, exhaling musk,
They tell me that thy charm will fade; ah well,
  The Rose itself grows hue-less in the Dusk."

Finally, there was a recognition of the Inevitable, a chill breath blowing across the poet's comfortable estimate of life—

"There is a sadness in each Dawn,
A sadness that you cannot rede,
The joyous Day brings in its train
The Feast, the Loved One, and the Steed.

Ah, there shall come a Dawn at last
That brings no life-stir to your ken,
A long, cold Dawn without a Day,
And ye shall rede its sadness then."

The verses of Ghurab came on the public at a moment when a comfortable, slightly quizzical philosophy was certain to be welcome, and their reception was enthusiastic. Elderly colonels, who had outlived the love of truth, wrote to the papers to say that they had been familiar with the works of Ghurab in Afghanistan, and Aden, and other suitable localities a quarter of a century ago. A Ghurab-of-Karmanshah Club sprang into existence, the members of which alluded to each other as Brother Ghurabians on the slightest provocation. And to the flood of inquiries, criticisms, and requests for information, which naturally poured in on the discoverer, or rather the discloser, of this long-hidden poet, the Rev. Wilfrid made one effectual reply: Military considerations forbade any disclosures which might throw unnecessary light on his nephew's movements.

After the war the Rector's position will be one of unthinkable embarrassment, but for the moment, at any rate, he has driven *The Forbidden Horsepond* out of the field.

The Square Egg

First Collected, 1924

THE SQUARE EGG

(A BADGER'S-EYE VIEW OF THE WAR MUD IN THE TRENCHES)

ASSUREDLY a badger is the animal that one most resembles in this trench warfare, that drab-coated creature of the twilight and darkness, digging, burrowing, listening; keeping itself as clean as possible under unfavourable circumstances, fighting tooth and nail on occasion for possession of a few yards of honeycombed earth.

What the badger thinks about life we shall never know, which is a pity, but cannot be helped; it is difficult enough to know what one thinks about, oneself, in the trenches. Parliament, taxes, social gatherings, economies, and expenditure, and all the thousand and one horrors of civilization seem immeasurably remote, and the war itself seems almost as distant and unreal. A couple of hundred yards away, separated from you by a stretch of dismal untidy-looking ground and some strips of rusty wire-entanglement, lies a vigilant, bullet-splitting enemy; lurking and watching in those opposing trenches are foemen who might stir the imagination of the most sluggish brain, descendants of the men who went to battle under Moltke, Blücher, Frederick the Great, and the Great Elector, Wallenstein, Maurice of Saxony, Barbarossa, Albert the Bear, Henry the Lion, Witekind the Saxon. They are matched against you there, man for man and gun for gun, in what is perhaps the most stupendous struggle that modern history has known, and yet one thinks remarkably little about them. It would not be advisable to forget for the fraction of a second that they are there, but one's mind does not dwell on their existence; one speculates little as to whether they are drinking warm soup and eating sausage, or going cold and hungry, whether they are well supplied with copies of the *Meggendorfer Blätter* and other light literature or bored with unutterable weariness.

Much more to be thought about than the enemy over yonder or the war all over Europe is the mud of the moment, the mud that at times engulfs you as cheese engulfs a cheesemite. In Zoological Gardens one has gazed at an elk or bison loitering at its pleasure more than knee-deep in a quagmire of greasy mud, and one has wondered what it would feel like to be soused and plastered, hour-long, in such a muck-bath. One knows now. In narrow-dug support-trenches, when thaw and heavy rain have come suddenly atop of a frost, when everything is pitch-dark around you, and you can only stumble about and feel your way against streaming mud walls, when you have to go down on hands and knees in several inches of soup-like mud to creep into a dug-out, when you stand deep in mud, lean against mud, grasp mud-slimed objects with mud-caked fingers, wink mud away from your eyes, and shake it out of your ears, bite muddy biscuits with muddy teeth, then at least you are in a position to understand thoroughly what it feels like to wallow—on the other hand the bison's idea of pleasure becomes more and more incomprehensible.

When one is not thinking about mud one is probably thinking about *estaminets*. An *estaminet* is a haven that one finds in agreeable plenty in most of the surrounding townships and villages, flourishing still amid roofless and deserted houses, patched up where necessary in rough-and-ready fashion, and finding a new and profitable tide of customers from among the soldiers who have replaced the bulk of the civil population. An *estaminet* is a sort of compound between a wine-shop and a coffee-house, having a tiny bar in one corner, a few long tables and benches, a prominent cooking stove, generally a small grocery store tucked away in the back premises, and always two or three children running and bumping about at inconvenient angles to one's feet. It seems to be a fixed rule that *estaminet* children should be big enough to run about and small enough to get between one's legs. There must, by the way, be one considerable advantage in being a child in a war-zone village; no one can attempt to teach it tidiness. The wearisome maxim, "A place for everything and everything in its proper place," can never be insisted on when a considerable part of the roof is lying in the backyard, when a bedstead from a neighbour's demolished bedroom is half buried in the beetroot pile, and the chickens are roosting in a derelict meat-safe because a shell has removed the top and sides and front of the chicken-house.

Perhaps there is nothing in the foregoing description to suggest that a village wine-shop, frequently a shell-nibbled building in a shell-gnawed street, is a paradise to dream about, but when one has lived in a dripping wilderness of unrelieved mud and sodden sandbags for any length of time one's mind dwells on the plain-furnished parlour with its hot coffee and *vin ordinaire* as something warm and snug and comforting in a wet and slushy world. To the soldier on his trench-to-billets migration the wine-shop is what the tavern rest-house is to the caravan nomad of the East. One comes and goes in a crowd of chance-foregathered men, noticed or unnoticed as one wishes; amid the khaki-clad, be-putteed throng of one's own kind one can be as unobtrusive as a green caterpillar on a green cabbage leaf; one can sit undisturbed, alone or with one's own friends, or if one wishes to be talkative and talked to one can readily find a place in a circle where men of divers variety of cap badges are exchanging experiences, real or improvised.

Besides the changing throng of mud-stained khaki there is a drifting leaven of local civilians, uniformed interpreters, and men in varying types of foreign military garb, from privates in the Regular Army to Heaven-knows-what in some intermediate corps that only an expert in such matters could put a name to, and, of course, here and there are representatives of that great army of adventurer purse-sappers, that carries on its operations uninterruptedly in time of peace or war alike, over the greater part of the earth's surface. You meet them in England and France, in Russia and Constantinople; probably they are to be met with also in Iceland, though on that point I have no direct evidence.

In the *estaminet* of the Fortunate Rabbit I found myself sitting next to an individual of indefinite age and nondescript uniform, who was obviously determined to make the borrowing of a match serve as a formal introduction and a banker's reference. He had the air of jaded jauntiness, the equipment of temporary amiability, the aspect of a foraging crow, taught by experience to be wary and prompted by necessity to be bold; he had the contemplative downward droop of nose and moustache and the furtive sidelong range of eye—he had all those things that are the ordinary outfit of the purse-sapper the world over.

"I am a victim of the war," he exclaimed after a little preliminary conversation.

"One cannot make an omelette without breaking eggs," I answered, with the appropriate callousness of a man who had seen some dozens of square miles of devastated country-side and roofless homes.

"Eggs!" he vociferated, "but it is precisely of eggs that I am about to speak. Have you ever considered what is the great drawback in the excellent and most useful egg—the ordinary, everyday egg of commerce and cookery?"

"Its tendency to age rapidly is sometimes against it," I hazarded; "unlike the United States of North America, which grow more respectable and self-respecting the longer they last, an egg gains nothing by persistence; it resembles your Louis the Fifteenth, who declined in popular favour with every year he lived—unless the historians have entirely misrepresented his record."

"No," replied the Tavern Acquaintance seriously, "it is not a question of age. It is the shape, the roundness. Consider how easily it rolls. On a table, a shelf, a shop counter, perhaps, one little push, and it may roll to the floor and be destroyed. What catastrophe for the poor, the frugal!"

I gave a sympathetic shudder at the idea; eggs here cost 6 sous apiece.

"Monsieur," he continued, "it is a subject I had often pondered and turned over in my mind, this economical malformation of the household egg. In our little village of Verchey-les-Torteaux, in the Department of the Tarn, my aunt has a small dairy and poultry farm, from which we drew a modest income. We were not poor, but there was always the necessity to labour, to contrive, to be sparing. One day I chanced to notice that one of my aunt's hens, a hen of the mop-headed Houdan breed, had laid an egg that was not altogether so round-shaped as the eggs of other hens; it could not be called square, but it had well-defined angles. I found out that this particular bird always laid eggs of this particular shape. The discovery gave a new stimulus to my ideas. If one collected all the hens that one could find with a tendency to lay a slightly angular egg and bred chickens only from those hens, and went on selecting and selecting, always choosing those that laid the squarest egg, at last, with patience and enterprise, one would produce a breed of fowls that laid only square eggs."

"In the course of several hundred years one might arrive at such a result," I said; "it would more probably take several thousands."

"With your cold Northern conservative slow-moving hens that might be the case," said the Acquaintance impatiently and rather angrily; "with our vivacious Southern poultry it is different. Listen. I searched, I experimented, I explored the poultry-yards of our neighbours, I ransacked the markets of the surrounding towns, wherever I found a hen laying an angular egg I bought her; I collected in time a vast concourse of fowls all sharing the same tendency; from their progeny I selected only those pullets whose eggs showed the most marked deviation from the normal roundness. I continued, I persevered. Monsieur, I produced a breed of hens that laid an egg which could not roll, however much you might push or jostle it. My experiment was more than a success; it was one of the romances of modern industry."

Of that I had not the least doubt, but I did not say so.

"My eggs became known," continued the *soi-disant* poultry-farmer; "at first they were sought after as a novelty, something curious, bizarre. Then merchants and housewives began to see that they were a utility, an improvement, an advantage over the ordinary kind. I was able to command a sale for my wares at a price considerably above market rates. I began to make money. I had a monopoly. I refused to sell any of my 'square-layers,' and the eggs that went to market were carefully sterilized, so that no chickens should be hatched from them. I was in the way to become rich, comfortably rich. Then this war broke out, which has brought misery to so many. I was obliged to leave my hens and my customers and go to the Front. My aunt carried on the business as usual, sold the square eggs, the eggs that I had devised and created and perfected, and received the profits; can you imagine it, she refuses to send me one centime of the takings! She says that she looks after the hens, and pays for their corn, and sends the eggs to market, and that the money is hers. Legally, of course, it is mine; if I could afford to bring a process in the Courts I could recover all the money that the eggs have brought in since the war commenced, many thousands of francs. To bring a process would only need a small sum; I have a lawyer friend who would arrange matters cheaply for me. Unfortunately I have not sufficient funds in hand; I need still about eighty francs. In war-time, alas! it is difficult to borrow."

I had always imagined that it was a habit that was especially indulged in during war-time, and said so.

"On a big scale, yes, but I am talking of a very small matter. It is easier to arrange a loan of millions than of a trifle of eighty or ninety francs."

The would-be financier paused for a few tense moments. Then he recommenced in a more confidential strain.

"Some of you English soldiers, I have heard, are men with private means: is it not so? It is perhaps possible that among your comrades there might be some one willing to advance a small sum—you yourself, perhaps—it would be a secure and profitable investment, quickly repaid—"

"If I get a few days' leave I will go down to Verchey-les-Torteaux and inspect the square-egg hen-farm," I said gravely, "and question the local egg-merchants as to the position and prospects of the business."

The Tavern Acquaintance gave an almost imperceptible shrug to his shoulders, shifted in his seat, and began moodily to roll a cigarette. His interest in me had suddenly died out, but for the sake of appearances he was bound to make a perfunctory show of winding up the conversation he had so laboriously started.

"Ah, you will go to Verchey-les-Torteaux and make inquiries about our farm. And if you find that what I have told you about the square eggs is true, Monsieur, what then?"

"I shall marry your aunt."

BIRDS ON THE WESTERN FRONT

CONSIDERING the enormous economic dislocation which the war operations have caused in the regions where the campaign is raging, there seems to be very little corresponding disturbance in the bird life of the same districts. Rats and mice have mobilized and swarmed into the fighting line, and there has been a partial mobilization of owls, particularly barn owls, following in the wake of the mice, and making laudable efforts to thin out their numbers. What success attends their hunting one cannot estimate; there are always sufficient mice left over to populate one's dug-out and make a parade-ground and race-course of one's face at night. In the matter of nesting accommodation the barn owls are well provided for; most of the still intact barns in the war zone are requisitioned for billeting purposes, but there is a wealth of ruined houses, whole streets and clusters of them, such as can hardly have been available at any previous moment of the world's history since Nineveh and Babylon became humanly desolate. Without human occupation and cultivation there can have been no corn, no refuse, and consequently very few mice, and the owls of Nineveh cannot have enjoyed very good hunting; here in Northern France the owls have desolation and mice at their disposal in unlimited quantities, and as these birds breed in winter as well as in summer, there should be a goodly output of war owlets to cope with the swarming generations of war mice.

Apart from the owls one cannot notice that the campaign is making any marked difference in the bird life of the country-side. The vast flocks of crows and ravens that one expected to find in the neighbourhood of the fighting line are non-existent, which is perhaps rather a pity. The obvious explanation is that the roar and crash and fumes of high explosives have driven the crow tribe in panic from the fighting area; like many obvious explanations, it is not a correct one. The crows of the locality are not attracted to the battlefield, but they certainly are not scared away from it. The rook is normally so gun-shy and nervous where noise is concerned that the sharp banging of a barn door or the report of a toy pistol will sometimes set an entire rookery in commotion; out here I have seen him sedately busy among the refuse heaps of a battered village, with shells bursting at no great distance, and the impatient-sounding, snapping rattle of machine-guns going on all round him; for all the notice that he took he might have been in some peaceful English meadow on a sleepy Sunday afternoon. Whatever else German frightfulness may have done it has not frightened the rook of North-Eastern France; it has made his nerves steadier than they have ever been before, and future generations of small boys, employed in scaring rooks away from the sown crops in this region, will have to invent something in the way of super-frightfulness to achieve their purpose. Crows and magpies are nesting well within the shell-swept area, and over a small beech-copse I once saw a pair of crows engaged in hot combat with a pair of sparrow-hawks, while considerably higher in the sky, but almost directly above them, two Allied battle-planes were engaging an equal number of enemy aircraft.

Unlike the barn owls, the magpies have had their choice of building sites considerably restricted by the ravages of war; the whole avenues of poplars, where they were accustomed to construct their nests, have been blown to bits, leaving nothing but dreary-looking rows of shattered and splintered trunks to show where once they stood. Affection for a particular tree has in one case induced a pair of magpies to build their bulky, domed nest in the battered remnants of a poplar of which so little remained standing that the nest looked almost bigger than the tree; the effect rather suggested an archiepiscopal enthronement taking place in the ruined remains of Melrose Abbey. The magpie, wary and suspicious in his wild state, must be rather intrigued at the change that has come over the erst-while fearsome not-to-be-avoided human, stalking everywhere over the earth as its possessor, who now creeps about in screened and sheltered ways, as chary of showing himself in the open as the shyest of wild creatures.

The buzzard, that earnest seeker after mice, does not seem to be taking any war risks, at least I have never seen one out here, but kestrels hover about all day in the hottest parts of the line, not in the least disconcerted, apparently, when a promising mouse-area suddenly rises in the air in a cascade of black or yellow earth. Sparrow-hawks are fairly numerous, and a mile or two back from the firing line I saw a pair of hawks that I took to be red-legged falcons, circling over the top of an oak-copse. According to investigations made by Russian naturalists, the effect of the war on bird life on the Eastern front has been more marked than it has been over here. "During the first year of the war rooks disappeared, larks no longer sang in the fields, the wild pigeon disappeared also." The skylark in this region has stuck tenaciously to the meadows and crop-lands that have been seamed and bisected with trenches and honeycombed with shell-holes. In the chill, misty hour of gloom that precedes a rainy dawn, when nothing seemed alive except a few wary waterlogged sentries and many scuttling rats, the lark would suddenly dash skyward and pour forth a song of ecstatic jubilation that sounded horribly forced and insincere. It seemed scarcely possible that the bird could carry its insouciance to the length of attempting to rear a brood in that desolate wreckage of shattered clods and gaping shell-holes, but once, having occasion to throw myself down with some abruptness on my face, I found myself nearly on the top of a brood of young larks. Two of them had already been hit by something, and were in rather a battered condition, but the survivors seemed as tranquil and comfortable as the average nestling.

At the corner of a stricken wood (which has had a name made for it in history, but shall be nameless here), at a moment when lyddite and shrapnel and machine-gun fire swept and raked and bespattered that devoted spot as though the artillery of an entire Division had suddenly concentrated on it, a wee hen-chaffinch flitted wistfully to and fro, amid splintered and falling branches that had never a green bough left on them. The wounded lying there, if any of them noticed the small bird, may well have wondered why anything having wings and no pressing reason for remaining should have chosen to stay in such a place. There was a battered orchard alongside the stricken wood, and the probable explanation of the bird's presence was that it had a nest of young ones whom it was too scared to feed, too loyal to desert. Later on, a small flock of chaffinches blundered into the wood, which they were doubtless in the habit of using as a highway to their feeding-grounds; unlike the solitary hen-bird, they made no secret of their desire to get away as fast as their dazed wits would let them. The only other bird I ever saw there was a magpie, flying low over the wreckage of fallen tree-limbs; "one for sorrow," says the old superstition. There was sorrow enough in that wood.

The English gamekeeper, whose knowledge of wild life usually runs on limited and perverted lines, has evolved a sort of religion as to the nervous debility of even the hardiest game birds; according to his beliefs a terrier trotting across a field in which a partridge is nesting, or a mouse-hawking kestrel hovering over the hedge, is sufficient cause to drive the distracted bird off its eggs and send it whirring into the next county.

The partridge of the war zone shows no signs of such sensitive nerves. The rattle and rumble of transport, the constant coming and going of bodies of troops, the incessant rattle of musketry and deafening explosions of artillery, the night-long flare and flicker of star-shells, have not sufficed to scare the local birds away from their chosen feeding grounds, and to all appearances they have not been deterred from raising their broods. Gamekeepers who are serving with the colours might seize the opportunity to indulge in a little useful nature study.

THE GALA PROGRAMME

AN UNRECORDED EPISODE IN ROMAN HISTORY

It was an auspicious day in the Roman Calendar, the birthday of the popular and gifted young Emperor Placidus Superbus. Every one in Rome was bent on keeping high festival, the weather was at its best, and naturally the Imperial Circus was crowded to its fullest capacity. A few minutes before the hour fixed for the commencement of the spectacle a loud fanfare of trumpets proclaimed the arrival of Cæsar, and amid the vociferous acclamations of the multitude the Emperor took his seat in the Imperial Box. As the shouting of the crowd died away an even more thrilling salutation could be heard in the near distance, the angry, impatient roaring and howling of the beasts caged in the Imperial menagerie.

"Explain the programme to me," commanded the Emperor, having beckoned the Master of the Ceremonies to his side.

That eminent official wore a troubled look.

"Gracious Cæsar," he announced, "a most promising and entertaining programme has been devised and prepared for your august approval. In the first place there is to be a chariot contest of unusual brilliancy and interest; three teams that have never hitherto suffered defeat are to contend for the Herculaneum Trophy, together with the purse which your Imperial generosity has been pleased to add. The chances of the competing teams are accounted to be as nearly as possible equal, and there is much wagering among the populace. The black Thracians are perhaps the favourites–"

"I know, I know," interrupted Cæsar, who had listened to exhaustive talk on the same subject all the morning; "what else is there on the programme?"

"The second part of the programme," said the Imperial Official, "consists of a grand combat of wild beasts, specially selected for their strength, ferocity, and fighting qualities. There will appear simultaneously in the arena fourteen Nubian lions and lionesses, five tigers, six Syrian bears, eight Persian panthers, and three North African ditto, a number of wolves and lynxes from the Teutonic forests, and seven gigantic wild bulls from the same region. There will also be wild swine of unexampled savageness, a rhinoceros from the Barbary coast, some ferocious man-apes, and a hyæna, reputed to be mad."

"It promises well," said the Emperor.

"It *promised* well, O Cæsar," said the official dolorously, "it promised marvellously well; but between the promise and the performance a cloud has arisen."

"A cloud? What cloud?" queried Cæsar, with a frown.

"The Suffragetæ," explained the official; "they threaten to interfere with the chariot race."

"I'd like to see them do it!" exclaimed the Emperor indignantly.

"I fear your Imperial wish may be unpleasantly gratified," said the Master of the Ceremonies; "we are taking, of course, every possible precaution, and guarding all the entrances to the arena and the stables with a triple guard; but it is rumoured that at the signal for the entry of the chariots five hundred women will let themselves down with ropes from the public seats and swarm all over the course. Naturally no race could be run under such circumstances; the programme will be ruined."

"On my birthday," said Placidus Superbus, "they would not dare to do such an outrageous thing."

"The more august the occasion, the more desirous they will be to advertise themselves and their cause," said the harassed official; "they do not scruple to make riotous interference even with the ceremonies in the temples."

"Who *are* these Suffragetæ?" asked the Emperor. "Since I came back from my Pannonian expedition I have heard of nothing else but their excesses and demonstrations."

"They are a political sect of very recent origin, and their aim seems to be to get a big share of political authority into their hands. The means they are taking to convince us of their fitness to help in making and administering the laws consist of wild indulgence in tumult, destruction, and defiance of all authority. They have already damaged some of the most historically valuable of our public treasures, which can never be replaced."

"Is it possible that the sex which we hold in such honour and for which we feel such admiration can produce such hordes of Furies?" asked the Emperor.

"It takes all sorts to make a sex," observed the Master of the Ceremonies, who possessed a certain amount of worldly wisdom; "also," he continued anxiously, "it takes very little to upset a gala programme."

"Perhaps the disturbance that you anticipate will turn out to be an idle threat," said the Emperor consolingly.

"But if they should carry out their intention," said the official, "the programme will be utterly ruined."

The Emperor said nothing.

Five minutes later the trumpets rang out for the commencement of the entertainment. A hum of excited anticipation ran through the ranks of the spectators, and final bets on the issue of the great race were hurriedly shouted. The gates leading from the stables were slowly swung open, and a troop of mounted attendants rode round the track to ascertain that everything was clear for the momentous contest. Again the trumpets rang out, and then, before the foremost chariot had appeared, there arose a wild tumult of shouting, laughing, angry protests, and shrill screams of defiance. Hundreds of women were being lowered by their accomplices into the arena. A moment later they were running and dancing in frenzied troops across the track where the chariots were supposed to compete. No team of arena-trained horses would have faced such a frantic mob; the race was clearly an impossibility. Howls of disappointment and rage rose from the spectators, howls of triumph echoed back from the women in possession. The vain efforts of the circus attendants to drive out the invading horde merely added to the uproar and confusion; as fast as the Suffragetæ were thrust away from one portion of the track they swarmed on to another.

The Master of the Ceremonies was nearly delirious from rage and mortification. Placidus Superbus, who remained calm and unruffled as ever, beckoned to him and spoke a word or two in his ear. For the first time that afternoon the sorely tried official was seen to smile.

A trumpet rang out from the Imperial Box; an instant hush fell over the excited throng. Perhaps the Emperor, as a last resort, was going to announce some concession to the Suffragetæ.

"Close the stable gates," commanded the Master of the Ceremonies, "and open all the menagerie dens. It is the Imperial pleasure that the second portion of the programme be taken first."

It turned out that the Master of the Ceremonies had in no wise exaggerated the probable brilliancy of this portion of the spectacle. The wild bulls were really wild, and the hyæna reputed to be mad thoroughly lived up to its reputation.

THE INFERNAL PARLIAMENT

In an age when it has become increasingly difficult to accomplish anything new or original, Bavton Bidderdale interested his generation by dying of a new disease. "We always knew he would do something remarkable one of these days," observed his aunts; "he has justified our belief in him." But there is a section of humanity ever ready to refuse recognition to meritorious achievement, and a large and influential school of doctors asserted their belief that Bidderdale was not really dead. The funeral arrangements had to be held over until the matter was settled one way or the other, and the aunts went provisionally into half-mourning.

Meanwhile, Bidderdale remained in Hell as a guest pending his reception on a more regular footing. "If you are not really supposed to be dead," said the authorities of that region, "we don't want to seem in an indecent hurry to grab you. The theory that Hell is in serious need of population is a thing of the past. Why, to take your family alone, there are any number of Bidderdales on our books, as you may discover later. It is part of our system that relations should be encouraged to live together down here.

From observations made in another world we have abundant evidence that it promotes the ends we have in view. However, while you are a guest we should like you to be treated with every consideration and be shown anything that specially interests you. Of course, you would like to see our Parliament?"

"Have you a Parliament in Hell?" asked Bidderdale in some surprise.

"Only quite recently. Of course we've always had chaos, but not under Parliamentary rules. Now, however, that Parliaments are becoming the fashion, in Turkey and Persia, and I suppose before long in Afghanistan and China, it seemed rather ostentatious to stand outside the movement. That young Fiend just going by is the Member for East Brimstone; he'll be delighted to show you over the institution."

"You will just be in time to hear the opening of a debate," said the Member, as he led Bidderdale through a spacious outer lobby, decorated with frescoes representing the fall of man, the discovery of gold, the invention of playing cards, and other traditionally appropriate subjects. "The Member for Nether Furnace is proposing a motion 'that this House do arrogantly protest to the legislatures of earthly countries against the wrongful and injurious misuse of the word "fiendish," in application to purely human misdemeanours, a misuse tending to create a false and detrimental impression concerning the Infernal Regions.'"

A feature of the Parliament Chamber itself was its enormous size. The space allotted to Members was small and very sparsely occupied, but the public galleries stretched away tier on tier as far as the eye could reach, and were packed to their utmost capacity.

"There seems to be a very great public interest in the debate," exclaimed Bidderdale.

"Members are excused from attending the debates if they so desire," the Fiend proceeded to explain; "it is one of their most highly valued privileges. On the other hand, constituents are compelled to listen throughout to all the speeches. After all, you must remember, we are in Hell."

Bidderdale repressed a shudder and turned his attention to the debate.

"Nothing," the Fiend-Orator was observing, "is more deplorable among the cultured races of the present day than the tendency to identify fiendhood, in the most sweeping fashion, with all manner of disreputable excesses, excesses which can only be alleged against us on the merest legendary evidence. Vices which are exclusively or predominatingly human are unblushingly described as inhuman, and, what is even more contemptible and ungenerous, as fiendish. If one investigates such statements as 'inhuman treatment of pit ponies' or 'fiendish cruelties in the Congo,' so frequently to be heard in our brother Parliaments on earth, one finds accumulative and indisputable evidence that it is the human treatment of pit ponies and Congo natives that is really in question, and that no authenticated case of fiendish agency in these atrocities can be substantiated. It is, perhaps, a minor matter for complaint," continued the orator, "that the human race frequently pays us the doubtful compliment of describing as 'devilish funny' jokes which are neither funny nor devilish."

The orator paused, and an oppressive silence reigned over the vast chamber.

"What is happening?" whispered Bidderdale.

"Five minutes Hush," explained his guide; "it is a sign that the speaker was listened to in silent approval, which is the highest mark of appreciation that can be bestowed in Pandemonium. Let's come into the smoking-room."

"Will the motion be carried?" asked Bidderdale, wondering inwardly how Sir Edward Grey would treat the protest if it reached the British Parliament; an *entente* with the Infernal Regions opened up a fascinating vista, in which the Foreign Secretary's imagination might hopelessly lose itself.

"Carried? Of course not," said the Fiend; "in the Infernal Parliament all motions are necessarily lost."

"In earthly Parliaments nowadays nearly everything is found," said Bidderdale, "including salaries and travelling expenses."

He felt that at any rate he was probably the first member of his family to make a joke in Hell.

"By the way," he added, "talking of earthly Parliaments, have you got the Party system down here?"

"In Hell? Impossible. You see we have no system of rewards. We have specialized so thoroughly on punishments that the other branch has been entirely neglected. And besides, Government by delusion, as you practise it in your Parliament, would be unworkable here. I should be the last person to say anything against temptation, naturally, but we have a proverb down here 'in bait-ing a mouse-trap with cheese, always leave room for the mouse.' Such a party-cry, for instance, as your 'ninepence for fourpence' would be absolutely inoperative; it not only leaves no room for the mouse, it leaves no room for the imagination. You have a saying in your country. I believe, 'there's no fool like a damned fool'; all the fools down here are, necessarily, damned, but—you wouldn't get them to nibble at ninepence for fourpence."

"Couldn't they be scolded and lectured into believing it, as a sort of moral and intellectual duty?" asked Bidderdale.

"We haven't all your facilities," said the Fiend; "we've nothing down here that exactly corresponds to the Master of Elibank."

At this moment Bidderdale's attention was caught by an item on a loose sheet of agenda paper: "Vote on account of special Hells."

"Ah," he said, "I've often heard the expression 'there is a special Hell reserved for such-and-such a type of person.' Do tell me about them."

"I'll show you one in course of preparation," said the Fiend, leading him down the corridor. "This one is designed to accommodate one of the leading playwrights of your nation. You may observe scores of imps engaged in pasting notices of modern British plays into a huge press-cutting book, each under the name of the author, alphabetically arranged. The book will contain nearly half a million notices, I suppose, and it will form the sole literature supplied to this specially doomed individual."

Bidderdale was not altogether impressed.

"Some dramatic authors wouldn't so very much mind spending eternity poring over a book of contemporary press-cuttings," he observed.

The Fiend, laughing unpleasantly, lowered his voice.

"The letter 'S' is missing."

For the first time Bidderdale realized that he was in Hell.

THE ACHIEVEMENT OF THE CAT

In the political history of nations it is no uncommon experience to find States and peoples which but a short time since were in bitter conflict and animosity with each other, settled down comfortably on terms of mutual goodwill and even alliance. The natural history of the social developments of species affords a similar instance in the coming-together of two once warring elements, now represented by civilized man and the domestic cat. The fiercely waged struggle which went on between humans and felines in those far-off days when sabre-toothed tiger and cave lion contended with primeval man, has long ago been decided in favour of the most fitly equipped combatant—the Thing with a Thumb—and the descendants of the dispossessed family are relegated today, for the most part, to the waste lands of jungle and veld, where an existence of self-effacement is the only alternative to extermination. But the *felis catus*, or whatever species was the ancestor of the modern domestic cat (a vexed question at present), by a master-stroke of adaptation avoided the ruin of its race, and "captured" a place in the very keystone of the conqueror's organization. For not as a bond-servant or dependent has this proudest of mammals entered the human fraternity; not as a slave like the beasts of burden, or a humble camp-follower like the dog. The cat is domestic only as far as suits its own ends; it will not be kennelled or harnessed nor suffer any dictation as to its goings out or comings in. Long contact with the human race has developed in it the art of diplomacy, and no Roman Cardinal of mediæval days knew better how to ingratiate himself with his surroundings than a cat with a saucer of cream on its mental horizon. But the social smoothness, the purring innocence, the softness of the velvet paw may be laid aside at a moment's notice, and the sinuous feline may disappear, in deliberate aloofness, to a world of roofs and chimney-stacks, where the human element is distanced and disregarded. Or the innate savage spirit that helped its survival in the bygone days of tooth and claw may be summoned forth from beneath the sleek exterior, and the torture-instinct (common alone to human and feline) may find free play in the death-throes of some luckless bird or rodent. It is, indeed, no small triumph to have combined the untrammelled liberty of primeval savagery with the luxury which only a highly developed civilization can command; to be lapped in the soft stuffs that commerce has gathered from the far ends of the world; to bask in the warmth that labour and industry have dragged from the bowels of the earth; to banquet on the dainties that wealth has bespoken for its table, and withal to be a free son of nature, a mighty hunter, a spiller of life-blood. This is the victory of the cat. But besides the credit of success the cat has other qualities which compel recognition. The animal which the Egyptians worshipped as divine, which the Romans venerated as a symbol of liberty, which Europeans in the ignorant Middle Ages anathematized as an agent of demonology, has displayed to all ages two closely blended characteristics—courage and self-respect. No matter how unfavourable the circumstances, both qualities are always to the fore. Confront a child, a puppy, and a kitten with a sudden danger; the child will turn instinctively for assistance, the puppy will grovel in abject submission to the impending visitation, the kitten will brace its tiny body for a frantic resistance. And dissociate the luxury-loving cat from the atmosphere of social comfort in which it usually contrives to move, and observe it critically under the adverse conditions of civilization—that civilization which can impel a man to the degradation of clothing himself in tawdry ribald garments and capering mountebank dances in the streets for the earning of the few coins that keep him on the respectable, or non-criminal, side of society. The cat of the slums and alleys, starved, outcast, harried, still keeps amid the prowlings of its adversity the bold, free, panther-tread with which it paced of yore the temple courts of Thebes, still displays the self-reliant watchfulness which man has never taught it to lay aside. And when its shifts and clever managings have not sufficed to stave off inexorable fate, when its enemies have proved too strong or too many for its defensive powers, it dies fighting to the last, quivering with the choking rage of mastered resistance, and voicing in its death-yell that agony of bitter remonstrance which human animals, too, have flung at the powers that may be; the last protest against a destiny that might have made them happy—and has not.

THE OLD TOWN OF PSKOFF

Russia at the present crisis of its history not unnaturally suggests to the foreign mind a land pervaded with discontent and disorder and weighed down with depression, and it is certainly difficult to point to any quarter of the Imperial dominions from which troubles of one sort or another are not reported. In the *Novoe Vremya* and other papers a column is now devoted to the chronicling of disorders as regularly as a British news-sheet reports sporting events. It is the more agreeable therefore occasionally to make the acquaintance of another phase of Russian life where the sombreness of political mischance can be momentarily lost sight of or disbelieved in. Perhaps there are few spots in European Russia where one so thoroughly feels that one has passed into a new and unfamiliar atmosphere as the old town of Pskoff, once in its day a very important centre of Russian life. To the average modern Russian a desire to visit Pskoff is an inexplicable mental freak on the part of a foreigner who wishes to see something of the country he is living in; Petersburg, Moscow, Kieff, perhaps, and Nijni-Novgorod, or the Finnish watering-places if you want a country holiday, but why Pskoff? And thus happily an aversion to beaten tracks and localities where inspection is invited and industriously catered for turns one towards the old Great Russian border town, which probably gives as accurate a picture as can be obtained of a mediæval Russian burgh, untouched by Mongol influence, and only slightly affected by Byzantine-imported culture.

The little town has ample charm of situation and structure, standing astride of a bold scarp of land wedged into the fork of two rivers, and retaining yet much of the long lines of ramparts and towers that served for many a hundred years to keep out Pagan Lithuanians and marauding Teuton knights. The powers of Darkness were as carefully guarded against in those old days as more tangible human enemies, and from out of thick clusters of tree-tops there still arise the white walls and green roofs of many churches, monasteries, and bell-towers, quaint and fantastic in architecture, and delightfully harmonious in colouring. Steep winding streets lead down from the rampart-girt heart of the town to those parts which lie along the shores of the twin rivers, and two bridges, one a low, wide, wooden structure primitively planted on piles, give access to the further banks, where more towers and monasteries, with other humbler buildings, continue the outstraggling span of the township. On the rivers lie barges with high masts painted in wonderful bands of scarlet, green, white, and blue, topped with gilded wooden pennons figured somewhat like a child's rattle, and fluttering strips of bunting at their ends. Up in the town one sees on all sides quaint old doorways, deep archways, wooden gable-ends, railed staircases, and a crowning touch of pleasing colour in the sage green or dull red of the roofs. But it is strangest of all to find a human population in complete picturesque harmony with its rich old-world setting. The scarlet or blue blouses that are worn by the working men in most Russian towns give way here to a variety of gorgeous-tinted garments, and the women-folk are similarly gay in their apparel, so that streets and wharves and market-place glow with wonderfully effective groupings of colour. Mulberry, orange, dull carmine, faded rose, hyacinth purple, greens, and lilacs and rich blues mingle their hues on shirts and shawls, skirts and breeches and waistbands. Nature competing with Percy Anderson was the frivolous comment that came to one's mind, and certainly a mediæval crowd could scarcely have been more effectively staged. And the business of a town in which it seemed always market day went forward with an air of contented absorption on the part of the inhabitants. Strings of primitively fashioned carts went to and from the riverside, the horses wearing their bits for the most part hung negligently under the chin, a fashion that prevails in many parts of Russia and Poland.

Quaint little booths line the sides of some of the steeper streets, and here wooden toys and earthenware pottery of strange local patterns are set out for sale. On the broad market-place women sit gossiping by the side of large baskets of strawberries, one or two long-legged foals sprawl at full stretch under the shade of their parental market carts, and an extremely contented pig pursues his leisurely way under the guardianship of an elderly dame robed in a scheme of orange, mulberry, and white that would delight the soul of a colourist. A stalwart peasant strides across the uneven cobbles, leading his plough-horse, and carrying on his shoulder a small wooden plough, with iron-tipped shares, that must date back to some stage of agriculture that the West has long left behind. Down in the buoyant waters of the Velikaya, the larger of the two rivers, youths and men are disporting themselves and staider washer-women are rinsing and smacking piles of many-hued garments. It is pleasant to swim well out into the stream of the river, and, with one's chin on a level with the wide stretch of water, take in a "trout's-eye view" of the little town, ascending in tiers of wharfage, trees, grey ramparts, more trees, and clustered roofs, with the old cathedral of the Trinity poised guardian-like above the crumbling walls of the Kremlin. The cathedral, on closer inspection, is a charming specimen of genuine old Russian architecture, full of rich carvings and aglow with scarlet pigment and gilded scrollwork, and stored with yet older relics or pseudo-relics of local hero-saints and hero-princes who helped in their day to make the history of the

Pskoff Commonwealth. After an hour or two spent among these tombs and ikons and memorials of dead Russia, one feels that some time must elapse before one cares to enter again the drearily magnificent holy places of St. Petersburg, with their depressing *nouveau riche* atmosphere, their price-list tongued attendants, and general lack of historic interest.

The heart knoweth its own bitterness, and maybe the Pskoffskie, amid their seeming contentment and self-absorption, have their own hungerings for a new and happier era of national life. But the stranger does not ask to see so far; he is thankful to have found a picturesque and apparently well-contented corner of a weary land, a land "where distress seems like a bird of passage that has hurt its wing and cannot fly away."

CLOVIS ON THE ALLEGED ROMANCE OF BUSINESS

"It is the fashion nowadays," said Clovis, "to talk about the romance of Business. There isn't such a thing. The romance has all been the other way, with the idle apprentice, the truant, the runaway, the individual who couldn't be bothered with figures and book-keeping and left business to look after itself. I admit that a grocer's shop is one of the most romantic and thrilling things that I have ever happened on, but the romance and thrill are centred in the groceries, not the grocer. The citron and spices and nuts and dates, the barrelled anchovies and Dutch cheeses, the jars of *caviar* and the chests of tea, they carry the mind away to Levantine coast towns and tropic shores, to the Old World wharfs and quays of the Low Countries, to dusty Astrachan and far Cathay; if the grocer's apprentice has any romance in him it is not a business education he gets behind the grocer's counter, it is a standing invitation to dream and to wander, and to remain poor. As a child such places as South America and Asia Minor were brought painstakingly under my notice, the names of their principal rivers and the heights of their chief mountain peaks were committed to my memory, and I was earnestly enjoined to consider them as parts of the world that I lived in; it was only when I visited a large well-stocked grocer's shop that I realized that they certainly existed. Such galleries of romance and fascination are not bequeathed to us by the business man; he is only the dull custodian, who talks glibly of Spanish olives and Rangoon rice, a Spain that he has never known or wished to know, a Rangoon that he has never imagined or could imagine. It was the unledgered wanderer, the careless-hearted seafarer, the aimless outcast, who opened up new trade routes, tapped new markets, brought home samples or cargoes of new edibles and unknown condiments. It was they who brought the glamour and romance to the threshold of business life, where it was promptly reduced to pounds, shillings, and pence; invoiced, double-entried, quoted, written-off, and so forth; most of those terms are probably wrong, but a little inaccuracy sometimes saves tons of explanation.

"On the other side of the account there is the industrious apprentice, who grew up into the business man, married early and worked late, and lived, thousands and thousands of him, in little villas outside big towns. He is buried by the thousand in Kensal Green and other large cemeteries; any romance that was ever in him was buried prematurely in shop and warehouse and office. Whenever I feel in the least tempted to be business-like or methodical or even decently industrious I go to Kensal Green and look at the graves of those who died in business."

THE COMMENTS OF MOUNG KA

MOUNG KA, cultivator of rice and philosophic virtues, sat on the raised platform of his cane-built house by the banks of the swiftly flowing Irrawaddy. On two sides of the house there was a bright-green swamp, which stretched away to where the uncultivated jungle growth began. In the bright-green swamp, which was really a rice-field when you looked closely at it, bitterns and pond-herons and elegant cattle-egrets stalked and peered with the absorbed air of careful and conscientious reptile-hunters, who could never forget that, while they were undoubtedly useful, they were also distinctly decorative. In the tall reed growth by the riverside grazing buffaloes showed in patches of dark slaty blue, like plums fallen amid long grass, and in the tamarind trees that shaded Moung Ka's house the crows, restless, raucous-throated, and much-too-many, kept up their incessant afternoon din, saying over and over again all the things that crows have said since there were crows to say them.

Moung Ka sat smoking his enormous green-brown cigar, without which no Burmese man, woman, or child seems really complete, dispensing from time to time instalments of worldly information for the benefit and instruction of his two companions. The steamer which came up-river from Mandalay thrice a week brought Moung Ka a Rangoon news-sheet, in which the progress of the world's events was set forth in telegraphic messages and commented on in pithy paragraphs. Moung Ka, who read these things and retailed them as occasion served to his friends and neighbours, with philosophical additions of his own, was held in some esteem locally as a political thinker; in Burma it is possible to be a politician without ceasing to be a philosopher.

His friend Moung Thwa, dealer in teakwood, had just returned down-river from distant Bhamo, where he had spent many weeks in dignified, unhurried chaffering with Chinese merchants; the first place to which he had naturally turned his steps, bearing with him his betel-box and fat cigar, had been the raised platform of Moung Ka's cane-built house under the tamarind trees. The youthful Moung Shoogalay, who had studied in the foreign schools at Mandalay and knew many English words, was also of the little group that sat listening to Moung Ka's bulletin of the world's health and ignoring the screeching of the crows.

There had been the usual preliminary talk of timber and the rice market and sundry local matters, and then the wider and remoter things of life came under review.

"And what has been happening away from here?" asked Moung Thwa of the newspaper reader.

"Away from here" comprised that considerable portion of the world's surface which lay beyond the village boundaries.

"Many things," said Moung Ka reflectively, "but principally two things of much interest and of an opposite nature. Both, however, concern the action of Governments."

Moung Thwa nodded his head gravely, with the air of one who reverenced and distrusted all Governments.

"The first thing, of which you may have heard on your journeyings," said Moung Ka, "is an act of the Indian Government, which has annulled the not-long-ago accomplished partition of Bengal."

"I heard something of this," said Moung Thwa, "from a Madrassi merchant on the boat journey. But I did not learn the reasons that made the Government take this step. Why was the partition annulled?"

"Because," said Moung Ka, "it was held to be against the wishes of the greater number of the people of Bengal. Therefore the Government made an end of it."

Moung Thwa was silent for a moment. "Is it a wise thing the Government has done?" he asked presently.

"It is a good thing to consider the wishes of a people," said Moung Ka. "The Bengalis may be a people who do not always wish what is best for them. Who can say? But at least their wishes have been taken into consideration, and that is a good thing."

"And the other matter of which you spoke?" questioned Moung Thwa, "the matter of an opposite nature."

"The other matter," said Moung Ka, "is that the British Government has decided on the partition of Britain. Where there has been one Parliament and one Government there are to be two Parliaments and two Governments, and there will be two treasuries and two sets of taxes."

Moung Thwa was greatly interested at this news.

"And is the feeling of the people of Britain in favour of this partition?" he asked. "Will they not dislike it, as the people of Bengal disliked the partition of their Province?"

"The feeling of the people of Britain has not been consulted, and will not be consulted," said Moung Ka; "the Act of Partition will pass through one Chamber where the Government rules supreme, and the other Chamber can only delay it a little while, and then it will be made into the Law of the Land."

"But is it wise not to consult the feeling of the people?" asked Moung Thwa.

"Very wise," answered Moung Ka, "for if the people were consulted they would say 'No,' as they have always said when such a decree was submitted to their opinion, and if the people said 'No' there would be an end of the matter, but also an end of the Government. Therefore, it is wise for the Government to shut its ears to what the people may wish."

"But why must the people of Bengal be listened to and the people of Britain not listened to?" asked Moung Thwa; "surely the partition of their country affects them just as closely. Are their opinions too silly to be of any weight?"

"The people of Britain are what is called a Democracy," said Moung Ka.

"A Democracy?" questioned Moung Thwa. "What is that?"

"A Democracy," broke in Moung Shoogalay eagerly, "is a community that governs itself according to its own wishes and interests by electing accredited representatives who enact its laws and supervise and control their administration. Its aim and object is government of the community in the interests of the community."

"Then," said Moung Thwa, turning to his neighbour, "if the people of Britain are a Democracy—"

"I never said they were a Democracy," interrupted Moung Ka placidly.

"Surely we both heard you!" exclaimed Moung Thwa.

"Not correctly," said Moung Ka; "I said they are what is called a Democracy."

II
THE NOVELS

The Unbearable Bassington

CHAPTER I

FRANCESCA BASSINGTON sat in the drawing-room of her house in Blue Street, W., regaling herself and her estimable brother Henry with China tea and small cress sandwiches. The meal was of that elegant proportion which, while ministering sympathetically to the desires of the moment, is happily reminiscent of a satisfactory luncheon and blessedly expectant of an elaborate dinner to come.

In her younger days Francesca had been known as the beautiful Miss Greech; at forty, although much of the original beauty remained, she was just dear Francesca Bassington. No one would have dreamed of calling her sweet, but a good many people who scarcely knew her were punctilious about putting in the "dear."

Her enemies, in their honester moments, would have admitted that she was svelte and knew how to dress, but they would have agreed with her friends in asserting that she had no soul. When one's friends and enemies agree on any particular point they are usually wrong. Francesca herself, if pressed in an unguarded moment to describe her soul, would probably have described her drawing-room. Not that she would have considered that the one had stamped the impress of its character on the other, so that close scrutiny might reveal its outstanding features, and even suggest its hidden places, but because she might have dimly recognized that her drawing-room was her soul.

Francesca was one of those women towards whom Fate appears to have the best intentions and never to carry them into practice. With the advantages put at her disposal she might have been expected to command a more than average share of feminine happiness. So many of the things that make for fretfulness, disappointment and discouragement in a woman's life were removed from her path that she might well have been considered the fortunate Miss Greech, or later, lucky Francesca Bassington. And she was not of the perverse band of those who make a rock-garden of their souls by dragging into them all the stony griefs and unclaimed troubles they can find lying around them. Francesca loved the smooth ways and pleasant places of life; she liked not merely to look on the bright side of things, but to live there and stay there. And the fact that things had, at one time and another, gone badly with her and cheated her of some of her early illusions made her cling the closer to such good fortune as remained to her now that she seemed to have reached a calmer period of her life. To undiscriminating friends she appeared in the guise of a rather selfish woman, but it was merely the selfishness of one who had seen the happy and unhappy sides of life and wished to enjoy to the utmost what was left to her of the former. The vicissitudes of fortune had not soured her, but they had perhaps narrowed her in the sense of making her concentrate much of her sympathies on things that immediately pleased and amused her, or that recalled and perpetuated the pleasing and successful incidents of other days. And it was her drawing-room in particular that enshrined the memorials or tokens of past and present happiness.

Into that comfortable quaint-shaped room of angles and bays and alcoves had sailed, as into a harbour, those precious personal possessions and trophies that had survived the buffetings and storms of a not very tranquil married life. Wherever her eyes might turn she saw the embodied results of her successes, economies, good luck, good management or good taste. The battle had more than once gone against her, but she had somehow always contrived to save her baggage train, and her complacent gaze could roam over object after object that represented the spoils of victory or the salvage of honourable defeat. The delicious bronze Fremiet on the mantelpiece had been the outcome of a Grand Prix sweepstake of many years ago; a group of Dresden figures of some considerable value had been bequeathed to her by a discreet admirer, who had added death to his other kindnesses; another group had been a self-bestowed present, purchased in blessed and unfading memory of a wonderful nine-days' bridge winnings at a country-house party. There were old Persian and Bokharan rugs and Worcester tea-services of glowing colour, and little treasures of antique silver that each enshrined a history or a memory in addition to its own intrinsic value. It amused her at times to think of the bygone craftsmen and artificers who had hammered and wrought and woven in far distant countries and ages, to produce the wonderful and beautiful things that had come, one way and another, into her possession. Workers in the studios of medieval Italian towns and of later Paris, in the bazaars of Bagdad and of Central Asia, in old-time English workshops and German factories, in all manner of queer hidden corners where craft secrets were jealously guarded, nameless unremembered men and men whose names were world-renowned and deathless.

And above all her other treasures, dominating in her estimation every other object that the room contained, was the great Van der Meulen that had come from her father's home as part of her wedding dowry. It fitted exactly into the central wall panel above the narrow buhl cabinet, and filled exactly its right space in the composition and balance of the room. From wherever you sat it seemed to confront you as the dominating feature of its surroundings. There was a pleasing serenity about the great pompous battle scene with its solemn courtly warriors bestriding their heavily prancing steeds, grey or skewbald or dun, all gravely in earnest, and yet somehow conveying the impression that their campaigns were but vast serious picnics arranged in the grand manner. Francesca could not imagine the drawing-room without the crowning complement of the stately well-hung picture, just as she could not imagine herself in any other setting than this house in Blue Street with its crowded Pantheon of cherished household gods.

And herein sprouted one of the thorns that obtruded through the rose-leaf damask of what might otherwise have been Francesca's peace of mind. One's happiness always lies in the future rather than in the past. With due deference to an esteemed lyrical authority one may safely say that a sorrow's crown of sorrow is anticipating unhappier things. The house in Blue Street had been left to her by her old friend Sophie Chetrof, but only until such time as her niece Emmeline Chetrof should marry, when it was to pass to her as a wedding present. Emmeline was now seventeen and passably good-looking, and four or five years were all that could be safely allotted to the span of her continued spinsterhood. Beyond that period lay chaos, the wrenching asunder of Francesca from the sheltering habitation that had grown to be her soul. It is true that in imagination she had built herself a bridge across the chasm, a bridge of a single span. The bridge in question was her schoolboy son Comus, now being educated somewhere in the southern counties, or rather one should say the bridge consisted of the possibility of his eventual marriage with Emmeline, in which case Francesca saw herself still reigning, a trifle squeezed and incommoded perhaps, but still reigning in the house in Blue Street. The Van der Meulen would still catch its requisite afternoon light in its place of honour, the Fremiet and the Dresden and Old Worcester would continued undisturbed in their accustomed niches. Emmeline could have the Japanese snuggery, where Francesca sometimes drank her after-dinner coffee, as a separate drawing-room, where she could put her own things. The details of the bridge structure had all been carefully thought out. Only—it was an unfortunate circumstance that Comus should have been the span on which everything balanced.

Francesca's husband had insisted on giving the boy that strange Pagan name, and had not lived long enough to judge as to the appropriateness, or otherwise, of its significance. In seventeen years and some odd months Francesca had had ample opportunity for forming an opinion concerning her son's characteristics. The spirit of mirthfulness which one associates with the name certainly ran riot in the boy, but it was a twisted wayward sort of mirth of which Francesca herself could seldom see the humorous side. In her brother Henry, who sat eating small cress sandwiches as solemnly as though they had been ordained in some immemorial Book of Observances, fate had been undisguisedly kind to her. He might so easily have married some pretty helpless little woman, and lived at Notting Hill Gate, and been the father of a long string of pale, clever, useless children, who would have had birthdays and the sort of illnesses that one is expected to send grapes to, and who would have painted fatuous objects in a South Kensington manner as Christmas offerings to an aunt whose cubic space for lumber was limited. Instead of committing these unbrotherly actions, which are so frequent in family life that they might almost be called brotherly, Henry had married a woman who had both money and a sense of repose, and their one child had the brilliant virtue of never saying anything which even its parents could consider worth repeating. Then he had gone into Parliament, possibly with the idea of making his home life seem less dull; at any rate it redeemed his career from insignificance, for no man whose death can produce the item "another by-election" on the news posters can be wholly a nonentity. Henry, in short, who might have been an embarrassment and a handicap, had chosen rather to be a friend and counsellor, at times even an emergency bank balance; Francesca on her part, with partiality which a clever and lazily-inclined woman often feels for a reliable fool, not only sought his counsel but frequently followed it. When convenient, moreover, she repaid his loans.

Against this good service on the part of Fate in providing her with Henry for a brother, Francesca could well set the plaguy malice of the destiny that had given her Comus for a son. The boy was one of those untamable young lords of misrule that frolic and chafe themselves through nursery and preparatory and public-school days with the utmost allowance of storm and dust and dislocation and the least possible amount of collar-work, and come somehow with a laugh through a series of catastrophes that has reduced every one else concerned to tears or Cassandra-like forebodings. Sometimes they sober down in after-life and become uninteresting, forgetting that they were ever lords of anything; sometimes Fate plays royally into their hands, and they do great things in a spacious manner, and are thanked by Parliaments and the Press and acclaimed by gala-day crowds. But in most cases their tragedy begins when they leave school and turn themselves loose in a world that has grown too civilized and too crowded and too empty to have any place for them. And they are very many.

Henry Greech had made an end of biting small sandwiches, and settled down like a dust-storm refreshed, to discuss one of the fashionably prevalent topics of the moment, the prevention of destitution.

"It is a question that is only being nibbled at, smelt at, one might say, at the present moment," he observed, "but it is one that will have to engage our serious attention and consideration before long. The first thing that we shall have to do is to get out of the dilettante and academic way of approaching it. We must collect and assimilate hard facts. It is a subject that ought to appeal to all thinking minds, and yet, you know, I find it surprisingly difficult to interest people in it."

Francesca made some monosyllabic response, a sort of sympathetic grunt which was meant to indicate that she was, to a certain extent, listening and appreciating. In reality she was reflecting that Henry possibly found it difficult to interest people in any topic that he enlarged on. His talents lay so thoroughly in the direction of being uninteresting, that even as an eye-witness of the massacre of St. Bartholomew he would probably have infused a flavour of boredom into his descriptions of the event.

"I was speaking down in Leicestershire the other day on this subject," continued Henry, "and I pointed out at some length a thing that few people ever stop to consider——"

Francesca went over immediately but decorously to the majority that will not stop to consider.

"Did you come across any of the Barnets when you were down there?" she interrupted; "Eliza Barnet is rather taken up with all those subjects."

In the propagandist movements of Sociology, as in other arenas of life and struggle, the fiercest competition and rivalry is frequently to be found between closely allied types and species. Eliza Barnet shared many of Henry Greech's political and social views, but she also shared his fondness for pointing things out at some length; there had been occasions when she had extensively occupied the strictly limited span allotted to the platform oratory of a group of speakers of whom Henry Greech had been an impatient unit. He might see eye to eye with her on the leading questions of the day, but he persistently wore mental blinkers as far as her estimable qualities were concerned, and the mention of her name was a skillful lure drawn across the trail of his discourse; if Francesca had to listen to his eloquence on any subject she much preferred that it should be a disparagement of Eliza Barnet rather than the prevention of destitution.

"I've no doubt she means well," said Henry, "but it would be a good thing if she could be induced to keep her own personality a little more in the background, and not to imagine that she is the necessary mouthpiece of all the progressive thought in the countryside. I fancy Canon Besomley must have had her in his mind when he said that some people came into the world to shake empires and others to move amendments."

Francesca laughed with genuine amusement.

"I suppose she is really wonderfully well up in all the subjects she talks about," was her provocative comment.

Henry grew possibly conscious of the fact that he was being drawn out on the subject of Eliza Barnet, and he presently turned on to a more personal topic.

"From the general air of tranquility about the house I presume Comus has gone back to Thaleby," he observed.

"Yes," said Francesca, "he went back yesterday. Of course, I'm very fond of him, but I bear the separation well. When he's here it's rather like having a live volcano in the house, a volcano that in its quietest moments asks incessant questions and uses strong scent."

"It is only a temporary respite," said Henry; "in a year or two he will be leaving school, and then what?"

Francesca closed her eyes with the air of one who seeks to shut out a distressing vision. She was not fond of looking intimately at the future in the presence of another person, especially when the future was draped in doubtfully auspicious colours.

"And then what?" persisted Henry.

"Then I suppose he will be upon my hands."

"Exactly."

"Don't sit there looking judicial. I'm quite ready to listen to suggestions if you've any to make."

"In the case of any ordinary boy," said Henry, "I might make lots of suggestions as to the finding of suitable employment. From what we know of Comus it would be rather a waste of time for either of us to look for jobs which he wouldn't look at when we'd got them for him."

"He must do something," said Francesca.

"I know he must; but he never will. At least, he'll never stick to anything. The most hopeful thing to do with him will be to marry him to an heiress. That would solve the financial side of his problem. If he had unlimited money at his disposal, he might go into the wilds somewhere and shoot big game. I never know what the big game have done to deserve it, but they do help to deflect the destructive energies of some of our social misfits."

Henry, who never killed anything larger or fiercer than a trout, was scornfully superior on the subject of big game shooting.

Francesca brightened at the matrimonial suggestion. "I don't know about an heiress," she said reflectively. "There's Emmeline Chetrof, of course. One could hardly call her an heiress, but she's got a comfortable little income of her own, and I suppose something more will come to her from her grandmother. Then, of course, you know this house goes to her when she marries."

"That would be very convenient," said Henry, probably following a line of thought that his sister had trodden many hundreds of times before him. "Do she and Comus hit it off at all well together?"

"Oh, well enough in boy and girl fashion," said Francesca. "I must arrange for them to see more of each other in future. By the way, that little brother of hers that she dotes on, Lancelot, goes to Thaleby this term. I'll write and tell Comus to be specially kind to him; that will be a sure way to Emmeline's heart. Comus has been made a prefect, you know. Heaven knows why."

"It can only be for prominence in games," sniffed Henry; "I think we may safely leave work and conduct out of the question."

Comus was not a favourite with his uncle.

Francesca had turned to her writing cabinet and was scribbling a letter to her son in which the delicate health, timid disposition and other inevitable attributes of the new boy were brought to his notice, and commended to his care. When she had sealed and stamped the envelope Henry uttered a belated caution.

"Perhaps on the whole it would be wiser to say nothing about the boy to Comus. He doesn't always respond to directions, you know."

Francesca did know, and already was more than half of her brother's opinion; but the woman who can sacrifice a clean unspoiled penny stamp is probably yet unborn.

CHAPTER II

Lancelot Chetrof stood at the end of a long bare passage, restlessly consulting his watch and fervently wishing himself half an hour older with a certain painful experience already registered in the past; unfortunately it still belonged to the future, and what was still more horrible, to the immediate future. Like many boys new to a school he had cultivated an unhealthy passion for obeying rules and requirements, and his zeal in this direction had proved his undoing. In his hurry to be doing two or three estimable things at once he had omitted to study the notice-board in more than a perfunctory fashion and had thereby missed a football practice specially ordained for newly-joined boys. His fellow-juniors of a term's longer standing had graphically enlightened him as to the inevitable consequences of his lapse; the dread which attaches to the unknown was, at any rate, deleted from his approaching doom, though at the moment he felt scarcely grateful for the knowledge placed at his disposal with such lavish solicitude.

"You'll get six of the very best, over the back of a chair," said one.

"They'll draw a chalk line across you, of course, you know," said another.

"A chalk line?"

"Rather. So that every cut can be aimed exactly at the same spot. It hurts much more that way."

Lancelot tried to nourish a wan hope that there might be an element of exaggeration in this uncomfortably realistic description.

Meanwhile in the prefects' room at the other end of the passage, Comus Bassington and a fellow-prefect sat also waiting on time, but in a mood of far more pleasurable expectancy. Comus was one of the most junior of the prefect caste, but by no means the least well known, and outside the masters' common-room he enjoyed a certain fitful popularity, or at any rate admiration. At football he was too erratic to be a really brilliant player, but he tackled as if that act of bringing his man headlong to the ground was in itself a sensuous pleasure, and his weird swear-words whenever he got hurt were eagerly treasured by those who were fortunate enough to hear them. At athletics in general he was a showy performer, and although new to the functions of a prefect he had already established a reputation as an effective and artistic caner. In appearance he exactly fitted his fanciful Pagan name. His large green-grey eyes seemed for ever asparkle with goblin mischief and the joy of revelry, and the curved lips might have been those of some wickedly-laughing faun; one almost expected to see embryo horns fretting the smoothness of his sleek dark hair. The chin was firm, but one looked in vain for a redeeming touch of ill-temper in the handsome, half-mocking, half-petulant face. With a strain of sourness in him Comus might have been leavened into something creative and masterful; fate had fashioned him with a certain whimsical charm, and left him all unequipped for the greater purposes of life. Perhaps no one would have called him a lovable character, but in many respects he was adorable; in all respects he was certainly damned.

Rutley, his companion of the moment, sat watching him and wondering, from the depths of a very ordinary brain, whether he liked or hated him; it was easy to do either.

"It's not really your turn to cane," he said.

"I know it's not," said Comus, fingering a very serviceable-looking cane as lovingly as a pious violinist might handle his Strad. "I gave Greyson some mint-chocolate to let me toss whether I caned or him, and I won. He was rather decent over it and let me have half the chocolate back."

The droll lightheartedness which won Comus Bassington such measures of popularity as he enjoyed among his fellows did not materially help to endear him to the succession of masters with whom he came in contact during the course of his schooldays. He amused and interested such of them as had the saving grace of humour at their disposal, but if they sighed when he passed from their immediate responsibility it was a sigh of relief rather than of regret. The more enlightened and experienced of them realized that he was something outside the scope of the things that they were called upon to deal with. A man who has been trained to cope with storms, to foresee their coming, and to minimize their consequences, may be pardoned if he feels a certain reluctance to measure himself against a tornado.

Men of more limited outlook and with a correspondingly larger belief in their own powers were ready to tackle the tornado had time permitted.

"I think I could tame young Bassington if I had your opportunities," a form-master once remarked to a colleague whose House had the embarrassing distinction of numbering Comus among its inmates.

"Heaven forbid that I should try," replied the housemaster.

"But why?" asked the reformer.

"Because Nature hates any interference with her own arrangements, and if you start in to tame the obviously untamable you are taking a fearful responsibility on yourself."

"Nonsense; boys are Nature's raw material."

"Millions of boys are. There are just a few, and Bassington is one of them, who are Nature's highly finished product when they are in the schoolboy stage, and we, who are supposed to be moulding raw material, are quite helpless when we come in contact with them."

"But what happens to them when they grow up?"

"They never do grow up," said the housemaster; "that is their tragedy. Bassington will certainly never grow out of his present stage."

"Now you are talking in the language of Peter Pan," said the form-master.

"I am not thinking in the manner of Peter Pan," said the other. "With all reverence for the author of that masterpiece I should say he had a wonderful and tender insight into the child mind and knew nothing whatever about boys. To make only one criticism on that particular work, can you imagine a lot of British boys, or boys of any country that one knows of, who would stay contentedly playing children's games in an underground cave when there were wolves and pirates and Red Indians to be had for the asking on the other side of the trap door?"

The form-master laughed. "You evidently think that the 'Boy who would not grow up' must have been written by a 'grown-up who could never have been a boy.' Perhaps that is the meaning of the 'Never-never land.' I daresay you're right in your criticism, but I don't agree with you about Bassington. He's a handful to deal with, as any one knows who has come in contact with him, but if one's hands weren't full with a thousand and one other things I hold to my opinion that he could be tamed."

And he went his way, having maintained a form-master's inalienable privilege of being in the right.

In the prefects' room, Comus busied himself with the exact position of a chair planted out in the middle of the floor.

"I think everything's ready," he said.

Rutley glanced at the clock with the air of a Roman elegant in the Circus, languidly awaiting the introduction of an expected Christian to an expectant tiger.

"The kid is due in two minutes," he said.

"He'd jolly well better not be late," said Comus.

Comus had gone through the mill of many scorching castigations in his earlier schooldays, and was able to appreciate to the last ounce the panic that must be now possessing his foredoomed victim, probably at this moment hovering miserably outside the door. After all, that was part of the fun of the thing, and most things had their amusing side if one knows where to look for it.

There was a knock at the door, and Lancelot entered in response to a hearty friendly summons to "come in."

"I've come to be caned," he said breathlessly; adding by way of identification, "my name's Chetrof."

"That's quite bad enough in itself," said Comus, "but there is probably worse to follow. You are evidently keeping something back from us."

"I missed a footer practice," said Lancelot.

"Six," said Comus briefly, picking up his cane.

"I didn't see the notice on the board," hazarded Lancelot as a forlorn hope.

"We are always pleased to listen to excuses, and our charge is two extra cuts. That will be eight. Get over."

And Comus indicated the chair that stood in sinister isolation in the middle of the room. Never had an article of furniture seemed more hateful in Lancelot's eyes. Comus could well remember the time when a chair stuck in the middle of a room had seemed to him the most horrible of manufactured things.

"Lend me a piece of chalk," he said to his brother prefect.

Lancelot ruefully recognized the truth of the chalk-line story.

Comus drew the desired line with an anxious exactitude which he would have scorned to apply to a diagram of Euclid or a map of the Russo-Persian frontier.

"Bend a little more forward," he said to the victim, "and much tighter. Don't trouble to look pleasant, because I can't see your face anyway. It may sound unorthodox to say so, but this is going to hurt you much more than it will hurt me."

There was a carefully measured pause, and then Lancelot was made vividly aware of what a good cane can be made to do in really efficient hands. At the second cut he projected himself hurriedly off the chair.

"Now I've lost count," said Comus; "we shall have to begin all over again. Kindly get back into the same position. If you get down again before I've finished Rutley will hold you over and you'll get a dozen."

Lancelot got back on to the chair, and was re-arranged to the taste of his executioner. He stayed there somehow or other while Comus made eight accurate and agonizingly effective shots at the chalk line.

"By the way," he said to his gasping and gulping victim when the infliction was over, "you said Chetrof, didn't you? I believe I've been asked to be kind to you. As a beginning you can clean out my study this afternoon. Be awfully careful how you dust the old china. If you break any don't come and tell me, but just go and drown yourself somewhere; it will save you from a worse fate."

"I don't know where your study is," said Lancelot between his chokes.

"You'd better find it or I shall have to beat you, really hard this time. Here, you'd better keep this chalk in your pocket, it's sure to come in handy later on. Don't stop to thank me for all I've done, it only embarrasses me."

As Comus hadn't got a study Lancelot spent a feverish half-hour in looking for it, incidentally missing another footer practice.

"Everything is very jolly here," wrote Lancelot to his sister Emmeline. "The prefects can give you an awful hot time if they like, but most of them are rather decent. Some are Beasts. Bassington is a prefect, though only a junior one. He is the Limit as Beasts go. At least, I think so."

Schoolboy reticence went no further, but Emmeline filled in the gaps for herself with the lavish splendour of feminine imagination. Francesca's bridge went crashing into the abyss.

CHAPTER III

On the evening of a certain November day, two years after the events heretofore chronicled, Francesca Bassington steered her way through the crowd that filled the rooms of her friend Serena Golackly, bestowing nods of vague recognition as she went, but with eyes that were obviously intent on focusing one particular figure.

Parliament had pulled its energies together for an Autumn Session, and both political Parties were fairly well represented in the throng. Serena had a harmless way of inviting a number of more or less public men and women to her house, and hoping that if you left them together long enough they would constitute a *salon*. In pursuance of the same instinct she planted the flower borders at her weekend cottage retreat in Surrey with a large mixture of bulbs, and called the result a Dutch garden. Unfortunately, though you may bring brilliant talkers into your home, you cannot always make them talk brilliantly, or even talk at all; what is worse you cannot restrict the output of those starling-voiced dullards who seem to have, on all subjects, so much to say that was well worth leaving unsaid. One group that Francesca passed was discussing a Spanish painter, who was forty-three, and had painted thousands of square yards of canvas in his time, but of whom no one in London had heard till a few months ago; now the starling-voices seemed determined that one should hear of very little else. Three women knew how his name was pronounced, another always felt that she must go into a forest and pray whenever she saw his pictures, another had noticed that there were always pomegranates in his later compositions, and a man with an indefensible collar knew what the pomegranates "meant." "What I think so splendid about him," said a stout lady in a loud challenging voice, "is the way he defies all the conventions of art while retaining all that the conventions stand for." "Ah, but have you noticed–" put in the man with the atrocious collar, and Francesca pushed desperately on, wondering dimly as she went what people found so unsupportable in the affliction of deafness. Her progress was impeded for a moment by a couple engaged in earnest and voluble discussion of some smouldering question of the day; a thin spectacled young man with the receding forehead that so often denotes advanced opinions, was talking to a spectacled young woman with a similar type of forehead, and exceedingly untidy hair. It was her ambition in life to be taken for a Russian girl-student, and she had spent weeks of patient research in trying to find out exactly where you put the tea-leaves in a samovar. She had once been introduced to a young Jewess from Odessa, who had died of pneumonia the following week; the experience, slight as it was, constituted the spectacled young lady an authority on all things Russian in the eyes of her immediate set.

"Talk is helpful, talk is needful," the young man was saying, "but what we have got to do is to lift the subject out of the furrow of indisciplined talk and place it on the threshing-floor of practical discussion."

The young woman took advantage of the rhetorical full-stop to dash in with the remark which was already marshalled on the tip of her tongue.

"In emancipating the serfs of poverty we must be careful to avoid the mistakes which Russian bureaucracy stumbled into when liberating the serfs of the soil."

She paused in her turn for the sake of declamatory effect, but recovered her breath quickly enough to start afresh on level terms with the young man, who had jumped into the stride of his next sentence.

"They got off to a good start that time," said Francesca to herself; "I suppose it's the Prevention of Destitution they're hammering at. What on earth would become of these dear good people if any one started a crusade for the prevention of mediocrity?"

Midway through one of the smaller rooms, still questing for an elusive presence, she caught sight of some one that she knew, and the shadow of a frown passed across her face. The object of her faintly signalled displeasure was Courtenay Youghal, a political spur-winner who seemed absurdly youthful to a generation that had never heard of Pitt. It was Youghal's ambition—or perhaps his hobby—to infuse into the greyness of modern political life some of the colour of Disraelian dandyism, tempered with the correctness of Anglo-Saxon taste, and supplemented by the flashes of wit that were inherent from the Celtic strain in him. His success was only a half-measure. The public missed in him that touch of blatancy which it looks for in its rising public men; the decorative smoothness of his chestnut-golden hair, and the lively sparkle of his epigrams were counted to him for good, but the restrained sumptuousness of his waistcoats and cravats was as wasted efforts. If he had habitually smoked cigarettes in a pink coral mouthpiece, or worn spats of Mackenzie tartan, the great heart of the voting-man, and the gush of the paragraph-makers might have been unreservedly his. The art of public life consists to a great extent of knowing exactly where to stop and going a bit farther.

It was not Youghal's lack of political sagacity that had brought the momentary look of disapproval into Francesca's face. The fact was that Comus, who had left off being a schoolboy and was now a social problem, had lately enrolled himself among the young politician's associates and admirers, and as the boy knew and cared nothing about politics, and merely copied Youghal's waistcoats, and, less successfully, his conversation, Francesca felt herself justified in deploring the intimacy. To a woman who dressed well on comparatively nothing a year it was an anxious experience to have a son who dressed sumptuously on absolutely nothing.

The cloud that had passed over her face when she caught sight of the offending Youghal was presently succeeded by a smile of gratified achievement, as she encountered a bow of recognition and welcome from a portly middle-aged gentleman, who seemed genuinely anxious to include her in the rather meagre group that he had gathered about him.

"We were just talking about my new charge," he observed genially, including in the "we" his somewhat depressed-looking listeners, who in all human probability had done none of the talking. "I was just telling them, and you may be interested to hear this——"

Francesca, with Spartan stoicism, continued to wear an ingratiating smile, though the character of the deaf adder that stoppeth her ear and will not hearken, seemed to her at that moment a beautiful one.

Sir Julian Jull had been a member of a House of Commons distinguished for its high standard of well-informed mediocrity, and had harmonized so thoroughly with his surroundings that the most attentive observer of Parliamentary proceedings could scarcely have told even on which side of the House he sat. A baronetcy bestowed on him by the Party in power had at least removed that doubt; some weeks later he had been made Governor of some West Indian dependency, whether as a reward for having accepted the baronetcy, or as an application of a theory that West Indian islands get the Governors they deserve, it would have been hard to say. To Sir Julian the appointment was, doubtless, one of some importance; during the span of his Governorship the island might possibly be visited by a member of the Royal Family, or at the least by an earthquake, and in either case his name would get into the papers. To the public the matter was one of absolute indifference; "who is he and where is it?" would have correctly epitomized the sum total of general information on the personal and geographical aspects of the case.

Francesca, however, from the moment she had heard of the likelihood of the appointment, had taken a deep and lively interest in Sir Julian. As a Member of Parliament he had not filled any very pressing social want in her life, and on the rare occasions when she took tea on the Terrace of the House she was wont to lapse into rapt contemplation of St. Thomas's Hospital whenever she saw him within bowing distance. But as Governor of an island he would, of course, want a private secretary, and as a friend and colleague of Henry Greech, to whom he was indebted for many little acts of political support (they had once jointly drafted an amendment which had been ruled out of order), what was more natural and proper than that he should let his choice fall on Henry's nephew Comus? While privately doubting whether the boy would make the sort of secretary that any public man would esteem as a treasure, Henry was thoroughly in agreement with Francesca as to the excellence and desirability of an arrangement which would transplant that troublesome young animal from the too restricted and conspicuous area that centres in the parish of St. James's to some misty corner of the British dominion overseas. Brother and sister had conspired to give an elaborate and at the same time cozy little luncheon to Sir Julian on the very day that his appointment was officially announced, and the question of the secretaryship had been mooted and sedulously fostered as occasion permitted, until all that was now needed to clinch the matter was a formal interview between His Excellency and Comus. The boy had from the first shown very little gratification at the prospect of his deportation. To live on a remote shark-girt island, as he expressed it, with the Jull family as his chief social mainstay, and Sir Julian's conversation as a daily item of his existence, did not inspire him with the same degree of enthusiasm as was displayed by his mother and uncle, who, after all, were not making the experiment. Even the necessity for an entirely new outfit did not appeal to his imagination with the force that might have been expected. But, however lukewarm his adhesion to the project might be, Francesca and her brother were clearly determined that no lack of deft persistence on their part should endanger its success. It was for the purpose of reminding Sir Julian of his promise to meet Comus at lunch on the following day, and definitely settle the matter of the secretaryship, that Francesca was now enduring the ordeal of a long harangue of the value of the West Indian group as an Imperial asset.

Other listeners dexterously detached themselves one by one, but Francesca's patience outlasted even Sir Julian's flow of commonplaces, and her devotion was duly rewarded by a renewed acknowledgment of the lunch engagement and its purpose. She pushed her way back through the throng of starling-voiced chatterers fortified by a sense of well-earned victory. Dear Serena's absurd *salons* served some good purpose after all.

Francesca was not an early riser, and her breakfast was only just beginning to mobilize on the breakfast-table next morning when a copy of *The Times,* sent by special messenger from her brother's house, was brought up to her room. A heavy margin of blue penciling drew her attention to a prominently-printed letter which bore the ironical heading: "Julian Jull, Proconsul." The matter of the letter was a cruel disinterment of some fatuous and forgotten speeches made by Sir Julian to his constituents not many years ago, in which the value of some of our Colonial possessions, particularly certain West Indian islands, was decried in a medley of pomposity, ignorance and amazingly cheap humour. The extracts given sounded weak and foolish enough, taken by themselves, but the writer of the letter had interlarded them with comments of his own, which sparkled with an ironical brilliance that was Cervantes-like in its polished cruelty. Remembering her ordeal of the previous evening Francesca permitted herself a certain feeling of amusement as she read the merciless stabs inflicted on the newly-appointed Governor; then she came to the signature at the foot of the letter, and the laughter died out of her eyes. "Comus Bassington" stared at her from above a thick layer of blue pencil lines marked by Henry Greech's shaking hand.

Comus could no more have devised such a letter than he could have written an Episcopal charge to the clergy of any given diocese. It was obviously the work of Courtenay Youghal, and Comus, for a palpable purpose of his own, had wheedled him into forgoing for once the pride of authorship in a clever piece of political raillery, and letting his young friend stand sponsor instead. It was a daring stroke, and there could be no question as to its success; the secretaryship and the distant shark-girt island faded away into the horizon of impossible things. Francesca, forgetting the golden rule of strategy which enjoins a careful choosing of ground and opportunity before entering on hostilities, made straight for the bathroom door, behind which a lively din of splashing betokened that Comus had at least begun his toilet.

"You wicked boy, what have you done?" she cried reproachfully.

"Me washee," came a cheerful shout; "me washee from the neck all the way down to the merrythought, and now washee down from the merrythought to—"

"You have ruined your future. *The Times* has printed that miserable letter with your signature."

A loud squeal of joy came from the bath. "Oh, Mummy! Let me see!"

There were sounds as of a sprawling dripping body clambering hastily out of the bath. Francesca fled. One cannot effectively scold a moist nineteen-year-old boy clad only in a bath-towel and a cloud of steam.

Another messenger arrived before Francesca's breakfast was over. This one brought a letter from Sir Julian Jull, excusing himself from fulfilment of the luncheon engagement.

CHAPTER IV

Francesca prided herself on being able to see things from other people's points of view, which meant, as it usually does, that she could see her own point of view from various aspects. As regards Comus, whose doings and non-doings bulked largely in her thoughts at the present moment, she had mapped out in her mind so clearly what his outlook in life ought to be, that she was peculiarly unfitted to understand the drift of his feelings or the impulses that governed them. Fate had endowed her with a son; in limiting the endowment to a solitary offspring Fate had certainly shown a moderation which Francesca was perfectly willing to acknowledge and be thankful for; but then, as she pointed out to a certain complacent friend of hers who cheerfully sustained an endowment of half a dozen male offsprings and a girl or two, her one child was Comus. Moderation in numbers was more than counterbalanced in his case by extravagance in characteristics.

Francesca mentally compared her son with hundreds of other young men whom she saw around her, steadily, and no doubt happily, engaged in the process of transforming themselves from nice boys into useful citizens. Most of them had occupations, or were industriously engaged in qualifying for such; in their leisure moments they smoked reasonably-priced cigarettes, went to the cheaper seats at music-halls, watched an occasional cricket match at Lord's with apparent interest, saw most of the world's spectacular events through the medium of the cinematograph, and were wont to exchange at parting seemingly superfluous injunctions to "be good." The whole of Bond Street and many of the tributary throughfares of Piccadilly might have been swept off the face of modern London without in any way interfering with the supply of their daily wants. They were doubtless dull as acquaintances, but as sons they would have been eminently restful. With a growing sense of irritation Francesca compared these deserving young men with her own intractable offspring, and wondered why Fate should have singled her out to be the parent of such a vexatious variant from a comfortable and desirable type. As far as remunerative achievement was concerned, Comus copied the insouciance of the field lily with a dangerous fidelity. Like his mother he looked round with wistful irritation at the example afforded by contemporary youth, but he concentrated his attention exclusively on the richer circles of his acquaintance, young men who bought cars and polo ponies as unconcernedly as he might purchase a carnation for his buttonhole, and went for trips to Cairo or the Tigris valley with less difficulty and finance-stretching than he encountered in contriving a week-end at Brighton.

Gaiety and good looks had carried Comus successfully and, on the whole, pleasantly, through schooldays and a recurring succession of holidays; the same desirable assets were still at his service to advance him along his road, but it was a disconcerting experience to find that they could not be relied on to go all distances at all times. In an animal world, and a fiercely competitive animal world at that, something more was needed than the decorative *abandon* of the field lily, and it was just that something more which Comus seemed unable or unwilling to provide on his own account; it was just the lack of that something more which left him sulking with Fate over the numerous breakdowns and stumbling-blocks that held him up on what he expected to be a triumphal or, at any rate, unimpeded progress.

Francesca was, in her own way, fonder of Comus than of any one else in the world, and if he had been browning his skin somewhere east of Suez she would probably have kissed his photograph with genuine fervour every night before going to bed; the appearance of a cholera scare or rumour of native rising in the columns of her daily news-sheet would have caused her a flutter of anxiety, and she would have mentally likened herself to a Spartan mother sacrificing her best-beloved on the altar of State necessities. But with the best-beloved installed under her roof, occupying an unreasonable amount of cubic space, and demanding daily sacrifices instead of providing the raw material for one, her feelings were tinged with irritation rather than affection. She might have forgiven Comus generously for misdeeds of some gravity committed in another continent, but she could never overlook the fact that out of a dish of five plovers' eggs he was certain to take three. The absent may be always wrong, but they are seldom in a position to be inconsiderate.

Thus a wall of ice had grown up gradually between mother and son, a barrier across which they could hold converse, but which gave a wintry chill even to the sparkle of their lightest words. The boy had the gift of being irresistibly amusing when he chose to exert himself in that direction, and after a long series of moody or jangling meal-sittings he would break forth into a torrential flow of small talk, scandal and malicious anecdote, true or more generally invented, to which Francesca listened with a relish and appreciation that was all the more flattering from being so unwillingly bestowed.

"If you chose your friends from a rather more reputable set you would be doubtless less amusing, but there would be compensating advantages."

Francesca snapped the remark out at lunch one day when she had been betrayed into a broader smile than she considered the circumstances of her attitude towards Comus warranted.

"I'm going to move in quite decent society tonight," replied Comus with a pleased chuckle; "I'm going to meet you and Uncle Henry and heaps of nice dull God-fearing people at dinner."

Francesca gave a little gasp of surprise and annoyance.

"You don't mean to say Caroline has asked you to dinner tonight?" she said; "and of course without telling me. How exceedingly like her!"

Lady Caroline Benaresq had reached that age when you can say and do what you like in defiance of people's most sensitive feelings and most cherished antipathies. Not that she had waited to attain her present age before pursuing that line of conduct; she came of a family whose individual members went through life, from the nursery to the grave, with as much tact and consideration as a cactus-hedge might show in going through a crowded bathing tent. It was a compensating mercy that they disagreed rather more among themselves than they did with the outside world; every known variety and shade of religion and politics had been pressed into the family service to avoid the possibility of any agreement on the larger essentials of life, and such unlooked-for happenings as the Home Rule schism, the Tariff-Reform upheaval and the Suffragette crusade were thankfully seized on as furnishing occasion for further differences and subdivisions. Lady Caroline's favourite scheme of entertaining was to bring jarring and antagonistic elements into close contact and play them remorselessly one against the other. "One gets much better results under those circumstances," she used to observe, "than by asking people who wish to meet each other. Few people talk as brilliantly to impress a friend as they do to depress an enemy."

She admitted that her theory broke down rather badly if you applied it to Parliamentary debates. At her own dinner table its success was usually triumphantly vindicated.

"Who else is to be there?" Francesca asked, with some pardonable misgiving.

"Courtenay Youghal. He'll probably sit next to you, so you'd better think out a lot of annihilating remarks in readiness. And Elaine de Frey."

"I don't think I've heard of her. Who is she?"

"Nobody in particular, but rather nice looking in a solemn sort of way, and almost indecently rich."

"Marry her" was the advice which sprang to Francesca's lips but she choked it back with a salted almond, having a rare perception of the fact that words are sometimes given to us to defeat our purposes.

"Caroline has probably marked her down for Toby or one of the grand-nephews," she said carelessly; "a little money would be rather useful in that quarter, I imagine."

Comus tucked in his underlip with just the shade of pugnacity that she wanted to see.

An advantageous marriage was so obviously the most sensible

course for him to embark on that she scarcely dared to hope that he would seriously entertain it; yet there was just a chance that if he got as far as the flirtation stage with an attractive (and attracted) girl who was also an heiress, the sheer perversity of his nature might carry him on to more definite courtship, if only from the desire to thrust other more genuinely enamoured suitors into the background. It was a forlorn hope; so forlorn that the idea even crossed her mind of throwing herself on the mercy of her *bête noire*, Courtenay Youghal, and trying to enlist the influence which he seemed to possess over Comus for the purpose of furthering her hurriedly conceived project. Anyhow, the dinner promised to be more interesting than she had originally anticipated.

Lady Caroline was a professed Socialist in politics, chiefly, it was believed, because she was thus enabled to disagree with most of the Liberals and Conservatives, and all the Socialists of the day. She did not permit her Socialism, however, to penetrate below stairs; her cook and butler had every encouragement to be Individualists. Francesca, who was a keen and intelligent food critic, harboured no misgivings as to her hostess's kitchen and cellar departments; some of the human side-dishes at the feast gave her more ground for uneasiness. Courtenay Youghal, for instance, would probably be brilliantly silent; her brother Henry would almost certainly be the reverse.

The dinner party was a large one, and Francesca arrived late with little time to take preliminary stock of the guests; a card with the name "Miss de Frey," immediately opposite her own place at the other side of the table, indicated, however, the whereabouts of the heiress. It was characteristic of Francesca that she first carefully read the menu from end to end, and then indulged in an equally careful, though less open, scrutiny of the girl who sat opposite her, the girl who was nobody in particular, but whose income was everything that could be desired. She was pretty in a restrained nut-brown fashion, and had a look of grave reflective calm that probably masked a speculative unsettled temperament. Her pose, if one wished to be critical, was just a little too elaborately careless. She wore such excellently set rubies with that indefinable air of having more at home that is so difficult to improvise. Francesca was distinctly pleased with her survey.

"You seem interested in your *vis-à-vis*," said Courtenay Youghal.

"I almost think I've seen her before," said Francesca; "her face seems familiar to me."

"The narrow gallery at the Louvre: attributed to Leonardo da Vinci," said Youghal.

"Of course," said Francesca, her feelings divided between satisfaction at capturing an elusive impression and annoyance that Youghal should have been her helper. A stronger tinge of annoyance possessed her when she heard the voice of Henry Greech raised in painful prominence at Lady Caroline's end of the table.

"I called on the Trudhams yesterday," he announced; "it was their Silver Wedding, you know, at least the day before was. Such lots of silver presents, quite a show. Of course there were a great many duplicates, but still, very nice to have. I think they were very pleased to get so many."

"We must not grudge them their show of presents after their twenty-five years of married life," said Lady Caroline gently; "it is the silver lining to their cloud."

A third of the guests present were related to the Trudhams.

"Lady Caroline is beginning well," murmured Courtenay Youghal.

"I should hardly call twenty-five years of married life a cloud," said Henry Greech lamely.

"Don't let's talk about married life," said a tall handsome woman, who looked like some modern painter's conception of the goddess Bellona; "it's my misfortune to write eternally about husbands and wives and their variants. My public expects it of me. I do so envy journalists who can write about plagues and strikes and Anarchist plots, and other pleasing things, instead of being tied down to one stale old topic."

"Who is that woman and what has she written?" Francesca asked Youghal; she dimly remembered having seen her at one of Serena Golackly's gatherings, surrounded by a little court of admirers.

"I forget her name; she has a villa at San Remo or Mentone, or somewhere where one does have villas, and plays an extraordinary good game of bridge. Also she has the reputation, rather rare in your sex, of being a wonderfully sound judge of wine."

"But what has she written?"

"Oh, several novels of the thinnish ice order. Her last one, *The Woman who wished it was Wednesday*, has been banned at all the libraries. I expect you've read it."

"I don't see why you should think so," said Francesca coldly.

"Only because Comus lent me your copy yesterday," said Youghal. He threw back his handsome head and gave her a sidelong glance of quizzical amusement. He knew that she hated his intimacy with Comus, and he was secretly rather proud of his influence over the boy, shallow and negative though he knew it to be. It had been, on his part, an unsought intimacy, and it would probably fall to pieces the moment he tried seriously to take up the *rôle* of mentor. The fact that Comus's mother openly disapproved of the friendship gave it perhaps its chief interest in the young politician's eyes.

Francesca turned her attention to her brother's end of the table. Henry Greech had willingly availed himself of the invitation to leave the subject of married life, and had launched forthwith into the equally well-worn theme of current politics. He was not a person who was in much demand for public meetings, and the House showed no great impatience to hear his views on the topics of the moment; its impatience, indeed, was manifested rather in the opposite direction. Hence he was prone to unburden himself of accumulated political wisdom as occasion presented itself—sometimes, indeed, to assume an occasion that was hardly visible to the naked intelligence.

"Our opponents are engaged in a hopelessly uphill struggle, and they know it," he chirruped defiantly; "they've become possessed, like the Gadarene swine, with a whole legion of——"

"Surely the Gadarene swine went downhill?" put in Lady Caroline in a gently inquiring voice.

Henry Greech hastily abandoned simile and fell back on platitude and the safer kinds of fact.

Francesca did not regard her brother's views of statecraft either in the light of gospel or revelation; as Comus once remarked, they more usually suggested exodus. In the present instance she found distraction in a renewed scrutiny of the girl opposite her, who seemed to be only moderately interested in the conversational efforts of the diners on either side of her. Comus, who was looking and talking his best, was sitting at the farther end of the table, and Francesca was quick to notice in which direction the girl's glances were continually straying. Once or twice the eyes of the young people met and a swift flush of pleasure and a half-smile that spoke of good understanding came to the heiress's face. It did not need the gift of the traditional intuition of her sex to enable

Francesca to guess that the girl with the desirable banking account was already considerably attracted by the lively young Pagan who had, when he cared to practise it, such an art of winning admiration. For the first time for many, many months Francesca saw her son's prospects in a rose-coloured setting, and she began, unconsciously, to wonder exactly how much wealth was summed up in the expressive label "almost indecently rich." A wife with a really large fortune and a correspondingly big dower of character and ambition, might, perhaps, succeed in turning Comus's latent energies into a groove which would provide him, if not with a career, at least with an occupation, and the young serious face opposite looked as if its owner lacked neither character nor ambition. Francesca's speculations took a more personal turn. Out of the well-filled coffers with which her imagination was toying, an inconsiderable sum might eventually be devoted to the leasing, or even perhaps the purchase of, the house in Blue Street when the present convenient arrangement should have come to an end, and Francesca and the Van der Meulen would not be obliged to seek fresh quarters.

A woman's voice, talking in a discreet undertone on the other side of Courtenay Youghal, broke in on her bridge-building.

"Tons of money and really very presentable. Just the wife for a rising young politician. Go in and win her before she's snapped up by some fortune hunter."

Youghal and his instructress in worldly wisdom were looking straight across the table at the Leonardo da Vinci girl with the grave reflective eyes and the over-emphasized air of repose. Francesca felt a quick throb of anger against her matchmaking neighbour; why, she asked herself, must some women, with no end or purpose of their own to serve, except the sheer love of meddling in the affairs of others, plunge their hands into plots and schemings of this sort, in which the happiness of more than one person was concerned? And more clearly than ever she realized how thoroughly she detested Courtenay Youghal. She had disliked him as an evil influence, setting before her son an example of showy ambition that he was not in the least likely to follow, and providing him with a model of extravagant dandyism that he was only too certain to copy. In her heart she knew that Comus would have embarked just as surely on his present course of idle self-indulgence if he had never known of the existence of Youghal, but she chose to regard that young man as her son's evil genius, and now he seemed likely to justify more than ever the character she had fastened on to him. For once in his life Comus appeared to have an idea of behaving sensibly and making some use of his opportunities, and almost at the same moment Courtenay Youghal arrived on the scene as a possible and very dangerous rival. Against the good looks and fitful powers of fascination that Comus could bring into the field, the young politican could match half a dozen dazzling qualities which would go far to recommend him in the eyes of a woman of the world, still more in those of a young girl in search of an ideal. Good-looking in his own way, if not on such showy lines as Comus, always well turned-out, witty, self-confident without being bumptious, with a conspicuous Parliamentary career alongside him, and Heaven knew what else in front of him, Courtenay Youghal certainly was not a rival whose chances could be held very lightly. Francesca laughed bitterly to herself as she remembered that a few hours ago she had entertained the idea of begging for his good offices in helping on Comus's wooing. One consolation, at least, she found for herself: if Youghal really meant to step in and try and cut out his young friend, the latter at any rate had snatched a useful start. Comus had mentioned Miss de Frey at luncheon that day, casually and dispassionately; if the subject of the dinner guests had not come up he would probably not have mentioned her at all. But they were obviously already very good friends. It was part and parcel of the state of domestic tension at Blue Street that Francesca should only have come to know of this highly interesting heiress by an accidental sorting of guests at a dinner party.

Lady Caroline's voice broke in on her reflections; it was a gentle purring voice, that possessed an uncanny quality of being able to make itself heard down the longest dinner table.

"The dear Archdeacon is getting *so* absent-minded. He read a list of box-holders for the opera as the First Lesson the other Sunday, instead of the families and lots of the tribes of Israel that entered Canaan. Fortunately no one noticed the mistake."

CHAPTER V

On a conveniently secluded bench facing the Northern Pheasantry in the Zoological Society's Gardens, Regent's Park, Courtenay Youghal sat immersed in mature flirtation with a lady, who, though certainly young in fact and appearance, was some four or five years his senior. When he was a schoolboy of sixteen, Molly McQuade had personally conducted him to the Zoo and stood him dinner afterwards at Kettner's, and whenever the two of them happened to be in town on the anniversary of that bygone festivity they religiously repeated the programme in its entirety. Even the menu of the dinner was adhered to as nearly as possible; the original selection of food and wine that schoolboy exuberance, tempered by schoolboy shyness, had pitched on those many years ago, confronted Youghal on those occasions, as a drowning man's past life is said to rise up and parade itself in his last moment of consciousness.

The flirtation which was thus perennially restored to its old-time footing owed its longevity more to the enterprising solicitude of Miss McQuade than to any conscious sentimental effort on the part of Youghal himself. Molly McQuade was known to her neighbours in a minor hunting shire as a hard-riding conventionally unconventional type of young woman, who came naturally into the classification, "a good sort." She was just sufficiently good-looking, sufficiently reticent about her own illnesses, when she had any, and sufficiently appreciative of her neighbours' gardens, children and hunters to be generally popular. Most men liked her, and the percentage of women who disliked her was not inconveniently high. One of these days, it was assumed, she would marry a brewer or a Master of Otter Hounds, and, after a brief interval, be known to the world as the mother of a boy or two at Malvern or some similar seat of learning. The romantic side of her nature was altogether unguessed by the countryside.

Her romances were mostly in serial form, and suffered perhaps in fervour from their disconnected course what they gained in length of days. Her affectionate interest in the several young men who figured in her affairs of the heart was perfectly honest, and certainly made no attempt either to conceal their separate existences, or to play them off one against the other. Neither could it be said that she was a husband hunter; she had made up her mind what sort of man she was likely to marry, and her forecast did not differ very widely from that formed by her local acquaintances. If her married life were eventually to turn out a failure, at least she looked forward to it with very moderate expectations. Her love affairs she put on a very different footing, and apparently they were the all-absorbing element in her life. She possessed the happily constituted temperament which enables a man or woman to be a "pluralist," and to observe the sage precaution of not putting all one's eggs into one basket. Her demands were not exacting; she required of her affinity that he should be young, good-looking, and at least moderately amusing; she would have preferred him to be invariably faithful, but, with her own example before her, she was prepared for the probability, bordering on certainty, that he would be nothing of the sort. The philosophy of the "Garden of Kama" was the compass by which she steered her barque, and thus far, if she had encountered some storms and buffeting, she had at least escaped being either ship-wrecked or becalmed.

Courtenay Youghal had not been designed by Nature to fulfil the *rôle* of an ardent or devoted lover, and he scrupulously respected the limits which Nature had laid down. For Molly, however, he had a certain responsive affection. She had always obviously admired him, and at the same time she never beset him with crude flattery; the principal reason why the flirtation had stood the test of so many years was the fact that it only flared into active existence at convenient intervals. In an age when the telephone has undermined almost every fastness of human privacy, and the sanctity of one's seclusion depends often on the ability for tactful falsehood shown by a club page-boy, Youghal was duly appreciative of the circumstance that his lady fair spent a large part of the year pursuing foxes, in lieu of pursuing him. Also the honestly admitted fact that, in her human hunting, she rode after more than one quarry, made the inevitable break-up of the affair a matter to which both could look forward without a sense of coming embarrassment and recrimination. When the time for gathering ye rosebuds should be over, neither of them could accuse the other of having wrecked his or her entire life. At the most they would only have disorganized a week-end.

On this particular afternoon, when old reminiscences had been gone through, and the intervening gossip of past months duly recounted, a lull in the conversation made itself rather obstinately felt. Molly had already guessed that matters were about to slip into a new phase; the affair had reached maturity long ago, and a new phase must be in the nature of a wane.

"You're a clever brute," she said suddenly, with an air of affectionate regret; "I always knew you'd get on in the House, but I hardly expected you to come to the front so soon."

"I'm coming to the front," admitted Youghal judicially; "the problem is, shall I be able to stay there? Unless something happens in the financial line before long, I don't see how I'm to stay in Parliament at all. Economy is out of the question. It would open people's eyes, I fancy, if they knew how little I exist on as it is. And I'm living so far beyond my income that we may almost be said to be living apart."

"It will have to be a rich wife, I suppose," said Molly slowly; "that's the worst of success, it imposes so many conditions. I rather knew, from something in your manner, that you were drifting that way."

Youghal said nothing in the way of contradiction; he gazed steadfastly at the aviary in front of him as though exotic pheasants were for the moment the most absorbing study in the world. As a matter of fact, his mind was centred on the image of Elaine de Frey, with her clear untroubled eyes and her Leonardo da Vinci air. He was wondering whether he was likely to fall into a frame of mind concerning her which would be in the least like falling in love.

"I shall mind horribly," continued Molly, after a pause, "but, of course, I have always known that something of the sort would have to happen one of these days. When a man goes into politics he can't call his soul his own, and I suppose his heart becomes an impersonal possession in the same way."

"Most people who know me would tell you that I haven't got a heart," said Youghal.

"I've often felt inclined to agree with them," said Molly; "and then, now and again, I think you have a heart tucked away somewhere."

"I hope I have," said Youghal, "because I'm trying to break to you the fact that I think I'm falling in love with somebody."

Molly McQuade turned sharply to look at her companion, who still fixed his gaze on the pheasant run in front of him.

"Don't tell me you're losing your head over somebody useless, some one without money," she said; "I don't think I could stand that."

For the moment she feared that Courtenay's selfishness might have taken an unexpected turn, in which ambition had given way to the fancy of the hour; he might be going to sacrifice his Parliamentary career for a life of stupid lounging in momentarily attractive company. He quickly undeceived her.

"She's got heaps of money."

Molly gave a grunt of relief. Her affection for Courtenay had produced the anxiety which underlay her first question; a natural jealousy prompted the next one.

"Is she young and pretty and all that sort of thing, or is she just a good sort with a sympathetic manner and nice eyes? As a rule that's the kind that goes with a lot of money."

"Young and quite good-looking in her way, and a distinct style of her own. Some people would call her beautiful. As a political hostess I should think she'd be splendid. I imagine I'm rather in love with her."

"And is she in love with you?"

Youghal threw back his head with the slight assertive movement that Molly knew and liked.

"She's a girl who I fancy would let judgment influence her a lot. And without being stupidly conceited I think I may say she might do worse than throw herself away on me. I'm young and quite good-looking, and I'm making a name for myself in the House; she'll be able to read all sorts of nice and horrid things about me in the papers at breakfast-time. I can be brilliantly amusing at times, and I understand the value of silence; there is no fear that I shall ever degenerate into that fearsome thing—a cheerful talkative husband. For a girl with money and social ambitions I should think I was rather a good thing."

"You are certainly in love, Courtenay," said Molly, "but it's the old love and not a new one. I'm rather glad. I should have hated to have you head-over-heels in love with a pretty woman, even for a short time. You'll be much happier as it is. And I'm going to put all my feelings in the background, and tell you to go in and win. You've got to marry a rich woman, and if she's nice and will make a good hostess, so much the better for everybody. You'll be happier in your married life than I shall be in mine, when it comes; you'll have other interests to absorb you. I shall just have the garden and dairy and nursery and lending library, as like as two peas to all the gardens and dairies and nurseries for hundreds of miles round. You won't care for your wife enough to be worried every time she has a finger-ache, and you'll like her well enough to be pleased to meet her sometimes at your own house. I shouldn't wonder if you were quite happy. She will probably be miserable, but any woman who married you would be."

There was a short pause; they were both staring at the pheasant cages. Then Molly spoke again, with the swift nervous tone of a general who is hurriedly altering the disposition of his forces for a strategic retreat.

"When you are safely married and honeymooned and all that sort of thing, and have put your wife through her paces as a political hostess, some time, when the House isn't sitting, you must come down by yourself, and do a little hunting with us. Will you? It won't be quite the same as old times, but it will be something to look forward to when I'm reading the endless paragraphs about your fashionable political wedding."

"You're looking forward pretty far," laughed Youghal; "the lady may take your view as to the probable unhappiness of a future shared with me, and I may have to content myself with penurious political bachelorhood. Anyhow, the present is still with us. We dine at Kettner's tonight, don't we?"

"Rather," said Molly, "though it will be more or less a throat-lumpy feast as far as I am concerned. We shall have to drink to the health of the future Mrs. Youghal. By the way, it's rather characteristic of you that you haven't told me who she is, and of me that I haven't asked. And now, like a dear boy, trot away and leave me. I haven't got to say good-bye to you yet, but I'm going to take a quiet farewell of the Pheasantry. We've had some jolly good talks, you and I, sitting on this seat, haven't we? And I know, as well as I know anything, that this is the last of them. Eight o'clock tonight, as punctually as possible."

She watched his retreating figure with eyes that grew slowly misty; he had been such a jolly comely boy-friend, and they had had such good times together. The mist deepened on her lashes as she looked round at the familiar rendezvous where they had so often kept tryst since the day when they had first come there together, he a schoolboy and she but lately out of her teens. For the moment she felt herself in the thrall of a very real sorrow.

Then, with the admirable energy of one who is only in town for a fleeting fortnight, she raced away to have tea with a world-faring naval admirer at his club. Pluralism is a merciful narcotic.

CHAPTER VI

ELAINE DE FREY sat at ease—at bodily ease, at any rate—in a low wicker chair placed under the shade of a group of cedars in the heart of a stately spacious garden that had almost made up its mind to be a park. The shallow stone basin of an old fountain, on whose wide ledge a leaden-moulded otter for ever preyed on a leaden salmon, filled a conspicious place in the immediate foreground. Around its rim ran an inscription in Latin, warning mortal man that time flows as swiftly as water and exhorting him to make the most of his hours; after which piece of Jacobean moralizing it set itself shamelessly to beguile all who might pass that way into an abandonment of contemplative repose. On all sides of it a stretch of smooth turf spread away, broken up here and there by groups of dwarfish chestnut and mulberry trees, whose leaves and branches cast a laced pattern of shade beneath them. On one side the lawn sloped gently down to a small lake, whereon floated a quartet of swans, their movements suggestive of a certain mournful listlessness, as though a weary dignity of caste held them back from the joyous bustling life of the lesser waterfowl. Elaine liked to imagine that they reembodied the souls of unhappy boys who had been forced by family interests to become high ecclesiastical dignitaries and had grown prematurely Right Reverend. A low stone balustrade fenced part of the shore of the lake, making a miniature terrace above its level, and here roses grew in a rich multitude. Other rose bushes, carefully pruned and tended, formed little oases of colour and perfume amid the restful green of the sward, and in the distance the eye caught the variegated blaze of a many-hued hedge of rhododendron. With these favoured exceptions flowers were hard to find in this well-ordered garden; the misguided tyranny of staring geranium beds and beflowered archways leading to nowhere, so dear to the suburban gardener, found no expression here. Magnificent Amherst pheasants, whose plumage challenged and almost shamed the peacock on his own ground, stepped to and fro over the emerald turf with the assured self-conscious pride of reigning sultans. It was a garden where summer seemed a part-proprietor rather than a hurried visitor.

By the side of Elaine's chair under the shadow of the cedars a wicker table was set out with the paraphernalia of afternoon tea. On some cushions at her feet reclined Courtenay Youghal, smoothly preened and youthfully elegant, the personification of decorative repose; equally decorative, but with the showy restlessness of a dragonfly, Comus disported his flannelled person over a considerable span of the available foreground.

The intimacy existing between the two young men had suffered no immediate dislocation from the circumstance that they were tacitly paying court to the same lady. It was an intimacy founded not in the least on friendship or community of tastes and ideas, but owed its existence to the fact that each was amused and interested by the other. Youghal found Comus, for the time being at any rate, just as amusing and interesting as a rival for Elaine's favour as he had been in the *rôle* of scapegrace boy-about-town; Comus for his part did not wish to lose touch with Youghal, who among other attractions possessed the recommendation of being under the ban of Comus's mother. She disapproved, it is true, of a great many of her son's friends and associates, but this particular one was a special and persistent source of irritation to her from the fact that he figured prominently and more or less successfully in the public life of the day. There was something peculiarly exasperating in reading a brilliant and incisive attack on the Government's rash handling of public expenditure delivered by a young man who encouraged her son in every imaginable extravagance. The actual extent of Youghal's influence over the boy was of the slightest; Comus was quite capable of deriving encouragement to rash outlay and frivolous conversation from an anchorite or an East End parson if he had been thrown into close companionship with such an individual. Francesca, however, exercised a mother's privilege in assuming her son's bachelor associates to be industrious in labouring to achieve his undoing. Therefore the young politician was a source of unconcealed annoyance to her, and in the same degree as she expressed her disapproval of him Comus was careful to maintain and parade the intimacy. Its existence, or rather its continued existence, was one of the things that faintly puzzled the young lady whose sought-for favour might have been expected to furnish an occasion for its rapid dissolution.

With two suitors, one of whom at least she found markedly attractive, courting her at the same moment, Elaine should have had reasonable cause for being on good terms with the world, and with herself in particular. Happiness was not, however, at this auspicious moment, her dominant mood. The grave calm of her face masked as usual a certain degree of grave perturbation. A succession of well-meaning governesses and a plentiful supply of moralizing aunts on both sides of her family, had impressed on her young mind the theoretical fact that wealth is a great responsibility. The consciousness of her responsibility set her continually wondering, not as to her own fitness to discharge her "stewardship," but as to the motives and merits of people with whom she came in contact. The knowledge that there was so much in the world that she could buy, invited speculation as to how much there was that was worth buying. Gradually she had come to regard her mind as a sort of appeal court before whose secret sittings were examined and judged the motives and actions, the motives especially, of the world in general. In her schoolroom days she had sat in conscientious judgment on the motives that guided or misguided Charles and Cromwell and Monck, Wallenstein and Savonarola. In her present stage she was equally occupied in examining the political sincerity of the Secretary for Foreign Affairs, the good-faith of a honey-tongued but possibly loyal-hearted waiting-maid, and the disinterestedness of a whole circle of indulgent and flattering acquaintances. Even more absorbing, and, in her eyes, more urgently necessary, was the task of dissecting and appraising the characters of the two young men who were favouring her with their attentions. And herein lay cause for much thinking and some perturbation. Youghal, for example, might have baffled a more experienced observer of human nature. Elaine was too clever to confound his dandyism with foppishness or self-advertisement. He admired his own toilet effect in a mirror from a genuine sense of pleasure in a thing good to look upon, just as he would feel a sensuous appreciation of the sight of a well-bred, well-matched, well-turned-out pair of horses. Behind his careful political flippancy and cynicism one might also detect a certain careless sincerity, which would probably in the long run save him from moderate success, and turn him into one of the brilliant failures of his day. Beyond this it was difficult to form an exact appreciation of Courtenay Youghal, and Elaine, who liked to have her impressions distinctly labelled and pigeon-holed, was perpetually scrutinizing the outer surface of his characteristics and utterances, like a baffled art critic vainly searching beneath the varnish and scratches of a doubtfully assigned picture for an enlightening signature. The young man added to her perplexities by his deliberate policy of never trying to show himself in a favourable light even when most anxious to impart a favourable impression. He preferred that people should hunt for his good qualities, and merely took very good care that as far as possible they should never draw blank; even in the matter of selfishness, which was the anchor-sheet of his existence, he contrived to be noted, and justly noted, for doing remarkably unselfish things. As a ruler he would have been reasonably popular; as a husband he would probably be unendurable.

Comus was to a certain extent as great a mystification as Youghal, but here Elaine was herself responsible for some of the perplexity which enshrouded his character in her eyes. She had taken more than a passing fancy for the boy—for the boy as he might be, that was to say—and she was desperately unwilling to see him and appraise him as he really was. Thus the mental court of appeal was constantly engaged in examining witnesses as to character, most of whom signally failed to give any testimony which would support the favourable judgment which the tribunal was so anxious to arrive at. A woman with wider experience of the world's ways and shortcomings would probably have contented herself with an endeavour to find out whether her liking for the boy outweighed her dislike of his characteristics; Elaine took her judgments too seriously to approach the matter from such a simple and convenient standpoint. The fact that she was much more than half in love with Comus made it dreadfully important that she should discover him to have a lovable soul, and Comus, it must be confessed, did little to help forward the discovery.

"At any rate he is honest," she would observe to herself, after some outspoken admission of unprincipled conduct on his part, and then she would ruefully recall certain episodes in which he had figured, from which honesty had been conspiciously absent. What she tried to label honesty in his candour was probably only a cynical defiance of the laws of right and wrong.

"You look more than usually thoughtful this afternoon," said Comus to her, "as if you had invented this summer day and were trying to think out improvements."

"If I had the power to create improvements anywhere I think I should begin with you," retorted Elaine.

"I'm sure it's much better to leave me as I am," protested Comus; "you're like a relative of mine up in Argyllshire, who spends his time producing improved breeds of sheep and pigs and chickens. So patronizing and irritating to the Almighty, I should think, to go about putting superior finishing touches to Creation."

Elaine frowned, and then laughed, and finally gave a little sigh.

"It's not easy to talk sense to you," she said.

"Whatever else you take in hand," said Youghal, "you must never improve this garden. It's what our idea of heaven might be like if the Jews hadn't invented one for us on totally different lines. It's dreadful that we should accept them as the impresarios of our religious dreamland instead of the Greeks."

"You are not very fond of the Jews," said Elaine.

"I've travelled and lived a good deal in Eastern Europe," said Youghal.

"It seems largely a question of geography," said Elaine; "in England no one really is anti-Semitic."

Youghal shook his head. "I know a great many Jews who are."

Servants had quietly, almost reverently, placed tea and its accessories on the wicker table, and quietly receded from the landscape. Elaine sat like a grave young goddess about to dispense some mysterious potion to her devotees. Her mind was still sitting in judgment on the Jewish question.

Comus scrambled to his feet.

"It's too hot for tea," he said; "I shall go and feed the swans."

And he walked off with a little silver basket-dish containing brown bread-and-butter.

Elaine laughed quietly.

"It's so like Comus," she said, "to go off with our one dish of bread-and-butter."

Youghal chuckled responsively. It was an undoubted opportunity for him to put in some disparaging criticism of Comus, and Elaine sat alert in readiness to judge the critic and reserve judgment on the criticized.

"His selfishness is splendid but absolutely futile," said Youghal; "now my selfishness is commonplace, but always thoroughly practical and calculated. He will have great difficulty in getting the swans to accept his offering, and he incurs the odium of reducing us to a bread-and-butterless condition. Incidentally, he will get very hot."

Elaine again had the sense of being thoroughly baffled. If Youghal had said anything unkind it was about himself.

"If my cousin Suzette had been here," she observed, with the shadow of a malicious smile on her lips, "I believe she would have gone into a flood of tears at the loss of her bread-and-butter, and Comus would have figured ever after in her mind as something black and destroying and hateful. In fact, I don't really know why we took our loss so unprotestingly."

"For two reasons," said Youghal; "you are rather fond of Comus. And I—am not very fond of bread-and-butter."

The jesting remark brought a throb of pleasure to Elaine's heart. She had known full well that she cared for Comus, but now that Courtenay Youghal had openly proclaimed the fact as something unchallenged and understood matters seemed placed at once on a more advanced footing. The warm sunlit garden grew suddenly into a heaven that held the secret of eternal happiness. Youth and comeliness would always walk here, under the low-boughed mulberry trees, as unchanging as the leaden otter that for ever preyed on the leaden salmon on the edge of the old fountain, and somehow the lovers would always wear the aspect of herself and the boy who was talking to the four white swans by the water steps. Youghal was right; this was the real heaven of one's dreams and longings, immeasurably removed from that Rue de la Paix Paradise about which one professed utterly insincere hankerings in places of public worship. Elaine drank her tea in a happy silence; besides being a brilliant talker Youghal understood the rarer art of being a non-talker on occasion.

Comus came back across the grass swinging the empty basket-dish in his hand.

"Swans were very pleased," he cried gaily, "and said they hoped I would keep the bread-and-butter dish as a souvenir of a happy tea-party. I may really have it, mayn't I?" he continued in an anxious voice; "it will do to keep studs and things in. You don't want it."

"It's got the family crest on it," said Elaine. Some of the happiness had died out of her eyes.

"I'll have that scratched off and my own put on," said Comus.

"It's been in the family for generations," protested Elaine, who did not share Comus's view that because you were rich your lesser possessions could have no value in your eyes.

"I want it dreadfully," said Comus sulkily, "and you've heaps of other things to put bread-and-butter in."

For the moment he was possessed by an overmastering desire to keep the dish at all costs; a look of greedy determination dominated his face, and he had not for an instant relaxed his grip of the coveted object.

Elaine was genuinely angry by this time, and was busily telling herself that it was absurd to be put out over such a trifle; at the same moment a sense of justice was telling her that Comus was displaying a good deal of rather shabby selfishness. And somehow her chief anxiety at the moment was to keep Courtenay Youghal from seeing that she was angry.

"I know you don't really want it, so I'm going to keep it," persisted Comus.

"It's too hot to argue," said Elaine.

"Happy mistress of your destinies," laughed Youghal; "you can suit your disputations to the desired time and temperature. I have to go and argue, or what is worse, listen to other people's arguments, in a hot and doctored atmosphere suitable to an invalid lizard."

"You haven't got to argue about a bread-and-butter dish," said Elaine.

"Chiefly about bread-and-butter," said Youghal; "our great preoccupation is other people's bread-and-butter. They earn or produce the material, but we busy ourselves with making rules how it shall be cut up, and the size of the slices, and how much butter shall go on how much bread. That is what is called legislation. If we could only make rules as to how the bread-and-butter should be digested we should be quite happy."

Elaine had been brought up to regard Parliaments as something to be treated with cheerful solemnity, like illness or family reunions. Youghal's flippant disparagement of the career in which he was involved did not, however, jar on her susceptibilities. She knew him to be not only a lively and effective debater but an industrious worker on committees. If he made light of his labours, at least he afforded no one else a loophole for doing so. And certainly the Parliamentary atmosphere was not uninviting on this hot afternoon.

"When must you go?" she asked sympathetically.

Youghal looked ruefully at his watch. Before he could answer, a cheerful hoot came through the air, as of an owl joyously challenging the sunlight with a foreboding of the coming night. He sprang laughing to his feet.

"Listen! My summons back to my galley," he cried. "The Gods have given me an hour in this enchanted garden, so I must not complain."

Then in a lower voice he almost whispered, "It's the Persian debate tonight."

It was the one hint he had given in the midst of his talking and laughing that he was really keenly enthralled in the work that lay before him. It was the one little intimate touch that gave Elaine the knowledge that he cared for her opinion of his work.

Comus, who had emptied his cigarette-case, became suddenly clamorous at the prospect of being temporarily stranded without a smoke. Youghal took the last remaining cigarette from his own case and gravely bisected it.

"Friendship could go no farther," he observed, as he gave one-half to the doubtfully appeased Comus, and lit the other himself.

"There are heaps more in the hall," said Elaine.

"It was only done for the Saint Martin of Tours effect," said Youghal; "I hate smoking when I'm rushing through the air. Good-bye."

The departing galley-slave stepped forth into the sunlight, radiant and confident. A few minutes later Elaine could see glimpses of his white car as it rushed past the rhododendron bushes. He woos best who leaves first, particularly if he goes forth to battle or the semblance of battle.

Somehow Elaine's garden of Eternal Youth had already become clouded in its imagery. The girl-figure who walked in it was still distinctly and unchangingly herself, but her companion was more blurred and undefined, as a picture that has been superimposed on another.

Youghal sped townward well satisfied with himself. Tomorrow, he reflected, Elaine would read his speech in her morning paper, and he knew in advance that it was not going to be one of his worst efforts. He knew almost exactly where the punctuations of laughter and applause would burst in, he knew that nimble fingers in the Press Gallery would be taking down each gibe and argument as he flung it at the impassive Minister confronting him, and that the fair lady of his desire would be able to judge what manner of young man this was who spent his afternoon in her garden, lazily chaffing himself and his world.

And he further reflected, with an amused chuckle, that she would be vividly reminded of Comus for days to come, when she took her afternoon tea, and saw the bread-and-butter reposing in an unaccustomed dish.

CHAPTER VII

TOWARDS four o'clock on a hot afternoon Francesca stepped out from a shop entrance near the Piccadilly end of Bond Street and ran almost into the arms of Merla Blathlington. The afternoon seemed to get instantly hotter. Merla was one of those human flies that buzz; in crowded streets, at bazaars and in warm weather, she attained to the proportions of a human bluebottle. Lady Caroline Benaresq had openly predicted that a special fly-paper was being reserved for her accommodation in another world; others, however, held the opinion that she would be miraculously multiplied in a future state, and that four or more Merla Blathlingtons, according to deserts, would be in perpetual and unremitting attendance on each lost soul.

"Here we are," she cried, with a glad eager buzz, "popping in and out of shops like rabbits; not that rabbits do pop in and out of shops very extensively."

It was evidently one of her bluebottle days.

"Don't you love Bond Street?" she gabbled on. "There's something so unusual and distinctive about it; no other street anywhere else is quite like it. Don't you know those ikons and images and things scattered up and down Europe, that are supposed to have been painted or carved, as the case may be, by St. Luke or Zaccheus, or somebody of that sort; I always like to think that some notable person of those times designed Bond Street. St. Paul, perhaps. He travelled about a lot."

"Not in Middlesex, though," said Francesca.

"One can't be sure," persisted Merla; "when one wanders about as much as he did one gets mixed up and forgets where one *has* been. I can never remember whether I've been to the Tyrol twice and St. Moritz once, or the other way about; I always have to ask my maid. And there's something about the name Bond that suggests St. Paul; didn't he write a lot about the bond and the free?"

"I fancy he wrote in Hebrew or Greek," objected Francesca; "the word wouldn't have the least resemblance."

"So dreadfully non-committal to go about pamphleteering in those bizarre languages," complained Merla; "that's what makes all those people so elusive. As soon as you try to pin them down to a definite statement about anything you're told that some vitally important word has fifteen other meanings in the original. I wonder our Cabinet Ministers and politicians don't adopt a sort of dog-Latin or Esperanto jargon to deliver their speeches in; what a lot of subsequent explaining away would be saved! But to go back to Bond Street—not that we've left it——"

"I'm afraid I must leave it now," said Francesca, preparing to turn up Grafton Street. "Good-bye."

"Must you be going? Come and have tea somewhere. I know of a cozy little place where one can talk undisturbed."

Francesca repressed a shudder and pleaded an urgent engagement.

"I know where you're going," said Merla, with the resentful buzz of a bluebottle that finds itself thwarted by the cold unreasoning resistance of a windowpane. "You're going to play bridge at Serena Golackly's. She never asks me to her bridge parties."

Francesca shuddered openly this time; the prospect of having to play bridge anywhere in the near neighbourhood of Merla's voice was not one that could be contemplated with ordinary calmness.

"Good-bye," she said again firmly, and passed out of earshot; it was rather like leaving the machinery section of an exhibition. Merla's diagnosis of her destination had been a correct one; Francesca made her way slowly through the hot streets in the direction of Serena Golackly's house on the far side of Berkeley Square. To the blessed certainty of finding a game of bridge, she hopefully added the possibility of hearing some fragments of news which might prove interesting and enlightening. And of enlightenment on a particular subject, in which she was acutely and personally interested, she stood in some need. Comus of late had been provokingly reticent as to his movements and doings; partly, perhaps, because it was his nature to be provoking, partly because the daily bickerings over money matters were gradually choking other forms of conversation. Francesca had seen him once or twice in the Park in the desirable company of Elaine de Frey, and from time to time she heard of the young people as having danced together at various houses; on the other hand, she had seen and heard quite as much evidence to connect the heiress's name with that of Courtenay Youghal. Beyond this meagre and conflicting and altogether tantalizing information, her knowledge of the present position of affairs did not go. If either of the young men was seriously "making the running," it was probable that she would hear some sly hint or open comment about it from one of Serena's gossip-laden friends, without having to go out of her way to introduce the subject and unduly disclose her own state of ignorance. And a game of bridge, played for moderately high points, gave ample excuse for convenient lapses into reticence; if questions took an embarrassingly inquisitive turn, one could always find refuge in a defensive spade.

The afternoon was too warm to make bridge a generally popular diversion, and Serena's party was a comparatively small one. Only one table was incomplete when Francesca made her appearance on the scene; at it was seated Serena herself, confronted by Ada Spelvexit, whom every one was wont to explain as "one of the Cheshire Spelvexits," as though any other variety would have been intolerable. Ada Spelvexit was one of those naturally stagnant souls who take infinite pleasure in what are called "movements." "Most of the really great lessons I have learned have been taught me by the Poor," was one of her favourite statements. The one great lesson that the Poor in general would have liked to have taught her, that their kitchens and sickrooms were not unreservedly at her disposal as private lecture halls, she had never been able to assimilate. She was ready to give them unlimited advice as to how they should keep the wolf from their doors, but in return she claimed and enforced for herself the penetrating powers of an east wind or a duststorm. Her visits among her wealthier acquaintances were equally extensive and enterprising, and hardly more welcome; in countryhouse parties, while partaking to the fullest extent of the hospitality offered her, she made a practice of unburdening herself of homilies on the evils of leisure and luxury, which did not particularly endear her to her fellow-guests. Hostesses regarded her philosophically as a form of social measles which every one had to have once.

The third prospective player, Francesca noted without any special enthusiasm, was Lady Caroline Benaresq. Lady Caroline was far from being a remarkably good bridge player, but she always managed to domineer mercilessly over any table that was favoured with her presence, and generally managed to win. A domineering player usually inflicts the chief damage and demoralization on his partner; Lady Caroline's special achievement was to harass and demoralize partner and opponents alike.

"Weak and weak," she announced in her gentle voice, as she cut her hostess for a partner; "I suppose we had better play only five shillings a hundred."

Francesca wondered at the old woman's moderate assessment of the stake, knowing her fondness for highish play and her usual luck in card holding.

"I don't mind what we play," said Ada Spelvexit, with an incautious parade of elegant indifference; as a matter of fact she was inwardly relieved and rejoicing at the reasonable figure proposed by Lady Caroline, and she would certainly have demurred if a higher stake had been suggested. She was not as a rule a successful player, and money lost at cards was always a poignant bereavement to her.

"Then as you don't mind we'll make it ten shillings a hundred," said Lady Caroline, with the pleased chuckle of one who has spread a net in the sight of a bird and disproved the vanity of the proceeding.

It proved a tiresome ding-dong rubber, with the strength of the cards slightly on Francesca's side, and the luck of the table going mostly the other way. She was too keen a player not to feel a certain absorption in the game once it had started, but she was conscious today of a distracting interest that competed with the momentary importance of leads and discards and declarations. The little accumulations of talk that were unpent during the dealing of the hands became as noteworthy to her alert attention as the play of the hands themselves.

"Yes, quite a small party this afternoon," said Serena, in reply to a seemingly casual remark on Francesca's part; "and two or three non-players, which is unusual on a Wednesday. Canon Besomley was here just before you came; you know, the big preaching man."

"I've been to hear him scold the human race once or twice," said Francesca.

"A strong man with a wonderfully strong message," said Ada Spelvexit, in an impressive and assertive tone.

"The sort of popular pulpiteer who spanks the vices of his age and lunches with them afterwards," said Lady Caroline.

"Hardly a fair summary of the man and his work," protested Ada. "I've been to hear him many times when I've been depressed or discouraged, and I simply can't tell you the impression his words leave——"

"At least you can tell us what you intend to make trumps," broke in Lady Caroline gently.

"Diamonds," pronounced Ada, after a rather flurried survey of her hand.

"Doubled," said Lady Caroline, with increased gentleness, and a few minutes later she was pencilling an addition of twenty-four to her score.

"I stayed with his people down here in Herefordshire last May," said Ada, returning to the unfinished theme of the Canon; "such an exquisite rural retreat, and so restful and healing to the nerves. Real country scenery; apple blossom everywhere."

"Surely only on the apple trees!" said Lady Caroline.

Ada Spelvexit gave up the attempt to reproduce the decorative setting of the Canon's home-life, and fell back on the small but practical consolation of scoring the odd trick in her opponent's declaration of hearts.

"If you had led your highest club to start with, instead of the nine, we should have saved the trick," remarked Lady Caroline to her partner in a tone of coldly gentle reproof; "it's no use, my dear," she continued, as Serena flustered out a halting apology, "no earthly use to attempt to play bridge at one table and try to see and hear what's going on at two or three other tables."

"I can generally manage to attend to more than one thing at a time," said Serena rashly; "I think I must have a sort of double brain."

"Much better to economize and have one really good one," observed Lady Caroline.

"*La belle dame sans merci* scoring a verbal trick or two as usual," said a player at another table in a discreet undertone.

"Did I tell you Sir Edward Roan is coming to my next big evening?" said Serena hurriedly, by way, perhaps, of restoring herself a little in her own esteem.

"Poor dear good Sir Edward! What have you made trumps?" asked Lady Caroline, in one breath.

"Clubs," said Francesca; "and pray, why these adjectives of commiseration?"

Francesca was a Ministerialist by family interest and allegiance, and was inclined to take up the cudgels at the suggested disparagement aimed at the Foreign Secretary.

"He amuses me so much," purred Lady Caroline. Her amusement was usually of the sort that a sporting cat derives from watching the Swedish exercises of a well-spent and carefully throught-out mouse.

"Really? He has been rather a brilliant success at the Foreign Office, you know," said Francesca.

"He reminds one so of a circus elephant—infinitely more intelligent than the people who direct him, but quite content to go on putting his foot down or taking it up as may be required, quite unconcerned whether he steps on a meringue or a hornet's nest in the process of going where he's expected to go."

"How can you say such things!" protested Francesca.

"I can't," said Lady Caroline; "Courtenay Youghal said it in the House last night. Didn't you read the debate? He was really rather in form. I disagree entirely with his point of view, of course, but some of the things he says have just enough truth behind them to redeem them from being merely smart; for instance, his summing up of the Government's attitude towards our embarrassing Colonial Empire in the wistful phrase 'Happy is the country that has no geography.'"

"What an absurdly unjust thing to say!" put in Francesca; "I daresay some of our Party at some time have taken up that attitude, but every one knows that Sir Edward is a sound Imperialist at heart."

"Most politicians are something or other at heart, but no one would be rash enough to insure a politician against heart failure. Particularly when he happens to be in office."

"Anyhow, I don't see that the Opposition leaders would have acted any differently in the present case," said Francesca.

"One should always speak guardedly of the Opposition leaders," said Lady Caroline, in her gentlest voice; "one never knows what a turn in the situation may do for them."

"You mean they may one day be at the head of affairs?" asked Serena briskly.

"I mean they may one day lead the Opposition. One never knows."

Lady Caroline had just remembered that her hostess was on the Opposition side in politics.

Francesca and her partner scored four tricks in clubs; the game stood irresolutely at twenty-four all.

"If you had followed the excellent lyrical advice given to the Maid of Athens and returned my heart we should have made two more tricks and gone game," said Lady Caroline to her partner.

"Mr. Youghal seems pushing himself to the fore of late," remarked Francesca, as Serena took up the cards to deal. Since the young politician's name had been introduced into their conversation the opportunity for turning the talk more directly on him and his affairs was too good to be missed.

"I think he's got a career before him," said Serena; "the House always fills when he's speaking, and that's a good sign. And then he's young and got rather an attractive personality, which is always something in the political world."

"His lack of money will handicap him, unless he can find himself a rich wife or persuade some one to die and leave him a fat legacy," said Francesca; "since M.P.'s have become the recipients of a salary rather more is expected and demanded of them in the expenditure line than before."

"Yes, the House of Commons still remains rather at the opposite pole to the Kingdom of Heaven as regards entrance qualifications," observed Lady Caroline.

"There ought to be no difficulty about Youghal picking up a girl with money," said Serena; "with his prospects he would make an excellent husband for any woman with social ambitions."

And she half sighed, as though she almost regretted that a previous matrimonial arrangement precluded her from entering into the competition on her own account.

Francesca, under an assumption of languid interest, was watching Lady Caroline narrowly for some hint of suppressed knowledge of Youghal's courtship of Miss de Frey.

"Whom are you marrying and giving in marriage?"

The question came from George St. Michael, who had strayed over from a neighbouring table, attracted by the fragments of small-talk that had reached his ears.

St. Michael was one of those dapper, bird-like, illusorily-active men, who seem to have been in a certain stage of middle-age for as long as human memory can recall them. A close-cut peaked beard lent a certain dignity to his appearance—a loan which the rest of his features and mannerisms were continually and successfully repudiating. His profession, if he had one, was submerged in his hobby, which consisted of being an advance-agent for small happenings or possible happenings that were or seemed imminent in the social world around him; he found a perpetual and unflagging satisfaction in acquiring and retailing any stray items of gossip or information, particularly of a matrimonial nature, that chanced to come his way. Given the bare outline of an officially announced engagement, he would immediately fill it in with all manner of details, true or, at any rate, probable, drawn from his own imagination or from some equally exclusive source. The *Morning Post* might content itself with the mere statement of the arrangement which would shortly take place, but it was St. Michael's breathless little voice that proclaimed how the contracting parties had originally met over a salmon-fishing incident, why the Guards' Chapel would not be used, why her Aunt Mary had at first opposed the match, how the question of the children's religious upbringing had been compromised, etc., etc., to all whom it might interest and to many whom it might not. Beyond his industriously-earned pre-eminence in this special branch of intelligence, he was chiefly noteworthy for having a wife reputed to be the tallest and thinnest woman in the Home Counties. The two were sometimes seen together in Society, where they passed under the collective name of St. Michael and All Angles.

"We are trying to find a rich wife for Courtenay Youghal," said Serena, in answer to St. Michael's question.

"Ah, there I'm afraid you're a little late," he observed, glowing with the importance of pending revelation; "I'm afraid you're a little late," he repeated, watching the effect of his words as a gardener might watch the development of a bed of carefully tended asparagus. "I think the young gentleman has been before you and already found himself a rich mate in prospect."

He lowered his voice as he spoke, not with a view to imparting impressive mystery to his statement, but because there were other table groups within hearing to whom he hoped presently to have the privilege of re-disclosing his revelation.

"Do you mean—?" began Serena.

"Miss de Frey," broke in St. Michael hurriedly, fearful lest his revelation should be forestalled, even in guesswork; "quite an ideal choice, the very wife for a man who means to make his mark in politics. Twenty-four thousand a year, with prospects of more to come, and a charming place of her own not too far from town. Quite the type of girl, too, who will make a good political hostess, brains without being brainy, you know. Just the right thing. Of course, it would be premature to make any definite announcement at present——"

"It would hardly be premature for my partner to announce what she means to make trumps," interrupted Lady Caroline, in a voice of such sinister gentleness that St. Michael fled headlong back to his own table.

"Oh, is it me? I beg your pardon. I leave it," said Serena.

"Thank you. No trumps," declared Lady Caroline. The hand was successful, and the rubber ultimately fell to her with a comfortable margin of honours. The same partners cut together again, and this time the cards went distinctly against Francesca and Ada Spelvexit, and a heavily piled-up score confronted them at the close of the rubber. Francesca was conscious that a certain amount of rather erratic play on her part had at least contributed to the result. St. Michael's incursion into the conversation had proved rather a powerful distraction to her ordinarily sound bridge-craft.

Ada Spelvexit emptied her purse of several gold pieces, and infused a corresponding degree of superiority into her manner.

"I must be going now," she announced; "I'm dining early. I have to give an address to some charwomen afterwards."

"Why?" asked Lady Caroline, with a disconcerting directness that was one of her most formidable characteristics.

"Oh, well, I have some things to say to them that I daresay they will like to hear," said Ada, with a thin laugh.

Her statement was received with a silence that betokened profound unbelief in any such probability.

"I go about a good deal among working-class women," she added.

"No one has ever said it," observed Lady Caroline, "but how painfully true it is that the poor have us always with them!"

Ada Spelvexit hastened her departure; the marred impressiveness of her retreat came as a culminating discomfiture on the top of her ill-fortune at the card-table. Possibly, however, the multiplication of her own annoyances enabled her to survey charwomen's troubles with increased cheerfulness. None of them, at any rate, had spent an afternoon with Lady Caroline.

Francesca cut in at another table, and with better fortune attending on her, succeeded in winning back most of her losses. A sense of satisfaction was distinctly dominant as she took leave of her hostess. St. Michael's gossip, or rather the manner in which it had been received, had given her a clue to the real state of affairs, which, however slender and conjectural, at least pointed in the desired direction. At first she had been horribly afraid lest she should be listening to a definite announcement which would have been the death-blow to her hopes, but as the recitation went on without any of those assured little minor details which St. Michael so loved to supply, she had come to the conclusion that it was merely a piece of intelligent guesswork. And if Lady Caroline had really believed in the story of Elaine de Frey's virtual engagement to Courtenay Youghal she would have taken a malicious pleasure in encouraging St. Michael in his confidences, and in watching Francesca's discomfiture under the recital. The irritated manner in which she had cut short the discussion betrayed the fact that, as far as the old woman's information went, it was Comus, and not Courtenay Youghal, who held the field. And in this particular case Lady Caroline's information was likely to be nearer the truth than St. Michael's confident gossip.

Francesca always gave a penny to the first crossing-sweeper or match-seller she chanced across after a successful sitting at bridge. This afternoon she had come out of the fray some fifteen shillings to the bad, but she gave two pennies to a crossing-sweeper at the north-west corner of Berkeley Square as a sort of thank-offering to the gods.

CHAPTER VIII

It was a fresh rain-repentant afternoon, following a morning that had been sultry and torrentially wet by turns: the sort of afternoon that impels people to talk graciously of the rain as having done a lot of good, its chief merit in their eyes probably having been its recognition of the art of moderation. Also it was an afternoon that invited bodily activity after the convalescent languor of the earlier part of the day. Elaine had instinctively found her way into her riding-habit and sent an order down to the stables—a blessed oasis that still smelt sweetly of horse and hay and cleanliness in a world that reeked of petrol, and now she set her mare at a smart pace through a succession of long-stretching country lanes. She was due some time that afternoon at a garden-party, but she rode with determination in an opposite direction. In the first place, neither Comus nor Courtenay would be at the party, which fact seemed to remove any valid reason that could be thought of for inviting her attendance thereat; in the second place about a hundred human beings would be gathered there, and human gatherings were not her most crying need at the present moment. Since her last encounter with her wooers, under the cedars in her own garden, Elaine realized that she was either very happy or cruelly unhappy, she could not quite determine which. She seemed to have what she most wanted in the world lying at her feet, and she was dreadfully uncertain in her more reflective moments whether she really wanted to stretch out her hand and take it. It was all very like some situation in an *Arabian Nights* tale or a story of Pagan Hellas, and consequently the more puzzling and disconcerting to a girl brought up on the methodical lines of Victorian Christianity. Her appeal court was in permanent session these last few days, but it gave no decisions, at least none that she would listen to. And the ride on her fast light-stepping little mare, alone and unattended, through the fresh-smelling leafy lanes into unexplored country, seemed just what she wanted at the moment. The mare made some small delicate pretence of being road-shy, not the staring dolt-like kind of nervousness that shows itself in an irritating hanging-back as each conspicuous wayside object presents itself, but the nerve-flutter of an imaginative animal that merely results in a quick whisk of the head and a swifter bound forward. She might have paraphrased the mental attitude of the immortalized Peter Bell into

A basket underneath a tree
A yellow tiger is to me,
If it is nothing more.

The more really alarming episodes of the road, the hoot and whir of a passing motor-car or the loud vibrating hum of a wayside threshing-machine, were treated with indifference.

On turning a corner out of a narrow coppice-bordered lane into a wider road that sloped steadily upward in a long stretch of hill, Elaine saw, coming toward her at no great distance, a string of yellow-painted vans, drawn for the most part by skewbald or speckled horses. A certain rakish air about these oncoming road-craft proclaimed them as belonging to a travelling wild-beast show, decked out in the rich primitive colouring that one's taste in childhood would have insisted on before it had been schooled in the artistic value of dulness. It was an unlooked-for and distinctly unwelcome encounter. The mare had already commenced a sixfold scrutiny with nostrils, eyes, and daintily-pricked ears; one ear made hurried little backward movements to hear what Elaine was saying about the eminent niceness and respectability of the approaching caravan, but even Elaine felt that she would be unable satisfactorily to explain the elephants and camels that could certainly form part of the procession. To turn back would seem rather craven, and the mare might take fright at the manœuvre and try to bolt; a gate standing ajar at the entrance to a farmyard lane provided a convenient way out of the difficulty.

As Elaine pushed her way through she became aware of a man standing just inside the lane, who made a movement forward to open the gate for her.

"Thank you. I'm just getting out of the way of a wild-beast show," she explained; "my mare is tolerant of motors and traction-engines, but I expect camels—hallo!" she broke off, recognizing the man as an old acquaintance, "I heard you had taken rooms in a farm-house somewhere. Fancy meeting you in this way!"

In the not very distant days of her little-girlhood, Tom Keriway had been a man to be looked upon with a certain awe and envy; indeed the glamour of his roving career would have fired the imagination, and wistful desire to do likewise, of many young Englishmen. It seemed to be the grown-up realization of the games played in dark rooms in winter firelit evenings, and the dreams dreamed over favourite books of adventure. Making Vienna his headquarters, almost his home, he had rambled where he listed through the lands of the Near and Middle East as leisurely and thoroughly as tamer souls might explore Paris. He had wandered through Hungarian horse-fairs, hunted shy crafty beasts on lonely Balkan hillsides, dropped himself pebble-wise into the stagnant human pool of some Bulgarian monastery, threaded his way through the strange racial mosaic of Salonika, listened with amused politeness to the shallow ultra-modern opinions of a voluble editor or lawyer in some wayside Russian town, or learned wisdom from a chance tavern companion, one of the atoms of the busy ant-stream of men and merchandise that moves untiringly round the shores of the Black Sea. And far and wide as he might roam, he always managed to turn up at frequent intervals, at ball and supper and theatre, in the gay Hauptstadt of the Habsburgs, haunting his favourite cafés and wine-vaults, skimming through his favourite news-sheets, greeting old acquaintances and friends, from ambassadors down to cobblers in the social scale. He seldom talked of his travels, but it might be said that his travels talked of him; there was an air about him that a German diplomat once summed up in a phrase: "a man that wolves have sniffed at."

And then two things happened, which he had not mapped out in his route; a severe illness shook half the life and all the energy out of him, and a heavy money loss brought him almost to the door of destitution. With something, perhaps, of the impulse which drives a stricken animal away from its kind, Tom Keriway left the haunts where he had known so much happiness, and withdrew into the shelter of a secluded farm-house lodging; more than ever he became to Elaine a hearsay personality. And now the chance meeting with the caravan had flung her across the threshold of his retreat.

"What a charming little nook you've got hold of!" she exclaimed with instinctive politeness, and then looked searchingly round, and discovered that she had spoken the truth; it really was charming. The farm-house had that intensely English look that one seldom sees out of Normandy. Over the whole scene of rickyard, garden, outbuildings, horsepond and orchard, brooded that air which seems rightfully to belong to out-of-the-way farm-yards, an air of wakeful dreaminess which suggests that here man and beast and bird have got up so early that the rest of the world has never caught them up and never will.

Elaine dismounted, and Keriway led the mare round to a little paddock by the side of a great grey barn. At the end of the lane they could see the show go past, a string of lumbering vans and great striding beasts that seemed to link the vast silences of the desert with the noises and sights and smells, the naphtha-flares and advertisement hoardings and trampled orange-peel, of an endless succession of towns.

"You had better let the caravan pass well on its way before you get on the road again," said Keriway; "the smell of the beasts may make your mare nervous and restive going home."

Then he called to a boy, who was busy with a hoe among some defiantly prosperous weeds, to fetch the lady a glass of milk and a piece of currant loaf.

"I don't know when I've seen anything so utterly charming and peaceful," said Elaine, propping herself on a seat that a pear-tree had obligingly designed in the fantastic curve of its trunk.

"Charming, certainly," said Keriway, "but too full of the stress of its own little life struggle to be peaceful. Since I have lived here I've learnt, what I've always suspected, that a country farm-house, set away in a world of its own, is one of the most wonderful studies of interwoven happenings and tragedies that can be imagined. It is like the old chronicles of mediæval Europe in the days when there was a sort of ordered anarchy between feudal lords and overlords, and burg-grafs, and mitred abbots, and prince-bishops, robber barons and merchant guilds, and Electors and so forth, all striving and contending and counter-plotting, and interfering with each other under some vague code of loosely-applied rules. Here one sees it reproduced under one's eyes, like a musty page of black-letter come to life. Look at one little section of it, the poultry-life on the farm. Villa poultry, dull egg-machines, with records kept of how many ounces of food they eat, and how many pennyworths of eggs they lay, give you no idea of the wonder-life of these farm-birds; their feuds and jealousies, and carefully maintained prerogatives, their unsparing tyrannies and persecutions, their calculated courage and bravado or sedulously hidden cowardice, it might all be some human chapter from the annals of the old Rhineland or mediæval Italy. And then, outside their own bickering wars and hates, the grim enemies that come up against them from the woodlands; the hawk that dashes among the coops like a moss-trooper raiding the border, knowing well that a charge of shot may tear him to bits at any moment. And the stoat, a creeping slip of brown fur a few inches long, intently and unstayably out for blood. And the hunger-taught master of craft, the red fox, who has waited perhaps half the afternoon for his chance while the fowls were dusting themselves under the hedge, and just as they were turning supper-ward to the yard one has stopped a moment to give her feathers a final shake and found death springing upon her. Do you know," he continued, as Elaine fed herself and the mare with morsels of currant-loaf, "I don't think any tragedy in literature that I have ever come across impressed me so much as the first one that I spelled out slowly for myself in words of three letters: the bad fox has got the red hen. There was something so dramatically complete about it; the badness of the fox, added to all the traditional guile of his race, seemed to heighten the horror of the hen's fate, and there was such a suggestion of masterful malice about the word 'got.' One felt that a countryside in arms would not get that hen away from the bad fox. They used to think me a slow dull reader for not getting on with my lesson, but I used to sit and picture to myself the red hen, with its wings beating helplessly, screeching in terrified protest, or perhaps, if he had got it by the neck, with beak wide agape and silent, and eyes staring, as if it left the farmyard for ever. I have seen blood-spilling and down-crushings and abject defeat here and there in my time, but the red hen has remained in my mind as the type of helpless tragedy." He was silent for a moment as if he were again musing over the three-letter drama that had so dwelt in his childhood's imagination.

"Tell me some of the things you have seen in your time," was the request that was nearly on Elaine's lips, but she hastily checked herself and substituted another.

"Tell me more about the farm, please."

And he told her of a whole world, or rather of several intermingled worlds, set apart in this sleepy hollow in the hills, of beast lore and wood lore and farm craft, at times touching almost the border of witchcraft—passing lightly here, not with the probing eagerness of those who know nothing, but with the averted glance of those who fear to see too much. He told her of those things that slept and those that prowled when the dusk fell, of strange hunting cats, of the yard swine and the stalled cattle, of the farm folk themselves, as curious and remote in their way, in their ideas and fears and wants and tragedies, as the brutes and feathered stock that they tended. It seemed to Elaine as if a musty store of old-world children's books had been fetched down from some cobwebbed lumber-room and brought to life. Sitting there in the little paddock, grown thickly with tall weeds and rank grasses, and shadowed by the weather-beaten old grey barn, listening to this chronicle of wonderful things, half fanciful, half very real, she could scarcely believe that a few miles away there was a garden-party in full swing, with smart frocks and smart conversation, fashionable refreshments and fashionable music, and a fevered undercurrent of social strivings and snubbings. Did Vienna and the Balkan Mountains and the Black Sea seem as remote and hard to believe in, she wondered, to the man sitting by her side, who had discovered or invented this wonderful fairyland? Was it a true and merciful arrangement of fate and life that the things of the moment thrust out the after-taste of the things that had been? Here was one who had held much that was priceless in the hollow of his hand and lost it all, and he was happy and absorbed and well content with the little wayside corner of the world into which he had crept. And Elaine, who held so many desirable things in the hollow of her hand, could not make up her mind to be even moderately happy. She did not even know whether to take this hero of her childhood down from his pedestal, or to place him on a higher one; on the whole she was inclined to resent rather than approve the idea that ill-health and misfortune could so completely subdue and tame an erstwhile bold and roving spirit.

The mare was showing signs of delicately-hinted impatience; the paddock, with its teasing insects and very indifferent grazing, had not thrust out the image of her own comfortable well-foddered loose-box. Elaine divested her habit of some remaining crumbs of bun-loaf and jumped lightly on to her saddle. As she rode slowly down the lane, with Keriway escorting her as far as its gate, she looked round at what had seemed to her, a short while ago, just a picturesque old farmstead, a place of bee-hives and hollyhocks and gabled cart-sheds; now it was in her eyes a magic city, with an undercurrent of reality beneath its magic.

"You are a person to be envied," she said to Keriway; "you have created a fairyland, and you are living in it yourself."

"Envied?"

He shot the question out with sudden bitterness. She looked down and saw the wistful misery that had come into his face.

"Once," he said to her, "in a German paper I read a short story about a tame crippled crane that lived in the park of some small town. I forget what happened in the story, but there was one line that I shall always remember: 'it was lame, that is why it was tame.'"

He had created a fairyland, but assuredly he was not living in it.

CHAPTER IX

In the warmth of a late June morning the long shaded stretch of raked earth, gravel-walk and rhododendron bush that is known affectionately as the Row was alive with the monotonous movement and alert stagnation appropriate to the time and place. The seekers after health, the seekers after notoriety and recognition, and the lovers of good exercise were all well represented on the galloping ground; the gravel-walk and chairs and long seats held a population whose varied instincts and motives would have baffled a social catalogue-maker. The children, handled or in perambulators, might be excused from instinct or motive; they were brought.

Pleasingly conspicuous among a bunch of indifferent riders pacing along by the rails where the onlookers were thickest was Courtenay Youghal, on his handsome plum-roan gelding Anne de Joyeuse. That delicately stepping animal had taken a prize at Islington and nearly taken the life of a stable-boy of whom he disapproved, but his strongest claims to distinction were his good looks and his high opinion of himself. Youghal evidently believed in thorough accord between horse and rider.

"Please stop and talk to me," said a quiet beckoning voice from the other side of the rails, and Youghal drew rein and greeted Lady Veula Croot. Lady Veula had married into a family of commercial solidity and enterprising political nonentity. She had a devoted husband, some blond teachable children, and a look of unutterable weariness in her eyes. To see her standing at the top of an expensively horticultured staircase receiving her husband's guests was rather like watching an animal performing on a music-hall stage. One always tells oneself that the animal likes it, and one always knows that it doesn't.

"Lady Veula is an ardent Free Trader, isn't she?" some one once remarked to Lady Caroline.

"I wonder," said Lady Caroline, in her gently questioning voice;

"a woman whose dresses are made in Paris and whose marriage has been made in heaven might be equally biased for and against free imports."

Lady Veula looked at Youghal and his mount with slow critical appraisement, and there was a note of blended raillery and wistfulness in her voice.

"You two dear things, I should love to stroke you both, but I'm not sure how Joyeuse would take it. So I'll stroke you down verbally instead. I admired your attack on Sir Edward immensely, though of course I don't agree with a word of it. Your description of him building a hedge round the German cuckoo and hoping he was isolating it was rather sweet. Seriously though, I regard him as one of the pillars of the Administration."

"So do I," said Youghal; "the misfortune is that he is merely propping up a canvas roof. It's just his regrettable solidity and integrity that makes him so expensively dangerous. The average Briton arrives at the same judgment about Roan's handling of foreign affairs as Omar does of the Supreme Being in his dealings with the world: 'He's a good fellow and 'twill all be well.'"

Lady Veula laughed lightly. "My Party is in power, so I may exercise the privilege of being optimistic. Who is that who bowed to you?" she continued, as a dark young man with an inclination to stoutness passed by them on foot; "I've seen him about a good deal lately. He's been to one or two of my dances."

"Andrei Drakoloff," said Youghal; "he's just produced a play that has had a big success in Moscow and is certain to be extremely popular all over Russia. In the first three acts the heroine is supposed to be dying of consumption; in the last act they find she is really dying of cancer."

"Are the Russians really such a gloomy people?"

"Gloom-loving, but not in the least gloomy. They merely take their sadness pleasurably, just as we are accused of taking our pleasures sadly. Have you noticed that dreadful Klopstock youth has been pounding past us at shortening intervals? He'll come up and talk if he half catches your eye."

"I only just know him. Isn't he at an agricultural college or something of the sort?"

"Yes, studying to be a gentleman farmer, he told me. I didn't ask if both subjects were compulsory."

"You're really rather dreadful," said Lady Veula, trying to look as if she thought so; "remember, we are all equal in the sight of Heaven."

For a preacher of wholesome truths her voice rather lacked conviction.

"If I and Ernest Klopstock are really equal in the sight of Heaven," said Youghal, with intense complacency, "I should recommend Heaven to consult an eye specialist."

There was a heavy spattering of loose earth, and a squelching of saddle-leather, as the Klopstock youth lumbered up to the rails and delivered himself of loud, cheerful greetings. Joyeuse laid his ears well back as the ungainly bay cob and his appropriately matched rider drew up beside him; his verdict was reflected and endorsed by the cold stare of Youghal's eyes.

"I've been having a nailing fine time," recounted the new-comer with clamorous enthusiasm; "I was over in Paris last month and had lots of strawberries there, then I had a lot more in London, and now I've been having a late crop of them in Herefordshire, so I've had quite a lot this year." And he laughed as one who had deserved well and received well of Fate.

"The charm of that story," said Youghal, "is that it can be told in any drawing-room." And with a sweep of his wide-brimmed hat to Lady Veula he turned the impatient Joyeuse into the moving stream of horses and horsemen.

"That woman reminds me of some verse I've read and liked," thought Youghal, as Joyeuse sprang into a light showy canter that gave full recognition to the existence of observant human beings along the side-walk. "Ah, I have it."

And he quoted almost aloud, as one does in the exhilaration of a canter:

> "How much I loved that way you had
> Of smiling most, when very sad,
> A smile which carried tender hints
> Of sun and spring,
> And yet, more than all other thing,
> Of weariness beyond all words."

And having satisfactorily fitted Lady Veula on to a quotation he dismissed her from his mind. With the constancy of her sex she thought about him, his good looks and his youth and his railing tongue, till late in the afternoon.

While Youghal was putting Joyeuse through his paces under the elm trees of the Row a little drama in which he was directly interested was being played out not many hundred yards away. Elaine and Comus were indulging themselves in two pennyworths of Park chair, drawn aside just a little from the serried rows of sitters who were set out like bedded plants over an acre or so of turf. Comus was, for the moment, in a mood of pugnacious gaiety, disbursing a fund of pointed criticism and unsparing anecdote concerning those of the promenaders or loungers whom he knew personally or by sight. Elaine was rather quieter than usual, and the grave serenity of the Leonardo da Vinci portrait seemed intensified in her face this morning. In his leisurely courtship Comus had relied almost exclusively on his physical attraction and the fitful drollery of his wit and high spirits, and these graces had gone far to make him seem a very desirable and rather lovable thing in Elaine's eyes. But he had left out of account the disfavour which he constantly risked and sometimes incurred from his frank and undisguised indifference to other people's interests and wishes, including, at times, Elaine's. And the more that she felt that she liked him the more she was irritated by his lack of consideration for her. Without expecting that her every wish should become a law to him, she would at least have liked it to reach the formality of a Second Reading. Another important factor he had also left out of his reckoning, namely the presence on the scene of another suitor, who also had youth and wit to recommend him, and who certainly did not lack physical attractions. Comus, marching carelessly through unknown country to effect what seemed already an assured victory, made the mistake of disregarding the existence of an unbeaten army on his flank.

Today Elaine felt that, without having actually quarrelled, she and Comus had drifted a little bit out of sympathy with one another. The fault she knew was scarcely hers, in fact from the most good-natured point of view it could hardly be denied that it was almost entirely his. The incident of the silver dish had lacked even the attraction of novelty; it had been one of a series, all bearing a strong connecting likeness. There had been small unrepaid loans which Elaine would not have grudged in themselves, though the application for them brought a certain qualm of distaste; with the perversity which seemed inseparable from his doings, Comus had always flung away a portion of his borrowings in some ostentatious piece of glaring and utterly profitless extravagance, which outraged all the canons of her upbringing without bringing him an atom of understandable satisfaction. Under these repeated discouragements it was not surprising that some small part of her affection should have slipped away, but she had come to the Park that morning with an unconfessed expectation of being gently wooed back to the mood of gracious forgetfulness that she was only too eager to assume. It was almost worth while being angry with Comus for the sake of experiencing the pleasure of being coaxed into friendliness again with the charm which he knew so well how to exert. It was delicious here under the trees on this perfect June morning, and Elaine had the blessed assurance that most of the women within range were envying her the companionship of the handsome merry-hearted youth who sat by her side. With special complacence she contemplated her cousin Suzette, who was self-consciously but not very elatedly basking in the attentions of her fiancé, an earnest-looking young man who was superintendent of a People's something-or-other on the south side of the river, and whose clothes Comus had described as having been made in Southwark rather than in anger.

Most of the pleasures in life must be paid for, and the chair-ticket vendor in due time made his appearance in quest of pennies. Comus paid him from out of a varied assortment of coins and then balanced the remainder in the palm of his hand. Elaine felt a sudden foreknowledge of something disagreeable about to happen, and a red spot deepened in her cheeks.

"Four shillings and fivepence and a halfpenny," said Comus reflectively. "It's a ridiculous sum to last me for the next three days, and I owe a card debt of over two pounds."

"Yes?" commented Elaine dryly and with an apparent lack of interest in his exchequer statement. Surely, she was thinking hurriedly to herself, he could not be foolish enough to broach the matter of another loan.

"The card debt is rather a nuisance," pursued Comus, with fatalistic persistency.

"You won seven pounds last week, didn't you?" asked Elaine; "don't you put any of your winnings to balance losses?"

"The four shillings and the fivepence and the halfpenny represent the rearguard of the seven pounds," said Comus; "the rest have fallen by the way. If I can pay the two pounds today I daresay I shall win something more to go on with; I'm holding rather good cards just now. But if I can't pay it, of course I shan't show up at the club. So you see the fix I am in."

Elaine took no notice of this indirect application. The Appeal Court was assembling in haste to consider new evidence, and this time there was the rapidity of sudden determination about its movement.

The conversation strayed away from the fateful topic for a few moments, and then Comus brought it deliberately back to the danger zone.

"It would be awfully nice if you would let me have a fiver for a few days, Elaine," he said quickly; "if you don't I really don't know what I shall do."

"If you are really bothered about your card debt I will send you the two pounds by messenger boy early this afternoon." She spoke quietly and with great decision. "And I shall not be at the Connors' dance tonight," she continued; "it's too hot for dancing. I'm going home now; please don't bother to accompany me, I particularly wish to go alone."

Comus saw that he had overstepped the mark of her good nature. Wisely he made no immediate attempt to force himself back into her good graces. He would wait till her indignation had cooled.

His tactics would have been excellent if he had not forgotten that unbeaten army on his flank.

Elaine de Frey had known very clearly what qualities she had wanted in Comus, and she had known, against all efforts at self-deception, that he fell far short of those qualities. She had been willing to lower her standard of moral requirements in proportion as she was fond of the boy, but there was a point beyond which she would not go. He had hurt her pride, besides alarming her sense of caution. Suzette, on whom she felt a thoroughly justified tendency to look down, had at any rate an attentive and considerate lover. Elaine walked towards the Park gates feeling that in one essential Suzette possessed something that had been denied to her, and at the gates she met Joyeuse and his spruce young rider preparing to turn homeward.

"Get rid of Joyeuse and come and take me out to lunch somewhere," demanded Elaine.

"How jolly!" said Youghal. "Let's go to the Corridor Restaurant. The head-waiter there is an old Viennese friend of mine and looks after me beautifully. I've never been there with a lady before, and he's sure to ask me afterwards, in his fatherly way, if we're engaged."

The lunch was a success in every way. There was just enough orchestral effort to immerse the conversation without drowning it, and Youghal was an attentive and inspired host. Through an open doorway Elaine could see the café reading-room, with its imposing array of *Neue Freie Presse*, *Berliner Tageblatt*, and other exotic newspapers hanging on the wall. She looked across at the young man seated opposite her, who gave one the impression of having centred the most serious efforts of his brain on his toilet and his food, and recalled some of the flattering remarks that the Press had bestowed on his recent speeches.

"Doesn't it make you conceited, Courtenay," she asked, "to look at all those foreign newspapers hanging there and know that most of them have got paragraphs and articles about your Persian speech?"

Youghal laughed.

"There's always a chastening corrective in the thought that some of them may have printed your portrait. When once you've seen your features hurriedly reproduced in the *Matin*, for instance, you feel you would like to be a veiled Turkish woman for the rest of your life."

And Youghal gazed long and lovingly at his reflection in the nearest mirror, as an antidote against possible incitements to humility in the portrait gallery of fame.

Elaine felt a certain soothed satisfaction in the fact that this young man, whose knowledge of the Middle East was an embarrassment to Ministers at question time and in debate, was showing himself equally well informed on the subject of her culinary likes and dislikes. If Suzette could have been forced to attend as a witness at a neighbouring table she would have felt even happier.

"Did the head-waiter ask if we were engaged?" asked Elaine, when Courtenay had settled the bill, and she had finished collecting her sunshade and gloves and other impedimenta from the hands of obsequious attendants.

"Yes," said Youghal, "and he seemed quite crestfallen when I had to say 'No.'"

"It would be horrid to disappoint him when he's looked after us so charmingly," said Elaine; "tell him that we are."

CHAPTER X

The Rutland Galleries were crowded, especially in the neighbourhood of the tea-buffet, by a fashionable throng of art-patrons which had gathered to inspect Mervyn Quentock's collection of Society portraits. Quentock was a young artist whose abilities were just receiving due recognition from the critics; that the recognition was not overdue he owed largely to his perception of the fact that if one hides one's talent under a bushel one must be careful to point out to every one the exact bushel under which it is hidden. There are two manners of receiving recognition: one is to be discovered so long after one's death that one's grandchildren have to write to the papers to establish their relationship; the other is to be discovered, like the infant Moses, at the very outset of one's career. Mervyn Quentock had chosen the latter and happier manner. In an age when many aspiring young men strive to advertise their wares by imparting to them a freakish imbecility, Quentock turned out work that was characterized by a pleasing delicate restraint, but he contrived to herald his output with a certain fanfare of personal eccentricity, thereby compelling an attention which might otherwise have strayed past his studio. In appearance he was the ordinary cleanly young Englishman, except, perhaps, that his eyes rather suggested a library edition of the *Arabian Nights;* his clothes matched his appearance and showed no taint of the sartorial disorder by which the bourgeois of the garden-city and the Latin Quarter anxiously seeks to proclaim his kinship with art and thought. His eccentricity took the form of flying in the face of some of the prevailing social currents of the day, but as a reactionary, never as a reformer. He produced a gasp of admiring astonishment in fashionable circles by refusing to paint actresses—except, of course, those who had left the legitimate drama to appear between the boards of Debrett. He absolutely declined to execute portraits of Americans unless they hailed from certain favoured States. His "water-colour line," as a New York paper phrased it, earned for him a crop of angry criticism and a shoal of Transatlantic commissions, and criticism and commissions were the things that Quentock most wanted.

"Of course he is perfectly right," said Lady Caroline Benaresq, calmly rescuing a piled-up plate of caviare sandwiches from the neighbourhood of a trio of young ladies who had established themselves hopefully within easy reach of it. "Art," she continued, addressing herself to the Rev. Poltimore Vardon, "has always been geographically exclusive. London may be more important from most points of view than Venice, but the art of portrait painting, which would never concern itself with a Lord Mayor, simply grovels at the feet of the Doges. As a Socialist I'm bound to recognize the right of Ealing to compare itself with Avignon, but one cannot expect the Muses to put the two on a level."

"Exclusiveness," said the Reverend Poltimore, "has been the salvation of Art, just as the lack of it is proving the downfall of religion. My colleagues of the cloth go about zealously proclaiming the fact that Christianity, in some form or other, is attracting shoals of converts among all sorts of races and tribes that one had scarcely ever heard of, except in reviews of books of travel that one never read. That sort of thing was all very well when the world was more sparsely populated, but nowadays, when it simply teems with human beings, no one is particularly impressed by the fact that a few million, more or less, of converts, of a low stage of mental development, have accepted the teachings of some particular religion. It not only chills one's enthusiasm, it positively shakes one's convictions when one hears that the things one has been brought up to believe as true are being very favourably spoken of by Buriats and Samoyeds and Kanakas."

The Rev. Poltimore Vardon had once seen a resemblance in himself to Voltaire, and had lived alongside the comparison ever since.

"No modern cult or fashion," he continued, "would be favourably influenced by considerations based on statistics; fancy adopting a certain style of hat or cut of coat, because it was being largely worn in Lancashire and the Midlands; fancy favouring a certain brand of champagne because it was being extensively patronized in German summer resorts! No wonder that religion is falling into disuse in this country under such ill-directed methods."

"You can't prevent the heathen being converted if they choose to be," said Lady Caroline; "this is an age of toleration."

"You could always deny it," said the Reverend Poltimore, "like the Belgians do with regrettable occurrences in the Congo. But I would go further than that. I would stimulate the waning enthusiasm for Christianity in this country by labelling it as the exclusive possession of a privileged few. If one could induce the Duchess of Pelm, for instance, to assert that the Kingdom of Heaven, as far as the British Isles are concerned, is strictly limited to herself, two of the under-gardeners at Pelmby, and, possibly, but not certainly, the Dean of Dunster, there would be an instant reshaping of the popular attitude towards religious convictions and observances. Once let the idea get about that the Christian Church is rather more exclusive than the Lawn at Ascot, and you would have a quickening of religious life such as this generation has never witnessed. But as long as the clergy and the religious organizations advertise their creed on the lines of 'Everybody ought to believe in us: millions do,' one can expect nothing but indifference and waning faith."

"Time is just as exclusive in its way as Art," said Lady Caroline.

"In what way?" said the Reverend Poltimore.

"Your pleasantries about religion would have sounded quite clever and advanced in the early 'nineties. Today they have a dreadfully warmed-up flavour. That is the great delusion of you would-be advanced satirists; you imagine you can sit down comfortably for a couple of decades saying daring and startling things about the age you live in, which, whatever other defects it may have, is certainly not standing still. The whole of the Sherard Blaw school of discursive drama suggests, to my mind, Early Victorian furniture in a travelling circus. However, you will always have relays of people from the suburbs to listen to the Mocking Bird of yesterday, and sincerely imagine it is the harbinger of something new and revolutionizing."

"*Would* you mind passing that plate of sandwiches?" asked one of the trio of young ladies, emboldened by famine.

"With pleasure," said Lady Caroline, deftly passing her a nearly empty plate of bread-and-butter.

"I meant the plate of caviare sandwiches. So sorry to trouble you," persisted the young lady.

Her sorrow was misapplied; Lady Caroline had turned her attention to a new-comer.

"A very interesting exhibition," Ada Spelvexit was saying; "faultless technique, as far as I am a judge of technique, and quite a master-touch in the way of poses. But have you noticed how very animal his art is? He seems to shut out the soul from his portraits. I nearly cried when I saw dear Winifred depicted simply as a good-looking healthy blonde."

"I wish you had," said Lady Caroline; "the spectacle of a strong, brave woman weeping at a private view in the Rutland Galleries would have been so sensational. It would certainly have been reproduced in the next Drury Lane drama. And I'm so unlucky; I never see these sensational events. I was ill with appendicitis, you know, when Lulu Braminguard dramatically forgave her husband, after seventeen years of estrangement, during a State luncheon party at Windsor. The old Queen was furious about it. She said it was so disrespectful to the cook to be thinking of such a thing at such a time."

Lady Caroline's recollections of things that hadn't happened at the court of Queen Victoria were notoriously vivid; it was the very widespread fear that she might one day write a book of reminiscences that made her so universally respected.

"As for his full-length picture of Lady Brickfield," continued Ada, ignoring Lady Caroline's commentary as far as possible, "all the expression seems to have been deliberately concentrated in the feet; beautiful feet, no doubt, but still, hardly the most distinctive part of a human being."

"To paint the right people at the wrong end may be an eccentricity, but it is scarcely an indiscretion," pronounced Lady Caroline.

One of the portraits which attracted more than a passing flutter of attention was a costume study of Francesca Bassington. Francesca had secured some highly desirable patronage for the young artist, and in return he had enriched her pantheon of personal possessions with a clever piece of work into which he had thrown an unusual amount of imaginative detail. He had painted her in a costume of the Great Louis's brightest period, seated in front of a tapestry that was so prominent in the composition that it could scarcely be said to form part of the background. Flowers and fruit, in exotic profusion, were its dominant note; quinces, pomegranates, passion-flowers, giant convolvulus, great mauve-pink roses, and grapes that were already being pressed by gleeful cupids in a riotous Arcadian vintage, stood out on its woven texture. The same note was struck in the beflowered satin of the lady's kirtle, and in the pomegranate pattern of the brocade that draped the couch on which she was seated. The artist had called his picture "Recolte." And after one had taken in all the details of fruit and flower and foliage that earned the composition its name, one noted the landscape that showed through a broad casement in the left-hand corner. It was a landscape clutched in the grip of winter, naked, bleak, black-frozen; a winter in which things died and knew no rewakening. If the picture typified harvest, it was a harvest of artificial growth.

"It leaves a great deal to the imagination, doesn't it?" said Ada Spelvexit, who had edged away from the range of Lady Caroline's tongue.

"At any rate one can tell who it's meant for," said Serena Golackly.

"Oh, yes, it's a good likeness of dear Francesca," admitted Ada; "of course, it flatters her."

"That, too, is a fault on the right side in portrait painting," said Serena; "after all, if posterity is going to stare at one for centuries it's only kind and reasonable to be looking just a little better than one's best."

"What a curiously unequal style the artist has!" continued Ada, almost as if she felt a personal grievance against him. "I was just noticing what a lack of soul there was in most of his portraits. Dear Winifred, you know, who speaks so beautifully and feelingly at my gatherings for old women, he's made her look just an ordinary dairy-maidish blonde; and Francesca, who is quite the most soulless woman I've ever met, well, he's given her quite——"

"Hush!" said Serena, "the Bassington boy is just behind you."

Comus stood looking at the portrait of his mother with the feeling of one who comes suddenly across a once-familiar, half-forgotten acquaintance in unfamiliar surroundings. The likeness was undoubtedly a good one, but the artist had caught an expression in Francesca's eyes which few people had ever seen there. It was the expression of a woman who had forgotten for one short moment to be absorbed in the small cares and excitements of her life, the money worries and little social plannings, and had found time to send a look of half-wistful friendliness to some sympathetic companion. Comus could recall that look, fitful and fleeting, in his mother's eyes when she had been a few years younger, before her world had grown to be such a committee-room of ways and means. Almost as a re-discovery, he remembered that she had once figured in his boyish mind as a "rather good sort," more ready to see the laughable side of a piece of mischief than to labour forth a reproof. That the by-gone feeling of good-fellowship had been stamped out was, he knew, probably in great part his own doing, and it was possible that the old friendliness was still there under the surface of things, ready to show itself again if he willed it, and friends were becoming scarcer with him than enemies in these days. Looking at the picture with its wistful hint of a long-ago comradeship, Comus made up his mind that he very much wanted things to be back on their earlier footing, and to see again on his mother's face the look that the artist had caught and perpetuated in its momentary flitting. If the projected Elaine marriage came off, and in spite of recent maladroit behaviour on his part he still counted it an assured thing, much of the immediate cause for estrangement between himself and his mother would be removed, or at any rate easily removable. With the influence of Elaine's money behind him, he promised himself that he would find some occupation that would remove from himself the reproach of being a waster and idler. There were lots of careers, he told himself, that were open to a man with solid financial backing and good connexions. There might yet be jolly times ahead, in which his mother would have her share of the good things that were going, and carking thin-lipped Henry Greech and other of Comus's detractors could take their sour looks and words out of sight and hearing. Thus, staring at the picture as though he were studying its every detail, and seeing really only that wistful friendly smile, Comus made his plans and dispositions for a battle that was already fought and lost.

The crowd grew thicker in the galleries, cheerfully enduring an amount of overcrowding that would have been fiercely resented in a railway carriage. Near the entrance Mervyn Quentock was talking to a Serene Highness, a lady who led a life of obtrusive usefulness, largely imposed on her by a good-natured inability to say "No." "That woman creates a positive draught with the number of bazaars she opens," a frivolously-spoken ex-Cabinet Minister had once remarked. At the present moment she was being whimsically apologetic.

"When I think of the legions of well-meaning young men and women to whom I've given away prizes for proficiency in art-school curriculum, I feel that I ought not to show my face inside a picture gallery. I always imagine that my punishment in another world will be perpetually sharpening pencils and cleaning palettes for unending relays of misguided young people whom I deliberately encouraged in their artistic delusions."

"Do you suppose we shall all get appropriate punishments in another world for our sins in this?" asked Quentock.

"Not so much for our sins as for our indiscretions; they are the things which do the most harm and cause the greatest trouble. I feel certain that Christopher Columbus will undergo the endless torment of being discovered by parties of American tourists. You see I am quite old-fashioned in my ideas about the terrors and inconveniences of the next world. And now I must be running away; I've got to open a Free Library somewhere. You know the sort of thing that happens—one unveils a bust of Carlyle and makes a speech about Ruskin, and then people come in their thousands and read *Rabid Ralph, or Should He Have Bitten Her?* Don't forget, please, I'm going to have the medallion with the fat cupid sitting on a sundial. And just one thing more—perhaps I ought not to ask you, but you have such nice kind eyes, you embolden one to make daring requests, *would* you send me the recipe for those lovely chestnut-and-chicken-liver sandwiches? I know the ingredients, of course, but it's the proportions that make such a difference—just how much liver to how much chestnut, and what amount of red pepper and other things. Thank you so much. I really am going now."

Staring round with a vague half-smile at everybody within nodding distance, Her Serene Highness made one of her characteristic exits, which Lady Caroline declared always reminded her of a scrambled egg slipping off a piece of toast. At the entrance she stopped for a moment to exchange a word or two with a young man who had just arrived. From a corner where he was momentarily hemmed in by a group of tea-consuming dowagers, Comus recognized the new-comer as Courtenay Youghal, and began slowly to labour his way towards him. Youghal was not at the moment the person whose society he most craved for in the world, but there was at least the possibility that he might provide an opportunity for a game of bridge, which was the dominant desire of the moment. The young politician was already surrounded by a group of friends and acquaintances, and was evidently being made the recipient of a salvo of congratulation—presumably on his recent performances in the Foreign Office debate, Comus concluded. But Youghal himself seemed to be announcing the event with which the congratulations were connected. Had some dramatic catastrophe overtaken the Government? Comus wondered. And then, as he pressed nearer, a chance word, the coupling of two names, told him the news.

CHAPTER XI

After the momentous lunch at the Corridor Restaurant, Elaine had returned to Manchester Square (where she was staying with one of her numerous aunts) in a frame of mind that embraced a tangle of competing emotions. In the first place she was conscious of a dominant feeling of relief; in a moment of impetuosity, not wholly influenced by pique, she had settled the problem which hours of hard thinking and serious heart-searching had brought no nearer to solution, and, although she felt just a little inclined to be scared at the head-long manner of her final decision, she had now very little doubt in her own mind that the decision had been the right one. In fact, the wonder seemed rather that she should have been so long in doubt as to which of her wooers really enjoyed her honest approval. She had been in love these many weeks past with an imaginary Comus, but now that she had definitely walked out of her dreamland she saw that nearly all the qualities that had appealed to her on his behalf had been absent from, or only fitfully present in, the character of the real Comus. And now that she had installed Youghal in the first place of her affections he had rapidly acquired in her eyes some of the qualities which ranked highest in her estimation. Like the proverbial buyer she had the happy feminine tendency of magnifying the worth of her possession as soon as she had acquired it. And Courtenay Youghal gave Elaine some justification for her sense of having chosen wisely. Above all other things, selfish and cynical though he might appear at times, he was unfailingly courteous and considerate towards her. That was a circumstance which would always have carried weight with her in judging any man; in this case its value was enormously heightened by contrast with the behaviour of her other wooer. And Youghal had in her eyes the advantage which the glamour of combat, even the combat of words and wire-pulling, throws over the fighter. He stood well in the forefront of a battle which however carefully stage-managed, however honeycombed with personal insincerities and overlaid with calculated mock-heroics, really meant something, really counted for good or wrong in the nation's development and the world's history. Shrewd parliamentary observers might have warned her that Youghal would never stand much higher in the political world than he did at present, as a brilliant Opposition free-lance, leading lively and rather meaningless forays against the dull and rather purposeless foreign policy of a Government that was scarcely either to be blamed for or congratulated on its handling of foreign affairs. The young politician had not the strength of character or convictions that keeps a man naturally in the forefront of affairs and gives his counsels a sterling value, and on the other hand his insincerity was not deep enough to allow him to pose artificially and successfully as a leader of men and shaper of movements. For the moment, however, his place in public life was sufficiently marked out to give him a secure footing in that world where people are counted individually and not in herds. The woman whom he would make his wife would have the chance, too, if she had the will and the skill, to become an individual who counted.

There was balm to Elaine in this reflection, yet it did not wholly suffice to drive out the feeling of pique which Comus had called into being by his slighting view of her as a convenient cash supply in moments of emergency. She found a certain satisfaction in scrupulously observing her promise, made earlier on that eventful day, and sent off a messenger with the stipulated loan. Then a reaction of compunction set in, and she reminded herself that in fairness she ought to write and tell her news in as friendly a fashion as possible to her dismissed suitor before it burst upon him from some other quarter. They parted on more or less quarrelling terms, it was true, but neither of them had foreseen the finality of the parting nor the permanence of the breach between them; Comus might even now be thinking himself half-forgiven, and the awakening would be rather cruel. The letter, however, did not prove an easy one to write; not only did it present difficulties of its own, but it suffered from the competing urgency of a desire to be doing something far pleasanter than writing explanatory and valedictory phrases. Elaine was possessed with an unusual but quite overmastering hankering to visit her cousin Suzette Brankley. They met but rarely at each other's houses and very seldom anywhere else, and Elaine for her part was never conscious of feeling that their opportunities for intercourse lacked anything in the way of adequacy. Suzette accorded her just that touch of patronage which a moderately well-off and immoderately dull girl will usually try to mete out to an acquaintance who is known to be wealthy and suspected of possessing brains. In return Elaine armed herself with that particular brand of mock humility which can be so terribly disconcerting if properly wielded. No quarrel of any description stood between them and one could not legitimately have described them as enemies, but they never disarmed in one another's presence. A misfortune of any magnitude falling on one of them would have been sincerely regretted by the other, but any minor discomfiture would have produced a feeling very much akin to satisfaction. Human nature knows millions of these inconsequent little feuds, springing up and flourishing apart from any basis of racial, political, religious or economic causes, as a hint perhaps to crass unseeing altruists that enmity has its place and purpose in the world as well as benevolence.

Elaine had not personally congratulated Suzette since the formal announcement of her engagement to the young man with the dissentient tailoring effects. The impulse to go and do so now overmastered her sense of what was due to Comus in the way of explanation. The letter was still in its blank unwritten stage, an unmarshalled sequence of sentences forming in her brain, when she ordered her car and made a hurried but well-thought-out change into her most sumptuously sober afternoon toilette. Suzette, she felt tolerably sure, would still be in the costume that she had worn in the Park that morning, a costume that aimed at elaboration of detail, and was damned with overmuch success.

Suzette's mother welcomed her unexpected visitor with obvious satisfaction. Her daughter's engagement, she explained, was not so brilliant from the social point of view as a girl of Suzette's attractions and advantages might have legitimately aspired to, but Egbert was a thoroughly commendable and dependable young man, who would very probably win his way before long to membership of the County Council.

"From there, of course, the road would be open to him to higher things."

"Yes," said Elaine, "he might become an alderman."

"Have you seen their photographs, taken together?" asked Mrs. Brankley, abandoning the subject of Egbert's prospective career.

"No; do show me," said Elaine, with a flattering show of interest; "I've never seen that sort of thing before. It used to be the fashion once for engaged couples to be photographed together, didn't it?"

"It's *very* much the fashion now," said Mrs. Brankley assertively, but some of the complacency had filtered out of her voice.

Suzette came into the room, wearing the dress that she had worn in the Park that morning.

"Of course, you've been hearing all about *the* engagement from mother," she cried, and then set to work conscientiously to cover the same ground.

"We met at Grindelwald, you know. He always calls me his Ice Maiden because we first got to know each other on the skating-rink. Quite romantic, wasn't it? Then we asked him to tea one day, and we got to be quite friendly. Then he proposed."

"He wasn't the only one who was smitten with Suzette," Mrs. Brankley hastened to put in, fearful lest Elaine might suppose that Egbert had had things all his own way. "There was an American millionaire who was quite taken with her, and a Polish count of a very old family. I assure you I felt quite nervous at some of our tea-parties."

Mrs. Brankley had given Grindelwald a sinister but rather alluring reputation among a large circle of untravelled friends as a place where the insolence of birth and wealth was held in precarious check from breaking forth into scenes of savage violence.

"My marriage with Egbert will, of course, enlarge the sphere of my life enormously," pursued Suzette.

"Yes," said Elaine; her eyes were rather remorselessly taking in the details of her cousin's toilette. It is said that nothing is sadder than victory except defeat. Suzette began to feel that the tragedy of both was concentrated in the creation which had given her such unalloyed gratification till Elaine had come on the scene.

"A woman can be so immensely helpful in the social way to a man who is making a career for himself. And I'm so glad to find that we've a great many ideas in common. We each made out a list of our idea of the hundred best books, and quite a number of them were the same."

"He looks bookish," said Elaine, with a critical glance at the photograph.

"Oh, he's not at all a bookworm," said Suzette quickly, "though he's tremendously well-read. He's quite the man of action."

"Does he hunt?" asked Elaine.

"No, he doesn't get much time or opportunity for riding."

"What a pity!" commented Elaine. "I don't think I could marry a man who wasn't fond of riding."

"Of course that's a matter of taste," said Suzette stiffly; "horsey men are not usually gifted with overmuch brains, are they?"

"There is as much difference between a horseman and a horsey man as there is between a well-dressed man and a dressy one," said Elaine judicially; "and you may have noticed how seldom a dressy woman really knows how to dress. As an old lady of my acquaintance observed the other day, some people are born with a sense of how to clothe themselves, others acquire it, others look as if their clothes had been thrust upon them."

She gave Lady Caroline her due quotation marks, but the sudden tactfulness with which she looked away from her cousin's frock was entirely her own idea.

A young man entering the room at this moment caused a diversion that was rather welcome to Suzette.

"Here comes Egbert," she announced, with an air of subdued triumph; it was at least a satisfaction to be able to produce the captive of her charms, alive and in good condition, on the scene. Elaine might be as critical as she pleased, but a live lover outweighed any number of well-dressed straight-riding cavaliers who existed only as a distant vision of the delectable husband.

Egbert was one of those men who have no small talk, but possess an inexhaustible supply of the larger variety. In whatever society he happened to be, and particularly in the immediate neighbourhood of an afternoon-tea table, with a limited audience of womenfolk, he gave the impression of some one who was addressing a public meeting, and would be happy to answer questions afterwards. A suggestion of gaslit mission-halls, wet umbrellas, and discreet applause seemed to accompany him everywhere. He was an exponent, among other things, of what he called New Thought, which seemed to lend itself conveniently to the employment of a good deal of rather stale phraseology. Probably in the course of some thirty odd years of existence he had never been of any notable use to man, woman, child, or animal, but it was his firmly-announced intention to leave the world a better, happier, purer place than he had found it;

against the danger of any relapse to earlier conditions after his disappearance from the scene, he was, of course, powerless to guard. 'Tis not in mortals to ensure succession, and Egbert was admittedly mortal.

Elaine found him immensely entertaining, and would certainly have exerted herself to draw him out if such a proceeding had been at all necessary. She listened to his conversation with the complacent appreciation that one bestows on a stage tragedy, from whose calamities one can escape at any moment by the simple process of leaving one's seat. When at last he checked the flow of his opinions by a hurried reference to his watch, and declared that he must be moving on elsewhere, Elaine almost expected a vote of thanks to be accorded him, or to be asked to signify herself in favour of some resolution by holding up her hand.

When the young man had bidden the company a rapid businesslike farewell, tempered in Suzette's case by the exact degree of tender intimacy that it would have been considered improper to omit or overstep, Elaine turned to her expectant cousin with an air of cordial congratulation.

"He is exactly the husband I should have chosen for you, Suzette."

For the second time that afternoon Suzette felt a sense of waning enthusiasm for one of her possessions.

Mrs. Brankley detected the note of ironical congratulation in her visitor's verdict.

"I suppose she means he's not her idea of a husband, but he's good enough for Suzette," she observed to herself, with a snort that expressed itself somewhere in the nostrils of the brain. Then with a smiling air of heavy patronage she delivered herself of her one idea of a damaging counterstroke.

"And when are we to hear of your engagement, my dear?"

"Now," said Elaine quietly, but with electrical effect; "I came to announce it to you but I wanted to hear all about Suzette first. It will be formally announced in the papers in a day or two."

"But who is it? Is it the young man who was with you in the Park this morning?" asked Suzette.

"Let me see, who was I with in the Park this morning? A very good-looking dark boy? Oh, no, not Comus Bassington. Some one you know by name, anyway, and I expect you've seen his portrait in the papers."

"A flying-man?" asked Mrs. Brankley.

"Courtenay Youghal," said Elaine.

Mrs. Brankley and Suzette had often rehearsed in the privacy of their minds the occasion when Elaine should come to pay her personal congratulations to her engaged cousin. It had never been in the least like this.

On her return from her enjoyable afternoon visit Elaine found an express messenger letter waiting for her. It was from Comus, thanking her for her loan—and returning it.

"I suppose I ought never to have asked you for it," he wrote, "but you are always so deliciously solemn about money matters that I couldn't resist. Just heard the news of your engagement to Courtenay. Congrats. to you both. I'm far too stony broke to buy you a wedding present so I'm going to give you back the bread-and-butter dish. Luckily it still has your crest on it. I shall love to think of you and Courtenay eating bread-and-butter out of it for the rest of your lives."

That was all he had to say on the matter about which Elaine had been preparing to write a long and kindly-expressed letter, closing a rather momentous chapter in her life and his. There was not a trace of regret or upbraiding in his note; he had walked out of their mutual fairyland as abruptly as she had, and to all appearances far more unconcernedly. Reading the letter again and again, Elaine could come to no decision as to whether this was merely a courageous gibe at defeat, or whether it represented the real value that Comus set on the thing that he had lost.

And she would never know. If Comus possessed one useless gift to perfection it was the gift of laughing at Fate even when it had struck him hardest. One day, perhaps, the laughter and mockery would be silent on his lips, and Fate would have the advantage of laughing last.

CHAPTER XII

A DOOR closed and Francesca Bassington sat alone in her well-beloved drawing-room. The visitor who had been enjoying the hospitality of her afternoon-tea table had just taken his departure. The *tête-à-tête* had not been a pleasant one, at any rate as far as Francesca was concerned, but at least it had brought her the information for which she had been seeking. Her rôle of looker-on from a tactful distance had necessarily left her much in the dark concerning the progress of the all-important wooing, but during the last few hours she had, on slender though significant evidence, exchanged her complacent expectancy for a conviction that something had gone wrong. She had spent the previous evening at her brother's house, and had naturally seen nothing of Comus in that uncongenial quarter; neither had he put in an appearance at the breakfast table the following morning. She had met him in the hall at eleven o'clock, and he had hurried past her, merely imparting the information that he would not be in till dinner that evening. He spoke in his sulkiest tone, and his face wore a look of defeat, thinly masked by an air of defiance; it was not the defiance of a man who is losing, but of one who has already lost.

Francesca's conviction that things had gone wrong between Comus and Elaine de Frey grew in strength as the day wore on. She lunched at a friend's house, but it was not a quarter where special social information of any importance was likely to come early to hand. Instead of the news she was hankering for, she had to listen to trivial gossip and speculation on the flirtations and "cases" and "affairs" of a string of acquaintances whose matrimonial projects interested her about as much as the nesting arrangements of the wildfowl in St. James's Park.

"Of course," said her hostess, with the duly impressive emphasis of a privileged chronicler, "we've always regarded Claire as the marrying one of the family, so when Emily came to us and said, 'I've got some news for you,' we all said, 'Claire's engaged!' 'Oh, no,' said Emily, 'it's not Claire this time, it's me.' So then we had to guess who the lucky man was. 'It can't be Captain Parminter,' we all said, 'because he's always been sweet on Joan.' And then Emily said——"

The recording voice reeled off the catalogue of inane remarks with a comfortable purring complacency that held out no hope of an early abandoning of the topic. Francesca sat and wondered why the innocent acceptance of a cutlet and a glass of indifferent claret should lay one open to such unsparing punishment.

A stroll homeward through the Park after lunch brought no further enlightenment on the subject that was uppermost in her mind; what was worse, it brought her, without possibility of escape, within hailing distance of Merla Blathlington, who fastened on to her with the enthusiasm of a lonely tsetse fly encountering an outpost of civilization.

"Just think," she buzzed inconsequently, "my sister in Cambridgeshire has hatched out thirty-three White Orpington chickens in her incubator!"

"What eggs did she put in it?" asked Francesca.

"Oh, some very special strain of White Orpington."

"Then I don't see anything remarkable in the result. If she had put in crocodiles' eggs and hatched out White Orpingtons, there might have been something to write to *Country Life* about."

"What funny fascinating things these little green park-chairs are," said Merla, starting off on a fresh topic; "they always look so quaint and knowing when they're stuck away in pairs by themselves under the trees, as if they were having a heart-to-heart talk or discussing a piece of very private scandal. If they could only speak, what tragedies and comedies they could tell us of, what flirtations and proposals!"

"Let us be devoutly thankful that they can't," said Francesca, with a shuddering recollection of the luncheon-table conversation.

"Of course, it would make one very careful what one said before them—or above them rather," Merla rattled on, and then, to Francesca's infinite relief, she espied another acquaintance sitting in unprotected solitude, who promised to supply a more durable audience than her present rapidly moving companion. Francesca was free to return to her drawing-room in Blue Street to await with such patience as she could command the coming of some visitor who might be able to throw light on the subject that was puzzling and disquieting her. The arrival of George St. Michael boded bad news, but at any rate news, and she gave him an almost cordial welcome.

"Well, you see I wasn't far wrong about Miss de Frey and Courtenay Youghal, was I?" he chirruped, almost before he had seated himself. Francesca was to be spared any further spinning-out of her period of uncertainty. "Yes, it's officially given out," he went on, "and it's to appear in the *Morning Post* tomorrow. I heard it from Colonel Deel this morning, and he had it direct from Youghal himself. Yes, please, one lump; I'm not fashionable, you see." He had made the same remark about the sugar in his tea with unfailing regularity for at least thirty years. Fashions in sugar are apparently stationary. "They say," he continued hurriedly, "that he proposed to her on the Terrace of the House, and a division bell rang and he had to hurry off before she had time to give her answer, and when he got back she simply said, 'The Ayes have it.'" St. Michael paused in his narrative to give an appreciative giggle.

"Just the sort of inanity that would go the rounds," remarked Francesca, with the satisfaction of knowing that she was making the criticism direct to the author and begetter of the inanity in question. Now that the blow had fallen and she knew the full extent of its weight, her feeling towards the bringer of bad news, who sat complacently nibbing at her tea-cakes and scattering crumbs of tiresome small-talk at her feet, was one of whole-hearted dislike. She could sympathize with, or at any rate understand, the tendency of Oriental despots to inflict death or ignominious chastisement on messengers bearing tidings of misfortune and defeat, and St. Michael, she perfectly well knew, was thoroughly aware of the fact that her hopes and wishes had been centred on the possibility of having Elaine for a daughter-in-law; every purring remark that his mean little soul prompted him to contribute to the conversation had an easily recognizable undercurrent of malice. Fortunately for her powers of polite endurance, which had been put to such searching and repeated tests that day, St. Michael had planned out for himself a busy little time-table of afternoon visits, at each of which his self-appointed task of forestalling and embellishing the newspaper announcements of the Youghal-de Frey engagement would be hurriedly but thoroughly performed.

"They'll be quite one of the best-looking and most interesting couples of the season, won't they?" he cried, by way of farewell. The door closed, and Francesca Bassington sat alone in her drawing-room.

Before she could give way to the bitter luxury of reflection on the downfall of her hopes, it was prudent to take precautionary measures against unwelcome intrusion. Summoning the maid who had just speeded the departing St. Michael, she gave the order: "I am not at home this afternoon to Lady Caroline Benaresq." On second thoughts she extended the taboo to all possible callers, and sent a telephone message to catch Comus at his club, asking him to come and see her as soon as he could manage before it was time to dress for dinner. Then she sat down to think, and her thinking was beyond the relief of tears.

She had built herself a castle of hopes, and it had not been a castle in Spain, but a structure well on the probable side of the Pyrenees. There had been a solid foundation on which to build. Miss de Frey's fortune was an assured and unhampered one, her liking for Comus had been an obvious fact; his courtship of her a serious reality. The young people had been much together in public, and their names had naturally been coupled in the match-making gossip of the day. The only serious shadow cast over the scene had been the persistent presence, in foreground or background, of Courtenay Youghal. And now the shadow suddenly stood forth as the reality, and the castle of hopes was a ruin, a hideous mortification of dust and debris, with the skeleton outlines of its chambers till standing to make mockery of its discomfited architect. The daily anxiety about Comus and his extravagant ways and intractable disposition had been gradually lulled by the prospect of his making an advantageous marriage, which would have transformed him from a ne'er-do-well and adventurer into a wealthy idler. He might even have been moulded, by the resourceful influence of an ambitious wife, into a man with some definite purpose in life. The prospect had vanished with cruel suddenness, and the anxieties were crowding back again, more insistent than ever. The boy had had his one good chance in the matrimonial market and missed it; if he were to transfer his attentions to some other well-dowered girl he would be marked down at once as a fortune-hunter, and that would constitute a heavy handicap to the most plausible of wooers. His liking for Elaine had evidently been genuine in its way, though perhaps it would have been rash to read any deeper sentiment into it, but even with the spur of his own inclination to assist him he had failed to win the prize that had seemed so temptingly within his reach. And in the dashing of his prospects, Francesca saw the threatening of her own. The old anxiety as to her precarious tenure of her present quarters put on again all its familiar terrors. One day, she foresaw, in the horribly near future, George St. Michael would come pattering up her stairs with the breathless intelligence that Emmeline Chetrof was going to marry somebody or other in the Guards or the Record Office, as the case might be, and then there would be an uprooting of her life from its home and haven in Blue Street and a wandering forth to some cheap unhappy far-off dwelling, where the stately Van der Meulen and its companion host of beautiful and desirable things would be stuffed and stowed away in soulless surroundings, like courtly *émigrés* fallen on evil days. It was unthinkable, but the trouble was that it had to be thought about. And if Comus had played his cards well and transformed himself from an encumbrance into a son with wealth at his command, the tragedy which she saw looming in front of her might have been avoided, or at the worst whittled down to easily bearable proportions. With money behind one, the problem of where to live approaches more nearly to the simple question of where do you wish to live, and a rich daughter-in-law would have surely seen to it that she did not have to leave her square mile of Mecca and go out into the wilderness of bricks and mortar. If the house in Blue Street could not have been compounded for there were other desirable residences which would have been capable of consoling Francesca for her lost Eden. And now the detested Courtenay Youghal, with his mocking eyes and air of youthful cynicism, had stepped in and overthrown those golden hopes and plans whose non-fulfilment would make such a world of change in her future. Assuredly she had reason to feel bitter against that young man, and she was not disposed to take a very lenient view of Comus's own mismanagement of the affair; her greeting when he at last arrived was not couched in a sympathetic strain.

"So you have lost your chance with the heiress," she remarked abruptly.

"Yes," said Comus coolly; "Courtenay Youghal has added her to his other successes."

"And you have added her to your other failures," pursued Francesca relentlessly; her temper had been tried that day beyond ordinary limits.

"I thought you seemed getting along so well with her," she continued, as Comus remained uncommunicative.

"We hit it off rather well together," said Comus, and added with deliberate bluntness, "I suppose she got rather sick at my borrowing money from her. She thought it was all I was after."

"You borrowed money from her!" said Francesca; "you were fool enough to borrow money from a girl who was favourably disposed towards you, and with Courtenay Youghal in the background waiting to step in and oust you!"

Francesca's voice trembled with misery and rage. This great stroke of good luck that had seemed about to fall into their laps had been thrust aside by an act or series of acts of wanton paltry folly. The good ship had been lost for the sake of the traditional ha'p'orth of tar. Comus had paid some pressing tailor's or tobacconist's bill with a loan unwillingly put at his disposal by the girl he was courting, and had flung away his chances of securing a wealthy and in every way desirable bride. Elaine de Frey and her fortune might have been the making of Comus, but he had hurried in as usual to effect his own undoing. Calmness did not in this case come with reflection; the more Francesca thought about the matter, the more exasperated she grew. Comus threw himself down in a low chair and watched her without a trace of embarrassment or concern at her mortification. He had come to her feeling rather sorry for himself, and bitterly conscious of his defeat, and she had met him with a taunt and without the least hint of sympathy; he determined that she should be tantalized with the knowledge of how small and stupid a thing had stood between the realization and ruin of her hopes for him.

"And to think she should be captured by Courtenay Youghal," said Francesca bitterly; "I've always deplored your intimacy with that young man."

"It's hardly my intimacy with him that's made Elaine accept him," said Comus.

Francesca realized the futility of further upbraiding. Through the tears of vexation that stood in her eyes she looked across at the handsome boy who sat opposite her, mocking at his own misfortune, perversely indifferent to his folly, seemingly almost indifferent to its consequences.

"Comus," she said quietly and wearily, "you are an exact reversal of the legend of Pandora's Box. You have all the charm and advantages that a boy could want to help him on in the world, and behind it all there is the fatal damning gift of utter hopelessness."

"I think," said Comus, "that is the best description that any one has ever given of me."

For the moment there was a flush of sympathy and something like outspoken affection between mother and son. They seemed very much alone in the world just now, and in the general overturn of hopes and plans there flickered a chance that each might stretch out a hand to the other, and summon back to their lives an old dead love that was the best and strongest feeling either of them had known. But the sting of disappointment was too keen, and the flood of resentment mounted too high on either side to allow the chance more than a moment in which to flicker away into nothingness. The old fatal topic of estrangement came to the fore, the question of immediate ways and means, and mother and son faced themselves again as antagonists on a well-disputed field.

"What is done is done," said Francesca, with a movement of tragic impatience that belied the philosophy of her words; "there is nothing to be gained by crying over spilt milk. There is the present and the future to be thought about, though. One can't go on indefinitely as a tenant-for-life in a fools' paradise." Then she pulled herself together and proceeded to deliver an ultimatum which the force of circumstances no longer permitted her to hold in reserve.

"It's not much use talking to you about money, as I know from long experience, but I can only tell you this, that in the middle of the season I'm already obliged to be thinking of leaving town. And you, I'm afraid, will have to be thinking of leaving England at equally short notice. Henry told me the other day that he can get you something out in West Africa. You've had your chance of doing something better for yourself from the financial point of view, and you've thrown it away for the sake of borrowing a little ready money for your luxuries, so now you must take what you can get. The pay won't be very good at first, but living is not dear out there."

"West Africa," said Comus reflectively; "it's a sort of modern substitute for the old-fashioned *oubliette*, a convenient depository for tiresome people. Dear Uncle Henry may talk lugubriously about the burden of Empire, but he evidently recognizes its uses as a refuse consumer."

"My dear Comus, you are talking of the West Africa of yesterday. While you have been wasting your time at school, and worse than wasting your time in the West End, other people have been grappling with the study of tropical diseases, and the West African coast country is being rapidly transformed from a lethal chamber into a sanatorium."

Comus laughed mockingly.

"What a beautiful bit of persuasive prose! It reminds one of the Psalms, and even more of a company prospectus. If you were honest you'd confess that you lifted it straight out of a rubber or railway promotion scheme. Seriously, mother, if I must grub about for a living, why can't I do it in England? I could go into a brewery, for instance."

Francesca shook her head decisively; she could foresee the sort of steady work Comus was likely to accomplish, with the lodestone of town and the minor attractions of race-meetings and similar festivities always beckoning to him from a conveniently attainable distance, but apart from that aspect of the case there was a financial obstacle in the way of his obtaining any employment at home.

"Breweries and all those sort of things necessitate money to start with; one has to pay premiums or invest capital in the undertaking and so forth. And as we have no money available, and can scarcely pay our debts as it is, it's no use thinking about it."

"Can't we sell something?" asked Comus.

He made no actual suggestion as to what should be sacrificed, but he was looking straight at the Van der Meulen.

For a moment Francesca felt a stifling sensation of weakness, as though her heart was going to stop beating. Then she sat forward in her chair and spoke with energy, almost fierceness.

"When I am dead my things can be sold and dispersed. As long as I am alive I prefer to keep them by me."

In her holy place, with all her treasured possessions around her, this dreadful suggestion had been made. Some of her cherished household gods, souvenirs and keepsakes from past days, would, perhaps, not have fetched a very considerable sum in the auction-room, others had a distinct value of their own, but to her they were all precious. And the Van der Meulen, at which Comus had looked with impious appraising eyes, was the most sacred of them all. When Francesca had been away from her town residence or had been confined to her bedroom through illness, the great picture with its stately solemn representation of a long-ago battle-scene, painted to flatter the flattery-loving soul of a warrior-king who was dignified even in his campaigns—this was the first thing she visited on her return to town or convalescence. If an alarm of fire had been raised it would have been the first thing for whose safety she would have troubled. And Comus had almost suggested that it should be parted with, as one sold railway shares and other soulless things.

Scolding, she had long ago realized, was a useless waste of time and energy where Comus was concerned, but this evening she unloosed her tongue for the mere relief that it gave to her surcharged feelings. He sat listening without comment, though she purposely let fall remarks that she hoped might sting him into self-defence or protest. It was an unsparing indictment, the more damaging in that it was so irrefutably true, the more tragic in that it came from perhaps the one person in the world whose opinion he had ever cared for. And he sat through it as silent and seemingly unmoved as though she had been rehearsing a speech for some drawing-room comedy. When she had had her say his method of retort was not the soft answer that turneth away wrath, but the inconsequent one that shelves it.

"Let's go and dress for dinner."

The meal, like so many that Francesca and Comus had eaten in each other's company of late, was a silent one. Now that the full bearings of the disaster had been discussed in all its aspects, there was nothing more to be said. Any attempt at ignoring the situation and passing on to less controversial topics would have been a mockery and pretence which neither of them would have troubled to sustain. So the meal went forward with its dragged-out dreary intimacy of two people who were separated by a gulf of bitterness, whose hearts were hard with resentment against one another.

Francesca felt a sense of relief when she was able to give the maid the order to serve her coffee upstairs. Comus had a sullen scowl on his face, but he looked up as she rose to leave the room, and gave his half-mocking little laugh.

"You needn't look so tragic," he said. "You're going to have your own way. I'll go out to that West African hole."

CHAPTER XIII

Comus found his way to his seat in the stalls of the Straw Exchange Theatre, and turned to watch the stream of distinguished and distinguishable people who made their appearance as a matter of course at a First Night in the height of the season. Pit and gallery were already packed with a throng, tense, expectant and alert, that waited for the rise of the curtain with the eager patience of a terrier watching a dilatory human prepare for outdoor exercises. Stalls and boxes filled slowly and hesitatingly with a crowd whose component units seemed for the most part to recognize the probability that they were quite as interesting as any play they were likely to see. Those who bore no particular face-value themselves derived a certain amount of social dignity from the near neighbourhood of obvious notabilities; if one could not obtain recognition oneself there was some vague pleasure in being able to recognize notoriety at intimately close quarters.

"Who is that woman with the auburn hair and a rather effective belligerent gleam in her eyes?" asked a man sitting just behind Comus. "She looks as if she might have created the world in six days and destroyed it on the seventh."

"I forget her name," said his neighbour; "she writes. She's the author of that book, *The Woman Who Wished it was Wednesday*, you know. It used to be the convention that women writers should be plain and dowdy; now we have gone to the other extreme and build them on extravagantly decorative lines."

A buzz of recognition came from the front rows of the pit, together with a craning of necks on the part of those in less favoured seats. It heralded the arrival of Sherard Blaw, the dramatist who had discovered himself, and who had given so ungrudgingly of his discovery to the world. Lady Caroline, who was already directing little conversational onslaughts from her box, gazed gently for a moment at the new arrival, and then turned to the silver-haired Archdeacon sitting beside her.

"They say the poor man is haunted by the fear that he will die during a general election, and that his obituary notices will be seriously curtailed by the space taken up by the election results. The curse of our party system, from his point of view, is that it takes up so much room in the Press."

The Archdeacon smiled indulgently. As a man he was so exquisitely worldly that he fully merited the name of the Heavenly Worldling bestowed on him by an admiring duchess, and withal his texture was shot with a pattern of such genuine saintliness that one felt that whoever else might hold the keys of Paradise he, at least, possessed a private latchkey to that abode.

"Is it not significant of the altered grouping of things," he observed, "that the Church, as represented by me, sympathizes with the message of Sherard Blaw, while neither the man nor his message find acceptance with unbelievers like you, Lady Caroline?"

Lady Caroline blinked her eyes. "My dear Archdeacon," she said, "no one can be an unbeliever nowadays. The Christian Apologists have left one nothing to disbelieve."

The Archdeacon rose with a delighted chuckle. "I must go and tell that to De la Poulett," he said, indicating a clerical figure sitting in the third row of the stalls; "he spends his life explaining from his pulpit that the glory of Christianity consists in the fact that though it is not true it has been found necessary to invent it."

The door of the box opened and Courtenay Youghal entered, bringing with him a subtle suggestion of chaminade and an atmosphere of political tension. The Government had fallen out of the good graces of a section of its supporters, and those who were not in the know were busy predicting a serious crisis over a forthcoming division in the Committee stage of an important Bill. This was Saturday night, and unless some successful cajolery were effected between now and Monday afternoon, Ministers would be, seemingly, in danger of defeat.

"Ah, here is Youghal," said the Archdeacon; "he will be able to tell us what is going to happen in the next forty-eight hours. I hear the Prime Minister says it is a matter of conscience, and they will stand or fall by it."

His hopes and sympathies were notoriously on the Ministerial side.

Youghal greeted Lady Caroline and subsided gracefully into a chair well in the front of the box. A buzz of recognition rippled slowly across the house.

"For the Government to fall on a matter of conscience," he said, "would be like a man cutting himself with a safety razor."

Lady Caroline purred a gentle approval.

"I'm afraid it's true, Archdeacon," she said.

No one can effectively defend a Government when it's been in office several years. The Archdeacon took refuge in light skirmishing.

"I believe Lady Caroline sees the makings of a great Socialist statesman in you, Youghal," he observed.

"Great Socialist statesmen aren't made, they're stillborn," replied Youghal.

"What is the play about tonight?" asked a pale young woman who had taken no part in the talk.

"I don't know," said Lady Caroline, "but I hope it's dull. If there is any brilliant conversation in it I shall burst into tears."

In the front row of the upper circle a woman with a restless starling-voice was discussing the work of a temporarily fashionable composer, chiefly in relation to her own emotions, which she seemed to think might prove generally interesting to those around her.

"Whenever I hear his music I feel that I want to go up into a mountain and pray. Can you understand that feeling?"

The girl to whom she was unburdening herself shook her head.

"You see, I've heard his music chiefly in Switzerland, and we were up among the mountains all the time, so it wouldn't have made any difference."

"In that case," said the woman, who seemed to have emergency emotions to suit all geographical conditions, "I should have wanted to be in a great silent plain by the side of a rushing river."

"What I think is so splendid about his music–" commenced another starling-voice on the farther side of the girl. Like sheep that feed greedily before the coming of a storm, the starling-voices seemed impelled to extra effort by the knowledge of four imminent intervals of acting during which they would be hushed into constrained silence.

In the back row of the dress circle a late-comer, after a cursory glance at the programme, had settled down into a comfortable narrative, which was evidently the resumed thread of an unfinished taxi-drive monologue.

"We all said, 'It can't be Captain Parminter, because he's always been sweet on Joan,' and then Emily said––"

The curtain went up, and Emily's contribution to the discussion had to be held over till the entr'acte.

The play promised to be a success. The author, avoiding the pitfall of brilliancy, had aimed at being interesting; and as far as possible, bearing in mind that his play was a comedy, he had striven to be amusing. Above all he had remembered that in the laws of stage proportions it is permissible and generally desirable that the part should be greater than the whole; hence he had been careful to give the leading lady such a clear and commanding lead over the other characters of the play that it was impossible for any of them ever to get on level terms with her. The action of the piece was now and then delayed thereby, but the duration of its run would be materially prolonged.

The curtain came down on the first act amid an encouraging instalment of applause, and the audience turned its back on the stage and began to take a renewed interest in itself. The authoress of *The Woman Who Wished it was Wednesday* had swept like a convalescent whirlwind, subdued but potentially tempestuous, into Lady Caroline's box.

"I've just trodden with all my weight on the foot of an eminent publisher as I was leaving my seat," she cried, with a peal of delighted laughter. "He was such a dear about it; I said I hoped I hadn't hurt him, and he said, 'I suppose you think, who drives hard bargains should himself be hard.' Wasn't it pet lamb of him?"

"I've never trodden on a pet lamb," said Lady Caroline, "so I've no idea what its behaviour would be under the circumstances."

"Tell me," said the authoress, coming to the front of the box, the better to survey the house, and perhaps also with a charitable desire to make things easy for those who might pardonably wish to survey her, "tell me, please, where is the girl sitting whom Courtenay Youghal is engaged to?"

Elaine was pointed out to her, sitting in the fourth row of the stalls, on the opposite side of the house to where Comus had his seat. Once during the interval she had turned to give him a friendly nod of recognition as he stood in one of the side gangways, but he was absorbed at the moment in looking at himself in the glass panel. The grave brown eyes and the mocking green-grey ones had looked their last into each other's depths.

For Comus this first-night performance, with its brilliant gathering of spectators, its groups and coteries of lively talkers, even its counterfoil of dull chatterers, its pervading atmosphere of stage and social movement, and its intruding undercurrent of political flutter, all this composed a tragedy in which he was the chief character. It was the life he knew and loved and basked in, and it was the life he was leaving. It would go on reproducing itself again and again, with its stage interest and social interest and intruding outside interests, with the same lively chattering crowd, the people who had done things being pointed out by people who recognized them to people who didn't—it would all go on with unflagging animation and sparkle and enjoyment, and for him it would have stopped utterly. He would be in some unheard-of-sun-blistered wilderness, where natives and pariah dogs and raucous-throated crows fringed round mockingly on one's loneliness, where one rode for sweltering miles for the chance of meeting a collector or police officer, with whom most likely on closer acquaintance one had hardly two ideas in common, where female society was represented at long intervals by some climate-withered woman missionary or official's wife, where food and sickness and veterinary lore became at last the three outstanding subjects on which the mind settled, or rather sank. That was the life he foresaw and dreaded, and that was the life he was going to. For a boy who went out to it from the dulness of some country rectory, from a neighbourhood where a flower show and a cricket match formed the social landmarks of the year, the feeling of exile might not be very crushing, might indeed be lost in the sense of change and adventure. But Comus had lived too thoroughly in the centre of things to regard life in a backwater as anything else than stagnation, and stagnation while one is young he justly regarded as an offence against nature and reason, in keeping with the perverted mockery that sends decrepit invalids touring painfully about the world and shuts panthers up in narrow cages. He was being put aside, as a wine is put aside, but to deteriorate instead of gaining in the process, to lose the best time of his youth and health and good looks in a world where youth and health and good looks count for much and where time never returns lost possessions. And thus, as the curtain swept down on the close of each act, Comus felt a sense of depression and deprivation sweep down on himself; bitterly he watched his last evening of social gaiety slipping away to its end. In less than an hour it would be over; in a few months' time it would be an unreal memory.

In the third interval, as he gazed round at the chattering house, some one touched him on the arm. It was Lady Veula Croot.

"I suppose in a week's time you'll be on the high seas?" she said. "I'm coming to your farewell dinner, you know; your mother has just asked me. I'm not going to talk the usual rot to you about how much you will like it and so on. I sometimes think that one of the advantages of hell will be that no one will have the impertinence to point out to you that you're really better off than you would be anywhere else. What do you think of the play? Of course one can foresee the end; she will come to her husband with the announcement that their longed-for child is going to be born, and that will smooth over everything. So conveniently effective to wind up a comedy with the commencement of some one else's tragedy. And every one will go away saying, 'I'm glad it had a happy ending.'"

Lady Veula moved back to her seat, with her pleasant smile on her lips and the look of infinite weariness in her eyes.

The interval, the last interval, was drawing to a close, and the house began to turn with fidgety attention towards the stage for the unfolding of the final phase of the play. Francesca sat in Serena Golackly's box listening to Colonel Springfield's story of what happened to a pigeon-cote in his compound at Poona. Every one who knew the Colonel had to listen to that story a good many times, but Lady Caroline had mitigated the boredom of the infliction, and in fact invested it with a certain sporting interest, by offering a prize to the person who heard it oftenest in the course of the season, the competitors being under an honourable understanding not to lead up to the subject. Ada Spelvexit and a boy in the Foreign Office were at present at the top of the list with five recitals each to their score, but the former was suspected of doubtful adherence to the rules and spirit of the competition.

"And there, dear lady," concluded the Colonel, "were the eleven dead pigeons. What had become of the bandicoot no one ever knew."

Francesca thanked him for his story, and complacently inscribed the figure 4 on the margin of her theatre programme. Almost at the same moment she heard George St. Michael's voice pattering out a breathless piece of intelligence for the edification of Serena Golackly and any one else who might care to listen. Francesca galvanized into sudden attention.

"Emmeline Chetrof to a fellow in the Indian Forest Department. He's got nothing but his pay, and they can't be married for four or five years: an absurdly long engagement, don't you think so? All very well to wait seven years for a wife in patriarchal times when you probably had others to go on with, and you lived long enough to celebrate your own tercentenary, but under modern conditions it seems a foolish arrangement."

St. Michael spoke almost with a sense of grievance. A marriage project that tied up all the small pleasant nuptial gossip items about bridesmaids and honeymoon and recalcitrant aunts and so forth for an indefinite number of years seemed scarcely decent in his eyes, and there was little satisfaction or importance to be derived from early and special knowledge of an event which loomed as far distant as a Presidential Election or a change of

Viceroy. But to Francesca, who had listened with startled apprehension at the mention of Emmeline Chetrof's name, the news came in a flood of relief and thankfulness. Short of entering a nunnery and taking celibate vows, Emmeline could hardly have behaved more conveniently than in tying herself up to a lover whose circumstances made it necessary to relegate marriage to the distant future. For four or five years Francesca was assured of undisturbed possession of the house in Blue Street, and after that period who knew what might happen? The engagement might stretch on indefinitely, it might even come to nothing under the weight of its accumulated years, as sometimes happened with these protracted affairs. Emmeline might lose her fancy for her absentee lover, and might never replace him with another. A golden possibility of perpetual tenancy of her present home began to float once more through Francesca's mind. As long as Emmeline had been unbespoken in the marriage market there had always been the haunting likelihood of seeing the dreaded announcement, "A marriage has been arranged and will shortly take place," in connexion with her name. And now a marriage had been arranged and would *not* shortly take place, might indeed never take place. St. Michael's information was likely to be correct in this instance; he would never have invented a piece of matrimonial intelligence which gave such little scope for supplementary detail of the kind he loved to supply. As Francesca turned to watch the fourth act of the play, her mind was singing a pæan of thankfulness and exultation. It was as though some artificer sent by the gods had reinforced with a substantial cord the horsehair thread that held up the sword of Damocles over her head. Her love for her home, for her treasured household possessions and her pleasant social life, was able to expand once more in present security, and feed on future hope. She was still young enough to count four or five years as a long time, and tonight she was optimistic enough to prophesy smooth things of the future that lay beyond that span. Of the fourth act, with its carefully held back but obviously imminent reconciliation between the leading characters, she took in but little, except that she vaguely understood it to have a happy ending. As the lights went up she looked round on the dispersing audience with a feeling of friendliness uppermost in her mind; even the sight of Elaine de Frey and Courtenay Youghal leaving the theatre together did not inspire her with a tenth part of the annoyance that their entrance had caused her. Serena's invitation to go on to the Savoy for supper fitted in exactly with her mood of exhilaration. It would be a fit and appropriate wind-up to an auspicious evening. The cold chicken and modest brand of Chablis waiting for her at home should give way to a banquet of more festive nature.

In the crush of the vestibule, friends and enemies, personal and political, were jostled and locked together in the general effort to rejoin temporarily estranged garments and secure the attendance of elusive vehicles. Lady Caroline found herself at close quarters with the estimable Henry Greech, and experienced some of the joy which comes to the homeward wending sportsman when a chance shot presents itself on which he may expend his remaining cartridges.

"So the Government is going to climb down, after all," she said, with a provocative assumption of private information on the subject.

"I assure you the Government will do nothing of the kind," replied the Member of Parliament with befitting dignity; "the Prime Minister told me last night that under no circumstances—"

"My dear Mr. Greech," said Lady Caroline, "we all know that Prime Ministers are wedded to the truth, but like other wedded couples they sometimes live apart."

For her, at any rate, the comedy had had a happy ending.

Comus made his way slowly and lingeringly from the stalls, so slowly that the lights were already being turned down and great shroud-like dustcloths were being swathed over the ornamental gilt-work. The laughing, chattering, yawning throng had filtered out of the vestibule, and was melting away in final groups from the steps of the theatre. An impatient attendant gave him his coat and locked up the cloak-room. Comus stepped out under the portico; he looked at the posters announcing the play, and in anticipation he could see other posters announcing its 200th performance. Two hundred performances; by that time the Straw Exchange Theatre would be to him something so remote and unreal that it would hardly seem to exist or to have ever existed except in his fancy. And to the laughing, chattering throng that would pass in under that portico to the 200th performance, he would be, to those that had known him, something equally remote and non-existent. "The good-looking Bassington boy? Oh, dead, or rubber-growing or sheep-farming, or something of that sort."

CHAPTER XIV

The farewell dinner which Francesca had hurriedly organized in honour of her son's departure threatened from the outset to be a doubtfully successful function. In the first place, as he observed privately, there was very little of Comus and a good deal of farewell in it. His own particular friends were unrepresented. Courtenay Youghal was out of the question; and though Francesca would have stretched a point and welcomed some of his other male associates of whom she scarcely approved, he himself had been opposed to including any of them in the invitations. On the other hand, as Henry Greech had provided Comus with this job that he was going out to, and was, moreover, finding part of the money for the necessary outfit, Francesca had felt it her duty to ask him and his wife to the dinner; the obtuseness that seems to cling to some people like a garment throughout their life had caused Mr. Greech to accept the invitation. When Comus heard of the circumstance he laughed long and boisterously; his spirits, Francesca noted, seemed to be rising fast as the hour for departure drew near.

The other guests included Serena Golackly and Lady Veula, the latter having been asked on the inspiration of the moment at the theatrical first night. In the height of the season it was not easy to get together a goodly selection of guests at short notice, and Francesca had gladly fallen in with Serena's suggestion of bringing with her Stephen Thorle, who was alleged, in loose feminine phrasing, to "know all about" tropical Africa. His travels and experiences in those regions probably did not cover much ground or stretch over any great length of time, but he was one of those individuals who can describe a continent on the strength of a few days' stay in a coast town as intimately and dogmatically as a palæontologist will reconstruct an extinct mammal from the evidence of a stray shinbone. He had the loud penetrating voice and the prominent penetrating eyes of a man who can do no listening in the ordinary way and whose eyes have to perform the function of listening for him. His vanity did not necessarily make him unbearable, unless one had to spend much time in his society, and his need for a wide field of audience and admiration was mercifully calculated to spread his operations over a considerable human area. Moreover, his craving for attentive listeners forced him to interest himself in a wonderful variety of subjects on which he was able to discourse fluently and with a certain semblance of special knowlledge. Politics he avoided; the ground was too well known, and there was a definite No to every definite Yes that could be put forward. Moreover, argument was not congenial to his disposition, which preferred an unchallenged flow of dissertation modified by occasional helpful questions which formed the starting-point for new offshoots of word-spinning. The promotion of cottage industries, the prevention of juvenile street trading, the extension of the Borstal prison system, the furtherance of vague talkative religious movements, the fostering of inter-racial *ententes,* all found in him a tireless exponent, a fluent and entertaining, though perhaps not very convincing, advocate. With the real motive power behind these various causes he was not very closely identified; to the spade-workers who carried on the actual labours of each particular movement he bore the relation of a trowel-worker, delving superficially at the surface, but able to devote a proportionately far greater amount of time to the advertisement of his progress and achievements. Such was Stephen Thorle, a governess in the nursery of Chelsea-bred religions, a skilled window-dresser in the emporium of his own personality, and needless to say, evanescently popular amid a wide but shifting circle of acquaintances. He improved on the record of a socially much-travelled individual whose experience has become classical, and went to most of the best houses—twice.

His inclusion as a guest at this particular dinner-party was not a very happy inspiration. He was inclined to patronize Comus, as well as the African continent, and on even slighter acquaintance. With the exception of Henry Greech, whose feelings towards his nephew had been soured by many years of overt antagonism, there was an uncomfortable feeling among those present that the topic of the black-sheep export trade, as Comus would have himself expressed it, was being given undue prominence in what should have been a festive farewell banquet. And Comus, in whose honour the feast was given, did not contribute much towards its success; though his spirits seemed strung up to a high pitch, his merriment was more the merriment of a cynical and amused onlooker than of one who responds to the gaiety of his companions. Sometimes he laughed quietly to himself at some chance remark of a scarcely mirth-provoking nature, and Lady Veula, watching him narrowly, came to the conclusion that an element of fear was blended with his seemingly buoyant spirits. Once or twice he caught her eye across the table, and a certain sympathy seemed to grow up between them, as though they were both consciously watching some lugubrious comedy that was being played out before them.

An untoward little incident had marked the commencement of the meal. A small still-life picture that hung over the sideboard had snapped its cord and slid down with an alarming clatter on to the crowded board beneath it. The picture itself was scarcely damaged, but its fall had been accompanied by a tinkle of broken glass, and it was found that a liqueur glass, one out of a set of seven that would be impossible to match, had been shivered into fragments. Francesca's almost motherly love for her possessions made her peculiarly sensible to a feeling of annoyance and depression at the accident, but she turned politely to listen to Mrs. Greech's account of a misfortune in which four soup-plates were involved. Mrs. Henry was not a brilliant conversationalist, and her flank was speedily turned by Stephen Thorle, who recounted a slum experience in which two entire families did all their feeding out of one damaged soup-plate.

"The gratitude of those poor creatures when I presented them with a set of table crockery apiece, the tears in their eyes and in their voices when they thanked me, would be impossible to describe."

"Thank you all the same for describing it," said Comus.

The listening eyes went swiftly round the table to gather evidence as to how this rather disconcerting remark had been received, but Thorle's voice continued uninterruptedly to retail stories of East End gratitude, never failing to mention the particular deeds of disinterested charity on his part which had evoked and justified the gratitude. Mrs. Greech had to suppress the interesting sequel to her broken crockery narrative, to wit, how she subsequently matched the shattered soup-plates at Harrod's. Like an imported plant species that sometimes flourishes exceedingly, and makes itself at home to the dwarfing and overshadowing of all native species, Thorle dominated the dinner-party and thrust its original purport somewhat into the background. Serena began to look helplessly apologetic. It was altogether rather a relief when the filling of champagne glasses gave Francesca an excuse for bringing matters back to their intended footing.

"We must all drink a health," she said. "Comus, my own dear boy, a safe and happy voyage to you, much prosperity in the life you are going out to, and in due time a safe and happy return——"

Her hand gave an involuntary jerk in the act of raising the glass, and the wine went streaming across the tablecloth in a froth of yellow bubbles. It certainly was not turning out a comfortable or auspicious dinner-party.

"My dear mother," cried Comus, "you must have been drinking healths all the afternoon to make your hand so unsteady."

He laughed gaily and with apparent carelessness, but again Lady Veula caught the frightened note in his laughter. Mrs. Henry, with practical sympathy, was telling Francesca two good ways for getting wine-stains out of tablecloths. The smaller economies of life were an unnecessary branch of learning for Mrs. Greech, but she studied them as carefully and conscientiously as a stay-at-home plain-dwelling English child commits to memory the measurements and altitudes of the world's principal peaks. Some women of her temperament and mentality know by heart the favourite colours, flowers, and hymn-tunes of all the members of the Royal Family; Mrs. Greech would possibly have failed in an examination of that nature, but she knew what to do with carrots that have been overlong in storage.

Francesca did not renew her speech-making; a chill seemed to have fallen over all efforts at festivity, and she contented herself with refilling her glass and simply drinking to her boy's good health. The others followed her example, and Comus drained his glass with a brief "Thank you all very much." The sense of constraint which hung over the company was not, however, marked by any uncomfortable pause in the conversation. Henry Greech was a fluent thinker, of the kind that prefer to do their thinking aloud; the silence that descended on him as a mantle in the House of Commons was an official livery of which he divested himself as thoroughly as possible in private life. He did not propose to sit through dinner as a mere listener to Mr. Thorle's personal narrative of philanthropic movements and experiences, and took the first opportunity of launching himself into a flow of satirical observations on current political affairs. Lady Veula was inured to this sort of thing in her own home circle, and sat listening with the stoical indifference with which an Eskimo might accept the occurrence of one snowstorm the more, in the course of an Arctic winter. Serena Golackly felt a certain relief at the fact that her imported guest was not, after all, monopolizing the conversation. But the latter was too determined a personality to allow himself to be thrust aside for many minutes by the talkative M.P. Henry Greech paused for an instant to chuckle at one of his own shafts of satire, and immediately Thorle's penetrating voice swept across the table.

"Oh, you politicians!" he exclaimed, with pleasant superiority; "you are always fighting about how things should be done, and the consequence is you are never able to do anything. Would you like me to tell you what a Unitarian horse-dealer said to me at Brindisi about politicians?"

A Unitarian horse-dealer at Brindisi had all the allurement of the unexpected. Henry Greech's witticisms at the expense of the Front Opposition bench were destined to remain as unfinished as his wife's history of the broken soup-plates. Thorle was primed with an ample succession of stories and themes, chiefly concerning poverty, thriftlessness, reclamation, reformed characters, and so forth, which carried him in an almost uninterrupted sequence through the remainder of the dinner.

"What I want to do is to make people think," he said, turning his prominent eyes on to his hostess; "it's so hard to make people think."

"At any rate you give them the opportunity," said Comus cryptically.

As the ladies rose to leave the table Comus crossed over to pick up one of Lady Veula's gloves that had fallen to the floor.

"I did not know you kept a dog," said Lady Veula.

"I could have sworn I saw one follow you across the hall this evening," she said.

"A small black dog, something like a schipperke?" asked Comus in a low voice.

"Yes, that was it."

"I saw it myself tonight; it ran from behind my chair just as I was sitting down. Don't say anything to the others about it; it would frighten my mother."

"Have you ever seen it before?" Lady Veula asked quickly.

"Once, when I was six years old. It followed my father downstairs."

Lady Veula said nothing. She knew that Comus had lost his father at the age of six.

In the drawing-room Serena made nervous excuses for her talkative friend.

"Really, rather an interesting man, you know, and up to the eyes in all sorts of movements. Just the sort of person to turn loose at a drawing-room meeting, or to send down to a mission-hall in some unheard-of neighbourhood. Given a sounding-board and a harmonium, and a titled woman of some sort in the chair, and he'll be perfectly happy; I must say I hadn't realized how overpowering he might be at a small dinner-party."

"I should say he was a very good man," said Mrs. Greech; she had forgiven the mutilation of her soup-plate story.

The party broke up early, as most of the guests had other engagements to keep. With a belated recognition of the farewell nature of the occasion they made pleasant little good-bye remarks to Comus, with the usual predictions of prosperity and anticipations of an ultimate auspicious return. Even Henry Greech sank his personal dislike of the boy for the moment, and made hearty jocular allusions to a home-coming, which, in the elder man's eyes, seemed possibly pleasantly remote. Lady Veula alone made no reference to the future; she simply said, "Good-bye, Comus," but her voice was the kindest of all, and he responded with a look of gratitude. The weariness in her eyes was more marked than ever as she lay back against the cushions of her carriage.

"What a tragedy life is!" she said aloud to herself.

Serena and Stephen Thorle were the last to leave, and Francesca stood alone for a moment at the head of the stairway watching Comus laughing and chatting as he escorted the departing guests to the door. The ice-wall was melting under the influence of coming separation, and never had he looked more adorably handsome in her eyes, never had his merry laugh and mischief-loving gaiety seemed more infectious than on this night of his farewell banquet. She was glad enough that he was going away from a life of idleness and extravagance and temptation, but she began to suspect that she would miss, for a little while at any rate, the high-spirited boy who could be so attractive in his better moods. Her impulse, after the guests had gone, was to call him to her and hold him once more in her arms, and repeat her wishes for his happiness and good-luck in the land he was going to, and her promise of his welcome back, some not too distant day, to the land he was leaving. She wanted to forget, and to make him forget, the months of irritable jangling and sharp discussions, the months of cold aloofness and indifference, and to remember only that he was her own dear Comus as in the days of yore, before he had grown from an unmanageable pickle into a weariful problem. But she feared lest she should break down, and she did not wish to cloud his light-hearted gaiety on the very eve of his departure. She watched him for a moment as he stood in the hall, settling his tie before a mirror, and then went quietly back to her drawing-room. It had not been a very successful dinner-party, and the general effect it had left on her was one of depression.

Comus, with a lively musical-comedy air on his lips, and a look of wretchedness in his eyes, went out to visit the haunts that he was leaving so soon.

CHAPTER XV

ELAINE YOUGHAL sat at lunch in the Speise Saal of one of Vienna's costlier hotels. The double-headed eagle, with its "K.u.K." legend, everywhere met the eye and announced the imperial favour in which the establishment basked. Some several square yards of yellow bunting, charged with the image of another double-headed eagle, floating from the highest flagstaff above the building, betrayed to the initiated the fact that a Russian Grand Duke was concealed somewhere on the premises. Unannounced by heraldic symbolism, but unconcealable by reason of nature's own blazonry, were several citizens and citizenesses of the great republic of the Western world. One or two Cobdenite members of the British Parliament, engaged in the useful task of proving that the cost of living in Vienna was on an exorbitant scale, flitted with restrained importance through a land whose fatness they had come to spy out; every fancied overcharge in their bills was welcome as providing another nail in the coffin of their fiscal opponents. It is the glory of democracies that they may be misled, but never driven. Here and there, like brave deeds in a dust-patterned world, flashed and glittered the sumptuous uniforms of representatives of the

Austrian military caste. Also in evidence, at discreet intervals, were stray units of the Semitic tribe that nineteen centuries of European neglect had been unable to mislay.

Elaine, sitting with Courtenay at an elaborately appointed luncheon table, gay with high goblets of Bohemian glassware, was mistress of three discoveries. First, to her disappointment, that if you frequent the more expensive hotels of Europe you must be prepared to find, in whatever country you may chance to be staying, a depressing international likeness between them all. Secondly, to her relief, that one is not expected to be sentimentally amorous during a modern honeymoon. Thirdly, rather to her dismay, that Courtenay Youghal did not necessarily expect her to be markedly affectionate in private. Some one had described him, after their marriage, as one of Nature's bachelors, and she began to see how aptly the description fitted him.

"Will those Germans on our left never stop talking?" she asked, as an undying flow of Teutonic small-talk rattled and jangled across the intervening stretch of carpet. "Not one of those three women has ceased talking for an instant since we've been sitting here."

"They will presently, if only for a moment," said Courtenay; "when the dish you have ordered comes in there will be a deathly silence at the next table. No German can see a *plat* brought in for some one else without being possessed with a great fear that it represents a more toothsome morsel or a better money's worth than what he has ordered for himself."

The exuberant Teutonic chatter was balanced on the other side of the room by an even more penetrating conversation unflaggingly maintained by a party of Americans, who were sitting in judgment on the cuisine of the country they were passing through, and finding few extenuating circumstances.

"What Mr. Lonkins wants is a real *deep* cherry pie," announced a lady in a tone of dramatic and honest conviction.

"Why, yes, that is so," corroborated a gentleman who was apparently the Mr. Lonkins in question; "a real *deep* cherry pie."

"We had the same trouble way back in Paris," proclaimed another lady; "little Jerome and the girls don't want to eat any more *crême renversée*. I'd give anything if they could get some real cherry pie."

"Real *deep* cherry pie," assented Mr. Lonkins.

"Way down in Ohio we used to have peach pie that was real good," said Mrs. Lonkins, turning on a tap of reminiscence that presently flowed to a cascade. The subject of pies seemed to lend itself to indefinite expansion.

"So those people think of nothing but their food?" asked Elaine, as the virtues of roasted mutton suddenly came to the fore and received emphatic recognition, even the absent and youthful Jerome being quoted in its favour.

"On the contrary," said Courtenay, "they are a widely-travelled set, and the man has had a notably interesting career. It is a form of homesickness with them to discuss and lament the cookery and foods that they've never had the leisure to stay at home and digest. The Wandering Jew probably babbled unremittingly about some breakfast dish that took so long to prepare that he had never time to eat it."

A waiter deposited a dish of Wiener Nierenbraten in front of Elaine. At the same moment a magic hush fell upon the three German ladies at the adjoining table, and the flicker of a great fear passed across their eyes. Then they burst forth again into tumultuous chatter. Courtenay had proved a reliable prophet.

Almost at the same moment as the luncheon-dish appeared on the scene, two ladies arrived at a neighbouring table, and bowed with dignified cordiality to Elaine and Courtenay. They were two of the more worldly and travelled of Elaine's extensive stock of aunts, and they happened to be making a short stay at the same hotel as the young couple. They were far too correct and rationally minded to intrude themselves on their niece, but it was significant of Elaine's altered view as to the sanctity of honeymoon life that she secretly rather welcomed the presence of her two relatives in the hotel, and had found time and occasion to give them more of her society than she would have considered necessary or desirable a few weeks ago. The younger of the two she rather liked, in a restrained fashion, as one likes an unpretentious watering-place or a restaurant that does not try to give one a musical education in addition to one's dinner. One felt instinctively about her that she would never wear rather more valuable diamonds than any other woman in the room, and would never be the only person to be saved in a steamboat disaster or hotel fire. As a child she might have been perfectly well able to recite "On Linden when the sun was low," but one felt certain that nothing ever induced her to do so. The elder aunt, Mrs. Goldbrook, did not share her sister's character as a human rest-cure; most people found her rather disturbing, chiefly, perhaps, from her habit of asking unimportant questions with enormous solemnity. Her manner of inquiring after a trifling ailment gave one the impression that she was more concerned with the fortunes of the malady than with oneself, and when one got rid of a cold one felt that she almost expected to be given its postal address. Probably her manner was merely the defensive outwork of an innate shyness, but she was not a woman who commanded confidences.

"A telephone call for Courtenay," commented the younger of the two women as Youghal hurriedly flashed through the room; "the telephone system seems to enter very largely into the young man's life."

"The telephone has robbed matrimony of most of its sting," said the elder; "so much more discreet than pen and ink communications which get read by the wrong people."

Elaine's aunts were conscientiously worldly; they were the natural outcome of a stock that had been conscientiously strait-laced for many generations.

Elaine had progressed to the pancake stage before Courtenay returned.

"Sorry to be away so long," he said, "but I've arranged something rather nice for tonight. There's rather a jolly masquerade ball on. I've 'phoned about getting a costume for you, and it's all right. It will suit you beautifully, and I've got my harlequin dress with me. Madame Kelnicort, excellent soul, is going to chaperon you, and she'll take you back any time you like; I'm quite unreliable when I get into fancy dress. I shall probably keep going till some unearthly hour of the morning."

A masquerade ball in a strange city hardly represented Elaine's idea of enjoyment. Carefully to disguise one's identity in a neighbourhood where one was entirely unknown seemed to her rather meaningless. With Courtenay, of course, it was different; he seemed to have friends and acquaintances everywhere. However, the matter had progressed to a point which would have made a refusal to go seem rather ungracious. Elaine finished her pancake and began to take a polite interest in her costume.

"What is your character?" asked Madame Kelnicort that evening, as they uncloaked, preparatory to entering the already crowded ball-room.

"I believe I'm supposed to represent Marjolaine de Montfort, whoever she may have been," said Elaine. "Courtenay declares he only wanted to marry me because I'm his ideal of her."

"But what a mistake to go as a character you know nothing about. To enjoy a masquerade ball you ought to throw away your own self and be the character you represent. Now Courtenay has been Harlequin since half-way through dinner; I could see it dancing in his eyes. At about six o'clock tomorrow morning he will fall asleep and wake up a member of the British House of Parliament on his honeymoon, but tonight he is unrestrainedly Harlequin."

Elaine stood in the ball-room surrounded by a laughing, jostling throng of pierrots, jockeys, Dresden-china shepherdesses, Rumanian peasant-girls, and all the lively make-believe creatures that form the ingredients of a fancy-dress ball. As she stood watching them she experienced a growing feeling of annoyance, chiefly with herself. She was assisting, as the French say, at one of the gayest scenes of Europe's gayest capital, and she was conscious of being absolutely unaffected by the gaiety around her. The costumes were certainly interesting to look at, and the music good to listen to, and to that extent she was amused, but the *abandon* of the scene made no appeal to her. It was like watching a game of which you did not know the rules, and in the issue of which you were not interested. Elaine began to wonder what was the earliest moment at which she could drag Madame Kelnicort away from the revel without being guilty of sheer cruelty. Then Courtenay wriggled out of the crush and came towards her, a joyous, laughing Courtenay, looking younger and handsomer than she had ever seen him. She could scarcely recognize in him tonight the rising young debater who made embarrassing onslaughts on the Government's foreign policy before a crowded House of Commons. He claimed her for the dance that was just starting, and steered her dexterously into the heart of the waltzing crowd.

"You look more like Marjolaine than I should have thought a mortal woman of these days could look," he declared, "only Marjolaine did smile sometimes. You have rather the air of wondering if you'd left out enough tea for the servants' breakfast. Don't mind my teasing; I love you to look like that, and besides, it makes a splendid foil to my Harlequin—my selfishness coming to the fore again, you see. But you really are to go home the moment you're bored; the excellent Kelnicort gets heaps of dances throughout the winter, so don't mind sacrificing her."

A little later in the evening Elaine found herself standing out a dance with a grave young gentleman from the Russian Embassy.

"Monsieur Courtenay enjoys himself, doesn't he?" he observed, as the youthful-looking harlequin flashed past them, looking like some restless gorgeous-hued dragon-fly. "Why is it that the good God has given your countrymen the boon of eternal youth? Some of your countrywomen, too, but all of the men."

Elaine could think of many of her countrymen who were not and never could have been youthful, but as far as Courtenay was concerned she recognized the fitness of the remark. And the recognition carried with it a sense of depression. Would he always remain youthful and keen on gaiety and revelling, while she grew staid and retiring? She had thrust the lively intractable Comus out of her mind, as by his perverseness he had thrust himself out of her heart, and she had chosen the brilliant young man of affairs as her husband. He had honestly let her see the selfish side of his character while he was courting her, but she had been prepared to make due sacrifices to the selfishness of a public man who had his career to consider above all other things. Would she also have to make sacrifices to the harlequin spirit which was now revealing itself as an undercurrent in his nature? When one has inured oneself to the idea of a particular form of victimization it is disconcerting to be confronted with another. Many a man who would patiently undergo martyrdom for religion's sake would be furiously unwilling to be a martyr to neuralgia.

"I think that is why you English love animals so much," pursued the young diplomat; "you are such splendid animals yourselves. You are lively because you want to be lively, not because people are looking on at you. Monsieur Courtenay is certainly an animal. I mean it as a high compliment."

"Am I an animal?" asked Elaine.

"I was going to say you are an angel," said the Russian, in some embarrassment, "but I do not think that would do; angels and animals would never get on together. To get on with animals you must have a sense of humour, and I don't suppose angels have any sense of humour; you see it would be no use to them as they never hear any jokes."

"Perhaps," said Elaine, with a tinge of bitterness in her voice, "perhaps I am a vegetable."

"I think you most remind me of a picture," said the Russian.

It was not the first time Elaine had heard the simile.

"I know," she said, "the Narrow Gallery at the Louvre: attributed to Leonardo da Vinci."

Evidently the impression she made on people was solely one of externals.

Was that how Courtenay regarded her? Was that to be her function and place in life, a painted background, a decorative setting to other people's triumphs and tragedies? Somehow tonight she had the feeling that a general might have who brought imposing forces into the field and could do nothing with them. She possessed youth and good looks, considerable wealth, and had just made what would be thought by most people a very satisfactory marriage. And already she seemed to be standing aside as an onlooker where she had expected herself to be taking a leading part.

"Does this sort of thing appeal to you?" she asked the young Russian, nodding towards the gay scrimmage of masqueraders and rather prepared to hear an amused negative.

"But yes, of course," he answered; "costume balls, fancy fairs, café chantant, casino, anything that is not real life appeals to us Russians. Real life with us is the sort of thing that Maxim Gorki deals in. It interests us immensely, but we like to get away from it sometimes."

Madame Kelnicort came up with another prospective partner, and Elaine delivered her ukase: one more dance and then back to the hotel. Without any special regret she made her retreat from the revel which Courtenay was enjoying under the impression that it was life and the young Russian under the firm conviction that it was not.

Elaine breakfasted at her aunts' table the next morning at much her usual hour. Courtenay was sleeping the sleep of a happy tired animal. He had given instructions to be called at eleven o'clock. from which time onward the *Neue Freie Presse*, the *Zeit*, and his toilet would occupy his attention till he appeared at the luncheon table. There were not many people breakfasting when Elaine arrived on the scene, but the room seemed to be fuller than it really was by reason of a penetrating voice that was engaged in recounting how far the standard of Viennese breakfast fare fell below the expectations and desires of little Jerome and the girls.

"If ever little Jerome becomes President of the United States," said Elaine, "I shall be able to contribute quite an informing article on his gastronomic likes and dislikes to the papers."

The aunts were discreetly inquisitive as to the previous evening's entertainment.

"If Elaine would flirt mildly with somebody it would be such a good thing," said Mrs. Goldbrook; "it would remind Courtenay that he's not the only attractive young man in the world."

Elaine, however, did not gratify their hopes; she referred to the ball with the detachment she would have shown in describing a drawing-room show of cottage industries. It was not difficult to discern in her description of the affair the confession that she had been slightly bored. From Courtenay, later in the day, the aunts received a much livelier impression of the festivities, from which it was abundantly clear that he, at any rate, had managed to amuse himself. Neither did it appear that his good opinion of his own attractions had suffered any serious shock. He was distinctly in a very good temper.

"The secret of enjoying a honeymoon," said Mrs. Goldbrook afterwards to her sister, "is not to attempt too much."

"You mean——?"

"Courtenay is content to try and keep one person amused and happy, and he thoroughly succeeds."

"I certainly don't think Elaine is going to be very happy," said her sister, "but at least Courtenay saved her from making the greatest mistake she could have made—marrying that young Bassington."

"He has also," said Mrs. Goldbrook, "helped her to make the next biggest mistake of her life—marrying Courtenay Youghal."

CHAPTER XVI

It was late afternoon by the banks of a swiftly rushing river, a river that gave back a haze of heat from its waters as though it were some stagnant steaming lagoon, and yet seemed to be whirling onward with the determination of a living thing, perpetually eager and remorseless, leaping savagely at any obstacle that attempted to stay its course; an unfriendly river, to whose waters you committed yourself at your peril. Under the hot breathless shade of the trees on its shore arose that acrid all-pervading smell that seems to hang everywhere about the tropics, a smell as of some monstrous musty still-room where herbs and spices have been crushed and distilled and stored for hundreds of years, and where the windows have seldom been opened. In the dazzling heat that still held undisputed sway over the scene, insects and birds seemed preposterously alive and active, flitting their gay colours through the sunbeams, and crawling over the baked dust in the full swing and pursuit of their several businesses; the flies engaged in Heaven knows what, and the fly-catchers busy with the flies. Beasts and humans showed no such indifference to the temperature; the sun would have to slant yet farther downward before the earth would become a fit arena for their revived activities. In the sheltered basement of a wayside rest-house a gang of native hammock-bearers slept or chattered drowsily through the last hours of the long midday halt; wide awake, yet almost motionless in the thrall of a heavy lassitude, their European master sat alone in an upper chamber, staring out through a narrow window-opening at the native village, spreading away in thick clusters of huts girt around with cultivated vegetation. It seemed a vast human ant-hill, which would presently be astir with its teeming human life, as though the Sun God in his last departing stride had roused it with a careless kick. Even as Comus watched he could see the beginnings of the evening's awakening. Women, squatting in front of their huts, began to pound away at the rice or maize that would form the evening meal, girls were collecting their water-pots preparatory to a walk down to the river, and enterprising goats made tentative forays through gaps in the ill-kept fences of neighbouring garden-plots; their hurried retreats showed that here at least some one was keeping alert and wakeful vigil. Behind a hut perched on a steep hill-side, just opposite to the rest-house, two boys were splitting wood with a certain languid industry; farther down the road a group of dogs were leisurely working themselves up to quarrelling pitch. Here and there, bands of evil-looking pigs roamed about, busy with foraging excursions that came unpleasantly athwart the borderline of scavenging. And from the trees that bounded and intersected the village rose the horrible, tireless, spiteful-sounding squawking of the iron-throated crows.

Comus sat and watched it all with a sense of growing aching depression. It was so utterly trivial to his eyes, so devoid of interest, and yet it was so real, so serious, so implacable in its continuity. The brain grew tired with the thought of its unceasing reproduction. It had all gone on, as it was going on now, by the side of the great rushing, swirling river, this tilling and planting and harvesting, marketing and store-keeping, feast-making and fetish-worship and love-making, burying and giving in marriage, child-bearing and child-rearing, all this had been going on, in the shimmering, blistering heat and the warm nights, while he had been a youngster at school, dimly recognizing Africa as a division of the earth's surface that it was advisable to have a certain nodding acquaintance with. It had been going on in all its trifling detail, as its serious intensity, when his father and his grandfather in their day had been little boys at school, it would go on just as intently as ever long after Comus and his generation had passed away, just as the shadows would lengthen and fade under the mulberry trees in that far-away English garden, round the old stone fountain where a leaden otter for ever preyed on a leaden salmon.

Comus rose impatiently from his seat, and walked wearily across the hut to another window-opening which commanded a broad view of the river. There was something which fascinated and then depressed one in its ceaseless hurrying onward sweep, its tons of water rushing on for all time, as long as the face of the earth should remain unchanged. On its farther shore could be seen spread out at intervals other teeming villages, with their cultivated plots and pasture clearings, their moving dots which meant cattle and goats and dogs and children. And far up its course, lost in the forest growth that fringed its banks, were hidden away yet more villages, human herding-grounds where men dwelt and worked and bartered, squabbled and worshipped, sickened and perished, while the river went by with its endless swirl and rush of gleaming waters. One could well understand primitive early races making propitiatory sacrifices to the spirit of a great river on whose shores they dwelt. Time and the river were the two great forces that seemed to matter here.

It was almost a relief to turn back to that other outlook and watch the village life that was now beginning to wake in earnest. The procession of water-fetchers had formed itself in a long chattering line that stretched riverwards. Comus wondered how many tens of thousands of times that procession had been formed since first the village came into existence. They had been doing it while he was playing in the cricket-fields at school, while he was spending Christmas holidays in Paris, while he was going his careless round of theatres, dances, suppers and card-parties, just as they were doing it now; they would be doing it when there was no one alive who remembered Comus Bassington. This thought recurred again and again with painful persistence, a morbid growth arising in part from his loneliness.

Staring dumbly out at the toiling, sweltering human ant-hill, Comus marvelled how missionary enthusiasts could labour hopefully at the work of transplanting their religion, with its home-grown accretions of fatherly parochial benevolence, in this heat-blistered, fever-scourged wilderness, where men lived like groundbait and died like flies. Demons one might believe in, if one did not hold one's imagination in healthy check, but a kindly all-managing God, never. Somewhere in the west country of England Comus had an uncle who lived in a rose-smothered rectory and taught a wholesome gentle-hearted creed that expressed itself in the spirit of "Little lamb, Who made thee?" and faithfully reflected the beautiful homely Christ-child sentiment of Saxon Europe. What a far-away, unreal fairy-story it all seemed here in this West African land, where the bodies of men were of as little account as the bubbles that floated on the oily froth of the great flowing river, and where it required a stretch of wild profitless imagination to credit them with undying souls! In the life he had come from Comus had been accustomed to think of individuals as definite masterful personalities, making their several marks on the circumstances that revolved around them; they did well or ill, or in most cases indifferently, and were criticized, praised, blamed, thwarted, or tolerated, or given way to. In any case, humdrum or outstanding, they had their spheres of importance, little or big. They dominated a breakfast table or harassed a Government, according to their capabilities or opportunities, or perhaps they merely had irritating mannerisms. At any rate it seemed highly probable that they had souls. Here a man simply made a unit in an unnumbered population, an inconsequent dot in a loosely-compiled death-roll. Even his own position as a white man exalted conspicuously above a horde of black natives did not save Comus from the depressing sense of nothingness which his first experience of fever had thrown over him. He was a lost, soulless body in this great uncaring land; if he died another would take his place, his few effects would be inventoried and sent down to the coast, some one else would finish off any tea or whisky that he left behind–that would be all.

It was nearly time to be starting towards the next halting-place where he would dine, or at any rate eat something. But the lassitude which the fever had bequeathed him made the tedium of travelling through interminable forest-tracks a weariness to be deferred as long as possible. The bearers were nothing loath to let another half-hour or so slip by, and Comus dragged a battered paper-covered novel from the pocket of his coat. It was a story dealing with the elaborately tangled love affairs of a surpassingly uninteresting couple, and even in his almost bookless state Comus had not been able to plough his way through more than two-thirds of its dull length; bound up with the cover, however, were some pages of advertisement, and these the exile scanned with a hungry intentness that the romance itself could never have commanded. The name of a shop, of a street, the address of a restaurant, came to him as a bitter reminder of the world he had lost, a world that ate and drank and flirted, gambled and made merry, a world that debated and intrigued and wire-pulled, fought or compromised political battles–and recked nothing of its outcasts wandering through forest paths and steamy swamps or lying in the grip of fever. Comus read and re-read those few lines of advertisement, just as he treasured a much-crumpled programme of a first-night performance at the Straw Exchange Theatre; they seemed to make a little more real the past that was already too shadowy and so utterly remote. For a moment he could almost capture the sensation of being once again in those haunts that he loved; then he looked round and pushed the book wearily from him. The steaming heat, the forest, the rushing river hemmed him in on all sides.

The two boys who had been splitting wood ceased from their labours and straightened their backs; suddenly the smaller of the two gave the other a resounding whack with a split lath that he still held in his hand, and flew up the hillside with a scream of laughter and simulated terror, the bigger lad following in hot pursuit. Up and down the steep bush-grown slope they raced and twisted and dodged, coming sometimes to close quarters in a hurricane of squeals and smacks, rolling over and over like fighting kittens, and breaking away again to start fresh provocation and fresh pursuit. Now and again they would lie for a time panting in what seemed the last stage of exhaustion, and then they would be off in another wild scamper, their dusky bodies flitting through the bushes, disappearing and reappearing with equal suddenness. Presently two girls of their own age, who had returned from the water-fetching, sprang out on them from ambush, and the four joined in one joyous gambol that lit up the hillside with shrill echoes and glimpses of flying limbs. Comus sat and watched, at first with an amused interest, then with a returning flood of depression and heartache. Those wild young human kittens represented the joy of life, he was the outsider, the lonely alien, watching something in which he could not join, a happiness in which he had no part or lot. He would pass presently out of the village and his bearers' feet would leave their indentations in the dust: that would be his most permanent memorial in this little oasis of teeming life. And that other life, in which he once moved with such confident sense of his own necessary participation in it, how completely he had passed out of it! Amid all its laughing throngs, its card-parties and race-meetings and country-house gatherings, he was just a mere name, remembered or forgotten, Comus Bassington, the boy who went away. He had loved himself very well and never troubled greatly whether any one else really loved him, and now he realized what he had made of his life. And at the same time he knew that if his chance were to come again he would throw it away just as surely, just as perversely. Fate played with him with loaded dice; he would lose always.

One person in the whole world had cared for him, for longer than he could remember, cared for him perhaps more than he knew, cared for him perhaps now. But a wall of ice had mounted up between him and her, and across it there blew that cold breath that chills or kills affection.

The words of a well-known old song, the wistful cry of a lost cause, rang with insistent mockery through his brain:

Better loved you canna be,
Will ye ne'er come back again?

If it was love that was to bring him back he must be an exile for ever. His epitaph in the mouths of those that remembered him would be: Comus Bassington, the boy who never came back.

And in his unutterable loneliness he bowed his head on his arms, that he might not see the joyous scrambling frolic on yonder hill-side.

CHAPTER XVII

THE bleak rawness of a grey December day held sway over St. James's Park, that sanctuary of lawn and tree and pool, into which the bourgeois innovator has rushed ambitiously time and again, to find that he must take the patent leather from off his feet, for the ground on which he stands is hallowed ground.

In the lonely hour of early afternoon, when the workers had gone back to their work, and the loiterers were scarcely yet gathered again, Francesca Bassington made her way restlessly along the stretches of gravelled walk that bordered the ornamental water. The overmastering unhappiness that filled her heart and stifled her thinking powers found answering echo in her surroundings. There is a sorrow that lingers in old parks and gardens that the busy streets have no leisure to keep by them; the dead must bury their dead in Whitehall or the Place de la Concorde, but there are quieter spots where they may still keep tryst with the living and intrude the memory of their bygone selves on generations that have almost forgotten them. Even in tourist-trampled Versailles the desolation of a tragedy that cannot die haunts the terraces and fountains like a blood-stain that will not wash out; in the Saxon Garden at Warsaw there broods the memory of long-dead things, coeval with the stately trees that shade its walks, and with the carp that swim today in its ponds as they doubtless swam there when "Lieber Augustin" was a living person and not as yet an immortal couplet. And St. James's Park, with its lawns and walks and water-fowl, harbours still its associations with a bygone order of men and women, whose happiness and sadness are woven into its history, dim and grey as they were once bright and glowing, like the faded pattern worked into the fabric of an old tapestry. It was here that Francesca had made her way when the intolerable inaction of waiting had driven her forth from her home. She was waiting for that worst news of all, the news which does not kill hope, because there has been none to kill, but merely ends suspense. An early message had said that Comus was ill, which might have meant much or little; then there had come that morning a cablegram which only meant one thing; in a few hours she would get a final message, of which this was the preparatory forerunner. She already knew as much as that awaited message would tell her. She knew that she would never see Comus again, and she knew now that she loved him beyond all things that the world could hold for her. It was no sudden rush of pity or compunction that clouded her judgment or gilded her recollection of him; she saw him as he was, the beautiful wayward laughing boy, with his naughtiness, his exasperating selfishness, his insurmountable folly and perverseness, his cruelty that spared not even himself, and as he was, as he always had been, she knew that he was the one thing that the Fates had willed that she should love. She did not stop to accuse or excuse herself for having sent him forth to what was to prove his death. It was, doubtless, right and reasonable that he should have gone out there, as hundreds of other men went out, in pursuit of careers; the terrible thing was that he would never come back. The old cruel hopelessness that had always chequered her pride and pleasure in his good looks and high spirits and fitfully charming ways had dealt her a last crushing blow; he was dying somewhere thousands of miles away without hope of recovery, without a word of love to comfort him, and without hope or shred of consolation she was waiting to hear of the end. The end; that last dreadful piece of news which would write "Nevermore" across his life and hers.

The lively bustle in the streets had been a torture that she could not bear. It wanted but two days to Christmas, and the gaiety of the season, forced or genuine, rang out everywhere. Christmas shopping, with its anxious solicitude or self-centred absorption, overspread the West End and made the pavements scarcely passable at certain favoured points. Proud parents, parcel-laden and surrounded by escorts of their young people, compared notes with one another on the looks and qualities of their offspring and exchanged loud hurried confidences on the difficulty or success which each had experienced in getting the right presents for one and all. Shouted directions where to find this or that article at its best mingled with salvos of Christmas good wishes. To Francesca, making her way frantically through the carnival of happiness with that lonely deathbed in her eyes, it had seemed a callous mockery of her pain; could not people remember that there were crucifixions as well as joyous birthdays in the world? Every mother that she passed happy in the company of a fresh-looking, clean-limbed schoolboy son sent a fresh stab at her heart, and the very shops had their bitter memories. There was the tea-shop where he and she had often taken tea together, or, in the days of their estrangement, sat with their separate friends at separate tables. There were other shops where extravagantly-incurred bills had furnished material for those frequently recurring scenes of recrimination, and the Colonial outfitters, where, as he had phrased it in whimsical mockery, he had bought grave-clothes for his burying-alive. The "oubliette"! She remembered the bitter petulant name he had flung at his destined exile. There at least he had been harder on himself than the Fates were pleased to will; never, as long as Francesca lived and had a brain that served her, would she be able to forget. That narcotic would never be given to her. Unrelenting, unsparing memory would be with her always to remind her of those last days of tragedy. Already her mind was dwelling on the details of that ghastly farewell dinner-party and recalling one by one the incidents of ill-omen that had marked it; how they had sat down seven to table and how one liqueur glass in the set of seven had been shivered into fragments, how her glass had slipped from her hand as she raised it to her lips to wish Comus a safe return; and the strange, quiet hopelessness of Lady Veula's "Good-bye"; she remembered now how it had chilled and frightened her at the moment.

The park was filling again with its floating population of loiterers, and Francesca's footsteps began to take a homeward direction. Something seemed to tell her that the message for which she waited had arrived and was lying there on the hall table. Her brother, who had announced his intention of visiting her early in the afternoon, would have gone by now; he knew nothing of this morning's bad news—the instinct of a wounded animal to creep away by itself had prompted her to keep her sorrow from him as long as possible. His visit did not necessitate her presence; he was bringing an Austrian friend, who was compiling a work on the Franco-Flemish school of painting, to inspect the Van der Meulen, which Henry Greech hoped might perhaps figure as an illustration in the book. They were due to arrive shortly after lunch, and

Francesca had left a note of apology, pleading an urgent engagement elsewhere. As she turned to make her way across the Mall into the Green Park a gentle voice hailed her from a carriage that was just drawing up by the sidewalk. Lady Caroline Benaresq had been favouring the Victoria Memorial with a long unfriendly stare.

"In primitive days," she remarked, "I believe it was the fashion for great chiefs and rulers to have large numbers of their relatives and dependents killed and buried with them; in these more enlightened times we have invented quite another way of making a great sovereign universally regretted. My dear Francesca," she broke off suddenly, catching the misery that had settled in the other's eyes, "what is the matter? Have you had bad news from out there?"

"I am waiting for very bad news," said Francesca, and Lady Caroline knew what had happened.

"I wish I could say something; I can't." Lady Caroline spoke in a harsh, grunting voice that few people had ever heard her use.

Francesca crossed the Mall, and the carriage drove on.

"Heaven help that poor woman," said Lady Caroline, which was, for her, startlingly like a prayer.

As Francesca entered the hall she gave a quick look at the table; several packages, evidently an early batch of Christmas presents, were there, and two or three letters. On a salver by itself was the cablegram for which she had waited. A maid, who had evidently been on the look-out for her, brought her the salver. The servants were well aware of the dreadful thing that was happening, and there was pity on the girl's face and in her voice.

"This came for you ten minutes ago, ma'am, and Mr. Greech has been here, ma'am, with another gentleman, and was sorry you weren't at home. Mr. Greech said he would call again in about half an hour."

Francesca carried the cablegram unopened into the drawing-room and sat down for a moment to think. There was no need to read it yet, for she knew what she would find written there. For a few pitiful moments Comus would seem less hopelessly lost to her if she put off the reading of that last terrible message. She rose and crossed over to the windows and pulled down the blinds, shutting out the waning December day, and then re-seated herself. Perhaps in the shadowy half-light her boy would come and sit with her again for awhile and let her look her last upon his loved face; she could never touch him again or hear his laughing petulant voice, but surely she might look on her dead. And her starving eyes saw only the hateful soulless things of bronze and silver and porcelain that she had set up and worshipped as gods; look where she would they were there around her, the cold ruling deities of the home that held no place for her dead boy. He had moved in and out among them, the warm, living, breathing thing that had been hers to love, and she had turned her eyes from that youthful comely figure to adore a few feet of painted canvas, a musty relic of a long-departed craftsman. And now he was gone from her sight, from her touch, from her hearing for ever, without even a thought to flash between them for all the dreary years that she should live, and these things of canvas and pigment and wrought metal would stay with her. They were her soul. And what shall it profit a man if he save his soul and slay his heart in torment?

On a small table by her side was Mervyn Quentock's portrait of her—the prophetic symbol of her tragedy; the rich dead harvest of unreal things that had never known life, and the bleak thrall of black unending Winter, a Winter in which things died and knew no re-awakening.

Francesca turned to the small envelope lying in her lap; very slowly she opened it and read the short message. Then she sat numb and silent for a long, long time, or perhaps only for minutes. The voice of Henry Greech in the hall, inquiring for her, called her to herself. Hurriedly she crushed the piece of paper out of sight; he would have to be told, of course, but just yet her pain seemed too dreadful to be laid bare. "Comus is dead" was a sentence beyond her power to speak.

"I have bad news for you, Francesca, I'm sorry to say," Henry announced. Had he heard, too?

"Henneberg has been here and looked at the picture," he continued, seating himself by her side, "and though he admired it immensely as a work of art, he gave me a disagreeable surprise by assuring me that it's not a genuine Van der Meulen. It's a splendid copy, but still, unfortunately, only a copy."

Henry paused and glanced at his sister to see how she had taken the unwelcome announcement. Even in the dim light he caught some of the anguish in her eyes.

"My dear Francesca," he said soothingly, laying his hand affectionately on her arm, "I know that this must be a great disappointment to you, you've always set such store by this picture, but you mustn't take it too much to heart. These disagreeable discoveries come at times to most picture fanciers and owners. Why, about twenty per cent. of the alleged Old Masters in the Louvre are supposed to be wrongly attributed. And there are heaps of similar cases in this country. Lady Dovecourt was telling me the other day that they simply daren't have an expert in to examine the Van Dykes at Columbey for fear of unwelcome disclosures. And, besides, your picture is such an excellent copy that it's by no means without a value of its own. You must get over the disappointment you naturally feel, and take a philosophical view of the matter. . . ."

Francesca sat in stricken silence, crushing the folded morsel of paper tightly in her hand and wondering if the thin, cheerful voice with its pitiless, ghastly mockery of consolation would never stop.

When William Came

A STORY OF LONDON UNDER
THE HOHENZOLLERNS

Chapter I

THE SINGING-BIRD AND THE BAROMETER

CICELY YEOVIL sat in a low swing chair, alternately looking at herself in a mirror and at the other occupant of the room in the flesh. Both prospects gave her undisguised satisfaction. Without being vain she was duly appreciative of good looks, whether in herself or in another, and the reflection that she saw in the mirror, and the young man whom she saw seated at the piano, would have come with credit out of a more severely critical inspection. Probably she looked longer and with greater appreciation at the piano-player than at her own image; her good looks were an inherited possession, that had been with her more or less all her life, while Ronnie Storre was a comparatively new acquisition, discovered and achieved, so to speak, by her own enterprise, selected by her own good taste. Fate had given her adorable eyelashes and an excellent profile. Ronnie was an indulgence she had bestowed on herself.

Cicely had long ago planned out for herself a complete philosophy of life, and had resolutely set to work to carry her philosophy into practice. "When love is over how little of love even the lover understands," she quoted to herself from one of her favourite poets, and transposed the saying into "While life is with us how little of life even the materialist understands." Most people that she knew took endless pains and precautions to preserve and prolong their lives and keep their powers of enjoyment unimpaired; few, very few, seemed to make any intelligent effort at understanding what they really wanted in the way of enjoying their lives, or to ascertain what were the best means for satisfying those wants. Fewer still bent their whole energies to the one paramount aim of getting what they wanted in the fullest possible measure. Her scheme of life was not a wholly selfish one; no one could understand what she wanted as well as she did herself, therefore she felt that she was the best person to pursue her own ends and cater for her own wants. To have others thinking and acting for one merely meant that one had to be perpetually grateful for a lot of well-meant and usually unsatisfactory services. It was like the case of a rich man giving a community a free library, when probably the community only wanted free fishing or reduced tram-fares. Cicely studied her own whims and wishes, experimented in the best method of carrying them into effect, compared the accumulated results of her experiments, and gradually arrived at a very clear idea of what she wanted in life, and how best to achieve it. She was not by disposition a self-centred soul, therefore she did not make the mistake of supposing that one can live successfully and gracefully in a crowded world without taking due notice of the other human elements around one. She was instinctively far more thoughtful for others than many a person who is genuinely but unseeingly addicted to unselfishness. Also she kept in her armoury the weapon which can be so mightily effective if used sparingly by a really sincere individual—the knowledge of when to be a humbug.

Ambition entered to a certain extent into her life and governed it perhaps rather more than she knew. She desired to escape from the doom of being a nonentity, but the escape would have to be effected in her own way and in her own time; to be governed by ambition was only a shade or two better than being governed by convention.

The drawing-room in which she and Ronnie were sitting was of such proportions that one hardly knew whether it was intended to be one room or several, and it had the merit of being moderately cool at two o'clock on a particularly hot July afternoon. In the coolest of its many alcoves servants had noiselessly set out an improvised luncheon table: a tempting array of caviare, crab and mushroom salads, cold asparagus, slender hock bottles and high-stemmed wine goblets peeped out from amid a sitting of Charlotte Klemm roses.

Cicely rose from her seat and went over to the piano.

"Come," she said, touching the young man lightly with a finger-tip on the top of his very sleek, copper-hued head, "we're going to have a picnic-lunch today up here; it's so much cooler than any of the downstairs rooms, and we shan't be bothered with the servants trotting in and out all the time. Rather a good idea of mine, wasn't it?"

Ronnie, after looking anxiously to see that the word "picnic" did not portend tongue sandwiches and biscuits, gave the idea his blessing.

"What is young Storre's profession?" some one had once asked concerning him.

"He has a great many friends who have independent incomes," had been the answer.

The meal was begun in an appreciative silence; a picnic in which three kinds of red pepper were available for the caviare, demanded a certain amount of respectful attention.

"My heart ought to be like a singing-bird today, I suppose," said Cicely presently.

"Because your good man is coming home?" asked Ronnie.

Cicely nodded.

"He's expected some time this afternoon, though I'm rather vague as to which train he arrives by. Rather a stifling day for railway travelling."

"And *is* your heart doing the singing-bird business?" asked Ronnie.

"That depends," said Cicely, "if I may choose the bird. A missel-thrush would do, perhaps; it sings loudest in stormy weather, I believe."

Ronnie disposed of two or three stems of asparagus before making any comment on this remark.

"Is there going to be stormy weather?" he asked.

"The domestic barometer is set rather that way," said Cicely. "You see, Murrey has been away for ever so long, and, of course, there will be lots of things he won't be used to, and I'm afraid matters may be rather strained and uncomfortable for a time."

"Do you mean that he will object to me?" asked Ronnie.

"Not in the least," said Cicely, "he quite broad-minded on most subjects, and he realizes that this is an age in which sensible people know thoroughly well what they want, and are determined to get what they want. It pleases me to see a lot of you, and to spoil you and pay you extravagant compliments about your good looks and your music, and to imagine at times that I'm in danger of getting fond of you; I don't see any harm in it, and I don't suppose Murrey will either—in fact, I shouldn't be surprised if he takes rather a liking to you. No, it's the general situation that will trouble and exasperate him; he's not had time to get accustomed to the *fait accompli* like we have. It will break on him with horrible suddenness."

"He was somewhere in Russia when the war broke out, wasn't he?" said Ronnie.

"Somewhere in the wilds of Eastern Siberia, shooting and bird collecting, miles away from a railway or telegraph line, and it was all over before he knew anything about it; it didn't last very long, when you come to think of it. He was due home somewhere about that time, and when the weeks slipped by without my hearing from him, I quite thought he'd been captured in the Baltic or somewhere on the way back. It turned out that he was down with marsh fever in some out-of-the-way spot, and everything was over and finished with before he got back to civilization and newspapers."

"It must have been a bit of a shock," said Ronnie, busy with a well-devised salad; "still, I don't see why there should be domestic storms when he comes back. You are hardly responsible for the catastrophe that has happened."

"No," said Cicely, "but he'll come back naturally feeling sore and savage with everything he sees around him, and he won't realize just at once that we've been through all that ourselves, and have reached the stage of sullen acquiescence in what can't be helped. He won't understand, for instance, how we can be enthusiastic and excited over Gorla Mustelford's début, and things of that sort; he'll think we are a set of callous revellers, fiddling while Rome is burning."

"In this case," said Ronnie, "Rome isn't burning, it's burnt. All that remains to be done is to rebuild it—when possible."

"Exactly, and he'll say we're not doing much towards helping at that."

"But," protested Ronnie, "the whole thing has only just happened. 'Rome wasn't built in a day,' and we can't rebuild our Rome in a day."

"I know," said Cicely, "but so many of our friends, and especially Murrey's friends, have taken the thing in a tragical fashion, and cleared off to the Colonies, or shut themselves up in their country houses, as though there was a sort of moral leprosy infecting London."

"I don't see what good that does," said Ronnie.

"It doesn't do any good, but it's what a lot of them have done because they felt like doing it, and Murrey will feel like doing it too. That is where I foresee trouble and disagreement."

Ronnie shrugged his shoulders.

"I would take things tragically if I saw the good of it," he said; "as matters stand it's too late in the day and too early to be anything but philosophical about what one can't help. For the present we've just got to make the best of things. Besides, you can't very well turn down Gorla at the last moment."

"I'm not going to turn down Gorla, or anybody," said Cicely with decision. "I think it would be silly, and silliness doesn't appeal to me. That is why I foresee storms on the domestic horizon. After all, Gorla has her career to think of. Do you know," she added, with a change of tone, "I rather wish you would fall in love with Gorla; it would make me horribly jealous and a little jealousy is such a good tonic for any woman who knows how to dress well. Also, Ronnie, it would prove that you are capable of falling love with some one, of which I've grave doubts up to the present."

"Love is one of the few things in which the make-believe is superior to the genuine," said Ronnie, "it lasts longer, and you get more fun out of it, and it's easier to replace when you've done with it."

"Still, it's rather like playing with coloured paper instead of playing with fire," objected Cicely.

A footman came round the corner with the trained silence that tactfully contrives to make itself felt.

"Mr. Luton to see you, madam," he announced. "Shall I say you are in?"

"Mr. Luton? Oh, yes," said Cicely, "he'll probably have something to tell us about Gorla's concert," she added, turning to Ronnie.

Tony Luton was a young man who had sprung from the people, and had taken care that there should be no recoil. He was scarcely twenty years of age, but a tightly packed chronicle of vicissitudes lay behind his sprightly insouciant appearance. Since his fifteenth year he had lived, Heaven knew how, getting sometimes a minor engagement at some minor music-hall, sometimes a temporary job as secretary-valet-companion to a roving invalid, dining now and then on plovers' eggs and asparagus at one of the smarter West End restaurants, at other times devouring a kipper or a sausage in some stuffy Edgwara Road eating-house; always seemingly amused by life, and always amusing. It is possible that somewhere in such heart as he possessed there lurked a rankling bitterness against the hard things of life, or a scrap of gratitude towards the one or two friends who had helped him disinterestedly, but his most intimate associates could not have guessed at the existence of such feelings. Tony Luton was just a merry-eyed dancing faun, whom Fate had surrounded with streets instead of woods, and it would have been in the highest degree inartistic to have sounded him for a heart or a heartache.

The dancing of the faun took one day a livelier and more assured turn, the joyousness became more real, and the worst of the vicissitudes seemed suddenly over. A musical friend, gifted with mediocre but marketable abilities, supplied Tony with a song, for which he obtained a trial performance at an East End hall. Dressed as a jockey, for no particular reason except that the costume suited him, he sang, "They quaff the gay bubbly in Eccleston Square" to an appreciative audience, which included the manager of a famous West End theatre of varieties. Tony and his song won the managerial favour, and were immediately transplanted to the West End house, where they scored a success of which the drooping music-hall industry was at the moment badly in need.

It was just after the great catastrophe, and men of the London world were in no humour to think; they had witnessed the inconceivable befall them, they had nothing but political ruin to stare at, and they were anxious to look the other way. The words of Tony's song were more or less meaningless, though he sang them remarkably well, but the tune, with its air of slyness and furtive joyousness, appealed in some unaccountable manner to people who were furtively unhappy, and who were trying to appear stoically cheerful.

"What must be, must be," and "It's a poor heart that never rejoices," were the popular expressions of the London public at that moment, and the men who had to cater for that public were thankful when they were able to stumble across anything that fitted in with the prevailing mood. For the first time in his life Tony Luton discovered that agents and managers were a leisured class, and that office boys had manners.

He entered Cicely's drawing-room with the air of one to whom assurance of manner has become a sheathed weapon, a court accessory rather than a trade implement. He was more quietly dressed than the usual run of music-hall successes; he had looked critically at life from too many angles not to know that though clothes cannot make a man they can certainly damn him.

"Thank you, I have lunched already," he said in answer to a question from Cicely. "Thank you," he said again in a cheerful affirmative, as the question of hock in a tall ice-cold goblet was propounded to him.

"I've come to tell you the latest about the Gorla Mustelford evening," he continued. "Old Laurent is putting his back into it, and it's really going to be rather a big affair. She's going to out-Russian the Russians. Of course, she hasn't their technique nor a tenth of their training, but she's having tons of advertisement. The name Gorla is almost an advertisement in itself, and then there's the fact that she's the daughter of a peer."

"She has temperament," said Cicely, with the decision of one who makes a vague statement in a good cause.

"So Laurent says," observed Tony. "He discovers temperament in every one that he intends to boom. He told me that I had temperament to the finger-tips, and I was too polite to contradict him. But I haven't told you the really important thing about the Mustelford début. It is a profound secret, more or less, so you must promise not to breathe a word about it till half-past four, when it will appear in all the six o'clock newspapers."

Tony paused for dramatic effect, while he drained his goblet, and then made his announcement.

"Majesty is going to be present. Informally and unofficially, but still present in the flesh. A sort of casual dropping in, carefully heralded by unconfirmed rumour a week ahead."

"Heavens!" exclaimed Cicely, in genuine excitement, "what a bold stroke. Lady Shalem has worked that, I bet. I suppose it will go down all right."

"Trust Laurent to see to that," said Tony, "he knows how to fill his house with the right sort of people, and he's not the one to risk a fiasco. He knows what he's about. I tell you, it's going to be a big evening."

"I say!" exclaimed Ronnie suddenly, "give a supper-party here for Gorla on the night, and ask the Shalem woman and all her crowd. It will be awful fun."

Cicely caught at the suggestion with some enthusiasm. She did not particularly care for Lady Shalem, but she thought it would be just as well to care for her as far as outward appearances went.

Grace, Lady Shalem, was a woman who had blossomed into sudden importance by constituting herself a sort of foster-mother to the *fait accompli*. At a moment when London was denuded of most of its aforetime social leaders she had seen her opportunity, and made the most of it. She had not contented herself with bowing to the inevitable, she had stretched out her hand to it, and forced herself to smile graciously at it, and her polite attentions had been reciprocated. Lady Shalem, without being a beauty or a wit, or a grand lady in the traditional sense of the word, was in a fair way to becoming a power in the land; others, more capable and with stronger claims to social recognition, would doubtless overshadow her and displace her in due course, but for the moment she was a person whose good graces counted for something, and Cicely was quite alive to the advantage of being in those good graces.

"It would be rather fun," she said, running over in her mind the possibilities of the suggested supper-party.

"It would be jolly useful," put in Ronnie eagerly; "you could get all sorts of interesting people together, and it would be an excellent advertisement for Gorla."

Ronnie approved of supper-parties on principle, but he was also thinking of the advantage which might accrue to the drawing-room concert which Cicely had projected (with himself as the chief performer), if he could be brought into contact with a wider circle of music patrons.

"I know it would be useful," said Cicely, "it would be almost historical; there's no knowing who might not come to it—and things are dreadfully slack in the entertaining line just now."

The ambitious note in her character was making itself felt at that moment.

"Let's go down to the library, and work out a list of people to invite," said Ronnie.

A servant entered the room and made a brief announcement.

"Mr. Yeovil has arrived, madam."

"Bother," said Ronnie sulkily. "Now you'll cool off about that supper-party, and turn down Gorla and the rest of us."

It was certainly true that the supper already seemed a more difficult proposition in Cicely's eye than it had a moment or two ago.

> "'You'll not forget my only daughter,
> E'en though Saphia has crossed the sea,'"

quoted Tony, with mocking laughter in his voice and eyes.

Cicely went down to greet her husband. She felt that she was probably very glad that he was home once more; she was angry with herself for not feeling greater certainty on the point. Even the well-beloved, however, can select the wrong moment for return. If Cicely Yeovil's heart was like a singing-bird, it was of a kind that has frequent lapses into silence.

Chapter II

THE HOMECOMING

Murrey Yeovil got out of the boat-train at Victoria Station, and stood waiting, in an attitude something between listlessness and impatience, while a porter dragged his light travelling kit out of the railway carriage and went in search of his heavier baggage with a hand-truck. Yeovil was a grey-faced young man, with restless eyes, and a rather wistful mouth, and an air of lassitude that was evidently only a temporary characteristic. The hot dusty station, with its blended crowds of dawdling and scurrying people, its little streams of suburban passengers pouring out every now and then from this or that platform, like ants swarming across a garden path, made a wearisome climax to what had been a rather wearisome journey. Yeovil glanced quickly, almost furtively, around him in all directions, with the air of a man who is constrained by morbid curiosity to look for things that he would rather not see. The announcements placed in German alternatively with English over the booking office, left-luggage office, refreshment buffets, and so forth, the crowned eagle and monogram displayed on the post boxes, caught his eye in quick succession.

He turned to help the porter to shepherd his belongings on to the truck, and followed him to the outer yard of the station, where a string of taxicabs was being slowly absorbed by an outpouring crowd of travellers.

Portmanteaux, wraps, and a trunk or two, much be-labelled and travel-worn, were stowed into a taxi, and Yeovil turned to give the direction to the driver.

"Twenty-eight, Berkshire Street."

"Berkschirestrasse, acht-und-zwanzig," echoed the man, a bulky spectacled individual of unmistakable Teuton type.

"Twenty-eight, Berkshire Street," repeated Yeovil, and got into the cab, leaving the driver to re-translate the direction into his own language.

A succession of cabs leaving the station blocked the roadway for a moment or two, and Yeovil had leisure to observe the fact that Viktoria Strasse was lettered side by side with the familiar English name of the street. A notice directing the public to the neighbouring swimming baths was also written up in both languages. London had become a bilingual city, even as Warsaw.

The cab threaded its way swiftly along Buckingham Palace Road towards the Mall. As they passed the long front of the Palace the traveller turned his head resolutely away, that he might not see the alien uniforms at the gates and the eagle standard flapping in the sunlight. The taxi driver, who seemed to have combative instincts, slowed down as he was turning into the Mall, and pointed to the white pile of memorial statuary in front of the palace gates.

"Grossmutter Denkmal, yes," he announced, and resumed his journey.

Arrived at his destination, Yeovil stood on the steps of his house and pressed the bell with an odd sense of forlornness, as though he were a stranger drifting from nowhere into a land that had no cognizance of him; a moment later he was standing in his own hall, the object of respectful solicitude and attention. Sprucely garbed and groomed lackeys busied themselves with his battered travel-soiled baggage; the door closed on the guttural-voiced taxi driver, and the glaring July sunshine. The wearisome journey was over.

"Poor dear, how dreadfully pulled-down you look," said Cicely, when the first greetings had been exchanged.

"It's been a slow business, getting well," said Yeovil. "I'm only three-quarter way there yet."

He looked at his reflection in a mirror and laughed ruefully.

"You should have seen what I looked like five or six weeks ago," he added.

"You ought to have let me come out and nurse you," said Cicely; "you know I wanted to."

"Oh, they nursed me well enough," said Yeovil, "and it would have been a shame dragging you out there; a small Finnish health resort, out of season, is not a very amusing place, and it would have been worse for any one who didn't talk Russian."

"You must have been buried alive there," said Cicely, with commiseration in her voice.

"I wanted to be buried alive," said Yeovil. "The news from the outer world was not of a kind that helped a despondent invalid towards convalescence. They spoke to me as little as possible about what was happening, and I was grateful for your letters because they also told me very little. When one is abroad, among foreigners, one's country's misfortunes cause one an acuter, more personal distress, than they would at home even."

"Well, you are at home now, anyway," said Cicely, "and you can jog along the road to complete recovery at your own pace. A little quiet shooting this autumn and a little hunting, just enough to keep you fit and not to overtire you; you mustn't overtax your strength."

"I'm getting my strength back all right," said Yeovil. "This journey hasn't tired me half as much as one might have expected. It's the awful drag of listlessness, mental and physical, that is the worst after-effect of these marsh fevers; they drain the energy out of you in bucketfuls, and it trickles back again in teaspoonfuls. And just now untiring energy is what I shall need, even more than strength; I don't want to degenerate into a slacker."

"Look here, Murrey," said Cicely, "after we've had dinner together tonight, I'm going to do a seemingly unwifely thing. I'm going to go out and leave you alone with an old friend. Doctor Holham is coming in to drink coffee and smoke with you. I arranged this because I knew it was what you would like. Men can talk things over best by themselves, and Holham can tell you everything that happened—since you went away. It will be a dreary story, I'm afraid, but you will want to hear it all. It was a nightmare time, but now one sees it in a calmer perspective."

"I feel in a nightmare still," said Yeovil.

"We all felt like that," said Cicely, rather with the air of an elder person who tells a child that it will understand things better when it grows up; "time is always something of a narcotic, you know. Things seem absolutely unbearable, and then bit by bit we find out that we are bearing them. And now, dear, I'll fill up your notification paper and leave you to superintend your unpacking. Robert will give you any help you want."

"What is the notification paper?" asked Yeovil.

"Oh, a stupid form to be filled up when any one arrives, to say where they came from, and their business and nationality and religion, and all that sort of thing. We're rather more bureaucratic than we used to be, you know."

Yeovil said nothing, but into the sallow greyness of his face there crept a dark flush, that faded presently and left his colour more grey and bloodless than before.

The journey seemed suddenly to have recommenced; he was under his own roof, his servants were waiting on him, his familiar possessions were in evidence round him, but the sense of being at home had vanished. It was as though he had arrived at some wayside hotel, and been asked to register his name and status and destination. Other things of disgust and irritation he had foreseen in the London he was coming to—the alterations on stamps and coinage, the intrusive Teuton element, the alien uniforms cropping up everywhere, the new orientation of social life; such things he was prepared for, but this personal evidence of his subject state came on him unawares, at a moment when he had, so to speak, laid his armour aside. Cicely spoke lightly of the hateful formality that had been forced on them; would he, too, come to regard things in the same acquiescent spirit?

Chapter III
"THE METSKIE TSAR"

"I WAS in the early stages of my fever when I got the first inkling of what was going on," said Yeovil to the doctor, as they sat over their coffee in a recess of the big smoking-room; "just able to potter about a bit in the daytime, fighting against depression and inertia, feverish as evening came on, and delirious in the night. My game tracker and my attendant were both Buriats, and spoke very little Russian, and that was the only language we had in common to converse in. In matters concerning food and sport we soon got to understand each other, but on other subjects we were not easily able to exchange ideas. One day my tracker had been to a distant trading-store to get some things of which we were in need; the store was eighty miles from the nearest point of railroad, eighty miles of terribly bad roads, but it was in its way a centre and transmitter of news from the outside world. The tracker brought back with him vague tidings of a conflict of some sort between the 'Metskie Tsar' and the 'Angliskie Tsar,' and kept repeating the Russian word for defeat. The 'Angliskie Tsar' I recognized, of course, as the King of England, but my brain was too sick and dull to read any further meaning into the man's reiterated gabble. I grew so ill just then that I had to give up the struggle against fever, and make my way as best I could towards the nearest point where nursing and doctoring could be had. It was one evening, in a lonely rest-hut on the edge of a huge forest, as I was waiting for my boy to bring the meal for which I was feverishly impatient, and which I knew I should loathe as soon as it was brought, that the explanation of the word 'Metskie' flashed on me. I had thought of it as referring to some Oriental potentate, some rebellious rajah perhaps, who was giving trouble, and whose followers had possibly discomfited an isolated British force in some out-of-the-way corner of our Empire. And all of a sudden I knew that 'Nemetskie Tsar,' German Emperor, had been the name that the man had been trying to convey to me. I shouted for the tracker, and put him through a breathless cross-examination; he confirmed what my fears had told me. The 'Metskie Tsar' was a big European ruler, he had been in conflict with the 'Angliskie Tsar,' and the latter had been defeated, swept away; the man spoke the word that he used for ships, and made energetic pantomime to express the sinking of a fleet. Holham, there was nothing for it but to hope that this was a false, groundless rumour, that had somehow crept to the confines of civilization. In my saner balanced moments it was possible to disbelieve it, but if you have ever suffered from delirium you will know what raging torments of agony I went through in the nights, how my brain fought and refought that rumoured disaster."

The doctor gave a murmur of sympathetic understanding.

"Then," continued Yeovil, "I reached the small Siberian town towards which I had been struggling. There was a little colony of Russians there, traders, officials, a doctor or two, and some army officers. I put up at the primitive hotel-restaurant, which was the general gathering-place of the community. I knew quickly that the news was true. Russians are the most tactful of any European race that I have ever met; they did not stare with insolent or pitying curiosity, but there was something changed in their attitude which told me that the travelling Briton was no longer in their eyes the interesting respect-commanding personality that he had been in past days. I went to my own room, where the samovar was bubbling its familiar tune and a smiling red-shirted Russian boy was helping my Buriat servant to unpack my wardrobe, and I asked for any back numbers of newspapers that could be supplied at a moment's notice. I was given a bundle of well-thumbed sheets, odd pieces of the *Novoe Vremya*, the *Moskovskie Viedomosti*, one or two complete numbers of local papers published at Perm and Tobolsk. I do not read Russian well, though I speak it fairly readily, but from the fragments of disconnected telegrams that I pieced together I gathered enough information to acquaint me with the extent of the tragedy that had been worked out in a few crowded hours in a corner of North-Western Europe. I searched frantically for telegrams of later dates that would put a better complexion on the matter, that would retrieve something from the ruin; presently I came across a page of the illustrated supplement that the *Novoe Vremya* publishes once a week. There was a photograph of a long-fronted building with a flag flying over it, labelled 'The new standard floating over Buckingham Palace.' The picture was not much more than a smudge, but the flag, possibly touched up, was unmistakable. It was the eagle of the Nemetskie Tsar. I have a vivid recollection of that plainly-furnished little room, with the inevitable gilt ikon in one corner, and the samovar hissing and gurgling on the table, and the thrumming music of a balalaika orchestra coming up from the restaurant below; the next coherent thing I can remember was weeks and weeks later, discussing in an impersonal detached manner whether I was strong enough to stand the fatigue of the long railway journey to Finland.

"Since then, Holham, I have been encouraged to keep my mind as much off the war and public affairs as possible, and I have been glad to do so. I knew the worst and there was no particular use in deepening my despondency by dragging out the details. But now I am more or less a live man again, and I want to fill in the gaps in my knowledge of what happened. You know how much I know, and how little; those fragments of Russian newspapers were about all the information that I had. I don't even know clearly how the whole thing started."

Yeovil settled himself back in his chair with the air of a man who has done some necessary talking, and now assumes the rôle of listener.

"It started," said the doctor, "with a wholly unimportant disagreement about some frontier business in East Africa; there was a slight attack of nerves in the stock markets, and then the whole thing seemed in a fair way towards being settled. Then the negotiations over the affair began to drag unduly, and there was a further flutter of nervousness in the money world. And then one morning the papers reported a highly menacing speech by one of the German Ministers, and the situation began to look black indeed. 'He will be disavowed,' every one said over here, but in less than twenty-four hours those who knew anything knew that the crisis was on us—only their knowledge came too late. 'War between two such civilized and enlightened nations is an impossibility,' one of our leaders of public opinion had declared on the Saturday; by the following Friday the war had indeed become an impossibility, because we could no longer carry it on. It burst on us with calculated suddenness, and we were just not enough, everywhere where the pressure came. Our ships were good against their ships, our seamen were better than their seamen, but our ships were not able to cope with their ships plus their superiority in aircraft. Our trained men were good against their trained men, but they could not be in several places at once, and the enemy could. Our half-trained men and our untrained men could not master the science of war at a moment's notice, and a moment's notice was all they got. The enemy were a nation apprenticed in arms, we were not even the idle apprentice: we had not deemed apprenticeship worth our while. There was courage enough running loose in the land, but it was like unharnessed electricity, it controlled no forces, it struck no blows. There was no time for the heroism and the devotion which a drawn-out struggle, however hopeless, can produce; the war was over almost as soon as it had begun. After the reverses which happened with lightning rapidity in the first three days of warfare, the newspapers made no effort to pretend that the situation could be retrieved; editors and public alike recognized that these were blows over the heart, and that it was a matter of moments before we were counted out. One might liken the whole affair to a snap checkmate early in a game of chess; one side had thought out the moves, and brought the requisite pieces into play, the other side was hampered and helpless, with its resources unavailable, its strategy discounted in advance. That, in a nutshell, is the history of the war."

Yeovil was silent for a moment or two, then he asked:

"And the sequel, the peace?"

"The collapse was so complete that I fancy even the enemy were hardly prepared for the consequences of their victory. No one had quite realized what one disastrous campaign would mean for an island nation with a closely packed population. The conquerors were in a position to dictate what terms they pleased, and it was not wonderful that their ideas of aggrandizement expanded in the hour of intoxication. There was no European combination ready to say them nay, and certainly no one Power was going to be rash enough to step in to contest the terms of the treaty that they imposed on the conquered. Annexation had probably never been a dream before the war; after the war it suddenly became temptingly practical. *Warum nicht?* became the theme of leader-writers in the German Press; they pointed out that Britain, defeated and humiliated, but with enormous powers of recuperation, would be a dangerous and inevitable enemy for the Germany of tomorrow, while Britain incorporated within the Hohenzollern Empire would merely be a disaffected province, without a navy to make its disaffection a serious menace, and with great tax-paying capabilities, which would be available for relieving the burdens of the other Imperial States. Wherefore, why not annex? The *warum nicht?* party prevailed. Our King, as you know, retired with his Court to Delhi, as Emperor in the East, with most of his overseas dominions still subject to his sway. The British Isles came under the German Crown as a *Reichsland,* a sort of Alsace-Lorraine washed by the North Sea instead of the Rhine. We still retain our Parliament, but it is a clipped and pruned-down shadow of its former self, with most of its functions in abeyance; when the elections were held it was difficult to get decent candidates to come forward or to get people to vote. It makes one smile bitterly to think that a year or two ago we were seriously squabbling as to who should have votes. And, of course, the old party divisions have more or less crumbled away. The Liberals naturally are under the blackest of clouds, for having steered the country to disaster, though to do them justice it was no more their fault than the fault of any other party. In a democracy such as ours was the Government of the day must more or less reflect the ideas and temperament of the nation in all vital matters, and the British nation in those days could not have been persuaded of the urgent need for military apprenticeship or of the deadly nature of its danger. It was willing now and then to be half-frightened and to have half-measures, or, one might better say, quarter-measures taken to reassure it, and the governments of the day were willing to take them, but any political party or group of statesmen that had said 'the danger is enormous and immediate, the sacrifices and burdens must be enormous and immediate,' would have met with certain defeat at the polls. Still, of course, the Liberals, as the party that had held office for nearly a decade, incurred the odium of a people maddened by defeat and humiliation; one Minister, who had had less responsibility for military organization than perhaps any of them, was attacked and nearly killed at Newcastle, another was hiding for three days on Exmoor, and escaped in disguise."

"And the Conservatives?"

"They are also under eclipse, but it is more or less voluntary in their case. For generations they had taken their stand as supporters of Throne and Constitution, and when they suddenly found the Constitution gone and the Throne filled by an alien dynasty, their political orientation had vanished. They are in much the same position as the Jacobites occupied after the Hanoverian accession. Many of the leading Tory families have emigrated to the British lands beyond the seas, others are shut up in their country houses, retrenching their expenses, selling their acres, and investing their money abroad. The Labour faction, again, are almost in as bad odour as the Liberals, because of having hob-nobbed too effusively and ostentatiously with the German democratic parties on the eve of the war, exploiting an evangel of universal brotherhood which did not blunt a single Teuton bayonet when the hour came. I suppose in time party divisions will reassert themselves in some form or other; there will be a Socialist Party, and the mercantile and manufacturing interests will evolve a sort of bourgeoisie party, and the different religious bodies will try to get themselves represented——"

Yeovil made a movement of impatience.

"All these things that you forecast," he said, "must take time, considerable time; is this nightmare, then, to go on for ever?"

"It is not a nightmare, unfortunately," said the doctor, "it is a reality."

"But, surely—a nation such as ours, a virile, highly-civilized nation with an age-long tradition of mastery behind it, cannot be held under for ever by a few thousand bayonets and machine guns. We must surely rise up one day and drive them out."

"Dear man," said the doctor, "we might, of course, at some given moment overpower the garrison that is maintained here, and seize the forts, and perhaps we might be able to mine the harbours; what then? In a fortnight or so we could be starved into unconditional submission. Remember, all the advantages of isolated position that told in our favour while we had the sea dominion, tell against us now that the sea dominion is in other hands. The enemy would not need to mobilize a single army corps or to bring a single battleship into action; a fleet of nimble cruisers and destroyers circling round our coasts would be sufficient to shut out food supplies."

"Are you trying to tell me that this is a final overthrow?" said Yeovil in a shaking voice; "are we to remain a subject race like the Poles?"

"Let us hope for a better fate," said the doctor. "Our opportunity may come if the Master Power is ever involved in an unsuccessful naval war with some other nation, or perhaps in some time of European crisis, when everything hung in the balance, our latent hostility might have to be squared by a concession of independence. That is what we have to hope for and watch for. On the other hand, the conquerors have to count on time and tact to weaken and finally obliterate the old feelings of nationality; the middle-aged of today will grow old and acquiescent in the changed state of things; the young generations will grow up never having known anything different. It's a far cry to Delhi, as the old Indian proverb says, and the strange half-European, half-Asiatic Court out there will seem more and more a thing exotic and unreal. 'The King across the water' was a rallying-cry once upon a time in our history, but a king on the farther side of the Indian Ocean is a shadowy competitor for one who alternates between Potsdam and Windsor."

"I want you to tell me everything," said Yeovil, after another pause; "tell me, Holham, how far has this obliterating process of 'time and tact' gone? It seems to be pretty fairly started already. I bought a newspaper as soon as I landed, and I read it in the train coming up. I read things that puzzled and disgusted me. There were announcements of concerts and plays and first-nights and private views; there were even small dances. There were advertisements of house-boats and week-end cottages and string bands for garden parties. It struck me that it was rather like merry-making with a dead body lying in the house."

"Yeovil," said the doctor, "you must bear in mind two things. First, the necessity for the life of the country going on as if nothing had happened. It is true that many thousands of our working men and women have emigrated and thousands of our upper and middle class too; they were the people who were not tied down by business, or who could afford to cut those ties. But those represent comparatively a few out of the many. The great businesses and the small businesses must go on, people must be fed and clothed and housed and medically treated, and their thousand-and-one wants and necessities supplied. Look at me, for instance; however much I loathe coming under a foreign domination and paying taxes to an alien government, I can't abandon my practice and my patients, and set up anew in Toronto or Allahabad, and if I could, some other doctor would have to take my place here. I or that other doctor must have our servants and motors and food and furniture and newspapers, even our sport. The golf links and the hunting field have been wellnigh deserted since the war, but they are beginning to get back their votaries because outdoor sport has become a necessity, and a very rational necessity, with numbers of men who have to work otherwise under unnatural and exacting conditions. That is one factor of the situation. The other affects London more especially, but through London it influences the rest of the country to a certain extent. You will see around you here much that will strike you as indications of heartless indifference to the calamity that has befallen our nation. Well, you must remember that many things in modern life, especially in the big cities, are not national but international. In the world of music and art and the drama, for instance, the foreign names are legion, they confront you at every turn, and some of our British devotees of such arts are more acclimatized to the ways of Munich or Moscow than they are familiar with the life, say, of Stirling or York. For years they have lived and thought and spoken in an atmosphere and jargon of denationalized culture—even those of them who have never left our shores. They would take pains to be intimately familiar with the domestic affairs and views of life of some Galician gipsy dramatist, and gravely quote and discuss his opinions on debts and mistresses and cookery, while they would shudder at 'D'ye ken John Peel?' as a piece of uncouth barbarity. You cannot expect a world of that sort to be permanently concerned or downcast because the Crown of Charlemagne takes it place now on the top of the Royal box in the theatres, or at the head of programmes at State concerts. And then there are the Jews."

"There are many in the land, or at least in London," said Yeovil.

"There are even more of them now than there used to be," said Holham. "I am to a great extent a disliker of Jews myself, but I will be fair to them, and admit that those of them who were in any genuine sense British have remained British and have stuck by us loyally in our misfortune; all honour to them. But of the others, the men who by temperament and everything else were far more Teuton or Polish or Latin than they were British, it was not to be expected that they would be heartbroken because London had suddenly lost its place among the political capitals of the world, and became a cosmopolitan city. They had appreciated the free and easy liberty of the old days, under British rule, but there was a stiff insularity in the ruling race that they chafed against. Now, putting aside some petty Government restrictions that Teutonic bureaucracy has brought in, there is really, in their eyes, more licence and social adaptability in London than before. It has taken on some of the aspects of a No-Man's-Land, and the Jew, if he likes, may almost consider himself as of the dominant race; at any rate he is ubiquitous. Pleasure, of the café and cabaret and boulevard kind, the sort of thing that gave Berlin the aspect of the gayest capital in Europe within the last decade, that is the insidious leaven that will help to denationalize London. Berlin will probably climb back to some of its old austerity and simplicity, a world-ruling city with a great sense of its position and its responsibilities, while London will become more and more the centre of what these people understand by life."

Yeovil made a movement of impatience and disgust.

"I know, I know," said the doctor, sympathetically; "life and enjoyment mean to you the howl of a wolf in a forest, the call of a wild swan on the frozen tundras, the smell of a wood fire in some little inn among the mountains. There is more music to you in the quick thud, thud of hoofs on desert mud as a free-stepping horse is led up to your tent door than in all the dronings and flourishes that a highly-paid orchestra can reel out to an expensively fed audience. But the tastes of modern London, as we see them crystallized around us, lie in a very different direction. People of the world that I am speaking of, our dominant world at the present moment, herd together as closely packed to the square yard as possible, doing nothing worth doing, and saying nothing worth saying, but doing it and saying it over and over again, listening to the same melodies, watching the same artistes, echoing the same catch-words, ordering the same dishes in the same restaurants, suffering each other's cigarette smoke and perfumes and conversation, feverishly, anxiously making arrangements to meet each other again tomorrow, next week, and the week after next, and repeat the same gregarious experience. If they were not herded together in a corner of western London, watching each other with restless intelligent eyes, they would be herded together at Brighton or Dieppe, doing the same thing. Well, you will find that life of that sort goes forward just as usual, only it is even more prominent and noticeable now because there is less public life of other kinds."

Yeovil said something which was possibly the Buriat word for the nether world.

Outside in the neighbouring square a band had been playing at intervals during the evening. Now it struck up an air that Yeovil had already heard whistled several times since his landing, an air with a captivating suggestion of slyness and furtive joyousness running through it.

He rose and walked across to the window, opening it a little wider. He listened till the last notes had died away.

"What is that tune they have just played?" he asked.

"You'll hear it often enough," said the doctor. "A Frenchman writing in the *Matin* the other day called it the 'National Anthem of the *fait accompli.*'"

Chapter IV
"ES IST VERBOTEN"

Yeovil wakened next morning to the pleasant sensation of being in a household where elaborate machinery for the smooth achievement of one's daily life was noiselessly and unceasingly at work. Fever and the long weariness of convalescence in indifferently comfortable surroundings had given luxury a new value in his eyes. Money had not always been plentiful with him in his younger days; in his twenty-eighth year he had inherited a fairly substantial fortune, and he had married a wealthy woman a few months later. It was characteristic of the man and his breed that the chief use to which he had put his newly-acquired wealth had been in seizing the opportunity which it gave him for indulging in unlimited travel in wild, out-of-the-way regions, where the comforts of life were meagrely represented. Cicely occasionally accompanied him to the threshold of his expeditions, such as Cairo or St. Petersburg or Constantinople, but her own tastes in the matter of roving were more or less condensed within an area that comprised Cannes, Homburg, the Scottish Highlands, and the Norwegian Fiords. Things outlandish and barbaric appealed to her chiefly when presented under artistic but highly civilized stage management on the boards of Covent Garden, and if she wanted to look at wolves or sand grouse, she preferred doing so in the company of an intelligent Fellow of the Zoological Society on some fine Sunday afternoon in Regent's Park. It was one of the bonds of union and good-fellowship between her husband and herself that each understood and sympathized with the other's tastes without in the least wanting to share them; they went their own ways and were pleased and comrade-like when the ways happened to run together for a span, without self-reproach or heart-searching when the ways diverged. Moreover, they had separate and adequate banking accounts, which constitute, if not the keys of the matrimonial Heaven, at least the oil that lubricates them.

Yeovil found Cicely and breakfast waiting for him in the cool breakfast-room, and enjoyed, with the appreciation of a recent invalid, the comfort and resources of a meal that had not to be ordered or thought about in advance, but seemed as though it were there, foreordained from the beginning of time in its smallest detail. Each desire of the breakfasting mind seemed to have its realization in some dish, lurking unobtrusively in hidden corners until asked for. Did one want grilled mushrooms, English fashion, they were there, black and moist and sizzling, and extremely edible; did one desire mushrooms *à la Russe,* they appeared, blanched and cool and toothsome under their white blanketing of sauce. At one's bidding was a service of coffee, prepared with rather more forethought and circumspection than would go to the preparation of a revolution in a South American Republic.

The exotic blooms that reigned in profusion over the other parts of the house were scrupulously banished from the breakfast-room; bowls of wild thyme and other flowering weeds of the meadow and hedgerow gave it an atmosphere of country freshness that was in keeping with the morning meal.

"You look dreadfully tired still," said Cicely critically, "otherwise I would recommend a ride in the Park, before it gets too hot. There is a new cob in the stable that you will just love, but he is rather lively, and you had better content yourself for the present with some more sedate exercise than he is likely to give you. He is apt to try and jump out of his skin when the flies tease him. The Park is rather jolly for a walk just now."

"I think that will be about my form after my long journey," said Yeovil, "an hour's stroll before lunch under the trees. That ought not to fatigue me unduly. In the afternoon I'll look up one or two people."

"Don't count on finding too many of your old set," said Cicely rather hurriedly. "I dare say some of them will find their way back some time, but at present there's been rather an exodus."

"The Bredes," said Yeovil, "are they here?"

"No, the Bredes are in Scotland, at their place in Sutherlandshire; they don't come south now, and the Ricardes are farming somewhere in East Africa, the whole lot of them. Valham has got an appointment of some sort in the Straits Settlement, and has taken his family with him. The Collards are down at their mother's place in Norfolk; a German banker has bought their house in Manchester Square."

"And the Hebways?" asked Yeovil.

"Dick Hebway is in India," said Cicely, "but his mother lives in Paris; poor Hugo, you know, was killed in the war. My friends the Allinsons are in Paris too. It's rather a clearance, isn't it? However, there are some left, and I expect others will come back in time. Pitherby is here; he's one of those who are trying to make the best of things under the new *régime*."

"He would be," said Yeovil, shortly.

"It's a difficult question," said Cicely, "whether one should stay at home and face the music or go away and live a transplanted life under the British flag. Either attitude might be dictated by patriotism."

"It is one thing to face the music, it is another thing to dance to it," said Yeovil.

Cicely poured out some more coffee for herself and changed the conversation.

"You'll be in to lunch, I suppose? The Clubs are not very attractive just now, I believe, and the restaurants are mostly hot in the middle of the day. Ronnie Storre is coming in; he's here pretty often these days. A rather good-looking young animal with something midway between talent and genius in the piano-playing line."

"Not long-haired and Semitic or Tcheque or anything of that sort, I suppose?" asked Yeovil.

Cicely laughed at the vision of Ronnie conjured up by her husband's words.

"No, beautifully groomed and clipped and Anglo-Saxon. I expect you'll like him. He plays bridge almost as well as he plays the piano. I suppose you wonder at any one who can play bridge well wanting to play the piano."

"I'm not quite so intolerant as all that," said Yeovil; "anyhow I promise to like Ronnie. Is any one else coming to lunch?"

"Joan Mardle will probably drop in, in fact I'm afraid she's a certainty. She invited herself in that way of hers that brooks of no refusal. On the other hand, as a mitigating circumstance, there will be a *point d'asperge* omelette such as few kitchens could turn out, so don't be late."

Yeovil set out for his morning walk with the curious sensation of one who starts on a voyage of discovery in a land that is well known to him. He turned into the Park at Hyde Park Corner and made his way along the familiar paths and alleys that bordered the Row. The familiarity vanished when he left the region of fenced-in lawns and rhododendron bushes and came to the open space that stretched away beyond the bandstand. The bandstand was still there, and a military band, in sky-blue Saxon uniform, was executing the first item in the forenoon programme of music. Around it, instead of the serried rows of green chairs that Yeovil remembered, was spread out an acre or so of small round tables, most of which had their quota of customers, engaged in a steady consumption of lager beer, coffee, lemonade and syrups. Farther in the background, but well within earshot of the band, a gaily painted pagoda-restaurant sheltered a number of more commodious tables under its awnings, and gave a hint of convenient indoor accommodation for wet or windy weather. Movable screens of trellis-trained foliage and climbing roses formed little hedges by means of which any particular table could be shut off from its neighbours if semi-privacy were desired. One or two decorative advertisements of popularized brands of champagne and Rhine wines adorned the outside walls of the building, and under the central gable of its upper story was a flamboyant portrait of a stern-faced man, whose image and superscription might also be found on the newer coinage of the land. A mass of bunting hung in folds round the flagpole on the gable, and blew out now and then on a favouring breeze, a long three-coloured strip, black, white, and scarlet, and over the whole scene the elm trees towered with an absurd sardonic air of nothing having changed around their roots.

Yeovil stood for a minute or two, taking in every detail of the unfamiliar spectacle.

"They have certainly accomplished something that we never attempted," he muttered to himself. Then he turned on his heel and made his way back to the shady walk that ran alongside the Row. At first sight little was changed in the aspect of the well-known exercising ground. One or two riding masters cantered up and down as of yore, with their attendant broods of anxious-faced young girls and awkwardly bumping women pupils, while horsey-looking men put marketable animals through their paces or drew up to the rails for long conversations with horsey-looking friends on foot. Sportingly attired young women, sitting astride of their horses, careered by at intervals as though an extremely game fox were leading hounds a merry chase a short way ahead of them; it all seemed much as usual.

Presently, from the middle distance a bright patch of colour set in a whirl of dust drew rapidly nearer and resolved itself into a group of cavalry officers extending their chargers in a smart gallop. They were well mounted and sat their horses to perfection, and they made a brave show as they raced past Yeovil with a clink and clatter and rhythmic thud, thud of hoofs, and became once more a patch of colour in a whirl of dust. An answering glow of colour seemed to have burned itself into the grey face of the young man, who had seen them pass without appearing to look at them, a stinging rush of blood, accompanied by a choking catch in the throat and a hot white blindness across the eyes. The weakness of fever broke down at times the rampart of outward indifference that a man of Yeovil's temperament builds coldly round his heart-strings.

The Row and its riders had become suddenly detestable to the wanderer; he would not run the risk of seeing that insolently joyous cavalcade come galloping past again. Beyond a narrow stretch of tree-shaded grass lay the placid sunlit water of the Serpentine, and Yeovil made a short cut across the turf to reach its gravelled bank.

"Can't you read either English or German?" asked a policeman who confronted him as he stepped off the turf.

Yeovil stared at the man and then turned to look at the small neatly-printed notice to which the official was imperiously pointing; in two languages it was made known that it was forbidden and *verboten*, punishable and *straffbar*, to walk on the grass.

"Three shilling fine," said the policeman, extending his hand for the money.

"Do I pay you?" asked Yeovil, feeling almost inclined to laugh; "I'm rather a stranger to the new order of things."

"You pay me," said the policeman, "and you receive a quittance for the sum paid," and he proceeded to tear a counterfoil receipt for a three shilling fine from a small pocket book.

"May I ask," said Yeovil, as he handed over the sum demanded and received his quittance, "what the red and white band on your sleeve stands for?"

"Bi-lingual," said the constable, with an air of importance. "Preference is given to members of the Force who qualify in both languages. Nearly all the police engaged on Park duty are bi-lingual. About as many foreigners as English use the parks nowadays; in fact, on a fine Sunday afternoon, you'll find three foreigners to every two English. The park habit is more Continental than British, I take it."

"And are there many Germans in the Police Force?" asked Yeovil.

"Well, yes, a good few; there had to be," said the constable; "there were such a lot of resignations when the change came, and they had to be filled up somehow. Lots of men what used to be in the Force emigrated or found work of some other kind, but everybody couldn't take that line; wives and children had to be thought of. 'Tisn't every head of a family that can chuck up a job on the chance of finding another. Starvation's been the lot of a good many what went out. Those of us that stayed on got better pay than we did before, but then of course the duties are much more multitudinous."

"They must be," said Yeovil, fingering his three shilling State document; "by the way," he asked, "are all the grass plots in the Park out of bounds for human feet?"

"Everywhere where you see the notices," said the policeman, "and that's about three-fourths of the whole grass space; there's been a lot of new gravel walks opened up in all directions. People don't want to walk on the grass when they've got clean paths to walk on."

And with this parting reproof the bi-lingual constable strode heavily away, his loss of consideration and self-esteem as a unit of a sometime ruling race evidently compensated for to some extent by his enhanced importance as an official.

"The women and children," thought Yeovil, as he looked after the retreating figure; "yes, that is one side of the problem. The children that have to be fed and schooled, the women folk that have to be cared for, an old mother, perhaps, in the home that cannot be broken up. The old case of giving hostages."

He followed the path alongside the Serpentine, passing under the archway of the bridge and continuing his walk into Kensington Gardens. In another moment he was within view of the Peter Pan statue and at once observed that it had companions. One one side was a group representing a scene from one of the Grimm fairy stories, on the other was Alice in conversation with Gryphon and Mockturtle, the episode looking distressingly stiff and meaningless in its sculptured form. Two other spaces had been cleared in the neighbouring turf, evidently for the reception of further statue groups, which Yeovil mentally assigned to Struwelpeter and Little Lord Fauntleroy.

"German middle-class taste," he commented, "but in this matter we certainly gave them a lead. I suppose the idea is that childish fancy is dead and that it is only decent to erect some sort of memorial to it."

The day was growing hotter, and the Park had ceased to seem a desirable place to loiter in. Yeovil turned his steps homeward, passing on his way the bandstand with its surrounding acreage of tables. It was now nearly one o'clock, and luncheon parties were beginning to assemble under the awnings of the restaurant. Lighter refreshments, in the shape of sausages and potato salads, were being carried out by scurrying waiters to the drinkers of lager beer at the small tables. A park orchestra, in brilliant trappings, had taken the place of the military band. As Yeovil passed the musicians launched out into the tune which the doctor had truly predicted he would hear to repletion before he had been many days in London; the "National Anthem of the *fait accompli.*"

Chapter V

L'ART D'ETRE COUSINE

Joan Mardle had reached forty in the leisurely untroubled fashion of a woman who intends to be comely and attractive at fifty. She cultivated a jovial, almost joyous manner, with a top-dressing of hearty good will and good nature which disarmed strangers and recent acquaintances; on getting to know her better they hastily re-armed themselves. Some one had once aptly described her as a hedgehog with the protective mimicry of a puffball. If there was an awkward remark to be made at an inconvenient moment before undesired listeners, Joan invariably made it, and when the occasion did not present itself she was usually capable of creating it. She was not without a certain popularity, the sort of popularity that a dashing highwayman sometimes achieved among those who were not in the habit of travelling on his particular highway. A great-aunt on her mother's side of the family had married so often that Joan imagined herself justified in claiming cousinship with a large circle of disconnected houses, and treating them all on a relationship footing, which theoretical kinship enabled her to exact luncheons and other accommodations under the plea of keeping the lamp of family life aglow.

"I felt I simply had to come today," she chuckled at Yeovil; "I was just dying to see the returned traveller. Of course, I know perfectly well that neither of you want me, when you haven't seen each other for so long and must have heaps and heaps to say to one another, but I thought I would risk the odium of being the third person on an occasion when two are company and three are a nuisance. Wasn't it brave of me?"

She spoke in full knowledge of the fact that the luncheon party would not in any case have been restricted to Yeovil and his wife, having seen Ronnie arrive in the hall as she was being shown upstairs.

"Ronnie Storre is coming, I believe," said Cicely, "so you're not breaking into a tête-à-tête."

"Ronnie, oh, I don't count him," said Joan gaily; "he's just a boy who looks nice and eats asparagus. I hear he's getting to play the piano really well. Such a pity. He will grow fat; musicians always do, and it will ruin him. I speak feelingly because I'm gravitating towards plumpness myself. The Divine Architect turns us out fearfully and wonderfully built, and the result is charming to the eye, and then He adds another chin and two or three extra inches round the waist, and the effect is ruined. Fortunately you can always find another Ronnie when this one grows fat and uninteresting; the supply of boys who look nice and eat asparagus is unlimited. Hullo, Mr. Storre, we were all taking about you."

"Nothing very damaging, I hope?" said Ronnie, who had just entered the room.

"No, we were merely deciding that, whatever you may do with your life, your chin must remain single. When one's chin begins to lead a double life one's own opportunities for depravity are insensibly narrowed. You needn't tell me that you haven't any hankerings after depravity; people with your coloured eyes and hair are always depraved."

"Let me introduce you to my husband, Ronnie," said Cicely, "and then let's go and begin lunch."

"You two must almost feel as if you were honeymooning again," said Joan as they sat down; "you must have quite forgotten each other's tastes and peculiarities since you last met. Old Emily Fronding was talking about you yesterday, when I mentioned that Murrey was expected home; 'curious sort of marriage tie,' she said, in that stupid staring way of hers, 'when husband and wife spend most of their time in different continents. I don't call it marriage at all.' 'Nonsense,' I said, 'it's the best way of doing things. The Yeovils will be a united and devoted couple long after heaps of their married contemporaries have trundled through the Divorce Court.' I forgot at the moment that her youngest girl had divorced her husband last year, and that her second girl is rumoured to be contemplating a similar step. One can't remember everything."

Joan Mardle was remarkable for being able to remember the smallest details in the family lives of two or three hundred acquaintances.

From personal matters she went with a bound to the political small talk of the moment.

"The Official Declaration as to the House of Lords is out at last," she said; "I bought a paper just before coming here, but I left it in the Tube. All existing titles are to lapse if three successive holders, including the present ones, fail to take the oath of allegiance."

"Have any taken it up to the present?" asked Yeovil.

"Only about nineteen, so far, and none of them representing very leading families; of course others will come in gradually, as the change of Dynasty becomes more and more an accepted fact, and of course there will be lots of new creations to fill up the gaps. I hear for certain that Pitherby is to get a title of some sort, in recognition of his literary labours. He has written a short history of the House of Hohenzollern, for use in schools you know, and he's bringing out a popular Life of Frederick the Great—at least he hopes it will be popular."

"I didn't know that writing was much in his line," said Yeovil, "beyond the occasional editing of a company prospectus."

"I understand his historical researches have given every satisfaction in exalted quarters," said Joan; "something may be lacking in the style, perhaps, but the august approval can make good that defect with the style of Baron. Pitherby has such a kind heart; 'kind hearts are more than coronets,' we all know, but the two go quite well together. And the dear man is not content with his services to literature, he's blossoming forth as a liberal patron of the arts. He's taken quite a lot of tickets for dear Gorla's début; half the second row of the dress-circle."

"Do you mean Gorla Mustelford?" asked Yeovil, catching at the name; "what on earth is she having a début about?"

"What?" cried Joan, in loud-voiced amazement; "haven't you heard? Hasn't Cicely told you? How funny that you shouldn't have heard. Why, it's going to be one of the events of the season. Everybody's talking about it. She's going to do suggestion dancing at the Caravansery Theatre."

"Good Heavens, what is suggestion dancing?" asked Yeovil.

"Oh, something quite new," explained Joan; "at any rate the name is quite new and Gorla is new as far as the public are concerned, and that is enough to establish the novelty of the thing. Among other things she does a dance suggesting the life of a fern; I saw one of the rehearsals, and to me it would have equally well suggested the life of John Wesley. However, that is probably the fault of my imagination—I've either got too much or too little. Anyhow it is an understood thing that she is to take London by storm."

"When I last saw Gorla Mustelford," observed Yeovil, "she was a rather serious flapper who thought the world was in urgent need of regeneration and was not certain whether she would regenerate it or take up miniature painting. I forget which she attempted ultimately."

"She is quite serious about her art," put in Cicely; "she's studied a good deal abroad and worked hard at mastering the technique of her profession. She's not a mere amateur with a hankering after the footlights. I fancy she will do well."

"But what do her people say about it?" asked Yeovil.

"Oh, they're simply furious about it," answered Joan; "the idea of a daughter of the house of Mustelford prancing and twisting

about the stage for Prussian officers and Hamburg Jews to gaze at i
a dreadful cup of humiliation for them. It's unfortunate, of course
that they should feel so acutely about it, but still one can under
stand their point of view."

"I don't see what other point of view they could possibly take,"
said Yeovil sharply; "if Gorla thinks that the necessities of art, or her
own inclinations, demand that she should dance in public, why
can't she do it in Paris or even Vienna? Anywhere would be
better, one would think, than in London under present conditions."

He had given Joan the indication that she was looking for as to
his attitude towards the *fait accompli*. Without asking a question
she had discovered that husband and wife were divided on the
fundamental issue that underlay all others at the present moment
Cicely was weaving social schemes for the future, Yeovil had
come home in a frame of mind that threatened the destruction of
those schemes, or at any rate a serious hindrance to their execu
tion. The situation presented itself to Joan's mind with an alluring
piquancy.

"You are giving a grand supper-party for Gorla on the night of
her début, aren't you?" she asked Cicely; "several people spoke to
me about it, so I suppose it must be true."

Tony Luton and young Storre had taken care to spread the
news of the projected supper function, in order to ensure against
a change of plans on Cicely's part.

"Gorla is a great friend of mine," said Cicely, trying to talk as
if the conversation had taken a perfectly indifferent turn; "also I
think she deserves a little encouragement after the hard work she
has been through. I thought it would be doing her a kindness to
arrange a supper party for her on her first night."

There was a moment's silence. Yeovil said nothing, and Joan
understood the value of being occasionally tongue-tied.

"The whole question is," continued Cicely as the silence became
oppressive, "whether one is to mope and hold aloof from the na
tional life, or take our share in it; the life has got to go on whether
we participate in it or not. It seems to me to be more patriotic to
come down into the dust of the marketplace than to withdraw
oneself behind walls or beyond the seas."

"Of course the industrial life of the country has to go on," said
Yeovil; "no one could criticize Gorla if she interested herself in
organizing cottage industries or anything of that sort, in which she

would be helping her own people. That one could understand, but I don't think a cosmopolitan concern like the music-hall business calls for personal sacrifices from young women of good family at a moment like the present."

"It is just at a moment like the present that the people want something to interest them and take them out of themselves," said Cicely argumentatively; "what has happened, has happened, and we can't undo it or escape the consequences. What we can do, or attempt to do, is to make things less dreary, and make people less unhappy."

"In a word, more contented," said Yeovil; "if I were a German statesman, that is the end I would labour for and encourage others to labour for, to make the people forget that they were discontented. All this work of regalvanizing the social side of London life may be summed up in the phrase '*travailler pour le roi de Prusse.*'"

"I don't think there is any use in discussing the matter further," said Cicely.

"I can see that grand supper-party not coming off," said Joan provocatively.

Ronnie looked anxiously at Cicely.

"You can see it coming on, if you're gifted with prophetic vision of a reliable kind," said Cicely; "of course as Murrey doesn't take kindly to the idea of Gorla's enterprise I won't have the party here. I'll give it at a restaurant, that's all. I can see Murrey's point of view, and sympathize with it, but I'm not going to throw Gorla over."

There was another pause of uncomfortably protracted duration.

"I say, this is a top-hole omelette," said Ronnie.

It was his only contribution to the conversation, but it was a valuable one.

Chapter VI
HERR VON KWARL

Herr von Kwarl sat at his favourite table in the Brandenburg Café, the new building that made such an imposing show (and did such thriving business) at the lower end of what most of its patrons called the Regentstrasse. Though the establishment was new it had already achieved its unwritten code of customs, and the sanctity of Herr von Kwarl's specially reserved table had acquired the authority of a tradition. A set of chess-men, a copy of the *Kreuz Zeitung* and the *Times,* and a slim-necked bottle of Rhenish wine, ice-cool from the cellar, were always to be found there early in the forenoon, and the honoured guest for whom these preparations were made usually arrived on the scene shortly after eleven o'clock. For an hour or so he would read and silently digest the contents of his two newspapers, and then at the first sign of flagging interest on his part, another of the café's regular customers would march across the floor, exchange a word or two on the affairs of the day, and be bidden with a wave of the hand into the opposite seat. A waiter would instantly place the chess-board with its marshalled ranks of combatants in the required position, and the contest would begin.

Herr von Kwarl was a heavily built man of mature middle-age, of the blond North-German type, with a facial aspect that suggested stupidity and brutality. The stupidity of his mien masked an ability and shrewdness that was distinctly above the average and the suggestion of brutality was belied by the fact that von Kwarl was as kind-hearted a man as one could meet with in a day's journey. Early in life, almost before he was in his teens, Fritz von Kwarl had made up his mind to accept the world as it was, and to that philosophical resolution, steadfastly adhered to, he attributed his excellent digestion and his unruffled happiness. Perhaps he confused cause and effect; the excellent digestion may have been responsible for at least some of the philosophical serenity.

He was a bachelor of the type that is called confirmed, and which might better be labelled consecrated; from his early youth onward to his present age he had never had the faintest flickering intention of marriage. Children and animals he adored, women and plants he accounted somewhat of a nuisance. A world without women and roses and asparagus would, he admitted, be robbed of much of its charm, but with all their charm these things were tiresome and thorny and capricious, always wanting to climb or creep in places where they were not wanted, and resolutely drooping and fading away when they were desired to flourish. Animals, on the other hand, accepted the world as it was and made the best of it, and children, at least nice children, uncontaminated by grown-up influences, lived in worlds of their own making.

Von Kwarl held no acknowledged official position in the country of his residence, but it was an open secret that those responsible for the real direction of affairs sought his counsel on nearly every step that they meditated, and that his counsel was very rarely disregarded. Some of the shrewdest and most successful enactments of the ruling power were believed to have originated in the brain-cells of the bovine-fronted *Stammgast* of the Brandenburg Café.

Around the wood-panelled walls of the Café were set at intervals well-mounted heads of boar, elk, stag, roebuck, and other game-beasts of a northern forest, while in between were carved armorial escutcheons of the principal cities of the lately expanded realm, Magdeburg, Manchester, Hamburg, Bremen, Bristol and so forth. Below these came shelves on which stood a wonderful array of stone beer-mugs, each decorated with some fantastic device or motto, and most of them pertaining individually and sacredly to some regular and unfailing customer. In one particular corner of the highest shelf, greatly at his ease and in nowise to be disturbed, slept Wotan, the huge grey house-cat, dreaming doubtless of certain nimble and audacious mice down in the cellar three floors below, whose nimbleness and audacity were as precious to him as the forwardness of the birds is to a skilled gun on a grouse moor. Once every day Wotan came marching in stately fashion across the polished floor, halted midway to resume an unfinished toilet operation, and then proceeded to pay his leisurely respects to his friend von Kwarl. The latter was said to be prouder of this daily demonstration of esteem than of his many coveted orders of merit. Several of his friends and acquaintances shared with him the distinction of having achieved the Black Eagle, but not one of them had ever succeeded in obtaining the slightest recognition of their existence from Wotan.

The daily greeting had been exchanged and the proud grey beast had marched away to the music of a slumberous purr. The *Kreuz Zeitung* and the *Times* underwent a final scrutiny and were pushed aside, and von Kwarl glanced aimlessly out at the July sunshine bathing the walls and windows of the Piccadilly Hotel. Herr Rebinok, the plumb little Pomeranian banker, stepped across the floor, almost as noiselessly as Wotan had done, though with considerably less grace, and some half-minute later was engaged in sliding pawns and knights and bishops to and fro on the chess-board in a series of lightning moves bewildering to look on. Neither he nor his opponent played with the skill that they severally brought to bear on banking and statecraft, nor did they conduct their game with the politeness that they punctiliously observed in other affairs of life. A running fire of contemptuous remarks and aggressive satire accompanied each move, and the mere record of the conversation would have given an uninitiated onlooker the puzzling impression that an easy and crushing victory was assured to both the players.

"Aha, he is puzzled. Poor man, he doesn't know what to do. . . . Oho, he thinks he will move there, does he? Much good that will do him. . . . Never have I seen such a mess as he is in . . . he cannot do anything, he is absolutely helpless, helpless."

"Ah, you take my bishop, do you? Much I care for that. Nothing. See, I give you check. Ah, now he is in a fright! He doesn't know where to go. What a mess he is in. . . ."

So the game proceeded, with a brisk exchange of pieces and incivilities and a fluctuation of fortunes, till the little banker lost his queen as the result of an incautious move, and, after several woebegone contortions of his shoulders and hands, declined further contest. A sleek-headed piccolo rushed forward to remove the board, and the erstwhile combatants resumed the courteous dignity that they discarded in their chess-playing moments.

"Have you see the *Germania* today?" asked Herr Rebinok, as soon as the boy had receded to a respectful distance.

"No," said von Kwarl, "I never see the *Germania*. I count on you to tell me if there is anything noteworthy in it."

"It has an article today headed, 'Occupation or Assimilation,'" said the banker. "It is of some importance, and well written. It is very pessimistic."

"Catholic papers are always pessimistic about the things of this world," said von Kwarl, "just as they are unduly optimistic about the things of the next world. What line does it take?"

"It says that our conquest of Britain can only result in a temporary occupation, with a 'notice to quit' always hanging over our heads; that we can never hope to assimilate the people of these islands in our Empire as a sort of maritime Saxony or Bavaria, all the teaching of history is against it; Saxony and Bavaria are part of the Empire because of their past history. England is being bound into the Empire in spite of her past history; and so forth."

"The writer of the article has not studied history very deeply," said von Kwarl. "The impossible thing that he speaks of has been done before, and done in these very islands, too. The Norman Conquest became an assimilation in comparatively few generations."

"Ah, in those days, yes," said the banker, "but the conditions were altogether different. There was not the rapid transmission of news and the means of keeping the public mind instructed in what was happening; in fact, one can scarcely say that the public mind was there to instruct. There was not the same strong bond of brotherhood between men of the same nation that exists now. Northumberland was almost as foreign to Devon or Kent as Normandy was. And the Church in those days was a great international factor, and the Crusades bound men together fighting under one leader for a common cause. Also there was not a great national past to be forgotten as there is in this case."

"There are many factors, certainly, that are against us," conceded the statesman, "but you must also take into account those that will help us. In most cases in recent history where the conquered have stood out against all attempts at assimilation, there has been a religious difference to add to the racial one—take Poland, for instance, and the Catholic parts of Ireland. If the Bretons ever seriously begin to assert their nationality as against the French, it will be because they have remained more Catholic in practice and sentiment than their neighbours. Here there is no such complication; we are in the bulk a Protestant nation with a Catholic minority, and the same may be said of the British. Then in modern days there is the alchemy of Sport and the Drama to bring men of different races amicably together. One or two sportsmanlike Germans in a London football team will do more to break down racial antagonism than anything that Governments or Councils can effect. As for the Stage, it has long been international in its tendencies. You can see that every day."

The banker nodded his head.

"London is not our greatest difficulty," continued von Kwarl. "You must remember the steady influx of Germans since the war; whole districts are changing the complexion of their inhabitants, and in some streets you might almost fancy yourself in a German town. We can scarcely hope to make much impression on the country districts and the provincial towns at present, but you must remember that thousands and thousands of the more virile and restless-souled men have emigrated, and thousands more will follow their example. We shall fill up their places with our own surplus population, as the Teuton races colonized England in the old pre-Christian days. That is better, is it not, to people the fat meadows of the Thames valley and the healthy downs and uplands of Sussex and Berkshire than to go hunting for elbow-room among the flies and fevers of the tropics? We have somewhere to go to, now, better than the scrub and the veldt and the thorn-jungles."

"Of course, of course," assented Herr Rebinok, "but while this desirable process of infiltration and assimilation goes on, how are you going to provide against the hostility of the conquered nation? A people with a great tradition behind them and the ruling instinct strongly developed, won't sit with their eyes closed and their hands folded while you carry on the process of Germanization. What will keep them quiet?"

"The hopelessness of the situation. For centuries Britain has ruled the seas, and been able to dictate to half the world in consequence; then she let slip the mastery of the seas, as something too costly and onerous to keep up, something which aroused too much jealousy and uneasiness in others, and now the seas rule her. Every wave that breaks on her shore rattles the keys of her prison. I am no fire-eater, Herr Rebinok, but I confess that when I am at Dover, say, or Southampton, and see those dark blots on the sea and those grey specks in the sky, our battleships and cruisers and aircraft, and realize what they mean to us, my heart beats just a little quicker. If every German was flung out of England tomorrow, in three weeks' time we should be coming in again on our own terms. With our sea scouts and air scouts spread in organized network around, not a shipload of food-stuff could reach the country. They know that; they can calculate how many days of independence and starvation they could endure, and they will make no attempt to bring about such a certain fiasco. Brave men fight for a forlorn hope, but the bravest do not fight for an issue they know to be hopeless."

"That is so," said Herr Rebinok; "as things are at present they can do nothing from within, absolutely nothing. We have weighed all that beforehand. But, as the *Germania* points out, there is another Britain beyond the seas. Supposing the Court at Delhi were to engineer a league——"

"A league? A league with whom?" interrupted the statesman.

"Russia we can watch and hold. We are rather nearer to its western frontier than Delhi is, and we could throttle its Baltic trade at five hours' notice. France and Holland are not inclined to provoke our hostility; they would have everything to lose by such a course."

"There are other forces in the world that might be arrayed against us," argued the banker; "the United States, Japan, Italy, they all have navies."

"Does the teaching of history show you that it is the strong Power, armed and ready, that has to suffer from the hostility of the world?" asked von Kwarl. "As far as sentiment goes, perhaps, but not in practice. The danger has always been for the weak, dismembered nation. Think you a moment, has the enfeebled scattered British Empire overseas no undefended territories that are a temptation to her neighbours? Has Japan nothing to glean where we have harvested? Are there no North American possessions which might slip into other keeping? Has Russia herself no traditional temptations beyond the Oxus? Mind you, we are not making the mistake Napoleon made, when he forced all Europe to be for him or against him. We threaten no world aggressions, we are satiated where he was insatiable. We have cast down one overshadowing Power from the face of the world, because it stood in our way, but we have made no attempt to spread our branches over all the space that it covered. We have not tried to set up a tributary Canadian republic or to partition South Africa; we have dreamed no dream of making ourselves Lords of Hindostan. On the contrary, we have given proof of our friendly intentions towards our neighbours. We backed France up the other day in her squabble with Spain over the Moroccan boundaries, and proclaimed our opinion that the Republic had as indisputable a mission on the North Africa coast as we have in the North Sea. That is not the action or the language of aggression. No," continued von Kwarl, after a moment's silence, "the world may fear us and dislike us, but, for the present at any rate, there will be no leagues against us. No, there is one rock on which our attempt at assimilation will founder or find firm anchorage."

"And that is–?"

"The youth of the country, the generation that is at the threshold now. It is them that we must capture. We must teach them to learn, and coax them to forget. In course of time Anglo-Saxon may blend with German, as the Elbe Saxons and the Bavarians and Swabians have blended with the Prussians into a loyal united people under the sceptre of the Hohenzollerns. Then we should be doubly strong, Rome and Carthage rolled into one, an Empire of the West greater than Charlemagne ever knew. Then we could look Slav and Latin and Asiatic in the face and keep our place as the central dominant force of the civilized world."

The speaker paused for a moment and drank a deep draught of wine, as though he were invoking the prosperity of that future world-power. Then he resumed in a more level tone:

"On the other hand, the younger generation of Britons may grow up in hereditary hatred, repulsing all our overtures, forgetting nothing and forgiving nothing, waiting and watching for the time when some weakness assails us, when some crisis entangles us, when we cannot be everywhere at once. Then our work will be imperilled, perhaps undone. There lies the danger, there lies the hope, the younger generation."

"There is another danger," said the banker, after he had pondered over von Kwarl's remarks for a moment or two amid the incense-clouds of a fat cigar; "a danger that I foresee in the immediate future; perhaps not so much a danger as an element of exasperation which may ultimately defeat your plans. The law as to military service will have to be promulgated shortly, and that cannot fail to be bitterly unpopular. The people of these islands will have to be brought into line with the rest of the Empire in the matter of military training and military service, and how will they like that? Will not the enforcing of such a measure infuriate them against us? Remember, they have made great sacrifices to avoid the burden of military service."

"Dear God," exclaimed Herr von Kwarl, "as you say, they have made sacrifices on that altar!"

Chapter VII
THE LURE

Cicely had successfully insisted on having her own way concerning the projected supper-party; Yeovil had said nothing further in opposition to it, whatever his feelings on the subject might be. Having gained her point, however, she was anxious to give her husband the impression of having been consulted, and to put her victory as far as possible on the footing of a compromise. It was also rather a relief to be able to discuss the matter out of range of Joan's disconcerting tongue and observant eyes.

"I hope you are not really annoyed about this silly supper-party," she said on the morning before the much-talked-of first night. "I had pledged myself to give it, so I couldn't back out without seeming mean to Gorla, and in any case it would have been impolitic to cry off."

"Why impolitic?" asked Yeovil coldly.

"It would give offence in quarters where I don't want to give offence," said Cicely.

"In quarters were the *fait accompli* is an object of solicitude," said Yeovil.

"Look here," said Cicely in her most disarming manner, "it's just as well to be perfectly frank about the whole matter. If one wants to live in the London of the present day one must make up one's mind to accept the *fait accompli* with as good a grace as possible. I do want to live in London, and I don't want to change my way of living and start under different conditions in some other place. I can't face the prospect of tearing up my life by the roots; I feel certain that I shouldn't bear transplanting. I can't imagine myself re-creating my circle of interests in some foreign town or colonial centre or even in a country town in England. India I couldn't stand. London is not merely a home to me, it is a world, and it happens to be just the world that suits me and that I am suited to. The German occupation, or whatever one likes to call it, is a calamity, but it's not like a molten deluge from Vesuvius that need send us all scuttling away from another Pompeii. Of course," she added, "there are things that jar horribly on one, even when one has got more or less accustomed to them, but one must just learn to be philosophical and bear them."

"Supposing they are not bearable?" said Yeovil; "during the few days that I've been in the land I've seen things that I cannot imagine will ever be bearable."

"That is because they're new to you," said Cicely.

"I don't wish that they should ever come to seem bearable," retorted Yeovil. "I've been bred and reared as a unit of a ruling race; I don't want to find myself settling down resignedly as a member of an enslaved one."

"There's no need to make things out worse than they are," protested Cicely. "We've had a military disaster on a big scale, and there's been a great political dislocation in consequence. But there's no reason why everything shouldn't right itself in time, as it has done after other similar disasters in the history of nations. We are not scattered to the winds or wiped off the face of the earth, we are still an important racial unit."

"A racial unit in a foreign Empire," commented Yeovil.

"We may arrive at the position of being the dominant factor in that Empire," said Cicely, "impressing our national characteristics on it, and perhaps dictating its dynastic future and the whole trend of its policy. Such things have happened in history. Or we may become strong enough to throw off the foreign connexion at a moment when it can be done effectually and advantageously. But meanwhile it is necessary to preserve our industrial life and our social life, and for that reason we must accommodate ourselves to present circumstances, however distasteful they may be. Emigration to some colonial wilderness, or holding ourselves rigidly aloof from the life of the capital, won't help matters. Really, Murrey, if you will think things over a bit, you will see that the course I am following is the one dictated by sane patriotism."

"Whom the gods wish to render harmless they first afflict with sanity," said Yeovil bitterly. "You may be content to wait for a hundred years or so, for this national revival to creep and crawl us back into a semblance of independence and world-importance. I'm afraid I haven't the patience or the philosophy to sit down comfortably and wait for a change of fortune that won't come in my time—if it comes at all."

Cicely changed the drift of the conversation; she had only introduced the argument for the purpose of defining her point of view and accustoming Yeovil to it, as one leads a nervous horse up to an unfamiliar barrier that he is required eventually to jump.

"In any case," she said, "from the immediately practical standpoint England is the best place for you till you have shaken off all traces of that fever. Pass the time away somehow till the hunting begins, and then go down to the East Wessex country; they are looking out for a new master after this season, and if you were strong enough you might take it on for a while. You could go to Norway for fishing in the summer and hunt the East Wessex in the winter. I'll come down and do a bit of hunting too, and we'll have house-parties, and get a little golf in between whiles. It will be like old times."

Yeovil looked at his wife and laughed.

"Who was that old fellow who used to hunt his hounds regularly through the fiercest times of the great Civil War? There is a picture of him, by Caton Woodville, I think, leading his pack between King Charles's army and the Parliament forces just as some battle was going to begin. I have often thought that the King must have disliked him rather more than he disliked the men who were in arms against him; they at least cared, one way or the other. I fancy that old chap would have a great many imitators nowadays, though, when it came to be a question of sport against soldiering. I don't know whether any one has said it, but one might almost assert that the German victory was won on the golf-links of Britain."

"I don't see why you should saddle one particular form of sport with a special responsibility," protested Cicely.

"Of course not," said Yeovil, "except that it absorbed perhaps more of the energy and attention of the leisured class than other sports did, and in this country the leisured class was the only bulwark we had against official indifference. The working classes had a big share of the apathy, and, indirectly, a greater share of the responsibility, because the voting power was in their hands. They had not the leisure, however, to sit down and think clearly what the danger was; their own industrial warfare was more real to them than anything that was threatening from the nation that they only knew from samples of German clerks and German waiters."

"In any case," said Cicely, "as regards the hunting, there is no Civil War or national war raging just now, and there is no immediate likelihood of one. A good many hunting seasons will have to come and go before we can think of a war of independence as even a distant possibility, and in the meantime hunting and horse-breeding and country sports generally are the things most likely to keep Englishmen together on the land. That is why so many men who hate the German occupation are trying to keep field sports alive, and in the right hands. However, I won't go on arguing. You and I always think things out for ourselves and decide for ourselves, which is much the best way in the long run."

Cicely slipped away to her writing-room to make final arrangements over the telephone for the all-important supper-party, leaving Yeovil to turn over in his mind the suggestion that she had thrown out. It was an obvious lure, a lure to draw him away from the fret and fury that possessed him so inconveniently, but its obvious nature did not detract from its effectiveness. Yeovil had pleasant recollections of the East Wessex, a cheery little hunt that afforded good sport in an unpretentious manner, a joyous thread of life running through a rather sleepy countryside, like a merry brook careering through a placid valley. For a man coming slowly and yet eagerly back to the activities of life from the weariness of a long fever, the prospect of a leisurely season with the East Wessex was singularly attractive, and side by side with its attractiveness there was a tempting argument in favour of yielding to its attractions. Among the small squires and yeoman farmers, doctors, country tradesmen, auctioneers and so forth who would gather at the covert-side and at the hunt breakfasts, there might be a local nucleus of revolt against the enslavement of the land, a discouraged and leaderless band waiting for some one to mould their resistance into effective shape and keep their loyalty to the old dynasty and the old national cause steadily burning. Yeovil could see himself taking up that position, stimulating the spirit of hostility to the *fait accompli*, organizing stubborn opposition to every Germanizing influence that was brought into play, schooling the youth of the countryside to look steadily Delhiward. That was the bait that Yeovil threw out to his conscience, while slowly considering the other bait that was appealing so strongly to his senses. The dry warm scent of the stable, the nip of the morning air, the pleasant squelch-squelch of the saddle leather, the moist earthy fragrance of the autumn woods and wet fallows, the cold white mists of winter days, the whimper of hounds and the hot restless pushing of the pack through ditch and hedgerow and undergrowth, the birds that flew up and clucked and chattered as you passed, the hearty greeting and pleasant gossip in farmhouse kitchens and market-day bar-parlours—all these remembered delights of the chase marshalled themselves in the brain, and made a cumulative appeal that came with special intensity to a man who was a little tired of his wanderings, more than a little drawn away from the jarring centres of life. The hot London sunshine baking the soot-grimed walls and the ugly incessant hoot and grunt of the motor traffic gave an added charm to the vision of hill and hollow and copse that flickered in Yeovil's mind. Slowly, with a sensuous lingering over detail, his imagination carried him down to a small, sleepy, yet withal pleasantly bustling market town, and placed him unerringly in a wide straw-littered yard, half-full of men and quarter-full of horses, with a bob-tailed sheep-dog or two trying not to get in everybody's way, but insisting on being in the thick of things. The horses gradually detached themselves from the crowd of unimportant men and came one by one into momentary prominence, to be discussed and appraised for their good points and bad points, and finally to be bid for. And always there was one horse that detached itself conspicuously from the rest, the ideal hunter, or at any rate, Yeovil's ideal of the ideal hunter. Mentally it was put through its paces before him, its pedigree and brief history recounted to him; mentally he saw a stable lad put it over a jump or two, with credit to all concerned, and inevitably he saw himself outbidding less discerning rivals and securing the desired piece of horseflesh, to be the chief glory and mainstay of his hunting stable, to carry him well and truly and cleverly through many a joyous long-to-be-remembered run. That scene had been one of the recurring half-waking dreams of his long days of weakness in the far-away Finnish nursing-home, a dream sometimes of tantalizing mockery, sometimes of pleasure in the foretaste of a joy to come. And now it need scarcely be a dream any longer, he had only to go down at the right moment and take an actual part in his oft-rehearsed vision. Everything would be there, exactly as his imagination had placed it, even down to the bob-tailed sheep-dogs; the horse of his imagining would be there waiting for him, or if not absolutely the ideal animal, something very like it. He might even go beyond the limits of his dream and pick up a couple of desirable animals—there would probably be fewer purchasers for good class hunters in these days than of yore. And with the coming of this reflection his dream faded suddenly and his mind came back with a throb of pain to the things he had for the moment forgotten, the weary, hateful things that were symbolized for him by the standard that floated yellow and black over the frontage of Buckingham Palace.

Yeovil wandered down to his snuggery, a mood of listless dejection possessing him. He fidgeted aimlessly with one or two books and papers, filled a pipe, and half filled a wastepaper basket with torn circulars and accumulated writing-table litter. Then he lit the pipe and settled down in his most comfortable arm-chair with an old notebook in his hand. It was a sort of disjointed diary, running fitfully through the winter months of some past years, and recording noteworthy days with the East Wessex.

And over the telephone Cicely talked and arranged and consulted with men and women to whom the joys of a good gallop or the love of a stricken fatherland were as letters in an unknown alphabet.

Chapter VIII
THE FIRST NIGHT

HUGE posters outside the Caravansery Theatre of Varieties announced the first performance of the uniquely interesting Suggestion Dances, interpreted by the Hon. Gorla Mustelford. An impressionist portrait of a rather severe-looking young woman gave the public some idea of what the *danseuse* might be like in appearance, and the further information was added that her performance was the greatest dramatic event of the season. Yet another piece of information was conveyed to the public a few minutes after the doors had opened, in the shape of large notices bearing the brief announcement, "House full." For the first-night function most of the seats had been reserved for specially invited guests or else bespoken by those who considered it due to their own importance to be visible on such an occasion.

Even at the commencement of the ordinary programme of the evening (Gorla was not due to appear till late in the list) the theatre was crowded with a throng of chattering, expectant human beings; it seemed as though every one had come early to see every one else arrive. As a matter of fact it was the rumour-heralded arrival of one personage in particular that had drawn people early to their seats and given a double edge to the expectancy of the moment.

At first sight and first hearing the bulk of the audience seemed to comprise representatives of the chief European races in well-distributed proportions, but if one gave it closer consideration it could be seen that the distribution was geographically rather than ethnographically diversified. Men and women there were from Paris, Munich, Rome, Moscow and Vienna, from Sweden and Holland and divers other cities and countries, but in the majority of cases the Jordan Valley had supplied their forefathers with a common cradle-ground. The lack of a fire burning on a national altar seemed to have drawn them by universal impulse to the congenial flare of the footlights, whether as artists, producers, impresarios, critics, agents, go-betweens, or merely as highly intelligent and fearsomely well-informed spectators. They were prominent in the chief seats, they were represented, more sparsely but still in fair numbers, in the cheaper places, and everywhere they were voluble, emphatic, sanguine or sceptical, prodigal of word and gesture, with eyes that seemed to miss nothing and acknowledge nothing, and a general restless dread of not being seen and noticed. Of the threatre-going London public there was also a fair muster, more particularly centred in the less expensive parts of the house, while in boxes, stalls and circles a sprinkling of military uniforms gave an unfamiliar tone to the scene in the eyes of those who had not previously witnessed a first-night performance under the new conditions.

Yeovil, while standing aloof from his wife's participation in this social event, had made private arrangements for being a personal spectator of the scene; as one of the ticket-buying public he had secured a seat in the back row of a low-priced gallery, whence he might watch, observant and unobserved, the much-talked-of début of Gorla Mustelford, and the writing of a new chapter in the history of the *fait accompli*. Around him he noticed an incessant undercurrent of jangling laughter, an unending give-and-take of meaningless mirthless jest and catchword. He had noticed the same thing in streets and public places since his arrival in London, a noisy, empty interchange of chaff and laughter that he had been at a loss to account for. The Londoner is not well adapted for the irresponsible noisiness of jesting tongue that bubbles up naturally in a Southern race, and the effort to be volatile was the more noticeable because it so obviously was an effort. Turning over the pages of a book that told the story of Bulgarian social life in the days of Turkish rule, Yeovil had that morning come across a passage that seemed to throw some light on the thing that had puzzled him:

"Bondage has this one advantage: it makes a nation merry. Where far-reaching ambition has no scope for its development the community squanders its energy on the trivial and personal cares of its daily life, and seeks relief and recreation in simple and easily obtained material enjoyment." The writer was a man who had known bondage, so he spoke at any rate with authority. Of the London of the moment it could not, however, be said with any truth that it was merry, but merely that its inhabitants made desperate endeavour not to appear crushed under their catastrophe. Surrounded as he was now with a babble of tongues and shrill mechanical repartee, Yeovil's mind went back to the book and its account of a theatre audience in the Turkish days of Bulgaria, with its light and laughing crowd of critics and spectators. Bulgaria! The thought of that determined little nation came to him with a sharp sense of irony. There was a people who had not thought it beneath the dignity of their manhood to learn the trade and discipline of arms. They had their reward; torn and exhausted and debt-encumbered from their campaigns, they were masters in their own house, the Bulgarian flag flew over the Bulgarian mountains. And Yeovil stole a glance at the crown of Charlemagne set over the Royal box.

In a capacious box immediately opposite the one set aside for royalty the Lady Shalem sat in well-considered prominence, confident that every Press critic and reporter would note her presence, and that one or two of them would describe, or misdescribe, her toilet. Already quite a considerable section of the audience knew her by name, and the frequency with which she graciously nodded towards various quarters of the house suggested the presence of a great many personal acquaintances. She had attained to that desirable feminine altitude of purse and position when people who go about everywhere know you well by sight and have never met your dress before.

Lady Shalem was a woman of commanding presence, of that type which suggests a consciousness that the command may not necessarily be obeyed; she had observant eyes and a well-managed voice. Her successes in life had been worked for, but they were also to some considerable extent the result of accident. Her public history went back to the time when, in the person of her husband, Mr. Conrad Dort, she had contested two hopeless and very expensive Parliamentary elections on behalf of her party; on each occasion the declaration of the poll had shown a heavy though reduced majority on the wrong side, but she might have perpetrated an apt misquotation of the French monarch's traditional message after the defeat of Pavia, and assured the world "all is lost save honours." The forthcoming Honours List had duly proclaimed the fact that Conrad Dort, Esquire, had entered Parliament by another door as Baron Shalem of Wireskiln, in the county of Suffolk. Success had crowned the lady's efforts as far as the achievement of the title went, but her social ambitions seemed unlikely to make further headway. The new Baron and his wife, their title and money notwithstanding, did not "go down" in their particular segment of county society, and in London there were other titles and incomes to compete with. People were willing to worship the Golden Calf, but allowed themselves a choice of altars. No one could justly say that the Shalems were either oppressively vulgar or insufferably bumptious; probably the chief reason for their lack of popularity was their intense and obvious desire to be popular. They kept open house in such an insistently open manner that they created a social draught. The people who accepted their invitations for the second or third time were not the sort of people whose names gave importance to a dinner party or a house gathering. Failure, in a thinly-disguised form, attended the assiduous efforts of the Shalems to play a leading rôle in the world that they had climbed into. The Baron began to observe to his acquaintances that "gadding about" and entertaining on a big scale was not much in his line; a quiet after-dinner pipe and talk with some brother legislator was his ideal way of spending an evening.

Then came the great catastrophe, involving the old order of society in the national overthrow. Lady Shalem, after a decent interval of patriotic mourning, began to look around her and take stock of her chances and opportunities under the new régime. It was easier to achieve distinction as a titled oasis in the social desert that London had become than it had been to obtain recognition as a new growth in a rather overcrowded field. The observant eyes and agile brain quickly noted this circumstance, and her ladyship set to work to adapt herself to the altered conditions that governed her world. Lord Shalem was one of the few Peers who kissed the hand of the new Sovereign, his wife was one of the few hostesses who attempted to throw a semblance of gaiety and lavish elegance over the travesty of a London season following the year of disaster. The world of tradesmen and purveyors and caterers, and the thousands who were dependent on them for employment, privately blessed the example set by Shalem House, whatever their feelings might be towards the *fait accompli*, and the august new-comer who had added an old Saxon kingdom and some of its accretions to the Teutonic realm of Charlemagne was duly beholden to an acquired subject who was willing to forget the bitterness of defeat and to help others to forget it also. Among other acts of Imperial recognition an earldom was being held in readiness for the Baron who had known how to accept accomplished facts with a good grace. One of the wits of the Cockatrice Club had asserted that the new earl would take as supporters for his coat of arms a lion and a unicorn oublié.

In the box with Lady Shalem was the Gräfin von Tolb, a well-dressed woman of some fifty-six years, comfortable and placid in appearance, yet alert withal, rather suggesting a thoroughly wide-awake dormouse. Rich, amiable and intelligent were the adjectives which would best have described her character and her life-story. In her own rather difficult social circle at Paderborn she had earned for herself the reputation of being one of the most tactful and discerning hostesses in Germany, and it was generally suspected that she had come over and taken up her residence in London in response to a wish expressed in high quarters; the lavish hospitality which she dispensed at her house in Berkeley Square was a considerable reinforcement to the stricken social life of the metropolis.

In a neighbouring box Cicely Yeovil presided over a large and lively party, which of course included Ronnie Storre, who was for once in a way in a chattering mood, and also included an American dowager, who had never been known to be in anything else. A tone of literary distinction was imparted to the group by the presence of Augusta Smith, better known under her pen-name of Rhapsodie Pantril, author of a play that had had a limited but well-advertised success in Sheffield and the United States of America, author also of a book of reminiscences, entitled *Things I Cannot Forget*. She had beautiful eyes, a knowledge of how to dress, and a pleasant disposition, cankered just a little by a perpetual dread of the non-recognition of her genius. As the woman, Augusta Smith, she probably would have been unreservedly happy; as the superwoman, Rhapsodie Pantril, she lived within the borderline of discontent. Her most ordinary remarks were framed with the view of arresting attention; some one once said of her that she ordered a sack of potatoes with the air of one who is making inquiry for a love-philtre.

"Do you see what colour the curtain is?" she asked Cicely, throwing a note of intense meaning into her question.

Cicely turned quickly and looked at the drop-curtain.

"Rather a nice blue," she said.

"Alexandrine blue—*my* colour—the colour of hope," said Rhapsodie impressively.

"It goes well with the general colour-scheme," said Cicely, feeling that she was hardly rising to the occasion.

"Say, is it really true that His Majesty is coming?" asked the lively American dowager. "I've put on my nooest frock and my best diamonds on purpose, and I shall be mortified to death if he doesn't see them."

"There!" pouted Ronnie, "I felt certain you'd put them on for me."

"Why no, I should have put on rubies and orange opals for you. People with our colour of hair always like barbaric display——"

"They don't," said Ronnie, "they have chaste cold tastes. You are absolutely mistaken."

"Well, I think I ought to know!" protested the dowager; "I've lived longer in the world than you have, anyway."

"Yes," said Ronnie with devastating truthfulness, "but my hair has been this colour longer than yours has."

Peace was restored by the opportune arrival of a middle-aged man of blond North-German type, with an expression of brutality on his rather stupid face, who sat in the front of the box for a few minutes on a visit of ceremony to Cicely. His appearance caused a slight buzz of recognition among the audience, and if Yeovil had cared to make enquiry of his neighbours he might have learned that this decorated and obviously important personage was the redoubtable von Kwarl, artificer and shaper of much of the statecraft for which other men got the public credit.

The orchestra played a selection from the "Gondola Girl," which was the leading musical-comedy of the moment. Most of the audience, those in the more expensive seats at any rate, heard the same airs two or three times daily, at restaurant lunches, teas, dinners and suppers, and occasionally in the Park; they were justified therefore in treating the music as a background to slightly louder conversation than they had hitherto indulged in. The music came to an end, episode number two in the evening's entertainment was signalled, the curtain of Alexandrine blue rolled heavily upward, and a troupe of performing wolves was presented to the public. Yeovil had encountered wolves in North Africa deserts and in Siberian forest and wold, he had seen them at twilight stealing like dark shadows across the snow, and heard their long whimpering howl in the darkness amid the pines; he could well understand how a magic lore had grown up round them through the ages among the peoples of four continents, how their name had passed into a hundred strange sayings and inspired a hundred traditions. And now he saw them ride round the stage on tricycles, with grotesque ruffles round their necks and clown caps on their heads, their eyes blinking miserably in the blaze of the footlights. In response to the applause of the house a stout, atrociously smiling man in evening dress came forward and bowed; he had had nothing to do either with the capture or the training of the animals, having bought them ready for use from a continental emporium where wild beasts were prepared for the music-hall market, but he continued bowing and smiling till the curtain fell.

Two American musicians with comic tendencies (denoted by the elaborate rags and tatters of their costumes) succeeded the wolves. Their musical performance was not without merit, but their comic "business" seemed to have been invented long ago by some man who had patented a monopoly of all music-hall humour and forthwith retired from the trade. Some day, Yeovil reflected, the rights of the monopoly might expire and new "business" become available for the knockabout profession.

The audience brightened considerably when item number five of the programme was signalled. The orchestra struck up a rollicking measure and Tony Luton made his entrance amid a rousing storm of applause. He was dressed as an errand-boy of some West End shop, with a livery and box-tricycle, as spruce and decorative as the most ambitious errand-boy could see himself in his most ambitious dreams. His song was a lively and very audacious chronicle of life behind the scenes of a big retail establishment, and sparkled with allusions which might fitly have been described as suggestive—at any rate they appeared to suggest meanings to the audience quite as clearly as Gorla Mustelford's dances were likely to do, even with the aid, in her case, of long explanations on the programmes. When the final verse seemed about to reach an unpardonable climax a stage policeman opportunely appeared and moved the lively songster on for obstructing the imaginary traffic of an imaginary Bond Street. The house received the new number with genial enthusiasm, and mingled its applause with demands for an earlier favourite. The orchestra struck up the familiar air, and in a few moments the smart errand-boy, transformed now into a smart jockey, was singing. "They quaff the gay bubbly in Eccleston Square" to an audience that hummed and nodded its unstinted approval.

The next number but one was the Gorla Mustelford début, and the house settled itself down to yawn and fidget and chatter for ten or twelve minutes while a troupe of talented Japanese jugglers performed some artistic and quite uninteresting marvels with fans and butterflies and lacquer boxes. The interval of waiting was not destined, however, to be without its interest; in its way it provided the one really important and dramatic moment of the evening. One or two uniforms and evening toilettes had already made their appearace in the Imperial box; now there was observable in that quarter a slight commotion, an unobtrusive reshuffling and reseating, and then every eye in the suddenly quiet semi-darkened house focused itself on one figure. There was no public demonstration from the newly-loyal, it had been particularly wished that there should be none, but a ripple of whisper went through the vast audience from end to end. Majesty had arrived. The Japanese marvel-workers went through their display with even less attention than before. Lady Shalem, sitting well in the front of her box, lowered her observant eyes to her programme and her massive bangles. The evidence of her triumph did not need staring at.

Chapter IX

AN EVENING "TO BE REMEMBERED"

To the uninitiated or unappreciative the dancing of Gorla Mustelford did not seem widely different from much that had been exhibited aforetime by exponents of the posturing school. She was not naturally graceful of movement, she had not undergone years of arduous tutelage, she had not the instinct for sheer joyous energy of action that is stored in some natures; out of these unpromising negative qualities she had produced a style of dancing that might best be labelled a conscientious departure from accepted methods. The highly imaginative titles that she had bestowed on her dances, the "Life of a fern," the "Soul-dream of a topaz," and so forth, at least gave her audience and her critics something to talk about. In themselves they meant absolutely nothing, but they induced discussion, and that to Gorla meant a great deal. It was a season of dearth and emptiness in the footlights and box-office world, and her performance received a welcome that would scarcely have befallen it in a more crowded and prosperous day. Her success, indeed, had been waiting for her, ready-made, as far as the managerial profession was concerned, and nothing had been left undone in the way of advertisement to secure for it the appearance, at any rate, of popular favour. And loud above the interested applause of those who had personal or business motives for acclaiming a success swelled the exaggerated enthusiasm of the fairly numerous art-satellites who are unstinted in their praise of anything that they are certain they cannot understand. Whatever might be the subsequent verdict of the theatre-filling public the majority of the favoured first-night audience was determined to set the seal of its approval on the suggestion dances, and a steady roll of applause greeted the conclusion of each item. The dancer gravely bowed her thanks; in marked contradistinction to the gentleman who had "presented" the performing wolves she did not permit herself the luxury of a smile.

"It teaches us a great deal," said Rhapsodie Pantril vaguely, but impressively, after the Fern dance had been given and applauded.

"At any rate we know now that a fern takes life very seriously," broke in Joan Mardle, who had somehow wriggled herself into Cicely's box.

As Yeovil, from the back of his gallery, watched Gorla running and ricochetting about the stage, looking rather like a wagtail in energetic pursuit of invisible gnats and midges, he wondered how many of the middle-aged women who were eagerly applauding her would have taken the least notice of similar gymnastics on the part of their offspring in nursery or garden, beyond perhaps asking them not to make so much noise. And a bitterer tinge came to his thoughts as he saw the bouquets being handed up, thoughts of the brave old dowager down at Torywood, the woman who had worked and wrought so hard and so unsparingly in her day for the well-being of the State—the State that had fallen helpless into alien hands before her tired eyes. Her eldest son lived invalid-wise in the South of France, her second son lay fathoms deep in the North Sea, with the hulk of a broken battleship for a burial-vault; and now the granddaughter was standing here in the limelight, bowing her thanks for the patronage and favour meted out to her by this cosmopolitan company, with its lavish sprinkling of the uniforms of an alien army.

Prominent among the flowers at her feet was one large golden-petalled bouquet of gorgeous blooms, tied with a broad streamer of golden riband, the tribute rendered by Cæsar to the things that were Cæsar's. The new chapter of the *fait accompli* had been written that night and written well. The audience poured slowly out with the triumphant music of Jancovius's *Kaiser Wilhelm* march, played by the orchestra as a happy inspiration, pealing in its ears.

"It has been a great evening, a most successful evening," said Lady Shalem to Herr von Kwarl, whom she was conveying in her electric brougham to Cicely Yeovil's supper party; "an important evening," she added, choosing her adjectives with deliberation. "It should give pleasure in high quarters, should it not?"

And she turned her observant eyes on the impassive face of her companion.

"Gracious lady," he replied with deliberation and meaning, "it has given pleasure. It is an evening to be remembered."

The gracious lady suppressed a sigh of satisfaction. Memory in high places was a thing fruitful and precious beyond computation.

Cicely's party at the Porphyry Restaurant had grown to imposing dimensions. Every one whom she had asked had come, and so had Joan Mardle. Lady Shalem had suggested several names at the last moment, and there was quite a strong infusion of the Teutonic military and official world. It was just as well, Cicely reflected, that the supper was being given at a restaurant and not in Berkshire Street.

"Quite like ole times," purred the beaming proprietor in Cicely's ear, as the staircase and cloakrooms filled up with a jostling, laughing throng.

The guests settled themselves at four tables, taking their places where chance or fancy led them, late comers having to fit in wherever they could find room. A babel of tongues in various languages reigned round the tables, amid which the rattle of knives and forks and plates and the popping of corks made a subdued hubbub. Gorla Mustelford, the motive for all this sound and movement, this chatter of guests and scurrying of waiters, sat motionless in the fatigued self-conscious silence of a great artist who has delivered a great message.

"Do sit at Lady Peach's table, like a dear boy," Cicely begged of Tony Luton, who had come in late; "she and Gerald Drowly have got together, in spite of all my efforts, and they are both so dull. Try and liven things up a bit."

A loud barking sound, as of fur-seals calling across Arctic ice, came from another table, where Mrs. Mentieth-Mendlesohnn (one of the Mendlesohnns of Invergordon, as she was wont to describe herself) was proclaiming the glories and subtleties of Gorla's achievement.

"It was a revelation," she shouted; "I sat there and saw a whole new scheme of thought unfold itself before my eyes. One could not define it, it was thought translated into action—the best art cannot be defined. One just sat there and knew that one was seeing something one had never seen before, and yet one felt that one had seen it in one's brain, all one's life. That was what was so wonderful—yes, please," she broke off sharply as a fat quail in aspic was presented to her by a questioning waiter.

The voice of Mr. Mauleverer Morle came across the table, like another seal barking at a greater distance.

"Rostand," he observed with studied emphasis, "has been called *le Prince de l'Adjectif Inopiné;* Miss Mustelford deserves to be described as the Queen of Unexpected Movement."

"Oh, I say, do you hear that?" exclaimed Mrs. Mentieth-Mendlesohnn to as wide an audience as she could achieve; "Rostand has been called—tell them what you said, Mr. Morle," she broke off, suddenly mistrusting her ability to handle a French sentence at the top of her voice.

Mr. Morle repeated his remark.

"Pass it on to the next table," commanded Mrs. Mentieth-Mendlesohnn. "It's too good to be lost."

At the next table, however, a grave impressive voice was dwelling at length on a topic remote from the event of the evening. Lady Peach considered that all social gatherings, of whatever nature, were intended for the recital of minor domestic tragedies. She lost no time in regaling the company around her with the detailed history of an interrupted week-end in a Norfolk cottage.

"The most charming and delightful old-world spot that you could imagine, clean and quite comfortable, just a nice distance from the sea and within an easy walk of the Broads. The very place for the children. We'd brought everything for a four days' stay and meant to have a really delightful time. And then on Sunday morning we found that some one had left the springhead, where our only supply of drinking water came from, uncovered, and a dead bird was floating in it; it had fallen in somehow and got drowned. Of course we couldn't use the water that a dead body had been floating in, and there was no other supply for miles round, so we had to come away then and there. Now what do you say to that?"

"'Ah, that a linnet should die in the Spring,'" quoted Tony Luton with intense feeling.

There was an immediate outburst of hilarity where Lady Peach had confidently looked for expressions of concern and sympathy.

"Isn't Tony just perfectly cute? Isn't he?" exclaimed a young American woman, with an enthusiasm to which Lady Peach entirely failed to respond. She had intended following up her story with the account of another tragedy of a smiliar nature that had befallen her three years ago in Argyllshire, and now the opportunity had gone. She turned morosely to the consolations of a tongue salad.

At the centre table the excellent von Tolb led a chorus of congratulation and compliment, to which Gorla listened with an air of polite detachment, much as the Sheikh Ul Islam might receive the homage of a Wesleyan Conference. To a close observer it would have seemed probable that her attitude of fatigued indifference to the flattering remarks that were showered on her had been as carefully studied and rehearsed as any of her postures on the stage.

"It is something that one will appreciate more and more fully every time one sees it. . . . One cannot see it too often. . . . I could have sat and watched it for hours. . . . Do you know, I am just looking forward to tomorrow evening, when I can see it again. . . . I knew it was going to be good, but I had no idea—" so chimed the chorus, between mouthfuls of quail and bites of asparagus.

"Weren't the performing wolves wonderful?" exclaimed Joan in her fresh joyous voice, that rang round the room like laughter of the woodpecker.

If there is one thing that disturbs the complacency of a great artist of the Halls it is the consciousness of sharing his or her triumphs with performing birds and animals, but of course Joan was not to be expected to know that. She pursued her subject with the assurance of one who has hit on a particularly acceptable topic.

"It must have taken them years of training and concentration to master those tricycles," she continued in high-pitched soliloquy. "The nice thing about them is that they don't realize a bit how clever and educational they are. It would be dreadful to have them putting on airs, wouldn't it? And yet I suppose the knowledge of being able to jump through a hoop better than any other wolf would justify a certain amount of 'side.'"

Fortunately at this moment a young Italian journalist at another table rose from his seat and delivered a two-minute oration in praise of the heroine of the evening. He spoke in rapid nervous French, with a North Italian accent, but much of what he said could be understood by the majority of those present, and the applause was unanimous. At any rate he had been brief and it was permissible to suppose that he had been witty.

It was the opening for which Mr. Gerald Drowly had been watching and waiting. The moment that the Italian enthusiast had dropped back into his seat amid a rattle of hand-clapping and rapping of forks and knives on the tables, Drowly sprang to his feet, pushed his chair well away, as for a long separation, and begged to endorse what had been so very aptly and gracefully, and, might he add, truly said by the previous speaker. This was only the prelude to the real burden of his message; with the dexterity that comes of practice he managed, in a couple of hurried sentences, to divert the course of his remarks to his own personality and career, and to inform his listeners that he was an actor of some note and experience, and had had the honour of acting under–and here followed a string of names of eminent actor managers of the day. He thought he might be pardoned for mentioning the fact that his performance of "Peterkin" in the "Broken Nutshell," had won the unstinted approval of the dramatic critics of the Provincial Press. Towards the end of what was a long speech, and which seemed even longer to its hearers, he reverted to the subject of Gorla's dancing and bestowed on it such laudatory remarks as he had left over. Drawing his chair once again into his immediate neighbourhood he sat down, aglow with the satisfied consciousness of a good work worthily performed.

"I once acted a small part in some theatricals got up for a charity," announced Joan in a ringing, confidential voice; "the

Clapham Courier said that all the minor parts were very creditably sustained. Those were its very words. I felt I must tell you that, and also say how much I enjoyed Miss Mustelford's dancing."

Tony Luton cheered wildly.

"That's the cleverest speech so far," he proclaimed. He had been asked to liven things up at his table and was doing his best to achieve that result, but Mr. Gerald Drowly joined Lady Peach in the unfavourable opinion she had formed of that irrepressible youth.

Ronnie, on whom Cicely kept a solicitous eye, showed no sign of any intention of falling in love with Gorla. He was more profitably engaged in paying court to the Gräfin von Tolb, whose hospitable mansion in Belgrave Square invested her with a special interest in his eyes. As a professional Prince Charming he had every inducement to encourage the cult of Fairy Godmother.

"Yes, yes, agreed, I will come and hear you play, that is a promise," said the Gräfin, "and you must come and dine with me one night and play to me afterwards, that is a promise, also, yes? That is very nice of you, to come and see a tiresome old woman. I am passionately fond of music; if I were honest I would tell you also that I am very fond of good-looking boys, but this is not the age of honesty, so I must leave you to guess that. Come on Thursday in next week, you can? That is nice. I have a reigning Prince dining with me that night. Poor man, he wants cheering up; the art of being a reigning Prince is not a very pleasing one nowadays. He has made it a boast all his life that he is Liberal and his subjects Conservative; now that is all changed—no, not all; he is still Liberal, but his subjects unfortunately are become Socialists. You must play your best for him."

"Are there many Socialists over there, in Germany I mean?" asked Ronnie, who was rather out of his depth where politics were concerned.

"*Ueberall*," said the Gräfin with emphasis; "everywhere, I don't know what it comes from; better education and worse digestions I suppose. I am sure digestion has a good deal to do with it. In my husband's family for example, his generation had excellent digestions, and there wasn't a case of Socialism or suicide among them; the younger generation have no digestions worth speaking of, and there have been two suicides and three Socialists within the last six years. And now I must really be going. I am not a Berliner and late hours don't suit my way of life."

Ronnie bent low over the Gräfin's hand and kissed it, partly because she was the kind of woman who naturally invoked such homage, but chiefly because he knew that the gesture showed off his smooth burnished head to advantage.

The observant eyes of Lady Shalem had noted the animated conversation between the Gräfin and Ronnie, and she had overheard fragments of the invitation that had been accorded to the latter.

"Take us the little foxes, the little foxes that spoil the vines," she quoted to herself; "not that that music-boy would do much in the destructive line, but the principle is good."

Chapter X

SOME REFLECTIONS AND A "TE DEUM"

Cicely awoke, on the morning after the "memorable evening," with the satisfactory feeling of victory achieved, tempered by a troubled sense of having achieved it in the face of a reasonably grounded opposition. She had burned her boats, and was glad of it, but the reek of their burning drifted rather unpleasantly across the jubilant incense-swinging of her *Te Deum* service.

Last night had marked an immense step forward in her social career; without running after the patronage of influential personages she had seen it quietly and tactfully put at her service. People such as the Gräfin von Tolb were going to be a power in the London world for a very long time to come. Herr von Kwarl, with all his useful qualities of brain and temperament, might conceivably fall out of favour in some unexpected turn of the political wheel, and the Shalems would probably have their little day and then a long afternoon of diminishing social importance; the placid dormouse-like Gräfin would outlast them all. She had the qualities which make either for contented mediocrity or else for very durable success, according as circumstances may dictate. She was one of those characters that can neither thrust themselves to the front, nor have any wish to do so, but being there, no ordinary power can thrust them away.

With the Gräfin as her friend Cicely found herself in altogether a different position from that involved by the mere interested patronage of Lady Shalem. A vista of social success was opened up to her, and she did not mean it to be just the ordinary success of a popular and influential hostess moving in an important circle. That people with naturally bad manners should have to be polite and considerate in their dealings with her, that people who usually held themselves aloof should have to be gracious and amiable, that the self-assured should have to be just a little humble and anxious where she was concerned, these things of course she intended to happen; she was a woman. But, she told herself, she intended a great deal more than that when she traced the pattern for her scheme of social influence. In her heart she detested the German occupation as a hateful necessity, but while her heart registered the hatefulness the brain recognized the necessity. The great fighting-machines that the Germans had built up and maintained, on land, on sea, and in air, were three solid crushing facts that demonstrated the hopelessness of any immediate thought of revolt. Twenty years hence, when the present generation was older and greyer, the chances of armed revolt would probably be equally hopeless, equally remote-seeming. But in the meantime something could have been effected in another way. The conquerors might partially Germanize London, but, on the other hand, if the thing were skilfully managed, the British element within the Empire might impress the mark of its influence on everything German. The fighting men might remain Prussian or Bavarian, but the thinking men, and eventually the ruling men, could gradually come under British influence, or even be of British blood. An English Liberal-Conservative "Centre" might stand as a bulwark against the Junkerdom and Socialism of Continental Germany. So Cicely reasoned with herself, in a fashion induced perhaps by an earlier apprenticeship to the reading of *Ninteenth Century* articles, in which the possible political and racial developments of various countries were examined and discussed and put away in the pigeon-holes of probable happenings. She had sufficient knowledge of political history to know that such a development might possibly come to pass, she had not sufficient insight into actual conditions to know that the possibility was as remote as that of armed resistance. And the rôle which she saw herself playing was that of a deft and courtly political intriguer, rallying the British element and making herself agreeable to the German element, a political inspiration to the one and a social distraction to the other. At the back of her mind there lurked an honest confession that she was probably overrating her powers of statecraft and personality, that she was more likely to be carried along by the current of events than to control or divert its direction; the political day-dream remained, however, as day-dreams will, in spite of the clear light of probability shining through them. At any rate she knew, as usual, what she wanted to do, and as usual she had taken steps to carry out her intentions. Last night remained in her mind a night of important victory. There also remained the anxious proceeding of finding out if the victory had entailed any serious losses.

Cicely was not one of those ill-regulated people who treat the first meal of the day as a convenient occasion for serving up any differences or contentions that have been left over from the day before or overlooked in the press of other matters. She enjoyed her breakfast and gave Yeovil unhindered opportunity for enjoying his; a discussion as to the right cooking of a dish that he had first tasted among the Orenburg Tartars was the prevailing topic on this particular morning, and blended well with trout and toast and coffee. In the cozy nook of the smoking-room, in participation of the after-breakfast cigarettes, Cicely made her dash into debatable ground.

"You haven't asked me how my supper-party went off," she said.

"There is a notice of it in two of the morning papers, with a list of those present," said Yeovil; "the conquering race seems to have been very well represented."

"Several races were represented," said Cicely; "a function of that sort, celebrating a dramatic first-night, was bound to be cosmopolitan. In fact, blending of races and nationalities is the tendency of the age we live in."

"The blending of races seems to have been consummated already in one of the individuals at your party," said Yeovil drily; "the name Mentieth-Mendlesohnn struck me as a particularly happy obliteration of racial landmarks."

Cicely laughed.

"A noisy and very wearisome sort of woman," she commented; "she reminds one of garlic that's been planted by mistake in a conservatory. Still, she's useful as an advertising agent to any one who rubs her the right way. She'll be invaluable in proclaiming the merits of Gorla's performance to all and sundry; that's why I invited her. She'll probably lunch today at the Hotel Cecil, and every one sitting within a hundred yards of her table will hear what an emotional education they can get by going to see Gorla dance at the Caravansery."

"She seems to be like the Salvation Army," said Yeovil; "her noise reaches a class of people who wouldn't trouble to read Press notices."

"Exactly," said Cicely. "Gorla gets quite good notices on the whole, doesn't she?"

"The one that took my fancy most was the one in the *Standard*," said Yeovil, picking up that paper from a table by his side and searching its columns for the notice in question. " 'The wolves which appeared earlier in the evening's entertainment are, the programme assures us, trained entirely by kindness. It would have been a further kindness, at any rate to the audience, if some of the training, which the wolves doubtless do not appreciate at its proper value, had been expended on Miss Mustelford's efforts at stage dancing. We are assured, again on the authority of the programme, that the much-talked-of Suggestion Dances are the last word in Posture dancing. The last word belongs by immemorial right to the sex which Miss Mustelford adorns, and it would be ungallant to seek to deprive her of her privilege. As far as the educational aspect of her performance is concerned we must admit that the life of the fern remains to us a private life still. Miss Mustelford has abandoned her own private life in an unavailing attempt to draw the fern into the gaze of publicity. And so it was with her other suggestions. They suggested many things, but nothing that was announced on the programme. Chiefly they suggested one outstanding reflection, that stage-dancing is not like those advertised breakfast foods that can be served up after three minutes' preparation. Half a lifetime, or rather half a youthtime is a much more satisfactory allowance.' "

"The *Standard* is prejudiced," said Cicely; "some of the other papers are quite enthusiastic. The *Dawn* gives her a column and a quarter of notice, nearly all of it complimentary. It says the report of her fame as a dancer went before her, but that her performance last night caught it up and outstripped it."

"I should not like to suggest that the *Dawn* is prejudiced," said Yeovil, "but Shalem is a managing director on it, and one of its biggest shareholders. Gorla's dancing is an event of the social season, and Shalem is one of those most interested in keeping up the appearance, at any rate, of a London social season. Besides, her début gave the opportunity for an Imperial visit to the theatre—the first appearance at a festive public function of the Conqueror among the conquered. Apparently the experiment passed off well; Shalem has every reason to feel pleased with himself and well-disposed towards Gorla. By the way," added Yeovil, "talking of Gorla, I'm going down to Torywood one day next week."

"To Torywood?" exclaimed Cicely. The tone of her exclamation gave the impression that the announcement was not very acceptable to her.

"I promised the old lady that I would go and have a talk with her when I came back from my Siberian trip; she travelled in Eastern Russia, you know, long before the Trans-Siberian railway was built, and she's enormously interested in those parts. In any case I should like to see her again."

"She does not see many people nowadays," said Cicely; "I fancy she is breaking up rather. She was very fond of the son who went down, you know."

"She has seen a great many of the things she cared for go down," said Yeovil; "it is a sad old life that is left to her, when one thinks of all that the past has been to her, of the part she used to play in the world, the work she used to get through. It used to seem as though she could never grow old, as if she would die standing up, with some unfinished command on her lips. And now I suppose her tragedy is that she has grown old, bitterly old, and cannot die."

Cicely was silent for a moment, and seemed about to leave the room. Then she turned back and said:

"I don't think I would say anything about Gorla to her if I were you."

"It would not have occurred to me to drag her name into our conversation," said Yeovil coldly, "but in any case the accounts of her dancing performance will have reached Torywood through the newspapers—also the record of your racially-blended supper-party."

Cicely said nothing. She knew that by last night's affair she had definitely identified herself in public opinion with the Shalem clique, and that many of her old friends would look on her with distrust and suspicion on that account. It was unfortunate, but she reckoned it a lesser evil than tearing herself away from her London life, its successes and pleasures and possibilities. These social dislocations and severing of friendships were to be looked for after any great and violent change in State affairs. It was Yeovil's attitude that really troubled her; she would not give way to his prejudices and accept his point of view, but she knew that a victory that involved estrangement from him would only bring a mockery of happiness. She still hoped that he would come round to an acceptance of established facts and deaden his political *malaise* in the absorbing distraction of field sports. The visit to Torywood was a misfortune; it might just turn the balance in the undesired direction. Only a few weeks of late summer and early autumn remained before the hunting season, and its preparations would be at hand, and Yeovil might be caught in the meshes of an old enthusiasm; in those few weeks, however, he might be fired by another sort of enthusiasm, an enthusiasm which would sooner or later mean voluntary or enforced exile for his part, and the probable breaking up of her own social plans and ambitions.

But Cicely knew something of the futility of improvising objections where no real obstacle exists. The visit to Torywood was a graceful attention on Yeovil's part to an old friend; there was no decent ground on which it could be opposed. If the influence of that visit came athwart Yeovil's life and hers with disastrous effect, that was "Kismet."

And once again the reek from her burned and smouldering boats mingled threateningly with the incense fumes of her *Te Deum* for victory. She left the room, and Yeovil turned once more to an item of news in the morning's papers that had already arrested his attention. The Imperial *Aufklärung* on the subject of military service was to be made public in the course of the day.

Chapter XI
THE TEA SHOP

Yeovil wandered down Piccadilly that afternoon in a spirit of restlessness and expectancy. The long-awaited *Aufklärung* dealing with the new law of military service had not yet appeared; at any moment he might meet the hoarse-throated newsboys running along with their papers, announcing the special edition which would give the terms of the edict to the public. Every sound or movement that detached itself with isolated significance from the general whir and scurry of the streets seemed to Yeovil to herald the oncoming clamour and rush that he was looking for. But the long endless succession of motors and buses and vans went by, hooting and grunting, and such newsboys as were to be seen hung about listlessly, bearing no more attractive bait on their posters than the announcement of an "earthquake shock in Hungary; feared loss of life."

The Green Park end of Piccadilly was a changed, and in some respects a livelier thoroughfare to that which Yeovil remembered with affectionate regret. A great political club had migrated from its palatial home to a shrunken habitation in a less prosperous quarter; its place was filled by the flamboyant frontage of the Hotel Konstantinopel. Gorgeous Turkey carpets were spread over the wide entrance steps, and boys in Circassian and Anatolian costumes hung around the doors, or dashed forth in un-Oriental haste to carry such messages as the telephone was unable to transmit. Picturesque sellers of Turkish delight, attar-of-roses, and brass-work coffee services, squatted under the portico, on terms of obvious good understanding with the hotel management. A few doors farther down a service club that had long been a Piccadilly landmark was a landmark still, as the home of the Army Aeronaut Club, and there was a constant coming and going of gay-hued uniforms, Saxon, Prussian, Bavarian, Hessian, and so forth, through its portals. The mastering of the air and the creation of a scientific aerial war fleet, second to none in the world, was an achievement of which the conquering race was pardonably proud, and for which it had good reason to be duly thankful. Over the gateways was blazoned the badge of the club, an elephant, whale, and eagle, typifying the three armed forces of the State, by land and sea and air; the eagle bore in its beak a scroll with the proud legend: "The last am I, but not the least."

To the eastward of this gaily-humming hive the long-shuttered front of a deserted ducal mansion struck a note of protest and mourning amid the noise and whirl and colour of a seemingly uncaring city. On the other side of the roadway, on the gravelled paths of the Green Park, small ragged children from the back streets of Westminster looked wistfully at the smooth trim stretches of grass on which it was now forbidden, in two languages, to set foot. Only the pigeons, disregarding the changes of political geography, walked about as usual, wondering perhaps, if they ever wondered at anything, at the sudden change in the distribution of park humans.

Yeovil turned his steps out of the hot sunlight into the shade of the Burlington Arcade, familiarly known to many of its newer frequenters as the Passage. Here the change that new conditions and requirements had wrought was more immediately noticeable than anywhere else in the West End. Most of the shops on the western side had been cleared away, and in their place had been installed an "open-air" café, converting the long alley into a sort of promenade tea-garden, flanked on one side by a line of haberdashers', perfumers', and jewellers' show windows. The patrons of the café could sit at the little round tables, drinking their coffee and syrups and *apéritifs,* and gazing, if they were so minded, at the pyjamas and cravats and Brazilian diamonds spread out for inspection before them. A string orchestra, hidden away somewhere in the gallery, was alternating grand opera with the *Gondola Girl* and the latest gems of Transatlantic melody. From around the tightly-packed tables arose a babble of tongues, made up chiefly of German, a South American rendering of Spanish, and a North American rendering of English, with here and there the sharp shaken-out staccato of Japanese. A sleepy-looking boy, in a nondescript uniform, was wandering to and fro among the customers, offering for sale the *Matin, New York Herald, Berliner Tageblatt,* and a host of crudely coloured illustrated papers, embodying the hard-worked wit of a world-legion of comic artists. Yeovil hurried through the Arcade; it was not here, in this atmosphere of staring alien eyes and jangling tongues, that he wanted to read the news of the Imperial *Aufklärung.*

By a succession of by-ways he reached Hanover Square, and thence made his way into Oxford Street. There was no commotion of activity to be noticed yet among the newsboys; the posters still concerned themselves with the earthquake in Hungary, varied with references to the health of the King of Roumania, and a motor accident in South London. Yeovil wandered aimlessly along the street for a few dozen yards, and then turned down into the smoking-room of a cheap teashop, where he judged that the flourishing foreign element would be less conspicuously represented. Quiet-voiced, smooth-headed youths, from neighbouring shops and whole-sale houses, sat drinking tea and munching pastry, some of them reading, others making a fitful rattle with dominoes on the marble-topped tables. A clean, wholesome smell of tea and coffee made itself felt through the clouds of cigarette smoke; cleanliness and listlessness seemed to be the dominant notes of the place, a cleanliness that was commendable, and a listlessness that seemed unnatural and undesirable where so much youth was gathered together for refreshment and recreation. Yeovil seated himself at a table already occupied by a young clergyman who was smoking a cigarette over the remains of a plateful of buttered toast. He had a keen, clever, hard-lined face, the face of a man who, in an earlier stage of European history, might have been a warlike prior, awkward to tackle at the council-board, greatly to be avoided where blows were being exchanged. A pale, silent damsel drifted up to Yeovil and took his order with an air of being mentally some hundreds of miles away, and utterly indifferent to the requirements of those whom she served; if she had brought calf's-foot jelly instead of the pot of China tea he had asked for, Yeovil would hardly have been surprised. However, the tea duly arrived on the table, and the pale damsel scribbled a figure on a slip of paper, put it silently by the side of the teapot, and drifted silently away. Yeovil had seen the same sort of thing done on the musical-comedy stage, and done rather differently.

"Can you tell me, sir, is the Imperial announcement out yet?" asked the young clergyman, after a brief scrutiny of his neighbour.

"No, I have been waiting about for the last half-hour on the look-out for it," said Yeovil; "the special editions ought to be out by now." Then he added: "I have only just lately come from abroad. I know scarcely anything of London as it is now. You may imagine that a good deal of it is very strange to me. Your profession must take you a good deal among all classes of people. I have seen something of what one may call the upper, or, at any rate, the richer classes, since I came back; do tell me something about the poorer classes of the community. How do they take the new order of things?"

"Badly," said the young cleric, "badly, in more senses than one. They are helpless and they are bitter—bitter in the useless kind of way that produces no great resolutions. They look round for some one to blame for what has happened; they blame the politicians, they blame the leisured classes; in an indirect way I believe they blame the Church. Certainly, the national disaster has not drawn them towards religion in any form. One thing you may be sure of, they do not blame themselves. No true Londoner ever admits that fault lies at his door. 'No, I never!' is an exclamation that is on his lips from earliest childhood, whenever he is charged with anything blameworthy or punishable. That is why school discipline was ever a thing repugnant to the schoolboard child and its parents; no schoolboard scholar ever deserved punishment. However obvious the fault might seem to a disciplinarian, 'No, I never' exonerated it as something that had not happened. Public schoolboys and private schoolboys of the upper and middle class had their fling and took their thrashings, when they were found out, as a piece of bad luck, but 'our Bert' and 'our Sid' were of those for whom there is no condemnation; if *they* were punished it was for faults that 'no, they never' committed. Naturally the grown-up generation of Berts and Sids, the voters and householders, do not realize, still less admit, that it was they who called the tune to which the politicians danced. They had to choose between the vote-mongers and the so-called 'scare-mongers,' and their verdict was for the vote-mongers all the time. And now they are bitter; they are being punished, and punishment is not a thing that they have been schooled to bear. The taxes that are falling on them are a grievous source of discontent, and the military service that will be imposed on them, for the first time in their lives, will be another. There is a more lovable side to their character under misfortune, though," added the young clergyman. "Deep down in their hearts there was a very real affection for the old dynasty. Future historians will perhaps be able to explain how and why the Royal Family of Great Britain captured the imaginations of its subjects in so genuine and lasting a fashion. Among the poorest and the most matter-of-fact, for whom the name of no public man, politician or philanthropist, stands out with any especial significance, the old Queen, and the dead King, the dethroned monarch and the young prince live in a sort of domestic Pantheon, a recollection that is a proud and wistful personal possession when so little remains to be proud of or to possess. There is no favour that I am so often asked for among my poor parishioners as the gift of the picture of this or that member of the old dynasty. 'I have got all of them, only except Princess Mary,' an old woman said to me last week, and she nearly cried with pleasure when I brought her an old *Bystander* portrait that filled the gap in her collection. And on Queen Alexandra's day they bring out and wear the faded wild-rose favours that they bought with their pennies in days gone by."

"The tragedy of the enactment that is about to enforce military service on these people is that it comes when they've no longer a country to fight for," said Yeovil.

The young clergyman gave an exclamation of bitter impatience.

"That is the cruel mockery of the whole thing. Every now and then in the course of my work I have come across lads who were really drifting to the bad through the good qualities in them. A clean combative strain in their blood, and a natural turn for adventure, made the ordinary anæmic routine of shop or warehouse or factory almost unbearable for them. What splendid little soldiers they would have made, and how grandly the discipline of a military training would have steadied them in after-life when steadiness was wanted. The only adventure that their surroundings offered them has been the adventure of practising mildly criminal misdeeds without getting landed in reformatories and prisons; those of them that have not been successful in keeping clear of detection are walking round and round prison yards, experiencing the operation of a discipline that breaks and does not build. They were merry-hearted boys once, with nothing of the criminal or ne'er-do-well in their natures, and now—have you ever seen a prison yard, with that walk round and round and round between grey walls under a blue sky?"

Yeovil nodded.

"It's good enough for criminals and imbeciles," said the parson, "but think of it for those boys, who might have been marching along to the tap of the drum, with a laugh on their lips instead of Hell in their hearts. I have had Hell in my heart sometimes, when I have come in touch with cases like those. I suppose you are thinking that I am a strange sort of parson."

"I was just defining you in my mind," said Yeovil, "as a man of God, with an infinite tenderness for little devils."

The clergyman flushed.

"Rather a fine epitaph to have on one's tombstone," he said, "especially if the tombstone were in some crowded city graveyard.

I suppose I am a man of God, but I don't think I could be called a man of peace."

Looking at the strong young face, with its suggestion of a fighting prior of bygone days more marked than ever, Yeovil mentally agreed that he could not.

"I have learned one thing in life," continued the young man, "and that is that peace is not for this world. Peace is what God gives us when He takes us into His rest. Beat your sword into a ploughshare if you like, but beat your enemy into smithereens first."

A long-drawn cry, repeated again and again, detached itself from the throb and hoot and whir of the street traffic.

"Speshul! Military service, spesh-ul!"

The young clergyman sprang from his seat and went up the staircase in a succession of bounds, causing the domino players and novelette readers to look up for a moment in mild astonishment. In a few seconds he was back again, with a copy of an afternoon paper. The Imperial Rescript was set forth in heavy type, in parallel columns of English and German. As the young man read a deep burning flush spread over his face, then ebbed away into a chalky whiteness. He read the announcement to the end, then handed the paper to Yeovil, and left without a word.

Beneath the courtly politeness and benignant phraseology of the document ran a trenchant searing irony. The British-born subjects of the Germanic Crown, inhabiting the islands of Great Britain and Ireland, had habituated themselves as a people to the disuse of arms, and resolutely excluded military service and national training from their political system and daily life. Their judgment that they were unsuited as a race to bear arms and conform to military discipline was not to be set aside. Their new Overlord did not propose to do violence to their feelings and customs by requiring from them the personal military sacrifices and services which were rendered by his subjects German-born. The British subjects of the Crown were to remain a people consecrated to peaceful pursuits, to commerce and trade and husbandry. The defence of their coasts and shipping and the maintenance of order and general safety would be guaranteed by a garrison of German troops, with the co-operation of the Imperial war fleet. German-born subjects residing temporarily or permanently in the British Isles would come under the same laws respecting compulsory military service as their fellow-subjects of German blood in the other parts of the Empire, and special enactments would be drawn up to ensure that their interests did not suffer from a periodical withdrawal on training or other military calls. Necessarily a heavily differentiated scale of war taxation would fall on British taxpayers, to provide for the upkeep of the garrison and to equalize the services and sacrifices rendered by the two branches of His Majesty's subjects. As military service was not henceforth open to any subject of British birth no further necessity for any training or exercise of a military nature existed, therefore all rifle clubs, drill associations, cadet corps and similar bodies were henceforth declared to be illegal. No weapons other than guns for specified sporting purposes, duly declared and registered and open to inspection when required, could be owned, purchased, or carried. The science of arms was to be eliminated altogether from the life of a people who had shown such marked repugnance to its study and practice.

The cold irony of the measure struck home with the greater force because its nature was so utterly unexpected. Public anticipation had guessed at various forms of military service, aggressively irksome or tactfully lightened as the case might be, in an event certain to be bitterly unpopular, and now there had come this contemptuous boon, which had removed, at one stroke, the bogey of compulsory military service from the troubled imaginings of the British people, and fastened on them the cruel distinction of being in actual fact what an enemy had called them in splenetic scorn long years ago—a nation of shopkeepers. Aye, something even below that level, a race of shopkeepers who were no longer a nation.

Yeovil crumpled the paper in his hand and went out into the sunlit street. A sudden roll of drums and crash of brass music filled the air. A company of Bavarian infantry went by, in all the pomp and circumstance of martial array and the joyous swing of rapid rhythmic movement. The street echoed and throbbed in the Englishman's ears with the exultant pulse of youth and mastery set to loud Pagan music. A group of lads from the tea-shop clustered on the pavement and watched the troops go by, staring at a phase of life in which they had no share. The martial trappings, the swaggering joy of life, the comradeship of camp and barracks, the hard discipline of drill yard and fatigue duty, the long sentry watches, the trench digging, forced marches, wounds, cold, hunger, makeshift hospitals, and the blood-wet laurels—these were not for them. Such things they might only guess at, or see on a cinema film, darkly; they belonged to the civilian nation.

The function of afternoon tea was still being languidly observed in the big drawing-room when Yeovil returned to Berkshire Street. Cicely was playing the part of hostess to a man of perhaps forty-one years of age, who looked slightly older from his palpable attempts to look very much younger. Percival Plarsey was a plump, pale-faced, short-legged individual, with puffy cheeks, over-prominent nose, and thin colourless hair. His mother, with nothing more than maternal prejudice to excuse her, had discovered some twenty odd years ago that he was a well-favoured young man, and had easily imbued her son with the same opinion. The slipping away of years and the natural transition of the unathletic boy into the podgy unhealthy-looking man did little to weaken the tradition; Plarsey had never been able to relinquish the idea that a youthful charm and comeliness still centred in his person, and laboured daily at his toilet with the devotion that a hopelessly lost cause is so often able to inspire. He babbled incessantly about himself and the accessory futilities of his life in short, neat, complacent sentences, and in a voice that Ronald Storre said reminded one of a fat bishop blessing a butter-making competition. While he babbled he kept his eyes fastened on his listeners to observe the impression which his important little announcements and pronouncements were making. On the present occasion he was pattering forth a detailed description of the upholstery and fittings of his new music-room.

"All the hangings, *violette de Parme,* all the furniture, rosewood. The only ornament in the room is a *replica* of the Mozart statue in Vienna. Nothing but Mozart is to be played in the room. Absolutely, nothing but Mozart."

"You will get rather tired of that, won't you?" said Cicely, feeling that she was expected to comment on this tremendous announcement.

"One gets tired of everything," said Plarsey, with a fat little sigh of resignation. "I can't tell you *how* tired I am of Rubenstein, and one day I suppose I shall be tired of Mozart, and *violette de Parme* and rosewood. I never thought it possible that I could ever tire of jonquils, and now I simply won't have one in the house. Oh, the scene the other day because some one brought some jonquils into the house! I'm afraid I was dreadfully rude, but I really couldn't help it."

He could talk like this through a long summer day or a long winter evening.

Yeovil belonged to a race forbidden to bear arms. At the moment he would gladly have contented himself with the weapons with which nature had endowed him, if he might have kicked and pommelled the abhorrent specimen of male humanity whom he saw before him.

Instead he broke into the conversation with an inspired flash of malicious untruthfulness.

"It is wonderful," he observed carelessly, "how popular that Viennese statue of Mozart has become. A friend who inspects County Council Art Schools tells me you find a copy of it in every class-room you go into."

It was a poor substitute for physical violence, but it was all that civilization allowed him in the way of relieving his feelings; it had, moreover, the effect of making Plarsey profoundly miserable.

Chapter XII

THE TRAVELLING COMPANIONS

THE train bearing Yeovil on his visit to Torywood slid and rattled westward through the hazy dreamland of an English summer landscape. Seen from the train windows the stark bare ugliness of the metalled line was forgotten, and the eye rested only on the green solitude that unfolded itself as the miles went slipping by. Tall grasses and meadow-weeds stood in deep shocks, field after field, between the leafy boundaries of hedge or coppice, thrusting themselves higher and higher till they touched the low sweeping branches of the trees that here and there overshadowed them. Broad streams, bordered with a heavy fringe of reed and sedge, went winding away into a green distance where woodland and meadowland seemed indefinitely prolonged; narrow streamlets, lost to view in the growth that they fostered, disclosed their presence merely by the water-weed that showed in a riband of rank verdure threading the mellower green of the fields. On the stream banks moorhens walked with jerky confident steps, in the easy boldness of those who had a couple of other elements at their disposal in an emergency; more timorous partridges raced away from the apparition of the train, looking all leg and neck, like little forest elves fleeing from human encounter. And in the distance, over the tree line, a heron or two flapped with slow measured wing-beats and an air of being bent on an immeasurably longer journey than the train that hurtled so frantically along the rails. Now and then the meadowland changed itself suddenly into orchard, with close-growing trees already showing the measure of their coming harvest, and then straw-yard and farm buildings would slide into view; heavy dairy cattle, roan and skewbald and dappled, stood near the gates, drowsily resentful of insect stings, and bunched-up companies of ducks halted in seeming irresolution between the charms of the horse-pond and the alluring neighbourhood of the farm kitchen. Away by the banks of some rushing mill-stream, in a setting of copse and cornfield, a village might be guessed at, just a hint of red roof, grey wreathed chimney and old church tower as seen from the windows of the passing train, and over it all brooded a happy, settled calm, like the dreaming murmur of a trout-stream and the far-away cawing of rooks.

It was a land where it seemed as if it must be always summer and generally afternoon, a land where bees hummed among the wild thyme and in the flower-beds of cottage gardens, where the harvest-mice rustled amid the corn and nettles, and the mill-race flowed cool and silent through water-weeds and dark tunnelled sluices, and made soft droning music with the wooden mill-wheel. And the music carried with it the wording of old undying rhymes, and sang of the jolly, uncaring, uncared-for miller, of the farmer who went riding upon his grey mare, of the mouse who lived beneath the merry mill-pin, of the sweet music on yonder green hill and the dancers all in yellow—the songs and fancies of a lingering olden time, when men took life as children take a long summer day, and went to bed at last with a simple trust in something they could not have explained.

Yeovil watched the passing landscape with the intent hungry eyes of a man who revisits a scene that holds high place in his affections. His imagination raced even quicker than the train, following winding roads and twisting valleys into unseen distances, picturing farms and hamlets, hills and hollows, clattering inn yards and sleepy woodlands.

"A beautiful country," said his only fellow-traveller, who was also gazing at the fleeting landscape; "surely a country worth fighting for."

He spoke in fairly correct English, but he was unmistakably a foreigner; one could have allotted him with some certainty to the Eastern half of Europe.

"A beautiful country, as you say," replied Yeovil; then he added the question, "Are you German?"

"No, Hungarian," said the other; "and you, you are English?" he asked.

"I have been much in England, but I am from Russia," said Yeovil, purposely misleading his companion on the subject of his nationality in order to induce him to talk with greater freedom on a delicate topic. While living among foreigners in a foreign land he had shrunk from hearing his country's disaster discussed, or even alluded to; now he was anxious to learn what unprejudiced foreigners thought of the catastrophe and the causes which led up to it.

"It is a strange spectacle, a wonder, is it not so?" resumed the other, "a great nation such as this was, one of the greatest nations in modern times, or of any time, carrying its flag and its language into all parts of the world, and now, after one short campaign, it is——"

And he shrugged his shoulders many times and made clucking noises at the roof of his voice, like a hen calling to a brood of roving chickens.

"They grew soft," he resumed; "great world-commerce brings great luxury, and luxury brings softness. They had everything to warn them, things happening in their own time and before their eyes, and they would not be warned. They had seen, in one generation, the rise of the military and naval power of the Japanese, a brown-skinned race living in some island rice-fields in a tropical sea, a people one thought of in connexion with paper fans and flowers and pretty tea-gardens, who suddenly marched and sailed into the world's gaze as a Great Power; they had seen, too, the rise of the Bulgars, a poor herd of *zaptieh*-ridden peasants, with a few students scattered in exile in Bucharest and Odessa, who shot up in one generation to be an armed and aggressive nation with history in its hands. The English saw these things happening around them, and with a war-cloud growing blacker and bigger and always more threatening on their own threshold they sat down to grow soft and peaceful. They grew soft and accommodating in all things; in religion——"

"In religion?" said Yeovil.

"In religion, yes," said his companion emphatically; "they had come to look on the Christ as a sort of amiable elder Brother, whose letters from abroad were worth reading. Then, when they had emptied all the divine mystery and wonder out of their faith naturally they grew tired of it, oh, but dreadfully tired of it. I know many English of the country parts, and always they tell me they go to church once in each week to set the good example to the servants. They were tired of their faith, but they were not virile enough to become real Pagans; their dancing fauns were good young men who tripped Morris dances and ate health foods and believed in a sort of Socialism which made for the greatest dullness of the greatest number. You will find plenty of them still if you go into what remains of social London."

Yeovil gave a grunt of acquiescence.

"They grew soft in their political ideas," continued the unsparing critic; "for the old insular belief that all foreigners were devils and rogues they substituted another belief, equally grounded on insular lack of knowledge, that most foreigners were amiable, good fellows, who only needed to be talked to and patted on the back to become your friends and benefactors. They began to believe that a foreign Minister would relinquish long-cherished schemes of national policy and hostile expansion if he came over on a holiday and was asked down to country houses and shown the tennis court and the rock-garden and the younger children. Listen. I once heard it solemnly stated at an after-dinner debate in some literary club that a certain very prominent German statesman had a daughter at school in England, and that future friendly relations between the two countries were improved in prospect, if not assured, by that circumstance. You think I am laughing; I am recording a fact, and the men present were politicians and statesmen as well as literary dilettanti. It was an insular lack of insight that worked the mischief, or some of the mischief. We, in Hungary, we live too much cheek by jowl with our racial neighbours to have many illusions about them. Austrians, Roumanians, Serbs, Italians, Czechs, we know what to think of them, we know what we want in the world, and we know what they want; that knowledge does not send us flying at each other's throats, but it does keep us from growing soft. Ah, the British lion was in a hurry to inaugurate the Millennium and to lie down gracefully with the lamb. He made two mistakes, only two, but they were very bad ones; the Millennium hadn't arrived, and it was not a lamb that he was lying down with."

"You do not like the English, I gather," said Yeovil, as the Hungarian went off into a short burst of satirical laughter.

"I have always liked them," he answered, "but now I am angry with them for being soft. Here is my station," he added, as the train slowed down, and he commenced to gather his belongings together. "I am angry with them," he continued, as a final word on the subject, "because I *hate* the Germans."

He raised his hat punctiliously in a parting salute and stepped out on to the platform. His place was taken by a large, loose-limbed man, with florid face and big staring eyes, and an immense array of fishing-basket, rod, fly-cases, and so forth. He was of the type that one could instinctively locate as a loud-voiced, self-constituted authority on whatever topic might happen to be discussed in the bars of small hotels.

"Are you English?" he asked, after a preliminary stare at Yeovil.

This time Yeovil did not trouble to disguise his nationality; he nodded curtly to his questioner.

"Glad of that," said the fisherman; "I don't like travelling with Germans."

"Unfortunately," said Yeovil, "we have to travel with them, as partners in the same State concern, and not by any means the predominant partner either."

"Oh, that will soon right itself," said the other with loud assertiveness, "that will right itself damn soon."

"Nothing in politics rights itself," said Yeovil; "things have to be righted, which is a different matter."

"What d'y'mean?" said the fisherman, who did not like to have his assertions taken up and shaken into shape.

"We have given a clever and domineering people a chance to plant themselves down as masters in our land; I don't imagine that they are going to give us an easy chance to push them out. To do that we shall have to be a little cleverer than they are, a little harder, a little fiercer, and a good deal more self-sacrificing than we have been in my lifetime or in yours."

"We'll be that, right enough," said the fisherman; "we mean business this time. The last war wasn't a war, it was a snap. We weren't prepared and they were. That won't happen again, bless you. I know what I'm talking about. I go up and down the country, and I hear what people are saying."

Yeovil privately doubted if he ever heard anything but his own opinions.

"It stands to reason," continued the fisherman, "that a highly civilized race like ours, with the record that we've had for leading the whole world, is not going to be held under for long by a lot of damned sausage-eating Germans. Don't you believe it! I know what I'm talking about. I've travelled about the world a bit."

Yeovil shrewdly suspected that the world travels amounted to nothing more than a trip to the United States and perhaps the Channel Islands, with, possibly, a week or fortnight in Paris.

"It isn't the past we've got to think of, it's the future," said Yeovil. "Other maritime Powers had pasts to look back on; Spain and Holland, for instance. The past didn't help them when they let their sea-sovereignty slip from them. That is a matter of history and not very distant history either."

"Ah, that's where you make a mistake," said the other; "our sea-sovereignty hasn't slipped from us, and won't do, neither. There's the British Empire beyond the seas; Canada, Australia, New Zealand, East Africa."

He rolled the names round his tongue with obvious relish.

"If it was a list of first-class battleships, and armoured cruisers and destroyers and airships that you were reeling off, there would be some comfort and hope in the situation," said Yeovil; "the loyalty of the colonies is a splendid thing, but it is only pathetically splendid because it can do so little to recover for us what we've lost. Against the Zeppelin air fleet, and the Dreadnought sea squadrons and the new Gelberhaus cruisers, the last word in maritime mobility, of what avail is loyal devotion plus half-a-dozen warships, one keel to ten, scattered over one or two ocean coasts?"

"Ah, but they'll build," said the fisherman confidently; "they'll build. They're only waiting to enlarge their dockyard accommodation and get the right class of artificers and engineers and workmen together. The money will be forthcoming somehow, and they'll start in and build."

"And do you suppose," asked Yeovil in slow bitter contempt, "that the victorious nation is going to sit and watch and wait till the defeated foe has created a new war fleet, big enough to drive it from the seas? Do you suppose it is going to watch keel added to keel, gun to gun, airship to airship, till its preponderance has been wiped out or even threatened? That sort of thing is done once in a generation, not twice. Who is going to protect Australia or New Zealand while they enlarge their dockyards and hangars and build their dreadnoughts and their airships?"

"Here's my station and I'm not sorry," said the fisherman, gathering his tackle together and rising to depart; "I've listened to you long enough. You and me wouldn't agree, not if we was to talk all day. Fact is, I'm an out-and-out patriot and you're only a half-hearted one. That's what you are, half-hearted."

And with that parting shot he left the carriage and lounged heavily down the platform, a patriot who had never handled a rifle or mounted a horse or pulled an oar, but who had never flinched from demolishing his country's enemies with his tongue.

"England has never had any lack of patriots of that type," thought Yeovil sadly; "So many patriots and so little patriotism."

Chapter XIII

TORYWOOD

Yeovil got out of the train at a small, clean wayside station, and rapidly formed the conclusion that neatness, abundant leisure, and a devotion to the cultivation of wallflowers and wyandottes were the prevailing influences of the station-master's life. The train slid away into the hazy distance of trees and meadows, and left the traveller standing in a world that seemed to be made up in equal parts of rock-garden, chicken coops, and whisky advertisements. The station-master, who appeared also to act as emergency porter, took Yeovil's ticket with the gesture of a kind-hearted person brushing away a troublesome wasp, and returned to a study of the *Poultry*

Chronicle, which was giving its readers sage counsel concerning the ailments of belated July chickens. Yeovil called to mind the station-master of a tiny railway town in Siberia, who had held him in long and rather intelligent converse on the poetical merits and demerits of Shelley, and he wondered what the result would be if he were to engage the English official in a discussion on Lermontoff —or for the matter of that, on Shelley. The temptation to experiment was, however, removed by the arrival of a young groom, with brown eyes and a friendly smile, who hurried into the station and took Yeovil once more into a world where he was of fleeting importance.

In the roadway outside was a four-wheeled dog-cart with a pair of the famous Torywood blue roans. It was an agreeable variation in modern locomotion to be met at a station with high-class horse-flesh instead of the ubiquitous motor, and the landscape was not of such a nature that one wished to be whirled through it in a cloud of dust. After a quick spin of some ten or fifteen minutes through twisting hedge-girt country roads, the roans turned in at a wide gateway, and went with dancing, rhythmic step along the park drive. The screen of oak-crowned upland suddenly fell away and a grey sharp-cornered building came into view in a setting of low growing beeches and dark pines. Torywood was not a stately, reposeful-looking house; it lay amid the sleepy landscape like a couched watch-dog with pricked ears and wakeful eyes. Built somewhere about the last years of Dutch William's reign, it had been a centre, ever since, for the political life of the countryside; a storm centre of discontent or a rallying ground for the well affected, as the circumstances of the day might entail. On the stone-flagged terrace in front of the house, with its quaint leaden figures of Diana pursuing a hound-pressed stag, successive squires and lords of Torywood had walked to and fro with their friends, watching the thunder-clouds on the political horizon or the shifting shadows on the sundial of political favour, tapping the political barometer for indications of change, working out a party campaign or arranging for the support of some national movement. To and fro they had gone in their respective generations, men with the passion for statecraft and political combat strong in their veins, and many oft-recurring names had echoed under those wakeful-looking casements, names spoken in anger or exultation, or murmured in fear and anxiety: Bolingbroke, Charles Edward, Walpole, the Farmer King, Bonaparte, Pitt, Wellington, Peel, Gladstone—echo and Time might have graven those names on the stone flags and grey walls. And now one tired old woman walked there, with names on her lips that she never uttered.

A friendly riot of fox terriers and spaniels greeted the carriage, leaping and rolling and yelping in an exuberance of sociability, as though horses and coachman and groom were comrades who had been absent for long months instead of half an hour. An indiscriminately affectionate puppy lay flat and whimpering at Yeovil's feet, sending up little showers of gravel with its wildly thumping tail, while two of the terriers raced each other madly across lawn and shrubbery, as though to show the blue roans what speed really was. The laughing-eyed young groom disentangled the puppy from between Yeovil's legs, and then he was ushered into the grey silence of the entrance hall, leaving sunlight and noise and the stir of life behind him.

"Her ladyship will see you in her writing-room," he was told, and he followed a servant along the dark passages to the well-remembered room.

There was something tragic in the sudden contrast between the vigour and youth and pride of life that Yeovil had seen crystallized in those dancing, high-stepping horses, scampering dogs, and alert, clean-limbed young men-servants, and the age-frail woman who came forward to meet him.

Eleanor, Dowager Lady Greymarten, had for more than half a century been the ruling spirit at Torywood. The affairs of the county had not sufficed for her untiring activities of mind and body; in the wider field of national and Imperial service she had worked and schemed and fought with an energy and a far-sightedness that came probably from the blend of caution and bold restlessness in her Scottish blood. For many educated minds the arena of politics and public life is a weariness of dust and disgust, to others it is a fascinating study, to be watched from the comfortable seat of a spectator. To her it was a home. In her town house or down at Torywood, with her writing-pad on her knee and the telephone at her elbow, or in personal counsel with some trusted colleague or persuasive argument with a halting adherent or half-convinced opponent, she had laboured on behalf of the poor and the ill-equipped, had fought for her idea of the Right, and above all, for the safety and sanity of her Fatherland. Spadework when necessary and leadership when called for, came alike within the scope of her activities, and not least of her achievements, though perhaps she hardly realized it, was the force of her example, a lone, indomitable fighter calling to the half-caring and the half-discouraged, to the laggard and the slow-moving.

And now she came across the room with "the tired step of a tired king," and that look which the French so expressively called *l'air défait*. The charm which Heaven bestows on old ladies, reserving its highest gift to the end, had always seemed in her case to be lost sight of in the dignity and interest of a great dame who was still in the full prime of her fighting and ruling powers. Now, in Yeovil's eyes, she had suddenly come to be very old, stricken with the forlorn languor of one who knows that death will be weary to wait for. She had spared herself nothing in the long labour, the ceaseless building, the watch and ward, and in one short autumn week she had seen the overthrow of all that she had built, the falling asunder of the world in which she had laboured. Her life's end was like a harvest home when blight and storm have laid waste the fruit of long toil and unsparing outlay. Victory had been her goal, the death or victory of old heroic challenge, for she had always dreamed to die fighting to the last; death or victory—and the gods had given her neither, only the bitterness of a defeat that could not be measured in words, and the weariness of a life that had outlived happiness or hope. Such was Eleanor, Dowager Lady Greymarten, a shadow amid the young red-blooded life at Torywood, but a shadow that was too real to die, a shadow that was stronger than the substance that surrounded it.

Yeovil talked long and hurriedly of his late travels, of the vast Siberian forests and rivers, the desolate tundras, the lakes and marshes where the wild swans rear their broods, the flower carpet of the summer fields and the winter ice-mantle of Russia's northern sea. He talked as a man talks who avoids the subject that is uppermost in his mind, and in the mind of his hearer, as one who looks away from a wound or deformity that is too cruel to be taken notice of.

Tea was served in a long oak-panelled gallery, where generations of Mustelfords had romped and played as children, and remained yet in effigy, in a collection of more or less faithful portraits. After tea Yeovil was taken by his hostess to the aviaries, which constituted the sole claim which Torywood possessed to being considered a show place. The third Earl of Greymarten had collected rare and interesting birds, somewhere about the time when Gilbert White was penning the last of his deathless letters, and his successors in the title had perpetuated the hobby. Little lawns and ponds and shrubberies were partitioned off for the various ground-loving species, and higher cages with interlacing perches and rockwork shelves accommodated the birds whose natural expression of movement was on the wing. Quails and francolins scurried about under low-growing shrubs, peacock-pheasants strutted and sunned themselves, pugnacious ruffs engaged in perfunctory battles, from force of habit now that the rivalry of the mating season was over; choughs, ravens, and loud-throated gulls occupied sections of a vast rockery, and bright-hued Chinese pond-herons and delicately stepping egrets waded among the water-lilies of a marble-terraced tank. One or two dusky shapes seen dimly in the recesses of a large cage built round a hollow tree would be lively owls when evening came on.

In the course of his many wanderings Yeovil had himself contributed three or four inhabitants to this little feathered town, and he went round the enclosures, renewing old acquaintances and examining new additions.

"The falcon cage is empty," said Lady Greymarten, pointing to a large wired dome that towered high above the other enclosures; "I let the lanner fly free one day. The other birds may be reconciled to their comfortable quarters and abundant food and absence of dangers, but I don't think all those things could make up to a falcon for the wild range of cliff and desert. When one has lost one's own liberty one feels a quicker sympathy for other caged things, I suppose."

There was silence for a moment, and then the Dowager went on, in a wistful, passionate voice:

"I am an old woman now, Murrey, I must die in my cage. I haven't the strength to fight. Age is a very real and very cruel thing, though we may shut our eyes to it and pretend it is not there. I thought at one time that I should never really know what it meant, what it brought to one. I thought of it as a messenger that one could keep waiting out in the yard till the very last moment.

I know now what it means. . . . But you, Murrey, you are young, you can fight. Are you going to be a fighter, or the very humble servant of the *fait accompli*?"

"I shall never be the servant of the *fait accompli*," said Yeovil. "I loathe it. As to fighting, one must first find out what weapon to use, and how to use it effectively. One must watch and wait."

"One must not wait too long," said the old woman. "Time is on their side, not ours. It is the young people we must fight for now, if they are ever to fight for us. A new generation will spring up, a weaker memory of old glories will survive, the *éclat* of the ruling race will capture young imaginations. If I had your youth, Murrey, and your sex, I would become a commercial traveller."

"A commercial traveller!" exclaimed Yeovil.

"Yes, one whose business took him up and down the country, into contact with all classes, into homes and shops and inns and railway carriages. And as I travelled I would work, work on the minds of every boy and girl I came across, every young father and young mother too, every young couple that were going to be man and wife. I would awaken or keep alive in their memory the things that we have been, the grand, brave things that some of our race have done, and I would stir up a longing, a determination for the future that we must win back. I would be a counter-agent to the agents of the *fait accompli*. In course of time the Government would find out what I was doing, and I should be sent out of the country, but I should have accomplished something, and others would carry on the work. That is what I would do. Murrey, even if it is to a losing battle, fight it, fight it!"

Yeovil knew that the old lady was fighting her last battle, rallying the discouraged, and spurring on the backward.

A footman came to announce that the carriage waited to take him back to the station. His hostess walked with him through the hall, and came out on to the stone-flagged terrace, the terrace from which a former Lady Greymarten had watched the twinkling bonfires that told of Waterloo.

Yeovil said good-bye to her as she stood there, a wan, shrunken shadow, yet with a greater strength and reality in her flickering life than those parrot men and women that fluttered and chattered through London drawing-rooms and theatre foyers.

As the carriage swung round a bend in the drive Yeovil looked back at Torywood, a lone, grey building, couched like a watch-dog with pricked ears and wakeful eyes in the midst of the sleeping landscape. An old pleading voice was still ringing in his ears:

Imperious and yet forlorn,
Came through the silence of the trees,
The echoes of a golden horn,
Calling to distances.

Somehow Yeovil knew that he would never hear that voice again, and he knew, too, that he would hear it always, with its message, "Be a fighter." And he knew now, with a shame-faced consciousness that sprang suddenly into existence, that the summons would sound for him in vain.

The weary brain-torturing months of fever had left their trail behind, a lassitude of spirit and a sluggishness of blood, a quenching of the desire to roam and court adventure and hardship. In the hours of waking and depression between the raging intervals of delirium he had speculated, with a sort of detached, listless indifference, on the chances of his getting back to life and strength and energy. The prospect of filling a corner of some lonely Siberian graveyard or Finnish cemetery had seemed near realization at times, and for a man who was already half dead the other half didn't particularly matter. But when he had allowed himself to dwell on the more hopeful side of the case it had always been a complete recovery that awaited him; the same Yeovil as of yore, a little thinner and more lined about the eyes perhaps, would go through life in the same way, alert, resolute, enterprising, ready to start off at short notice for some desert or upland where the eagles were circling and the wild-fowl were calling. He had not reckoned that Death, evaded and held off by the doctors' skill, might exact a compromise, and that only part of the man would go free to the West.

And now he began to realize how little of mental and physical energy he could count on. His own country had never seemed in his eyes so comfort-yielding and to-be-desired as it did now when it had passed into alien keeping and become a prisonland as much as a homeland. London with its thin mockery of a Season, and its chattering horde of empty-hearted self-seekers, held no attraction for him, but the spell of English country life was weaving itself round him, now that the charm of the desert was receding into a mist of memories. The waning of pleasant autumn days in an

English woodland, the whir of game birds in the clean harvested fields, the grey moist mornings in the saddle, with the magical cry of hounds coming up from some misty hollow, and then the delicious abandon of physical weariness in bathroom and bedroom after a long run, and the heavenly snatched hour of luxurious sleep, before stirring back to life and hunger, the coming of the dinner hour and the jollity of a well-chosen house-party.

That was the call which was competing with that other trumpet-call, and Yeovil knew on which side his choice would incline.

Chapter XIV

"A PERFECTLY GLORIOUS AFTERNOON"

It was one of the last days of July, cooled and freshened by a touch of rain and dropping back again to a languorous warmth. London looked at its summer best, rain-washed and sun-lit, with the maximum of coming and going in its more fashionable streets.

Cicely Yeovil sat in a screened alcove of the Anchorage Restaurant, a feeding-ground which had lately sprung into favour. Opposite her sat Ronnie, confronting the ruins of what had been a dish of prawns in aspic. Cool and clean and fresh-coloured, he was good to look on in the eyes of his companion, and yet, perhaps, there was a ruffle in her soul that called for some answering disturbance on the part of that superbly tranquil young man, and certainly called in vain. Cicely had set up for herself a fetish of onyx with eyes of jade, and doubtless hungered at times with an unreasonable but perfectly natural hunger for something of flesh and blood. It was the religion of her life to know exactly what she wanted and to see that she got it, but there was no possible guarantee against her occasionally experiencing a desire for something else. It is the golden rule of all religions that no one should really live up to their precepts; when a man observes the principles of his religion too exactly he is in immediate danger of founding a new sect.

"Today is going to be your day of triumph," said Cicely to the young man, who was wondering at the moment whether he would care to embark on an artichoke; "I believe I'm more nervous than you are," she added, "and yet I rather hate the idea of you scoring a great success."

"Why?" asked Ronnie, diverting his mind for a moment from the artichoke question and its ramifications of *sauce hollandaise* or *vinaigre.*

"I like you as you are," said Cicely, "just a nice-looking boy to flatter and spoil and pretend to be fond of. You've got a charming young body and you've no soul, and that's such a fascinating combination. If you had a soul you would either dislike or worship me, and I'd much rather have things as they are. And now you are going to go a step beyond that, and other people will applaud you and say that you are wonderful, and invite you to eat with them and motor with them and yacht with them. As soon as that begins to happen, Ronnie, a lot of other things will come to an end. Of course I've always known that you don't really care for me, but as soon as the world knows it you are irrevocably damaged as a plaything. That is the great secret that binds us together, the knowledge that we have no real affection for one another. And this afternoon every one will know that you are a great artist, and no great artist was ever a great lover."

"I shan't be difficult to replace, anyway," said Ronnie, with what he imagined was a becoming modesty; "there are lots of boys standing round ready to be fed and flattered and put on an imaginary pedestal, most of them more or less good-looking and well turned out and amusing to talk to."

"Oh, I dare say I could find a successor for your vacated niche," said Cicely lightly; "one thing I'm determined on though, he shan't be a musician. It's so unsatisfactory to have to share a grand passion with a grand piano. He shall be a delightful young barbarian who would think Saint-Saëns was a Derby winner or a claret."

"Don't be in too much of a hurry to replace me," said Ronnie, who did not care to have his successor too seriously discussed. "I may not score the success you expect this afternoon."

"My dear boy, a minor crowned head from across the sea is coming to hear you play, and that alone will count as a success with most of your listeners. Also, I've secured a real Duchess for you, which is rather an achievement in the London of today."

"An English Duchess?" asked Ronnie, who had early in life learned to apply the Merchandise Marks Act to ducal titles.

"English, oh certainly at least as far as the title goes; she was born under the constellation of the Star-spangled Banner. I don't suppose the Duke approves of her being here, lending her countenance to the *fait accompli,* but when you've got republican blood in your veins a Kaiser is quite as attractive a lodestar as a King, rather more so. And Canon Mousepace is coming," continued Cicely, referring to a closely-written list of guests; "the excellent von Tolb has been attending his church lately, and the Canon is longing to meet her. She is just the sort of person he adores. I fancy he sincerely realizes how difficult it will be for the rich to enter the Kingdom of Heaven, and he tries to make up for it by being as nice as possible to them in this world."

Ronnie held out his hand for the list.

"I think you know most of the others," said Cicely, passing it to him.

"Leutnant von Gabelroth?" read out Ronnie; "who is he?"

"In one of the hussar regiments quartered here; a friend of the Gräfin's. Ugly but amiable, and I'm told a good cross-country rider. I suppose Murrey will be disgusted at meeting the 'outward and visible sign' under his roof, but these encounters are inevitable as long as he is in London."

"I didn't know Murrey was coming," said Ronnie.

"I believe he's going to look in on us," said Cicely; "it's just as well, you know, otherwise we should have Joan asking in her loudest voice when he was going to be back in England again. I haven't asked her, but she overheard the Gräfin arranging to come and hear you play, and I fancy that will be quite enough."

"How about some Turkish coffee?" said Ronnie, who had decided against the artichoke.

"Turkish coffee, certainly, and a cigarette, and a moment's peace before the serious business of the afternoon claims us. Talking about peace, do you know, Ronnie, it has just occurred to me that we have left out one of the most important things in our *affaire;* we have never had a quarrel."

"I hate quarrels," said Ronnie, "they are so domesticated."

"That's the first time I've ever heard you talk about your home," said Cicely.

"I fancy it would apply to most homes," said Ronnie.

"The last boy-friend I had used to quarrel furiously with me at least once a week," said Cicely reflectively; "but then he had dark slumberous eyes that lit up magnificently when he was angry, so it would have been a sheer waste of God's good gifts not to have sent him into a passion now and then."

"With your excursions into the past and the future you are making me feel dreadfully like an instalment of a serial novel," protested Ronnie; "we have now got to 'synopsis of earlier chapters.'"

"It shan't be teased," said Cicely; "we will live in the present and go no further into the future than to make arrangements for Tuesday's dinner-party. I've asked the Duchess; she would never have forgiven me if she'd found out that I had a crowned head dining with me and hadn't asked her to meet him."

A sudden hush descended on the company gathered in the great drawing-room at Berkshire Street as Ronnie took his seat at the piano; the voice of Canon Mousepace outlasted the others for a moment or so, and then subsided into a regretful but gracious silence. For the next nine or ten minutes Ronnie held possession of the crowded room, a tense slender figure, with cold green eyes aflame in a sudden fire, and smooth burnished head bent low over the keyboard that yielded a disciplined riot of melody under his strong deft fingers. The world-weary Landgraf forgot for the moment the regrettable trend of his subjects towards Parliamentary Socialism, the excellent Gräfin von Tolb forgot all that the Canon had been saying to her for the last ten minutes, forgot the depressing certainty that he would have a great deal more than he wanted to say in the immediate future, over and above the thirty-five minutes or so of discourse that she would contract to listen to next Sunday. And Cicely listened with the wistful equivocal triumph of one whose goose has turned out to be a swan and who realizes with secret concern that she has only planned the rôle of goosegirl for herself.

The last chords died away, the fire faded out of the jade-coloured eyes, and Ronnie became once more a well-groomed youth in a drawing-room full of well-dressed people. But around him rose an explosive clamour of applause and congratulation, the sincere tribute of appreciation and the equally hearty expression of imitative homage.

"It is a great gift, a great gift," chanted Canon Mousepace. "You must put it to a great use. A talent is vouchsafed to us for a purpose;

you must fulfil the purpose. Talent such as yours is a responsibility; you must meet that responsibility."

The dictionary of the English language was an inexhaustible quarry, from which the Canon had hewn and fashioned for himself a great reputation.

"You must gom and blay to me at Schlachsenberg," said the kindly-faced Landgraf, whom the world adored and thwarted in about equal proportions. "At Christmas, yes, that will be a good time. We still keep the Christ-Fest at Schlachsenberg, though the 'Sozi' keep telling our schoolchildren that it is only a Christ myth. Never mind, I will have the Vice-President of our Landtag to listen to you; he is 'Sozi' but we are good friends outside the Parliament House; you shall blay to him, my young friendt, and gonfince him that there is a Got in Heaven. You will gom? Yes?"

"It was beautiful," said the Gräfin simply; "it made me cry. Go back to the piano again, please, at once."

Perhaps the near neighbourhood of the Canon inspired this command, but the Gräfin had been genuinely charmed. She adored good music and she was unaffectedly fond of good-looking boys.

Ronnie went back to the piano and tasted the matured pleasure of a repeated success. Any measure of nervousness that he may have felt at first had completely passed away. He was sure of his audience and he played as though they did not exist. A renewed clamour of excited approval attended the conclusion of his performance.

"It is a triumph, a perfectly *glorious* triumph," exclaimed the Duchess of Dreyshire, turning to Yeovil, who sat silent among his wife's guests; "isn't it just *glorious?*" she demanded, with a heavy insistent intonation of the word.

"Is it?" said Yeovil.

"Well, isn't it?" she cried, with a rising inflection, "isn't it just *perfectly* glorious?"

"I don't know," confessed Yeovil; "you see, glory hasn't come very much my way lately." Then, before he exactly realized what he was doing, he raised his voice and quoted loudly for the benefit of half the room:

"'Other Romans shall arise,
Heedless of a soldier's name,
Sounds, not deeds, shall win the prize,
Harmony the path to fame.'"

There was a sort of shiver of surprised silence at Yeovil's end of the room.

"Hell!"

The word rang out in a strong voice.

"Hell! And it's true, that's the worst of it. It's damned true!"

Yeovil turned, with some dozen others, to see who was responsible for this vigorously expressed statement.

Tony Luton confronted him, an angry scowl on his face, a blaze in his heavy-lidded eyes. The boy was without a conscience, almost without a soul, as priests and parsons reckon souls, but there was a slumbering devil-god within him, and Yeovil's taunting words had broken the slumber. Life had been for Tony a hard school, in which right and wrong, high endeavour and good resolve, were untaught subjects; but there was a sterling something in him, just that something that helped poor street-scavenged men to die brave-fronted deaths in the trenches of Salamanca, that fired a handful of apprentice boys to shut the gates of Derry and stare unflinchingly at grim leaguer and starvation. It was just that nameless something that was lacking in the young musician, who stood at the farther end of the room, bathed in a flood of compliment and congratulation, enjoying the honey-drops of his triumph.

Luton pushed his way through the crowd and left the room, without troubling to take leave of his hostess.

"What a strange young man," exclaimed the Duchess; "now do take me into the next room," she went on almost in the same breath, "I'm just dying for some iced coffee."

Yeovil escorted her through the throng of Ronnie-worshippers to the desired haven of refreshment.

"Marvellous!" Mrs. Menteith-Mendlesohnn was exclaiming in ringing trumpet tones; "of course I always knew he could play, but this is not mere piano playing, it is tone-mastery, it is sound magic. Mrs. Yeovil has introduced us to a new star in the musical firmament. Do you know, I feel this afternoon just like Cortez, in the poem, gazing at the newly discovered sea."

"'Silent upon a peak in Darien,'" quoted a penetrating voice that could only belong to Joan Mardle; "I say, can any one picture Mrs. Menteith-Mendlesohnn silent on any peak or under any circumstances?"

If any one had that measure of imagination, no one acknowledged the fact.

"A great gift and a great responsibility," Canon Mousepace was assuring the Gräfin; "the power of evoking sublime melody is akin to the power of awakening thought; a musician can appeal to dormant consciousness as the preacher can appeal to dormant conscience. It is a responsibility, an instrument for good or evil. Our young friend here, we may be sure, will use it as an instrument for good. He has, I feel certain, a sense of his responsibility."

"He is a nice boy," said the Gräfin simply; "he has such pretty hair."

In one of the window recesses Rhapsodie Pantril was talking vaguely but beautifully to a small audience on the subject of chromatic chords; she had the advantage of knowing what she was talking about, an advantage that her listeners did not in the least share. "All through his playing there ran a tone-note of malachite green," she declared recklessly, feeling safe from immediate contradiction; "malachite green, *my* colour–the colour of striving."

Having satisfied the ruling passion that demanded gentle and dexterous self-advertisement, she realized that the Augusta Smith in her craved refreshment, and moved with one of her over-awed admirers towards the haven where peaches and iced coffee might be considered a certainty.

The refreshment alcove, which was really a good-sized room, a sort of chapel-of-ease to the larger drawing-room, was already packed with a crowd who felt that they could best discuss Ronnie's triumph between mouthfuls of fruit salad and iced draughts of hock-cup. So brief is human glory that two or three independent souls had even now drifted from the theme of the moment on to other more personally interesting topics.

"Iced mulberry salad, my dear, it's a *spécialité de la maison,* so to speak; they say the roving husband brought the recipe from Astrakhan, or Seville, or some such outlandish place."

"I wish my husband would roam about a bit and bring back strange palatable dishes. No such luck, he's got asthma and has to keep on a gravel soil with a south aspect and all sorts of other restrictions."

"I don't think you're to be pitied in the least; a husband with asthma is like a captive golf-ball, you can always put your hand on him when you want him."

"All the hangings, *violette de Parme,* all the furniture, rosewood.

Nothing is to be played in it except Mozart. Mozart only. Some of my friends wanted me to have a replica of the Mozart statue at Vienna put up in a corner of the room, with flowers always around it, but I really couldn't. I *couldn't.* One is *so* tired of it, one sees it everywhere. I couldn't do it. I'm like that, you know."

"Yes, I've secured the hero of the hour, Ronnie Storre, oh, yes, rather. He's going to join our yachting trip, third week of August. We're going as far afield as Fiume, in the Adriatic—or is it the Ægean? Won't it be jolly? Oh, no, we're not asking Mrs. Yeovil; it's quite a small yacht, you know—at least, it's a small party."

The excellent von Tolb took her departure, bearing off with her the Landgraf, who had already settled the date and duration of Ronnie's Christmas visit.

"It will be dull, you know," he warned the prospective guest; "our Landtag will not be sitting, and what is a bear-garden without the bears? However, we haf some wildt schwein in our woods, we can show you some sport in that way."

Ronnie instantly saw himself in a well-fitting shooting costume, with a Tyrolese hat placed at a very careful angle on his head, but he confessed that the other details of boar-hunting were rather beyond him.

With the departure of the von Tolb party Canon Mousepace gravitated decently but persistently towards a corner where the Duchess, still at concert pitch, was alternatively praising Ronnie's performance and the mulberry salad. Joan Mardle, who formed one of the group, was not openly praising any one, but she was paying a silent tribute to the salad.

"We were just talking about Ronnie Storre's music, Canon," said the Duchess; "I consider it just perfectly glorious."

"It's a great talent, isn't it, Canon," put in Joan briskly, "and of course it's a responsibility as well, don't you think? Music can be such an influence, just as eloquence can; don't you agree with me?"

The quarry of the English language was of course a public property, but it was disconcerting to have one's own particular barrow-load of sentence-building material carried off before one's eyes. The Canon's impressive homily on Ronnie's gift and its possibilities had to be hastily whittled down to a weakly acquiescent, "Quite so, quite so."

"Have you tasted this iced mulberry salad, Canon?" asked the

Duchess; "it's perfectly luscious. Just hurry along and get some before it's all gone."

And her Grace hurried along in an opposite direction, to thank Cicely for past favours and to express lively gratitude for the Tuesday to come.

The guests departed, with a rather irritating slowness, for which perhaps the excellence of Cicely's buffet arrangements was partly responsible. The great drawing-room seemed to grow larger and more oppressive as the human wave receded, and the hostess fled at last with some relief to the narrower limits of her writing-room and the sedative influences of a cigarette. She was inclined to be sorry for herself; the triumph of the afternoon had turned out much as she had predicted at lunch-time. Her idol of onyx had not been swept from its pedestal, but the pedestal itself had an air of being packed up ready for transport to some other temple. Ronnie would be flattered and spoiled by half a hundred people, just because he could conjure sounds out of a keyboard, and Cicely felt no great incentive to go on flattering and spoiling him herself. And Ronnie would acquiesce in his dismissal with the good grace born of indifference—the surest guarantor of perfect manners. Already he had social engagements for the coming months in which she had no share; the drifting apart would be mutual. He had been an intelligent and amusing companion, and he had played the game as she had wished it to be played, without the fatigue of keeping up pretences which neither of them could have believed in. "Let us have a wonderfully good time together" had been the single stipulation in their unwritten treaty of comradeship, and they had had the good time. Their whole-hearted pursuit of material happiness would go on as keenly as before, but they would hunt in different company, that was all. Yes, that was all. . . .

Cicely found the effect of her cigarette less sedative than she was disposed to exact. It might be necessary to change the brand.

Some ten or eleven days later Yeovil read an announcement in the papers that, in spite of handsome offers of increased salary, Mr. Tony Luton, the original singer of the popular ditty *Eccleston Square,* had terminated his engagement with Messrs. Isaac Grosvenor and Leon Hebhardt of the Caravansery Theatre, and signed on as a deck hand in the Canadian Marine.

Perhaps, after all, there had been some shred of glory amid the trumpet triumph of that July afternoon.

Chapter XV
THE INTELLIGENT ANTICIPATOR OF WANTS

Two of Yeovil's London clubs, the two that he had been accustomed to frequent, had closed their doors after the catastrophe. One of them had perished from off the face of the earth, its fittings had been sold and its papers lay stored in some solicitor's office, a tidbit of material for the pen of some future historian. The other had transplanted itself to Delhi, whither it had removed its early Georgian furniture and its traditions, and sought to reproduce its St. James's Street atmosphere as nearly as the conditions of a tropical Asiatic city would permit. There remained the Cartwheel, a considerably newer institution, which had sprung into existence somewhere about the time of Yeovil's last sojourn in England; he had joined it on the solicitation of a friend who was interested in the venture, and his bankers had paid his subscription during his absence. As he had never been inside its door there could be no depressing comparisons to make between its present state and aforetime glories, and Yeovil turned into its portals one afternoon with the adventurous detachment of a man who breaks new ground and challenges new experiences.

He entered with a diffident sense of intrusion, conscious that his standing as a member might not be recognized by the keepers of the doors; in a moment, however, he realized that a rajah's escort of elephants might almost have marched through the entrance hall and vestibule without challenge. The general atmosphere of the scene suggested a blend of the railway station at Cologne, the Hotel Bristol in any European capital, and the second act in most musical comedies. A score of brilliant and brilliantined pages decorated the foreground, while Hebraic-looking gentlemen, wearing tartan waistcoats of the clans of their adoption, flitted restlessly between the tape machines and telephone boxes. The army of occupation had obviously established a firm footing in the hospitable premises; a kaleidoscopic pattern of uniforms, sky-blue, indigo and bottle-green, relieved the civilian attire of the groups that clustered in lounge and card-rooms and corridors. Yeovil rapidly came to the conclusion that the joys of membership were not for him. He had turned to go, after a very cursory inspection of the premises and their human occupants, when he was hailed by a young man, dressed with strenuous neatness, whom he remembered having met in past days at the houses of one or two common friends.

Hubert Herlton's parents had brought him into the world, and some twenty-one years later had put him into a motor business. Having taken these pardonable liberties they had completely exhausted their ideas of what to do with him, and Hubert seemed unlikely to develop any ideas of his own on the subject. The motor business elected to conduct itself without his connivance; journalism, the stage, tomato culture (without capital), and other professions that could be entered on at short notice were submitted to his consideration by nimble-minded relations and friends. He listened to their suggestions with polite indifference, being rude only to a cousin who demonstrated how he might achieve a settled income of from two hundred to a thousand pounds a year by the propagation of mushrooms in a London basement. While his walk in life was still an undetermined promenade his parents died, leaving him with a carefully-invested income of thirty-seven pounds a year. At that point of his career Yeovil's knowledge of him stopped short; the journey to Siberia had taken him beyond the range of Herlton's domestic vicissitudes.

The young man greeted him in a decidedly friendly manner.

"I didn't know you were a member here," he exclaimed.

"It's the first time I've ever been in the club," said Yeovil, "and I fancy it will be the last. There is rather too much of the fighting-machine in evidence here. One doesn't want a perpetual reminder of what has happened staring one in the face."

"We tried at first to keep the alien element out," said Herlton apologetically, "but we couldn't have carried on the club if we'd stuck to that line. You see we'd lost more than two-thirds of our old members so we couldn't afford to be exclusive. As a matter of fact the whole thing was decided over our heads; a new syndicate took over the concern, and a new committee was installed, with a good many foreigners on it. I know it's horrid having these uniforms flaunting all over the place, but what is one to do?"

Yeovil said nothing, with the air of a man who could have said a great deal.

"I suppose you wonder, why remain a member under those conditions?" continued Herlton. "Well, as far as I am concerned, a place like this is a necessity for me. In fact, it's my profession, my source of income."

"Are you as good at bridge as all that?" asked Yeovil; "I'm a fairly successful player myself, but I should be sorry to have to live on my winnings, year in, year out."

"I don't play cards," said Herlton, "at least not for serious stakes. My winnings or losings wouldn't come to a tenner in an average year. No, I live by commissions, by introducing likely buyers to would-be sellers."

"Sellers of what?" asked Yeovil.

"Anything, everything; horses, yachts, old masters, plate, shootings, poultry-farms, week-end cottages, motor-cars, almost anything you can think of. Look," and he produced from his breast pocket a bulky notebook illusorily inscribed "Engagements."

"Here," he explained, tapping the book, "I've got a double entry of every likely client that I know, with a note of the things he may have to sell and the things he may want to buy. When it is something that he has for sale there are cross-references to likely purchasers of that particular line of article. I don't limit myself to things that I actually know people to be in want of, I go further than that and have theories, carefully indexed theories, as to the things that people might want to buy. At the right moment, if I can get the opportunity, I mention the article that is in my mind's eye, and I frequently bring off a sale. I started a chance acquaintance on a career of print-buying the other day merely by telling him of a couple of good prints that I knew of, that were to be had at a quite reasonable price; he is a man with more money than he knows what to do with, and he has laid out quite a lot on old prints since his first purchase. Most of his collection he has got through me, and of course I net a commission on each transaction. So you see, old man, how useful, not to say necessary, a club with a large membership is to me. The more mixed and socially chaotic it is, the more serviceable it is."

"Of course," said Yeovil, "and I suppose, as a matter of fact, a good many of your clients belong to the conquering race."

"Well, you see, they are the people who have got the money," said Herlton; "I don't mean to say that the invading Germans are usually people of wealth, but while they live over here they escape the crushing taxation that falls on the British-born subject. They serve their country as soldiers, and we have to serve it in garrison money, ship money and so forth, besides the ordinary taxes of the State. The German shoulders the rifle, the Englishman has to shoulder everything else. That is what will help more than anything towards the gradual Germanizing of our big towns; the comparatively lightly-taxed German workman over here will have a much bigger spending power and purchasing power than his heavily taxed English neighbour. The public-houses, bars, eating-houses, places of amusement and so forth, will come to cater more and more for money-yielding German patronage. The stream of British emigration will swell rather than diminish, and the stream of Teuton immigration will be equally persistent and progressive. Yes, the military-service ordinance was a cunning stroke on the part of that old fox, von Kwarl. As a civilian statesman he is far and away cleverer than Bismarck was; he smothers with a feather-bed where Bismarck would have tried to smash with a sledge-hammer."

"Have you got me down on your list of noteworthy people?" asked Yeovil, turning the drift of the conversation back to the personal topic.

"Certainly I have," said Herlton, turning the pages of his pocket directory to the letter Y. "As soon as I knew you were back in England I made several entries concerning you. In the first place it was possible that you might have a volume on Siberian travel and natural history notes to publish, and I've cross-referenced you to a publisher I know who rather wants books of that sort on his list."

"I may tell you at once that I've no intentions in that direction," said Yeovil, in some amusement.

"Just as well," said Herlton cheerfully, scribbling a hieroglyphic in his book; "that branch of business is rather outside my line—too little in it, and the gratitude of author and publisher for being introduced to one another is usually short-lived. A more serious entry was the item that if you were wintering in England you would be looking out for a hunter or two. You used to hunt with the East Wessex, I remember; I've got just the very animal that will suit that country, ready waiting for you. A beautiful clean jumper. I've put it over a fence or two myself, and you and I ride much the same weight. A stiffish price is being asked for it, but I've got the letters D.O. after your name."

"In Heaven's name," said Yeovil, now openly grinning, "before I die of curiosity tell me what D.O. stands for."

"It means some one who doesn't object to pay a good price for anything that really suits him. There are some people of course who won't consider a thing unless they can get it for about a third of what they imagine to be its market value. I've got another suggestion down against you in my book; you may not be staying in the country at all, you may be clearing out in disgust at existing conditions. In that case you would be selling a lot of things that you wouldn't want to cart away with you. That involves another set of entries and a whole lot of cross-references."

"I'm afraid I've given you a lot of trouble," said Yeovil dryly.

"Not at all," said Herlton, "but it would simplify matters if we take it for granted that you are going to stay here, for this winter anyhow, and are looking out for hunters. Can you lunch with me here on Wednesday, and come and look at the animal afterwards? It's only thirty-five minutes by train. It will take us longer if we motor. There is a two-fifty-three from Charing Cross that we could catch comfortably."

"If you are going to persuade me to hunt in the East Wessex country this season," said Yeovil, "you must find me a convenient hunting-box somewhere down there."

"I *have* found it," said Herlton, whipping out a stylograph, and hastily scribbling an "order to view" on a card; "central as possible for all the meets, grand stabling accommodation, excellent water-supply, big bathroom, game larder, cellarage, a bakehouse if you want to bake your own bread——"

"Any land with it?"

"Not enough to be a nuisance. An acre or two of paddock and about the same of garden. You are fond of wild things; a wood comes down to the edge of the garden, a wood that habours owls and buzzards and kestrels."

"Have you got all those details in your book?" asked Yeovil; " 'wood adjoining property, O.B.K.' "

"I keep those details in my head," said Herlton, "but they are quite reliable."

"I shall insist on something substantial off the rent if there are no buzzards," said Yeovil; "now that you have mentioned them they seem an indispensable accessory to any decent hunting-box. Look," he exclaimed, catching sight of a plump middle-aged individual crossing the vestibule with an air of restrained importance, "there goes the delectable Pitherby. Does he come on your books at all?"

"I should say!" exclaimed Herlton fervently. "The delectable P. nourishes expectations of a barony or viscounty at an early date. Most of his life has been spent in streets and squares, with occasional migrations to the esplanades of fashionable watering-places or the gravelled walks of country house gardens. Now that *noblesse* is about to impose its obligations on him, quite a new catalogue of wants has sprung into his mind. There are things that a plain esquire may leave undone without causing scandalized remark, but a fiercer light beats on a baron. Trigger-pulling is one of the obligations. Up to the present Pitherby has never hit a partridge in anger, but this year he has commissioned me to rent him a deer forest. Some pedigree Herefords for his 'home farm' was another commission, and a dozen and a half swans for a swannery. The swannery, I may say, was my idea; I said once in his hearing that it gave a baronial air to an estate; you see, I knew a man who had got a lot of surplus swan stock for sale. Now Pitherby wants a heronry as well. I've put him in communication with a client of mine who suffers from superfluous herons, but of course I can't guarantee that the birds' nesting arrangements will fall in with his territorial requirements. I'm getting him some carp, too, of quite respectable age, for a carp pond; I thought it would look so well for his lady-wife to be discovered by interviewers feeding the carp with her own fair hands, and I put the same idea into Pitherby's mind."

"I had no idea that so many things were necessary to endorse a patent of nobility," said Yeovil. "If there should be any miscarriage in the bestowal of the honour at least Pitherby will have absolved himself from any charge of contributory negligence."

"Shall we say Wednesday, here, one o'clock, lunch first, and go down and look at the horse afterwards?" said Herlton, returning to the matter in hand.

Yeovil hesitated, then he nodded his head.

"There is no harm in going to look at the animal," he said.

Chapter XVI

SUNRISE

Mrs. Kerrick sat at a little teakwood table in the veranda of a low-pitched teak-built house that stood on the steep slope of a brown hill-side. Her youngest child, with the grave natural dignity of nine-year-old girlhood, maintained a correct but observant silence, looking carefully yet unobtrusively after the wants of the one guest, and checking from time to time the incursions of ubiquitous ants that were obstinately disposed to treat the table-cloth as a foraging ground. The wayfaring visitor, who was experiencing a British blend of Eastern hospitality, was a French naturalist, travelling thus far afield in quest of feathered specimens to enrich the aviaries of a bird-collecting Balkan King. On the previous evening, while shrugging his shoulders and unloosing his vocabulary over the meagre accommodation afforded by the native rest-house, he had been enchanted by receiving an invitation to transfer his quarters to the house on the hill-side, where he found not only a pleasant-voiced hostess and some drinkable wine, but three brown-skinned English youngsters who were able to give him a mass of intelligent first-hand information about the bird life of the region. And now, at the early morning breakfast, ere yet the sun was showing over the rim of the brown-baked hills, he was learning something of the life of the little community he had chanced on.

"I was in these parts many years ago," explained the hostess, "when my husband was alive and had an appointment out here. It is a healthy hill district and I had pleasant memories of the place, so when it became necessary, well, desirable let us say, to leave our English home and find a new one, it occurred to me to bring my boys and my little girl here—my eldest girl is at school in Paris. Labour is cheap here and I try my hand at farming in a small way. Of course it is very different work to just superintending the dairy and poultry-yard arrangements of an English country estate. There are so many things, insect ravages, bird depredations, and so on, that one only knows on a small scale in England, that happen here in wholesale fashion, not to mention droughts and torrential rains and other tropical visitations. And then the domestic animals are so disconcertingly different from the ones one has been used to; humped cattle never seem to behave in the way that straight-backed cattle would, and goats and geese and chickens are not a bit the same here that they are in Europe—and of course the farm servants are utterly unlike the same class in England. One has to unlearn a good deal of what one thought one knew about stock-keeping and agriculture, and take note of the native ways of doing things; they are primitive and unenterprising of course, but they have an accumulated store of experience behind them, and one has to tread warily in initiating improvements."

The Frenchman looked round at the brown sun-scorched hills, with the dusty empty road showing here and there in the middle distance and other brown sun-scorched hills rounding off the scene; he looked at the lizards on the veranda walls, at the jars for keeping the water cool, at the numberless little insect-bored holes in the furniture, at the heat-drawn lines on his hostess's comely face. Notwithstanding his present wanderings he had a Frenchman's strong homing instinct, and he marvelled to hear this lady, who should have been a lively and popular figure in the social circle of some English county town, talking serenely of the ways of humped cattle and native servants.

"And your children, how do they like the change?" he asked.

"It is healthy up here among the hills," said the mother, also looking round at the landscape and thinking doubtless of a very different scene; "they have an outdoor life and plenty of liberty. They have their ponies to ride, and there is a lake up above us that is a fine place for them to bathe and boat in; the three boys are there now, having their morning swim. The eldest is sixteen and he is allowed to have a gun, and there is some good wild-fowl shooting to be had in the reed beds at the farther end of the lake. I think that part of the joy of his shooting expeditions lies in the fact that many of the duck and plover that he comes across belong to the same species that frequent our English moors and rivers."

It was the first hint that she had given of a wistful sense of exile, the yearning for other skies, the message that a dead bird's plumage could bring across rolling seas and scorching plains.

"And the education of your boys, how do you manage for that?" asked the visitor.

"There is a young tutor living out in these wilds," said Mrs. Kerrick; "he was assistant master at a private school in Scotland, but it had to be given up when—when things changed; so many of the boys left the country. He came out to an uncle who has a small estate eight miles from here, and three days in the week he rides over to teach my boys, and three days he goes to another family living in the opposite direction. Today he is due to come here. It is a great boon to have such an opportunity for getting the boys educated, and of course it helps him to earn a living."

"And the society of the place?" asked the Frenchman.

His hostess laughed.

"I must admit it has to be looked for with a strong pair of field-glasses," she said; "it is almost as difficult to get a good bridge four together as it would have been to get up a tennis tournament or a subscription dance in our particular corner of England. One has to ignore distances and forget fatigue if one wants to be gregarious even on a limited scale. There are one or two officials who are our chief social mainstays, but the difficulty is to muster the few available souls under the same roof at the same moment. A road will be impassable in one quarter, a pony will be lame in another, a stress of work will prevent some one else from coming, and another may be down with a touch of fever. When my little girl gave a birthday party here her only little girl guest had come twelve miles to attend it. The Forest officer happened to drop in on us that evening, so we felt quite festive."

The Frenchman's eyes grew round in wonder. He had once thought that the capital city of a Balkan kingdom was the uttermost limit of social desolation, viewed from a Parisian standpoint, and there at any rate one could get *café chantant,* tennis, picnic parties, an occasional theatre performance by a foreign troupe, now and then a travelling circus, not to speak of Court and diplomatic functions of a more or less sociable character. Here, it seemed, one went a day's journey to reach an evening's entertainment, and the chance arrival of a tired official took on the nature of a festivity. He looked round again at the rolling stretches of brown hills; before he had regarded them merely as the background to this little shut-away world, now he saw that they were foreground as well. They were everything, there was nothing else. And again his glance travelled to the face of his hostess, with its bright, pleasant eyes and smiling mouth.

"And you live here with your children," he said, "here in this wilderness? You leave England, you leave everything, for this?"

His hostess rose and took him over to the far side of the veranda. The beginnings of a garden were spread out before them, with young fruit trees and flowering shrubs, and bushes of pale pink roses. Exuberant tropical growths were interspersed with carefully-tended vestiges of plants that had evidently been brought from a more temperate climate, and had not borne the transition well. Bushes and trees and shrubs spread away for some distance, to where the ground rose in a small hillock and then fell away abruptly into bare hill-side.

"In all this garden that you see," said the Englishwoman, "there is one tree that is sacred."

"A tree?" said the Frenchman.

"A tree that we could not grow in England."

The Frenchman followed the direction of her eyes and saw a tall, bare pole at the summit of the hillock. At the same moment the sun came over the hill-tops in a deep, orange glow, and a new light stole like magic over the brown landscape. And, as if they had timed their arrival to that exact moment of sunburst, three brown-faced boys appeared under the straight, bare pole. A cord shivered and flapped, and something ran swiftly up into the air, and swung out in the breeze that blew across the hills—a blue flag with red and white crosses. The three boys bared their heads and the small girl on the veranda steps stood rigidly to attention. Far away down the hill, a young man, cantering into view round a corner of the dusty road, removed his hat in loyal salutation.

"That is why we live out here," said the Englishwoman quietly.

Chapter XVII

THE EVENT OF THE SEASON

In the first swelter room of the new Osmanli Baths in Cork Street four or five recumbent individuals, in a state of moist nudity and self-respecting inertia, were smoking cigarettes or making occasional pretence of reading damp newspapers. A glass wall with a glass door shut them off from the yet more torrid regions of the further swelter chambers; another glass partition disclosed the dimly-lit vault where other patrons of the establishment had arrived at the stage of being pounded and kneaded and sluiced by Oriental-looking attendants. The splashing and trickling of taps, the flip-flap of wet slippers on a wet floor, and the low murmur of conversation, filtered through glass doors, made an appropriately drowsy accompaniment to the scene.

A new-comer fluttered into the room, beamed at one of the occupants, and settled himself with an air of elaborate languor in a long canvas chair. Cornelian Valpy was a fair young man, with perpetual surprise impinged on his countenance, and a chin that seemed to have retired from competition with the rest of his features. The beam of recognition that he had given to his friend or acquaintance subsided into a subdued but lingering simper.

"What is the matter?" drawled his neighbour lazily, dropping the end of a cigarette into a small bowl of water and helping himself from a silver case on the table at his side.

"Matter?" said Cornelian, opening wide a pair of eyes in which unhealthy intelligence seemed to struggle in undetermined battle with utter vacuity; "why should you suppose that anything is the matter?"

"When you wear a look of idiotic complacency in a Turkish bath," said the other, "it is the more noticeable from the fact that you are wearing nothing else."

"Were you at the Shalem House dance last night?" asked Cornelian, by way of explaining his air of complacent retrospection.

"No," said the other, "but I feel as if I had been; I've been reading columns about it in the *Dawn*."

"The last event of the season," said Cornelian, "and quite one of the most amusing and lively functions that there have been."

"So the *Dawn* said; but then, as Shalem practically owns and controls that paper, its favourable opinion might be taken for granted."

"The whole idea of the Revel was quite original," said Cornelian, who was not going to have his personal narrative of the event forestalled by anything that a newspaper reporter might have given to the public; "a certain number of guests went as famous personages in the world's history, and each one was accompanied by another guest typifying the prevailing characteristic of that personage. One man went as Julius Cæsar, for instance, and had a girl typifying Ambition as his shadow, another went as Louis the Eleventh, and his companion personified Superstition. Your shadow had to be some one of the opposite sex, you see, and every alternate dance throughout the evening you danced with your shadow-partner. Quite clever idea; young Graf von Schnatelstein is supposed to have invented it."

"New York will be deeply beholden to him," said the other; "shadow-dances, with all manner of eccentric variations, will be the rage there for the next eighteen months."

"Some of the costumes were really sumptuous," continued Cornelian; "the Duchess of Dreyshire was magnificent as Aholibah, you never saw so many jewels on one person, only of course she didn't look dark enough for the character; she had Billy Carnset for her shadow, representing Unspeakable Depravity."

"How on earth did he manage that?"

"Oh, a blend of Beardsley and Bakst as far as get-up and costume, and of course his own personality counted for a good deal. Quite one of the successes of the evening was Leutnant von Gabelroth, as George Washington, with Joan Mardle as his shadow, typifying Inconvenient Candour. He put her down officially as Truthfulness, but every one had heard the other version."

"Good for the Gabelroth, though he does belong to the invading Horde; it's not often that any one scores off Joan."

"Another blaze of magnificence was the loud-voiced Bessimer woman, as the Goddess Juno, with peacock tails and opals all over her; she had Ronnie Storre to represent Green-eyed Jealousy. Talking of Ronnie Storre *and* of jealousy, you will naturally wonder whom Mrs. Yeovil went with. I forget what her costume was, but she'd got that dark-headed youth with her that she's been trotting round everywhere the last few days."

Cornelian's neighbour kicked him furtively on the shin, and frowned in the direction of a dark-haired youth reclining in an adjacent chair. The youth in question rose from his seat and stalked into the farther swelter room.

"So clever of him to go into the furnace room," said the unabashed Cornelian; "now if he turns scarlet all over we shall never know how much is embarrassment and how much is due to the process of being boiled. La Yeovil hasn't done badly by the exchange; he's better looking than Ronnie."

"I see that Pitherby went as Frederick the Great," said Cornelian's neighbour, fingering a sheet of the *Dawn*.

"Isn't that exactly what one would have expected Pitherby to do?" said Cornelian. "He's so desperately anxious to announce to all whom it may concern that he has written a life of that hero. He had an uninspiring-looking woman with him, supposed to represent Military Genius."

"The Spirit of Advertisement would have been more appropriate," said the other.

"The opening scene of the Revel was rather effective," continued Cornelian; "all the Shadow people reclined in the dimly-lit centre of the ball-room in an indistinguishable mass, and the human characters marched round the illuminated sides of the room to solemn processional music. Every now and then a shadow would detach itself from the mass, hail its partner by name, and glide out to join him or her in the procession. Then, when the last shadows had been found their mates and every one was partnered, the lights were turned up in a blaze, the orchestra crashed out a whirl of nondescript dance music, and people just let themselves go. It was Pandemonium. Afterwards every one strutted about for half an hour or so, showing themselves off, and then the legitimate programme of dances began. There were some rather amusing incidents throughout the evening. One set of lancers was danced entirely by the Seven Deadly Sins and their human exemplars; of course seven couples were not sufficient to make up the set, so they had to bring in an eighth sin, I forget what it was."

"The sin of Patriotism would have been rather appropriate, considering who were giving the dance," said the other.

"Hush!" exclaimed Cornelian nervously. "You don't know who may overhear you in a place like this. You'll get yourself into trouble."

"Wasn't there some rather daring new dance of the 'bunny-hug' variety?" asked the indiscreet one.

"The 'Cubby-Cuddle,'" said Cornelian; "three or four adventurous couples danced it towards the end of the evening."

"The *Dawn* says that without being strikingly new it was strikingly modern."

"The best description I can give of it," said Cornelian, "is summed up in the comment of the Gräfin von Tolb when she saw it being danced: 'if they *really* love each other I suppose it doesn't matter.' By the way," he added with apparent indifference, "is there any detailed account of my costume in the *Dawn*?"

His companion laughed cynically.

"As if you hadn't read everything that the *Dawn* and the other morning papers have to say about the ball hours ago."

"The naked truth should be avoided in a Turkish bath," said Cornelian; "kindly assume that I've only had time to glance at the weather forecast and the news from China."

"Oh, very well," said the other; "your costume isn't described; you simply come amid a host of others as 'Mr. Cornelian Valpy, resplendent as the Emperor Nero; with him Miss Kate Lerra, typifying Insensate Vanity.' Many hard things have been said of Nero, but his unkindest critics have never accused him of resembling you in feature. Until some very clear evidence is produced I shall refuse to believe it."

Cornelian was proof against these shafts; leaning back gracefully in his chair he launched forth into that detailed description of his last night's attire which the *Dawn* had so unaccountably failed to supply.

"I wore a tunic of white Nepaulese silk, with a collar of pearls, real pearls. Round my waist I had a girdle of twisted serpents in beaten gold, studded all over with amethysts. My sandals were of gold, laced with scarlet thread, and I had seven bracelets of gold on each arm. Round my head I had a wreath of golden laurel leaves set with scarlet berries, and hanging over my left shoulder was a silk robe of mulberry purple, broidered with the signs of the zodiac in gold and scarlet; I had it made specially for the occasion. At my side I had an ivory-sheathed dagger, with a green jade handle, hung in a green Cordova leather——"

At this point of the recital his companion rose softly, flung his cigarette end into the little water-bowl, and passed into the farther swelter room. Cornelian Valpy was left, still clothed in a look of ineffable complacency, still engaged, in all probability, in reclothing himself in the finery of the previous evening.

Chapter XVIII

THE DEAD WHO DO NOT UNDERSTAND

THE pale light of a November afternoon faded rapidly into the dusk of a November evening. Far over the countryside housewives put up their cottage shutters, lit their lamps, and made the customary remark that the days were drawing in. In barnyards and poultry-runs the greediest pullets made a final tour of inspection, picking up the stray remaining morsels of the evening meal, and then, with much scrambling and squawking, sought the places on the roosting-pole that they thought should belong to them. Labourers working in yard and field began to turn their thoughts homeward or tavernward as the case might be. And through the cold squelching slush of a water-logged meadow a weary, bedraggled, but unbeaten fox stiffly picked his way, climbed a high bramble-grown bank, and flung himself into the sheltering labyrinth of a stretching tangle of woods. The pack of fierce-mouthed things that had rattled him from copse and gorse-cover, along fallow and plough, hedgerow and wooded lane, for nigh on an hour, and had pressed hard on his life for the last few minutes, receded suddenly into the background of his experience. The cold, wet meadow, the thick mask of woods, and the oncoming dusk had stayed the chase—and the fox had outstayed it. In a short time he would fall mechanically to licking off some of the mud that caked on his weary pads; in a shorter time horsemen and hounds would have drawn off kennelward and homeward.

Yeovil rode through the deepening twilight, relying chiefly on his horse to find its way in the network of hedge-bordered lanes that presumably led to a high road or to some human habitation. He was desperately tired after his day's hunting, a legacy of weakness that the fever had bequeathed to him, but even though he could scarcely sit upright in his saddle his mind dwelt complacently on the day's sport and looked forward to the snug cheery comfort that awaited him at his hunting-box. There was a charm, too, even for a tired man, in the eerie stillness of the lone twilight land through which he was passing, a grey shadow-hung land which seemed to have been emptied of all things that belonged to the daytime, and filled with a lurking, moving life of which one knew nothing beyond the sense that it was there. There, and very near. If there had been wood-gods and wicked-eyed fauns in the sunlit groves and hill-sides of old Hellas, surely there were watchful, living things of kindred mould in this dusk-hidden wilderness of field and hedge and coppice.

It was Yeovil's third or fourth day with the hounds, without taking into account a couple of mornings' cub-hunting. Already he felt that he had been doing nothing different from this all his life. His foreign travels, his illness, his recent weeks in London, they were part of a tapestried background that had very slight and distant connexion with his present existence. Of the future he tried to think with greater energy and determination. For this winter, at any rate, he would hunt and do a little shooting, entertain a few of his neighbours and make friends with any congenial fellow-sportsmen who might be within reach. Next year things would be different;

he would have had time to look round him, to regain something of his aforetime vigour of mind and body. Next year, when the hunting season was over, he would set about finding out whether there was any nobler game for him to take a hand in. He would enter into correspondence with old friends who had gone out into the tropics and the backwoods–he would do something.

So he told himself, but he knew thoroughly well that he had found his level. He had ceased to struggle against the fascination of his present surroundings. The slow, quiet comfort and interest of country life appealed with enervating force to the man whom death had half conquered. The pleasures of the chase, well-provided for in every detail, and dovetailed in with the assured luxury of a well-ordered, well-staffed establishment, were exactly what he wanted and exactly what his life down here afforded him. He was experiencing, too, that passionate recurring devotion to an old loved scene that comes at times to men who have travelled far and willingly up and down the world. He was very much at home. The alien standard floating over Buckingham Palace, the Crown of Charlemagne on public buildings and official documents, the grey ships of war riding in Plymouth Bay and Southampton Water with a flag at their stern that older generations of Britons had never looked on, these things seemed far away and inconsequent amid the hedgerows and woods and fallows of the East Wessex country. Horse and hound-craft, harvest, game broods, the planting and felling of timber, the rearing and selling of stock, the letting of grasslands, the care of fisheries, the upkeep of markets and fairs, they were the things that immediately mattered. And Yeovil saw himself, in moments of disgust and self-accusation, settling down into this life of rustic littleness, concerned over the late nesting of a partridge or the defective draining of a loose-box, hugely busy over affairs that a gardener's boy might grapple with, ignoring the struggle-cry that went up, low and bitter and wistful, from a dethroned dispossessed race, in whose glories he had gloried, in whose struggle he lent no hand. In what way, he asked himself in such moments, would his life be better than the life of that parody of manhood who upholstered his rooms with art hangings and rosewood furniture and babbled over the effect?

The lanes seemed interminable and without aim or object except to bisect one another; gates and gaps disclosed nothing in the way of a landmark, and the night began to draw down in increasing shades of darkness. Presently, however, the tired horse quickened its pace, swung round a sharp corner into a broader roadway, and stopped with an air of thankful expectancy at the low doorway of a wayside inn. A cheerful glow of light streamed from the windows and door, and a brighter glare came from the other side of the road, where a large motor-car was being got ready for an immediate start. Yeovil tumbled stiffly out of his saddle, and in answer to the loud rattle of his hunting crop on the open door the innkeeper and two or three hangers-on hurried out to attend to the wants of man and beast. Flour and water for the horse and something hot for himself were Yeovil's first concern, and then he began to clamour for geographical information. He was rather dismayed to find that the cumulative opinions of those whom he consulted, and of several others who joined unbidden in the discussion, placed his destination at nothing nearer than nine miles. Nine miles of dark and hilly country road for a tired man on a tired horse assumed enormous, far-stretching proportions, and although he dimly remembered that he had asked a guest to dinner for that evening he began to wonder whether the wayside inn possessed anything endurable in the way of a bedroom. The landlord interrupted his desperate speculations with a really brilliant effort of suggestion. There was a gentleman in the bar, he said, who was going in a motor-car in the direction for which Yeovil was bound, and who would no doubt be willing to drop him at his destination; the gentleman had also been out with the hounds. Yeovil's horse could be stabled at the inn and fetched home by a groom the next morning. A hurried embassy to the bar parlour resulted in the news that the motorist would be delighted to be of assistance to a fellow-sportsman. Yeovil gratefully accepted the chance that had so obligingly come his way, and hastened to superintend the housing of his horse in its night's quarters. When he had duly seen to the tired animal's comfort and foddering he returned to the roadway, where a young man in hunting garb and a liveried chauffeur were standing by the side of the waiting car.

"I am so very pleased to be of some use to you, Mr. Yeovil," said the car-owner, with a polite bow, and Yeovil recognized the young Leutnant von Gabelroth, who had been present at the musical afternoon at Berkshire Street. He had doubtless seen him at the meet that morning, but in his hunting kit he had escaped his observation.

"I, too, have been out with the hounds," the young man continued; "I have left my horse at the 'Crow and Sceptre' at Dolford. You are living at Black Dene, are you not? I can take you right past your door, it is all on my way."

Yeovil hung back for a moment, overwhelmed with vexation and embarrassment, but it was too late to cancel the arrangement he had unwittingly entered into, and he was constrained to put himself under obligation to the young officer with the best grace he could muster. After all, he reflected, he had met him under his own roof as his wife's guest. He paid his reckoning to mine host, tipped the stable lad who had helped him with his horse, and took his place beside von Gabelroth in the car.

As they glided along the dark roadway and the young German reeled off a string of comments on the incidents of the day's sport, Yeovil lay back amid his comfortable wraps and weighed the measure of his humiliation. It was Cicely's gospel that one should know what one wanted in life and take good care that one got what one wanted. Could he apply that test of achievement to his own life? Was this what he really wanted to be doing, pursuing his uneventful way as a country squire, sharing even his sports and pastimes with men of the nation that had conquered and enslaved his Fatherland?

The car slackened its pace somewhat as they went through a small hamlet, past a schoolhouse, past a rural police-station with the new monogram over its notice-board, past a church with a little tree-grown graveyard. There, in a corner, among wild-rose bushes and tall yews, lay some of Yeovil's own kinsfolk, who had lived in these parts and hunted and found life pleasant in the days that were not so very long ago. Whenever he went past that quiet little gathering-place of the dead Yeovil was wont to raise his hat in mute affectionate salutation to those who were now only memories in his family; tonight he somehow omitted the salute and turned his head the other way. It was as though the dead of his race saw and wondered.

Three or four months ago the thing he was doing would have seemed an impossibility, now it was actually happening; he was listening to the gay, courteous, tactful chatter of his young companion, laughing now and then at some joking remark, answering some question of interest, learning something of hunting ways and traditions in von Gabelroth's own country. And when the car turned in at the gate of the hunting lodge and drew up at the steps the laws of hospitality demanded that Yeovil should ask his benefactor of the road to come in for a few minutes and drink something a little better than the wayside inn had been able to supply. The young officer spent the best part of a half-hour in Yeovil's snuggery, examining and discussing the trophies of rifle and collecting gun that covered the walls. He had a good knowledge of woodcraft, and the beasts and birds of Siberian forests and North African deserts were to him new pages in a familiar book. Yeovil found himself discoursing eagerly with his chance guest on the European distribution and local variation of such and such a species, recounting peculiarities in its habits and incidents of its pursuit and capture. If the cold observant eyes of Lady Shalem could have rested on the scene she would have hailed it as another root-fibre thrown out by the *fait accompli*.

Yeovil closed the hall door on his departing visitor, and closed his mind on the crowd of angry and accusing thoughts that were waiting to intrude themselves. His valet had already got his bath in readiness and in a few minutes the tired huntsman was forgetting weariness and the consciousness of outside things in the languorous abandonment that steam and hot water induce. Brain and limbs seemed to lay themselves down in a contented waking sleep, the world that was beyond the bathroom walls dropped away into a far unreal distance; only somewhere through the steam clouds pierced a hazy consciousness that a dinner, well chosen, was being well cooked, and would presently be well served–and right well appreciated. That was the lure to drag the bather away from the Nirvana land of warmth and steam. The stimulating after-effect of the bath took its due effect, and Yeovil felt that he was now much less tired and enormously hungry. A cheery fire burned in his dressing-room and a lively black kitten helped him to dress, and incidentally helped him to require a new tassel to the cord of his dressing-gown. As he finished his toilet and the kitten finished its sixth and most notable attack on the tassel a ring was heard at the front door, and a moment later a loud, hearty, and unmistakably hungry voice resounded in the hall. It belonged to the local doctor, who had also taken part in the day's run and had been bidden to enliven the evening meal with the entertainment of his inexhaustible store of sporting and social reminiscences. He knew the countryside and the countryfolk inside out, and he was a living unwritten chronicle of the East Wessex hunt. His conversation seemed exactly the right accompaniment to the meal; his stories brought glimpses of wet hedgerows, stiff ploughlands, leafy spinneys and muddy brooks in among the rich old Worcester and Georgian silver of the dinner service, the glow and crackle of the wood fire, the pleasant succession of well-cooked dishes and mellow wines. The world narrowed itself down again to a warm, drowsy-scented dining-room, with a productive hinterland of kitchen and cellar beyond it, and beyond that an important outer world of loose-box and harness-room and stable-yard; farther again a dark hushed region where pheasants roosted and owls flitted and foxes prowled.

Yeovil sat and listened to story after story of the men and women and horses of the neighbourhood; even the foxes seemed to have a personality, some of them, and a personal history. It was a little like Hans Andersen, he decided, and a little like the *Reminiscences of an Irish R.M.*, and perhaps just a little like some of the more probable adventures of Baron Munchausen. The newer stories were evidently true to the smallest detail, the earlier ones had altered somewhat in repetition, as plants and animals vary under domestication.

And all the time there was one topic that was never touched on. Of half the families mentioned it was necessary to add the qualifying information that they "used to live" at such and such a place; the countryside knew them no longer. Their properties were for sale or had already passed into the hands of strangers. But neither man cared to allude to the grinning shadow that sat at the feast and sent an icy chill now and again through the cheeriest jest and most jovial story. The brisk run with the hounds that day had stirred and warmed their pulses; it was an evening for comfortable forgetting.

Later that night, in the stillness of his bedroom, with the dwindling noises of a retiring household dropping off one by one into ordered silence, a door shutting here, a fire being raked out there, the thoughts that had been held away came crowding in. The body was tired, but the brain was not, and Yeovil lay awake with his thoughts for company. The world grew suddenly wide again, filled with the significance of things that mattered, held by the actions of men that mattered. Hunting-box and stable and gun-room dwindled to a mere pin-point in the universe, there were other larger, more absorbing things on which the mind dwelt. There was the grey cold sea outside Dover and Portsmouth and Cork, where the great grey ships of war rocked and swung with the tides, where the sailors sang, in doggerel English, that bitter-sounding adaptation, "Germania rules t'e waves," where the flag of a World-Power floated for the world to see. And in oven-like cities of India there were men who looked out at the white sun-glare, the heat-baked dust, the welter of crowded streets, who listened to the unceasing chorus of harsh-throated crows, the strident creaking of cart-wheels, the buzz and drone of insect swarms and the rattle call of the tree lizards; men whose thoughts went hungrily to the cool grey skies and wet turf and moist ploughlands of an English hunting country, men whose memories listened yearningly to the music of a deep-throated hound and the call of a game-bird in the stubble. Yeovil had secured for himself the enjoyment of the things for which these men hungered; he had known what he wanted in life, slowly and with hesitation, yet nevertheless surely, he had arrived at the achievement of his unconfessed desires. Here, installed under his own roof-tree, with as good horse-flesh in his stable as man could desire, with sport lying almost at his door, with his wife ready to come down and help him to entertain his neighbours, Murrey Yeovil had found the life that he wanted–and was accursed in his own eyes. He argued with himself, and palliated and explained, but he knew why he had turned his eyes away that evening from the little graveyard under the trees; one cannot explain things to the dead.

Chapter XIX
THE LITTLE FOXES

"Take us the foxes, the little foxes, that spoil the vines"

On a warm and sunny May afternoon, some ten months since Yeovil's return from his Siberian wanderings and sickness, Cicely sat at a small table in the open-air restaurant in Hyde Park, finishing her after-luncheon coffee and listening to the meritorious performance of the orchestra. Opposite her sat Larry Meadowfield, absorbed for the moment in the slow enjoyment of a cigarette, which also was not without its short-lived merits. Larry was a well-dressed youngster, who was, in Cicely's opinion, distinctly good to look on—an opinion which the boy himself obviously shared. He had the healthy, well-cared-for appearance of a country-dweller who has been turned into a town dandy without suffering in the process. His blue-black hair, growing very low down on a broad forehead, was brushed back in a smoothness that gave his head the appearance of a rain-polished sloe; his eyebrows were two dark smudges and his large violet-grey eyes expressed the restful good temper of an animal whose immediate requirements have been satisfied. The lunch had been an excellent one, and it was jolly to feed out of doors in the warm spring air—the only drawback to the arrangement being the absence of mirrors. However, if he could not look at himself a great many people could look at him.

Cicely listened to the orchestra as it jerked and strutted through a fantastic dance measure, and as she listened she looked appreciatively at the boy on the other side of the table, whose soul for the moment seemed to be in his cigarette. Her scheme of life, knowing just what you wanted and taking good care that you got it, was justifying itself by results. Ronnie, grown tiresome with success, had not been difficult to replace, and no one in her world had had the satisfaction of being able to condole with her on the undesirable experience of a long interregnum. To feminine acquaintances with fewer advantages of purse and brains and looks she might figure as "that Yeovil woman," but never had she given them justification to allude to her as "poor Cicely Yeovil." And Murrey, dear old soul, had cooled down, as she had hoped and wished, from his white heat of disgust at the things that she had prepared herself to accept philosophically. A new chapter of their married life and man-and-woman friendship had opened; many a rare gallop they had had together that winter, many a cheery dinner gathering and long bridge evening in the cozy hunting-lodge. Though he still hated the new London and held himself aloof from most of her Town set, yet he had not shown himself rigidly intolerant of the sprinkling of Teuton sportsmen who hunted and shot down in his part of the country.

The orchestra finished its clicking and caracoling and was accorded a short clatter of applause.

"The *Danse Macabre*," said Cicely to her companion; "one of Saint-Saëns' best known pieces."

"Is it?" said Larry indifferently; "I'll take your word for it. 'Fraid I don't know much about music."

"You dear boy, that's just what I like in you," said Cicely; "you're such a delicious young barbarian."

"Am I?" said Larry. "I dare say. I suppose you know."

Larry's father had been a brilliantly clever man who had married a brilliantly handsome woman; the Fates had not had the least intention that Larry should take after both parents.

"The fashion of having one's lunch in the open air has quite caught on this season," said Cicely; "one sees everybody here on a fine day. There is Lady Bailquist over there. She used to be Lady Shalem, you know, before her husband got the earldom—to be more correct, before she got it for him. I suppose she is all agog to see the great review."

It was in fact precisely the absorbing topic of the forthcoming Boy-Scout march-past that was engaging the Countess of Bailquist's earnest attention at the moment.

"It is going to be an historical occasion," she was saying to Sir Leonard Pitherby (whose services to literature had up to the present received only a half-measure of recognition); "if it miscarries it will be a serious set-back for the *fait accompli*. If it is a success it will be the biggest step forward in the path of reconciliation between the two races that has yet been taken. It will mean that the younger generation is on our side—not all, of course, but some, that is all we can expect at present, and that will be enough to work on."

"Supposing the Scouts hang back and don't turn up in any numbers," said Sir Leonard anxiously.

"That of course is the danger," said Lady Bailquist quietly; "probably two-thirds of the available strength will hold back, but a third or even a sixth would be enough; it would redeem the parade from the calamity of fiasco, and it would be a nucleus to work on for the future. That is what we want, a good start, a preliminary rally. It is the first step that counts, that is why today's event is of such importance."

"Of course, of course, the first step on the road," assented Sir Leonard.

"I can assure you," continued Lady Bailquist, "that nothing has been left undone to rally the Scouts to the new order of things. Special privileges have been showered on them, alone among all the cadet corps they have been allowed to retain their organization, a decoration of merit has been instituted for them, a large hostelry and gymnasium has been provided for them in Westminster, His Majesty's youngest son is to be their Scoutmaster-in-Chief, a great athletic meeting is to be held for them each year, with valuable prizes, three or four hundred of them are to be taken every summer, free of charge, for a holiday in the Bavarian Highlands and the Baltic Seaboard; besides this the parent of every scout who obtains the medal for efficiency is to be exempted from part of the new war taxation that the people are finding so burdensome."

"One certainly cannot say that they have not had attractions held out to them," said Sir Leonard.

"It is a special effort," said Lady Bailquist; "it is worth making an effort for. They are going to be the Janissaries of the Empire; the younger generation knocking at the doors of progress, and thrusting back the bars and bolts of old racial prejudices. I tell you, Sir Leonard, it will be an historic moment when the first crops of those little khaki-clad boys swings through the gates of the Park."

"When do they come?" asked the baronet, catching something of his companion's zeal.

"The first detachment is due to arrive at three," said Lady Bailquist, referring to a small time-table of the afternoon's proceedings; "three, punctually, and the others will follow in rapid succession. The Emperor and Suite will arrive at two-fifty and take up their positions at the saluting base—over there, where the big flag-staff has been set up. The boys will come in by Hyde Park Corner, the Marble Arch, and the Albert Gate, according to their districts, and form in one big column over there, where the little flags are pegged out. Then the young Prince will inspect them and lead them past His Majesty."

"Who will be with the Imperial party?" asked Sir Leonard.

"Oh, it is to be an important affair; everything will be done to emphasize the significance of the occasion," said Lady Bailquist, again consulting her programme. "The King of Württemberg, and two of the Bavarian royal Princes, an Abyssinian Envoy who is over here—he will lend a touch of picturesque barbarism to the scene—the general commanding the London district and a whole lot of other military bigwigs, and the Austrian, Italian and Roumanian military attachés."

She reeled off the imposing list of notables with an air of quiet satisfaction. Sir Leonard made mental notes of personages to whom he might send presentation copies of his new work *Frederick-William, the Great Elector, a Popular Biography,* as a souvenir of today's auspicious event.

"It is nearly a quarter to three now," he said; "let us get a good position before the crowd gets thicker."

"Come along to my car, it is just opposite to the saluting base," said her ladyship; "I have a police pass that will let us through. We'll ask Mrs. Yeovil and her young friend to join us."

Larry excused himself from joining the party; he had a barbarian's reluctance to assisting at an Imperial triumph.

"I think I'll push off to the swimming-bath," he said to Cicely; "see you again about tea-time."

Cicely walked with Lady Bailquist and the literary baronet towards the crowd of spectators, which was steadily growing in dimensions. A newsboy ran in front of them displaying a poster with the intelligence "Essex wickets fall rapidly"—a semblance of county cricket still survived under the new order of things. Near the saluting base some thirty or forty motor-cars were drawn up in line, and Cicely and her companions exchanged greeting with many of the occupants.

"A lovely day for the review, isn't it?" cried the Gräfin von Tolb, breaking off her conversation with Herr Rebinok, the little Pomeranian banker, who was sitting by her side. "Why haven't you brought young Mr. Meadowfield? Such a nice boy. I wanted him to come and sit in my carriage and talk to me."

"He doesn't talk, you know," said Cicely; "he's only brilliant to look at."

"Well, I could have looked at him," said the Gräfin.

"There'll be thousands of other boys to look at presently," said Cicely, laughing at the old woman's frankness.

"Do you think there will be thousands?" asked the Gräfin, with an anxious lowering of the voice, "really, thousands? Hundreds, perhaps; there is some uncertainty. Every one is not sanguine."

"Hundreds, anyway," said Cicely.

The Gräfin turned to the little banker and spoke to him rapidly and earnestly in German.

"It is most important that we should consolidate our position in this country; we must coax the younger generation over by degrees, we must disarm their hostility. We cannot afford to be always on the watch in this quarter; it is a source of weakness, and we cannot afford to be weak. This Slav upheaval in south-eastern Europe is becoming a serious menace. Have you seen today's telegrams from Agram? They are bad reading. There is no computing the extent of this movement."

"It is directed against us," said the banker.

"Agreed," said the Gräfin; "it is in the nature of things that it must be against us. Let us have no illusions. Within the next ten years, sooner perhaps, we shall be faced with a crisis which will be only a beginning. We shall need all our strength; that is why we cannot afford to be weak over here. Today is an important day; I confess I am anxious."

"Hark! The kettledrums!" exclaimed the commanding voice of Lady Bailquist. "His Majesty is coming. Quick, bundle into the car."

The crowd behind the police-kept lines surged expectantly into closer formation; spectators hurried up from side-walks and stood craning their necks above the shoulders of earlier arrivals.

Through the archway at Hyde Park Corner came a resplendent cavalcade with a swirl of colour and rhythmic movement and a crash of exultant music; life-guards with gleaming helmets, a detachment of Württemberg lancers with a flutter of black and yellow pennons, a rich medley of staff uniforms, a prancing array of princely horsemen, the Imperial Standard, and the King of Prussia, Great Britain, and Ireland, Emperor of the West. It was the most imposing display that Londoners had seen since the catastrophe.

Slowly, grandly, with thunder of music and beat of hoofs, the procession passed through the crowd, across the sward towards the saluting base, slowly the eagle standard, charged with the leopards, lion and harp of the conquered kingdoms, rose mast-high on the flag-staff and fluttered in the breeze, slowly and with military precision the troops and Suite took up their position round the central figure of the great pageant. Trumpets and kettledrums suddenly ceased their music, and in a moment there rose in their stead an eager buzz of comment from the nearest spectators.

"How well the young Prince looks in his scout uniform. . . ." "The King of Württemberg is a much younger man than I thought he was. . . ." "Is that a Prussian or Bavarian uniform, there on the right, the man on a black horse? . . ." "Neither, it's Austrian, the Austrian military attaché. . . ." "That is von Stoppel talking to His

Majesty; he organized the Boy Scouts in Germany, you know. . . ." "His Majesty is looking very pleased." "He has reason to look pleased; this is a great event in the history of the two countries. It marks a new epoch. . . ." "Oh, do you see the Abyssinian Envoy? What a picturesque figure he makes. How well he sits his horse. . . ." "That is the Grand Duke of Baden's nephew, talking to the King of Württemberg now."

On the buzz and chatter of the spectators fell suddenly three sound strokes, distant, measured, sinister; the clang of a clock striking three.

"Three o'clock and not a boy scout within sight or hearing!" exclaimed the loud ringing voice of Joan Mardle; "one can usually hear their drums and trumpets a couple of miles away."

"There is the traffic to get through," said Sir Leonard Pitherby in an equally high-pitched voice; "and of course," he added vaguely, "it takes some time to get the various units together. One must give them a few minutes' grace."

Lady Bailquist said nothing, but her restless watchful eyes were turned first to Hyde Park Corner and then in the direction of the Marble Arch, back again to Hyde Park Corner. Only the dark lines of the waiting crowd met her view, with the yellow newspaper placards flitting in and out, announcing to an indifferent public the fate of Essex wickets. As far as her searching eyes could travel the green stretch of tree and sward remained unbroken, save by casual loiterers. No small brown columns appeared, no drum-beat came throbbing up from the distance. The little flags pegged out to mark the positions of the awaited scout-corps fluttered in meaningless isolation on the empty parade ground.

His Majesty was talking unconcernedly with one of his officers, the foreign attachés looked steadily between their chargers' ears, as though nothing in particular was hanging in the balance, the Abyssinian Envoy displayed an untroubled serenity which was probably genuine. Elsewhere among the Suite was a perceptible fidget, the more obvious because it was elaborately cloaked. Among the privileged onlookers drawn up near the saluting point the fidgeting was more unrestrained.

"Six minutes past three, and not a sign of them!" exclaimed Joan Mardle, with the explosive articulation of one who cannot any longer hold back a truth.

"Hark!" said some one; "I hear trumpets!"

There was an instant concentration of listening, a straining of eyes.

It was only the toot of a passing motor-car. Even Sir Leonard Pitherby, with the eye of faith, could not locate as much as a cloud of dust on the Park horizon.

And now another sound was heard, a sound difficult to define, without beginning, without dimension; the growing murmur of a crowd waking to a slowly dawning sensation.

"I wish the band would strike up an air," said the Gräfin von Tolb fretfully; "it is stupid waiting here in silence."

Joan fingered her watch, but she made no further remark; she realized that no amount of malicious comment could be so dramatically effective now as the slow slipping away of the intolerable seconds.

The murmur from the crowd grew in volume. Some satirical wit started whistling an imitation of an advancing fife and drum band; others took it up and the air resounded with the shrill music of a phantom army on the march. The mock throbbing of drum and squealing of fife rose and fell above the packed masses of spectators, but no answering echo came from beyond the distant trees. Like mushrooms in the night a muster of uniformed police and plain clothes detectives sprang into evidence on all sides; whatever happened there must be no disloyal demonstration. The whistlers and mockers were pointedly invited to keep silence, and one or two addresses were taken.

Under the trees, well at the back of the crowd, a young man stood watching the long stretch of road along which the Scouts should come. Something had drawn him there, against his will, to witness the Imperial Triumph, to watch the writing of yet another chapter in the history of his country's submission to an accepted fact. And now a dull flush crept into his grey face; a look that was partly new-born hope and resurrected pride, partly remorse and shame, burned in his eyes. Shame, the choking, searing shame of self-reproach that cannot be reasoned away, was dominant in his heart. *He* had laid down his arms–there were others who had never hoisted the flag of surrender. He had given up the fight and joined the ranks of the hopelessly subservient; in thousands of English homes throughout the land there were young hearts that had not forgotten, had not compounded, would not yield.

The younger generation had barred the door.

And in the pleasant May sunshine the Eagle standard floated and flapped, the black and yellow pennons shifted restlessly, Emperor and Princes, Generals and guards, sat stiffly in their saddles, and waited.

And waited. . . .

The Westminster Alice

THE WESTMINSTER ALICE

INTRODUCTION

"ALICE," Child with dreaming eyes,
Noting things that come to pass
Turvey-wise in Wonderland
Backwards through a Looking-Glass.

Figures flit across thy dream,
Muddle through and flicker out
Some in cocksure blessedness,
Some in Philosophic Doubt.

Some in brackets, some in sulks,
Some with latchkeys on the ramp,
Living (in a sort of peace)
In a Concentration Camp.

Party moves on either side,
  Checks and feints that don't deceive,
Knights and Bishops, Pawns and all,
  In a game of Make-Believe.

Things that fall contrariwise,
  Difficult to understand
Darkly through a Looking-Glass
  Turvey-wise in Wonderland.

ALICE IN DOWNING STREET

"HAVE you ever seen an Ineptitude?"[1] asked the Cheshire Cat suddenly; the Cat was nothing if not abrupt.

"Not in real life," said Alice. "Have you any about here?"

"A few," answered the Cat comprehensively. "Over there, for instance," it added, contracting its pupils to the requisite focus, "is the most perfect specimen we have."

Alice followed the direction of its glance and noticed for the first time a figure sitting in a very uncomfortable attitude on nothing in particular. Alice had no time to wonder how it managed to do it, she was busy taking in the appearance of the creature, which was something like a badly-written note of interrogation and something like a guillemot, and seemed to have been trying to preen its rather untidy plumage with whitewash. "What a dreadful mess it's in!" she remarked, after gazing at it for a few moments in silence. "What is it, and why is it here?"

"It hasn't any meaning," said the Cat, "it simply *is*."

"Can it talk?" asked Alice eagerly.

"It has never done anything else," chuckled the Cat.

"Can you tell me what you are doing here?" Alice inquired politely. The Ineptitude shook its head with a deprecatory motion and commenced to drawl, "I haven't an idea."

"It never has, you know," interrupted the Cheshire Cat rudely,

[1] "The Ineptitude"—Mr. A. J. (later Earl) Balfour, First Lord of the Treasury in Lord Salisbury's third Administration, 1895–1900.

"but in its leisure moments" (Alice thought it must have a good many of them) "when it isn't playing with a gutta-percha ball it unravels the groundwork of what people believe—or don't believe, I forget which."

"It really doesn't matter which," said the Ineptitude with languid interest.

"Of course it doesn't," the Cat went on cheerfully, "because the unravelling got so tangled that no one could follow it. Its theory is," he continued, seeing that Alice was waiting for more, "that you mustn't interfere with the Inevitable. Slide and let slide, you know."

"But what do you keep it here for?" asked Alice.

"Oh, somehow you can't help it; it's so perfectly harmless and amiable and says the nastiest things in the nicest manner, and the King just couldn't do without it. The King is only made of pasteboard, you know, with sharp edges; and the Queen"—here the Cat sank its voice to a whisper—"the Queen comes from another pack, made of Brummagem ware, without polish, but absolutely indestructible; always pushing, you know; but you can't push an Ineptitude. Might as well try to hustle a glacier."

"That's why you keep so many of them about," said Alice.

"Of course. But its temper is not what it used to be. Lots of things have happened to worry it."

"What sort of things?"

"Oh, people have been dying off in round numbers, in the most ostentatious manner, and the Ineptitude dislikes fuss—but hush, here's the King coming."

His Majesty was looking doleful and grumpy, Alice thought, as though he had been disturbed in an afternoon nap. "Who is this, and what is that Cat doing here?" he asked, glancing gloomily at Alice and her companion.

"I really must ask you to give me notice of these questions," said the Ineptitude with a yawn.

"There's a dragon loose somewhere in the garden," the King went on peevishly, "and I am expected to help in getting it under control. Do I look as if I could control dragons?"

Alice thought he certainly did not.

"What do you propose doing?" drawled the Ineptitude.

"That's just it," said the King. "I say that whatever is done must be done cautiously and deliberately; the Treasurer says that whatever is done must be done cheaply–I am afraid the Treasurer is the weakest member of the pack," he added anxiously.

"Only made of Bristol board, you know," explained the Cat aside to Alice.

"What does the Queen say about it?" asked the Ineptitude.

"The Queen says that if something is not done in less than no time there'll be a Dissolution."

Both looked very grave at this, and nothing was said for some minutes. The King was the first to break the silence. "What are you doing with that whitewash?" he demanded. "The Queen said everything was to be painted khaki."

"I know," said the creature pathetically, "but I had run out of khaki; the Unforeseen again, you know; and things needed whitewash so badly."

The Cat had been slowly vanishing during the last few minutes, till nothing remained of it but an eye. At the last remark it gave a wink at Alice and completed its eclipse.

When Alice turned round she found that both the King and the Ineptitude were fast asleep.

"It's no good remaining here," she thought, and as she did not want to meet either the Queen or the dragon, she turned to make her way out of the street.

"At any rate," she said to herself, "I know what an Ineptitude is like."

ALICE IN PALL MALL

"The great art in falling off a horse," said the White Knight,[1] "is to have another handy to fall on to."

"But wouldn't that be rather difficult to arrange?" asked Alice.

"Difficult, of course," replied the Knight, "but in my Depart-

[1] The White Knight—The Marquess of Lansdowne, Secretary of State for War, 1895–1900; became Foreign Secretary November, 1900, in succession to Lord Salisbury, who till then had been both Prime Minister and Foreign Secretary.

The inscription on the name of the Foreign Office horse is an allusion to Lord Lansdowne's reputed facility in the French language.

ment one has to be provided for emergencies. Now, for instance, have you ever conducted a war in South Africa?"

Alice shook her head.

"I have," said the Knight, with a gentle complacency in his voice.

"And did you bring it to a successful conclusion?" asked Alice.

"Not exactly to a *conclusion*—not a *definite* conclusion, you know—nor entirely successful either. In fact, I believe it's going on still. . . . But you can't think how much forethought it took to get it properly started. I dare say, now, you are wondering at my equipment?"

Alice certainly was; the Knight was riding rather uncomfortably on a sober-paced horse that was prevented from moving any faster by an elaborate housing of red-tape trappings. "Of course, I see the reason for that," thought Alice; "if it were to move any quicker the Knight would come off." But there were a number of obsolete weapons and appliances hanging about the saddle that didn't seem of the least practical use.

"You see, I had read a book," the Knight went on in a dreamy faraway tone, "written by some one to prove that warfare under modern conditions was impossible. You may imagine how disturbing that was to a man of my profession. Many men would have thrown up the whole thing and gone home. But I grappled with the situation. You will never guess what I did."

Alice pondered. "You went to war, of course——"

"Yes; *but not under modern conditions.*"

The Knight stopped his horse so that he might enjoy the full effect of this announcement.

"Now, for instance," he continued kindly, seeing that Alice had not recovered her breath, "you observe this little short-range gun that I have hanging to my saddle? Why do you suppose I sent out guns of that particular kind? Because if they happened to fall into the hands of the enemy they'd be very little use to him. That was my own invention."

"I see," said Alice gravely; "but supposing you wanted to use them against the enemy?"

The Knight looked worried. "I know there is that to be thought of, but I didn't choose to be putting dangerous weapons into the enemy's hands. And then, again, supposing the Basutos had risen, those would have been just the sort of guns to drive them off with. Of course they *didn't* rise; but they might have done so, you know."

At this moment the horse suddenly went on again, and the Knight clutched convulsively at its mane to prevent himself from coming off.

"That's the worst of horses," he remarked apologetically; "they are so Unforeseen in their movements. Now, if I had had my way I would have done without them as far as possible—in fact, I began that way, only it didn't answer. And yet," he went on in an aggrieved tone, "at Crécy it was the footmen who did the most damage."

"But," objected Alice, "if your men hadn't got horses how could they get about from place to place?"

"They couldn't. That would be the beauty of it," said the White Knight eagerly; "the fewer places your army moves to, the fewer maps you have to prepare. And we hadn't prepared very many. I'm not very strong at geography, but," he added, brightening, "you should hear me talk French."

"But," persisted Alice, "supposing the enemy went and attacked you at some other place——"

"They did," interrupted the Knight gloomily; "they appeared in strength at places that weren't even marked on the ordinary maps. But how do you think they got there?"

He paused and fixed his gentle eyes upon Alice as she walked beside him, and then continued in a hollow voice:

"They rode. Rode and carried rifles. They were no mortal foes—they were Mounted Infantry."

The Knight swayed about so with the violence of his emotion that it was inevitable that he should lose his seat, and Alice was relieved to notice that there was another horse with an empty saddle ready for him to scramble on to. There was a frightful dust, of course, but Alice saw him gathering the reins of his new mount into a bunch, and smiling down upon her with increased amiability.

"It's not an easy animal to manage," he called out to her, "but if I pat it and speak to it in French it will probably understand where I want it to go. And," he added hopefully, "it may go there. A knowledge of French and an amiable disposition will see one out of most things."

"Well," thought Alice as she watched him settling down uneasily into the saddle, "it ought not to take long to see him out of that."

ALICE AND THE LIBERAL PARTY

Quite a number of them were going past, and the noise was considerable, but they were marching in sixes and sevens and didn't seem to be guided by any fixed word of command, so that the effect was not so imposing as it might have been. Some of them, Alice noticed, had the letters "I.L." embroidered on their tunics and headpieces and other conspicuous places ("I wonder," she thought, "if it's marked on their underclothing as well"); others simply had a big "L," and others again were branded with a little "e." They got dreadfully in each other's way, and were always falling over one another in little heaps, while many of the mounted ones did not seem at all sure of their seats. "They won't go very far if they don't fall into better order," thought Alice, and she was glad to find herself the next minute in a spacious hall with a large marble staircase at one end of it. The White King[1] was sitting on one of the steps, looking rather anxious and just a little uncomfortable under his heavy crown, which needed a good deal of balancing to keep it in its place.

"Did you happen to meet any fighting men?" he asked Alice.

"A great many—two or three hundred, I should think."

"Not quite two hundred, all told," said the King, referring to his notebook.

"Told what?" asked Alice.

"Well, they haven't been told anything, exactly—yet. The fact is," the King went on nervously, "we're rather in want of a messenger just now. I don't know how it is, there are two or three of them about, but lately they have always been either out of reach or else out of touch. You don't happen to have passed any one coming from the direction of Berkeley Square?"[2] he asked eagerly.

Alice shook her head.

"There's the Primrose Courier,[3] for instance," the King continued reflectively, "the most reliable Messenger we have; he understands all about Open Doors and Linked Hands and all that sort of thing,

[1] The White King—Sir Henry Campbell-Bannerman.

[2] Berkeley Square, Lord Rosebery's residence (No. 38).

[3] The Primrose Courier—Lord Rosebery, leader of the Liberal Imperialists.

and he's quite as useful at home. But he frightens some of them nearly out of their wits by his Imperial Anglo-Saxon attitudes. I wouldn't mind his skipping about so if he'd only come back when he's wanted."

"And haven't you got any one else to carry your messages?" asked Alice sympathetically.

"There's the Unkhaki Messenger,"[4] said the King, consulting his pocket-book.

"I beg your pardon," said Alice.

"You know what Khaki means, I suppose?"

"It's a sort of colour," said Alice promptly; "something like dust."

"Exactly," said the King; "thou dost—he doesn't. That's why he's called the Unkhaki Messenger."

Alice gave it up.

"Such a dear, obliging creature," the King went on, "but so dreadfully unpunctual. He's always half a century in front of his times or half a century behind them, and that puts one out so."

Alice agreed that it would make a difference.

"It's helped to put us out quite six years already," the King went on plaintively; "but you can't cure him of it. You see he will wander about in by-ways and deserts, hunting for Lost Causes, and whenever he comes across a stream he always wades against the current. All that takes him out of his way, you know; he's somewhere up in the Grampian Hills by this time."

"I see," said Alice; "that's what you mean by being out of touch. And the other Messenger is——"

"Out of reach," said the King. "Precisely."

"Then it follows," said Alice——

"I don't know what you mean by 'it,'" interrupted the King sulkily. "No one follows. That is why we stick in the same place. DON'T," he suddenly screamed, jumping up and down in his agitation. "Don't do it, I say."

[4] The Unkhaki Messenger—Mr. John (afterwards Viscount) Morley, who had been active as an anti-Imperialist. Mr. Morley had recently produced his book on Oliver Cromwell, and Lord Rosebery his book on Napoleon at St. Helena, entitled *Napoleon; The Last Phase*. Lord Rosebery had resigned the leadership of the Liberal Party in 1896, and Mr. Morley had retired from the "councils of the party" in 1898. But both had reappeared on the scene and the allusions are to Sir Henry Campbell-Bannerman's perplexities at their disappearances and reappearances.

"Do what?" asked Alice in some alarm.

"Give advice. I know you're going to. They've all been doing it for the last six weeks. I assure you the letters I get——"

"I wasn't going to give you advice," said Alice indignantly, "and as to letters, you've got too much alphabet as it is."

"Why, you're doing it now," said the King angrily. "Good-bye."

As Alice took the hint and walked away towards the door she heard him calling after her in a kinder tone: "If you *should* meet any one coming from the direction of Berkeley Square——"

ALICE AT LAMBETH

There was so much noise inside that Alice thought she might as well go in without knocking.

The atmosphere was as noticeable as the noise when Alice got in, and seemed to be heavily charged with pepper. There was a faint whiff of burning incense, and some candles that had just been put out were smouldering unpleasantly. Quite a number of Articles were strewn about on the floor, some of them more or less broken. The Duchess was seated in the middle of the kitchen, holding, as well as she could, a very unmanageable baby that kept wriggling itself into all manner of postures and uncompromising attitudes. At the back of the kitchen a cook was busily engaged in stirring up a large cauldron, pausing every now and then to fling a reredos or half a rubric at the Duchess, who maintained an air of placid unconcern in spite of the combined fractiousness of the baby and cook and the obtrusiveness of the pepper.

"Your cook seems to have a very violent temper," said Alice, as soon as a lull in the discord enabled her to make herself heard.

"Drat her!" said the Duchess.

"I beg your pardon," said Alice, not quite sure whether she had heard aright; "your Grace was remarking——"

"'*Pax vobiscum,*' was what I said," answered the Duchess; "there's nothing like a dead language when you're dealing with a live volcano."

"But aren't you going to do something to set matters straight a bit?" asked Alice, dodging a whole set of Ornaments that went skimming through the air, and watching with some anxiety the contortions of the baby, which was getting more difficult to hold every moment.

"Of course something must be done," said the Duchess, with decision, "but quietly and gradually—the leaden foot within the velvet shoe, you know."

Alice seemed to recognize the quotation, but she did not notice that anything particular was being done. "At the rate you're going, it will be years before you get settled," she remarked.

"Perhaps it will," said the Duchess resignedly. "I'm paid by the year, you know. *Festina lente*, say I."

"But surely you can keep some sort of order in your Establishment?" said Alice. "Why don't you exert your authority?"

"My dear, it takes me all the exertion I can spare to have any authority. I give orders, and it's my endeavour not to see that they're disobeyed. I'm sure I've given this child my Opinion—but there, you might as well opine to a limpet. As to the cook——"

Here the cook sent the pepper-pot straight at the Duchess, who broke off in a violent fit of sneezing. In the midst of the commotion the baby suddenly disappeared, and as the cook had taken up a new caster labelled "cayenne" Alice thought she might as well go and see where it had gone to. As she slipped out of the kitchen she heard the Duchess gasping between her sneezes, "Must . . . be done . . . quietly . . . and . . . gradually."

"What happened to the baby?" asked the Cheshire Cat, appearing suddenly a few minutes later.

"It went out—to roam, I think," said Alice.

"I always said it would," said the Cat.

ALICE AT ST. STEPHEN'S

"It's very provoking," said Alice to herself; she had been trying for the previous quarter of an hour to attract the attention of a large and very solemn caterpillar that was perched on the top of a big mushroom with a Gothic fringe. "I've heard that the only chance of speaking to it is to catch its eye," she continued, but she found out that however perseveringly she thrust herself into the Caterpillar's[1]

[1] The Caterpillar—Mr. Speaker Gully.

range of vision its eye persistently looked beyond her, or beneath her, or around her—never at her. Alice had read somewhere that little girls should be seen and not heard; "but," she thought, "I'm not even seen here, and if I'm not to be heard, what am I here at all for?" In any case she determined to make an attempt at conversation.

"If you please——" she began.

"I don't," said the Caterpillar shortly, without seeming to take any further notice of her.

After an uncomfortable pause she commenced again.

"I should like——"

"You shouldn't," said the Caterpillar with decision.

Alice felt discouraged, but it was no use to be shut up in this way, so she started again as amiably as she could.

"You can't think, Mr. Caterpillar——"

"I can, and I often do," he remarked stiffly; adding, "You mustn't make such wild statements. They're not relevant to the discussion."

"But I only said that in order——"

"You didn't," said the Caterpillar angrily. "I tell you it was not in order."

"You are so dreadfully short," exclaimed Alice; the Caterpillar drew itself up.

"In manner, I mean; no—in memory," she added hastily, for it was thoroughly angry by this time.

"I'm sure I didn't mean anything," she continued humbly, for she felt that it was absurd to quarrel with a caterpillar.

The Caterpillar snorted.

"What's the good of talking if you don't mean anything? If you've talked all this time without meaning anything you're not worth listening to."

"But you put a wrong construction——" Alice began.

"You can't discuss Construction now, you know; that comes on the Estimates. Shrivel!"

"I don't understand," said Alice.

"Shrivel. Dry up," explained the Caterpillar, and proceeded to look in another direction, as if it had forgotten her existence.

"Good-bye," said Alice, after waiting a moment; she half hoped that the Caterpillar might say "See you later," but it took not the slightest notice of her remark, so she got up reluctantly and walked away.

"Well, of all the gubernatorial——" said Alice to herself when she got outside. She did not quite know what it meant, but it was an immense relief to be able to come out with a word of six syllables.

ALICE IN DIFFICULTIES[1]

"How are you getting on?" asked the Cheshire Cat.

"I'm not," said Alice.

Which was certainly the truth.

It was the most provoking and bewildering game of croquet she had ever played in. The other side did not seem to know what they were expected to do, and, for the most part, they weren't doing anything, so Alice thought she might have a good chance of winning —though she was ever so many hoops behind. But the ground she had to play over was all lumps and furrows, and some of the hoops were three-cornered in shape, which made them difficult to get through, while as for the balls (which were live hedgehogs and very opinionated), it was all she could do to keep them in position for a minute at a time. Then the flamingo which she was using as a mallet kept stiffening itself into uncompromising attitudes, and had to be coaxed back into a good temper.

"I think I can manage *him* now," she said; "since I let him have a latchkey and allowed him to take up the position he wanted he has been quite amiable. The other flamingo I was playing with," she added regretfully, "strayed off into a furrow. The last I saw of it, it was trying to bore a tunnel."

"A tunnel?" said the Cat.

"Yes; under the sea, you know."

[1] The difficulties are those of the Liberal Party in 1901. The first flamingo (p. 318) is Sir Edward Grey, the second (p. 319) Lord Rosebery.

The "furrow' is an allusion to a speech in which Lord Rosebery had said, "I must plough my furrow alone" (July, 1901). "Cross-currents" was the term usually employed for differences in the Liberal Party.

One of the hedgehogs (p. 318) is labelled "Rattigan," and the other "I.L.P." (Independent Labour Party) on one side and L.I. (Liberal Imperialist) on the other. This is an allusion to the North-East Lanark by-election in September, 1901, when Sir W. H. Rattigan secured the seat through a split in the Liberal and Radical vote, Mr. Cecil Harmsworth standing as a Liberal Imperialist and Mr. R. Smillie as an Independent Labour candidate.

"I see; to avoid the cross-current, of course."

Alice waited till the Cat had stopped grinning at its own joke, and then went on:

"As for the hedgehogs, there's no doing anything with them; they've got such prickly tempers. And they're *so* short-sighted; if they don't happen to be looking the same way they invariably run against each other. I should have won that last hoop if both hedgehogs hadn't tried to get through at the same time."

"Both?"

"Yes, the one I was playing with and the one I wasn't. And every one began shouting out all sorts of different directions till I scarcely knew which I *was* playing with. Really," she continued plaintively, "it's the most discouraging croquet-party I was ever at; if we go on like this there soon won't be any party at all."

"It's no use swearing and humping your back," said the Cat sympathetically. (Alice hadn't done either.) "Keep your temper and your flamingo."

"Is that all?"

"No," said the Cat; "keep on playing *with the right ball.*"

"Which *is* the right ball?" asked Alice.

But the Cat had discreetly vanished.

ALICE ANYWHERE BUT IN DOWNING STREET

"I DON'T know what business you have here," the Red Queen[1] was saying, "if you don't belong to the Cabinet; of course," she added more kindly, "you may be one of the outer ring. There are so many of them, and they're mostly so unimportant, that one can't be expected to remember *all* their faces."

"What is *your* business?" asked Alice, by way of evading the question.

"There isn't any business really," said the White Queen.[2] "Her Red Majesty sometimes says more than she means. Fancy," she added eagerly, "I went round in 85 yesterday!"

"Round what?" asked Alice.

[1] The Red Queen—Mr. Joseph Chamberlain.

[2] The White Queen—Mr. Balfour whose favourite occupation was supposed to be golf.

"The Links, of course."

"Talking about a Lynx," said the Red Queen, "are you any good at Natural History? Take prestige from a Lion, what would remain?"

"The prestige wouldn't, of course," said Alice, "and the Lion might not care to be without it. I suppose nothing——"

"*I* should remain, whatever happened," said the Red Queen with decision.

"She's no good at Natural History," observed the White Queen. "Shall I try her with Christian Science? If there was a sort of warfare going on in a kind of a country, and you wanted to stop it, and didn't know how to, what course of inaction would you pursue?"

"Action, you mean. Her White Majesty occasionally muddles things," interposed the Red Queen.

"It amounts to much the same thing with us," said the White Queen.

Alice pondered. "I suppose I should resign," she hazarded.

Both Queens gasped and held up their hands in reprobation.

"A most improper suggestion," said the White Queen severely. "Now I should simply convince my reasoning faculty that the war didn't exist—and there'd be an end of it."

"But," objected Alice, "supposing the war was to assume that your reasoning faculty was wanting, and went on all the same?"

"The child is talking nonsense," said the Red Queen; "she doesn't know anything of Christian Science. Let's try Political Economy. Supposing you were pledged to introduce a scheme for Old Age Pensions,[3] what would be your next step?"

Alice considered. "I should think——"

"Of course you'd think," said the White Queen, "ever so much. You'd go on thinking off and on for years. I can't tell you how much I've thought about it myself; I still think about it a little, just for practice—principally on Tuesdays."

"I should think," continued Alice, without noticing the interruption, "that the first thing would be to find the money."

"Dear, no," said the Red Queen pityingly, "*that* wouldn't be Political Economy. The first thing would be to find an excuse for dropping the question."

[3] Old Age Pensions: Mr. Chamberlain had pledged himself to a scheme of Old Age Pensions, and he was much criticized by the Opposition in these years for postponing or evading the fulfilment of this pledge.

"What a dreadful lot of unnecessary business we're talking!" said the White Queen fretfully. "It makes me quite miserable—carries me back to the days when I was in Opposition. Can't she sing us something?"

"What shall I sing you?" asked Alice.

"Oh, anything soothing; the 'Intercessional,' if you like."

Alice began, but the words didn't come a bit right, and she wasn't at all sure how the Queens would take it:

Voice of the People, lately polled,
Awed by our broad-cast battle scheme,
By virtue of whose vote we hold
Our licence still to doze and dream,
Still, falt'ring Voice, complaisant shout,
Lest we go out, lest we go out.

Alice looked anxiously at the Queens when she had finished, but they were both fast asleep.

"It will take a deal of shouting to rouse them," she thought.

ALICE LUNCHES AT WESTMINSTER

"I THINK I would rather not hear it just now," said Alice politely.

"It is expressly intended for publication," said Humpty Dumpty[1]; "I don't suppose there'll be a paper tomorrow that won't be talking about it."

1 Humpty Dumpty—General Sir Redvers Buller, V.C. On his return from South Africa in 1901, Sir Redvers was appointed to command the first Army Corps at Aldershot in pursuance of a new Army Reorganization Scheme. There was much criticism of the appointment and on October 10 he answered his critics in a singular speech at the Queen's Hall, Westminster, in which he specially defended himself against the charge that he had counselled the surrender of Ladysmith. His defence was that in heliographing instructions to Sir George White, when he was locked up in Ladysmith, he had "spatchcocked" a passage which would have relieved Sir George of responsibility in case he had found it necessary to surrender, and that this passage had been ungenerously twisted into an instruction to surrender. The speech was so confused and eccentric that it greatly perplexed the public, and ten days later the Government cancelled his appointment on the ground that he had committed a breach of regulations in making it. Sir Redvers suggested in his speech that the Boers had put dead horses into the river Tugela, in order to poison the water for the besieged garrison.

"In that case I suppose I may as well hear it," said Alice with resignation.

"The scene," said Humpty Dumpty, "is Before Ladysmith, and the time—well, the time is After Colenso:

I sent a message to the White
To tell him—if you must, *you might.*
But then, I said, you p'raps might not
(The weather was extremely *hot).*
This query, too, I spatchcock-slid,
How would you do it, if you did?
I did not know, I rather thought—
And then I wondered if I ought."

"It's dreadfully hard to understand," said Alice.

"It gets easier as it goes on," said Humpty Dumpty, and resumed:

They tried a most malignant scheme,
They put dead horses in the stream;
(With One at home I saw it bore
On preference for a horseless war).
But though I held the war might cease,
At least I never held my peace.
I held the key; it was a bore
I could not hit upon the door.
Then One suggested, in my ear,
It would be well to persevere.
The papers followed in that strain,
They *said it very loud and plain.*
I simply answered with a grin,
"Why, what a hurry they are in."
I went and played a waiting game;
Observe, I got there just the same.
And if you have *a better man,*
Well, show him to me, if *you can.*

"Thank you very much," said Alice; "it's very interesting, but I'm afraid it won't help to cool the atmosphere much."

"I could tell you lots more like that," Humpty Dumpty began, but Alice hastily interrupted him.

"I hear a lot of fighting going on in the wood; don't you think I had better hear the rest some other time?"

ALICE IN A FOG

"THE Duke and Duchess!"[1] said the White Rabbit nervously as it went scurrying past; "they may be here at any moment, and I haven't got it yet."

"Hasn't got what?" wondered Alice.

"A rhyme for Cornwall," said the Rabbit, as if in answer to her thought; "borne well, yawn well"—and he pattered away into the distance, dropping in his hurry a folded paper that he had been carrying.

"What have you got there?" asked the Cheshire Cat as Alice picked up the paper and opened it.

"It seems to be a kind of poetry," said Alice doubtfully; "at least," she added, "some of the words rhyme and none of them appear to have any particular meaning."

"What is it about?" asked the Cat.

"Well, some one seems to be coming somewhere from everywhere else, and to get a mixed reception:

. . . Your Father smiles,
Your Mother weeps."

"I've heard something like that before," said the Cat; "it went on, if I remember, 'Your aunt has the pen of the gardener.'"

"There's nothing about that here," said Alice; "supposing she didn't weep when the time came?"

"She would if she had to read all that stuff," said the Cat.

"And then it goes on:

You went as came the swallow."

"That doesn't help us unless we know how the swallow came," observed the Cat. "If he went as the swallow usually travels he would have won the Deutsch Prize."[2]

[1] The Duke of York (now King George V) visited Australia accompanied by the Duchess to open the first session of the Australian Commonwealth Parliament on May 7, 1901, and the Poet Laureate (Mr. Alfred Austin) improved the occasion by writing a royal and loyal ode to greet him on his return. Mr. Austin's poems had been frequently the subject of Gould's satire, and "Saki" takes up the theme.

[2] A prize given for aviation in its early days.

". . . homeward draw
Now it hath winged its way to winters green.

"There seems to have been some urgent reason for avoiding the swallow," continued Alice. "Then all sorts of things happened to the Almanac:

Twice a hundred dawns, a hundred noons, a hundred eves.

"You see there were two dawns to every noon and evening—it must have been dreadfully confusing."

"It would be at first, of course," agreed the Cat.

"I think it must have been that extra dawn that

Never swallow or wandering sea-bird saw

or else it was the Flag."

"What flag?"

"Well, the flag that some one found,

Scouring the field or furrowing the sea."

"Would you mind explaining," said the Cat, "which was doing the scouring and furrowing?"

"The flag," said Alice, "or the some one. It isn't exactly clear, and it doesn't make sense either way. Anyhow, wherever the flag was unfurled it floated o'er the Free."

"Come, that tells us something. Whoever it was must have avoided Dartmoor and St. Helena."

"You, wandering, saw,
Young Commonwealths you found."

"There's a great deal of wandering in the poem," observed the Cat.

"You sailed from us to them, from them to us," continued Alice.

"That isn't new, either. It *should* go on: 'You all returned from him to them, though they were mine before.'"

"It doesn't go on quite like that," said Alice; "it ends up with a lot of words that I suppose were left over and couldn't be fitted in anywhere else:

Therefore rejoicing mightier hath been made
Imperial Power."

"That," said the Cat, "is the cleverest thing in the whole poem. People see that at the end, and then they read it through to see what on earth it's about."

"I'd give sixpence to any one who can explain it," said Alice.

ALICE HAS TEA AT THE HOTEL CECIL[1]

The March Hare and the Dormouse and the Hatter were seated at a very neglected-looking tea-table; they were evidently in agonized consideration of something—even the Dormouse, which was asleep, had a note of interrogation in its tail.

"No room!" they shouted, as soon as they caught sight of Alice.

"There's lots of room for improvement," said Alice, as she sat down.

"You've got no business to be here," said the March Hare.

"And if you had any business you wouldn't be here, you know," said the Hatter; "I hope you don't suppose this is a business gathering. What will you have to eat?" he continued.

Alice looked at a long list of dishes with promising names, but nearly all of them seemed to be crossed off.

"That list was made nearly seven years ago, you know," said the March Hare, in explanation.

"But you can always have patience," said the Hatter. "You begin with patience and we do the rest." And he leaned back and seemed prepared to do a lot of rest.

"Your manners want mending," said the March Hare suddenly to Alice.

"They don't," she replied indignantly.

"It's very rude to contradict," said the Hatter; "you would like to hear me sing something."

Alice felt that it would be unwise to contradict again, so she said nothing, and the Hatter began:

Dwindle, dwindle, little war,
How I wonder more and more,
As about the veldt you hop
When you really mean to stop.

1 Lord Salisbury's Government was frequently spoken of in popular jest as the "Hotel Cecil" in allusion to the supposed predominance of the Cecil family in its composition. The March Hare is Mr. Balfour, the Mad Hatter, Mr. Chamberlain, and the Dormouse, Lord Salisbury. The Boer War, supposed to have been over in September, 1900, is still going on, and the Irish question has again begun to trouble the Government.

"Talking about stopping," interrupted the March Hare anxiously, "I wonder how my timepiece is behaving."

He took out of his pocket a large chronometer of complicated workmanship, and mournfully regarded it.

"It's dreadfully behind the times," he said, giving it an experimental shake. "I would take it to pieces at once if I was at all sure of getting the bits back in their right places."

"What is the matter with it?" asked Alice.

"The wheels seem to get stuck," said the March Hare. "There is too much Irish butter in the works."

"Ruins the thing from a dramatic point of view," said the Hatter; "too many scenes, too few acts."

"The result is we never have time to get through the day's work. It's never even time for a free breakfast-table; we do what we can for education at odd moments, but we shall all die of old age before we have a moment to spare for social duties."

"You might lose a lot if you run your business in that way," said Alice.

"Not in this country," said the March Hare. "You see, we have a Commission on everything that we don't do."

"The Dormouse must tell us a story," said the Hatter, giving it a sharp pinch.

The Dormouse awoke with a start, and began as though it had been awake all the time: "There was an old woman who lived in a shoe——"

"I know," said Alice, "she had so many children that she didn't know what to do."

"Nothing of the sort," said the Dormouse, "you lack the gift of imagination. She put most of them into Treasuries and Foreign Offices and Boards of Trade, and all sorts of unlikely places where they could learn things."

"What did they learn?" asked Alice.

"Painting in glowing colours, and attrition, and terminology (that's the science of knowing when things are over), and iteration (that's the same thing over again), and drawing——"

"What did they draw?"

"Salaries. And then there were classes for foreign languages. And such language!" (Here the March Hare and the Hatter shut their eyes and took a big gulp from their tea-cups.) "However, I don't think anybody attended to them."

The Dormouse broke off into a chuckle which ended in a snore, and as no one seemed inclined to wake it up again Alice thought she might as well be going.

When she looked back the Hatter and the March Hare were trying to stiffen the Dormouse out into the attitude of a lion guardant. "But it will never pass for anything but a Dormouse if it will snore so," she remarked to herself.

ALICE GOES TO CHESTERFIELD[1]

ALICE noticed a good deal of excitement going on among the Looking-Glass creatures; some of them were hurrying off expectantly in one direction, as fast as their legs would carry them, while others were trying to look as if nothing in particular was about to happen.

"Those mimsy-looking birds," she said, catching sight of a group that did not look in the best of spirits, "those must be Borogoves. I've read about them somewhere; in some parts of the country they have to be protected. And, I declare, there is the White King coming through the Wood."

Alice went to meet the King, who was struggling with a very unwieldy pencil to write something in a notebook. "It's a memorandum of my feelings, in case I forget them," he explained. "Only," he added, "I'm not quite sure that I meant to put it that way."

Alice peeped over his shoulder and read: "The High Commissioner may tumble off his post; he balances very badly."

"Could you tell me," she asked, "what all the excitement is about just now?"

"Haven't an idea," said the White King, "unless it's the awakening."

"The what?" said Alice.

"The Red King, you know; he's been asleep for ever so long, and

1 Lord Rosebery's speech at Chesterfield on December 16 was the chief event in Liberal politics in the winter of 1901. It caused extraordinary interest and commotion both before and after, and though the South African parts of it were hailed equally by both sections of the party, it opened a new line of division in domestic policy, to the great embarrassment of Sir Henry Campbell-Bannerman (the White King).

he's going to wake up today. Not that it makes any difference that I can see—he talks just as loud when he's asleep."

Alice remembered having seen the Red King, in rose-coloured armour that had got a little rusty, sleeping uneasily in the thickest part of the wood.

"The fact is," the White King went on, "some of them think we're only a part of his dream, and that we shall all go 'piff' when he wakes up. That is what makes them so jumpy just now. Oh," he cried, giving a little jump himself, "there go some more!"

"What are they?" asked Alice, as several strange creatures hurtled past, like puff-balls in a gale.

"They're the Slithy Toves," said the King, "Libimps and Jubjubs and Bandersnatches. They're always gyring and gimbling wherever they can find a wabe."

"Where are they all going in such a hurry?" Alice asked.

"They're going to the meeting to hear the Red King," the White King said in rather a dismal tone. "They've all got latchkeys," he went on, "but they'd better not stay out too late."

Here the White King gave another jump. "What's the matter?" asked Alice.

"Why, I've just remembered that I've got a latchkey too, my very own! I must go and find it." And away went the White King into the wood.

"How these kings do run about!" thought Alice. "It seems to be one of the Rules of the Game that when one moves the other moves also."

The next moment there was a deafening outburst of drums, and Alice saw the Red King rushing through the wood with a big roll of paper.

"Dear me!" she heard him say to himself as he passed, "I hope I shan't be late for the meeting, and I wonder how they'll take my speech."

Alice noticed that the Borogoves made no attempt to follow, but tried to look as if they didn't care a bit. And away in the distance she heard a sort of derisive booing with a brogue in it. "That must be the Mome Raths outgribing," she thought.

THE AGED MAN

I shook him well from side to side
Until his face was blue.
"Come, tell me where's the Bill," I cried,
"And what you're going to do."
He said, "I hunt for gibes and pins
To prick the Bishops' calves,
I search for Royal Commissions, too,
To use as safety valves."

[*See the Debate on Temperance Legislation in the House of Lords, May 14, 1901.*[1]]

SPADES IN WONDERLAND

THE RED KING: Harcourt, Grey, and Lloyd George are all putting their own colours on, I think I'd better paint it myself.

1 Lord Salisbury chaffed the Bishops and suggested another Royal Commission as the next step, thereby evoking a spirited reply from Lord Rosebery. (See footnote p. 837.)

III
THE PLAYS

The Death-Trap

THE DEATH-TRAP

CHARACTERS

DIMITRI. (*Reigning Prince of Kedaria.*)

Dr. STRONETZ	*Officers of the Kranitzki Regiment of Guards.*
Col. GIRNITZA	
Major VONTIEFF	
Captain SHULTZ	

SCENE:–*An Ante-chamber in the Prince's Castle at Tzern.*

TIME:–*The Present Day. The scene opens about ten o'clock in the evening.*

An ante-chamber, rather sparsely furnished. Some rugs of Balkan manufacture on the walls. A narrow table in centre of room, another table set with wine bottles and goblets near window, R. *Some high-backed chairs set here and there round room. Tiled stove,* L. *Door in centre.*

GIRNITZ, VONTIEFF *and* SHULTZ *are talking together as curtain rises.*

GIRNITZA. The Prince suspects something: I can see it in his manner.

SHULTZ. Let him suspect. He'll know for certain in half an hour's time.

GIR. The moment the Andrieff Regiment has marched out of the town we are ready for him.

SHULTZ (*drawing revolver from case and aiming it at an imaginary person*). And then—short shift for your Royal Highness! I don't think many of my bullets will go astray.

GIR. The revolver was never a favourite weapon of mine. I shall finish the job with this. (*Half draws his sword and sends it back into its scabbard with a click.*)

VONTIEFF. Oh, we shall do for him right enough. It's a pity he's such a boy, though. I would rather we had a grown man to deal with.

GIR. We must take our chance when we can find it. Grown men marry and breed heirs and then one has to massacre a whole family. When we've killed this boy we've killed the last of the dynasty, and laid the way clear for Prince Karl. As long as there was one of this brood left our good Karl could never win the throne.

VONT. Oh, I know this is our great chance. Still I wish the boy could be cleared out of our path by the finger of Heaven rather than by our hands.

SHULTZ. Hush! Here he comes.

(*Enter, by door, centre,* PRINCE DIMITRI, *in undress cavalry uniform. He comes straight into room, begins taking cigarette out of a case, and looks coldly at the three officers.*)

DIMITRI. You needn't wait.

(*They bow and withdraw,* SHULTZ *going last and staring insolently at the* PRINCE. *He seats himself at table, centre. As door shuts he stares for a moment at it, then suddenly bows his head on his arms in attitude of despair. . . . A knock is heard at the door.* DIMITRI *leaps to his feet. Enter* STRONETZ, *in civilian attire.*)

DMITRI (*eagerly*). Stronetz! My God, how glad I am to see you!

STRONETZ. One wouldn't have thought so, judging by the difficulty I had in gaining admission. I had to invent a special order to see you on a matter of health. And they made me give up my revolver; they said it was some new regulation.

DIM. (*with a short laugh*). They have taken away every weapon I possess, under some pretext or another. My sword has gone to be reset, my revolver is being cleaned, my hunting-knife has been mislaid.

STRON. (*horrified*). My God, Dimitri! You don't mean–?

DIM. Yes, I do. I am trapped. Since I came to the throne three years ago as a boy of fourteen I have been watched and guarded against this moment, but it has caught me unawares.

STRON. But your guards!

DIM. Did you notice the uniforms? The Kranitzki Regiment. They are heart and soul for Prince Karl; the artillery are equally disaffected. The Andrieff Regiment was the only doubtful factor in their plans, and it marches out to camp tonight. The Lonyadi Regiment comes in to relieve it an hour or so later.

STRON. They are loyal surely?

DIM. Yes, but their loyalty will arrive an hour or so too late.

STRON. Dimitri! You mustn't stay here to be killed! You must get out quick!

DIM. My dear good Stronetz, for more than a generation the Karl faction have been trying to stamp our line out of existence. I am the last of the lot; do you suppose that they are going to let me slip out of their claws now? They're not so damned silly.

STRON. But this is awful! You sit there and talk as if it were a move in a chess game.

DIM. (*rising*). Oh, Stronetz! if you knew how I hate death! I'm not a coward, but I do so want to live. Life is so horribly fascinating when one is young, and I've tasted so little of it yet. (*Goes to window.*) Look out of the window at that fairyland of mountains with the forest running up and down all over it. You can just see Grodvitz where I shot all last autumn, up there on the left, and far away beyond it all is Vienna. Were you ever in Vienna, Stronetz? I've only been there once, and it seemed like a magic city to me. And there are other wonderful cities in the world that I've never seen. Oh, I do so want to live. Think of it, here I am alive and talking to you, as we've talked dozens of times in this grey old room, and tomorrow a fat stupid servant will be washing up a red stain in that corner–I think it will probably be in that corner. (*He points to corner near stove,* L.)

STRON. But you mustn't be butchered in cold blood like this, Dimitri. If they've left you nothing to fight with I can give you a drug from my case that will bring you a speedy death before they can touch you.

DIM. Thanks, no, old chap. You had better leave before it begins; they won't touch you. But I won't drug myself. I've never seen any one killed before, and I shan't get another opportunity.

STRON. Then I won't leave you; you can see two men killed while you are about it.

(*A band is heard in distance playing a march.*)

DIM. The Andrieff Regiment marching out! Now they won't waste much time! (*He draws himself up tense in corner by stove.*) Hush, they are coming!

STRON. (*rushing suddenly towards* DIMITRI). Quick! An idea! Tear open your tunic! (*He unfastens* DIMITRI's *tunic and appears to be testing his heart. The door swings open and the three officers enter.* STRONETZ *waves a hand commanding silence, and continues his testing. The officers stare at him.*)

GIR. Dr. Stronetz, will you have the goodness to leave the room? We have some business with His Royal Highness. Urgent business, Dr. Stronetz.

STRON. (*facing round*). Gentlemen, I fear my business is more grave. I have the saddest of duties to perform. I know you would all gladly lay down your lives for your Prince, but there are some perils which even your courage cannot avert.

GIR. (*puzzled*). What are you talking of, sir?

STRON. The Prince sent for me to prescribe for some disquieting symptoms that have declared themselves. I have made my examination. My duty is a cruel one. . . . I cannot give him six days to live!

(DIMITRI *sinks into chair near table in pretended collapse. The officers turn to each other, nonplussed.*)

GIR. You are certain? It is a grave thing you are saying. You are not making any mistake?

STRON. (*laying his hand on* DIMITRI's *shoulder*). Would to God I were!

(*The officers again turn, whispering to each other.*)

GIR. It seems our business can wait.

VONT. (*to* DIMITRI). Sire, this is the finger of Heaven.

DIM. (*brokenly*). Leave me.

(*They salute and slowly withdraw.* DIMITRI *slowly raises his head, then springs to his feet, rushes to door and listens, then turns round jubilantly to* STRONETZ.)

DIM. Spoofed them! Ye gods, that was an idea, Stronetz!

STRON. (*who stands quietly looking at* DIMITRI). It was not altogether an inspiration, Dimitri. A look in your eyes suggested it. I had seen men who were stricken with a mortal disease look like that.

DIM. Never mind what suggested it, you have saved me. The Lonyadi Regiment will be here at any moment and Girnitza's gang daren't risk anything then. You've fooled them, Stronetz, you've fooled them.

STRON. (*sadly*). Boy, I haven't fooled them. . . . (DIMITRI *stares at him for a long moment.*) It was a real examination I made while those brutes were waiting there to kill you. It was a real report I made; the malady *is* there.

DIM. (*slowly*). Was it *all* true, what you told them?

STRON. It was all true. You have not six days to live.

DIM. (*bitterly*). Death has come twice for me in one evening. I'm afraid he must be in earnest. (*Passionately.*) Why didn't you let them kill me? That would have been better than this "to-be-left-till-called-for" business. (*Paces across to window,* R., *and looks out. Turns suddenly.*) Stronetz! You offered me a way of escape from a cruel death just now. Let me escape now from a crueler one. I am a monarch. I won't be kept waiting by death. Give me that little bottle.

(STRONETZ *hesitates, then draws out a small case, extracts bottle and gives it to him.*)

STRON. Four or five drops will do what you ask for.

DIM. Thank you. And now, old friend, good-bye. Go quickly. You've seen me just a little brave—I may not keep it up. I want you to remember me as being brave. Good-bye, best of friends, go.

(STRONETZ *wrings his hand and rushes from the room with his face hidden in his arm. The door shuts.* DIMITRI *looks for a moment after his friend. Then he goes quickly over to side table and uncorks wine bottle. He is about to pour some wine into a goblet when he pauses as if struck by a new idea. He goes to door, throws it open and listens, then calls, "Girnitz, Vontieff, Shultz!" Darting back to the table he pours the entire phial of poison into the wine bottle, and thrusts phial into his pocket. Enter the three officers.*)

DIM. (*pouring the wine into four goblets*). The Prince is dead —long live the Prince! (*He seats himself.*) The old feud must be healed now, there is no one left of my family to keep it on, Prince Karl must succeed. Long life to Prince Karl! Gentlemen of the Kranitzki Guards, drink to your future sovereign.

(*The three officers drink after glancing at each other.*)

GIR. Sire, we shall never serve a more gallant Prince than your Royal Highness.

DIM. That is true, because you will never serve another Prince. Observe, I drink fair! (*Drains goblet.*)

GIR. What do you mean, never serve another Prince?

DIM. (*rises*). I mean that I am going to march into the next world at the head of my Kranitzki Guards. You came in here tonight to kill me. (*They all start.*) You found that Death had forestalled you. I thought it a pity that the evening should be wasted, so I've killed *you*, that's all!

SHULTZ. The wine! He's poisoned us!

(VONTIEFF *seizes the bottle, and examines it.* SCHULTZ *smells his empty goblet.*)

GIR. Ah! Poisoned! (*He draws his sword and makes a step towards* DIMITRI, *who is sitting on the edge of the centre table.*)

DIM. Oh, certainly, if you wish it. I'm due to die of disease in a few days and of poison in a minute or two, but if you like to take a little extra trouble about my end, please yourself. (GIRNITZA *reels and drops sword on table and falls back into chair groaning.* SHULTZ *falls across table and* VONTIEFF *staggers against wall. At that moment a lively march is heard approaching.* DIMITRI *seizes the sword and waves it.*)

DIM. Aha! the Lonyadi Regiment marching in! My good loyal Kranitzki Guards shall keep me company into the next world. God save the Prince! (*Laughs wildly.*) Colonel Girnitza, I never thought death . . . could be . . . so amusing.

(*He falls dying to the ground.*)

CURTAIN

Karl-Ludwig's Window

KARL-LUDWIG'S WINDOW

A Drama in One Act

CHARACTERS

KURT VON JAGDSTEIN.
THE GRÄFIN VON JAGDSTEIN (*his mother*).

ISADORA (*his betrothed*) PHILIP (*Isadora's brother*) VIKTORIA (*niece of the Gräfin*) BARON RABEL (*a parvenu*)	*Guests at Schloss Jagdstein*

AN OFFICER.

SCENE:—*"Karl-Ludwig's Room" in the Schloss Jagdstein, on the outskirts of a town in Eastern Europe.*

TIME:—*An evening in Carnival Week, the present day.*

A room furnished in medieval style. In the centre a massive tiled stove of old-German pattern, over which, on a broad shelf, a large clock. Above the clock a painting of a man in sixteenth-

century costume. Immediately to Left, *in a deep embrasure, a window with a high window-seat. Immediately on* Right *of stove an old iron-clamped door, approached by two steps. The* Walls *to* Left *and* Right *are hung with faded tapestry. In the foreground a long oak table, with chairs right, left and centre, and a low armchair on* Left *of stage. On the table are high-stemmed goblets and wine bottles, and a decanter of cognac with some smaller glasses.*

THE GRÄFIN, *in an old Court costume, and* BARON RABEL, *also in some Court attire of a bygone age, are discovered. Both wear little black velvet masks. The* BARON *bows low to the lady, who makes him a mock curtsy. They remove their masks.*

GRÄFIN (*seating herself at left of table*). Of course we old birds are the first to be ready. Light a cigar, Baron, and make yourself at your ease while the young folks are completing their costumes.

BARON (*seating himself at table*). At my ease in this room I could never be. It makes my flesh creep every time I enter it. I am what the world calls a parvenu (*lights cigar*), a man of today, or perhaps I should say of this afternoon, while your family is of the day before yesterday and many yesterdays before that. Naturally I envy you your ancestry, your title, your position, but there is one thing I do not envy you.

GRÄF. (*helping herself to wine*). And that is—?

BAR. Your horrible creepy traditions.

GRÄF. You mean Karl-Ludwig, I suppose. Yes, this room is certainly full of his associations. There is his portrait, and there is the window from which he was flung down. Only it is more than a tradition: it really happened.

BAR. That makes it all the more horrible. I am a man who belongs to a milder age, and it sickens me to think of the brutal deed that was carried through in this room. How his enemies stole in upon him and took him unawares, and how they dragged him screaming to that dreadful window.

GRÄF. Not screaming, I hope; cursing and storming, perhaps. I don't think a Von Jagdstein would scream even in a moment like that.

BAR. The bravest man's courage might be turned to water, looking down at death from that horrid window. It makes one's breath go even to look down in safety; one can see the stones of the courtyard fathoms and fathoms below.

GRÄF. Let us hope he hadn't time to think about it. It would be the thinking of it that would be so terrible.

BAR. (*with a shudder*). Ah, indeed! I assure you the glimpse down from that window has haunted me ever since I looked.

GRÄF. The window is not the only thing in the room that is haunted. They say that whenever one of the family is going to die a violent death that door swings open and shuts again of its own accord. It is supposed to be Karl-Ludwig's ghost coming in.

BAR. (*with apprehensive glance behind him*). What an unpleasant room! Let us forget its associations and talk about something more cheerful. How charming Fräulein Isadora is looking tonight. It is a pity her betrothed could not get leave to come to the ball with her. She is going as Elsa, is she not?

GRÄF. Something of the sort, I believe. She's told me so often that I've forgotten.

BAR. You will be fortunate in securing such a daughter-in-law, is it not so?

GRÄF. Yes, Isadora has all the most desirable qualifications: heaps of money, average good looks, and absolutely no brains.

BAR. And are the young people very devoted to each other?

GRÄF. I am a woman of the world, Baron, and I don't put too high a value on the sentimental side of things, but even I have never seen an engaged couple who made less pretence of caring for one another. Kurt has always been the naughty boy of the family, but he made surprisingly little fuss about being betrothed to Isadora. He said he should never marry any one he loved, so it didn't matter whom I married him to.

BAR. That was at least accommodating.

GRÄF. Besides the financial advantages of the match the girl's aunt has a very influential position, so for a younger son Kurt is doing rather well.

BAR. He is a clever boy, is he not?

GRÄF. He has that perverse kind of cleverness that is infinitely more troublesome than any amount of stupidity. I prefer a fool like Isadora. You can tell beforehand exactly what she will say or do under any given circumstances, exactly on what days she will have a headache, and exactly how many garments she will send to the wash on Mondays.

BAR. A most convenient temperament.

GRÄF. With Kurt one never knows where one is. Now, being in the same regiment with the Archduke ought to be of some advantage to him in his career, if he plays his cards well. But of course he'll do nothing of the sort.

BAR. Perhaps the fact of being betrothed will work a change in him.

GRÄF. You are an optimist. Nothing ever changes a perverse disposition. Kurt has always been a jarring element in our family circle, but I don't regard one unsatisfactory son out of three as a bad average. It's usually higher.

(*Enter* ISADORA, *dressed as Elsa, followed by* PHILIP, *a blond loutish youth, in the costume of a page, Henry III period.*)

ISADORA. I hope we haven't kept you waiting. I've been helping Viktoria; she'll be here presently.

(*They sit at table.* PHILIP *helps himself to wine.*)

GRÄF. We mustn't wait much longer; it's nearly half-past eight now.

BAR. I've just been saying, what a pity the young Kurt could not be here this evening for the ball.

ISA. Yes, it is a pity. He is only a few miles away with his regiment, but he can't get leave till the end of the week. It is a pity, isn't it?

GRÄF. It is always the way: when one particularly wants people they can never get away.

ISA. It's always the way, isn't it?

GRÄF. As for Kurt, he has a perfect gift for never being where you want him.

(*Enter* KURT, *in undress Cavalry uniform. He comes rapidly into the room.*)

GRÄF. (*rising with the others*). Kurt! How come you to be here? I thought you couldn't get leave.

(KURT *kisses his mother's hand, then that of* ISADORA, *and bows to the two men.*)

KURT. I came away in a hurry (*pours out a glass of wine*) to avoid arrest. Your health, everybody. (*Drains glass thirstily.*)

GRÄF. To avoid arrest!

BAR. Arrest!

(KURT *throws himself wearily into armchair,* Left *of Stage, The others stand staring at him.*)

GRÄF. What *do* you mean? Arrest for what?

KURT (*quietly*). I have killed the Archduke.

GRÄF. Killed the Archduke! Do you mean you have murdered him?

KURT. Scarcely that: it was a fair duel.

GRÄF. (*wringing her hands*). Killed the Archduke in a duel! What an unheard-of scandal! Oh, we are ruined!

BAR. (*throwing his arms about*). It is unbelievable! What, in Heaven's name, were the seconds about to let such a thing happen?

KURT (*shortly*). There were no seconds.

GRÄF. No seconds! An irregular duel? Worse and worse! What a scandal! What an appalling scandal!

BAR. But how do you mean—no seconds?

KURT. It was in the highest degree desirable that there should be no seconds, so that if the Archduke fell there would be no witnesses to know the why and wherefore of the duel. Of course there will be a scandal, but it will be a sealed scandal.

GRÄF. Our poor family! We are ruined.

BAR. (*persistently*). But *you* are alive. You will have to give an account of what happened.

KURT. There is only one way in which my account can be rendered.

BAR. (*after staring fixedly at him*). You mean—?

KURT (*quietly*). Yes. I escaped arrest only by giving my *parole* to follow the Archduke into the next world as soon as might be.

GRÄF. A suicide in our family! What an appalling affair. People will never stop talking about it.

ISA. It's very unfortunate, isn't it?

GRÄF. (*crossing over to* ISADORA). My poor child!

(ISADORA *dabs at her eyes.*)

(*Enter* VIKTORIA, *dressed in Italian peasant costume.*)

VIK. I'm so sorry to be late. All these necklaces took such a time to fasten. Hullo, where did Kurt spring from?

(KURT *rises.*)

GRÄF. He has brought some bad news.

VIK. Oh, how dreadful. Anything very bad? It won't prevent us from going to the ball, will it? It's going to be a particularly gay affair.

(*A faint sound of a tolling bell is heard.*)

KURT. I don't fancy there will be a ball tonight. The news has come as quickly as I have. The bells are tolling already.

BAR. (*dramatically*). The scandal is complete!

GRÄF. I shall never forgive you, Kurt.

VIK. But what has happened?

KURT. I should like to say a few words to Isadora. Perhaps you will give us till nine o'clock to talk things over.

GRÄF. I suppose it's the proper thing to do under the circumstances. Oh, why should I be afflicted with such a stupid son!

(*Exit the* GRÄFIN, *followed by the* BARON, *who waves his arms about dramatically, and by* PHILIP *and* VIKTORIA. PHILIP *is explaining matters in whispers to the bewildered* VIKTORIA *as they go out.*)

ISA. (*stupidly*). This is very unfortunate, isn't it?

KURT. (*leaning across table with sudden animation as the door closes on the others*). Isadora, I have come to ask you to do something for me. The search party will arrive to arrest me at nine o'clock and I have given my word that they shall not find me alive. I've got less than twenty minutes left. You *must* promise to do what I ask you.

ISA. What is it?

KURT. I suppose it's a strange thing to ask of a woman I'm betrothed to, but there's really no one else who can do it for me. I want you to take a message to the woman I love.

ISA. Kurt!

KURT. Of course it's not very conventional, but I knew her and loved her long before I met you, ever since I was eighteen. That's only three years ago, but it seems the greater part of my life. It was a lonely and unhappy life, I remember, till she befriended me, and then it was like the magic of some old fairy-tale.

ISA. Do I know who she is?

KURT. You must have guessed that long ago. Your aunt will easily be able to get you an opportunity for speaking to her, and you must mention no name, give no token. Just say "I have a message for you." She will know who it comes from.

ISA. I shall be dreadfully frightened. What is the message?

KURT. Just one word: "Good-bye."

ISA. It's a very short message, isn't it?

KURT. It's the longest message one heart ever sent to another.

Other messages may fade away in the memory, but Time will keep on repeating that message as long as memory lasts. Every sunset and every night-fall will say good-bye for me.

(*The door swings open, and then slowly closes of its own accord.* KURT *represses a shiver.*)

ISA. (*in a startled voice*). What was that? Who opened the door?

KURT. Oh, it's nothing. It does that sometimes when—when—under circumstances like the present. They say it's old Karl-Ludwig coming in.

ISA. I shall faint!

KURT (*in an agonized voice*). Don't you do anything of the sort. We haven't time for that. You haven't given me your promise; oh, do make haste. Promise you'll give the message! (*He seizes both her hands.*)

ISA. I promise.

KURT. (*kissing her hands*). Thank you. (*With a change to a lighter tone.*) I say, you haven't got a loaded revolver on you, have you? I came away in such a hurry I forgot to bring one.

ISA. Of course I haven't. One doesn't take loaded revolvers to a masquerade ball.

KURT. It must be Karl-Ludwig's window then. (*He unbuckles his sword and throws it into the armchair.*) Oh, I forgot. This miniature mustn't be found on me. Don't be scandalized if I do a little undressing. (*He picks up an illustrated paper from a stool near stove and gives it to* ISADORA *to hold open in front of her.*) Here you are. (*He proceeds to unbutton his tunic at the neck and breast and removes a miniature which is hung round his neck. He gazes at it for a moment, kisses it, gazes again, then drops it on the floor and grinds it to pieces with his heel. Then he goes to window, opens it and looks down.*) I wish the night were darker; one can see right down to the flagstones of the courtyard. It looks awful, but it will look fifty times more horrible in eight minutes' time. (*He comes back to table and seats himself on its edge.*) As I rode along on the way here it seemed such an easy thing to die, and now it's come so close I feel sick with fear. Fancy a Von Jagdstein turning coward. What a scandal, as my dear mother would say. (*He tries to pour out some brandy, but his hand shakes too much.*) Do you mind pouring me out some brandy? I can't steady my hand. (ISADORA *fills a glass for him.*) Thanks. No (*Pushing it away*), I won't take it; if I can't have my own courage I won't have that kind. But I wish I hadn't looked down just now. Don't you know what it feels like to go down too quickly in a lift, as if one was racing one's inside and winning by a neck? That's what it will feel like for the first second, and then– (*He hides his eyes a moment in his hands.* ISADORA *falls back in her chair in a faint.* KURT *looks up suddenly at clock.*)

KURT. Isadora! Say that the clock is a minute fast! (*He looks towards her.*) She's fainted. Just what she would do. She isn't a brilliant conversationalist, but she was some one to talk to. How beastly lonely it feels up here. Not a soul to say, "Buck up, Kurt, old boy!" Nothing but a fainting woman and Karl-Ludwig's ghost. I wonder if his ghost is watching me now. I wonder if I shall haunt this room. What a rum idea. (*Looks again at clock and gives a start.*) I *can't* die in three minutes' time. O God! I can't do it. It isn't the jump that I shrink from now–it's the ending of everything. It's too horrible to think of. To have no more life! Isadora and the Baron and millions of stupid people will go on living, every day will bring them something new, and I shall never have one morsel of life after these three minutes. I *can't* do it. (*Falls heavily into chair,* left *of table.*) I'll go away somewhere where no one knows me; that will be as good as dying. I told them they should not find me here alive. Well, I can slip away before they come. (*He rises and moves towards door; his foot grinds on a piece of the broken miniature. He stoops and picks it up, looks hard and long at it, then drops it through his fingers. He turns his head slowly towards the clock and stands watching it. He takes handkerchief from his sleeve and wipes his mouth, returns handkerchief to sleeve, still watching the clock. Some seconds pass in silence. . . . The clock strikes the first stroke of nine.* KURT *turns and walks to the window. He mounts the window-seat and stands with one foot on the sill, and looks out and down. He makes the sign of the Cross . . . throws up his arms and jumps into space.*)

(*The door opens and the* GRÄFIN *enters, followed by an* OFFICER. *They look at the swooning* ISADORA, *then round the room for* KURT.)

GRÄF. He is gone!

OFFICER. He gave me his word that I should find him here at nine o'clock, and that I should come too late to arrest him. It seems he has tricked me!

GRÄF. A Von Jagdstein always keeps his word.

(She stares fixedly at the open window. The OFFICER *follows the direction of her gaze, goes over to window, looks out and down. He turns back to the room, straightens himself and salutes.)*

CURTAIN

The Watched Pot

THE WATCHED POT

(*Alternative Title*)

THE MISTRESS OF BRIONY

"THE WATCHED POT" was written in collaboration with Mr. Charles Maude, who has sent me the following account concerning the play:

"The circumstances of our writing 'The Watched Pot' were: Mr. Frederick Harrison was very interested in your brother's original 'Watched Pot,' but found it unsuitable for the stage, and brought Saki and myself together in the hope that our joint efforts would make it suitable. My share was shortening it, giving it incident, and generally adapting it for stage purposes. Saki used to write more as a novelist than a playwright.

"He and I used to have many friendly quarrels, as he was so full of witty remarks that it was a cruel business discarding some of his *bons mots*. We always used to terminate such quarrels by agreeing to use his axed witticisms in our next play. . . . Shortly before the war Saki at last gave in on the question of plot, and we had practically completed an entirely new story, still retaining the characters which he loved so dearly and which were so typical of his brain."

The character of Hortensia Bavvel is from life, but the tyranny of her prototype was confined to her own family. She died many years ago.

E. M. M.

CHARACTERS

TREVOR BAVVEL.
HORTENSIA. (*Mrs. Bavvel, his mother.*)
LUDOVIC BAVVEL. *His uncle.*
RENÉ ST. GALL.
AGATHA CLIFFORD
CLARE HENESSEY
SYBIL BOMONT
MRS. PETER VULPY
STEPHEN SPARROWBY
(Agatha Clifford, Clare Henessey, Sybil Bomont, Mrs. Peter Vulpy, Stephen Sparrowby: *Guests at Briony.*)
COL. MUTSOME.
THE YOUNGEST DRUMMOND BOY.
WILLIAM. *Page-boy at Briony.*
JOHN. *Under Butler at Briony.*

ACT I. *Briony Manor Breakfast Room.*
ACT II. *Briony Manor Hall (the next evening).*
ACT III. *Briony Manor Breakfast Room (the next morning).*

ACT I

Breakfast Room at Briony Manor.

LUDOVIC *fidgeting with papers at escritoire,* L., *occasionally writing.* MRS. VULPY *seated in armchair,* R., *with her back partially turned to him, glancing at illustrated papers.*

MRS. VULPY (*with would-be fashionable drawl*). So sweet of your dear cousin Agatha to bring me down here with her. Such a refreshing change from the dust and glare of Folkestone.

LUD. (*absently*). Yes, I suppose so.

Mrs. V. And so unexpected. Her invitation took me quite by surprise.

Lud. Dear Agatha is always taking people by surprise. She was born taking people by surprise; in Goodwood Week, I believe, with an Ambassador staying in the house who hated babies. So thoroughly like her. One feels certain that she'll die one of these days in some surprising and highly inconvenient manner; probably from snake-bite on the Terrace of the House of Commons.

Mrs. V. I'm afraid you don't like your cousin.

Lud. Oh, dear, yes. I make it a rule to like my relations. I remember only their good qualities and forget their birthdays. (*With increased animation, rising from his seat and approaching her.*) Excuse the question, Mrs. Vulpy, are you a widow?

Mrs. V. I really can't say with any certainty.

Lud. You can't say?

Mrs. V. With any certainty. According to latest mail advices from Johannesburg my husband, Mr. Peter Vulpy, was not expected by his medical attendants to last into the next week. On the other hand, a cablegram from the local mining organ to a City newspaper over here congratulates that genuine sportsman, Mr. P. Vulpy, on his recovery from his recent severe illness. There happens to be a Percival Vulpy in Johannesburg, so my present information is not very conclusive in either direction. Doctors and journalists are both so untrustworthy, aren't they?

Lud. Could your Mr. P. Vulpy be correctly described as a genuine sportsman?

Mrs. V. There was nothing genuine about Peter. I've never heard of his hitting even a partridge in anger, but he used to wear a horse-shoe scarf-pin, and I've known him to watch football matches, so I suppose he might be described as a sportsman. For all I know to the contrary, he may by this time have joined the majority, who are powerless to resent these intrusions, but my private impression is that he's sitting up and taking light nourishment in increasing doses.

Lud. How extremely unsatisfactory.

Mrs. V. Really, Mr. Bavvel, I think if any one is to mourn Mr. Vulpy's continued existence I should be allowed that privilege. After all, he's my husband, you know. Perhaps you are one of those who don't believe that the marriage tie gives one any proprietary rights.

LUD. Oh, most certainly I do. I am a prospective candidate for Parliamentary honours, and I believe in all the usual things. My objection to Mr. Vulpy's inconvenient vitality is entirely impersonal. If you were in a state of widowhood there would be no obstacle to your marrying Trevor. (*Resumes seat at escritoire, but sits facing her.*)

MRS. V. Marrying Trevor! Really, this is interesting. And why, pray, should I be singled out for that destiny?

LUD. My dear Mrs. Vulpy, let me be absolutely frank with you. Honoured as we should be to welcome you into the family circle, I may at once confess that my solicitude is not so much to see you married to my nephew as to see him married to somebody; happily and suitably married of course, but anyhow—married.

MRS. V. Indeed!

LUD. Briefly, the gist of the business is this. Like most gifted young men, Trevor has a mother.

MRS. V. Oh, I fancy I know *that* already.

LUD. One could scarcely be at Briony for half an hour without making that discovery.

MRS. V. Hortensia, Mrs. Bavvel, is not exactly one of those things that one can hide under a damask cheek, or whatever the saying is.

LUD. Hortensia is a very estimable woman. Most estimable women are apt to be a little trying. Without pretending to an exhaustive knowledge on the subject, I should say Hortensia was the most trying woman in Somersetshire. Probably without exaggeration one of the most trying women in the West of England. My late brother Edward, Hortensia's husband, who was not given to making original observations if he could find others ready-made to his hand, used to declare that marriage was a lottery. Like most popular sayings, that simile breaks down on application. In a lottery there are prizes and blanks; no one who knew her would think of describing Hortensia as either a prize or a blank.

MRS. V. Well, no: she doesn't come comfortably under either heading.

LUD. My brother was distinguished for what is known as a retiring disposition. Hortensia, on the other hand, was dowered with a commanding personality. Needless to say she became a power in the household, in a very short time the only power—a sort of Governor-General and Mother Superior and political Boss rolled into one. A

Catherine the Second of Russia without any of Catherine's redeeming vices.

MRS. V. An uncomfortable sort of person to live with.

LUD. Hortensia did everything that had to be done in the management of a large estate—and a great deal that might have been left undone: she engaged and dismissed gardeners, decided which of the under-gamekeepers might marry and how much gooseberry jam should be made in a given year, regulated the speed at which perambulators might be driven through the village street and the number of candles which might be lighted in church on dark afternoons without suspicion of Popery. Almost the only periodical literature that she allowed in the house was the *Spectator* and the *Exchange and Mart*, neither of which showed any tendency to publish betting news. Halma and chess were forbidden on Sundays for fear of setting a bad example to the servants.

MRS. V. If servants knew how often the fear of leading them astray by bad example holds us back from desperate wickedness, I'm sure they would ask for double wages. And what was poor Mr. Edward doing all this time?

LUD. Edward was not of a complaining disposition, and for a while he endured Hortensia with a certain philosophic calm. Later, however, he gave way to golf.

MRS. V. And Hortensia went on bossing things?

LUD. From the lack of any organized opposition her autocracy rapidly developed into a despotism. Her gubernatorial energies overflowed the limits of the estate and parish, and she became a sort of minor power in the moral and political life of the county, not to say the nation. Nothing seemed to escape her vigilance, whether it happened in the Established Church or the servants' hall or the Foreign Office. She quarrelled with the Macedonian policy of every successive Government, exposed the hitherto unsuspected Atheism of the nearest Dean and Chapter, and dismissed a pageboy for parting his hair in the middle. With equal readiness she prescribed rules for the better management of the Young Women's Christian Association and the Devon and Somerset Staghounds. Briony used to be a favourite rendezvous for the scattered members of the family. Under the Hortensia *régime* we began to find the train service less convenient and our opportunities for making prolonged visits recurred at rare intervals.

Mrs. V. Didn't her health wear out under all that strain of activity?

Lud. With the exception of an occasional full-dress headache, Hortensia enjoyed implacable good health. We resigned ourselves to the prospect of the good lady's rule at Briony for the rest of our natural lives. Then something happened which we had left out of our calculations. Edward caught a chill out otter-hunting and in less than a week Hortensia was a widow. We are what is known as a very united family, and poor dear Edward's death affected us acutely.

Mrs. V. Naturally it would, coming so suddenly.

Lud. At the same time, there was a rainbow of consolation irradiating our grief. Edward's otherwise untimely decease seemed to promise the early dethronement of Hortensia. Trevor was twenty years of age and in the natural course of things he would soon be absolute master of Briony, and the relict of Edward Bavvel would be denuded of her despotic terrors and become merely a tiresome old woman. As I have said, we were all much attached to poor Edward, but somehow his funeral was one of the most cheerful functions that had been celebrated at Briony for many years. Then came a discovery that cast a genuine gloom over the whole affair. Edward had left the management of the estate and the control of his entire and very considerable fortune to Hortensia until such time as Trevor should take unto himself a wife. (*Rises from seat and takes short steps up and down.*) That was six long years ago and Trevor is still unmarried, unengaged, not even markedly attracted towards any eligible female. Hortensia, on the other hand, has—well, ripened, without undergoing any process of mellowing; rather the reverse.

Mrs. V. Aha! I begin to spot the nigger in the timber-yard.

Lud. I beg your pardon?

Mrs. V. I begin to twig. Deprived by Trevor's marriage of her control of the money-bags, Hortensia, as a domestic tyrant, would shrink down to bearable limits.

Lud. (*seating himself*). Hortensia under existing circumstances is like a permeating dust-storm, which you can't possibly get away from or pretend that it's not there. Living with a comparatively modest establishment at the dower-house, she would be merely like Town in August or the bite of a camel—a painful experience which may be avoided with a little ordinary prudence.

MRS. V. I don't wonder that you're keen on the change.

LUD. Keen! There is no one on the estate or in the family who doesn't include it in his or her private litany of daily wants.

MRS. V. And I suppose Mrs. Bavvel is not at all anxious to see herself put on the shelf and does her best to head Mr. Trevor off from any immediate matrimonial projects?

LUD. Of course Hortensia recognizes the desirability of Trevor ultimately finding a suitable consort, if only for carrying on the family. I've no doubt that one day she'll produce some flabby little nonentity who will be flung into Trevor's arms with a maternal benediction.

MRS. V. Meantime you haven't been able to get him to commit himself in any way. But perhaps his mother would break off any engagement she didn't approve of?

LUD. Oh, no fear of that. With all his inertness, Trevor has a wholesome strain of obstinacy in his composition. If he once gets engaged to a girl, he'll marry her. The trouble is that his obstinacy takes the form of his refusing to be seriously attracted by any particular competitor. If patient, determined effort on the part of others would have availed he would have been married dozens of times, but a touch of real genius is required. That is why I appeal to you to help us.

MRS. V. I suppose Agatha considers herself in the running?

LUD. Poor Agatha has a perfect genius for supporting lost causes. I've no doubt she fancies she has an off chance of becoming Mrs. Trevor Bavvel. I've equally no doubt that she never will. Agatha is one of those unaccountable people who are impelled to keep up an inconsequent flow of conversation if they detect you trying to read a book or write a letter, and if you should be suffering from an acknowledged headache she invariably bangs out something particularly triumphant on the nearest piano by way of showing that she at least is not downhearted. Or if you want to think out some complicated problem she will come and sit by your side and read through an entire bulb catalogue to you, with explanatory comments of her own. No, we are all very fond of Agatha, but strictly as a cheerful inane sort of person to have about the house —some one else's house for preference.

MRS. V. And what about Miss Henessey?

LUD. Oh, Clare; she's a rattling good sort in her way, and at one time I used to hope that she and Trevor might hit it off. I think in his own sleepy way he was rather attracted to her. Unfortunately, she only pays rare visits here, and even that she has to keep dark. You see, she's the favourite grandniece and prospective heiress of old Mrs. Packington—you've heard of Mrs. Packington?

MRS. V. No; who is she?

LUD. She lives near Bath, and she's fabulously old, and fabulously rich, and she's been fabulously ill for longer than any living human being can remember. I believe she caught a chill at Queen Victoria's coronation and never let it go again. The most human thing about her is her dislike for Hortensia, who, I believe, once advised her to take more exercise and less medicine. The old lady has ever since alluded to her as a rattlesnake in dove's plumage, and has more than once, with her dying breath, cautioned Clare against intercourse with Briony and its inhabitants. So, you see, there's not much to be hoped for in that direction.

MRS. V. Awfully provoking, isn't it? What about Sybil Bomont?

LUD. Ah, Sybil is the one ray of hope that I can see on the horizon. Personally, she's rather too prickly in her temperament to suit me. She has a fatal gift for detecting the weak spots in her fellow humans and sticking her spikes into them. Matrimony is not reputed to be an invariable bed of roses, but there is no reason why it should be a cactus-hedge. However, she is clever enough to keep that side of her character to the wall whenever Trevor is alongside.

MRS. V. And you think she's got a good sporting chance with him?

LUD. She isn't losing any opportunities that come along, and I'm naturally trying my best to drive the game up her way, but the daily round at Briony doesn't give us much help. We begin the day with solid breakfast businesses; then there are partridges to be tramped after, and Trevor takes his birds rather solemnly, as though it hurt him more than it does them, you know. In the evening a solid dinner, and then Bridge for such small stakes that even Agatha can't lose enough in a fortnight to convince her that she can't play. Then bed.

MRS. V. Well, that's not a very promising programme for any one who's working a matrimonial movement. Couldn't we get up something that would supply a few more openings? Why not theatricals?

LUD. Theatricals? At Briony! You might as well suggest a massacre of Christian villagers. Hortensia looks on the stage and everything that pertains to it as a sort of early door to the infernal regions.

MRS. V. What about a gymkhana?

LUD. Infinitely worse. The mention of a gymkhana would suggest to Hortensia's mind the unchastened restlesssness of the Anglo-Saxon grafted on to the traditional licentiousness of the purple East. The very word "gymkhana" reeks with an aroma of long drinks, sweepstakes, and betrayed husbands, and the usual things that are supposed to strew the social horizon east of Suez.

MRS. V. Well, I'm afraid it's hopeless. I give it up.

LUD. (*rising hastily from his seat*). Dear Mrs. Vulpy, on no account give it up. I rely so much on your tact and insight and experience. You *must* think of something. I'm not a wealthy man, but if you help me to pull this through I promise you my gratitude shall take concrete shape. A commemorative bracelet, for instance—have you any particular favourite stones?

MRS. V. I love all stones—except garnets or moonstones.

LUD. You think it unlucky to have moonstones?

MRS. V. Oh, distinctly, if you've the chance of getting something more valuable. I adore rubies; they're so sympathetic.

LUD. I'll make a note of it. (*Writes in pocketbook.*)

MRS. V. I gather that we're to concentrate on Sybil?

LUD. Sybil, certainly. And of course if there's anything I can do to back you up— (*Enter* CLARE *and* SYBIL *by door:* Left *back*) . . . no, I don't know that part of Switzerland; I once spent a winter at St. Moritz.

(CLARE *seats herself on couch,* R. SYBIL *takes chair in centre stage.*)

CLARE. You needn't pretend you're discussing Swiss health resorts, because you're not.

MRS. V. Oh, but we are, Miss Henessey. I was just saying Montreux was so——

CLARE. You were discussing Trevor and possible Mrs. Trevors. My dear Mrs. Vulpy, it's our one subject of discussion here.

SYBIL. It's a frightfully absorbing subject, especially for me.

CLARE. Why for you especially?

SYBIL. Oh, well, dear.

LUD. We did touch on the subject, I admit, and Mrs. Vulpy has very kindly offered to help matters along in that direction if she can find an opportunity.

SYBIL. Have you had bad news from South Africa?

MRS. V. Oh, dear, no. My offer is quite disinterested.

SYBIL. How noble of you. How do you propose to begin?

MRS. V. Well, I was just suggesting a little departure from the usual routine of life here, something that would give an opening for a clever girl to bring a man to the scratch. But it seems that Mrs. Bavvel is rather against any of the more promising forms of entertainment.

SYBIL. We've had the annual harvest thanksgiving, but Trevor was seedy and couldn't help with the decorations.

MRS. V. Harvest thanksgiving?

CLARE. Yes, it's one of our rural institutions. We get our corn and most of our fruit from abroad, but we always assemble the local farmers and tenantry to give thanks for the harvest. So broad-minded of us. It shows such a nice spirit for a Somersetshire farmer to be duly thankful for the ripening of the Carlsbad plum.

MRS. V. Is Mrs. Bavvel never absent at dinner parties or anything of that sort? A little impromptu frolic is sometimes a great success.

LUD. Now if you're going to plot anything illicit I must really leave you. Hortensia is not in very great demand as a dinner guest, but she is taking me tomorrow to a meeting at Panfold in connexion with the opening of a Free Library there, and there will be a reception of some sort in the Town Hall afterwards. I entirely disapprove of anything of a festive nature taking place here behind her back, but—we shan't be home much before midnight. It's a fairly long drive. Understand, I entirely disapprove.

(*Gathers papers and Exits, door* Left *front.*)

SYBIL. This threatens to be rather sporting. What have you got up your sleeve?

MRS. V. Oh, nothing, only why not beat up your men and girl friends at short notice and have a Cinderella? There's a lovely floor in the morning room and a good piano, and you could have a scratch supper.

CLARE. And how about the servants? Are we to beg them all individually to hold their tongues about the affair?

MRS. V. Oh, of course Mrs. Bavvel would have to know about it next day.

CLARE. It's very well for you to talk like that, you're a comparative stranger here, and I dare say you'd find a certain amount of amusement in the situation. Those of us who know what Hortensia is like when anything displeases her—well, it would simply be a case of Bradshaw at breakfast and a tea-basket at Yeovil.

MRS. V. But then we're playing to win; it's a sort of *coup d'état.* With the fun and excitement of the dancing and the music, and of course the sitting-out places, and, above all, the charming sense of doing something wrong, the betting is that Trevor will be engaged to one of you girls before the night's out. And then the morrow can be left to take care of itself.

SYBIL. It sounds *lovely*. I'm horribly frightened of Hortensia, but I'm game to get up this dance.

CLARE. A *coup d'état* is a wretchedly messy thing. It's as bad as cooking with a chafing-dish; it takes such ages to clean things up afterwards.

(*Enter* AGATHA *door* Right *back, with two large baskets piled with asters, dahlias, etc., and long trails of ivy and brambles.*)

AGATHA. Hullo, you idle people. I'm just going to arrange the flowers. (*Puts baskets down on escritoire.*)

SYBIL. Are you? Why?

AGATHA. Oh, I always do when I'm here. (*Begins slopping flowers and leaves about in inconvenient places.*)

MRS. V. We're plotting to have a little impromptu dance here tomorrow night.

AGATHA (*spilling a lot of dahlias over* MRS. VULPY). Oh, you dear things, how delightful! But whatever will Hortensia say?

SYBIL. Hortensia is opening an Ear Hospital or Free Library or some such horror at Panfold, and won't know about it till it's all over, and then it will be too late to say much.

CLARE. I fancy you'll find that Hortensia's motto will be "better late than never."

AGATHA. Oh, I fancy she'll be rather furious. But what fun, all the same. But who will we get to come?

SYBIL. Oh, we can get nine couples easily. There's all the Abingdon house party, they'll be dead nuts on it And Evelyn Bray plays dance music like a professional.

AGATHA. What a lovely joke. I say—let's make it a fancy dress affair while we're about it.

SYBIL. Oh, let's have fireworks on the lawn and Salome dances and a looping-the-loop performance.

AGATHA. That's talking nonsense. But fancy dress is so easily managed. I went to a ball in North Devon three years ago as Summer, and it was all done at a moment's notice. Just a dress of some soft creamy material with roses in my hair and a few sprays of flowers round the skirt. I've got the dress with me somewhere, and it wouldn't need very much alteration.

SYBIL. It will only want letting out a bit at the waist, and you can call yourself "St. Martin's Summer."

AGATHA. How dare you say such things! Really, you're the most spiteful tongued person I know. I should think you'd better go as an East Wind.

SYBIL. My dear Agatha, I'm not one of the Babes in the Wood, so I wish you'd stop covering me with leaves. And don't let us start quarrelling. Of course you're as jumpy as a grasshopper at the idea of this dance, and I suppose you flatter yourself that you're going to pull it off with Trevor. Because a man has refused you twice there's no particular reason for supposing that he'll accept you at the third bidding. It's merely a superstition.

AGATHA (*furiously*). You utterly odious fablemonger! I suppose it's considered clever to say ill-natured, untrue things about people you happen to be jealous of.

MRS. V. My dear girls, don't waste time in a sparring match. There's no sense quarrelling when we want to get our little scheme started.

SYBIL. *I* don't want to quarrel; I'm only too ready to be accommodating all round. If I *do* chance to land a certain eligible individual in my net I'm quite willing to turn my second-best prospect over to any one that applies for him; quite a darling, with a decent rent roll, and a perfect martyr to asthma; ever so many climates that he can't live in, and you'll have to keep him on a gravel soil. Awfully good arrangement. A husband with asthma has all the advantages of a captive golf-ball; you always know pretty well where to put your hand on him when you want him.

AGATHA. But if I had a really nice man for a husband I should want him to be able to come with me wherever I went.

SYBIL. A woman who takes her husband about with her everywhere is like a cat that goes on playing with a mouse long after she's killed it.

MRS. V. First catch your mouse. Which brings us back to the subject of the dance. I think we agree that fancy dress is out of the question?

CLARE. There wouldn't be time.

MRS. V. Well, why not make it a sheet-and-pillow-case dance? (*They all stare at her.*) Quite simple, every one drapes themselves in sheets, with a folded pillow-case arranged as a head-dress, and a little linen mask completes the domino effect. No trouble, only takes ten minutes to arrange, and at a given time every one sheds their masks and headgear, and the sheets make a most effective sort of Greek costume. Lulu Duchess of Dulverton gave quite a smart sheet-and-pillow-case at Bovery the other day.

AGATHA. Was it respectable?

MRS. V. Absolutely. Oh, do take your blessed bramble-bush somewhere else. (AGATHA, *who has impaled* MRS. VULPY'S *skirt on a trail of briars, makes violent efforts to disentangle her.*) No, please leave my skirt where it is. I only want the brambles removed.

AGATHA. That's the worst of briars, they do catch on to one's clothes so.

MRS. V. That is one of the reasons why I never sit down in a bramble patch for choice. Of course, if one has a tame hedge following one about the house, one can't help it.

AGATHA (*gathering up remains of her foliage*). Well, I shall go and do the dining-room vases now and leave you irritable things to work out the dance programme. I'll think out a list of people we can invite.

[*Exit, door* Left *front.*

CLARE. Agatha would be almost tolerable in the Arctic regions where the vegetation is too restricted to be used as house decoration.

SYBIL. Look here, I'll bike over to the Abingdons' and get things in marching order there. I've just time before lunch. You're going to help us, I suppose, Clare?

CLARE. Oh, if you are all bent on having a domestic earthquake, I'll stand in with you. I'll send notes over to Evelyn and the Drummond boys. But I know the whole thing will be a horrid fizzle.

SYBIL. You dear old thing. You always turn up trumps when it comes to the pinch.

CLARE. If you dare to call me a dear old thing I'll allude to you in public as a brave little woman. So there.

MRS. V. Well, if you two are going to start sparring, I shall go and write letters.

[*Exit,* MRS. VULPY, *door R. back.*

CLARE. There's something I don't like about that woman. She looks at me sometimes in a way that's almost malicious. What on earth did Agatha bring her down here for?

Sybil. Mrs. Vulpy is somewhat of a rough diamond, no doubt.

Clare. So many people who are described as rough diamonds turn out to be merely rough paste.

Sybil. Even paste has its uses.

Clare. Oh, afflictions of most kinds have their uses, I suppose, but one needn't go out of one's way to import them. (*Exit* Sybil, R. *back; Enter* Trevor, L. *back; he is about to sit on couch.*) Be careful where you sit, Trevor. Agatha has been shedding bits of bramble all over the room. (*They both begin picking bits of leaf, etc., off the couch.*) When that parable was being read at prayers this morning about going to the hedges and by-ways to fetch in the halt and the blind, I couldn't help thinking Agatha wouldn't have stopped at that: she'd have brought in the hedges as well.

Trevor (*seating himself with caution on couch*). I've just had about a wheelbarrow-load of gorse prickles removed from the cozy corner in the smoking-room.

Clare. Gorse prickles? (*Seats herself on couch.*)

Trevor. Agatha said it was a Japanese design. If it had been an accident I could have forgiven it. I say, Clare, do you know you have got rather beautiful eyes?

Clare. How should I know, you've never mentioned it before.

Trevor. Oh, well, I noticed it long ago, but it takes me ages to put my thoughts into words.

Clare. That's rather unfortunate where compliments are concerned. By the time it occurs to you to tell me that I've got a nice profile I shall probably have developed a double chin.

Trevor. And that will be the time when you'll be best pleased at being told you've got a nice profile. So you see there's some sense in holding back a compliment.

Clare. Well, don't be horrid and sensible, just when you were beginning to be interesting. It's not often one catches you in the mood for paying compliments. Please begin over again.

Trevor. Item, a pair of beautiful eyes, one rather nice chin, with power to add to its number. Quite a lot of very pretty hair, standing in its own grounds—or is it semi-detached?

Clare. I don't think your compliments are a bit nice; I don't mind how long you keep them back.

Trevor. I haven't finished yet. (*Takes her hand.*) Do you know, Clare, you've got the most charming hand in the world, because it's a friendly hand. I think if you were once friends with a fellow you'd always be friends with him, even——

CLARE. Even–?

TREVOR. Even if you married him, and that's saying a great deal.

CLARE. I think if I liked a man well enough to marry him I should always be the best of friends with him.

(*Enter* LUDOVIC, *bustles over to escritoire.*)

LUD. (*as they let go each other's hands*). Hullo, has Trevor been telling you your fortune?

CLARE (*rising*). Nothing so romantic; he's been explaining the finger-print system of criminal investigation. If I ever strangle Agatha in a moment of justifiable irritation Trevor will be a most damaging witness.

(LUDOVIC *rings bell and then seats himself at escritoire.*)

TREVOR. Shall I be disturbing you if I smoke a cigarette here?

LUD. Not in the least. I like seeing people idle when I'm occupied. It gives me the impression that I'm working so much harder than I am.

CLARE. Don't be long over your cigarette, Trevor, you've got to be let into a conspiracy that Mr. Ludovic isn't supposed to know anything about. [*Exit* CLARE.

TREVOR. Are they plotting to give you a birthday present or something of that sort?

LUD. Nothing so laudable.

(*Enter* WILLIAM, R. *front.*)

WILL. Did you ring, sir?

LUD. Yes, just arrange the flowers.

WILL. Yes, sir. (*Gathers up flowers and foliage from various places where* AGATHA *has stacked and strewn them and proceeds to re-arrange them with considerable taste.*)

LUD. (*to* TREVOR). No, it's your despotic mother who mustn't get wind of the plot. I am merely the innocent by-stander.

TREVOR. I'm awfully fond of my mother of course, but I must admit things would be a little more comfortable if she wasn't quite so–so——

LUD. Exactly. But she always has been and she always will be. As regards household affairs, of course I've no right to express an opinion, but her constant supervision of the political affairs of the neighbourhood is extremely embarrassing to the Party. My prospective candidature down here is becoming more and more doubtful under the circumstances. Hortensia is not content with having her finger in the pie, she wants to put the whole dish into her pocket.

WILL. (*who is standing near doorway*). Mrs. Bavvel is crossing the hall, sir.

LUD. (*becomes violently busy at escritoire*). The factory system in East Prussia presents many interesting points of comparison—(*Enter* HORTENSIA, R. LUDOVIC *rises.*) Ah, Hortensia.

HOR. William, what are you doing here?

WILL. Arranging the flowers, ma'am.

HOR. They don't want arranging every day. They were arranged only yesterday. (*Seats herself on chair in centre of stage.* LUDOVIC *resumes seat.*)

WILL. It was brought on prematurely, ma'am.

LUD. Agatha had been trying some new effects in autumnal foliage; I told William to put things straight a bit.

HOR. I see. And where is Adolphus?

WILL. The cockatoo, ma'am? She's drying in the pantry after her bath.

HOR. It's not his day for a bath. He always bathes on Thursday.

WILL. She seemed restless, as if she wanted it, ma'am.

HOR. In future, remember he bathes on Thursdays only. And, William——

WILL. Yes, ma'am.

HOR. I think I've spoken about it before. You always hear me allude to the cockatoo as he, or Adolphus, therefore you are not to speak of him in the feminine gender.

WILL. Yes, ma'am. [*Exit,* L. *front.*

HOR. A quiet-mannered boy and always behaves reverently at prayers, but I'm afraid he's inclined to be opinionated. What coverts are you shooting this afternoon, Trevor?

TREVOR. The other side of the long plantation.

HOR. I understand that you are employing one of the Brady boys as a beater. I do not approve of the selection. Kindly discontinue his services.

TREVOR. But, mother, the Bradys are dreadfully poor.

HOR. Not deservingly poor. Mrs. Brady is the most thriftless woman in the parish. Some people can't help being poor, but Mrs.

Brady is poor as if she enjoyed it. I'm not going to have that sort of thing encouraged.

LUD. (*rising from seat*). There is another aspect of the matter which I think you are losing sight of, Hortensia. Mrs. Brady may be poor in this world's goods, but she is rich in relatives. She has a husband and one or two uncles, and at least three brothers, and they all have votes. The non-employment of the Brady boy may lose us all those votes at the next election.

HOR. My dear Ludovic, I am not inattentive to local political needs. I supervise the issue of pamphlets dealing with the questions of the day to all electors, in monthly instalments. When the next election comes you may be sure it won't take me by surprise.

LUD. No, but the result may. (*Resumes his seat.*)

HOR. Trevor, oblige me by taking an amended list of beaters to the head-keeper, with the Brady boy left out. Go now, or you will forget.

TREVOR (*rising unwillingly*). As you will, mother. He made a very good beater, you know.

HOR. But not a suitable one. (*Exit* TREVOR. LUDOVIC *throws up his hands.*) Who is this Mrs. Vulpy that Agatha has brought down? I don't care for the look of her.

LUD. I believe Agatha met her at Folkestone.

HOR. That doesn't make it any better. Agatha says she's seen trouble, but she doesn't explain what sort of trouble. Some women see trouble with their eyes open.

LUD. I believe she has a husband in Johannesburg.

HOR. To have a husband in Johannesburg might be a source of anxiety or inconvenience, but it can hardly be called seeing trouble.

LUD. Agatha is so good-natured that she's very easily imposed on.

HOR. I wish her good nature would occasionally take the form of consulting other people's interests. I suppose this Mrs. Vulpy is married after a fashion, though we really know nothing about her. She may be merely a husband-hunting adventuress, and of course Trevor is sufficiently important as a matrimonial prize to attract that sort of woman. Agatha ought to be more careful.

LUD. Wouldn't it be as well, in view of such dangers, if Trevor were to bestir himself to find a suitable wife?

HOR. Nothing of the sort. I must ask you not to give him any advice of that sort. Trevor is far younger than his years, and there is no need to suggest marriage to him for a long while to come. If I thought he had any present intentions that way I should be far more particular what sort of girls I had staying down here. Sybil Bomont and Miss Henessey, for instance, I've no objections to them as guests, but I should require quite a different type of young woman for a daughter-in-law.

LUD. Trevor may have his own views on the subject.

HOR. Hitherto he has expressed none. I must go and write to the Bishop.

LUD. About Trevor?

HOR. (*rising*). *No.* About the Dean of Minehead.

LUD. What has the Dean been doing?

HOR. He has treated me with flippancy. I had written asking if he could give me any material for a lecture I am going to give next week on the Puritan movement in England. He replies on a post-card (*reads*): "The Puritan movement was a disease, wholesome though irritating, which was only malignant if its after effects were not guarded against." Things have come to a disgraceful pass when a Church dignitary can treat the Puritan movement in that spirit.

LUD. Perhaps the Dean was only exercising a little clerical humour.

HOR. I don't think the subject lends itself to jest, and I certainly don't intend that my lecture shall be regarded in a spirit of frivolity. I've something better to do than provide an outlet for Deanery humour. My letter to the Bishop will contain some pretty plain speaking.

LUD. My dear Hortensia, the Dean of Minehead is one of the few churchmen in these parts who give us political support. It would be rather unfortunate to fall out with him.

HOR. In my opinion, it would be still more unfortunate to tolerate post-card flippancies on serious subjects from men in his position. I shall ask the Bishop, among other things, whether it is not high time that certain clerical clowns ceased their unfair competition with the music-halls.

(*Exit* HORTENSIA, R. *back.* LUDOVIC *goes through pantomime of tragic disgust.*)

(*Enter* BUTLER, L. *back.*)

BUTLER. Mr. St. Gall to see you, sir.

LUD. René! What on earth brings him down here? Show him in.

(*Exit* BUTLER, L. *back. Enter* RENÉ, L. *back, crosses stage without shaking hands, looks at himself in mirror,* R.)

RENÉ. I've lost my mother.

LUD. (*wheeling round in chair*). Do I understand you to mean that your mother is dead?

RENÉ (*who has carefully settled himself in armchair,* R.). Oh, nothing so hackneyed. I don't think my mother will ever die as long as she can get credit. She was a Whortleford, you know, and the Whortlefords never waste anything. No, she's simply disappeared and I was wired for. It was most inconvenient.

LUD. But can't she be found?

RENÉ. The butler says she can't. Personally I haven't tried. Only got down late last night. And I've had to come away with simply nothing to wear. I've been in Town for the last three days having some clothes made, and I was to have had two new lounge suits tried on this morning for the first time. Naturally I'm a bit upset.

LUD. But about your mother's disappearance—aren't you doing anything?

RENÉ. Oh, everything that could be done at short notice. We've notified the police and the family solicitors and consulted a crystal-gazer, and we've told the dairy to send half a pint less milk every day till further notice. I can't think of anything else to do. It's the first time I've lost a mother, you know.

LUD. But do you mean to say there's absolutely no trace of her? Why, I saw her in church only last Sunday.

RENÉ. I expect they've looked for her there; but the butler says they've searched everywhere. The servants have been awfully kind and helpful about it. They say they must put their trust in Christian Science, and go on drawing their wages as if nothing had happened. That's all very well, but no amount of Christian Science will help me to be fitted on when I'm here and my clothes are in Sackville Street, will it?

LUD. I think you might show a little natural anxiety and emotion.

RENÉ. But I am showing emotion in a hundred little ways if you'd only notice them. To begin with, I'm walking about practically naked. This suit I've got on was paid for last month, so you may judge how old it is. And that reminds me, I wish you'd do something for me. Something awfully kind and pet-lamb in my hour of trouble. Lend me that emerald scarf-pin that you hardly ever wear. It would go so well with this tie and I should forget how shabbily I'm dressed.

LUD. It would go so well that it would forget to find its way back again. Things that are lent to you, René, are like a hopeless passion, they're never returned. In the light of past experience I absolutely refuse to lend you a thirty-guinea scarf-pin.

RENÉ. How true it is that when one weeps one weeps alone. Anyway, you might lend me your pearl and turquoise one; the pearl is a very poor one, and it can't be worth anything like thirty guineas.

LUD. I don't see why I should be expected to make you a present of it, even if it only cost five.

RENÉ. Oh, well, after all, I've lost a mother. I make less fuss about that than you do at the prospect of separation from a five-guinea scarf-pin. You might show a little kindness to a poor grass orphan. And, Ludovic, now that you've practically given way on that matter, I want you to turn your attention to something that's been worrying me dreadfully of late.

LUD. Gracious, what have you been doing now?

RENÉ. Oh, it isn't now, the mischief was done twenty-three years ago, and then it wasn't exactly my doing. It's just this, that I'm twenty-three years old. If my mother had only held me over a matter of four years I should be nineteen now, which is the only age worth being. Women always rush things so. I shouldn't mind so much being twenty-three if I had the money to carry it off well. The mater does the best she can for me; she can't afford me an allowance, but she borrows money whenever she can from friends and acquaintances, and sends me haphazard cheques. It's quite exciting getting a letter from home. Of course that sort of thing can't go on indefinitely, and now that my only source of income has disappeared without leaving a postal address things have nearly come to a crisis. One can't treat life indefinitely as a prolonged Saturday-to-Monday. There are always the Tuesdays to be reckoned with.

LUD. I don't like to suggest anything so unbecoming as an occupation, but can't you manage to get entangled with a salary of some sort?

RENÉ. It's not so beastly easy. I've tried designing posters, and for three weeks I was assistant editor of a paper devoted to fancy mice. The devotion was all on one side. Now, Ludovic, if you'd only do what you sometimes half promised to do, and make me your personal private secretary, and let me do Parliamentary correspondence for you, and tell female deputations that they can't see you because you're in your bath, and all that sort of thing that a busy man can't do for himself——

LUD. My dear boy, I'm not at the present moment a member of Parliament, I'm not even standing as a candidate.

RENÉ. But, Ludo, why aren't you? You know you've had a hankering that way for a long time, and you can easily afford it. And it isn't a difficult job. All one has to do is to boil with indignation at discreet intervals over something—the Jews in Russia or impurity in beer or lawlessness in the Church of England. It doesn't matter particularly what, as long as you really boil. The public likes a touch of the samovar about its representatives. And, then, if you want to be a Parliamentary wit, *that* isn't difficult nowadays. If the Government is making a mess of Persian affairs just mew like a Persian kitten whenever a Minister gets up to speak. It isn't anything really hard I'm asking of you.

LUD. Thanks very much for coaching me. But an indispensable preliminary to all this brilliance is that I should be elected.

RENÉ. You could easily get a seat down here if you wanted to. They've always wanted one of the Bavvels to stand, and old Spindleham is not likely to last another session, so the ball is practically at your feet.

LUD. My dear René, under present circumstances Briony would be an impossible headquarters from which to conduct an election campaign. Have you considered that Hortensia would have her finger in the pie all the time? She would speak at my meetings and pledge me to the most appalling social and political doctrines. She would get down the most unfortunate specimens of the party to support me—in fact, by the time election day came round I should feel inclined to vote against myself. I should very probably be defeated, and if I got in Hortensia would look on me as her nominee, sent to Westminster to represent her views on every subject under the sun. I shouldn't have half an hour's peace. No, as long as Hortensia remains in the foreground I shan't contest a seat in this part of the country. That's absolutely certain.

RENÉ. Ludovic, this Hortensia business is getting to be absurd. Everything you want to do down here you run up against Hortensia, Mrs. Bavvel. When *are* you going to get Trevor married and the old woman dethroned?

LUD. My dear René, as if we hadn't tried! Talk about bringing a horse to the water, we've brought water to the horse, gallons of it, and put it right under his nose. We've advertised eligible young women as if they had been breakfast foods.

RENÉ. And here am I, twenty-three years old, expecting to wait indefinitely for my secretaryship and my daily bread until Trevor chooses to suit himself with a wife. It's really ridiculous. That's the worst of you middle-aged folks, if I may say so without offence. You're so jolly well content to wait for things to happen. It's only the old and the quite young who really know the value of hurry.

LUD. But, bless my soul, we can't compel Trevor to marry.

RENÉ. It's absurd of him to persist in celibacy that he isn't qualified for. He's decent enough in his way, but he hasn't got the strength of character to fit him for the graver responsibilities of bachelorhood. Can't he be rushed into marrying somebody?

LUD. Rushing Trevor is not exactly a hopeful operation. It's rather suggestive of stampeding a tortoise; at the same time, I may tell you in confidence that something desperate of that nature is going to be tried tomorrow night in the absence of Hortensia and myself at Panfold.

RENÉ. Oh, Ludovic! What?

LUD. You must ask Sybil or some of the others for details. I know nothing about it and entirely disapprove, but the idea originated with me. Hush!

(*Enter* HORTENSIA, *door* R. *back.*)

(LUDOVIC *and* RENÉ *rise to their feet.*)

HOR. I want you to read my letter to the Bishop. Oh, Mr. St. Gall. I didn't know the neighbourhood was honoured with your presence. I needn't ask if you're on a holiday; that is a permanent condition with you, I believe.

LUD. Mr. St. Gall has lost his mother—she's disappeared.

HOR. Disappeared! What an extraordinary thing to do. Had she any reasons for disappearing?

RENÉ. Oh, several, but my mother would never do anything for a reason.

HOR. But was anything troubling her? (*Sits chair centre of stage.*)

RENÉ. Oh, nothing of that kind. She's one of those people with a conscience silk-lined throughout.

LUD. Has she any relatives that she might have gone to?

RENÉ. Relatives? None that she's on speaking terms with. She was a Whortleford, you know, and the Whortlefords don't speak. There is a cousin of hers, a Canon, somewhere in the Midlands; he's got peculiar views—he believes in a future life, or else he doesn't, I forget which. The mater and he used to be rather chummy, but a hen came in between them.

Hor. A hen?

René. Yes, a bronze Orpington or some such exotic breed; the mater sold it to him at a rather exotic price. It turned out afterwards that the bird was an abstainer from the egg habit, and the Canon wanted his money back. I read some of the letters that passed between them. I don't think the mater is likely to have gone *there.*

Hor. But there is an alarming side to this disappearance which you don't seem to appreciate. Something dreadful may have happened.

René. It has. I had been measured for two lounge suits, one of them in a rather taking shade of copper beech, and they were to have been tried on for the first time this morning——

Lud. (*hurriedly*). As everything is naturally rather at sixes and sevens at the Oaks, I have asked St. Gall to stay to lunch. I suppose we can give him a bite of something?

Hor. (*coldly*). I am always glad to show hospitality to your friends, Ludovic. I'll read you my letter to the Bishop at a more convenient moment. I'm just going to see Laura Gubbings; she's going out to Afghanistan as a missionary, you know. That country has been scandalously neglected in the way of missionary effort.

Lud. There are considerable political and geographical difficulties in the way.

Hor. Not insuperable, however.

Lud. Perhaps not, but extremely likely to expand. We usually set out on these affairs with the intention of devoting a certain amount of patient effort in making the natives reasonably glad at the introduction of mission work; then we find ourselves involved in a much bigger effort to make them reasonably sorry for having killed the missionaries.

Hor. Really, Ludovic, your reasoning is preposterous. I should be the first to oppose anything in the shape of armed aggression in Central Asia.

Lud. If you would oppose Miss Gubbings' missionary designs on that region I should feel more comfortable.

René. I say, can't she take me with her?

HOR. I don't really see in what capacity you could be included in a mission party.

RENÉ. I could give my famous imitation of a nautch-girl. That would fetch the Afghans in shoals, and then Miss Gubbings could hold overflow meetings and convert them.

HOR. A nautch-girl?

RENÉ. Yes, I did it for some friends at St. Petersburg and they just loved it. They said I got as far East as any one could be expected to go. If I wasn't suffering under a domestic bereavement I'd do it for you now.

HOR. Not at Briony, thank you! St. Petersburg may applaud such performances if it pleases. From the things I've heard from there——

RENÉ. Oh, for the matter of that, the things one hears about the Afghans—there is a proverb in that country——

LUD. (*hurriedly*). In any case Miss Gubbings is hardly likely to accept your collaboration in her labours.

HOR. Miss Gubbings is going out with a religious mission, not with a *café chantant*. From your description of your performance and from what I can guess of its nature, I don't think it would be likely to enhance either our moral or national reputation in the eyes of the Ameer's subjects. (*Rises from chair.*) A boy masquerading as a nautch-girl!

[*Exit* HORTENSIA, *door* L. *front.*

RENÉ. Another avenue of employment closed to me. By the way, where is Trevor? I want to ask him to lend me some sleeve-links. These ones won't go at all with the scarf-pin you're lending me.

LUD. You'll probably find him at the headkeeper's lodge. Lunch is at one sharp..

[*Exit* RENÉ, *door* L. *back.*

Now perhaps I can have a few moments to myself and the Prussian Factory Acts.

(*Enter* SPARROWBY, R. *back.*)

SPAR. (*seating himself astride of chair, centre*). I say, I wish you'd do something to help me.

LUD. (*looks over shoulder and then back to pamphlet*). If it's anything in the way of sleeve-links or scarf-pins you're too late.

SPAR. Oh, nothing of that sort——

LUD. Or are you looking for a strayed relative? I can get you the address of a crystal-gazer.

Spar. Oh, no, I haven't lost any one; quite the reverse, dear old chap, I've *found* her.

Lud. (*half turning round*). Not Mrs. St. Gall?

Spar. Mrs. St. Gall! Dear, no. I've found the one woman I could ever want to make my wife, and I want you to help me to pull it off.

Lud. (*returning to the perusal of his pamphlet*). Oh, I see. Delighted to be of any use to you. I don't quite know how you pull these things off, and I'm rather occupied these days, but on Wednesday next, in the early part of the afternoon, I can spare you an hour or two. (*Cuts page of pamphlet and continues reading.*)

Spar. Oh, but one can't fix a precise time for that sort of thing. The trouble I'm in is that she won't be serious about it. She——

Lud. What does "Bewegungslosigkeit" mean in English?

Spar. Oh, I don't know, it's a German word, isn't it? I don't know any German. (Ludovic *consults dictionary.*) She treats it as a sort of temporary infatuation on my part. She won't realize how hopelessly I'm in love with her.

Lud. (*yawning*). I thought it was the hopelessness of your suit that she did realize. Who is the lady?

Spar. Sybil Bomont.

Lud. (*leaping round in his seat and letting dictionary fall*). Impossible! Out of the question. You mustn't think of marrying Sybil Bomont.

Spar. But I can think of nothing else. Why mustn't I marry her?

Lud. You must dismiss the matter completely from your mind. Go fishing in Norway or fall in love with a chorus girl. There are heaps of chorus girls who are willing to marry commoners if you set the right way about it. But you mustn't think of Sybil Bomont.

Spar. But what is the objection? Surely there's no madness in her family?

Lud. (*contemplatively*). Madness, no. Oh, no. At least not that one knows of. Certainly her father lives at West Kensington, but he is sane on most other subjects.

Spar. Then what is this mysterious obstacle? There is nothing against me, I suppose? I am fairly well off as far as income is concerned.

Lud. Ah! And to what sort of environment are you proposing to take this young girl, who has been carefully brought up and kept shielded from the coarser realities of life?

SPAR. Well, I live very quietly in the country and farm a few acres of my own.

LUD. Precisely: I had heard stories to that effect. Now, my dear Sparrowby, the moral atmosphere of a farm, however amateur and non-paying the farm may be, is most unsuitable for a young woman who has been brought up in the seclusion of a town life. Farming involves cows, and I consider that cows carry the maternal instinct to indelicate excess. They seem to regard the universe in general as an imperfectly weaned calf. And then poultry—you must admit that the private life of the domestic barn-door fowl—well, there's remarkably little privacy about it.

SPAR. But, my dear Bavvel——

LUD. And are you quite sure that you are free to pay court to Miss Bomont—that you have no other entanglements?

SPAR. Entanglements? Why, certainly not.

LUD. Think a moment. What about Miss Clifford?

SPAR. Agatha Clifford! You must be dreaming. I haven't the ghost of an entanglement with her.

LUD. I thought I saw you both on rather intimate terms at breakfast this morning.

SPAR. (*indignantly*). She upset a sardine on to my knees.

LUD. I suppose you encouraged her to.

SPAR. Encouraged her! Why, it ruined a pair of flannel trousers.

LUD. Well, I expect her sardine was just as irrevocably damaged. Anyway, you condoned her action; I heard you tell her that it didn't matter.

SPAR. Oh, I had to say that. What else could one say?

LUD. If any one upset a sardine on to my lap I should find no difficulty in keeping the conversation from flagging. The difficulty would be to avoid saying too much. In your case I think you were rather too eloquently silent. The spilling of a sardine on to your lap may seem a small thing to you, but you must remember that women attach more importance to these trifles than we do. Believe me, I have watched your perhaps unconscious attentions to Miss Clifford with interest, and if anything I can do——

SPAR. But I assure you——

(*Enter* AGATHA *and* SYBIL, *door* L. *back*.)

AGATHA. Everything's going splendidly. Every one whom we've asked is coming, and Cook has been given a dark hint to have some fruit salads and mayonnaise and that sort of thing accidentally on hand– Oh, I forgot you weren't to know anything about it. Promise that you'll forget that you heard anything.

LUD. I assure you I heard nothing. I was struggling with some technicalities in a German pamphlet. Dear Miss Bomont, do show me where I can find a better dictionary than this one.

SYBIL. Come along. There's one somewhere in the library.

LUD. And, Agatha—Mr. Sparrowby wants you to help him to dig up some ferns for a rockery he's making at home.

(LUDOVIC *holds door,* L. *front, open for* SYBIL, *both Exit.*)

SPAR. I say——

AGATHA (*cheerfully*). By all means; let's come now. I love rooting up ferns. Here are some baskets. (*Fishes three large garden baskets out of chest.*)

SPAR. But it's nearly lunch-time, and I don't really——

AGATHA. Never mind lunch. There's sure to be something cold that we can peck at if we're late. Come on; the trowels are out in the tool-shed. I know a lovely damp wood where we can grub about for hours.

SPAR. But I've got rheumatism.

AGATHA. So have I. Come on.

(*Gives him two baskets to carry and leads the way off by door,* R. *back.*)

CURTAIN

ACT II

The Hall. Briony Manor.

(CLARE *and* TREVOR *seated on couch, centre of stage. Enter* AGATHA, *door* L., *passes behind them. All three dressed in sheet costume, with hood thrown back, no masks.*)

AGATHA. I say, Trevor, it's going splendidly!

[*Exit* AGATHA, *door* R. *back.*

CLARE. If you ask me, it's going as flat as can be. No one seems to want to dance, and Cook is scared to death and has only sent us up half the amount of supper that we asked for.

TREVOR. There's enough to drink, anyhow; I saw to that. I went down to the cellar myself.

CLARE. Yes, and the result will be that just when we want to be hurrying every one off the premises they'll be getting festive and reckless, and your august and awful mother will run up against half of them on the doorstep, or meet them in the drive. (*Enter door,* R. *back, veiled figure, who glides up to them.*) Hallo, who's this? (SYBIL *unmasks and throws back hood.*) Oh, Sybil, I might have guessed.

SYBIL (*seating herself armchair centre of stage*). I fled away from that tiresome Sparrowby person who keeps on pestering me to sit out with him. Clare dear, do go and relieve Evelyn, she's played about six dances running.

CLARE. Oh, Evelyn would play all night without feeling tired. (*Rises.*) But one excuse is as good as another, I suppose. (*Walks towards door,* R.)

SYBIL. I don't know what you mean. (*Exit* CLARE, *door* R. *back.*) It's going awfully flat.

TREVOR (*lighting cigarette*). Oh, a frightful fizzle. I think every one is a bit scared at what they're doing.

SYBIL. I know I am. There'll be fine fireworks tomorrow when Her Majesty gets to hear of it.

TREVOR. Fireworks! There'll be a full-sized earthquake. I think I shall go cub-hunting if there's a meet within reasonable distance.

SYBIL. You won't find many of us here when you return. We shall be cleared out in a batch, like Chinese coolies. Trevor, why on earth don't you marry and get rid of this one-woman rule at Briony? With all due respect, your mother is no joke. She's perfectly awful.

TREVOR. Oh, I suppose I shall marry somebody some day, but it's the choosing business that is so beastly complicated. Think of the millions and millions of nice women there are in the world, and then of the fact that one can only marry one of them—it makes marrying an awfully ticklish matter. It's like choosing which puppies you're going to keep out of a large litter; you can never be sure that you haven't drowned the wrong ones.

SYBIL. Oh, but if you go on those lines you'll never marry any one. You should just have a look round at the girls you personally know and like and make your choice from one of them. You'd soon find out whether she responded or not. I believe in grasping one's nettle.

TREVOR. But supposing there are half a dozen nettles and you don't know which to grasp?

SYBIL. Oh, come, we're getting on. Half a dozen is better than millions and millions. And there must always be some one whom you prefer out of the half-dozen. There's Agatha, for instance. Of course she is your cousin, but that doesn't really matter. And in her way she's not a bad sort.

TREVOR. She passed through the hall just before you came in. If I'm to ask her to marry me I'd better go and do it now before I forget it.

SYBIL (*alarmed*). Oh, don't go and propose to her just because I suggested it. You'd make me feel an awful matchmaker, and I should never forgive myself if it turned out wrong. Besides, I doubt very much if she'd make the sort of mistress you'd want for Briony. One has to think of so many things, hasn't one?

TREVOR. Precisely my standpoint. And if Agatha turned out a disappointment I couldn't give her away to the gardener's boy, like an unsatisfactory puppy. You see, it isn't so easy to grasp the nettle when you really come to do it.

SYBIL. Oh, well, Agatha doesn't exhaust the list. There's Clare, for instance, she's got some good points, don't you think?

TREVOR. You don't say so with much conviction.

SYBIL. I'm awfully good pals with Clare, but that doesn't prevent me from recognizing that she's got rather a queer temper at times; the things that she says sometimes are simply hateful, and she's not a bit straightforward. I could tell you of little things she's done— (*Enter from door centre veiled figure.*) Who on earth is this?

(SPARROWBY *throws off hood and mask and seats himself on small chair facing* SYBIL.)

SPAR. I've been following all sorts of figures about, thinking they were you. But I knew all the time they couldn't be you, because I didn't feel a thrill when I was near them. I always feel a thrill when I'm near you.

SYBIL (*viciously*). I wish you never felt thrills, then.

SPAR. You're dreadfully unkind, Sybil, but I know you don't mean what you say.

SYBIL. Sorry you find my conversation meaningless.

SPAR. Oh, I didn't mean that!

SYBIL. We seem equally unfortunate in our meanings.

SPAR. I say, Sybil, I wish you'd take me a little more seriously.

SYBIL. One would think you were an attack of measles.

(*Enter* Mrs. Vulpy *with* Drummond, door L., *both unhooded. She catches sight of trio and rushes up.*)

Mrs. V. (*to* Drummond). Excuse me one moment. (*To* Spar) Naughty man, you know you promised me the kitchen lancers. Come along. Hurry.

Spar. (*rising unwillingly*). But they're playing a waltz now.

Mrs. V. They're getting ready for the lancers. Come on.

[*Exeunt* Mrs. Vulpy, Sparrowby *and* Drummond, *door* R. *back.*

Sybil. The Vulpy woman is rather a brick at times. I say, *Trevor.*

(*During* Sparrowby *duologue* Trevor *has fallen asleep. Wakes hurriedly.*)

Trevor. I nearly went off to sleep. Please excuse my manners. I was up awfully early this morning.

Sybil. Well, do keep awake now. We're in the middle of a most interesting conversation.

Trevor. Let's see, you were recommending me to marry Clare Henessey.

Sybil. Oh, well—I don't think I went as far as that. Clare and I are first-rate pals, and I should awfully like to see her make a good marriage; but I'd be rather sorry for her husband all the same. If anything rubs her the wrong way her temper goes queer at once, like milk in thunder-time, and she simply says the most ill-natured things.

Trevor. That's another ungraspable nettle, then. I told you it wasn't so jolly easy.

Sybil. But, Trevor, there are surely others, only you're too lazy to think of them.

Trevor. As to thinking of them, I am not too lazy to do that; it's the further stages I'm deficient in.

Sybil. Of course I sympathize with your difficulty. I wish I could find you some one really nice, some one who would enter into all your pursuits and share your ambitions and be a genuine companion to you.

Trevor. I hate that sort.

Sybil. Do you? How funny? At least, I don't know, I rather think I agree with you. Some women make dreadful nuisances of themselves that way. Well, you don't give me much help in choosing you a wife.

Trevor. What do you think of Mrs. Vulpy?

SYBIL. What! That woman with nasturtium-coloured hair and barmaid manners. Surely you're not attracted by her.

TREVOR. I didn't say I was. I asked you what you thought of her.

SYBIL. Oh, as to that; not a bad sort in her way, I suppose. Some people call her a rough diamond. If it was my declaration I should call her a defensive spade. But anyhow she's married, so she doesn't come into our discussion.

TREVOR. I want to tell you something, something that concerns you alone.

SYBIL. What is it?

TREVOR. Your hair's coming down behind.

SYBIL. Oh, bother! It's that horrid hood arrangement. I'll fly upstairs and put it right. (*Rises.*) I say, Trev, there's a much nicer sitting-out place on the landing, near that old carved press, where the tiresome Sparrowby person won't find me. Come up in two minutes' time, there's a dear.

TREVOR. Right-oh!

SYBIL. Now don't go to sleep.

[*Exit* SYBIL, *up staircase* L.

(*Enter* AGATHA *door* R. *back, passes along back of stage.*)

AGATHA. Everything's going swimmingly; it's a huge success.

[*Exit* AGATHA, *door* L. *back.*

(*Enter* RENÉ, *door centre, in evening dress with smoking jacket; carrying bottle of wine, wine-glass, some grapes and peaches. Seats himself on armchair near small table.*)

RENÉ. Going rather flat, isn't it?

TREVOR. Frightful fizzle. I'm so sleepy myself that I can only just keep my eyes open. Was up at the farm awfully early this morning.

RENÉ. Some shorthorn or bantam was going to have young ones, I suppose. In the country animals are always having young ones; passes the time away, I suppose. I know a lady in Warwickshire who runs a rabbit farm. She has musical boxes set up over the hutches.

TREVOR. Musical boxes?

RENÉ. Yes, they play the wedding march from "Lohengrin" at decent intervals. I'm going to ask you an extremely personal question.

Trevor. If it has anything to do with spare shirt-studs——

René (*who is delicately feeding himself while talking*). Don't be silly. It hasn't. I want to know—are you happy?

Trevor. Immensely.

René (*disappointedly*). Are you? Why?

Trevor. One never has any definite reason for being happy. It's simply a temperamental accident in most cases. I've nothing to worry me, no money troubles, no responsibilities; why should I be anything else but happy?

René. You ought to marry.

Trevor. You think that would improve matters?

René. It would elevate you. Suffering is a great purifier.

Trevor. You're not a very tempting advocate of matrimony.

René. I don't recommend it, except in desperate cases. Yours is distinctly a desperate case. You ought to marry if only for your mother's sake.

Trevor. My mother? I don't know that she is particularly anxious to see me mated just yet.

René. Your mother is one of those proud silent women who seldom indicate their wishes in actual words.

Trevor. My dear René, my mother may be proud, but where her wishes are concerned she is not inclined to be silent.

René. At any rate, an unmarried son of marriageable age is always a great anxiety. There's never any knowing what impossible person he may fix his fancy on. As old Lady Cloutsham said to me the other day, *à propos* of her eldest son: "If Robert chooses a wife for himself, it's certain to be some demi-mondaine with the merest superficial resemblance to a lady; whereas if I choose a wife for him I should select some one who at least would be a lady, with a merely superficial resemblance to a demi-mondaine.

Trevor. Poor Lady Cloutsham, her children are rather a trial to her, I imagine. Her youngest boy had to leave the country rather hurriedly, hadn't he?

René. Yes, poor dear. He's on a ranch somewhere in the wilds of Mexico. Conscience makes cowboys of us all. Unfortunately, it's other people's consciences that give all the trouble; there ought to be a law compelling every one to keep his conscience under proper control, like chimneys that have to consume their own smoke. And then Gladys, who was the most hopeful member of the family, went and married a Colonial Bishop. That really finished Lady

Cloutsham. As she said to me: "I always classed Colonial Bishops with folksongs and peasant industries and all those things that one comes across at drawing-room meetings. I never expected to see them brought into one's family. This is what comes of letting young girls read Ibsen and Mrs. Humphry Ward.

(*An unearthly long-drawn-out howl is heard.*)

TREVOR (*sitting up*). What on *earth—?*

RENÉ. Only the idiotic Drummond boy, who pretends he's the Hound of the Baskervilles.

(*Enter* AGATHA, *door* L., *runs giggling across stage pursued by* DRUMMOND *in sheet with phantom-hound mask on head. Exeunt both, door* R. *back.*)

TREVOR (*rising slowly*). By Jove, forgot I'd promised to go upstairs. Sybil will be fuming her head off.

RENÉ. We can't get a rubber of Bridge presently, can we?

TREVOR. 'Fraid not. The women would be rather mad if we shirked dancing.

(*Draws himself slowly together and lounges up staircase,* L. *Exit.*)

(*Enter* SPARROWBY, *door* R. *back.*)

SPAR. Why aren't you rigged out like the rest of us, St. Gall?

(*Takes* TREVOR'S *seat on couch.*)

RENÉ. Well, for one thing I'm in platonic mourning, having partially lost a mother, so it would hardly be the thing. And another reason is that the hood arrangement would ruffle one's hair so.

SPAR. As if that mattered a bit. You're absurdly particular about your appearance and your clothes and how your tie is tied and about your hair. Look at me; it doesn't take me two minutes in the morning to do my hair.

RENÉ. So I should imagine. Isn't there a proverb, a fool and his hair are soon parted?

SPAR. I say, you're beastly rude!

RENÉ. I know I am. My mother was a Whortleford, and the Whortlefords have no manners. I'm sorry I called you a fool, though, because I want you to do something really kind for me. Trevor has suggested a game of Bridge and I don't want to back out of playing. The trouble is that I haven't a coin worth speaking about on me. If you'd be awfully pet-lamb and lend me something——

SPAR. I dislike lending on principle. It generally leads to unpleasantness.

RENÉ. Really this worship of Mammon is getting to be the curse of the age. People make more fuss about lending a few miserable guineas than the Sabine women did at being borrowed by the Romans. I know a lady of somewhat mature age who took rather a fancy to me last season and in a fit of sheer absence of mind she lent me ten pounds. She's got quite a comfortable income, but I declare she thinks more of that lost tenner than of the hundreds and hundreds that she's never lent me. It is become quite a monomania with her. It's her one subject of conversation whenever we meet.

SPAR. Don't you intend paying her back?

RENÉ. Certainly not. Her loss makes her beautiful. It brings an effective touch of tragedy into an otherwise empty life. I could no more think of her apart from her mourned-for loan than one could think of Suez without the canal or Leda without the swan.

SPAR. If that's your view of your obligations I certainly shan't lend you anything. By the way, where is Sybil Bomont? She's been sitting out about four dances with Trevor. It's about my turn now.

RENÉ (*with sudden energy*). Sybil has got a bad headache. She's lying down for a few minutes.

SPAR. Where? I particularly want to see her.

RENÉ. In the billiard-room, and she particularly doesn't want to see any one.

SPAR. But I only want——

(*Enter* CLARE *and* AGATHA, *door* R. *back.*)

RENÉ. Agatha! Sparrowby is complaining that he's got no one to dance with.

AGATHA. Come along, they're just going to try that new Paris dance; I can't pronounce it.

SPAR. But I can't dance it!

AGATHA. Neither can I. Come on.

SPAR. But I say——

[*Exit* AGATHA *dragging* SPARROWBY *off, door* R. *back.*

RENÉ. Thank goodness, he's out of the way. People who make a principle of not lending money are social pests.

CLARE (*seating herself on couch*). This is going to be a dismal failure. By the way, have you seen Trevor anywhere?

RENÉ. Yes, he turned rather giddy with the dancing, I suppose, so he's taking a turn or two out in the air.

CLARE. Is he alone?

RENÉ. Oh, quite. So am I for the moment. Do stay and talk to me.

CLARE. You must be interesting, then. After sitting out successfully with Sparrowby and the two Drummond boys, I feel that there's nothing left in the way of dull and trivial conversation to listen to.

(*While she is talking* RENÉ *hands her half of the remaining peach and resumes his seat.*)

RENÉ. Let's talk about ourselves; that's always interesting.

CLARE. I suppose you mean, let's talk about yourself.

RENÉ. No, I'd much rather dissect your character; I find some good points in it.

CLARE. Do tell me what they are.

RENÉ. You have a rich aunt who is childless.

CLARE. She's a great-aunt.

RENÉ. All the better. That sort of thing doesn't spoil by being kept in the family for a generation or two. The greater the aunt the greater the prospect.

CLARE. And what other good points do you find in me?

RENÉ. I think I've nearly exhausted the list.

CLARE. I don't find you a bit interesting.

RENÉ. Well, be patient for a moment, I'm going to say something quite personal and interesting. Will you marry me? The question is sudden, I admit, but these things are best done suddenly. I suppose it was the mention of your great-aunt that suggested it.

CLARE. The answer is equally sudden. It's "No."

RENÉ. Are you quite sure you mean that?

CLARE. Convinced.

RENÉ. How thoroughly sensible of you. So many girls in your place would have said "Yes."

CLARE. I dare say. Our sex hasn't much reputation for discrimination. I didn't know that marrying was in your line.

RENÉ. It isn't. I dislike the idea of wives about a house: they accumulate dust. Besides, so few of the really nice women in my set could afford to marry me.

CLARE. From the point of view of reputation?

RENÉ. Oh, I wasn't thinking of that. At twenty-three one is supposed to have conquered every earthly passion: of course it's the fashion in statesmanship nowadays to allow the conquered to have the upper hand.

CLARE. A convenient fashion and saves a lot of bother. Tell me, taking me apart from my great-aunt, are you pleased to consider that I should make a satisfactory wife?

RENÉ. Satisfactory wives aren't made: they're invented. Chiefly by married men. But as things go I think we should have made what is called a well-assorted couple. I should have taught you in time to be as thoroughly selfish as myself, and then each would have looked after our own particular interests without having need to fear that the other was likely to suffer from any neglect.

CLARE. There is much to be said for that point of view. It's the imperfectly selfish souls that cause themselves and others so many heart-burnings. People who make half sacrifices for others always find that it's the unfinished half that's being looked at. Naturally they come to regard themselves as unappreciated martyrs.

RENÉ. By the way, I may as well tell you before you find out. Trevor isn't out of doors. He's sitting out with Sybil somewhere on the landing.

CLARE (*half rising from seat*). You beast! Why did you tell me he'd gone out?

RENÉ. Well, the fact of the matter is, I thought that if those two were left together undisturbed for half an hour or so, one or other of them might propose.

CLARE (*resuming seat*). Oh, that's the game, is it? And has Sybil enlisted your services in this precious stalking movement?

RENÉ. Oh, dear, no: I'm merely working in a good cause. Some one's got to marry Trevor, you know, and the sooner the better. Personally, I don't think it's very hopeful, but the whole motive of this otherwise idiotic dance is to head Trevor into a matrimonial ambush of some sort. He's so superbly sleepy that there's just a chance of it coming off, but I'm not sanguine.

CLARE. If he *is* to be rushed into marrying some one, I don't see why I shouldn't be in the running as well as any one else.

RENÉ. Exactly what William was saying to me this morning.

CLARE. William! The page-boy?

RENÉ. Yes, he's rather keen on seeing you Mrs. Trevor Bavvel.

CLARE. That's very sweet of him, but I didn't know he took such an intelligent interest in the matter.

RENÉ. It's not altogether disinterested. It seems they've got a half-crown sweepstake on the event, in the servants' hall, and he happened to draw you, so naturally he's in a bit of a flutter on your behalf.

CLARE. I didn't know we were the centre of so much speculation. Mercy on us, what would Hortensia say if she knew that she was nurturing a living sweepstake under her roof! And is William good enough to consider that I have a fair sporting chance of pulling it off?

RENÉ. I fancy he's rather despondent. He said you didn't seem to try as hard as some of the others were doing. He puts your chair as near Trevor's as possible at prayers, but that's all he's able to do personally.

CLARE. The little devil!

RENÉ. I believe that if the Vulpy woman wasn't handicapped with a preliminary husband, she'd carry Trevor off against all competitors. She's just got the bounce that appeals to a lazy, slow-witted bachelor.

CLARE. There's something I particularly object to in that woman. She always talks to me with just a suspicion of a furtive sneer in her voice that I find extremely irritating. I don't know why Agatha inflicted her on us.

(*Enter* AGATHA, R. *back.*)

AGATHA. What's that you're saying about me?

CLARE. Only wondering what induced you to cart Mrs. Vulpy down here.

AGATHA. Oh, come, she's not a bad soul, you know, taking her all round. (*Seats herself on couch.*) We are all of us as God made us.

RENÉ. In Mrs. Vulpy's case some recognition is due to her maid as a collaborator.

AGATHA. You're all very ill-natured about her. Anyway, this dance was her idea.

CLARE. Yes, and a horrid mess it's going to land us all in. I daren't think of tomorrow. By the afternoon the news will have spread over the greater part of Somersetshire that a costume ball has been given at Briony in the temporary absence of Mrs. Bavvel.

AGATHA. I say, do you think she'll be very furious?

CLARE. If Hortensia is more intolerant on one question than on any other, it's on the subject of what she calls mixed dancing. I remember a county fête at Crowcoombe where she vetoed the project of a maypole dance by children of six and seven years old until absolutely assured that the sexes would dance apart. Some of the smaller children were rather ambiguously dressed and were too shy to tell us their names, and the curate and I had a long and delicate task in sorting the he's from the she's. One four-year-old baffled our most patient researches, and finally had to dance by itself round a maypole of its own.

AGATHA. I'm beginning to get dreadfully frightened about to-morrow. Can't we water it down a bit and pretend that we had games and Sir Roger de Coverley and that sort of thing?

CLARE. We shall have to tone things down as much as possible, but Hortensia will hold an inquiry into the whole matter, and drag the truth out by inches. She'll probably dismiss half the servants and have the morning-room repapered; as for us—

RENÉ. There's a very good up train at 3.15.

AGATHA. But I haven't made arrangements for going anywhere; it will be most inconvenient.

CLARE. On the morrow of an unsuccessful *coup d'état* one generally travels first and makes one's arrangements afterwards.

(*A prolonged howl heard.*)

RENÉ. The idiotic Drummond boy again.

(*Enter* DRUMMOND, *door* R. *back.*)

DRUMMOND. I say, you make nice cheerful hosts, sitting there like a lot of moping owls. Do come and buck things up a bit; there are only two couples dancing.

RENÉ (*tragically*). Yes, let us go and dance on the edge of our volcano.

AGATHA. Oh, don't, I feel quite creepy. It reminds me of that Duchess person's ball on the eve of Waterloo.

[*Exeunt* DRUMMOND, RENÉ, AGATHA, *door* R. *back.*

(CLARE *remains seated. Enter* MRS. VULPY, *centre.*)

MRS. V. All alone, Miss Henessey? By the way, where is that dear boy, Trevor?

CLARE. I believe he's upstairs, and I don't think he wishes to be disturbed.

MRS. V. I suppose that means that you are waiting to catch him when he comes down, and that *you* don't want to be disturbed.

CLARE. Oh, please put that construction on it if it amuses you. I shouldn't like to think you weren't enjoying yourself.

MRS. V. Oh, I'm enjoying myself right enough, *Miss* Henessey, watching some of the little by-play that's goin' on. (*Seats herself.*) It is *Miss* Henessey, isn't it? (*Gives a little laugh.*)

CLARE. What do you mean?

MRS. V. Oh, well, only that we've met before, you know, at least

I've seen you before, though you probably didn't see me. You were writing your name in the visitors' book at the Grand Anchor Hotel at Bristol, just about six weeks ago.

CLARE. I did stop there one night about six weeks ago. I don't remember seeing you there.

MRS. V. I remember not only seeing you, but the names you wrote in the book: Henessey wasn't one of them, nor Miss Anything either.

CLARE. How clever of you to remember. You seem to have a good head for business—other people's business.

MRS. V. Oh, well, I suppose it was the innocent vagueness of the names you had put down that arrested my attention. "Mr. and Mrs. Smith," London. Your companion had gone upstairs with the luggage, so I didn't see Mr. Smith, and somehow at the time I had a feeling that I wasn't seeing Mrs. Smith—at least not the permanent Mrs. Smith.

CLARE. It sounds rather crude and compromising as you put it, I admit, but the explanation is not really very dreadful. Only——

MRS. V. Only you don't feel disposed to give an explanation at such short notice. You're quite right. Second thoughts are usually more convincing in such cases.

CLARE. Well, to be candid, I don't see that my travelling adventures are any particular concern of yours.

MRS. V. Perhaps you're right. I dare say they more immediately concern the lady whose guest you are. Shall I raise her curiosity on the subject? As you've got such a satisfactory explanation ready, you can have no objection, I suppose.

CLARE. You know Mrs. Bavvel well enough to know that what might seem a harmless escapade to ordinary judges would not be regarded so leniently by her.

MRS. V. And Mr. Trevor? He doesn't share his mother's prejudices. You won't mind if I let him into our little secret about the Smith *ménage*?

CLARE (*rising from her seat*). Mrs. Vulpy, what particular gratification do you find in threatening to make mischief between me and my friends? It shows you up in rather a bad light, and I don't really see what you expect to gain by it.

MRS. V. Simply, my dear girl, we happen to be interested in the same man.

CLARE. You mean Trevor?

Mrs. V. Of course. I know perfectly well that all you girls are hanging round here for a chance of snapping him up, and I'm clever enough to see which of you is likely to succeed. It won't be Sybil Bomont, whatever any one may say.

Clare. In any case, you can scarcely regard yourself as a competitor.

Mrs. V. Because of being already married, you mean? Well, I don't mind telling you I've more definite news about my husband's condition than I've been pretending to have. He was past all chance of recovery when the last mail went out. I'm too honest to pretend to be anything but glad. If you knew the life we've had! I've been a lonely woman since the day I married Peter, and now I don't intend being lonely any more. As soon as I set eyes on Trevor Bavvel I knew he was just the sort of man I wanted to begin life with over again.

Clare. And do you suppose that you are so obviously *his* conception of the ideal life-mate that he'll throw himself at your feet as soon as he knows you are free to marry him?

Mrs. V. Oh, my dear, most things in life that are worth having have to be worked for. I've made a good beginning by enlisting his sympathy as a fellow-conspirator over this dance. The worse row we get into over it the better. Then, when my husband's estate has been straightened out, I shan't be badly off, and I shall come to this neighbourhood and do a little hunting and give Bridge parties and all that sort of thing. Provided nothing happens in the meantime, I fancy I stand a very fair chance of pulling it off.

Clare. I see.

Mrs. V. Ah, you do see, do you? You understand now why I want your flirtation with Trevor to be nipped in the bud, and why I'm prepared to nip it myself if necessary with that little story of the Grand Anchor Hotel?

Clare. You are making one little miscalculation, Mrs. Vulpy. Trevor was a public-school boy, and in English public-school tradition the spy and the tale-bearer don't occupy a very exalted position.

Mrs. V. Oh, you may call me hard names, but you can't wriggle away from me in that fashion. I've got you in my grip–so! Either you leave the field clear for me or the story of your visit to the Grand Anchor Hotel with a gentleman, whom, for want of fuller information, we will call Mr. Smith, becomes public property.

CLARE. Some one is coming downstairs. Shall we go and see how the dancing is going on? They're playing that Bulgarian March.

MRS. V. Oh, yes, let's go and hear it. I love Slav music, it takes one out of oneself so.

CLARE. Which is sometimes an advantage.

[*Exeunt* VULPY *and* CLARE.

(*Enter down staircase*, L., SYBIL *and* TREVOR.)

TREVOR. I say, it's getting nearly time to call this off.

SYBIL. Oh, nonsense, it's only just ten. They can't be back before eleven. Your mother is delivering an address, and she's not given to cutting her words short on these occasions, I believe.

TREVOR. Well, half an hour more, then. And let's make it go with a bit more fling for the wind-up.

SYBIL. Right-oh! (*Enter* SPARROWBY, L.) Lord, here's that pestering idiot again.

SPAR. Ah, at last I've found you! Are you better?

SYBIL. Better?

SPAR. I was told you were lying down in the billiard-room with a bad headache.

SYBIL. Who on earth told you that?

SPAR. St. Gall.

SYBIL. Oh, René! Never believe a word he says. I'm in my usual health, but I'm frightfully hungry. Trevor, do go and forage for something edible. I'll wait for you here. I was too excited to eat much at dinner, and I know I shan't dare to come down to breakfast tomorrow.

TREVOR. I'll go and parley with Cook.

[*Exit* TREVOR, *door centre*.

SPAR. What have you been doing all this time?

SYBIL (*seating herself on couch*). Oh, don't ask me. Sitting upstairs with Trevor and trying to keep him from going to sleep. I assure you it wasn't amusing.

SPAR. I should never want to go to sleep if I were by your side.

SYBIL. What an inconvenient husband you would be.

SPAR. Oh, I wish you wouldn't be always fooling. (*Seats himself beside her*.) You don't know how much I love you!

SYBIL. Of course I don't; I've only got your word for it that you care in the least bit for me. Now if you were to do something to prove it—

SPAR. I'd do anything.

SYBIL. Well, do something that would give you a name in the world. For instance, paint pictures and have them exhibited in the Royal Academy: it would be something to talk about when one went there.

SPAR. But I can't paint.

SYBIL. Oh, I don't think that matters as long as you exhibited. Of course, they wouldn't sell. Or why not found a religion, like Mahomet and Wesley and those sort of people did.

SPAR. But you can't found religions off-hand. You want inspiration and enthusiasm and disciples, and all manner of special conditions.

SYBIL. Well, then, you could invent a new system of scoring at county cricket, or breed a new variety of fox-terrier.

SPAR. But it would take years and years to produce a new variety.

SYBIL. I would wait—oh, so patiently.

SPAR. *Sybil,* if I was successful in breeding a new kind of fox-terrier, would you really marry me?

SYBIL. I wouldn't exactly marry you, but I would buy some of the puppies from you. I've got an awfully jolly little fox-terrier at home. If you tell her "the Kaiser's coming," or "Roosevelt's coming," she lies quite still, but if you say, "King Edward's coming," she jumps up at once. Isn't it clever? I taught her myself with gingerbread biscuits.

SPAR. Won't you realize that I'm asking you to be my wife?

SYBIL. Of course I realize it; you've asked me so often that I'm getting to expect nothing else. I wish you would vary it a little and ask me something different. Only don't ask me that dreadful thing about "this man's father was my father's only son," it nearly gives me brain fever.

SPAR. I wonder if you have a heart at all?

SYBIL. Of course I've got the usual fittings. It's very rude of you to suggest that I'm jerry-built. But look here, joking apart, do do something to oblige me. Go and dance with poor Evelyn Bray; she's been at the piano all the evening and hasn't had a scrap of dancing herself.

SPAR. If I do, will you give me a dance afterwards?

SYBIL. I'll give you two.

SPAR. (*rising from his seat*). You angel. I wish you'd always be as kind.

[*Exit* SPARROWBY, *door* R. *back.*

SYBIL (*hearing some one coming*). Is that you, Trevor? I'm getting ravenous. (*Enter* AGATHA, *door centre.*) Oh, Lord!

AGATHA. Hullo, Sybil, have you seen Trevor?

SYBIL. No, I think he's dancing.

AGATHA. He hasn't been in the dancing room for about an hour; neither have you. (*Seats herself on chair right of couch.*)

SYBIL. I'm so hot, I'm sitting out here to get cool. I suppose it's the excitement. I say, do go and help Evelyn at the piano, she's getting quite fagged out, poor child.

AGATHA (*acidly*). I've just played them a polka; Evelyn hasn't been near the piano for the last half-hour. If you hadn't been sticking to Trevor like a drowning leech you might have known that.

SYBIL (*furiously*). I haven't been sticking on him, and leeches don't drown, anyway.

AGATHA. Oh, I'm not up in their natural history. I only know they stick like mud. I'll say a floating leech if you like.

SYBIL. It so happens I've been listening to marriage proposals from that pestering Sparrowby all the evening.

AGATHA. I've had the infliction of dancing with him no fewer than four times, my dear, and he kept on complaining that he couldn't find you. Don't be disheartened: accidents will happen to the most accomplished fibbers.

SYBIL. Why is it that plain women are always so venomous?

AGATHA. Oh, if you're going to be introspective, my dear. (*Laughs.*)

(*Enter* TREVOR, *door centre.*)

TREVOR. All I could raise was some cold rice pudding and a bottle of pickled walnuts. If there's anything I detest in this world it's rice pudding.

AGATHA (*going over to table*). I loathe rice pudding, it's so wholesome. On the other hand, I simply adore pickled walnuts. (*Helps herself.*)

TREVOR. Won't you have some, Sybil? (*Helps himself.*)

SYBIL (*rising from seat*). I'm not going to stay here to be insulted. I've been called a liar and a leech.

AGATHA. I said fibber, my dear, not liar.

[*Exit* SYBIL, *door* R. *back.*

TREVOR. Have you two been having a slanging match?

AGATHA. Oh, no, only poor Sybil is so dreadfully short-tempered, she can't take anything in good part. She's a dear, sweet girl, one of the very best, but I should be awfully sorry for any fellow who married her. That reminds me, Trevor—you ought to marry.

(*Helps herself to another walnut.*)

TREVOR. There's a great deal to be said for that point of view: and as far as I can see there's no particular likelihood of it's being left unsaid.

(*Helps himself to walnut.*)

AGATHA. I suppose the difficulty is to think of any one you care for sufficiently.

TREVOR. Have you anything to say against Mrs. Vulpy?

AGATHA. Good heavens! Mrs. Vulpy? That vulgar, overdressed parrot, with the manners of a cockney sparrow. I should think she began life in a cheap-jack store. Surely you can't be thinking seriously of her?

TREVOR. I asked you if you had anything to say against her. Considering the short notice you managed very well. Wasn't it you who brought her down here?

AGATHA (*helping herself to walnut*). Well, yes, I suppose I did. Somehow in Folkestone she didn't seem such an awful rotter. Anyway, she's got a husband. No, the woman for you must be one with great similarity of tastes——

TREVOR. On the contrary, I avoid that kind. At the present moment I regard you with something bordering on aversion. (*Stirs frantically in jar.*)

AGATHA. Regard me with aversion! My dear Trevor!

TREVOR. If it hadn't been for our duplicate passion for pickled walnuts this cruel tragedy wouldn't have happened. There's not one left.

AGATHA. Oh, Trevor, not one? (*Stirs mournfully in jar.*)

TREVOR. No, the woman I marry must have an unbridled appetite for rice pudding.

AGATHA (*dubiously*). I dare say some rice pudding, nicely cooked, wouldn't be bad eating. (*Begins agitating spoon listlessly through rice pudding dish.*)

TREVOR. That is not the spirit in which my ideal woman must approach rice pudding. She must eat it with an avidity that will almost create scandal; she must devour it secretly in dark corners, she must buy it in small quantities from chemists on the plea that she has neuralgia. Such a woman I could be happy with.

AGATHA. She might be odious in other respects. (*While talking is waving spoon in air.*)

TREVOR. One must not expect to find perfection.

AGATHA. I wish you would be serious when we are discussing a serious subject. I suppose matrimony is a more serious affair for us poor women than for you men.

TREVOR. How can I discuss anything seriously when you're covering me with fragments of rice pudding?

AGATHA. Oh, you poor dear, I'm so sorry. Let me rub you down.

TREVOR. No, don't you; I won't be massaged with rice pudding.

(*Enter* MRS. VULPY, *door centre.*)

MRS. V. What *are* you two people playing at?

TREVOR. Only trying to find new uses for cold rice pudding. I was firmly convinced as a child that it couldn't be primarily intended as a food.

MRS. V. René is just going to do his nautch-girl dance. He wants you to go and play tom-tom music, Agatha.

AGATHA. Bother René. Why was I born good-natured?

[*Exit* AGATHA, R.

TREVOR. Stay and talk to me, Mrs. Vulpy. I've seen the nautch-dance before.

MRS. V. You are such a sought-after young man that I feel I oughtn't to be taking you away from the others.

TREVOR. I'd rather sit and talk with you than with any of the others.

MRS. V. Dear me! I thought you never worked up the energy to make pretty speeches.

TREVOR. I don't; it's my mere sheer laziness that makes me blurt out the truth on this occasion.

MRS. V. And am I really to suppose that it is truth that you would rather sit with me than with any of the others?

TREVOR. You are the only woman of the lot that it is safe to sit out with. Perhaps you are not very securely married, but you're not exactly floating loose ready to take advantage of the artless innocence of a young bachelor.

MRS. V. And is that where my superior fascination begins and leaves off?

TREVOR. That's where it begins. I didn't say it left off there.

MRS. V. Now don't try to talk pretty. You know you're not capable of sustained effort in that direction. Nothing is more discouraging than to have a man say that you've ruined his life, and then to find that you haven't even given him after-dinner insomnia.

TREVOR. Oh, I promise to keep awake—only it's rather soothing and sedative to talk to a charming woman who has no intention of marrying one. You don't intend to marry me, do you?

MRS. V. My dear Trevor, I have intended marrying you ever since I first saw you.

TREVOR. They say the road to matrimony is paved with good intentions, don't they?

MRS. V. I have heard it put in a more roundabout manner.

TREVOR. In your case isn't there rather a big obstacle in the road?

MRS. V. You mean Peter?

TREVOR. I suppose he *is* a factor in the situation?

MRS. V. Of course he's my husband, and it's my duty to think of him before any one else. But I am not going to be a hypocrite and waste sentiment in that direction. Our married life has been about as odious an experience as I wish to go through.

TREVOR. Still, I suppose even an unsatisfactory marriage has to be taken into account. There is no First Offender's clause in our marriage system. However uncongenial he may be, Peter remains your husband.

MRS. V. Well, that's the question. Peter was always selfish, but double pneumonia on the top of nervous breakdown may have overcome even his obstinate temperament. Why, at any moment I might get what I should be obliged to call in public "bad news." So you see I'm not so safe a person to sit and make pretty speeches to as you thought. And now I suppose my fascination has melted into thin air?

TREVOR. No, I shall merely have to label you "dangerous" along with the others.

MRS. V. Ah, Trevor, I'm much more dangerous than any of the others, if you only knew it.

TREVOR. Why so?

MRS. V. Because I really want you for your own self. The others are all after you for family reasons and general convenience and that sort of thing. I want you because—well, I've seen a bit of the world, and I know the worth of a man like you, who can't be flattered or humbugged or led by the nose——

TREVOR. Hush! Some one's coming. (*Enter* WILLIAM, *door* L.) Just clear these things away, William; I should like my mother to find the hall in its usual state. Now, Mrs. Vulpy, I must be going in to the dance. I've shirked my duty most horribly.

MRS. V. Well, let's have a dreamy waltz together, to set the seal on what we've been talking about. We are friends, aren't we?

(*Exeunt* TREVOR *and* MRS. VULPY, *door* R. WILLIAM *gathers up empty plates. Enter* RENÉ, *door centre.*)

RENÉ (*helping himself to wine*). William, can you find me any more peaches?

WILL. No, sir, I brought you the last.

RENÉ (*arranging himself comfortably on couch*). Well, try to discover a fig or banana somewhere, do; and if you remind me tomorrow I'll ask Mr. Ludovic to give you that yellow striped waistcoat that he hardly ever wears.

WILL. Thank you, sir. You don't know of no one wanting a page, do you, sir?

RENÉ. Why, are you thinking of leaving?

WILL. I expect I shall have to leave without having time to do any thinking about it, sir. When Mrs. Bavvel comes to hear about our goings on behind her back she'll behave like one of those cyclops that sweeps away whole villages.

RENÉ. Cyclone, William, not cyclops.

WILL. That's it, sir, cyclone, and I expect I shall be among the sweepings. I've no particular fancy to be going home out of a situation just now, sir. Home life is a different thing with you gentry, you're so comfortable and heathen.

RENÉ. When one comes think of it, I suppose we are. It's a rather overcrowded profession all the same. (*While* WILLIAM *is talking* RENÉ *is helping himself to* TREVOR's *Russian cigarettes and filling his case.*)

WILL. Ah, sir, *you* haven't known what it was to be brought up by respectable parents.

RENÉ. Really, William!

WILL. My father is Plymouth Brethren, sir. Not that I've anything to say against Plymouth as a religion, but in a small cottage it takes up a lot of room. My father believed in smiting sin wherever he found it; what I complained of was that he always seemed to find it in the same place. Plymouth narrows the prospective. Between gentry religion and cottage religion there's the same difference as between keeping ferrets and living in a hutch with one.

[*Exit* WILLIAM, *door centre.*

(*Enter the first four in couples by door* R. *back,* TREVOR *and* MRS. VULPY, DRUMMOND *and* CLARE *and* SYBIL, SPARROWBY *and* AGATHA, *prancing through hall and singing "Non je ne marcherai pas," which is heard being played on piano off.*)

AGATHA (*to* RENÉ). You slacker! Come and join in.

(*They Exeunt in same order through door* L., *still singing.*)

RENÉ (*to himself*). I'm of far too tidy a disposition to leave half-emptied bottles lying about. Did I hear wheels? (*Rises and listens.*) Stop your squalling, you people. I fancied I heard wheels. (*Listens again.*) My nerves are getting quite jumpy. (*Reseats himself.*)

(*Hall door* R. *thrown open. Enter* HORTENSIA, *who turns to some one in porch.*)

HOR. Ludovic, quick, catch the carriage; I've left my pamphlets and notes in it. (*Catches sight of* RENÉ, *who is regarding her with helpless stare.*) Mr. St. Gall! May I ask what you are doing here at this hour?

RENÉ. Such a silly mistake. Old Colonel Nicholas asked me to go over to Bowerwood after dinner, as I was all alone. I distinctly told the groom Bowerwood, but he drove me here instead, and I didn't see where I was till he had driven off. So I've had to wait here till he comes to fetch me.

HOR. (*who has been staring fixedly at him and at the wine bottles and siphons on the table*). Will you repeat your story, please? I didn't quite follow.

RENÉ. Colonel Nicholas, thinking I might be lonely——

HOR. I hear music!

RENÉ. I've been thinking I heard harps in the air all the evening. I put it down to the state of my nerves. (SYBIL *with hood over head runs through laughing, from door* L., *and Exit door centre, without noticing* HORTENSIA.) Ah! Did you see *that!* Did you see *that!* (HORTENSIA *stares at doorway where figure vanished. Howl heard off. Enter* DRUMMOND *with phantom hound mask on, door* L., *runs through and Exit centre.*) Oh, say something or we shall . . . both . . . go . . . mad! (*Sobs convulsively.*)

HOR. (*furiously*). Ludovic!

(*Enter* LUDOVIC, *hall door* R.)

LUD. What is happening?

(René *has collapsed in fit of pretended hysterics in arm-chair.*)

Hor. The boy is either drunk or mad! Something disgraceful is taking place in this house!

Lud. Something disgraceful here! René, what *is* all this?

René (*sitting rigid in chair and staring straight in front of him*). Only were-wolves chasing goblins to the sound of unearthly music. Will some one kindly see if my carriage has come? I refuse to stay another moment in this house.

(*Enter* Trevor, Clare, Mrs. Vulpy, *from door* L. Sybil *and* Drummond, *door centre, all unhooded.*)

Trevor. Oh, good God!

(René *pours out glass of wine and drains it, then lies back composedly in his chair. A prolonged pause, during which* Hortensia *surveys sheepish group of revellers.*)

Sybil (*weakly*). We were having games.

Mrs. V. Old English games.

Drum. Charades.

Clare. Historical charades.

Sybil
Trevor
Mrs. V.
Drum. } (*together*). Yes, historical charades.

(*Enter* Agatha *and* Sparrowby, *door* R. *back, prancing in together singing with fatuous exuberance "Non je ne marcherai pas." They stop horror-stricken in centre of stage.*)

Hor. (*seating herself in high-backed chair, her voice trembling with rage*). May I ask who has organized this abominable and indecent orgy in my house? Will somebody enlighten me?

Clare. It was something we got up on the spur of the moment; there was nothing organized.

Hor. And what brought people in from outside? I've heard a contemptibly ridiculous story about Mr. St. Gall's accidental arrival here; how do you account for Mr. Drummond's presence? Was he also trying to make his way to Bowerwood?

Drum. (*blunderingly*). Yes.

René (*decisively*). No. That's my story. I won't be plagiarized.

Sybil. He dropped in by chance.

Drum. Yes, quite by chance.

Hor. Also on the spur of the moment! A moment, be it observed, when I happened to be temporarily absent. And knowing my strong objection to the questionable form of entertainment involved in promiscuous dancing you choose this moment for indulging in an aggravated and indecent kind of dance which I can only describe as a brawl.

MRS. V. But, dear Mrs. Bavvel, I assure you there is nothing indecent in a sheet-and-pillow-case dance. Lulu Duchess of Dulverton gave one at——

HOR. Lulu Duchess of Dulverton is not a person whose behaviour or opinions will be taken as a pattern at Briony as long as I am mistress here. While you are still under my roof, Mrs. Vulpy, I trust you will endeavour to remember that fact. Whether, after this deplorable error of taste, you will see fit to prolong your visit, of course I don't know. Apparently this monstrous misuse of the bed-linen which is intended for the sleeping accommodation of my guests was carried out at your suggestion.

MRS. V. (*bursting into tears*). I think, considering the mental anxiety and strain through which I am passing, with a husband hovering between Johannesburg and Heaven, I'm being most unfairly treated.

[*Exit* MRS. VULPY, *door* L.

HOR. I've refrained from complaining, Agatha, at the inconsiderate way in which you bring brambles and hedge weeds and garden refuse into the house, but I must protest against your introducing individuals of the type of Mrs. Vulpy as guests at Briony. Who is that playing the piano?

SYBIL. I think it's Evelyn Bray.

HOR. Ah! Who also dropped in accidentally, I suppose. Ludovic, will you kindly tell Miss Bray that we don't require any more music this evening. (*Exit* LUDOVIC, *door* R. *back.*) Had we not returned unexpectedly early, I presume this outrageous entertainment would have been kept from my knowledge. I may inform you that the mayor took upon himself to cancel the reception at the Town Hall, at which I was to have delivered a brief address, for the rather far-fetched reason of showing respect and sympathy at the sudden disappearance of Mrs. St. Gall.

RENÉ. I say, that was rather pet-lamb of him.

HOR. Mrs. St. Gall's son appears to treat the incident as of less serious importance.

RENÉ. I came here for rest and sympathy, with the faint possibility of a little Bridge to distract my thoughts; I wasn't to be expected to know that historical charades would be going on all round me. My nerves won't recover for weeks.

HOR. I am a persistent advocate of the abolition of corporal punishment in the Navy and in Board Schools, but I must confess, Mr. St. Gall, that a good birching inflicted on you would cause me no displeasure.

RENÉ. A most indelicate wind-up to a doubtful evening's amusement. I should insist on its being done *in camera.*

(*Enter* LUDOVIC, *door* R. *back.*)

SYBIL. Really, Mrs. Bavvel, we must plead guilty to having planned this semi-impromptu affair just a little, but we thought it would be such a good occasion for making an announcement.

AGATHA. An announcement?

HOR. What announcement?

SYBIL (*looking at* TREVOR). An announcement that I'm provisionally—well, engaged——

SPAR. Oh, Sybil, you angel! Let me announce it! Sybil and I are engaged!

LUD. Engaged! You and Sybil? Impossible. I congratulate you, of course, but it's—most unexpected.

CLARE. You dear thing. Congratulations.

SYBIL (*furiously*). You misunderstand me. I'm not engaged! Do you hear?

SPAR. Oh, Sybil, but you just said you were!

SYBIL. You fool! I was talking about something quite different.

[*Exit* SYBIL, *door* L.

HOR. There seems to be some confusion about this wonderful announcement.

LUD. I gathered that Miss Bomont was talking about something she's engaged on. Anyhow, she distinctly stated that she is not engaged to Mr. Sparrowby.

HOR. In any case this is hardly a fortunate moment in which to make announcements of secondary interest. (*Enter* WILLIAM, *door centre, carrying plate with banana. Stops horrified on seeing* MRS. BAVVEL, *who rises from chair.*) What are you carrying there, William?

WILL. (*miserably*). A banana, ma'am.

HOR. What are you doing with a banana at this time of night?

WILL. It's for her—him, the cockatoo, ma'am.

HOR. For Adolphus? At a quarter to eleven! He's never fed at this hour.

WILL. She–he seemed disturbed and restless as if he was asking for something, ma'am.

HOR. Disturbed? I am not surprised. In the fourteen years that he has lived here he has never before experienced such an evening of disgraceful disorder. Trevor, perhaps you will see that your neighbours who dropped in so unexpectedly will leave with as little delay as possible. Those of you who are at present my guests will kindly retire to their sleeping apartments. William!

WILL. Yes, ma'am.

HOR. Tell Cook to send a cold supper for myself and Mr. Ludovic to the dining-room. Some beef and pickled walnuts and a few peaches.

WILL. (*weakly*). Yes, ma'am.

HOR. Tomorrow I shall have a good deal to say on the subject of these deplorable proceedings. Tonight I am too upset. I left Briony an orderly English home, I return to find it a casino.

(*Exit* HORTENSIA *up staircase* L., *followed by* LUDOVIC, *who holds up his hands in mock despair. The others stand blankly watching them disappear.* RENÉ *seizes banana which* WILLIAM *is holding on plate and exits* R. *eating it. He is followed by* DRUMMOND *and* AGATHA. WILLIAM *Exit, door* L., *leaving* CLARE *and* TREVOR *alone.*)

CURTAIN

ACT III

Breakfast Room at Briony.

(LUDOVIC, *having just breakfasted, is still seated, chair pushed back from table, reading paper.* BUTLER *about to clear away breakfast things.*)

BUTLER. Shall I remove the breakfast things, sir?

LUD. (*glancing at clock*). Is no one else coming down? Where is Miss Clare?

BUTLER. Miss Clare complained of a headache, sir, and had breakfast in her room.

LUD. And Mr. Trevor?

BUTLER. Mr. Trevor breakfasted very early and went up to the farm. Miss Sybil breakfasted in her room.

LUD. Had she a headache also?

BUTLER. She complained of a headache, sir. Mrs. Vulpy breakfasted in her room.

LUD. The same—complaint?

BUTLER. No, sir, anxiety and nervous depression. She made a very big breakfast, sir. I don't know whether Miss Agatha has had her breakfast sent up. She wasn't awake half an hour ago.

LUD. By the way, do you know whether Mrs. Vulpy received any telegrams this morning?

BUTLER. She received one, sir, that she seemed to be expecting.

LUD. Ah!

BUTLER. She held it for a long while looking at it, sir, theatrical like, and then said there was no answer.

LUD. Did she seem less depressed after she'd received it?

BUTLER. She ordered some more kidneys and toast. I should say she was a lot more cheerful.

(*Enter* AGATHA *hastily, door* L.)

AGATHA. Hullo, Ludovic, only you here? I meant to have breakfast upstairs, but I saw Hortensia go out to the rose garden, so I skipped down.

BUTLER. Shall I warm some of the breakfast dishes for you, miss?

AGATHA. No, just make me some fresh tea, and leave the ham and sardines. (*While speaking has both arms on the table.*) I don't see any butter.

BUTLER. Your sleeve's in the butter, miss.

AGATHA. Oh, so it is. And you might bring in some more toast.

BUTLER. Yes, miss.

AGATHA. Isn't there any honey?

LUD. Your other sleeve is in the honey.

AGATHA. Oh, bother. (*Exit* BUTLER, *door centre.*) I say, did you breakfast with Hortensia? Was she very awful?

LUD. She told me she had lain awake most of the night boiling with indignation. She's now in the hard-boiled state of cold vindictiveness.

AGATHA. Mercy on us, whatever shall we do?

LUD. Personally I intend going for a few weeks on a visit to Ireland.

AGATHA. But we can't all go to Ireland.

LUD. One of the great advantages of Ireland as a place of residence is that a large number of excellent people never go there.

AGATHA. You're disgustingly selfish; you don't think what is to become of the rest of us.

LUD. On the contrary, it's you that are selfish and inconsiderate. If one of you would only marry Trevor all this Hortensia discomfort and forced marching would be avoided.

AGATHA. But how absurd you are, Ludovic! One can't marry Trevor without his consent. No really nice girl would make advances to a man unless he showed himself attracted to her first; and, as regards Trevor, it wouldn't be the slightest good anyway; one might as well make advances to the landscape. We poor women are so dreadfully handicapped. If I were only a man——

LUD. If you were a man you couldn't marry Trevor, so that wouldn't help us. Your sleeve's in the honey again.

(*Enter* BUTLER, *door centre, with tea and toast.*)

BUTLER. Is there anything else I can bring you, miss?

AGATHA. No, thank you. Oh, tell Cook, in case I should be travelling later in the day, to cut me some ham sandwiches. No mustard.

BUTLER. Yes, miss. Shall you want the dogcart ordered?

LUD. You had better say the waggonette and the luggage cart; there may be others leaving this afternoon.

BUTLER. The 3.20 up or the 4.15 down, miss?

AGATHA. I'm not quite sure. I'll let you know later.

BUTLER. Yes, miss.

[*Exit* BUTLER, *door centre.*

AGATHA. If Hortensia is in a never-darken-my-doors-again kind of temper I shall go right off to Town and on somewhere from there. On the other hand, if it's the kind of outbreak that blows over in a week or two, I shall merely go and stay with some people I know at Exeter.

LUD. Nice people?

AGATHA. Oh, dear, no. Quite uninteresting. I met them somewhere in Switzerland; they helped to find some luggage that had gone astray. I always lose luggage when I travel. They have porridge in the mornings, but they live close to the station, so one hasn't got to take a cab.

LUD. Perhaps it won't be convenient for them to have you at a moment's notice.

AGATHA. It's not at all convenient for me to go there, but at a time like this one can't stop to think of convenience. Especially other people's.

(*Enter* SPARROWBY *cautiously, door* L.)

SPAR. I've been afraid to come in before for fear of meeting Hortensia. I'm awfully hungry: I suppose everything's cold.

LUD. As a matter of public convenience I request you to be sparing with the ham; it may be required later in the day for an emergency ration of sandwiches. Have you booked a seat in the waggonette?

SPAR. I say, is it as bad as all that? I hoped Mrs. Bavvel might have cooled down a bit.

LUD. She has. She has settled comfortably into a glacial epoch which will transform Briony into a sub-arctic zone in which I, for one, am not tempted to remain.

SPAR. (*seating himself at table and beginning to eat*). What an awful nuisance; I don't at all want to leave Briony just now. I say, do you think I'm engaged to Sybil or not? She certainly seemed to say that we were engaged last night.

LUD. I really haven't given it a thought. I don't think it matters particularly. The important question is, is Trevor engaged to anybody?

SPAR. I think you're awfully unsympathetic.

LUD. It's absurd to expect sympathy at breakfast-time. Breakfast is the most unsympathetic meal of the day. One can't love one's neighbour with any sincerity when he's emptying the toast-rack and helping himself lavishly to the grilled mushrooms that one particularly adores. Even at lunch one is usually in rather a quarrelsome frame of mind; you must have noticed that most family rows take place at lunch-time. At afternoon tea one begins to get polite, but one isn't really sympathetic till about the second course at dinner.

SPAR. But the whole future happiness of my life is wrapped up in Sybil's acceptance of my offer.

LUD. People who wrap up their whole future happiness in one event generally find it convenient to unwrap it later on.

(*Enter* CLARE, *door* L.)

CLARE. Morning, everybody. Have you brave things breakfasted with Hortensia?

AGATHA. No, only Ludovic. He reports her as being pretty bad. It's a regular case of *sauve qui peut.*

CLARE. Such disgusting weather to travel in. Fancy being cooped up in a stuffy railway carriage all the afternoon. Anything in the papers, Ludovic?

LUD. Very possibly there may be. Agatha and Sparrowby have kept me so pleasantly engaged in discussing their plans that I've scarcely been able to grapple with the wider events of the day.

AGATHA. Oh, I can always read and carry on a conversation at the same time. I suppose I've got a double brain.

CLARE. Why don't you economize and have one good one.

LUD. (*rising*). If you two are going to quarrel, I'm off. Other people's quarrels always make me feel amiable, and a prospective Parliamentary candidate can't afford to be amiable in private life. It's like talking shop out of hours. (LUDOVIC *walks towards door* L.)

SPAR. (*jumping up and following him*). I say, Ludovic, I want to ask you—do you really think——

[*Exit* LUDOVIC *and* SPARROWBY, *door* L.

(*Enter* MRS. VULPY, *door centre.*)

MRS. V. Is the coast clear? I'm scared to death of meeting that Gorgon again.

AGATHA. Had breakfast?

MRS. V. Nothing worth speaking of. Oh, is there tea? How adorable. (*Seats herself at table.*) Well, has anything happened?

AGATHA. The luggage cart has been requisitioned, and if you want anything in the way of sandwiches or luggage labels an early order will prevent disappointment.

MRS. V. Gracious, what an earthquake. And all because of a little harmless dance. If any of you girls do succeed in marrying that young man, you'll have to break him of the farmyard habit. A husband who is always going to earth is rather a poor sort of investment.

CLARE. As long as one marries him, what *does* it matter? One can afford to be neglected by one's own husband; it's when other people's husbands neglect one that one begins to talk of matrimonial disillusion.

MRS. V. Other people's husbands are rather an overrated lot. I prefer unmarried men any day; they've so much more experience.

CLARE. I don't agree with you. Isn't there a proverb: "A relapsed husband makes the best rake"?

AGATHA. You're positively disgraceful, both of you. We used to be taught to be content with the Ten Commandments and one husband; nowadays women get along with fewer commandments and want ten husbands.

MRS. V. It's no use scolding. It's the fault of the age we live in. The perfection of the motor-car has turned the country into a vast prairie of grass-widowhood. How can a woman be expected to cleave to some one who's at Lancaster Gate one minute and at North Berwick the next?

AGATHA. She can stay at home and lavish her affections on her babies.

CLARE. I hate babies. They're so human—they remind one of monkeys.

(*Enter* SYBIL, *door* L., *throws herself into chair* L. *centre of stage.*)

MRS. V. Well, it's no use taking a tragic view of yesterday's fiasco. There are thousands of as good men as Trevor in the world, waiting to be married.

SYBIL. That's just it; they don't seem to mind how long they wait. And when you come to have a closer look at the thousands there are very few of them that one could possibly marry.

AGATHA. Oh, nonsense; I don't see why one should be so dreadfully fastidious. After all, we're told all men are brothers.

SYBIL. Yes; unfortunately, so many of them are younger brothers.

AGATHA. Oh, well, money isn't everything.

SYBIL. It isn't everything, but it's a very effective substitute for most things.

MRS. V. By the way, tell me which is the nearest and cleanest way to the farm.

AGATHA (*who is about to leave room*). Through the white gates into the fir plantation, and past the potting sheds. You can't miss it. (*Suddenly turning back and sitting down abruptly.*) What do you want to go there for?

MRS. V. Merely to say my good-byes to Mr. Trevor, and while he is showing me round the farm buildings I dare say I'll find an opportunity to tell him how badly he's treated you all, and what an uncomfortable situation he's created, and generally work on his better feelings.

SYBIL. You might as well work on superior blotting-paper. (*Exit* MRS. VULPY.) I don't trust that woman a little atom.

CLARE. I believe she's had bad news from South Africa, and she's keeping it dark and going for Trevor on her own account.

SYBIL. He spoke very curiously about her to me last night, asked what I thought of her and all that.

AGATHA. Exactly what he did to me. I say, can't we stop her?

CLARE. Are you proposing to use violence? If so I think I'll watch from a distance; when you used to play hockey you were noted for hitting more people than you ever aimed at.

SYBIL (*jumping to her feet*). Hortensia's voice!

(CLARE *and* SYBIL *scurry out of the room by door* R. AGATHA *blunders into the arms of* HORTENSIA, *who enters by door* L.)

AGATHA (*trying to look at her ease*). Oh, good morning. Did it rain in the night?

HOR. I lay awake most of the night; I did not hear any rain. (*Rings bell.*)

AGATHA. Oh, I'm *so* sorry you didn't sleep well. Oak leaves soaked in salt water and put under the bed are an awfully good remedy. Let me get you some.

HOR. (*coldly*). Thank you, we don't want any more decaying vegetation brought into the house. My sleeplessness was not due to insomnia. Under normal circumstances I sleep excellently.

AGATHA. I feel that I ought to explain about last night.

HOR. You will have to explain. Every one will have to give an account of his or her share in the disgraceful affair, including the servants, who seem to have connived at it. I have ordered a gathering of the household for 4 o'clock in the library, which you will kindly attend. (*Enter* WILLIAM, *door centre.*) William, at this hour of the morning I expect the breakfast things to be cleared away.

[*Exit* HORTENSIA, R.

AGATHA. William, tell John that I shall have to leave here well before four to catch the 4.15. I've got lots of luggage to register at the station.

WILL. Yes, miss; the waggonette's ordered already.

AGATHA. I expect it will have to be the dogcart as well; there will probably be a lot of us wanting to catch trains this afternoon.

WILL. Yes, miss. What I envy about you, miss, is your play-going way of taking things.

AGATHA. Play-going way?

WILL. Yes, miss. You just sit and wait till things has been brought to a climax and then you put on your hat and gloves and walk outside. It's different for those who've got to go on living with the climax.

AGATHA. I hadn't thought of that; I suppose it is rather horrid.

[*Exit* WILLIAM *by door centre, carrying off breakfast things on tray.*

[*Exit* AGATHA, *door* L.

(*Enter* LUDOVIC, *door* R. *He takes newspaper packet off table* L., *opens wrapper, throws himself into a chair and begins reading.*)

(*Enter* RENÉ, *door* R.)

RENÉ. Ludovic! Aren't you all feeling like a lot of drowned kittens?

LUD. I don't know what a lot of drowned kittens feel like. I hope I'm not looking like a lot of drowned kittens.

RENÉ. Oh, don't talk about looks. (*Looks himself carefully over in the mirror.*) I felt so jumpy last night that I scarcely dared put the light out. I had a hot-water bottle in my bed.

LUD. A hot-water bottle? Surely it's too warm for that.

RENÉ. Oh, there was no hot water in it, it was merely to give a sense of protection. I suppose there's a general stampede? (*Seats himself, chair centre stage.*)

LUD. The house resounds with the cutting of sandwiches and the writing of luggage labels.

RENÉ. And what does *he* say to it all?

LUD. Who? Trevor? He made a strategic move to the farm at an early hour.

RENÉ. I believe he was so sleepy last night that he doesn't really know whether he proposed to Sybil or not.

LUD. Sybil did her best, but that miserable Sparrowby ruined whatever chance she had.

RENÉ. I've no use for that person; he's just the kind of idiot who comes up to you in a Turkish bath and says, "Isn't it hot?" Meanwhile, what are you going to do?

LUD. I shall pay a long-projected visit to an old chum who lives in Kildare.

RENÉ. Nonsense, Ludo, you can't. Nobody really lives in Kildare; I don't believe there are such places. And old Spindleham is really at the last gasp. The *Western Morning News* says he can't live out the week.

LUD. Under present circumstances, René, I've no intention of standing.

RENÉ. Oh, don't be so provoking. Go and see Trevor and tell him he must marry Sybil. Explain the circumstances to him. A wife is a sort of thing that can happen any day. But a Parliamentary vacancy is a different matter. There's your career to think of.

LUD. He will naturally retort that his whole future happiness has got to be thought of.

RENÉ. Oh, damn! what about my whole future income?

LUD. My dear René, the question is, whether we have not hunted Trevor into the wrong net. I have just met that Vulpy woman in full cry up to the farm, and something in her manner tells me that she's running a trail of her own.

RENÉ. But her husband——

LUD. I asked her if she had had any news of him. She was careful to tell me that she hadn't received any letters this morning. She was equally careful *not* to inform me that she did get a telegram. I fancy that telegram announced her promotion to the rank of widowhood.

RENÉ. But you surely don't think that Trevor would——

LUD. That's exactly what I do think. We've tried to badger and harry him into a matrimonial entanglement with all sorts of eligible and likely young women, and it's quite in the nature of things that he'll turn round and perversely commit himself to this wholly impossible person. You must remember that Trevor is a fellow who has seen comparatively little of the world, and what he's seen has been more or less of one pattern. Now that he's suddenly confronted with a creature of quite another type, with whom he isn't expected to interest himself, naturally he at once becomes interested.

RENÉ. Well, if this stumbling-block of a husband of hers has really been good-natured enough to migrate to another world, everything is plain sailing. Trevor can go ahead and marry the lady—after a decent interval, of course.

LUD. Absolutely out of the question. I should never forgive myself if such a thing happened.

RENÉ. But why—haven't we been moving heaven and earth to get him married?

LUD. Married, yes, but not to Mrs. Vulpy. After all, Trevor is my only brother's only son, and if I can help it I'm not going to sit still and let him tie himself to that bundle of scheming vulgarity. Besides, a woman like that installed as mistress of Briony would only mean a prolongation of Hortensia's influence. Trevor would be driven to consult his mother in everything, from the sheer impossibility of putting confidence in his wife.

RENÉ. I think we're being absurdly fastidious about Trevor's wife. We've given him heaps of opportunities for marrying decent nonentities, so I don't see why we should reproach ourselves if he accidentally swallows a clumsier bait. Anyhow, I don't see how you're going to stop it if there's really anything in it.

LUD. That's just what's worrying me. To speak to him about it would be to clinch matters. With rare exceptions the Bavvels are devilishly obstinate.

RENÉ. Well, it would be rather a delicate subject to broach to her. She would scarcely relish being told that she's impossible.

LUD. I should put it more tactfully. I should tell her she wouldn't harmonize with local surroundings, that she has too much dash and go, and—help me out with some tactful attribute.

RENÉ. Too flamboyant.

LUD. I asked you for tact, not truth.

RENÉ. Too much individuality. I don't know what that means. But it sounds well.

LUD. Thank you, that will do nicely. A woman always respects a word that she can't spell.

RENÉ. You'd better jot it all down on your cuff. You'll forget it in a sudden panic when you're talking to her.

(*Enter* BUTLER, R.)

BUTLER. Colonel Mutsome.

(*Enter* COL. MUTSOME, R.)

[*Exit* BUTLER, *same door.*

COL. How do you do? (*Shakes hands with* LUDOVIC, *bows to* RENÉ.) What unpleasant weather. Quite damp. I hope dear Hortensia is well. I've a great admiration for Hortensia. I always say she's the first lady in Somersetshire.

RENÉ. Everything must have a beginning.

COL. I hear our member is not expected to live. (*Seats himself in chair,* R.)

LUD. I saw something to that effect in the local papers.

COL. I suppose we shall be having an election in a few weeks' time. Is it true that you are the prospective Party candidate?

LUD. I saw it suggested in the local papers. There has always been some idea of getting a Bavvel to stand.

COL. I suppose you would accept!

LUD. That will depend very largely on family considerations.

RENÉ. Of course Ludovic means to stand. I caught him yesterday being ostentatiously sympathetic to the local chemist, a man with a hare-lip and personal reminiscences and a vote. No one listens to the personal reminiscences of a man with a hare-lip unless they've got some imperative motive; when the man also has a vote the motive is unmistakable.

LUD. René, as a private secretary, you would have to be very private.

COL. I suppose you subscribe to all the principal items of the Party programme?

LUD. Oh, I believe so—and to most of the local charities. That is the really important thing. It is generally understood that a rich man has some difficulty in entering the Kingdom of Heaven; the House of Commons is not so exclusive. Our electoral system, however, takes good care that the rich man entering Parliament shall not remain rich. It is simply astonishing the number of institutions supported by involuntary contributions that a candidate discovers in his prospective constituency. At least he doesn't discover them —they discover him. For instance, I don't keep bees, I don't know how to, and don't want to know how to. I don't eat honey. I never go near a hive except at an agricultural show when I am perfectly certain there are no bees in it. Yet I have already consented to be vice-president and annual subscriber to the local beekeepers' association. On consulting a memorandum book I find I am vice-president of seven bell-ringers' guilds and about twenty village football clubs. I cannot remember having been so enthusiastic about football when I was at school. I am a subscribing member of a botanical ramble club. Can you imagine me doing botanical rambles? Of course you quite understand that there's no bribery in all this.

COL. Oh, of course not. Bribery is not tolerated nowadays.

LUD. At any rate, one gives it another name. Let us call it altruism in compartments; very intense and comprehensive where it exists, but strictly confined within the bound of one's constituency.

COL. I suppose you're sound on religious questions? There is no truth in the story that you have leanings towards agnosticism?

LUD. My dear Colonel, no one can be Agnostic nowadays. The Christian Apologists have left one nothing to disbelieve.

RENÉ. Personally I am a pagan. Christians waste too much time in professing to be miserable sinners, which generally results in their being merely miserable and leaving some of the best sins undone; whereas the pagan gets cheerfully to work and commits his sins and doesn't brag so much about them.

COL. I trust you are only talking in theory.

RENÉ. In theory, of course. In practice, every one is pagan according to his lights.

LUD. René, as a private secretary, I'm afraid you would become a public scandal. I shouldn't dare to leave you alone with an unprotected deputation.

(*Enter* TREVOR, *door* L.)

TREVOR. Morning, Ludovic. Hullo, Colonel, I didn't know you were here. (*Shakes hands with* COLONEL MUTSOME.) Morning, René. I distinctly heard you all talking politics. (TREVOR *seats himself in chair, centre stage.*)

COL. Politics are rather in the air. It seems we are threatened with a Parliamentary vacancy.

LUD. By way of meeting trouble half-way, Colonel Mutsome has come to ascertain whether there is any probability of my standing.

COL. I should have expressed it differently.

LUD. Things do not point at present to the probability of my becoming a candidate, but the Colonel has taken things betimes and has been doing a little preliminary heckling.

COL. Not heckling, exactly. My position as Vice-Chairman of the local Party Association gives me some opportunity for gauging opinion down here. Collectively the Government has, perhaps, lost some of its prestige, but individually I think Ministers are popular.

LUD. Including the irrepressible Bumpingford.

COL. Oh, certainly. Rather an assertive personality, perhaps, but of undeniable ability. He comes into the category of those who are born to command.

LUD. Possibly. His trouble so far is that he hasn't been able to find any one who was born to obey him. So you think Ministers are in general popular?

COL. Compared with the leaders of the Opposition——

LUD. One should be careful not to say disparaging things of Opposition leaders.

COL. Because they may one day be at the head of affairs?

LUD. No, because they may one day lead the Opposition. One never knows.

COL. There is the question of Votes for Women.

LUD. Personally I see no reason why women shouldn't have votes. They're quite unfit to have votes, but that's no argument against their having them. If we were to restrict the right of voting to those of the male sex who were fitted for it we should have to enlarge Hyde Park to accommodate the protesting hordes of non-voters. Government by democracy means government of the mentally unfit by the mentally mediocre tempered by the saving grace of snobbery.

COL. You will be very unpopular if you say that sort of thing down here.

LUD. I have no intention of saying it. Some poet has remarked, "To think is to be full of sorrow." To think aloud is a luxury of sorrow which few politicians can afford to indulge in.

COL. (*suddenly*). By the way—was there some dancing at Briony last night?

LUD. (*in nervous haste*). Oh, no, just some Shakespeare readings and a little music. I wonder you haven't asked me about land values.

COL. I was coming to that.

TREVOR (*eagerly*). It's rather an important question, particularly down here.

LUD. Most important.

RENÉ (*same eagerness*). It's quite one of the questions of the immediate future. An aunt of a Cabinet Minister was speaking to me about it only last week. She said it kept her awake at nights.

COL. Really—I quite understood that there was a Cinderella dance——

LUD. Oh, no, dear no, nothing of that kind. Some Shakespeare reading, in costume.

COL. In costume—but how very interesting. What scenes did you give?

RENÉ. The Ghost scenes from what-do-you-call-it.

COL. The Ghost scene from "Hamlet"? That must have needed a lot of rehearsal.

RENÉ. No, we had a lot of ghosts, so that if one forgot his lines another could go on with them.

Col. What an odd idea. What a very odd idea. But they couldn't all have been in costume.

René. They were, rows of them. All in white sheets.

Col. How very extraordinary. It couldn't have been a bit like Shakespeare.

René. It wasn't, but it was very like Maeterlinck. Whoever really wrote "Hamlet," there can be no doubt that Maeterlinck and Maxim Gorki ought to have written it, in collaboration.

Col. But how could they? They weren't born at that time.

René. That's the bother of it. Ideas get used up so quickly. If the Almighty hadn't created the world at the beginning of things Edison would probably have done it by this time on quite different lines, and then some one would have come along to prove that the Chinese had done it centuries ago.

Col. (*acidly, to* Trevor, *turning his back on* René). How is your cold, Mr. Trevor? You had a cold before we went to Worcestershire.

Trevor. That one went long ago. I've got another one now, which is better, thank you.

Col. We had such a lot of asparagus in Worcestershire.

Trevor. Yes?

Col. We got our earliest asparagus in London, then we got more down here, and then we had a late edition in Worcestershire, so we've had quite a lot this year.

René. The charm of that story is that it could be told in any drawing-room.

Col. (*rising from seat*). I think I saw Hortensia pass the window. If you don't mind I'll go and meet her.

Lud. Let me escort you.

[*Exeunt* Ludovic *and* Colonel Mutsome, *door* R.

René (*lighting cigarette*). You've heard the story that's going about?

Trevor. That we held unholy revels here last night.

René. Well, *à propos* of that; people are saying that you and Sparrowby proposed to the same girl and that Sparrowby threatened to break your neck if you didn't give way to him; and that you gave way rather than have any unpleasantness.

Trevor. What an infernal invention. I am damned if I let that go about.

René. I don't see what you can do to stop it.

TREVOR. I might break Sparrowby's neck.

RENÉ. No one could have any reasonable objection to that course; Sparrowby is one of those people who would be enormously improved by death. Unfortunately, he is your guest, and on that account it wouldn't be quite the thing to do. He's sure to have a parent or aunt or some one who'd write letters to *The Times* about it: "Fatal ragging in country houses," and so on. No, your only prudent line of action would be to marry the girl, or any girl who came handy, just to knock the stuffing out of the story. Otherwise you'll have to take it recumbent, as the saying is.

TREVOR. I'm not fool enough to rush off and perpetrate matrimony with the first person I meet in order to put a stop to a ridiculous story.

RENÉ. My dear Trevor, I quite understand your situation.

TREVOR. You don't.

RENÉ. Of course I do. You don't want to interrupt an agreeable and moderately safe flirtation with a woman who has just got husband enough to give her the flavour of forbidden fruit. I'm not one of those who run the Vulpy down just because she's a trifle too flamboyant for the general taste. As a wife I dare say she'd be rather an experiment down here, but I've no doubt you'd be tolerably happy. She'd be more at her ease at a suburban race meeting than at a county garden party, but still—you could travel a good deal. And if you find her sympathetic it doesn't matter so very much whether she's intelligent or not. But all that is beside the point, because she's not available. Inconvenient husbands don't come to timely ends in real life like they do in fiction. If you seriously want to put your foot down on the gossip that is going about, and make an end of this uncomfortable domestic situation, your only course is to go straight ahead and propose to the first available girl that you run up against. If it's the bother of the thing that you shirk let me open negotiations for you—my mission in life is to save other people trouble, on reasonable terms. (RENÉ *becomes suddenly aware that* TREVOR *has gone to sleep, and rises angrily from his seat.*) Of all the exasperating dolts! I don't know how match-making mothers manage to grow fat on the business; a week of this would wear me to a shadow.

[*Exit* RENÉ *in a fury, door* R.

(*Enter* LUDOVIC, L.)

LUD. Hullo, is René here?

TREVOR. He was, a minute or two ago. I think I heard him leave the house.

LUD. Has anything been heard of his mother? So many distracting things have been happening that I clean forgot to ask about her.

TREVOR. By Jove, so did I. He'll think us rather remiss, but anyhow he seemed more concerned about finding me a suitable wife than about retrieving his lost parent. Have you heard anything of the story that he says is going about?

LUD. (*seating himself*). About last night, you mean?

TREVOR. Yes, that Sparrowby and I proposed to the same girl, and that Sparrowby bounced me into taking a back seat.

LUD. Ah! no—at least, probably what I heard had reference to that. What an unpleasant scandal. Unfortunately, the fact that Sybil is leaving Briony in such a hurry will give colour to it.

TREVOR. Was it Sybil, then?

LUD. I suppose so. I think I heard her name mentioned. What shall you do then?

TREVOR. Do? I don't know. What do you suggest?

LUD. My suggestion would be so simple that you are not likely to accept it for a moment. If one shows people an intricate and risky way out of a difficulty they are becomingly grateful: if you point out a safe and obvious exit they regard you with resentment. In your case the resentment would probably take the form of going to sleep in the middle of my advice.

TREVOR. I wasn't going to sleep! I was wondering which particular girl you were going to recommend to my notice. There seems to be a concentration on Sybil Bomont.

LUD. It's scarcely my place to fill in the details for you; I suppose matrimony is an eventuality which begins to present itself rather prominently to you, and when you've settled that point the details soon fit themselves in. If the Bomont girl doesn't meet with your requirements there is your neighbour Evelyn Bray, whom you entangled in last night's entertainment—I shall never forget her face when I told her that Hortensia didn't require any more music —and there's Clare Henessey; you used to get on famously with Clare.

TREVOR. Clare and Evelyn are very good sorts——

LUD. (*raising his hand*). Good sorts— Oh, my dear Trevor, you are still in the schoolboy stage as regards women. The schoolboy divides womenkind broadly into two species, the decent sort and the holy horror, much as the naturalist, after a somewhat closer investigation of his subject, classifies snakes as either harmless or poisonous. The schoolboy is usually fairly well informed about things that he doesn't have to study, but as regards women he is altogether too specific. You can't really divide them in a hard-and-fast way.

TREVOR. At least there are superficial differences.

LUD. But nothing deeper. Woman is a belated survival from a primeval age of struggle and cunning and competition; that is why, wherever you go the world over, you find all the superfluous dust and worry being made by the gentler sex. If you are on a crowded P. and O. steamer, who is it that wages an incessant warfare over the cabin accommodation? Who is it that creates the little social feuds that divide benighted country parishes and lonely hill stations? Who is it that raises objections to smoking in railway carriages, and who writes to housemasters to complain of the dear boys' breakfast fare? Man has moved with the historic progression of the ages. But woman is a habit that has survived from the period when one had to dispute with cave bears and cave hyenas whether one ate one's supper or watched others eat it, whether one slept at home or on one's doorstep. The great religions of the world have all recognized this fact and kept womankind severely outside of their respective systems. That is why, however secular one's tendencies, one turns instinctively to religion in some form for respite and peace.

TREVOR. But one can't get along without women.

LUD. Precisely what I have been trying to impress upon you. Granted that woman is merely a bad habit, she is a habit that we have not grown out of. Under certain circumstances a bad habit is first-cousin to a virtue. In your case it seems to me that matrimony is not only a virtue but a convenience.

TREVOR. It's all very well for you to talk about convenience. What may be convenient for other people may be highly inconvenient for me.

LUD. That means that you're involved in some blind-alley affair with a married woman. Precisely what I feared. Men like yourself of easy-going, unsuspecting temperament, invariably fall victims to the most rapacious type of cave woman, the woman who already has a husband and who merely kills for the sake of killing. You pick and choose and dally among your artificial categories of awfully good sorts and dear little women, and then some one of the Mrs. Vulpy type comes along and quietly annexes you.

TREVOR. I seem to have been annexed to Mrs. Vulpy by popular delimitation. Critically speaking, she isn't a bit my style, but I don't see anything so very dreadful about her. She's a trifle pronounced, perhaps—she tells me she had a Spanish grandfather.

LUD. Ancestors will happen in the best-intentioned families. Every social sin or failing is excused nowadays under the plea of an artistic temperament or a Sicilian grandmother. As poor Lady Cloutsham once told me, as soon as her children found out that a Hungarian lady of blameless moral character had married into the family somewhere in the reign of the Georges, they considered themselves absolved from any further attempts to distinguish between good and evil—except by way of expressing a general preference for the latter. When her youngest boy was at Winchester he made such unblushing use of the Hungarian strain in his blood that he was known as the Blue Danube. "That," said Lady Cloutsham, "is what comes of letting young children read Debrett and Darwin."

TREVOR. As regards Mrs. Vulpy's temperament, I don't fancy one need go very far afield.

LUD. Oh, no, Greater London is quite capable of turning her out without having recourse to foreign blending.

TREVOR. Still, I don't see that she's anything worse than a flirt.

LUD. Oh, on her best behaviour, I've no doubt she's perfectly gentle and frolicsome; for the matter of that, the cave hyenas probably had their after-dinner moments of comparative amiability. But, from the point of view of an extremely marriageable young bachelor, she simply isn't safe to play with. I don't want to run her down on the score of her rather common personality, but I wish to warn you that she is one of those people gifted with just the sort of pushing, scheming audacity—(*Enter* MRS. VULPY, *door centre.*) Ah, good morning, Mrs. Vulpy (TREVOR *looks round and jumps to his feet*), just the sort of pushing, scheming audacity that makes them dangerous. Once we let them wriggle their way into the Persian Gulf they'll snap up all our commerce under our eyes.

MRS. V. You dreadful men, always talking politics.

LUD. Politics are rather in the air just now.

MRS. V. I feel as if we were all in the air after the dreadful explosion of last night. I am just wondering where I am going to come down.

TREVOR. It seems an awful shame, driving all you charming people away. My mother goes to absurd lengths about some things.

MRS. V. It's poor us who have to go the absurd lengths. I shan't feel safe till I have put two fair-sized counties between Mrs. Bavvel and myself. Oh, Mr. Trevor, before I leave you *must* show me the model dairy.

TREVOR. Right-oh, I'll take you there now if you like.

MRS. V. Do, please. I just love dairies and cheese-making and all that sort of thing. I think it's so clever the way they make those little blue insertions in Gorgonzola cheese. I always say I ought to have been a farmer's wife. We'll leave Ludovic to his horrid politics.

LUD. Before I forget, Trevor, go and get me those trout flies you promised me, and I'll have them packed. Mrs. Vulpy won't mind, I dare say, waiting for you here for a few minutes.

TREVOR. Right you are. I won't be a second.

[*Exit* TREVOR.

LUD. I hope you don't despise me too much.

MRS. V. Despise you! Oh, Mr. Ludovic, what ever should I despise you for?

LUD. For being fool enough to put confidence in you as a fellow conspirator.

MRS. V. Why, I am sure I have been loyal enough to our compact. If the results haven't been brilliant, you can scarcely blame me for the breakdown.

LUD. The compact was that you should help in an endeavour to get Trevor engaged to one of the girls of the house party. I don't think I'm mistaken in saying that the game you are playing is to secure him for yourself.

MRS. V. Never more mistaken in your life. Really, you seem to forget that I'm a married woman.

LUD. Your memory is even shorter. You seem to forget that you received a telegram this morning to say that your husband is dead.

MRS. V. Whatever will you say next? You don't know what you're talking about.

LUD. Oh, it's correct enough; I read it.

MRS. V. (*raising her voice*). How dare you intercept my correspondence. The telegram was marked plain enough, "Vulpy, c/o Bavvel." You're simply a common sneak.

LUD. I didn't read the intelligence in your telegram. I read it in your manner. You've just been obliging enough to confirm my deductions.

MRS. V. Oh, you're trying amateur detective business on me, are you? (*With sudden change of manner.*) Now, look here, Mr. Ludovic, don't you set yourself against me. Why shouldn't I marry Trevor? You said yourself two days ago that it was a pity I wasn't a widow, so that I could be eligible for marrying him.

LUD. Of course, I spoke jestingly.

MRS. V. Well, it isn't a jest to me. I have had a wretched, miserable time with my late husband; I can't tell you what a time I've had with him.

LUD. Because you have had a miserable time with the late Mr. Vulpy is precisely, my dear lady, the reason why I don't wish you to try the experiment of being miserable with my nephew. You are so utterly unsuited to him and his surroundings that you couldn't fail to be unhappy and to make him unhappy into the bargain.

MRS. V. I don't see why I should be unsuited to him. Trevor is a gentleman, and I am a lady, I suppose. Perhaps you wish to suggest that I am not.

LUD. You are, if you will permit me to say so, a very charming and agreeable lady, but you would not fit in with the accepted ideals of the neighbourhood. You have too much dash and go and—in—indefinable—characteristics. I don't know if you've noticed it, but in Somersetshire we don't dash.

MRS. V. Oh, don't fling your beastly county set and its prejudices in my face. I am as good as the lot of you and a bit better. I mix in far smarter circles than you've got here. Lulu Duchess of Dulverton and her set are a cut above the pack of you, and as for you, if you want my opinion, you're a meddling, interfering, middle-aged toad.

LUD. You asked me a moment ago why you shouldn't marry Trevor. You're supplying one of the reasons now. You're flying into something very like a rage. In Somersetshire we never fly into a rage. We walk into one, and when necessary we stay there for weeks, perhaps for years. But we never fly into one.

MRS. V. Oh, I've had enough of your sarcasms. You've had my opinion of you. You're a mass of self-seeking and intrigue. You're mistaken if you think I'm going to let a middle-aged toad stand in my path.

(*Enter* Trevor.)

Trevor. Here are all the flies I could find. Sorry to have kept you waiting, but I had to hunt for them.

Lud. Don't mention it; we've been having such an interesting talk, about the age toads live to. Mrs. Vulpy is quite a naturalist.

Mrs. V. I've got all my packing to do, so we'd better not lose any more time.

Trevor. Right you are, we will go at once.

[*Exit* Trevor *and* Mrs. Vulpy, R.

(*Enter* Agatha, L.)

(Ludovic *flings himself down savagely at writing table.*)

Agatha. Have you seen Trevor anywhere?

Lud. He was here a minute ago. I believe he's now in the dairy.

Agatha. The dairy! What's he doing in the dairy?

Lud. I don't know. What does one do in dairies?

Agatha. One makes butter and that sort of thing. Trevor can't make butter.

Lud. I don't believe he can. We spend incredible sums on technical education, but the number of people who know how to make butter remains extremely limited.

Agatha. Is he alone?

Lud. I fancy Mrs. Vulpy is with him.

Agatha. That cat! Why is she with him?

Lud. I don't know. There's a proverb—isn't there?—about showing a cat the way to the dairy, but I forget what happens next.

Agatha. I call it rather compromising.

Lud. It's a model dairy, you know.

Agatha. I don't see that that makes it any better. Mrs. Vulpy is scarcely a model woman.

Lud. She's a married woman.

Agatha. A South African husband is rather a doubtful security.

Lud. Then you can scarcely blame her for taking a provident interest in West of England bachelors.

Agatha. It's simply indecent. She might wait till one husband is definitely dead before trying to rope in another.

Lud. My dear Agatha, brevity is the soul of widowhood.

Agatha. I loathe her. She promised she would try to get Trevor to put an end to all this muddle and row by getting him engaged to —to Sybil or any one else available.

LUD. How do you know she's not trying now?

AGATHA. Oh, I say, do you think she is?

LUD. I think it's quite possible; also I think it's quite possible that Trevor is discoursing learnedly on the amount of milk a Jersey cow can be induced to yield under intelligent treatment. Frankly, I consider these milk and egg statistics that one is expected to talk about in the country border on the indelicate. If I were a cow or hen I should resent having my most private and personal actions treated as a sort of auction bridge. The country has no reticence.

(*Enter* SYBIL, R.)

SYBIL. Well, I've packed.

AGATHA. Oh, dear, I haven't begun. I know I shall be late for the train; I'm always late for trains. I must go and dig up some foxglove roots in the plantation to take away with me.

SYBIL. I refuse to let you bring more than five cubic feet of earth mould and stinging nettles into the carriage.

AGATHA. Don't excite yourself, my dear. I'm going by a down train and you're going by an up, I presume.

SYBIL. Don't be a pig. You must come with us to make a four for Bridge; there'll be Clare and myself and you and the Vulpy. Otherwise we'll have to let that wearisome Sparrowby in, and I'd rather have a ton of decaying hedge and compressed caterpillar in the carriage than have Sparrowby inflicted on me for three mortal hours.

AGATHA. I'm not going to upset all my visiting plans just to suit your Bridge arrangements. Besides, you said the last time we played that I had no more notion of the game than an unborn parrot. I haven't got such a short memory, you see.

SYBIL. I wish you hadn't got such a short temper.

AGATHA. Me short-tempered! My good temper is proverbial.

SYBIL. Not to say legendary.

LUD. Please don't start quarrelling. You're making me feel amiable again.

(*Enter* MRS. VULPY, R., *trying not to look crest-fallen.*)

MRS. V. I never knew a dairy could be so interesting. All the latest improvements. Such beautiful ventilation—and such plain dairymaids. What it is to have a careful mother.

LUD. You weren't very long in going over it.

MRS. V. Oh, I had to rush it, of course. I must go and superintend my packing. It doesn't do to leave everything to one's maid.

SYBIL. Hortensia! It's no use bolting, we're cornered.

(*Enter*, R., HORTENSIA *and* COLONEL MUTSOME.)

MRS. V. Good morning, Mrs. Bavvel. (*She bows to the* COLONEL.) (*Pause.*)

COL. MRS. Bavvel has just been showing me the poultry yard. I've been admiring the black minorcas. How many eggs did you say they've laid in the last six months, Hortensia?

HOR. I don't think Mrs. Vulpy is much interested in such matters.

MRS. V. Oh, I adore poultry. There's something so Omar Khayyám about them. Lulu Duchess of Dulverton keeps white peacocks. (*Pause.*)

COL. Such a disappointment to us not to have had Mrs. Bavvel's lecture last night. All on account of Mrs. St. Gall's extraordinary disappearance. People are talking of a suicide. Others say it's a question of eluding creditors. Her debts, I believe, are simply enormous.

HOR. One must be careful of echoing local gossip, but from the improvident way in which that household is managed one is justified in supposing that financial difficulties are not unknown there.

COL. In any case, I feel convinced that we shan't see Mrs. St. Gall in these parts again.

(*Enter* RENÉ, *door* R., *followed by* TREVOR.)

RENÉ. I've found my mother!

COL. Mrs. St. Gall found? You've seen her?

RENÉ. No, but I've spoken to her. She was having a bath when I got back, so we conversed through the bath-room door. Touching scene of filial piety. Return of the prodigal mother, son weeping over bath-room door-handle. We don't run to a fatted calf, but I promised her she should have an egg with her tea.

COL. But where had she been all this time?

RENÉ. Principally at Cardiff.

COL. Cardiff! Whatever did she want to go to Cardiff for?

RENÉ. She didn't want to go. She was taken.

HOR. Taken!

RENÉ. She was doing a stroll on the Crowcoombe road when Freda Tewkesbury and her husband swooped down on her in their road car. They live at Warwick, at least they've got a house and some children there, but since they've gone mad on motoring they spend most of their time on the highway. The poor we have always in our midst, and nowadays the rich may crash into us at any moment.

Col. Your mother wasn't run over?

René. Oh, no, but Freda took her up for a spin and then insisted on her coming on just as she was for a day or two's visit to Monmouth and Cardiff. Freda is always picking up her friends in that impromptu way; she keeps spare tooth-brushes and emergency night-things of various sizes on her car. Of course, you can't dress for dinner, but that doesn't matter very fundamentally in Cardiff.

Lud. But surely your mother might have telegraphed to say what had become of her.

René. She did, from Monmouth, with long directions about charcoal biscuits for the chows' suppers, and again from Cardiff to say when she was coming back. Freda gave the wires to her husband to send off, which accounts for their never having reached us. None of the Tewkesburys have any memories. Their father got a knock on the head at Inkermann and since then the family have never been able to remember anything. I love borrowing odd sums from Tewkesbury; both of us are so absolutely certain to forget all about it.

Hor. And it was on account of this madcap freak that last night's function was postponed and my address cancelled.

Col. This promiscuous gadding about in motors is undermining all home life and sense of locality. One scarcely knows nowadays to which county people belong.

Hor. I trust that Mrs. St. Gall showed some appreciation of the anxiety and alarm caused by her disappearance.

René. I don't know. I wasn't in a position to see.

Hor. Altogether a most extraordinary episode—a fitting sequel to last night's Saturnalia.

Col. Saturnalia! At Briony?

Hor. Advantage was taken of my absence at Panfold last night to indulge in an entertainment which I describe as a Saturnalia for fear of giving it a worse name.

Lud. Perhaps we are judging it a little too seriously. A little dancing——

HOR. Dancing of a particularly objectionable character, in costumes improvised from bed-linen.

COL. Bed-linen!

HOR. To an accompaniment of French songs.

COL. *French* songs! But how horrible. I was told that it was merely Shakespeare readings.

HOR. I regret to say that some of the servants appear to have lent themselves to the furtherance of this underhand proceeding. Among others it will be my unpleasant duty to ask Cook to find another place; I shall give her a good character as a cook, but I shall be very restrained as to what I say about her trustworthiness.

TREVOR. But, mother, isn't that being rather extreme? She's an awfully good cook.

HOR. I put conduct before cookery.

TREVOR. After all, she did nothing more than make two or three supper dishes for us; she couldn't be expected to know that there would be French songs to follow.

HOR. It was her duty to consult me as to these highly unusual preparations. I had given my customary orders for the kitchen department and they did not include chicken mayonnaise or pêches melba. Had she informed me of these unauthorized instructions that she had received the mischief would have been detected and nipped in the bud.

TREVOR. I think it's scarcely fair that she should be punished for what we did. (TREVOR *rises and goes to window,* R. *centre.*)

LUD. I confess I think it's rather unfortunate that such an eminently satisfactory cook should be singled out for dismissal.

HOR. Scarcely singled out, Ludovic; two or three of the other servants will also have to go.

COL. One must see that one's orders are respected, mustn't one?

(*Enter* WILLIAM, L., *with card.*)

WILL. (*to* LUDOVIC). The reporter of the *Wessex Courier* would like to speak with you, sir.

LUD. Tell him I am unable to see any pressmen at present.

WILL. (*handing card to* LUDOVIC). He's written a question which he would feel obliged if you'd answer, sir.

HOR. What is the question?

LUD. He wants to know if I intend standing in the event of a Parliamentary vacancy. (*To* WILLIAM.) You can tell him that I have not the remotest intention of standing.

(RENÉ *groans tragically.*)

WILL. Yes, sir.

[*Exit* WILLIAM, L

HOR. Really, Ludovic, I think you are rather precipitate in your decisions. Differing though we do on more than one of the secondary questions of the day, I am nevertheless inclined to think that the Briony influence would be considerably augmented by having one of the family as Member for the division. Subject to certain modifications of your political views, I am distinctly anxious to see you representing this district in Parliament. I consider this impending vacancy to be a golden opportunity for you.

LUD. There are some people whose golden opportunities have a way of going prematurely grey. I am one of those.

COL. I must say we rather counted on having you for a candidate. I think I may voice a very general disappointment.

RENÉ. There are some disappointments that are too deep to be voiced.

(*Enter* WILLIAM, *door centre.*)

WILL. If you please, ma'am.

HOR. What is it?

WILL. Adolphus has laid an egg.

RENÉ. Oh, improper little bird.

HOR. An egg! How very extraordinary. In all the years that we've had that bird such a thing has never happened. I must admit that I'm rather astonished. See that she has everything she wants and is not disturbed.

WILL. Yes, ma'am.

[*Exit* WILLIAM, *centre.*

(*Enter* CLARE, R., *with telegram in hand.*)

CLARE. My great-aunt, Mrs. Packington, died at nine o'clock this morning.

(TREVOR *goes into fit of scarcely suppressed laughter.*)

COL. A great age, was she not?

HOR. A great age and for longer than I can remember a great invalid. At any rate, a great consumer of medicines. I suppose her death must be regarded as coming in the natural order of things. At the same time, I scarcely think, Trevor, that it is a subject for unbridled amusement.

TREVOR. I'm awfully sorry, but I couldn't help it. It seemed too—too unexpected to be possible. Please excuse me. (*Goes to window and opens it. The others stare at him.*)

CLARE. The fact is, I was Mrs. Packington's favourite niece. There were things in her will which I couldn't afford to have altered. On the other hand, as I dare say you know, Mrs. Bavvel, she had a very special dislike for you.

HOR. I am aware of it. We had some differences of opinion during my husband's lifetime.

CLARE. It was a favourite observation of hers that you reminded her of a rattlesnake in dove's plumage.

COL. Oh, but what unjust imagery!

CLARE. She hated Briony and everything connected with it, and I had to keep my visits here a dark secret.

COL. How very embarrassing.

CLARE. Not at all. I like duplicity, when it's well done. But when Trevor asked me to marry him it did become embarrassing.

(*All the others start up from their seats. Enter* WILLIAM, L., *stands listening.*)

HOR. Trevor asked you—to marry him?

CLARE. Two months ago. Mrs. Packington wasn't expected to live for another fortnight, but she'd been in that precarious condition, off and on, for five years. At the same time, I couldn't risk letting Trevor slip; he'd have forgotten everything and married some one else in sheer absence of mind.

TREVOR. I don't altogether admit that, you know. A thing of that sort I should have remembered.

CLARE. Anyhow, we married on the quiet.

TREVOR. By special licence. It was rather fun, it felt so like doing wrong.

LUD. Do you mean to tell us that you are Mrs. Trevor Bavvel?

CLARE. Of Briony, in the County of Somerset, at your service.

RENÉ (*shouts*). William!

WILL. Yes, sir.

RENÉ. Has that journalist man gone?

WILL. A minute ago, sir.

RENÉ. Quick, send some one after him. Stop him. Tell him——

LUD. That in the event of a vacancy——

RENÉ. Mr. Ludovic Bavvel——

LUD. Will place himself at the disposal of the Party leaders.

RENÉ. Fly! (*Almost pushes* WILLIAM *out of the door,* L.)

CLARE. And, William—tell John to bring up some bottles of Heidsieck.

WILL. Yes, miss, ma'am.

SYBIL. You dear old thing, you've taken all our breaths away; I always said you and Trevor ought to make a match of it. (*Kisses her.*)

AGATHA. I shall put up evergreens all over the house. (*Kisses her.*)

HOR. On a subject of such primary importance as choosing a wife I should have preferred and certainly expected to be consulted. As you have *chosen* this rather furtive method of doing things, I don't know that there is anything for me to do beyond offering my congratulations, which in the nature of things must be rather perfunctory. I congratulate you both. I trust that the new mistress of Briony will remember that certain traditions of conduct and *decorum* have reigned here for a generation. I think without making undue pretensions that Briony has set an example of decent domestic life to a very large neighbourhood.

CLARE. My dear Hortensia, I think Briony showed last night what it could do in the way of outgrowing traditions. Trevor and I have had plenty of time during the last two months to think out the main features of the new *régime*. We shall keep up the model dairy and the model pigsties, but we've decided that we won't be a model couple.

(*Enter* JOHN *with four bottles of fizz.*)

JOHN (*to* CLARE). If you please, madam, will the wagonette and luggage cart be required as ordered?

CLARE. No, I don't think any one will be leaving today. I shall expect you all to prolong your visits in our honour. Oh, of course, I was forgetting Mrs. Vulpy has to go up to Tattersall's to see about some hunters. Just the dogcart then.

HOR. I shall require the carriage for the 4.15 down. There is a conference at Exeter which I think I ought to attend.

JOHN. Very well, madam. [*Exit,* L.

[*Exeunt* HORTENSIA *and* COLONEL MUTSOME, R.

AGATHA (*holding up glass*). You dear things, here's your very good health, and may you have lots and lots of——

RENÉ. Oh, hush!

AGATHA. I was going to say lots of happiness.

RENÉ. Oh, I was afraid you were going to lecture against race suicide.

LUD.
SYBIL
MRS. V.
RENÉ
} (*speaking together*). "Mr. and Mrs. Trevor Bavvel." (*They drink.*)

TREVOR. Thank you all, and here's to the success of the future Member for the Division——

CLARE. Coupled with that of his charming secretary.

(LUDOVIC *and* RENÉ *bow.*)

(*Enter* WILLIAM, *centre, with enormous pile of sandwiches.*)

WILL. Please, Cook thought that as the sandwiches wouldn't be wanted for this afternoon you might like them now. Those with mustard on the right, without on the left, sardine and egg in the middle. And, please, I'm asked to express the general rejoicing in the servants' hall, and Cook says that if marriages are made in heaven the angels will be for putting this one in the window as a specimen of their best work.

CLARE. Thank Cook and all of you very much. (*She whispers to* TREVOR.)

TREVOR. Of course, certainly.

CLARE. And tell John to open some Moselle in the servants' hall for you all to drink our healths. We're coming in presently to get your congratulations.

WILL. Yes, ma'am; thank you, ma'am.

(WILLIAM *turns to go.*)

CLARE. And, William——

WILL. (*turning back*). Yes, ma'am.

CLARE. How much did you win on the sweepstake?

(WILLIAM *turns and flies in confusion.*)

CURTAIN